LaVyrle Spencer

Three Complete Novels

Three Complete Novels

LaVyrle Spencer

The Endearment
Bitter Sweet
Forgiving

G. P. PUTNAM'S SONS   NEW YORK

G. P. Putnam's Sons
Publishers Since 1838
200 Madison Avenue
New York, NY 10016

The Endearment © 1982, © 1983 by LaVyrle Spencer
Bitter Sweet © 1990 by LaVyrle Spencer
Forgiving © 1991 by LaVyrle Spencer

Published simultaneously in Canada
Library of Congress Cataloging-in-Publication Data
Spencer, LaVyrle.
    [Selections. 1995]
    Three complete novels / LaVyrle Spencer.
        p. cm.
    Contents: The endearment—Bitter sweet—Forgiving.
    ISBN 0-399-14021-2
    I. Title. II. Title: 3 complete novels.
PS3569.P4534A6   1995   94-22682 CIP
813'.54—dc20

Printed in the United States of America
    2   3   4   5   6   7   8   9   10

Contents

THE
ENDEARMENT

Historical Note

During the years immediately preceding Minnesota's declaration of statehood, while it was still considered the frontier, few women ventured into her depths, particularly not north of St. Anthony Falls. Frontier life made the woman pay too dearly for her place in the North Country. Although newspapers in the East carried tempting descriptions of all the Minnesota Territory had to offer men, along with open invitations to settle there, no such invitation was extended to women. Instead, those newspapers ran articles discouraging women from that rough, untamed land. Thus, most men who came as pioneers to pluck a living out of the wilderness of the Minnesota Territory came, at first, womanless.

And so was necessitated the practice of sending for women, sight unseen.

And these were called "mail-order brides."

L.S.

Chapter 1

Anna Reardon had done the unforgivable. She had lied through her teeth to get Karl Lindstrom to marry her! She had intentionally deceived the man in order to get him to send her passage money to Minnesota as his mail-order bride. He was expecting her to be twenty-five years old, an able cook, an experienced housekeeper, a willing farm worker and . . . a virgin.

Furthermore, he was expecting her to arrive alone.

The only thing Anna hadn't lied about was her looks. She had accurately described herself as whiskey-haired, Irish, about as tall as a mule's withers, on the thin side, with brown eyes, flat ears, a few freckles, passable features, all her teeth and no pox marks.

But the rest of Anna's letters were a passel of lies good enough to finagle the unsuspecting Lindstrom into sending her fare, enabling her to escape Boston.

Still, lie though she had, those fabrications had not come easy for Anna. They were dictated by a desperate, homeless girl, written by her youngling brother and had lain like a hair shirt upon Anna's conscience ever since. Indeed, every time she recounted her lies, she was punished by a dull pain in the pit of her stomach until now, only minutes away from meeting Karl Lindstrom, Anna had a stomachache the likes of which she'd never suffered before.

The pain had gotten worse and worse all through their long and tedious trip west, a trip that began a month ago after the ice floes had broken up on the Great Lakes. Anna and her brother, James, had traveled throughout June by train from Boston to Albany, then by canal boat to Buffalo. There they'd boarded a lake steamer bound for a mudhole called Chicago, a town that in 1854 consisted of not more than a plank road leading from the boat landing to a hotel. Beyond lay the wilderness country that Anna and James had crossed.

A teamster drove them to Galena in the Illinois Territory, this leg of the trip taking an entire week while mosquitoes, weather and the bumpy ox-cart trail joined forces in making everyone miserable. At Galena, they boarded a steamboat for St. Paul, where they transferred to an ox team that took them the few miles to St. Anthony Falls.

Alas, compared to Boston, the town was utterly disillusioning—not much more than a smattering of roughhewn, unpainted buildings. It made Anna wonder what to expect at the outpost settlement of Long Prairie where she was to meet her future husband.

For more than a month now, she'd had nothing more to do than watch miles of earth and water slip by and worry about what Karl Lindstrom would do when he learned of her countless deceits. Her nerves shattered, Anna wondered why she'd ever thought she could get by with such a scheme in the first place.

One lie would be apparent immediately—James. Never had Anna told her future husband that she had a brother for whom she felt responsible. She had no idea what the man's reaction would be when presented with an adolescent brother-in-law along with his bride-to-be.

The second of Anna's lies was her age. Karl Lindstrom had stated in his advertisement that he wanted an experienced, mature woman, so Anna knew beyond a doubt that had she admitted she was only seventeen, Lindstrom would've known she was greener than spring corn! And so, instead, Anna had told him she was twenty-five, the same age as Lindstrom himself. Anna figured any woman of twenty-five would have the practical experience a man out here needed in a frontier wife. But Lord help her when he found out different!

For the first time in her life Anna Reardon wished she had some wrinkles in her skin, some crow's feet about the eyes, maybe some fat around the waist—anything to make her look a little older than seventeen! He'd take one look and know the truth. And what would he say then? Take your brother and pack yourselves straight back to Boston? With what? thought Anna.

What would they do if Lindstrom left them high and dry out here in the middle of nowhere? Anna had been forced once to earn passage money—she'd had to get James to Minnesota without Lindstrom knowing—and she shuddered now at the memory, the knot in her stomach growing sickeningly fierce. Not again, she thought. Never again!

She and her brother were completely at Lindstrom's mercy. It helped calm Anna's roiling stomach to wonder if Lindstrom might've told a few lies of his own. She had no guarantee he'd been truthful with her. He'd told her all this stuff about his place and his plans for the future, but what bothered her was that he'd said so little about himself. Maybe because there wasn't much to tell!

He'd written endlessly about Minnesota, Minnesota, Minnesota! Apologizing for his lack of originality and his inadequate English, Karl had instead quoted newspapers, which were trying to entice immigrants and settlers to this untamed place.

Minnesota is better than the plains. Here is a spot where one can live in rude but generous plenty. Here there are trees for fuel and building materials. Here, too, wild fruits grow in profusion, while game of all kinds range the forests and prairies; lakes and streams swarm with fishes. Noble forests, fertile prairies, hills and sky-tinted lakes and streams provide well their yields of necessity and beauty.

These descriptions, Karl wrote, had reached even as far as his native Sweden where a sudden explosion in the population had caused a land shortage. Minnesota, sounding so much like his beloved Skåne, had lured Karl with its invitation.

Thus, he crossed the ocean, and hoped his brothers and sisters might soon follow. But neither brother nor sister nor neighbor had come to alleviate his loneliness.

How idyllic it had sounded when James read to Anna all Karl said about Minnesota. But when it came to describing himself, Lindstrom was far less adept.

All he'd said was that he was Swedish, with blond hair, blue eyes, and that he was "pretty big." Of his face, he'd said, "I do not think it would make milk curdle."

Anna and James had both laughed when he read that, and agreed that Karl Lindstrom sounded like a man with a sense of humor. Riding now toward her first meeting with him, Anna fervently hoped he did, for he'd need it sooner than he knew!

In an effort to dispel her misgivings, Anna again began to wonder what Karl Lindstrom would be like. Would he be handsome? What would be the timbre of his voice? The bent of his disposition? What kind of husband would he be—considerate or unkind? Gentle or rough? Forgiving or intolerant?

This, above all, worried Anna, for what man would not be angry to learn that his wife was not a virgin? At the thought, Anna's cheeks burned and her stomach grew worse. Of all her lies, this was the greatest and least forgivable. It was the one she could most easily conceal from Karl Lindstrom until it was too late for him to do anything about it, but the one that made her break out in a cold, clammy sweat.

James Reardon had been made a willing accomplice in his sister's scheme. As a matter of fact, he was the first one who found Lindstrom's ad and showed it to Anna. But because Anna couldn't read or write, it had fallen to James to pen the letters to Lindstrom. At first it had been easy to write a glib description of the kind of woman they thought Lindstrom wanted. Yet as time went on, James realized they were becoming caught in a web of their own making. Repeatedly he had argued that they should at least let Lindstrom know he, James, was coming along. But Anna had won. She had insisted that if Lindstrom learned the truth, their hopes of escaping Boston would be lost.

Riding now atop the packing crates, barrels and sacks, James wore a deep furrow between his brows. Bouncing along the ill-kept government road, he worried about his fate should Lindstrom hold Anna to her promise to marry but be unwilling to accept James in the bargain. He frowned into the lowering sun, a worn hat pulled low over his eyes, a fringe of auburn hair showing above his ears, the lines of worry too deep for such a boyish face.

"Hey," Anna said, reaching out to lightly rap one of his knuckles, knuckles that seemed to outproportion the length of fingers, "it's gonna be all right."

But James only stared toward the west as before, his head resting against the side of the wagon, bumping there as the wheels thudded into each pothole. "Oh yeah? And what if he sends us packin'? What'll we do then?"

"I don't think he will. And anyway, we agreed, didn't we?"

"Did we?" he asked, giving her a brief glance. "We should've told him I was coming, Anna. We should've told him that much of the truth."

"And end up rotting in Boston!" Anna replied for the hundredth time.

"So, we end up rotting in Minnesota. What's the difference?"

But Anna hated it when they argued like this. She tweaked a bit of hair on his arm. "Aw, come on, you're just getting cold feet."

"And I suppose you aren't," James returned, refusing to be humored. He'd seen the way Anna'd been clutching her stomach over there. Her face crumpled a little, making him sorry he'd started arguing again.

"I'm just as scared as you," she finally admitted, all pretense of brightness now gone. "My stomach hurts so bad I feel like I could throw up."

There was absolutely no doubt whatsoever in the mind of Karl Lindstrom that Anna Reardon would be every bit as good as she sounded in her letters. He took her words at face value. He paced back and forth in front of Morisette's store, looking east for sign of the approaching supply wagon. He polished his boot tops on the backs of his calves yet another time. He removed his small-billed, black, woolen cap and thwacked it against his thigh, eyed the road, and settled the hat back on his fair hair. He tried whistling a little between his teeth, but became critical of the notes, and stopped. He cleared his throat and jammed his hands into his pockets and thought of her again.

He had taken to thinking of her as his "little whiskey-haired Anna." It did not matter that she'd said she was tall, nor that she said she had trouble controlling her hair. Karl pictured her as he remembered all the women from back home—pink-cheeked, vigorous, with a becoming face framed in blonde, Swedish braids. Freckles, she'd said. Passable, she'd said. What did that mean—passable? He wanted her to be more than passable, he wanted her to be pretty!

Then, feeling guilty at placing too much value upon such a superficial thing, he took up pacing again, telling himself, "So, what is in a face, Karl Lindstrom? It is what is inside that matters." In spite of himself, Karl still hoped that his Anna might be comely. But he realized beauty was much to expect when she would be able to help so much on the farm.

The only thing that worried him was the fact that she was Irish. He had heard that the Irish had short tempers. Living where they would, so far from others, with only each other, would turn out to be a fine fix if she proved to be quick to anger. He himself, being Swedish, was an amiable fellow—at least he thought himself so. He did not think his temper was anything to put a woman off, although sometimes, looking in the mirror, he worried about his face doing so. He had told Anna it would not make milk curdle, but the closer he came to meeting her the more he fretted. Yet he knew beyond a doubt she'd love the place.

He thought of his land, much land, so much more than in Sweden. He thought of his team of horses, a rare thing here where most had oxen, which cost a full two hundred dollars less than his beautiful Percheron team. He had named them the most American of names—Belle and Bill— in honor of his newly adopted land. He thought of his sod house, which he had cleaned so meticulously today before leaving it, and of the log house already begun. He thought of his grainfields ripening in full sun, which only two short years ago had been solid forest. He thought of his spring, his creek, his pond, his maples, his tamaracks. And even though he set small store by himself or his appearance, Karl Lindstrom thought, yes, I have much to offer a woman. I am a man with plenty.

Yet he dreamed of having more.

He pulled Anna's letters out of his deep pants pocket and studied the script again with great pride, thinking how lucky he was to be getting a woman who was lettered. How many men could claim a thing like that? Here, a man was lucky to have any woman, let alone a lettered one. But his Anna had learned her letters in Boston, and so could teach their children some day. Touching the coarse paper upon which she had written, thinking of her hands touching it—those hands he had never seen— and of the children they would one day make together, a lump clotted his throat. Thinking that no more would he have only his animals to talk to, only his own solitary company at mealtime, only his own warmth in the bed at night, he felt his heart beat crazily.

Anna, he thought, my little whiskey-haired Anna. How long I have waited for you!

Anna peered around the backs of the half-breed drivers as long as she dared, before hiding behind them, wiping her palms on her hand-me-down dress and telling James to alert her when he saw what he thought was the store.

"I see it!" James croaked, stretching his neck while Anna tried to shrink lower in the wagon.

"Oh nooo," she moaned under her breath.

"There's something standing out front!" James said excitedly.

"Is it him? Do you think it's him?" Anna whispered nervously.

"I don't know yet, but he's looking this way."

"James, do I look all right?"

He glanced at her garish, royal blue dress with its ruffled skirt. James didn't much care for it. It revealed too much of her breasts, though she'd done her best to make tucks to draw its bodice protectively closer to decency. But he answered, "You look fine, Anna."

"I wish I had a hat," she said wistfully, touching her flyaway locks, absently smoothing them while her inadequacies loomed ever more obvious.

"Maybe he'll buy you one. He had one. It's a funny little cap like a pie plate with a bill."

"Wh . . . what else? What does he . . . what does he look like?"

"He's big, but I can't make out much. The sun's in my eyes."

Anna's eyes slid closed. She clasped her hands tightly between her knees and wished she knew how to pray. She rocked forward and backward, then resolutely opened her eyes again and took a deep breath that did nothing whatever to stop the quivering in her stomach.

"Tell me what he looks like as soon as you can make him out better," she whispered. One of the Indian drivers heard the whispering and turned around questioningly. "Just drive!" she said testily, flapping an impatient hand at him, and he faced front again, chuckling.

"I can see now!" James said excitedly. "He's awful big, and he's wearing a white shirt and dark britches tucked into his boots and—"

"No, his face! What does his face look like!"

"Well, I can't tell from here. Why don't you look for yourself?" Then James, too, sat down so he wouldn't be caught gaping when they pulled in.

At the last minute Anna warned, "Remember, don't say anything about who you are until I have a chance to talk to him. I'll . . . I'll try to get him used to me a little bit before he has to get used to you." She dusted at her skirt and gave it a useless fluff, then looked down at her chest and placed a trembling hand there, hoping he would not notice the patch of skin she couldn't quite cover when she'd altered the dress.

James swallowed hard, his youthful Adam's apple looking pronounced in his gangly neck. "Good luck, Anna," he said, but his voice cracked in the way it did so often lately. Those unexpected falsettos usually made the two of them laugh, but neither Anna nor James laughed now.

As the wagon approached, Karl Lindstrom suddenly wondered what to do with his hands. What will she think of these hands, such big, clumsy things? He jammed them into his pockets and felt her letters there, and grabbed onto one of them for dear life. His ears seemed suddenly filled with the sound of his own swallowing. He could see the two drivers clearly now. Behind them bobbed two other heads, and Karl fixed his sights on one of them, trying to make out the color of its hair.

A man, Karl thought, should not appear to be shaking in his big Swedish boots when he comes to meet his woman. What will she think if she sees my fright? She will expect a moose like me to act like I know what I am doing, to be sure of myself. Calm down, Karl! But the trembling in his gut could not be talked away so simply.

The wagon slowed, then stopped. The Indians secured the reins, and Anna heard a deep voice say to them, "You are here in good time. You have had a good trip?" The voice had the faint musicality of a Swedish accent.

"Good enough," one driver answered.

Footsteps came slowly around the rear of the wagon bringing a broad, blond giant of a man. In that first moment she felt like her whole body wanted to smile. There was a boyish hesitation before his mouth dropped open just a little. A big, calloused hand moved up in slow motion to doff the little pie-plate hat from his wheat-colored hair. His Adam's apple bobbed once, but still he said nothing, just stood smashing that poor cap into a tight little twist in his two outsized fists, his eyes all the while locked on her face.

Anna's tongue felt swollen, and her throat wouldn't work right. Her heart was clubbing the bejesus out of the wall of her chest.

"Anna?" he spoke at last, charming her by his old-world pronunciation that made of the word a warmer thing than it had ever been before. "*Onnuh?*" he questioned again.

"Yes," she finally managed, "I am Anna."

"I am Karl," he said simply, and up went his eyes to her hair. And up went hers, also, to his.

Yellow, she thought, such very yellow hair. All this time she had wondered, imagined. Now here it was, the one thing that had had color in her thoughts of him. But she found her imagination had not done it justice. This was the most magnificent blond hair she had ever beheld on a man. Thick and healthy it was, with a hint of curl at the nape of his neck and around his face where tiny beads of perspiration formed.

Her hair, Karl found, was indeed the color of rich, Irish whiskey, as when the sun glances through it and lights its depths with shafts of sienna. It flew free in scarcely manageable wavelets; there were no Swedish braids in sight.

When his glance went wandering, so did her hand, to touch an unruly lock at her temple. The way Karl was staring, Anna wished once again that she had a hat. Then suddenly her hand dropped down and self-consciously clutched her other as she realized what she'd done, touching her hair as if frightened to have his gaze rove over her.

Once again their eyes met, his the color of the Minnesota sky, hers like the darkest brown stripes in the agates he so often plowed up from his soil. His glance dropped to her mouth. He wondered what it would look like when she stopped biting her upper lip. And just then it slipped free of her teeth, and he beheld a lovely mouth with the curve of a leaf, sweet but unsmiling.

And so he smiled a little himself, and she tried a shaky one in return. She was afraid to smile as wide as his appearance merited, for he was as handsome a man as she'd ever seen. His nose was perfectly straight, and symmetrical, with fine nostrils like halves of a heart. His cheeks were long, and just concave enough to make him look young and eager. His chin bore a shallow cleft, and his lips—still fallen open as if he too was having difficulty breathing—were beautifully sculptured and bowed up at crest and corners. His skin held the richness of color put there by the sun.

Guiltily, Anna dropped her gaze, realizing how freely she'd allowed her eyes to travel his face.

And Anna thought, no, he would not make milk curdle.

And Karl thought, yes, she is much more than passable.

At last Karl cleared his throat and settled his little cap back on his head. "Come, let me help you down, Anna, but pass me your things first." When he reached, his arm filled his white sleeve as fully as fifty pounds of wheat fills a grainsack.

She turned and reached beyond James who had sat through all that feeling like an eavesdropper—for all they'd hardly spoken to one another. When Anna got to her feet, she found her muscles stiff and unreasonable after the long ride, and feared Karl would find her clumsy and graceless. But he didn't seem to notice the hitch in her hip, only reached up his large hands to help her over the heckboard. His shirt-sleeves were rolled up to the elbow, exposing thick, sturdy forearms. His shoulders, too, filled his shirt until it was taut against his skin. When she braced upon them, she found them like rocks. Effortlessly, he took the distance from her leap, then his two wide hands lingered at her waist.

His hands are so big, she thought, her stomach going light at his touch.

Karl felt how little there was to her, and at closer range his suspicion was confirmed. She was no twenty-five years old!

"It is a very long ride. You must be very tired," he said, noticing that—young or not—she was very tall, indeed. The top of her head came nearly to the tip of his nose.

"Yes," she mumbled, feeling stupid at being unable to think of more to add, but his hands were still on her waist, the warmth of them seeping through and touching her, while he acted like he'd forgotten they were there. Suddenly, he yanked them away.

"Well, tonight you will not have to sleep beneath a wagon. You will be in a warm, safe bed at the mission." Then he thought, fool! She will think that this is all you can think of—bed! First you must show concern for her. "This is the store of Joe Morisette I told you about. If there are things that you need, we can get them here. It is best if we do the trading now because in the morning we will start early for my place."

He turned and walked beside her, watching the tips of her shoes flare her flouncy skirt out. She wore a dress that was not to his liking. It was sheeny, and too bright, with gussets at the breast as if made for an older woman of far fuller figure. It was an odd thing, with too much ruffle and too little chest, ill-suited for a place like Minnesota.

He was suddenly sure she wore it to make herself appear older. She could not be more than eighteen, he guessed, watching her askance as she walked a step ahead of him toward the store. There was a hint of breast camouflaged within the tawdry bodice, but what did he know of such?

She moved through the door ahead of him and he saw her from behind for the first time. There was nothing to her. Oh, she was tall all right, but far too thin for Karl's taste. He thought of the poles upon which his mother's green beans climbed, and decided the only thing this Anna of his needed was a little fattening up.

Morisette looked up as soon as they entered, calling out in a robust French accent, "So, she is here and the bridegroom can stop his nervous pacing and whiskey drinking!"

You have a big mouth, Morisette, Karl thought. But when Anna turned sharply and glanced back at Karl, she found him red to the ears. She'd seen enough whiskey drinkers in Boston to last her a lifetime. The last thing she wanted was to be married to one.

Must I deny such a thing to her right here before Morisette? Karl wondered. No, the girl will just have to learn that I am honorable once she has lived with me for a while.

Anna gazed around the store, wondering what he would say if she told him she would like to own a hat. Never had she owned a new hat of her own, and he *had* asked her if there was anything she needed. But she dared not ask for anything, knowing James still waited outside, thoroughly unnoticed by Karl Lindstrom. A hand at her elbow urged her toward the storekeeper. The swarthy French-Canadian wore a ready smile and a somewhat teasing grin.

"This is Anna, Joe. She is here at last."

"But of course it is Anna. Who else could it be?" Morisette laughed infectiously, flinging his palms wide. "You have had quite a ride up the government road, eh? It is not the best road, but it is not the worst. Wait until you have seen the road to Karl's house, then you will appreciate the one you have just come down. Do you know, young lady, that the newspapers warn women not to come here because the life is so hard?"

It was not at all what Karl would have had Morisette tell Anna. He did not want to scare her away before she even had a chance to see his wonderful Minnesota and let it speak for itself.

"Yes, of course, I've . . . read them for myself," Anna lied. "But Karl thinks there is no place better to settle because there is so much land and it is so rich and . . . and there's everything a man could want here."

Morisette laughed. Karl had filled her head already, he could tell.

Pleased with her reply, Karl answered, "See there, Morisette, you cannot scare Anna away with your foolish talk. She has come this far, and she is here to stay." Anna's heart grew a little lighter. So far she seemed to be passing muster, seventeen or not, wrinkles or none.

"And so the good *père* is marrying you at the mission?" Morisette asked.

"Yes, in the morning," Karl said, looking at the back of Anna's shoulders where those tumblecurls were rioting over her collar.

Just then the half-breed drivers came into the store, each with a barrel hoisted on his shoulder. One of them set his load down with a thud, then said, "That boy stands in the road as if he is lost. Did you not tell him this is the end of the run?" There was no doubt that he was directing his question to Anna. But she stood dumbstruck.

"What boy?" Lindstrom asked.

Seeing no way out, Anna looked him square in the eye and answered, "My brother, James."

Baffled for a moment, Karl stared back at her, the truth dawning on him even as Morisette and the drivers looked on. "Ya, of course . . . James." Lindstrom stalked to the door, and for the first time looked fully at the lad who had been the other passenger on the supply wagon. Karl had been so intent upon Anna that he'd scarcely realized the boy was there.

"James?" Lindstrom spoke, trying to make it sound as if he'd known all along.

"Yes?" James replied, then amended it to, "Yes, sir," wanting to create a good impression on the tall man.

"Why do you stand in the road? Come in and meet my friend, Morisette."

Surprised, the boy's feet seemed rooted momentarily, then he jammed his hands in his pockets and entered the store. When he passed before Karl, the man noted some similarity between the boy's looks and Anna's. The lad was gangly and thin, too, with similar coloring, but the freckles were missing, and the eyes, although large like his sister's, were green instead of brown.

Karl expertly concealed his surprise, moving about the store methodically, loading supplies on his wagon out front. James and Anna explored the shop, catching each other's eye now and then, quickly looking away, wondering at Karl's reaction or lack of it. They were both amazed at how unconcerned the man seemed to be with James being here. He just went about calmly loading supplies onto his wagon, bantering with Morisette.

When things were firmly lashed on behind the pair of blinking Percherons, Karl came back inside, announcing that it was time to leave. But Anna noticed he did not repeat his offer to buy her anything she needed. He bid goodbye to Morisette and took Anna stiffly by the elbow to guide her outside, but there was a pressure there that warned her this new husband-to-be was not as complacent as she'd thought earlier.

Chapter 2

❧

Anna thought Karl would dislocate her arm before he let go of it. Without a word he herded her along, Anna taking two steps to every one of his, but he ignored all but her elbow with which he finally pushed her up to the wagon seat. She ventured a peek at his face, and his expression made her stomach take to quaking something awful. She rubbed her misused shoulder socket, wishing more than ever that she had written the truth in all those letters.

Karl's voice was as controlled as ever as he spoke to his horses, gave them a cluck and started them up the road. But when they were around a bend, beyond earshot of the store, the wagon lurched to a sudden halt. Lindstrom's voice bit the air in a far different tone than he had used thus far. His words were as slow as always, but louder.

"I do not air my arguments before Joe Morisette down at his store. I do not let that tease Morisette see that Karl Lindstrom has had a fast one pulled on him. But I think this is what has happened! I think you, Anna Reardon, have tried to take in a stupid Swede, eh? You have not been honest and would make a fool of Karl Lindstrom before his friend Morisette!"

Her back stiffened. "Wh . . . what do you mean?" she stammered, growing sorrier by the minute.

"What do I mean?" he repeated, the accent more pronounced. "Woman, I am no fool!" he exploded. "Do not take me for one! We have made a bargain, you and me. All these months we make the plan for you to come to me, and not once do you mention your brother in your letters! Instead, you bring a little surprise for Karl, huh, that will make people laugh when they know that it is the first time I have heard of my bride bringing an extra passenger I have not been expecting!"

"I . . . I guess I should have told you, but—"

"You guess!" he shouted, totally frustrated. "You do more than guess! You *know* long ago you are planning this trick on me, and you probably think Karl Lindstrom is such a big dumb Swede that it will work!"

"No, I didn't think that at all. I wanted to tell you but I thought once you saw James, you'd see what a help he'll be to you. James is a good, strong boy. Why, he's almost a man!" she pleaded.

"James is a stripling! He is another mouth to feed and another set of winter clothes to buy."

"He's thirteen years old, and in another year or two he'll be full-grown. Then he'll be twice the help that I'll be."

"I did not put the advertisement in the Boston paper for a hired boy, I advertised for a wife."

"And I'm here, aren't I?"

"Ya, you sure are. But you, plus this brother, is more than I bargained for."

"He's a good worker, Lindstrom."

"This is not Boston, Anna Reardon. Here an extra person means extra provisions. Where will he sleep? What will he wear? Will there be enough food to feed three during the coming winter? These are things a man must consider in order to survive here."

She pleaded in earnest now, words rushing out. "He can sleep on the floor. He has enough clothing for one winter. He'll help you raise extra crops during the summer ahead."

"The crops area already in the ground, and you were supposed to help me tend them. I only needed one—you."

"I *will* help you. Just think of how much more three of us could raise! Why, we'd have so much—"

"I told you, the crops are already in! Right now I do not even think it is the crops I am concerned with. It is the fact that you have lied to me and what I must do about that. Never would I willingly choose a liar for a wife."

Anna sat smitten into silence. There seemed no argument against that.

James, who had gotten onto the wagon without a word, spoke up at last. "Mr. Lindstrom, we didn't have any choice. Anna thought that if you knew I was part of the deal you'd turn her down flat." James' voice cracked from tenor to soprano, then back again.

"And you think right!" Karl exploded. "That is exactly what I would do, and I am thinking I might still do just that!"

Anna found her voice again, but fear made it tremble. Her eyes were wide in her too thin face, and they sparkled with threatening tears.

"You . . . you wouldn't send us back? Oh, please don't send us back."

"When you lie to me, you break our agreement. I do not think I am responsible for you any longer. I did not bargain for a wife who was a liar."

He sounded so self-righteous, sitting there all sated and healthy-looking, so obviously well-fed, that Anna's temper suddenly flared.

"No, you don't have to bargain at all, do you!" she lashed, then gestured with hands thrown wide toward the earth in general. "Not when you have your precious Minnesota to yield all its *nectar* and *wood* and *fruit!*" Her voice fairly oozed with sarcasm. "Not when you're warm and fat and cozy! You wouldn't know the first thing about going cold and hungry, would you? I'd like to see you that way, Karl Lindstrom. Maybe then you'd find out how easy it is to lie a little to improve your station in life. Boston would teach you quick how to be a blinkin' artist at lying!"

"So you make a habit of lying? Is that what you are saying?" He glared at her then, finding her cheeks pinked beneath their sprinkling of freckles.

"You're damn right," she cursed with fierce intensity, looking him square in the eye. "I lied so I could eat. I lied so James could eat. First, we tried it without lying, but we got no place fast. Nobody wanted to hire James 'cause he was too skinny and undernourished. And nobody wanted to hire me because I was a girl. Finally, when trying for an honest living didn't work, we decided it was time to try a little dishonesty and see if it'd work out better for us."

"Anna!" he exclaimed, disappointed as much by her cussing as by her lying. "How could you do such a thing? There have been times I have been hungry, too. But never have I been hungry enough to make lies. Nothing makes Karl Lindstrom into a liar!''

"Well, if you're so almighty honest, you'll keep your half of the bargain and marry me!'' she spouted.

"Bargain! I said the bargain is broken by your deceit. I paid good money for your passage. What of that? Can you return it to me? Can you do that, or have I been fool enough to get you here and end up with no wife and no money?''

"I can't pay you back in money, but if you'll take us, both of us, we'll work hard. That's the only way we can pay you back.'' She looked away from the genuine shock in Karl Lindstrom's eyes, the kind that comes from gentle rearing where black and white are clearly defined.

"Mr. Lindstrom,'' James interjected, "I'll pay my way, too, you'll see. I'm stronger than I look. I can help you build that cabin you're planning on, and I can help you clear land, and . . . and plant it and harvest it.''

Karl's eyes bored straight ahead between Belle's ears. His jaw was so taut it looked swollen.

"Can you manage a team, boy?'' he snapped.

"N . . . no.''

"Can you handle a plow?''

"I've never tried.''

"Can you lift a logging chain or handle a flail or fell with an axe?''

"I . . . I can learn,'' James stammered.

"Learning takes time. Out here time is precious. Our growing season is short and the winters are long. You come to me unskilled and expect me to make you teamster, logger and farmer all in one summer?''

Anna began to see the shortsightedness of her plan, but she couldn't give up now. "He learns fast, Lindstrom,'' she promised. "You wouldn't be sorry.''

Karl looked at her sideways, shook his head despondently and studied his boots. "I am already sorry. I am sorry I ever had such an idea, to send for a wife through the mail. But I waited two years thinking there would be other settlers coming, other women. In Sweden there is much talk about this Minnesota, and I believed other Swedes would follow me. But nobody comes and I can wait no longer. This you know, too. This I think you have planned to use against me to get your way.'' He sounded sad.

"Maybe I did, but I thought you'd see that an extra person would be useful.'' Anna picked at a piece of loose cuticle while she said this.

There was another point Karl wanted to make, but he did not know how to say it without seeming to be a man of great sexual demands. He could not imagine taking a wife to bed in the same room with a brother. If he said as much, Anna would undoubtedly be horrified. All he could do was tiptoe around the issue by saying, with his eyes now on Belle's neck, "I live in a house of only one room, Anna.''

Anna quit picking at her cuticle. She felt her face warming, understanding fully what Karl implied. His courteous way of implying they would need more privacy touched her. He was different from any man she had ever met. She'd never before met a human being who was totally good, but it looked as if perhaps Karl Lindstrom was. That goodness filled her with self-recriminations that she could not have come to him a better person herself.

Had Karl dared to look at Anna that moment, he would have seen a faint blush beneath her freckles. But he did not. He stared absently, preoccupied with another disillusioning thought. Suppose Anna had been wily enough to reckon on using their lack of privacy to keep her from performing the duty that some wives—he'd been told—found distasteful. This, of course, he could not accuse her of, especially not in front of the lad.

Karl only wanted to take his new wife to his little home, which was waiting in readiness for their return. There he would have had time and privacy to woo her as in any normal courtship. Ah, thought Karl, what a strange way we have come together, Anna and me.

Within the heart of Karl Lindstrom fell a heavy sadness. How he had looked forward to this day, thinking always how proud he would be when he took his little whiskey-haired Anna into his sod house for the first time. He would proudly show her the fireplace he had built of fieldstone from his own soil, the table and chairs he had fashioned of sturdy black walnut from his own trees. He remembered the long hours spent braiding buffalo grass into ropes to restring the log frame of the bed for her. How carefully he had dried last season's corn husks to make the softest tickings a woman could want. He'd spent precious hours collecting cattails, plucking their down to fill pillow ticks for her. The buffalo robes had been aired and shaken and rubbed with wild herbs to make them smell sweet. Lastly, he had picked a sheaf of sweet clover, its fragrance headier than any other, and had lain it on the spot where their two pillows met, in the center of the bed.

In all these ways Karl Lindstrom had sought to tell his Anna that he prized her, welcomed her and strove to please her. Only now that she was here, he found her a liar, perhaps not worthy of his lofty concern, a liar who brought a brother who would be sleeping on the floor on the night Karl Lindstrom took a bride to his bed for the first time.

Karl pondered long and silently, while Anna and James held their tongues. At last, unable to bear the strained silence any longer, Anna bit the inside of her cheek and said, "You keep me and I won't lie no more."

Karl looked at her finally. There was the stain of guilt upon her skin, which in itself was pleasing to him. It told him she did not lie without feeling small at getting caught. Her cheek had turned the color of the wild roses that graced Karl's land in June. And, just like coming upon one of them unexpectedly at a turn of the trail, coming upon that rosy color in Anna's cheeks now made him want to pick it and take it home with him.

He was a man to whom loneliness was a dread thing. Again he thought of awakening to find the bloom of her cheek on the pillow of cattail down beside him, and his own face felt warm. He found he had been studying her golden freckles, too; they seemed to lessen the severity of her guilt. They made her look utterly innocent. In that moment he thought of her lies as childish tales, told by a youngster to turn things her way.

"You promise me that?" he asked, looking straight into her eyes. "That you will not lie to me anymore?" His voice was soft again, disarming.

"I promise, yes," she vowed, matching his steady gaze with a steadiness of her own, matching his quiet tone, too.

"Then I want you to tell me how old you really are."

Her eyes dropped, she bit her lip, and Karl knew he had her cold again!

"Twenty," she said. But the color in her cheeks had deepened to the heliotrope hue of the prairie thistle blossom, which Karl had never desired to pick and take home.

"And if I say I do not believe you?"

She only shrugged her shoulders, but avoided his eyes.

"I would ask your brother to tell me the truth, but I see that the two of you are in cahoots together with this pack of lies you have cooked up for me." The gentle tone of his voice did not deceive her this time. Beneath it was an iron stubbornness to get at the truth.

Anna threw up both hands at once. "Oh, for heaven's sake! *All right.* I'm seventeen! So what!" She glared bravely into Karl's face, her sudden spunk making him want to smile, which he carefully did not do.

"So what?" he repeated, raising his eyebrows, leaning back relaxedly—a cat playing with a mouse before sinking his teeth in. "So I wonder if you are the cook and housemaid that you said you are."

She puckered up her pretty mouth tight and sat staring stonily ahead.

"Do not forget, you said you are done with lying," he reminded her.

"I said I'm seventeen. What more do you want?"

"I want a wife who knows how to cook. Can you cook?"

"A little."

"A little?"

"Well, not much," she spit, "but I can learn, can't I?"

"I do not know. How will you learn? Will I have to teach this, too?"

She elected not to answer.

"How much housework do you know?"

Silence.

He nudged her. "How much?"

She jerked her arm away. "About as much as I know about cooking!"

"Can you make soap?"

No answer.

"Can you make tallow dips?"

No answer.

"Bake bread?"

No answer.

"I guess that you have never done much farming either, or gardening or caring for a house."

"I can stitch!" was all she'd say.

"Stitch . . ." he repeated, quite sarcastically for Karl Lindstrom. "She can stitch," he said to the wagon wheel. Then Karl began talking to himself in Swedish, and that really riled Anna, for she couldn't understand a word he said.

At last he fell silent, studying the wagon wheel, his head turned away from her. She sat ramrod stiff, her arms crossed over her chest.

"I reckon you should've waited for those Swedish girls to come to Minnesota, huh?" she asked sourly, taking her turn at staring down the horses' necks.

"Ya, I think I should have," Karl said in English. Then he muttered, once more for good measure, "Seventeen and she knows nothing but how to stitch."

He mulled silently for some time, then finally turned to face her, wondering how a man of his age could take to bed a child of seventeen without feeling like a defiler of innocence. His eyes flickered down to her breasts, over to James, then back to Anna's face. "There seems to be a lot you do not know how to do."

"I can damn well do anything you set me to, seventeen or not!" But she prayed her face was not flushed.

"You can sure cuss real good, but I don't need no woman to cuss." He wondered how he'd survive the rest of his life with her Irish temper. He wondered how he'd survive another year or two womanless. All he said was, "I must think."

"Sir . . ." James began, "Anna and me—"

"*Do not disturb me when I think,*" Karl ordered. James and Anna looked at each other out of the corners of their eyes. They thought he'd set the horses to walking, but he continued to brood in silence. It was his way, the way his father had taught him, the way his grandfather had taught his father. He spent time meditating a situation first, pondering before making a decision, so that when he tackled a problem, he almost always solved it. He sat quiet as a stone while the birds twittered, soft evening talk as if putting their young ones to nest for the night.

The summer evening imposed itself on Anna, and she thought how bird-talk wasn't often heard in Boston. There, at this time of day, came the music from the taverns opening for the evening. Already Anna found she preferred the birds. In his letters Karl had said there were more birds here than anyone could name. She wondered now if she'd ever get the chance to try.

"Anna!" he said, making her jump, "you must tell me now what other lies you have told. I think I am entitled to know if there are any more."

Anna felt James jab her in the side with his elbow.

"I didn't tell any other lies. Heaven's sake! What more could there possibly be?" Oh, she sounded so convincing she thought she should be on the stage.

"There better not be more!" he warned. But still he did not give a clue what else he was thinking. He picked up the reins, started the horses on their way again and drove to the mission.

He pulled the horses up before the pair of log buildings with well-worn earth between them. The larger building had a crude cross atop the door, while the other had none. It was the school, Anna knew.

"I have much thinking to do yet," Karl said. "We will sleep here tonight as planned, and I will seek the wisdom of Father Pierrot to guide me. In the morning I will decide about everything—whether to keep you or send you back to Boston on the next Red River cart train that comes through."

Suddenly Anna realized the significance of the term, "Father."

"*Father* Pierrot?" she inquired. "Is this a Catholic mission?" Already her mind was racing ahead, wondering how she'd get out of this one.

"Yes, of course. In my letters I told you we would be married here."

"But . . . but you never said it was Catholic."

"Of course it is Catholic. Are you worried that Father Pierrot will not be willing to witness our marriage because I am Lutheran and you are Catholic? It is all fixed and Father has received a special dispensation from Bishop Cretin to witness the vows we will speak ourselves. But think no more about it because perhaps we will say no vows after all."

Anna was not sure which prospect scared her more, being sent away, or having Karl unearth her other deceptions.

Karl jumped down, tied the reins, then helped Anna alight. But this time, when he put his hands on her thin waist, he could not help recalling what she'd said about his always having plenty to eat. She was reed-thin.

They were greeted at the door of the smaller building by Father Pierrot himself. "Ah, Karl, what a pleasant thing it is to greet you, my friend. And this must be Anna."

"Hello, Father."

Anna bobbed her head while the dark-haired priest broke into an even deeper smile. "Do you know how this young man has been waiting for you? Each time I see him, all he can talk of is his Anna. His little whiskey-haired Anna. I thought if you did not get here soon, he would abandon that place he's always bragging about and run looking for you."

Irreverently, Karl thought, you, too, Father, have a big mouth, even if you are a man of the cloth! Karl had been raised to have great respect for the clergy. It was natural for him to radiate toward the friendship of the only cleric within a hundred miles, no matter what denomination he was.

"Do I brag, Father?" Karl inquired.

"Oh, do not look so worried, Karl. I enjoy teasing you." Eyeing James, the priest next asked, "And who might this young man be?"

"James, sir," the boy replied, "James Reardon."

"He's my brother," Anna declared forthrightly.

"Your brother . . . mmm . . . Karl neglected to tell me you had a brother. This is good news. Minnesota can use strong young settlers like you, James. It is not a bad place for a boy to grow into a man either. Do you think you will like it here, James?"

"Yes, sir," James quickly answered, "but I have lots to learn."

Father raised his head and laughed. "Well, you pick a good man to come to, son. If you have any doubts about Minnesota, this big Swede will soon put them out of your head."

Karl suddenly cleared his throat and said, "I must tend my horses, Father. You will perhaps like to talk to Anna and James about Boston and the East."

"Can I help you?" James asked immediately.

Karl looked at the lad, so stringy, so lean, so young, so eager. Karl found himself not wanting to have the tug of the boy's willingness influencing his decision regarding Anna. "You go with Father and your sister. You have had a long trip, and it is not over yet. You rest." The look in the boy's eyes seemed to ask, but will the rest of my trip take me back to Boston or forward to your place? Karl looked away, for he did not yet know the answer.

Watching his broad shoulders going through the door, Anna felt a sudden longing to please him for James' sake. James had never known a father, and this man would be the best influence a boy of his age could possibly have. When Karl was gone, the image of his sturdy back lingered in Anna's mind.

An Indian woman served a delicious mixture of corn and meat. Anna and James fairly wolfed supper down. From across the table Karl now studied Anna more thoroughly. Her face was appealing enough, but he truly disliked her dress, and her hair seemed wild and disorderly, nothing like the neat coronets of braids he was used to on Swedish women.

Anna looked up unexpectedly and caught him watching her. Immediately, she slowed her eating.

But the word "hungry" stayed in his mind, just as she'd said it earlier.

Her shoulders were peaked beneath her dress, and her knuckles were large on otherwise thin hands, making him wonder just how hungry she had been in Boston. The boy, too, was painfully thin, with eyes that looked too large for their sockets. Karl tried to dismiss these thoughts as he ate his meal, but again and again they forced their way upon him.

After dinner, Father Pierrot asked the Indian woman to prepare pallets for his three guests on the floor of the schoolroom.

This done, the woman returned and led Anna and James to their beds, while Karl stayed behind to talk to Father Pierrot.

Brother and sister found comfortable makeshift beds of straw and buffalo robes, and they settled down drearily to worry about what was to become of them. It was quiet and dark, the night rampant with unspoken thoughts.

Finally, James asked, "Do you think he'll send us back?"

"I don't know," Anna admitted. He could tell by her voice that she was really worried.

"I'm scared, Anna," he confessed.

"So am I," she confessed.

"But he seems like a fair man," James put in, needing some hope.

"We'll know in the morning."

Again silence fell, but neither of them was remotely sleepy.

"Anna?" came James' small, worried voice.

"What now?"

"You shouldn't have lied to him about the other things. You should've admitted them when he asked."

"About what other things?" she asked, holding her breath for fear he knew her worst, most unforgivable secret.

But he only listed the others. "About knowing how to write, and that I was the one wrote those letters, and where we lived."

"I was afraid to tell the truth."

"But he'll find out. He's bound to find out."

"But he'll find out too late, if we're lucky."

"That ain't right, Anna."

Anna stared up into the darkness above her, feeling tears gathering in her throat. "I know. But since when's right ever worked on our side?"

No, James admitted to himself, right had never been on their side at all. Still, he didn't think two wrongs made a right either. He knew what a shock it must've been to Karl Lindstrom to see him arrive today with Anna—a kid Karl hadn't even known existed! And then poor Karl learned that Anna was only seventeen instead of twenty-five, and that she couldn't do a blame thing around the place. James acknowledged that Karl had taken it all better than most men would have.

"What'd you think of him, Anna?" he asked quietly.

"Oh, shut up and go to sleep!" she exclaimed in a choked voice. Then she buried her head in her arms to stifle a sob as she thought of the bald look of innocent expectation that had greeted her on Karl's face. And of how he had helped her down from the wagon at first, and offered to buy her anything she needed in the store. Oh, she liked him all right. But at the same time she was scared to death of him. He was, after all, a man.

Chapter 3

♣

"Father Pierrot, I must speak to you as a friend as much as a priest. I have a problem regarding Anna." The two had settled in Father's little sitting room at the rear of the school building, companionably smoking fragrant pipes of Indian tobacco.

"Ah, Karl, I could tell you were troubled as soon as you arrived. Are you having last-minute thoughts?"

"Ya, I am, but not in the way you might think." Karl sighed. "You know how many months it has taken to get Anna here. You know I have prepared a good home for her, and I have plans for an even better one. I have been much more than ready for a wife for some time now. All this time I have dreamed of her coming. But I think I have been a little foolish, Father. I dreamed her to be something she is not. I find out today she has lied to me about many things."

"Was it not a risk you took, courting her by letter?"

"Ya, a risk it was. But still, not a good way to begin married life. I think I do not want a wife who is a liar, yet I want a wife, and she is the only one available."

"About what has she lied, my friend?"

"The first is a lie of omission. This brother James was a complete surprise to me today. She did not tell me of him. I think she knew I would not want a lad of that age living with us when we are newly married."

"Would you send them back because of this?"

"I threatened to do just that, but I do not think I could stand the loneliness for another year while I try to find another wife. Forgive me, Father . . . I should perhaps not speak of it, but I am already twenty-five years old. I have been alone since I left Sweden, two years already. I am eager to begin building a family. There have been times, especially in the winter when I am snowed in for days at a time with nobody for company when I . . ." Karl cupped the bowl of his pipe in a big hand, rubbing the glossed wood with a large thumb, watching the slow curl of smoke rise from it. He remembered only too wrenchingly the emptiness of those winter nights.

He looked up to find the eyes of his friend upon him, and laughing sheepishly, Karl leaned his elbow on a knee and rested his chin in his palm. "You know, Father, sometimes I bring the goat inside to keep her from freezing in the bad blizzards and so I have somebody to talk to. But poor Nanna, I think she grows tired of hearing her foolish master pining for human companionship."

"I understand, Karl. You need not apologize for your needs. There is no dishonor in wanting a wife for long winter nights, and for beginning a family. Neither is there dishonor in wanting to begin married life with time to get accustomed to each other in privacy.''

"But I feel small for resenting the boy.''

"What man wouldn't?''

"You would not, Father, if you were in my place?'' Karl was reluctant to think a priest could feel such human failings.

"I think perhaps I would. On the other hand, I would weigh it against the boy's value to me in this wilderness. He could be more than a helper. He could, in time, be a friend, perhaps even a buffer.''

"What does this mean, Father—buffer.''

"Let me put it to you this way, Karl,'' the priest said, sitting back with a philosophical air. "Do you think that if you marry Anna, all your troubles will be magically over and she will be all those things you dreamed she'd be? I think not. I think that—beginning as strangers, as it were— the two of you will cross swords many times before you truly know and accept each other for what you are. Sometimes in the crossing of swords it is good to have a third party to act as conciliator or mediator, or as I said before, just a plain friend.''

"This I had not thought of before, but I see you are wise. It is almost like you heard Anna's temper flare today, to say nothing of my own.''

"You had words, you two?''

"Ya, words. But the lad was there, so I think we both said less than we maybe thought.''

"Aside from the fact that the lad came unannounced, what do you think of him?''

"He seems eager to learn and has promised to work hard.''

"The boy could do worse than end up with you as a teacher, Karl. Under your tutelage I believe young James would learn quickly. Had you thought there might be reward in teaching him, too?''

The two puffed at their pipes in companionable silence again. Karl thought of all the priest had said about the boy. The idea of having the lad to teach, to nurture, became an inviting challenge. Karl thought of the log house and all it would take to erect it, imagined himself and the lad working side by side, bare-chested in the sun, imagined the first . . . then second, then third . . . tier of logs going up, and the two of them bantering as they worked side by side skidding, notching. He could teach the lad much about building and about woods, just as his papa had taught him.

"Karl?'' A lazy curl of smoke floated upward with the word.

"Hm?'' Karl replied absently, quite lost in thought.

"There is something I must ask, but I ask it to make you think realistically about all of this.''

"Ya, well ask, then.''

"Have you been considering sending the girl back because you are disappointed in what you saw when she arrived? I think you must consider this aspect of marrying her equally as much as all the others. You brought her here sight unseen, with high hopes. If you find her repugnant, it could bring much difficulty to your marriage. You must look at this realizing you are a human being, Karl. As such, you are subject to doubt and skepticism. Maybe even outright dislike. I think you are a man whose principles would speak louder than his dislikes, though, and would keep her with you out of duty, if you thought you were obliged to do so.''

Karl was learning a new side of Father Pierrot tonight, a human side that Karl deeply needed. "Oh, no, Father, I truly do not find her unattractive, only a little thin. But her face . . . she . . . I . . ." It was difficult for Karl to express to this priest the feelings that had swept over him when he'd first seen Anna, when he had taken her hand in his to help her down from the wagon, or the feeling of her slim hips and waist as she jumped down. It was difficult for Karl himself to equate those feelings with anything but lustfulness. Naturally, he did not wish to appear crude before his friend, this priest.

"My eye is pleased, truly, Father, but I have tried to use good reason. It should not matter to me if her looks please me, I should instead—"

"But of course it should matter!" the priest interrupted, jumping to his feet. "Karl, don't turn fool on me now. If you do, it will be for the first time since I've known you. You will look at the woman for many years if you marry her. What fool would not want to be pleased with what he sees?"

Karl laughed. "You surprise me, Father. In the time I have know you I would not have thought you to be a man with such sympathy when it comes to matters of the heart."

Father, too, laughed. "I was a man first, a priest second."

Karl now looked his friend straight in the eye, all laughter faded. "Then I admit to you I am pleased by her appearance. I am perhaps too pleased. Perhaps I will not use good judgment about her other lies."

"Tell me," the priest said simply, sitting down again.

"She is only a child. I was expecting a full-grown woman of twenty-five. But Anna lied about this, too. She is only seventeen years old."

"But did she not make the choice of her own free will to come here and be your wife?"

"Not exactly. I think she and the boy were destitute. I was their last resort. Yes, she came to be married, but I think it was the lesser of two evils."

"Has she told you that?"

"Not exactly in those words. She has begged me not to send them away, but while she is begging I see how very young and scared she is, and I do not think she realizes all that is entailed in being a wife."

"Karl, you are placing a burden of worry on yourself that perhaps is not necessary. Why not let her be the judge of whether or not she is old enough to marry?"

"But seventeen, Father . . . She has admitted she knows almost nothing about being housekeeper and cook. There would be much I would have to teach her, too."

"It would be a challenge, Karl, but it could be fun with a spirited girl."

"It could also be a mistake with a spirited girl."

"Karl, have you considered why she lied? If she and the boy came to you as a last hope, I can see why she felt the need to lie to get here. I do not condone the lies, Karl, not at all. But I think perhaps they are forgivable, perhaps her circumstances make them so. I think you must ask yourself if she could not, underneath, be an honest woman who was forced into lying by her circumstances. Perhaps, Karl, you are judging her too harshly for your own good."

"You leave me much to consider, my friend," Karl said, rising and stretching. "All my life I have been taught what is right and what is wrong, and I have been warned that the path runs narrowly. Never before have I had to consider circumstances that lessen the degree of wrongness. I think you have helped me tonight to look at things from another person's viewpoint. I will try to do this."

He paused, glanced across the room toward the doorway. "Anna and the boy have had plenty of time to get themselves settled for the night. I think I will join them and finish my considerations there."

"Sleep well, Karl," the priest wished.

Karl scraped the ashes from his pipe. "You know, Father," he said thoughtfully, "she has assured me these are the only lies she told, and made me the promise never to lie to me again. That promise is worth something."

Father Pierrot smiled, placed a hand on Karl Lindstrom's shoulder and understood how a man of his nature would be torn by uncertainty at a time like this. Most men who had lived alone for two years on the frontier would not stop to think of anything but their own need for a woman, both in and out of bed. But Karl was a man of rare quality, rare honesty. Anna Reardon would be a lucky woman to marry such a man.

It was dark, dusty and dry in the schoolroom. Karl found his empty pallet and stretched out on his back with both hands behind his head. He thought about all Father Pierrot had said, and for the first time, and guiltlessly now, would have allowed himself to consider Anna as a woman. But he could not do this; he found he thought of her as a child instead. She was tall, but so thin it gave her a look of almost boyish callowness.

Her wide-eyed fright at times today made him think of her as a green young girl who perhaps did not even know what was the duty of the marriage bed. In some ways this pleased him, but in others it frightened him, too. It was one thing to take to bed a woman of twenty-five who knew what to expect. It was quite another to bed a child of seventeen whose luminous dark eyes might burn up at him in fear when she learned what was expected of her. She seemed so frail her little bones might snap were he even to hug her against his chest.

But even as he thought this, the hair on his chest prickled teasingly. He ran his hand over his shirt, sliding it across the breadth of his chest. It was a wide chest. His arms were thick and fully muscled from using the axe all his life. His thighs were heavy, long from knee to hip. He had the tall, muscular stature of his father. Always before, he had taken for granted what women thought as they looked at him.

Now, for the first time, as he thought of Anna, he realized that to a girl, perhaps his size seemed frightening. Perhaps he did not please her. It struck him quite suddenly that tonight he had been selfishly concerned with what he, Karl, thought of her, Anna. Perhaps he should have given equal time to wondering what she thought of him! Yes, she had pleaded with him not to send them back. But had she pleaded with him out of fear? Penniless and scared, what else would the girl do when threatened with abandonment in the middle of the wilderness?

He thought once again of his sod hut, of the bed he had prepared for her with the most honorable intentions. He tried to imagine what she would think when she saw that sheaf of sweet clover. His own heart hammered with uncertainty now. Perhaps it had been a stupid blunder to prepare the bed in so obvious a manner for her coming, as if the only thing on his mind all these months was getting her into it! She would see the full, plump tick, the freshly stuffed pillows, the clover meant as a welcome only, and she would shy away like a foolish spring colt shies from a rabbit, never knowing the rabbit could not and would not do it harm.

Anna, he thought, what should I do with you? How can I send you away? Yet how can I ask you to stay? And if I do, how far we have to go together, and how much we have to learn of one another.

He awakened in the morning when the sunlight was but a promise. It was the time when day hesitates before nudging the night away, the pale light tiptoeing into the room with scarcely the strength to threaten the shadows that lay heavily upon Anna as she slept on her side, facing Karl. She had an arm tucked beneath her ear, her chin tucked down childishly upon her chest. She wore a look of such innocence, that again he wondered if he were doing the right thing.

But his mind was settled. He had thought well and long about what was right, for both of them, and within the heart of Karl Lindstrom beat the conviction that together, he and Anna and the boy could make this thing work. They must make a marriage in which this unfortunate beginning was forgotten. If it took patience on his part, it would take courage on hers. If it took forgiveness on his part, it would take humility on hers. Each of them, he was sure, would need to have strengths the other lacked, for this was the foundation of a marriage.

Anna had, so far, shown the kind of strength many women lacked. Just coming here, braving it the way she had, with the boy she was responsible for, meant she had determination. A quality like that could be priceless here.

Karl rolled from his pallet, fully dressed, and knelt down on a single knee beside Anna. He had never before awakened a sleeping woman, except for his sisters and mother, and wondered if it were too intimate to touch her arm and shake her gently. Her arm lay relaxed over the buffalo robe, thin and long. He could see pale freckles upon the back of her hand. Despite the thin light, he saw more freckles dancing across the bridge of her nose, across her cheeks. Childishly she slept, unaware of how he studied her, and he thought it was somehow an unfair thing of him to do.

"Anna?" he whispered, and saw her eyelids move as if she were dreaming. "Anna?"

Her eyes flew open. In the instant she awoke they took on the look of startled wariness already so familiar to Karl. She stared at him for a moment, gathering her senses. He could tell by her expression the moment in which recollection stirred and she remembered where she was and who he was.

Because she looked so young and helpless and wary, he asked, "Did you know you have sandman in your eyes?"

She continued to stare at him as if surprised speechless. She blinked and felt the grit grinding against her eyelids, knowing it was there because she had been crying last night before going to sleep.

"It is time you get up and wash them out. Then I want to talk to you," Karl said.

The boy awoke at the sound of Karl's voice, so the man stood and spoke again. "Time to get up, boy. Let us leave your sister to get herself together." Then he stalked from the room.

"Anna?" James croaked, a little disoriented, too.

She rolled over to look at him. "You sound like a bullfrog this morning," she teased.

But he didn't smile. "Did he say what he decided?"

"No. He said he wants to talk to me. That's all. He's coming back as soon as he gives us time to get up."

"Hurry, then, let's get ready."

But although James scurried from the room, Anna lay for a moment, hesitant to leave the warm protection of the buffalo robes, wondering what Karl planned to do with her and James.

She thought of the curious words he'd used as he awakened her. They were gentle words, those used with a child. Perhaps he was usually a kind man whose temper had been tested in an extreme way yesterday by all her and James' revelations. Perhaps, given the chance, given time, Lindstrom would be less fierce and fault-finding, perhaps even gentle, as he'd been a moment ago. But when she thought of awakening in the same bed with him where he could note more than just the sandman in her eyes, Anna shivered.

She arose and tried to whisk the wrinkles out of her dress, rinsed her face and tied her hair back. A knock on the door told her Karl had returned, and she glanced up from where she knelt, gathering up the heavy buffalo robes.

He apparently had washed his face and combed his hair. He wore his little strange cap again. He came to stand beside her, gazing down at her wide, brown eyes that always wore that too open look whenever he came near.

"How did you sleep, Anna?"

"Fi . . ." But her voice croaked almost as James' had, and she cleared her throat before trying again. "Fine." Her hands lay idle on the furs, as if she'd forgotten what she was about.

His simple question was meant to put her at ease, but he could see she was tense and apprehensive. It broke his heart to think that she might be this way because of him. He knelt down on one knee upon the buffalo robe she'd been folding. "Anna, I did not sleep so well. I spent a long time thinking. Do you know what I learned while I thought?"

She shook her head no, saying nothing.

"I learned that I thought only of myself yesterday, and of what I wanted in a wife. Selfishly, I did not consider your opinion of me. All the time I think only of what Karl thinks of Anna, never what Anna thinks of Karl. But this is not right, Anna. Today, this must be a decision that both of us make, not just me."

She studied his golden arm braced across one upraised knee, knowing he studied her face while he spoke.

"We start out backward, Anna, yes? First we agree to marry, and it is only after this that we meet each other. And when I meet you, all I can do is get angry because you have lied to me, without considering why it was you lied. Father Pierrot made me see I must understand your side and realize you had to get out of Boston where things were bad for you and the boy." He studied the freckles on her cheeks and saw the pink glow beneath them, and could feel the thrum of his heart in strange places in his body. He wished she would raise her eyes. It was hard to read her feelings when she avoided looking at him.

Anna's heart skittered and leapt in her breast at his unexpected gentleness and selflessness. Considerateness of this sort was foreign to her. She wanted terribly to meet the blue depths of his eyes, but had she done so, she thought she might start crying. She could only stare at the strong, brown hand draped over a wide kneecap as he went on speaking.

"Anna, it is not too late for you to go back. It is not too late for either of us to change our minds. I thought that now you have met me, maybe . . . maybe you might not want to get married. Knowing how young you are and how you had to think of some way for you and the boy to live, I see you had to act quick, but maybe you think now you made a mistake, now that you see Karl Lindstrom. I think, Anna, that I must give you two choices. I must promise you first that if you want to go back, Father Pierrot and I will find a way to get you to Boston safely. Only if you are very sure this is not what you want, then I must give you the second choice to marry me."

The callus on his thumb grew wavery. Anna felt the tears form upon her lashes and quiver there, just short of dropping. "I told you, I have nobody to go back to, no place to go back to." Still she did not look up at him.

"Father and I will try to think of something else if this is what you want. Some place for you to go and live here in Minnesota."

"Your place sounded pretty good to me," she braved timorously.

Yes, she was afraid of him. He knew it now because of the tremble in her voice.

"You are sure, Anna?"

She nodded at the buffalo robes.

"In that case, a girl should have the right to say she has been given a proper proposal of marriage, and that she truly had a choice in the matter, *after* she has met the man, not *before*."

Now she did look up. Her eyes flew to his face, so close above hers. His intense eyes had never left hers, were only waiting for her to raise her glance to his. Those eyes were liquid blue, shining with sincerity. She wondered how many girls had gazed into them and found them as heartstopping as she did at this moment. The lashes were darker than the perfectly shaped eyebrows, which beckoned her fingers to trace their curve. That silly compulsion prompted her to close her fist about a handful of buffalo fur, to keep it from doing such an outrageous thing.

"*Onnuh* . . ." he began, and during the long hesitation before he continued, she wanted to say, yes, yes, I am *Onnuh* now, say it once more just like that. And as if he heard her thought, he did. "*Onnuh,* if I am not what you thought I would be, I will understand. But if you think that we could forget this poor start we had yesterday, I promise I will be good to you, *Onnuh.* I will take both you and the boy with me."

Slowly one big hand went up to slide the cap from his hair, the old-country courtesy tearing at her heartstrings. He reached to take her elbow in his free hand. The warmth of his flesh, the look of need she read in his eyes, the feathertouch upon her elbow, all combined to make Anna feel light-headed and dizzy.

"*Onnuh* Reardon, will you marry me?"

She felt like she had awakened in the midst of some fantastic dream, to find this handsome blond giant kneeling upon one knee to her, rubbing her inner elbow with his thumb, an expression of intense hope and promise upon his sun-bronzed face.

Anna's lips fell open, a quickly drawn breath told the secret mingling of emotions she was experiencing: relief, fear, and—yes—a new, beating exhilaration that made her breasts seem tight and brought a film of perspiration to the palms of her hands.

"Yes," she breathed at last.

Karl smiled, a relieved tilting of the corners of his lips. He glanced at her hair once, then gave her elbow a light squeeze of reassurance.

"Good. We will make this our beginning then, right here. And everything else is forgotten, right?"

"Yes," she agreed, wondering wildly if she should confess the rest to him here and now. Yet she was terrified lest he withdraw his proposal and the security it offered. She gave him a wavering smile.

"We will make a good start . . . just Karl and Anna . . ." Then, with a full wide smile, he added, "and James."

"Karl and Anna and James," she repeated, almost like a vow.

Karl stood before her then. As she looked up, she noticed for the first time what straight teeth he had. *Has he no flaws whatsoever?* she wondered. Anna became ever more aware of a feeling of inferiority as she compared herself to him.

"Come," he said nicely, "I will help you roll up these robes, then we will go tell Father Pierrot the decision is made and we are ready."

Outwardly, Father Pierrot beamed as he shook their hands with great enthusiasm, saying, "I have every confidence that you will build a good and lasting marriage."

Inwardly, he was troubled. Although he had led Karl to believe he'd received a special dispensation from the diocese to act as a witness while these two spoke their own vows, this was not altogether true. Bishop Cretin had sympathized with the couple's plight, but had adamantly refused, saying such dispensation must come from the Holy Father himself in Rome and could take one to two years to get. Father Pierrot found this attitude hard. After all, he was not asking to perform the Sacrament—this he knew would be entirely out of the question!

So Father Pierrot had faced the dilemma of which dictates to follow, those of Holy Mother the Church or those of his own heart. Surely, it was a more Christian act to witness the sealing of vows between two such well-meaning souls and sanctify the union than to send them away to live in sin. *This is the frontier,* argued Michael Pierrot, the man within the ordained priest. *This is the only church within a hundred miles, and these people have turned to it and to me with the best of intentions.*

Michael Pierrot's human side was swayed also by the fact that Karl Lindstrom was a good friend. Their relationship surmounted any differences of faith. Leading the way toward the humble sacristy, the priest thought of this marriage as wholly right, perhaps the most fitting he might ever perform.

"Come, Anna, I will hear your confession now without delay, for I know you are both anxious to be on your way."

Totally taken off guard, Anna came up short behind the black cassock. "My . . . my confession?" she blurted out, appalled.

"Yes, Anna, come," the priest said as he continued into the incense-scented vestry.

Anna's legs seemed to have turned to mush. She had instructed James to tell Karl that they were devout Catholics, knowing that the man wanted a wife of Christian bent. Never had Karl told her in his letters this mission was Catholic. If he had, she would obligingly have told him she was some other religion, to avoid having to prove Catholicism. As it was, she was now entangled in another lie.

"But can't I just . . . I mean . . . well, I don't want to go to confession."

"Anna," the priest chided, turning around, "forgive me for being direct, but last night Karl and I talked. He said you admitted telling him lies. These are sins, my child. You must confess them, so you will be in a state of grace before entering the state of marriage. Surely you know this."

Of course she didn't know this. All she knew about the Catholic church was that it was warm inside St. Mark's, and they refused no one entry there.

"But . . . but I've told Karl I'm sorry and I've promised I won't lie any more. Isn't that enough?"

"It is not enough for a Catholic. You know that confession is necessary, Anna, to cleanse the soul." The priest truly didn't understand her reluctance.

She fidgeted and shifted from foot to foot, refusing to look at him while Karl, too, wondered at Anna's hesitation. With growing trepidation, Anna realized the only confession she would be making here today was the truth. She bit the inside of her lip, clasped her hands tightly behind her back, then, big-eyed and brave, admitted, "I'm not a Catholic."

Karl couldn't believe his ears. He took her by the elbow—it seemed to Anna that her elbow was certainly being over-worked lately—and forced her to look up into his face. "But Anna, you told me you were Catholic. Why did you tell me this?"

"Because you said in your advertisement that you wanted a God-fearing woman."

"Another lie, Anna?" Karl asked, dismayed anew.

"That's not a lie, that's the truth. You said you wanted the truth, so I gave it to you this time. But what does it matter anyway, as long as we're going to be saying our vows ourselves?"

Caught now himself by the half-truth he had let Karl believe, Father Pierrot suffered pangs of remorse. What was he to do? If he witnessed the union, he would be liable for excommunication should his bishop ever learn of it. At this point the priest was wishing that Long Prairie boasted just one justice of the peace, so he could send these two to get themselves legally married without all this confusion.

But the staunch Irish girl looked her betrothed in the eye and kept a stiff upper lip. "Well, if it's still all right with you, Karl, it's all right with me."

This was all too much for Karl. He had spent most of the night carefully reflecting in order to decide it was the right thing to marry Anna. Now another of his delusions about her lay shattered. He was acutely embarrassed to have this newest lie come to light in front of Father Pierrot. Karl found he could not abase himself further by standing there and arguing. And the day was moving on. So much time had been wasted already on this trip, it was folly wasting more, and there were no other churches nearby. But a godless woman! thought the beleaguered Swede. What have I gotten into?

"It does not matter," Karl said tightly, and everyone in the room could see it mattered a great deal. "We will be married as we agreed." He turned to his friend in the black robes.

Father Pierrot hadn't the heart to say, no, Karl, I cannot witness this marriage after all, nor record it in my books. The strength of the vow rests within the heart, he thought, not in witnesses nor penned words. If these two were ready to accept each other, he would not stand in their way.

Anna felt a flood of relief wash over her as the ceremony was agreed upon. Her knees were weak. Her tongue stuck to the roof of her mouth. She squeezed her eyes shut and silently promised the man beside her that she'd make it up to him, one way or another.

But Karl's heart was heavy as he stepped to the altar. He had, in his own halting way, achieved his amnesty with her this morning. Peace should be the feeling in a man's heart as he spoke his vows, not this resentment that now lay coldly inside. It is difficult enough to promise love, Karl thought, when the one you promise it to is a stranger. To promise it with such a feeling of foreboding is less than good.

Father had donned his surplice, alb and stole, and the time was at hand.

"James will be our witness," Anna said, wishing to please Karl in some small way. Karl, she could see, was very dissatisfied with her. He avoided her glance, and studied the distance as if ruminating the deepest of thoughts. Also, when he'd last spoken, his voice had become devoid of its usual musicality. It told her in no uncertain terms that he was displeased.

The pair stood so stiff and erect that Father Pierrot felt certain things must be said. He could sense the animosity, which had sprung up so quickly. Karl's mouth was pursed and Anna stared at the little bouquet of lemon lilies and wild roses at the feet of St. Francis of Assisi.

"Anna," he began, "I speak to you first, and I speak with the hope that you will take to heart everything I say. You are young, Anna. You are taking on a grave responsibility when you marry Karl here. The two of you have a long life ahead of you, and it can be a good life if you work to make it so. But goodness must be built upon mutual respect, and this respect must stem from trust. Trust, in return, must spring from truthfulness. I believe you have done what you thought necessary to get here to Karl. But henceforth I caution you to be truthful with him in all ways. You will find him to be understanding and patient. This much I know of him. But you will find, too, that he is rigid in his honor. I caution you once more always to tell him the truth. When you make your vow here to love, honor and obey, I ask you to add in your heart that you, Anna, will always be truthful with Karl."

She looked up at him with her girlish face and said guilelessly, "Yes, Father, I was." Father Pierrot could not help the tiny curve of his lips at her reply. He noted, too, the way Karl glanced briefly sideways.

"Good. So be it. And Karl, there are things not expressed in the vows, about which I must caution you. It falls onto your shoulders to protect Anna and provide for her. In your case, here in the wilderness, and with the added responsibility for James, this job is a far greater one than for most men." Karl glanced at the boy, and the priest saw a perceptible softening of Karl's expression. "The wilderness is new to them, and there will be much they have to learn. Patience will be required of you time and again. But you have the gift of knowledge to give them. You must be teacher as well as protector, father as well as husband, almost from the start. If at times this task falls heavy upon you, I ask you to remember that on your wedding day you silently added the vow of patience."

"Yes, Father."

"And while it is not written in the vows either, there is an old adage I firmly believe in, which I would repeat here and ask you both to remember on days when perhaps you have not seen eye to eye. 'Never let the sun set on your anger.' There will be disagreements between you, and these cannot be avoided—you are human beings with much to learn about each other. But differences incurred during the day become lodged in stubbornness if held throughout the night. By remembering this, you will perhaps not cling to your opinions when it is long past the time you should have conceded or compromised. Will the two of you remember this?''

''Yes, Father,'' they said in unison.

''So be it. Then let us begin.''

Father Pierrot began praying.

The soft tonal inflections of Latin brought back to Anna the memories of nights she and James had sheltered in St. Marks's. Nights when all the rooms above the tavern were busy and they were told to get out and not show their faces till the last customer had staggered home. Anna tried to push the hurtful memory aside, but the priest's flowing Latin brought back the anguish all over again, the anguish of huddling in the scented dusk—beeswax, incense, candlelights—vowing that she would find a way out of a life where, since her mother's death, nobody cared whether Barbara's brats lived or died.

They'd hung on, she and James, by the skin of their teeth, but all the while Anna was determined to get them away from the hopeless situation somehow. Well, she was doing it now. She and James would never go homeless again. Never would they be chased away by the ''ladies'' and their ''gentlemen'' customers. But knowing what she'd done to get here, knowing that she was duping a man who truly didn't deserve it, an engulfing guilt washed over her.

She felt her hand taken into the large hand of Karl Lindstrom, felt the calluses of labor there, and felt the firm grip that told of his intensity, and she knew beyond a doubt that this big, honorable man would never, never understand a thing like she'd done. His palm was warm and dry and as hard as oak. The way he squeezed her knuckles she thought they might shatter in a moment, but his grip told her he meant all he promised here today. She found herself looking up into blue eyes, then watching sensitive lips speaking the words from the book Father Pierrot held open upon his palms. Karl's voice came lilting, and she watched his mouth, memorizing the words as best she could.

And the long months of hoping, dreaming and planning for this day would become part of the fabric that wove Karl to Anna in the words he spoke aloud. Nor would the thoughts, which had so long lived in Karl Lindstrom, now be denied their part in all he promised.

''I, Karl, take thee, Anna . . .'' *My little whiskey-haired Anna . . .*

''for my lawful wedded wife . . .'' *How I have waited for you . . .*

''to have and to hold . . .'' *Not yet have I even held you, Anna . . .*

''from this day forward . . .'' *Forward to this night, and tomorrow and tomorrow . . .*

''For better, for worse . . .'' *In spite of everything, I know I could do far worse . . .*

''for richer, for poorer . . .'' *Ah, how rich we can be, Anna, rich with life . . .*

"in sickness and in health . . ." *And I will see this thin hand grow strong . . .*

"till death do us part." *These things I promise with my life—these things and the promise of patience, as Father, my friend, said.*

As Anna's eyes roved over Karl's face, a shaft of golden sun came through the open door, gilding his features as if nature itself bestowed the blessing Father Pierrot could not. In the tiny outpost mission of Long Prairie only wildflowers adorned the altar. Only the cooing of mourning doves provided song. But to Anna's ears and eyes it was as fine as any cathedral hosting a hundred-voice choir. She could feel the beats of their hearts joined where her slight, pale hand rested in his wide, dark one. As she took her turn at vows, Anna felt a willingness she had certainly not expected when she'd thought of this moment through the dreary winter, waiting to come to an unknown husband.

"I, Anna, take thee, Karl . . ." *Forgive me, Karl, for tricking you . . .*

"for my lawful wedded husband . . ." *But James and I didn't know what else to do . . .*

"from this day forward . . ." *Never again will we be homeless . . .*

"for better, for worse . . ." *I promise I will never, never tell another lie . . .*

"for richer, for poorer . . ." *Riches we do not need. A home will be enough . . .*

"in sickness and in health . . ." *I'll learn all I said I knew . . .*

"till death do us part." *I'll make up for everything, Karl, somehow I promise I'll make up for everything.*

She saw Karl swallow and detected a tremble in his eyelids.

Then, still squeezing her hand, he looked at Father Pierrot. "There is no gold ring, Father. I could not afford gold, and there was nothing else at Morisette's store. But I have simple ring because it doesn't seem right without a ring."

"A simple ring is fine, Karl."

From his pocket he extracted a horseshoe nail curled into a circle. It was on his lips to say, I'm sorry, Anna, but she was smiling down at the ring as if it were burnished gold.

Anna saw Karl's hands shake, and her own, as she extended her fingers and he slid the heavy iron circlet over her knuckle. He had misjudged in bending it, and she had to curl her fingers quickly to keep it from slipping off. Then Karl's hand recaptured hers again. Gently, he spread her fingers and lay the banded hand upon his open palm, the fingers of his other hand lightly touching the ring as if to seal it upon her flesh for life.

"Anna Reardon, with this ring I make you my wife forever." His voice cracked faintly upon the last word, bringing her eyes up to his once more.

Then she put her free hand over his and the ring, and said into his eyes, "Karl Lindstrom, with this ring I accept you for my husband . . . forever."

He looked down at her turned-up freckled nose, her pretty, waiting lips. His heart became a wild thing within him. Now she is really my Anna, he thought, suddenly timid and eager all at once.

Fleetingly, Anna's eyelids quivered, and she felt his hold upon her hands tighten a fraction of a second before he bent to kiss her lightly, forgetting to close his eyes as he brushed her lips uncertainly, then straightened again.

"So be it," Father Pierrot said softly, while bride and groom nervously cast about for something upon which to settle their gazes. Anna's turned to her brother, and the two hugged quickly.

"Oh, Anna, Anna . . ." he said.

She whispered in his ear, "We'll be safe now, James."

He squeezed her extra hard. "I'll do my part." But he looked at Karl as he said it, though it was Anna's hand he still held.

"I know," Anna said, now looking at Karl.

Father Pierrot surprised her by warmly embracing her, then planting a congratulatory kiss on her cheek. "I wish you health, happiness and the blessing of many children." Then, turning to Karl with a firm handshake of four hands instead of two, the priest said emotionally, "And the same to you, my friend."

"Thank you, Father. It seems that I already have one of those things." Karl looked meaningfully at James, who smiled broadly.

"Yes," Father Pierrot said, shaking James' hand in a manful way. "Now, young man, it will be your job to see that these two do as I have ordered. There may be times it will be the hardest job of all."

"Yes, sir!" James replied, and everyone laughed.

"So be it, and so it is done. Now all that remains is for you two to put your signatures on the document, to be witnessed by James here and myself. Then you may be on your way. You have a long ride ahead."

Karl turned, placing Anna's hand in the crook of his elbow, then reached to include James, who stood uncertainly. "We have a long ride ahead, eh, James?"

"Yes, sir!" the boy beamed.

"But we go together, you and Anna and I."

While Father led them once again to his tiny rooms at the rear of the school building, Anna moved beside Karl, her hand on his solid arm, worried sick once again. Father produced ink and quill, then dipped the tip and handed it to her, indicating the parchment on the desk.

"You may sign first, Anna."

But Karl was right there, smiling broadly, watching her. She didn't know how to write her name!

"Let Karl sign first," she said ingeniously.

"Very well." Agreeably, Karl carefully placed his name on the paper.

She stood behind him, eyeing the back of his neck while he formed the letters. She glanced at James, who shrugged covertly in reply. Anna exchanged places with Karl and made a grand X on the paper while he looked over her shoulder.

And so quickly was the next deception exposed.

He saw her make the mark, and was naturally surprised, knowing she was a lettered woman. But she smiled brightly into his face in an effort to disarm him.

But Karl was not disarmed. And so, he thought, I learn one more truth about Anna. But he did not let Father Pierrot know what little drama was being acted out here. Instead, he took Anna's arm stiffly, steered her toward the door and led her out.

"Wait here. I must get the wagon," was all he said. Then he stalked off, leaving her with James.

"Anna, I didn't know what to do," her brother sympathized. "I couldn't sign that one for you. I told you we shoulda told him."

"It's all right. At least now he knows."

"But why didn't he say anything? Maybe he's not too mad about it."

"Oh, he's mad all right. He nearly cracked my elbow leading me out of there, but I promised never to lie to him again and I'm never going to. But I didn't promise to tell him every lick of truth about myself all at once. I'm not sure he could take it all in one gulp."

"I'll rest easier when he knows it all," James said.

Anna looked at him sharply, wondering again if he suspected anything about how she'd earned money for his passage and his clothes. But just then Father Pierrot came out with a bundle of food for their journey, and Karl appeared with the wagon. It was time for fond farewells, handshakes and the ride into their uncertain, married future.

Chapter 4

They had not traveled a mile up the road before Karl pursued the subject which could not be avoided. But he drove his team, and when he drove his team he was not one to raise his voice, so he spoke now with stilted patience, glowering at the reins that stretched ahead of him through the checkrings.

"I think you have more to tell me, Anna. Do you want to tell me now?"

She peeked sideways. Sure enough—that jaw bulged out like a rock. "You know already, so why make me tell you?" she asked her lap.

"It is true then? The letters were not written by you?"

With a shake of the head she answered no.

"And you do not know how to read or write?"

Again she shook her head negatively.

"Who wrote the letters?" he asked, recalling all the times he had touched them, lingered over them, thinking of his Anna's hands having touched them first.

"James."

"James?" Karl looked across Anna to the boy who stared straight ahead. "You set the boy to writing deliberate lies because you could not write them yourself?"

"I didn't *set* him to writing them."

"Well, what would you call it, teaching a young boy like him such lessons?"

"We agreed, that's all. We had to get out of Boston and find a way to live. James was the one who found your advertisement in the paper and read it to me. We decided together to try to get you to marry me."

"You decided together to get Karl Lindstrom to marry a twenty-five-year-old woman, a good Catholic girl who could read and write and teach our children to read and write, who could cook and make soap and garden.''

The two guilty parties sat silent.

"And who will do that, Anna? Who will teach our children to read and write? Am I supposed to take the time to come in from the fields and teach them?"

His casual reference to *their children* brought roses to Anna's cheeks, still she answered, hopefully, "James can teach them."

"James, you said, is to be my helper in the woods and in the fields. How can James be in two places at once?"

She had no answer.

"How is it that James learned to read and write, but you did not?" he asked.

"Sometimes, when our mother got a fit of conscience, she'd make him go to school, but she didn't see any girl needing to know her letters, so she left me alone."

"What kind of mother would only send a boy to school now and then, when she had a fit of conscience? Conscience over what?"

This time James saved Anna from lying or revealing the full truth. He burst in. "We didn't have much, even before Barbara got sick and died. We lived with . . . with friends of hers most of the time, and I had to go out and try to find work to help. I guess she thought I was kind of young to be out working, and sometimes she'd get . . . well, sorry, kind of. That's when I'd have to go to school. I managed to go enough to learn to read and write a little."

Puzzled, Karl asked, "Barbara? Who is Barbara?"

"That was our ma's name."

"You called your mother *Barbara*?" Karl could not conceive of a child calling his mother by her given name. What kind of mother would allow such a thing? But since neither of them answered, Karl pressed on. "You told me there was no work for you in Boston and that is why you needed to get away."

"Well, there wasn't. I mean . . . well—"

"Well, what, boy?" Karl demanded. "Which is the truth? Did you work or not?"

James took a gulp of air and braved it, in a strange falsetto. "Mostly I picked pockets."

Karl was stunned again. He looked at the fledgling's profile, trying to imagine a boy that young doing such a dishonest thing. Then he glanced at Anna, who sat sullenly staring at the narrow road ahead.

"Did your mother know this?" he asked, watching Anna's face carefully for signs of lies. But there was no sign, just a resigned sadness that expressed age far older than her actual years.

"She knew," Anna said. "She wasn't really much of a mother."

Something in her tone of voice melted Karl. The resigned way she said it made him suddenly sorry for both of them, having such a mother. Karl thought of his own mother, of the warm and loving family she had raised, teaching the value of honesty and of all the old beatitudes. Father Pierrot had been right to admonish him that he must be prepared to be their teacher. It seemed he would have to make up to both Anna and the boy all the teachings that this lax mother of theirs had not bothered to instill in them. Now more than ever Anna seemed but a child to him, a wayward child much like her brother.

"Here in the wilderness you will not find many pockets to pick," Karl said. "Here, instead, there is much honest work to keep a boy's hands busy from sunup to sundown. It is a good place to forget that you ever learned how to pick pockets."

Brother and sister both turned and looked at Karl at the same time, then with growing smiles, at each other, realizing they'd once again been forgiven. Anna ventured a brief study of Karl's profile, the nose so straight and Nordic, his burnished cheek, his bleached hair curling like a sun-washed wave over his shell-like ear, his lips that had brushed her own such a short time ago. Oh, he was magnificent in every way, it seemed. And she wondered how a person came to be so good. What manner of man is this, she asked herself, who faces each new hurdle and moves past it with such forbearance?

He turned a ghost of a glance down at her. In that moment she could have sworn she saw a smile aborning upon his lips. Then he scanned the woods on his far side.

Some weight seemed to turn to warm, summer-scented air and drift away from Anna's shoulders like a dandelion seed in the wind. She clasped each knee, and smiled at the rutted road. For the first time, she looked around, fully aware of the surrounding beauties.

They were passing through a place of green magnificence. The forest was built of verdant walls, broken here and there by peaceful embrasures where prairie grasses fought for a stronghold. Trees of giant proportions canopied above saplings vying for the sky. The sky was embroidered with stitches of leafy design. Anna leaned her head way back to gaze at the dappled emerald roof above.

Karl eyed her arched throat, smiling at her childish but pleasing pose. "So what do you think of my Minnesota?"

"I think you were right. It's much better than the plains."

"Far better," Karl seconded, pleased by her answer. Suddenly, he felt expansive and glib.

"There is wood here for every purpose a man could name. Maples! Why, we have maples aplenty, and they are filled with nectar such as you will find no place else." He pointed, stretching a long arm in front of Anna's nose. "See? That is the white maple, a hundred feet of wood and twelve gallons of sap every year. And such grains it has—fiddleback, burl, birds-eye, leaf . . ." He chuckled deep in his throat. "When you cut into a maple it is always full of surprises. And hard . . . why, it can be polished to shine like still water."

Anna had never thought about trees as anything but trees before. She was amused at his rapport with them. They drove a little farther before he pointed again.

"See that one there? Yellow locust. Splits as smooth and true as the flight of an apple falling from a tree. And that chestnut there? Another smooth splitter, to make boards as flat as milk on a plate."

They passed through a little patch of sun just then. Anna shaded her eyes and peered up at Karl. He looked down at her piquantly cocked head, the squint, the crinkled-up nose, the cute smile. He found it all thoroughly delightful, and was pleased she didn't seem to find this subject too profound nor too boring.

Anna searched all around, with a sudden intuition of how to please him. She discovered a new variety, pointed and asked, "What's that one?"

Karl followed her finger. "That's a beech tree."

"And what's it good for?" she asked, following it with her eyes as they came abreast of it.

"Beech? The beech you whittle. It takes to the carving knife like no other wood I know. And when it is rubbed smooth, no wood is prettier."

"You mean you can't carve just any old wood?" James interjected.

"You can try, but some will disappoint you. You see, some people don't understand about trees. They think wood is wood, and they ask of some trees things they cannot do. You must ask a tree to do what it does best, then it will never disappoint you. And so I split the locust, carve the beech and make boards from pine and chestnut. It is the same with people. I would not ask a blacksmith to bake me a pie, would I? Or a baker to shoe my horse." Karl tipped a little grin their way. "If I did, I would perhaps have to eat my horseshoe and tack the pie to my horse's hoof."

James and Anna laughed gaily, making Karl feel truly clever and more optimistic than ever before about this family of his.

"Tell us more," James said. "I like hearing about the trees."

Anna looked up, studying Karl's jaw while he constantly played his eyes back and forth as they jogged up the road. She thought that she had never seen a person so alert while looking as if he weren't.

"Soon we will come to the oaks," he continued. "Oaks like to grow in groves. The white oak makes shingles that will keep a roof tight for fifty years. You must think of that—fifty years! It is a long time, fifty years. Longer than the life of my *morfar* who—"

"Your *what*?" Anna interrupted, crunching up her face.

"My *morfar,* my mother's father. He taught me much about trees, as he did my *far* . . . my father, too. My *morfar* gave me my first lessons in riving."

Anna digested the idea of being taught to love the land and its fruits by a grandfather. "But your . . . your *morfar*?" It sounded ridiculously English to Anna, but Karl nodded approvingly at her attempt. "He is dead now?"

"Yes, he died years ago, but not before he teaches me much of what he has learned about the woods. My *morfar,* she is still alive in Sweden though."

A wistful note had crept into Karl's voice. Anna wanted more than anything to lay her hand comfortingly upon his forearm. He seemed lost in thought, then momentarily glanced over his shoulder, as if sorry he'd burdened them with his memories or his lonesomeness.

It's all right—Anna smiled the tacit message, then urged, "Go on . . . I interrupted. You were talking about the oaks."

"Ya, the oaks . . . ." Again he looked glad, and Anna liked him better that way. "Do you know that when you rive shingles from oak, there are natural and beautiful grains which catch the rain and send it running in channels as true as the course of a river over a falls? It's true. But when I need fence rails I use red oak. Once I made an axe handle of white oak, but it was not good. Too hard. Hickory is best for axe handles, but this I do not have here. But ash does almost as well. It is light and strong and springy."

"Springy?" James asked, mystified at the idea of wood being springy.

"It must be, to absorb the shock from the hands when it strikes the tree trunk."

"What other kinds of trees do you have?"

"Not too many dogwood here, but one here and there. With dogwood I make gluts and mauls. Willows I split into withes. Elder is for shade and beauty." Karl smiled. "We must not forget that some trees are given to us for nothing more than shade and beauty, and if this is all we ask of them, they are happy."

James smiled crookedly. "Aw, Karl, trees can't be happy." He leaned his elbows on his lap and peered around Anna at the blond man, who only grinned as if he knew something special. "Boy, Karl, you sure know a lot about them though," James said, sitting up again and looking around in a wide arc, wondering how a man could ever learn as much as Karl knew. And Karl was only twenty-five!

"Like I said, I learn from my *morfar* and my *far* in Sweden, which is much like Minnesota. That is why I came here instead of Ohio. Also, I learn from my older brothers. We have all worked with wood since we are much younger than you are now. I think we get a late start teaching you, eh, boy? You will have to learn twice as fast as Karl did."

But James detected a teasing lilt in Karl's voice, which made him all the more eager. "So tell me more about the trees," he demanded almost giddily, getting caught up in the magic of learning, already catching the contagious love that flowed from Karl to the woods.

"Here are the pines, the best friend the axeman has."

"Why?"

"Because they save him trouble. Most trees have sapwood and heartwood that must be cut away before he can make boards. But the pine has only bark to strip off, then there lays the wood, ready to make a batch of fine boards. Have you heard of the brake and froe, boy?"

"No, sir," James replied, eyeing the lofty pines, which swayed with fairy-wing tips into the blue firmament above.

"I will teach you about them. They are the tools of shingle-making."

"When?"

Karl laughed a little at the boy's impatience. "In time. First comes the axe, and when you have mastered that you will be able to carve your way to survival in any forest. A man worth his salt can survive with no other tool but his axe in the deepest wilderness nature ever made."

"I never used one."

"Can you shoot a rifle, boy?" Karl asked, with a sudden change of subject.

"No, sir."

"Do you think you could if you had to?"

"I don't know."

Something made Anna look sharply at Karl now. The tone of his voice had not changed, but something told her that the last question was not as casual as the others had been. Sure enough—Karl's eyes shifted watchfully from side to side.

"What is it?" Anna asked, a tingle fingering its way up her spine.

"Boy, climb into the back," Karl said calmly but intensely. "There is a rifle there. Get it, but be careful. It is loaded."

"Is something wrong?" James asked.

"Your first lesson in this woods is that when I tell you to get a rifle, you move as if your life depended on it, because most often it does." James scrambled to the rear of the wagon without further ado, even though the words had not been harsh or critical. They were spoken with a quiet evenness while Karl cautiously continued to scan the woods. "Now come back up here, but point that rifle well away from our heads while you are climbing."

James did as he was told, quickly this time.

"What is it?" Anna insisted, growing nervous now.

"That smell," Karl answered. "Do you smell it? It is the scent of cat."

She sniffed repeatedly, tasting only the pleasant aroma of the pines. "I don't smell anything but pines," she said.

"At first it was the pines only, but now there is the smell of cat, too. There are cougars in these woods. They are wily, and leave their scent where the pines can disguise it. So we must be wilier and be ready if one of them stalks us. Keep your eyes on the trees ahead. When we break into the oak grove, we must be most cautious. The branches are high, and the cougar can perch there in wait to pounce on anything that moves below."

He spoke as calmly as he had when discussing the attributes of the trees that grew here. Even so, ripples of fear threaded through Anna's blood. She realized suddenly how totally dependent she and James were upon this man's knowledge of the woods.

"The gun will kick if you must shoot it, so remember to pull the stock up tight against your shoulder before you pull the trigger or you will end up with bruised bones. It is a good rifle. It is a Sharps breechloader—the best, made right here in America—Windsor, Vermont. It will not fail you, but you must learn to use it properly. Once the lever is raised, you have sheared off the end of the cloth cartridge, leaving the powder exposed. She's got no flint, boy. She doesn't need it with that percussion cap, so you are holding a live thing in your hands right now. When you are holding it, that means you are respecting it. Now lift it to your shoulder and sight along the barrel. Get used to the feel of it there, and do not be afraid to fire it if you must."

The gun was sleek, simple, only the thumbnotch of the hammer breaking its long, smooth line as James lifted it to his shoulder. Anna heard his breath coming in short jerks, and sensed both excitement and fear emanating from him. She wished Karl would take the gun himself, but no sooner had the thought appeared than he said, "If you must fire the gun, be ready to hold tight, because at the report, the horses will panic. I can control them, but it is best if I keep the reins. Are you all right, boy?"

"Y . . . yessir."

The horses nickered and Karl soothed them, "Shoo-ey, Belle. Shoo-ey, Bill. Easy does it." There was a jingle of harness, as if the horses understood and nodded their agreement. Again Karl cooed, "Eeeasy." Then he spoke to James. "Ease up on that gun, boy. You are wound up as tight as a three-day clock. When you do not know what is out there and you do not know how long you must wait to find out, you can get so tense that nothing works when you want it to. Relax a little and let your eyes do the guarding as much as the gun."

"But . . . but I never saw a cougar before," James said, swallowing.

"We do not know if it is cougar. Could be lynx. If it is cougar it will be golden brown, like a nicely turned pancake, with a long graceful tail. If it is lynx he will be buff gray, spotted and harder to see up there in the dark green leaves. Sometimes we see bobcat here, too, with just a stub of a tail and reddish brown. He is much smaller than the cougar, but is harder to spy.''

There was a sudden popping sound. Anna jumped!

''It is only acorns popping beneath the wheels,'' Karl explained. ''We are in the oaks now. You can see what I meant about the high branches.'' James noticed the way Karl scanned left, then right, then above, studying the woods constantly. Karl sat upright, his entire body taut with caution. ''Lots of oak woods here in Minnesota, and plenty of acorns for the pigs to eat. They grow fat and good on acorns. The trouble is pigs are too stupid to stay at home, and sometimes they wander off into the woods and get lost. Then we must go in search of them.''

''Why don't you fence them in?'' James asked.

Anna thought the two of them had gone crazy, talking of pigs and acorns at a time like this.

''In Minnesota we build fences to keep the animals out, not in. The woods are so rich with foods for livestock, we let them wander wherever they will. It is our own vegetable garden that must be fenced in, so the greedy pigs will not eat up our winter supply of food. I have seen pigs root up an entire turnip patch in short time, and eat the whole thing. Oh, pigs love turnips! If a family loses its turnip crop, it could mean much hunger during the winter.'' There was a subtle relaxing of Karl's posture. Both James and Anna sensed it before the man said, ''It is all right now. You can rest easy.''

''How do you know?'' inquired James.

''By the squirrels. See the squirrels?''

Anna looked but didn't see any squirrels. ''Where?'' she asked, squinting.

''There.'' Following Karl's brown finger, she at last saw a bushy tail lithely leaping through the oaks. ''The squirrels hide in their nests when cats are near. When you see the squirrels busy scampering free through the oaks, the threat is gone. Still, you will hold that gun for a while yet, but rest it on your lap now, boy. You did fine.''

A thrill of pride such as he'd never before felt filled James' chest. The exhilaration caused by the danger was something new to him, too. It was totally different from anything he had experienced in his life. To hold the gun like a man, to be trusted enough by Karl to do this, to feel that if danger approached he would have been their defender—all this created a blossoming sense of maturity in the boy.

''And so you have learned your first lesson about the woods,'' Karl noted.

''Yessir,'' James replied, his cheeks puffed out.

''So, tell me what it is you have learned.''

''To be careful in the pines because the cats use them to cover their scent. That the oaks are pretty good places for cougars to perch. To watch the squirrels and keep the gun ready till they show up again. And . . .'' James had saved the best for last, ''that a lot of loud talking helps keep a prowling cat at bay.''

Anna was amazed! Without it being said in so many words, James had learned such a lesson only from Karl's example. She had never before realized her brother was so quick-witted.

As if he read her mind, Karl praised, "You are quick with your wits, boy. Do you think your sister is as quick?" He glanced at Anna momentarily.

She cocked her head quite saucily his way, then aside to find more squirrels while she said, "She's quick enough to learn she'll probably have the insufferable job of chasing pigs through the woods when they need rounding up, and she'll be eating lots of turnips, which she despises."

For the first time Karl laughed without holding back. It was a sonorous, baritone sound that pleased and surprised Anna, and made James laugh, too. There had been so much strain between Karl and Anna, it was a relief to hear this first billowing laughter.

"In that case," Karl said, "we had better check the wild hops, so while James and I are eating turnips, his sister can eat bread, eh, James?"

"Yessir!" James agreed eagerly, then made them all laugh again by adding, "What for?"

Karl explained that hops were necessary for making yeast. Each summer he came to this spot to pick enough hops to last the entire year. "I think these are the longest hops in the world. I also think they will not be ready—it is early yet—but we will check them just the same, as long as we are passing. It will tell me when to come back for the picking."

Karl pulled to a stop at a point in the road that looked no different from any other.

"How do you know where to stop?" Anna asked.

Again he pointed. "By the notch," he answered. "I know enough to start looking for it just beyond the oaks."

A wide, white gash showed on a tree trunk, telling Karl the whereabouts of the hops, which could not be seen from the road. He led them into the brush, the gun cradled in the crook of his arm. He took them into fragrant shade, holding back branches now and then, turning to watch Anna dip her way through the thick press of elderwood, with its pink flowers that would turn to black berries come fall. She bent and led with her elbow, sidetracked a branch and looked up unexpectedly into blue eyes that were waiting for her to pass.

"Be careful," he said.

Quickly she looked away, wondering when was the last time anyone admonished her with the simple phrase that meant so much more than it said. "What are these?" she asked, distracted by her thought.

"Elderbrush."

"And what is elderbrush good for?"

"Not much," he answered, walking along behind her. 'In the autumn it berries, but the fruit is much too bitter to eat. Why should we eat bitter berries when there are plenty sweet ones to be had?"

"Like what?"

"Many," he answered. "Strawberry, raspberry, blackberry, gooseberry, pincherry, grapes, blueberry. Blueberry is my favorite. I have never seen a land with so much wild fruit. The blueberries grow to the size of plums here. Oh, there are wild plums, too."

They arrived at the place of the hops then, twining vines that clung to the elderbrush and cascaded from it in grape-shaped leaves. Although they were not coning yet, Karl seemed pleased. "There will be plenty of hops again this summer. Perhaps my Anna will not have to eat turnips after all."

For so long he had thought of her as "my Anna" that the term had slipped out without warning.

Anna flashed him a quick look of surprise, but she felt the heat creep up her cheeks.

Karl quickly concerned himself with the hops again. He picked a large, perfectly formed leaf, saying, "Here, study it well. If ever you find another like it, mark the spot well. It would save time if we did not have to come this far for the hops. Maybe you will find some nearer to our place."

Our place, she thought. She peeked up to find a band of deeper color rising from his open, white collar. She stared at the hollow of his throat. Suddenly, his Adam's apple jumped convulsively. He was playing with the leaf, staring at it, twirling it by its stem as if he had forgotten he'd picked it. She reached out a palm, and Karl twitched as if waking up. Guiltily, he laid it on her hand. Her eyes lingered on his for a moment longer, then she dropped them again and smoothed the leaf.

He was beguiled by her freckled nose. Standing there studying his Anna while shadows dappled her brow, he pictured his sod house and the sheaf of sweet clover lying on the bed in welcome. His chest tightened like new rawhide. Why did I dream up such an idea, he wondered miserably. At the time it seemed gracious, but now it just seems foolish and misleading.

"I think we had better go," he said softly, glancing briefly at James who was exploring big beige mushrooms. Karl suddenly wished that the boy were not here at all so he could touch Anna's cheek.

She glanced up then. Her heart started thumping and she immediately took up leaf studying again.

Karl cleared his throat and called to James, "You pick a leaf, too, boy. It will be your second lesson." Then he turned and led the way from the woods, while thoughts of freckles on Anna's perky little nose dotted his mind.

Chapter 5

❧

It was near day's end before they finally swerved off the main road and turned into a trace where the trees formed a closer tunnel overhead. Here there was room for only one wagon to scrape through the infringing forest. The underbrush pressed so close that the horses sometimes snuffled when the weeds touched their noses. The horses made the harness sing again, throwing their great heads in exaggerated nods of recognition. "Ya, you are impatient. You know we are nearly home, but I cannot let you run away with us. Slow down."

Neither Anna nor James had ever heard a person speak to beasts as if they were human. Unbelievably, Bill angled a blinker at the sound of his name. "The lane is as narrow as it was yesterday," Karl said, "so slow down, Bill."

In a way much like the horses, James and Anna raised their heads, sensing home, wondering what it would be like. Karl had announced this was his land, and already every leaf, limb and loam took on greater importance to her. It even seemed to smell more pungent, of things burgeoning, ripening while others decayed, adding their own secret scent of nature's continuing cycle.

This is my road, thought Anna—my trees, my wildflowers, the place where my life will be joyous or sad. Come winter, the snows will seal me in with this man who speaks to horses and trees. Her eyes tracked over everything as fast as they could take it all in. The space broadened and before them lay the home of Karl and Anna Lindstrom, this place of plenty about which the bride had heard so much.

There was a wide clearing, with a vegetable garden planted within a split rail fence. Anna smiled to see how sturdily the fence was built so their pigs would not root up Karl's turnips. Turnips! she thought . . . yukk!

The house lay off to the left, a nearly rectangular dwelling made of large cubes of sod, pasted with mortar of white clay and buffalo grass. A stone chimney ran up its side, and it had a roof of split logs, covered with blocks of sod. It had two small windows and a plank door against which a large length of wood was wedged. Anna's heart sank as she looked at this place where Karl had already lived for two years. It was so tiny! And so . . . so crude! But she could see his eyes scan it to make sure all was as he'd left it, the look rife with the pride of ownership. She must be careful not to hurt his feelings.

Beside the sod house stood the most enormous woodpile Anna had ever seen, its rank and file as straight as if a land surveyor had shot it with his transit. She marveled that the hands of her husband had chopped all that wood and piled it so precisely. There were smaller buildings, too. One looked to be a smokehouse, for it had a clay chimney sticking out of its center. The enclosure for the horses was made of vertical split wood, its roof of bark secured with willow withes. Anna experienced a queer thrill of pride because already she knew that withes were cut of willow. But, looking around, she knew suddenly how much—how very, very much— she would have to learn to survive here and be any help to Karl.

The clearing extended to the east to include tilled patches where new corn, wheat and barley sprang up. Directly opposite where the road entered, a broad avenue had been cleared of trees, and upon it lay a double track of logs with their bark removed, running up a gentle slope like a wooden railroad track, disappearing into the trees around a wide curve in the distance.

Never did Karl Lindstrom leave this place without returning to it filled with wonder and pride. His sod house hovered in welcome, the vegetables seemed to have grown immeasurably in two such short days, the corn clicked in the wind as if asking where he'd been while it had been busy growing, the barn seemed impatient to gather in Belle and Bill between its bark walls. The skid trail beckoned like the road to his dreams.

It was difficult for Karl not to throw his chest out and crow like a rooster upon seeing his place again. His place? No, their place now. His heart beat with gladness at the sight of it, and at last he let Belle and Bill have their heads and hurry the last fifty yards to the barn. When he stopped them just short of it, their heavy hooves pawed the earth, impatiently. And suddenly it was far easier for Karl to speak to his horses than to face Anna.

Suppose she does not like it, he thought. He jerked the brake home, tied the reins to it. It will not seem to a woman what it seems to me. She will not feel the love with which I have done all this. She will perhaps see only that it is very lonely here for her with nobody near enough to be a friend to her except the boy and me.

To the horses he said, "I think maybe you will be jealous because I make you wait, but first I must take Anna and the boy to the house." She saw Karl nervously wipe his palms upon his thighs, and read the silent plea for her approval in his eyes. Softly, he said, "We are home, Anna."

She swallowed, wanting to say something to please him; but all that she could think of was if the outside of the house was so miserable, what was the inside going to look like? She might spend the rest of her life there. And, if not that long, at least her wedding night, which was fast coming on.

Karl's eyes skittered to the house. He was remembering that sheaf of sweet clover and wishing to high heaven he had never put it there! It was a stupid move, he was sure now, made when he had thought to please her. It was meant as a symbol of welcome only, one which spoke not only from the heart of the man, but from his land and his home, which had no voices of their own.

But would she know his intention? Or would she perhaps see the clover as only a decoration of a bed and the eagerness of the man to take her to it? There was little he could do about it now. It was there, and she would see it as soon as she walked in.

He leaped from the wagon, while James went off the other side and gawked at the surroundings.

Anna stood up, again finding Karl waiting to help her down. As usual, his shirt-sleeves were rolled up to the elbow as he raised his arms to her. She avoided his eyes and let herself swing down to his grasp. The touch of his hands on her waist made the coming night loom up before her in a formidable way. She would have turned quickly from Karl, but he gently held her, the butts of his hands resting lightly on her slim hipbones. He glanced quickly at the boy, but James was paying little attention to them.

"Anna, do not be afraid," Karl said, dropping his hands. "It will be good here, I promise you. I welcome you to my home and to all that is mine. All of it is yours now, too."

"I have a lot to learn and to get used to," she said. "I probably won't be good at much and you'll be sorry you brought me."

There were things that Karl, too, had to learn and he thought with racing heart of the coming night. But, he thought, this we will learn together. "Come, I will show you the house, then I must tend Belle and Bill."

He wished he could take her into the house alone, but the boy was running toward them. It was his home, too, and he was eager to see inside.

Crossing the clearing, Anna noticed a bench beside the door with a bucket on it, a leather strop hanging on a peg above, apparently where Karl did his washing and shaving. There was a stump beside the woodpile where he must do the chopping.

He walked just behind her. When they reached the door, he leaned around her to remove the chunk of wood wedged against the outside of the door. "It keeps the Indians from stealing everything in the place," he explained, and walked to the side of the house to fling it toward the chopping block. "Indians have a curious sense of honor. If you leave and they discover you gone, they will take whatever they can lay their hands on. But if you place the block of wood before the door to tell them you are gone, they would not take so much as a wild plum from the bush beside your door."

"Are there many Indians around here?"

"Many. But they are my friends, and you need not fear them. One of them is taking care of my goat while I am gone. I will have to go fetch her."

But he'd avoided taking Anna inside as long as he could. He reached for the latchstring. She'd never seen such a thing before. It hung outside the door, leading from a small hole in the puncheons, tied to the latch itself which was on the other side. When he pulled the string, she heard the klunk as a heavy oak bar lifted, then the door swung open. He leaned with the door, his shoulder blade against it, letting both Anna and the boy pass in front of him.

The interior was dark and smelled of musty earth and wood smoke. She wondered how he had stood it to live in such a burrow for two years! But he quickly found a tallow candle, his flint and steel, while she stood waiting to see what was beyond the arc of fading afternoon light created by the open door.

She heard the scratch as the tinder lit, then the candle flared. She saw a wooden table and chairs with pegged legs; another bench like the one outside; a curious thing that appeared to be a section of tree trunk on four legs; a fireplace with its iron cauldron suspended above the dead ashes, brass containers hanging on hooks, various earthenware dishes on the hearth; barrels raised off the floor on wooden slabs; dried foods hanging from the ceiling; an earthen floor with fresh swirls telling her he'd swept it last thing before he left.

Karl stood expectantly, watching her glance from one thing to the next. His throat filled with heartbeats as he saw her slowly turn in the opposite direction and find the bed. He wanted to reach out and take her slim shoulders and say, "I meant it as a welcome, nothing more." He saw her hand go up to her throat before she looked quickly away to his clothing hanging on pegs behind the door, then to the wooden trunk nearby.

James turned, too, to eye the bed, and Karl longed more than ever to snatch up the sheaf of sweet clover and run outside with it. Instead, he excused himself, saying, "Belle and Bill are anxious to be free of the harness."

When he was gone, James explored the place further, saying, "It's not so bad, is it, Anna?"

"It's not so bad if you're a badger who expects to live in a burrow. I don't see how he could live here all this time."

"But Anna, he built it all by himself!" James was intrigued by everything, examining the set of the stones in the fireplace, the way the legs of the table were set into the puncheon boards, the windows covered with waxed sheets of opaque cloth that let in only negligible amounts of light. While Anna wondered how anyone could possibly mistake them for windows, James seemed pleased by everything. "Why, I'll bet this place is as snug as a rabbit's nest in the winter. He's got these walls so thick that no snow or rain could ever get in."

She took their rolls of clothing and laid them on the bed and began untying them, trying to pretend she wasn't crestfallen. James charged out the door saying he was going to help with the horses. She sat down on one of the chairs and clasped her hands between her knees, staring at the bed across the room, at the flowers that were drying there on their stalks. Something at once inviting and foreboding flooded her veins at the sight of them.

She thought about Karl, his first displeasure with her, his later acceptance and forgiveness, his hesitancy at times; his seeming kindness. She imagined him picking these flowers all alone, getting this hut ready for her. She remembered how he had slipped and called her "my Anna" and it raised goose bumps on her skin. She shivered and hugged her arms, still wondering about the clover, the sight of it somehow prompting a surge of guilt in her.

This was not a man who took a wife lightly to his bed with no thought of what it all meant. His words of welcome by the wagon came back to her now, telling her again how he felt about sharing all that was his. These were words of a man who was doing his best to please, who offered all that he had as a kind of dowry to his bride. But the only dowry she brought was deceit.

Already she knew how her lies had disillusioned Karl, and how very difficult it had been for him to accept her in spite of them. Thinking of lying with him, of his discovering the one lie she was most afraid to reveal, she knew with unerring certainty that a man like Karl Lindstrom would be totally unable to accept a used wife.

He came in with a barrel on his shoulder, filling the doorway with his bulk before leaning to set it on the floor, then turning to find her huddled on the chair.

"Anna, you are shivering. I will light a fire. It is always cool in the place. The sod keeps it so. Why do you not go outside where it is warmer?"

"Karl?" she asked hesitantly. His head snapped around.

She realized it was the first time she had used his first name. "Don't you have a stove?"

"I have never needed a stove," he answered. "The fireplace is good and I can do everything with it—cook, keep warm, dry herbs, heat water, make soap, melt wax. I have never thought too much about a stove. Morisette sells them, but they cost dearly."

She wondered how in the world she was going to use that black pit of a fireplace when the little she suspected of how to cook was all based upon doing so on an iron stove like everybody had back East.

He studied her a moment. He himself liked a fireplace. For the long, dreary nights of the winter there was nothing so heartening as blazing flames to stare into, especially a fire kindled of logs from one's own land. How many times he had envisioned this night when he would bring her here, his Anna, and of building up the fire high, and by its light laying her down on a buffalo robe before it. Yes, he thought, a house should have a fireplace. A house with love should have a fireplace.

"So you want a stove, Anna?" he asked anyway.

She shrugged. "A stove would be nice."

"Perhaps in the log house we will have a stove," he offered. She smiled then and he felt better. "Come," he said. "You can gather the woodchips for kindling while I bring in the logs." He took down a willow basket and handed it to her, leading the way outside.

James called from across the clearing, "Hey, Karl, what's all this stuff in your garden?"

"A little bit of everything," he called back. He liked the sound of the boy's voice calling him Karl.

"What's all this stuff here?" James called.

"Those are turnips."

"All these?"

"All those. But do not say it so loud. You will make your sister want to run away." He smiled sideways at Anna, and she realized how hard he was trying to put her at ease.

"I can tell the peas and beans and stuff," James said proudly.

"Did you see the watermelon there at the end? Do you like watermelon, boy?"

"Watermelons? Really?" With arms flapping, James went to the far end of the vegetable plot. "Hey, Anna, did you hear that? Watermelons!"

Karl laughed and continued watching as James explored the garden. "It does not take much to gain that one's interest, does it?"

"I guess not. He seems as happy as you are to be here." But she made no mention of her own feelings as she started to pick up wood chips and place them in the basket. The fragrance of freshly chopped wood seemed to hang around Karl Lindstrom all the time. She recalled the way he had spoken of the trees on their ride home, and the woodsmell seemed right.

Inside the cabin, Karl knelt with his back to her, a small hatchet in his hands. He shaved curls of wood off one of the pieces he'd brought in. They were much the same color as the hair at the back of his neck, which she studied. He finished, then reached up to her for the basket. Again, his eyes lingered on her in a way that made her mind stray to bedtime. He took a small scoop and cleaned the ashes from the fireplace into a pail. He found a large chunk of charcoal at the bottom of the ashes and carefully placed it aside as if it were quite precious.

Anna watched all this from behind, observing the play of muscles as he reached up for the scoop, leaned forward to use it, swiveled at the hips toward the pail, pivoted on the balls of his feet to take the charcoal up, straightened, then knelt again with a cracking of knees. He turned abruptly to look up at her, and she wondered if he knew she'd been wondering what the muscles beneath his shirt looked like.

"Hand me the candle," he said.

She reached to put it in his outstretched hand. Their fingers carefully avoided touching.

He pivoted again toward the fireplace, readjusting the fleecy mound of wood curls. It kindled and flamed under Karl's watchful eye. He added chips. He squatted before the growing fire, unmoving, lost in thought, elbows braced upon knees. The blaze before him brightened and turned his hair to the color of flame.

Anna stared fixedly at the spot where his shirt disappeared into the back of his pants.

"You can put your things in the trunk," he said, not turning around.

"I don't have much."

"What you have you can put there. There is room for them, and the trunk will keep them from getting damp. You can put the boy's things in it, too."

He heard her move, heard the lid of the trunk squeak open. He arose, the fire now burning satisfactorily. He turned to find her laying her clothing into the trunk, partially hidden by the door.

"Would you like me to show you the spring?" he asked. "I have a wonderful spring, and there is watercress growing near it." Such a foolish thing to say, Karl told himself. Why do you not say what it is you want to say about the spring? But if I mention washing, she might think I am criticizing her—or worse—she might think I want her clean for bedtime and this is the only reason I bring up the spring.

"I've never tasted watercress before. What's it like?" The clothes were all in the trunk and she had to stand up fully now and act as though her mind were on what she was saying.

"It tastes like . . . like watercress," he ended, then laughed nervously. "A little like collard, a little like dandelion, but mostly like watercress. Sweeter than other greens." Karl picked up the chunk of charcoal and took it with him outside, saying, "Come, you have to see my spring."

"Hey, Karl," James hollered, "where's all this water come from?" He was already studying the bubbling flow that came from beneath the walls of the springhouse.

"It comes from deep in the earth. It runs all year long, no matter how cold the weather gets. We are lucky. Never will we have to chop holes in the ice of the pond for water, or melt down snow or ice, which takes much time."

"You mean all we have to do is come right here and have a cold drink, any time?"

"Ya, that is so, boy," Karl said proudly, hoping Anna, too, would be impressed with this spot he had chosen for their home. "This is a springhouse. Open the door and look inside."

It was built of wood, with a latched door that swung on hand-carved wooden hinges. When James opened it, he was surprised at how very cool it was inside. The soft sand around the spring had been hollowed out, shored up and formed a wide bowl in which earthen jugs and crocks were partially submerged. The crystal-clear water purled with a whisper around the jugs, then wended its way out below the walls again. In one corner was a leather bag hanging above a pail where Karl placed his chunk of charcoal.

"What're you saving that for?" James asked.

"This is my lye leach. The water drips from the bag onto the charcoal, and slowly lye is made. The bag is empty again, so I must refill it." He stooped to do so. "With it we make soap and tan leather and many other things. You could be a help to me if you would check the water bag when you come in here, and always keep it filled and dripping. But I must warn you, there are times when we must test the lye to see if it is strong enough. Then I must find a prairie chicken egg and float it. When it sinks, this tells me the lye is ready. The lye in the cup will look so much like tea a person could not tell the difference. Never leave it in that cup. If it was mistaken for tea and somebody drank it, this would be a disaster." The bag was again filled and hung. The regular plops of the dripping water accented the constant music of the spring, the smell of the damp wood.

"Gosh, Karl, did you think this up all by yourself?" James asked, taking in the entire structure.

"No. My father taught me this, too, how to make a springhouse, when I am only a tad like you."

"In Boston we got water from out back in barrels where they came and filled them every other day or so. Seems like it never tasted fresh. This water's the best I ever had. Hey, Anna, come and try some."

James passed the dipper to his sister, while Karl looked on expectantly. It was water such as she'd never tasted in her life. It was so icy it hurt her teeth, making Karl laugh when she grabbed them with her fingers to warm them. But that didn't stop her from drinking again and again while Karl watched with pleasure in his eye.

"It's good," she said, when she'd finally drunk her fill.

"It is plenty close to the house, and even closer to where the new log house will be. Enough good, fresh water, and close enough to the house that a lad has little excuse for not keeping clean with it, huh? I think maybe it is time we filled a couple of these buckets and let the water lose its chill for later. What do you say, James?"

"You mean for washing?" the boy asked.

The tone of his question made Karl ask, "Do you object to washing?"

"Well, I never been much for bath-taking," James admitted.

"Such a reply for a tadpole. Anna, what have you taught the lad? In Sweden a boy learns right from the start that in all of nature, animals clean themselves to keep healthy. A boy must do the same."

But James said, "Anna's not much for baths either."

"She's not?" Karl said before he could stop himself. He was beginning to realize that a lad of thirteen could be an embarrassment to an older sister. "Well, when you have only a barrel in your backyard it is a problem. Here there is no such problem. There is the spring here, and the pond and the creek. Plenty water for everything."

Anna could have kicked James into the spring! It was true she hated baths, but did he have to spew out the fact to Karl first thing?

"Come. Fill yourself a pail, boy, and take it back to the house. Tonight we will baby you a little bit and heat the water. Most times I will not warm it up. It is refreshing, and makes you want to work hard to get warm fast."

With filled pails they trudged back to the house, and the subject of baths was blessedly dropped. Anna, however, was well aware that Karl was outside at what she'd guessed to be the washbench. He shaved before supper while she explored things around the kitchen end of the house, peeking inside barrels and tins and crocks. There were odd-looking foods, some of which Anna could not identify. Others held basic staples.

She heard a yelp outside and realized that James must be following Karl's suit. They both came in, shiny-faced and combed, making her realize she would surely be expected to wash as well. But there was no privacy, and she had no inclination to let the icy water touch her skin.

Their supper was simple. Karl laid it all on the table, showing Anna where things were kept. They had cold meat, which he brought from a crock in the springhouse; bread, which he said he baked himself, although Anna couldn't for the life of her figure out where; cheese he'd made from his own goat's milk. Anna had never eaten goat's cheese before, and found it sweet and full-flavored.

Naturally, James again brought up what Anna would have avoided. "You don't expect Anna to know how to make cheese, do you, Karl?"

"No," he answered, avoiding her eyes. "But I will have to teach her. It is not too hard. There is a corner of the chimney that keeps the milk just warm enough to curdle good and slow. In the morning I will walk to get my goat from my friend, Two Horns. Then we will have fresh milk for breakfast. Have you ever milked a goat, boy?"

"Never," James answered. "Are you gonna teach me?"

"First thing in the morning. Maybe Anna would like to learn, too."

Then again, maybe Anna would not, thought the one in question, while her brother went on with his questions. "Why do you keep a goat? Why not a cow like everybody else?"

"Cows are truly expensive here, and they like to stray away into the woods like the pigs. Then you must find them each day when it is time to milk them. Goats are like pets. They do not stray as far, and they are good company."

"I never thought about a goat being like a pet before."

"Goats make maybe the best pets of all. They are loyal and quiet and do not eat much. During the winter blizzards, there were many times when I was grateful for the company of my Nanna to listen to me talk and never complain when I tell her how impatient I am to have neighbors, and how I miss my family back in Sweden and how I think spring will never come. Nanna, she just chews her cud and puts up with me." His eyes strayed to Anna as he spoke, then back to the boy.

"Is that your goat's name—Nanna?"

"Ya. You will love her when you meet her."

"I can't wait! Tell me about the rest. Tell me what else we're gonna do tomorrow besides milk the goat."

Karl laughed softly at the boy's eagerness, so like his own since he had come here. "Tomorrow we begin felling trees for the log house, but by the end of the day I do not think you will be as pleased as you are right now."

"Will Anna help, too?"

"That is up to Anna," Karl said.

She looked up quickly, anxious to be included in anything that would get her out of this dingy cabin and into the sun. "Could I, Karl?" she asked, fearing he meant to leave her to watch goat's milk turn into cheese on the chimney corner. But Karl read only happiness into her question.

"Anna will help, too," Karl said. "Even for three the work will be hard."

"So we were right, and you'll be glad I'm here," James boasted a little.

"Ya, I think so. Tomorrow I will be glad you are here."

But tonight was a different matter. Even though Karl enjoyed talking with the boy, he was ever aware of bedtime drawing near. The fire was spitting and settling. Karl stretched his legs out toward it, forcing himself to relax back into his chair. From his pocket he fished a pipe and leather pouch.

Anna watched his movements, learning something new—he smoked a pipe.

He filled it slowly, while he and James talked about the cabin and all it would take to build it. The smell of the tobacco smoke drifted lazily, and James leaned his chin more and more heavily upon his hand. Now and then Karl's gaze moved toward Anna, but she would look quickly away toward the fire. There, on the hob, hung the black cauldron Karl had filled with water after supper.

James revived when Anna arose to clear away their few dishes, but soon he nodded heavily once more.

The squeak of Karl's chair called out as he got up, saying, "The boy will fall off his bench soon if I do not make a bed for him. I will go to the barn and bring back a forkful of hay."

She turned her eyes to Karl, trying not to look skittish and seventeen. "Yes," she said.

He left her standing gawkily, and within minutes returned, bringing a wooden fork laden with sweet-smelling hay. "It grows wild in the meadows," Karl said, looking squarely at Anna, then back down to his chore of piling it high and spreading it with a buffalo robe.

James dove for the shakedown immediately, while Karl leaned on the fork and watched him. "Do you think you have time to take your shoes off before you sleep, lad?" James doggedly removed his shoes.

Again Karl's eyes met Anna's briefly, and he said, "I will take the fork back where it belongs." When he left, she turned and stared at the pot of water, tested it quickly and found it was getting warm much too fast.

"Anna?" She jumped at the softly spoken word and turned, unaware that Karl had returned.

"Yes?"

He realized they had never had a chance to talk alone, to acquaint themselves with each other. Wildly, he searched his mind for something to give them time to do so. A woman should not jump so when she hears her man's voice, he thought. "Would you like a cup of tea?"

"Tea?" she repeated stupidly, then quickly added, "Oh, tea . . . yes." The relief was evident in her voice.

"Sit down. I will make it for you. I will teach you how."

She sat, watching him move about the room, now and then casting an anxious glance at her brother who was snuggled comfortably on his makeshift bed. At last Karl brought their two cups to the table and pushed hers over to her.

"Rose hips," he said quietly.

"What?" She looked up, startled.

"The tea is made of rose hips. First you must squash them in the cup, then add the hot water."

"Oh."

"Have you never had tea of rose hips before?"

"The only tea I ever had was . . . well, tea. Real tea. But not too often."

"Here there is little real tea or coffee either. But rose hip is almost better. When winters get long, rose hips will keep you from getting scurvy." Achingly, he wondered why he rambled on about rose hips. But his tongue had a mind of its own. "Wild mulberry hips will do the same, but they are not so plentiful here as rose." She took a sip of her drink. "How do you like it?"

She found it delightful, which gratified him.

"Anna," he said, leaning on an elbow across the table from her, "there is so much here in Minnesota, I cannot tell you how good a life we will have. Why, I could walk out into the woods right now and pick you more herbs for tea than you could remember by morning. There is wild strawberry, chamomile, basswood, salsify . . . Have you ever tasted comfrey, Anna?'' She shook her head no. Karl promised, "I will show you how to make comfrey tea. Comfrey is so good I grow it in my garden. I will show you, too, how to dry it. You will love comfrey tea.''

"I'm sure I will, Karl,'' she said, realizing all of a sudden that he was just as nervous as she.

"I have so much to show you, Anna. Have you ever caught a bass on a line and felt him fight you so hard the line would cut your hand if you let him take it through your palm? You will love to fish, Anna, and so will the boy. In Skäne where I grew up, my papa and I fished much, and my brothers, too. Here there are as many fish and more than in Sweden, and wild fowl and deer and elk. Anna, I have seen an *elk* in my woods! I did not know what it was, but my friend Two Horns told me. It was magnificent. Did you ever imagine a place with so much? In the autumn when geese fly south from Canada, there are battalions of them. So many a man can bring down one with each shot. And the way things grow here, Anna, you will not believe it. Potatoes grow to be the size of squash and squash grow to the size of pumpkins and pumpkins—''

Suddenly Karl stopped, realizing he was rambling on about his favorite subject, quite carried away by it. "I think I chatter on like the squirrels,'' he said sheepishly, dropping his eyes to the tabletop only to find her hands tense upon her cup.

"It's all right. You had forgotten to mention the squirrels anyway.'' Her reply brought smiles to both of their faces before she again dropped her gaze to her cup and said quietly, "It's very different here from Boston. Already I'm beginning to see the difference. I think it'll be good here for James. He seems to like it already.''

A moment of silence went quivering by before Karl quietly asked, "And you, Anna . . . how about you?''

They studied each other across the table while the fire lit a single side of each of their faces, the far sides cast into complete shadow. And so it seemed to Karl and Anna, as if only half of what each was, was illuminated for the other to see so far. There was yet much that remained in shadow, but only time would bring it to light.

"It . . . it takes some getting used to . . .'' Anna dropped her eyes. "But little by little I think I am.''

He wondered what she would like for him to say, what was the best way. After some time he could only think to ask, "Are you tired, Anna?''

She looked sharply at James, but he was still. "A little,'' she answered uncertainly.

"The water is warm.'' Of course it was warm. It was hot enough to have steeped rose hip tea. Together they looked at the pale threads of steam rising from the kettle. "But I have only homemade lye soap.''

"Oh, that . . . that's fine!'' she said too brightly. He made no move to leave and she sat glued to her chair.

"The basin is on the bench outside. I will fill it for you.''

"Thank you.''

He took the kettle from the hook and went outside.

By the time she followed him out, he was gone somewhere into the dark. She washed herself faster than she ever had in her life. In spite of how she hated baths, she had to admit it felt more than tolerable to be rid of the travel grit. She glanced toward the clearing, but there were only fireflies skipping in the dark. From the barn came a gentle nicker, then all was quiet.

She slipped back into the house, found her nighty in the trunk, put it on and stood uncertainly, looking first at James asleep on the floor, then at the bed. Resolutely, she crossed to it, flung the buffalo robe back and put one knee on the mattress. But she stopped still at a crackling noise—cornhusks filling the mattress. My God! What is that! Gingerly, she moved her knee and the crackling sounded again. There was nowhere else to go. So with her mind set, she scampered the rest of the way in and pulled the robe up to her neck.

The door moved, its shadow widening, then narrowing on the sod walls, before Karl closed it with the wooden thud of the latch falling into place. Carefully, he drew the latchstring in. He came to the side of the bed, no longer able to ignore the sheaf of sweet clover, which still lay where he'd placed it yesterday morning. Her eyes followed him as he leaned to pick it up from beside her head.

"This is sweet clover," he said dumbly.

"It smells good," she choked.

"There is no sweeter smell in all of Minnesota." Then he swallowed. "Oh, Anna, I meant it as a welcome, but after I left it here I thought perhaps I should not have done so. I thought . . ." He looked down at the clover in his hands. ". . . I thought it might scare you."

"No . . . no, it didn't." But her body was shaking so beneath the buffalo robe, its nap of hairs was trembling.

He turned and went to the fireplace and thrust the stalk of sweet clover into it. She watched it flare, brightening the room momentarily, throwing Karl's silhouette into sharp relief. Hands on hips, he studied the fire while she studied his back. Then he bent to bank the coals, sending sparks popping their way up the chimney. He hesitated, kneeling there in thought, while the room's illumination waned to a gentle glow. But there was no more to be done, nowhere to go but to bed. He ran a hand through his hair.

Her eyes stayed fixed on the pale fireglow as he returned to the side of the bed and, with his back to her, slipped from his clothing and into the spot beside her. The husks crackled. The ropes creaked. The tick readjusted to his weight, and she found a new force threatening to roll her in his direction. She tightened her shoulder muscles to keep it from happening.

They lay on their backs, staring at the logs of the ceiling. At last Karl turned his face to her, studied her profile, then whispered, "Look at me, Anna, while there is still enough light left to see by."

She did, wide-eyed and undeniably frightened, remembering that other time. She tried to focus on Karl Lindstrom's face, but only the scalding memory of Saul McGiver came to her, and with it dread and shame.

"It is hard for me to believe you are here at last," Karl whispered. "The way we started—I want to forget all that. I want to do things right with you. I want this to be right."

She was afraid even to swallow, let alone talk.

He wondered if she knew his turmoil. He found her hand and brought it to his chest and pressed it palm down upon his hammering heart, surprising her.

His heart is going crazy just like mine is! she thought disbelievingly.

"You are so young, Anna. Seventeen . . . no more than a child, when I had expected a woman."

"Seventeen is . . . is old enough," she whispered in a strained little tone.

"Do you know what you say, Anna?" He wondered if she truly understood.

She wondered if she truly understood. She said what she felt compelled to say to a husband who had all rights to her. Knowing what her duty was, she had answered as she did. But she did not know what Karl's response would be. Memories of the past and fear of the future gripped her. As long as they talked, nothing else happened, so she went on, "I know lots of girls who got married at seventeen." But she really didn't. She only knew lots of slatternly women who—at thirty, thirty-five and forty—had long ago given up hope of marrying out of their profession.

"Anna, in Sweden things like this are not done—two strangers agreeing to marry as we have done. If we lived in Sweden and I could meet you first in the village, I would buy for you a silk hair ribbon and maybe tease and laugh with you a bit. You would have a chance to say to yourself, 'yes, I think I like getting a silk hair ribbon from Karl' or 'I will take no more hair ribbons from Karl.' But if you took the ribbons with a smile and tucked them into your little hanging pocket on your waist belt, I would next take you to meet my *mor* and *far* so you could see for yourself where I come from. I had always thought to court a girl in the way I remember my brothers doing in Skåne." He rubbed his palm over the back of her hand, remembering, while his heartbeat thundered on.

Anna's only opinion of men in this element—in bed— was tainted too vividly by growing up where she had, among people with whom flesh was a business and nothing more. But slowly the realization was dawning that Karl was just as uncertain about this as she was, that his heart was hammering not solely from arousal, but in hesitancy, too.

"I used to imagine something like that," she admitted, "when I was younger."

"Ya, I think all girls do. I thought to marry a golden-haired girl whose braids were pulled up beneath a small white starched hat with deep pleats, and who wore her embroidered apron on Midsummer's Eve, with the laces tied criss-cross upon her waist girdle. Our families would be there, and there would be dancing and laughter, much laughter." His voice had grown reminiscent, wistful.

Anna somehow found herself, too, growing wistful. But the dancing and laughter, she had observed in her tender years, were nothing of which she wanted a part. She had not observed them in such a heartwarming setting as Karl's homeland. She had never had a starched hat, nor a girlish apron and cross-ties. She had never been courted by young swains on the village green, nor had she been given ribbons or smiles or invitations to their homes to meet their mamas and papas. She was not a girl given to fits of self-pity, but at the moment she was fighting the urge to indulge in it.

But Karl was handsome and earnest and sincere, and the murmur of his voice in the gloaming made it somehow easy for Anna to voice some of her girlhood dreams.

"I thought to get married in St. Mark's. I always felt good in St. Mark's. Sometimes I would dream of marrying a soldier in high boots and braids, with epaulettes on his shoulders."

"A soldier, Anna?" He knew he was far from a soldier.

"Well, there were always soldiers around Boston. Sometimes I'd see them."

It grew still—both the nightshadows and Karl's hand grew still.

"There are no soldiers here," Karl said, disappointed.

"There are no blonde braids either," she said timorously, surprising her husband once again.

Karl swallowed. "I think I can get along without blonde braids," he whispered. Beneath Anna's hand his flesh rose and fell more rapidly.

Despite his seeming gentleness, she was afraid to give him the reply he sought, even though a soldier in epaulettes was at this moment the farthest thing from her mind.

He rolled onto his side, facing her. "I think I go too fast, Anna. I am sorry." He lifted her hand to his mouth and kissed its palm—warm lips, soft breath for the briefest moment touching her—then laid it on the pillow between them, quite where the sweet clover had lain before. "But I have been alone so long, Anna. There has been no one to talk with, no one to touch, no one to touch me, and at times I thought I would die of it. I would sometimes bring the goat inside, when the blizzards blew fierce in the winter, and to her I would talk, and often I talk to my horses. And to touch their velvet noses is good, or to stroke the ears of the goat, but it is not the same. Always I dream of the day when I have more than the animals to talk to. More than the bleat of my goat for an answer."

Again, he took her hand to his lips, but differently this time, as if its warmth were the cure of him. The way he placed her fingers upon his lips, then moved the hand upward as if to wash himself with its touch, she felt glorified and undeserving. He whispered throatily, "Anna, oh Anna, do you know how good just your fingers on me feel?"

Then he pulled her palm against the length of his long cheek. It was warm, smooth, and she remembered its appearance as her hands fit its contours. Her fingertips brushed his eyebrow and, for a moment, his closed eyelid, and she felt a faint quiver there that made her yearn for light so she might see such a surprising vision as a man who held deep-pent emotions within.

"I never knew . . . You never told me all these things in your letters."

"I thought I would scare you away. Anna, I do not mean to scare you. You are such a child and I have been alone too long."

"But I made the agreement, Karl," she said, determinedly.

"But you shake so, Anna."

"So do you," she whispered.

Yes, Karl thought, I shake from a little eagerness, a little timidity, maybe a little fright of scaring her off. It was his first time, and he wanted it to be by mutual consent—but more—by mutual love. He could wait a while to earn those things from her, but he had been alone too long to take away nothing with him this night. He reached to curl a hand around her neck, stroking her chin with his thumb, filled with wonder at the softness of her skin after feeling only his own for so long.

"Would it be all right if I kiss you, Anna?"

"A man doesn't need permission to kiss his own wife," she whispered.

But he took it—slow-leaning on an elbow beside her, grazing her lips with the thumb, wishing she was not so afraid.

Anna lay rigidly, waiting for the bad part to begin. But it didn't. Everything was different about Karl. Different, the way he waited and touched her gently first, as if assuring her he meant well. Different, as he leaned so slowly closer, making the corn husks rustle in hushed tones. Different, as he hovered on an elbow, pausing, giving her time with his thumb still on her lips to say no. Different, as he touched his lips to her lightly, lightly.

There was no force, no fight, no fear, only a light lingering of flesh upon flesh, a blending of breaths, an introduction. And her name, "Anna . . ." whispered upon her mouth in a way no person had ever before spoken it. His fingers slid into her hair at the back of her head, tenderly, not clutching, while she understood new things about this man. Patiently, he waited for some sign from her. It came in the tiniest lifting of her chin, bringing her lips closer to his. Again, his lips touched hers, warmer, nearer, a little fuller, letting her ease into the newness of him.

For the first time ever, Anna found a willingness to let a man know this much of her. But when he moved his hand slowly to her ribs, she stiffened, quite unable to control the reaction. He raised his mouth from hers, anxious to do the right thing with her, for he could feel the way her forearms were tightly guarding her chest.

"Anna, I would not hurry you. We have time now, if we did not have before."

Reprieved, Anna nevertheless felt silly and inadequate. Her heart raced wildly while she searched for the right thing to say. He still hovered above her, and she felt his warm breath caressing her face. He smelled of clean shaving soap and tobacco, but he had tasted faintly of rose hips.

How can I be afraid of a man who tastes like roses? she thought. Yet she was. She knew very well what it was that men did to women. This man, with his might, could do it with tolerable ease, should he choose. But instead, he backed farther away, so she could no longer feel the touch of his breath on her nose.

"I . . . I'm sorry, Karl," she said, then added, shakily, "and thank you."

Disappointment swept through Karl's veins. But he touched her jaw with the back of a callused index finger, a brief, reassuring brush upon her downy flesh.

"We have plenty time. Sleep now, Anna." Then he lay back on his own side of the bed, but unrelaxed, for now he knew what her skin felt like.

Anna rolled onto her side facing the wall, curling her spine and tugging the buffalo robe up securely between shoulder and jaw. But a strange feeling crept over her, as if she'd done something wrong but she wasn't sure what. She felt much like just before she started to cry. Finally, she rolled slightly backward, looked over her shoulder and whispered, "Goodnight, Karl."

"Goodnight, Anna," he said thickly.

But for Karl it was not a good night. He lay stiff as a board, wanting to leap from the bed and run into the dewy damp night air and cool off, talk to his horses, dip his head in the icy basin of water in the springhouse—something! But he lay instead like a ramrod—sleepless—for now he knew the feel of her skin, the taste of her tongue, the tug of her diminutive body making its furrow into the other half of the husk mattress. How long, he wondered miserably. How long? How long must I court my own wife?

Chapter 6

In the morning Karl was gone to fetch his goat before James and Anna awoke. By the time he returned, they were up and dressed and already making nuisances of themselves. They heard a bell tinkling, and looked at each other hopelessly through the billowing smoke. Anna fanned her hand before her eyes and nose uselessly.

"Oh, no, I think he's back," she wailed.

"It's a good thing, too," James observed.

A moment later Karl stepped to his doorway. "What are you two doing? Burning our house down?"

"Sod doesn't—" Anna coughed. "Sod doesn't burn."

"And so I am a lucky man or I would be homeless by now. Have you ever heard of a damper?" Of course they'd heard of a damper. All the cast-iron stoves had dampers in their pipes, but they hadn't considered that Karl's fireplace would have one. He stepped to the smoking mouth of the fireplace, made the necessary adjustment, then herded the two of them outside while the air cleared.

"I can see I will have to watch you two every minute to keep you out of trouble," he said good-naturedly.

"We thought it'd help if we got the fire going."

"Ya, it would help if you built a fire instead of a smudge. But you will come in handy when the mosquitoes need chasing away."

Karl, it seemed, was prepared to practice the patience he'd promised to exercise. "Tonight I will teach you to build a proper fire. Now, come and meet Nanna."

James took to the goat at once, and there seemed an answering friendliness in the animal.

"Nanna, this is James," Karl said affectionately, folding the goat's ear backward. "And if he milks a goat like he builds a fire, I would run back to the Indians, if I were you," he whispered into Nanna's ear.

Anna laughed, and at last Karl looked directly at her, his hand still toying with the soft, pink ear. Smiling, he said, "Good morning, Anna."

"Good morning, Karl," she replied, her eyes sliding back to his fingers, which scratched affectionately as the animal nudged and bent her head for more. But while he scratched, Karl's eyes stayed on Anna.

"Can you make biscuits?" he asked.

"No," she answered.

"Can you milk the goat then?"

"No."

"Can you fry salt pork and make corn mush in the drippings?"

"Maybe. I'm not sure."

"Now we are getting somewhere!"

And this is how it became James' job to milk the goat in the mornings, once Karl showed the boy how. And to Anna fell the chore of cooking mush in drippings, while Karl brought water from the springhouse for the horses, for use in the house and for washing outside.

He washed at the bench by the door. From the beginning it intrigued Anna how he would strip off his shirt and suffer the freezing water without so much as a shiver. Karl brought out his straightedge razor and honed it on the strop while the boy eyed his every movement.

"Does it hurt to shave, Karl?" he asked.

"Only if the blade is not sharp enough. A sharp blade makes all cutting easier. Wait till I show you how to sharpen the axe. Everywhere a logger goes he should carry his stone and use it perhaps once each hour. I have much to teach you."

"Oh boy! I can't wait."

"You will have to. At least until we finish your sister's cornmeal mush and salt pork."

"Hey, Karl?"

"Ya?"

James lowered his voice. "I don't think Anna ever cooked that before. It'll probably be pretty bad."

"If it is, you must not tell her so. And if your first sharpening is bad, I will not tell you so, either."

It was bad, all right. The poor salt pork had had the life fried out of it, and the cornmeal was lumpy. Amazingly, Karl made no comment. Instead, he talked of what a beautiful day it was, and of how much he hoped to get done and of how pleasant it was to be eating his meal with company. But Karl and James seemed to be enjoying some private little joke Anna was not asked to share. Still, she was pleased the way Karl seemed to be accepting her brother.

It was a jeweled day of brilliant color—blue of sky, green of tree, bedazzled by gilt the sun lay upon them. The sun had not yet topped the periphery of the clearing before the three went out. From hooks above the mantel Karl withdrew his broadaxe, handed the hatchet to Anna. James proudly accepted the rifle once again.

"Come," he said. "First I will show you the place where our cabin will be." He stalked across the clearing to the basework of stones laid in a rectangle of some sixteen by twelve feet. As he stepped to the foundation, he placed a foot upon one of its stones and pointed with the sharpest tip of his axe. "There will be the door, facing east . . . due east. I have used my compass, for a worthy house should sit square with the earth itself."

Turning his head toward Anna, he stated, "No dirt floors in this house, Anna. Here we will have real plank floors. I have hauled the stones from the fields and along the creek, the flattest I could find, to hold the foundation logs."

Then he turned, flipped the axe up until the smooth, curved ash handle slipped through his hand. Pointing again with it, he said, "I have cleared that path and put down the skids from here to the tamaracks." The double track of skinned logs led away like a wooden railroad track running north into the trees. "On my land I have the straightest virgin tamarack anywhere. With logs that straight we will have a tight house, you will see.

No half-timbers for us. I will use the whole log, only flattened a little to make it fit tight so the walls will be thick and warm."

Skids and half-timbers meant nothing to Anna, but she could see by the density of the forest what it had taken him to clear that wide skid path.

"Come, we will harness Bill and Belle and get started."

As they walked toward the barn, Karl asked, "Have you ever harnessed a pair, boy?"

"No . . . nossir," James answered, still looking over his shoulder at the skids.

"If you want to be a teamster, you must first learn about harnessing. You will learn now," Karl said with finality. "Your sister, too. There could come a time when she might need to know."

They entered the barn, and Karl spoke in soft greeting to the animals. Nearing them, he patted them on rump, shoulder and finally on their wide foreheads, giving each horse a scratch between the eyes. It was a small building, and the space was narrow.

"Get over," Karl said to Bill. But the horse stood contentedly, waiting for more scratching. "Get over!" Karl repeated more sternly, wedging his body between the animal and the wall, giving Bill a solid slap that commanded but did not hurt. Bill moved over, while Anna marveled at the man's assuredness in putting his mere body between the awesome bulk of the horse and a solid barn wall.

Karl seemed unconcerned, confident. To James he said, "A horse who does not know what 'get over' means, needs a wider vocabulary." But even as he said it, a smile tugged his cheek, and his big hands smoothed the horse's hide affectionately. "Remember that, boy. And remember that you talk to a horse with more than words. Your terms are only as good as your tones. Tones say much.

"Hands talk most of all. A horse gets to trust a man's hands first, and the man himself second." All the while he spoke, Karl's hands rode the horse's hide, resting on the withers, gliding over the shoulders, patting the flanks, returning to the high poll. He looked Bill in the eye as he said, "You know what I am talking about, ya, Bill?"

He led the horse near the wall where the harnesses hung on two thick wooden pegs. "A horse is nearsighted, did you know that, boy? This is why the horse shies away from movement that is a ways off—because he cannot see it clear enough to trust it. But you show him what it is, up close, and he rewards you by being still.

"First comes the collar," Karl went on. He lifted the flanged leather oval. "This one is Bill's." At his name, Bill jerked his head and Karl spoke to the animal. "Ya, you know I am talking about you. Here is your collar, my curious friend." Patiently, he showed the animal the leather before placing it over the horse's head, all the while instructing the two novices. "You must make sure never to get the collars mixed up, for if you put the wrong one on a horse, he gets a sore neck and shoulders. A horse gets used to his own collar, just as you get used to your own shoes. You would not give a marching soldier someone else's boots now, would you, James?"

"Nossir, of course not," James answered, his eyes never leaving Karl as the man buckled the collar beneath Bill's neck, then slipped it firmly back against the Percheron's massive shoulders.

Sliding his big hand between the horse and collar, he said, "It should fit snug. Make sure it is not too tight, for if it presses against his windpipe, the horse will choke. If it is too long, it will rub and chafe the poor boy and cause shoulder galls.''

From two hooks on the wall, Karl withdrew the first harness, his muscles straining as he lifted it down. Approaching Bill from the left, Karl seated the hames on the collar, buckled the hame strap, walked to the horse's flank, adjusted the breaching seat. Then he walked forward again to connect breast strap to hame. Never did he move without first running his hand ahead of him along the horse's flesh or pacifying Bill with low words. The animal stood motionless, only a slow blink of his eyes indicating he was even awake.

Karl instructed the watching pair in the same tone of voice with which he spoke to Bill. Instruction and lulling words blended into a feeling of serenity. Next, he adjusted the belly band, and through it all, Anna found she was mesmerized by the gentle movements of his hands upon horseflesh, his voice in the animal's ear, in her own. She found herself thinking of the coming night, of what it would be like should he handle her as he now handled the horse.

She came to with a start, realizing that Karl had put the bit into the horse's mouth. As he led the reins through the various checkrings, he was asking her if she thought she could do all that.

"I . . . I don't know. I suppose if I could lift that heavy thing down from the wall, I could do the rest."

"I will have to feed you well to put some muscle on your bone," Karl said. She found he could look at her in an amused way that made his comment playful instead of critical.

But James was confidently boasting, "I think I could do it, Karl! Can I try?"

With a silent chuckle, Karl turned the job of harnessing Belle over to the lad. James struggled beneath the weight of the harness, but with a little help from his teacher, made surprisingly few mistakes in dressing the horse in its loggingwear.

"You have a quick memory," Karl complimented, when the boy had finished. James beamed at Anna as if he'd just invented the craft of harnessing.

Next, Karl patiently explained the why and wherefore of attaching the round oak singletree to the two smaller doubletrees. In the exact center of the doubletree went the clevis, and finally they were ready for the massive logging chain. It was an enormous thing.

Again, Anna realized the power behind the man as Karl hefted a coil of it and dragged it over to attach to the clevis. He knelt down, securing the slip hook up into a link of the chain. "When you are going out empty like we are now, never let the slip hook dangle at the end of the chain. It likes to catch on roots, and the horses can be hurt that way." He rose, touching the nearest warm flank again. "Always, the horses must be your first consideration. Without them a man is powerless here."

"Yessir," James responded.

Karl's eyes touched Anna momentarily, and she gave a soldierlike salute, repeating, "Yessir!"

Karl smiled. She seemed a game thing, in spite of her narrow shoulders and willow thinness. Today she wore a dress no more suited to outside work than yesterday's had been. She would soon learn. Once the work began, she would realize that simple clothes suited best, and would choose differently.

Meanwhile, the moment Karl had dreamed of during the long winter alone had come at last—the time of turning toward his trees, husband and wife together, to work in the sun toward their future. The three of them headed out into the Minnesota morning. They walked behind the team in the heightening sun, up the skid path. The horses, with their nodding gait and long stride, set the pace. With sleeves rolled up to the elbow, Karl held the four reins, leaning backward from the waist against the tug and strut of the horses. There was a look of oneness about the man and his team, each of them well-toned and thick-muscled, with a big job to be done.

Anna, long-legged though she was, had to stretch her steps to keep up. Her long skirt swept the morning grass and soon was wet to the knees. She ignored it, listening, smelling, tasting the day. The morning had a music of its own, played out by the awakening wildlife, the squeak of leather, the chink of chains, the clop of the horses' hooves. The dew was still heavy, and the earth redolent with summerscent. There was the ever-present mustiness of leaves decaying, and the crisp flavor of vegetation renewing itself. Birch, beech, maple, black walnut, elm, poplar and willow burgeoned with life.

Karl pointed and named each tree, saying, "A wood for each purpose a man could have," as if he could never get over the bounty he owned, no matter how often he measured it.

"It's funny," Anna mused, "I always thought before that wood was just wood."

"Ah, how much you have to learn. Each wood has a personality. Each tree has a trait that makes it . . . like a man, an individual. Here in Minnesota, a man need not worry that he will not have the proper tree for each need."

They came to the place of the tamaracks, tall, spindly pines with scaly trunks and tapering tips swaying into the morning clouds. "And these are my tamaracks," Karl said with pride, looking up. "A full sixteen feet of log before the taper begins," he boasted. "See what I mean? The best. Will a sixteen-foot cabin be big enough for you?" He eyed Anna sideways, wondering if she believed he could build her a house so big.

"Is that a big one?" she asked, leaning, also, to look at the top of the tamaracks.

"Most are twelve. Some fourteen. It depends upon the trees. Here, where a man has tamaracks . . . here a man has plenty." Again Karl paused. "More than plenty."

Dropping her gaze down the tamarack trunks, Anna found Karl's eyes upon her. Something warm and expectant fluttered through her limbs, making her concur. "Plenty," she said softly. "Sixteen feet will be plenty."

Karl suddenly glanced at James, as if remembering he was there. "And plenty work. Come, boy, I will show you how to fell a tree."

He took the broadaxe and approached a tamarack, walked in a full circle around it, gauging, reckoning the course of its fall, glancing up, then back down, checking it for weighty limbs. After some deliberation, he said, "Ya, this is a good one. It is a perfect fourteen inches in diameter. Remember that now, boy. It will make your task easier if each tree is the same size. Before you start, you must consider the wind.''

James looked skyward, saying, "But there isn't any."

"Good! Now you have considered it. If there is wind, we must allow for it with the very first cut of the axe.''

Anna watched and listened with only half an ear as Karl patiently explained the rudiments of tree-felling. She was far more taken by the effect Karl was having on her brother.

James doted upon his every word, even unconsciously imitating his wide-legged stance as the pair gazed up the towering trunk and planned the course of the fall. And when James asked a question, Karl's boot scraped aside pine needles to clear a small spot on the forest floor. He broke off a sturdy twig and knelt down to make a rude drawing in the dirt.

Anna smiled as James again imitated the big man, kneeling on a single knee, leaning to brace an elbow on the other in manly fashion. But James' thin back looked all the thinner when posed beside Karl's as the pair hunched forward, studying the sketch. It showed the placement of the notches, which Karl called "kerfs." Karl explained that the first kerf they'd make would be on the opposite side of the tree from the direction of its fall.

Anna's attention to instructions suffered further as Karl reached to point, causing the back of his shirt to stretch so tightly it looked as if it would split up the center. Her eyes followed it downward to his waist, mesmerized by the sight of a tiny width of exposed skin where the shirttails had shinnied up. Karl's hips were narrow, but his thighs bulged, kneeling down that way.

He swiveled half around. Anna's eyes darted toward the tamaracks.

Just then James surprised Karl by pronouncing the word "kerfs" and asking where they should go and how deep they should be. Karl grinned at the boy, then lifted his glance to Anna while he teased and taught in one and the same breath.

"I know from cutting down many trees—many, many trees—in Sweden with my papa and brothers, and right here before you came. It takes much practice to know these things."

What patience he has, admired Anna. Even his voice and pose were patient, as well as the expression on his face. Even if she could read and write, she thought, any child would be luckier to be taught by a man like him. She herself had little tolerance. James' face radiated pure pleasure as he studied the rude sketch, committing Karl's instructions to memory.

Karl stood up, using the axe handle to push himself. When he moved, it was with easy grace, always with the axe an integral part of his pose. Anna was beginning to understand that where the man went, the axe went. He used it as a natural extension of himself.

The tool was terribly heavy, but even so Karl now held it straight out by the end of its handle, measuring the distance between himself and the bole of the tree as he took up a spraddled stance at a right angle to it. As he held the extended axe the veins along his inner elbow stood out like blue rivers, disappearing into a shirt-sleeve rolled up just above the elbow. The powerful muscles of the forearm appeared to have square edges as he poised. He explained that the first cut must be perfectly horizontal, at waist level, and he took a slow-motion swing, demonstrating. He swiveled at hip and shoulder, the muscles beneath his shirt tensing one by one while Anna watched, realizing what strength lay within the man's well-toned body.

Karl raised the axe and let its handle slip through his palm until the poll rested against the rim of his hand. He pointed with the honed edge. "Now take your sister over there. When a tree comes down, it can be a killer if you underestimate it. The trunk can snap and jump farther and faster than even a spry boy like you could get away from."

He turned his blue eyes on Anna, and she dropped her own and quickly followed James.

Once they were a safer distance away, Karl called across the cleared space words he had been hearing since he was only a tadpole. "A man who is worth his salt should know exactly where a tree will fall. Some say that you can set a spike in the ground and a worthy Swede can drive it clear in with the trunk of a falling tree."

He smiled teasingly, spotted a gnarled root and pointed at it, again with his axe. "See that root on that oak over here? It will break in half where it humps up out of the round."

Again, he turned toward the tamarack. From his first movement, something magical happened within Anna. He hefted his axe, swung, first left, then right, while she looked on. With a fluid movement, he wielded the tool in perfect rhythm, his right hand slipping down to meet his left at the exact moment of impact. In a grace born of long practice, he shifted the bite of each swing, left and right, left and right, sending woodchips flying high into the air. The rhythm never slowed, and Karl's eyes never wavered from the trunk of the tree. The axe made a whistling song as it cut through the air, a thud of percussion as each measure ended with steel meeting wood.

It was impossible for Anna and James not to look up as the deepening kerfs set the tree atremble. A tremble of sorts began, too, in Anna's belly. The man, the axe, the motion, the tree—all created a dizzying spectacle that heightened her heartbeat and made her hold tightly to her stomach with both hands. There began the final anguished packing, and slowly the scaly trunk tilted.

Karl placed the axe poll against it, gave a push, then backed off himself. He glanced over to see his two, with their chins in the air. Anna clutched her stomach, while the boy had his hands clasped upon the top of his head in a sort of ecstasy. The head of the axe slid to rest against Karl's hand as the bole shuddered, hesitated, then gave way with a final popping of bark and core, until there came the roar of limbs and foliage as the tree plunged downward with a magnificent, resounding crash onto the needle-sewn earth.

There followed the small nicker of the horses, then the mightiest stillness Anna had ever heard. She looked at Karl through the dust motes caught in shafts of sunlight, and found him watching her with a small smile on his face. He stood at ease, Karl and his axe, as if it had been someone else who'd chopped down that tree—relaxed, one knee bent, fingers curled around the axe handle, a film of barkdust settling upon his shoulders, a sprinkling of tamarack twigs drifting down near him.

And everywhere . . . everywhere . . . the stunning fragrance of tamarack—sweet, fresh and vital.

Before she could control it, the full sensation of what she had witnessed flashed in Anna's eyes. For perhaps the first time in her life she had seen a thing of total beauty. For that brief moment, Karl Lindstrom read it in her face and knew she felt what he felt when the tree hit the earth, landing with its farthest tip upon the gnarled root of the oak—satisfaction.

James broke the spell to come back to Karl, leaping, arms flapping, exclaiming, "Wow! That was really something! When can I do that?"

Karl laughed in his slow way and nudged the boy lightly in the stomach with the poll of his axe. "I think you will not fell many before you are asking when you can stop. Right, Anna?" He was reluctant to break the feeling of affinity he'd sensed between the two of them.

"How many can *you* do before you stop?" she asked, coming nearer, still awed by what she'd seen.

"As many as I must," he answered, "while my two helpers take care of smaller branches and pulling the logs down the skid trail. Now we must trim the tree and do the bucking."

"Bucking?" James ventured.

"Chopping the tree into the length we want."

Together they set to work using axe and hatchet to trim the scraggly branches from the tamarack. Anna was assigned the task of dragging the branches away to form a scrub pile.

When the tree was stripped, Karl measured it by axe lengths, marked the sixteen-foot spot with a small notch, then mounted the trunk at that spot. Grasping his axe, he bounded up to a stance upon the rough bark. He stood with feet perfectly balanced, about half an axe handle's width apart, the notch halfway between his boots. This time he talked between swings, explaining to James that the two kerfs he would cut, one on each side of the log, must form a perfect forty-five-degree angle to one another.

The axe went soaring and swooping again and again. With each stroke Karl bent lower, lower, lower, until he was doubled over at the waist, chopping so near to the ground. Then, with the agility of a monkey, he turned, scarcely needing to curl his toes to keep abreast of the log as the opposite kerf was honed away with precise strokes. He leapt from the tree, leaving behind the severed sections, each with a perfect V-shaped tip.

Four more trees were felled and bucked. "A good logger does not raze the forest, but only thins it," Karl explained. "Therefore we take one tree from here, one from there and one from over there."

The logs trimmed and ready now for skidding, Karl demonstrated the proper technique of lifting, bending the knees rather than the back. With a powerful effort he raised the end of one log off the earth, and James slung the heavy chain beneath it.

When the team was brought over, Karl instructed, "Attach the load close to the singletree, boy, like this, then the skidding is easier for the horses." Accompanied by the chink of chain as the big hook fell into a link, Karl warned, "But when you do this yourself, you must stand to the side as you work. Only a fool gets between his team and the load."

Then Karl gave a single command and the horses lugged the log toward the top of the skid trail to be deposited. Even as they moved, Karl instructed the lad who matched the big man step for step, stretching his youthful legs unnaturally to do so. "When you are skidding, you must think ahead before giving the command to turn. Always keep the draft angle wide, out of consideration for your horseflesh. The straighter the course, the easier the work is for them."

Heading the horses back for a second log, Karl's voice changed; nothing more than a faint cluck set the team on the move. But when their load was heavy, Karl spoke to them in melodic tones. "*Eee-easy*, now." And the tractable animals flexed their huge shoulders, leaning into their burden with muscle wrought patiently, as ordered. And so it was for each new log—advice for the boy, an order for the team, each treated with respect to individual intelligence and ability.

Never in her life had Anna seen James this happy. He absorbed every word Karl spoke, kneeling when Karl knelt, rising when Karl rose, watching when Karl demonstrated, striding when Karl strode. When, at last, Karl handed James the reins, telling him to take the team to the next log, the boy looked up with anxious uncertainty in his eyes. "Really, Karl?"

"Really. You want to be a teamster, do you, boy?"

"Yessir . . . but—"

"The horses must learn to get used to you, too. Now is as good a time as any."

James wiped his palms on his thighs.

"I will be right beside you," Karl assured him. "Just hold the reins like I showed you and do not pull on them. Bill and Belle know what to do. They will teach you as much as I will, you will see."

The boy took the sweat-smooth leathers into his smaller hands, cooing, "*Eaaasy now.*" With the horses' initial steps, James' eyes grew wide.

But Karl spoke reassuringly to the boy, much as he did to Belle and Bill. "You are doing good, lad, let them have their heads . . . Ya . . . good . . . Now rein left . . . light, light . . . good." By the time the horses drew nigh the next log, James was smiling. His chest jutted in satisfaction.

Karl, too, seemed pleased. "You will do good as long as you remember *never* ride the logs, and *never* walk beside them once we start skidding down the trail and the logs ride sideways. If the end of a log strikes a tree, it can swing away and crack your legs like they were no more than kindling. Only walk behind the load!"

"Yessir, I'll remember."

More instructions were necessary as the load of logs was bound with a chain at each end, then towed down the skid trail to the cabin site. They went down together with the first load. Karl allowed James to handle the reins, showing him the correct speed and the importance of avoiding stumps, which edged near the open way and were hazardous to both horse and driver. He also explained how the downward slope had been kept gentle to avoid the risk of a load sliding into the horses' hocks.

When the logs were dropped at the clearing, Karl watered the horses, saying that a hot horse should never be fed icy water. Instead, he used water he'd drawn that morning. Next, the horses were fed—hay before grain—then watered again. Finally, the animals were allowed to rest, while the three went inside for their noonday meal.

After dinner, James took the team out empty and headed back up the trail. He pleased Karl by remembering to hook the gaff into the links before starting. Karl and Anna came behind, he sweat-stained, bearing his axe and gun, she pink-nosed, bearing a basket in which to collect woodchips and carrying the hatchet.

"You're a fine teacher, Karl," she said, watching his boots whisk the grass with each step, unable to look him in the eye.

"The boy is quick and willing," Karl replied modestly, looking ahead.

"I've never seen him quite so happy." Anna peeked up at Karl.

"No?" His blue gaze fell on her face, which moved beside him in his noontime shadow.

"No," she said, thoughtfully. "He's never been around a man before."

"What about his father?" He gave Anna a sidelong look, but she quickly turned her gaze to James and the horses.

"James never knew his father."

"Did you?"

She flashed him a quick eye before admitting, "Me neither." Then she bent down, never breaking stride, and whisked up a little stick and started fraying its end with her fingernail.

"I am sorry, Anna. Children should know their fathers. I myself could not have come here and started such a life without the wise teachings of my own father."

"And now you teach it all to James," she said reflectively.

"Ya. I am lucky."

"Lucky?" she questioned.

"What man is not lucky who has learned so much and can keep all these good ways alive forever by passing them on to another willing pupil?"

"And so I am forgiven, Karl, for bringing him and not telling you before?"

"You are many times forgiven, Anna," he said, stalking along beside her, wondering if he had ever really resented the boy.

"And you really enjoy teaching him?"

"Ya. Very much."

"He learned a lot this morning. So did I."

"It has been a memorable morning. The teaching has been part of what made it so." Then, looking from the thin shoulders of the lad who drove the team ahead of them, to the glorious woodland surrounding them and, lastly, to Anna's face, he finished, "The morning in which we have begun building our log house."

His face wore a look of serenity, the look of a man who knows where he's been, where he is and where he's heading.

To Anna, who'd never been blessed with such knowledge, the look spoke loudly of the inner peace garnered from the simple knowing of one's self. No, Anna thought, I do not know who my father was. I do not know where I came from. I do not know where I'll be headed once Karl learns my secret. But now is mighty good. Yes, now is mighty good, she thought, walking beside her husband to continue their work in the sun-strewn day, woodchips once again flying and perfuming the air, the song of the axe careening back to them from the green forest walls around them.

Chapter 7

❧

The trio melded into a routine of chopping, trimming, hauling, hitching and driving as the day wore on. The sun was high upon their shoulders. Karl stripped off his shirt and worked bare to the waist.

Anna had difficulty keeping her eyes from sliding time and again to the golden head, the tanned torso, the lean hips, the flexing arms. He performed with a fluidity akin to a dance. He was tapered like the tamaracks themselves, from shoulder to hip. The muscles in his arms bunched and hardened with the flow of his work, the cords of his neck stood out. The veins of his arms became defined each time he poised with the axe at its apex above his head. From behind, she watched his shoulder muscles gather in ridges at each fall of the blade, relax with the release, then hunch again.

He would bend to brush away some errant woodchip or branch, leaning on the axe handle, one foot balanced behind him. And Anna would find her eye drawn to the spot where the shadow of his spine widened and disappeared into the back of his britches. Sometimes, without warning, he would turn and find her watching him, and she would quickly lower her gaze from the sparkle of sun off the gold hairs of his chest and the line where it tapered down his abdomen.

"Are you tired, Anna?" he would ask. "Are you hot, Anna? Have a drink," he would say. Always she glanced down the skid path, away from him.

Soon another tree would go crashing down, and the two would find themselves enjoying the exhilaration of the moments just afterward. Always their eyes met then, if only briefly, before they found themselves working side by side, he with the axe, she with the hatchet, removing branches, while James continued to skid with the team.

Then Karl straightened from his task, saying, "Your cheeks will be burned. Here, take my hat." He plopped his soiled straw hat on her head, carrying with it the smell of him.

"I had a straw hat once," she said, concentrating on her chopping. "One of the women at—someone I knew gave it to me, but it was almost a goner when she decided she was done with it." She whacked another branch off, then added, "It had a pink ribbon around the crown."

"Hats with pink ribbons are scarce here in Minnesota."

"Doesn't matter," she said. "I'll get along." She started dragging a load of branches to the scrub pile.

He noticed the dark rings beneath her arms and said, "There is a deep spot in my creek where we can all go to cool off at the end of the day."

"How deep?" she asked, wondering just what he meant by "cool off."
Wearing what?

"Over your head."

"I can't swim."

"I will teach you."

"How cold is it?"

"Not as cold as the spring."

"Oho! It better not be!"

"You will try it then?"

At last she stopped tugging at the branches and looked over at him.
"We'll see."

"You really do not like to bathe, then?"

Embarrassed now, she lunged again at a bough. "It's just that we never
had to before. I mean, nobody ever made us. There was nobody to tell us
what to do."

"What about your mother?" Karl asked, amazed.

Anna gave a tug that sent her quick-footing it in reverse to keep from
tumbling. "She couldn't have cared less," she said expressionlessly.

By the time Anna and James made their last trip down the hill, the shadows had lengthened and their strides had shortened. They stumbled along
after Karl, who still strode sure and long and vigorously.

Looking at the wilted pair of helpers, Karl laughed. "Go to the house,
you two, but do not start any fires. I will come in as soon as I have seen
to the horses." He knew how tired they were after the day they'd put in.

The fire-making and supper-making fell to him. He showed James the
proper way to build a blaze, then showed Anna the proper way to build
a stew. Alas, the two observed him listlessly, nearly asleep on their chairs.
When the venison and turnips and wild onions were bubbling away on
the hob, Karl could not help laughing again at his sapped companions.

"If I do not do something quick to keep you two awake I will be eating
all that stew by myself. And I have had my fill of solitary meals. Come!"
He nudged each of them. "I think it is time we went for that swim."

The two sat disconsolately, while he gathered up clean clothing and
flannels for drying. "Come along. Get your dry things and follow me."

"Karl, you're a merciless mule!" Anna complained, feeling a rush of
intimacy in the criticizing.

"Ya, I am," he smilingly agreed. "And you, Anna, are a musty one."

Shamed, she could only follow him, ordering James to do the same.

The trail followed the bank of the creek, a narrow footpath worn by
Indians and animals in the long past. The creek was a purling brook that
bubbled over stones in some spots, ran smooth in others. In most places
it could be leaped in a single bound. The spot to which Karl led them
had had the help of the beavers in creating a serene pond above a dam.
Maidenhair and bracken ferns brushed their knees, while beneath the
thick press of fronds, feathergrass sprang up. The smooth water was dotted
with wild violets, shaded by tall virgin elms that stepped back to give
sprawling black willow bushes first chance at the stream's edge.

The last thing in the world Anna wanted to do was climb into the frigid
water. "Do you do this every day?" she asked Karl.

He was already stripping off his shirt. "Every day in the summer. In the
winter I use my bathhouse where I sweat myself clean like in Sweden."

"Do you have some kind of fetish for cleanliness?"

He stared at her, shirt hanging in his hands, while she stood without making any move to remove her clothing. "A person keeps clean," he said simply.

"Yes," she agreed lamely.

"Why do you not—" He felt suddenly shy. "Why do you not go put your things in the willow thicket there while James and I get in?"

Mutely, she turned and headed for cover.

"Come on, James," she heard after two splashes. "We will hide behind the beaver dam while your sister gets in."

She shucked down to her shift and crept out of hiding. The two were gone; all their clothes lay in heaps.

Anna hesitated. A toe in the water confirmed her suspicion. It was freezing! A person keeps clean, she said to herself, grimacing as she took the hated plunge.

At her shriek, laughter sounded, then James called, "Come on in, Anna. It ain't so bad once you get used to it and move around some."

She sat down, screamed again. "James Reardon and Karl Lindstrom, you're both a pair of liars and I hate you!"

For an answer came a big laugh answered by calls from birds perched nearby, watching these foolish humans who removed their plumage before bathing.

"I'm in now, you can come out!" she called. When Karl and James emerged and moved toward her, she had no choice but to dip in up to her neck. She didn't want either one of them seeing her puckered nipples through the flimsy shift.

"James, you little traitor!" she teased. "You never liked bathing any more than I did."

"It's different when you can get clear in." His head disappeared, popped up with a big grin on it. "I dare you to duck under, Anna!"

"Oh yeah?" Gamely, she dipped, only to come up sputtering and shuddering. Eyes still closed, she playfully nagged, "I hate your pool, Karl Lindstrom! Can't you heat it up for me?"

"I will go down and ask it." He flipped his feet, dove and with a flash of white skin was gone. He emerged across the way and yelled, "Sorry, Anna. The beavers do not agree. It is as warm as it is going to get."

He struck out in long, even strokes, effortlessly swimming the distance to her. "Come, I will take you to where the ledge angles down, then we will swim back toward shore. Do not be afraid."

He took her hands under the water and pulled her slowly off her feet. She glided, mouthing water. He smiled at the way the droplets clung to her eyelashes and hair.

"Don't take me too far," she begged.

"Do not worry. Do you think I would risk you now that you are here?"

"Maybe!" she sputtered. "What are you going to do with a woman who can't cook stew?"

"There are uses I can think of," he said quietly, so James could not hear. His mouth, like hers, was halfway beneath the surface. They bobbed, weightless, holding hands and learning each other's eyes, with eyelashes stuck wetly together, hair swept back in furrows and skin jeweled by occasional runnels.

"How about a woman who cannot bake bread?"

"She can be taught," he burbled, the water lapping about his lips.

"Or make soap?"

"She can be taught," he repeated.

"To make it or to use it?"

"Both." And he opened his mouth, took in a mouthful of water and spit it right between her eyes.

"You big Swedish bully!" she yelped, coming after him. But he was gone like quicksilver to the deep near James.

"Be good and I will come and teach you to swim," he backtalked.

"Why? I don't like your miserable pond, anyway!"

But a serious look came over his face. Then he pointed just behind her, asking James, "Is that a snapping turtle?"

Poor Anna almost broke her neck wrenching around. Her hands dug wildly at the water as she scrambled to get out. On her way up the bank, her pantaloons sagged, revealing one white cheek before she snatched angrily at them and turned with hands on hips, bellering, "Karl Lindstrom, see if I come in there again! That wasn't funny!"

But Karl and James were slapping the surface of the water in disgusting merriment, falling over backward like fools, while Anna fumed. She sat miserably on shore, hugging her arms, shivering while the two took up surface diving, racing and exploring the outer perimeter of the beaver dam. Stubbornly she sat until Karl swam toward her. "Come on, Anna. I won't tease any more."

She crossed her arms over her chest. Her nipples were like spearpoints now.

"Should I come and get you?" he threatened, taking one more step. Her eyes dropped to the level where the water sliced across his hips, revealing the hollows just below the hipbones.

"No! I'm coming!" She leaped up and plunged in, venturing farther than before. Karl taught her to roll on her back and flap her hands at her sides, like a fish using its fins. But lying that way with his arm slung beneath her back, her breasts became islands with no more than a cloud-thin veil of clinging cotton to disguise their darker centers. She quickly flipped onto her stomach again.

Anna and Karl bobbed out to the ledge and swam toward shore many times. Once, heading back out, she overshot the shallows and panicked when her feet touched nothingness. Karl grabbed her from behind with one swift flexing of his steely arm, and again her feet touched sand. But his arm lingered long after she was safe, spanning her ribs, touching the bottom of her breasts, pulling her back against his nakedness below the water.

Then James came near, and Karl released her. The trio broke for shore.

When Karl announced their stew must now be done, Anna was surprised to find she had forgotten her tiredness while they were frolicking. They each went their separate ways to dry and dress, then met back on the path to walk home. On their way they were accompanied by night peepers and frogs who'd tuned up to orchestrate dusk.

Fragrant aroma greeted them at their door. Karl enjoyed supper, especially watching Anna and James polish off enough food for a pair of grizzlies. Before the bowls were emptied for the last time, James drooped and wilted, then his sister followed suit. Karl scooted them off to bed.

With full night fallen, Karl lit his pipe and wandered out to the barn.

Belle and Bill, their great breaths pumping slowly, shifted contentedly, thumping hello in their stalls. They knew who entered, knew a oneness with their visitor. His gentle hand stroked the wide heads between the eyes. Finally, when the pipe coals turned pungent, dying away, came the deep voice. "She is a spunky one, my Anna. What do you think, Bill? Not as easy to break to the halter as your Belle, here."

In the dark sod house Karl lay aside his pipe, then his clothes. He settled into the enveloping cornhusks. Automatically, he reached out to encircle the slumbering Anna. He pulled her into his curve, knowing at once content and want. He thought about her breasts and how they had looked in the water. They lay now so close above his arm. All he need do was shift his arm slowly, slide his hand upward and he would be touching her breast at last. How badly he wanted to caress her, to know that first feel of her.

But she slept in utter exhaustion while Karl's sense of fairness rankled. When he explored Anna for the first time, he wanted it to be a shared thing. He wanted her awake, aware, receptive and responsive.

He could hold off. He had waited all this time to ease his loneliness. What they'd shared today—the three of them—would be enough for now. That and the feel of her sleeping body curved against his belly, the texture of her hair where he pressed his face against it upon her back.

Chapter 8
♣

Anna awakened to a myriad of sounds: bird-song so involved it became tuneless chatter, the crack of the axe, male voices, a short spurt of laughter. The bed beside her was empty. So was the pallet on the floor. The cabin door stood open, beckoning the long sun to cascade across the floor in a welcome rush of gold. She clenched her fists and stretched, lynxlike and twisting, savoring the goodness of everything—the sounds, the sun, the snugness.

Arising, she found a blanket had been strung up across one corner to act as her dressing room.

When Karl came inside, he saw only her backside. He eyed it appreciatively as she poked her head around the drape to investigate her niche of privacy.

"Good morning, Anna."

She whirled around to find him smiling at her, sunshafts at his back, hugging a burden of firewood against his chest. In his other hand was the axe again, looking ever so right.

"Good morning, Karl." She stood with bare toes curled against the dirt floor, her nighty wrinkled, her hair in terrible disarray.

Karl couldn't have been more pleased with her appearance.

Suddenly, Anna realized that they'd both been stupidly smiling at one another, he with perhaps thirty pounds of wood on his arm, she with a blanket pulled across her front. She looked at the rope from which it hung, patted the cloth to make it wave a little and asked, "Did you remodel your house for me?"

He laughed and answered, "I guess I did." Then he went to the fireplace with his load.

"Thank you," she said to his strong back as it bent, sending the wood clattering.

He turned, his eyes flicked momentarily over her breasts, then back to her face. "I should have thought of it yesterday, with the boy here and all."

Having followed the path of his eyes, she grew flustered, so asked quickly, "Were you teaching him to use the axe?"

"Ya, on something a little smaller than a standing tamarack."

"How did he do?"

James sailed in just then, answering her question. "Lookit, Anna! I split nearly all the wood Karl brought in."

"Nearly all?" Karl repeated, with a cock of his head.

"We-e-e-ll . . . half anyway."

All three laughed at once, then James asked, "Which pail should I use for the milk?"

"Any one from the springhouse." Karl nodded toward it.

Before James darted away again, excited, eager, he bubbled, "You were right, Karl. Nanna came home all by herself to get milked, and she came right up to me and nuzzled my hand as if she knew I was the one who'd be taking care of that job from now on."

Within Anna grew the realization of what this place, these duties, this man, meant to a boy of thirteen, and just how good it would be for her brother to grow to manhood learning a life such as this. "He's awful happy, Karl," she said, knowing no other way to express it.

"So am I," Karl answered, turning to look over his shoulder at her from where he hunkered to his fire-making again.

As she slipped behind the drape, Karl found himself intrigued by the sight of her bare feet peeping below it and lost track of what he was supposed to be doing. He watched her nightgown fall in a heap around her ankles. The blanket billowed here and there. Anna's feet turned around toward the trunk, which was also behind the blanket now. Then she seemed to balance on a single foot.

"Ow!" Anna heard from the direction of the fireplace.

"Karl? What's wrong?"

"Nothing."

"Then why did you say 'ow'?"

"I think there will be a little skin burning with the kindling, that's all."

Anna's hands fell still. *Karl* made a mismove with his axe? she thought wonderingly. *Karl?* Then, looking down at her bare feet and the space between the floor and the blanket, she smiled widely to herself.

When his fire was started, he called, "Do you know how to build a pancake?"

"No."

"You will after today. I thought I could give up these kitchen duties once you came, and be a woodsman instead. But I think I must teach you how to make pancakes first."

Anna grimaced. She herself already liked the woods far better than the kitchen, but she buttoned the last button and stepped out to meet her domestic fate.

"So, teach me how to build a pancake," she ordered in an affected tone of command.

"Annuuuh!" he exclaimed when he saw her, drawing but her name. "What is this you wear?"

"Britches." She flapped her hands.

"Britches? Ya, I see it is britches but . . . but you are a woman."

"Karl, my skirts were wet to the knees before we got halfway out to the tamaracks yesterday. And they caught on the branches and made me trip, and got pitch all over them from dragging across the scrub. And . . . and they made my work harder, so I decided to try on a pair of James' britches. Look!" She spun around. "They fit!"

"Ya, I see, but I do not know what to think. In Sweden no lady would be caught hiding in her pantry in britches."

"Oh, fiddle!" she snapped lightly. "In Sweden I'll bet there are so many men to build your houses the women don't have to help, right?"

"Ya, that is right," he reluctantly admitted. "But, Anna, I do not know about these britches."

"Well, I know. I know I'm not tripping over soggy skirts. Besides, who's gonna see me except you and James?"

He couldn't actually think of a logical argument. He had thought her dresses inappropriate. But britches? He could not resist asking, "I suppose in Boston there was no one to stop you from running loose in britches any time you wanted either?"

She looked sideways at him, then away. She found the still-rumpled bed and made herself busy flipping the covers smooth. "I did pretty much as I pleased there."

"Ya. I think you sure did. And it did not please you to learn pancake batter?"

"Here I am," she flipped her hands palms up, "ready to learn. But I'm not promising just how much I'll like it."

Karl explained that he had to adapt his mama's recipe for filmy, light Swedish pancakes because he had to do without eggs here.

He looked so utterly ridiculous, her great big Karl, standing there at the table, mixing up pancakes, she could not help teasing him. Throughout the lesson she refused to be serious, while he instructed her in odd measurements.

"Two palms full of flour."

"Whose palms? Yours or mine?" she kidded him.

"Two pinches of salt."

"I might have to borrow your palms and your fingers when it's my turn, because yours are a different size than mine."

"Enough saleratus—leavening—to fill perhaps the half shell of a hazelnut."

"And if I've never seen a hazelnut?" she asked mischievously, eliciting his promise to show her one soon, and an order to straighten up and pay attention, though he tried hard to hold a straight face.

"A lump of lard the size of two walnuts or so."

"Now—walnuts—at last, I know! It is the first useful measurement you have given me."

"No eggs," he said hopelessly. "No chickens, no eggs!"

"No eggs!" she exclaimed, pretending chagrin. "Whatever shall I do? I'm sure my pancakes will be tough as calluses without my eggs!"

He was having the utmost difficulty getting through this without kissing her teasing little face. He promised that soon they would hunt for prairie chicken eggs. Then came goat's milk.

"Enough to make it the right thickness," which she observed at extremely close range, getting her head in his way so he could not see, telling him ignorantly when she thought the batter was "just right."

The eggless pancakes proved sumptuous fare, indeed, especially when topped with syrup, which Karl explained proudly, was tapped and boiled down right here just this spring, from his own maples, which he promised to show her soon.

Anna was forced to miss the harnessing of the horses that morning, for she was left behind to clean up the dishes and scour the wooden pail from the goat's milk, using the disgusting yellow lye soap, which burned her skin. It was becoming increasingly apparent to Anna why a man needed help out here in the wilderness. Who in his right mind would not want someone to take care of these unpalatable household tasks?

But once again free of the cabin, her spirits blossomed. Outside was where she loved it best, with the wind lifting her hair, and the horses snorting and tossing their heads impatiently, and James pleased because he'd helped with the harnessing again today and had remembered everything quite clearly, and Karl seizing up his axe and the five of them all heading out to the tamaracks again.

They flushed a covey of grouse that morning, and Karl brought down one of the elusive darting birds with a single shot, laughing when he lowered the gun to find Anna squatted down in terror with her elbows over her ears.

"It is only a grouse," he said, "my little brave boy in britches."

"Only a grouse? It sounded like a hurricane!"

"Next time you hear it, you will know it is only wings, and you will not need to hide like a mouse."

The ease with which Karl brought the bird down convinced Anna that he was a practiced marksman, along with everything else. He gutted the kill immediately. At noon he completed the dressing of the bird, while James watched and learned, and Anna gagged.

Karl beamed with pride when he showed her where he kept his wild rice. It, too, was harvested off a slough on his own land in the northeast section. He set the rice to soak in boiling water, promising them a delightful supper. Later he taught them how to stuff the grouse with the musty-smelling rice, and how to wrap it all up in damp plantain leaves and plunge it into the coals along with yams wrapped likewise. He showed them how to sweeten the yams with maple syrup. Their meal would be truly delicious when they returned from their swim.

Anna was less tired that night, and also somewhat less unwilling to dip into the cold water. While Karl and James stood in chest-high water, throwing pink rocks into the drop-off, concentrating hard on just where they'd have to dive to retrieve them again, Anna took an enormous breath, glided underwater from behind Karl and bit him on the ankle, touching nothing else of his skin. Karl yelped. Anna heard him clear underwater, and came up howling and sputtering, the sand all awhirl where Karl had jumped and kicked at the underwater menace.

"Oh, Karl, you're so funny!" she gasped. "Scared of a little fish that doesn't make half the commotion of a bunch of dumb ruffed grouse!"

But one glance at Karl, and she knew the play war was on. He crouched. He narrowed his eyes menacingly, and lowered his face till it rode the water like a crocodile, only his eyes showing as he glided silently in pursuit. She backed away, hands spread to fend him off.

"Karl . . . no, Karl . . . I was just teasing, Karl!" She thrashed wildly, laughing and screaming, trying to get away from him.

James hollered, "Git her, Karl! Git her!"

"James, you little turd! I'm your sister! You're supposed to be on my side!" she yelled, clumsily plowing water. She looked over her shoulder and found she was getting nowhere fast.

"Git her, Karl! She called me a turd!"

"I heard her. Do you think a woman with such a nasty tongue should be punished?"

"Yeah! Yeah!" cheered the disloyal James, loving every minute of it.

"Traitor!" she badgered while Karl advanced, a feral gleam in his eye. Suddenly, he disappeared. Anna turned a circle, but the surface was broken only by little ripples. "Where'd he go? Karl? Where are—"

Like a whale surfacing, Karl lunged up and out of the water, catching Anna with a shoulder behind her knees, pitching her high in the air while the forest reverberated with her shriek. She flipped butt-up and landed with an ignominious splat! Up she came, with hair every place but where it should be, to the tune of James and Karl guffawing in great camaraderie.

"I think I just made a new kind of sea monster!" Karl pointed at Anna, who was coming on with fingers gnarled, snarling beautifully through the mop of dripping hair. Karl feigned helplessness when she caught him with both hands from behind his waist and wrestled him off his feet. She got the worst of it, naturally, for she went down backward and Karl sat on top of her. Under the water her arms slipped down on his water-slicked body and came into contact with more than just his belly. Swiftly, he turned in that liquid world, caught her against his chest and together they shot up like geysers, laughing into each other's faces.

"Oh, Anna, my little sea monster," he said, "what did I do before you were here?"

They all went to bed at the same time that night, in the room flavored with tobacco smoke and fellowship. When the cornhusks quit rustling, James' voice came lazily. " 'Night, Karl. 'Night, Anna."

"Goodnight, James," the two wished together.

Then Karl found Anna's hand and made patterns on its palm with his thumb. At last he pulled her nearer, making her roll on her side to face him, while he did likewise. "Are you tired?" he whispered very near her lips.

"No," she whispered back, thinking, no, no, no, no, no! I'm not at all tired.

"Last night I was disappointed you went to sleep so fast."

"So was I," she whispered, thrilled by his simple words and the feel of his hard thumb softly brushing. Her heart beat in double time while the palm of Anna's hand grew hot where Karl stroked it. They lay so still, with eyes wide open, noses almost touching, breathing upon each other.

James sighed, and Karl's thumb stopped moving. His breath warmed her face. With a slight movement, he touched the tip of his nose to hers. Silently, he let the touch speak for him while feelings of greater need coursed through his body. His grip on her hand became almost painful. A hint of movement brought Karl's lips lightly to hers.

Do that again, Karl—harder, she thought, while her heart hammered wildly. They lay unmoving, childlike, knees to knees, nose to nose, lips to lips, breath to breath, absorbed in the growing feeling of goodness at such simple nearness.

"Today was so good, Anna, having you and the boy here. I . . . I feel such things," he whispered.

"What kind of things?"

"Things about all three of us," he whispered hoarsely, wishing he knew better how to tell her what he meant. "Working together on the logs—it is good. Eating together, swimming. I feel . . . I feel full, Anna."

"Is . . . is that what makes it? Working together and all the rest?" She nudged his thumb aside so hers could stroke his palm. Briefly his warm breath stopped falling upon her face, then she heard him swallow.

"You feel it, too, Anna?"

"I think so. I . . . I don't know, Karl. I just know it's different here from Boston. It's better. We never had to work before. Working here, helping you . . . I don't know. It doesn't really seem like work." She wanted to add things she didn't know how to say, things about his smile, his teasing, his patience, his love of his place, which somehow had started to seep into her, even the sweet peace of weariness last night, a satisfied weariness she had never before known. But these were things she yet only sensed but could not put voice to.

"For so long I dreamed of you being here to help with the cabin. Now it is just like I thought it would be. Going out all together in the morning, working all day, relaxing together in the evenings. I feel . . . how good it is to laugh again, to laugh with you."

"You make me laugh so easy, Karl."

"Good. I like to see you laughing. You and the boy, too."

"Karl?"

"Hm?"

"We never had much reason to laugh before. Here, though, it's different."

It pleased him that he should have provided this nicety, one he had not consciously sought to provide. He felt her admission was more than a simple statement of enjoyment, sensed it as her invitation for affection. Soundlessly, he moved, taking a piece of her upper lip between his, tugging lightly at it, as if to say, come nearer.

She obliged, and their mouths met softly, each of them slightly open, hesitant, hopeful, yet infinitely childish in their slowness, their willingness to let the other move first. There had been only that chaste kiss the first night. But this kiss had been born on the rising sun, had been foretold by their first "good mornings" while Karl stood holding an armload of wood and Anna stood holding her curtain. Through the day the certainty of this kiss had grown, enriched by their teasing and good humor and their growing sense of familiarity with each other.

He slowly straightened his knees to move nearer. This time he took her lips fully, undemandingly at first, but his wet, warm tongue came seeking, riding upon the seam of her lips as if dissolving some sugar stitches he tasted there. Dissolve them he did, feeling beneath his tongue a first opening of her own mouth. Emboldened, he cradled the back of her neck, pulling her into the kiss, using his tongue to tease her away from passivity. What Karl waited for was some first sign, a movement, a touch of encouragement. His exploration touched a response in Anna and she, too, straightened her legs.

Cautiously, she laid her hand upon his cheek. Never before had she caressed him in any way. The touch of her hand upon his skin raised an ardor in Karl that became difficult to control. Beneath her palm Anna felt his cheek muscles stretch as his mouth widened. His tongue entered her mouth more forcefully while she felt the strokes of it through her palm and his cheek.

Never had Anna experienced kissing as an enjoyable thing. Now was awakened in her the knowledge that things like this could be different from the way she had always thought them. About this there was nothing sordid or ugly. There was no compulsion to push this man away, no crawling of skin, no stinging of tears. There was instead a feeling that he honored her, and thereby honored the act upon which they embarked. She sensed in Karl the unfolding wonder he experienced in taking her nearer fulfillment one slow step at a time. Anna felt herself unfolding, too, like the petals of a flower until the full beauty of the blossom is revealed.

With a slow relaxing of muscle, he lowered his chest across hers, resting there upon her breast to see what she'd do. But she only laid her hand on the bare skin of his shoulder blade, testing again the rightness of what she felt, training her hand to move down the ridge beneath her palm. How well she remembered it after watching it flex in the sun these two days.

Karl collapsed with his face buried in the pillow he'd filled for her with cattail down, basking in the first tentative exploration of her hand upon his back. Needing more, he arched away, freeing her pinned hand. But when she didn't seem to understand what he needed, he found the hand there beneath him and nudged it onto his shoulder, then settled down upon her, his face lost once more in the pillow beside her head.

Anna could not help vividly recalling the expression on his face when he had told of bringing Nanna inside the house for company during winter. She remembered, too, the way Karl's hand had toyed with the goat's ear. She had never known before that men needed simple touching.

The years of aloneness slid away with each pass of her hands along his skin. Their hearts, pressed tightly together, spoke of the human need both had harbored for so long. Within Anna, to whom such a feeling had also been denied for long years, a desperate voice warned she could lose all this warmth that radiated to her once Karl carried this act to its climax. But it was a good thing to feel so at one with another human being. She could not stop her hands from playing upon his back just a little longer.

"Oh, Anna, what you do to me," he said huskily, suddenly raising up, pinning her down with both hands on her arms. "Do you know what you do to me?'' he whispered with a kind of vehemence that warned her she had perhaps already gone too far. But at Karl's movement, the cornhusks rustled, and they heard James make a sound as he rolled over. Karl's head jerked up in alert.

They waited a moment before Anna whispered, ''I think I know, Karl, but . . .'' She had received the reprieve she needed, from James. She was confused herself, liking everything so far, still afraid to let it go further. ''Karl, I wish . . .'' Never before had she felt such dread of hurting someone's feelings. It was a new thing to Anna, this concern she had for Karl. She knew she must pick her way carefully. ''It's only been three days. I feel like each day we've gotten to know each other a little better, but I think we need more time.''

He'd done the thing he most wanted to avoid: he'd pushed her too fast. By now Karl liked Anna so much, and felt she liked him, too. Still, he tried to look at it from her point of view. She was perhaps afraid of being hurt. For this Karl could not blame her. ''I should not have pushed you this way,'' he admitted. ''I only thought to touch you, but I find it is hard to hold back.''

''Karl, please don't be so hard on yourself. I liked it and it's all right you touched me and kissed me. I'm only getting to know you better when I return the touches, like any woman wants to know her husband. Please understand, Karl . . .''

She wondered exactly how to say what she meant. She wanted him— yes—yet she wanted to put off the time of consummation because she feared afterward he would find her repugnant, and that would be the end of this interlude of adjustment she was so enjoying.

Also, Anna wanted more time to be wooed. It had nothing to do with whether or not she was a virgin. She was a woman, and as such had had dreams of soldiers with braids and epaulettes. How could she make him understand that braids and epaulettes mattered little, but that she wanted the joy of anticipation to go on a while longer? She wanted to be courted when she was already married. How absurd it sounded, even to her. Still, she had to try to explain.

''Do you know what I want?''

''No, Anna, what?'' He thought he would give her anything if she would only not deny him interminably.

''I want some more days like today . . . first. I want laughing and teasing and looking at each other across the way and . . . oh, I don't know. The things we'd have done if we had met in Sweden and you had bought me that hair ribbon, I guess. All girls want that sort of thing, like we talked about the other night. Do you understand, Karl?''

''I understand, but for how long do you want such a thing?'' The intensity was waning from his voice, and she thought perhaps she had succeeded in keeping from alienating him.

''Oh, a little while, Karl. Just a little while for you to be my suitor instead of my husband. A little while to enjoy getting to know each other.''

''So you like some teasing and some . . .'' Karl could not think of the right word.

''Flirting?'' she filled in.

''A true American word—flirting.''

''Yes, Karl, maybe I do. For both of us.''

"You are a strange girl, Anna, writing letters to me to agree to be my wife sight unseen, now demanding me to flirt with you. What am I to do with such a whiskey-haired girl anyway?"

"Do as she asks," Anna said coquettishly, something quite new to her.

"You will have your way, Anna. But before you do, let me have another kiss like the last one. Just one."

Chapter 9

♣

If Anna wanted flirting, she got it in subtle ways during the following days. Karl could do things in the most offhand manner, making her turn red, or away, or look quickly to see if James saw. Karl could draw his oversize red handkerchief out of his hip pocket and dry his neck and chest in the sun, never laying an eye on Anna, but knowing full well she watched his every shimmering muscle.

Anna could bend to pick up a load of branches and point the hind pockets of James' britches at Karl in as equally an innocent manner. He could remove his straw hat—she had taken time to stitch a sunbonnet for herself realizing Karl needed his hat—and wipe his forehead with his forearm, then, squint at the sun and say, "It is hot today." Guilelessly?

Anna didn't think so.

Raising the hair from the back of her neck, she would agree casually, "It sure is."

In the pond their frolicking became sensitized by more frequent brushing against each other, under the guise of dunking, learning to swim, being teacher and student.

Those sun-splashed days in the tamaracks were harbingers of more to come. But one day when the three awakened to rain, the tamaracks were forgotten for the time being. Karl checked the gray drizzle after breakfast, lit his pipe thoughtfully, then went to the barn to fetch a pitchfork and dig worms. Soon afterward he and James left with fishing poles in hand.

Anna was alone in the springhouse washing vegetables, displeased at being left behind. She muttered to herself and threw the beans from pail to pan in irritation. Beans! she silently griped. I'm left to clean beans while those two go off to fish bass!

Suddenly the light from outside was dimmed even more. Anna looked up and screamed. A bunch of Indians stood crowding around the doorway of the springhouse, somber faces impassive while she jumped up and spilled green beans everywhere. They all had oiled hair, pulled back into braided tails, and were dressed in fringed buckskin.

The one nearest the doorway smiled in a toothy grin at the sound of her fright. They all acted like they were waiting for her to step outside.

What else could she do? She squelched her fears and stepped into the misty day.

"Foxhair," Toothy Grin grunted.

She stood in the drizzle, wondering what to do, while they all stared at her hair. Should she act as if it were totally natural to stand in the rain carrying on a conversation with an Indian, or stalk off toward the cabin where they were sure to follow?

"Anna," she corrected. "Anna Lindstrom." The name surprised even her.

Toothy Grin shot a curious glance to one of his friends who had the face of an old buffalo on the body of a young deer.

"Foxhair," Toothy Grin repeated, nodding now.

Buffalo Face grinned. He had magnificent teeth for such an ugly face. "Foxhair marry Whitehair, together make baby striped like skunk kitten."

They all laughed in great amusement at this.

"What do you want?" she snapped. "If all you've come here to do is make fun of my hair, you can leave! If you want to see my husband, he's not here. You'll have to come back another time." She was trembling in her britches, but she was damned if she was going to let them come sneaking here into her own yard and ridicule her!

"Tonka Squaw!" one of them said, in a tone she could have sworn was approving, although why was beyond her guess.

"What do you want?" she asked again, none too gently.

"Tonka Squaw?" one Indian asked Buffalo Face. "How you know she squaw?" They seemed to be amused by her britches, all pointing and jabbering in their unrecognizable jargon while eyeing her clothing. She grew angrier by the moment at being talked past like she wasn't even there.

"Talk English!" she spit. "If you're going to come around here, you can just by-damn talk English! I know you know how because Karl told me!"

"Tonka Squaw!" one said again, with a broad grin.

"Spit fire!" another said.

Then they laughed again at her britches.

"Well, if you weren't all so rude, I'd invite you inside to wait for Karl, but I'll be darned if I'll have you in when all you came to do is laugh at me!"

She spun and headed for the cabin, and they all silently followed. In the doorway, she turned to challenge them. "Anybody who comes in here had just better forget about my britches and keep his smart comments to himself!"

But in they came, right behind her. Silently, they squatted and sat cross-legged on the floor before the fireplace. She wondered what she was expected to do to entertain them.

She decided the best course of action was action. She would pretend to be very busy preparing dinner, and maybe they would get tired of watching her and go away. She had struggled once before through the making of a kind of mince cake, baked in the spider instead of in an oven. She struggled to remember the ingredients Karl had taught her, and in her preoccupation thought she was probably ruining it entirely. But she didn't care. Anything to look busy and distract the Indians. But they muttered among themselves, now and then breaking into laughter, as if what she did were the funniest thing in the world.

She began mixing the cake ingredients, found the mince made of pumpkin and vinegar and put the crock on the table while she reached for a clean spoon. Turning around, she found an Indian, with a nose like a beaver, reaching into her jar with his bare hand. Without thinking, she whacked him a good one across the knuckles with her wooden spoon.

"Git!" she spit at him. "Where are your manners? You don't come into my house and reach your big dirty hands into my mincemeat and eat it behind my back! Sit down and keep out of my way and maybe, just maybe, I'll give you some cake when it's done! Meanwhile, keep your hands where they belong!"

Beaver Nose's companions had a jolly good laugh at that one. While he held his smitten knuckles, the others held their sides and rocked in raucous laughter, repeating over and over, "Tonka Squaw, Tonka Squaw."

"Quiet! You're no better than him," she warned the rest brandishing her spoon, "you all came in here uninvited!"

She tended to her cake-mixing, discomfited by having five Indian men sitting and watching her. So far they seemed to respect her spunk. As long as it worked, she'd keep it up. She had no other defense against her fear anyway.

She knew before the batter was done she'd made a mess of it again. But she went about putting it on the spider to fry into cakes as if it were an epicurean delicacy. The Indians watched her and mumbled as if intrigued by this involved cooking method. The little patties were flatter than Beaver Nose's nose, but she couldn't stop now. She fried away until all the batter was cooked. Such as they were, she ceremoniously put all the cakes on her largest wooden platter, and said, "Now, if you will be patient, I'll make some rose hip tea for you."

She set the platter on the table, keeping a corner of an eye on the Indians, lest they reach out for one of her sad confections before she bid them do so. Hungrily, they eyed the cakes, but not one of them made a move toward them, remembering the fury of her spoon on Beaver Nose's knuckle.

She mashed and steeped the rose hips, all the time remembering that Karl said rose hips prevented scurvy, wondering why in the world she was keeping the disease from befalling this group that had won her wrath. When the tea was steeped, she had a problem of where to find enough containers to serve all five Indians at the same time, but she would by-gum do this thing right!

She went to the doorway, stopped and turned an admonishing finger at the sitting men. "Don't you dare touch those cakes till I get back!" Then she ran to the springhouse to get the dipper and a couple of small, empty crocks.

She came back to the sound of their guttural mumblings, and made a big show of putting rose hip tea into the dipper, the two crocks and her three mugs. She was darned if she'd drink out of that dipper herself. She handed it to Buffalo Face, since he was the one who had poked fun at her britches. Let him drink out of the dipper! She was a lady and would drink from the mug, britches or not!

This, then, was the sight that greeted Karl and James when they returned from the creek, dripping, but bearing a stunning catch of wide-mouth bass. Anna reigned supreme, the only one of the group sitting on a chair. At her feet were five oily-haired, buckskinned Indians, drinking rose hip tea, of all things, and eating the most miserable-looking mince cakes Karl had ever seen in his life—eating them and nodding in appreciation as if they were angel's food!

Anna turned startled eyes to him as he entered. He could almost see her shoulders sag in relief at his appearance. He wondered how long the Indians had been there.

"Whitehair! Hah!" one of the Indians greeted.

"Hello, Two Horns," Karl replied, "I see you have met my wife." It was Karl's best friend, Two Horns, that Anna had insulted by making him drink his tea from the dipper. But he didn't seem to mind.

"Tonka Squaw!" Two Horns said again.

"Tonka Squaw!" they all chimed in, if you could call all that guttering "chiming."

"Yes, she is," Karl agreed, smirking and cocking an eyebrow, raising Anna's temperature a notch.

"Tonka Squaw dress like Whitehair. How you know she squaw?"

Karl laughed. "I know by what is inside."

So, thought Anna, Tonka Squaw means a woman who wears britches! Just wait until I get you alone, Karl Lindstrom!

But they were all laughing at Karl's remark. The ominous look on Anna's face told him he'd been a little precipitous in making jokes about her britches before his friends.

"I have fish. You will all stay for supper," Karl said.

Oh, great! thought Anna. I've been entertaining his rude Indian friends all afternoon. So what does he do but make sure I have to put up with them through supper, too!

"Anna can throw a few more potatoes into the fire," Karl added.

That's just what Anna did. She was downright huffy by this time. She stomped out to get more potatoes from the root cellar. She knew the Indians loved potatoes and the white wheat bread so different from that which the Indians themselves made of corn. She returned to thrust the potatoes into the coals, not even bothering to wrap them in plantain leaves. She wasn't going to get all soaking wet gathering up plantain for the benefit of a bunch of outspoken Indians!

Karl had begun cleaning the fish on the tabletop. The Indians expressed their disapproval of this, adding heat to Anna's already fiery anger. "Why Tonka Squaw not clean fish? Whitehair sit and smoke pipe with his friends."

"Anna is not very good at cleaning things," Karl explained, embarrassing her further. "She has never learned how to clean fish anyway. These are the first fish we have had since she has been here."

"Bad start to marriage," was the general consensus among the group.

Anna gathered that no self-respecting Indian would be caught dead cleaning fish when he had a wife to do it for him. She began to resent Karl a little less for not expecting her to perform that loathsome duty. She went to the spring house for water, came back and conceded to wash each fillet after it was scraped free by his knife.

The Indians had taken James into their circle, already having dubbed him One-Who-Has-Eye-Of-Cat because he had green eyes, something new to them. When they brought out their pipes, they included James in their offer to smoke.

"Oh no, you don't!" Anna objected. "You're not teaching him any of your bad habits at his age. He's still a growing boy."

They saw the way James withdrew the hand he'd been reaching toward the pipe, and once more nodded in approval, saying "Tonka Squaw." But when it was time for the frying of the fish, they became amused at the big white Swede whose woman did not even know a simple thing like that. Nevertheless, they ate their fill, relishing in particular those potatoes. The only potatoes they usually ate were wild ones, not nearly as delicious as these the white man cultivated.

When the meal was over, Anna was left to clean up while the men sat around with their pipes again. She wondered if the Indians would ever leave, for she was getting sick and tired of being called Tonka Squaw at every move she made, and having her britches closely scrutinized and being criticized because she didn't perform all the duties these big bullies let their women perform.

But they left at last, long after dark, and she wondered how they would find their way home in the blackness. Karl bid them goodbye at the door, and they all raised their palms to him. They did the same to James, but never gave Anna so much as a glance, which nettled her to a snit again, after it was she who'd invited them in in the first place!

Karl came back inside and could tell she was in a lather, so left her alone. He and James talked about the Indians, Karl saying he'd known all along they'd come around to have a look at his new squaw sooner or later.

She flounced into bed and faced the wall, really puckered now because Karl had called her a squaw! She'd had enough of it from those redskins!

When the fire was banked and the cabin dark, Karl laid down beside her. Instead of taking her hint and leaving her alone, he leaned over her shoulder to whisper into her ear, "Is my Tonka Squaw upset with her husband?"

In a forced whisper she sizzled, "Don't you dare call me a squaw one more time! I've had about all of it I can stand for one day! You and your big bully Indian friends!"

"Ya. We are some big bullies, calling you Tonka Squaw. Maybe you do not deserve it, after all."

Now he had her wondering. She turned her face a little his way, asking over her cold shoulder, "Deserve it?"

"Ya. Do you think you do?"

"Well, how should I know? What does it mean?"

"It means Big Woman, and it is the highest compliment an Indian can pay. You must have done something to make them think you were really tough."

"Tough?" At last her pent-up emotions of the afternoon and evening began evaporating. "Karl, I was so scared when I saw them standing in the door of the springhouse that I threw beans all over forty acres!"

"So that's why those beans are covering the springhouse step."

"I was scared," she repeated, seeking his sympathy now.

"I told you they were my friends."

"But I never saw them before, Karl. I didn't know who they were. The one with the toothy grin made fun of my hair, then Two Horns poked fun at my britches. All I could think to do was put them in their places for being so rude to me . . . and in my own home, too!''

"I thought as much. You just are not used to their ways. The Indian respects authority. When you put them in their places, you fix yourself in yours, and they look up to you."

"They do?'' she asked, surprised.

"So they call you Tonka Squaw, Big Woman, because you make them behave, when Indian men are used to having their own way with their women."

"They are?''

"They are."

Anna couldn't help laughing. "Oh, Karl, do you know what I did? I smacked old Beaver Nose so hard with my wooden spoon that before the end of the night he had black and blue marks on his knuckles."

"You did such a thing, Anna?'' he asked, amazed at this wife of his.

"Well, he stuck his dirty hand right in my mincemeat pot!''

"So you smacked him with your wooden spoon?''

"I did. Oh, Karl, I did,'' she giggled now. "That was an awful thing to do, wasn't it?'' Her giggling grew louder at the thought of her own temerity.

"It seems you are the kind of squaw those Indians would like to have, but make sure they don't! One who keeps her men in line!''

"Oh you!'' Anna spouted. "You just forget about calling me Tonka Squaw, right this minute. I like *Anna* just fine, no matter what kind of squaw I am!''

"Tonka,'' Karl reiterated.

"Well, you might have thought I was enjoying it all, but let me tell you I was plenty scared. Besides, I was put out with them for teasing me about my britches and my hair."

"They teased you about your hair, too, Anna?'' Karl asked now.

"Yours and mine both, I gather." Too late she realized she had led herself toward a subject that would better have been avoided.

"Well, what did they say?'' Obviously, Karl was eager to hear the rest.

"Nothing.''

"Nothing?''

"Nothing, I said.''

But in the dark, he leaned and teased at her earlobe. "When you say it is nothing, I know it is something. But maybe something you do not want your husband to know." Anna stifled a giggle as he lightly nipped her jaw.

"Something like that,'' she admitted.

"How would you like to gut the fish the next time I bring the catch home?'' he teased. "You would just love it, I bet.''

He could feel her cheeks round up in a smile against his teasing lips.

"How would you like a rap in the knuckles with my spoon? After all, it is Tonka Squaw you are threatening."

"I am not very scared, as you can tell." He was whispering against her cheek now. "That is not why I am shaking."

"Why are you shaking then, Whitehair?'' she whispered back.

His hand came seeking.

"I am shaking with laughter at those foolish Indians who think I have such a Big Woman." His hand found her breast. There was scarcely a spoonful of it.

She grabbed his hand and took it to her mouth, saying, "I guess I'll just have to prove those Indians right." Then she bit it.

When he yelped out loud, James asked what was going on up there.

"Tonka Squaw is just trying to prove she is more tonka than she really is."

"One of the reasons I first got mad at your big red friends was because they made themselves at home without asking," she informed Karl merrily.

He got her good and tight this time in a mighty hug that subdued her. The cornhusks were carrying on something awful as the two of them scrapped and rolled, laughing and teasing. They ended in a kiss, with Karl saying into her ear, "Ah, Anna, you are something."

"But not tonka?" she whispered, knowing that the bosom pressed against his chest was anything but ample.

"It does not matter," came his voice in the dark. And Anna smiled happily.

In the morning when they got up they found two pheasants hanging on their door. How the Indians had shot them before sunup remained a mystery. But Karl explained the Indians had chosen this way of thanking Anna for her hospitality. It was, too, their tribute to her, their approval of "Tonka Woman," their welcome and their utterly predictable sense of honor. The Indians never took anything without giving something in return.

Chapter 10

❧

Anna and Karl had been married for two weeks. They found they were compatible in countless ways, but disparate in others. Like all newlyweds, they revealed pieces of themselves to each other daily. Perhaps the similarity they found most enticing was their appreciation of fresh, healthy teasing, which went on daily.

The chief shortcoming Karl found in Anna was the way she hated all domestic work. If she had her way, she'd be outside from sunup to sundown and let the housework go to the devil. When she had to stay behind to perform household tasks, she tended to sulk, and often gave him the honed edge of her Irish tongue just to let him know she didn't appreciate this aspect of wifehood.

If there was one thing that bothered Anna about Karl, it was only that he was too perfect. Silly as it sometimes sounded, even to herself, it rankled her that beside him she must seem nearly ignorant. Anna had yet to find the thing Karl could not do or figure out how to do or couldn't teach either James or herself how to do. He had every virtue a man could possibly have: he was loving, patient, gentle . . . oh, the list went on and on in her mind until sometimes, beside him, she felt positively inadequate by comparison.

But Karl never complained. When her temper flared, he soothed her with his own good humor. When she became irritable at her own incapacities, he patiently told her there was much to learn around a house and it would take time. He took precious hours out from the cabin work to teach the never-ending lessons Father Pierrot had admonished him to teach, even though Anna knew how badly Karl wanted to devote all his time to the raising of the new house.

But above all, at bedtime Karl practiced more patience than any new wife had a right to ask of her husband, and Anna knew it. The flirting and innuendo could not go on endlessly. It came to a head one night after they'd had a particularly carefree session in the pond where Anna had been even more playful than usual. In bed, later, she was still feeling sportive and coquettish.

"Know what, Karl?" she whispered.

"What?"

"I've never kissed you."

"But we have kissed every night."

"You've kissed me every night. Now it's time for me to kiss you." She'd been thinking about it, about what it would be like to be the instigator. But she knew she'd better be careful. Any active move on her part raised ever-greater response in Karl as the days went by.

Karl was totally surprised, wondering what impish thing she could think of next. "Come then, kiss me and I'll be good." He lay back with both arms crossed behind his head. Anna amazed him further by sitting up on her knees beside him. Although it was dark, he pictured her there, childlike, kneeling beside him in her nighty with those freckles dancing across her nose. If he thought of her that way, as a child, perhaps he could make it through one more night of the torture he now suffered at this time each day.

Thankfully, she gave him only a childlike peck. But she braced both hands on his chest to do it. After the peck, they stayed there.

I am playing with fire, thought Anna, but it is such fun. His skin was bare, warm, covered with a fine mat of hair. Beneath her palms she could feel the thrum of his heart, and for a moment she was confused. Did she want him to make love to her or not? Times during the day, watching him with the axe or stroking the horses or splashing water over his neck she often quelled the desire to reach out and caress his beautiful flesh.

In the dark he was only a shadow, a voice, but a warm shadow, a throaty voice. By now she knew the color of the skin concealed by darkness, the shine of the hair resting on the pillow so near her. She need not even touch them to remember them, but the memories tempted her hands, and they strayed lightly across the rises of his chest while she spoke.

"Karl?"

"Hm?"

How could a single syllable sound so strained, she wondered.

"What did you think when you first saw me?"

"That you were too young and too thin."

She tugged at a couple of hairs, and he winced, but kept his arms behind his head. "Do you want an old, fat wife?" she teased.

"In Sweden girls are a little plumper."

"A little plumper, huh?" She felt him shrug apologetically, and promised with mock sincerity, "I'll try to get fat for you, Karl. I think I can do that quite fast, the way I've been eating. But it will take me awhile longer to get old."

In the dark he smiled. "Have I married a girl who will tease me to death?"

She pushed against his chest one time, as if it were a lump of dough she was kneading. "Yes, a skinny, young tease I am. I will tease you mercilessly." She sat back on her heels, but left her palms lightly on his ribs, for she could tell more about him by what was going on beneath her touch than ever she'd seen in broad daylight.

Karl chuckled softly, pleased as usual by this bent of hers toward humor. Again it grew quiet, and Karl battled to keep his tongue from asking what he'd always thought was supposed to be of little importance. Lately though, since she had played this game of keeping him at bay, the question had grown significant, until now he could not help asking.

"What did you think when you saw me?" His low voice sounded slightly hoarse.

She remembered that first day, his face appearing around the wagon, the large hand sliding his cap from his head in slow motion, the look of boyish wonder upon his handsome features as his eyes wandered over her for the first time. She remembered that her heart had raced then just like it did now.

"That you lied," she answered softly.

"Me!"

"Yes, by making less of your looks than you should have in your letters to me."

Her finger brushed against his nipple. It was as hard as a pebble, and with a start she thought, do men's get hard like that, too? Quickly, she slid her fingertips away from it, wondering if it was hard because he was aroused or if it was that way all the time. Her own breasts were puckered so tightly they hurt.

A swell of self-satisfaction washed through Karl at Anna's last words. And the tiny things she was doing to his chest . . . Ah, she does find me pleasing, he thought. But then, feeling guilty for the thought, he said gruffly, "It is what is inside that matters."

"What's inside matters, but other things matter, too." By the minute these other things were coming to matter more and more and more as Anna's hands played upon Karl.

"What other things?" he couldn't resist asking.

"Size, shape, colors, features, faces."

"I . . . I guess maybe you are right," Karl admitted, remembering Father Pierrot's lecture on this subject the night before their marriage.

"I thought so much about what you would look like while James and I were on our way to Minnesota. When I got here and saw you for the first time, I was pleased. I liked what I saw, but I remember being . . . well, surprised at your size. It . . . well, it rather scared me."

Her hand sailed lightly across his chest, raising goose bumps up the lengths of both his arms.

"You're a big man, Karl," she whispered into the dark.

"Like my father," he got out.

Then, hand over hand, she measured his breadth, burning a path across his skin. "Seven hands wide," she counted.

"From using the axe." Where her touch lingered, his heart thudded dangerously. Still, he did not move, so she slid her hands up to encircle one of his biceps.

"And you're strong."

Stridently, he whispered, "I have cleared much land."

"Like your father?" quietly.

"Yes, like my father," shakily.

"And is this your father's neck?" she asked, placing both hands around it, falling just short of spanning it, making the hair on the back of it prickle with awareness.

"I guess so."

"I can't even reach around it. I've wanted to try it for the longest time, just to know what it felt like."

He thought if she continued this way much longer, she would learn the feel of more than just his neck. But next she found his hair.

"You have such blond hair. I never saw such blond hair."

"I am Swedish," he reminded her unnecessarily.

"And do all Swedes think so little of their looks?" she asked, thinking, now, Karl, please, now.

He lay unmoving, stunned by the sensations her exploration invoked.

"I can only speak for myself," he croaked.

"That your face would not make milk curdle?"

"Ya."

She found his temple, laid a palm against his long cheek and followed the line of one eyebrow with a fingertip. "What kind of thing is that to say about a face like this? That it would not make milk curdle."

There followed a long, intense silence, and it seemed as if the thunder of two hearts reverberated off the cabin walls into the trembling night.

"Would it?"

"No, Karl, it most certainly would not," she whispered, her fingertips passing lightly across his lips, then disappearing.

His chest was so taut he could scarcely find the breath to whisper, "My mother's face."

"Your mother is a beautiful woman." Karl's chest expanded like never before.

Anna knew exactly what she was doing, what was happening to Karl. And she knew, too, that it was unfair. But she had discovered the universal power of femininity and could not resist wielding it. I *am* merciless, she thought. I know what is happening to his body, and I know it can lead nowhere tonight, yet I cannot resist plying him, knowing I have bent him to my will.

Bent him, she surely had, to an angle that would bear little more force before snapping. He had lain all this time with both hands folded behind his head, but now he brought one to her shoulder in the dark, squeezing it forcefully. The grip was like iron before he moved in one smooth flow, coming up, turning her, pushing her onto her back with a kiss that told her he was done with her games.

Oh God, Karl, I thought you would take till morning, she thought.

His mouth was warm, wide, and his kiss hungry. His tongue touched hers, then moved in a circle upon her lips. She felt the soft silken skin of his inner lips beneath her tongue, and deep in her body a pulsing made her lower parts feel ready to burst from want. His tongue washed her teeth, explored the warm crevice between them and her upper lip. The turn of her waist was his undoing as he found it, then moved his hand upward to slake its emptiness and fill his palm with her breast while his other cupped the back of her head.

He rested his lips against the side of her nose as he pleaded hoarsely, "Anna, do not play games with me this way. I have waited long enough."

Tell him now, she ordered herself. But it was heavenly being touched at last by him, fully, intimately. The hand that lifted trees, harnessed horses and held an axe as if it were a child's toy now was gentle in its insistence, provoking a yearning in Anna's breasts to be bared to that callused palm. Yes, yes, she thought, just this. For tonight, just this joy of knowing your touch and tingling to it and tasting the sweetness of my body yearning for more.

"Oh, Anna, are you child or woman? You are so warm." Gently, he fondled her breasts, carried away by touching them at last, feeling her nipples hard and aroused.

"Oh, Karl, I fear I am both. Wait, Karl!"

"No more waiting, Anna. Do not be afraid." His hand slid down her ribs and kneaded her hip while he covered her mouth with his.

Anna realized she had tricked not only Karl, but herself. She wanted him so badly, all thought of playing him any longer fled, for as she played him, she played herself, and it had become torturous. She grabbed his hand.

"Karl, I'm sorry . . . wait! I . . . I shouldn't have started this tonight. I— it's my time of month."

His hand stopped kneading, and he tensed away from her. She heard his sharp, indrawn breath before he fell aside with an audible groan, throwing the back of a wrist across his forehead. She thought she actually heard his teeth gritting.

"Why didn't you tell me, Anna?" he asked tightly. "Why did you start this tonight of all nights?" His displeasure was evident.

She could sense how he'd withdrawn from her with scarcely controlled anger as he lay back again, arms crossed behind his head.

"I'm sorry, Karl. I didn't realize."

Only cold silence greeted her.

"Don't be mad. I . . . I don't like it any more than you do." Defensively, she drew herself over to her side of the bed, fluffed the covers over her chest and pinned them with her arms.

"You knew all the time and still you started this."

"I said I was sorry, Karl."

"I have played along with this game of yours for two weeks already. I think I have had enough of it. I do not think what you just did was such fun."

"Don't be mad."

"I am not mad."

"Yes you are, Karl. I won't do anything like this again."

He studied the blackness above him a long time, obviously put out at her. Finally, he asked, "How long does this thing last with women?"

"A couple more days," she whispered.

"A couple more? Two more, Anna?" he asked deliberately.

She was cornered, but could only answer, "Yes, two more," realizing that with the words she at last committed herself to a definite time. Two nights from now would be either her doing or her undoing, depending upon what Karl would or would not realize about her past, once they made love.

"All right," he said now with finality, "two more days."

Anna didn't put her fears into precise pigeonholes. She didn't actually think to herself, if Karl realizes the truth about me he'll send me away. Somehow she knew he wouldn't do that. Still, guilt and uncertainty provoked her to arm herself against his possible displeasure. Her only insurance was to prove her worth around the place beyond a doubt, to make Karl think of her as indispensable. That, she admitted, was a lot to prove over the next couple of days.

She began the next morning by attempting to make pancakes. When Karl and James came in from morning chores they found the intrepid Anna ready to pour batter in the griddle.

"So, I can be a full-time logger at last?" Karl asked smilingly, while Anna nervously wiped her hands on the thighs of her britches.

"Maybe," she quavered, and would have poured the batter into the ungreased spider had Karl not reminded her to lard it first. When she had the cakes baked on one side, then turned them, she realized they looked nothing like his had. These were flat and lifeless. But she served him the first ones anyway, hurrying to pour the second batch for James.

Karl eyed the flat specimens with their wavy edges. Too much milk, he thought, and not enough saleratus. But he ate the helping, then another, kindly withholding criticism. When Anna took her first bite, her jaws stopped. Karl and James eyed each other sideways and tried not to snicker. Then she spit the mouthful back onto her plate with disgust.

"Ish!" she spouted. "That's like a slice of a cow's hoof!"

The other two at last burst out laughing, while Anna railed at herself in disgust. "I thought I'd surprise you, but I'm too *stupid* to remember the simplest recipe. It's awful! I don't know how you ever ate so many!"

"It was hard, wasn't it, James?" Karl managed between gusts of laughter.

James curled his tongue out and rolled his eyes upward.

"Don't you dare poke fun at me for failing, Karl Lindstrom! At least I tried! And you can put your tongue back in now, you little brat!" she yelled at her brother.

Karl silenced his laughter at once, but his chest still shook.

"You were the one who said it was like a cow's hoof," James reminded her.

"*I* can say it!" she snapped. "You don't have to!" She whisked her plate from the table, turning her back on the both of them.

"Tell your sister not to throw away the leftovers," Karl whispered loudly behind her. "We can use them to shoe the horses with."

But when she whirled on him, he had already made it to the door. The pancake missed his head and sailed out into the yard where Nanna came and nosed at it inquisitively, then—unbelievably!—turned away in disinterest. Anna stood in the door with her hands on her hips, yelling across the clearing at Karl's retreating back, "All right, smarty, what'd I do wrong?"

"You probably forgot the saleratus," he called merrily without so much as turning around.

She kicked viciously at the pancake lying in the dirt, then swung back to the door, mumbling, "Saleratus! A nincompoop forgets saleratus!"

For good measure, Karl turned now, and added, "And you put in too much milk!" He watched her feisty little backside swivel into the house again. He'd had a sneaking suspicion last night she'd fibbed to him again just to put him off for a while longer. But now he was sure she'd been telling the truth. He had enough sisters to remember their bursts of temper and inexplicable irritability that came and went in mysterious cycles.

Anna was so disgusted with herself she could have cried. After all her promises to try her best to please Karl, look what she'd done! Flying off the handle at him and throwing the pancake like it was his fault. But, oh, those pancakes had been so miserable!

Noon dinner was worse, because it should have been easier. All she had to do was slice bread and fry venison steaks. She volunteered to go back down the skid trail early and get the fire stoked up and the meal begun so it'd be ready when Karl and James brought the load of wood.

Her bread slices were wedge-shaped. The venison, which had looked so appetizing when raw, was charred to a curl on the outside, oozing cold blood on the inside. Nobody mentioned the inept preparation of the food. But the steaks were scarcely touched.

Anna's ineptitude in the kitchen served a purpose after all. She was so furious with herself she worked like a dynamo to get rid of her frustration. That afternoon, because of her excessive energy, she and James kept up, tree-for-tree, with Karl. In the twenty minutes or so it took Karl to fell one tree, Anna could skin another tamarack of its branches, while James could skid a load down the hill from the siding. Time of the month or not, Anna would show Karl she was good for something!

By the end of the day Anna's stomach was growling like a riled hedgehog. Once it chose to growl when she was so near Karl, he heard it and could not resist a little corner-of-the-mouth smile. But he kept on working, bare-chested and amused.

Anna could not stand it any longer. When the next tree went crashing down, she looked at Karl across the roaring silence and, even though it was earlier than usual, asked, "Karl, could we go back early today?"

"Why?" he asked, already seizing his axe, moving to the next tree.

"Because I'm so hungry I haven't got enough strength to whack one more limb off."

"Me, too," James put in from his spot at the far end of the tamarack. Still, he cast a wary glance at his sister while he admitted it.

"Me, too," Karl said, trying not to smirk.

Suddenly, the humor of the situation struck Anna. All of them working away here while she grumbled and mumbled and was the worst kind of spitfire! She knew she had to be the first one to laugh. It started as a thin, self-conscious giggle, but before she knew what was happening, James chuckled, then Karl. Then a most unladylike snort came through her nose, and all three of them let go fully!

She collapsed in the sawdust in an uncontrollable fit of mirth. Karl stood with one foot on a stump, one hand braced on the axe, hooting at the azure sky, while James came whisking through the branches of the downed tree to Anna's side, where he, too, settled onto his knees in the sawdust. The crows must have heard, for they started up a cacophony of their own from the woods. The trio laughed until their stomachs growled all the more. Anna finally sat up, weak, exhausted in the nicest way. Karl eyed her appreciatively, her hair now salted with sawdust, dark circles of sweat beneath her arms, smudges of bark lichens on her chin. He'd never seen anything prettier.

"I think I was right the first time when I took you for a whelp still wet behind the ears, Anna. Look at you. No wife of mine could look like that, sitting there in her britches with sawdust all over everything."

But the way he smiled at her, she knew she was forgiven for last night. Making a face at him, she asked, "Can we go down right now, Karl?"

"Right now?"

"Right this very now!"

"But we should trim and buck this tree first, and—"

"And by that time you will have to bury me! Please, let's go now. I'm starving, Karl, starving!"

"All right," Karl laughed, pulling his axe from its slice in the stump, extending it toward Anna. "Let's go."

She squinted up at this husband of hers, his tanned, smiling face framed by damp, unruly curls near his temples. She wondered how she'd managed to get so lucky. Her heart tripped in gay excitement at the very sight of him, holding the axe in his powerful grip, with that blue-eyed smile slanting down at her. With a coy smile of her own, she grabbed the cheeks of the axe with both hands, and he tugged her to her feet in a shower of woodchips. She came flying to land lightly against him, and he caught her with his free arm, pulling her up against his hip, then laughed down into her eyes as she peered up at him.

James smiled, watching them, then scampered off, saying, "I'll get Belle and Bill."

Karl dropped his arm, but raised his eyes to Anna's hair, then reached out to pick a piece of pine from it. "You are a mess," he said smilingly, and flicked the fragment away.

She touched her index finger to his temple and followed the track of a bead of sweat that trailed downward at the edge of his hair. "So are you," she returned. Then she put the finger to the tip of her tongue, her brown eyes never leaving his, which widened a little in surprise before she coquettishly whirled away.

They started down the hill, the five of them, Anna declaring that the team had never moved this slow before; surely she would fall dead in her tracks halfway to the table if they didn't hustle. But Karl reminded her with a smirk that for safety's sake the horses must not be hurried. She strode half a pace ahead of Karl with impatient steps, making sure her hips swung a little come-hither message into the bargain.

"What are you cooking for supper?" asked the husband behind her.

She fired him a withering look over her shoulder, then faced front again as she scolded, "Don't be smart, Karl."

"I think it is someone else who is being smart here, and if she doesn't watch her teasing she will end up doing the cooking yet."

Anna turned around and skipped a few steps backward while pleading in her most earnest voice, "I'd do *anything* for a decent meal cooked by somebody else for a change."

"Anything?" he questioned suggestively, stretching his steps to gain on Anna, who suddenly whirled around, ignored his innuendo, continuing to march vigorously toward supper.

"Come back here, Anna," he ordered mildly.

"What?"

"I said come back here. You have sawdust on your britches."

She stuck her rear out to inspect it as best she could while still down-hilling it. But Karl caught up to her, and she felt his hand swipe her seat, sending little shivers of anticipation through her belly and breasts. Then, his sweeping done, Karl left his hand around her waist, pulling her lightly against his hip. With the axe swung over his other shoulder, they walked down to the clearing.

That night they splurged on precious sliced ham because it was the fastest thing Karl could think of. He plucked it down from the rafter of the springhouse where it had been hanging upside down like a bat. He showed Anna how to make red-eye gravy of flour and milk. With it they had crystalline boiled potatoes, which she managed to peel quite nicely for Karl—this first small domestic success filling her with pride.

During the supper preparations, Karl warned her, "We're almost out of bread. Tomorrow I think I must show you how to bake more."

Disheartened, she wailed, "Ohhh, no! If I couldn't handle pancakes, I'll for sure kill the bread!"

"It will take time but you must learn."

She threw out her hands hopelessly. "But there's so much to remember, Karl. Everything you show me has different stuff in it. I can't possibly get it all straight."

"Give yourself time and you will."

"But you'll be sick and tired of me ruining all your precious food when you have to work so hard for every bit of it."

"You are too impatient with yourself, Anna. Have I complained?" He raised his blue eyes to hers.

"No, Karl, but I only wish I could learn quicker so you didn't have to do it all. If I could get things right the first time, you could leave me without worrying I'll burn the house down and your supper with it. Why, I still haven't got the spider clean from dinner!"

"A little sand will work it clean," he advised, nonplussed.

The sand worked beautifully, and she displayed the rejuvenated pan with pride. But later, when the ham was spitting and smelling unendurably delicious, Anna stopped in the door, clutching the bowl of potato parings against her stomach.

"Karl?"

He looked up to find her playing with a curl of potato peeling, twisting it around an index finger distractedly.

"What is it, Anna?"

She studied the peeling intently. "If I knew how to read, you could write things down for me so I'd be able to cook stuff right. I mean . . ." She looked up expectantly. "I mean, then it wouldn't matter if my memory's not so good." Again, she dropped her eyes to the bowl.

"There is nothing wrong with your memory, Anna. It will all smooth out in time."

"But would you teach me to read, Karl?" Her eyes wandered back to his. "Just enough to know the names of things like flour and lard . . . and saleratus?"

A soft, understanding smile broke across his face. "Anna, I will not send you packing because you have forgotten the leavening in the pancakes. You should know that by now, little one."

"I know. It's just that you can do everything so good, and I can't do anything without you watching every move. I want to do better for you."

He wanted nothing so badly as to step to the doorway and pitch the bowl of potato parings aside and take her in his arms and kiss her until the ham burned.

"Anna, do you not know that it is enough for me that you wish this?"

"It is?" Her childish, large eyes opened wide.

"Of course it is." He was rewarded with her smile.

"But would you teach me to read anyway, Karl?"

"Perhaps in the winter when time grows long."

"By then I will have burned up all your valuable flour," she said mischievously.

"By then we will have a new crop."

She turned with her bowl to leave, happy now.

"Anna?"

"What?"

"Save the parings. We will plant those with eyes and see if the season is long enough to give us a second crop. We will need it."

She turned to study him thoughtfully. "Is there anything you don't know, Karl?"

"Ya," he answered. "I do not know how I will make it till tomorrow night."

That evening he showed Anna how to make yeast from the potato water, which he saved from supper, and a handful of dried hops. To this he added a curious syrup, which he said was made of the pulp of watermelons, a plentiful source of sugar. The maple sugar, which he harvested, had too strong a flavor for bread, he said. So instead he boiled watermelon pulp each summer and preserved it in crocks by pouring melted beeswax over it.

With the yeast ingredients set in the warm chimney corner for the night, they all enjoyed cups of the remaining watermelon nectar, a treat Anna and James had never known before.

"Can I have more, Karl?" James asked. Karl emptied the jug into the boy's mug.

"It's delicious," Anna agreed.

"I have many more delicious things to introduce you to. Minnesota knows no end of such delights."

"You were right, Karl. It really does seem to be a land of plenty."

"Soon the wild raspberries will be ripe. Then you will have a treat!"

"What else?" James asked.

"Wild blackberries, too. Did you know that when a wild blackberry is green, it is red?"

James puzzled a moment, then laughed. "It's a riddle in reverse—what's red when it's green."

"But when it is ripe, it turns as black as the pupil of a rattlesnake's eye," Karl said.

"Have you got rattlesnakes here?" Anna asked, wideeyed.

"Timber rattlers. But I have not seen many. I have had to kill only two since I am here. Snakes eat the pesky rodents in the grainfields, so I do not like killing a snake. But the rattler is a devil, so I must."

Anna shivered. They had not gone for their swim before supper because they'd been in too much of a hurry to eat. Karl suggested a swim now, but the mention of rattlesnakes made Anna opt for the washstand instead. James, too, agreed for this one night he'd put off their swim.

When they were tucked in bed, Anna spoke first, in a whisper, as usual.

"Karl?"

"Hm?"

"Have you thought any more about a stove for the new house?"

"No, Anna. I have been busy and it slipped my mind."

"Not mine."

"Do you think a stove will make you a better cook?" he asked, amused.

"Well, it might," she ventured.

But Karl laughed a little.

"Well, it might!" she repeated.

"And then again, it might not, and Karl Lindstrom will have spent his good money for nothing."

A little fist clunked him one in the chest.

"Perhaps we make a bargain, you and I. First Anna learns to cook decent, then Karl buys her the stove."

"Oh, do you mean it, Karl?" Even in a whisper her voice was enthused.

"Karl Lindstrom is no liar. Of course I mean it."

"Oh, Karl . . ." She grew excited just thinking of it.

"But I will be the judge of when your cooking is decent."

She lay there smiling in the dark.

"I'm going to make good bread tomorrow. You'll see!"

"*I* am making good bread tomorrow. You are watching me make it."

"All right. I'm watching. But this time I'm gonna remember everything," she vowed, "just like James does. You'll be going off to buy that new stove before the month is out, you'll see." She imagined how it would be to own an iron stove, and how glorious it would be to find cooking not a hateful job, to have things turn out right.

"Karl?"

"Hm?"

"How do you bake bread without an oven?"

"In a kiln in the yard. Have you never seen it?"

"No. Where is it?"

"Back by the woodpile."

"You mean that mound of dried mud?"

"Ya."

"But it has no door!"

"I will make a door by sealing up the hole with wet clay after the loaves are inside."

"You mean you want me to goop around with wet clay every time I make bread, for the rest of my life?"

"What I want is for you to come over here and shut your little mouth. I said I would think about the stove, and I will. I grow tired of talking about bread and clay and stoves now."

So she found a spot to nestle in Karl's arm, and she did what she was told: she shut her mouth. When his kiss found it, she refused to open up. He backed off, tried again in his most persuasive fashion, but could only feel her smiling with lips sealed.

"What is this?" he asked.

"I'm only doing what I promised to do. I vowed to obey my husband, didn't I? So when I'm told to shut my mouth, I do it."

"Well, your husband is ordering you to open it again."

And she did. Willingly.

Chapter 11

The bread-making was a larger undertaking than Anna had imagined, made so mostly by the fact that they were to make fourteen loaves at once, enough for two weeks.

In the morning the hop tea had turned into a crock of effervescent bubbles, which had to be strained through a horsehair strainer into the hollowed-out black walnut log with legs, which Karl called a dough box. Water and lard were added, and much, much flour. Anna got into the act at this point by kneading, elbow-to-elbow with Karl. Before the flour was all mixed in, her arms ached as if she'd been wielding Karl's axe instead of his bread dough. The dough box had a concave cover, also made of hollowed-out wood, and when at last it was in place, the whole thing was left beside the fireplace where it was warm and the dough could rise.

"And now you know how to mix bread," Karl said.

"Do you always make so much?"

"It is easier in the long run than having to mix dough more often. Are your arms tired?"

"No," she lied—a little white lie—not wanting him to think her too weak for such a task.

"Good, then let us go see about that tamarack we left lying on its side yesterday."

The day was different from any so far. Between Anna and Karl there was none of the light banter. There was, instead, a concerted avoiding of eyes, of touch, even of speech.

For this was the day!

They mounted the skid trail behind Belle and Bill. Today Karl took the reins instead of turning them over to James. The familiar reins felt comforting in Karl's palms. The familiar rumps of the horses were good to set his eyes upon when they felt like wandering to Anna. The words of command flowed in gentle but gruff tones to the horses, though Karl found little to say to his wife.

He was attuned to her every motion, though. He need not even look her way to sense each movement, each sound she made. The sigh of her pant legs through the damp morning grass, the quick tilt of her head at the bark of a pheasant, the accented swing of the basket she carried, the natural swing of her hips, the perk of alertness when a gopher caught her eye, the way she watched the small animal as she walked past it, the determination in her stance as she set to work on the branches, the way she raised the jug to her lips when she broke for water, the way she backhanded her mouth after taking the drink, the curl of her back as she bent to fill the basket, the way she put the first chip to her nose before dropping it in, the pause to push her hair back when the nape of her neck grew warm, the way she smiled reassuringly at James when he seemed to be questioning silently, why this sudden change between you and Karl?

Anna, too, knew a sense of content with Karl, as if suddenly, a tuning fork had been struck in her body and its vibrations matched his as they played out this new movement of a symphony started two weeks ago.

That first movement, with its light allegrolike gaity, echoed and was gone now, high among the tamaracks. It was replaced by this sensual adagio that caught them in its slowly measured beat. Even Karl's axe seemed to match that slower rhythm, its mellow thud counting away the minutes until nightfall. It was as if Anna stood beside Karl, elbow-to-elbow, as she had earlier.

She knew his every movement, though she never looked squarely at him the entire morning. The brush of his hand upon Belle's haunch, the way it absently eased down to her thigh, the pat on her shoulder before leaving her in favor of curved ash, the squaring of shoulders and that last gaze skyward before hefting the axe for the first time that day, the great breath, the way he held it in his thick chest before that initial fluid swing, then the symmetry of motion, the flash of yellow hair back and forth in the sun as he nodded into each stroke, the rise of chin at the measure of trembling tree, the squint of eye as the bark cracked, the near shudder of satisfaction as it plunged, the one-handed way he unbuttoned his shirt, the rolling backward of shoulders to be free of it, the axe handle leaning upon his groin as he shrugged from the confines of cotton, the shirt flying through the air, his hands flexing wide before taking up the axe once more, making it sing, the sudden silence when James pointed wordlessly, Karl walking with catlike stealth to reach for the rifle and raise it, aiming at the squirrel who perched in mesmerized silence waiting to be their supper, the recoil that scarcely rocked Karl's shoulder, his look of amazement as the butt of the gun slid down to rest beside his foot while the squirrel scampered free, untouched.

And for one of the few times that day, Karl's eyes meeting Anna's, hers falling away, her head turning so she could smile at his missed shot without his knowing.

And all day long their thoughts ranged over parallel themes.

"What will she think of me?"

"What will he think of me?"

"Will she come along swimming?"

"He will want to go swimming."

"I had best shave again."

"I had best wash my hair."

"I wish I had better than lye soap to offer."

"I wish I had better than homespun to wear."

"Supper will seem endless."

"I'll hardly be hungry."

"Shall I go to the barn?"

"Shall I go to bed first?"

"When have two days been this long?"

"When have two days been this short?"

"Will she resist?"

"Will he demand?"

"She is so slight."

"He is so big."

"What do women need?"

"Will he be gentle?"

"Will she know it is my first time?"

"He will know it's not my first time!"

"I must wait till the boy sleeps."

"James, fall asleep early!"

"She will sure want the fire low."

"James will see in the fireglow!"

"Blast those cornhusks!"

"Oh! Those crackling cornhusks!"

"Should I take off her gown?"

"Will he take off my gown?"

"My hands are so callused."

"My hands have grown rough."

"What if I hurt her?"

"Will it hurt like the first time?"

"Will she know all my doubts?"

"Will he know all my fears?"

"There will be blood."

"There'll be no blood!"

"Let me do it right."

"Let him not suspect."

At noon they punched down the dough and Karl showed Anna how to shape the loaves. He sprinkled the hand-forged iron pan with cornmeal before placing the first loaf in it. He said they had enough tamaracks to begin hewing, so they need not return to the woods that afternoon. If she wanted, Anna could tend to some weeding in the vegetable garden, which had been sadly neglected lately. Also, those potato peelings needed planting if they were not to dry into uselessness. And the hardwood fire in the kiln would bear tending in readiness for the baking.

So Karl went to his hewing and Anna to her weeding. Alas, Anna could not tell the weeds from the herbs and pulled up Karl's comfrey, so much taller than the rest, and looking ever so unvegetablelike. Unaware of her mistake, she continued on with her task until Karl came to show her how deep to plant the potato parings. Eyeing the plot, then the weedpile, Karl asked, "Where is my comfrey?"

"Your what?" Anna asked.

"My comfrey. A little while ago it was growing right up along the end of this row."

"You mean that big, tall, gangly stuff?"

"Ya."

"That's . . . comfrey?"

Karl again eyed the weed pile, then Anna bent to fetch up the abused comfrey. "Is this it?"

"I'm afraid so. It was."

"Oh no."

Another day they would have laughed joyously at what she'd done. Today they were too aware of each other. Anna shrugged, Karl smiled, not at her face but at the wilted comfrey. "Comfrey is tough," he said, reaching for it. "I think it can survive in spite of your gardening. I will put it back where it came from, but it will need a little drink to get it going again."

"I'll get it, Karl," she offered, and scampered away, jumping the vegetable rows, running toward the springhouse while he watched her whiskey-hair fly untethered with each leap and bound, the limp comfrey forgotten in his hand.

She returned with her pailful. Karl dug a hollow, stood back while she poured water in, then knelt on one knee to replace the herb and tamp moist earth upon its roots with the sole of his big foot. Above him, Anna grasped the rope handle of the wooden bucket with both hands, mesmerized by the sight of his bare back and the shallows of his spine diving into the back of his pants. He'd been hewing in the sun before he came over; his shoulders gleamed with a film of sweat. The hair at the back of his neck was wet, curling in rebellion at the heat. He stood up, took the pail from her, lifted it and drank deeply, wiped his mouth with the back of his hand and said, "I must get back to my hewing."

She wished she could help with hewing instead of poking potato peelings into the ground. At the same time, it was disconcerting being near Karl today. It was probably a good thing, their working separately.

The sun wore low and the pigeons began moving again. The day cooled slightly as the birds fluttered to the edges of the clearing, then to the roof of the springhouse with throaty clucks and soothing coos. At the spring the chipping sparrows dipped their rust caps for an evening drink. Barn swallows swooped out across the open, darting in blue-gray flashes on their evening pursuit of bugs, cutting sharply to scatter the gray haze of gnats. Dragonflies left the potato blossoms, disappearing somewhere to fold away their jaconet wings for the night. The inchworms gave up their incessant measuring of the cabbage plants, flexed their backs one last time and disappeared within the leaves where the hungry birds wouldn't find them.

Karl, too, flexed his back one last time. The ash handle of his axe slid through his palm and he scanned the first tier of logs, which lay now in place. Anna had gone from the garden to the springhouse.

"Well, boy, what do you think?"

"I think I'm tired."

"Too tired to take a walk to the clay pit?"

"Where is it?"

"Up along the creek a little ways. We need fresh clay to seal up the kiln."

"Sure, I'll come with you, Karl."

"Good. Ask your sister if she wants to come along, too. And tell her to bring an empty pail from the springhouse."

James thought Karl could have asked Anna as easily as not, but the two had acted strangely standoffish all day long as if they'd had a tiff or something. Anyway, James called, "Hey, Anna, Karl says do you wanna come with us to get clay!"

She turned from latching the springhouse door. Karl was standing just behind James, watching her.

"Tell Karl yes," she called back.

"He says to bring a pail."

She went back in to get it.

Anna carried the bucket, James the spade and Karl the rifle. Karl led the way, explaining, "The pheasants are feeding now, filling their crops with gravel along the creek bank. I want you behind me if I flush one up." Both he and Anna remembered how he'd missed that sitting target this morning.

They walked in single file along the worn footpath to the creek. But halfway there they overtook a sluggish porcupine headed the same place they were. He waddled along unconcernedly on stout, bowed legs, sniffing his way with a flat nose until he realized he had company. Then, giving a warning snort, he tucked his head between his front feet and brandished his tail, protecting his barbless little belly.

"Give this fellow wide berth," Karl warned, leading the way around the quilled rodent. "It pays to remember we share the woods with him and he likes the salt from a man's hands. He is the reason why I always teach you to hang up our axe at the end of the day. He will eat up the sweaty handle in short time if you let him. It takes a man some time to fashion his axe handle."

They continued walking and came to where the yellow clay lay thickly at the feet of the willows. There were countless footprints in it. Intrigued, James at once knelt, asking what they all were. He and Karl squatted a long time, inspecting the markings while Karl patiently identified each one. Raccoon, skunk, mouse, otter, long-clawed porcupine. But no rabbit or woodchuck, for they, Karl said, needed only the moisture they took in with the dew-laden leaves of early morning. At last Karl had satisfied all of James' questions. They filled the pail with clay and started back through the emerald caress of the forest light.

When they returned to the clearing, they found the kiln aglow with hardwood coals, which Karl scooped out, leaving only the heated brick radiating within. After the loaves were inserted, he quickly sealed the opening, packing it with handfuls of damp clay, smoothing, shaping, watering, then smoothing again, with the thick yellow rivulets oozing between his fingers, running down the backs of his hands.

There was something sensual about the sight and Anna could not tear her eyes away. She was reminded again of the many times she'd watched his hands stroke the horses, and of the night he had fondled her breast. Something wild and liquid and surging happened within her as she stood above and behind Karl's shoulder, watching the task he performed. She looked down at the back of his neck, his shoulders, which shifted sinuously as he made wide circles on the new kiln wall he was building. She remembered the salt of him upon her tongue from the droplet she had taken from his temple.

Suddenly, Karl swiveled around to glance up at Anna from his hunkered pose. He watched her face turn the color of ripe watermelon, and quickly she looked aside, then down at her own hands with dirt from the gardening still imbedded beneath the nails.

A thrill of anticipation shot through Karl, and he turned to give the kiln one last pat. "We will open it in the morning and there will be fresh bread for our breakfast."

"That sounds good," Anna said, but her face had not faded yet, and she studied the barn wall across the way.

Karl stood up and stretched. "Probably every Indian for ten miles will be here, too. They can smell that bread baking clear across forty acres."

"Really?" James put in excitedly. "I like the Indians. Can we go swimming now?"

Karl answered the boy, but watched his wife. "Anna is afraid of snakes since I mentioned the timber rattlers."

"No I'm not!" she quickly interjected. "Yes, I am, but . . . I mean . . . well, let's go. I'm full of the garden anyway."

Karl controlled an impulse to smile. Nothing made Anna react like a challenge thrown her way. He watched her face carefully while he noted, "And I am full of our kiln." But she swung around, away from him, and he could not tell if she still blushed or not.

"Let's go then!" James said, leading the way.

An honest sense of shyness had sprung up between Karl and Anna now. It heightened their anticipation as well as their apprehension at the coming of night.

Whatever must James be thinking? Anna worried, knowing exactly how stilted she and Karl had acted toward each other most of the day. But there was no cure for it. James was given to think whatever he might. But in a way James became the blessing Father Pierrot had predicted. For while they talked *to* him, they communicated *through* him.

As is often true with breathless lovers, it was not the things they did say that mattered, but those they didn't.

"I've never seen a timber rattler at this time of evening. They hunt for food during the day, and they are not swimmers."

"I'm not the one who's worried about them, Karl. Anna is."

"If I thought there was danger, we would not be going to the pond."

"James, slow down! You're walking too fast!"

"It's not me, it's Karl. Slow down, Karl! Anna can't keep up."

"Oh, was I hurrying?"

"Hey, Anna! Come on out here in the deep part with us!"

"No, not tonight."

"How come?"

"I'm going to wash my hair instead."

"Wash your hair! But you always said you hated that lardy soap!"

"Leave your sister alone, boy."

"You shaving again, Karl? You shaved once this morning."

"Leave him alone, James."

"Man! I'm starved after that swim! Pass me the stew."

"Sure . . . here."

"Hey, how come you two ain't eating tonight?"

"I'm not very hungry."

"Me either."

"Hey, Anna, you sure been quiet all day."

"Have I?"

"Seems like it. How come?"

"I pulled up Karl's comfrey and I think he's disgusted with me."

"Is that why you two are mad at each other?"

"I am not mad at her."

"I'm not mad at him."

"Help your sister clean up the supper things, James. She's had a hard day."

"So have I!"

"Just do as I say, James."

"I'll see to the horses."

"What in the world is there to see to out there when they're all put away for the night?"

"Leave Karl alone, James."

"Well, heck, I just asked is all."

"Get your bed ready, okay?"

In the barn, Karl lit his pipe, but it lay fragrantly forgotten in his hand.

"Hello, Belle. Just came to say goodnight." Karl stroked the heavy neck and mane, running the coarse hairs through his fingers until Belle turned her giant head curiously. "What do you think, old girl? Do you think she's ready for bed by now?"

Belle blinked slow, there in the dark. But tonight, her presence and Bill's soothed Karl less than usual.

"Ah, well . . ." the man sighed. "Goodnight you two." He gave them each a pat on the rump, then walked slowly to the house. He took the latchstring in his fingers. He paused thoughtfully, then turned to the washbench and cleaned the smell of the horses from his hands.

Back inside, Karl found James still up. Time moved like the soft-shelled snails on a dewy morning. Anna brushed her hair, while James seemed more interested than ever in erecting log walls. His questions went on interminably. Karl answered them all, but finally arose and raised his elbows in the air, twisting at the waist and yawning most convincingly.

"Don't tell me," James warned Karl, "tomorrow is another day . . . I know! But I don't feel sleepy at all."

Anna's stomach flipped sideways. "Well, Karl is. And he can't entertain you here all night, so get to bed, little brother."

At last James hit the floor.

"I will bank the coals," Karl said. He knelt, heard the lid of the trunk squeak behind him and stayed where he was, poking at the fire, fiddling until finally the cornhusks spoke.

Karl stood up, pulled his shirttails out, stepped over James' feet and slipped into the deep shadows cast upon his and Anna's bed. Karl wondered if the hammering of his heart might make the ropes creak. Surely a commotion like the one inside him would rock the world!

His entire life had come to this, to lying beside this woman, this girl, this virgin; and his Papa had taught him well and fully how to be a man in this world in all ways but this. Papa had given him a deep and abiding respect for women, but beyond that, little more. From his older brothers Karl had gathered that this aspect of marriage was distasteful to some women, chiefly because it brought them pain, especially the first time. How to make this pleasant for her, this was what Karl wondered. How to lead her slowly, how to soothe her. What is Anna thinking, lying over there so still? Did she put that nightgown on? Don't be asinine, man, of course she put it on! It is no different tonight. Oh, yes it is! How long have I been lying here like a quaking schoolboy?

"Come here," Anna heard him whisper, and felt him raise his arm to put around her. She lifted her head and his arm slipped close, gathered her in and passed downward along her back. Softly, he rubbed in ever-widening circles through her nightgown. Shivers danced along her spine. Fleetingly, he hesitated at the base of her spine, moved again in gentle motions until he felt her relax a little. Deftly, he had rolled her onto her side until her ear was pressed upon his biceps.

Within her head resounded her own thumping heart. How long had she lain stiffly on her back, telling her locked muscles to relax? Now, slowly, his hand began to achieve what her will had not. Close your mouth, she told herself, or he will hear you breathing like a jackrabbit and know how scared you are. But breathing through her nose was worse. And so when Karl's lips touched hers, they were already parted.

He pulled her fully into his kiss. Her lips were soft and seeking. Halfway through the kiss he swallowed. Fool, he thought! Surely the boy heard you swallow clear over there! Saliva pooled in his mouth and he was forced to swallow again. But when Anna, too, swallowed, Karl quit worrying about it. And the problem took care of itself.

One-armed he'd captured her, rolled her toward him so her hands rested lightly upon his chest. As the kiss lingered and lengthened, her fingers timidly began to move, as if she'd only now realized his skin lay beneath them. She glided lightly over the silken hairs she'd so often seen in the sun. It felt like thistledown, so softly textured in contrast to the firm muscle from which it sprang. Her tiny movements set his senses on edge, awakening nerves he'd not guessed he possessed. Inadvertently, she brushed his nipple, quickly passing it by. He captured her hand to place it again where the touch had brought pleasing sensations. Again her fingers fanned his chest in butterfly movements of encouragement, while she wondered what it was he waited for.

He waited for her arms to encircle him, to free the breasts she protected so virginally. Finally, he whispered, "Put your arms around me, Anna." Her arms found their way, her hands played over his muscled back. Slowly, Karl drew a pattern on her flesh that brought his palm to the gentle swelling of her breasts. Her hands fell still. All of her lay expectant, waiting, waiting, breath falling warmly on his cheek, until his caress found its way like the fall of a feather.

Lightly, he rubbed the backs of his fingers upon the cockled tip. The universe held its breath with Karl and Anna as he slowly eased his touch in search of buttons, finding them, slipping them free, one by one, in slow, slow motions. Don't move, Anna, he thought. Let me feel your warmth. She lay unresisting, receptive to his touch. He smoothed his hand within the loosened garment, riding his palm from the shallows of her ribs upward to rest on her breastbone. He stroked her jaw with his thumb, caressed her neck, encircled it fleetingly, then again rested the heel of his hand just above and between her breasts, savoring the delight of making them both wait, want.

She closed her eyes, sighing as his touch fell upon her bare breast, cupping it, contouring it, making fire build in its nerve endings. In a wonder of discovery his hand roved her skin, so different from his own. Her breasts were soft, like the petals of the wild rose, unbelievably soft. Yet, here, puckered tightly with a contraction so unexpectedly powerful. "Anna," he breathed, his lips skimming hers, "you are so warm, so soft here," he gently squeezed the resilient flesh; "so hard here," he took the firmly aroused nipple to stroke it gently, roll it between his fingers rapturously. "How I have wondered."

She lay with her mouth a mere inch away from his, feeling his words on her skin, finding no answer but to lie beneath his touch while he learned the beautiful mystery of man and woman. As if she were his altar, he came to adore in profound awe the goodness of this offering.

Within Anna grew the incredulous knowledge of this man's innate respect for the act upon which they embarked, so that when he soothed her gown from her shoulders there was goodness flowing already between them, even before their bodies joined. He touched her hair, her shoulder, took her hand from behind him and kissed its palm, then pressed her back into the pillows.

Then he leaned to do what he'd thought of for so long; he kissed her breasts, stunning both Anna and himself with sensations that gushed through them. Warm, wet, hungry tongue swooped, swept, stroked. Ardent, eager lips encircled, engulfed, enflamed.

To Anna came an incredible thirst at the tugging of his kiss upon her breast. She knew physical thirst that brought unexpected cravings for cool, flowing water. She knew emotional thirst that brought visions of warm, quivering flesh. It built in a marvelous anguish until her head pressed back of its own accord. Her ribs rose, her back arched, her hands found his hair. He groaned softly as her fingers threaded the strands. Her hands tugged impatiently, then fell to his cheeks to hold their hollows, the better to feel his open-mouthed possession of her flesh. His searching, suckling mouth created within Anna such a confusion of warring sensations. She was at once slaked but thirsty, filled but hungering, sapped but fortified, languid but vital, relaxed but tensile.

His face traveled her body while Anna luxuriated in the leisurely pace he'd set. Beneath his lips he felt her stretching like a cat as he touched the hollow between her ribs. His hands stroked the curve of her waist. As if this triggered some magic, she raised her hands above her head, arching further upward in a languor he had not expected. Her hips were hilled and warm, their hollows small and soft beneath his palm. Slowly, fluidly he stretched himself beside her, finding her lips with his again while the circle of her arms came down to press his shoulders to her.

"Karl," she murmured, lying in wait until at last he found the mystery of her in treasured folds of warmth.

"Oh, Anna," his voice came raspy, his mouth buried between the pillow and her ear. "I cannot believe you." Hosannas filled his mind at the newness of this woman and her reaction to his touches. He rubbed his ear across her mouth, his touch taken at last within her.

"It's so different," she whispered. "I was so afraid."

"Anna, never will I hurt you." Glorying in her acceptance, he explored her until his body's forces could be denied no longer. He covered her with the length of his own body, thinking, Anna, Anna, that you should be such as you are! You do not reject me or make me feel callow as I feared. His hips thrust against her of their own accord, bringing a rustle to the room. Fiercely, he cupped the back of her neck, pulling her ear roughly against his throaty whisper. "Anna, let's go outside . . . please." He bent his ear to her lips again.

"Yes," she whispered huskily.

And he was out of the bed, finding his discarded clothing in the dark while she thrust her trembling arms back into sleeves, found buttons, felt Karl's hand reaching to pull her from the bed. At their sounds of departure James' sleepy voice came from the floor.

"Karl, is that you?"

"Ya. Anna and me. We want to talk a while so we are going for a walk. Go to sleep, James."

They stole barefoot onto the night grass, latching the door behind them, limbs quivering with each step. The liquid moon fell upon their heads like rich cream while they walked, untouching, in disciplined slowness, toward the barn. Anna felt a tugging at her arm and looked up to find Karl's face and hair alight with moonglow, the seam of his lips etched in moonshadow. He stopped and swept an arm around her shoulders, mantling them with the blanket he had hastily pulled from where it hung in the corner as they fled to privacy. Her arms took his broad neck in a tight, clinging loop while he picked her up off the ground, spreading his feet and leaning back for balance. His hastily donned shirt hung unbuttoned between them. She plunged both hands into the back of it, rubbing his high-muscled shoulders while he kissed her throat which arched into the night sky.

"I would have this first time last all night if I could," he groaned. The curves and planes of her body were pressed beguilingly against his as he held her aloft. "Just your touch, Anna . . ." She kissed away his words, her hands playing over his back until at last he eased her down. Her toes touched dew, then she and Karl were running toward the barn with hands joined and the blanket flaring behind them.

He tugged her hand in the hay-scented dark, showing her the way. She heard the flip of the blanket, the vague rushing sound of it settling upon the hay. She reached for the buttons of her nightgown, but his hands came seeking, stopping hers, taking her wrists in a commandeering grasp. Relentlessly, he forced them down to her sides, then his fingers plied her buttons.

"This is my job," he said. "I want every joy of this night to be mine." He brushed the gown from her shoulders and found her wrists again and brought them to his stomach. "Right from the beginning, Anna, the way it ought to be."

Wordlessly, she did his bidding, with trembling hands, until they stood in naked splendor before each other. Blood beat in their ears. They savored that moment of hesitation before Karl reached out with strong hands to grip her shoulders and take her against him, drawing her down to the hay, the blanket.

He was lithe and engulfing and impassioned, rolling with her, kissing her with an ardor she had not imagined, everywhere, everywhere. Her arms clung. Her lips sought. Her body arched. Above her he braced, poised.

"Anna, I do not want to hurt you, little one."

Never had she expected such sensitive and pained concern. "It's all right, Karl," she said, gone past thoughts of waiting longer for the final blending of their bodies.

He hovered, quivering, then placed himself lightly in her. He felt her hands seek his hips and wielded her in shallow movements. Again he waited for her sign, slowly, lingeringly. She moved, flowing into his being, gently, thrusting up. Together they found rhythm. Their breaths came in labored draughts through the dusky night, uttering each other's names. Their motion became ballet, graceful, flowing, smooth, choreographed by the master hand of nature into a synchronization unlike either had imagined. Karl heard the sound of his own moans of pleasure as heat and height built. An unintelligible cry broke from Anna and he stopped moving, agonized.

"No . . . don't . . ." she cried out.

He moved back, stricken. She pulled at him.

"What is it, Anna?"

"It's good . . . please . . ."

She told him, too, with some obscure language of centuries to flex now, until time and tone and tempo reached deeply to bring Anna reason for being. And at her grip and flow, Karl, too, shuddered, collapsed, lowering his head to cradle in exhaustion at her neck.

She held him there, fiercely stroking the damp hair at the back of his neck, wondering if it would be all right to cry, fearing it was not a choice left up to her. For her chest was filled to bursting. A stinging bit in the depths of her nose. The warning glands in her jaws filled. Then, horrified, she burst forth with a shattering, single sob that filled the barn with sound and Karl with alarm.

"Anna!" he cried, fearful at something he'd done to hurt her after all. He fell to his side, taking her with him. But she forced her face sharply aside and covered her eyes with a forearm.

"What is it, Anna? What have I done?" Regretfully, he withdrew from her, stroked the arm she held over her eyes.

"Nothing," she choked.

"Why do you cry, then?"

"I don't know . . . I don't know." Truly she didn't.

"You don't know?" he asked.

Silently, she shook her head, unable to delve this mystery herself.

"Did I hurt you?"

"No . . . no."

His big hand stroked her hair helplessly. "I thought it was . . ." He begged, "Tell me, Anna."

"Something good happened, Karl, something I didn't expect."

"And this makes you cry?"

"I'm silly."

"No, no, Anna . . . do not say that."

"I thought you would be displeased with me, that's all."

"No, Anna, no. Why would you think such a thing?"

But she couldn't tell him the real reason. Unbelievably, he did not seem to know.

"It is I who wondered if I did right. All day long I thought of this and worried. And now it has happened and we knew, Anna. We knew. Is it not incredible how it was? How we knew?"

"Yes, it's incredible."

"Your body, Anna, how you are made, how we fit." He touched her reverently. "Such a miracle."

"Oh, Karl, how did you get this way?" She clutched him against her almost desperately, as if he'd threatened to leave.

"How am I?"

"You're . . . I don't know . . . you're filled with such wonder at everything. Things mean so much to you. It's like you're always looking for the good in things."

"Do you not look for the good? Did you not look for this to be good then?"

"Not like you, I don't think, Karl. My life hasn't had much good in it until I met you. You are the first truly good thing that has happened to me. All except for James."

"That makes me happy. You have made me happy, Anna. Everything is so much better since you are here. To think that I will never have to be lonely again." Then he sighed, a pleasured, full sigh, and snuggled his face into her neck again.

They lay silently for some time, basking. She touched the arm he'd flung tiredly across her and rubbed its hair up, smoothed it down. He idled his foot upon the back of her calf, using it to hold her near. They began talking lazily into each other's chins, necks, chests, anywhere their mouths happened to be.

"I thought I would die before this day was over."

"You too, Anna?"

"Mm-hmmm. Me, too. You too?"

"I worried about the craziest things."

"I didn't know if I should look at you or ignore you."

"I worried about those cornhusks all day."

"You did?"

He nodded his head. She laughed softly.

"Didn't you?"

Again she laughed softly.

"I did not know what I would do if you would not come out here."

"I was so relieved when you asked me."

"I will hurry to finish the log cabin, then James will have a loft to himself."

They fell silent, thinking of it.

Soon she asked, "Karl, guess what?"

"What."

"You lied tonight."

"I?"

"You told James we were going for a walk. You said 'nothing makes a liar out of Karl Lindstrom' but something did."

"And something might again," he warned.

And something certainly did.

Chapter 12

❧

James could tell the minute he opened his eyes that things were okay again between Karl and Anna. For one thing, today was the first day Karl hadn't risen before Anna and gone outside to keep out of the way while she got up and washed and dressed. When James opened his eyes and stretched to look over his shoulder, he found both his sister and brother-in-law tucked up in bed yet. They were whispering, and James thought he heard giggles. A pleasant sense of security enfolded the boy. It was always terrible when things were strained between Karl and Anna. But today, James knew, would be one of those good, good days he liked best.

Karl was at the moment lying nose to nose with his wife. He had her by both breasts. "There is not a handful in both of these together," he was whispering.

"You didn't seem to mind last night," she whispered back.

"Did I say I minded?"

She faked a heavy Swedish accent and whispered, "If *you-u-u* vant a vife *who-o-o* is shaped like a *moo-o-ose* and has *bu-u-u*-soms like vatermelons, you vill haff to go back to Sveden. This vun has only *two-o-o* little *blu-u-u*-berries."

Karl had to put his face somewhere to stifle the laughter, so he plunged it into her two little bu-u-soms.

"But, Anna, I told you, blueberries are my favorite," he said when he was able.

"*You-u-u* don't *foo-o-o-l* me! I know *you-u-u!*"

"A man cannot help having a favorite."

"Ya, favorite, says this *foo-o-o-l*. He should remember that if he did not have hands like *sou-u-u-p* plates, they would be *fu-u-u-ll* right now!"

Another spasm of laughter grabbed Karl. Beneath his hands, he felt Anna's breasts bounce with laughter, too. "And if you were not so busy being smart to your new husband, you might have your hands full, too." He captured her hand and placed it upon his genitals.

"*Ya, su-u-u-re,*" Anna said, her Swedish accent beautiful by this time, "like I said, he is a *foo-o-o-l*. Vith the sun up and his brother-in-law on the floor, he vakes up like a ripe *cu-u-u*-cumber!"

This time they couldn't keep it quiet any more. They laughed in audible snorts while Karl engulfed Anna in his big, powerful arms and they rolled back and forth, bubbling over with joy.

"What are you two doing up there?" James asked from the floor.

"We are talking about gardening," Karl answered.

"So early in the morning?" James wasn't misled. He knew things were going to be *great* around here from now on!

"Ya. I was just telling Anna how much I love blueberries and she was telling me how she loves cu—" The rest of Karl's word was muffled as Anna clapped her hand over Karl's mouth.

Then James heard more giggling, and the cornhusks snapping like they'd never snapped before and many grunts and sounds of playful battle. But James wisely kept his back to the bed as he got up and went outside to the washbench. He was smiling from ear to ear.

Karl was right; the Indians showed up in the clearing before breakfast, looking longingly at the kiln. What else could they do but invite them to stay for breakfast? Thankfully, there were only three this time, so only one of their precious loaves had to be shared. Karl took his axe outside. Anna, James and the three visitors watched as he rapped on the kiln and broke it open. The fourteen loaves were gloriously brown and still warm.

"Tonka Squaw cook good bread," Two Horns complimented when he tasted it.

"Two Horns shoots fat pheasants," she returned. And with her words, peace was made between Anna and the Indians. Karl did not find it necessary to clear up who had made the bread. Instead, he let Anna bask in the Indians' obvious admiration of her. To them she would always be Tonka Squaw, Big Woman, and Karl was proud of her for earning the honorary title. Now that Anna understood the import of it, she was congenial to them.

She found it strange that Karl still said in spite of their friendship the Indians would steal food if the house was left untended. Just as the Indians believed no man owned the birds of the air, they believed no man owned the wheat of the land. If they wanted white bread, they would come in and take it. If they wanted white potatoes, they would come in and take them. But their sense of honor would keep them out if they saw the warning block of wood wedged against the door.

Breakfast with the Indians made for a late start that day, but it didn't matter. The trio were in high spirits, for this was the day the hewing began in earnest, and nothing could rival the excitement they all felt. Anna was glowing. Karl was energetic. James was eager. All in time for the day the actual walls began going up.

Karl brought out his keenly sharpened foot adz and began hewing, explaining the art that seemed dangerous to both Anna and James. Standing upon a tamarack log, Karl used short strokes, which swept toward the toe of his boot. Anna was horrified to realize the blade actually bit into the wood beneath Karl's boot with each swipe. He moved forward a mere three inches after each stroke, making his way along the length of the log to leave behind a creamy, flat surface.

"Karl, you'll hurt yourself!" she scolded.

"Do you think so?" he questioned, eyeing the cleanly hewed wood, then curling his boot toes up. "A proper adzman can split the sole of his boot into two layers without touching either the timber beneath it or the toes inside it. Shall I show you?"

"No!" she yelped. "You and your logger's ego!"

"But it is so, Anna."

"I don't care. I would rather have you with ten toes than an award for splitting soles!"

"Your sister likes my toes," Karl said smilingly to James, "so I guess I cannot prove to her they are in no danger." Then, to Anna again, he said, "Come, help James and me roll this log over."

Together the three of them strained, using braces with which to roll the log onto its flat side so Karl could adz the topside. Then, with no more than six deft strokes, he removed a cleanly rectangular half notch some eight inches from one end of the log. He did the same at the other end, and together the trio worked to raise it onto the foundation. Always there was a perfect fit to receive, a perfect fit to enter.

During those days, as the walls grew higher, Karl made sexual innuendo out of even the fit of the notches. These were days of grueling work, of sweat-stained clothing, of hot, stinging muscles, but of satisfaction.

Everything to Karl was a source of satisfaction. Whether he was showing James the proper way to drive the blunt side of an axe poll into a kerf to hold it secure for sharpening or measuring the distance between notches by axe lengths or fitting the newly notched log securely onto the last or pausing for a drink of spring water—to Karl the living of life was a precious thing. In all he did, he taught the most important lesson of all: life must not be squandered. A person got from life what he put into it. If even the most arduous labor was looked upon benevolently, it would offer countless rewards.

He would raise one more level of logs, sit straddling the wall up above their heads, slap that log soundly, and say, "This will be a magnificent house! See how straight these tamaracks lie?" Sweating, hair plastered to the sides of his head, muscles hot and trembling from the massive effort of placing the log just perfectly, he found glory in this honorable task.

Below him, Anna would gaze up, shading her eyes with an arm, tired beyond any tiredness she had ever imagined, but still ready to help raise one more log, knowing that when it was up, she would feel swelling in her chest again, the glorious satisfaction only Karl had taught her to feel.

One day, standing thus, she called up to her husband, "Oh, this is a magnificent thing all right, but I think it is a magnificent birdcage!" Indeed, it did look like a birdcage. Even with Karl's deeply cleft notches the logs did not quite meet. By now Anna knew perfectly well that all log cabins were made this way, but Karl's infectious teasing had by this time rubbed off on her.

"And I know a little bird I will put inside and keep there and feed her good to try to fatten her up!"

"Like a hen for market?"

"Oh no! This hen is not for sale."

"Even so, if you want to fatten her up in this cage, you'll have trouble getting her in, since you forgot the door."

He laughed fully, raising his golden head till the sun caught it brightly against the blue sky. "Such a smart little hen she is that she noticed a thing like that. Such a foolish Swede I am that I forgot to build a door."

"Or windows either!"

"Or windows either," he acknowledged playfully. "You will just have to peek out between the logs."

"How can I peek out when I can't get in?"

"You will just have to get in over the top, I guess."

"That should be easy enough on a roofless house!"

"Does the little hen want to try it?"

"Try what?"

"Try out her birdcage?"

"You mean go inside?"

"Ya, I mean go inside."

"But how?"

"Come up here, my scrawny little chick, and I will show you how."

"Come up there?" It looked mighty high from where she stood.

"I have had to look at you in those awful britches all this time. This is the first time I see some advantage in you wearing them. You can climb the walls easily. Come on."

Anna was not one to waver before a challenge. Up she went! Hand over hand, toe over toe. "Be careful," he called down, "chickens cannot fly!" Twelve logs high she went, and Karl leaned to grab her arm and help her swing a leg over the top of the wall. Of course, she swung the leg out behind instead of before her, almost knocking poor Karl off his perch. But he skittered backward and Anna made it safely up. The world seemed magnificent from this height! She could see the straight rows of the vegetable garden and their corn crop. The wheat lay like a green waving sea below her. The backs of Bill and Belle were so wide! She'd never realized how wide! The roof of the sod hut had a squirrel's nest up against the chimney. The road out of the clearing was so straight and shaded.

From behind her Karl's voice came. "All this is ours, Anna. Have we not plenty?" He edged forward, put an arm around her waist and drew her back into his spraddled thighs, pulling her tightly till she was forced to lean her head sideways against his shoulder. He smelled of fresh wood and sweat and horses and leather and all things wonderful.

He rubbed her ribs, just beneath her breasts, while she reached behind her to put a hand on his neck. "Yes, Karl, I know now what you mean when you talk about having plenty. It has nothing to do with amounts, does it?"

For answer, he squeezed her ribs a little harder, then whispered, "Come, we will go down inside," and swung to do so.

Together they climbed down until they stood within the four new walls. The sun coming through the timbers fell upon the interior in bars of light and shadow that angled across their faces, shoulders, hair. It was like a cool, green cathedral with a blue sky ceiling. It was encompassing, private, pungent with the clean, crisp scent of wood. Automatically, they both looked up. Above the walls a fringe of branches swayed lightly in the summer breeze. Instantly, they both looked down. The wind sighed softly through the fretted walls, lazy birds chirped in the elms outside, the gurgle of the brook spoke quietly from the spring. And everywhere were those bands of sun and shadow, crossing Karl's shirtless chest, Anna's freckled face, their humble house where soon would be door, window, fireplace, loft and bed. His arms opened and his eyes closed as she pressed against him. Her arms entwined round his sun-striped body, which sprang to life at her touch against his limbs. Mouths joined, they turned in a slow circle, not thinking about what they did, but answering some need to move with each other, against each other, in harmony with each other.

"Oh, Anna, how happy we will be here," he said at last against her hair.

"Show me where our bed will be," she said. He led her to a corner where sticks and leaves and grass were its only furnishings.

"Here," he pointed, envisioning it. "And here I will cut the hole for the fireplace. And here will be the ladder to James' loft. And here I will put a dresser. Would you like a dresser in your kitchen, Anna? I can build it of maple. I have already chosen a good maple tree. And I thought of a chair that rocks. Always I have wanted a chair that rocks. With my adz I can hollow out a smooth seat and make spindles for the back of it of willow whips. What a chair that will be, Anna."

She could not help smiling at him, with him. She thought she would rather have an iron stove than a rocking chair or dresser put together, but did not say so. His enthusiasm was too fine to dampen.

"When can we start chinking?" Anna asked.

"Soon," he answered. "First I must bring in the ridgepole from the woods. I have it chosen, too."

"When will it all be done, Karl? When can we move in?"

"You are anxious, my little one?"

"I am tired of lying to James about all these walks we've been taking lately."

He hugged her against his chest again, chuckling into her neck, placing his mouth there, tasting salt of her labors, loving it. He dropped his arm to her hips, drew them against his own. Then he placed both hands upon her buttocks and cupped them handily, though there was no need for him to pressure her against her will. Her will was now his own. She had come to love the feel of his body molded against hers, sought it out as eagerly as he did here.

"If my Tonka Squaw keeps it up, she will be lying to her brother again and he will know perfectly well this time that we are not going for a walk in broad daylight with a cabin only half built."

"Since he will know the truth anyway, perhaps this little Tonka Squaw will just go ahead and tell him the truth, that his big, hot-blooded brother-in-law is off to the cucumber patch again."

His laughter sailed up over the fretwork walls, and hers along with it.

The raising of the ridgepole was an auspicious occasion, for it was James' first real chance to prove his mettle as a teamster. It was a tricky business, and as Anna watched his eyes darted time and again to the height of the walls. He pulled in huge gulps of breath, then blew them out exaggeratedly, cheeks puffed, raising the hair off his forehead.

The tamarack Karl had chosen was of necessity a stately old giant longer than any used so far. It lay now in wait beside the cabin wall. Four thinner trees were skinned and shone whitely, leaning up against the topmost tier of logs in the sun.

The great chains were attached to the clevises, and James felt his palms sweat. Never in his life had he wanted to please a man more than he wanted to please Karl today. Wiping his forehead, James again raised his eyes to the top of the cabin, wishing suddenly there were another man here to help Karl, so he could be excused. Yet at the same time, the challenge filled the boy with the will to do his best.

James scoured his memory, recalling every lesson Karl had taught him about the importance of soothing the horse with quiet words before and while it was worked. But his voice cracked to a high falsetto when he tried to speak reassuringly to Belle. The horses were accustomed to working closely, side by side, and were uneasy now at this unaccustomed separation as one animal was attached to each end of the long ridgepole. Only rarely were they asked to respond singly to any command, thus Belle unconsciously swerved toward Bill, and James ordered, "Haw! Haw!" But nervousness made his voice too sharp.

From across the way, Karl explained. "Boy, do not forget you are commanding only Belle now, but Bill can hear your orders, too. When you give a command, use her name."

James swallowed the lump in his throat, going over all the things Karl had taught him—horses have a keen sense of hearing; if you shout at a horse you only shout to relieve yourself; quiet but firm commands are best.

"Keep the reins tight until I give you the nod, then we will start them out together," Karl instructed. "Remember, if you let her ease up too much we will lose the ridgepole in a sideslip!"

Unconsciously, Anna balled up her fists, as if the reins were in her hands rather than in her brother's. Her heart beat as quickly as she was sure his did. She spared a glance at Karl. The trust he had in James showed in his casual stance and the relaxed expression upon his face as he turned one last time to reassure the boy.

"How many times have you handled the team, boy?" Karl asked now.

"Lots of times. Every day since I been here."

"And have they ever let you down?"

"Nossir."

"And you ever let them down?"

"Nossir."

"How many are in a team?"

"What?" James's face registered surprise at such a question.

"A team. How many in a team?"

"T . . . two, of course."

"You handled two overgrown Percherons all this time. Now you have to handle only half as many, right?"

After a hesitation, James replied, "Right," even though he realized this was part of the problem.

"A man who can skid a ridgepole into place can do anything with his team." And with these words Karl squared his stance behind Bill.

Never before had Karl used the term "man" in regard to James. Hearing it now, knowing that this truly was a man's job, James tried mightily to reflect the confidence Karl placed in him.

The reins seemed greased. The sweat trickled down the hollow at the back of James' neck while shivers ran up his calves. Belle's haunches looked so massive that no puny hanks of leather could stop that power, should it decide to flesh itself at will. Grasping the reins, James frantically wondered if he could possibly have missed a weak link in the chain somehow when he'd checked it over. Were Belle's tug straps, which bore the vast stress of the load, really thick and unworn? But it was too late to make any further corrections as the chains pulled taut and the slack disappeared with a musical chink.

James looked over at Karl. The big man gave him a great wink. Then came Karl's silent nod, and together the man and boy spoke: "Get up, Belle. Get up, Bill." There was a first grating denial, then a clunk, as the ridgepole settled on the green skids. The chests of the Percherons strained in their harnesses, and James took his first step, leaning back, as he'd seen Karl do. The squeak of green wood sang through the clearing, then the groan of the skids as they bent beneath their burden.

"Get up, Belle," James ordered, as Belle felt the stress build upon her chest. The horse's head arose with the effort, and her step became shorter, higher. "Get up, Belle. Attagirl, Belle!" The ridgepole—twenty feet of deadly, crushing weight should it go awry—slid steadily, horizontally, skyward.

The horses moved forward and were cut off from each other's range of vision by the cabin. Then the drivers were cut off likewise. Now they could see only an end of the ridgepole, could only envision the rest of it going up level, moving, nearing its mooring, until, when it seemed the lungs of the horses would implode from their efforts, there came the soft thud, and Karl's voice from the other side of the cabin, "We made it, boy! We made it!"

James forgot himself then, and let out a whoop and a holler and jumped in the air, scaring poor Belle into skittering sideways.

Anna let out the breath she'd been holding and ran forward gleefully, nearly as excited as James by his success. "You did it! You did it!" she sang, enormously pleased by his ever-growing prowess as a teamster.

"I did, didn't I?"

"With a little help from Belle."

"A little," James agreed, but then laughed again. "Belle, you big old sweetheart!" James exclaimed, and foolishly kissed the rounded side of Belle's belly.

Just then, Karl came around the corner. "What is this? My brother-in-law kissing my horse!" That brought another round of laughter.

"I did it, Karl," James said again proudly.

"Ya, you sure did. You could show a thing or two to some Swedes I know about skidding up a ridgepole." James knew that from Karl there was no higher praise. They both looked up at the pole lying securely in place.

"I was plenty scared though, Karl."

"Sometimes we must do things, plenty scared or not. To be able to say afterward, 'I was plenty scared' makes a man a bigger man, not a smaller one."

"I didn't want to tell you how scared I was when I took those reins."

Karl could not help being amused by such an admission. He smiled and nodded. "And I was plenty scared myself. I always am when a ridgepole goes up. But we did it, eh?"

"We sure did."

Chapter 13

The raising of the ridgepole was the catalyst in the nurturing relationship between Karl and James. After that day there developed a compatibility between them such as James had never experienced with another man, and unlike Karl had shared with any but his older brothers.

They found they could speak on more equal terms since James had passed muster as a teamster. The ease with which they worked, learned and taught together created an ease of discourse, too. Soon they found themselves talking of more intimate feelings, memories and hopes.

Karl told James countless tales about his life in Sweden, about the family that had been so close and loving, about the desolate loneliness he had experienced during his two years before Anna and James had come here. Karl even confessed openly how wonderful it was not having to sleep alone any more, to eat alone.

Often they spoke of Anna. There was no doubt in James' mind that Karl loved his sister. The knowledge made for a security that had been lacking in James' life. Warm beneath it, he began unfolding into a man.

Slowly, Karl drew him out about the life he and Anna had known before they came here. But there was only so much James would say. There were gaps he left unfilled, as if they were too unpleasant to remember. One of those gaps was their mother. Whenever she was mentioned, he would withdraw behind a barrier as palpable as the walls of the new cabin. Neither would Anna speak much about her mother.

But Karl learned bits here and there that made him certain the two did not want him to know about the woman they called "Barbara." He did not force the issue, but merely brought the word "Boston" into his conversations with James now and then as encouragement for the boy to tell anything he wanted about their past.

During this time there were countless chores Karl had to teach James or Anna or sometimes both of them. There was the gathering of wax from honeycombs. Wax, it seemed, was as essential as lye. They would save it till autumn in hopes of killing a fat bear to provide them with plenty of tallow to melt with the wax for candles. It was used also in treating the horse harnesses, in preserving various foods and in medicinal concoctions.

Karl taught Anna how to boil the laundry, rub it on the washboard and hang it over the bushes to dry. The laundry was a very difficult chore for Anna. She complained about the lye soap burning her hands until finally Karl examined them more closely and discovered that she had acquired the malaise commonly called "prairie dig," which most newcomers to the plains states contracted. It was a mystery that had no solution but to wait out the itching and puffiness, which made Anna—and soon James—scratch irritably. Karl told Anna it had nothing to do with lye soap, but with digging in the garden. This did not lift her spirits any. Both laundry and gardening were basically her chores.

Karl sought out help from the Indians and did as Two Horns' wife advised. He made an ointment of lard and laurel, hunting for the lance-shaped evergreen branches, then working the dried leaves into a fine powder to be mixed with lard. Anna put this on at bedtime. So did James. At other times they used a weak wash made of the laurel powder and water.

There seemed to be no end to the things a man must learn about horses. The upkeep of the harnesses alone was demanding. They were carefully kept washed clean of sweat, which rotted the leather almost as fast as the urine fumes if the barn was not kept clean. Karl had no forge, so Belle and Bill were not shod. Thus it was necessary always to keep their hooves and feet in tip-top condition. Countless ailments could lame a horse whose feet were not kept clean, whose hooves were not kept trim, or who stood in an unkempt stall.

Karl and James were working over the horses' feet in the barn one day. James, as usual, was leaning close to watch every move the big man made as Karl demonstrated the proper way to grasp the horse's cannon and force the knee to bend. He squatted, holding the giant foreleg in his lap, demonstrating the use of the hoof pick to remove soil and pebbles out of the hollow, spongy part of the hoof called the frog.

"I am very pleased with your progress as a farrier," Karl praised. "You have learned it almost as fast as you have learned to drive the team. If I did not know better, I would say you drove many horses before you came here."

"Nope, never," said James. Then, remembering something, he quickly added, "Well, once I did. There was this man in Boston who let me drive his horse and shay just once."

"And all this time I thought you had never handled a team," Karl teased.

"Well, it was no team. It was just a single bay. But what a bay! It was one of the most beautiful horses I ever saw, and pulling the fanciest red leather rig in the world. Sometimes, I'd just hang around the livery barn to see if I could catch sight of it. After all that time I got my chance. I never could figure out why Saul let me take her out that day. Up till then he never let me get within a mile of her, even if I offered to lead her to the livery for free. You coulda knocked me over with a toothpick when he ups and says I could take that bay and rig out for a ride."

Karl continued the lesson and the conversation simultaneously, carefully keeping his questions casual. "You must see that the frog of the hoof is free of dirt or the horse will develop a disease called thrush. So . . . if you knew this man . . . this Saul, why would he not let you take care of his horse before?"

"Well, I didn't really *know* him, actually. Well, sort of . . . I don't really know. He was a friend of Barbara's and he sort of took to Anna after Barbara died."

"He was a young man then, Anna's age?"

"No, he was at least as old as Barbara."

"Once the frog is cleaned out, you must check the hoof wall for cracks." Karl picked up his cutter, bending, couching the big hoof in his lap. "But even so, when your mother was gone, this Saul remained your friend?"

"I told you, he was no friend. He never used to like us underfoot when he came to see Barbara. She'd usually send us packing whenever Saul was around."

"Once the hoof is trimmed, it must be made level with the rasp." Karl picked up his rasp. "But that day Saul offered to let you drive his fancy bay and fancy shay, eh?"

"Yup! I took 'er for a sprint around the commons. She was a high-stepper and you shoulda seen the blokes stare. There I came—Barbara's Brat—behind that pretty little bay. It was somethin', Karl, I tell you!"

Barbara's Brat? thought Karl. But he didn't want to interrupt the first insight into James' Boston life. Instead of questioning the queer phrase, Karl only agreed, "Ya, I bet it was something. Now you watch here and see how I shape this hoof so Bill will balance on it right. What did Anna think of riding behind that high-stepper?"

"Oh, she wasn't along."

"No? Poor Anna missed out on a treat like that?"

"She acted nervous and said she didn't trust that bay. Said he was too spirited for her taste and sent me off by myself."

"Anna should have had more sense than to let you take that horse out alone if it was so spirited."

"She figured I'd be okay, I guess. She said it was too good of a chance for me to miss, so I oughta go without her. That time she stayed behind even though Saul was there."

The rasp croaked quietly as Karl shaped the hoof. "Anna, what did she think of this man, Saul?"

"She never liked him much."

"But he took to Anna, huh?"

"Oh, Karl, are you jealous? That's funny. You don't have to be jealous of Saul. Why, Anna used to run and hide when he came around. She said he gave her the willies." James smiled at Karl's concerned expression, knowing he had no cause to frown so. Anna had never even *liked* any man before Karl. Of this James was sure.

But Karl was not relieved. He forced a smile and laughed for James' benefit, but the sound was strangely unfamiliar, coming from high in his throat. He tried to picture Anna standing with a man who gave her the willies, a man from whom she had always hidden, while James drove away in the fancy rig. Once he had pictured it, he tried not to.

To all outward appearances, he seemed absorbed in the hoof, studying it critically while he asked, "I guess he was a pretty rich man, this Saul, huh? That was some fancy rig he owned."

"I guess. He wore fancy clothes most of the time, too."

A hot, sick feeling crept through Karl.

"Here, boy, you try trimming this next hoof and I will watch to see you do it right." But it was not the boy working the hoof that Karl saw. It was Anna, standing beside some dandy named Saul while James drove away.

Karl seemed withdrawn that night. When Anna asked him how James had done at hoof-trimming, he gazed at her vacantly until she had to ask him a second time.

They all went to the pond, as usual, but Karl was not his usual playful self. He swam with singular intense vigor, driving himself back and forth across the deep end of the water, leaving Anna and James to cavort in the shallows if they wanted to. By now Anna could swim out above her head. But when she did and tried to coax Karl into a corner against the beaver dam, he told her to leave him alone tonight; he wasn't in the mood for playing.

In bed later, he muttered something to the same effect, saying he'd had a hard day. He sighed and rolled over, facing away from her. Immediately, she hugged him from behind, settling her lap around his posterior. But he did not take her hand for a long, long time. He only took it when she reached to fondle him, squeezing it then so tightly she had to pull her fingers out of his grip with a sharp sound of complaint. The ointment on the prairie dig was all over his hand and he got up to find a rag and wipe it off his skin, making an unmistakable sound of irritation at the bother.

Anna slept at last, but Karl dozed fitfully. Every time he drifted off, some past comment of Anna's or James' would come tearing through his mind, bringing with it an ulterior meaning. Like pieces of a puzzle, various things fit into place. But as the picture formed, always it was the vision of Anna standing beside a fancily dressed man as old as her mother, while James rode off in the man's rig.

Guiltily, Karl opened his eyes wide in the darkness to dispel the picture that intimated something about Anna of which he should be shot for thinking! But then again would come James' words, "he gave her the willies." Then again, "that time she stayed behind even though Saul was there."

By the time dawn was hovering on the horizon, Karl had finally begun the deep search of the thing he had resisted all night long: his memory of the first night Anna and he had made love. It was terrible he should even be suspecting her of such things. Still, he allowed that night to come back fully. Things he'd been too overwrought to see at the time became significant now. Most significantly, three things had been missing from Anna: pain, resistance and blood.

Karl wondered if he was right. How could he know if she suffered pain? Perhaps she had hidden it from him. But he remembered again saying to her, "I don't want to hurt you, Anna." What had she said? Exactly what had she said? He thought it had been something like, "It's all right, Karl."

Then he remembered something else she had said afterward: "Something good happened, Karl, something I didn't expect." He laid his arm across his forehead and found he was perspiring. Another memory came, again too vividly. In the house, before they had run out to the barn, she had said, "It's so different, Karl . . ." Different from what? he wondered now. Oh God, different from what?

When he could stand the torment no longer, he got up and went out to the barn where Belle and Bill turned inquiring eyes on him. But he did not touch them, only stood with hands in his pockets, staring ahead with unseeing eyes.

"When're we gonna cut out the door, Karl?" Anna asked, just as gay and carefree as ever.

"After the roof is finished," he answered.

"Hurry, huh?" she said piquantly, tilting her head sideways.

Instead of his usual chuck under the chin or teasing pinch, he turned on his heel and left her staring at James for the answer as to why her husband had become so distant all of a sudden.

James scanned his memory for anything he himself might have done to displease Karl. But there was nothing. He'd come pretty close to giving away their secret about Barbara, but he didn't really think Karl was the kind of man who'd blame them if he did find out what Barbara was. Not Karl. Karl was too good to do a thing like that. Still, James wondered about the conversation in which he'd mentioned Saul. Could Karl be jealous of Saul after all? But it couldn't be that! After all, he'd as much as told Karl that Anna couldn't stand Saul's guts. If anything, that should have put his mind at ease.

Karl's taciturn distraction became more noticeable with each passing day. Anna tried to bring Karl out of his "drears" as she called it. But he would not be cajoled by her, or persuaded to smile. He made excuses not to make love until one night he changed his mind only to handle Anna so roughly she lay stunned by his lack of tenderness throughout the act. Crushed and hurt, she dared not ask what was bothering him again. She had asked before, but he wouldn't say anything.

Meanwhile, Karl himself was suffering sleepless nights and torturous days. More and more evidence built in his mind against Anna. In his typical way, he said nothing to her, continuing to mull it all over until he had given her every conceivable benefit of doubt. Yet at long last, he could see it no other way than that what he suspected was true. Too many things now fit, things he had never associated before with Anna's previous life or her mother. Karl realized he could not go on this way, for even his face was beginning to show the ravages of sleeplessness and worry. Dreading it, yet needing it, he must know the truth.

Anna was scrubbing clothes on the washboard in the yard, wearing a pair of James' pants again. Karl could scarcely remember the dress she'd worn the day she came on the supply wagon to Long Prairie. He hadn't remembered until this morning when he'd gone to the trunk and looked while Anna was busy in the yard.

He studied her now as she worked. Her hair was tumbling around her as she scrubbed. Oh, that whiskey hair he had dreamed of during the months alone waiting for her. He pushed the thought aside and quietly came up behind his wife.

"Anna, who is Saul?" he asked simply. He saw her shoulders suddenly stiffen and her head snap up as her hands idled.

Anna felt as if a giant fist had unexpectedly smashed into her stomach. She realized she was clutching the top of the washboard, and forced her hands to move again, dropping her eyes to the tub.

"Saul?" she inquired in what she hoped was a casual tone.

"Who is he?"

"He was a . . . a friend of Barbara's."

"James says he had an eye for you."

"J . . . James said that?" Anna's chin was tucked hard against her chest. She had become too intent upon washing.

Karl stepped to her side and grasped her elbow, making her turn so he could see her face.

It was deep scarlet and her chin quivered beneath slightly open lips.

Her horrified gaze trembled down to the top button on Karl's shirt, but was drawn inexorably up to his haunted eyes.

"Did he?" Karl asked, his voice strange, hurt.

"I said he was a friend of Barbara's, not mine."

"What kind of a friend?" His thumb dug into her soft skin.

"Just a friend," she said, jerking her arm free and turning back to the washbench.

Karl tried to make her look at him by leaning partially in front of her, but she stubbornly kept her eyes cast down and had plunged into her washing once more with frantic energy.

"A friend who sent you and James away when he wanted to be alone with your mother?"

The old pain clutched her stomach muscles. "Did James say that?"

"Ya, James said that!"

Damn you, James! How could you? Anna's teeth grasped the soft skin of her inner bottom lip to keep it from quivering.

"He also said you were afraid of this Saul . . . that he gave you the willies."

"He did! He made my skin crawl every time I looked at him." She was scrubbing violently now, her insides repulsed by sordid memories Karl's questions were dredging up.

"And so you sent James away for a ride in his fancy carriage and stayed behind with this man who made your skin crawl? Why?"

She didn't know what to say. What could she say? Please, help me . . . James . . . somebody, help me make him understand.

But Karl understood only too well. In a steely voice he went on. "Tell me why a rich man with a fine high-strutting bay horse and red leather shay would let a lad of thirteen take his rig out for a ride after never letting the boy so much as stable the horse before."

Her eyelids had begun to tremble. "How should I know?"

"Would you know, then, why this boy's sister would not jump at the chance to ride along when she knew it would mean avoiding the man who makes her skin crawl?"

"Please, Karl . . ." Her eyelids slid closed. But this time he forced her to face him fully.

"Anna, rich men like that do not court seamstresses and their orphaned daughters for no reason."

"He was not courting me!" Anna's eyes flew open and she met his defensively. In Karl's face she read the truth—that he felt as sick about this as she did.

He spoke resignedly. "I did not think he was courting you—a man the age of your mother, this mother who you call nothing but Barbara. Why did you not call her 'mother' like other children call their mothers?"

She would not answer.

"Was it because she was not a simple seamstress? Was it because she did not care to have men like this Saul know she had two children? Was it because it would be bad for her business if they knew?"

Anna's eyelids closed. She could not look into the honest face of Karl Lindstrom while he guessed her guilt.

"Was she a seamstress, Anna, or was that a lie, too?"

When she did not answer he went on. "Where did you get the money for James' passage and those new clothes of his?"

Her cheeks were afire and her stomach hurt so bad she was afraid she would retch on the spot.

Karl grasped her cheeks in the vise of one huge hand. "What kind of dresses are those you refuse to wear before me?"

As the tears slid from Anna's closed eyes and rolled to wet Karl's fingers where they grasped her cheek, the last and most horrifying truth was revealed. For by now it was evident these questions were already answered. Because they were answered, they need not even be asked.

Still, Karl tried one more halting beginning. "The first night you and I made love, Anna . . ." But he could not make himself go the full distance of discovering what he did not want to discover. His voice fell still. He dropped his hand from her face, turned away from her and strode across the clearing to the barn, where James was today working on Belle's hooves.

When Karl burst in, James looked up, expecting perhaps a word of praise. Instead, Karl said grimly, "Boy, I need the truth out of you."

James looked up from the big, shaggy leg that was cradled in his lap.

"Was your mother a seamstress?"

The rasp hung uselessly in James' hand. His eyes were like saucers. "Nossir," he whispered.

"Do you know what she did to earn a living?" The question was fired like a load from a rifle.

James swallowed. Belle's foot clacked onto the floor. "Y . . . yessir," he whispered again, this time dropping his gaze to Karl's feet.

Karl could not, need not ask further. How could he force this winsome lad of thirteen to identify his own mother as a prostitute, much less his sister, whom James loved so much better than he ever had the mother?

Karl's voice gentled perceptibly. "That's all, boy. You got that hoof nice and level. I can tell from here how the hoof is the same angle as the pastern. When you are done with her, you can turn her out to forage for a while. It will be her little treat after standing so still for you."

"Yessir." But the word was mumbled, James' eyes still set on the floor.

Anna stumbled through the remainder of the day in a blur of emotions. At first she avoided Karl's eyes, but then tried to catch his glance, only to realize he would not even so much as look at her. In the close confines of the cabin his careful withdrawal cut deeply, for he gave her wide berth, cautiously avoiding even the brush of her clothing against his. She knew self-disgust at having disappointed him so utterly.

By the time dusk fell, Anna's trepidation had spread its tentacles about her, squeezing the life from the small amount of self-confidence she'd slowly gleaned through her days as Karl's wife.

That night when his weight finally joined hers on the cornhusks, not so much as a single crackle sounded. Karl lay rigidly upon his back. After what seemed a lifetime he crossed his arms behind his head. His elbow brushed Anna's hair, and she felt him carefully move farther away to avoid even the slightest contact.

After lying beside his stiff form for as long as she could stand it, she realized someone must make the first move toward reconciliation. Gathering up her courage, she turned and lay her palm entreatingly along the underside of his biceps.

As if her touch were now a vile thing, he immediately jerked away and rolled to face the outside, leaving her stricken, with thick throat and flowing eyes.

Oh God, my God, what have I done? Karl, Karl, turn back to me. Let me show you how sorry I am. Let me feel your strong arms around me, forgiving me. Please, love, let's be like before.

But his withdrawal was complete. She suffered it not only that night, but also during the days and nights that followed. She suffered it in resigned silence, knowing she fully deserved this misery. The days were torture, but bedtime was worse, for the dark held remembrance of their former closeness, the joy they had given and found in intimacy, the passion foregone, gone . . . gone . . .

James knew it had been several nights since Karl and Anna had gone out for their late-night walk, so it surprised him to hear the door opening after they'd already settled into bed. Then he realized it was only Karl who'd gone out. Anna was still there. She turned over and sighed.

Sick at heart for having started this whole thing, James thought he would maybe be able to put things straight. Maybe if he went out and explained to Karl it was none of their fault what their mother had been, maybe if he told Karl for sure how Anna had hated knowing, how she'd vowed to James she'd see he had a better life, maybe then Karl wouldn't be so bitter about it.

James slipped into his britches and out the door. He crossed the clearing to the barn, but once inside, realized that the horses were still tethered outside where he himself had put them that afternoon. He was sure Karl would be with the horses.

He was right. Even from here he could see the outline of Karl, standing beside one of their necks. As he approached on the silent grass, he saw it was Bill by whom the big man stood. The moon picked out the marking on Bill's forehead, and the whiteness of Karl's hair in the night. James saw how Karl had his face buried in Bill's neck, his two fist clutching the coarse mane.

Before James could let Karl know he stood there, Karl's sobs came to him, sounding muffled against the horse and the night. Never had James seen a man cry. He didn't know men cried. He thought he himself was the only boy in the world who had ever cried. But now Karl stood before him, Karl whom he loved almost more than Anna, sobbing wretchedly, pathetically, gripping Bill's mane.

The sound shattered James' bubble of security, which had sheltered him with ever-increasing sureness since he had come to live here in the only home he had ever known. Fearful, not knowing what to do, he turned and fled back to the house, to his pallet on the floor to lie with hammering heart, swallowing back the tears he, too, now wanted to shed, waiting to hear the reassuring footsteps of Karl going back to his bed with Anna. But he didn't cry. He didn't cry. Somebody around here had to not cry.

Chapter 14

Anna and James worked on the chinking. They made trip after trip to the pit for clay to mix with dry prairie grass. With this they packed the spaces between the logs. Their prairie dig got worse. Karl, meanwhile, continued to work on the roof, using smaller willows for the first layer. These were joined to the ridgepole by boring holes, pegging them in place with small lengths of saplings.

Since Karl had put forth his questions about Saul, there was no more pleasantry at bedtime to break the monotony and lighten the load of the hard-working days. James, ever aware of the distance between sister and brother-in-law, suffered under the strain as much as Karl and Anna. He lay on his pallet listening for the sounds of their whispers, their soft laughter, even for the sounds of the cornhusks trembling secretly.

In her spot beside Karl, Anna felt him turn away from her again and pretended to go straight to sleep. She came to expect the tears, which nightly became her companions, but she swallowed them back and gulped down the threatening sobs until Karl's breathing turned deep and even. Only then did those tears stream down her face, puddling in her ears before wetting the pillow case, until, desperately, she would roll over and bury her face, letting the racking sobs come.

Behind her, Karl was fully awake, his empty arms longing for the Anna he'd known before. But stony Swedish pride held him aloof and hurting.

It was not at all the way Karl had imagined it would be the day he cut the opening for the door. This, he'd thought, would be a time of great celebration—the day Anna and James and I walk into our house for the first time. But she was gaunt and tired, with purple smudges beneath her eyes. James was quiet and plodding, unsure how to act between the two of them. Karl himself was efficient, quiet and polite.

The doorway was opened, facing due east as Karl had promised. But when they stepped inside for the first time, it was not into bands of sun and shadow as before. The roof poles were in place now, and much of the chinking was packed. The only solid light penetrated from the doorway. Inside, Anna found the cabin dismal. Assiduously, she avoided going near the corner where she and Karl had stood kissing, or the spot where he had told her the bed would be.

James put on an interested air, walking around the confined space, exclaiming, "Wow! It's three times as big as the sod house!"

"More than three times with the loft, too."

James said, "I never had a spot of my own before."

"It is time we get back to work and stop daydreaming about lofts. There is much to be done before we come to loft-building. Are you ready to bring those stones in, boy?"

"Yessir."

"Good! Then hitch up Belle and Bill, and I will walk out with you and show you where the pile is."

With a sense of doom, Anna set out with the two of them to help James load rocks onto a carrier bogan, which Karl told them was the bunk and runners of his wintertime conveyance, the bobsled. Karl showed them where his rock pile was, east of the cleared grainfields, then returned to the cabin, leaving them to struggle with their morning's drudgery. Yes, that's what it seemed to Anna today—drudgery. All the beautiful meaning had gone out of their work.

When James drove the bogan back to the clearing with Anna trailing beside, they were both tired and sore.

She dragged herself into the clearing, then to the door of the cabin. It was brighter inside now, for Karl was chopping out a hole for a fireplace.

Sensing she was behind him, he turned and found her staring at his handiwork.

"You're building a fireplace then, Karl?" she asked.

"Ya. A house should have a fireplace."

And a bride should be a virgin, she thought. Is that it, Karl? So she was doomed to cook and heat water and boil soap and boil clothes using only a fireplace for the rest of her life. So Karl, whom she had not guessed could be vindictive, was getting even with her. She longed to cry out, don't do this, Karl! I had no choice, and I'm sorry . . . so sorry!

Karl, heart swollen in hurt, returned to his chopping, recalling how he'd always thought of the joy of building this fireplace. How he had thought to bring his Anna to it, to lay her before it in the deep of winter when the flames blazed high, to toy with her, to take her body against his, to wrap them both in the buffalo robe later and fall asleep uncaringly, there on the floor.

The stones of the fireplace went up, one by lonely one.

The day came when Karl announced they must drive back to check the wild hops. He announced it to James. He spoke little to Anna now, although when he did, he was always polite. Politeness was not what Anna wanted. She wanted the Karl who had teased and cajoled and been so vocal about her disastrous cooking. Now, though her cooking was no better than before, he made no remarks about it, just ate it stolidly, arose from the table and left with his axe or his gun over his shoulder. He continued teaching her the things she needed to know, but all the playfulness and mirth had gone from the lessons.

So it was to James that Karl announced, "I think we must go to the wild hops and check them again. If we want bread next winter, we had best go now."

"Should I hitch up Belle and Bill?" James asked eagerly. These days he tried to do anything he could think of to make Karl smile, but nothing did the trick.

"Yes. We will leave as soon as you have finished milking Nanna."

When the time came for them to leave, Anna sensed they were not simply heading out to skid a load of building supplies into the clearing. The horses were pointed toward the road for the first time since she had arrived. She stepped to the doorway, staying back in the shadows so Karl couldn't see her. She wondered where they were going. Suddenly, she feared they might leave her here alone, for nobody had said anything to her. Karl had fetched willow baskets and put them in the wagonbed. She saw him turn to James, then James came toward the sod house at a trot. Anna backed away from the door.

"Karl says it's time to go check the wild hops again. He says to see if you're coming, too."

Her heart sang and cried, both at once. He did not mean to leave her then, but neither did he come to invite her himself. She dropped the scoop in the hod and went with James, hesitating only long enough to close the door behind her.

When she reached the wagon, Karl was already perched on the seat. He glanced back at the house, and Anna's hopes that he would reach a hand down to help her up were dashed. Instead, while she climbed aboard one side, Karl clambered down the other, walked back to the woodpile, got a stout log and braced it against the door.

"Why didn't you remind me, Karl?" she asked, wondering if she would ever learn to be the kind of wife he needed. She couldn't even remember a simple thing like bracing the wood against the door.

"It does not matter," he said.

Dismally, she thought, no it doesn't matter. Nothing matters any more, does it, Karl?

The wild hops were ripe this time. The heavy stems clung to their supporting trees with hooked hairs, each vine twining in the clockwise direction peculiar to the hop plant, which Karl explained was one way to identify it. The yellow-green flowers were crisp, papery, sticky, bearing hard purple seeds. They all picked, filling the baskets until they had harvested what they needed and more.

"We'll be eating an awful lot of bread this winter, from the looks of it," Anna said.

"I will sell most of the hops. They bring in fair money," Karl explained.

"At Long Prairie?" she asked.

"Ya, at Long Prairie," he answered, giving her no clue as to when he intended to make the trip.

When the baskets were overflowing and the three were ready to go, Anna bent to touch a newly sprouted growth, stemming up near the mother plant. Karl had called the sprouts "bines."

"Karl? Since there are no hops on your land, why don't we try taking a bine and starting some there?"

"I have tried it before. They have not lived for me."

"Why don't we try it again?"

"We can, if you want to, but I brought nothing to dig it up with."

"What about your axe? Couldn't we chop it out with that?"

Karl's expression was horrified. "With my axe?" He sounded appalled at the thought of his precious axe digging into the dulling grains of the earth. "No man willingly sets his axe in the soil. An axe is made for wood."

Feeling stupid, she looked at the bines, saying, "Oh," in a small voice. But she knelt down, determined to get a plant some way. "I'll see if I can dig one up with my hands then."

Surprisingly, he knelt beside her, and together they tunneled, trying to reach the bottom of the root. It was the closest they had worked together in days, and each was conscious of the other's hands, burrowing and scraping to free the root of the hop bine. There was in Anna a desperate need to please Karl in some small way. If the root were to take hold and grow, she knew it would be like giving Karl a gift.

"I'll water it every day," she promised.

He looked up to find her kneeling there with other promises in her eyes. Then he looked away, saying, "We had better pack this root in some moss or it will dry up before we reach home." He went in search of moss, leaving Anna with the promise dying in her eyes and her heart.

James came back from a trip to the wagon with a basket. "Did you get one up?"

"Yes, Karl helped me."

"It probably won't grow for you if it didn't grow for him," James returned.

James' heedless opinion made Anna feel like crying. He's probably right, she thought. Still, it cut her to the quick to realize James was so devoted to Karl he scarcely spent time caring about what she felt or boosting her spirits like he'd always done in the past.

Karl returned with moss, packed it around the root, then arose, saying, "It is best you take two, Anna."

"Two?"

"Ya." He seemed self-conscious all of a sudden. "Hops grow in both male and female plants. The one you picked is a female, but if you take one male, too, you will have a better crop if they decide to grow."

"How do you know this is female?" she asked.

His eyes met hers momentarily, wavered away, then he stepped nearer to show her the remaining few cones that hung on the mother plant. "By the catkins," he explained. Reaching out a fingertip he touched the nubbin. "The female's are short, only a couple inches long." He stepped to another plant that clung to a nearby tree and reached to stroke a panicle remaining there. It was about six inches in length. "The males are much longer." Then quickly he turned, picked up a basket and left her to dig up a male bine by herself, if she would.

Resolutely, she freed the second bine and took it to the wagon, carefully avoiding Karl's eyes. She wrapped it in the moss with the female, while Karl waited patiently for her to board the wagon. Come hell or high water she would make those two plants grow!

When they had traveled more than halfway home, Karl pulled the horses to a stop. "I have made up my mind to have cedar shingles," he announced. "Although the trees are not my own, I do not think this land is owned by anyone else, so I would be taking nobody's timber. It will take no more than a single tree to make shingles for the entire house, and I will have it down in no time."

To Anna, all conifers looked the same. But once Karl started chopping, she smelled the difference. The cedar fragrance was so heady she wondered if one might become intoxicated by it. Again, she was watching the beauty and grace of Karl's body as he wielded the axe. She had not seen him do any felling since they had become estranged. It moved her magically, creating a longing in the pit of her stomach for this fence to be mended between them.

Suddenly, she realized that Karl had slowed his axefalls, changed the rhythm somehow, which was something he *never* did!

He took two more swings, and each was answered by an echo. But when he stopped chopping, the echo went on. He stood alert, like a wild turkey cock at the cluck of a hen. He twisted his head around, thinking he was hearing things, but the chopping continued somewhere off to the north.

Anna and James heard it, too, and poised in alert.

"Do you hear that?" Karl asked.

"It's just an axe," James said.

"Just an axe, boy? Just an axe! Do you know what this means?"

"Neighbors?" ventured James, a smile growing on his face.

"Neighbors," confirmed Karl, "if we are lucky."

It was the first genuine smile Anna had seen on Karl's face in days. He hefted the axe again, this time forcing himself to keep his own measured beat, forcing himself not to hurry, which tired a man and only slowed him down in the long run.

The answering echo stopped momentarily. The trio imagined a man they had never met, pausing in his felling to listen to the echo of Karl's axe making its way through the woods to him.

The far-off beat joined Karl's again, but this time as a backbeat, set evenly between Karl's axefalls, and the two axemen spoke to each other in a language only a man of the woods understood. They measured their paces into a regularity that beat out a steady question and answer, back and forth.

Clack! went Karl's axe.

Clokk! came the answer.

Clack!

Clokk!

Clack!

Clokk!

The wordless conversation drummed on, and Karl worked now with a full smile on his face. When he stepped back to watch the cedar plummet, Anna felt the same exhilaration she'd felt the first time she witnessed the spectacle.

Karl's eagerness affected her, too. When the roaring silence boomed in their ears, his eyes were drawn to her, as always. He found her beaming in the scented silence and could do no less than smile back.

Into their silence started the other woodsman's axe.

"He heard!" James said.

"Get a basket and take the cedar chips," Karl said, "while I buck the tree. Cedar chips are good for keeping the bugs away. A few in the trunk will keep the moths out. Hurry!"

Never since she'd known him had she seen Karl Lindstrom hurry. But he did now. She hurried, too.

While she was picking up the chips, Karl again surprised her by suggesting, "Try sucking on a chip."

She did. So did James. "It's sweet!" Anna exclaimed, amazed.

"Yes, plenty sweet," agreed Karl, but he was thinking of the sweet sound of the distant axe.

It took little doing to find the source of the sound. There was a new road carved in such a way that the hazelbrush had hidden it from view when they'd passed it earlier in the day. Now, approaching it from the other direction, it was clearly visible. Led, too, by the sound of the axe as they neared, they were as metal shavings to a magnet.

And so it was that they came upon a stocky, middle-aged man working his stand of tamarack along his newly cleared road. They pulled the wagon to a halt while the man let his axe poll slip down to rest against his hand, just like Karl did when he stopped chopping. He pushed back a small woolen cap much like the one Karl owned. Then, seeing Anna, he removed the cap and came toward the wagon.

Karl alone alighted, walking toward the man with hand already extended. "I heard your axe."

"Ya! I heard yours, too!"

Their two outsized hands met.

Swedish! Karl thought.

Swedish! Olaf Johanson thought.

"I am Karl Lindstrom."

"And I am Olaf Johanson."

"I live perhaps four, five miles up this road here."

"I live a few hundred rods up this road here."

Anna watched in amazement as the two greeted each other with disbelief at finding another Swede so close by. They laughed aloud together, pumping those big, axemen's hands in a way that raised a response of happiness within Anna, for she knew how deeply Karl had missed his countrymen.

"You are homesteading here?" Karl asked.

"Ya. Me and my whole family."

"I hear other axes." Karl looked off in the direction of the sound.

"Ya. Me and my boys are clearing for the cabin." Johanson's Swedish accent was far more pronounced than Karl's.

"We have been raising our cabin, too. This . . . this is my family." Karl turned to the wagon. "This is my wife, Anna, and her brother, James."

Olaf Johanson, with hat still doffed, nodded his head repeatedly, coming to shake their hands before donning the little wool thing again.

"Oh, my Katrene will be happy to see you-u-u! She and our girls, Kerstin and Nedda, have been saying, 'What if there are no neighbors or friends?' They think they will die of loneliness, those three. How could a person die of loneliness in a big family like ours?" He finished with a chuckle.

"You have a really big family?" Karl asked.

"Ya. I have three overgrown boys and two daughters, maybe not so overgrown, but pretty big girls, I tell you. We will need a big cabin, that is for sure."

Karl laughed, overjoyed at the news.

"Come, you must meet my Katrene and the children. They will not believe what I am bringing home for dinner!"

"You will ride in my wagon."

"Su-u-ure!" Johanson agreed, climbing aboard the load of cedar. "Wait till they see you! They will think they are dreaming!"

Again Karl laughed. "We cut down a cedar tree for shingles, but I think we have cut it from your land. I did not know you had settled here or I would have asked first."

"What is one cedar tree among neighbors, I ask you!" Olaf boomed vibrantly. "What is one cedar among so plenty?" His hand swept, gesturing toward the woods.

"It is a good land, this Minnesota. It is much like Sweden."

"I think it is better, maybe. I have never seen such tamaracks."

"They make a wall straight, all right," Karl agreed.

By the time they reached the narrow clearing where the axes were still ringing, the two men were in their glory.

There was a canvas-covered wagon in the clearing, and evidence of the family's having lived by roughing it since they'd arrived. There were homewares scattered around an open fire, furniture looking hapless out in the elements, makeshift pens to hold an assortment of animals. Trunks, bedding and clothing were airing on the earth, draped over wagon wheels or strewn over bushes.

A woman was stirring something in a pot that hung on a tripod over the fire. Another was climbing down from the back of the covered wagon. A girl about James' age was sorting blueberries. At the edge of the clearing, three broad backs were swinging axes. Everyone seemed to stop what they were doing at once. Olaf called and waved to the entire assemblage, bringing them all from far corners to stand around the wagon as it pulled to a halt.

"Katrene, look what I have found for you," Olaf bellered, climbing down over the back of the wagon. "Neighbors!"

"Neighbors!" exclaimed the woman, wiping her hands on her copious apron.

"Swedish neighbors!" Olaf bellered again, as if he were responsible for the existence of the nationality.

Indeed, the clearing was filled with Swedish. Everyone seemed to be yaa-ing and ooo-ing at once. Everyone except Anna and James, that is. At last Karl broke away from the eager handshakes to reach up and help Anna down.

"This is my wife, Anna," he said, "but she does not speak Swedish."

Sounds of pity issued like a swoon.

"And this is her brother, James."

There was no doubt of the welcome, although it irritated Anna the way they all broke into the foreign language she could not understand. But to her and James, they spoke English. "You will stay here and have dinner with us. There is plenty for everyone!"

"Thank you," Anna returned.

Olaf introduced his entire brood, from oldest to youngest. Katrene, his wife, was a rotund woman who chuckled gaily at everything she said. She looked much like Anna imagined Karl's own mother looked, from past descriptions Karl had given. Katrene was braided, aproned, apple-cheeked and jolly, and had dancing eyes that never seemed to dull.

Erik, the oldest son, seemed to be about Karl's age. Actually, he seemed like Karl in many ways, but was a little shorter and not quite as handsome.

Kerstin, the oldest daughter, came next. She was a young replica of her mother.

Then came Leif and Charles, strapping young men of perhaps twenty and sixteen years.

Last came Nedda, fourteen years old, who made James' voice go falsetto when he said hello to her.

Anna thought never in her life had she seen a more robust bunch of people. Pink-cheeked and vigorous and built solidly, even the women. Blond heads, all, nodded and beckoned the newcomers near the fire to have a seat on the felled logs that were the only chairs there. Excited voices exchanged news about Sweden with Karl, who reciprocated with bits about Minnesota.

While the conversations went on, Anna and James were left to listen to the unintelligible jargon and smile at everybody's enthusiasm. She glanced around the circle at all the blond heads. One in particular caught Anna's eye, making her self-conscious of the way her hair flew at will, untethered, around her head.

The oldest daughter, Kerstin, turned to stir up the smell of tantalizing food cooking in the big cast-iron pot. From behind, Anna watched the head with those flawless braids that looked stitched onto Kerstin's scalp, they were so painfully neat. The braids came away from a center part, ended like the wreath of a Roman goddess in a flawless coronet at the back of her head. Kerstin wore a meticulously clean dress and apron, which she protected from the fire when she leaned over to stir whatever it was that smelled so delicious in the pot.

Anna, in her brother's britches, felt suddenly like a tomboy. She hid her hands behind her back. They were filthy from digging up the hop bines. Kerstin's hands were as clean as her dress. She moved efficiently around the fire, obviously knowing what she was doing with food.

It was unbelievable what materialized for the meal! Where it all came from, Anna was wont to guess. There was Swedish crusty rye bread that had Karl drooling in no time. *Limpa!* went up the hosanna! Butter! There was actually butter, for the Johansons owned several cows. The stew pot produced the most delicious sausage Anna had ever tasted, and though Katrene said it was made of venison, it was nothing like any venison Anna had ever had. It was spicy and rich and full of flavor. They had barley cooked in the meat juices, and a tempting pan of cobbler dumplings steamed atop wild blueberries, crowned with rich cream.

Karl was dipping into his second dish of cobbler when Katrene chuckled at him, asking, "You like that cobbler, Karl?"

Already it was Karl instead of Mr. Lindstrom!

"Kerstin, she made that cobbler. She is some cook, that Kerstin," Katrene crooned.

Anna had all she could do to keep the smile pasted on her face.

Karl nodded in Kerstin's direction, acknowledging her talent politely, then went back to eating again.

Nothing would do but that Karl share their harvest of hops with the Johansons. He gave Katrene a whole bushel.

When the meal was done and the three Johanson women began making motions toward dish-washing, Anna offered to help, but they declined, saying she was their guest and they would have no such thing. Today they would only enjoy each other's company. There seemed to be no question that any help Karl wanted to give them with his axe would not be turned down. But the following day, of course. Today they would make a holiday. They all agreed that when they lit into cabin-raising, there would be a building standing in record time. "Like in Sweden," they all said, happily deciding that once the Johansons' cabin was livable, they would pitch in together to complete the loft and roof and floor over at Karl and Anna's place.

They ended up staying for supper and left for home with the promises of returning early the next day to whip the cabin up. Katrene waved them away with her apple cheeks rounded in their usual smile, shouting something to Karl in Swedish.

"What did she say?" Anna asked.

"She said we should not eat breakfast before we come tomorrow because she will be making Swedish pancakes with lingonberries they have brought from Sweden!"

The joy in Karl's voice brought such a pang of jealousy to Anna, she didn't know what to do with it. It didn't help any when James added, "Boy! I hope they're as good as that blueberry cobbler was. That was really something, wasn't it, Karl?"

"Just like my mama used to make," he said.

"Where'd they get the berries?" James asked.

"They grow all over around here. Why, there is a thick patch of them up on the northwest section of my land, but since we have been so busy with our cabin, I have not been up that way to check them. I suppose they are ripe, too."

"Gosh, Karl, could Anna make cobbler with our berries?"

"I do not think it would be quite the same without that rich cream from Olaf's cows." Then he added, "I had forgotten how much sweeter is the milk from the cows than from goats."

"If Nanna could hear you, she'd probably stop giving out, just to get even," James teased.

Karl laughed. "Ya. That Nanna, she is one smart goat. But I do not think she is quite that smart."

"Are we going back tomorrow for sure?" James asked, clearly anxious to do so.

"Ya. Of course we are. Just like in Sweden it will be one for all and all for one. With our help the Johansons will have their cabin up in two or three days."

"Two or three days!" James sounded disbelieving.

"With six men and two teams, it will rise like hop yeast," Karl predicted.

"I just hope it doesn't go up too fast. I sure like eating at their place," James said with enthusiasm. "I can't wait to taste them lingonberries."

"Ya. You will love them. They taste like Sweden."

At those words Anna vowed that no matter how delicious Swedish pancakes and lingonberries were, she would definitely not like them!

When they went to bed, Karl spoke to Anna, something he had not done in bed since their falling out. "It is wonderful to have neighbors again, and wonderful to hear Swedish."

"Yes, they were nice," Anna said, feeling she must add something.

"I will be going early in the morning to help them with their cabin. Are you coming along, Anna?"

He didn't say, be ready early in the morning, Anna. Or, we must leave early in the morning, Anna. But, are you coming, Anna? Half of her wanted to screech at him that he could go alone to his Swedish-speaking friends who could make him laugh and smile when his wife could not. But she was too lonely to face a day without anyone for company, too jealous of the entire Johanson family already to entrust Karl to them for the entire day without her.

"Of course I'm coming. I wouldn't dream of missing Swedish pancakes and lingonberries!"

Karl detected a sarcastic note in her voice, but attributed it to nothing more than her usual shortness whenever the subject of cooking came up.

Again, Anna promised herself that if those pancakes were so light they floated off the griddle to her plate unaided, if the lingonberries were so flavorful they made her drool in her dish, she would absolutely not admit she liked them!

Yet she did—the very next day.

The morning meal at the Johansons was a success. The pancakes were eggy and light and delicious, and the berries were the perfect complement to Katrene's superb cooking. Anna found she couldn't help but tell Katrene so. No matter how jealous of their Swedishness Anna was, it was impossible for her to dislike any of the Johansons. They were indeed a joyful family to be around. Even the capable Kerstin had a guileless charm.

Laughter, Anna was learning, was as common to these Swedes as liking lingonberries. Swedes seemed to laugh in all they did. Teasing, too, was natural, even between the two elder Johansons. Among the sisters and brothers, of course, it ran rampant. Undoubtedly, Nedda took more than her share when James was around, but she accepted it with rosy blushes that made everyone the more gay.

Work, too, came as naturally to these blond giants as breathing. If Anna had been mesmerized by the sight of Karl with his axe, she was hypnotized by the sight of all five men—Olaf, Erik, Leif, Charles and Karl—swinging axes and adzes as if they were shooing bugs away. During the following two days Anna saw a cabin-raising done in the tradition of a bunch of hard-working, companionable Swedes.

They meshed like cogs of a gear as they worked, skidding, hewing, notching, raising, sometimes two logs going up at once on opposite walls. Karl, she was to learn, was a master shingle-maker and took great pride in tapping shingles off the cedar heartwood with his maul and froe nearly as fast as they could be hauled up to the roof and pegged on.

Leif, at age twenty, was a close second to Karl, and between the two of them, the shingles quite flew to the roofpoles!

Erik, it seemed, had a touch with heartwood, and could size up a piece of heartpine with a deadly eye of accuracy. When he drove his wedge into the piece, it split into planks that looked as if they'd been smoothed by running water for fifty years.

Olaf saw to the cutting of the fireplace hole and the door space.

To James fell the task of rock-hauling again. But Nedda worked with him, and he seemed to enjoy his job immensely.

Anna and Kerstin gathered mud for the daubing, for now Anna was allowed to help, too. Katrene did the cooking, and supplied the workers with the water bucket and dipper periodically, bringing it around to inspect the progress and add her lilting Swedish comments to the feeling of goodwill already there.

At the end of the first day, Charles produced his fiddle, and they danced in the clearing while the orange and purple blended in the west behind the trees. Olaf and Katrene cut delightful steps. Kerstin danced with her brothers, and so did Nedda. It took some persuading on her part to get James to give it a try. Olaf and Leif both tried to persuade Anna to dance, but she declared she'd never been taught how and wasn't as brave as her brother, though she wanted ever so much to learn. But she wanted to learn with Karl, not with Olaf or Leif.

Karl danced with all the Johanson women. When he paired off with Kerstin, Anna continued clapping to the fiddle, forcing herself to bite back the storm of emotion that sprang up whenever the two spoke to each other. Watching them spin gaily around the firelit clearing, laughing, with Kerstin's full skirts flitting high as she lifted them, Anna again felt dismay at this newest talent she discovered in Kerstin, which she herself lacked.

Even after Anna had turned Karl down, Erik at last made her try it, pulling her out into the festivities with the others. She really didn't do half bad, although she felt far from feminine, swooping around the circle in her britches. She wished she had a dress like Kerstin's, but resolutely refrained from wearing the inappropriate ones she owned.

The work on the cabin went on the next day, and at the end of it the floor was completely laid. The fiddle was tuned again, to christen the new house with music and dancing. This time, Anna participated whenever invited to do so. Karl asked her to dance many times, but she felt clumsy when she compared herself to any of the other women there, particularly Kerstin, who could pick up her skirts and laugh without reserve while she spun and cut figures with her light steps.

Karl danced with Kerstin no more often than he did with any of the others, but it seemed to Anna that each time she looked up, Kerstin was bobbing around in the crook of Karl's arm. At the end of one particularly carefree jig with a fast-paced rhythm, everyone was breathless and laughing as they twirled an end to the song. Anna glanced over Olaf's shoulder to see Karl whirling Kerstin, his arms locked around her, until her feet left the floor and her skirts went sailing. She was laughing unabashedly as he released her. Then she reached to pat her forehead and straighten a wisp of hair that wasn't even out of place.

"Oh, Anna," she said, coming to take Anna's arm, "that Karl is some dancer. He wears me right out!"

Anna bit her tongue to keep from saying what had crossed her mind. "Ya! He used to wear me right out, *too-o-o!*"

That night Anna lay awake a long time after Karl was sleeping soundly. She rehashed everything about the last two days with the Johansons. Each word between Karl and Kerstin took on an increasingly personal note. Each compliment Karl paid Kerstin's cooking rankled mercilessly. Each light footstep during the dancing seemed flirtatious. Each memory of that last whirling hug became more intimate. There was no doubt about it. Beside Kerstin, Anna felt as inferior as a ragweed in a rosebed.

Well, she thought angrily, if he wants his perfect, plump Kerstin, let him have her! I'll be damned if I'll stand by and watch while he fawns over every move she makes. They said they'll finish in a short day's work tomorrow and they don't need me anyhow, so why should I go and get in their way anyway? Even when I'm there, I might as well be a stump, for all the attention I get. They talk Swedish around me as if I *am* a stump!

Nothing more than the useless stump left when they're done chopping down their precious tamaracks! Well, I might be as useless, but I don't need to stand around and let them lean their big Swedish boots and their precious Swedish axes on me!

Chapter 15

The following day, Anna woke early enough to prepare breakfast for Karl and James. She did it before they could protest. Let them eat my cooking whether they like it or not! They can just do without their lingonberries for one morning! Anna threw a baleful eye at James. He was rarin' to go. Seems he's hooked on one of the Swedish lovelies, too, Anna thought bitterly, making herself all the more miserable.

When Karl said, "Hurry up, Anna, we must get going," it wasn't quite as satisfying as she'd thought it'd be to answer, "I'm not going today."

"Not going?" To his credit, Karl sounded dismayed. "Why not, Anna?"

"I think I had better stay home and tend to my weeding. The vegetables are getting lost out there. Anyway, there's not much left to do on their cabin, so you won't even miss me."

"Come on, Karl!" James called from the wagon. "Hurry up!"

"Are you sure, Anna?" Karl asked. "I do not like to leave you here alone, Anna."

She needed to show him she was just as capable as the capable Kerstin Johanson . . . even more so, staying all day without a man to depend on for every ounce of protection.

"Don't be silly, Karl, I've got the gun, haven't I?"

It was the longest day of Anna's life. She cried and dried up, dried up and cried, until she thought she would kill the poor vegetables with salt tears! She worked fiendishly, but all day she bludgeoned herself with images of Karl and Kerstin. She imagined him nodding to Kerstin to tell her how good her blueberry cobbler was. She imagined him telling her how he loved her golden braids, so neatly wrapped upon her fine, Swedish head. She even imagined the two of them speaking together in Swedish, and felt a greater anguish at not being able to share his beloved language with Karl. Time and again, Anna remembered Karl calling her "my skinny little hen," and she berated herself for her thinness. There was little Anna could do about her thinness or her wretched cooking, but at least she could take a bath! If Karl wanted his women smelling like lye soap, so be it!

She bathed, then waited, but the sun was still far above the horizon. It was then, with the sun just beginning to filter through the western tree-line, when Anna had the splendid idea of how to please Karl.

She would find his precious blueberry patch and pick him blueberries till he got hives from them! Bolstered by the idea of a way to keep busy till he returned, and at the same time do *something* right, she grabbed a wooden pail and took off, following the familiar path to the beaver pond and heading north along the creek until she reached the shallows where she crossed, heading northwest in search of berries.

She kept a close eye on the sun, gauging its descent, knowing when it rimmed the horizon, she had better start for home so she'd be there when Karl and James returned.

Not twenty minutes from the creek she found the berries. They were fat and purple and thick as the mosquitoes that hovered above them. Never in her life had Anna suffered mosquitoes like this! She swatted and slapped, and still they stung her faster than she could swoosh them away. At last she was forced to move out of the thicket for a while. But Karl wanted blueberries, and she was determined he'd have them. She moved from thicket to thicket, continuing to pick until her pail was nearly two-thirds full and heavier than she'd imagined mere blueberries could be.

The sun was as low as she'd decided she should let it get before starting back. She heard the gurgle of the creek and headed for it. The mosquitoes were coming out worse than ever now as evening drew on. But she tried to ignore them, carrying her bucket and following the meandering stream toward home, until she reached a sharp curve that took the creek northward.

On her way out to the berries, she had not passed this bend in the water! Well, with the sun at her right, she ought to be going in the proper direction. But when she retraced her steps, she came to a fork where this creek met another, and they both seemed to be flowing due north. Their own little creek flowed south by southwest!

The pail became leaden, the sun slipped down, dusk came on. Anna picked a willow switch to keep the mosquitoes fanned off herself as best she could. The tree frogs started up, and the mosquitoes kept it up. Finally, Anna thought she could stand neither the singing nor the stinging one more minute! By the time she admitted she was abysmally lost, the western sky was tinted with only a faint hint of orange, making the stark silhouettes of the trees loom like threatening black fingers.

Karl and James returned from the Johansons expecting to find woodsmoke rising from the chimney and a pleasant supper warm on the hob. But the ashes were scarcely warm, and there was no sign of supper cooking. Karl walked out to the vegetable garden, found it freshly weeded. He walked to the new log house and stepped inside. It was dark, for the sun was gone. He could see nothing in the far corners.

"Anna?" he called. "Are you in here?" But there was only the soft tittering of the birds, chirping through the partially opened chimney hole. "Anna?"

He met James in the clearing. "She's not in the springhouse," James said. "I checked."

"There is still the barn."

"She's not there either. I searched there, too."

Karl's heart began hammering harder. "She might have gone down to the pond."

"Alone?" James asked disbelievingly.

"It is the only other place I can think of."

They grabbed the gun and headed for the pond. Why hadn't Anna taken the gun if she went out alone into the woods? It was feeding time for the wild animals. Karl knew the pond was the likeliest place to come upon any number of various creatures drinking—creatures with claws and teeth and horns and—But at the pond there were no animals. There was no Anna.

He could think of no place she might be. Sadly, he headed back down the trail for home. James was on the verge of tears. He walked ahead of Karl and kept peering into the darkening woods on either side, hoping to see his sister appear out of the shadows. By the time they reached the cabin, the sun had fully set, and there was a scant hour of dimming light left by which to see.

"Would she have walked out along the road toward Johanson's?" James asked hopefully.

"We would have seen her if she was headed that way to join us." Karl's eyebrows were blond question marks of worry.

"What's the other way up the road?"

"Nothing. It is only the trail that goes all the way to Fort Pembina in Canada. Why would she go that way?"

"Karl, I'm scared," James said, his eyes wide with bewilderment.

"When you are scared is the best time to keep your wits about you, boy."

"Karl, I know Anna's been crying a lot lately."

Karl felt like James had taken a hot poker and branded him in the middle of his chest. He gritted his teeth together and stared. "Be quiet and let me think."

James did as he was bid, but it didn't settle his nerves any to have Karl pacing back and forth, rubbing his forehead and saying absolutely nothing. Karl built a fire, knelt before it staring. At last, when James thought he wouldn't be able to stand the silence another second, Karl leapt up and exploded. "Count the buckets!"

"What?"

"Count the pails in the springhouse, boy! Now!"

"Yessir!" James ran out the door while Karl sprinted to the barn to see if there were any pails there.

They met in the clearing again, and it was almost full dark by this time.

"Four," James reported.

"Three," said Karl. "There is one missing!"

"One missing?"

"If she took a pail, she must have gone to get something. What? A load of clay for chinking? No, we have already been down to the clay pit. Berries? No. She does not know where any berries grow—Wait!"

They both thought of it at once.

"You told us blueberries grow on the northwest corner of your property."

"That's it! Get the team back out, James, and ride to the Johansons. If Anna is lost in the woods, it will take every person to find her. These woods are deadly at night."

Karl rigged a flare of cattails for James to take along, lit it and handed it to him, ordering, "Get the Johansons back here as fast as you can. Tell them to bring guns and flares. Hurry, boy!"

"Yessir!"

Knowing there was no sense in going out alone, that one man could do little against these wilds, Karl forced himself to remain calm while waiting for James to return with the Johansons. In the meantime he continued binding the cattails into slow-burning torches the search party could carry through the woods. He tied them into clusters of eight, so each member of the party would have a supply to sling on his back. At last James returned with the Johansons.

They wasted no time on questions, except for those Karl needed to answer to make sure nobody else got lost while hunting for Anna.

"We will quarter the creek," Karl explained, meaning they would walk at a ninety-degree angle to it. "Walk fanned out with only the distance of the torchlight between us. Never get so far away you lose sight of the torches next to you. If your torch goes out, signal the person next to you. If you find Anna, pass the word along the line. When we have gone as deep into the woods as I believe she could have gotten, I will fire a single shot. That means everybody turns to his right and walks eight hundred paces before turning back toward the creek again."

"Do not worry, Karl," Olaf said, "we will find her."

"Everybody take ashes from the bucket and rub them on your face and hands," Karl ordered, "or the mosquitoes will eat you alive. When you get to Anna, you will have to use your own face and hands to rub ashes on her. She will be in bad shape from bites, I fear."

They followed Karl and James into the woods, along the babbling creek, deeper and deeper, until Karl gave the instruction to fan out. They quartered the creek, walking in the buzzing night with only the far-off torch flickers to brave fearful hearts.

Each of them thought of how it must be for Anna somewhere out here alone, with no ashes to protect her from the vicious mosquitoes, no torchlight to remind her there were others within shouting distance, no gun to protect her from the nocturnal prowlers ranging the forests. They strained their eyes and ears, called out until their throats were raw, their voices hoarse.

Karl and James searched with frantic pictures in their minds of Anna hurt, Anna crying, Anna dead.

Karl berated himself for leaving her home alone today when he should have insisted she come along. He thought of the cleanly weeded garden, and swallowed hard at the lump in his throat. He thought of their estrangement and the reason for it, and of how long it had been since they had made love. He thought of James saying earlier, "I know Anna's been crying a lot lately, Karl." He knew Anna had been crying a lot lately, too.

Why hadn't he done as Father Pierrot so wisely advised? Why had he not talked this thing over more fully with Anna when he had the chance? Instead, he had not only let the sun set on his anger; tonight he had also let it set on Anna, lost somewhere in the woods with all this enmity between them. And if he never found her again, or if it was too late when he found her, it would be entirely his fault.

Anna, where are you? I promise I will try to work this thing out of my system, Anna, if you are only here and safe. At least we will talk about it and find some way to work at forgetting it. Anna, where are you? Anna, answer me.

. . .

But it was not Karl who found her. It was Erik Johanson. He found her not by spying her running toward the torchlight in the woods, but by spying the red eyes of the wolves, by hearing their nipping yaps ahead of him long before their eyes pierced the night.

The wolves were circling the tree where Anna perched in terror, afraid her numb limbs would give out, afraid she would fall asleep and tumble down. Underneath, the jaws snapped and the canine mewls told her the animals were still trying to get to her by leaping at the tree trunk. There were only three of them.

When Erik bared his own teeth and whirled his torch above his head, the wolves retreated. Still, all three hovered until Erik jabbed at a pair of red eyes with his torch, and at last they slinked off like shifting shadows.

"Over here!" Erik shouted to the search party members nearest, then raised his eyes and arms. "Anna, are you all right?"

Before she could answer or slip down the tree to him, she saw one of the wolves advancing again toward Erik and she shrieked his name.

He swung about sharply, stabbing at the hungry, glowing eyes, singeing fur upon the beast who thought his threat empty. At the smell, the animal withdrew farther into the woods to join the other two before they disappeared into the blackness for good.

By this time another torch had come to help ward off the attackers, then another. Karl had stationed himself in the center of the flank, so by the time the word got to him, four other torches were there and Anna had been safely brought down from the tree.

Karl came into the circle of torchlight to find a sobbing Anna clutched in the strong arms of Erik Johanson. Tears streamed down her face, rinsing it clean. Thin rivulets of tears and ashes washed down her skin. Erik had done as instructed, had used his own face and hands, rubbing them upon Anna as soon as he found her. But she had clutched Erik about the neck in a locked grip, which she would not relinquish.

Erik looked across her head as Karl came into the torchlight, helplessly bound by Anna's arms, not knowing what to do or say. Karl was smitten with mental pictures of Erik's cheeks and hands rubbing his Anna's face. His stomach turned curiously tight, and he wanted to shout at Erik to get his arms away from her.

"She seems to be all right," Eric assured him, then his voice became gentler as he spoke near Anna's ear. "Anna, Karl is here now. You can go to Karl now."

But Anna didn't seem to hear, and if she did the words weren't registering. She clung to Erik as if her life depended upon him.

Karl watched with heart so utterly relieved that the sudden release from fear caused his stomach to tremble. James came plummeting out of the woods to fling himself against Anna, hugging her from behind with his face against her back, fighting away the tears. And all the while Anna clung to Erik Johanson.

Kerstin saw the way Karl hung back, strangely reluctant to take his wife from her brother's arms. It confirmed the suspicion she'd had all along that all was not right between the Lindstroms.

At last Karl spoke. "Anna, you are going to choke poor Erik." But it was Karl who sounded like he was being choked. He approached, waiting for her to turn to him.

At the sound of his voice, she did. He saw her ash-smeared face wavering in the torchlight while she, too, saw his. When his familiar voice came from behind the gray mask, she whimpered, "Karl?"

"Yes, Anna."

And still they hesitated. She stood forlornly, like a ragged, dirty waif, her face smeared and ashen, puffed beneath the gray from bites and from crying. Her hair was an explosion of whiskey strands and blueberry twigs. In the torchlight her red-rimmed eyes were frighteningly enormous. Her tears rolled silently and plopped off her cheeks onto her shirt, making dirty blobs where the garment hung loosely on her thin frame. She struggled to hold her chest still, but could not breathe without shuddering. The back of one hand came up and swiped at her nose, then dropped down forlornly.

Never in her life had Anna wanted a person to touch her . . . just touch her . . . as badly as she now needed Karl to. Bitten, abject, frightened, penitent, she stood before him, her insides trembling, her limbs quaking, knowing she had fallen short of his expectations again.

"You have given us such a fright, Anna," Karl said tiredly, but relieved.

Between sobs she choked pitifully on her words. "I wa . . . wanted to p . . . pick you suh-hum blueb . . . herries . . . fo . . . hoar your . . . suh . . . hupper."

At her wracked appeal, Karl was overcome by pity. Opening his arms, he clutched her against his thick chest, with James somewhere in the hug, too, and Karl's hard, cold rifle pressing into the back of Anna's head, pulling her hard against him.

"The wol . . . wolves . . . ca . . . came . . . Karl," she sobbed, "a . . . hand . . . I—"

"It's all right, Anna. It's all right," he soothed, but she went on.

"And the . . . mos . . . mosque . . . heetoes . . . were . . . s . . . so bad."

"Shh, shh."

"I just wa . . . haunted to . . . get . . . s . . . some blue . . . berries for you, K . . . Karl."

"Anna, you don't have to talk now."

"The p . . . pail . . . spilled, K . . . Karl."

He squeezed his eyelids tight shut. "I know, I know," he said, rocking her.

"But . . . but the blue . . . blueb . . . berries."

"There will be more."

"The creek . . . it flowed north and . . . and I . . . I couldn't—"

"Anna, Anna, you are safe now."

"Oh, Karl, I'm . . . s . . . sorry. I'm s . . . sorry, Karl."

"Yes, Anna, I know." The tears were gathering on the rims of his eyes.

"Don't I . . . let . . . me . . . g . . . go, Karl. I'm s . . . sorry."

"I will not let you go. Come, Anna, we must go home now."

But she would not give up her grip. She sobbed out of control against his neck until he finally handed his rifle to James and picked Anna up in his arms.

Encircled by the torches, he carried her home. Before they got there, she was asleep in his arms, though her hold around his neck was as tight as ever. In spite of his stature and physical condition, Karl was in a quivering state himself by the time they reached the cabin.

Everyone hovered after Karl had laid Anna down on the bed, wanting the best for both of them, hesitant to leave for fear they might yet be needed. Karl assured them they had done more than enough, and once outside thanked them all with handclasps and squeezes.

Before going Olaf suggested, "Karl, perhaps we should not come to-morrow to help with the cabin. We can wait and come the next day. Anna is in a bad state and maybe would like to rest one day. You spend the day with her until she feels better, and we will come the next day."

Katrene advised, "You put a thick saleratus paste on those bites so Anna will not feel so awful."

"Ya, Katrene. I will do as you say. And I think you are right, too, Olaf. One day more or less will not matter. We will finish the work on my cabin day after tomorrow."

"We will all be here then, don't you worry," Erik assured him.

Each Johanson made a comforting comment as the family parted.

Charles said, "You rest now and take it easy tomorrow, too. You can use it."

In Swedish Katrene said, "Now do not forget—saleratus will take away that itching."

Karl smiled and promised he would not forget.

Leif said, "I sure hope she's all right, Karl. We'll all be thinking about her till we see you again."

Olaf said, "We will be here with sharp axes, bright and early day after tomorrow, boy." He clapped a big paw around the back of Karl's neck, much as he might to one of his own sons.

Erik lingered. "I am sorry you were not the one to find her, Karl." His eyes said, she was not thinking of who she clung to, think nothing of it, my friend. Karl's eyes rewarded the young man with a tired smile, telling him he must not worry about it.

Kerstin came last. She laid her hand upon Karl's forearm and looked directly into his troubled blue eyes. She, too, spoke in Swedish.

"Karl," she said, "Mama is right about saleratus, but I think saleratus will not fix all that is wrong with Anna. I can see there is something that needs fixing in her heart. Whatever it is, I think you could help her fix it, Karl."

"We have not been married long, Kerstin," he muttered. "There are things between us we are still getting used to."

"I will not say more now. I can see you are troubled, too, Karl. Just remember, differences cannot be overcome if they continue to be held inside."

Her words were essentially the same as Father Pierrot's.

"I will remember. Thank you, Kerstin."

Nedda was the only one not to bid goodbye to Karl, for she and James had strolled near the barn when the others crowded outside the tiny sod house. In the soft late-summer night they stood beneath the starshine. A whippoorwill called a repetitious song from the dark of the trees. Bats swooped and darted, squeaking in mouselike voices, while the cheep of the ever-present crickets scraped away like fiddles with single strings.

Nedda bravely put her hand over the back of James' where it lay on the top rail of the fence. "I am happy we found her. I did not know before how terrible it would actually be to lose a sister or brother."

"I didn't either. Anna and me, we been together all our lives. I mean,

she's just always been there takin' care of me. I never stopped to think
how horrible it would be without her.''

Nedda removed her hand from his, but watched his face. "Where's your
mama and papa, James?''

"Our ma is dead and our—" He swallowed, making the sudden manful
decision to trust Nedda with the truth, no matter what she'd feel. He had
seen his and Anna's lies hurt Karl enough. For himself now, he chose to
be straightforward right off and avoid the long-reaching tentacles of lies.
"We never knew our pa, Anna and me. And you might as well know the
truth, Nedda. It's a pretty sure bet we each had a different pa. See, our
ma really was never too glad to have either of us. That's why Anna and
me had to stick together so close, else we wouldn't have anybody.''

Nedda was stricken by the idea of a mother who didn't want her children. "I guess Anna's awful special to you, huh?''

"Ya, she sure is.'' James didn't even realize that his answer sounded like
Karl's might have. "I mean, golly, it's almost more special when somebody
isn't your full blood and they still . . . they—" James couldn't finish. He
was recalling all the times Anna had bundled him protectively off to St.
Mark's, or promised she'd find them a better life. He remembered how
she had refused to leave him behind to come here to Karl. He thought,
too, of her recent misery, helpless to find any answer for it himself.

"I guess what you say is Anna's not even your whole sister but she loves
you like as if she was. Ya, James?''

He scuffed at nothing with the toe of his boot, looked down with a
strange uncomposed feeling upon him. He nodded his head. He thought
for a moment, then asked plaintively, while looking up at the stars,
"Nedda, what makes people who love each other not want each other to
know it?''

"You mean your ma?''

"No, not her! I never cared a fig about her. It's Karl and Anna I'm
talkin' about. There . . . there's something wrong between them and I'd
give anything to fix it, but I don't know how. Heck, I don't even know
what it is.''

"Do they fight?''

"That's just it. No!'' James sounded frustrated. "If they did, maybe
they'd straighten it out. Instead, they just treat each other—I don't know
what to call it. Polite, I guess. You know how your ma and pa laugh and
he pinches her and everything?''

"Ya, but my papa is a big tease.''

"Don't you see? That's how Karl and Anna used to be when we first came
here. See, they've only been married since the beginning of summer. They
seemed to get along so good and then I said something and—" He swallowed, thinking he would give anything if he could take back the truth he'd
revealed when he thoughtlessly spewed out all he had to Karl. "I think I
caused all this trouble between them because I told Karl something one day
that he can't forget.''

"About Anna?''

"No. That's why I can't figure out the whole mess. It was about our ma.
She was . . . She was a . . .''

"A what, James?''

"A prostitute,'' he finally got out, waiting for Nedda to run in shocked
disapproval back to her family.

Instead, she remained steadfastly beside him. "I don't know what that is."

"But Nedda, you're a year older than me!"

"I still don't know what it is. My English is not so good yet. Some words I haven't learned."

He searched for some way to say it.

She sensed his struggle and said, "It doesn't matter, James."

"Well, it matters to Karl. And if he didn't know, I think everything would still be okay between him and Anna. At the same time, I just can't believe he would hold it against her if he didn't like our ma. He's a fair man. He just wouldn't do that."

"You really like Karl, don't you?"

"Almost as much as Anna. He's . . ." But it was impossible to encapsulate all he felt for Karl. "He gave us the only home we ever had. I just wish whatever is between him and Anna would get straightened out so they'd be happy again."

"It will, James, I just know it will."

He turned to look at her face squarely. "Thanks for listening anyway, and for coming to help us find Anna."

"Don't be silly."

"I guess . . . I guess I did look pretty silly, how I acted when we found Anna, but, golly . . ." He felt sheepish to have had Nedda see him clinging to his sister's skirts like such a baby.

But then Nedda said something quite wonderful that made him forget how he'd clung to Anna and cried.

"You know something, James?"

"What?"

"I'm kind of glad all this happened."

"Glad?"

"Ya. Because you rode all that way to our house in the dark by yourself."

"It's not that far," James said in a hushed pride.

"In the dark alone it is," she insisted.

"So, why are you glad?"

"Because now that you did it once, you can do it any time—come over, I mean."

"I can?"

"Sure. You don't have to wait for Karl and Anna to come. See you day after tomorrow, James." Then she was gone to join her family, and Karl bade them goodbye at their wagon.

When the Johansons left, Karl clapped a big hand on James' shoulder. "You did a man's job tonight," he praised.

"Yessir," James replied, so much more in his heart he was unable to say.

They stood a while in silence before Karl added, "She is a cute little thing, that Nedda."

"Yessir," James said again, swallowing. Then he wisely offered, "I'd like to go out and see to Belle and Bill tonight if you don't mind, Karl."

"I do not mind. Just make sure you do not smoke any pipes out there like I do. Your sister would not like it."

"Don't worry. I just got some thinking to do."

"I will leave the latchstring out."

"Goodnight, Karl."

"Goodnight, boy."

* * *

Anna watched Karl as he entered. He walked to the fireplace and stood facing it. He cradled both of his cheeks in his hands, dug his fingertips into his eyes, then sighed heavily as he rubbed his hands downward and dropped them from his cheeks. His shoulders drooped.

"Karl?"

He whirled around. "Anna, you are awake," he said, coming to the bedside.

"I have been for some time now. All the while you and Kerstin were whispering in Swedish outside. What were you talking about, Karl?"

"About you."

"What about me?"

"She said you will need some saleratus for those bites."

But Anna didn't believe him. Tears sprang to her eyes. "I am nothing but trouble to you, Karl. I'm even trouble to the Johansons."

"They are good people. They do not mind."

"But *I* mind, Karl, I mind. I never should have come here." She lay on her side, watching his knees as he stood beside the bed.

He did not know what to reply. On one hand was a great engulfing sympathy for her. On the other, that great engulfing hurt she had caused him. Yes, it was still there. He longed to go back to the days before he had guessed the truth.

"It is too late to think of that now," he said. "Your face is still all streaked with ashes, Anna. You had better wash it before you fall asleep again. There is warm water for you."

She struggled to sit up, and he came to take her by an elbow and help her. To have him touch her thus—with polite consideration, even though he had not even argued when she'd said she should never have come here—took her apart at the fringes again. But she bit back the tears and went out to the washbench and cleaned her face, hands and neck in the dark.

She came back inside and ducked behind the blanket to change into her nightgown. The curtain hung now like a gonfalon, a constant reminder of the night Karl had pulled it down and taken it with them to the barn.

He was waiting for her when she emerged. "I have made a paste of saleratus and water," he said. "It will relieve the itching for tonight."

She raised her hands to her face self-consciously, touching it, testing it. Even without a mirror, she could tell it was puffed and swollen. "I'm really a mess."

"Here, this will help."

"Thank you, Karl."

She sat down on the edge of the bed and patted the paste onto her face.

"Take care you do not get it into your eyes," he warned.

"I'll be careful."

Karl hovered listlessly, feeling awkward standing there waiting for her to be finished and get into bed so he, too, could lie down.

She covered her face, neck and the backs of her hands. But the paste needed drying to be effective. Sitting there waiting for it, she started twitching. She tried to reach to the center of her back, but couldn't.

"Karl, they got me all over. Scratch me back there," she said, wriggling.

He sat down on the edge of the bed behind her. While he scratched her back, she began scratching her ankle, then her arms and soon her chest.

"Ya, they got you good, little one," he agreed. When he realized what he'd said, his fingers stopped moving.

Suddenly she too fell still, the bites forgotten momentarily, while she let the endearment wash over her.

But the itching started again, so she asked, "Karl, could you put some paste on my back?"

There followed a long pause while he looked at her shoulder blades, remembering times his palms had run over them while he was carried away by passion. At last he swallowed hard and said, "Hand me the cup."

When she had, she unbuttoned the front of her gown and lowered it, exposing her back to him, holding the front over her breasts. It was more skin than she had bared to him since their estrangement had begun. She pictured his eyes scanning her bareness, remembered his hands, gentle in the midst of love, caressing her in the way she now yearned for with daily-increasing fervor. She waited with hammering heart and tingling nerves for his first touch upon her, after all this lonely time. When it came, it was cold, and she flinched, then silently cursed herself, wanting to appear calm before him.

There were welts as big as peas all over her back, white-centered, rimmed with red. When he touched the first one with the clammy paste, her shoulders twitched away.

"Sorry," he muttered, the sight of her bare back raising old, yearning memories within him. He forced himself calmly to continue his ministrations, keeping his eyes from dropping to the shadow of her spine where the gown sagged, swagged, far enough adroop that he knew there was an inviting shadow there. He dabbed all the bites he could see, then—his stomach went tight and his heart went crazy—he lifted the fringe of hair from her neck and found two more bites beneath it.

She reached an arm back, lifting the hair aside so he could get at the rest hidden there. With racing heart she wondered if he would think her wanton posing so seductively. As if to repudiate his possible thought, she clutched the front of her nighty more tightly to her breasts that ached for the sensual way he had touched them so well, days past.

The hair that grew in the hollow of her neck was fine and curly. He had never seen it before, for she always let her hair hang free.

"You must let them dry," he rasped.

She sat there holding the hair up, feeling his thigh against her buttock on the edge of the bed, wondering if he was experiencing any of the same overwhelming feelings as she—sexual, pulsing, throbbing. But he sat as still as a statue, and finally the hair dropped. Anna reached blindly over her shoulder, saying, "There are a few more up here. Hand me the cup."

Wordlessly, he placed it into her hand, carefully avoiding her fingers. He saw her gown drop to her waist, saw her chin lower as she looked down at herself, watched her elbows moving as she touched the paste to her skin. He need not see the front of her to remember. He felt blood surge through his loins, and a tightening contract his chest. He tried to think of her as he had when he was writing letters to her, as his little whiskey-haired Anna. But even as want crept over him, he found himself wondering how many others had seen her brush the back of her hair away from her neck so seductively. No matter how many others there had been, he could not help placing his hand around her neck, squeezing her hair lightly against it.

Anna's eyes drifted closed and she leaned back, lifting her chin, pushing more firmly into his spanning hand. It was warm, even through her hair, speaking of desperation and hope, making her want to turn quickly and be taken into his forgiving arms. But it had to be him beckoning her to return to them.

"Anna," he whispered in a choked voice, "there are things we must talk about."

"I can't go on like this much longer," she managed, tears in her voice.

"Neither can I."

"Then why do you?" She could feel her own breath, battling its way up her throat past the heart, which threatened to choke her with its clamor.

"I cannot forget it, Anna," he despaired.

"You don't want to forget it. You want to keep remembering it and keep me remembering it, too, so I will always know I was once bad." Her eyes still remained closed.

"Is that what I am doing?"

"I . . . I think so."

A very long, silent minute eased by, nothing more than crickets, fire and breath speaking.

"Can you blame me?" he asked.

The pain in his question became magnified within her own heart. She leaned yet against his hold, the hair now hot where he enclosed it about her neck. "No," she whispered.

"Did you think that if I guessed, I would let it pass?"

"No."

"I have tried to put it from my mind. But it is there, Anna. Every minute I am awake it is waiting there and I cannot forget it."

"Do you think I can?"

"I do not know. I do not know you well enough to know such things about you."

"Well, I can't, Karl. I can't forget it either. But I'd give anything if I could make it so it had never happened."

"But that cannot be."

"So will you hold it against me forever?"

"You are my wife, Anna! My wife!" he said intensely, squeezing her neck. "I took you to me believing you were pure. Do you know what it means to a man to learn that others have gone before him?"

Stung, shamed, she felt his words pierce her heart. So he had thought all this time that her scruples were that low. "Not *others*, Karl, only one."

Anger and hurt surged through him. "*Only* one? To me you say *only one!* You might as well say lightning is only fire after it has struck me down. Do you know that is how I felt that day?" His hand tightened painfully for a moment. "I felt like I was struck by lightning, only it was not kind enough to kill me. It only left me burned and blistered instead." The hand dropped from her hair as if the sensation were upon him presently.

"Karl, I never meant for you to find out," she said, ineptly. "I thought—"

"Don't you think I know that? There is no need for you to say it now.

I know what a fool you must have thought me when I did not even guess that night in the barn. Green Karl! Green as the spring grass. I thought we were learning together that night.''

Misery swept through Anna, coupled by her need to have him believe her. "We were."

"Do not lie to me any more. I forgave you all the other lies I discovered. But this one I have great trouble forgiving. I do not know if I ever can."

"Karl, you don't understand—"

"No, I do not understand, Anna." His voice quivered with intensity. "I am a person who does not understand the selling of what should only be won with love. I have thought to myself so many times, why did Anna do such a thing? How could she? Do you know that I have even started to think that if you had done this with a man you loved I was wrong not to forgive you? But to do it for money, Anna . . ." His voice trailed away. When it came again, it was heavy with defeat. "He did pay you, Anna, didn't he?"

She only nodded, then her chin dropped down to her chest.

"A man old enough to be your father . . ." His words had the woeful tune of a lament.

"Don't do this to yourself, Karl," she whispered at last.

"It is not Karl who does it to himself, it is you who have done it to me." His agonized voice drove on, killing her, making her bleed with regret. "How I thought of you as my little whiskey-haired Anna. All those months, waiting for you, thinking of how it would be to have you here, to build the log house and have you here so I would not have to be alone ever again. Do you know how alone I feel now? It was much better—the kind of being alone I felt before you came. This now—some days I do not think I can bear it."

Dread surged through Anna, but she knew she must ask the question which followed. "Do you want me to leave, Karl?"

He sighed. "I do not know what I want any more. I have spoken vows to love and honor you, and have sealed those vows with an act of love. I do not believe this vow can be sidestepped by turning you away. Yet I cannot honor you. I am torn in pieces, Anna."

As it had the first time she'd heard him pronounce it, her name falling from his lips with that beloved accent, endeared him to her as never before. "As soon as I met you, that very first day, I knew that this was how you'd feel if you ever learned the truth."

"Could you not tell by my letters that I am . . ."

"That you are forgiving, Karl?"

They both realized how utterly untrue that sounded right now.

"Accepting, Anna. Accepting. Do you understand? If you had told me beforehand I would have accepted."

"No, you wouldn't have, Karl. Even you aren't that big. You think if I had written to you and told you I was a prostitute's daughter and I had a kid brother I felt responsible for, you'd have brought us here willingly?"

Hearing it put that way, Karl, too, doubted what his reaction would have been.

"Karl, I think it's time I told you about Boston, all about Boston."

"I do not want to hear it. I have heard enough about Boston to last me a lifetime. I hate the word."

"If you hate it, imagine what I feel when I talk about it."

"Then do not!"

"I must. Because if I don't, you'll never understand about my mother."

"It is not your mother who disappointed me, Anna, it was you."

"But she's part of it, Karl. You have to know about her to understand me."

When he sat silently, she took it for assent. Gulping a shaky breath, she began.

"She never had much time for us. We were only two of her miscalculations, two of her mistakes. And in her profession, we were the biggest mistakes she could have made. She never let us forget it. 'Where are those two brats of mine now?' she'd holler, until everybody who knew us took to calling us Barbara's Brats.

"We were never told for sure, but it didn't take much figuring to know that it's a pretty slim chance James and I are even full brother and sister. Chances are we had different fathers. But where we came from, that didn't matter to us. We learned early to depend on each other. Nobody else gave us support of any kind, so we got it from just ourselves.

"You were right about something else, Karl. She never wanted us calling her 'mother' for fear it'd scare away her customers. She needed to look young and act young to keep the men interested. Sometimes, we'd forget and call her mom, and she'd fly into a rage. The last time it happened was when I was about ten or eleven, I think. One of the other women had given me a cast-off feather for my hair, and I went running to her to tell her about it.

"That's the first time I ever saw . . . saw Saul. He was with her when I went charging outside as she came home, calling her. Only, I was so excited, I forgot to call her Barbara. When she heard me saying 'ma' she tied into me right there in front of that man. Strangely enough, it proved one thing—she wouldn't lose her customers as quick as she thought, once they learned she had two kids.

"Saul was around from that time on, more than I'd have liked him to be. He watched and waited while I grew up, only I never knew he was waiting until I was about fifteen or so. That's when I started staying out of his way. You don't grow up in a place like that without knowing the hungry look on a man's face at too young an age.

"It was about that same time Barbara got the disease all women of her profession fear. She went downhill really fast, and lost her looks, her strength and her customers. After she died, her friends—if you want to call them that—let James and me stay at the place nights. But when the rooms were full, they sent us packing. That's why I knew what the inside of St. Mark's looked like. We holed up there when there was no place else to go. At least nobody threw us out of there.

"We did look for work, Karl, honest we did. I used to keep the women's dresses mended at the place—they always had to have their clothes just so, of course—and that's how I learned a little seamwork. They paid me a little to do it, but not nearly enough. When I started writing to you, that's why I told you I was a seamstress. It was the only thing I could think of.

"And you guessed right about the dresses, too. They're cast-offs from the ladies. They were better than nothing, so I took them. I guess you understand now why I'd rather wear James' britches.

"Well, we hung on by our teeth, James and I. Then he started picking pockets and stealing food from the market stalls, and the ladies at the house were starting to encourage me to join their ranks.

"It was about then that James found your advertisement in the paper. It seemed like the first lucky break we'd ever had in our lives. And when you actually answered his first letter, we couldn't believe something had finally gone our way. We knew perfectly well I was no prime candidate for your wife. But all we could think of to do was to lie about my qualifications until I got to you and it was too late for you to do anything but accept.

"Naturally, I was afraid to tell you I had a brother. I had enough strikes against me without saddling you with that fact, too. I was afraid you would say all the things you *did* say that first day when you realized he was with me—he's an extra mouth to feed, an extra body to clothe, but mostly, he's an invasion of your privacy. The men I've seen all my life always liked their privacy. Both James and I knew that from the time we were tykes. When the men came, we went! I only knew I couldn't leave him.

"So James and I set out to get him here to you without your guessing he was coming along. My problem was that you mailed money for only my passage, and I had no way to earn his. He's thirteen and growing like a weed, out of his clothes almost overnight. I managed with my cast-offs, but there was nobody to hand things down to James. He needed boots, britches, shirts and passage money. But the time came for us to leave, and I didn't have it.

"He . . ." Anna took a shuddering breath. "He was a very rich man, Saul was. He'd hung around after Barbara died, and I knew one of the reasons was me." All this time Anna had been sitting with her nightgown hugged against her front, draped down at her back. Now, she pulled it up and clutched it protectively closed.

Behind her, Karl put his hand on her shoulder, his fingers folding over into the shallow well in front. "Don't, Anna."

But she had to finish. If she wanted Karl to forgive her, he had to know exactly what it was he was forgiving her for.

"I got word to him, and he came in that red leather shay of his, thinking his money made him desirable. But I had hated him for as long as I could remember, and that day was no different, only worse."

From behind, Karl could tell when she started to cry softly again. "Don't," he whispered fiercely, reaching an arm high across the front of her, grasping her upper arm. His forearm rested against her throat, and he felt her swallow. He pulled her back against him, against the lurching pity in his heart, holding her with the steel band of his arm, willing her to stop saying things he did not want to hear.

"He paid for the use of one of the rooms that had been our only home all our lives, James and mine. When he took me into it, I knew all the others knew and I wanted to scream I was not like them, not at all. But there was nothing else I could do. I thought if I was lucky, some last-minute miracle would save me, but there was no miracle. He was big and overweight and his hands were sweaty and he kept saying how long it had been since he'd had a virgin and how much he would pay me and he . . . he—"

"Anna, stop, please stop! Why do you go on?"

"Because you have to know. Even though I agreed to do it, I did it against my will. You have to know how sick it made me feel! You have to know it was horrible and joyless and painful and degrading and when it was done I wanted to die. Instead, I took his money and came to you, bringing my brother along.

"When I got here, even though you seemed a gentle and kind person, Karl, I went through the whole thing again, worrying about how it would hurt, how awful it would be again. Only it was none of those things, Karl. With you, it was wholesome and good. With you it made . . . it made more of me instead of less. Oh, Karl, with you I *was* learning. You have to believe me. You taught me, you took away my fear, and you made it all beautiful. And when it was all over, I was so relieved you didn't guess the truth about me."

They allowed silence to settle over them. Thick, unwanted thoughts were their companions, too, as they sat on the edge of the bed with Karl's arm still clasped across Anna's chest.

She felt sapped, overcome by a weariness that made the work of the cabin or the garden pale by comparison. Her head fell forward, and her lips came to rest upon the thick muscle of Karl's forearm, feeling the silken hairs and the firmness beneath them. How long it had been since her lips had touched him.

His voice, when at last it came, was slow, tired, in a way defeated. "Anna, I understand better now. But I must ask you to understand about me, too, about the way I was raised to believe, and the way my mama and papa were. It was a far different upbringing than yours. The rules I lived by were rules that did not allow for a way of life such as your mother's to exist. I was as old as you are now before I knew about such existence, Anna. Now, I have learned so much so fast about you and James. I must sift it all through and get used to it. To come up against such truths about you puts battles inside me, and I must find my answers. I need some time, Anna. I ask you to give me more time, Anna." He had the urge to kiss her hair, but could not make himself do it. The pictures she had just drawn were too fresh and hurting. They had opened wounds, which needed healing.

"James kept telling me you were a fair man, that I should tell you everything at once—all the truth, I mean. But James doesn't know about all this."

"He is a good lad. I have never been sorry a day that you brought him to me."

"Whatever it takes, Karl, to make you feel the same about me, I'll do it. I'm not very good at most things around here, but I'll try hard to learn." Anna could not help thinking of the golden-haired Kerstin, braided and spotless and capable and Swedish. And . . . in all likelihood . . . a virgin. All those things Karl might have had in a wife if only he'd waited another month before bringing Anna here.

He sighed heavily. "I know you will, Anna. You already have. You have learned much, and you try as hard as the boy does. I can see that for myself."

"But that's not enough, is it?"

For an answer Karl only squeezed her arm, then removed his own from around her. "We must get some sleep, Anna. This day has been too long."

"All right, Karl," she said meekly.

"Come, get in and try to go to sleep." He held back the cover, and she slid to her side. Then he slipped his clothes off and lay on his back with a weary sigh. These days, Karl wore his underwear to bed like armor.

For Anna, it was not the bite of the mosquitoes alone that kept her awake. It was also the bite of regret.

Chapter 16

If Anna and Karl had not reached a reconciliation, they had at least reached a status quo, which they maintained all through the following day. Anna's unvarnished truth about Boston was a laying down of arms after which she waited for full amnesty. But Karl was biding his time, thinking over everything she had said, trying to accept it.

He took Anna and James fishing. It was the perfect activity Karl needed to give himself time to think. They spent a day that was, in Karl's estimation, far from unpleasant, all but for Anna's mosquito bites. He credited her sour mood to her discomforts at the gnawing itch as her body reacted to the toxins it was unaccustomed to, being an Easterner. It didn't help Anna's disposition any when Karl told her the longer she lived here, the greater would be her body's immunity to the bites. But by midday the bites were itching like scabies. She tried saleratus paste again, but it did little good. Finally, by late afternoon when raw spots were beginning to appear on her skin from the continued scratching, Karl took pity on her and announced he would walk over to ask Two Horns' wife what could be done to relieve Anna's bites.

He came back carrying a sheaf of Indian corn, which he shucked, shelled, then ground in a spice quern. He scrubbed a flat spade until it was perfectly clean, then sprinkled the grains of ground corn upon it and laid it in the coals until the kernels were dancing from the heat. Then he took a cold flatiron and pressed the hot corn until it emitted a light, pleasant-smelling oil. When the oil cooled, he instructed Anna to put it on her skin.

But he didn't volunteer to help her reach the bites on her back. She had to ask him, which annoyed her. He knew darn well she couldn't reach them! Standing with her shirt raised up, holding it behind her neck, she heard Karl say behind her, "Two Horns' wife said to tell Tonka Woman to soak Indian tobacco in water and wash with it the next time she goes berry picking, then the mosquitoes will not bite her."

"I hope you told her it won't be necessary because Tonka Woman will not be quite as anxious to pick berries from now on."

When they went to bed, Anna was sorry for her cutting remark. To make up for it she thanked Karl for going to the Indians and finding out about the corn oil. She thought maybe he would kiss her lightly and say it was no trouble.

He only said, "The Indians have an answer for everything. Goodnight, Anna."

She wondered angrily if the Indians had an answer for a husband who was so stubborn he would not bend! She had apologized, explained, appealed, and still he would not forgive her. His polite consideration was killing her!

Damn him and his corn oil! She didn't want his corn oil, she wanted his sweat! And she wanted it on her own skin!

The following day when the Johansons came, as promised, to help with the Lindstroms' cabin, Anna was ripe with irritability. After Karl's dismissive goodnight the evening before, she had alternately hated him and herself. She had worried about what an inept little nincompoop she would seem when it came time to prepare food for the battalion of people. She worried about what a tomboy she looked like next to Kerstin with her impeccable grooming. She worried about how Irish she looked next to Kerstin's blonde Swedishness. She worried about how English she sounded next to all the Johansons.

But Katrene and Kerstin took one look at her the following day, and the first of her worries was solved. She looked so pitiful with her blotched skin now scabbing in places, her hands still a mess from prairie dig, they said she was to let them prepare the meal and do the work around the kitchen. Watching the pair of Swedish women perform in her kitchen as if they were born to it, Anna felt once again clumsy, stupid and more cranky than ever. She allowed them full sway, taking over the smaller duties.

Katrene suggested that Anna try a mixture of warm beeswax and sweet oil on her hands, making Anna again feel guilty at her irritability with the well-meaning woman. When Anna said she didn't know if Karl had any sweet oil, Kerstin at once said, "If he does not, you just come to me and I will give you some." Anna's defenses crumbled with her generous offer. Kerstin was a warm lady, thoroughly undeserving of the mental acerbations Anna had been heaping upon her.

"Thank you, Kerstin. You're always helping me out of one scrape or another."

"This is what neighbors are for."

After that, Anna and the women spent a more pleasant day in conversation about countless things.

Meanwhile the men labored outside, completing the work on the shingles and the floors. At the end of the day the fiddle was tuned again, and the dancing christened yet another floor. Even the dancing annoyed Anna, though. Again, she felt second-rate next to the other females. Moreover, when Karl danced with her, he held his distance, as if she would burn him or something. She could only sizzle in silence.

What does he think? That my sinfulness will rub off on him if he gets too close? she thought.

They were catching their breaths between dances when Katrene asked, "When will you move in, Karl?"

"Not till the windows are installed and the door is on."

"Windows!" Katrene exclaimed.

"Are you going to have windows?" Nedda asked. "*Glass* windows?"

"Of course I will have windows, just as soon as I make the trip to Long Prairie to buy the sashes and panes," declared Karl.

This was a complete surprise to Anna. She had assumed they would have the same opaque sort as in the sod house. Karl had never mentioned he intended to get glass windows.

"Oh, how lucky you are, Anna," Kerstin said, obviously impressed.

Of all the luxuries on the frontier, the glass window was the greatest. It was no secret how the Indians could not even believe such a thing as a pane a person could see right through. The Indians spent hours staring into any glass window they came upon with the greatest of awe.

"I should say you are lucky," Kerstin's mother echoed. "I would think I was living in a castle if Olaf bought me glass windows."

"You did not tell me you wanted glass windows when we came through Long Prairie, Mother," Olaf said.

"I thought they would cost more money than we should spend."

"But I asked you what it was you wanted when we were there. You should have said, 'Glass windows, Olaf.' " He winked at Nedda who winked back. "If your mother plays her cards right, she could get glass windows yet."

"Olaf Johanson, you are teasing me! Have you decided we will have glass windows?"

"No, I think I ride along with Karl just to take the air."

"Olaf Johanson, you are a stubborn Swede if I ever saw one. You know I hinted about windows when I was in Long Prairie." But she was laughing in her usual merry way.

"But I did not think we would have neighbors to keep up with then."

She went after him with a fist raised to his head, and when the tussle was over they were dancing again to their son's fiddle.

In bed later Anna said quietly, "Karl?"

"Hm?"

She imitated Katrene Johanson's Swedish accent as she said, "*You-u-u did not tell me vee vould haff glass vindows.*"

"You did not ask me," he answered. There was a smile in his voice, but still he remained aloof.

Anna's attempt to win him with humor was unsuccessful, and her impatience grew. Once again it came to matter very much that Katrene and Kerstin had done a much better job than Anna could ever dream of doing in her own kitchen.

A trip to town was not made without due planning. The ride was long and was not made often. Summer was drawing to a close. Though they were anxious to have their glass windows, one did not make the trip after them without taking care of all other vital business in Long Prairie at the same time. And so the harvesting must come first.

Karl's wheat crop was ripe and needed cradling so he could take it to the mill to have their winter supply of flour ground while he was in town. Wild rice and cranberries were cash crops readily available on Karl's land. Cranberries in particular were in demand in the East and brought a dollar a bushel, compared to the fourteen cents a bushel brought in by potatoes. Potatoes, therefore, were kept for the family's own winter use, along with turnips and rutabagas, all of which could be dug up later. The cash crops and table grains must be harvested first.

They cradled and raked the wheat field first, Karl, James and Anna. It was a backbreaking chore even though they had only a few acres in wheat. Karl handled the cradle, crossing and recrossing the plot with its giant, curved fingers sweeping out before him while his shoulders swayed rhythmically in the sun. The rake's fingers were fashioned of weighty steel. Its handle was shaped from sturdy green ash and was abominably heavy, too.

Again, Anna marveled at the stamina of her husband. The massive cradle seemingly became an extension of the man. Like a switch that turned his power on, once it touched his hands he could wield it uncomplainingly in that unbreaking rhythm for endless hours.

The bundling of the grain was done by gathering it in clusters and using loose hanks of it as a self-tie. *Self*-tie? thought Anna tiredly—if only it would. This required much bending and stooping, though not as much muscle as cradling or raking.

If cradling and bundling were backbreaking, flailing was soulbreaking. Flogging the grains on smooth, cloth-covered earth in the clearing, Anna vowed that henceforth she would eat bread only once every other day to save on flour, if it took all this to produce it! Never had she experienced such aching shoulders as the day after flailing.

But at last the gunny sacks were filled, ready for loading, and Karl announced that all they had left was to gather wild cranberries, then he could make the trip to town.

The cranberry bog was deep in the woods where no trails had yet been cut. Karl fashioned a travois, which a single horse could pull easily through the woods with the baskets of berries loaded on it. Karl and his two helpers picked cranberries by hand and had many inquisitive visitors during the days they spent at the chore. The bogs, it seemed, were the favorite feeding grounds of many wild creatures who were perhaps put out at having their dinner table usurped by the marauding humans. Karl kept his gun close at his side while they garnered the berries, ever on the lookout for the black bears that considered this territory their own.

The group was busily picking the cranberries one day when James asked, "Why don't we move into the cabin, Karl?"

"Because it is not yet finished."

"It is, too! All but the windows and door."

"We cannot live in a house without a door, and I have been too busy to make one yet. And without windows it is too dark inside. We would use too many tallow dips."

"The windows in the sod house are so thick not much light comes through them. Besides, we use tallow dips there, too."

"It is customary to make the door last," Karl said adamantly, "and I cannot make the door last if I must yet make windows."

"Well, I'd move into the cabin all by myself even without windows and a door. I can't wait!"

Karl threw a look at Anna, but she was picking cranberries as if she didn't hear anything. "When the door closes on us for the first time, it will be on a finished house. I have promised Anna a dresser for her kitchen, which I have not yet made."

Anna glanced up sharply.

"Well, I wish you'd hurry so we can move in," James went on. "I wish I could sleep in there tonight."

"Without a door the wild animals could come right in and sleep with you."

"Not in the loft! They couldn't get up there!" James was suddenly excited by the idea, thinking he was only a few hours away from using his loft for the first time. But Karl remained firmly opposed to the idea.

"You will wait until we have a proper door fashioned, and windows and furniture. Then we will all move into the log house together." Karl's face now felt as red as the cranberries. Actually, he wanted James to stay in the sod house in his place on the floor for other reasons, too. Whether or not he admitted them to himself, he had spoken more harshly to the boy than he'd intended. The boy looked aside while Anna, too, turned her attention back to the berries.

"It won't be long now," Karl said in a more kindly tone. "We have only to finish the cranberries and Olaf and I can make the trip to town."

"Can I go with you?" James asked.

Anna longed to ask the same thing.

"No, you will stay here with your sister. Olaf and I will have a wagonful by the time we buy windows and bring back our winter flour. There are things you and Anna can do here that will be more useful than riding to town."

Anna was so disappointed she had to turn her back on Karl to hide the glint in her eyes. Karl had treated her kindly since their talk, but now she felt he was eager to get away from her for a couple of days. She turned to peek at Karl again, but froze. Across the clearing, at the edge of the willow bushes stood a massive black bear. He was standing on his hind legs, sniffing the air as if it had flavor.

"Karl," Anna whispered.

He looked up to find her startled eyes riveted on something behind him. Instinctively, Karl knew what he'd find. But he had worked his way several feet from his gun, and there was a basket of berries between him and it.

James, unaware, was picking away. "How long will it take you to get your flour milled?"

"Pass me the rifle, boy," Karl said, his voice silken, unequivocal.

James looked up, then glanced to where the other two were already staring. The blood dropped from his face.

"Pass me the rifle, boy. Now!" Karl snapped in strained, hushed tones.

But James stood stricken by the sight before him. The bear caught sight of them and dropped down on all fours and lumbered off into the pressing thicket of willows with a grumble that raised shivers up Anna's arms.

"Boy, when I tell you to pass me the rifle, I don't mean next Tuesday!" Karl snapped in a tone such as neither James nor Anna had ever heard from him before.

"I . . . I'm sorry, Karl."

"There might come a day when sorry will not be good enough!" Karl went on in the same dissecting voice that somehow made his Swedish accent far more pronounced than usual.

James stood defenseless before the big man, frozen, a palmful of cranberries forgotten in his hand.

"Do you know how fast a bear can run?" The question was rifled at the boy unmercifully.

"N . . . nossir."

"The first lesson I ever taught you was that when I give the order to get the rifle you do not tie your shoelaces first! Your life and your sister's life might depend on how quick you move! If that bear had decided he did not like us helping ourselves to his cranberry patch he would not have stopped to tie his shoelaces! Besides that, you have just watched our entire winter's supply of candles and meat run off into the brush!"

"I . . . I'm sorry, Karl," James quavered. The blood that had earlier fallen from his countenance now scorched it to a deep, burning red. In his stomach burned a molten trail of shame.

But still Karl continued his attack. "I warned you the bears come to this spot, so if this happened you would be prepared!"

James stared at Karl's knees, speechless before this barrage that had flared up so quickly out of nowhere. It was doubly effective in cutting the boy because from Karl, who was normally so patient, so understanding, it was totally unprecedented. Defenseless, James turned to pick up his heels and run.

"Come back here, boy!" Karl shouted. "Where do you think you will go? To find that bear again?"

James stopped, brought up sharp by Karl's command, yet unwilling to turn around and be chastised in this unfair manner before his sister. Karl's unnecessary wrath brought tears to his eyes.

"He said he was sorry!" Anna snapped.

"Sorry is not enough, I said!"

Suddenly, the dam broke in Anna and she was answering Karl with venomous indignation of her own. "No, it never is for you, is it, Karl? What is enough? Do you want him to take the gun and go after the bear singlehanded? Would that be enough for you, Karl?"

His face was redder than Anna had ever seen it. "I expect him to do no such thing. I expect him to act like a man when it is necessary, not to freeze into his boots on the spot!"

"Well, he's not a man," Anna shouted, defying her husband with hands on her hips. "He's a boy of thirteen and he's never seen a bear in his life. How did you expect him to act?"

"Do not tell me how to teach the boy, Anna! This is a job for a man!"

"Oh, sure, this is a job for a man all right. If you had your way you'd stand there and yell at him about your stupid bear until he was in tears, but I won't let you! He's my brother and if I don't defend him nobody will. He won't talk back to you and you know it!"

"I said keep out of this, Anna."

"Like *hell* I will!" she spit, glaring at Karl, defying him. "He's trailed after you all summer, doing everything you ever asked him to do, and now when he does the first little thing wrong, you jump on him as if he was an ignorant fool. How do you think he feels? How could he possibly know how fast a bear could run? How could he possibly be thinking about your precious tallow candles when all he sees is a black monster standing on his hind legs, for the first time in his life?"

"It would have been the last time in his life, if that bear had decided to run in our direction instead of into the woods. You do not seem to realize that, Anna!"

"And you don't seem to realize that you're treating him like he committed the biggest crime of the century when he only reacted like any thirteen-year-old boy would.''

"He has cost us enough meat to feed us and the Johansons for the entire winter!''

"Ah, the Johansons! Naturally, you'd have to bring them into this!''

"It is true! That meat was enough for them, too.''

"And I just bet you'd love to haul a bear carcass over there and present it to Kerstin with some little pink ribbons tied on its head!''

"What is that supposed to mean, Anna? Just what are you saying?'' His fists were clenched and he glowered menacingly.

"It means exactly what you think it means! That you're more concerned with running over to fawn over Kerstin than you are about staying here with us. Of course, who could blame you when Kerstin does all that lovely cooking, and has those lovely yellow Swedish braids?''

Karl raised his nose to the sky and let out a solid snort. "At least when I am at the Johansons I do not have a senseless woman chewing on me when I take a boy in hand for what he deserves!''

"He doesn't deserve it and you know it, Karl Lindstrom!''

"How would you know? Just how would you know? He came to me as green as these cranberry leaves and I have taught him well all summer. So far he has not done too bad listening to me!''

"So far! But not now. He doesn't have to listen to you now! Why should he when you're being an *unreasonable, stubborn, bullheaded fool!*''

Karl threw his hands up in the air. Both had forgotten that James stood by listening to them, watching them face each other like fighting cocks with their necks arched. "Ya, you can call me a fool and know what you are talking about. You are good at finding a fool, aren't you, Anna? An eager, blushing fool!''

Her mouth was pinched and her eyes slitted as she spit, "You can go straight to hell, Karl Lindstrom!''

"Is that the way they teach you to talk in that place you come from? Some lady I married, with a mouth like a sailor. Well, let me tell you something, Anna. I have been in hell. I have been in hell for weeks now! You think Boston was hell for you—''

"You leave Boston out of this! It's got nothing to do with it!''

"It has everything to do with it!''

"You just can't forget it, can you? I can work until I get dizzy around here. I can cook over your . . . your stupid smoky fireplace and flail your *damn* wheat till I can't straighten my shoulders, and scrub clothes with your rotten lye soap and pick blueberries till I'd like to die, and it doesn't matter one bit to you! I'm still the same fallen Anna, isn't that right? No matter what I do you want to punish me because you can't admit to yourself that maybe . . . just maybe . . . I was justified. Maybe, just maybe you are wrong to hold it against me all this time. But you can't back down and admit maybe the holier-than-thou, selfrighteous Karl Lindstrom should lower himself! Well, let me tell you something! You're just a big, stubborn, *stupid* Swede, and I don't know for one minute why I slave my britches off to try to please you!''

"What kind of wife thinks she pleases her man in britches. Ya, you have britches all—''

"You leave my britches out of this!'' she hissed. "You know why I wear these britches. I'll wear them until they fall off my bones before I'll put one of those dresses on! I remember a time when you didn't exactly cry over the way I look in britches!''

"That was a long time ago, Anna," he said more quietly.

"*Ya-a-a, you-u-u bet it vas!*" she retorted, using the exaggerated Swedish accent now as a hurting weapon. "It vuz before the *beau-u-u*-tifful Kerstin *mu-u-uves* in next door vitt her *blu-u-u*-berry cobbler and her big *bu-u-u*-som." Anna put a hand on her hip and swayed it provocatively while she drew out the vowel sounds, taunting Karl until his rage became fury.

"Anna, you go too far!" he shouted.

"Me?" she shouted back. "I go too far?" Then she kicked viciously at a basket of cranberries, upsetting it so the berries rolled around Karl's feet. "I can't go far enough to get away from you! But you just watch me try, Karl! You just watch me try!"

She swung around and strode across the lumpy earth and grabbed James by the arm. "Come on, James, we don't have to stay here and take any more of this!"

Karl stood in his mound of cranberries, shouting at their backs. "Anna, you come back here!"

But Anna only pulled James along, forcing him to walk faster.

"Anna, that bear is out there! Get back here!"

"No bear would want to touch a paw to me any more than you would!" she threw back over her shoulders.

"Anna . . . get—Dammit! Get back here!" swore Karl, who had never sworn at a woman in his life. But she only swooped away, riding on her wave of anger.

He tore his hat from his head and threw it on the ground, but knew nothing would make Anna turn around now. He bent to scoop the spilled berries back into the basket, glancing up at the diminishing figures disappearing across the bog. If he left the cranberries the bear would surely return and eat up Karl's most valuable cash crop, and all his richest earnings along with it. Karl could hardly leave the horse either, with the travois attached behind and loaded with the day's pick. The best he could do was hastily take what he could slap into the basket, load it as fast as possible and follow the willful wife who was striding away with her britched backside defying him with every step.

Anger and concern turned Karl's face a mottled red. The woman had no idea of the danger she'd just put herself and the boy into by running off through the woods with that bear around! Karl finally got the baskets somewhat secured and led poor Belle off across the bog at such a pace that the horse resisted on the precarious footing and got herself unjustly yelled at for the first time in her life.

By the time he reached the clearing James and Anna had been there for some time. Relieved to find them safe when he arrived, everything exploded inside Karl's head as he strode into the sod house like a war lord.

"Woman, don't you ever do a thing like that again!" he shouted, pointing a finger at Anna.

"I'm not deaf!" she spit back at him.

"You are not deaf, but you are certainly *dumb*! Do you know what that bear could have done to you? You put not only yourself in danger but the boy, too. It was a stupid, senseless thing you did, Anna!"

"Well, what do you expect from a stupid, senseless woman?"

"That bear could have torn you to ribbons!" he exploded.

Hands on hips, defiance in eyes, sneer on lips, Anna flung words at him she didn't mean. "And would you have cared, Karl?"

His face looked like he'd been slapped with a dirty rag for offering to wipe dishes. Anna knew immediately she had gone too far, but there was too much anger and pride and pain built up inside of her to pull back the words. Karl's blue eyes opened in surprise, then the lids lowered in hurt. The golden cheeks became mottled beneath his expression of disbelief.

They stared at each other across the rough-hewn table and it seemed like a lifetime passed in those few strained moments. Certainly, an entire marriage did. Anna saw the forced relaxing of muscles as one by one they eased from the tight hold Karl had upon himself. And by the time he turned to grab a canvas bag and stuff it with some food, too much time had passed for Anna to apologize gracefully. She watched as Karl silently went to the trunk, raised its lid and found a couple pieces of clean clothing and jammed them into the sack as well. He brushed around Anna to reach the spot above the fireplace where he kept his extra shot. He grabbed a handful of lead balls, thrust them into a leather pouch that lay on the mantel. Then he shouldered his way around Anna, picked up his gun, which he'd braced beside the door as he entered, and resolutely left the house.

Anna watched his back as he strode angrily across the clearing. Then, halfway across, he stopped, did an abrupt about-face and marched back into the hut, slammed the gun onto its hooks above the fireplace, slapped the bag of balls onto the mantel again and once more strode outside.

She continued watching him from the deep shadows of the dwelling. He disappeared into the barn, then came out with Bill and Belle, hitched the team to the wagon, loaded up all the sacks of grain, the hops, then all the baskets of cranberries—and left the yard without so much as a backward glance.

It was nearly evening. There was no question in Anna's mind where Karl would spend the night before starting out for town. That realization finally made Anna collapse onto the cornhusks and sob her heart out.

Poor James stood with his hands dangling at his sides until finally he couldn't stand listening to her and watching her any more. Helplessly, he went out to climb the ladder to his loft. There he, too, cried at last.

Chapter 17

Karl left his home, glad to be doing so for the first time since he'd built it. He watched the broad rumps of Belle and Bill, time and again forcing himself to loosen his hold on the reins. He tried to put Anna's harsh words from his mind, then tried even harder to remember them exactly as she'd said them. He tried to put his own angry responses from his mind. Then, in the most human of ways, thought of sharper, wittier, truer retorts he might have made that would have put her in her place far better.

He wondered what her place was. He told himself he had made a mistake bringing her here. Thinking of the boy, he told himself he was wrong. The cruel words he had spoken to James made Karl ache in a way he had not remembered aching for a long, long time. How unfair he had been to the boy when it was the thing between himself and Anna that was what he railed against. About that much Anna had been right. He had treated her brother unforgivably.

Karl admitted that he loved the boy as much as any father might. Throughout the summer it had been a sweet thing to have the lad working beside him, following him with those wide eyes that always said how anxious he was to learn, to please. And how well the lad had done. There was not a thing for which Karl could fault James.

But when he thought about Anna, Karl found he could more readily place the brunt of the blame on her instead of himself. The cutting things she had said burned his innards. She had called him a big, *stupid* Swede, taunting him with an imitation of his dialect.

I am Swede, he thought. Is this wrong, to speak my native language with the Johansons? To bring back only a little bit of the place I loved, still love—the place where I was born? Is it wrong for me to sit at their table and eat foods which bring back the picture of Mama cooking, putting food on our table, slapping lightly any hand that reached for a bowl before Papa had come to his seat?

He longed for the solace of his deep-seeing father, who was a teacher such as Karl never thought to be. If his papa was here, he would make Karl see things clearer. His papa would puff on his pipe and think long and hard, weighing one side against the other before offering any advice. Papa had taught him this was the wisest way. Yet, today Anna had taunted him for this very deliberate slowness, had called him dumb.

But most painful of all had been the last thing Anna had said about the bear, intimating he cared so little about her that such a thing would not bother him. Her words were weapons, he knew, weapons wielded by instinct, not by premeditation. Still, like all people when they are hurt by the tongue of another, Karl flayed himself with her words instead of admitting why she had spoken them.

At the Johansons', candles were burning in the new log house and everyone was at the supper table. When they heard Karl's wagon pull in, the entire family left its meal to come outside and gather him in.

"Why, Karl, this is a surprise," Olaf greeted.

"I thought we would get an earlier start in the morning if I came up this way and maybe slept in your wagon tonight."

"Why, sure, Karl, sure! But you will sleep in no wagon, you will sleep in the cabin you helped us build!"

"No, I do not want to put nobody out," he assured them.

"You want to see somebody put out, you try sleeping in our wagon, Karl Lindstrom!" Katrene scolded, shaking a finger at him as if he were a naughty child.

Their table was like his own family's table had been in Sweden. There was much laughter, much food, many smiles, big hands reaching this way and that, the fire glowing, and all around Karl's ears, his beloved Swedish.

Karl found himself more aware of Kerstin than he had ever been before. He had never singled her out any more than the others. But Anna's unfair accusation now made him do so. Kerstin laughed while fetching more food from the ledge of the fireplace, tweaking Charles' hair when he scolded her for letting the bowls grow empty. The firelight reflected off the gold coronet of her braids, and Karl found himself wondering if Anna had been right and he had been conscious of Kerstin's femininity all along. When she stretched between two broad shoulders to place the wooden bowl on the table, he caught the outline of her full breast against the firelight. But Kerstin caught his eye as she swung back, and he put his thoughts in order where they belonged.

When the meal was over, there came the supreme joy of sharing pipes together, man to man. The fragrant smoke drifted through the cabin—postlude to mealtime, prelude to evening, while the women put the cabin in order, washing dishes, sweeping the wood floor with willow broom. Talk slowed. Katrene, Kerstin and Nedda removed their aprons for the night, a thing Karl remembered so well his mother and sisters doing. Always they had worn a copious apron such as Kerstin had just removed.

"Papa," she said now, "you have filled Karl's nose with smoke long enough. I want to take him outside in the fresh air for a little while."

Karl looked up at Kerstin, startled. Never before had the two of them been alone together. To be so tonight, after he had been thinking what he had been thinking, during supper, was not a good idea, he thought.

"Come, Karl. I want to show you the new pen we have made for the geese," she said casually, and grabbed up her shawl and walked out of the cabin, leaving Karl little choice but to follow.

What could he do but excuse himself and trail behind her down where the new split rails showed white in the blueing evening. Yes, there was a new pen all right, but it was not about it which they spoke.

"How is Anna?" Kerstin opened, without preamble.

"Anna?" Karl said. "Oh, Anna is just fine."

"Anna is just fine?" Kerstin repeated, but her inflection made her meaning clear. "Karl, your place is no more than a half-hour's ride up the road. There was no need for you to save a half hour by staying at our house tonight."

"No, there was not," he admitted.

"So," Kerstin said quietly, "I was right. Anna is not so fine as you would have me believe."

Karl nodded. The geese were making soft clucks, settling down with their plump breasts looking plumper as they squatted to the ground. They were a pair, a goose and a gander. Karl watched as they wriggled themselves into comfort, closely nestled beside each other before the goose tucked her head beneath her wing.

"Karl, I must ask you something," Kerstin said in a matter-of-fact tone.

"Ya," he said, absently studying the fowl.

"Do you like me?"

Karl could feel the red creeping up his collar even before he turned to look squarely at Kerstin. "Well . . . ya, of course I like you," he answered, not knowing what else to say.

"And now I am going to ask you something else," she said, meeting his eyes with a steadiness that unsteadied him. "Do you love me?"

Karl swallowed. Never in his experience had any woman been so bold with him. He didn't know what to say without hurting her feelings.

Kerstin smiled, unchagrined, turning her palms up. "There, you have given me your answer. You have given yourself your answer. You do not love me." She turned aside and leaned her arms on the top of the fence. "Forgive me, Karl, if I speak to you in a straightforward manner. But I think it is time. Tonight at the supper table I thought I saw you looking at me in a way a woman senses is—Let me say *different*. But I think it is because of something between you and Anna, not something between you and me."

"I . . . I am sorry, Kerstin, if I offended you."

"Oh, for heaven's sake, Karl, do not be so foolish. I was not offended. If things were different, I would be outright proud. But I do not bring it up to make you feel uncomfortable. I bring it up to get you to talk about whatever is wrong between you and Anna."

"We have had terrible words," he admitted.

"I thought as much. And, forgive me again, Karl. I do not mean to sound as if I think so much of myself. It is not that. But as soon as I met Anna, I knew this fight was coming. I felt a kind of jealousy from her. Between women this is something that can be felt almost immediately. I thought right away it might bring about disagreements between you and her. Tonight when you rode in, I thought to myself, it has happened. Anna has said something to Karl at last. Am I right, Karl?"

"Ya," he said, looking down again at the geese.

"And you have stomped off like a stubborn Swede and come here to pout?"

It was all right for Kerstin to call him a stubborn Swede, because she was one, too. She was proving it right now by not letting up on him. He found enough goodwill in him to laugh lightly at her badgering. Then he sighed and said, "I am a little mixed up about Anna right now. I needed to get away to think."

"It is all right to think, as long as you think things that are true. What I believe you were thinking inside our house at the supper table, that was not true, Karl."

"I did not know that what I was thinking showed so much, and I am sorry, Kerstin. It was wrong of me. It was Anna who put those things in my head." But suddenly he stopped, contrite, a little embarrassed. "Oh, it is not like it sounds . . . not that I do not admire you, Kerstin, but—"

"I know what it is you are saying, Karl. I understand. Go on about Anna."

"What Anna and I fought about . . ." But Karl's words trailed away.

"You do not need to tell me, I think some of the things that bother Anna, I have already guessed. I guessed them when you came here with her the first time. But, Karl, you must look at us with her eyes. I could tell how she felt that day, coming in here and all of us so excited we were talking in Swedish, and she not understanding a word of it. All that talk about the homeland, and things we all loved back there. When we talk in English, this is what she hears. And then, when we came to your place I learned even more things about your Anna. She feels like she does not please you because things around her house come hard for her. I could tell when Mama and I worked in her kitchen she wished to feel comfortable in it, like we did. Something tells me Anna has not had much experience at the things I have been taught since I was a little girl."

"She has had a much different bringing up than us."

"I guessed that. The way she dresses tells that and more."

"She grew up in Boston and did not have a mother that was like yours and mine." Even the word Boston was hard for him to say now.

"Boston is far from here. How did you meet her?"

"This is part of our trouble. Anna and I did not meet before we got married. I . . . we agreed to get married through letters we wrote to each other. Here in America they would call Anna my mail-order bride."

"I have heard of such things, but I did not know this about you two."

"We were only married at the beginning of this summer."

"Why, Karl, you are newlyweds!"

Karl thought that over a moment. "I guess this is true," he said, though it seemed like the strain between Anna and himself was years old.

"And you are having some troubles like all newlyweds have, getting used to each other, is all."

"There seems to be much that neither of us will ever get used to in each other."

"Oh, Karl, I think you are looking on the dark side. So you have had your first fight. You are being too hard on both Anna and yourself. Things take time, Karl. You and Anna have not had much of that yet."

"Why would she say such a thing about . . . about . . . well, about you and me?"

Kerstin was a girl who met things head-on. "What was it she said, Karl? I do not know."

"That I—" He leaned on the fence rail, too, rubbing one big hand in the palm of the other. "That I would rather be here with you and your blueberry cobbler and your braids than with her."

Kerstin laughed, surprising Karl. "Oh, Karl, it is so plain! You are just a little bit foolish, I think. She sees you coming here to everything that is familiar, and I can do all the things and be all the things you have left behind in Sweden. Naturally, Anna is going to think you want those things when she sees how happy and gay you are here with us. She does not see that it is all of us who make you happy instead of just me. Do you know what she asked me to do when we were at your house?"

"No, but I hope it was to teach her how to make decent bread, though."

"There, Karl! You see! She tries very much to please you, but things like that come hard for her. No, it was not that which she asked me. It was to teach her how to put her hair up in braids."

Karl turned to Kerstin genuinely startled. "Braids?" he repeated. "On my Anna?"

"Yes, braids, Karl. Now why do you think a woman with such lovely curling hair as Anna would want to put it up in these awful braids?"

He remained silent.

"Karl, why do you think she went out picking blueberries for you?"

But he was busy trying to imagine Anna in braids, which would certainly not suit her at all.

"Do not be a fool," Kerstin went on. "Anna loves you very much. An Irish girl who tries so hard to be a Swede because she thinks it is what her man wants . . . Why, Karl, don't you see?"

"But I never told her she needed to pick blueberries or wear her hair in braids to please me. Once, a long time ago, I even told her braids were not important."

"A long time ago, Karl? How long ago? Before I came here?"

"Why, sure, but what does that matter?"

"What matters is that she sees you happier at our place than at your own. Even I see that. It should be the other way around."

"There are things you do not know, Kerstin."

"There always are, Karl. There always are. But I know a woman in love when I see one, and I know she tries very hard to please you. But I also know you hold yourself back from being pleased by her for some reason. This is why Anna accused you of liking me more than you do."

Karl lowered his face and covered it with callused hands, his elbows braced upon the fence rail.

"Anna should know better," he admitted raggedly.

"Why? When you have left her in anger? It is she who is maybe suffering more than you right now, wondering where you are and when you will come back. You need to go back and make things right with her, Karl."

He knew she was right. Knowing this, he admitted the rest of his day's transgressions. "I shouted at the boy today, too. I fixed it real good with both of them, I think."

"So, what is wrong with saying you are sorry when you get back, Karl? James needs to learn that people make mistakes. People do not always use good sense in everything they do. Surely the boy . . . and Anna, too . . . will see that and forgive you."

"She said she could not get far enough away from me and said I would not care if she was killed by a bear."

"Sure, I'll bet she did. But that is only part of the story. The part you left out is what went before. I do not even need to hear all of it to know you both said things you did not mean. But, Karl, you must remember Anna is human, too. She makes mistakes. She is probably sorry right now she made that one."

Yes, she is sorry for that one and the other one she cannot live with until I forgive her. Karl leaned his face in his hands, remembering Anna the night they had found her treed by the wolves. He remembered her sobbing in his arms, saying over and over again, "I'm sorry, Karl, I'm sorry."

He had known then it was not the getting lost, not that alone, for which she was sorry. She was telling him how sorry she was for everything, all the lies, all the things she saw as failures in herself, but mostly, for the thing he could not—no, now Karl knew the fact was that he would not—forgive.

And he, stubborn Swede that he was, had deliberately rejected her apology and held himself higher than her by doing so. How well he'd been taught by his mama that self-praise stinks. By refusing to accept Anna's honest efforts to please him, he had made himself better than her. And he'd clung to his stubbornness because of something she had done in desperation long before he had even met her.

"You know, Karl," Kerstin was saying, "I have reconsidered, and I think you could not go to buy windows at a better time. I think that a couple days away from Anna is going to do you both a world of good."

Chapter 18

🌹

James could build a beautiful fire by now. He could curl shavings off a piece of wood and make them as thin as paper, just like Karl. He could get a spark off his flint with the very first stroke. He could lay on the kindling without smothering the first flame, and add split logs until there was a hearty blaze. And through all this, not so much as a wisp of smoke backed up into the sod house.

But he caught himself squatting on his haunches, gazing into his freshly built fire as he'd so often seen Karl do, and immediately he arose and turned his back on it.

"Why'd he do it, Anna?" he asked defeatedly at last.

"Oh, James, it had nothing to do with you," she said in a soft, sorry voice. "It's something between Karl and me. Something we need to get straightened out, is all."

"But he was so mad at me, Anna." The hurt was intense, tangible in his voice.

"No, he wasn't. He was mad at me." Anna gazed ruminatively into the fire, seeing Karl's angry back as he drove out of the clearing, wishing she could call him back and apologize for her words which had hurt him cruelly when he deserved her love and respect instead.

"For what?"

"I can't tell you everything about it. Come and eat your supper."

Brother and sister sat in dismal companionship unable to eat, each of them at once angry at yet longing for the presence of the man who made this . . . who *undeniably* made this . . . *home.*

"It's got something to do with Barbara being what she was, doesn't it?"

"In a way, yes."

"I never would've guessed it about Karl. I mean . . ." James paused, confused, then went on. "Well, he's just about . . . he's just about the most perfect person I ever knew. He just doesn't seem like he'd blame us for what she was."

Anna reached to touch his hand. "Oh, James, he doesn't. Honest, he doesn't. It's not because of that, really. It's mostly me. I can't—well, I can't do much of anything around this place. I can't cook right or dress right or wear my hair right or any of the stuff that a wife oughta be able to do. Barbara didn't teach me much of that and every time I try to do something for him, it turns out bad." She stared into the fire and tears glimmered on her lids as she remembered all the disasters resulting from her attempts to please Karl.

"Like the blueberries." She raised her palms in a gesture of futility, then dropped them back between her knees. "I mean, I wanted to pick him those blueberries so bad, James. I just wanted to do that for him. So what do I end up doing but getting lost, and he's got to come searching for me and carry me all the way home and put stuff on my mosquito bites like I was some baby."

"But that wasn't your fault, Anna," James put in loyally. "He wasn't mad about that."

She shrugged and sighed. "It's not that he is really mad at me, James. It's more that he's disappointed with me. He thought he could get over all the disappointments he found in me when he learned about all the lies from those letters. But he can't. I'm nothing like he really needs a wife to be."

"But we had lots of fun in the beginning and he didn't seem to mind if it took you time to learn to do things around here."

"That was before the Johansons moved in up the road. Ever since Kerstin came he'd rather be up at her place than at home."

"That ain't true, Anna. I don't think that's true."

"Well, Kerstin can do everything. She can cook blueberry cobbler and she's not skinny and she's got braids and blonde hair and talks Swedish."

"Is that what's got you all hot under the collar, Anna?" James said, wide-eyed. "Why, shoot, that day we were up at their place without you, Karl hardly paid her any attention at all. They asked us to stay for supper and he said no, he thought he'd better get back here for supper."

"He did?" She brightened a little.

"Well, of course he did."

But then her face fell again. "See? I didn't have anything ready for him the very first time he goes away and comes home expecting a hot meal. Instead, he finds me sitting up in some godforsaken maple tree with a pack of wolves at my heels." It made her want to cry again at the thought of her failure. "He never even got any supper that night," she chastised herself.

"Supper was the last thing on his mind. I know that for sure. When we came home and you weren't here, why, I never saw Karl so upset. He pretended he wasn't, but I could tell. He ran all over, out to the log house and into the barn and everywhere, looking for you. When you didn't turn up and it was getting dark, I thought for a while Karl was gonna cry again."

"Again?" Anna interrupted, big-eyed now, disbelieving.

"Oh, forget it." James suddenly became engrossed in scratching a dab of dry gravy from the knee of his britches.

"You saw Karl cry once?"

"It don't matter, Anna." He scratched all the harder, keeping his eyes carefully lowered.

"When?" she insisted, and James threw her a look of appeal.

"Anna, he doesn't know I saw him and I don't think I should be telling you about it."

"James, you've got to tell me. There are so many things Karl and I need to straighten out between us that can't be straightened out until we know things like . . . like how we've made each other cry."

James still looked doubtful, but after considering what Anna had said he decided it would be all right to tell her. "It was the night after he came stomping out to the barn and asked me point-blank if Barbara was a seamstress. Then, when I said no, he asked me if I knew what she did to earn a living. All I said was yes, and I thought he'd make me say what it was. But he just told me I did a good job on Belle's hooves, and walked out. I never told him, Anna. Honest, I didn't. Later on I went outside when I heard him get up in the middle of the night. I'd made up my mind I was gonna tell him, and explain to him how you hated what Barbara was, and how you only lied because of me. But I never got a chance to tell him because I come on him out by the garden. He was just standing there by the horses and when I got up behind him I heard him crying. He . . . he was holding onto Bill's mane . . . and . . ." James' voice had softened until it was a pale whisper. He scratched at something on the table-top with his thumbnail. "Anna, I never seen a man cry before that. I didn't know men cried. Don't tell him I said so, okay?"

"No, James, I won't. Promise." She reached out and patted his hand.

"Anna, I know Karl likes you more than Kerstin. Otherwise, why would he cry?"

"I don't know." She thought about it for a while. "Kerstin's sure pretty though," Anna admitted wistfully. "And she's got some meat on her bones like Karl likes."

"Nothin's wrong with you, and if Karl thinks so, he's the one that's got somethin' wrong with him!"

There it was, what she'd thought she'd lost from her brother. She realized she had been silly to think that just because he admired Karl with increasing fervor, his feeling for her had waned. But when it came down to the wire, when it came to Karl finding fault with her, there was James, ready to stand up and fight for her, just as he'd always done.

"Oh, James, thank you, baby," she said, using the name she used to call him when he was a runny-nosed toddler tagging after her dresstails through the Boston streets.

"Anna?" James asked, after studying the fire intently to avoid the confusing rush of feelings that had made him feel so much like a man when she called him *baby,* "do you think he'll come back?"

"Of course he'll come back. This is his home."

"He didn't take the rifle, Anna. He left it here for us."

"Oh, don't be silly. If you're worrying about that . . . that *cougar* out there in the pines, you know perfectly well Olaf will be with him and Olaf will have his gun."

"Well, you're one to call me silly, since it looks like the same thing's been on your mind, too, or you wouldn't have brought it up."

"Karl is the most careful person I've ever met in my life. And one of the most cautious woodsmen, too. Now, believe me, that cougar is the last thing we have to worry about.''

Yet after Anna went to bed, she lay in the dark for long hours imagining the very scent of those pines, her nostrils pricking as if searching here in the dark cabin for the musk of cat, as if she could warn Karl should she detect it. His pillow lay beside her, puffed and empty. She punched it and made a hollow in the center of it and pretended that he had only gone outside for a minute. For the thousandth time since he had learned the truth, she cried out silently, from her aching throat, "I'm sorry, Karl. I'm sorry. Forgive me.'' Tonight, she added, "Please don't go to her, Karl. Please come back to me.''

She slept. She awakened, thinking of Karl crying into a horse's mane, knowing he had cried because of her. I'm sorry, Karl, she thought, tortured.

She'd been sound asleep again, but sat up as if she were attached to the ceiling by a spring. Something was wrong! No sooner had she coherently thought it than James' voice came to her, strident, panicked.

"Anna, are you awake? There's something out there! Listen!''

She sat stone still, listening to the scraping and thumping that came from beyond the door. It sounded like something was trying to eat the panel itself.

"James, come here!'' she begged in a whisper, wanting him near enough so she could put her arms around him and know he was with her in the dark.

"I gotta get the rifle,'' he whispered back. "I gotta get it like Karl said to.''

She heard him kick against a bowl or bucket on the hearth. She heard him pick up the bag of shot Karl had slapped down when he'd come wheeling back in the house this afternoon.

"James, it's already loaded!'' she warned. "Karl always keeps it loaded and he didn't shoot at that bear today!''

"I know, but I gotta be ready to load fast if I need to take a second shot.''

"Oh, James,'' she wailed, "do you think you'll even have to take a first one?''

"I don't know, Anna, but I gotta be ready. Karl said.''

Outside the door they heard a grunt, like when a man lifts something heavy.

"Do you think it's a man, James?''

"No. Shhh!''

But when she sat quiet, she could hear the intruder scraping around again on the puncheons.

"James, is the latchstring in?'' Panic hit her afresh. If the latchstring were hanging outside, all the intruder needed to do was pull it to lift the heavy bar that secured the door. She heard James make his way carefully through the dark to the door while she held her breath at the mere thought of his being so near whatever was on the opposite side of it.

"It's in,'' he whispered, and backed away from the door again.

Relieved somewhat, she swung her feet to the earthen floor and said, "I'm coming, James, don't point the gun this way.''

"Don't worry, it's pointed straight at the door.''

"But you can't see anything. What are you gonna do?"

"What I can't see, I can hear. I'll know if he breaks it down."

"B . . . breaks it down? How big—what to do you think it is?"

"I think it's that bear, Anna."

"But . . . but there's never been a bear here before. Why would he come now?"

"I don't know, but it sounded like something big."

"Shhh! Listen, it sounds like he's going away."

They heard thumping sounds again, then the unmistakable loud grunt and whine of a bruin. There was some clattering, then the sound of earthenware crashing, then a louder groan.

"He's in the springhouse, Anna. He's eating stuff in the springhouse!"

"Well, let him eat. Who cares? At least he's not eating us!"

"Anna, I gotta go out and shoot him."

"For God's sake, don't be stupid! Let him take anything he wants, but don't go out there."

"Karl says once a bear finds food he'll come back and raid you time after time as long as he knows where it is. He'll come back unless I shoot him."

"James, please don't go out there. Forget what Karl said about you not getting the gun fast enough today. He didn't mean it. It was me he was upset with. I told you that."

"I gotta go. It's got nothin' to do with Karl today. That's darn sure a bear out there. What if he decides to come back some day when we're not safe inside the house?"

From outside come the sound of splintering wood.

"No, James, don't go. It's so dark you won't be able to see him anyway."

"There's enough moonlight."

"No, there isn't."

"Then get the torches, Anna. Get the torches that Karl made when you were lost. They're leaning in the corner behind the ash bucket. Get one and light it and when I say the word, you're gonna have to do just what I tell you to. You're gonna have to lift the latchstring and take the torch outside a little bit ahead of me, so the bear won't be able to see anything behind it. As soon as I get the first shot off, you drop it and run, though, Anna!"

"No, I won't! We're not goin' outside with any torches and I'm not dropping it and running. We're staying right here."

"I'll do it without you if I have to, Anna," her baby brother said. The steel determination in his voice made her realize that he meant every word.

"Okay, I'll get the torch, but, James, if you miss him the first time, you gotta run with me!"

"Okay, Anna, I promise. Now hurry and light the torch before he goes away!"

She struck the flint and steel, and the spark grew to orange flame upon the cattails while the two big-eyed nightwalkers stared momentarily into each other's faces.

"We can do it, Anna," James said. "We got the rifle, not him."

"Be . . . be careful, James. Promise you'll run the minute the shot goes off?"

"I promise. But, Anna?"

"What?"

"We ain't gonna need to. I promise that, too."

She raised the heavy latch with every fiber of her body trembling so violently she thought it would rattle the door in spite of her efforts at silence. The door squeaked softly once. She nudged it open and thrust the torch out before her.

The bear was slurping watermelon syrup as if he was in bear heaven. When the light caught his eyes, he sluggishly nodded his head and looked quite human, as if torn between finishing this delightful drink or being put off by the intrusion. He made the wrong choice; his long tongue snaked out into the pink drink one more time, and the gun exploded and knocked James clear off his feet. He was up and running for the door of the sod house before the stunning reaction had truly registered, keeping up step-for-step with Anna, who had completely forgotten to drop the torch. They slammed the door, barred it and leaned against it, chests heaving, hugging, trying to hold perfectly still, listening . . . listening . . . listening.

All they heard was silence.

"I think you got him," Anna whispered.

"He could be just stunned. Wait awhile longer."

They hugged for what seemed an hour.

"Anna?" James whispered at last.

"What?"

"Don't burn my hair with that thing!"

They'd been standing there for so long the torch had burned down. James' remark broke their tension somewhat, and they agreed to light another torch and go outside to check and see if the bear was really dead. Anna got the torch and James reloaded the gun before they crept back out.

When they saw what they had done, they both broke into relieved laughter. The bear lay half in and half out of what used to be the springhouse. The massive black body was sprawled across the little pool where they'd always gotten their water. The blood from the hole in his head flowed downstream with the current. The crocks and pots were lying in pieces all around. The bear had made mincemeat of some wooden pails, too. What walls of the springhouse had not been splintered by the animal had been blown to kingdom come by the blast from the gun, which Karl had "loaded for bear."

"James, you did it!"

"I did it," he repeated, now quite breathless at the realization. "I did it?"

"You did it, baby brother!" Anna squealed, throwing her arms around him again.

"By golly, I did!" he exclaimed.

"And you know what?"

"Ya, I know what. My backside hurts. That gun kicks like a mule." James rubbed himself back there while they both giggled.

"No, that's not what I was going to say. I was going to say there lies our winter supply of tallow dips and enough to feed our family and the Johansons all winter long."

James beamed and couldn't resist slapping his knee like Olaf was fond of doing.

"Guess what else?" Anna went on.

"What else?"

"We got no horses to budge this monster with and he's laying in our spring and he's gonna start rotting before Karl gets back and both him and our spring will never be the same again."

James started laughing. Then Anna started laughing at James because he was out of control. Then James started laughing at Anna out of control and before long they were on their knees, tired from the vast relief after their petrifying fright, and the fact that it was somewhere around four o'clock in the morning.

After some time Anna said, "Tomorrow we'll have to walk over to Olaf's house and see if one of the boys can come over and help us gut this big fellow and get his carcass strung up and tell us what else we have to do with him."

"I'm not sure, Anna, but I don't think we can wait till then. I think we have to gut him now or the meat will foul."

"Now?" Anna exclaimed with disgust in her expression.

"I think so, Anna."

"But, James, he's laying in that cold spring water. Won't that keep him fresh?"

"The meat's got to be bled right away. I know that much because Karl told me. He says what you do in the first half hour after an animal is shot makes the difference between good meat and bad meat."

"Oh, James! *Ish!* Do we really have to get our hands in that thing?"

"I don't see how else we're gonna get him gutted. If we don't, Karl will just come home to another mess we've made."

That finally convinced Anna what must be done, must be done. "There are still some torches left in the corner. I'll get them."

"And bring some knives, too, and I'll go get Karl's oilstone that he uses for sharpening his axe. I think we're gonna need it."

Anna turned back before she was at the doorway of the house and called to her brother, "Karl's gonna be so proud of you, James." She was proud herself in a way she'd never dreamed she could be of her baby brother.

"Of you too, Anna. I just know it."

For some inexplicable reason, Anna remembered she had forgotten to water her hop bines that day, and promised herself she'd do it first thing in the morning. Soon as that bear was gutted and she got a little sleep and they'd gone over to get one of the boys to help hoist that bear up and they'd taken care of digging the potatoes and the turnips and the rutabagas and . . .

No, she thought, the hop bines will come first. First thing when I get up. Those hop bines *will not* fail!

Chapter 19

Three days later Karl Lindstrom rode northward along the trail that was now showing evidence of autumn coming on. The first sumac glowed brilliantly in startling scarlet from the edges of the forest trail. The hazelnuts were brown and thick. Karl remembered he'd promised Anna he would show them to her. As soon as the cabin was finished, he would bring her back here and do just that. In the meantime, he pulled the team up and picked a stem of the nuts and put it in his pocket. Once again on his way, he passed through the place of the wide heartpine, which he knew would make thick planks for Anna's kitchen dresser. He must come back here and fell it and split it as soon as he had a free day, and begin making the piece of furniture, which, too, he had promised Anna.

A pheasant lifted itself, disturbed from its dust bath at the edge of the road as Karl's team came clopping. The bird flashed in brilliant bars of rust and black, and iridescent green head, as it scaled quickly up toward cover in a graceful swoop, scolding, "C-a-a-a!"

I would shoot it and take it home for supper, Karl thought, but I do not have my gun. The pheasant can wait for James to bring it down.

No, Karl did not have his own rifle. He had a gun all right, but when it was shot for the first time, it would be shot by James. It was a Henry repeater that made Karl smile in anticipation. He had much to make up for with the lad. The gun would be a start. Karl thought about himself and the boy walking out in the amber autumn mornings, their guns slung on their arms, companionably silent as they stalked pheasants, brought them down and carried them home to Anna.

Then he would teach Anna how to stuff it with bread stuffing enhanced by their own wild hazelnuts. Karl supposed he would have to teach her to make bread all over again, now that she would be doing it in the cast-iron stove.

Karl smiled. He flicked the reins. But Belle and Bill each turned a blinder in his direction, as if asking him what the hurry was. They were already cutting a good pace toward home, and they were as anxious to be there as he was.

When the team turned into their own lane a short time later, Karl wanted to slow them instead of hurrying them. But now they obstinately refused to be slowed. Karl saw the familiar opening in the trees up ahead, then his skid trail, and at its base, the beautiful log house he and Anna and James had built together. Leaning beside it were neatly placed sacks of potatoes. Out on the grass by the garden were willow baskets with grapes drying in them, shriveling themselves into raisins. There was smoke coming from the chimney of the sod house.

But there was something missing. Karl scanned the clearing again and realized with a start that it was the springhouse! His springhouse was gone! There were two pails sitting where it had been before, and some rutabagas that looked half-washed. Some crocks were submerged in the sand, as usual. But the building itself had disappeared into thin air. There was a smell in the air that made Karl's nostrils twitch, but he couldn't figure out what it could be that smelled so much like bear. The horses seemed to smell it, too, for they threw their heads and flicked their manes until Karl had to say, "Eaaasy. We are home. You know home when you see it."

Neither Anna nor James was in sight as Karl drove the team up near the log house. There it stood—the house of his dreams. While he reined in his team before it, he wondered once more if he had shattered those dreams beyond repair or if he and the boy and Anna could patch them up. He forced a calm into his limbs as he tied the reins to the wooden brake handle, and spoke to Belle and Bill.

"You will have to wait a while till I get these things unloaded."

The horses told him in no uncertain terms they were impatient to get to their barn.

Coming around the rear of the wagon, Karl glanced toward the sod house. James stood just outside its door, his hands in his pockets, staring at Karl. Karl stopped short and looked back at the boy. A sudden stinging burned the back of Karl's eyes, seeing how James just stood there, making no move to come forward or greet him in any way. Karl tried to speak, but his tongue felt like it was stuck to the roof of his mouth. Finally, he just raised his hand in a silent gesture of hello. His heart beat high in his throat as he waited for a return greeting from the boy. At last James removed a hand from his pocket and raised it silently, too.

"I could use a little help unloading this wagon, boy," Karl called.

Without a word, James came toward him, watching his feet scuff up puffs of dust on his way. At the rear of the wagon he stopped, looked up at Karl, silent as before.

Inanely, Karl managed to get out, "I got the wheat ground."

"Good," said James. But the note escaped him in a high contralto. "Good," he repeated, deeper this time.

"We will have plenty flour for winter." Karl remembered how he had once told the boy he was an extra mouth to feed.

"Good."

"Got those windows for the log house."

James nodded his head as if to say, yes, so I see.

"Everything all right here?" Karl's eyes flickered toward the cabin, then back to the boy's face.

"Ya." After a pause, he went on. "We thought you'd be back yesterday."

"It took a day to get the flour milled. They were busy at the mill and we had to wait our turn." Did they think I wouldn't come back, Karl wondered. Is that what they thought?

"Oh."

Tentatively they hovered, brawny man and gangly boy, hearts surging with remorse and love, neither of them yet having said what he wanted so desperately to say.

"Well, we'd best get it unloaded," Karl said.

"Ya."

Karl stepped to the wagon to remove the backboard, but when his hands were upon it he did not pull it loose. He stood instead braced that way, gripping the rough wood as if it were his security. He closed his eyes. The boy stood unmoving, near Karl's elbow.

"Boy, I . . . I'm sorry," Karl croaked. Then he leaned his head back and looked up at the autumn sky. The sharp edges of the clouds were blurry.

"Me, too, Karl," James said. And for once in his life his voice came out strong and masculine.

"You got nothing to be sorry for, boy. It was all me. Me! Karl!"

"No, Karl. I shoulda got that gun like you said."

"The gun had nothing to do with it."

"Yes it did. It was the first lesson you taught me. Move for the gun like your life depends on it, cause it probably does."

"I was wrong that day. I was mad . . . I had things on my mind about Anna and we weren't getting along, so I took it out on you."

"It don't matter, really."

"Ya. It matters, boy. It matters."

"Not to me, not any more. I learned a lesson that day. I figure I needed it."

"I learned a lesson, too," Karl said.

Karl looked up then, found the boy's wide green eyes filled to the brim and understood how his own father had felt when he waved to him for the last time.

"I missed you, boy. I missed you these last three days."

James blinked and a tear rolled down, unchecked, for his hands were still stuffed in his pockets. "We mi—we missed you, too."

Karl took the plunge, loosening his hold on the wagon and turning in one heart-filling motion to sweep the boy into his arms and hug him to his chest. James' arms came clinging to Karl. Karl took James by the sides of his hair, holding him back to look into his face, saying, "I'm sorry, boy. Your sister was right. You did everything right that I ever asked you to learn. A man couldn't ask for anything better than a boy like you."

James pitched roughly against Karl's chest, releasing all his pent-up anguish in a torrent of words that came muffled against Karl's shirt. "We didn't think you were coming back. We looked for you all day yesterday, and then nighttime came, and you didn't have your rifle and we knew about the cougar."

Karl thought his heart would explode. "Olaf was with me, boy, you knew that." But he was rocking James, feeling the boy's heart beat against his own. "And he had his gun. Besides . . . a man would be a fool not to come back to a place like this, with all this plenty."

"Oh, Karl, don't ever go away again. I was so scared. I . . ." Standing there against the big man's chest, against the smell of him, that mixture of horses and tobacco and security, the words that ached in James' throat could be denied no longer. "I love you, Karl," he said, then backed away, his eyes cast earthward, and dried them sheepishly on his sleeve.

Karl pushed James' arm down and held him by the shoulders, forcing him to look square into his face as he said, "When you say to a man that you love him, there is no need to hide behind your sleeve. I love you, too, boy, and don't you ever forget it."

At last they both smiled. Then Karl swiped his own sleeve across his eyes and turned to the wagon again. "Now are you going to help me unload this wagon or do I need to get your sister to help me?"

"I'll help you, Karl."

"Can you lift a sack of flour?" Karl asked.

"Just watch me!"

They unloaded the flour and the windows, which were protectively couched between the sacks. Lifting a precious glass pane, Karl said, "I bought five of them. One for each side of the door and one for each of the other walls. A man should be able to look out and see his land all around him," he said, entering the log cabin.

Coming back outside, Karl said, "I see you picked potatoes while I was gone."

"Ya. Me and Anna."

"Where is she?" Karl inquired while his heart danced against his rib cage.

"She's getting some supper."

Now it was Karl's turn to say, "Oh." Then he jumped onto the wagon-bed again and said, "Help me move these last couple sacks, boy. We will take them to the sod house for Anna."

James pulled a sack away, revealing a long wooden box. He could see the words, "New Haven Arms Company" stamped on the front of it. He pulled the second sack away, and the words "Norwich, Connecticut" became visible. His hands fell loose upon the sack, and it would have tipped over sideways if Karl hadn't caught it. James' green eyes flashed up to Karl's blue ones.

"A man does best with his own gun," Karl said simply.

"His own gun?" James repeated doubtfully.

"Do you not agree?"

"Su . . . sure, Karl." James looked back down, wanting to touch the box, afraid to. He looked up again.

"I picked one with a stock of hand-shaped walnut that will fit your grip like your pants fit your seat. It is just right for a boy of your size."

"Really, Karl?" James asked disbelievingly, still not pulling the crate out. "Is it really for me?"

"I have taught you everything except how to be a hunter. It is time we got started. Winter is coming on."

James had the carton slipped free and in his arms. He leaped from the wagon and was running across the clearing, long legs bounding toward the sod house as he bellered, "Anna! Anna! Karl bought me a gun! Of my own, Anna, my own!"

Karl waited for her to appear in the doorway of the sod house, but she didn't. He shouldered a sack of flour and headed that way, for James had disappeared inside.

James was going crazy, talking far too loud, repeating that Karl had bought the gun to be his own. Anna was overjoyed for her brother.

"Oh, James, I told you, didn't I?" She had seen from the depths of the cabin how Karl and James had made their peace out there. It was not necessary for her to know what they had said. To see the two of them hugging that way in broad daylight had filled her heart to bursting.

Anna glanced up now as Karl's form filled the doorway, shutting out the daylight behind his wide shoulders. A queer, weak sensation flooded through her. He looked like a blond Nordic god, bigger than life, with that sack of flour on his shoulder and the muscles of his chest bulging as he paused uncertainly before coming all the way in. Sudden shyness overwhelmed her. She longed to rush to him and say, "Hold me, Karl," to feel his strong, tan arms take her against his chest.

"Hello, Anna," he said quietly. He had not thought he'd missed her this much, but the things his heart was doing told him how empty the last two days had been. He could tell she, too, was very tense and nervous.

When she spoke, her voice trembled. "Hello, Karl."

She wondered if he would stand in the doorway all evening.

"You're home," she at last thought to say. It sounded inane.

"Ya. I am home."

"And James says you've brought the gun for him?"

"Ya. A boy needs his own gun, so I bought him the best . . . a Henry repeater. But he had better not be thinking of using that hatchet to open the crate. Go out to the tack room and get a clawhammer, boy, like I taught you."

"Yessir!" James obeyed, and nearly knocked Karl back out the door.

There was a fire and something was cooking. Anna turned to stir it. The sack on Karl's shoulder grew heavy, and he passed just behind her to set it on a free spot on the floor.

His very nearness made her pulse throb faster, but she stirred the pot in order to appear busy, then clapped the cover on, saying, "I'll get some sticks from the woodpile to put under that sack."

"It can wait," Karl said, straightening.

"But the bugs will get it." She headed for the door.

"Not that fast."

His words and their boyish note of appeal stopped her halfway to the door. She turned to face Karl, then stood looking at him, and he at her, while time roared backward to the last time they had faced each other across this confined space.

"I have some small things in the wagon you could carry in for me." He glanced apologetically at the simmering pot. "It wouldn't take but a minute."

She nodded dumbly, then whirled toward the door, leaving him with his heart in a turmoil.

Is she afraid of me? thought Karl with fading hope. Have I fixed it so she wants nothing but to run from me like a brown-eyed chipmunk every time I come near her? Does she think I ran off to Kerstin to spite her?

When he came within inches of her to climb on the wagonbed, she skittered sideways to give him wide berth. He picked up a parcel from behind the seat, walked back to the open end of the wagon and stood above her, looking down at the top of her whiskey-hair.

"Here," he said, waiting for her to look up so he could toss the parcel down to her, "these are some things I thought you would need." Finally, she lifted her eyes, and he dropped it.

"What is it?" she asked as she caught it.

"Necessities," was all he would say.

Her eyes became wide with surprise, while he turned away with the picture of her undisguised delight in his mind.

Anna tried not to feel giddy, but it was hard. Nobody had ever given her a gift before. But Karl did not say it was a gift, she thought. Perhaps it's only some spices or things for the new kitchen. But it's soft, she thought. It bends and there is a lump in the middle of it!

An iron clank interrupted her notions as Karl dragged something black and heavy from the front of the wagon. It made another metallic chink as it scraped on the other pieces resting against it. One by one he pulled all of the black iron sections of the stove to the tail of the wagon, before leaping lightly down and heisting up the largest.

Anna gawked.

James came out of the barn then, polishing the stock of his new rifle with the sleeve of his shirt. He stopped long enough to watch Karl disappearing into the new cabin with his burden.

"What's that?" James called.

Karl swung around slowly, the iron sheet turning with him until his face appeared from behind it. "It is Anna's new stove," he answered. Then, without another word, he disappeared into the log cabin with the first of it.

Anna's new stove? thought Anna.

Anna's new stove!

Anna's new stove!

Had Karl answered, "It is Anna's new diamond tiara," he could not have surprised his wife more. Her eyes followed Karl's every step, back and forth, as he carried the pieces into the new house. Gladness filled her chest until she felt she would pop the seams of her shirt! She fought the urge to follow along at Karl's heels each step of the way to see where he was setting the pieces, if he was putting them up, connecting them together. Instead, she just stood in the yard while Karl marched to and fro, carefully attending to his stove-carrying and keeping his eyes from his wife. At last came the pipe from under the wagon seat. It was silvery black, shiny, clean. Anna could stand it no longer.

"Could I carry those for you, Karl?" she asked. Could I touch my stove? Could I touch this gift? Even this much of it—to make sure my eyes are not playing tricks on me?

"You do not need to help with this. It was only that little package I wanted you to carry."

"Oh, but I want to!"

He stopped, understood, handed her the sections of the stovepipe, pleasure growing in him at sight of her pleasure. Her freckles looked delightful beneath her excited brown eyes.

"There is more, Anna," he said.

"More?"

"More. When you buy a new stove, it seems they give you these newfangled kettles with it. They say they cook even better than cast-iron ones and they are lighter to lift. They are in the carton."

"Newfangled kettles?" Anna asked, incredulous.

"In the carton," he repeated, enjoying her disbelief.

"Are they copper?"

"No. Something called japanned ware."

"Japanned ware?"

"They say things don't burn in it as easy as copper, and it does not rust like iron because it is covered with lacquer."

At the mention of burned food, Anna's eyes skittered down to the package. She picked at the wrapping absently with a fingernail, remembering all those times she had charred poor Karl's dinners. He saw her eyes drop and wondered what he had said to disappoint her.

Then James intervened. "Wow, Karl! Anna gets a stove and all them kettles, and I get a gun! I wish you'd go to town more often!"

Karl forced a laugh. "The kettles are no good without food to cook in them."

"When can we go hunting?"

"When the cabin is done and the vegetables are all dug."

"The vegetables are all dug, Karl. Me and Anna did it while you were gone."

"The turnips, too?" Karl asked, amazed.

"Of course, the turnips, too. We already got 'em washed and down in the root cellar and Anna's cooking some for supper."

"She is, huh?" Karl eyed his wife again, finding a pleasing blush creeping upon her cheeks. "My Anna is cooking turnips?"

Always, when Karl called her "my *Onnuh*" that way, it made the blood beat at her cheeks. But James was still babbling away.

"You were sure right about the turnips. I never saw such big ones in my life!"

"What did I tell you?" Karl chided James good-naturedly. Then, lowering his voice, turning away, he repeated, "Turnips, huh?"

But while Karl went to the cabin with the box of japanned ware on his shoulder, Anna turned quickly to James and ordered in a feisty whisper, "James Reardon, you just keep your nose out of my turnip-cooking, do you hear!"

"What did *I* say?" he asked, stunned by her sudden attack on his innocent comment.

"You never mind!" she whispered back. "My turnips are my business!"

Just then Karl returned. He hitched his britches up at the waist a little, then turned toward the empty place where the springhouse used to be.

"I have been waiting to be told where my springhouse is, but since nobody tells me, I guess I must ask."

Turnips were forgotten as Anna and James smirked at each other conspiratorially.

"The springhouse got wrecked, Karl," James said in a masterpiece of simplicity.

"How does a springhouse get wrecked, just sitting there holding pails?"

"I blasted 'er to kingdom come when I shot the bear."

Should he live to be as old as Karl's virgin maples and their abundance of nectar, James would never forget the sweet nectar of that moment— the look on Karl's face, the jawfall of disbelief, James' own billowing pride, his self-pleasure at dropping the comment so casually, so manfully.

And if Karl lived to be as old as his maples, he would clearly remember forever the shock of that moment—the way the boy stood holding the new Henry lever action repeater, trying to look nonchalant when the pride was beaming from his face in shafts, when his knuckly hands squared the rifle before him as if to say, "nothing to it, Karl."

"A bear?"

"That's right."

"You shot a bear?"

"Well, not alone. Anna and me, we shot him together," James confirmed. There was no pretended nonchalance now. The words came tumbling from behind his widely smiling lips in a grand rush. "Didn't we, Anna? We were sleeping and we heard all these scraping noises and it sounded like something was trying to eat our door down, so we tried to figure out what it was, and pretty soon it moved to the springhouse and you shoulda heard all that racket, Karl. I think he had trouble gettin' through the doorway and by the time he did, why, he had it splintered five ways from Sunday and then we heard all this crashing and cracking and he got busy eatin' watermelon syrup after he broke most of the crocks and stuff, so I told Anna to light one of them torches that was left over from when she got lost, and she did and took it out in front of us to blind the bear so I could get off one good shot before he had a chance to think twice. 'Cause once you said that when a bear knows where to find free food he never fails to come back time after time and the only way to stop him is to kill him, so that's just what I did, Karl. I beaned 'im right between the eyes and there wasn't much left of his head when I was done, either!"

At last James stopped, breathless.

Karl was flabbergasted. He hunched his head and shoulders forward. "You and Anna did that?"

"We sure did, but you loaded that shot a little heavy and it blew the back wall clear off the springhouse. Blew me clear off my feet, too, didn't it, Anna?" But before she could even nod, James hurried on, "But Anna, she made me promise that as soon as I fired that first shot I'd run back in the sod house fast as my feet would carry me! I swear, Karl, I hardly knew if I had any feet left after that gun smacked me over, though. You said she'd kick, but I wasn't expecting 'er to kick like a mule!"

The import of all this was beginning to register on Karl. Suppose James had missed? Suppose the gun hadn't fired? Countless dire probabilities gripped Karl's gut.

"Boy, you knew it was just my temper out in the bog that day when I got on you for being slow to the gun. You could have let that bear eat everything on the place and I would not have scolded, just so I come home and find you and Anna safe."

"But we *are* safe," the boy reasoned.

"Ya, you are safe, but because of my silly scolding I make you take such a risk to prove yourself when you have proved yourself all along."

"It wasn't cause of what happened in the bog, Karl, honest. It was . . . well . . . I don't know how to say it. It was kinda like when you say to Anna, 'A person keeps clean,' or when you say to me 'A door faces east.' All I could think of was 'A man protects his home.' " Once said, the adultness of his simple statement struck James fully. He had taken his first steps across the threshold of manhood.

"Karl," James said now, suddenly very sure of the truth in what he was about to say, "I'd have done it anyway, even if I'd never seen a cranberry bog in my life before."

Anna watched the only two men she had ever loved coming to terms with each other, setting their tack toward a course of future respect and sharing. Joyful though she was for them, her heart ached to reach a similar plane of understanding with Karl. But their private truce would have to be put off for a while yet, for Karl was saying with an appealing half grin, "So show me this bear with his head shot off, who only bargained for a little watermelon syrup."

James broke into a grin and a jog at the same time. "He's out here behind the sod house. We wanted to put him where you couldn't see him at first, and spring the surprise on you when we were good and ready."

Karl began to follow him, but realized that Anna hung back. He turned, asking, "Aren't you coming, Anna?" She hesitated a moment, until he added, "The fireman must come along, too. If it had not been for you there would have been no torches in the house."

Was he teasing her? Anna wondered with a little skip of her heart. Oh, he was teasing her about getting lost in the blueberry patch! How long had it been since Karl had teased her?

He turned to follow James, and she studied his high boots, remembering the first day they'd met, how she'd wanted to look up at his face but had only walked along, like now, with her eyes on his boots, wondering what he thought of her.

Coming around the sod house, Karl was confronted not only by the carcass of the black bear hoisted into a tree. Beside it, hanging from its heel tendons, hung a twelve-point buck whitetail deer. Karl stopped dead in his tracks. He stared incredulously while Anna and James shared another conspiratorial pair of smiles. Karl's reaction was exactly what they'd hoped it would be. "But where did the deer come from?"

"Oh, that's Anna's," James said offhandedly, stifling a smirk.

"You two are just full of surprises today."

"Well, the deer was a surprise to us, too," James revealed.

Anna was poking around in the dirt with the toe of her shoe.

"Do you want to tell me about it?" He leveled his eyes on his wife.

"You tell him, James."

"Somebody tell me. I do not care who."

"The reason Anna doesn't want to tell you is 'cause she's scared you'll be mad at her about the potatoes."

"What potatoes?"

"The ones the Indians stole."

Karl was getting more confused by the minute. Still, Anna kept poking her shoe in the dirt, and he knew he wasn't going to get anything out of her.

"I see I must ask again," Karl said, playing their game. "What potatoes did the Indians steal?"

James completed the story. "The ones from the garden. We dug up all the potatoes and got them all washed and in gunny sacks, but we forgot how you always said the Indians would steal anything that wasn't tacked down if they wanted it. I guess, to tell the truth, we never really believed you. So we got all those sacks of potatoes lined up against the wall of the log house, but we figured there was no hurry getting them into the root cellar. We left 'em there overnight and when we got up yesterday morning, one of the sacks was gone. All we could figure out was that the Indians took it. Anna was pretty sure you'd be mad because you said we need all the potatoes we can raise for the winter ahead. Anyway, she was really upset about it and we didn't know how to get them potatoes back. Then, this morning when we got up, here hangs this deer in the tree next to the bear. I guess the Indians are pretty much like you had 'em pegged, Karl. They have the strangest sense of honesty I ever heard of. The deer has to be their way of paying us back for the potatoes they stole."

"I'm sure it is. I guess we will just have to eat more meat than potatoes this winter, that's all. Could I ask one question?"

"Sure," James answered.

"If Anna was so scared about the sack of potatoes that was gone, why are the rest still sitting there?"

"Because neither one of us could lift them down the steps of the root cellar. We figured we'd bruise them all up if we dragged 'em down and dropped 'em over the side. We had all we could do to get 'em this far. So Anna took a chunk of wood from the woodpile and leaned it against each sack during the night. She said that if the Indians want the potatoes that bad, let them take 'em and she'd eat turnips!"

"But I thought Anna hates turnips," Karl said, eyeing her.

Relieved that Karl didn't seem too upset about the stolen spuds, Anna finally braved a glance at him, but stubbornly didn't answer.

Karl again turned his attention to the pair of trees. "So, that takes care of the deer. But how did you get this other monster up?"

Warming to the game now, James answered, "Oh, we had a hard time pulling him up there, didn't we, Anna?" He had been around Karl long enough that he was unable to resist such an opportunity for teasing!

"Now do not try to tell me that you strung that bear up there, not two skinny little—" But Karl quickly amended, "Not two young pups like you!"

James couldn't wait to finish his story. As before, the words came bubbling out like the spring bubbled out of the earth near them. There was no stopping either.

"When we shot him he fell back into the springhouse and we knew we were in a terrible fix. He'd lay there and foul up the water in no time, I figured, so I took your axe and knocked away the walls that were left standing and Anna and me we gutted him right then and there. Anna, she got pretty queasy, but I told her if we didn't do it that meat'd be pure spoiled by morning. We washed the carcass out real good and let it lay, then first thing in the morning we walked up to Olaf's place and Erik come back with the team and got him hung up here with the block and tackle. Erik says he thinks this fellow would go three hunnert fifty pounds anyway. What do you think, Karl?"

But what Karl was thinking was, *Anna* gutted that bear? In the middle of the night, by torchlight, probably dressed in her nighty? My *Anna* gutted that bear? Anna, who retched at the sight of a prairie chicken being dressed? "I would say closer to four hundred, myself," Karl finally answered James.

"He mighta gone four hunnert with his head on. Course, Erik never saw him with his head on. We all had a pretty good laugh when he come down here to the spring and sees that headless bear. All the while we were stringin' him up, Erik keeps sayin', 'Yup! You two sure fixed one mighty beautiful bear rug!' "

Pleased as punch, getting into his story better all the time, James rambled on. It was "Erik this" and "Erik that" until Karl got quite peeved at hearing the man's name so much. Then, when Karl learned that Erik had stayed for dinner, he couldn't help but remember the way Anna had clung to Erik's neck the night he'd rescued her from the wolves. But just about the time James began telling about Erik staying to supper, Anna remembered she had those turnips cooking and took off for the sod house.

Damn you, James! she thought as she scurried away, do you have to go on and on and make it sound like Erik stayed here all day!

All through supper Karl and James talked bears and guns. They dissected the Henry forty-four caliber lever-action repeater and how she could hold fifteen rounds in her tubular magazine, and how she had a breech so tight she never leaked gas and how she would soon put Karl's own single-shot Sharps out to graze in obsolescence. When the meal was done, the Henry came to take the place of the dishes. The two of them took the gun apart, piece by piece, then put it back together, while Anna listened to foreign words again and was left out of the conversation: chamber, breechblock, wedge bar, finger lever, magazine spring. She grew fidgety.

Night came on, and Anna wondered what was in the package Karl had brought for her. In all the excitement over the stove and the kettles and the gun and the bear and the deer, the package had been eclipsed, and by the time they were all in the house for supper, Anna decided she wanted to open it when she was alone. Meanwhile, the package lay on the bed unopened.

At last Karl arose in his customary way and stretched, twisting at the waist with elbows raised. He picked up his tobacco pouch from the table. Now, Anna thought, while he is out there in the barn, and when James is already in bed, I will open the package.

But Karl startled her by saying, "I must check the horses. Will you come with me, Anna?"

She took a jacket. Nights were getting cooler now. It helped to have some place to stick her useless hands. She jammed them into the pockets and folded the jacket fronts deeply across one another. Karl lit his pipe and they sauntered toward the barn. Halfway there he noted, "You were very busy while I was gone."

"It just happened that way."

"I thought I would have to come home and dig potatoes and turnips."

"Oh, that was James' idea, to dig them. He said you told him they were ready for digging or I never would've known. I'm sorry about the potatoes the Indians took, Karl."

"I can see we will not be in need of them. I can tell just how busy you were when I look around and see how good the crops were. There will be plenty for winter. Plenty."

"Well, that's a relief. I really wasn't sure how much one sack of potatoes meant. But James forgot to tell you that we still have a few rutabagas and carrots left to take up. We didn't quite finish them."

"Ya, I see them out there, but they will keep. Carrots like to be in the earth to sweeten after the first frosts, my papa always used to say. We have plenty of time yet."

They swerved, nearing the barn. Anna's feet quite refused to take her into it. She turned and began sauntering with careless steps toward the vegetable garden, which was washed in moonlight, the carrot tops and rutabaga leaves and pumpkin vines clearly defined in the blue-white beams.

"That was something to come home and find that bear hanging in the tree. You were just as brave as the boy, Anna, to go outside not knowing for sure what was out there."

"I didn't feel very brave at all. If it had been up to me, we would've stayed right where we were and kept wondering what was out there. It wasn't my idea to open the door."

"But you did, Anna. The point is, you did."

She shrugged her narrow shoulders. "Well, what else could I do? Let James go out there by himself? I tell you, he's got a stubborn streak in him a mile long. You didn't see him, Karl. He was bound and determined to go out there alone if I refused to go along. I told him to let the bear eat everything in the place for all I cared, but he was determined. He kept saying 'Karl says this' and 'Karl says that,' and there was no way I was going to change his mind."

Karl's heart warmed, realizing the extent of his influence over the boy, just how fully James respected his teachings.

"He is something," Karl said ruminatively.

"Yes, he's something."

"Anna, if something had gone wrong and that bear had harmed either one of you, I could not live with myself."

The bitter, thoughtless words she'd thrown at Karl about the bear came back to plague her. They hurt her now more than they had hurt him at the time they were spoken. She struggled for the right words, needing so badly for things to be set right between them again.

"Karl . . . what I said before you left . . . about the bear—"

"Listen to me, Anna. It was my own stupidity that brought it here. I have thought about it and wondered why a bear would come nosing around when I have never been bothered by one before. It is because I was so angry when I left the cranberry bog that I did not use good sense. I think I must have left a trail of cranberries straight to our door. When a man loses his head that way, he uses bad sense. I think this is what I did that day. I even put my own good horse in danger by making her hurry where the footing was bad. And when I make her hurry, I spill cranberries. I should have covered the baskets, but I didn't. Instead, I foolishly led that bear to the door by inviting him with cranberries. Then I ran away and left you two to take care of him."

"That's not true, Karl. I think you say it now because of what I said before you left. I never should have said that and I knew it as soon as the words were out of my mouth. I didn't mean it, Karl." She glanced up at him penitently.

"That is what Kerstin said."

"Kerstin?" Anna's eyebrows shot up irritatedly. "You told Kerstin what I said?" Already Anna's face felt like it would glow in the dark.

"We had a talk, Kerstin and I, and she said you were only human and spoke without thinking, like we all do sometimes."

The idea of Karl exchanging confidences with Kerstin wounded Anna so fiercely that she climbed up on the top fence rail and sat down, facing away from Karl so he couldn't see her face in the moonlight. *He must be closer to Kerstin than I guessed,* she thought, *to speak with her about our private affairs.*

"You spent the night at Johansons, Erik said."

Erik said, thought Karl dismally.

"Ya. They were only too glad to take me in."

I'll bet! Anna thought sourly, *especially one.*

"Karl," Anna began, wanting the subject of Kerstin dropped once and for all so they could get on to mending their differences, "thank you for the stove."

"There is no need to thank me, Anna. Kerstin called me a stubborn

Swede, and I guess I have been, saying all the time that we do not need a stove. We talked a long time, Kerstin and I, and she made me see that we should have a stove.''

Something inside Anna turned to stone with those words. She was hurt beyond words to think that Karl came around to buying a stove only when the delectable Kerstin thought he should! Not because his own wife wanted one. All the joy went out of her at the thought of the stove now. She found herself wanting to lash out and hurt Karl in return, in any little way she could.

"You really gutted that bear, Anna?" Karl asked in admiration.

"I hated every minute of it!" she snapped coldly. "I never want to smell another bear as long as I live!"

Confused by her abrupt chilling, he went on, "You will have to smell this one a little longer. Tomorrow James and I will have to take care of the meat. Then there is still the melting down of tallow to be done before we can make winter candles."

"I guess that means you won't get to making the door for the cabin yet for a couple days. How long will it be, Karl?"

"Tomorrow I will work with the meat. It will take a day to put the windows in. And perhaps another day to make the door and put up the stove. And we have to move things out of the sod house, too, and I will have to make the new rope beds, and I promised you that dresser for the kitchen."

Anna had climbed down from the fence and was brushing off her seat as she curtly stated, "Well, you can skip the dresser. Just get me out of that sod house as fast as you can. I'm sick to death of that stinkin' fireplace and living like a badger in a burrow!"

Bewildered, Karl could only stand wondering what had so suddenly changed Anna while she sat on that fence. She had been almost too sweet to resist when they had first come outside. And she hadn't mentioned anything about the package he'd brought her.

When he went in to bed she was already there. He wanted desperately to turn and take her in his arms and put an end to their enmity. But she lay far over on her side. Seeking to soften her, he whispered, "Anna, how did you like what I brought you in the little package?"

"Oh, I haven't had time to open it yet," she said brusquely. And Karl withdrew the hand that had been planning to touch her back.

Anna could smell the aroma of Karl's pipe still in his hair. She lay miserably beside him, listening to the long-eared owl who sat with his yellow eyes and rusty face, on a limb above the woodpile, calling in a slurred whistle, "Whee-you, whee-you."

When Anna could no longer stand pretending she was asleep, she fluffed over onto her back like Karl.

It was then that the question came.

"You made dinner for Erik then?" he asked.

Anna's heart kicked up its pace, pattered in double time like the owl's.

"Well, Erik had helped with that bear. What else could I do?"

But some new welling of hope was reborn in Anna. Karl, it seemed, was jealous.

Chapter 20

The next morning Karl and James left the house to set up a butchering slab near the spring. As soon as they were gone, Anna took the package and pulled it open with anxious fingers. Inside was what she had hoped for. She found a length of delightful pink gingham, several hanks of thread and a bar of camomile soap. The material was wrapped around the bar, and when it dropped out Anna caught it in a surprised hand. She raised it to her nose. It smelled of flowers and freshness and femininity. She raised the gingham to her nose and it, too, smelled of these things.

She looked down at her britches. She glanced out the door at the new log house. She thought of the new glass windows and wondered if Karl meant the material for curtains when he said *necessities.* Who was there to look into the windows out here in the wilderness except an occasional raccoon or a passing swallow?

Anna was honestly torn by what Karl had meant the material to be used for. She wanted very badly to think the fabric was intended for something personal. Remembering Karl's last comment last night, the way he'd asked about Erik staying for supper, she could have sworn Karl was jealous. Yet, why was he so all-fired taken with Kerstin if he could be jealous of Erik? It didn't make any sense.

There was no denying the personal implication of the scented soap. And, after all, Karl had given her the material without putting any restrictions on it. Maybe she could put them both to use to end this breach between herself and Karl once and for all. She was the one who had coldly snubbed his gift; and thereby snubbed him. Could it be possible he waited for her to make the first move?

A plan formed in Anna's head.

Excitedly, she flipped the length of gingham out across the bed and began measuring it by scant yards—nose to outstretched hand equaling one yard. She found there were more yards of the stuff than she'd guessed. Enough for both curtains and a dress? Smiling to herself, she thought: Goodness! If there is, I will look like my windows!

Karl saw Anna cross the clearing and go into the log house. He wondered what she was doing in there. Maybe admiring the stove, he thought hopefully. He had been so proud of the fact he bought her that stove. With it he sought to win her favor back again, to tell her he accepted her. At first she had seemed very gratified by it. But later, out there by the garden, something had happened. He remembered Anna's eyes, as big and round as a cocker spaniel's when she'd first seen him unloading the stove. He remembered the hard edge on her voice later and knew his gift had not done the trick.

He turned back to his butchering but kept an eye on the log house to see when Anna left it again.

Inside, Anna was measuring the glass panes as they leaned against the fireplace wall. Marching back across the clearing, she saw Karl stop his meat-cutting to look her way. She braved a little wave of hello and continued on into the sod house to begin cutting curtain lengths. When Karl and James came in for lunch there was gingham all over everything. She had two lengths cut for each window and was busy with needle and thread.

"Thank you for the necessities, Karl," she said with renewed sweetness. "They will make lovely curtains."

Karl felt his heart fall. Curtains? Out here in the middle of nowhere? But he could not say to Anna that he'd meant her to have the gingham to use for dresses. If he said so, she would only feel like she'd disappointed him again by already cutting the fabric into pieces for the windows. He returned to his afternoon's work gravely disheartened. Would he have to look at her in those britches for the remainder of the winter then? Or could he find time for another trip to town before the snow flew?

As soon as Karl and James were gone, Anna found the pieces of the dress she'd been tearing apart to use as a pattern. She would follow it loosely, adding to the height of the neckline, making the sleeves looser, more serviceable, making the skirt less clinging, more like the dresses Kerstin and Katrene wore. During the afternoon she got the pieces of the new dress all cut out. But whenever Karl entered the house during the next few days, all he saw was his wife stitching curtains. She hid the dress pieces, easily camouflaged, beneath the plain panels on her lap.

For Karl and James there was not only the butchering to be done, but also the processing of the two hides. Karl showed James how to flesh out the hide, draping it over a felled tree, lying at an angle, still attached to its stump. Together they removed all the fat and sinew. They scraped away with their fleshing tools while Karl warned James not to puncture or score the hide, nor to expose the hair roots. It was a malodorous and tiring job. By the time the hides were placed in a lye solution to soak for two days, both Karl and James were well ready for a bath in the pond.

Anna refused their invitation to go along. She said she'd stay behind and get their supper ready. Karl, with disappointment threading his veins, wondered how to get her to do any of the things they used to so enjoy. He wanted to ask Anna if she had found the soap in the gingham, but was afraid she might think he was intimating she needed it. So Karl said nothing about camomile soap, and neither did Anna. But he detected the smell of their homemade lye soap, and figured she spurned the scented bar and used the stuff she still adamantly called "lardy" just to spite him.

Still, the next day, Karl thought he detected something about Anna, which he chose to think of as "saucy." It was as if she was teasing him about something he didn't quite catch. She walked around with an undeniable air of self-satisfaction. About what, he could not guess.

That day he began inserting the windows. It was a delicate job, requiring great accuracy when Karl cut each hole. If the openings were cut too large, it meant losing tightness when the weather caused the frames to expand. But if they were cut too small, it meant broken panes when the frames contracted. After Karl cut the first opening, he went to where the yellow poplar billets were stacked on the skid trail. Although the autumn air was crisping, Karl loosened his shirt, for it was warm in the sun. Finding his axe needed sharpening, he took out his oilstone and was working the steel upon it when Anna came out of the springhouse with a dipper and started up the hill toward him. He watched her approach, paying only cursory attention to the honing of the blade. He wondered what it was that made Anna tick these days. At times she seemed to be artfully flirting with him. Yet when she hit the bed last night, she'd been first to turn on her side away from him. He was terribly confused about what she wanted out of him. Now here she came, up the hill with a dipperful of water, wearing those abominable britches again. Karl was getting mighty tired of those pants.

When she neared, she handed him the dipper, saying, "Here, Karl, I thought you might be thirsty out here in the sun." She raised her wide eyes coyly to assess his beaded brow and the damp tendrils of hair across it.

"Thank you, Anna, I am." He took the dipper, studying her across the lip of it as he raised his head and drank. "How are your curtains coming?" He handed the dipper back to her.

"Fine." She hooked the dipper over her index finger and swung it like the pendulum of a clock, with her other hand still resting on her cocked hip. "So how are your windows coming?"

"Fine." He had all he could do to keep from smiling.

She looked around innocently, glancing at the billets, his axe, the pile of chips. "What are you working on up here?"

"I am splitting window edgings from yellow poplar."

She glanced around, spied the pile of rocks nearby, then asked, "Do you mind if I watch for a while?"

For the life of him he couldn't figure out why she would want to, but he nodded. He used two wedges and a small wooden sledge. She sat on the rock pile left over from their chimney, watching as Karl worked. It was disconcerting having her sitting there with that innocent look plastered all over her face. He wished that he knew what she was up to.

He picked up his axe, drove it into the edge of a billet, inserted the wedge, watching carefully for knots, which could make the cleavage go awry. When the first board fell free, Karl picked it up, looked at Anna and said, "Yellow poplar splits smooth as anything. The only thing you must remember is to watch for knots where branches grew before."

Anna lounged casually upon her rock, knees crossed, one foot swinging. "I'm not James, Karl," she said in a voice as smooth as warm honey. "I won't be needing to learn the art of board-making. I just came out to watch, that's all. I like to watch you work with the wood."

"You do?" Karl asked, his eyebrows lifting in astonishment.

She swung a foot, and let her eyes wander over him in a most suggestive fashion. "Yes, I do. It seems there's nothing you can't do with wood. I like to watch your hands on a piece that way. You sometimes look like you're caressing it."

Karl dropped his hand from the newly hewn plank as if it had suddenly developed nipples. Anna laughed lightly and settled more comfortably onto the rock pile, leaning her elbows back so her breasts thrust forward.

"Don't your shoulders ever get tired, Karl?"

"My shoulders?" he parroted.

"Sometimes I watch you and I can't believe how long you can work with an axe without tiring." Somehow she was toying with her hair, lifting it off the back of her neck and letting it flop back down repeatedly.

"A man does what must be done," Karl said, trying to concentrate on his board-making.

"But you never complain."

"What good would complaining do? A job takes so many hours of work, complaining will not shorten those hours."

Her eyes followed his every flex of muscle as he worked—every movement sinuous and inviting as her voice rippled on provocatively. "But with you, Karl, I think there's no complaining because you like what you're doing so much."

He kept his eyes and hands busy with the poplar, but a giddy sensation was tingling his nerve endings. He knew now that she was playing him like a northern pike on a long, strong line. He had avoided being caught by her for some time now, but this was the first she had ever retaliated with such obvious flirting.

She leaned back and studied him from behind half-closed lids awhile longer before murmuring in a low tone, "It's like watching a dancer when I watch you with your axe. From the first day I saw you with it, I thought so. You make every motion smooth and graceful."

The only thing Karl could think of to say was, "That's how my papa taught me. That is how I teach the boy." He wondered if his face was as red as it felt. He continued working while she just sat there, stretching in the sun, lazing, eyeing him up and down until he thought he'd lose control of his own axe.

At last she sighed. Then she clenched both fists and stretched her arms straight out at her sides in one last sinuous pose. "Oops!" she squeaked with a little giggle, for she'd knocked one of the rocks off the pile behind her and it went tumbling, taking a couple others with it. She stood up, bracing hands on knees and thrusting out her breasts and derrière, sighing, "Well, I guess I'd better get back down to—"

"Don't move, Anna!" he whispered, a fierce warning in his voice. His eyes had veered down to the base of the rock pile. They remained glued to the spot while he reached blindly, feeling for his axe.

The rattler had not made a sound, had given no indication it was sunning itself on the rock pile. But when the stones became dislodged and went rolling, the snake was suddenly exposed. Startled, the reptile curled into its fighting coil, raised its neck into the sharply oblique bow that warned of an imminent strike.

Anna looked down, following the path of Karl's gaze just as the stout tail began its warning buzz. Her stomach tightened and her limbs tensed as she confronted the snake's sulphur yellow eyes with their demonic elliptical pupils.

It happened so fast Anna scarcely had time to become mesmerized by shock. Karl's blind hand found the axe handle, and the next second the timber rattler was in two pieces, each leaping and coiling while Anna screamed, unable to take her eyes from the streaks of dark brown and yellow that writhed through the air in grotesque death twirls. Before the severed snake fell lifelessly to the earth, Karl's arms were around Anna, one of his big hands cupping the back of her head as he picked her up that way and set her away from the rock pile.

"Anna . . . Oh my God, Anna," he spoke into her hair.

She sobbed, followed by frightful spasms of quaking.

"It is all right, Anna. I have killed it."

"Your axe, Karl," she wailed senselessly.

"Yes, I killed it with my axe. Don't cry, Anna."

James was running up the hill by this time, alerted by Anna's scream, which had carried through the still air over the clearing like the shriek of a screech owl.

"Karl, what's wrong?" he called.

"There was a timber rattler, but it is all right now. I killed it."

"Is she okay?" James asked, frightened instantly.

"Ya, she is safe." But Karl did not relinquish his hold on her.

Anna continued to mutter senselessly something about Karl's axe while he attempted to soothe her. He tried to take her over to the woodpile and set her down, but she was too panicked to go near it.

"Your axe," she cried again.

"Anna, the snake is dead now. You are all right."

"But, K . . . Karl . . ." she sobbed, "your axe is . . . is in the dirt . . . your axe is in the d . . . dirt."

It was. Karl's precious honed steel, which never touched anything but worthy wood, had half of its poll buried in the earth. He looked at it over Anna's head, then squeezed his eyes shut and held her trembling body against his chest.

"Shh, Anna, it does not matter," he whispered.

"But you . . . s . . . said—"

"Anna, please," he entreated, "shut up and let me hold you."

There was no question of trying anything intimate with Anna that night. She was in such a shaken state when Karl tucked her into bed, he would have felt guilty even to lay a hand on her.

He and James sat up examining the rattles the boy had cut off the carcass. When James asked why a rattler would show up this late in the season, Karl explained that contrary to popular belief, they could not stand the hot sun. During the height of the summer they hid beneath their stone piles. But when the autumn sun grew less fierce, they came out once again to warm themselves, as if storing up heat before hibernating.

"They are getting ready for winter, too," he ended, glancing at the bed where Anna tossed fitfully.

"Like us, Karl, huh?"

"Ya. Like us, boy."

James looked at Anna, too, then asked, "Karl? When will we move into the cabin?"

"How about tomorrow? I must put up the stove and finish putting in one more window and make the door. But I can do that if you will wash the hides and get them ready for stretching. I think it is time we get Anna into a wooden house."

But they did not get everything finished the next day, though each worked like a dynamo.

Something told Karl that tonight was not the right night to make his final peace with Anna. One more night . . . one more night and they would be in the cabin for the first time. Then, then he would do what he now longed more than ever to do.

During that day and the next, he looked up often to find Anna watching him, whether from across the clearing, or from across the cabin, it was always the same. He knew that she, too, was waiting for the first night they would sleep in the house they had built together.

She brought him a drink again while he sat in the sun of the cabin door, smoothing the planks for the door. She stepped inside and after she'd been in there quietly for some time, Karl turned around to find her standing there, unmoving, studying the new floor of the loft above her, white and sweet-smelling and with its own ladder that rose to the hatchway across the way.

During that last day Karl put the stove up. It fit together like pieces of a jigsaw puzzle, but Anna did not rejoice over it as he thought she would. She remained almost timid now since he had killed that rattler and held her while she cried and trembled.

James worked at stringing the ropes for his own bed while Anna worked on those for her and Karl's bed. Karl showed them how to weave and splice the tough fibers of the prairie grass into tough, thick-gauged rope.

Once when James' fingers got tangled up and his weaving slipped loose, he asked Anna how she could do it so smoothly.

"Don't ask me," she answered. "Ask Karl. If anyone knows his way around a bed rope it's Karl." But she never glanced up, just kept weaving away at her own rope, sitting cross-legged in those britches in the middle of the cabin floor. Even James might have suspected a play on words had Anna looked amused or sprightly. But she only pulled her lip between her teeth, concentrating hard on her chore.

Meanwhile, Karl finished the door. He used the undauntable oak, which took more work splitting than any other wood because of its hardness. Karl worked away patiently, shaping and rubbing the panels smooth, then fashioning cross braces onto which the panels would be pegged.

In the early afternoon James and Anna began carrying their belongings from the sod house into the log house. They lugged dishes and bowls and barrels that were half empty, leaving the full flour barrels for Karl to fetch. Karl watched them parade past him, while he hinged the door, then tightened the final wooden pins. Then he set about tying the loosely placed ropes that needed only fastening to become beds.

Anna, a little withdrawn, sometimes almost shy, continued carrying their goods to the log cabin. Once, as she paused across the way to stretch her back after a heavy load, Karl watched her tuck her shirt into her britches, pulling in a deep breath and thrusting her breasts forward, standing that way, unaware that he watched her. Then she looked as if she sighed, though he heard no sigh from this distance, and she ran her hand deeply into the recesses of those pants, both front and back, ostensibly tucking in her shirttails again. She did all this in full profile to Karl. Just when he began to ask himself if Anna knew that he watched her, she looked up and discovered him with his hands idle upon his work, his eyes busy on her silhouette. She snapped almost guiltily away and fled into the sod house.

After she was gone, Karl contemplated what he had seen. When had her sharp-boned thinness mellowed and molded? How long had this contoured woman been hiding in boy's britches? Karl smiled, thinking of Anna's cooking, realizing she'd done all right eating it herself, in spite of all the self-criticism she heaped upon it.

Anna watched James taking down the blanket that had served as her dressing room ever since they'd lived here. He stepped off the trunk and she offered, "Here, I'll help you fold that."

"All right," he said. They each took two corners and stretched them out; there was scarcely room to do so in the cramped sod hut.

"James, I have a favor to ask you."

"Sure. What is it, Anna?"

"It's a very selfish one," she warned.

"Don't kid *me*, Anna. I know you better than that." He angled her a knowing smile.

"Oh, but it is! Especially because I ask it today, of all days."

"Well, ask!" he demanded brightly.

"I want you to ask Karl if you can take the team and ride over to the Johansons as soon as all the work is finished."

"You mean tonight?"

"No, this afternoon," Anna declared, feeling uncomfortable at this suggestion, for surely James would guess her intentions.

"What do you need from over there?"

They came nearly chest to chest, folding the blanket.

"I don't need anything from over there."

"Well then, what am I going for?"

"Just to get away from the house for a while." Her face went pink.

"But, Anna—"

"I know, I know. Today we're moving into the log cabin and everything. I told you it was selfish. You'd have to miss our first supper on the new stove and our first meal in the cabin together."

"But why?" James balked, and Anna despaired of ever enlightening him without drawing pictures.

"James, things have been—I need some time alone with Karl."

"Oh," he said shortly, the light suddenly dawning. "Well . . . in that case, sure. I'll be gone just as soon as I can."

"Listen, little brother," she said, reaching out to touch his arm, "I know it's unfair of me to ask it tonight, but believe me, it's got to be tonight. Karl and I have to straighten out some differences between us that have been festering for too long already. I'm afraid that if we don't get things ironed out now, they may drag on forever, and I couldn't stand—Oh, James, I feel just awful asking you tonight." She suddenly plopped down on the bare rope bed and looked at the floor dejectedly. "I know you've been looking forward to moving in just as much as we have. Believe me, I wouldn't ask if it wasn't absolutely necessary. I can't explain it all, James . . ." She looked up beseechingly. "But it's got to be today, tonight."

"What should I tell Karl? I mean, I never asked to take the team out alone before."

"Tell him you want to go calling on Nedda."

"Nedda?" James' Adam's apple did monkeyshines.

"Am I too far wrong in thinking you won't mind?"

"Go calling on Nedda?" James seemed thunderstruck by the idea, even though he, himself, had been toying with it ever since Nedda suggested it herself. "No! No, I won't mind a bit. But do you think Karl will let me?"

"Why not? He made you a teamster himself. He trusts you with Belle and Bill. Anyway, you went to Johansons the night I got lost in the woods, and made it just fine."

"I did, didn't I?" He remembered how proud Nedda had been of him then.

"That's not all I need you to do, James."

"What else?"

"I need for you to get Karl away from the house first, for at least an hour, longer if you can."

"How can I do that? He won't want to leave the log house."

"Make him go to the pond with you for a bath. Try to get him playing like we used to do all together, remember? That should keep him there a while."

"What are you going to do while we're gone?"

Anna arose with the blanket folded over her arm. She ran her hand over it with a little look of slyness. Then she smiled at her brother in a way he was soon to learn meant some fellow was going to meet his match. "James, that is a woman's secret. If you're old enough to go calling on Nedda, you're old enough to know a man doesn't ask a woman to tell all her secrets."

James colored a little, but he was unsure of something and didn't know what to do but ask about it.

"Anna, do I—should I ask the Johansons if I can stay all night?"

"No, James, I wouldn't ask that of you. I know how you've been waiting to sleep in your own loft for the first time. There's no need for you to stay out long past mid-evening. We'll be looking for you to come back then."

"Okay, Anna."

"You'll do it?" she asked breathlessly.

"'Course, I'll do it. I'm sorry I didn't think of it myself. From now on, if Karl lets me go this once, I'll go more often. I like visiting at their place. Besides," James added, hooking a thumb in his back pocket, gazing down at the floor almost guiltily, "I'd do darn near anything to see you and Karl the way you were before. I know things've been sour between you for a long time and I hate it. I just . . . I just want us all to be happy like before."

Anna smiled and reached to lay her hand on the long hard forearm and force him to take his hand from his back pocket so she could hold it. "Listen, baby brother, if I haven't said it for a long time, it's been my fault, not yours . . . but, I love you."

"Gosh, I know that," he said with a sideways smile lining his face. "Same goes for you."

Anna put her arms around him, taking the blanket into her hug as she pressed him to her. She had to reach up now to get her arm around his neck, he was so tall. She could sense James' having grown up not only physically but also emotionally this summer, for he made no attempt to pull away in embarrassment. He allowed himself to be hugged, and returned the pressure with a silent wish that whatever Anna had planned for tonight, it would work.

She pulled away. "Thanks, baby brother."

"Good luck, Anna," replied James.

"You, too. That's one stubborn Swede out there, and if he decides he doesn't want to go to the pond, you'll have your work cut out for you getting him away from the clearing."

The hanging of the freshly hewn door was symbolic to all of of them, but mostly to Karl. When it swung on its wooden hinges at last, he stood in its opening, looking first into the cabin, and then out of it.

"Due east," he said, glancing contentedly off across his cleared grain-fields to the rim of the woods, which waited yet to be cleared.

"Just like you always said," James confirmed.

Karl turned to rub his hand over the panels of the door. "Oak," he said, "good, tough oak." And he gave the door a slap.

"Just like you said, too."

"Just like I said, boy, and do not ever forget it."

"I won't, Karl."

Karl now looked at Anna. "And you have not forgotten you made me promise to let you be the first to pull the latchstring in."

Pleased he had remembered this from the days of early summer when they had lain in the dark whispering of such dreams to each other, Anna beamed and turned pleasantly rosy. But she hung back yet, wondering if this meant a reconciliation. The way he gazed at her, the way he stood with the light from the doorway behind him making his hair into a golden halo, the way he reminded her of those whispered secrets from long ago . . .

"So, Mrs. Lindstrom," Karl said, "why do you not try out your new door?"

Flustered now, she hastened to do so, saying, "Well, come on in, both of you. I'm certainly not going to take the latchstring in against my two favorite men, leaving them on the doorstep for the first time!"

Karl and James went inside to join her. James closed the door. Karl raised the bar and dropped it in place. Anna pulled at the latchstring, finger over finger, until a little round ball filled the hole and dropped inside.

"Did you carve this?" she asked Karl, holding the small wooden ball in her fingers. It was so perfectly round!

"No. It is a hazelnut. I promised I would show you a hazelnut."

She smiled mischievously. "But the squirrels will eat it right off the string."

"The squirrels must eat, too. So, let them. I will get another. I have plenty."

She looked up into Karl's face, keeping her own carefully expression-less, yet sincere, as she said, "Yes, Mr. Lindstrom, I believe you do."

James observed the way both Karl and Anna seemed to have forgotten he was there. Suddenly, with high heart, he believed he *would* have trouble getting Karl away from the clearing, but not for the reason Anna had predicted. He broke into their reverie, suggesting, "Karl, why don't you get that stove stoked up and then we'll go down and have a swim?"

"A swim? When we only just got into the log cabin? A man needs time to get acquainted here first."

"But I'm in kind of a hurry, Karl."

Karl was reluctant to tug his eyes away from Anna, but the boy was persistent. "You are in a hurry? What is it that makes you hurry? All these days we rush to finish the cabin. Now it is done and it is the time to ease up and enjoy it."

"Well, I want to—I got something I need to ask you."

"Ya, well ask then." Anna had turned away and had started fiddling with the stove lids. She'd probably never built a fire in a stove either, Karl thought, seeing what she was doing. So he went to do it.

"Could I take the team down to Johansons by myself?" James asked.

Karl turned around from the stove, genuine surprise on his face. "The team?"

"Yeah . . . I . . . I wanna go calling on Nedda."

"Today?"

"Well, yeah . . . what's the matter with today?" James had his thumbs hooked in his rear pockets again.

"But this is the day we are going to have our first supper in the cabin. Anna's going to cook on the new stove."

"Today's the first chance you give me to set down, too. We've been working on this cabin practically all summer. And when it wasn't the cabin keeping us busy, it was harvesting or trimming hooves or something else. What else have you got for me to do today?" James sounded genuinely irked.

Anna turned away, smiling at her brother's ingenuity, thinking, good for you, James! You can be a little shyster if you want!

Karl was truly surprised. He hadn't realized the boy had been hankering to get away from the place. If there was one thing Karl was gullible about, it was about James' deserving some time away. Without realizing it, James had tripped upon the weakest spot in the big Swede.

"Why nothing," Karl admitted. "There's nothing for you to do here. We are finished with everything."

"Then why can't I go?" James actually managed to sound persecuted.

"I did not say you could not go."

"Is it the team, Karl? Don't you trust me to take 'em out alone?"

"Sure, I trust you with the team."

"Well, can I take 'em, then?"

"Ya, I suppose you can. But what about supper?"

"I'd just as soon eat with the Johansons if it's all the same to you. That way I can get an early start over there."

"But, Anna was maybe planning something on the new stove."

"No offense, Anna, but if it takes you as long to get used to cooking on the new stove as it did to get used to the fireplace, I'd just as soon eat at Katrene's. Do you mind?"

Anna almost giggled out loud. Here all this time she'd thought her brother had forgotten how to be a little con man, but James was a genius at it!

"No, I don't mind. There'll be other meals at home."

"I don't think Katrene will mind either, and I sure do like her cooking."

To herself, Anna thought, all right, *brother,* enough is enough!

"I'd like to go as soon as possible, Karl, but first I need to talk to you. I thought maybe you'd come down to the pond with me. I want to clean up before I go, anyway."

"I was not planning on going down to the pond. Could we talk here?"

"I . . . I wanted to sort of . . . you know, talk man to man."

Bravo! thought Anna.

"Well . . . well, sure." Karl looked hesitantly at Anna.

At the look Karl gave her, Anna encouraged, "Listen, you two go. The water is too much for me now. I don't think I could stand getting into it when it's that cold. I'll stay here and play with my new toy," she said, indicating the stove.

Karl could only go along with the boy's request. "Get your clean things, James. We'll go now and you can get to their place before supper, like you want."

James climbed the ladder to the loft where his articles were neatly laid out, next to his own rope bed with its new tick of cornhusks.

Downstairs, Karl turned his eyes again to Anna. "I wish you would come with us today, but I think the boy has something on his mind."

He's not the only one, Karl, thought Anna, before she said, "It's his first time going to call on a girl. He's probably nervous and the swim will calm him down a bit. You remember your first time, Karl."

There was something different about Anna today. Something almost provocative as she laid that seemingly innocent reminder on her husband. She merely continued doing little things around the stove while she said it, but at her words Karl certainly did remember his first time, quite vividly. His first time with Anna. The incredible wonder of his first time with Anna.

"Ya, I remember," he said. "I was plenty nervous."

"Tell him that then, Karl, so he'll know he's not the only one to feel that way," Anna said.

At last she looked at him. Was it a challenge in her eye now? The words were spoken in simplicity, but what ulterior meaning was behind them? She was talking about herself and her first time with him, Karl was sure of it. She had kindling in her hands, a look of utter artlessness upon her face. With all this talk, that fire had never been built. That first fire in the stove had never been built.

"I will build the fire before we go," Karl said, breaking the invisible grip that had him clutched by his windpipe. He reached out, and she placed the pieces of kindling in his hand. He turned to build the fire in the stove which he had brought home for his Anna, thinking to her, I will build my fire always for you, Anna. What a fool I have been to keep it banked for so long.

James came clattering down the ladder and crossed to Anna. He put an arm loosely around her shoulders, casually, in a grown-up brotherly way.

"So, you have your stove at last. I just hope it does the trick."

Anna thought, don't you worry, baby brother, it will. I'm sure of it!

When the fire was going strong, the two left the cabin. Karl had carefully refrained from eyeing his wife too much in the presence of the boy. Things had suddenly kindled in himself, things that he was sure would show if he wasn't careful.

She watched them walk across the clearing. When they reached the far side, Anna called, "Karl?"

He turned to see her standing in the open cabin door with a hand shading her eyes.

"Ya, Anna?"

"Would you take a little water with you and water my hop bines as you pass them in the woods?"

He raised his hand—a silent salute of consent—and went to the spring for a pail. Anna knew that the hop bines had already taken root out there in the woods.

Chapter 21

❧

Anna sprang into action the minute their backs disappeared up the trail to the pond. Her stomach hurt with the old familiar ache of unsureness. Every nerve in her body, every muscle, every fiber wanted this to work. All she could think about was pleasing Karl. How much time did she have? Enough to wait for the water to warm on the stove?

She listened for the first sizzle of the kettle while she put their house in order. She hurried to hang the curtains at the windows on arching willow withes. Next she laid a matching gingham cloth upon the table, then their dishes, knives, mugs. She used precious minutes to pick the wildflowers, running all the way out to the edge of the field where they grew. These she placed in the center of the table in a thick pottery milk pitcher: clusters of Karl's beloved Minnesota. There were the late-blooming lavender asters, brown-eyed susans, lacy white northern bed-straw, feathery goldenrod, rich purple loosestrife, brilliant pink blazing star and lastly . . . most importantly . . . she interspersed the bouquet with fragrant stalks of yellow sweet clover. Standing back, she took a moment to assess her handiwork, wondering what Karl would say when he walked in and saw it.

But time was fleet-footed; the water was warmed now. She bathed, using the fragrant camomile soap for the first time. Then she hurried to don the new dress. Her stubborn hair thwarted her fingers, its willful curls resisting her efforts to bend it to her will. But she persisted with trembling fingers.

When at last both she and the cabin were in order, she gave herself one last look in their tiny mirror. Peeping into it critically, she closed her eyes, feeling the blood raddle her cheeks. She put the mirror down. She pressed both hands upon her stomach, fighting for calm, for reassurance that what she was doing was the right thing. Again doubt assailed her. Suppose Karl was not wooed by her efforts? How could she ever face him again? Suddenly, she thought about James entering the cabin and seeing the evidence of her attempted seduction, and knew she couldn't face him while he took in the curtains, the table, her dress.

When she heard them returning, she hid behind the curtain in the corner. She sat down on the trunk and pulled her feet up off the floor so they wouldn't know she was back there. Agonized, she hugged her knees to her chest, waiting with closed eyes to hear what was said when they first walked in.

James was speaking as they entered. ". . . because it gets dark earlier these nights, so I'll be sure to start back—" She didn't need to see him to know that James came up short at the sight of that table. The silence spoke volumes before James said in an awed tone, "Gosh, Karl, look at that!"

Not a word came from Karl. She imagined him, stopped in the doorway, holding his dirty clothes, maybe with a hand on the edge of the new door.

"Flowers, Karl," James said almost reverently, while Anna's heart threatened to choke her. "And the curtains. She hung the curtains."

Still not a word from Karl.

"I thought she was kind of silly to spend all that time on curtains, but they sure look good, don't they?"

"Ya. They sure look good," Karl said at last.

Anna leaned her head against the wall in her little corner, breathing as shallowly as possible so they wouldn't suspect she was there.

"I wonder where she is," James said.

"I . . . I guess she is around somewhere."

"I . . . I guess she is. Well, I better get my hair combed before I leave."

"Ya, you do that. I will get Belle and Bill harnessed for you."

"You don't need to, Karl. I can do it myself."

"It is all right, boy. I have nothing else to do until Anna gets back from wherever she is."

"Okay, I sure appreciate it."

An eternity passed while James whistled softly through his teeth, going up the ladder, coming back down. When Anna thought she couldn't stand it a minute longer, she heard his footsteps echo across the floor toward the door, then disappear. From outside came their voices again.

"Thanks, Karl."

"Ya, it was nothing. You have harnessed them plenty times for me. It was nothing."

"Well, this might be, too, but here goes."

They laughed together, then Anna heard Karl say, "Just remember what I said." She smiled to herself.

"Now you say hello to Olaf and everybody for Anna and me."

"I will. And don't worry, I'll take good care of Belle and Bill."

"That is one thing I do not worry about. Not any more."

"See you later then, Karl."

"Ya. Have a good time."

"I will. Bye."

Now is the time, thought Anna. Now, while Karl is still outside, I should go out and maybe be waiting by the stove when he comes in. But she couldn't make her limbs move. I've wrinkled my skirt by sitting here hugging my knees so tight, she thought wildly. I should have an apron like Katrene's. Oh, why didn't I think of making an apron?

She waited too long and heard Karl's heels on the floor. A few steps, then he paused. Was he studying the table? Is he wondering where I am? Will he think me stupidly childish when he discovers I have been hiding behind the curtain all this time? She pressed her hands to her cheeks again, but her palms seemed as hot as her face. She swung her feet to the floor and pulled the curtain open. In the pit of her stomach things were jumping and twitching like there were live frogs in there.

He was standing with his hands in his pockets, studying the table. The movement of the blanket as it was drawn aside caught his eye, and he looked up. Slowly, he withdrew his hands. Slowly, he lowered them to his sides.

Anna paused, holding onto the blanket.

The right thing to say eluded both of them, especially Karl.

Upon what should he make comment? Her table, set beguilingly with that crisp flowered cloth and the fresh blossoms she had gathered and placed in the homespun way his own mother used to do? Or should he mention the curtains she'd hung at the windows; they charmed him when at first he'd been so disappointed she was wasting the pink gingham on such things? Or the dress she had stitched as a surprise for him—simple, long-sleeved, full-skirted, matching those crisp, pink curtains? Or maybe her hair, her lovely, curling, Irish, whiskey-hair drawn severely into braids and wound into a coronet at the top of her head.

Karl searched his mind for the proper word. But, much like the first time he had ever laid eyes on her there was only one word he could say. It came out, as it had so often, questioning, wondering, telling, a response to all he saw before him, a question about all he saw before him. All he had, all he was, all he hoped to be was wrapped up in that single word: "Onnuh?"

She swallowed but her eyes stayed wide and unsure. She dropped the curtain, then clutched her hands behind her back.

"How was your swim, Karl?" she asked.

Unbelievably, he didn't answer.

"Was the water cold?" she tried again nervously.

Thankfully, he spoke, at last. "Not too cold." His cheeks and forehead were shiny clean, lean and tanned. His hair was freshly combed. The late afternoon sunlight came slanting in one of their precious glass windows, reflecting off his clean skin and hair, turning it even more golden. From clear across the room she thought she could smell his freshness.

"I see James got off all right."

"Ya. He is gone."

Her hands hurt. She suddenly realized her hands hurt. With a conscious effort she loosed them and brought them out of hiding. "Well . . ." she said, flipping them palms up in a nervous, little gesture.

Karl swallowed. "You have been busy while the boy and I were at the pond."

"A little," she said stupidly.

"More than a little, I think."

"Well, it's our first meal and all."

"Ya."

Silence again.

"So, did you and James get things talked over?"

"Ya. I don't know what good I did him, though. I am not so good at courting myself." He stuffed his hands into his pockets again.

Anna felt as if her tongue were paralyzed.

They stood there with only the sound of the fire snapping in the new wood stove, until finally Karl added, "He seemed to be a little less nervous by the time he left. The talk must have done him good."

"I thought it would."

"Ya."

Anna searched frantically for something to say. "Well, he sure didn't seem to mind missing supper with us."

"No, he didn't."

"Thank heavens for Nedda." Once she said it, she could have pinched her tongue!

"Well . . ." Karl said, much like she had a moment ago.

"Are you hungry, Karl?" she asked.

Hunger was the farthest thing from his mind, but he answered, "Ya, I am always hungry."

"I have supper started, but I need to do some last-minute things."

"There is no hurry."

"We could have some tea, though, while we wait."

"That would be good."

"Rose hip?" She saw Karl's Adam's apple lunge as he swallowed.

"Ya. Rose hip is fine."

"Well, sit down and I'll make it." She flapped one clumsy hand toward the ostentatious table and finally forced her feet to carry her to the stove.

Karl pulled out his chair, but stood next to it, watching as she reached for the container from the makeshift shelf on the wall next to the stove. "I wanted to have that dresser done for the kitchen by the time we moved in." he said.

"Oh, it doesn't matter. There's plenty of time to get it made when the weather turns cold and there's not much else to do. I think I'd enjoy the smell of the wood while you're working in the house."

"I have a tree picked out for it."

"Oh? What kind?"

"I decided on knotty pine. The knots look like jewels when they are polished up. Unless you would rather have oak or maple, Anna. I could use oak or maple."

He watched the sway of her skirts as she took the kettle and filled the pot with steaming water. She whirled around then, saying, "Oh, no, Karl, pine will be fine." But she whirled too fast and had to slap quickly at the lid of the teapot to keep it from flying off. He flinched as if to catch it if it came his way.

"Sit down, Karl, and I'll try not to scald you with the tea."

He thought about pulling her chair out for her, but she didn't go over to it. She stood beside his, waiting for him to roost. When he did, she bent to pour his tea, and he caught the distinct drift of camomile about her.

While she poured his tea, she apologized, "I'm sorry it's not comfrey. I know you like comfrey best. But I have a feeling you wouldn't have asked for it anyway, just because we don't have much left."

"It doesn't matter that the comfrey died. We can find more of it wild in the woods and transplant it in the spring."

"But you told me comfrey is your favorite."

"I like rose hip just as much."

She poured her own tea, then sat down opposite him. "The first drink you taught me to make," she said, raising her mug. "Here is to rose hips," she toasted, waiting with her mug aloft.

He followed her head and clicked his mug against hers, remembering the first night. He'd made her rose hip tea to calm her down before bedtime. "Here is to rose hips," he seconded.

They lifted the cups to their lips, looking first at each other, then sharply away, over the rims of their mugs.

"When did you get all this done?" he asked, scanning the cabin.

She shrugged her shoulders, limp yet from the hurrying.

"The flowers are . . . I like the flowers in the milk pitcher that way."

"Thank you."

"And the cloth on the table, too."

"Thank you," she repeated.

"And the curtains. You match the curtains, Anna," he said with a smile.

She too smiled. Funny, how they thought alike.

"I am a little camouflaged at that. You might have to search to find me."

"I do not think so, Anna," he said. "The gingham does not look the same on the windows and on the table as it does on you."

Damn my hands! she thought as one of them went up to brush down her collar like a simpering school girl.

"I was beginning to think I would have to make another trip to town for gingham if I did not want to see you in britches all winter."

"You did mean it for dresses, then?"

"I guess I was a little disappointed to see you using it all for curtains."

"Not quite all."

He lifted his cup toward her as a fencer might touch the tip of his sword to his fencing master. She lifted the tea pot to refill.

"The dress is lovely, Anna." The tea jiggled a bit on its way to his cup.

"It is?" she asked, as if she'd only now discovered it.

"Much better than the britches."

She couldn't help badgering him some more. "I kind of got used to those britches, though."

"I kind of did, too."

"Don't tease me, Karl," she said.

"Was I teasing?" he asked.

"I don't know. I think so."

"And you do not want me to tease you any more?"

Oh yes, her heart cried, like you used to do. But she had to say, "Not tonight," hoping he would read the rest in her eyes.

He nodded silently.

"I have some things to do. You sit here and enjoy your tea while I get things . . ." But her words trailed off. She got up self-consciously, knowing he would be watching everything she did. She took down the new japanned frying pan and placed it on the stove. She took up the bowl and the whisk and began breaking eggs, cracking them against the edge of the crock.

"Where did you get the eggs?" he asked.

"From Katrene, the other day when we went over there to fetch Erik to help with the bear. But I was saving them for tonight."

Again he fell silent, watching her as she whisked the eggs, then added them to the other dry things she had gotten ready in another bowl beforehand. She added milk, feeling his eyes on her back. When the batter was ready, she almost forgot and poured it into the pan without grease. But at the last minute she remembered, put a blob in the pan and sneaked a peek behind her to find Karl, indeed, watching her every move. The batter went sizzling into the pan, and she suddenly stamped her foot, remembering the jar of lingonberry jam still hidden in the root cellar.

"Oh! I forgot something. I'll be right back!" She ran at a most unladylike clip out the door, around the corner, and struggled with the ground-level door of the cellar. Down the steps she went, her skirts hindering her, worrying all the way how long it took Swedish pancakes to fry. The jar of jam was there, and she hurried back with it, dropped the cellar door in place and flew into the house to be greeted by the smell of scorching batter. She forgot to take up a pot holder, so the handle of the frying pan burned her hand when she reached to slide it to a cooler part of the stove.

Karl watched all this happening, not knowing if he should get up and flip the pancake over or let her do this her own way. It took every effort to stay where he was and let the pancake burn.

But when the japanned pan sang out in the quiet house, it echoed into too deep a silence. Anna's chin dropped down onto her chest, and from behind he saw the tender curls in the nape of her neck fighting to be free of the braids. Karl saw her pull up a forearm and swipe it across her eyes, realizing she was crying.

He got up from his chair and picked up the pot holders, took the frying pan and flipped the pancakes out the door. He came back and set the pan down on the stove, then stood behind Anna and placed both of his hands on her upper arms, squeezing lightly.

"I make a mess of everything I do," she wailed pitifully.

"No, Anna," he said encouragingly. "You have not made a mess of the curtains or the table or your dress, have you?"

"But look at this. Katrene showed me just how to do it, and I did everything like she said, but still, for me it's a disaster."

"You worry too much, Anna. You try too hard, and things upset you. Is there more batter you can fry?"

She nodded her head, dismally trying not to sniffle.

"Then put more on and start again."

"What for? They'll just be another disaster. Nothing I do ever turns out right."

He hated seeing her so defeated. If he could not get her to succeed at this attempt, which was so vital for both of them, he was afraid the beautiful beginning she had created would lead to nothing but defeat. He had to get her to smile a bit and try again. So, even though she had said she did not want to be teased tonight, he had to tease anyway.

"Perhaps the first ones were not such a disaster as you think. Nanna ate them this time."

She turned to look out the door, and sure enough! There stood Nanna, her happy face turned their way while she ground her teeth against the last of the burned pancakes. Anna gave a sorry little snuffle of laughter, wiped her eyes with the back of her wrists and resolutely picked up the batter and began pouring cakes again while Karl took his chair at the table.

This batch turned out perfectly, but Karl didn't know it until she brought the plate to him.

"I would like to wait until yours are done, then we will both eat together," he said.

"But these are all hot."

"Use the warming oven of your new stove to keep them that way while you cook yours."

"All right, Karl, if you say so."

Her failure to produce perfection immediately lost some of its sting as she placed the lovely cakes into the oven, then poured more. While she did this, she heard Karl get up and light tallow dips flanking the pitcher of flowers. She turned with the two plates again. The sun had gone away; the candles were welcome now as dusk settled.

"There now . . . see?" he said sensibly when she was seated across from him again, "these are beautiful pancakes you have made."

"Oh, Karl, you don't have to say that. The biggest dolt in the world can make pancakes."

"You are not the biggest dolt in the world, Anna," he said, so painfully sorry he'd called her dumb the day of their fight, realizing how those stinging words must have added to her sense of inadequacy.

"Well, almost," she said, staring at her plate.

"No," he insisted, "not even almost." They gazed at each other for some time before Karl asked, "Is that lingonberry jam you have there, or are you not going to let me find out?"

"Oh! Sure . . . here!" She handed it to him. "But I didn't make it. Katrene did. She gave it to me."

"Quit apologizing, Anna," he ordered gently.

Unconcernedly, he garnished his pancakes with lingonberry jam and began eating, looking at her across the table with his shining face as placid as the surface of the pond. Never in his life had Karl had to force himself to eat like he did now. For all he cared, the goat could come in and eat up pancakes, jam and all, right off the plates, and it would not concern him one bit. But for Anna, he knew he must eat these pancakes, and ask for more.

She picked at her food with pitiful interest; Karl was much better at acting than she was. She jumped up gratefully to fry more, when he asked for them. By the time she brought the second batch, the candlelight was intimate and disconcerting, limning as it did every expression that passed their faces as they stared—silently, most of the time now—at each other, across the pancakes and lingonberries, the cups and rose hips, the asters and loosestrife, the gingham and sweet clover.

When he finished, he leaned back and slung one arm around the backpost of his chair. "You never told me, Anna, what you thought of my gifts." Those blue eyes studied her in a way that turned her calves to the texture of Katrene's jam.

"I thanked you for the stove, Karl. I love the stove, you know that."

"I am not talking about the stove."

"The gingham?"

"Ya. The gingham."

"The gingham . . . I love the gingham. It's really made the place cheerful."

"I wanted to buy you a hat with a pink ribbon, but Morisette did not have any at this time of year."

"You did?" She was surprised and warmed by his even wanting to.

"Ya, I did. But I had to get you the soap instead."

She studied the tablecloth, picked at the edge of it absently with her thumbnail.

"I do like the soap, Karl. It's . . . it's very special."

"It took some doing to get that out of you."

"It took some doing to get that soap out of you," she said softly, thinking of all those bitter words they'd said the day he ran off in such anger.

"The night I brought it home, you did not seem to care much about it."

"I was saving it."

"For tonight?"

"Yes." She looked down at her lap.

"Like the eggs for the pancakes?"

She made no reply.

"How long have you been planning tonight?"

She only shrugged her shoulders.

"How long?" he repeated.

Her tear-filled eyes flashed in the candlelight as she looked beseechingly at him. "Oh, Karl, you came home that night and all you could talk about was Kerstin."

"And I will perhaps talk about Kerstin often. She is our friend, Anna. Do you understand that? She made me see things, made me talk about things that only a true friend could make me see."

Anna put her forehead in her hand and fought the tears. "I don't want to talk about Kerstin," she said wearily.

"But to talk about us, I must talk about Kerstin."

"Why, Karl?" She looked him squarely in the face again. "Because she's the one between us? Because she's the one you want?"

"Is that what you think, Anna?"

"Well, what am I supposed to think when ever since she came you have everything down the road you could have had if you'd only waited a few more weeks before bringing me here and marrying me?"

"Those are your words, Anna, not mine."

"Well, they're true," she accused with a touch of petulance. "Do you think I don't know how you feel when you're at their place? It shows, Karl. You . . . you're happy and smiling and talking Swedish and eating Swedish pancakes like you were back in Skåne again!"

Karl leaned forward, placing his forearms against the table edge, looking deep into her eyes. "Listen to me, Anna, and listen to yourself. You just said *their* place. That is what Kerstin made me see. It is *their* place that makes me happy. Yes, I am happy there, but it has nothing to do with Kerstin any more than the others there. But she made me see how it must look to you. That is why I must talk of her."

She sat across from him with her narrow shoulders pulled forward as she clasped her hands tightly between her knees. "Karl," she said plaintively, "I can never be Kerstin, not if I try for a thousand years."

His heart seemed broken and healed at once, broken for all the insecurity he had made her feel, but healed by the love that had driven her so far as to try to become what she thought he wanted. "Anna, Anna," he said with deep feeling, "I do not want you to be."

Suddenly she seemed confused. "But you said—"

"I have said many things that were better left unsaid, Anna."

"But Karl, she is everything you wanted for yourself, everything I lied about being . . . and more! She is twenty-four years old, and she can cook and keep house and raise gardens and talk Swedish and—"

"And wear her hair in braids?" Karl finished smilingly, raising his eyes briefly to her hair.

"Yes!" Anna answered wretchedly, "and wear braids."

"And so you thought you would try to be like her and it did not work?"

"Yes! I didn't know what else to do anymore." She sounded utterly miserable, felt utterly miserable. Karl was so tempting, sitting there in the candleglow talking all nice that way. Every time she met his eyes, she wanted to fly around the table and kiss him. Instead, she looked at her lap, clenching her hands tightly in bonds of pink gingham to keep them from reaching out to him.

"Did you think, Anna, that maybe it was not you who needed to change, but me?" he asked now, so softly.

"You?" Her head snapped up and she laughed a little too harshly. "Why, you're so perfect, Karl, any woman would be a fool to want you to change. There's not a single thing on this earth that you can't do or won't try or can't learn. You're patient, and you have a . . . a grand sense of humor, and you care about things so much, and you're honest and . . . and I have yet to see you defeated by anything. Why, I haven't found a single thing you don't know how to do."

"Except forgive, Anna," he admitted before the dusky room grew silent.

Flustered, she reached for her cup only to find it empty. But Karl captured her hand for a moment, then she pulled it away, clutched it between her knees again while she said, "Even that, Karl, you would not have had to do if you had waited for Kerstin. I'm sure of it."

"But I did not wait for Kerstin. That is the point. I had you, and I could not look past the one and only thing you could not change and try to forgive it. I have held onto my stubborn Swedish pride all these weeks, long after I could see that until I forgave you that one thing, you would not find pride in anything else you did."

"Karl, I can't change what I did." Her luminous eyes looked to him in supplication, which he knew she should not need to be feeling.

"I know that, Anna. It is something that Kerstin made me see. She made me see that I was wrong to hold it against you all this time."

"You . . . you talked with Kerstin about that, too?" she asked, aghast.

"No, Anna, no," he assured her. "It was about other things that we talked. About things like blueberry cobbler and an Irish girl who wants to have Swedish braids. She made me see you were trying to make up for things that did not need making up for, you were trying to be things you do not need to be. She made me see you were trying so hard to please me, you even try to be Swedish for me."

He arose from his chair and came to bend on one knee beside hers. "Anna," he said, putting both hands on her knees, "Anna, look at me." When she wouldn't he put a finger beneath her chin and raised it. He saw into the wide, brown eyes with the luminous teardrops quivering on their rims.

"Tonight you have done all this to please me. All the pretty gingham curtains and the flowers and this dress." His hand rose to her collar, and he took it between two fingers. His eyes rose to her hair, and an infinitely tender tone crept into his voice. "And these terrible braids that do not suit you at all because you have beautiful whiskey-hair that wants to curl its own way, flying free like it should be. All of this you do to win what was yours by rights from the first. Only I was too stubborn to give it to you. Do you know what that is, Anna?"

She thought he meant the right to his body, his lovemaking, but could hardly answer either of those. Instead, she remained silent.

"It is your pride, Anna," he went on. "Do you understand what I am saying?"

She shrugged her shoulders in a childish way.

"I am saying that when I walked into this cabin today I felt small and guilty at what I have made you do here. You have tried in all the good ways that make you my special little own Anna, to please me. All these weeks you have tried. But I make you do a thing like this."

"Don't . . . don't you like it, Karl?"

"Oh, Anna, my little Anna, I like it so much that it makes me want to cry. But I do not deserve it."

"Oh, Karl, you're wrong. You deserve so mu—"

He reached to cover her lips with his fingertips, stopping her words. "You are the one who deserves, Anna. More than I have given. It is not enough that I have taken up my axe and cut trees to build you a home and that I have cleared land and raised food for its table and bought you a stove and a bar of soap. A home is only a home because of the people in it. A home is only a home when it has love. And so if I give you all these things, what does it matter when I withhold myself?"

In his own fiercely honorable way, Karl kept his eyes glued to her face while he said all this. *When a man speaks of things which mean much to him, he does not hide it from showing in his face.* There, before Anna, all the pain and longing and want of Karl Lindstrom lay naked in the expression of his eyes upon hers, of his lips as he spoke, even in the hands that now stroked her hair, her collarbone, then the gingham skirt draped upon her knees.

"All these months, Anna, while I have planned this log house, I have dreamed about this first night in it and how it would be. I have thought of having you here and sitting with you at our table, and talking about things the way we would do after our supper was done. And always I dream of a fire in my hearth, and of loving you before it. Now, Anna, I find I have, by my own foolishness, almost lost all those things I worked so hard for. But I want them, Anna. I want them all, just like it is tonight. This beautiful table you have set, and you in your starchy little dress, and—"

But this time it was Anna who placed her trembling fingers over his lips, stilling them. "Then, why do you talk so long, Karl?" she whispered, her voice soft and quavering and yearning.

The hunger in his eyes spoke passionately, even before he reached to take her face between his two hands and bring it slowly toward his own. Lips parted, eyes closing, he touched her mouth hesitantly with his own while she sat too stunned to move.

"Forgive me, Anna," he whispered hoarsely, "forgive me for all these weeks."

Into his azure eyes Anna gazed wonderingly, wanting this moment to draw on into the forever of their years. "Oh, Karl, there is nothing to forgive. I'm the one who should be asking."

"No," he uttered, "you asked long ago, on the night you picked blueberries for me."

Still kneeling, he took her hands apart and lowered his face into them where they lay on her lap. He needed so badly to be touched by her, to be assured of her forgiveness now. She looked down at the back of his head, at the blond wisps that waved into the shadowed hollow of his neck. Her love surged in devastating swells that overflowed from her eyes, blurring Karl's image before her.

To Anna came the intrinsic understanding that he must have the words she alone could give. Karl. Karl who in all ways was good and loving and kind. Karl needed her absolution from a transgression of her own making. She felt his flesh upon her palm and moved her other hand to twine her fingers in his hair. "I forgive you, Karl," she said softly, knowing utter fullness at the words, at the look in his eyes as he raised them to her face again.

Then the expression on his countenance changed, beautified, intensified. He rose to his feet and grasped her upper arms to draw her inexorably up, up, too. He pulled her to his chest, leaning to kiss her, clutching her arms like they were his salvation. Then, suddenly he freed them, placed them around his neck, hungry for the clinging to start.

She came against him in a grasping, wild, tumultuous kiss that touched his body from nose to knees. Within her open mouth his tongue tasted salt tears mingling with the kiss, and he took them from her, stroking her tongue with his, swallowing the salt of her sadness, taking it into himself, that she should never again know tears because of him.

"Don't cry, Anna," he crooned, covering her face with kisses, holding the back of her head in both hands, as if she might slip away. "Never again, Anna," he promised, wiping away tears with his lips, then seeking the warmth of her neck, bending to her again, his face in the hollow of her gingham breasts now. Downward he kissed until he knelt on one knee with his face pressed to her stomach, drowning in the fragrance of camomile.

"Anna," he said against her, "I have loved you longer than you know."

She leaned her head back and her eyes slid closed as he cradled his head against her and held her with one arm while he ran a hand warmly, firmly, possessively, from the hollow of her back to the hollows behind her knees, then up again.

"How long, Karl?" she asked greedily, drifting in sensuousness while his hands played over her. "Tell me . . . Tell me everything you dreamed of telling me long before I came to you." Her voice was a joy-wracked whisper as his hands continued their reacquaintance with her curves.

"I have loved you when I did not know you existed, Anna. I have loved the dream of you. I have begun loving you before I left my mother's arms. I have loved you while I find this land to which I would bring you and while I cut its timbers to build this home for you and while I reap my grains for you and build my fire for you . . . I know all my life you are waiting somewhere for me."

"Karl, stand up," she whispered, she begged. "I have been waiting so long to feel you against me again."

He rose to his full height, running his hands up her legs, up her hips, up her ribs. She was waiting with seeking mouth for his return.

Together they clung and touched: faces, hair, shoulders, breasts, tongues, hips. Even the hollow of his spine was hers at last as she ran her hand down inside the back of his pants. "I can't believe you are letting me touch you at last," she said breathily, her voice a strange thing in both their ears: aroused, eager, throaty.

"Never ask. You never have to . . . Never, Anna." His eyes were closed, his breathing strained.

"Karl, how I used to watch you when you would lean to build the fire, and think of running my hands over you this way."

"And I watched you in those britches and wanted to put my hands here . . ." He fondled her breast, her stomach. "And here . . . and here . . ."

"You never have to ask either, Karl," she whispered, while his hands made free with her.

"Anna, I want to build a fire now. Do you want to watch me lean to build a fire?"

"Yes," she whispered.

"Always have I dreamed of a fire."

"Yes . . . yes . . ." she whispered, the waiting now a joyous agony.

"But I do not want you to ask anything while I do it."

"I won't ask, Karl," she whispered against his lips. "Go build your fire for me, but if I cannot ask, you cannot either."

"Only one thing, Anna, but now . . ."

Instead of asking what, she moved sinuously against him, blending her curves against his while her body promised what her words did not.

"Pull in our latchstring, Anna, and close our curtains that I did not think we needed."

He had to put her from him, turning her toward the door while he went to the fireplace and knelt before it. He shaved golden curls from the hardwood logs. And he heard the swish of one curtain after another whispering upon their willow withe curtain rods. He leaned to touch steel to flint and heard the gentle rap of the hazelnut swinging upon its string against the sturdy oak panels of his door. Keeping his face to the hearth he laid kindling to the growing flame, hearing the rustle of cornhusks behind him, then a strange brushing sound that whispered along the floor. But he gazed into the fire, kneeling upon one knee until her hand slid slowly down from his neck onto his shoulder, then down, down across his back and into the back of his pants to pull his shirttail up. She caressed his warm skin there, fanning her fingers upon him until he closed his eyes to the fire, basking instead in the heat of her touch.

"How I watched these shoulders in the sun," she whispered, raising his shirt as high as it would go, riding her hands up his back, then lowering her lips to the warm skin near a shoulder blade. Hunkered there on one knee, an arm cast out loosely, he dropped his forehead onto his biceps as she touched her tongue to his exposed back. "How I watched them, you'll never know."

He pivoted to face her then, finding her on both knees behind him, kneeling upon the heavy buffalo robe she had dragged over from the bed.

His hands moved onto her hips, pressing seductively. "Did you watch them like I watched these hips, bending over in those britches?" Now his hands swam upward along her ribs to her breasts again. "And how I wondered if I was mistaken about what was inside that shirt of your brother's."

She pressed against his palm, heat rising everywhere through her body now. "Were you mistaken?" she asked.

He had a handful of her firm breast, yet he answered, "There is only one way to find out when memory is dim."

He teased her buttons while she took lipfuls of his mouth, nipping gently at his lower lip.

"Memory can't recall what the eyes haven't seen, Karl," she whispered, braving a hand upon the inside of his knee as he knelt before her.

"But you have worked so hard on your pretty gingham dress. It is a shame it got so little use." Buttons came open one by breathtaking one.

"It would rather lie peacefully on the floor than get wrinkled and crushed," she whispered against his lips.

"Would it?" he asked through his kiss.

"You said no questions, Karl."

"These are not questions, Anna, these are answers."

Then Karl's hand found the warmth of her breast and followed the valley between her ribs to the warm, low place that hungered for his touch.

Her eyes blinked once, slowly, as the contact of his hand swept the breath from her. Open-eyed again, she moved her hand to cup him, taking her turn at answers.

They leaned into each other's hands. Karl's moved exploringly. Anna's followed suit. They kissed, touching, learning each other, asking questions with only their hands.

"Warm . . ." Karl murmured in her ear.

"Hard . . ." Anna murmured in answer.

"Beautiful . . ." he said, knowing before he saw.

"Beautiful . . ." she answered, knowing, too.

They lost their balance and clung. They regained it and separated, looking deeply into each other's faces by the fire that blazed. And then there were only vivid sensations.

Light and heat accompanying his hands as they moved down the remaining dress buttons, then fell away in invitation as he knelt with knees slightly apart before her. Heat and light on the movement of her fingers as they opened the line of his shirt buttons, then dropped obediently to her sides to wait. Gilded shoulder as he pushed the dress back and the fireplay danced along one side of her body. Golden skin as she answered by taking his shirt in her hands and wresting it from his shrug. Adoring eyes as he took the hem of her shift in both hands and pulled it upward until she raised her arms. Roving glances as they knelt, resplendent in the fire's light, letting the goodness build. Time holding its breath as he slowly plied her last barrier, curving his palms to the shape of her hips as he rustled her naked. Time beating at her breast as he dropped his hands to his thighs again, kneeling before her expectantly, waiting in the gold hue of the burning logs. The force of a long summer's love, moving her to reach out to this man and free him from the last restraint of woven threads.

And then there were only two lovers, kneeling in the glow that limned their bodies in fireshine, that splashed a half of each with orange, that picked the radiance from one pair of eyes and sent it dancing to another, eyes that wandered and worshiped, widened and wondered.

When Karl at last raised his eyes to Anna's, he beheld there a breathless wonder to match his own. Moved by it he forgot himself and spoke to her in Swedish. The lilting mellifluousness fell from his tongue as a song in Anna's ears, although she did not know what he said.

How ever could she have taunted him for this mellow, musical richness? It was, she knew now, a part of Karl she loved as much as his muscled body, his golden face, his patience and inherent goodness. She suddenly wished to understand the songful words he spoke to her in such a reverent tone.

"What did you say, Karl?" she asked, her misty eyes lifting to his.

Running a finger beneath her jaw, down the rim of light that gilded her chin, neck, breast, stomach, thigh and knee, he spoke this time in English. "Anna, you are beautiful."

"No, say it in Swedish. Teach me to say it in Swedish."

She watched his lips form the strange sounds. He had beautiful, bowed lips, a little full, very sensual now as he repeated, "*Du ar vacker, Anna.*"

Touching his lips, searching his face, she repeated, "*Du ar vacker, Karl.*" With her fingertips still touching his skin, he said, "*Jag älskar dig.*" The way his eyes closed when the words were gone, the way he pursed his lips and cupped her palm hard against his mouth, she knew even before he repeated it, what it meant.

"*Jag älskar dig, Anna,*" he said, the beautiful pronunciation, *Onnuh,* making her heart dance crazily.

"*Jag älskar dig,*" Anna said softly, her Swedish sounding Yankee, but the meaning ringing forth, no matter what the language. "What did I say, Karl?" she asked in a whisper.

"You said that you love me."

She took his face between her hands to kiss it. "*Jag älskar dig,*" she repeated, "*Jag älskar dig, Jag älskar dig, Karl,*" planting fevered kisses across his skin until she again forced his eyes closed.

Their warm flesh met. He took her tumbling down and over, until she felt soft fur below, firm flesh above, sandwiched between the two textures.

He clasped her, caressed her, kissing, learning what pleasured her when she smiled and nuzzled, then arched and moaned. With hands and tongue he brought her to a precipice where she trembled, waiting for the plunge that would carry her over. But the low sounds from her throat told him then to play her more slowly, extending the pleasure they found, each in the other.

He rolled over onto his back and stretched, taking every touch she gave, savoring the feel of her hands and lips becoming intimate with his honed body.

And then Anna slipped down and lay atop him, pressing warm and firm against him with breasts, belly, hips. Her braids had fallen down, the strands of her hair like filaments of the fire itself, surrounding her girlish face. He found a loose end, his fingers working it looser while she lay above him, kissing his neck and chest, meandering downward, downward. Soon he forgot her braids.

The two of them curled their bodies together, changed directions, kissing, tasting, trying to get enough, unable to. They gave each part of themselves freely, letting their senses expand beneath the joy. And when they hovered near their climaxes, righted again, shivering with anticipation, he made her say it one more time to compound his joy.

"Tell me again, Anna," he uttered fiercely, one hand twined in her hair, the other touching her depths as she moved rhythmically against it. "Tell me you love me like I love you."

"*Jag älskar dig.* I love you, Karl," she said, almost savagely, underlining the meaning of this act they now shared.

Once again they found the remembered magnificence from their first time, the grace in the blending of their bodies as he entered her, the litheness of movement as they flowed into a rhythm of mutual thrust and ebb.

They passed the bounds of language, creating a new one of their own, built of lovesounds—wordless murmurs, racked breathing, throbbing silences, pleasured moans. When their strength and suppleness brought them to the limits of fulfillment, they spoke the universal language: the deep, masculine shudder and groan, the strangled female response. Then together they collapsed, spent, in sated silence, with only the pop and titter of the fire sharing their communion.

He rested in her, at peace after all this time. She stroked the damp hair at the nape of his neck. His shoulders were drying now, beneath the touch of her fingers and the fire. His mouth rested in the depth of her neck.

When they had rested so for a long time, she spoke to the ceiling where the shadows danced. "Karl, do you know what you are like?"

He spoke to her neck. "What am I like?"

She wondered if she dared tell him, yet it was there on her mind, had been there since she first touched him, since before she had first touched him.

"You're like your axe handle when you have just laid it down."

He braced himself up to look into her face. "Like my axe handle?" he asked, puzzled.

"Smooth, warm, long, hard, curved . . . and like you once said, springy."

"Not any more, I am not," he said, smiling.

"I knew you would tease me if I told you."

"Yes," he said, kissing her nose. "From now on I shall tease my Anna so she will never forget the feel of an axe handle."

"Oh, Karl . . ." But her laugh came splashing.

"How I have missed that laugh," he said.

"How I've missed your teasing."

They smiled into each other's faces.

"Oh, Anna, you are something," he said, gloriously happy. He let his eyes wander all over her face and hair.

"What am I?" she probed.

But he could not liken her to anything he knew. Nothing else was as good as she. "I do not know what you are. I only know what you are not. You are not Swedish, and so you must not put these awful braids in that Irish hair of yours ever again. I tried to get them out, but I have only made them worse." Then seeing her concern, soothed it. "No, not now, Anna. You are a tempting little mess, so just leave it. And you are not fat and you are not the best cook and you are not the best gardener, but I do not care, Anna. I want you just as you are."

"All right, Karl," she said, looping her arms about his neck. "I promise I won't ever change."

"Good," he said.

"But, Karl?"

"Ya?"

"If you're going to the trouble of teaching me to read and write this winter, you might as well teach me in both languages, right off the bat."

He could only laugh and kiss her again, saying, "Oh, Anna, you are something."

When the night sounds were hushed and even the nocturnal creatures seemed abed, Anna and Karl joined them.

"Put the latchstring out for the boy, Anna," Karl said, while he lifted the heavy buffalo robe and took it to their rope bed in the corner.

Anna opened the door and stood gazing out at the night for a moment. "Karl, I really never felt what you did about this place and all its plenty until I thought I had lost you. But I know now. I really know."

"Come to bed, Anna."

She smiled over her shoulder, then closed the door and padded across the newly hewn boards of the floor to the candlelight at their bedside.

Karl stood waiting there for her.

And in the center of the bed, between their two pillows, lay a single shaft of sweet clover, plucked from the bouquet that had graced their dinner table, where lingonberry jam now dried on two forgotten plates.

BITTER SWEET

Chapter 1

❧

The room held a small refrigerator stocked with apple juice and soft drinks, a two-burner hot plate, a phonograph, a circle of worn, comfortable chairs and a smeared green chalkboard that said GRIEF GROUP 2:00–3:00.

Maggie Stearn entered with five minutes to spare, hung up her raincoat and helped herself to a tea bag and hot water. Bobbing the bag in a Styrofoam cup, she ambled across the room.

At the window she looked down. On the ship canal below, the water, pocked by the first of the August monsoons, seemed brooding and oily. The buildings of Seattle registered only in memory while Puget Sound hid behind a rainy curtain of gray. A rust-streaked tanker lumbered along the murky canal, ocean-bound, its rails and navigational aerials obscured by the downpour. On its weatherstained deck merchant marines stood motionless—blurred yellow blobs wrapped head to hip in oilskin slickers.

Rain. So much rain, and the entire winter of it ahead.

She sighed, thinking of facing it alone, and turned from the window just as two other members of the group arrived.

"Hi, Maggie," they said in unison from the door: Diane, thirty-six, whose husband had died when a blood vessel burst in his brain while they were clamming on Whidbey Island with their three kids; and Nelda, sixty-two, whose husband fell from a roof he was shingling and never got up again.

Without Diane and Nelda, Maggie wasn't sure how she'd have survived this last year.

"Hi," she returned, smiling.

Crossing the room, Diane asked, "How did the date go?"

Maggie grimaced. "Don't ask."

"That bad, huh?"

"How do you get over feeling married when you're not anymore?" It was a question all of them were striving to answer.

"I know what you mean," Nelda put in. "I finally went to bingo with George—you remember, I told you about him, the man from my church? All night long I felt like I was cheating on Lou. Playing *bingo*, mind you!"

While they commiserated, a man joined them, thin and balding, in his late fifties, wearing unfashionable pleated pants and a decrepit sweater that hung on his bony frame.

"Hi, Cliff." They widened their circle to let him in.

Cliff nodded. He was the newest member of the group. His wife had died when she ran a red light during her first time out driving after carotid surgery that had left her with no peripheral vision.

"How was your week?" Maggie asked him.

"Oh . . ." The word came out with a sigh and a shrug, but he offered no more.

Maggie rubbed his back. "Some weeks are better than others. It takes time." She'd had her own back rubbed more than once in this room and knew the healing power of a human touch.

"What about you?" Nelda turned the focus on Maggie. "Your daughter leaves for college this week, right?"

"Yup," Maggie replied with false brightness. "Two more days."

"I've been through that with three of my own. You call if it gets rough, will you? We'll go out and see some male strippers or something."

Maggie laughed. Nelda would no more go see a stripper than she would become one herself. "I wouldn't even know what to do with a stripped male anymore." All of them laughed. It was easier to laugh about the dearth of sex in their lives than it was to do something about it.

Dr. Feldstein walked in, a clipboard in one hand and a mug of steaming coffee in the other, talking with Claire, who'd lost her sixteen-year-old daughter in a motorcycle accident. Amid an exchange of greetings Dr. Feldstein shut the door and headed for his favorite chair, setting his coffee on a nearby table.

"Looks like everyone's here. Let's get started."

They all took seats, conversation trailing off, a group of healing people who cared about one another. Maggie sat on the brown sofa between Cliff and Nelda, Diane on the floor on a fat blue cushion and Claire in a chair to Dr. Feldstein's right.

It was Maggie who noted the absence. Glancing around she asked, "Shouldn't we wait for Tammi?" Tammi was their youngest, only twenty, unmarried, pregnant, abandoned by the father of the baby and struggling to overcome the recent loss of both of her parents. Tammi was everybody's darling, a surrogate daughter to everyone in the group.

Dr. Feldstein set his clipboard on the floor and replied, "Tammi won't be with us today."

Every eye fixed on him but nobody asked.

With his elbows resting on the wooden arms of his chair, Dr. Feldstein linked his hands over his stomach.

"Tammi took an overdose of sleeping pills two days ago and she's still in intensive care. We're going to be dealing with that today."

The shock hit them full force, stunning them into silence. Maggie felt it explode like a small bomb in her stomach and spread to her extremities. She stared at the doctor with his long, intelligent face, slightly hooked nose and full, cranberry-colored lips within a thick black beard. His eyes touched every member of the group—shrewd black eyes with flat violet planes beneath—watching their reaction.

Maggie finally broke the silence to ask what they were all wondering. "Will she live?"

"We don't know that yet. She's developed Tylenol poisoning so it's touch and go."

From outside came the faint bellow of a foghorn on the ship canal below. Inside, the group sat motionless, their tears beginning to build.

Claire leapt to her feet and stormed to the window, thumping the ledge with both fists. "Goddamn it! Why did she do it!"

"Why didn't she call one of us?" Maggie asked. "We would have helped her."

They'd struggled with it before—the helplessness, the anger in the face of that helplessness. Every person in the circle felt the same, for a setback suffered by one of them was a setback suffered by all. They had invested time and tears in each other, had trusted each other with their innermost hurts and fears. To think they could work this hard and have it backfire was tantamount to being betrayed.

Cliff sat motionless, blinking hard.

Diane sniffed and lowered her forehead to her updrawn knees.

Dr. Feldstein reached behind his chair and snagged a box of Kleenex from the top of the phonograph, stretched to place it on the table in the middle of the circle.

"All right, let's start with the basics," he said in a no-nonsense tone. "If she chose not to call any of us, there was no way we could have helped her."

"But she *is* us," Margaret reasoned, spreading her hands. "I mean, we're all striving for the same things here, aren't we? And we thought we were making headway."

"And if she could do it, none of you are safe, right?" Dr. Feldstein demanded before answering his own question. "Wrong! That's the first thing I want to fix in your minds. Tammi made a choice. Each of you makes choices every day. It's all right for you to be angry that she's done this, but it's not all right to see yourself in her place."

They talked about it, a long discussion filled with passion and compassion, that grew more animated as it lengthened. They worked past their anger until it became pity, and past the pity until it became renewed ardor to do all they could to make their own lives better. When they'd worked through their feelings, Dr. Feldstein announced, "We're going to do an exercise today, something I believe each of you is ready for. If you're not, you only have to pass—no questions asked. But for those of you who want to turn around that feeling of helplessness you've experienced because of Tammi's suicide attempt, I believe it will help."

He rose and placed a hard wooden chair in the center of the room. "We're going to say good-bye today to someone or something that has hindered our getting better. Someone who's left us through death, or maybe voluntarily, or something we haven't been able to face. It could be someplace we haven't been able to go to or an old grudge we've carried around for too long. Whatever it is, we're going to put it in that chair and say good-bye to it aloud. And when we've said good-bye, we're going to let that person or that thing know what we're going to do now to make ourselves happier. Do you all understand?" When nobody replied, Dr. Feldstein said, "I'll be first."

He stood before the vacant chair, opened his jaws wide and ran both palms down his beard. He drew a deep breath, looked at the floor, then at the chair.

"I'm going to say good-bye once and for all to my cigarettes. I gave you up over two years ago but I still reach toward my breast pocket for you, so I've put you in that chair and to you I say, so long, Dorals. I'm going to make myself happier in the future by giving up my resentment at quitting smoking. From now on, every time I reach for my pocket, instead of silently cursing because I find it empty, I'm going to silently thank myself for the gift I've given me." He waved at the chair. "Good-bye, Dorals."

He moved back to his own place and sat.

The tears were gone from the faces around him. In their place was candid introspection.

"Claire?" Dr. Feldstein said softly.

Claire sat a full minute without moving. No one spoke a word. Finally she rose and faced the chair.

When no words came, Dr. Feldstein asked, "Who's in the chair, Claire?"

"My daughter, Jessica," she managed.

"And what would you like to say to Jessica?"

Claire wiped her hands on her thighs and swallowed. Everyone waited. At length she began. "I miss you a lot, Jess, but after this I'm not going to let it control my life anymore. I've got a lot of years left, and I need to make me happy before your dad and your sister can be happy, too. And the thing I'm going to do to start is to go home and take your clothes out of your closet and give them to the Goodwill. So this is good-bye, Jess." She headed for her chair, then turned back. "Oh, and I'm also going to forgive you for not wearing your helmet that day because I know now that's been getting in the way of my getting well, too." She raised a hand. "Bye, Jess."

Maggie felt her eyes sting and watched through a blur as Claire sat down and Diane took her place.

"The person in the chair is my husband, Tim." Diane wiped her eyes hard with a tissue. She opened her mouth, closed it and dropped her head into one hand. "This is so hard," she whispered.

"Would you rather wait?" Dr. Feldstein asked.

Again she swabbed her eyes with stubborn determination. "No. I want to do it." She fixed her gaze on the chair, hardened her chin and began. "I've been really pissed off at you, Tim, for dying. I mean, you and I went together since high school, and I'd planned on another fifty years, you know?" The Kleenex hit her eyes once more. "Well, I just want you to know I'm not pissed off anymore, because you probably planned on fifty, too, so what right have I got, huh? And what I'm going to do . . ." She opened one palm wide and scratched at it with the opposite thumbnail, then looked up. ". . . what I'm going to do to make myself better is to take the kids and go up to our cabin on Whidbey this weekend. They've been begging to go and I keep saying no, but now I will, because until I'm better, how can they be happy? So, bye, Tim. Hang loose, huh, guy?"

She hurried to her place and sat down.

Everyone around the circle dried their eyes.

"Cliff?" Dr. Feldstein invited.

"I want to pass," Cliff whispered, looking at his lap.

"Fine. Nelda?"

Nelda said, "I said my good-byes to Carl a long time ago. I'll pass."

"Maggie?"

Maggie rose slowly and approached the chair. Upon it sat Phillip, with the ten extra pounds he could never seem to lose after reaching age thirty, with his green eyes that bordered on brown and his sandy hair in need of cutting (as it had been when he'd gotten on that plane) and his favorite Seahawks sweatshirt that she hadn't washed yet but occasionally took from the hook in the closet and smelled. She felt terrified of giving up her grief, terrified that when it left there'd be nothing in its stead and she'd be an apathetic shell incapable of feeling in any way at all. She rested an open hand on the top oak rung of the chair and drew an unsteady breath. "Well, Phillip," she began, "it's been a whole year, so it's time. I'm like Diane I guess, a little pissed off because you went on that plane for such a stupid reason—a gambling junket, when your gambling was the only thing I ever resented. No, that's not true. I've also resented the fact that you died just when Katy was about to graduate from high school and we could start traveling more and enjoying our freedom. But I promise I'll get over that and start traveling without you. Soon. Also, I'm going to stop thinking of the insurance money as blood money so I can enjoy it a little more, and I'm going to try again with Mother because I think I'm going to need her now that Katy will be gone." She stepped back and fanned an open hand. "So, good-bye, Phillip. I loved you."

After Maggie was finished they sat a long time in silence. Finally Dr. Feldstein asked, "How do you feel?" It took some time before they answered.

"Tired," Diane said.

"Better," Claire admitted.

"Relieved," Maggie said.

Dr. Feldstein gave them a moment to acclimate to these feelings before leaning forward and speaking in his rich, resonant voice. "They're bygones now, all those old feelings that you've been carrying around long enough that have been keeping you from getting better. Remember that. I think, without them, you're going to be happier, more receptive to healthy thoughts."

He sat back.

"In spite of all that, it's not going to be an easy week. You're going to worry about Tammi, and that worry is going to translate into depression, so I'm going to give you another prescription for when that happens. This is what I want you to do. Look up old friends, the older the better, friends you've lost touch with—call them, write to them, try to get together with them."

"You mean high school friends?" Maggie inquired.

"Sure. Talk about old times, laugh about the ridiculous things you did when you were too young to have more sense. Those days represent a time in life when most of us were at our most carefree. All we had to do, basically, was go to school, pull fairly respectable grades, handle a part-time job maybe, and have a lot of fun. By going back into the past we can often pull our present into perspective. Try it and see how you feel." He glanced at his watch. "Then we'll talk about it at our next session. Okay?"

The room became filled with the soft shuffle of movement signaling the end of the hour. People stretched and hitched themselves to the edges of their chairs and tucked away their sodden Kleenexes. "We've covered a lot of ground today," Dr. Feldstein said, rising. "I think we did very well."

Maggie walked to the elevator with Nelda. She felt closer to her than to any of the others, for their situations were most similar. Nelda could be a bit twittery and vacant at times, but she had a heart of gold and an unfailing sense of humor.

"Have you kept in touch with friends from that long ago?" Nelda asked.

"No, it's been a while. Have you?"

"Lord, girl, I'm sixty-two years old. I'm not even sure I can find some of mine anymore."

"Do you intend to try?"

"I might. I'll see." In the lobby they paused to adjust their rain gear and Nelda reached up for a parting hug. "Now you remember what I said. When your daughter leaves, you just give me a call."

"I will. I promise."

Outside, the rain drummed heavily, lifting miniature explosions in the puddles on the street. Maggie snapped open her umbrella and headed for her car. By the time she reached it her feet were wet, her raincoat streaming, and she was chilled clear through. She started the engine and sat a minute, her hands folded between her knees, watching her breath condense on the windows before the defroster could clear it.

It had been a particularly draining session. So much to think about: Tammi, her good-bye to Phillip, how she was going to carry out the promises she'd made, Katy's leaving—she hadn't even had a chance to bring it up, but it loomed above all other concerns, threatening to undo each bit of progress she'd made in the past year.

The weather didn't help any. Lord, she got so tired of the rain.

But Katy was still home and they had two more suppers together. Maybe tonight she'd make Katy's favorite, spaghetti and meatballs, and afterward they could build a fire in the fireplace and make plans for Thanksgiving when Katy would come home on break.

Maggie turned on the windshield wipers and headed home, out across Montlake Bridge that hummed beneath the tires like a dentist's drill, then north toward Redmond. As the car began climbing into the foothills, the sharp, resinous scent of pines was drawn inside by the ventilation system. She passed the entrance to Bear Creek Country Club, where she and Phillip had been members for years, where, since his death, more than one of their married male friends had made advances toward her. The country club had lost its appeal in more than one way since Phillip's death.

On Lucken Lane she pulled into a driveway before a ranch-style house constructed of weathered cedar and burnt orange brick, situated on the side of a wooded hill, a middle-class house with neatly tended marigolds lining the front walk and potted geraniums standing sentinel on either side of the front steps. A touch of the activator lifted the garage door and Maggie saw with disappointment that Katy's car was gone.

In the kitchen, the silence was broken only by the sound of rain dropping through the downspout outside the window and the garage door rumbling to a stop. On the table beside a half-eaten English muffin and a hot-pink hair clamp lay a note scrawled on a pad shaped like a blue foot.

Gone shopping with Smitty and to pick up a few more empty boxes. Don't fix supper for me. Love, K.

Stifling her disappointment, Maggie removed her coat and hung it in the front closet. She wandered down the hall and stopped in the doorway of Katy's room. Clothing lay everywhere, stacked, boxed, thrown across half-filled suitcases. Two giant black plastic bags, plump with discards, lay between the bifold closet doors. A pile of jeans and another of brightly colored sweatshirts waited at the foot of the bed to be laundered. Only the top half of the dresser mirror showed; the lower portion was hidden behind a stack of *Seventeen* magazines and a laundry basket filled with neatly folded towels and new bed linens, still in their plastic wrappers, waiting to make the move to Chicago. Strewn across the floor, separated only by narrow paths lay seventeen years' worth of memories: a pile of portfolios fat with old school papers, their top sides covered with graffiti; a softball cap and a mitt for a twelve-year-old hand; two corsages, one dried and yellowed, the other with tea roses still pink; a dusty poster of Bruce Springsteen; a shoebox full of graduation cards and unused thank-you notes; another of perfume bottles; a bill-cap full of tangled earrings and cheap plastic rope beads; a pile of stuffed animals; a French horn case; a mauve basket holding recent correspondence from Northwestern University.

Northwestern, her and Phillip's alma mater, halfway across America. Why hadn't Katy chosen the U here instead? To get away from a mother who hadn't been the most cheerful company during the past year?

Feeling tears build in her throat, Maggie turned away, determined to make it through the remainder of the day without breaking down. In her own bedroom she avoided glancing at the queen-sized bed and the memories it evoked. Marching straight to the mirrored closet, she slid open a door, pulled out Phillip's Seahawks sweatshirt and returned to Katy's room where she buried it in one of the bags of discards.

Back in her own room she pulled on an oversized set of red-and-white Pepsi sweats, then marched into the adjacent bathroom where she found a miniature pot of makeup and began dabbing some on the purple shadows beneath her eyes.

Midway through the task, tears began to build and her hands dropped. Who was she kidding? She looked like a forty-year-old scarecrow. Since Phillip's death she'd dropped from a size 12 to a size 8, lost a full bra size, and her auburn hair had lost its luster because she never ate right anymore. She didn't give a damn about cooking, or going back to work, or cleaning the house, or dressing decently. She did it because she knew she had to and because she didn't want to end up like Tammi.

She stared at the mirror.

I miss him and I want so damned badly to cry.

After fifteen seconds of self-pity she slammed the makeup into a drawer, switched off the light and spun from the room.

In the kitchen she wet a dishcloth and wiped up Katy's muffin crumbs. But on her way to the garbage disposal she made the mistake of taking a bite of the cold muffin. The taste of cinnamon and raisin spread with peanut butter—a favorite of both Katy and her father—keyed a reaction too powerful to fight any longer. Once more the dreaded tears came— hot, burning.

She threw the muffin into the sink with such force it ricocheted off the opposite side and landed beside the flour canister. She gripped the edge of the counter and doubled forward at the waist.

Damn you, Phillip, why did you go on that plane? You should be here now. We should be going through this together!

But Phillip was gone. And Katy soon would be. And what then? A lifetime of suppers alone?

Two days later Maggie stood in the driveway beside Katy's car, watching her daughter stuff one last tote bag behind the seat. The predawn air was chill, and mist formed a nimbus around the garage lights. Katy's car was new, expensive, a convertible with every conceivable option, paid for with a minute fraction of the insurance money from Phillip's death: a consolation prize from the airline for Katy's having to go fatherless for the remainder of her life.

"There, that's it." Katy straightened and dropped the seat back into place. She turned to Maggie—a pretty, young woman with her father's brown eyes, Maggie's cleft chin, and a cosmic hairdo appropriate for the cover of a science fiction novel, a look to which her mother had never grown accustomed. Viewing it now, at the hour of parting, Maggie recalled with a pang of nostalgia when it had been downy and she'd combed it in a top curl.

Katy broke the sad silence. "Thanks for the peanut-butter muffins, Mom. They'll taste good around Spokane or so."

"I put some apples in there, too, and a couple cans of cherry Coke for each of you. Now are you sure you've got enough money?"

"I've got everything, Mom."

"Remember what I said about speeding on the interstates."

"I'll use the cruise control, don't worry."

"And if you get sleepy—"

"Let Smitty drive. I know, Mom."

"I'm so glad she's going with you, that you'll be together."

"So am I."

"Well . . ."

The reality of parting crowded in; they had grown so close in the last year, since Phillip's death.

"I'd better go," Katy said quietly. "I told Smitty I'd be at her house at five-thirty sharp."

"Yes, you'd better."

Their eyes met, misty with good-bye, and sorrow created an awesome gulf between them.

"Oh, Mom . . ." Katy dove into her mother's arms, clinging hard, her blue jeans lost in the folds of Maggie's long quilted robe. "I'm going to miss you."

"I'll miss you, too, honey." Pressed breast to breast, with the scent of marigolds hanging musty-strong in the air and droplets of moisture plopping off the house roof onto the flower beds below, they exchanged a heartrending good-bye.

"Thanks for letting me go, and for everything you bought."

A mere movement of Maggie's head answered; her throat was too constricted to emit a sound.

"I hate leaving you here alone."

"I know." Maggie held her daughter fast, feeling the tears—her own? Katy's?—run in warm trickles down her neck, and Katy clinging hard and rocking her from side to side.

"I love you, Mom."

"I love you, too."

"And I'll be home for Thanksgiving."

"I'll count on that. Be careful, and call really often."

"I will. I promise."

They walked to the car, hip to hip, chins down, idling. "You know, it's hard to believe you're the same little girl who threw such a fit when I left her the first day of kindergarten." Maggie rubbed Katy's arm.

Katy gave the obligatory laugh as she slid into the driver's seat.

"I'm going to be one hell of a child psychologist though, 'cause I understand days like that." She looked up at her mother. "And days like this."

Their eyes exchanged a final good-bye.

Katy started the engine, Maggie slammed the door and leaned on it with both hands. The headlights came on, throwing a cone of gold into the dense haze of the wooded yard. Through the open window, Maggie kissed her daughter's lips.

"Keep mellow," Katy said.

Maggie gave their familiar all-level sign.

"Bye," Katy mouthed.

"Bye," Maggie tried to say, but only her lips moved.

The car engine purred a dolorous note as the vehicle backed down the driveway, turned, stopped, changed gears. Then it was gone, the tires hissing softly on the wet pavement, leaving a last memory of a young girl's hand waving out the open window.

Left behind in the quiet, Maggie gripped her arms, tilted her head back to its limits and searched for a hint of dawn. The tips of the pines remained invisible against the ebony sky. Droplets still fell into the marigold bed. She experienced a slight lightheadedness, a queer out-of-body sensation, as if she were Maggie Stearn, but standing apart, watching for her own reaction. To fall apart would mean certain disaster. Instead, she walked around the house, soaking her slippers in the wet grass and collecting scratchy pine needles in the hem of her robe. Heedless of them she moved past trapezoids of incandescence slanting into the yard from the windows of the bathroom, where Katy had taken her last shower, and from the kitchen, where she'd eaten her last breakfast.

I will get through this day. Just this one. And the next will be easier. And the next easier yet.

At the rear of the house she straightened a clump of petunias that had been flattened by the rain; brushed two fallen pinecones off the redwood deck; replaced three pieces of firewood that had tumbled from the tier against the rear garage wall.

The aluminum extension ladder lay on the north side of the garage. *You must put that away. It's been there since you cleaned the pine needles out of the gutters last spring. What would Phillip say?* But she walked on, leaving the ladder where it was.

In the garage her car was parked, a new luxurious Lincoln Town Car, purchased with Phillip's death money. She passed it, heading up the walk between the marigold borders. On the front step she sat, huddled, wrapped in her own arms, the moisture from the wet concrete seeping through her robe.

Afraid. Lonely. Despairing.

Thinking about Tammi and how loneliness like this had driven her over the edge. Afraid she wouldn't recognize it if she ever got that bad.

She made it through that first day by going to Woodinville High School and puttering around the home ec rooms. The building felt deserted, only the office staff working, the other faculty members not due back for another week and a half. Alone in the neat, spacious rooms, she oiled the sewing machines, scoured some sinks that had been used for summer school, unearthed dittoes and ran off copies of several first-day handouts, and decorated a bulletin board: TRUE BLUE—DENIM CLOTHING CONSTRUCTION FOR FALL.

She didn't give a damn about denim or its construction. The prospect of another year of teaching the same thing she'd been teaching for fifteen years seemed as pointless as cooking for one.

In the afternoon the house waited, permanently empty, filled with wrenching memories of the place astir with the daily activities of three. She called the hospital to check on Tammi and learned that her condition was still critical.

For supper she fried two slices of French toast and sat down to eat them at the kitchen counter, accompanied by the evening news on a ten-inch TV. In the middle of her meal the phone rang and she leapt to answer it, expecting to hear Katy's voice saying she was all right and in a motel somewhere near Butte, Montana. Instead Maggie heard a recorded voice, a trained baritone with canned conviviality following a mechanical pause. ". . . Hello! . . . I have an important message for you from . . ."

She slammed down the receiver and stared at it in revulsion, as if its message had been obscene. She spun away angrily, feeling somehow threatened by the fact that the instrument whose ring had often been a source of irritation in the past could now raise her pulse with anticipation.

The remaining half-slice of French toast swam before her eyes. Without bothering to throw it away she wandered into the study and sat in Phillip's large green leather chair, gripping the arms, pressing her head against its padded back, as he had often sat.

If she'd had Phillip's Seahawks sweatshirt, she'd have put it on, but it was gone, so instead she dialed Nelda. The phone rang thirteen times without an answer. Next she tried Diane, but it rang and rang and Maggie finally realized Diane had probably gone up to Whidbey Island with her kids. At Claire's she got an answer, but Claire's daughter said her mother had gone to a meeting and wouldn't be back until late.

She hung up and sat staring at the phone with a thumbnail between the teeth.

Cliff? She threw her head back in the chair. Poor Cliff couldn't resolve his own loss much less help anyone else resolve theirs.

She thought about her mother, but the thought brought a shudder.

Only when all her other possibilities were exhausted did Maggie remember Dr. Feldstein's prescription.

Call old friends, the older the better, friends you've lost touch with . . .

But who?

The answer came as if preordained: Brookie.

The name brought a flash of memory so vivid it seemed as if it had happened only yesterday. She and Glenda Holbrook—both altos—were standing side by side in the front row of the Gibraltar High School Choir, mercilessly aggravating the choir director, Mr. Pruitt, by softly humming an unauthorized note on the final chord of the song, making of an unadulterated C-major, an impertinent, jazzy C-seventh.

Ain't-a that good news, lord, ain't-a that good newwwwws?

Sometimes Pruitt would let their creativity pass, but more often he'd frown and wag a finger to restore purity to the chord. One time he'd stopped the entire choir and ordered, "Holbrook and Pearson, go stand out in the hall and sing your dissonant notes to your hearts' content.

When you're ready to sing the music the way it's written, you can come back in.''

Glenda Holbrook and Maggie Pearson had been first graders together. They had been stood in the corner for whispering on the second day of school. In the third grade they'd received scoldings from the school principal for breaking off Timothy Ostmeier's front tooth when a rock was thrown in the middle of an acorn fight, though neither girl would divulge who'd thrown it. In the fifth grade they'd been caught by Miss Hartman during noon recess with pointed Dixie cups inside their blouses. Miss Hartman, a flat-chested, sour-faced spinster with one crossed eye, opened the door of the girls' lavatory at the very moment Glenda had said, "If we had titties like this we could probably be movie stars!" In the sixth grade the girls along with Lisa Eidelbach had won praises for singing in three-part harmony, "Three White Doves Went Seaward Flying" for a monthly meeting of the PTA. In junior high they had attended Bible Study Class together and had penciled into their Bible Study books clever, irreverent answers to the questions. In the margins of their health books they'd drawn stupendous male body parts, years before they knew what those parts really looked like.

In senior high they'd been cheerleaders, nursing aching muscles after the first practice of the season, making blue-and-gold pom-poms, riding on pep buses and attending postgame dances in the school gym. They had double-dated, worn each other's clothes, shared a thousand teenage confidences, and slept at each other's houses with such regularity that each began keeping a spare toothbrush in the other family's medicine cabinet.

Brookie and Maggie—friends forever, they'd thought back then.

But Maggie had gone to Northwestern University in Chicago, married an aeronautical engineer and moved to Seattle, while Glenda attended beauty school in Green Bay, married a Door County, Wisconsin, cherry grower, moved out to his farm, bore six—or was it seven?—of his children and had never cut hair in a beauty shop again.

How long had it been since they'd lost touch? For a while after their ten-year class reunion they'd corresponded regularly. Then time had grown longer between letters, which had dwindled to annual Christmas cards until eventually those, too, had stopped. Maggie had missed their twenty-year reunion, and on her infrequent visits to her parents she and Brookie had always managed to miss bumping into each other.

Call Brookie? And say what? What could they possibly have in common anymore?

Out of mere curiosity, Maggie leaned forward in Phillip's green chair and selected H on the metal telephone index. The top popped open revealing Phillip's neat handwriting, done in mechanical lead pencil.

Sure enough, it was still there, under her maiden name: Holbrook, Glenda (Mrs. Eugene Kerschner), R.R. 1, Fish Creek, WI 54212.

On impulse, Maggie picked up the phone and dialed.

Someone answered after the third ring. "Hullo?" A male voice, young and booming.

"Is Glenda there?"

"Ma!" the voice shouted. "It's for you!" The phone clunked as if dropped on a wooden surface, and after a brief pause someone picked it up.

"Hello?"

"Glenda Kerschner?"

"Yo!"

Maggie was already smiling. "Brookie, is that you?"

"Who's . . ." Even across the wire Maggie sensed Brookie's surprise. "Maggie, is that you?"

"It's me."

"Where are you? Are you in Door? Can you come over?"

"I wish I could but I'm in Seattle."

"Oh, shit. Just a minute." To someone at the other end she shouted, "Todd, unplug that damn thing and take it in the other room so I can hear. Sorry, Maggie, Todd is making popcorn here with a bunch of his friends, and you know how loud a pack of boys can be. Gol, how *are* you?"

"I'm okay."

"Are you really, Mag? We heard about your husband dying in that plane crash. The *Advocate* ran an article. I meant to send you a sympathy card, I even bought one, but somehow the time got away from me and I never got it in the mail. It was cherry season, and you know how crazy things get around here at picking time. Maggie, I'm so sorry about it. I've thought of you a thousand times."

"Thanks, Brookie."

"So how are you doing?"

"Oh. Some days are better than others."

"Bad day today?" Brookie asked.

"Sort of . . . yeah. I've had worse, but . . ." Suddenly Maggie caved in. "Oh shit, Brookie." She propped an elbow on the desk and covered her eyes. "It's awful. Katy just left for Northwestern in Chicago and a woman in my grief group tired to commit suicide last week and I'm sitting here in this empty house wondering what the hell happened to my charmed life."

"Aw, Maggie . . ."

Sniffing against her knuckles, Maggie said, "My psychiatrist said it sometimes helps to talk to old friends, . . . laugh about old times. So here I am, crying on your shoulder just like when we were sophomores with boy troubles."

"Oh, Maggie, I should be shot for not getting to you first. When you've got as many kids as I do you sometimes forget there's a world beyond the kitchen and the laundry room. I'm sorry I didn't call or get in touch with you. I've got no excuse at all. Maggie, are you still there?" Brookie sounded alarmed.

"Yes," Maggie managed.

"Aw, Maggie . . . jeez, I wish I were closer."

"So do I. Some days I'd g-give anything to be able to sit down with you and just b-bawl my guts out."

"Aw, Maggie . . . gol, don't cry."

"I'm sorry. It seems like that's all I've done for the last year. It's so damned hard."

"I know, honey, I know. I wish I were there . . . but you go on and tell me everything. I've got all the time in the world."

Maggie dried her eyes with the heels of her hands and drew in a steadying breath.

"Well, we had to do this exercise in our grief group this week where we set a person in a chair and said good-bye to him. I put Phillip in the chair and said my good-byes, and I guess it really worked because it's finally hitting me that he's gone and he's not coming back." It was so easy to talk to Brookie. The years of separation might never have happened. Maggie told her everything—how happy she'd been with Phillip, how she'd tried to convince him not to go on the gambling junket, how he'd finally talked her into capitulating by promising they'd plan a trip to Florida together for Easter vacation, the shock of hearing that the plane had gone down with fifty-six people aboard, the agony of sending dental records and waiting for the names of the dead to be confirmed, the bizarre sense of fantasm attending a memorial service without a body while television cameras panned her and Katy's faces.

And of what happened afterward.

"It's really strange what happens when you're widowed. Your best friends treat you as if you have leprosy. You're the one who creates an odd number of table settings, you know? The fifth at bridge. The one without a seat belt. Phillip and I belonged to a country club but even there things have changed. Our friends—well, I thought they were our friends until he died and I got propositioned by two of them while their wives teed off less than twenty feet away. After that I gave up golf. Last spring I finally let one of the faculty members talk me into going out on a blind date."

"How was it?"

"Disastrous."

"You mean like Frankie Peterson?"

"Frankie Peterson?"

"Yeah, you remember Frankie Peterson, don't you? A finger in every hole?"

Maggie burst out laughing. She laughed to the point of weakness until she was lying back in the chair with the phone caught on her shoulder.

"Good lord, I'd forgotten about Frankie Peterson."

"How could any girl from Gibraltar High forget Frank the Crank? He stretched out more elastic than the Green Bay Packers!"

They laughed some more, and when it ended, Brookie said seriously, "So tell me about this guy they lined you up with. Tried to put the shaft to you, did he?"

"Exactly. At one o'clock in the morning. On my doorstep, for pete's sake. It was horrible. You get out of practice at fighting them off, you know? It was embarrassing, and belittling and . . . and . . . well, honest to God, Brookie, it made me so angry!"

"So what'd you do, punch him out, or what?"

"I slammed the door in his face and came in the house and made meatballs."

"M-meatballs!" Brookie was laughing so hard she could scarcely get the word out.

For the first time Maggie found the humor in the situation that had seemed so insulting at the time. She laughed with Brookie, great shaking gutlaughs that robbed her of breath and left her nursing a sore stomach while she curled low on her spine and grinned at the ceiling.

"God, it's good to talk to you, Brookie. I haven't laughed like this in months."

"Well, at least I'm good for something besides spawning."

Still more laughter before the line grew quiet and Maggie turned serious again. "It's a real change." Slumping comfortably, she rocked on the leather chair, toying with the phone cord. "You're so hard up—not just for sex, but for affection. Then you go out on a date and when he tries to kiss you you stiffen up and make a fool of yourself. I did it again last week."

"Another blind date?"

"Well, not quite blind. A man who works at my supermarket who lost his wife several years ago, too. I've known him as a passing acquaintance for years, and I could kind of sense that he liked me. Anyway, my grief group kept after me to ask him to do something, so I finally did. You don't want to think *that* doesn't feel awkward! The last time I dated it was the men who did the asking. Now it's everybody. So I asked, and he tried to kiss me, and I just . . . I just froze."

"Hey, don't rush it, Mag. They say it takes a while, and that's only two dates."

"Yeah . . . well . . ." Maggie sighed, braced her temple with a finger and admitted, "A person gets horny, you know. It clouds the judgment."

"Well, listen, you horny old broad, now that you've admitted it and I haven't died of shock, do you feel better?"

"Infinitely."

"Well, that's a relief."

"Dr. Feldstein was right. He said talking with people from the past was healthy, that it takes us back to a time when we didn't have much to worry about. So I called, and you didn't let me down."

"I'm so glad you did. Have you called any of the others? Fish? Lisa? Tani? I know they'd love to hear from you."

"It's been so many years since I talked to any of them."

"But we were the Senior Scourges, all five of us. I *know* they'd want to help if they thought they could. I'll give you their phone numbers."

"You mean you have them? All of them?"

"I've been in charge of the class reunion invitations twice already. They pick on me because I still live around here and I've got more than a half dozen kids of my own to help me address envelopes. Fish lives in Brussels, Wisconsin; Lisa lives in Atlanta; and Tani's in Green Bay. Here, hang on a minute and I'll give you their numbers."

While Brookie searched, Maggie pictured their faces: Lisa, their homecoming queen, who resembled Grace Kelly; Carolyn Fisher, a.k.a. Fish, with a turned-up nose which she'd always hated, and across which she'd written in everyone's yearbook; Tani, a freckled redhead.

"Maggie, you there?"

"I'm here."

"You got a pencil?"

"Go ahead."

She reeled off the girls' phone numbers, then added, "I've got a couple more here. How about Dave Christianson's?"

"Dave Christianson?"

"Well, hell, who says you can't call the guys? We were all friends, weren't we? He married a girl from Green Bay and runs some kind of ball bearing factory, I think."

Maggie took down Dave's number, then those of Kenny Hedlund (married to an underclassman named Cynthia Troy and living in Bowling

Green, Kentucky), Barry Breckholdt (from upstate New York, married with two children), and Mark Mobridge (Mark, Brookie said, was a homosexual, lived in Minneapolis, and had married a man named Greg).

"Are you making this up?" Maggie demanded, wide-eyed.

"No, I'm not making it up! I sent them a wedding card. What the hell— live and let live. I had a lot of laughs with Mark on band trips."

"You weren't kidding when you said you kept track of them all."

"Here, I've got one more for you. Eric Severson."

Maggie sat up straighter in her chair. The laughter left her face. "Eric?"

"Yeah, KL 5-3500, same area code as mine."

After several mute seconds Maggie declared, "I can't call Eric Severson."

"Why not?"

"Well . . . because." Because long ago, when they were seniors in high school, Maggie Pearson and Eric Severson had been lovers. Groping, green, first-time lovers, terrified of getting caught, or pregnant, lucky on both counts.

"He lives right here in Fish Creek. Runs a charter boat out of Gills Rock, just like his old man did."

"Brookie, I said I can't call Eric."

"Why not? Because you used to go all the way with him?"

Maggie's jaw dropped. "Brook*ieee!*"

Brookie laughed. "We didn't tell each other *quite* everything back then, did we? And don't forget, I was on his dad's boat the day after prom, too. What else could you two have been doing down in that cabin all that time? But what does it matter now? Eric's still around, and he's just as nice as he ever was, and I know he'd love to hear from you."

"But he's married, isn't he?"

"Yup. He's got a beautiful wife. A real stunner, and as far as I know they're very happy."

"Well, there." Amen.

"Maggie, for cripe's sake, *grow up*. We're adults now."

Maggie heard the most surprising words leave her mouth. "But what would I say to him?"

"How about, hi, Eric, how they hangin'?" Maggie could almost see Brookie flip a hand in the air. "How the hell should I know what you'd say to him! I just gave you his number along with all the rest. I didn't think it would be such a big deal."

"It's not."

"Then don't make it one."

"I . . ." On the verge of arguing further, Maggie thought better of it. "Listen . . . thanks, Brookie. Thanks so much, and that comes straight from the heart. You were exactly what the doctor ordered tonight."

"Blow it out your ear, Pearson. You don't thank a friend for something like this. You gonna be okay now? You won't flush yourself down the john or anything, will you?"

"I feel a hundred percent better."

"You sure?"

"I'm sure."

"Okay, then, I gotta go. I got kids to get to bed. Call me anytime, okay?"

"I will, and you do the same."

"I will. See y', Mag."

"See y', Brookie."

After hanging up, Maggie slouched in the chair, smiling lazily for a long time. A montage of pleasant memories reeled through her mind, of herself and the girls in high school—Fish, Tani, Lisa and Brookie. Especially Brookie—not particularly bright but liked by everyone because she had a terrific sense of humor and treated everyone equitably, never indulging in criticizing or backbiting. How wonderful to know she hadn't changed, that she was still there in Door County, a ready link with the past, the keeper of contacts.

Maggie rolled her chair closer to the desk and glanced at the telephone numbers highlighted in the beam of the banker's lamp. Fish's, Lisa's, Tani's, Dave Christianson's, Kenny Hedlund's.

Eric Severson's.

No, I couldn't.

She sat back, rocked, thought a little longer. Finally, she rose and searched the bookshelves, selecting a thin, padded volume of cream leather stamped with imitation gold that had long since tarnished.

Gibraltar, 1965.

She opened the cover and saw her own squarish handwriting, with the parenthetical instruction *(Save for Brookie)* and Brookie's abysmal chickenscratching.

Dear Maggie,

Well, we made it, huh? God, I didn't think we ever would. I thought Morrie-baby would catch us drinking beer and expel us before we ever graduated. Boy, we sure drank a few, huh? I'll never forget all the fun we had cheering and dancing and driving thru all those cornfields in Fish's panel truck with the Senior Scourges. Remember the time we stopped it and took a leak in the middle of Main Street? God, what if we'd got caught!! Don't forget the choir trip and that green slime we put in Pruitt's thermos bottle, and all the times we drove him nuts adding notes to songs, and the time we put that poster of the nude in the boys' locker room with you-know-who's name on it! (My mother still hasn't found out about all the trouble we got into over that!) Prom was the greatest with Arnie and Eric, and the day after out in Garrett's Bay in Eric's boat. (Sigh!) I sure hope everything works out for you and Eric, and I know it will because you're such a neat couple. Even though you'll be at Northwestern and I'll be in Green Bay at Beauty School, we'll still get together weekends and pork out with Fish and Lisa and Tani so let's all keep in touch ... fer sure, fer sure! Take it easy on the guys in Chi-town, and good luck in whatever you do. You're the one with all the brains and talent, so I know you'll be a success, no matter what. You've been the best friend ever, Mag, so whatever you do, don't change. And don't forget me. Promise!

Love, Brookie

Reaching the end of Brookie's monologue, Maggie found herself smiling wistfully. She didn't remember putting green slime in Mr. Pruitt's thermos or whose name they'd written on the poster of the nude. And who was Morrie-baby? So many lost memories.

She checked out Brookie's class picture, Tani's, Lisa's, Fish's, her own (wrinkling her nose in chagrin)—all of them so girlish and unsophisticated. But the one whose picture she'd really opened the book to see was Eric Severson.

And there he was. Extraordinarily good-looking at seventeen—tall, blond and Nordic. Though the yearbook was done in black and white, Maggie imagined color where there was none—the startling blue of his eyes, true as a field of Door County chicory in August; the sun-bleached blond of his hair, streaked like dry cornhusks; the perennial teak of his skin baked in by summers of helping his father on the fishing boat.

Eric Severson, my first lover.

She found his handwriting on the flyleaf at the end of the book.

Dear Maggie,

I never would have guessed at the beginning of this year how hard it'd be to write this to you. What a great year we had together. I remember that first night I asked if I could take you home, and when you said yes, I thought, Maggie Pearson with me, Wow!! And now look at us, graduating with a jillion memories. I'll never forget that first dance when you told me not to chew gum in your ear, and the first time I kissed you on the snowmobile trail down below Old Bluff Road, and all the times when coach Gilbert would be talking to us guys during the time-outs and I'd sneak a look at you on the other side of the gym while you were cheering. I liked you for a long time before I got up enough nerve to ask you out, and now I only wish I'd asked you about three years sooner. I'm going to miss you to beat hell this fall when I'm at Stout State, but we've got a date for Thanksgiving in The Door, and for Christmas, too. I'll never forget the day after the prom on the Mary Deare, and the night in old man Easley's orchard. Don't forget Felicity and Aaron, and we've got a date in the spring of '69 to talk about you know what. Keep wearing pink (but only when you got a date at home with me). I never saw a woman who looked so great in pink. I'll never forget you, Maggie M'girl.

Lots of love, Eric

Felicity and Aaron—the names they had picked for their future children. Heavens, she'd forgotten. And the date in the spring when they had agreed to talk about getting married. And how he'd always favored her in pink. And his own special endearment, Maggie M'girl.

Remembering him, she was gripped by nostalgia. Looking back on those giddy days through the perspective of maturity she thought, Brookie is right. He's happily married to a very beautiful wife, and we're all grown-ups now. How could a call from a girl twenty-three years in his past threaten either his marriage or my well-being? It'll be a friendly hello, that's all.

Following Dr. Feldstein's orders, Maggie picked up the phone and dialed.

Chapter 2

❧

The phone jarred Eric Severson out of a sound sleep. Beside him, Nancy mumbled and rolled over as he reached for the nightstand and answered in the dark.

"Hul—" He cleared his throat. "Hullo?"

"Hello, is this Eric Severson?"

"Who's this?" he asked ungraciously, peering at the red numbers on the digital clock.

"It's Margaret Stearn . . . ah, Pearson."

"Who?"

Nancy thumped a hip into the mattress and gave the covers an irritated jerk. "Who in the world is calling at this hour of the night?"

"It's Maggie, Eric," the woman on the phone said. "Maggie Pearson?"

"Mag—" He struggled to think who Maggie Pearson was.

"Oh, I woke you didn't I? I'm really sorry. How thoughtless of me. But I'm in Seattle and it's only nine o'clock here. Listen, Eric, I'll call some other time during the day when—"

"No, it's all right. Who . . . Maggie? You mean Maggie Pearson from Gibraltar High? Class of '65?" He recognized her laughter and settled onto his back, wider awake. "Well, I'll be damned."

Nancy rolled over and asked, "Who is it?"

Shielding the mouthpiece, he answered, "A girl I went to school with, Maggie Pearson."

"Oh, great," Nancy grumbled and rolled away again.

"There's someone with you?"

Into the phone Eric said, "Yes, my wife."

"I really am sorry, Eric. It was an impetuous call, anyway. Please apologize to your wife for my waking her and go back to sleep, both of you."

"Wait a minute!" he ordered, sitting up, dropping his feet over the edge of the bed. "Maggie?"

"Yes?"

"I'll change phones. Hang on a minute." He rose in the dark, flipped the covers over, leaned on them with both hands and kissed Nancy's cheek. "Hang this up when I get downstairs, will you, honey? Sorry to disturb you."

"What does she want?"

"I don't know," he said, leaving the room. "I'll tell you in the morning."

The only other phones were downstairs. He moved familiarly along the dark hall and down the steps, across the living room carpet and onto the cool, vinyl floor of the kitchen where he switched on the fluorescent light above the sink. In its sudden glare he squinted and reached for the phone on the counter.

"Hello?"

"Yes," Maggie replied.

"There, we can talk now. I'm downstairs. Well, Maggie, what a surprise to hear from you."

"I really am sorry, Eric. It was stupid of me not to consider the time difference. You see, I just finished talking to Brookie—she's the one who gave me your number and suggested I call you. We had such a great talk, by the time I hung up I never gave a second thought to the time."

"Stop apologizing."

"But what will your wife think?"

"She's probably already gone back to sleep." Eric heard the click as Nancy hung up the bedside phone. Dressed only in Jockey shorts, he settled gingerly on a kitchen chair, taking the phone with him. "She travels a lot, so she's used to sleeping in hotels and on planes, wherever she needs to. When she's here in her own bed, sleeping's no problem for her, believe me."

"Brookie told me you were married, and to a very beautiful wife."

"Yes, she is, thanks. Her name is Nancy."

"She's not from Door County?"

"No, she's from Estherville, Iowa. I met her my last year in college. How about you? You're living in Seattle and—?" His inflection left an open blank.

"And I was married for eighteen years. He died a year ago."

"I'm sorry, Maggie . . . I read a mention of it in the *Advocate*." After a pause, he inquired, "How about kids?"

"One. A daughter, Katy, seventeen. You?"

"No, unfortunately, none."

His reply left a gap. Groping for something to fill in, she put in, "Brookie says you're running your dad's charter boat."

"Yup. Out of Gills Rock with my brother Mike. You remember Mike, don't you? He was two years ahead of us?"

"Of course I remember Mike. We used his car to go to the prom."

"That's right, I'd forgotten. We've got two boats now, and Ma mans the radio for us and does all the shore work and the bookings and sells the licenses."

"Your mother—I smile when I think of her. How is she?"

"Unstoppable. Looks the same as ever—like a cross between Burgess Meredith and a Persian lamb coat."

Maggie laughed. The sound, coming across the wire, seemed to roll time backwards. "Ma never changes. She's still full of sass," Eric added, settling more comfortably in the chair.

"Your mother was such a spunky lady. I liked her so much. And your dad . . . he's gone now, I think my mother wrote."

"Yes, six years ago."

"You were always so close to him. I'm sure you must miss him."

"We all do." It was true. Even after six years, Eric still felt the loss. The values he had learned had been taught to him by the old man. He'd come by his occupation wrapped in the old man's arms, with his powerful hands covering Eric's own on the rod and reel, and his voice in Eric's ear, ordering, "Never jerk back on the line, son! Keep 'er steady!" More than

half of Eric's charter customers were old-time repeaters who'd been fishing on the *Mary Deare* since the early days of Severson Charters. Eric's
voice held gruff affection as he added, "Ah, well . . . he had a hell of a
good life, drove the boat till the end and died right here at home, holding
Ma's hand with all four of us kids around the bed."

"That's right—I forgot about your other brother and sister—where are
they?"

"Ruth lives in Duluth and Larry's in Milwaukee. I see your folks around
every now and then, your dad mostly when I go into the store. He always
wants a report on how the fish are biting."

"I'm sure he envies you, fishing for a living."

Eric chuckled. "I was in there about a month ago or so and I told him
to drive up sometime and I'd take him out."

"I suppose he never came."

"No, he didn't."

"Mother apparently wouldn't give him permission," Maggie remarked
sardonically.

Maggie's mother had been a harridan for as long as Eric had known
her. He remembered his fear of Vera Pearson when he'd dated Maggie
and how the area women, in general, disliked her.

"I take it she hasn't changed."

"Not much. At least she hadn't the last time I was home which was . . .
oh, three years ago, I guess. She's still got a ring in Daddy's nose, and
she'd like to see one in mine. Consequently, I don't come home very
often."

"You didn't make the last class reunion."

"No . . . Phillip and I lived out here in Seattle then and . . . well, it's a
long way. We just somehow never made it. We travel a lot, though . . . or
. . . well, we did, I mean."

Her slip caused a moment's awkwardness. "Sorry," she inserted. "I try
not to do that, but sometimes it slips out."

"No, that's . . . that's okay, Maggie." He paused, then admitted, "You
know, I'm trying to picture you. Funny, isn't it, how hard it is to picture
a person older than we remember them?" In his mind she was still seventeen, thin and auburn-haired, with brown eyes, a delicate face and an
attractively cleft chin. Vivacious. And laughing. He'd always been able to
make her laugh so easily.

"I'm older. Definitely older."

"Aren't we all?"

Eric picked up a teakwood pear from a wooden bowl in the center of
the table and rubbed it with his thumb. He'd never understood why Nancy
put wooden fruit on the table when the genuine article grew all over Door
County.

"You miss your husband a lot?"

"Yes, I do. We had a model marriage."

He tried to think of some reply but none came. "I'm afraid I'm not
much good at this, Maggie, I'm sorry. When my dad died it was the same
way. I didn't know what the hell to say to my mother."

"It's all right, Eric. It makes a lot of people uncomfortable, even me
sometimes."

"Maggie, can I ask you something?"

"Of course."

He paused uncertainly. "No, I guess I'd better not."

"No, go ahead. What?"

"I'm curious, that's all. It's . . . well . . ." Perhaps it was an impertinent question, but he couldn't stop himself from asking. "Why did you call?"

His question startled her, too; he could tell by the seconds of silence that followed.

"I don't know. Just to say hi."

After twenty-three years, just to say hi? It seemed odd, yet there appeared no other logical reason.

She rushed on. "Well . . . it's late, and I'm sure you have to be up early tomorrow. Saturday in The Door . . . I remember it well. Always a lot of tourists around then, and they probably all want to go fishing for salmon, right? Listen, forgive me for waking you, and please apologize to your wife. I know I woke her, too."

"No problem, Maggie. Hey, I'm really glad you called. I mean that."

"So am I."

"Well . . ." Eric waited, uneasy for no good reason he could name, finally coming up with a closing remark. "Next time you come home, give us a call. I'd like you to meet Nancy."

"I'll do that. And greet your mom and Mike for me."

"I will."

"Well, good-bye, Eric."

"Good-bye."

The line clicked immediately but he sat for long moments, perplexed, gazing at the phone.

What the hell?

He hung up, returned the phone to the cabinet and stood staring at it. *Eleven o'clock at night after twenty-three years Maggie calls. Why?* He slipped his hands inside the elastic waistband of his shorts and scratched his belly, wondering. He opened the refrigerator and stood a while with the chill air fanning his bare legs, registering little but the repetitive thought: *Why?*

Just to say hi, she'd said, but that sounded fishy.

He took out a container of orange juice, uncapped it and swilled half of it straight from the bottle. Backhanding his mouth, he continued standing in the wedge of light from the open door, baffled. He'd probably never know the real reason. Loneliness, maybe. Nothing more.

He put the juice away, snapped out the kitchen light and returned to his bedroom.

Nancy was sitting up cross-legged with the light on, dressed in a peach satin teddy and tap pants, her shapely limbs gleaming in the lamplight.

"Well, that took a while," she remarked dryly.

"Surprised the hell out of me."

"Maggie Pearson?"

"Yup."

"The one you took to the prom?"

"Yup."

"What did she want?"

He dropped onto the bed, braced his hands beside her hips and kissed her left breast above an inviting edge of peach-colored lace. "My body, what else?"

"Eric!" Grabbing a fistful of his hair, she lifted his head. "What did she want?"

He shrugged noncommittally. "Damned if I know. She said she talked to Brookie and Brookie gave her my phone number and told her to call me. I still haven't figured it out."

"Brookie?"

"Glenda Kerschner. Her maiden name was Holbrook."

"Oh. The cherry picker's wife."

"Yeah. She and Maggie were best friends in high school. We were all friends, a whole gang of us who ran around together."

"That still doesn't answer my question. What is your old girlfriend doing calling you in the middle of the night?"

With his inner wrists brushing her jutting knees he smiled smugly into her face. "Jealous?"

"Curious."

"Well, I don't know." He kissed Nancy's mouth. "Her husband died." He kissed her throat. "She's lonely, that's all I can figure out." He kissed her breast. "She said to tell you she's sorry she woke you up." He bit her nipple, silk and all.

"Where does she live?"

"Seattle." The word was muffled against Nancy's lingerie.

"Oh . . . in that case . . ." Nancy uncrossed her legs, slid onto her back and pulled him down on top of her, linking her arms and ankles behind him. They kissed, long and lazily, rocking against each other. When he lifted his head she looked into his eyes and said, "I miss you when I'm gone, Eric."

"Then stop going."

"And do what?"

"Keep the books for me, open a boutique and sell all your fancy cosmetics to the tourists here in Fish Creek . . ." He paused before adding, ". . . be a hausfrau and raise a pack of brats." *Or even one brat would do.* But he knew better than to push the subject.

"Hey," she scolded, "we're starting something interesting here. Let's not spoil it with that old epistle."

She drew his head down, invited his tongue inside her mouth and became the aggressor, stripping him of his briefs, rolling him onto his back and slithering from her own skimpy lingerie. She was adept, very adept, and infallibly desirable. She saw to her desirability the way some wives see to their daily housework, expending much time and energy upon it, allotting it a fixed time in her schedule.

Lord, she was a beautiful creature. While she reversed their roles and seduced him, he admired her at close range, her skin with the exquisite texture of an eggshell, incredibly unaged for a woman of thirty-eight, cared for twice a day with the expensive French cosmetics she sold; her nails, professionally groomed and artificially lengthened, painted a gleaming raspberry; her hair, which was presently a deep mahogany color, shining with highlights added by some costly beautician in some far-off city where she'd been this past week. Orlane paid their sales reps a hair and nail allowance and gave them unlimited gratis merchandise with the understanding that they present themselves as walking testimonials for their products. The company got its money's worth with Nancy Macaffee. She was the most beautiful woman he knew.

She ran one long nail across his lips and inside them. He bit it lightly, then, still lying beneath her, reached up to stroke her hair.

"I like the new color," he murmured, threading his fingers back along her skull, combing her hair toward the ceiling, then letting it fall. She had hair as coarse as a mare's tail, thick and healthy. Daytime, she wore it drawn back to the nape in a classic, smooth, tucked tail, held by a sixty-dollar gold barrette. Tonight it bunched around her high cheekbones, making her look like Cleopatra in an updraft.

She sat on his abdomen, svelte, nude, shaking her head until the hair slapped the corners of her eyes, flexing her fingers in the hair on his chest like a dozing cat.

"Maurice did it . . . in Chicago."

"Maurice, hm?"

She gave her head a final shake and let an insinuating smile tease her lips as she studied him with hooded eyes.

"Mm-hmm . . ."

On her hips his hands flexed repeatedly. "You know, you're incredible."

"Why?" She scratched a dim white line from his throat down his pelvic arch and watched it return to its natural color.

"You wake up in the middle of the night looking as if you just got up from Maurice's chair."

Her eyebrows were brushed upward, her eyelashes thick and black around deep brown eyes. Long ago, when she'd been in training to learn her trade, she'd told him a fact she'd learned: that most people are born with a single row of lashes, but some are blessed with a double. Nancy had a double and then some. She had incredible eyes. Lips, too.

"Come here," he ordered gruffly, catching her by the armpits and tipping her down. "We've got five days to make up for." He flipped her over neatly and slipped a hand between her legs, touched her inside, found her wet and swollen with desire equaling his own. He felt her cool hand surround him at last and shuddered with her first stroke. They knew each other's sexual temperaments intrinsically, knew what the other needed, wanted, liked best.

But at the moment when he reached to place himself inside her, she pressed him away, whispering, "Wait, sweetheart, I'll be right back."

He stayed where he was, pinning her down. "Why don't you forget it tonight?"

"I can't. It's too risky."

"So what?" He continued enticing her, stroking her shallowly, strewing kisses across her face. "Take a chance," he murmured against her lips. "Would it be the end of the world if you got pregnant?"

She chuckled, bit the end of his chin and repeated, "I'll be right back," then escaped and padded across the carpet to the bathroom down the hall.

He sighed, flopped to his back and closed his eyes. *When?* But he knew the answer. Never. She pampered her body not only for the benefit of Orlane cosmetics, not only for him, but for herself. She was afraid of jeopardizing that perfection. He had taken a chance, introducing the subject tonight. Most times when he mentioned having a baby, she grew indignant and found something in the room to occupy her attention. Afterward, for the remainder of their weekend together, the atmosphere would be strained. So he'd learned not to badger her about it. But the years were on a downhill run. In October he'd be forty-one; another two years or so and he'd be too old to want to start a family. A kid deserved an old man with a little zip and zest, one he could scrimmage and wrestle with, reel in the big ones with.

Eric recalled his earliest memory, of riding above his father's head, seated on the old man's wide, cupped palm while the gulls wheeled overhead. "See them birds, son? Follow them and they'll tell you where there's fish." In sharp contrast came the memory of himself and his brothers and sister standing around the bed when his father died, all with tears streaming down their faces as one by one they kissed the old man's lifeless cheek, then their ma's, before leaving her alone with him.

More than anything in the world, he wanted a family.

The mattress shifted and Eric opened his eyes.

Nancy knelt above him. "Hi, I'm back."

They made love, quite expertly if the books were any criteria. They were inventive and agile. They sampled three different positions. They verbalized their wishes. Eric experienced one orgasm; Nancy, two. But when it was over and the room dark, he lay studying the shadowed ceiling, cradling his head on his arms and pondering how empty the act could be when not used for its intended purpose.

Nancy rolled close, threw an arm and a leg over him and tried to finesse him into cuddling. She commandeered his arm and drew it around her waist.

But he had no desire to hold her as they drifted off to sleep.

In the morning Nancy rose at 5:30 and Eric at quarter to six, the moment the shower was free. He thought she must be the last woman in America who still used a vanity table. The house, prairie-styled, circa 1919, had never pleased Nancy. She had moved into it under duress, complaining that the kitchen was unsatisfactory, the plug-ins inadequate and the bathroom a joke. Thus the vanity table in the bedroom.

It sat against a narrow stretch of wall between two windows, accompanied by a large round makeup mirror circled by lights.

While Eric showered and dressed, Nancy went through her morning beauty rite: pots and tubes and bottles and wands; jellies and lotions, sprays and cremes; hair blowers and curlers and teasers and lifters. Though he'd never been able to understand how it could take her an hour and fifteen minutes, he'd watched her often enough to know it did. The cosmetic ritual was as deeply ingrained in Nancy's life as dieting; she did both as a matter of rote, finding it unthinkable to appear even at her own breakfast table without looking as flawless as she would if she were flying into New York to meet the Orlane hierarchy.

While Nancy sat at the makeup mirror, Eric moved about the bedroom, listening to the weather on the radio, dressing in white jeans, white Reeboks and a sky-blue knit pullover with the company logo, a ship's wheel, and his name stitched on the breast pocket.

Tying his sneakers, he asked, "Want anything from the bakery?"

She was drawing fine auburn eyelashes onto her lower lids. "You eat too much of that stuff. You should have some wholegrain instead."

"My only vice. Be right back."

She watched him leave the room, proud of his continued leanness, his eye-catching good looks. He had been displeased last night, she knew,

and it worried her. She wanted their relationship—just the two of them—
to be enough for him, as it was for her. She'd never been able to understand why he thought he needed more.

In the kitchen he put coffee on to perk before stepping outside and
pausing on the front stoop, studying the town and the water below. Main
Street, a mere block away, contoured the shoreline of Fish Creek Harbor,
which lay this morning beneath a patchy pink-tinged mist, obscuring the
view of Peninsula State Park, due north across the water. At the town docks
sailboats sat motionlessly, their masts piercing the fog, visible above the
treetops and the roofs of the businesses along Main. He knew that street
and the establishments on it as well as he knew the waters of the bay,
from the stately old White Gull Inn on the west end to the sassy new Top
of the Hill Shops at the east. He knew the people down there, too, hometown folks who waved when they saw his pickup go by and knew what time
the mail came into the post office each day (between 11:00 and 12:00)
and how many churches the town had, and who belonged in which congregation.

These first few minutes outside were some of the best of his day, casting
a weather eye at the water and the eastern sky above the woods which
crowded the town, listening to a mourning dove mimic itself from a
highwire nearby, inhaling the scent of the giant cedars behind the house
and the aroma of fresh bread, lifting from the bakery at the bottom of
the hill.

Why did Maggie Pearson call me after twenty-three years?

Out of nowhere the thought intruded. Startled by it, Eric set his feet in
motion and jogged down the hill, hollering hello to Pete Nelson through
the back screen door of the bakery as he passed it and headed around
the building. It was a pretty little place, set back from the street with a
grassy front lawn, surrounded by a white-railed porch and beds of bright
flowers that gave it a homey look. Inside, he nodded to two early tourists
buying bismarcks, exchanged good mornings with the pretty, young Hawkins girl behind the counter and asked after her mother, who'd had a
gallbladder operation, then exchanged pleasantries with Pete, who stuck
his head out of the back room, and with Sam Ellerby, who was out collecting his usual tray of assorted rolls and breads to serve at the Summer-
time Restaurant on Spruce Street, two blocks away.

To Eric, this ritual trip to the bakery had become as enjoyable as Pete
Nelson's pastries. He returned up the hill in blithe spirits, carrying a white
waxed bag, bounded into the house and poured two cups of coffee just
as Nancy entered the kitchen.

"Good morning," she said, for the first time that day. (To Nancy it was
never a good morning until her makeup ritual was complete.)

"Good morning."

She wore a bone-colored linen skirt and a boxy shirt with dropped
shoulders, immense sleeves, and an upturned collar, covered all over with
tiny purple and green cats. Who but Nancy could wear purple and green
cats and look chic? Even her belt—a twisted hank of purple sisal with a
buckle the size of a hubcap—would have looked stupid on anyone else.
But his wife had panache, and indubitable style, and access to the discount
rooms in the most elegant department stores across America. Any room
Nancy Macaffee entered became eclipsed by her presence.

Watching her cross the kitchen in purple shoes, her hair confined in a neat, low tail, her eyes shaded and mascaraed, her lips painted one color and outlined with another, Eric sipped his coffee and grinned.

"Thanks." She accepted the cup he handed her and took a careful sip. "Mmm . . . you look like you're in a good mood."

"I am."

"What brought the smile?"

He leaned against the cupboard, eating a fat, glazed doughnut, occasionally sipping. "Just trying to imagine you as a polyester mama—say, two hundred pounds, wearing double-knit slacks and hair rollers every morning."

"Don't hold your breath." She raised one eyebrow and gave him a smirk. "See anybody at the bakery?"

"Two tourists, Sam Ellerby, the Hawkins girl, and Pete stuck his head out of the kitchen."

"Any news?"

"Nuh-uh." He licked his fingers and downed the last of his coffee. "What are you going to do today?"

"Weekly sales reports, what else? This job would be ideal if it weren't for all the paperwork."

And the travel, he thought. After a full five days on the road, she spent her sixth, and often half of her seventh, doing paperwork—she was one damned hard worker, he'd give her that. But she loved the glamour associated with such stores as Bonwit Teller, Neiman-Marcus and Rocco Altobelli—all her accounts. And if traveling came along with the job, she accepted its drawbacks in exchange for that glamour.

She'd had the Orlane job when they moved back to Door County, and he'd thought she'd give it up, stay home and have a family. But instead, she'd put in longer hours both at home and on the road in order to keep the job.

"How about you?" she inquired, slipping on a pair of glasses, studying the weekly newspaper.

"We're full today, so is Mike. Taking three charter groups out." He rinsed his cup, put it into the dishwasher and donned a white skipper's cap with a shiny black bill.

"So you won't be home till seven?"

"Probably not."

She looked up through her oversized horn-rimmed glasses. "Try to make it earlier."

"I can't promise."

"Just try, okay?"

He nodded.

"Well, I'd better get to work," Nancy said, snapping the paper closed.

"Me, too."

Coffee and juice in hand, she touched her cheek to his.

"See you tonight."

She headed for her small downstairs office while he left the house and crossed a short stretch of sidewalk to a clapboard garage. He raised the door by hand, glanced at Nancy's ultra-respectable steel gray Acura and clambered into a rusty Ford pickup that twelve years ago had been white, had possessed a left rear fender and had not required wire to hold its tailpipe up. The vehicle was an embarrassment to Nancy, but Eric had grown fond of The Old Whore, as he affectionately called it. The engine was still reliable; the company name and phone number were still legible on the doors; and the driver's seat—after all these years—was shaped precisely like his backside.

Turning the key, he mumbled, "All right, you old whore, come on."

It took a little encouraging, but after less than a minute on the starter, the old 300 straight-six rumbled to life.

He gunned her, smiled, shifted into reverse and backed from the garage.

The ride from Fish Creek to Gills Rock covered nineteen of the prettiest miles in all of creation, Eric believed, with Green Bay intermittently visible off to his left; farms, orchards and forests to his right. From the flower-flanked Main Street of Fish Creek itself the road climbed, curved and dipped between thick walls of forest, past private cottages and resorts, heading northeast but swinging to the shore again and again: at the picturesque little village of Ephraim with its two white church steeples reflected in glassy Eagle Harbor; at Sister Bay where Al Johnson's famous goats were already grazing on the grassy roof of his restaurant; at Ellison Bay with its panoramic view from the hill behind the Grand View Hotel; and finally at Gills Rock beyond which the waters of Lake Michigan met those of Green Bay and created the hazardous currents from which the area extracted its name: Death's Door.

Eric had often wondered why a town and a rock had been named for a long-forgotten settler named Elias Gill when Seversons had been here earlier and longer, and were still here, for that matter. Why, hell, the name Gill had long ago disappeared from the area tax rolls and telephone book. But the heritage of the Seversons lived on. Eric's grandfather Severson had built the farm on the bluff above the bay, and his father had built the house tucked beneath the cedars beside Hedgehog Harbor as well as the charter boat business which he and Mike had expanded to provide a good living for two families—three if you counted Ma.

Some might not call Gills Rock a town at all. It was little more than a smattering of weatherbeaten buildings stretched like a gap-toothed smile around the southeast side of the harbor. A restaurant, a gift shop, several wooden docks, a boat landing and Ma's house were the primary obstacles keeping the trees from growing clear to the water's edge. Scattered among these were smaller buildings and the usual paraphernalia peculiar to a fishing community—boat trailers, winches, gasoline pumps and the cradles in which the big boats were dry-docked over the winter.

Turning into the driveway, the truck pitched steeply downhill and bumped over the stony earth. Maples and cedars grew haphazardly between patches of gravel and among the collection of huts near the docks. The roof of the fish-cleaning shack already sported a line of gulls whose droppings had permanently streaked the green shingles with white. Smoke from the fish-smoking shack hung in the air, pungent and blue. Permeating it all was the ever-present odor of decaying wood and fish. Pulling up beneath his favorite sugar maple, Eric noted that Mike's sons, Jerry Joe and Nicholas, were already aboard the *Mary Deare* and *The Dove*, vacuuming the decks, icing up the fish coolers and putting in a supply of refreshments. Like himself and Mike, the boys had grown up around the water and had been going out on the boats since their hands were big enough to grip a rail. At eighteen and sixteen Jerry Joe and Nicholas made responsible, knowledgeable mates on the two boats.

Slamming the truck door, he waved to the boys and headed for the house.

He'd grown up in the place and was unbothered by its doubling as the charter fishing office. The front door might be closed at times, but it was never locked; already at 6:55 it was shoved back as far as the buckled wood floor would allow and propped open by a six-pack of Coca-Cola. The walls of the office, paneled with knotty pine, were covered with lures, spoons, insect repellent, a two-way radio, fishing license forms, Door County maps, landing nets, two mounted chinook salmon and dozens of photos of tourists with their prize catches. On one rack hung yellow slickers for sale, on another a rainbow of sweatshirts lauding SEVERSON'S CHARTER FISHING, GILLS ROCK. Piled on the floor were more six-packs of canned soft drinks while on a card table in the corner a twenty-five-cup coffeepot was already steaming with free brew for the customers.

Circling the counter with its vintage brass cash register, Eric headed for the back, through a narrow door into a room that had once been a side porch but now housed a supply of Styrofoam coolers and the ice machine.

On the far side of the porch another door led into the kitchen.

"Mornin', Ma," he said, walking in.

"Mornin' yourself."

He reached into the cupboard for a thick, white cup and poured himself coffee from a chipped enamel pot on a chipped enamel gas range— the same one that had been there since he was a boy. Its grates were thick with charred boilover, and the paint on the wall behind it wore a yellow halo, but Ma was unapologetically undomestic—with one exception: she baked bread twice each week, refusing to put store-bought bread in her mouth, claiming, "That stuff'll kill you!"

She was mixing bread dough this morning, on an old gateleg table covered with blue oilcloth. To the best of Eric's memory that oilcloth was the only thing that had been replaced in the room since 1959 when the antique wooden icebox had gone and Ma had bought the Gibson refrigerator, which now was a yellowed relic, but still running.

Ma never threw away anything with a day's use left in it.

She was dressed in her usual getup, blue jeans and a tight aqua-blue T-shirt that made her resemble a stack of three inner tubes. Anna Severson loved T-shirts with slogans. Today's bore the words I DO IT WITH YOUNGER MEN, and a picture of an old woman and a young man fishing. Her tight, nickel-colored curls held the fresh shape of home-permanent rods, and her nose—what there was of it—held up a pair of glasses that were nearly as old as the Gibson and their lenses nearly as yellowed.

Turning with the cup in his hand, Eric watched her move to a cupboard to unearth bread pans.

"How're you today?" he inquired.

"Hah."

"That ornery, huh?"

"You come in here just to drink my coffee and give me grief?"

"That what you call this?" He looked into the cup. "It'd make a truck driver wince."

"Then drink that colored water in the office."

"You know I hate those buffalo board cups."

"Then drink your coffee at home. Or don't that wife of yours know how to make it? She get home last night?"

"Yup. About ten-fifteen."

"Ha."

"Ma, don't start in with me."

"That's some kind of life, you living there and her living all over the U.S. of A." She smeared lard in a bread pan and clunked it down on the oilcloth. "Your dad would of come and dragged me home by the hair if I'd've tried something like that."

"You haven't got enough hair. What'd you do to it, by the way?" He pretended a serious assessment of her ugly, tight curls.

"Went over to Barbara's last night and had her kink me up." Barbara was Mike's wife. They lived in the woods not fifty feet up the shoreline.

"Looks like it hurts."

She slapped him with a bread pan, then plopped a loaf into it. "I ain't got time for hair fussing and you know it. You had your breakfast?"

"Yup."

"What? Glazed doughnuts?"

"Ma, you're meddling again."

She stuck the loaf in the oven. "What else are mothers for? God didn't make no commandment named 'thou shalt not meddle,' so I meddle. That's what mothers are for."

"I thought they were for selling fishing licenses and booking charters."

"If you want that leftover sausage, eat it." She nodded toward an iron skillet on top of the stove and began wiping the flour off the oilcloth with the edge of her hand.

He lifted a cover and found two nearly cold Polish sausages—one for him, one for Mike as usual—picked one up with his fingers and leaned against the stove, eating it, pondering. "Ma, you remember Maggie Pearson?"

"Of course I remember Maggie Pearson. My hair ain't kinked up that tight. What brought her up?"

"She called me last night."

For the first time since he'd entered the room his mother stopped moving. She turned from the sink and looked back over her shoulder.

"She called you? For what?"

"Just to say hello."

"She lives out west someplace, doesn't she?"

"Seattle."

"She called you from *Seattle* just to say hello?"

Eric shrugged.

"She's widowed, ain't she?"

"Yes."

"Ah, that's it then."

"What's it then?"

"She always was sweet on you. Sniffin' around, that's what she's doing. Widows get to sniffin' when they need a man."

"Oh, Ma, for cryin' out loud, Nancy was right beside me when she called."

"When who called?" Mike interrupted, arriving in the middle of the exchange. He had thirty pounds and two years on his brother, plus a full brown beard.

"His old flame," Anna Severson answered.

"She's not my old flame!"

"Who?" Mike repeated, going straight to the cupboard for a coffee cup and filling it at the stove.

"That Pearson girl, the one he used to trade spit with on that back porch right there when he thought the rest of us had gone to bed."

"Oh, Judas," Eric groaned.

"Maggie Pearson?" Mike's eyebrows shot up.

"Vera and Leroy Pearson's daughter—you remember her," Anna clarified.

Testing the steaming coffee with his lips, Mike grinned at his brother. "Hoo-ey! You and old Maggie used to nearly set that old daybed on fire back in high school."

"If I'd've known I was going to take all this flak I wouldn't have told you two."

"So what did she want?" Mike found the leftover sausage and helped himself.

"I don't know. She and Glenda Holbrook keep in touch, and she just . . ." Eric shrugged. "Called, that's all. Said hi, how y' doing, are you married, you got kids, that sort of thing."

"Sniffin'," Anna put in again from the sink, her back to the boys.

"Ma!"

"Yeah, I heard you. Just to say hi."

"She said to say hi to both of you, too, but I don't know why the hell I bother."

"Mmm . . . something's missing here," Mike speculated.

"Well, when you figure out what it is, I'm sure you'll let me know," Eric told his brother sarcastically.

Out in the office the radio crackled and Jerry Joe's voice came on.

"*Mary Deare* to base, you up there, Grandma?"

Eric, closest to the office, went out to answer. "This is Eric. Go ahead, Jerry Joe."

"Mornin', Cap'n. Our seven o'clock parties are here. Just sent 'em up to the office. Nick and me could use some help down here."

"Be right there."

Eric glanced through the open office door and saw a group of men crossing the blacktop from the dock, heading in to register, pay and buy licenses—Ma's department. Beyond the fish-cleaning tables he saw Tim Rooney, their handyman, directing a boat that was being backed into the water on their ramp, while another pickup and boat had just pulled into the parking lot.

Switching off the mike, Eric called, "Ma? Mike? Customers coming from all directions, I'm heading for the boat."

At precisely 7:30 A.M. the *Mary Deare*'s engines chortled to life with Eric at the wheel. Jerry Joe released the mooring lines and leapt aboard as Eric pulled the cord for the air horn and it split the silence in a long, deafening blast. From the cockpit of *The Dove*, Mike answered with a matching blast as he, too, revved his engines.

Beneath Eric's hands the wide wooden wheel shuddered as he threw the engine from reverse into forward and headed at a crawl out of Hedge-hog Harbor.

This was the time of day Eric liked best, early morning, with the sun coming up behind him and fingers of steam rising from the water, parting and curling as the boat nudged through; and overhead, a battalion of herring gulls acting as escort, screaking loudly with their white heads cocked in the sun; and to the west Door Bluff rising sharp and green against a violet horizon.

He pointed the bow northward, leaving behind the damp-wood-and-fish smells of the harbor for the bracing freshness of the open water. Switching on the depth sounder, he plucked the radio mike off the ceiling.

"This is the *Mary Deare* on ten. Who's out there this morning?"

A moment later a voice came back. "This is the *Mermaid* off Table Bluff."

"Hi, Rog, any luck this morning?"

"Nothing yet but we're marking 'em at fifty-five feet."

"Anyone else out?"

"*Mariner* was heading toward Washington Island, but she's under fog, so they pulled line and went east."

"Maybe I'll head around Door Bluff then."

"Might as well. No action out here."

"What depth you running?"

"My deep line is shallow—oh, forty-five or so."

"We'll try a little deeper, then. Thanks, Rog."

"Good luck, Eric."

Among Door County guides it was customary to share information lib-erally in an effort to help each fishing party fill out, for successful trips brought fishermen back.

Eric made one more call. "*Mary Deare* to base."

Ma's voice came on, scratchy and gruff. "Go ahead, Eric."

"Heading out around Door Bluff."

"I hear you."

"See you at eleven. Have that bread baked, okay?"

She clicked on in the middle of a chuckle. "Aye-aye, brat. Base out."

Smiling over his shoulder as he hung up the mike, Eric heralded Jerry Joe. "Take over here while I set the lines."

For the next thirty minutes he was busy baiting rods and reels with shiny lures, attaching them to the downriggers on the stern, counting the times each line crossed the reel as it payed out, setting the depth accordingly. He assigned lines, checked the multicolored radar screen for sign of bait-fish or salmon and kept a constant eye on the tips of the reels in their scabbards along the side and rear rails. All the while he bantered with his customers, getting to know the first-timers, rehashing past catches with the repeaters, joshing and charming them all into coming back again.

He was good at his job, good with people, good with the lines. When the first fish was hooked his enthusiasm added as much to the excitement as the bowed rod. He plucked it from its holder, bellowing out instruc-tions, putting it in the hands of a thin, bald man from Wisconsin, then hurriedly buckling around the man's waist a heavy leather belt to hold the butt of the rod, shouting the directives his father had issued years before: "Don't jerk back! Stay close to the rail!" and to Jerry Joe, "Throt-tle down, circle right! We got him!" He scolded and encouraged with equal likability, as excited as if this were the first catch he'd ever overseen, manning the landing net himself and hauling the catch over the rail.

He'd been fishing these waters all his life so it was no surprise that they filled out: six salmon for six fishermen.

Returning to port at eleven, he weighed the fish, hung them on a hook board reading SEVERSON'S CHARTERS, GILLS ROCK, lined the proud fishermen up behind their catch, took the customary series of Polaroid photographs, gave one to each customer, cleaned the fish, sold four Styrofoam coolers and four bags of ice and went up to Ma's for dinner.

By seven o'clock that night he'd repeated the same routine three times. He'd baited lines a total of forty-two times, had met eight new customers and eleven old ones, helped them land fifteen chinook salmon and three brown trout, had cleaned all eighteen fish and had still managed to think of Maggie Pearson more times than he cared to admit. Odd, what a call like hers began. Old memories, nostalgia, questions like, *what if?*

Climbing the incline to Ma's house for the last time, he thought of Maggie again. He checked his watch. Seven-fifteen and Nancy would have supper waiting, but his mind was made up. He was going to make one phone call before heading home.

Mike and the boys had gone home, and Ma was closing up the front office as he went through.

"Big day," Ma said, unplugging the coffeepot.

"Yeah."

In the kitchen the Door County phone book hung on a dirty string from the wall phone beside the refrigerator. Looking up the number, he knew Ma would be coming in right behind him, but he had nothing to hide. He dialed. The phone rang in his ear and he propped an elbow against the top of the refrigerator. Sure enough, Ma came in with the percolator and started emptying coffee grounds into the sink while he listened to the fourth ring.

"Hello?" a child answered.

"Is Glenda there?"

"Just a minute." The phone clunked loudly in his ear. The same child returned and said, "She wants to know who this is."

"Eric Severson."

"Okay, just a minute." He heard the child shout, "Eric Severson!" while Ma moved about the room and listened.

Moments later Glenda came on. "Eric, hello! Speaking of the devil."

"Hi, Brookie."

"Did she call you?"

"Maggie? Yeah. Surprised the hell out of me."

"Me, too. I'm sure worried about her."

"Worried?"

"Well, yeah, I mean, gosh . . . aren't you?"

He did a mental double take. "Should I be?"

"Well, couldn't you tell how depressed she was?"

"No. I mean, she didn't say a word. We just—you know—caught up, sort of."

"She didn't say anything about this group she's working with?"

"What group?"

"She's in a bad way, Eric," Brookie told him. "She lost her husband a year ago, and her daughter just came back east to college. Apparently she's been going through counseling with some grief group and everything sort of came down on her at once. She was going through this struggle to accept the fact that her husband was dead, and in the middle of it all, somebody from the group tried to commit suicide."

"Suicide!" Eric's elbow came away from the refrigerator. "You mean she might possibly be that bad, too?"

"I don't know. All I know is that her psychiatrist told her that when she starts getting depressed the best thing to do is to call old friends and talk about the old days. That's why she called us. We're her therapy."

"Brookie, I didn't know. If I had . . . but she didn't say anything about a psychiatrist or therapy or anything. Is she in the hospital or what?"

"No, she's at home."

"How did she seem to you? I mean, was she still depressed or . . ." His troubled gaze was fixed on Anna, who had stopped her work and stood watching him.

"I don't know. I got her laughing some, but it's hard to tell. How did she seem when you talked to her?"

"I don't know either. It's been twenty-three years, Brookie. It's pretty hard to tell from just her voice. I got her laughing, too, but . . . hell, if only she'd have said something."

"Well, if you can spare the time, give her a call now and then. I think it'll help. I've already talked to Fish and Lisa and Tani. We're going to kind of take turns."

"Good idea." Eric considered for less than two seconds before making his decision. "Have you got her number, Brookie?"

"Sure. You got a pencil?"

He caught the one hanging on the dirty string. "Yeah, go ahead."

With his mother watching, he wrote Maggie's phone number among the dozens scrawled on the cover of the phone book.

"206–555–3404," he repeated. "Thanks, Brookie."

"Eric?"

"Yeah?"

"Tell her hi, and tell her I'm thinking about her and that I'll be calling her soon."

"I will."

"And say hi to your mom."

"I'll do that. I'm at her house now. Bye, Brookie."

"Bye."

When he hung up, his gaze locked with Anna's. He felt like a herd of horses was galloping through his insides.

"She's in some counseling group for people who are suicidal. Her doctor told her to call old friends." He released a tense breath and looked harried.

"Well, the poor, poor thing."

"She never told me, Ma."

"Can't be an easy thing to make yourself say."

He wandered to a kitchen window, stared out, seeing Maggie as he remembered her, a gay young girl who laughed so easily. He stood for a long time, filled with a startling amount of concern, considering what was proper.

Finally he turned back to Anna. He was forty years old, but he needed her approval before doing what was on his mind. "I've got to call her back, Ma."

"Absolutely."

"You care if I call from here?"

"You go right ahead. I got to take a bath." She abandoned the percolator and coffee grounds in the sink, crossed the room to him and gave him a rare hug and several bluff thumps on the back. "Sometimes, son, we got no choice," she said, then left him standing in the empty room beside the waiting telephone.

Chapter 3

♣

On the day following her conversations with Brookie and Eric, Maggie's phone made up for its usual silence. Her first call came at six A.M.

"Hi, Mom."

Maggie shot up and checked the clock. "Katy, are you all right?"

"I'm fine, which you would have known last night, except your phone was busy all night long."

"Oh, Katy, I'm sorry." Maggie stretched and settled into her pillow. "I had two of the most wonderful conversations with old high school friends." She filled Katy in on the highlights, asked where she was, told her to be sure to call again tonight, and said good-bye without any of the loneliness she'd expected upon ending her first long-distance conversation with her daughter.

Her next call came as she was bobbing her first tea bag of the day. It was Nelda.

"Tammi's going to make it and Dr. Feldstein says it would be good for her to see us."

Maggie put a hand to her heart, breathed, "Oh, thank God," and felt the day's promise brighten within her.

At 10:30 A.M. her next call came, this one wholly unexpected.

"Hello," she answered, and a voice out of her past said, "Hello, Maggie, this is Tani."

Jolted by surprise, Maggie smiled and held the receiver with both hands.

"Tani. Oh, Tani, how *are* you? Gosh, it's good to hear your voice."

Their conversation lasted forty minutes. Within an hour after it ended, Maggie answered the phone again, this time to hear a squeaky cartoon-mouse voice that could hardly be mistaken.

"Hi, Maggie. Guess who?"

"Fish? Fish, it's you, isn't it?"

"Yup. It's the fish."

"Oh my gosh, I can't believe this! Brookie called you, right?"

By the time Lisa called, Maggie was half expecting it. She was putting on the last of her makeup, preparing to go to the hospital and see Tammi when the phone rang yet again.

"Hello, stranger," a sweet voice said.

"Lisa . . . oh, Lisa . . ."

"It's been a long time, hasn't it?"

"Too long. Oh, goodness . . . I'm not sure I won't break down in tears here in a minute." She was half laughing, half crying.

"I'm a little choked up myself. How are you, Maggie?"

"How would you be if four of your dearest old friends rallied round when you put out the call? I'm overwhelmed."

Half an hour later, when they'd reminisced and caught up, Lisa said, "Listen, Maggie, I had an idea. Do you remember my brother, Gary?"

"Of course. He was married to Marcy Kreig."

"Was. They've been divorced for over five years. Well, Gary is getting remarried next week and I'll be in Door for the wedding. I was thinking, if you could come home, I'm sure Tani and Fish could drive up, and we could all get together out at Brookie's house."

"Oh, Lisa, I can't." Disappointment colored Maggie's voice. "It sounds wonderful, but I'm due to start teaching in less than two weeks."

"Just a quick trip?"

"I'm afraid it would be too quick, and at the beginning of the term like this . . . I'm sorry, Lisa."

"Oh, shoot. That's a disappointment."

"I know. It would have been so much fun."

"Well, listen . . . will you think about it? Even if it's only for the weekend. It would be so great to get everybody together again."

"All right," Maggie promised. "I'll think about it."

She did, on her drive in to the hospital to visit Tammi—about Brookie calling all the girls, and each of them concerned enough to make contact after all these years, and how her own outlook had brightened in so short a time. She thought about the curious rhythms in life, and how the support she'd just been given she would now pass on to another.

At 2:55 that afternoon she sat flipping the pages of a *Good Housekeeping* magazine in the family lounge of the intensive care unit of Washington University Hospital, waiting to be summoned. A television with its volume lowered murmured from its perch on the far wall. In a corner by the window a father and two sons waited for news of a mother who had undergone bypass surgery. From a Formica niche in the wall the smell of strong coffee drifted through the room.

A nurse entered, thin, pretty, walking briskly in on her silent, white shoes.

"Mrs. Stearn?"

"Yes?" Maggie dropped her magazine and jumped to her feet.

"You can go in and see Tammi now, but only for five minutes."

"Thank you."

Maggie wasn't prepared for the sight that greeted her upon entering Tammi's room. So much machinery. So many tubes and bottles; screens of various sizes bleeping out vital signs; and a thin, gaunt Tammi lying on the bed with a network of IV's threaded into her arms. Her eyes were closed, her hands lying wrist-up, her arms dotted by purple bruises where previous IVs had been. Her apricot-blond hair, which she'd always kept with meticulous teenage pride and wore in a style much like Katy's, lay brittle and spiky as a bird's nest on the pillow.

Maggie stood beside the bed for some time before Tammi opened her eyes and found her there.

"Hi, little one." Maggie leaned close and touched the girl's cheek. "We've all been so worried about you."

Tammi's eyes filled with tears and she rolled her face away.

Maggie brushed back Tammi's hair from her forehead. "We're so happy you're still alive."

"But I'm so ashamed."

"Noooo . . . noooo." Cupping Tammi's face, Maggie gently turned it toward herself. "You mustn't be ashamed. Think ahead, not behind. You're going to get stronger now, and we're all going to work together to get you happy."

Tammi's tears continued building and she tried to lift a hand to wipe them away. The hand was shaky, tethered by the IVs, and Maggie gently pushed it down, took a tissue from a nearby box and dried Tammi's eyes.

"I lost the baby, Maggie."

"I know, honey, I know."

Tammi turned her brimming gaze away while Maggie stayed close, brushing her temple.

"But you're alive, and it's your happiness we all care about. We want to see you up and smiling again."

"Why should anyone care about me?"

"Because you are you, an individual, and special. Because you've touched lives in ways you didn't realize. Each of us does that, Tammi. Each of us has worth. Can I tell you something?" Tammi turned back to Maggie who went on. "Last night I was so blue. My daughter had left for college, and you were in the hospital, and the house was so empty. Everything seemed hopeless. So I called one of my old high school friends, and do you know what happened?"

Tammi's eyes showed a spark of interest. "What?"

"She called some others, and started this wonderful chain reaction going. Today I had calls from three of them— wonderful old friends I haven't heard from in years, people I would never have suspected cared one way or the other about whether I was happy or not. That's how it will be with you, too. You'll see. Why, by the time I was getting ready to leave the house to come and see you, I was hoping the phone would stop ringing."

"Really?"

"Really." Maggie smiled, and received a glimmer of a smile in return. "Now, listen, little one . . ." She took Tammi's hand, careful not to disturb any of the plastic tubes. "They said I could stay for only five minutes, and I think my time is up. But I'll be back. Meanwhile, you think about what you'd like me to bring when you get into your own room. Malts, magazines, nachos—whatever you want."

"I know one thing right now."

"Just name it."

"Could you bring me some Nexxus shampoo and conditioner? I want my hair washed worse than anything."

"Absolutely. And my dryer and curling iron. We'll fix you up like Tina Turner."

Tammi almost laughed.

"That's what I like to see, those dimples showing." She kissed Tammi's forehead and whispered, "I've got to go. Get strong."

Leaving the hospital, Maggie felt charged with optimism: When a twenty-year-old girl asked to have her hair done, she was rounding the corner toward recovery! She stopped at a beauty shop on the way home and bought the things Tammi had asked for. Carrying the bag, she entered her kitchen to find her phone ringing again.

She charged across the room, whisked up the receiver and answered breathlessly, "Hello?"

"Maggie? It's Eric."

Surprise took her aback. She held the paper sack of shampoo against her stomach and stood tongue-tied for a full five seconds before realizing she must make some response. "Eric—well, heavens, this is a surprise."

"Are you okay?"

"Okay? I . . . well, yes. A little breathless is all. I just came in the door."

"I talked to Brookie and she told me the real reason you called last night."

"The real reason?" She set the bag on the cupboard in slow motion. "Oh, you mean my depression."

"I should have figured it out last night. I knew you weren't calling just to say hello."

"I'm much better today."

"Brookie said someone in your group tried to commit suicide. I just got so scared—I mean . . ." He heaved in a deep breath and expelled it loudly. "Christ, I don't know what I mean."

Maggie touched the receiver with her free hand. "Oh, Eric, you mean you thought I might be suicidal, too—that's why you're calling?"

"Well . . . I didn't know what to think. I just—hell, I couldn't get you off my mind today, wondering why you'd called. Finally, I had to call Brookie, and when she told me you'd been depressed and in therapy my gut clinched up. Maggie, you were always laughing when we were young."

"I'm not suicidal or even close to it. Honest, I'm not, Eric. It was a young woman named Tammi, but I just got back from visiting her in the hospital and she's not only going to make it, I got her to smile and almost laugh."

"Well, that's a relief."

"I'm sorry I wasn't completely truthful with you last night. Maybe I should have told you that I've been in group therapy, but after you answered the phone I felt—I don't know how to describe it—self-conscious, I guess. With Brookie it was a little easier, but with you, well . . . it seemed like an imposition after so many years, to call you up and wail about my difficulties."

"An imposition? Hell, that's silly."

"Maybe it was. Anyway, thanks for saying so. Listen, guess who else called today? Tani *and* Fish *and* Lisa. Brookie called every one of them. And now you. This has really been old home week."

"How are they? What are they doing?"

Maggie filled him in on the girls and as they talked, the constraints of last night disappeared. They reminisced a little. They laughed. As the conversation lengthened, Maggie found herself bent over the kitchen cabinet propped on both elbows, wholly at ease talking with him. He told her about his family, she told him about Katy. When a lull finally fell, it was comfortable. He ended it by saying, "I thought about you a lot today while I was out on the boat."

She traced a blue figure on a canister and said, "I thought about you, too." Insulated by distance, she found it easy to say. Harmless.

"I'd look out over the water and see you in a blue-and-gold letter sweater cheering for the Gibraltar Vikings."

"With my hair in some horrible beehive I suppose, and Cleopatra eye makeup."

He chuckled. "That's about it, yeah."

"Want to know what I see when I close my eyes and think of you?"

"I'm afraid to hear it."

She turned and braced her spine against the cabinet edge.

"I see you wearing a baby-blue sweater and dancing to the Beatles with a cigarette between your teeth."

He laughed. "The cigarette is gone but I'm still wearing a blue shirt, only now it says Captain Eric on the pocket."

"*Captain* Eric?"

"The customers like it. Gives them the illusion they're going seafaring."

"I'll bet you're good at it, aren't you? I'll bet the fishermen love you."

"Well, I can usually make them laugh and come back next year."

"Do you like it, what you do?"

"I love it."

She settled more comfortably against the cabinet. "So tell me about Door today. Was it sunny, did you catch fish, were there lots of sails on the water?"

"It was beautiful. Remember how you'd get up some mornings and the fog would be so thick you couldn't see across the harbor to Peninsula Park?"

"Mmmm . . ." she replied dreamily.

"It started out that way, with a heavy mist, then the sun came up over the trees and tinted the air red, but by the time we'd been on the water an hour the sky was as blue as a field of chicory."

"Oh, the chicory! Is it blooming now?"

"Full bloom."

"Mmm, I can just see it, a whole field of it, looking like the sky fell in. I loved this time of year back home. We don't have chicory here, not like in Door. Go on. Did you catch fish?"

"Eighteen today—fifteen chinook and three browns."

"Eighteen, wow," she breathed.

"We filled out."

"Hooray. And were there sails?"

"Sails . . ." he teased, perpetuating the long-standing raillery between power-and sail-boaters they'd inherited when they'd been born in Door County. "Who cares about sails?"

"I do."

"Yeah, I seem to remember you always were a ragman."

"And you always were a stinkpotter."

Maggie smiled and imagined him smiling, too. After seconds, her smile became whimsical. "I haven't been on the water for so long."

"Living in Seattle, I thought you'd have a boat."

"We do. A sailboat, naturally. But I haven't taken it out since Phillip died. I haven't fished either."

"You should come home and let me take you out with your dad. We'll hook you a big twenty-four pounder or so, and you'll get your share of fishing in one catch."

"Mmm, sounds heavenly."

"Do it."

"I can't."

"Why not?"

"I'm a teacher and school begins in less than two weeks."

"Oh, that's right. What do you teach again?"

"Home economics—food, clothing, family life, career planning. It's a mixed bag these days. We even have a unit where we turn the department into a nursery school and bring in preschoolers so the kids can study child development."

"Sounds noisy."

She shrugged. "Sometimes."

"So . . . are *you* good at it?"

"I suppose. I get along well with the kids, I think I make class interesting for them. But . . ." She paused.

"But what?"

"Oh, I don't know." She turned again and bent over the cabinet as before. "I've been doing the same thing for so many years it gets rather stagnant. And since Phillip's death . . ." Maggie put a hand to her forehead. "Oh, heavens, I get so tired of that phrase. *Since Phillip's death*. I've said it so often you'd think the calendar began that day."

"Sounds like you need a change."

"Maybe."

"I made a change six years ago. It was the healthiest thing I ever did for myself."

"What did you do?"

"Moved back to Door after living in Chicago since right after college. When I left here after high school I thought it was the last place on earth I'd come back to, but after sitting at a desk all those years, I was feeling claustrophobic. Then Dad died and Mike kept badgering me to come back and run the boat with him. He had these ideas about expanding our services, buying a second boat. So finally I said yes, and I haven't regretted it a day."

"You sound very happy."

"I am."

"In your marriage, too?"

"In my marriage, too."

"That's wonderful, Eric."

Another silence fell. It seemed they had said all that needed saying. Maggie straightened and checked the kitchen clock. "Listen, I'd better let you go. Gosh, we've been talking a long time."

"Yeah, I guess so . . ." An indistinguishable sound followed, the kind accompanied by a stretch. It ended abruptly. "I'm still up at Ma's house and Nancy's probably holding supper."

"Eric, thank you so much for calling. It's been wonderful talking to you."

"Same here."

"And please don't worry about me anymore. I'm happier than I've been in weeks."

"That's great to hear, and listen . . . call anytime. If I'm not around call out here and talk to Ma. She'd love to hear from you."

"Maybe I will, and tell her hello again. Tell her nobody in the world ever made bread as good as hers. I remember going to your house after school and polishing off about half a loaf at a time."

He laughed. "She still bakes, still claims store-bought bread will kill you. She'll get smug, but I'll give her your message anyway."

"Eric, thanks again."

"No thanks necessary. I enjoyed it. Now you take it easy, all right?"

"I will."

They both paused, uneasy for the first time in over thirty minutes.

"Well . . . good-bye," he said.

"Good-bye."

When Maggie hung up, her hand lingered on the phone, then fell away slowly. Studying the receiver, she stood motionless for a long time. The late afternoon sun slanted across the kitchen floor and from outside came the muffled sound of a neighbor mowing his lawn. From long ago came images of the same sun shining on other lawns, other trees, other water—not Puget Sound but Green Bay. In time Maggie slowly turned away from the telephone and wandered to the patio door. She rolled it open, leaned a shoulder against the casing and stood staring out, remembering. Him. Them. Door. That last year of high school. First love.

Ah, nostalgia.

But he was a happily married man. And if she saw him again he'd probably be twenty-five pounds overweight and balding and she'd be happy he was married to someone else.

Nevertheless, talking to him brought back thoughts of home, and as she stood staring at the evening yard she saw not a redwood deck surrounded by evergreens, but a sunbaked carpet of azure chicory. Nothing was as intense a blue as a field of blooming chicory stretched out beneath the August sun. And at evening it turned violet, sometimes creating the illusion that sky and earth were one. The Queen Anne's lace would be in full bloom, too, rioting in the high country fields and roadsides, sharing the rocky earth with black-eyed Susans and clumps of white yarrow. Was there another place on earth where wildflowers bloomed so profusely as in the Door?

She saw, too, gambrel-roofed red barns and rows of green corn and century-old log cabins with white-painted caulking; split rail fences and stone walls bordered by thick spills of orange lilies. White sails on blue water and unspoiled beaches that stretched for miles. She tasted home-baked bread and heard the growl of inboard motors coming home at dusk and caught the aroma of fishboils lifting over the villages on a Saturday night such as this one, coming from the backyards of restaurants where guitars played and red-and-white-checked tablecloths flitted in the evening breeze.

From two thousand miles away Maggie remembered it all and felt a surge of homesickness she had not known in years.

She thought of calling home. But Mother might answer, and if anyone could wreck a mellow mood, it was Mother.

Instead, she drew away from the door and went into the den where she took down a book called *Journeys to Door County*. For nearly half an hour she sat in Phillip's desk chair turning the full-color pages until the glossy photos of lighthouses and log cabins and landscapes prompted her to finally pick up the phone.

Dialing her parents' phone number she hoped her father would answer. Instead, she heard her mother's voice answer, "Hello?"

Hiding her disappointment Maggie said, "Hello, Mother."

"Margaret?"

"Yes."

"Well, it's about time you called. It's been over two weeks since we've heard from you, and you said you'd let us know when we could expect Katy. I've been waiting and waiting for you to call!"

Not, *Hello, dear, it's good to hear from you,* but *It's about time you called!* forcing Maggie to begin the conversation with an apology.

"I'm sorry, Mother, I know I should have called, but I've been busy. And I'm afraid Katy won't be stopping there on the way. It's out of her way, and she had her roommate with her and the car was loaded to the roof so they decided they'd better go straight to school and check into their dorm."

Maggie closed her eyes and waited for the list of grievances she was certain would follow. True to form, Vera came through with them.

"Well, I won't say I'm not disappointed. After all, I've been cooking and baking here all week. I put two apple pies in the freezer and bought a big beef roast. I don't know what I'll do with a piece of meat that big with only your dad and I to eat it up, and I cleaned your old room from top to bottom and did up the bedding and the curtains, and they're real devils to iron!"

"Mother, I told you we'd call if she was going to make it to your place."

"Well, I know, but I was so sure she would. After all, we're the only grandparents she has."

"I know, Mother."

"I guess young people don't have time for their grandparents like they did when I was a girl," Vera remarked petulantly.

Maggie rested her forehead on four fingertips and felt herself getting a headache.

"She said she'll drive up from Chicago in a couple weeks, after she gets settled in school. She mentioned maybe coming up in October when the leaves are turning."

"What is she driving? You didn't buy her that convertible, did you?"

"Yes, I did."

"Margaret, that child is too young to own an extravagant car like that! You should have bought her something sensible or better yet made her wait until she's out of college. How is she ever going to learn to appreciate things if you give her everything on a silver platter?"

"I think Phillip would have wanted her to have it, and heaven knows I can afford it."

"That's no reason to overdo it with her, Margaret. And speaking of money, you be careful about who you see. These divorced men are out there just looking for a rich, lonely widow. They'll take you for everything you've got and use your money to pay child support, mark my words!"

"I'll be careful, Mother," Maggie promised tiredly, feeling the headache intensify.

"Why, I remember a few years back when that young Gearhart fellow was stepping out on his wife and who was he seeing but some summer tourist who came up here from down in Louisiana someplace on a flashy cabin cruiser. They say the two of them were seen on the deck kissing on a Saturday night, and then Sunday morning he showed up at church all pious and pure with his wife and kids. Why, if Betty Gearhart knew what—"

"Mother, I said I'll be careful. I'm not even dating anyone, so you don't have to worry."

"Well, you can't be too careful, you know."

"I know."

"And speaking of divorcés, Gary Eidelbach is getting remarried next Saturday."

"I know, I talked to Lisa."

"You did? When?"

"Today. I've been in touch with all the girls lately."

"You didn't tell me that." Vera's voice held a trace of coolness, as if she expected to be told everything before it transpired.

"Lisa wants me to come home for the wedding. Well, not exactly for the wedding, but she's coming up from Atlanta so she thought all us girls could get together out at Brookie's."

"Are you coming?"

Then you could use up your beef roast and your apple pie, couldn't you, Mother?

"No, I can't."

"Why not? What else are you going to do with all that money? You know your father and I can't afford to travel out there on a plane and, after all, you haven't been home for three years."

Maggie sighed, wishing she could hang up the phone without a further word. "It isn't a question of money, Mother, it's a question of time. School will be starting soon and—"

"Well, we're not getting any younger you know. Your dad and I would appreciate a visit from you every now and then."

"I know. Is Daddy there?"

"He's here someplace. Just a minute." The phone clunked down and Vera went off, shouting, "Roy, where are you? Margaret is on the phone!" Her voice crescendoed as she returned and picked up the receiver. "Just a minute. He's outside puttering in the garage, sharpening the mower again. It's a wonder the thing has any blades left, as much time as he spends out there. Here he is now." As the phone exchanged hands Maggie heard Vera order, "Keep your hands off the counter, Roy, they're filthy!"

"Maggie, honey?" Roy's voice held all the warmth Vera's didn't. Hearing him, Maggie felt her homesickness return.

"Hi, Daddy."

"Well, this is a nice surprise. You know, I was just thinking about you today, about when you were a little girl and you'd come around asking for a nickel to buy a Dixie Cup."

"And you always gave me one, didn't you?"

He laughed and Maggie pictured his round face and balding head, his slightly stooped shoulders and the hands that never stopped working.

"Well, my head is turned by a pretty girl, same as the next man's. It's sure good to hear your voice, Maggie."

"I thought I'd better call and let you know Katy's not coming. She's going straight to school."

"Well, she'll be in our neck of the woods for four years. We'll see her when she's got time." It had always been this way—all the petty concerns Vera blew out of proportion, Roy put back into perspective. "And how about you?" he asked. "I suppose it's a little lonely around there with her gone."

"It's terrible."

"Well, honey, you get out of the house. Go to a movie or something. You shouldn't be there alone on a Saturday night."

"I won't be. I'm going to the club for dinner," she lied to ease his worry.

"Good . . . good. That's what I like to hear. School starting pretty soon, is it?"

"In less than two weeks."

"Here, too. Then the streets will be quiet during the week again. You know how it is. We cuss the tourists when they're here and miss 'em when they're gone."

She smiled. How many times in her life had she heard the equivalent of his remark? "I remember."

"Well, listen, honey, your mother's waiting to talk to you again."

"Here's a kiss, Daddy."

"And here's one for you. Be good now."

"Bye, Daddy."

"Good-b—"

"Margaret?" Vera had taken the receiver before Roy had a chance to finish.

"I'm here, Mother."

"Did you get rid of that sailboat yet?"

"No, but I've still got it listed with the agent at the marina."

"Don't you go out on it alone!"

"I won't."

"And be careful who you invest that money with."

"I will. Mother, I've got to go now. I'm going out to the club for dinner and I'm running a little late."

"All right, but don't wait so long to call next time."

"I won't."

"You know we'd call more often if we could, but these long distance rates are absolutely ridiculous. Now, listen, if you talk to Katy tell her her grandpa and I are anxious for her to come up."

"I will."

"Well . . . good-bye then, dear." Vera never failed to include one perfunctory endearment as their conversations ended.

"Bye, Mother."

By the time Maggie hung up, she needed a hot drink to soothe her nerves. She made a cup of herb tea and took it into the bathroom while she brushed her hair. Viciously.

Was it too much to expect a mother to inquire about her daughter's welfare? Her happiness? Her friends? Concerns? As always, Vera had turned the focus on herself. *Vera's* hard work. *Vera's* disappointments. *Vera's* demands. The entire *world* should consider Vera's wishes before it made its next move!

Return to Door County? Even for a vacation? No way on God's green earth!

Maggie was still punishing her scalp when the phone rang again. This time it was Brookie, opening without an introduction.

"We've got it all arranged. Lisa is getting in on Tuesday and she'll be spending a week or so at her mother's. Tani's right in Green Bay, and Fish's got only a three-hour drive from Brussels, so we're all getting together out here at my house on Wednesday noon and we plan on you being here, too. What do you say? Can you come?"

"Not within a hundred miles of my mother! Absolutely not!"

"Oh-oh. Sounds like I called at a bad time."

"I was talking to her. I just hung up."

In a conversational tone Brookie inquired, "How is the old bat?"

A snort of laughter caught Maggie by surprise. "Brookie, she's my *mother*!"

"Well, that's not *your* fault. And it shouldn't keep you from coming home to see your friends. Now what do you say—all five of us, a few bottles of vino, a few laughs and a good long gab session. All it takes is a plane ticket."

"Oh, damn, it sounds good."

"Then say you'll come."

"But I've—"

"But shit. Just come. Just drop everything and jump on a plane."

"Damn you, Brookie!"

"I'm a devil, ain't I?"

"Yes." Maggie thumped a foot on the floor. "Oh, I want to come so badly."

"Well, what's holding you back?"

Maggie's excuses tumbled out, as if she were trying to convince herself. "It's such short notice, and I'd only have five days, and teachers have to be back in school three days before the students, and I'd have to stay at my mother's and I can't even carry on a *telephone* conversation with her without wanting to put myself up for adoption!"

"You can stay with me. I can always throw a sleeping bag on the floor and another bone in the soup. Hell, there are so many bodies around this house one more will hardly be noticed."

"I couldn't do that—come all the way to Wisconsin and stay at your house. I'd never hear the end of it."

"So stay at your mother's nights and make sure you're gone all day. We'll go swimming and walk across the bar to Cana Island and poke around the antique shops. Heck, we can do anything we feel like. I've got one last week of vacation before school starts and I lose my built-in babysitters. God, could I use the escape. We could have a great time, Maggie. What do you say?"

"Oh, Brookie." The words conveyed Maggie's wilting determination.

"You said that before."

"Oh, Brookieeee!" Even as they laughed Maggie's face became distorted by frustration and longing.

"I suspect you've got plenty of money to buy a ticket," Brookie added.

"So much that you'd gag if I told you."

"Good for the woman. So come. Please."

Maggie lost her struggle with temptation.

"Oh, all right, you pest, I will!"

"Eeeyiiiiiiiiyow!" Brookie broke off the banshee yell to tell someone

nearby, "Maggie's coming!" To Maggie she said, "I'm getting off this phone so you can call the airport. Call me as soon as you get into town, or better yet, stop here first before going to your folks'. See you Tuesday!"

Maggie hung up and said to the wall, "I'm going to Door County." She rose from the chair and *exclaimed* to the wall, her palms raised in amazement, "I'm going to Door County! Day after tomorrow, I'm actually going to Door County!"

The sense of surprise remained, augmented. Maggie accomplished nothing on Sunday. She packed and unpacked five assortments of clothes, finally deciding she needed something new. She styled and restyled her hair deciding, too, on a trip to the beauty shop. She called for plane reservations and booked a seat in first class. She had almost a million and a half dollars in the bank and decided—for the first time ever—that it was time she started enjoying it.

At Gene Juarez the following day she told the unfamiliar hair designer, "Do something state of the art. I'm going home to get together with my high school girlfriends for the first time in twenty-three years." She came out looking like something that had been boiled and hung upside down to dry. The odd thing was, it exhilarated her as nothing had in years.

Next she stopped at Nordstrom's and asked the clerk, "What would my daughter wear if she were going to a Prince concert?" She came out with three pairs of acid-washed blue jeans and a selection of strappy undershirts that looked like something old man Niedzwiecki would wear selling used auto parts in his junk yard.

At Helen's Of Course she bought a couple of refined dresses—one for travel, one for any exigencies that might arise—sniffed the favorite perfumes of everyone from Elizabeth Taylor to Lady Bird Johnson, but wound up in Woolworth's dime store merrily paying $2.95 for a bottle of Emeraude which remained her perennial favorite.

On Tuesday morning she stepped out of a cab at Sea-Tac International Airport into a driving rain, deplaned four hours later in Green Bay beneath a blinding sun, and rented a car in a state of disbelief. During all her years of travel with Phillip they had always planned their trips weeks, months in advance. Impulsiveness was new to Maggie; it was exhilarating. Why had she never tried it before?

She made the drive north with a renewed sense of emerging and crossed the canal at Sturgeon Bay with an onrushing feeling of home. Door County at last, and within miles her first glimpse of cherry orchards. The trees—already shorn of their bounty—marched in formation across rolling green meadows rimmed with limestone walls and green forests. Apple and plum orchards hung heavy with fruit which shone like beacons in the August sun. At intervals along the highway open-air markets displayed colorful crates of fruit, berries, vegetables, juices and jams.

And of course there were the barns, telling the nationality of those who'd built them: the Belgian barns made of brick; the English ones of frame construction with gabled rooves and side doors; the Norwegians' variety of square-cut logs; the German ones of round logs; tall Finnish barns of two stories; German bank barns built into the earth, others half-timbered with the spaces between the timbers filled with brick or stovewood. And one grand specimen painted with a gay floral design against a red ground.

In Door County log structures were as common as frame ones. Sometimes entire farms remained as they had been a hundred years ago, their log buildings lovingly preserved, the cabins enhanced by modern bay windows and dormers, trimmed with white door-and window-frames. Yards were surrounded by split rail fences and abundant flowers— daylilies in grand, thrusting clumps of yellow and orange; petunias in puddles of pink; and hollyhocks, tipping their showy stalks at roadside culverts.

At Egg Harbor Maggie slowed to a crawl, amazed to see how it had grown. Tourists dawdled everywhere, crossing the road licking ice cream cones; on sidewalks before antique displays; in the doorways of craft shops. She passed the Blue Iris Restaurant, and the Cupola House, standing tall and white and unchanging, feeling their familiarity seep into her spirit and excite it. Then out onto the highway toward Fish Creek, between rich, tan wheat fields and more orchards and great stands of birches that stood out like chalk marks upon green velvet.

She reached the high bluff above her hometown, a last cherry orchard on the left, then the sharp downswing of the highway around the base of a sheer limestone cliff, into the town itself. Coming upon it was forever a pleasing surprise. One minute you were in the farmland above with no inkling the town lay below; the next you were sitting at a stop sign looking straight ahead at the sparkling waters of Fish Creek Harbor with Main Street stretching off to your left and right.

It was exactly as she remembered, tourists everywhere, and cars inching along while pedestrians jaywalked wherever they pleased; gaily decorated shops built in old houses along a shady Main Street whose east and west ends were both visible from where she sat. How long had it been since she'd been in a town without a traffic light or a turn lane? Or one whose Main Street needed mowing in the summer and raking in the fall? Where else did the Standard Gas Station look like Goldilocks's cottage? And the bakery have a front veranda? And the alleys between the buildings need regular watering to keep the petunias and geraniums healthy?

Across Main an old false-fronted building drew her attention: the Fish Creek General Store where her father worked. She smiled, imagining him behind the long white butcher case where he'd been cutting meat and making sandwiches for as long as she remembered.

Hi, Daddy, she thought. *I'll be right back.*

She turned west and drove at a snail's pace beneath the boulevard maples, past flowered lawns and gabled houses that had been transformed into gift shops, past the Whistling Swan, an immense white clapboard inn with its great east porch replete with wicker chairs. Past the confectionery and Founders Square, and the cottage of Asa Thorp, the town's founder, and the community church where the doves and morning glories on the three stained glass windows were exactly as she remembered. Out past the White Gull Inn to the end of the road where a tall stand of cedars marked the entrance to Sunset Beach Park. There the trees opened up and gave a majestic view of Green Bay, sparkling in the late afternoon sun.

She stopped the car, got out and stood in the lee of the open door, shading her eyes, admiring the sails—dozens of sails—far out on the water.

Home again.

In the car once more, she drove back the way she'd come.

The traffic crawled, and parking spots were at a premium, but she snagged one in front of a gift shop called The Dove's Nest and walked back a block and a half, past the stone retaining walls where tourists sat and sipped cool drinks.

Raising a hand to stop traffic she sneaked between two bumpers to the other side of the street.

The concrete steps of the Fish Creek General Store were as pitted as ever, leading up to doors set in an inverted bay. Inside, the floors squeaked, the lighting was less than adequate, and the smell was rich with memory: years of fruit that had grown too old to sell, and home-cured sausage and the sweeping compound Albert Olson still used when he swept the floors at night.

At five o'clock in the afternoon the place was crowded. She passed the busy counter up front, waving to Albert's wife, Mae, who called a surprised hello, and worked her way to the rear where a knot of customers surrounded the shoulder-high meat and delicatessen counter. Behind it, her father, dressed in a long white bibbed apron, was busy charming the customers as he ran the meat slicer.

"Fresh?" he was saying, above the whine of the machine. "Why, I went out and killed the cow myself at six o'clock this morning." He reached down and switched off the motor, swinging into the next motion without a wasted movement. "That's one French with mustard and Swiss. One pumpernickel with mustard and American." He sliced a French roll, slapped down two slices of pumpernickel, slathered them with butter and mustard, clapped on two stacks of corned beef, rolled open the glass door of the display case, peeled off two slices of cheese, plopped the ingredients into stacks and snapped the finished sandwiches into plastic containers. The entire process had taken him less than thirty seconds.

"Anything else?" He stood with the butts of his hands braced on the shoulder-high counter. "Potato salad's the best you'll find anywhere on the shores of Lake Michigan. My grandma grew the potatoes herself." He winked at the couple who were waiting for their sandwiches.

They laughed and said, "No, that'll be all."

"Pay up front. Next!" Roy bellowed.

A sixtyish man in Bermuda shorts and a terrycloth beach jacket ordered two pastrami sandwiches.

Watching her father make them, Maggie was amazed anew at his business persona, so different from the one he displayed around home. He was amusing and startlingly efficient. People loved him on sight. He could make them laugh and come back for more.

She stood back, remaining inconspicuous, watching him work the crowd like a barker in a sideshow, scarcely appearing to glance at them as he rushed from spot to spot. She listened to the sound of butcher paper tearing, of his hands slapping down beef roasts, of the heavy rolling doors on the meat case—the same one that had been here since she was a child. There was a wait—in summer there always was—but he kept tempers off edge with his efficiency and showmanship.

When she had watched for several minutes, she stepped up to the counter while his back was turned.

"I'll have a nickel from your pocket to buy a Dixie Cup," she said quietly.

He glanced over his shoulder and his face went blank with surprise.

"Maggie?" He swung around, wiping his hands on his white apron. "Maggie-honey, am I seeing things?"

She laughed, happy she'd come. "Nope, I'm really here." If the meat case had been any lower he might have vaulted over it. Instead he came around the end where he scooped her up in a jarring hug.

"Well, Maggie, this is a surprise."

"To me, too."

He held her away by both shoulders. "What are you doing here?"

"Brookie talked me into coming."

"Does your mother know yet?"

"No, I came straight to the store."

"Well, I'll be." He laughed jubilantly, hugged her again, then remembered his customers. With an arm around her shoulders, he turned to them. "For those of you who think I'm just a dirty old man, this is my daughter, Maggie, from Seattle. Just gave me the surprise of my life." Releasing her, he said, "Are you going up to the house now?"

"I guess so."

He checked his watch. "Well, I've got another forty-five minutes here yet. I'll be home at six. How long are you staying?"

"Five days."

"That's all?"

"I'm afraid so. I have to go back Sunday."

"Well, five's better than nothing. Now go on so I can take care of this crowd." He headed back toward his duties, calling after Maggie, "Tell your mother to call if she needs anything extra for supper."

As Maggie started her car and headed home, her enthusiasm waned. She drove slowly, wondering as she often did whether it was her tendency to expect too much of her mother that always made homecoming a disappointment. Pulling up before the house where she'd grown up, Maggie leaned over and peered at it a moment before leaving the car. Completely unchanged. Prairie-styled, two-storied, with a low-pitched hipped roof and widely overhanging eaves, it would have been perfectly square were it not for the front porch with its massive native limestone supports. Sturdy and stolid, with bridal wreath bushes on either side of the stone steps and matched elms in the side yards, the house looked as if it would be standing a hundred years from now.

Maggie turned off the engine and sat awhile: for as long as she could remember her mother had rushed to the front window at the sound of any action on the street. Vera would stand back from the curtains and watch neighbors unload their passengers or purchases and at supper would give a blow-by-blow, laced with aspersions. "Elsie must have been to Sturgeon Bay today. She had bags from Piggly Wiggly. Why she'd want to shop in *that* store is beyond me. It has the worst smell! I swear things are never fresh in there. But of course you can't tell *Elsie* anything."

Or, "Toby Miller brought that Anderson girl home in the middle of the afternoon when I know perfectly well his mother was working. Only sixteen years old and in the house all alone for a good hour and a half— Judy Miller would have a fit if she knew!"

Maggie closed the car door with little more than a click and walked up the front sidewalk almost reluctantly. On the parapets at the foot of the steps a pair of stone urns held the same pink geraniums and vinca vines as always. The wooden porch floor gleamed with its annual coat of gray paint. The welcome mat looked as if no shoe had ever scraped over it. The aluminum screen door had the same "P" on its grille.

She opened it quietly and stood in the front hall, listening. At the far end of the house a radio played softly and the kitchen water ran. The living room was quiet, tasteful, spotless. It had never been allowed to be otherwise, for Vera let it be known that shoes were to be left at the door, feet kept off the coffee table, and no smoking was allowed anywhere near her draperies. The fireplace had the same stack of birch logs it had had for thirty years because Vera never allowed them to be burned: fires made ashes and ashes were dirty. The andirons and fan-shaped firescreen had never been tarnished by smoke nor had the cinnamon-red bricks been discolored by heat. The mahogany mantel and woodwork gleamed, and through a square archway the cherry dining-room table held the same lace runner and the same silver bowl as always—one of Vera and Roy's wedding gifts.

Maggie found the changelessness simultaneously comforting and stifling.

Down the strips of varnished floor beside the hall runner, reflected light gleamed from the kitchen at the rear, and to the left the mahogany stairway climbed the wall and took a right turn at a landing with a high window. A thousand times Maggie had come running down only to hear her mother's voice ordering from below, "Margaret! *Walk* down those stairs!" Maggie was standing looking up at the landing window when Vera entered the opposite end of the hall, came up short, gasped and screamed.

"Mother, it's me, Maggie."

"Oh my word, girl, you scared the daylights out of me!" She had fallen back against the wall with a hand on her heart.

"I'm sorry, I didn't mean to."

"Well, what in the world are you doing here anyway?"

"I just came. Just . . ." Maggie spread her hands and shrugged. ". . . jumped on a plane and came."

"Well, my word, you could let a person know. What in the *world* have you done to your hair?"

"I tried something new." Maggie reached up, unconsciously trying to flatten the moussed strands that only yesterday had made her feel jaunty.

Vera looked away from the hair and took to fanning her face with a hand. "Gracious, my heart is still in my throat. Why, a person my age could have a stroke from a shock like that—standing there in front of the screen door where a person can't even see your face. All I could see was that hair sticking up. Why, for all I know you could have been a burglar looking for something to grab and run with. These days, from the things you read in the papers you never know anymore, and this town is full of strangers. A person should almost keep their doors locked."

Maggie moved toward Vera. "Don't I get a hug?"

"Why, of course."

Vera was much like her house: stout and stocky, meticulously neat and unmodish. She'd worn the same hairstyle since 1965—a backcombed French roll with two neat crescent curls up above the corners of her forehead. The hairdo got lacquered in once a week at Bea's Beauty Nook by Bea herself who had as little imagination as her customers. Vera wore a homogenized outfit of polyester aqua-blue double-knit slacks, a white shell and white nurse's shoes with thick crepe soles, rimless glasses with a silver slash across the top, and an apron.

As Maggie moved toward her she gave more of a hug than she received. "My hands are wet," Vera explained. "I was peeling potatoes."

As the hug ended, Maggie experienced the vague disappointment she always felt when she reached for any affection from her mother. With her father she'd have sauntered toward the kitchen arm in arm. With her mother she walked apart.

"Mmm . . . it smells good in here." She would try *very hard*.

"I'm making pork chops in cream of mushroom soup. Goodness, I hope I have enough for supper. I just *wish* you had called, Margaret."

"Daddy said for you to call and he'd bring home anything you need."

"Oh? You've seen him already?" There it was—the subtle jealous undertone Maggie always sensed at the mention of Roy.

"Just for a minute. I stopped at the store."

"Well, it's too late to put your pork chops in with the others. They'll never get done. I guess I'll just have to fry them for you." Vera headed directly for the kitchen phone.

"No, Mom, don't bother. I can run up and get a sandwich."

"A sandwich, why don't be silly!"

Maggie rarely ate pork anymore and would have preferred a turkey sandwich but Vera was dutifully dialing the phone before Maggie could state a preference. While she spoke she used her apron to polish the top of the spotless telephone. "Hello, Mae? This is Vera. Will you tell Roy to bring two pork chops home?" Next she polished the adjacent countertop. "No, two will be fine, and tell him to get here at six or everything else will be all dried up like it was last night. Thanks, Mae." She hung up and turned toward the sink, rushing on without a pause. "I swear you wouldn't know that father of yours owns a watch. He's supposed to get off at six on the dot, but he doesn't give a rip if he walks in here half an hour late or not. I said to him the other day, I said, 'Roy, if those customers at the store are more important than coming home to supper on time, maybe you should just move in down there.' Do you know what he did?" Vera's wattle shook as she picked up a peeler and began slashing at a potato. "He went out to the garage without so much as a word! Sometimes you wouldn't even think I lived here, for all he talks to me. He's out in the garage all the time. Now he even took a TV out there to watch his baseball games while he putters."

Maybe he'd watch it in the house, Mother, if you'd let him set his popcorn bowl where he wants to, or put his feet up on your precious coffee table.

Returning to her mother's realm, Maggie wondered how her father had tolerated living with her for forty-odd years. Maggie herself had been in the house only five minutes and already her nerves felt frayed.

"Well, you didn't come home to hear about that," Vera said in a tone that warned Maggie would hear plenty more in the next four days. Vera finished her peeling and put the pan of potatoes on the stove. "You must have some suitcases in the car. Why don't you bring them in and put them upstairs while I set the table?"

How badly Maggie wanted to say, "I'm staying out at Brookie's," but Vera's dominance could not be shrugged off. Even at age forty, Maggie hadn't the courage to cross her.

Upstairs, she forgot and set her suitcase on the bed. A moment later she plucked it off and set it on the floor, glancing cautiously toward the door, then smoothing the spread, relieved to see she hadn't left a mark on it.

The room looked the same. When Vera bought furniture, she bought it to last. Maggie's maple bed and dresser sat in the same spots as always. The subtle blue-flowered wallpaper through which Maggie had never been allowed to put thumbtacks would serve for years yet. Her desk was back in place; during the years when Katy had been a baby Vera had installed a crib in the spot for their convenience.

The memory brought a stab of longing. At the window Maggie held back the curtain and gazed down at the tidy backyard.

Phillip, I miss you so much. It was always easier to face Mother with you beside me.

She sighed, dropped the curtain into place and knelt to unpack.

Inside the closet some of her father's old suits hung beside a sealed plastic bag holding her formal from senior prom. Pink. Eric had asked her to wear pink and had given her a wrist corsage of pink tea roses.

Eric is married, and you're acting like a middle-aged idiot, standing here staring at a musty old dress.

She changed from her linen traveling suit into a pair of new Guess jeans and two of her rib-knit tank tops, blue over white. Around her throat she tied a twisted cotton scarf and added a pair of oversized lozenge-shaped earrings.

When she entered the kitchen, Vera took one look at her ensemble and said, "Those clothes are a little young for you, aren't they, dear?"

Maggie dropped a glance at the blotchy blue-and-white denim and answered, "There was no age restriction on the tag when I bought them."

"You know what I mean, dear. Sometimes when a woman is middle-aged she can make herself look ridiculous by trying to appear younger than she really is."

Rage formed a lump in Maggie's throat, and she knew if she didn't get away from her mother soon she'd blow up and make the next four days intolerable.

"I'm going out to Brookie's tonight. I doubt that she'll mind what I wear."

"Going to Brookie's! I don't see why you have to run out there the minute you get here."

No, Mother, I'm sure you don't, Maggie thought, and headed for the back door to escape her for a few minutes.

"Need anything from the garden?" she asked with forced lightness.

"No. Supper is all ready. All we need is your dad."

"Think I'll go out anyway."

Maggie slipped outside and wandered around the impeccably neat backyard, past the tidy strips of marigolds bordering the house, into the garage where her dad's vise and tools were arranged with military neatness. The floor was ridiculously clean, and the television set was perched above the workbench on a newly constructed shelf.

Poor Daddy.

Closing the service door of the garage she trailed around the vegetable garden where the beans and pea vines were already pulled up and gone, the tops of the onions drying. In all of her life she never remembered her mother putting off a single job that needed doing. Why did she resent even that?

Vera called out the back door. "On second thought, dear, pick me a couple of ripe tomatoes for slicing."

Maggie stepped between the tomato stakes and picked two to take to the house. But when she delivered them to the kitchen and stepped off the back rug, Vera scolded, "Take your shoes off, dear. I just waxed the floor yesterday."

By the time Roy got home Maggie felt ready to explode. She met him halfway up the sidewalk from the garage and walked with him, arm in arm, to the house.

"It's good to see you running out to meet me," he said fondly.

She smiled and squeezed his arm, feeling her frayed emotions smooth. "Ah, Daddy!" she sighed, tipping her face to the sky.

"I suppose you surprised the daylights out of your mother."

"She nearly had a stroke, or so she claimed."

"Your mother will never have a stroke. She wouldn't abide it."

"You're late, Roy," Vera interrupted from the doorway, opening the screen door and gesturing impatiently toward the white package in his hand. "And I still have to fry those pork chops. Hurry up and bring them up here."

He handed her the package and she disappeared. Left on the steps, Roy shrugged and smiled dolefully at his daughter.

"Come on," she said, "show me what's new in your workshop."

Inside the room with its scent of fresh wood, she asked, "Why do you let her do that to you, Daddy?"

"Aw, your mother's a good woman."

"She's a good *cook* and a good *housekeeper*. But she drives us both crazy. I don't have to live with it anymore, but you do. Why do you put up with it?"

He considered a moment and said, "I guess I never thought it was worth the trouble to buck her."

"Instead, you just come out here."

"Well, I enjoy it out here. I've been making a few birdhouses and bird-feeders to sell at the store."

She put a hand on his arm. "But don't you ever want to tell her to shut her mouth, to let you think for yourself? Daddy, she runs all over you."

He picked up a piece of planed oak and rubbed it with his fingertips. "Do you remember Grandma Pearson?"

"Yes, a little."

"She was the same way. Ran my dad like a drill sergeant runs new recruits. It's all I ever knew."

"But that doesn't make it right, Daddy."

"They celebrated their golden wedding anniversary before they died."

Their gazes caught and held for several seconds. "That's perseverance, Daddy, not happiness. There's a difference."

His fingers stopped rubbing the oak and he set it neatly aside. "It's what my generation believes in."

Perhaps he was right. Perhaps his life was peaceful enough, out here in his workshop, uptown at his job. Certainly his wife provided an immaculate home, good meals and clean clothing—the traditional wifely duties in which his generation also believed. If he accepted these as enough, who was she, Maggie, to foment dissatisfaction?

She reached for his hand. "All right, forget I mentioned it. Let's go in and have supper."

Chapter 4

♣

Glenda Holbrook Kerschner lived in a ninety-year-old farmhouse surrounded by twenty acres of Montmorency cherry trees, sixty acres of untilled meadow and woods, a venerable old red barn, a less venerable steel pole barn and a network of paths worn by children, machinery, dogs, cats, horses, cows, deer, raccoon and skunks.

Maggie had been here years before, but the house was larger now, with a clapboard addition jutting off the original limestone structure. The veranda, once railed in white, had been enclosed with glass and had become part of the living space. An immense vegetable garden stretched down an east-facing hill behind the house and on a clothesline (nearly as big as the garden) hung four rag rugs. Maggie drove into the yard shortly before eight o'clock that evening.

The engine was still running when the back door flew open and Brookie sailed out, shouting, "Maggie, you're here!"

Leaving the car door open, Maggie ran. They met in the yard, off-balance, hugging, glisteny-eyed.

"Brookie, it's so good to see you!"

"I can't believe it! I just can't believe it!"

"I'm here! I'm really here."

Pulling back at last, Brookie said, "My God, look at you! Thinner than a rake handle. Don't they feed you back in Seattle?"

"I came back here to get fattened up."

"Well, this is the place, as you can see."

Pirouetting, Glenda displayed her newel-post shape. Each of her pregnancies had left her five pounds heavier, but she was middle-age cute, with short brown hair curling around her face, an infectious smile and attractive hazel eyes.

She clapped both hands on her ample width and looked down at herself. "As Gene would say—heat in the winter and shade in the summer." Before Maggie finished laughing she was being herded to the house, tight against Brookie's side. "Come and meet him."

On the back step Gene Kerschner waited, tall, angular, dressed in blue jeans and a faded plaid shirt, holding the hand of a barefoot little girl in a nightgown, no taller than his hip. He looked the part of a contented farmer, a happy father, Maggie thought as he released the child's hand to give her a welcoming hug. "So this is Maggie. It's been a long time."

"Hello, Gene." She smiled up at the slow-spoken man.

"Maybe now that you're here Glenda can stop fretting."

The little girl tugged his jeans. "Daddy, who's that?"

He lifted the child and perched her on his arm. "This is Mommy's friend, Maggie." And, to Maggie, "This is our second youngest, Chrissy."

"Hi, Chrissy." Maggie extended a hand.

The child stuck a finger in her mouth and shyly laid her forehead against her father's jaw.

Laughing, they all moved inside while Glenda added, "The rest of the kids are scattered around. Justin's two, he's already down for the night, thank heavens. Julie and Danny are out riding Penelope, our horse. Erica's out on a date—she's sweet sixteen and madly in love. Todd's working in town, waiting tables at The Cookery. He's nineteen and he's trying to decide whether he should join the Air Force. And Paul, our oldest, has already gone back to college."

The house was spacious and serviceable with a farm-size kitchen dominated by a clawfoot table surrounded by eight chairs. The living room extended the kitchen, great-room style, and was furnished with worn davenports, a console TV and, at the end where the porch had been enclosed, an antique iron daybed flanked by two rocking chairs. The decor was unglamorous, a combination of Sears Roebuck, children's school art projects, and K Mart wall plaques and houseplants, but the moment Maggie walked in she felt at home.

She could tell immediately, Brookie's family was handled with a firm but loving hand.

"Kiss Mommy," Gene told Chrissy, "you're going to bed."

"Nooooo!" Chrissy flailed her feet against his stomach and draped her backside over his arm in token resistance.

"Yup, 'fraid so."

She took her father's face in both hands and tried a little female wile. "Pleeeeze, Daddy, can't I stay up for a little while longer?"

"You're a flirt," he said, tipping her toward her mother. "Kiss her quick if you want one."

Chrissy's straight long hair swayed around her mother's chin as the two exchanged a kiss and hug.

" 'Night, sweetie."

With no further complaint the child went upstairs on her father's arm.

"There," Glenda said, "now we can be alone. And true to my word . . ." With a flourish she opened the refrigerator and produced a long-necked green bottle. "I got a jug of zinfandel for the occasion. How 'bout that!"

"I'd love some. Especially after being with my mother for the last three hours."

"How is old Sergeant Pearson?" The name went way back to the days when Brookie would step onto the Pearsons' front porch and salute crisply at the "P" on the screen door before walking in with Maggie.

"Exasperating as ever. Brookie, I don't know how my dad lives with her. She probably watches when he goes to the bathroom to make sure he doesn't splatter the lid!"

"Too bad, because your dad's such a great guy. Everybody loves him."

"I know." Maggie accepted a goblet of wine and sipped. "Mmm, thank you." She followed Brookie to the far end of the great room where Brookie sat on a rocker and Maggie on the daybed hugging a plump throw pillow. Maggie gave Brookie a rundown of the criticism she and Roy had received in the brief time she'd been home. Gene came back downstairs, took a sip of Glenda's wine, kissed the top of her head, said, "Enjoy yourselves," and discreetly left the pair alone.

Within five minutes, however, Julie and Danny slammed in, smelling like horses, uncomfortable with introductions but suffering them politely before retreating to the kitchen where they began mixing up Kool-Aid. Erica and her boyfriend came in with another couple their age, boisterous and giddy, searching for the newspaper to find out what was playing at the drive-in theater. "Oh, hi!" Erica said when introduced to Maggie. "We've heard lots of stories about what you and Mom did together in high school. These are my friends, Matt and Karlie and Adam. Mom, can we make some popcorn to take to the movie?"

While the popping was in progress, Todd came home, teased his siblings on his way through the kitchen, said, "Hi, Mom, is this Maggie? She looks just like her picture in your yearbook." He shook Maggie's hand, then appropriated his mother's wineglass and took a sip.

"That stuff'll stunt your growth. Give me that."

"Doesn't look like it stunted yours," he teased, and leaped aside when she took a swat at his derriere.

"Is it always like this around here?" Maggie asked when Todd had gone back to the kitchen to steal popcorn and aggravate his younger siblings.

"Most of the time."

The contrast between Maggie's life and Brookie's was so sharp it prompted a series of comparisons, and when the house finally quieted down and the two were left alone, they talked as if the years of separation had never happened, comfortable and frank with one another.

Maggie described what it was like to have a husband die in a plane crash and learn the news when you switched on your TV in the morning; Brookie described what it was like to discover you were pregnant at thirty-eight.

Maggie told how lonely it felt having an only child go off to college; Brookie admitted the frustrations of having seven underfoot all the time.

Maggie spoke of her suppers alone in the silent, empty house with only MacNeil and Lehrer for company; Brookie described cooking for nine when it was ninety-five degrees and the house had no air conditioning.

Maggie told of her chagrin at being propositioned by a married friend of hers and Phillip's at a golf club whose greens were shaped like bear paws, complete with individual toes; Brookie said, meanwhile, she was mowing beneath twenty acres of cherry trees to keep the ground weeds under control.

Maggie described the loneliness of facing an empty bed after years of snuggling into the warmth of someone you loved. Brookie replied, "We still sleep three in a bed—sometimes four—whenever there's a thunderstorm."

"I envy you, Brookie," Maggie said. "Your house is so full of life."

"I wouldn't trade a one of them, even though there were times I thought my uterus would drop off."

They laughed. They had polished off the bottle of zinfandel and felt woozy and relaxed as they slumped in their chairs. The room was lit by only one floor lamp and the house was quiet, inspiring confidences.

"Phillip and I tried to have more," Maggie admitted, her feet updrawn on the daybed, the empty goblet swinging upside down between two fingers. "We tried twice, but I miscarried both times, and now I've started my change."

"Already?"

"About three months after Phillip died I was lying in bed at about eleven o'clock one night when I thought I was having a heart attack. I mean, it really felt like what I thought a heart attack must feel like, Brookie. It started in my chest and ran like electrical impulses down my arms and legs, out my fingers and toes and left my palms and soles damp. I was terrified. It happened again and I woke Katy and she drove me to the hospital. Guess what it was."

"I don't know."

"A hot flash."

Brookie tried to hold back a grin but couldn't.

"Brookie, if you laugh, I'll slug you!"

"A hot flash?"

"I was sitting in an examination room waiting for a doctor when the nurse who was taking my vital signs asked me to describe what had happened. As I was describing it, it happened again. I told her, here comes one now. She watched my face and said, Mrs. Stearn, how old are you? I thought she was crazy to be asking me a question like that when I was having a heart attack, but I told her thirty-nine and she said, you're not having a heart attack, you're having a hot flash. I'm watching the redness climb your chest and neck right now."

Glenda could hold back her snickers no longer. One came out. Then another. Soon she was leaning back in her rocking chair, hooting.

Maggie stretched a stocking foot off the daybed and kicked her.

"You think it's so funny, wait till you get one!"

Brookie quieted, caught her nape on the back of the rocking chair and crossed her hands on her belly. "Crimeny, can you believe we're getting that old?"

"Not we. Just me. *You're* still producing babies."

"Not anymore, I'm not! I keep a candy dish of condoms on the dining-room table."

They laughed again, drifted into amiable silence, and Maggie reached out a hand for Brookie's. "It's so good to be here with you. You're better than Dr. Feldstein. Better than group therapy. Better than any friends I've made in Seattle. Thank you so much."

"Aw, now we're getting sappy."

"No, I mean it, Brookie. I wouldn't be here in Door if you hadn't called everyone and started the round of telephoning. First Tani, then Fish and Lisa, and even Eric."

"So he *did* call you!"

"Yes. I was so surprised."

"What did he say?"

"That he'd found out from you the real reason I'd called him. He was worried I might be suicidal, but I assured him I wasn't."

"And?"

"And . . . the usual. We talked about his business, how the fishing had been, and about my teaching, and how long we'd both been married, and how many kids we had or didn't have, and he told me he's very happily married."

"Wait'll you see his wife. She's a knockout. Model material."

"I doubt that I will, or Eric either."

"Yeah, maybe not when you're here for such a short time."

"Why do you suppose they didn't have a family? It seems odd because when I went with Eric he always said he wouldn't mind having a half dozen."

"Who knows?"

"Well, it's none of my business anyway." Maggie yawned and stretched. Her doing so seemed to trigger a yawn in Brookie. Dropping her feet to the floor, Maggie said, "If there was ever a signal for a guest to go home . . ." Checking her watch, she exclaimed, "Oh, my gosh, it's nearly one o'clock!"

Brookie walked Maggie to her car. The night was warm and filled with scent from the petunia beds and the horse corral. Overhead the stars were showy on a blue-black firmament.

"It's funny about hometowns," Maggie mused.

"They call you back, huh?"

"Mmm . . . they really do. Especially when friends are there. And tomorrow it'll be all of us."

They hugged.

"Thank you for being here when I needed you. And for caring."

For once Glenda made no humorous comment. "It's good to have you back. I wish you'd stay forever."

Forever. Maggie thought about it on her way home through the cool August night, its scent of cut grain and ripening apples reminding that autumn stood poised. Nowhere was autumn more magnificent than in Door County, and it had been over two decades since she'd been here to witness the change of leaves. She'd love to experience a Door County autumn again. But forever? With Vera in the same town? Hardly.

At home, Vera had managed to leave one last order. Propped against Maggie's dresser lamp was a note: *Turn out the nightlight in the bathroom.*

The following day at eleven A.M. four mature adults descended upon Brookie's house, reducing themselves to a quintet of giggly, giddy throwbacks.

They hugged. They bounced. They cried. They kissed. They all talked at once. They called one another by their long-unused teenage nicknames. They dropped profanities with surprising ease after years of trimming these unladylike expletives from their speech. They admired Lisa (still the prettiest), commiserated with Maggie (the widowed), teased Brookie (the most prolific) and Carolyn (already a grandmother) and Tani (the grayest).

They compared family pictures, children's dispositions, and obstetric memories; wedding rings, husbands and jobs; travels, house styles and health setbacks; ate chicken salad and drank wine and grew giddier; caught up on extended-family history—mothers, fathers, sisters and brothers; gossiped about former classmates; relived teenage memories. They got out Brookie's yearbook and laughed at themselves in unflattering hairdos and heavy-lidded makeup; criticized the teachers they had disdained and praised those they had liked back in 1965; tried to sing the school song but couldn't remember the words (except for Brookie who still attended games). In the end they settled for a rendition of "Three White Doves

Went Seaward Flying" sung by Lisa, Brookie and Maggie in dubious three-part harmony.

They played scratchy Beatles records and danced the watusi. They walked through Brookie's meadow five abreast, arms linked, singing raunchy songs they would have punished their own children for singing, songs the boys had taught them clear back in high school.

At suppertime they went to town and ate at The Cookery where they were waited on by Brookie's son, Todd, who received the largest tip of his career. They walked along Main Street among the late summer tourists, down to the city beach where they sat on rocks and watched the sun drape itself across the water.

"Why haven't we done this before?" one of them said.

"We should make a pact to get together every year this way."

"We should."

"Why are you all sounding so sad all of a sudden?" Lisa asked.

"Because it *is* sad, saying good-bye. It's been such a fun day."

"But it's not good-bye. You're all coming to Gary's wedding, aren't you?"

"We're not invited."

"Of course you are! Oh, I almost forgot!" Lisa zipped open her handbag. "Gary and Deb sent this for all of you." She produced a pale gray invitation with all their names on the envelope, which she passed around.

"Gene and I will be there," Brookie confirmed, glancing around at the circle of faces. "Small town . . . everybody goes."

"And Maggie's not going home until Sunday," Lisa reasoned, "and you two live close enough to drive down. Honest, Gary and Deb want you all to come. He made it a point to remind me. The reception's going to be out at Bailey's Harbor Yacht Club."

They glanced at one another and shrugged, wanting to say yes.

"I'll come," Tani agreed. "I love the food at the yacht club."

"So will I," Fish seconded. "How about you, Maggie?"

"Well, of course I'll come if all the rest of you are going to be there."

"Great!"

They rose from the rocks, brushed off their clothing and ambled toward the street.

"What about tomorrow, Maggie?" Brookie inquired. "Let's do something. Swim? Shop? Walk out to Cana Island? What?"

"I feel guilty, taking you away from your family again."

"Guilty!" Brookie spouted. "When you've had as many as I have, you learn to snatch every opportunity to get away by yourself. Gene and I do plenty for our kids, they can do this for me, give me a day to myself now and then."

The plan was cemented and they set a time before wishing each other goodnight.

The following morning Maggie sat in the kitchen drinking tea, attempting to carry on a conversation with her mother without losing her temper.

"Brookie has a wonderful family, and I love her home."

"It's a shame the way she let herself go to fat though," remarked Vera. "And as for family, I'd say she could stand a little less of it. Why, she must have been thirty-eight when she had the last one."

Maggie bit back her exasperation and defended her friend. "They get along so well, though. The older ones look after the younger ones and they've been trained to pick up after themselves. They're a wonderful family."

"Nevertheless, when a woman's near forty she should be more careful. Why, she could have had a retarded child!"

"Even after forty, pregnancies aren't nearly as rare as they used to be, Mother, and Brookie said she wanted every one of her babies. Her last one was no mistake."

Vera's lips pruned and she raised one eyebrow.

"So what about Carolyn?" she asked.

"Carolyn seems happy being a farmer's wife. She and her husband are going to raise ginseng."

"Ginseng! Who in the world eats ginseng?"

Once again, Maggie had to fight down a sharp retort. Vera grew more opinionated the older she got. Whatever the subject, unless Vera used it, or owned it or approved it, the rest of the world was screwed up to do so. By the time Vera asked about Lisa, Maggie wanted to shout, Why do you even ask, Mother, when you don't care? Instead, she answered, "Lisa's just as beautiful as ever, maybe more so. Her husband is a pilot so they've traveled all over the world. And remember Tani's bright-red hair? It's the prettiest peach color you've ever seen. Like a silver maple leaf in the fall."

"I heard her husband started up a machine shop of his own and lost it a few years back. Did she say anything about it?"

Just shut up and get out of here before you blow, Maggie thought.

"No, Mother, she didn't."

"And I'll bet not a one of them has the money that you've got."

How did you get this way, Mother? Is there no generosity in your spirit at all? Maggie rose to set her cup in the sink. "I'm going to do some things with Brookie today, so don't plan lunch for me."

"With Brookie . . . but you haven't spent more than a two-hour stretch at home since you've been here!"

For once Maggie refused to apologize. "We're going to do some shopping and take a picnic out to Cana Island."

"What in the world do you want to go out there for? You've been there a hundred times."

"It's nostalgic."

"It's useless. Why, that old lighthouse is going to fall right over one of these days and when it does the county will have to pay for—"

Maggie walked out in the middle of Vera's diatribe.

Maggie drove. She picked up Brookie and together they went to the Fish Creek General Store where Roy made them towering sandwiches of turkey and cheese and smilingly said, "Have fun!"

They spent the morning poking through antique shops out on Highway 57—restored log cabins whose charm came alive behind white shutters and hollyhock borders. One was a great red barn, its doors thrown open to immense splashes of sun which fell across painted pine floors. Its rafters were hung with clusters of herbs, and dried flowers, the loft filled with hand-tied quilts and candles with uncut wicks. They examined pitchers and bowls, tin toys, antique lace, sleds with wooden runners, crocks and rockers and urns and armoirs.

Brookie found a charming blue basket filled with baby's breath and dried cornflowers with an immense pink bow on its handle.

"Oh, I love this." She suspended it on one finger.

"Buy it," Maggie suggested.

"Can't afford it."

"I can." Maggie took it from Brookie.

Brookie retrieved it and set it back on a pierced tin pie safe. "Oh, no you don't."

Maggie snatched the basket again. "Oh, yes, I do!"

"Oh, no you don't!"

"Brookie," Maggie scolded while they held the basket between them. "I have so much money and nobody to spend it on. Please . . . let me."

Their eyes met in a friendly face-off while above their heads a wind chime rang softly.

"All right. Thanks."

An hour later when they had walked across the rocky shoal to Cana Island, had visited the lighthouse, explored the shore, swam, and eaten their picnic looking out at Lake Michigan, Maggie lay on her back on a blanket, her eyes shielded by sunglasses.

"Hey, Brookie?" Maggie said.

"Hm?"

"Can I tell you something?"

"Sure."

Maggie pulled her sunglasses half-off and peered at a cloud through them, her elbows hanging in the air. "It's true, you know, what I said back at the antique store. I'm filthy rich and I don't even care."

"I wouldn't mind trying it for a while."

"It's the *reason*, Brookie." She slammed the glasses firmly on her face. "They gave me over a million dollars for Phillip's life, but I'd give every penny of it if I could have him back again. It's an odd feeling . . ." Maggie rolled to her side facing Brookie and propped her jaw on a hand. "From the moment that FAA ruling came in—pilot error, the ground crew left a flap open on the plane—I knew I'd never have to worry about money again. You wouldn't believe what settlements like this cover." She counted them on her fingers. "Grief of the children, their support and college education, the pain and suffering of the survivors, even the suffering of the *victim* while the plane was falling out of the sky. I get paid for that, Brookie . . . me!" She touched her chest in exasperation. "Can you imagine what it feels like to take money for Phillip's suffering?"

Brookie inquired, "Would you rather have taken nothing?"

Maggie's mouth drooped as she stared thoughtfully at Brookie. She flopped to her back with an arm over her forehead.

"I don't know. No. It's stupid to say I would. But, don't you understand? Everything is paid for—the house in Seattle, Katy's schooling, new cars for both of us. And I'm tired of teaching tenth-graders how to roll out pie crust when they'll probably buy pre-made crusts anyway. And I'm tired of noisy preschoolers, and of teaching child development when statistics show that a third of the couples who marry these days decide against having children, and most of the rest of them will probably end up in divorce court. I have all this money and nobody to spend it with, and I'm not ready to go out on dates yet, and even if I did, any man who'd ask me out would become suspect because I'd be afraid he was after my money. Oh, God, I don't know what I'm trying to say."

"I do. You need motivation. You need a change." Brookie sat up.

"That's what everybody keeps telling me."

"Who's everybody?"

"My psychiatrist. Eric Severson."

"Well, if everybody's saying it, it must be true. All we need to do is come up with what." Brookie scowled at the water, deep in thought.

Maggie peeked at her with one eye, then closed it, mumbling, "Oh, this should be good."

"Now let's see . . . all we have to do is think of what you'd be good at. Just a minute . . . just a minute . . . it's coming . . ." Brookie sprang up onto her knees. "I've got it! The old Harding place out on Cottage Row! We were talking about it last week at supper. Did you know old man Harding died this spring and the house has been sitting empty ever since? It would make a perfect bed-and-breakfast inn. It's just waiting for—"

"Are you crazy? I'm no innkeeper!"

". . . somebody to come along and fix the place up."

"I don't want to be tied down."

"Summers. You'd be tied down summers. Winters you could take your piles of money and go to the Bahamas in search of a man richer than you. You said you were lonely. You said you hate your empty house, so buy one you can put people in."

"Absolutely not."

"You always loved Cottage Row, and the old Harding house probably has piles of potential charm oozing from between the floorboards."

"Along with drafts and mice and termites, more than likely."

"You're a natural. Hell, what is home economics about anyway? Running a home economically—cooking, cleaning, decorating—I'll bet you've even taught a few charm courses to those greasy-headed little punks, haven't you?"

"Brookie, I don't want—"

"And you love antiquing. You'd go euphoric antiquing for real, to fill that place. We'd go to Chicago to the flea markets and auctions. To Green Bay to the junk dealers. Up and down Door County to all the boutiques and antique shops. With all your money you could furnish the place like the Biltmore mansion and—"

"I refuse to live within less than a thousand miles of my mother! Good heavens, Brookie, it wouldn't even be a long distance phone call away!"

"That's right, I forgot. Your mother is a problem . . ." Brookie squeezed her lower lip thoughtfully. Abruptly she brightened. "But we'd work that out. Put her to work cleaning, scrubbing, something like that. Nothing makes old Vera happier than when she's got a dustcloth in her hand."

"Are you kidding? I wouldn't have my mother on the place under any circumstances."

"Okay then, Katy can clean." Brookie's face grew even more avid. "Of course, it's perfect! Katy can come home summers from college and help you. And if you lived this close she could drive down weekends and holidays, which is what you want, isn't it?"

"Brookie, don't be silly. No woman without a man would be in her right mind to take on a house that old."

"Men, hell. You can buy men. Handymen, gardeners, plasterers, carpenters, even teenagers looking for summer jobs. Even my *own* teenagers looking for summer jobs. You can leave all the dirty work to the hired help and take care of the business yourself. And the timing would be perfect. You buy it now, spend the winter getting the place fixed up, and it gives you time to advertise and open for next year's tourist season."

"I don't want to run a bed and breakfast."

"What a setting, right on the Bay! I'll bet the place has a view from every room. You'd have customers beating down your door to stay in a place like that."

"I don't want customers beating down my door."

"And if I'm not mistaken, it has a gardener's apartment above the garage, remember? Tucked back into the hill across the road. Oh, Maggie, it'd be perfect."

"It'll have to be perfect for somebody else then. You're forgetting, I'm a home ec teacher from Seattle and I return to work on Monday."

"Oh, yes, Seattle. The place where it rains all winter long, and where your best friends' husbands proposition you at the country club, and where you get so depressed you have to talk about it in group therapy sessions."

"Now you're being crass."

"Well, don't you? What friends came rushing in to help you when you needed it? *This* is where your friends are. This is where your roots are, whether you want them to be or not. What has Seattle got to make you stay?"

Nothing. Maggie tightened her lips to keep from replying.

"What are you being so stubborn about? You're going back to a job that bores you, back to a house with no people in it, back to ... hell, I don't know what it *is* you're going back to. Your shrink says you need a change and the problem is, what change? Well, how are you ever going to find out until you start shopping around for a new life? Maybe it's not running a bed and breakfast, but what harm can there be in checking it out? And when you get back to Seattle, who have you got there to fire you up and make you start looking? Well, what are you sitting there for? Pack up your things, we're going to see the Harding house!"

"Brookie!"

Brookie was already on her feet, wadding up a beach towel. "Pack up, I said. What else have we got to do this afternoon? You can stay here if you want to. *I'm* going to see Harding House by myself if I have to."

"Brookie, wait!"

But Brookie was already ten yards away with her beach towel under one arm and her empty white sack under the other, heading for the mainland. While Maggie sat up on her heels and looked after her exasperatedly, Brookie yelled back over her shoulder, "I'll bet that place is a hundred years old or more, old enough to be on the National Register! Just think, you could be listed in *Bed-and-Breakfast Inns of America!*"

"For the last time, I don't want to be listed in *Bed-and-Break*—" Maggie thumped both fists on her thighs. "Damn you, Brookie," she called and scrambled up to follow.

At Homestead Realty, Althea Munne looked up while licking and sealing an envelope.

"Be right with you ladies. Oh, hello, Glenda."

"Hi, Mrs. Munne. You remember Maggie Pearson, don't you?"

"I certainly do." Althea rose and came forward, studying Maggie through eyeglasses whose rims had more angles than the roofline of the Vatican. The lenses were tinted cranberry with exposed, polished edges, and upon the left, a tiny gold A rested just above Althea's cheek. The spectacles were set with what appeared to be the crown jewels, and Althea glittered like a mirrored ballroom. The heavy glasses rested on a tiny owl-nose above a pair of lips ludicrously enlarged with Pepto-Bismol-pink lipstick that had bled into the cracks about her mouth.

A former teacher, she studied Maggie and recalled, "Class of '64. Honor society, school choir, cheerleader."

"All correct except the year. It was the class of '65."

The phone rang, and while Althea excused herself to answer, Maggie glanced at Brookie who flashed a smug grin and said under her breath, "See if you can top that with a Seattle realtor."

Mrs. Munne returned momentarily and asked, "What can I do for you?"

"Do you have the listing on the Harding house?" Brookie asked.

"The Harding house . . ." Althea licked her lips. "Yes. Which one of you is interested in seeing it?"

"She is."

"She is."

Maggie pointed at Brookie and Brookie pointed at Maggie.

Althea's lips pursed. She waited as one might expect an ex-teacher to wait for a class to silence.

Maggie sighed and lied. "I am."

"The house lists for ninety-six, nine. It has one and a half acres and 150 feet of shoreline." Althea turned away to get the listing sheets and Maggie flung a withering glare at Brookie. The realtor returned and asked, "Would that be in your price range?"

"Ah . . ." Maggie jumped. "Yes, that's . . . that's within my price range."

"It's vacant. It needs a little repair, but it has limitless possibilities. Would you like to take a ride over and see it?"

"Ahh . . ." Maggie balked and received a discreet thump on the knee from Brookie. "Yes, I . . . well, of course!"

Althea drove, giving a brief history of the house as they rode toward it.

The Harding place had been built in 1901 by a Chicago shipping magnate named Throckmorton for his wife, who had died before the building was complete. Inconsolably saddened by her death, Throckmorton sold the house to one Thaddeus Harding whose descendants had occupied it until the demise of old Thad's grandson, William, last spring. William's heirs lived in scattered parts of the country and showed no interest in maintaining the white elephant. All they wanted was their share of the money from its sale.

In the backseat, Maggie rode stubbornly beside Brookie—her mind closed—to the west end of Main Street, then south up Cottage Row on a picturesque road that twisted and climbed a steep limestone bluff; through thick cedar forest between old estates that had been established in the early 1900s by Chicago's wealthy who rode the shoreline up Lake Michigan to spend summers in the cool lake breezes of Door Peninsula. The wooded road gave glimpses of genteel homes—no two alike—behind rows of stacked stone walls. Some were perched below road level, their garages backed up against the stone cliff on the left, across the road from the houses themselves. Others lifted above dappled lawns. Many were glimpsed through tangles of old shrubbery and trellises. Occasionally the brilliant blue waters of Green Bay glittered, bringing images of panoramic views from the houses.

Maggie's first impression came not from Harding House itself, but from an abandoned tennis court nestled at the base of the cliff across the road. Moss had taken hold between the limestone paving blocks, some of which had cracked and buckled. The playing surface was covered with the slough of the infringing woods: dead leaves, twigs and pinecones and aluminum cans tossed by uncaring tourists from passing autos.

But along the south edge of the court a weathered arbor seat covered with grapevines spoke of days when the *wump* of tennis balls had resounded from the cliff wall, and players had rested on the curved wooden bench between sets. The vine had grown so heavy it had broken the wooden structure, but it evoked images of a grander day. At the opposite end of the court there was a garage with an apartment above, built in later years but still a relic itself, with cumbersome wooden doors, hinged at the sides. Maggie found her eyes drawn back to the arbor seat as she followed Althea through the break in a thick row of arborvitae that sheltered the yard and house from the road.

"We'll walk around the outside first," Althea directed.

The house was a Queen Anne cottage, gray with age and disrepair, and from the landward side seemed to offer little save a small rear veranda with a rotting floor, gap-toothed railing, and a lot of wooden siding badly in need of painting. But as Maggie followed Althea around the structure, she looked up and saw an enchanting collection of asymmetrical shapes covered in fish-scale shingles, with tiny porches tucked at all levels, exposed cornice brackets, carved bargeboards with finials and pendants in the gable peaks, a sweeping front veranda overlooking the lake and on the second story of the southwest corner the most fanciful veranda of all, rounded, with turned wood columns beneath a witch-hat roof.

"Oh, Brookie, look!" she exclaimed, pointing up at it.

"The belvedere," Althea clarified. "Off the largest bedroom. Would you like to go in and see it?"

Althea was no dummy. She took them in through the front door, across the wide front veranda whose floor was in much better shape than that of the rear; through a carved-oak door with a leaded, stained-glass window and matching sidelights; into a spacious entry hall with a staircase that brought a gasp of delight from Maggie. Looking up, she saw it turn at two landings around a shaft of open space leading to the upper hall.

Her heart began hammering even as her nostrils smelled the mould.

"The wood throughout the house is maple. It's said that Mr. Throckmorton had it custom milled in Sturgeon Bay."

From a doorway to the left Brookie said, "Maggie, look at this." From between the walls she rolled a pocket door, and with it came dust, spider webs and a loud creak of rusty hardware.

Althea quickly explained, "Mr. Harding lived here alone for nearly twenty years after his wife died and I'm afraid he let the place fall into disrepair. Many of the rooms he simply closed off. But anyone with a good eye will recognize the quality underneath the dirt."

The main floor contained the formal parlor with a small stone fireplace and an adjoining "music room." Across the hall was the dining room which connected, through a butler's pantry, with the kitchen at the rear. Opposite the pantry was the maid's room. When Althea opened the door a chipmunk scurried down between voluminous stacks of old newspapers that appeared to have gotten wet and dried many times over the years.

"The place would need a little tightening up," Althea said sheepishly, and proceeded into the kitchen.

The room was horrendous with bile-green paint flaking off the walls in one corner, giving evidence of bad plumbing. The sink was rustier than an ocean-bound tanker and the cupboards—a mere five-foot length of them—were made of tongue-and-groove beadboard, painted the same digestive hue as the walls. Two long narrow windows held shredded lace curtains that had turned the color of an old horse's tooth, while behind them hung tattered window shades of army green. Between the two windows a battered, windowless door led to the small rotting veranda they'd first glimpsed from outside.

The kitchen brought Maggie to her senses.

"Mrs. Munne, I'm afraid we're wasting your time. This is just not what I had in mind."

Althea proceeded, undaunted. "One has to picture it as it could be, not as it is. I'm sorry about this kitchen, but as long as we're here, we might as well take a look upstairs."

"I don't think so."

"Yes, let's." Brookie commandeered Maggie's arm and forced her to comply. Climbing the stairs behind Mrs. Munne, Maggie pinched Brookie's arm and whispered through clenched teeth, "This place is a wreck and it smells like bat shit."

"How do you know what bat shit smells like?"

"I remember from my aunt Lil's attic."

"There are five bedrooms," Mrs. Munne said. "Mr. Harding had them all closed off but one."

The one he'd used turned out to be the Belvedere Room and the moment Maggie stepped into it she had the sinking feeling she was lost. Not the water-stained wallpaper, nor the musty-smelling carpet, nor the obscene collection of ancient mouse-chewed furniture could hide the room's appeal. It came from the view of the lake, seen through tall, deep-silled windows and the exquisitely turned columns of the belvedere itself. As one upon whom a spell has been cast, Maggie opened the door and stepped out. She pressed her knees against the wooden railing, gazing westward as the sun jeweled the surface of the Green Bay. Below, the lawn lay in neglect, a rotting wooden dock listing to one side, half in the water, half out. But the trees were maples, lacy and ancient. The belvedere was solid, graceful, evocative, a place where women perhaps had once watched for steamships to bring their husbands home.

Maggie experienced a sense of loss for her own husband who would never stride up that long lawn, would never share the room behind her or clatter down the magnificent staircase.

But she knew as surely as she knew she'd regret it dozens of times that she would do this insane thing Brookie had suggested: She would live in Harding House.

"Show me the rest of the bedrooms," she ordered, returning inside.

They mattered not a whit. Each of the four had charms of its own, but all paled beside the belvedere room. Returning from the attic (which proved Maggie right—she'd be sharing the place with hundreds of bats) she stepped into her favorite room one more time.

I have come home, she thought unreasonably, and shivered.

Following Althea back downstairs she said, "I'd be making it into a bed-and-breakfast inn. Would there be any zoning problems?"

Brookie grabbed Maggie from behind and spun her by an arm, presenting bulging eyes and a mouth gaping in amazement.

"Are you serious?" she whispered.

Maggie pressed a palm to her stomach, whispering, "I'm trembling inside."

"A bed and breakfast—hmm . . . " Althea said, reaching the main floor. "I'm not sure. I'd have to check into that."

"And I'd want to have an architectural engineer look the place over to make sure it's structurally sound. Does it have a basement?"

"After a fashion. We're on bedrock here, you know, so it's really only a tiny cellar."

The Spanish Inquisition might have taken place in the cellar, so dank and black was it. But the place had a furnace and Althea claimed it worked. A re-examination of the kitchen wall and the maid's quarters which abutted it showed that the plumbing surely had leaked. Probably the bathroom fixtures overhead were ready to drop through the ceiling. But even as Maggie quavered Brookie called from the front parlor, "Maggie, come here! You've got to see this!"

Brookie had rolled back a moth-eaten rug and was on her hands and knees. She was rubbing the floor with a dampened Kleenex. She spit, rubbed again and exclaimed, "It is! It's parquet!"

Maggie's emotional barometer soared once more.

Together, on their hands and knees, dressed yet in bathing suits and beach jackets, the two discovered what Althea had not guessed: The parlor was paved with inch-wide quartersawn maple strips, laid in a bird's-nest design. In the dead center of the room they found the smallest piece; a perfect square. From it the strips telescoped to the outer edges of the room growing longer and longer until they disappeared beneath the high, delicately-coved mopboards that languished beneath years of crust and dust.

"Glory be. Imagine this sanded and polyurethaned," Brookie said. "It'd gleam like a new violin."

Maggie needed no more convincing. She was heading back upstairs to have one more look at the belvedere room before she had to bid it a temporary goodbye.

One hour from the time they had stepped foot into the Homestead Realty office Maggie and Brookie were back in the rented Toyota, gaping at each other and suppressing whoops of excitement.

"What in the name of God am I doing?" Maggie said.

"Curing yourself of your depression."

"Oh lord, Brookie, this is insane."

"I know! But I'm so excited I'm ready to pee my pants!"

They laughed, whooped and pounded their feet on the floorboards. "What day is it?" Maggie asked, too exhilarated to sort out such incidentals.

"Thursday."

"That gives me two days to do some fast footwork, one and a half if I go to that wedding. Damn, I wish I hadn't told Lisa I'd go. Do you have any idea where I'd find out what the zoning would be on a bed and breakfast?"

"We could try town hall."

"Does this town have any architects or engineers?"

"There's an architect up in Sister Bay."

"How about a lawyer?"

"Carlstrom and Nevis, same as always. My God, you're serious, Maggie. You really are serious!"

Maggie pressed a hand to her hammering heart. "Do you know how long it's been since I felt this way? I'm hyperventilating, almost!" Brookie laughed. Maggie squeezed the steering wheel, threw her head back and forced her shoulder blades deep into the seat cushions. "Oh, Brookie, it feels good."

Belatedly Brookie warned, "It'd cost a bundle to fix that relic up."

"I'm a millionaire. I can afford it."

"And you might not be able to buck the residential zoning out there."

"I can try! There are B and Bs in residential areas all over America. How did they manage?"

"You'd be living in the same area code as your mother."

"Oh," Maggie groaned, "don't remind me."

"What should we do first?"

Maggie started the engine, smiling, and felt her zest for life restored. "Go tell my dad."

Roy beamed and said, "I'll help you every way I can."

Vera scowled and said, "You're crazy, girl."

Maggie chose to believe her dad.

During the last business hour of that day Maggie made tracks to the town hall and verified that Cottage Row was, as expected, zoned residential and that an appeal would need to be made to get that zoning changed, but the clerk said the zoning was regulated by the county, not the township. Next Maggie contacted Burt Nevis with an order to draw up papers—conditional—to accompany earnest money. She spoke with the Sister Bay architect, Eames Gillard, who said he was all tied up for two weeks, but who directed her to a Sturgeon Bay structural engineer named Thomas Chopp. Chopp said he could examine the house and would give an *opinion* on its soundness, but would give no written warrantees nor did he know of any engineer or architect who *would* on a house ninety years old. Lastly, she called Althea Munne and said, "I'll have earnest money and a conditional purchase agreement for you by five o'clock tomorrow afternoon."

After supper Maggie sat down with Roy who worked up a generic checklist for the house: furnace, plumbing, wiring, termite condition, plat survey and water test if it was a private well, which, he said, it would be since Fish Creek had no city water.

Next he prepared a list of consultants from whom she might get estimates and advice.

All the while Vera carped, "I don't see why you don't have a pretty new house built up on top of the bluff, or move into one of the new condominiums. They're springing up all over the county, that way you'd have close neighbors and you wouldn't have to put up with leaky pipes and termites. And taking in lodgers—for heaven's sake, Maggie—it's beneath you! Plus the fact that a woman alone has no business opening her door to strangers. Who knows what kind of weirdos might walk in? And to have them sleeping under your roof! Why, it gives me the shivers to think of it!"

To Maggie's surprise Roy lowered his chin, leveled his gaze and said, "Why don't you find something to clean, Vera?"

Vera opened her mouth to retort, snapped it shut and spun from the room, red-faced with anger.

The next day and a half were a frantic merry-go-round of telephoning, exacting promises and dates from contractors, comparing real estate values, meeting lawyers; contacting the chamber of commerce, Althea Munne, the county, the state . . . and the state . . . again and again and again in an effort to obtain a Wisconsin state code book regulating bed-and-breakfast inns. After being misdirected no less than nine times, Maggie finally reached the person under whose jurisdiction B and Bs fell: the state milk inspector.

The state milk inspector, for God's sake!

After exacting his promise to send the pamphlet first class to her Seattle address, she raced to pick up the purchase agreement her lawyer had drawn up, then to Althea Munne's office where she paid the earnest money in spite of the fact that she still had no answer regarding the zoning permit. As she shook hands with Althea she glanced at her watch and stifled a shriek. She had fifty minutes to get back home, bathe, dress, and be at the community church for Gary Eidelbach's wedding.

Chapter 5

🍂

There could have been no more perfect day for a wedding. The temperature was in the low eighties, the sky clear, and shade dappled the front steps of the Fish Creek Community Church where the wedding party had gathered after the ceremony.

Eric Severson knew every person in the receiving line and most of the guests. His mother and Nancy moved ahead of him while behind him came Barbara and Mike, followed by businessmen, neighbors, and friends he'd known for years. He shook hands with the parents of the groom and made introductions. "Honey, this is Gary's mom and dad. Carl, Mary, my wife Nancy."

While they exchanged small talk he watched their admiring eyes linger on his wife and felt proud, as always, to have her at his side. Wherever he took her people stared. Women, children, old men and young: all were susceptible. Not even at a wedding did the bride receive more admiring glances.

Moving through the line, he kissed the bride's cheek. "You look beautiful, Deborah. Think you can keep this rounder in line?" he teased, cocking a grin at the groom who was ten years older than the woman in white beside him. The smiling groom drew his new wife firmly against his side and laughed into her eyes.

"No problem," he replied.

Eric shook Gary's hand. "Congratulations, fella, you deserve it." Everyone in town knew Gary's first wife had abandoned him with two children five years ago to run off with a cinematographer from L.A. who'd been in Door County on a shoot. The children were now eleven and thirteen and stood beside their father, dressed in their first formal wear.

"Sheila," Eric teased, taking the girl's hands. "Don't you know it's not polite to be prettier than the bride?" He kissed her cheek and made it turn the same bright pink as her first ankle-length dress.

She smiled, revealing a mouth full of braces, and replied shyly, "Your wife is prettier than all the brides in the world."

Eric grinned, dropped a hand on Nancy's neck and let his appreciative gaze touch her face. "Why, thank you, Sheila. I think so, too."

Next came Brett, the eleven-year-old. Eric fingered the silk lapel of Brett's tuxedo and whistled through his teeth. "Would you look at those threads! Michael Jackson, *sit down!*"

"I'd rather be wearing my football jersey," Brett grumbled, reaching inside his tux jacket to tug up his cummerbund. "This thing keeps fallin' down all the time."

They laughed and moved on to the end of the line where Eric broke into a wide smile at the sight of a familiar face he hadn't seen in years. "Well, I'll be darned. Lisa . . . hello!"

"Eric!"

He hugged the pretty, dark-haired woman, then backed away to make introductions. "Nancy, this is Gary's sister, Lisa. Homecoming queen, class of '65. You can see why. She and I were friends way back when Gary was just a little punk who always wanted us guys to throw him some passes or tag along on the boat. Lisa, this is my wife, Nancy."

The two women greeted one another and Eric added, "Lisa, I mean it. You look sensational." The line edged forward behind him and he was forced to move on, adding, "We'll talk more later, okay?"

"Yes, let's. Oh, Eric . . ." Lisa caught his arm. "Did you see Maggie?"

"Maggie?" His bearing snapped alert.

"She's here someplace."

Eric scanned the wedding guests milling about the sidewalk and boulevard.

"Over there . . ." Lisa pointed. "With Brookie and Gene. And that's my husband, Lyle, with them, too."

"Thanks, Lisa. I'll go over and say hi." To Nancy he said, "You don't mind, do you, honey?"

She did but refrained from saying so. He touched her shoulder and left her with his mother, saying, "Excuse me, honey, I'll be right back."

Watching him go, Nancy felt a shot of trepidation, realizing he was walking toward his old high school steady. The woman was a rich widow who'd recently called him in the dead of night, and Eric was an attractive man in a new gray suit and white shirt that accented his trimness and his healthy summer tan. As he moved through the crowd two teenagers and one woman a good seventy years old let their eyes follow him as he passed. If they looked twice, what would his old girlfriend do?

Eric saw Maggie for the first time from behind, dressed in white with a splash of watermelon pink thrown around her neck and over one shoulder, still dark-haired, still thin. She was involved in an animated exchange with the others, raising both hands, clapping once, then settling her weight on one foot and tilting the opposite high heel against the sidewalk.

Approaching her, he felt a smack of tension—anticipation and curiosity. She poked Brookie in the chest, still apparently talking, and the group laughed. As he reached her she was exclaiming, ". . . the Wisconsin state milk inspector, of all people!"

He touched her shoulder. "Maggie?"

She glanced back and went motionless. They both stared. Years had gone by, but past intimacy held them trapped in a moment's beat while neither knew quite what to do or say next.

"Eric . . ." she said, recovering first, smiling.

"I thought it was you."

"Well, Eric Severson, it's so good to see you." Anyone else she would have hugged, but to Eric she only extended her hands.

He took them, squeezing hard. "How are you?"

"Fine. Much better." She shrugged and smiled broadly. "Happy."

She was wand thin. The cleft still gave her chin the shape of a heart but had been joined by two deep grooves that parenthesized her mouth when she smiled. Her eyebrows were thinner and at the corners of her eyes crow's-feet had appeared. Her clothing was chic and her hair—still auburn—a study in stylish indifference.

"Happy—well, that's a relief. And looking wonderful."

"So do you," she replied.

The blue of Lake Michigan still tinted his eyes, and his skin was smooth and dark. His hair, once nearly yellow and well past his collar, had darkened to the hue of apple cider, and was now trimmed short and neat. He had matured beyond the boyish good looks of his teenage years into a honed, handsome man. His trunk had broadened; his face had filled out; his hands were hard and wide.

She dropped them discreetly.

"I didn't know you'd be here," Eric said.

"I didn't know myself. Brookie talked me into coming home, and Lisa insisted I attend the wedding. But you . . ." She laughed as if in happy surprise. "I didn't expect to see you here either."

"Gary and I are members of the Fish Creek Civic Association. We worked together to save the old town hall from being demolished. When you stick with a project that long you either become friends or enemies. Gary and I became friends."

At that moment Brookie stepped forward and interrupted. "And what about the rest of your friends, Severson—not even a hello for us?"

Belatedly Eric turned to greet them. "Hi, Brookie. Gene."

"And this is Lisa's husband, Lyle."

The two shook hands. "I'm an old school friend, Eric Severson."

"Tell him your news, Maggie," Brookie demanded smugly.

Eric glanced down as Maggie smiled up at him. "I'm buying the old Harding house."

"You're kidding!"

"No. I just put earnest money on it today and signed a conditional purchase agreement."

"That big old monstrosity?"

"If all goes well it'll be Fish Creek's first bed-and-breakfast inn."

"That was fast."

"Brookie coerced me into looking at it." She touched her forehead as if dizzy. "I still can't believe I've done it . . . I *am doing* it!"

"That old place looks like it's ready to crumble."

"You could be perfectly right. I'm having an architectural engineer take a look at it next week, and if it's anything less than structurally sound, the deal's off. But for now, I'm excited."

"Well, I don't blame you. So, how long have you been home?"

"I got here Tuesday. I'm going back tomorrow."

"Short trip."

"But fateful."

"Yes." They found themselves studying each other again—two old friends, slightly more, realizing they would always be slightly more.

"Listen," he said abruptly, glancing over his shoulder. "Come and say hello to my mother. I know she'd love to see you."

"She's here?" Maggie asked eagerly.

A grin climbed Eric's left cheek. "Got her hair all kinked up for the occasion."

Maggie laughed as they turned toward a group several feet away. She picked out Anna Severson immediately, curly-headed, gray, and stacked like a double-decker ice cream cone. She stood with Eric's brother, Mike, and his wife, Barbara, whom Maggie remembered as an upper classman who'd played a murderer in the class play. With them, too, was a beautiful woman Maggie immediately took to be Eric's wife.

Eric ushered Maggie forward with a touch on her elbow. "Ma, look who's here."

Anna cut herself off in mid-sentence, turned, and threw her hands up. "Well, for the cry-eye!"

"Hi, Mrs. Severson."

"Margaret Pearson, come here!"

Anna took Maggie in a gruff hug and thwacked her on the back three times before pushing her away and holding her in place. "You don't look much different than when you'd come in my kitchen and clean me out of half a batch of warm bread. A little skinnier is all."

"And a little older."

"Yeah, well, who ain't? Every winter I say I ain't going to run the business again next spring, but every spring at ice-out I start getting itchy to see those tourists come in all excited over the big one they caught, and to see the boats coming and going. You watch for them boats your whole life, you don't know what you'd do if you didn't have to anymore. The boys got two of them now, you know. Mike, he runs one. You remember Mike, don't you? And Barb."

"Yes, hello."

"And this," Eric interrupted, resting a proprietary hand on the nape of the most awesomely beautiful woman Maggie had ever seen. ". . . is my wife, Nancy." Her features had a natural symmetry almost startling in their perfection, enhanced by flawlessly applied makeup whose shadings blended like air-brushed art. Her hairstyle was chosen for its simplicity so as not to distract from her beauty. Added to what nature had provided was a carefully-honed thinness enhanced by costly clothing worn with an insouciant flair.

"Nancy . . ." Maggie extended a warm, lingering handshake, looking square into the woman's eyes, noting the hair-fine lashes drawn on her lower eyelids. "I've been told by a good half dozen people how beautiful you are, and they were certainly right."

"Why, thank you." Nancy withdrew her hand. Her nails were garnet, sculptured, the length of almonds.

"And I want to immediately apologize for waking you up the other night when I called. I should have checked the time first."

Nancy tipped up her lips but the smile stopped short of her eyes. Neither did she offer any conciliatory nicety, leaving an unpleasant void in the conversation.

"Maggie's got some news," Eric announced, filling the gap. "She tells me she's put in a bid on the old Harding place. Wants to be an innkeeper. What do you think, Mike, will that old house stand up long enough to make it worth her while?"

Anna answered. "Why of course it'll stand! They built that house back when they knew how to build houses. Milled the lumber down in Sturgeon Bay and hired a Polish carver from Chicago to come and live here while it was going up, to hand carve all the newel posts and spandrels and fireplace mantels and what not. Why, the floors in the place alone are worth their weight in gold." Anna interrupted herself to peer at Maggie. "An innkeeper, huh?"

"If I can get a zoning permit. So far I haven't even been able to find out where I have to go to apply for one."

"That's easy," put in Eric. "The Door County Planning Board. They meet once a month at the courthouse in Sturgeon Bay. I know because I used to be on it."

Elated to learn this much at last, Maggie turned eagerly to Eric. "What do I have to do?"

"Go before them and appeal for a conditional use permit and tell them what it's for."

"Do you think I'll have any trouble?"

"Well . . ." Eric's expression turned dubious as he reached up and ran a hand down the back of his head. "I hope not, but I may as well warn you, it's possible."

"Oh, no." Maggie looked crestfallen. "But Door County's economy depends on tourism, doesn't it? And what better facility to attract tourists than a B and B?"

"Well, I agree, but unfortunately I'm not on the board any longer. Five years ago I was, and we had a situation where—"

Brookie interrupted at that moment. "We're taking off for the reception now, Maggie. Are you riding with us? Hi, everybody. Hi, Mrs. Severson. Anyone mind if I haul Maggie away?"

"Yes, but—" Maggie glanced between Brookie and Eric who ended her consternation by saying, "Go ahead. We'll be at the reception, too. We can talk more there."

The yacht club was on the Lake Michigan side of the peninsula, a twenty-minute drive away. All the way there Maggie talked animatedly with Brookie and Gene, formulating plans, projecting into next spring and summer when she hoped to be open for business, worrying about her teaching contract and what difficulties she might have getting out of it, and the sale of her home in Seattle. Reaching the yacht club and marina where dozens of sailboats were moored, she exclaimed, "And my boat! I forgot about my boat! I've got to get that sold, too!"

"Easy, honey-child, easy," Brookie advised with a crooked smile. "First we're going to go in here and have us a wedding feast, *then* you can start worrying about your new business and making the move."

Bailey's Harbor Yacht Club had always been one of Maggie's favorite places, and entering it again she felt its familiarity impose itself upon her. Ceiling-to-floor windows wrapped around the broad, low-slung building giving a captivating view of the marina and docks where cabin cruisers, down from Chicago for the weekend, shared the slips with more modest sailboats. Beside the bleached-gray planking of the docks their white decks gleamed like a string of pearls floating upon the crystal-blue water. Between the club and the docks, pampered lawns inclined gently to the water's edge.

Inside, the carpet was plush and the air filled with the odor of freshly-ignited Sterno from a twenty-foot stretch of buffet tables placed against the windows. Blue flames swayed beneath gleaming silver chafing dishes. A line of cooks in tall, white mushroom hats waited with their hands crossed behind their backs, nodding to the arriving guests. In the adjacent lounge a three-piece combo played lazy jazz which filtered into the dining room, adding to the ambience. The tables were draped with white linen; coral napkins stood, pleated, upon each white plate; and crystal goblets awaited filling.

As the wedding guests meandered in, Maggie recognized many familiar faces—a little older now, but unmistakable. Old Mrs. Huntington, who years ago had been a cook at the high school, approached Maggie for a fond hello and offered an expression of condolence over her recent widowhood. Dave Thripton, who pumped gas at the Fish Creek docks, came up and said, "I remember you—you're Roy Pearson's daughter. You used to sing for the PTA meetings, didn't you?" Mrs. Marvella Peterson, one of the members of her mother's ladies' aid group, offered, "We live up on the top of the bluff now just two houses off the highway. Stop in sometime." Clinton Stromberg and his wife, Tina, who ran a resort near Sister Bay, already knew about Maggie's bid on the Harding place and wished her luck with her undertaking.

She was standing discussing the Door County lodging situation with the Strombergs when from the corner of her eye she saw Eric and his party arrive. With one ear on what Clinton was saying she watched Eric exchange handshakes and accept a glass of champagne from a circulating waitress, seat his wife, his mother and himself on the opposite side of the room.

There had been little mistaking Nancy Severson's cool reception of her, and though Maggie was eager to resume her conversation with Eric, she felt it expedient to refrain from approaching him again. She found a seat with her own group clear across the dining room from Eric.

Their eyes met once, during the course of the dinner. Eric flashed an impersonal smile, and Maggie broke the contact by turning to say something to Brookie, on her left.

They dined on the yacht club's renowned seafood extravaganza—scallops Mornay, stuffed flounder, Cajun catfish, marinated shrimp and steamed crab claws. Afterward, when the mingling and socializing resumed, Maggie found a moment alone. The dancing had begun as she stood at the immense window, watching the westering sun glint upon the blue water of the bay. A pair of sailboats appeared, white and nonchalant as gulls. The waiters had carried off their dripping silver pans and extinguished the blue flames. The strong smell of the Sterno, so peculiar to posh restaurants, reminded Maggie of the Bear Creek Country Club where she had last attended a wedding reception. Phillip had been alive then, and they had sat with friends, talked, laughed, danced. Six months after his death she had declined the invitation to another wedding, unwilling to face it alone. Now here she was, having an enjoyable day, another barrier of widowhood broken. Perhaps, as she'd been told in her classes on grief, she had been the one to withdraw from her friends. At the time she had adamantly argued, "No, *they've* abandoned *me!*"

Here, among familiar surroundings and remembered faces, and exhilarated by the imminent changes in her life, she finally admitted to herself a truth that had been a full year coming.

If I'd reached out earlier, I'd have been less lonely and miserable.

The sun had relaxed. It sat atop the water like a great golden coin. Across its path the pair of sailboats gave the illusory appearance of hovering inches above the water. Nearer, about the moored boats, the undisturbed water lay like cerulean silk, wrinkled only by a pair of mallards out for a last evening swim.

"It's beautiful, isn't it?" Eric remarked quietly at Maggie's shoulder.

She controlled the impulse to glance back at him, realizing his wife was in the room somewhere, probably watching them. "Beautiful and familiar, which is even better."

"You really needed this trip home."

"Yes. I didn't realize how badly until I got back. I've been standing here admitting that during the past year I pushed a lot of people away. I don't understand why, but it happens. All the time I thought they had abandoned me when actually it was the other way around. What made me finally see it was coming here, doing the reaching out myself. Do you know that this is the first sizable social function I've attended since Phillip's death?"

"And you're enjoying it?"

"Oh, very much. If I'd had time to consider the invitation I probably wouldn't have come. As it happened, I was caught off guard by Lisa. And here I am, suddenly not feeling sorry for myself anymore. Do you know what else I've discovered?"

"What?"

She turned to find him near, holding his glass without drinking, watching her. "That I don't feel like a fifth wheel the way I thought I would without a man at my side."

"Progress," he said simply.

"Yes, definite progress."

A lull fell. They studied each other while he stirred his drink with an olive-studded toothpick, took a sip and lowered the glass.

"You look good, Maggie." The words emerged quietly, as if he could not keep himself from saying them.

"So do you."

They stood close, tallying the changes in one another, pleased, suddenly, that they had aged gracefully. In their eyes were memories which would more wisely have been veiled.

He was the one to pull them out of their absorption with one another, shifting to put additional distance between them. "After you called, Ma dug out our yearbook and we laughed at how skinny and long-haired I look. Then I tried to imagine you thirty-nine . . ."

"Forty."

"That's right. Forty. I don't know what I imagined. An old wrinkled gray-haired dowager in orthopedic shoes and a shawl or something."

She laughed, released by his frankness to admit, "I did some wondering, too—if you'd gone bald or fat or had developed boils on your neck."

He tipped back his head and laughed.

"I'd say we've both weathered well."

She smiled and held his gaze. "Your wife is very beautiful."

"I know."

"Will she mind our talking like this?"

"She might. I don't know. I don't talk to many single women anymore."

Maggie glanced across the room to find Nancy watching them. "I don't want to cause any friction between you but I have dozens of questions to ask."

"Ask away. May I get you a drink?"

"No, thank you."

"A glass of white wine, maybe, or something soft?"

"On second thought, wine would be nice."

While he was gone she made a decision to make it unquestionably clear to Nancy Severson that she had no designs on her husband. She skirted the dancers, made her way to Eric's table and said, "Excuse me, Mrs. Severson?"

Nancy looked up, regarding Maggie with lukewarm detachment and replied, "It's Macaffee."

"I beg your pardon?"

"My *name* is Nancy Macaffee. I kept it when I married Eric."

"Oh," Maggie returned, nonplussed. "Ms. Macaffee. May I sit down?"

"Of course." Nancy removed her small beaded bag from the seat of a chair but added no welcoming smile.

"I hope you don't mind if I pick Eric's brain for a while. I have so very little time before I have to fly back to Seattle, and so much I need to learn."

Flourishing the flat of her hand and giving her returning husband a trenchant glare, Nancy said, "He's all yours."

"Here you are." Handing Maggie a glass of chilled wine, he looked at his wife, amazed at her undisguised brittleness, which fell just short of outright rudeness. What he'd told Maggie was true—he seldom socialized with single women. He was a married man and the thought never entered his mind. Furthermore, it felt peculiar to be the one observing jealous reactions instead of squelching them. Given Nancy's traffic-stopping face, he had to do little more than appear in public with her to witness males following her with beguiled glances, sometimes saluting her silently with a raised glass across a dining room. He had come to accept it without feeling threatened, to take it as a compliment to his good taste in choosing her for his wife.

But here he was, on the receiving end of a cool draft of jealousy, and he was male enough—and faithful enough—to appreciate its origins and regard them as healthy in a marriage of eighteen years.

He chose a seat beside Nancy and draped a wrist over the back of her chair.

"So you're really going to go for it, huh?" he said to Maggie, reopening the topic of earlier.

"Do you think it's a crazy idea? Opening a bed and breakfast in the Harding place?"

"No, not at all. If the house is sound."

"If it is, and if I came back to get a business established, tell me what I'd have to face when I come up against the planning board."

"They may grant your permit immediately or there may be outright hostility."

"But why?"

He leaned forward and propped both elbows on the table. "Five years ago a big conglomerate called Northridge Development came in and started secretly dealing on land, using what later was called 'kid-glove tactics' to persuade the owners to sell, even though they at first resisted. They applied for a conditional use permit and after we granted it, Northridge put up a thirty-two-unit condominium on a half-acre site, creating problems right and left, starting with parking. Fish Creek's barely got enough room for tourist parking, crowded against the bluff as it is, and we're trying damned hard to avoid paved lots, which would ruin the Grandma Moses atmosphere. When the new units were occupied the businesses nearby claimed their foot traffic had fallen off because people couldn't find a place to park. They claimed the conglomerate had intentionally ignored our density requirements, and raised particular hell with the board over the appearance of the place, which has a few too many skylights and sheer walls for local taste. We had the environmentalists on our backs, too, yelling about flora and fauna and sprawl and preservation of our shoreline. And they're right, they're all right. Door County's appeal lies in its provincialism. It's the board's duty to preserve not only what space we have left, but the rural atmosphere of the entire peninsula. That's what you'll be up against when you go in there and ask for rezoning to open another tourist facility."

"But I wouldn't be putting up thirty-two units. I'd only be opening four or five rooms to the public."

"And you'd be dealing with a cross-section of Door citizens that only hear the word 'motel.' "

"But a bed and breakfast isn't a motel! Why, it's . . . it's . . ."

"It's sprawl, some of them would say."

"And I have adequate parking! There's an old tennis court across the road that'll make the perfect parking lot."

"The board would take that into consideration, I'm sure."

"And I'm not some . . . some sly eastern conglomerate trying to buy up valuable property and make a killing selling condo units. I'm a hometown girl."

"Which should work in your favor, too. But you have to remember—" Eric was pointing a toothpick at Maggie's nose when Nancy grew tired of the animated conversation and drolly pushed his hand aside. "Excuse me. I think I'll go listen to the music awhile."

Pausing with a breath half-drawn, obviously stimulated by the conversation, he let her go, then pointed the toothpick again. "You have to remember, you're appealing to a group of Door residents who've been entrusted to look out for all interests. Right now sitting on the board there's a farmer from Sevastopol, a teacher from the high school, a newspaper reporter, a restaurant owner, a commercial fisherman and Loretta McConnell. Do you remember Loretta McConnell?"

Maggie's optimism flagged. "I'm afraid I do."

"What she didn't own in Fish Creek she coveted. Her people have been here since Asa Thorpe built his cabin. If she decides to vote against your zoning permit, you'll have a battle on your hands. She's got money and power, and unless I miss my guess, eighty or not, she gets off on wielding them both."

"What'll I do if they refuse me?"

"Re-appeal. But the best way to avoid that is to come before them armed with as many facts and figures as you can. Tell them how much you're willing to spend to renovate the place. Bring in the actual quotes. Get statistics on the number of lodging units that are filled here at peak seasons, and how many potential tourists get turned away for lack of lodging. Reassure them about the parking. Get local residents to speak up for you and talk to the board."

"Would you?"

"Would I what?"

"Speak up for me?"

"Me?"

"You were a board member. They know you, respect you. If I can make you believe I'll blend my business into the environment with as few changes as possible, and that I won't crowd Cottage Row with cars, would you come before the board with me and encourage them to give me the zoning change I'd need?"

"Well, I don't see why not. I might want to be reassured myself about what you're going to do to the place."

"Absolutely. As soon as I have estimates and plans, you'll be the first to see them."

"One other thing."

"What?"

"I'm not trying to pry, and you don't have to answer if you'd rather not, but have you got the money to carry this thing through? When Northridge came applying, the thing that convinced the board was the amount of money they had allotted for the project."

"Money is no problem, Eric. When an airliner that size goes down the survivors are paid well."

"Good. Now tell me who you've got lined up to give you estimates on the work."

The talk moved on to engineers, workmen, architecture, nothing more personal. She told him she'd get in touch with him when the time came that she'd need his help again, thanked him and they bid good-bye with a very proper handshake.

Shortly after midnight that night, Eric and Nancy were undressing on opposite sides of their bedroom when she remarked, "Well, Maggie whatever-her-name-is didn't waste any time coming on to you, did she?"

Eric paused with his tie half-loosened. "I figured this was coming."

"I'll bet you figured!" Nancy glanced at him in the mirror while removing her earrings. "I could have curled up with mortification. My husband flirting with his old flame and half the town looking on!"

"I wasn't flirting any more than she was."

"Well, what would you call it then?" She threw the earrings into a cut glass dish and yanked a bangle bracelet off her wrist.

"You were there, you heard. We were talking about the business she wants to open up."

"And what were you talking about over by the window? Don't tell me that was business, too!"

Eric turned to her, holding up both palms to forestall her. "Listen, I've had a couple martinis and so have you. Why don't we just shelve this discussion until morning?"

"Oh, you'd like that, wouldn't you!" She pulled her dress over her head and flung it aside. "Then you could run off to your precious boat in the middle of it and not have to answer me at all!"

Eric yanked his tie from under his collar and hung it on the closet door, followed by his suit jacket. "We were friends in high school. What did you expect me to do? Ignore her?"

"I didn't expect you to fawn over her right out in front of the damned church and to leave me alone in the middle of a wedding reception to go make calf eyes at her!"

"Calf eyes!" His head thrust forward. He stood still with his shirttails half-out of his trousers.

"Don't lie, Eric, I saw you! I never took my eyes off the pair of you!"

"She was telling me about how she missed her husband and that it was the first time she's been able to face going out without him."

"She didn't seem to be missing him very badly when she made calf eyes back at you!"

"Nancy, what the hell's gotten into you! In all the years we've been married, when have I ever so much as looked at another woman?" With his shoulders atilt, he propped both hands on his hips and faced her.

"Never. But then you didn't have any old flames around till now, did you?"

"She's not my old flame." He returned to undressing.

"You could've fooled me. Were you lovers in high school?" Nancy asked brittlely, dropping to the bed to remove her nylons.

"Nancy, for God's sake, drop it."

"You were, weren't you? I knew it the minute I saw you walk over to her on the church steps. When she turned around and saw you it was as plain as the dent in her chin." Dressed in a pair of brief navy-blue satin undergarments Nancy moved to the vanity mirror, raised her chin and ran four fingertips up her throat. "Well, I'll say one thing for you, you've got good taste. You pick 'em pretty."

It struck him as he watched her that she was too beautiful for her own good. The idea of his paying even minimal attention to another woman became a disproportionate threat. As he watched, she went on reassuring herself, running her fingers up her taut throat, admiring her reflection.

Apparently finding her beauty intact, she dropped her chin and reached to her nape to free the gold barrette, then began brushing her hair violently.

"I don't want you helping that woman."

"I already told her I would."

"That's it then? You'll do it whether I object or not?"

"You're blowing this thing all out of proportion, Nancy."

She threw down the brush and spun to face him. "Oh, am I? I'm on the road five days a week and I should leave you here to squire your old lover around to committee meetings while I'm gone?"

"You're on the road five days a week by choice, my dear!" Angrily, he pointed a finger at her.

"Oh, now we're going to start that old whining, are we?"

"Not we. You! You started the whole thing, so let's finish it once and for all. Let's get it nice and clear that I'd like my wife to *live* with me, not just drop in on weekends!"

"And what about what *I* want!" She spread a hand on her chest. "I married a man who said he wanted to be a corporate executive and live in Chicago, and all of a sudden he announces that he's going to pitch it all and become a . . . a *fisherman!*" She threw up her hands. "A *fisherman*, for Chrissake! Did you ask me if I wanted to be a fisherman's wife?" She splayed a hand on her chest and leaned forward from the waist. "Did you ask me if *I* wanted to live in this godforsaken no-man's land, eighty miles from civilization and—"

"Your idea of civilization and mine are two different things, Nancy. That's our trouble."

"Our trouble, Mr. Severson, is that you changed course in the middle of our marriage, and all of a sudden it no longer mattered to you that I had a blossoming career that mattered as much to me as your precious fishing mattered to you!"

"If you'll strain your memory, my dear, you'll recall that we did talk about your career, which, at the time, we thought would only last a couple more years and then we'd start a family."

"No, that was what *you* thought, Eric, not me. *You* were the one who outlined the five year plan, not me. Anytime I indicated that I wasn't interested in having a family you turned a deaf ear."

"And obviously that's what you expect me to keep doing. Well, time's running out, Nancy. I'm already forty years old."

She turned away. "You knew it when we got married."

"No." He grabbed her by an arm and made her stay. "No, I never knew it. I assumed—"

"Well, you assumed wrong! I *never* said I wanted children! Never!"

"Why, Nancy?"

"You know why."

"Yes, I do, but I'd like to hear you say it."

"Make sense, Eric. What do you think we've been talking about here? I've got a job I love, with perks a thousand women would kill to have—trips to New York, a red-air travel card, sales meetings at Boca Raton. I've worked hard to get every one of them and you're asking me to give that up to stick myself here in this . . . this cracker box and raise babies?"

Her chosen phrasing cut deep. As if they'd be just anybody's babies, as if it scarcely mattered to her the babies would be his and hers. He sighed and gave up. He could throw her narcissism in her face, but what purpose would it serve? He loved her and had no desire to hurt her. To be truthful, he, too, had loved her beauty. But as the years went by that physical pulchritude mattered less and less. Long ago, he had realized he would love her as much—perhaps even more—if her hips widened and she lost the ultra-chic thinness she so carefully safeguarded by dieting. He'd love her as much if she appeared in the kitchen at seven in the morning with a squalling infant on her shoulder and her makeup still in the pots on her vanity. If she dressed in jeans and a sweatshirt instead of couturier creations from Saks and Neiman-Marcus.

"Let's go to bed," he said disconsolately, scraping down the covers, then dropping heavily to the edge of the mattress to pull his socks off. He flung them aside and sat staring at them, slump-shouldered.

She watched him for a long time from across the room, feeling the framework of their marriage cracking, wondering what, short of children, would hold it together. She padded to him barefoot and knelt between his knees. "Eric, please understand." She circled him with both arms and pressed her face to his chest. "A woman has no business conceiving a baby she'd resent."

Put your arms around her, Severson, she's your wife and you love her and she's trying to make peace between you. But he couldn't. Or wouldn't. He sat with his hands folded over the edge of the mattress, feeling the awful weight of finality settle in his vitals. In the past when they'd had this same argument it had had no succinct end, but had taken days petering out while she nursed her displeasure with him. But that very open-endedness had always left him feeling they'd talk—argue—about it again before the issue was settled.

Tonight, however, Nancy presented a calm, reasonable defense against which there was no arguing. For he would no more wish his child onto a resentful mother than she would.

Chapter 6

🍀

Upon Maggie's return to Seattle her life became a frenzy. The school principal said he was sorry to see her leave, but he'd have no trouble hiring another full-time teacher to replace her. Before she left the building she had cleaned out her desk. At home she raked the dead pine needles, trimmed the shrubs, called an acquaintance and realtor, Elliott Tipton, and before he left the house a lockbox hung on her door. At Elliott's suggestion, she contacted workers to repaint the trim on the outside of the house, and repaper one bathroom. She called Waterways Marina and told them to shear two thousand dollars off the price of the boat: she wanted to unload it fast. She called Allied Van Lines and got a moving estimate. She heard from Thomas Chopp who informed her Harding House had dry rot in the porch floors, wet rot in one of the walls (the maid's room corner where the plumbing had leaked and carpenter ants had been busy), no insulation, inadequate wiring, too small a furnace, and would need new flashings and roof vents. The roof, however, he said, was in surprisingly good shape, as were the floor stringers and interior-bearing walls, therefore it was his opinion the place could be renovated but it would be costly.

She received the Health and Social Services pamphlet governing bed-and-breakfast establishments for the state of Wisconsin, and discovered she would need one additional bathroom and a fire exit upstairs to meet code, but found no other glaring reasons she would be denied a license.

She called Althea Munne and gave her the order to have papers prepared for the final purchase and hold them until further notice.

She contacted three Door County contractors and arranged for them to submit drawings and bids on the remodeling.

She called her father who said she was welcome at their house for as long as it took to make her own livable.

She spoke to her mother who gave her a string of orders, including the warning not to cross those mountains herself if there was snow.

And finally she called Katy.

"You're going to what!"

"Move back to Door County."

"And sell the house in Seattle?" Katy's voice rose with dismay.

"Yes."

"Mother, how could you!"

"What do you mean, how could I? It would be senseless to keep two houses."

"But it's the house where I was born and raised! It's been my home for as long as I remember! You mean I'll never have a chance to see it again?"

"You'll be able to come to my house in Fish Creek anytime."

"But it's not the same! My friends are in Seattle. And my old room will be gone, and . . . and . . . well, just everything!"

"Katy, *I'll* still be there for you, no matter where I live."

Katy's voice grew angry. "Don't pull your parental psychology on me, Mother. I think it's a lousy thing to do, sell the house right out from under me the minute I'm gone. You wouldn't like it either."

Maggie hid her dismay at Katy's anger. "Katy, I thought you'd be happy to have me closer, so you could come home more often. Why, it's close enough that you can even drive up on weekends, and on holidays we can be with Grandpa and Grandma, too."

"Grandpa and Grandma. I hardly even know them."

For the first time Maggie's voice grew sharp. "Well, perhaps it's time you got to! It seems to me, Katy, that you're being rather selfish about this whole thing."

At the other end of the line an astonished silence hummed. After moments Katy said tightly, "I gotta go, Mom. I've got a class in ten minutes."

"All right. Call anytime," Maggie ended coolly.

When she'd hung up she stood beside the phone pressing her stomach. Inside, it trembled. She could count on one hand the number of times she had put her own wishes before those of Katy, and she couldn't remember the last time the two of them had snapped at each other. She felt a sharp disappointment. How incredibly selfish one's children could be at times. As far as Katy was concerned Maggie might do whatever was necessary to bring happiness back into her life . . . as long as it didn't inconvenience Katy.

I was there for you your whole life, Katy. I was a good, attentive mother who made sure quality time with you was never sacrificed to my career. And now, when I need your approval to make my excitement complete you withhold it. Well, young woman, whether you like it or not, the time has come for me to please myself and not you.

Maggie's resoluteness startled even herself. Standing in the kitchen where Katy had sat in a high chair and been spoon-fed, where years later she had left muffin crumbs for her mother to wipe up, Maggie felt like a moth emerging from a chrysalis.

My goodness, she thought, *I'm forty years old and I'm still growing up.*

She realized something else in that moment, something Dr. Feldstein had said on numerous occasions: She had within herself the power of either creating or defeating happiness by choice. *She* had done it. *She* had gone to Door County, *she* had renewed old friendships, *she* had explored an old house and put anticipation back into her life. And anticipation made the difference. A life without it made a parent lean too hard on her children, a patient lean too hard on her psychiatrist, and a widow lean too hard on herself.

She walked into the family room and stood in the center of it, turning a slow circle, studying the room that held hundreds of memories. *I'll leave here without regrets, looking back only in fondness. You won't mind, Phillip, I know you won't. You would not have wanted me to keep the house as a shrine in exchange for my own happiness. Katy will come to realize this in time.*

She made the move to Door County in mid-September. The Seattle house had not sold so she left the furnishings behind and took along only what personal possessions her car would hold.

She had never been an alert long-distance driver and amazed herself again by remaining wide awake through ten-hour stretches without anyone to spell her. In the past she had been the relief driver and even as such had become mesmerized during the first hour behind the wheel. Now, knowing she had to do it on her own, she did.

Neither had she ever stayed in a motel alone. Always, Phillip had been there to lift the suitcases out of the trunk, a partner with whom to scout out a place for dinner, and afterward, a warm familiar body in a cold, strange bed. She settled the dinner issue by going through the drive-in window of a McDonald's and eating her hamburger and fries in her motel room. Exhausted after her day of driving, she fell asleep almost before the last french fry was eaten, and slept like a newborn, scarcely missing Phillip.

Idaho was rugged, Montana beautiful, North Dakota endless, and Minnesota exciting, for she was nearing home. But the moment she crossed the St. Croix River into Hudson, she felt the difference. *This* was Wisconsin! The clean, rolling farms with immense herds of black and white holsteins. The proud old two-story farm houses beside red gambrel-roofed barns. Vast tracts of yellow field corn meeting vast tracts of green woods. Cheese shops and antique shops, and a tavern at every country crossroad. Once, near Neillsville she saw a farmer—Amish, no doubt—harvesting behind a team of draft horses. And farther east, the ginseng farms with their shade frames stretched out like patchwork quilts.

She rounded Green Bay and headed north, feeling the same surge of elation as the last time she'd entered Door County, appreciating its changelessness, understanding the need to preserve it. It looked like a bit of Vermont misplaced. The wild sumac—harbinger of autumn—had begun to turn scarlet. The first apples of the season were being picked. The woodpiles were high and straight beside cottage doors.

Approaching Fish Creek, she decided to drive past *her* house first. A left turn off the highway led her onto a road known as the switchback which dropped in a series of tight curves to Cottage Row and her new neighborhood. She rolled down the window and savored the smells—the pungent scent of cedars and the herbal perfume of poplars at certain times of year when their sap is moving. Her heart plunged as she rounded a curve and caught sight of her own row of arborvitaes. She pulled off onto the tennis court beside the rickety arbor seat and looked down toward the house. Little more than its roof showed beyond the untended shrubbery, but a mere glimpse of it charged her with fresh anticipation. Beside the road a sold board had been added to the Homestead Realty sign.

Sold . . . to Maggie Stearn, the start of her new life.

She settled temporarily—very temporarily, she promised herself—into her parents' house and called Katy to let her know she'd arrived safely. Katy's response was, "Yeah, good, Mom. Listen, I can't talk right now, the girls are waiting to go down to the dining room." Hanging up, she thought, *Wise up, Maggie, kids don't worry about parents the way parents worry about kids.*

Vera bore out the fact by hounding Maggie incessantly. "Now make sure your lawyer looks over all the fine print so you know what you're getting into. Whatever you do, don't hire that Hardenspeer bunch to do the remodeling. They'll come to work half drunk and fall off a ladder and sue you for every cent you've got. Maggie, are you sure you're doing the right thing? It just seems to me a woman alone could get taken twenty ways trying to remodel a house that big. I almost wish you'd stayed in Seattle, much as I like having you here! I don't know what your father was thinking to encourage you!"

Maggie tolerated Vera's needling by keeping busy. She drove to Sturgeon Bay and filled out an application for a conditional use permit to open a bed-and-breakfast establishment in Fish Creek. She arranged for a water inspection which was required by law before the resale of any home that had its own well; she opened a checking account in the Fish Creek Bank, arranged for phone and electric service, and a box at the post office, since Fish Creek had no home mail delivery within its township limits. She met each of the three contractors she'd contacted by phone and collected their estimates, the lowest of which hovered just below the $60,000 mark.

Common sense said, wait until the county board gives you the permit before proceeding with the purchase of the house, but weather became a primary consideration: frost would be coming soon. Given the amount of plumbing that would have to be reworked, and the fact that an entire wall would have to be torn out and the furnace replaced, Maggie made a decision to go ahead with the purchase and hope for the best.

The closing took place during the last week of September, and two days later the Lavitsky brothers—Bert and Joe—knocked a hole in the maid's room wall big enough to drive their truck through: the refurbishing had begun.

Maggie received the call from the Door County Board of Adjustments— commonly called the planning board—that same week, instructing her to appear before them the following Tuesday night.

Which meant she must contact Eric.

She had neither seen nor talked to him since she'd been back, and felt a distinct ambivalence about dialing his number. On a chilly Friday morning with the maples outside her window tinged with frost, she stood in her noisy kitchen dressed in a thick red sweater with her hand on the phone. Inside, Bert Lavitsky was tearing the cupboards off the wall. Outside, his brother was replacing the back veranda floor. KL 5-3500. For some strange reason, she knew his number by heart but she withdrew her hand without dialing and crossed her arms tightly, frowning at the phone. *Don't be silly, Maggie, remember what Brookie said. It's no big deal, so don't make it one. And anyway, Anna will probably answer.*

She grabbed the receiver and punched out the number before she could change her mind. The voice that greeted hers was definitely not Anna's.

"Severson Charters."

"Oh . . . hello . . . Eric?"

"Maggie?"

"Yes."

"Well, hello! I heard you were back and you closed the deal on the house."

She plugged one ear. "Could you talk a little louder, Eric? I'm at the house and there's a lot of hammering going on here."

"I said, I heard you were back and that you closed the deal on the house."

"Sooner than might have been wise, but the snow could be flying in four weeks so I thought I'd better get the Lavitsky boys tearing into the walls without delay."

"The Lavitskys, huh?"

"That's who's making all the racket here. I checked around. They seem to have a good reputation," she said above the pounding of hammers.

"They're honest and they do good work. How fast they do it is another matter."

"Forewarned is forearmed. I'll keep that in mind and see what I can do to light a fire under them." At that moment Bert slipped his hammer into a loop on his overalls and went out to sit with Joe on the veranda step and have their morning coffee.

"Oh, what a relief," Maggie said as the welcome silence fell. "It's break time so you can stop shouting at me."

She heard Eric laugh.

After a pause, she added, "I've heard from the county board. They want me to be at their meeting this Tuesday night."

"Would you still like me to come with you?"

"If it's not too much trouble."

"No. No trouble at all. I'll be happy to."

She released a breath slowly, forcing herself to relax. "Good. I really appreciate it, Eric. Well, I'll see you there then. Seven-thirty at the court-house."

"Wait a minute, Maggie. Are you driving down alone?"

"I'd planned on it."

"Well, there's no sense in two of us driving. Do you want to ride with me?"

Unprepared for the suggestion, Maggie stammered. "Well . . . I . . . sure, I guess so."

"Should I pick you up at your parents' house?"

Vera would have a fit, but what could Maggie say? "That'll be fine."

On Tuesday night she left the mousse out of her hair and chose her clothing carefully in hope of favorably impressing the board. She wanted to appear mature, tasteful and— admittedly—well off enough to have the funds to restore a place the size of Harding House. Yet not too flashy. She chose a softly-pleated challis skirt in a mixture of autumn hues from rust to ruby, an ivory blouse with a tucked bodice and embroidery trim, a soft leather belt with an oversized buckle and, at her throat, an oval pin set with an amethyst crystal. Over the ensemble she wore a cropped-waisted jacket of burgundy suede.

When she came downstairs her mother gave her a cursory glance and remarked, "Dressing rather fancy for a town meeting, aren't you?"

"It's not a town meeting, Mother, it's an appearance before a board who'll pass judgment on me as much as on the business I'm proposing. I wanted to hint that I'd know how to make a decrepit old house attractive again. I thought the oval pin was a nice quaint touch, wouldn't you say?"

"It's quaint, all right," Vera replied. "I don't know what the world's coming to when a single woman runs all over the countryside with a married man, and right under her mother's nose."

Maggie felt herself blushing. "Mother!"

"Now, Vera," put in Roy, but she ignored him.

"Well, that's what you're doing, isn't it?"

"Eric is going to try to convince the board in my favor, nothing more!"

"Well, you know what people will say. His wife gone more than she's home, and him squiring a new widow around."

"He is not *squiring* me around! And I resent your implications!"

"You might very well resent them, Margaret, but I'm your mother, and as long as you're in this house—"

The doorbell interrupted Vera and she hurried forward to answer it before anyone else could. To Maggie's chagrin it was Eric, standing on the porch in a blue windbreaker that said SEVERSON'S CHARTERS on the breast. Had he only pulled up at the curb and honked the horn Maggie would have felt less culpable. But there he stood, smiling and congenial, much as he had in the days when he'd come to pick her up for a date. "Hello, Mrs. Pearson. How're you?"

"Hello," Vera replied without a smile.

"Maggie's riding down to Sturgeon with me."

"Yes, I know."

Maggie picked up her purse and brushed past Vera. "I'm all ready, Eric. We'd better hurry or we'll be late." She passed him like a streak and trotted down the porch steps at full steam. She was standing at the truck door, pulling fruitlessly on the handle when he reached around her and pushed her hand aside. "This old beater is a little spunky. Sometimes you've got to talk to 'er and coax 'er a little." Putting his body into it, he opened the door. Climbing in, Maggie could feel her mother's eyes dissecting every move from the living room window. Eric slammed the door, walked around and got in.

"Sorry about the truck," he said, putting the vehicle in gear. "It's kind of like an old family pet—you know you ought to put it to sleep, but it's hard to make yourself do it."

Maggie remained stiff and silent, glaring out the windshield.

As the truck began rolling, Eric glanced at her and said, "What's the matter?"

"My mother!" she answered in a voice tight with indignation. "She's a shrew."

"It's hard to live with them once you've been away."

"It was hard to live with her *before* I went away!"

"I'll admit, I've received warmer receptions in my life than I did tonight. Is she upset about us riding to Sturgeon together?" At her stubborn silence, he realized he'd guessed right. "Maggie, you should have said something, you should have called and we could have gone down separately. I just thought as long as we were both going to the same place—"

"Why should I say something? Why should I let her cast aspersions on a perfectly innocent meeting? We're riding to the courthouse together and I *refuse* to let her make me feel guilty about it! Damn it, I *have* nothing to feel guilty about! It's just her mind, her nosiness—she thinks everybody in town is like her, anxious to think the worst about people."

Eric looked at her intently. "The trouble is, they probably are and I never considered it until this moment. Do you want to go back, Maggie, and get your own car?"

"Absolutely not!"

"Everybody in the county knows this old truck. Hell, my name is right on the door."

"I wouldn't give my mother the satisfaction. And besides, like Brookie said, can't two adults be friends? I need your help tonight. I'm happy to have it. Let's leave it at that and let my mother work out her own hang-ups." Anxious to change the subject, Maggie glanced around curiously. "So this is your old truck." She took in the worn seats, the cracked side window, the dusty dash.

"I have a name for her, but I'd better not tell you what it is. It's not very polite."

Maggie grinned and said, "I can just about imagine."

"I didn't stop to think about your being all dressed up. Maybe you *would* have preferred to take your own car."

"My own car's got no character. This does."

Their banter eased the tension between them, and as they rolled south out of town beneath the great dome of evening, where the first bright star hung in the southwest sky, they spoke of other subjects: the autumn weather; the tourist trade which would reach its peak along with the autumn colors within two weeks; how the salmon were tougher to catch now that fall was here, but the brown trout were hot at Portage Park and Lily Bay; when Eric and Mike would take their boats out of the water, and how the Lavitsky boys were doing.

Then Eric said, "Maggie, I've been thinking a lot about Loretta Mc-Connell and her . . . shall we call it conservativism. If anyone on the board raises objections to your permit, she'll be the one. I've thought of a way to soften her up."

"How?"

"Have you come up with a name for your inn yet?"

"A name? No."

"Well, I was talking to Ma, and it came out that Loretta McConnell is a shirttail relative of the original Harding who owned the place. As close as we can figure it, her mother's side of the family would have been the third generation removed from Thaddeus Harding, though the lineage is somewhat obscured by married names. But my guess is, Loretta would know exactly, and if there's anyone who's rabid to preserve heritage, it's Loretta McConnell. She's an active member of the historical society, and gives them a good chunk of money every year. Supposing we appeal to her family pride. We tell her you've decided to keep the name Harding House to preserve as much of the place's heritage as possible."

"Oh, Eric, that's a wonderful idea! Harding House . . . I love it. And it's so common sense. After all, everyone in town has called it that for years, so why change it now?"

"I thought you might want your name on it."

"Stearn House . . ." She pondered, then shook her head. "Uh-uh. It doesn't have the ring that Harding House has. I can see it now, done in graceful copperplate on a swinging sign at the top of the walk. A wooden sign, I think, on a single post with a finial at the top." She gestured in the air as if the sign hung before her. "Harding House. A Bed-and-Breakfast Inn. Maggie Stearn, Proprietress."

He chuckled, charmed by her enthusiasm.

"You love it all, don't you—planning it, working on it?"

"Absolutely. I owe so much to Brookie for talking me into going there in the first place. I find myself fantasizing more and more about the day the first guest signs in. If this board says no tonight I'll probably burst into tears."

"I have a feeling you'll come out of that courthouse smiling."

The courthouse at Sturgeon Bay was a combination of old and new—the old Victorian building surrounded by the newer one of beige brick and gray stone. They parked on 4th Street and walked along the sidewalk beneath a row of mountain ash whose red berries had dropped onto the walkway. Between a pair of round red maples and green front lawns, into a doorway flanked by stone planters in which the marigolds and salvias lay black and wilted after the previous week's frosts.

Inside, Eric knew his way to the correct room. Entering it, Maggie felt nervous and expectant. She recognized Loretta McConnell immediately, a singularly unattractive woman with two missing bottom teeth, crooked eyeglasses and straight undressed hair, crudely cropped like that of an Elizabethan page boy. "There she is," she whispered, taking a seat in a wooden folding chair beside Eric.

"Don't be misled by her looks. She's a brilliant woman, privy to the doings of more politicians, musicians and artists than you've probably ever heard of. She's a great supporter of the arts and gives enormous endowments to everything from violin prodigies to our own Ridges Nature Sanctuary. Her name is as familiar in Washington as it is in Door County. But for all her power, she's a reasonable woman. Just remember that if she challenges you.''

They waited through a variety of appeals—a landowner unwilling to move his new fence although it would cause problems for the county snowplow; the owner of lakeshore property seeking a variance to have a new well drilled; a woman applying for a permit to open an antique shop in one of the county's original log cabins; a restaurant owner seeking a liquor license; a seedy, emaciated young man demanding that the county buy him a new pair of glasses because his had been sat on by the operator of the county bookmobile. (The latter was advised by Loretta McConnell that he was barking up the wrong county tree.)

Then it was Maggie's turn.

"Margaret Stearn," the chairman read off her application. "Wants to open a bed-and-breakfast inn on Cottage Row in Fish Creek."

Maggie rose and moved to the front of the room. The chairman lifted his eyes from the paper. He was a rawboned man who appeared much more suited to riding a tractor than sitting on a board such as the one he chaired. Obviously, he was the farmer from Sevastopol. He had large ears with tufts of hair springing from them. His suit—apparently a concession—was liver brown and dated; the knot in his tie, beneath a crinkled yellowy collar, skewed to one side. Maggie took one look at him and thanked herself for wearing her hair in a tidy downsweep.

"You're Maggie Stearn?" he asked.

"Yes, sir. My maiden name was Pearson. My father is Leroy Pearson. He's been a butcher at the Fish Creek General Store for forty-two years. I was born and raised in Fish Creek."

"Yes, of course. I know Roy Pearson." His glance passed over her suede jacket and returned to the paper.

"You've been living elsewhere?"

"In Seattle for eighteen years. My husband died a year ago and my daughter is a freshman at Northwestern in Chicago, so I decided to move back to Door County."

"It says here you've already bought the property in question."

"That's right." Since homes in Fish Creek had no street addresses, only fire numbers, she identified the house by its common name. "The old Harding house. I hired an architectural engineer to assess the house for soundness. Here is his report." On the table before the chairman she laid the letter from Thomas Chopp. "I'm investing sixty thousand dollars in refurbishing the house, and the work is already under way. Here's a copy of the contract between myself and the Lavitsky Brothers of Ephraim, who are doing the renovation on the structure itself. Here's another from Workman Electric who'll be replacing the furnace and bringing the electrical up to code. And this one is from Kunst Plumbing who'll be putting in an extra bathroom to meet state lodging codes for bed and breakfasts. This is a copy of the legal survey showing that the property covers one and a half acres, which would mean, if my rooms were full, and if I had one hired hand and myself, we would more than meet the density requirements. The ratio, as you can see, would be one person to every point-one-five-zero acres. I also have an estimate from J & B Blacktopping for tarring the tennis court on the opposite side of the road, which will provide ample parking for my guests. And here, from the Door County Chamber of Commerce, I have figures on the number of inquiries for lodging which they cannot accommodate—you'll notice it works out to approximately ten percent annually, which represents a significant loss of revenue not only for the hotel-and motel-keepers but for other retail businesses as well. Next I have a letter from the office of the county health inspector outlining what requirements I'd have to meet to pass inspection—not all of them are met at this point, but I assure you, they will be. Next—fire code regulations. You'll note in the estimate from the Lavitsky Brothers that an additional exit and exterior stairway is planned on the second floor to meet fire code. Here I have a room-by-room estimate for wallpaper, towels, bed linens, curtains and furnishings. And I've done a breakdown of daily costs for laundry services which would be provided by Evenson's at Sturgeon Bay—they'll do the sheets only. We'll do the towels ourselves. And a much rougher estimate on supplies such as soaps, toilet paper, paper cups, cleaning supplies and the like, although I'm still shopping for a better bargain on those items. I've also done a breakdown of the cost per serving of certain foods I'd be serving such as muffins, coffee cakes, coffee and juice. With those foods, which could be home made, you'll notice I've done a comparison between using the services of a bakery and making them myself. And lastly, I have a copy of my last six months' Merrill Lynch statement and I've circled in red the telephone number where you can verify my investments and average monthly balance, which I trust you'll hold in confidence. All this to show you that I'm very much in earnest, that I know very closely what it will cost to open and run this place, and that I can afford it. I want to assure you, ladies and gentlemen, that I won't be opening one season and closing the next. I think my inn would be a great asset to Fish Creek and Door County."

Maggie retreated one step and stood waiting. The courtroom was so silent you could have heard the hair growing in the board chairman's ears. A titter sounded at the rear of the room. The chairman blinked once and seemed to draw himself out of a daze.

"How long did you say you've been back in Door County?"

"A little less than three weeks."

He angled a wry grin to his constituents, both left and right, then said with a glint of humor in his eyes, "I imagine by now you know whether any of the members of this board have had a parking ticket in the last year."

Maggie smiled. "No, sir, I don't. But I know how much you make for sitting on the board. Since I'm a taxpayer here now, I thought it prudent to find out."

Laughter broke out throughout the room, even at the front table.

"Do you mind my asking, Mrs. Stearn, what you did in Seattle?"

"I was a home economics teacher, which I consider an additional advantage. I know how to cook and sew and decorate—all prerequisites for running an inn, and I think I'd have little trouble learning to manage the business end of things."

"There's no doubt in my mind." He glanced at the application form, then back to Maggie. "I imagine there's a question of zoning out there."

"I thought so, too, sir, until I received the Health and Social Services regulations for B-and-B establishments which states clearly that if I were to have five guest rooms or more I'd be considered a hotel, and I could only operate in an area that's zoned commercial. But as long as I stick to four guest rooms or less I'll be considered a bed and breakfast, and they are allowed in residential zones. There's a copy of the pamphlet there for you, too, somewhere. You'll find the ruling in paragraph three under HSS 197.03, the section called Definitions.''

The leader of the group looked as if he'd been poleaxed. His eyebrows nearly touched his hairline, and his lips hung open. "I'm almost afraid to ask . . . is there anything else you'd like to add?''

"Only that I have a former member of this board, Eric Severson, here with me tonight to give me a character reference.''

"Yes, I noticed him sitting next to you. Hello, Eric.''

Eric lifted a palm in hello.

At last Loretta McConnell spoke up. "I have a few questions for Mrs. Stearn.''

"Yes, ma'am.'' For the first time Maggie faced the woman whose gaze was shrewd and intimidating.

"Where would you advertise?''

"Primarily in the Chamber of Commerce publications, and I intend to make an appeal to Norman Simsons, the author of *Country Inns and Backroads*, in the hope that my inn will be included in the next edition of his book. And, of course, I'd have a discreet sign in front of the house itself.''

"No road signs?''

"Cluttering up Door County? Absolutely not. I'm a native, Miss McConnell. I want to see it kept as unspoiled as possible. I can live without billboards.''

"And the exterior of the house—are there any changes planned there?''

"The one stairway, which I mentioned, to meet fire code. And a new rear veranda because the original one was falling off, but the new one will be an exact replica of the old. The exterior painting has already begun, and the house will be restored to its original colors, which, as you know, is being required by law in some areas of the country. The house will be the same colors chosen by Thaddeus Harding—saffron yellow with tarnished-gold window trim, Prussian blue cornice brackets and a paler China blue on the bargeboards. The fretwork and porch rails will be all white. Those are the only changes I have planned. When I hang out the sign that says Harding House, the people who've known it all these years will find it just as they remember it in its early days.''

Loretta McConnell took the subtly-dangled bait. "Harding House?''

"I intend to keep the name, yes. It's every bit as much a landmark as this courthouse is. Landmarks ought not to be renamed, don't you think?''

Five minutes later Maggie and Eric left the courthouse with the Conditional Use Permit in hand.

They held in their hallelujahs as they moved down the echoey halls, but once outside, they both bellowed at once. She rejoiced while he let out a war whoop, picked her up and swung her off her feet.

"Holy balls, woman, did you have 'em bulldozed! Where in God's name did you get all that information so fast?''

She laughed, still amazed, and exclaimed, "Well, you told me to present them with facts!''

He set her down and smiled into her face. "Facts, yes—but they weren't expecting the World Almanac, and neither was I! Maggie, you were magnificent!''

"Was I?" She chuckled and felt her knees beginning to wobble. "Oh, Eric, I was so scared."

"You didn't look scared. You looked like Donald Trump putting up another building in New York, or Iacocca announcing a new model."

"I did?" she asked disbelievingly.

"You should have seen yourself."

"I think I have to sit down. I'm shaking." She fell back onto the edge of the concrete planter beside the front door and pressed a hand to her belly.

He perched beside her.

"You didn't have a thing to worry about, not from minute one. I've sat on that board, Maggie. Do you know how many people come in there asking for permits to build this or that, and they don't know wild honey from baby shit about what it would take to open it up, the cost of operating it, its chances for success, nothing! You knocked 'em right off their pins, Maggie. Hell, you didn't need me there at all."

"But I'm so happy you were. When I turned around and saw you smiling, I . . ." She interrupted herself and ended, "I'm so glad you're here to help me celebrate."

"So am I." He extended a hand. "Congratulations, Maggie M'girl."

She gave him her hand and he squeezed it. And held it. A little longer than prudent. The name had come out of nowhere, an echo of a bygone time. Their eyes met and held while the October night pressed near, and beside them the light fell through the window of the courthouse door. It felt too good, having her narrow hand in his much wider one.

She sensibly withdrew hers.

"So you're an innkeeper now," Eric remarked.

"I still can't believe it."

"Believe it."

She rose, joined her hands and hung them over the top of her head and turned a slow circle, looking at the stars. "Wow," she breathed.

"Did you see Loretta McConnell's face when you were slapping all those papers on the table?"

"Lord, no. I was afraid to look at her."

"Well, I did, and I could count her missing teeth, her mouth was open so wide. And then when you laid that color scheme on her—Maggie, how in the hell did you find out what color the place was?"

"I read an article in the *New York Times* on paint restoration and analysis. It named paint manufacturers who specialize in analyzing the old paint on buildings and producing authentic Victorian colors. I contacted one in Green Bay. What I didn't tell Loretta McConnell is that I didn't accomplish all this in the last three weeks. I started the moment I got back to Seattle. I ran up a long distance bill that would make you quiver and wince."

He chuckled and grinned at the stars. "Harding House Bed-and-Breakfast Inn," he mused. "I can see it already."

"You want to?" The question popped out of nowhere, prompted by Maggie's excitement.

"Now?"

"Now. I've just *got* to go see it now that I know it's really going to happen! Want to go with me?"

"Absolutely. I've been waiting for you to ask."

He had to stretch his legs to keep up with her on their way to the truck. "I'm going to run the classiest inn you ever saw!" she proclaimed as they hurried along. "Sour cream scones and Battenberg lace and eyelet bedding and antiques everywhere! Just you wait and see, Eric Severson!"

He laughed. "Maggie, slow down, you'll break your neck in those high heels."

"Not tonight. Tonight I'm charmed!"

She chattered all the way back to Fish Creek, spilling plans, from the most major such as where the laundry facilities would be, to the most minor—a dish of candy always available in the parlor, and cordials for the guests at bedtime. Amaretto, perhaps, or crème de cacao with cream floated on top. She had always been partial to crème de cacao and cream, she told him, and loved to watch the two colors swirl together after taking the first sip.

At her house he parked beside the thick wall of arborvitaes and followed her down a set of broad steps to the newly-restored back veranda where she unlocked the door and led the way inside.

"Stay there till I find the lightswitch."

Eric heard a click, but all remained black. The switch sounded again, four times in rapid succession. "Oh, damn, they must have disconnected something. The Lavitskys were using their electric tools when I left today, but . . . just a minute—wait here while I go try another light." A moment later he heard a dull thud and the scrape of wood on wood. "Ouch!"

"Maggie, you all right?"

"It's just a little bruise." More clicking. "Oh, shoot, I guess nothing's working."

"I've got a flashlight in the truck. Wait, I'll get it."

He returned in a minute, shining a light into the kitchen, catching Maggie in its beam. She looked incongruous, wearing high heels and suede, standing beside a sawhorse with a pile of broken plaster at her feet.

They stood in the dark room, their features highlighted by the dim flashlight, much as they'd been highlighted by dash lights years ago when they'd parked until the wee hours.

He thought, *You shouldn't be here, Severson.*

And she thought, *You'd better move. Fast.*

"Come on, let's go look at the house."

He handed her the flashlight. "Lead on."

She showed him the kitchen where there would soon be white cabinets with glass doors; the maid's room where the exterior wall had already been replaced; the tiny bathroom which would be for her private use, tucked beneath a stairway just off the kitchen, with its angled ceiling and beadboard wainscot; the main parlor with its fine quartersawn maple floor which she would use for her guests, and the music room which would become her own parlor; the pocket doors which could close to divide the two; the dining room where she would serve hot scones and coffee at breakfast time; the main stairway with its dramatic bannister and newels; three upstairs guest bedrooms, and a fourth, which would be divided to create the new exit and an additional guest bath.

"I saved the best for last," Maggie told Eric, leading him through one last doorway. "This . . ." She stepped inside. ". . . is the Belvedere Room." She flashed the light around the walls and crossed to a door on the opposite wall. "Look." She opened it and stepped out into the cool night air. "This is the belvedere. Isn't it lovely? In the daytime you can see the bay and the boats and Chambers Island from here."

"I've seen this from the water many times and always imagined it must have an impressive view."

"It'll be my best room. I'd love to have it for my own but I've come to realize that doesn't make a whole lot of sense. Not when I can use the maid's room downstairs, and have my own small bathroom, with access to the kitchen and second parlor. So, I've decided to make the Belvedere Room the honeymoon suite." She led the way back inside. "I'm going to put in a big brass bed and pile it with mountains of lacy pillows. Maybe an armoire on that wall, and over there a cheval mirror, and white lace on the windows so the view is never completely cut off. Of course, all the hardwood floors and woodwork will have to be refinished. Well, what do you think?"

"I think you're going to have a busy winter."

She laughed. "I don't mind. I'm looking forward to it."

"And . . ." He glanced at the illuminated face of his watch. "I think it's time I got you back home before your mother has a fit."

"I guess you're right. She'll probably be waiting up, ready to treat me as if I were fourteen years old again."

"Ah, mothers—they're all a thorn in the side at times."

They headed downstairs together with the light bobbing before them. "I can't imagine yours being one."

"Not often, but she has her moments. She gets on my case about Nancy working and being gone all the time. She thinks that's no way for a marriage to run." Reaching the bottom of the steps, Eric added, "The trouble is, neither do I."

In the dark, Maggie halted. It was the first time Eric had hinted at anything being amiss with his marriage, and it left Maggie searching for a graceful reply.

"Listen, Maggie, forget I said that. I'm sorry."

"No . . . no, it's all right, Eric. I just didn't know what to say."

"I love Nancy, honest to God, I do. It's just that we seem to have become so remote from one another since we moved back here. She's gone five days a week, and when she's home I'm out on the boat. She resents the boat and I resent her job. It's something we have to work out, that's all."

"Every marriage has its troubles."

"Did yours?"

"Of course."

"What? If you don't mind my asking."

They remained where they'd stopped, with Maggie aiming the flashlight at the floor between them.

"He liked gambling and I resented it. I still go on resenting it because it's what finally killed him. The plane he was on when he died was heading for a gambling junket in Reno. He went there once a year with a group from Boeing."

"And you never went with him?"

"Once. But I didn't like it."

"So he went without you."

"Yes."

"Was he addicted to it?"

"No, which left a lot of gray area between the two of us. It was simply a getaway for him, something he enjoyed that I didn't. He was always quick to point out that the money he gambled with was his own. Money he'd saved for that purpose. And he'd say, is there anything you want that you don't have? There wasn't, of course, so what could I say? But I always felt it was money we could have used together—to travel more, or . . . or . . ."

Silence fell around them. Seconds passed while they stood close enough to touch, but didn't. At last Maggie drew a shaky breath. "God, I loved him," she whispered. "And we did have everything. We *did* travel, and we *did* have luxuries—a sailboat, membership in an exclusive country club. And we'd still have all that—together—if he only hadn't gone on that last trip. You can't imagine the guilt I carry for still being angry with him when *he*'s the one who's dead."

Eric reached out and squeezed her arm. "I'm sorry, Maggie. I didn't mean to dredge up unwanted memories."

She moved and he knew she'd wiped her eyes in the dark. "It's all right," she said. "I learned in my grief group that it's perfectly normal for me to feel angry with Phillip. Just as it's probably perfectly normal for you to feel angry with Nancy."

"I *do* feel angry with her, but guilty, too, because I know she loves her job, and she's so damned good at it. And she works so hard. When she's flying all over the country she sometimes doesn't get into her hotel before nine or ten at night, and when she's home on weekends there's a horrendous amount of paperwork for her to do. But I find myself resenting that, too. Especially in the winter when we could be together on Saturdays. Instead, she's doing sales reports." He sighed and added despondently, "Oh, Christ . . . I don't know."

Silence returned and with it came a peculiar intimacy.

"Maggie, I never talked to anyone about this before," he admitted.

"Neither have I. Except in my group."

"My timing stinks—I'm sorry. You were so happy and excited before I started turning over stones."

"Oh, Eric, don't be silly. What are friends for? And I'm still happy and excited . . . underneath."

"Good."

In unison they turned and followed the beam of light toward the kitchen veranda door where they paused while Maggie flashed the light around the room once more.

"I like your house, Maggie."

"So do I."

"I'd like to see it when it's all done, sometime."

In an effort to buoy their deflated mood, she said, "I'll make sure I have you in for high tea in the parlor."

They stepped out onto the back veranda and Maggie locked the door. On their way to the truck Eric asked, "Will you be here tomorrow?"

"And the next day, and the next. I've started painting the upstairs woodwork and after that it's wallpapering and curtains."

"I'll sound the air horn when I go by in the boat."

"And I'll wave from the belvedere if I hear you."

"It's a deal."

They rode the short distance to her parents' house in silence, aware that a subtle change had taken place during the course of the evening.

The attraction was back. Curbed, but back. They told themselves it did not matter because tonight was an isolated dot of time which would not be repeated. She would go about the opening of her business and he about the continuation of his own, and if they occasionally met on the street they would pass each other with a friendly hello, and neither would admit how good it had felt being together one October night, how close they had felt celebrating her victory outside a courthouse. They would forget that he had unwittingly called her Maggie M'girl, and admitted things could be better with his marriage.

At her parents' house he pulled to the curb and shifted into neutral. The seat shimmied beneath them. Maggie sat as far away from him as possible, her right hip touching the door. In the living room the draperies were closed but the light was on.

"Thank you so much, Eric."

"My pleasure," he said softly.

They studied each other in the meager light from the dashboard, she with a portfolio against her side, he with his hands draped over the wheel.

She thought, it would be so easy.

He thought, get out, Maggie, quick.

"Good-bye," she said.

"Good-bye . . . and good luck."

She looked down, found the door handle and pulled, but the door stuck as it always did. He leaned across her lap and for that one brief moment while he opened the door, his shoulder grazed her breast.

The door swung open and Eric pushed himself upright. "There you go."

"Thanks again . . . goodnight," she said, clambering out, slamming the door before he could reply.

The truck changed gears and rolled away without delay, and she walked up the porch steps touching her hot face, thinking, Mother will know! Mother will know! She'll be waiting on the other side of this door.

She was.

"Well?" was all Vera said.

"I'll tell you in a minute, Mother. I have to go up to the bathroom first."

Maggie hurried upstairs, closed the bathroom door and leaned against it with her eyes closed. She walked to the medicine chest and studied her reflection in the mirror. It remained remarkably normal and unflushed, considering the charged emotions that had filled the truck only moments ago.

He's married, Maggie.

I know.

So that's the end of it.

I know.

You'll stay away from him.

I'll stay away.

But even as she made the promise she realized it should not have been necessary.

Chapter 7

♣

The air horn of the *Mary Deare* sounded the following afternoon, a great resonating bellow worthy of an antebellum riverboat.

Awoooooooozhhhhhh!

Even from a distance, it made the floors and windows vibrate.

Maggie's head came up. She sat back on her heels with a paintbrush in her hand, alert and tingling. It sounded again and she scrambled to her feet and ran along the upstairs hall, through the southwest bedroom and out onto the belvedere. But her view of the water was obstructed by the maples, still in full leaf. She stood in the thick shade, her hips pressed against the railing as her pulse slowed and disappointment settled in.

What are you doing, Maggie?

She backed up a step, composing herself.

What are you doing, running at the sound of his boat whistle?

As if someone had scolded her aloud, she turned sedately and went back inside.

After that, once each day, the air horn beckoned, always startling her, making her stop what she was doing and glance toward the front of the house. But she never ran again, as she had that first day. She told herself her fixation with Eric was simply a reaction to being back on familiar ground again. He was part of her past, Door County was part of her past, the two went together. She told herself she had no right to be thinking of him, to feel a jolt of reaction at the idea that he was thinking of her. She reminded herself of the low opinion she'd always held for single women who picked up married men.

Chasers, her mother had called them.

"That Sally Bruer is a chaser," Vera had said years ago of a young woman Maggie remembered as red-haired and blousy, a chatterbox who worked behind the ice cream counter at the corner store. She had always been particularly nice to the kids, though, giving them extra big scoops.

When Maggie was seven years old she overheard her mother talking with some ladies from her sewing circle about Sally Bruer. "That's what you get when you chase," Vera had said. "Pee-gee. And no telling whose baby it is because she runs with every Tom, Dick and Harry in the county. But they're saying it's Curve Rooney's." Curve Rooney was the town's baseball pitcher whose nickname was derived from his wicked curveball. Curve's pretty young wife came to every home game with their three apple-cheeked children and Maggie had seen them many times when she'd gone to games with her father. Sometimes she played with the oldest Rooney boy under the bleachers. Not until Maggie was twelve did she learn what pee-gee meant, and ever after she felt sorry for Curveball Rooney's children and for his pretty wife.

No, Maggie did not want to be a chaser. But the boat whistle called her every day, and she felt a pang of guilt at her reaction to it.

In mid-October she got away for two days. She drove to Chicago to choose furnishings for the house. At the Old House Store she bought a pedestal sink, clawfoot tub and brass hardware for the new bathroom. At Heritage Antiques she found a magnificent hand-carved oak bed for one of the bedrooms, and at Bell, Book and Candle, a mahogany marble-topped table and a pair of high-button shoes as unmarked as the day they'd been made, which she bought on a whim—period flavor for one of the guest rooms, she thought, picturing them side by side on the floor beside a cheval glass.

That evening, she took Katy out to dinner. Katy chose the spot—a small pub down on Asbury, frequented by the college crowd—and acted remote all the way there. When they were seated across the booth from one another she immediately immersed herself in the menu.

Maggie said, "Could we talk about it, Katy?"

Katy looked up, her brows sharply arched. "Talk about what?"

"My leaving Seattle. I take it that's what's kept you silent ever since I picked you up."

"I'd rather not, Mother."

"You're still angry."

"Wouldn't you be?"

The discussion started antagonistically on Katy's part, and resolved nothing. When the meal ended Maggie's emotions were a mixture of guilt and repressed exasperation at Katy's refusal to give her blessings to Maggie's move to Door County. As they said good-bye in front of Katy's dorm Maggie said, "You're coming home for Thanksgiving, aren't you?"

"Home?" Katy repeated sardonically.

"Yes. Home."

Katy glanced away. "I guess so. Where else would I go?"

"I'll make sure I have a room ready for you by then."

"Thanks." There was no warmth in the word as Katy reached for the door handle.

"Don't I get a hug?"

It was perfunctory, at best, perhaps even reluctant, and when they said good-bye Maggie headed away experiencing again an obscure guilt that she knew perfectly well she should not be feeling.

She returned to Door County the following day to the news that her Seattle house had sold. There was a message to call Elliott Tipton immediately. Dialing him, she expected to hear the news that there would be another delay while the buyers waited for their loan to be approved. Instead he told her the buyers had cash and were living out of a rented motel room, having undergone a company transfer from Omaha. They wanted to close as soon as possible.

She flew to Seattle within the week.

Leaving the Seattle house proved as unemotional as she had predicted, largely because it happened so fast. Upon her arrival she worked in the house for two frantic days, throwing away half-filled ketchup and mayonnaise bottles from the refrigerator, disposing of the turpentine and other combustibles the movers could not transport, dumping dirt and dead houseplants out of planters, giving away several pieces of furniture and cursorily sorting castoffs for the Salvation Army. On the third day the movers came and began packing. On the fourth, Maggie signed her name twenty-four times and turned over her house keys to the new owners. On the fifth she flew back to Door County to find a remarkable transformation had taken place at Harding House.

The exterior painting was finished, the scaffolding gone. In its new coat of original Victorian colors, Harding House dazzled. Maggie set her suitcase on the back sidewalk and walked clear around it, smiling, sometimes touching her mouth, wishing someone were with her to share her excitement. She looked up at the belvedere, down at the window ledges, up at the gingerbread gables, back down at the wide front porch. The painters had been forced to cut down the bridal-wreath bushes to get at the foundation, revealing the latticework wrapping the base of the porch. She imagined a cat slipping under there to sleep on the cool dirt on a hot summer day. She retreated to the lakeshore to view the house through the half-denuded maples whose brilliant orange leaves littered the lawn in a rustling carpet. She completed the circle and entered via the kitchen where the sheet rocking was finished, the walls smooth, white and empty, waiting for cabinets.

She set down her suitcase and listened.

From somewhere in the depths of the house came the sound of a radio playing a George Strait song, accompanied by the rhythmic swish of sandpaper on a plastered wall. She followed the sound along the front hall where the sun, enriched by its journey through stained glass, streamed across the entry and music room floors.

Tilting her head, she called up the stairs, "Hello?"

"Hello!" a man returned, "I'm up here!"

She found him in one of the smaller bedrooms, his clothes dusted with white, standing on a plank between two stepladders, sanding a replastered wall.

"Hello," she repeated from the doorway in a tone of surprise. "Where are the Lavitsky brothers?"

"Gone to do a short job somewhere else. I'm Nordvik, the plasterer."

"I'm Maggie Stearn, the owner."

He motioned with the sandpaper. "House is coming along fine."

"It certainly is. When I left there was no heat in here, and no kitchen walls. And, my goodness, the bathroom and fire exit are all in!"

"Yup, it's comin' right along. Plumber got the furnace in first of the week and the rockers started hanging the same day. Oh, by the way, there was a delivery came this morning from Chicago. We told 'em to put it in the living room. Hope that's okay."

"Fine, thank you."

Maggie rushed downstairs to find her antique furniture in the main parlor, and experienced one of those minutes where everything seemed so right, and the future so rosy, she simply had to be with somebody.

She called Brookie.

"Brookie, you've got to come and see my house! It's all painted outside and nearly ready for paint on the inside, and I've just come back from Seattle and the house there is all sold and my first pieces of antique furniture just arrived from Chicago and . . .'' She paused for a breath. "Will you come, Brookie?''

Brookie came to share her excitement, bringing—out of necessity—Chrissy and Justin, who explored the vast, empty rooms and played hide-and-seek in the closets while Maggie gave their mother a brief tour. Nordvik left for the day. The place became quiet, permeated by the cardboardy smell of new plaster and the sharper tang of glue from the tiles in the new bathroom. Maggie and Brookie walked through all the upstairs rooms, pausing finally in the Belvedere Room where they stood in a warm patch of sunlight while the voices of the children drifted in from down the hall.

"It's a great house, Maggie.''

"It is, isn't it? I think I'm going to love living here. I'm so glad you forced me to come and look at it.''

Brookie sauntered to the window, turned and perched on its low sill. "I hear you saw Eric a couple weeks ago.''

"Oh, Brookie, not you, too.''

"What do you mean, not me, too?''

"My mother nearly freaked out because we rode to Sturgeon Bay together for that board meeting.''

"Oh . . . I *didn't* hear that. Did anything happen?'' Brookie grinned impishly.

"Oh, Brookie, honestly! You're the one who told *me* to grow up.''

Brookie shrugged. "Just thought I'd ask.''

"Yes, something did happen. I got my permit to open a bed and breakfast.''

"I already found that out, even though my *best friend* didn't bother to call and tell me.''

"I'm sorry. Everything got crazy—the trip to Chicago, then to Seattle. I can't tell you how happy I'll be to get my own belongings back. As soon as I have so much as a frying pan and a bucket to dip lake water I intend to move out of my mother's house.''

"It's been bad, huh?''

"We don't get along any better now than we did when I was in school. Do you know she hasn't even come to see the house?''

"Oh, Maggie, I'm sorry.''

"What is it with my mother and me? I'm her only daughter. We're supposed to be close, but sometimes I swear, Brookie, she acts like she's jealous of me.''

"Of what?''

"I don't know. My relationship with Dad. My money, this house. The fact that I'm younger than she. Who knows? She's a hard woman to figure out.''

"I'm sure she'll come to see the house soon. Everyone else has, that's for sure! This place is the talk of Fish Creek. Loretta McConnell's been bragging hither and yon that you intend to name it after *her* forefathers, and about how you restored it to its original colors. You can't talk to a soul who hasn't driven past to look at it. It really looks beautiful, Maggie.''

"Thanks.'' Maggie crossed to the wide window and sat down beside Brookie. "But you know what, Brookie?'' Maggie studied the new plaster while the sound of the children's play echoed from the distance. "When

I see it changing—something new finished, like today when I got here—I get this . . .'' Maggie pressed a fist beneath her breast. ''. . . this big lump of emptiness because there's nobody to share it with. If Phillip were alive . . .'' She dropped her fist and sighed. ''But he's not, is he?''

''No.'' Brookie got to her feet. ''And you're going to do it all alone, and everyone in town including your mother is going to admire you for it.'' She hooked an elbow through Maggie's and drew her up.

Maggie's lips lifted into a grateful smile. ''Thanks so much for coming. I don't know what I'd do without you.'' Arm in arm, the two sauntered toward an adjacent room to scout up the children.

In the days that followed, as Maggie watched the house take shape, the lump of dejection appeared sporadically, particularly at the end of the day when the workers left and she'd wander the rooms alone, wishing for someone to share her sense of accomplishment. She couldn't call Brookie every day; Brookie had her own family responsibilities to keep her busy. Roy came often, but his enthusiasm was always counterposed by the fact that Vera never came with him.

The kitchen cabinets were hung, the Formica countertops set, the new bathroom fitted with its antique fixtures and the water turned on at last. Maggie's furniture arrived from Seattle and she moved out of her parents' house with a sense of great relief. On her first night in Harding House she slept in the Belvedere Room, though it contained only Katy's twin bed, a table and a lamp. The bulk of her belongings were piled into the crowded garage and the apartment above it until the floors in the main house could be refinished. An antique door for the new upstairs exit was located; Maggie stripped and varnished it, watched Joe Lavitsky hang it and as the light fell through its etched window for the first time she wished anew for someone with whom to share such moments.

October, viewed from the deck of the *Mary Deare*, was a season without rival, the sky-blue water reflecting the change in color that intensified daily as the trees turned in familiar sequence—first the butternuts, then the black walnuts, green ash, basswood, sugar maples, and finally the Norway maples. As the days progressed, Eric watched the breathtaking spectacle with a veneration that returned each year on cue. No matter how many times he witnessed it, autumn's impact never dulled.

This year Eric watched the season's change with an added interest, for each descending leaf exposed another bit of Maggie's house. It became anathema, this misplaced preoccupation with a woman not his wife. Yet he found himself passing Harding House daily, watching it appear section by section behind the maple trees, and he sounded his horn wondering if she ever stepped to a window to watch him pass, or onto the belvedere after he had.

Often he thought about the night they'd moused around in the blackness of her house with only a cone of light between them. It had been unwise, the kind of thing which, if discovered, could start tongues wagging. Yet it had been wholly innocent. Or had it? There had been a nostalgic feeling about the entire night, picking her up at her house just as he had when they were in high school, the hug on the courthouse steps, the ride back to Fish Creek and the confidences they'd exchanged in that black, black house.

In moments of greater clarity, he recognized the danger of putting himself anywhere near her, but at other times he'd ask himself what harm could come from sounding a whistle clear out on the bay.

By the last week of October the branches of her maples were nearly bare and he thought he saw her once, in a window of the belvedere room, but he wasn't sure if it was she or only a bright reflection off the glass.

November arrived, the waters of Green Bay turned cold and bare, its flotilla of autumn leaves sunk like shipwrecked treasures. There came that dreaded and anticipated day when the last of the fishermen had come and gone, and it was time to lay up the *Mary Deare* for the winter. Every year it was the same, looking forward to the slack time yet feeling forlorn when it arrived. Hedgehog Harbor, too, seemed forlorn, quiet with inactivity—no boat trailers unloading, no fishermen in misshapen caps posing for snapshots, no engines, horns, or shouting anywhere. Even the gulls—fickle birds—had disappeared now that their ready supply of food had stopped. Jerry Joe and Nicholas were back in school, and Ma had shut off the two-way radio till spring. She spent her days watching soap operas and shaping pieces of colored foam rubber into butterflies with magnetic bellies that perched on refrigerator doors. In those silent, crisp days that preceded snow, Eric cleaned the *Mary Deare* for the last time, winterized her engine, swaddled her up in canvas, lifted her from the water and blocked her up on a cradle. Mike laid up *The Dove* then disappeared into his back twenty to put up next winter's stovewood. The sound of the engine on his log-splitter sometimes drifted through the quiet from a half-mile away, revving and idling, revving and idling with monotonous regularity, adding to the melancholy.

Eric had told him to go; he'd finish the rest. When the fish-cleaning shed was scoured, and the docks out of the water, the rods and reels stored for the winter and all the outbuildings padlocked, Eric spent a few restless days at home, eating doughnuts and drinking coffee alone, doing what little laundry had accumulated, straightening spice cans in the kitchen cupboards. The coming winter loomed long and lonely, and he imagined Nancy at home with him, or the two of them going south, to Florida maybe, as so many of the other Door fishermen did in the winter.

Then one day when the house got too lonely, he went out to the woods to help Mike.

He found his brother beside the log-splitter, working alone over the noisy gasoline engine mounted on a knee-high trailer. Eric waited through the crescendo of sound while the powerful pneumatic ram slowly pushed the log against the wedge. The log creaked, tore, and finally fell to the earth in two pieces.

As Mike leaned over to pick up one, Eric called, "Yo, brother!"

Mike straightened, tossing the firewood aside. "Hey, what're you doing here?"

"Thought you might like a little help." Tugging worn leather gloves more tightly on his hands, Eric stepped to the far side of the rig. He tossed aside the other half of the log then reached for a whole one and placed it on the splitter.

"I'd never turn that down. It takes a mountain of wood to heat that house all winter." Mike engaged the clutch and the sound swelled as the log began moving. Above it, Eric shouted, "Thought you were going to put in a gas furnace this year."

"So did I but Jerry Joe decided to go to college so it'll have to wait."

"You need extra, Mike? I'd do damn near anything for that kid, you know."

"Thanks, Eric, but it's not just Jerry Joe. There's something else."

"Oh?"

Another log split, fell, and the engine quieted.

Mike picked up a piece of oak and said, "Barbara is pregnant again." He gave the wood a ferocious heave, then stood glowering at it.

Eric stood motionless, letting the news settle, feeling a wad of jealousy lodge in his chest: another one for Mike and Barb when they already had five scattered in ages from six to eighteen while he and Nancy had none. As quickly as it came, the jealousy fled. He picked up the piece of oak from his side of the splitter and tossed it onto the pile, grinning. "Well, smile, man."

"Smile! Would you smile if you'd just found out you were expecting your sixth one?"

"Damn right, especially if they were all like Jerry Joe."

"In case you hadn't heard, they don't come out that way, all raised and wearing size-ten shoes. First they need shots and they get ear infections and colic and measles and they go through about two thousand damned expensive diapers. Besides, Barb's forty-two already." He stared morosely at the naked trees nearby, then muttered, "Christ."

Between the two men the engine idled, forgotten.

"We're too damn old," Mike said at last. "Hell, we thought we were too old last time, when Lisa was born."

Eric leaned down and killed the engine, then stepped over it to grip Mike's shoulder.

"Listen, don't worry. You read all the time about how people are younger at forty than ever before, how women are having babies later and later in life, and everything's turning out fine. Hell, a couple years ago I remember reading about a woman in South Africa fifty-five years old who had a baby."

Mike laughed ruefully and dropped down to sit on a log. He sighed and mumbled "Aw, shit . . ." then stared a long time before raising a look of dismay to Eric. "You know how old I'll be when that kid graduates from high school? Retirement age, that's how old. Barb and I were looking forward to having a little time to ourselves before then."

Eric dropped to a squat, inquiring, "So, if you didn't want it, how did it happen?"

"Hell, I don't know. I guess we're just one of those statistics. What is it? Ten out of a thousand, even *with* birth control?"

"I don't know if it'll help, but I think you and Barb are the best parents I've ever known. The way your kids turned out—why, hell, the world ought to be grateful to have one more."

The remark finally raised a partial grin on Mike's face.

"Thanks."

The two brothers sat in silence for some time before Eric spoke again. "You want to know something ironic?"

"What?"

"While you're sitting there upset about having another baby, I'm sitting here envying the hell out of you because you're going to. I *know* how damned old you are because I'm only two years behind you and my time's running out."

"Well, what's holding you up?"

"Nancy."

"I thought so."

"She doesn't want one."

After several seconds of silence, Mike admitted, "Everyone in the family guessed as much. She doesn't want to give up her job, does she?"

"Nope." Eric let that settle before adding, "I don't think she's too crazy about the idea of losing her shape either. That's always been so important to Nancy."

"Have you talked to her about it, told her you wanted a family?"

"Yeah, for about six years now. I just kept waiting, thinking she'd say yes one of these times, but it's not going to happen. I know that now and it's gotten to the point where we fight about it."

Again the two sat ruminating while a noisy flock of sparrows settled in a nearby sumac copse. "Aw, hell, it's more than that. It's Fish Creek. She hates it here. She's happier when she's out on the road traveling than when she's home."

"You could be imagining that."

"Yeah, I could be, but I don't think so. She never wanted to move here."

"That might be so, but that doesn't mean she hates coming home."

"She always used to say how she hated leaving on Mondays, but I don't hear that anymore." Eric studied the sparrows a while. They were pecking on the ground beneath the sumac, murmuring soft *cheep-cheeps*. He'd grown up with lots of birds around, both water and land birds. The first Christmas after they were married, Nancy had given him a beautiful Audubon book and had written on the flyleaf, *because you miss them*. Before moving here from Chicago she'd boxed up the book with a bunch of others and had given it to the Goodwill without his knowledge. Watching the sparrows on the chill autumn day he grieved not over the loss of the book but over the loss of affection it represented.

"You know what I think happened?"

"What?"

Eric turned to look at his brother. "I think we stopped giving." After a stretch of profound silence, Eric went on. "I think it started when we moved here. She was deadset against it and I wouldn't have it any other way. I wanted a family and she wanted a career, and it started this cold war between us. On the surface everything appears fine, but underneath it's all turned sour."

The flock of sparrows flew away. Off in the distance a pair of crows called. In the clearing all was still beneath a steely gray sky that seemed to reflect Eric's morose mood.

"Hey, Mike," he said after some moments of silence, "do you think people without kids get sort of selfish after a while?"

"That's a pretty broad generalization."

"I think it happens though. When you've got kids you're forced to think about them first, and sometimes, even though you're bone tired, you get up and you relieve the other one. When kids are sick, or whiny, or when they need you for one thing or the other. But when there are just the two of you . . . aw, hell, I don't know how to say it." Eric picked up a piece of bark and started flaking off bits with his thumbnail. After some time he forgot his preoccupation and gazed into the distance.

"Remember how it was with Ma and the old man? How at the end of a busy day after she'd manned the office all day long and washed clothes in that old wringer washer and hung them on the line between customers and fed us kids and probably acted as referee in about a dozen fights, she'd go out there and help him scour down the fish shed? And the next thing you know they'd be laughing down there. I used to lay in my bed and wonder what they found to laugh about in the fish-cleaning shack at ten-thirty at night. The crickets would be squawking, and the water would be lapping down by the boats, and I'd lay there and listen to them laugh and feel so damned good. Secure, I guess. And one time—I remember this so clearly, it's as if it just happened yesterday—I came into the kitchen late at night when all of us kids were supposed to be asleep and you know what he was doing?"

"What?"

"He was washing her feet."

The two brothers exchanged a long, silent glance before Eric continued. "She was sitting on a kitchen chair and he was on his knees in front of her washing her feet. She had her head back and her eyes were closed and neither one of them said a word. He was just holding her soapy foot above a wash basin and rubbing it real slow with his hands." Eric paused thoughtfully. "I'll never forget that. Her lumpy old feet that always hurt her so much, and the way the old man was doing that for her."

Once more the two brothers sat in silence, bound by the memory. In time Eric went on quietly. "That's the kind of marriage I want, and I don't have it."

Mike settled his elbows on his knees. "Maybe you're too idealistic."

"Maybe."

"Different marriages work for different reasons."

"Ours isn't working at all, not since I forced her to move back here to Fish Creek. I realize now, that's when our trouble really started."

"So what are you going to do about it?"

"I don't know."

"You going to give up fishing?"

"I can't do that. I love it too much."

"Is she going to give up her job?"

Disconsolately, Eric shook his head.

Mike scooped up two twigs and began snapping them into pieces. "So . . . you scared?"

"Yeah . . ." Eric glanced over his shoulder. "It's scary as hell the first time you bring it out into the open." He chuckled ruefully. "As long as you don't admit your marriage is falling apart, maybe it isn't . . . right?"

"Do you love her?"

"I should. She's still got a lot of the qualities I married her for. She's beautiful, and smart, and hard working. She's really made something of herself at Orlane."

"But do you love her?"

"I don't know anymore."

"Things okay in bed?"

Eric cursed softly and threw away the bark. He propped his elbows on his knees and shook his head at the ground. "Hell, I don't know."

"What do you mean, you don't know. Does she play around?"

"No, I don't think so."

"Do you?"

"No."

"Then what is it?"

"It all harks back to the same old problem. When we're making love . . ." It was hard to say.

Mike waited.

"When we're making love everything is okay until she gets out of bed to use that goddamned contraceptive foam, then I feel like . . ." Eric's lips narrowed and his jaw tensed. "Like taking the can and throwing it through the goddamned wall. And when she comes back, I want to push her away."

Mike sighed. He considered at length before advising, "The two of you ought to talk to somebody—a doctor or a marriage counselor."

"When? She's gone five days a week. Besides, she doesn't know how I feel about the sex part."

"Don't you think you should tell her?"

"It'd kill her."

"It's killing you."

"Yeah . . ." Eric replied despondently, staring off through the skeletal trees at the tarnished silver sky. He sat for a long time, hunched like a cowboy before a campfire. Finally he sighed, stretched out his legs and studied the buckled knees of his blue jeans. "Hell of a deal, isn't it? You with more kids than you want and me without any?"

"Yeah. Hell of a deal."

"Does Ma know yet?" Eric glanced at Mike.

"That Barb's pregnant? No. She'll have something to say, I'm sure."

"She's never said anything about our not having any. But she says plenty about Nancy being gone all the time, so I suppose it's the same thing."

"Well, she was raised on old-fashioned ways, and since she worked beside the old man her whole life long she thinks that's the way it ought to be."

They pondered awhile, thinking about their lives as they were now and as they were when they were younger. Presently, Eric said, "You want to know something, Mike?"

"What?"

"Sometimes I wonder if Ma is right."

Three days later, on a Saturday night after a late supper at home, Nancy sat back, toying with a glass of Chablis and eating the last of her green grapes. The atmosphere was intimate, the mood lazy. Outside the wind plucked at the shingles and sent the cedars swaying against the metal rain gutters, sending out a muted screech that filtered through the walls. Inside, candlelight reflected off the surface of the teakwood table and enriched the texture of the cutwork linen place mats.

She studied her husband appreciatively. He'd showered before supper and had come to the table uncombed. With his hair loose and unstyled, he made an arresting sight. He was dressed in jeans and a new designer sweatshirt she'd brought him from Neiman-Marcus, an oversized pewter gray slop-top with a rolled collar and immense raglan sleeves that made him look rugged and negligent as he sat slant-shouldered, drinking Irish coffee.

He was a handsome thing, as handsome as any man she'd ever seen, and she'd seen many. In her job, she bumped shoulders with them in every town, in the best department stores, dressed like fashion plates and smelling good enough to stuff into a dresser drawer with your lingerie. They had haircuts like girls and wore wool scarves over their suitjackets and dressed in flat Italian slippers of exquisitely thin leather, without socks. Some were gay, but some were overtly heterosexual and made it no secret.

She had grown accustomed to parrying their advances, and on the few occasions when she returned them, she made sure the *tête-à-tête* lasted only one night; for, once in bed, those men never quite measured up to Eric. Their bodies were small where his was large, their hands soft where his were hard, their skin white where his was brown, and with none of them could she achieve the sexual harmony it had taken her and Eric eighteen years to achieve together.

She studied him, relaxed and appealing across the table and hated to mar the mood she had so carefully cultured with the candlelight, linens and wine. But she had cultured it for a purpose, and the time had come to test its effectiveness.

She slipped one nylon-covered foot onto Eric's chair. "Honey?" she murmured, rubbing the inside of his knee.

"Hm?"

"Why don't you put the boat up for sale?"

He studied her impassively for some moments, tipped up and emptied his cup of coffee and silently turned to study a woven wood shade.

"Please, honey." She leaned forward provocatively with her forearms lining the table edge. "Advertise it now, and by spring you'll have it sold and we can move back to Chicago. Or any other major city you like. How about Minneapolis? It's a beautiful town, lakes everywhere and it's a mecca for the arts. You'd love Minneapolis. Eric . . . please, can't we discuss it?" She watched a muscle tic in his jaw while he continued avoiding her eyes. Finally he faced her, speaking with careful control.

"Tell me something. What do you want out of this marriage?"

Her foot stopped caressing his knee. This was not going at all as she'd hoped. "What do I want?"

"Yes, want. Besides me, or . . . or having sex with me on the Saturdays and Sundays when you don't have your period. What do you want, Nancy? You don't want this house, you don't want this town, you don't want me to be a fisherman. And you've made it perfectly clear you don't want a family. So what *do* you want?"

Instead of answering, she demanded sharply, "When are you going to get over this?"

"Get over what?"

"You know what I mean, Eric. Playing the Old Man and the Sea. When we left Chicago I thought you'd play fisherman with your brother for a couple of years and get it out of your system, then we'd move back to the city so we could spend more time together."

"When we left Chicago I thought you'd want to give up your job with Orlane and stay here with me to start a family."

"I make a lot of money. I love my work."

"So do I."

"And you're wasting a perfectly good college degree, Eric. What about your business degree, don't you intend to use it again?"

"I use it every day."

"You're being stubborn."

"What will change if we live in Chicago or Minneapolis? Tell me."

"We'd have a city—art galleries, orchestra halls, theaters, department stores, new—"

"Department stores, ha! You spend five days out of seven in department stores as it is! How the *hell* can you want to spend any more time there!"

"It's not the department stores alone and you know it. It's urbanity! Civilization! I want to live where things happen!"

He studied her a long time, his expression arctic and unapproachable. "All right, Nancy, I'll make you a deal." He pushed back his cup, crossed his forearms on the table edge and fixed her with unrelenting eyes. "You have a baby and we'll move to the city of your choice."

She drew back as if he'd swung at her. Her face grew white, then red as she struggled with a compromise she was incapable of accepting. "You're not being fair!" Her anger flared and she rapped a fist on the table. "I don't *want* a damn baby, and you know it!"

"And I don't want to leave Door County, and you know it. If you're going to be gone five days a week at least I want to be near my family."

"I'm your family!" She pressed her chest.

"No, you're my wife. A family includes progeny."

"So we're at the same old impasse."

"Apparently so, and it's been on my mind so much since our last argument that I finally talked to Mike about it the other day."

"To Mike!"

"Yes."

"Our personal problems are no business of Mike's, and I resent your spilling them to him!"

"It just came up. We were talking about babies. They're going to have another one."

Nancy's expression became one of distaste. "Oh, Christ, that's obscene."

"Is it?" he retorted sharply.

"Don't you think it is? Those two spawn as regularly as salmon! My God, they're old enough to be grandparents! Why in heaven's name would they want another baby at their age?"

Eric threw his napkin onto the table and lurched to his feet. "Nancy, sometimes you really piss me off!"

"And you run right to your brother and tell him so, don't you? So, naturally the world's best father has some choice opinions about a wife who'd *choose* not to have babies."

"Mike has never said *one* negative thing about you!" He pointed a finger at her nose. "Not one!"

"So what did he say when he found out the reason we don't have a family?"

"He advised us to see a marriage counselor."

Nancy stared at Eric as if she had not heard.

"Would you?" he asked, watching her closely.

"Sure," she replied sarcastically, sitting back in her chair with her hands joined at her midriff. "Tuesday nights are usually reasonably free when I'm in St. Louis." Her tone changed, became exacting. "What's going on

here, Eric? All of a sudden this talk about marriage counselors and mal-
content. What's wrong? What's changed?"

He picked up his coffee cup, spoon and napkin and took them into
the kitchen. She followed, standing behind him as he set the dishes in
the sink and stood staring down at them, afraid to answer her question
and start the tumult he knew he must start if he was ever to make his life
happier.

"Eric," she appealed softly, touching his back.

He drew a deep breath and with his insides trembling, stated the thing
that had been eating at him for months. "I need more out of this marriage
than I'm getting, Nancy."

"Eric, please . . . no, don't . . . Eric, I love you." She coiled her arms
around his trunk and rested her face on his back. He stood unyielding,
facing the sink.

"I love you, too," he told her quietly. "That's why this hurts so much."

They stood awhile, wondering what to say or do next, neither of them
prepared for the heartbreak already setting in.

"Let's go to bed, Eric," she whispered.

He closed his eyes and felt a wave of emptiness that terrified him worse
than anything thus far.

"You just don't understand, do you, Nancy?"

"Understand what? That part has always been good. Please . . . come
upstairs."

He sighed and for the first time ever, turned her down.

Chapter 8

❧

Nancy left for work again on Monday. Their parting kiss was filled with
uncertainty and he watched her drive away with a sense of desolation.
When she was gone, he spent the days on winter work, tallying the number
of feet of fishing line used during the season, the number of lures lost,
searching through the hundreds of suppliers' catalogues for the best re-
placement prices. He sent in preregistration fees for display booths at the
Minneapolis, Chicago and Milwaukee Sportsmen's Shows and ordered
brochures to pass out there. He tallied up the number of Styrofoam coolers they'd sold out of the office and contracted to buy an entire truckload
of them for the next year's season.

In between times, he wondered what to do about his marriage.

He ate alone, slept alone, worked alone, and asked himself how many
more years it would be this way. How many more years could he tolerate
this solo existence?

He went uptown for a haircut before he actually needed one because the house was so quiet and there was always pleasant company at the barbershop.

He called Ma every day and went out to check her fuel oil barrel well before he knew it was empty, because he knew she'd ask him to stay for supper.

He changed the oil in the pickup and tried to fix the sticking passenger door but couldn't. It reminded him of Maggie, of leaning across her lap the night he'd dropped her off at her mom and dad's. He thought of her often. How was she doing, how was her house progressing, had she found all those antiques she talked about? Rumor had it the outside paint job was done and her house looked like a showplace. Then one day he decided to drive by himself, just to take a look.

Just to take a look.

The leaves were all down, lying in battered windrows along the edge of Cottage Row as his pickup climbed the hill. The evergreens appeared shaggy and black against a late afternoon sun. It had turned cold, the sky taking on a haze almost like sun dogs, warning it would be colder tomorrow. Most of the houses along the Row were deserted now, their wealthy owners gone back to the southern cities where they wintered. As he approached Maggie's place he noted a Lincoln Town Car with a Washington license plate parked beside her garage—undoubtedly hers. The cedars at the edge of her property were still untrimmed and cut off much of the view; he rolled by slowly, glancing down the break between them, catching a glimpse of the gaily colored house. They'd been right: it was a showplace.

That night, at home, he turned on the television and sat before it for nearly an hour before realizing he hadn't heard a word. He'd been sitting motionless, staring at the shifting figures on the screen, thinking of Maggie.

The second time he drove past her place he was armed with a registration form from the chamber of commerce and a copy of their summer tourist booklet. Her car was parked in the same place as before as he pulled up beside the cedars, killed the engine and stared at the booklet on the seat. For sixty seconds he stared, then started the engine and tore up the hill without glancing at her house.

The next time he drove by, a green panel truck was parked at the top of her walk, its rear doors open and an aluminum ladder hanging from its side. If the truck hadn't been there he might have driven right by again, but it would be okay with a workman in the house.

It was late afternoon again, chilly with a cutting wind that snapped at the papers he carried as he slammed his truck door. Rolling them into a cylinder, he passed the panel truck and peered inside—conduit, coils of wire and tools—good, he was right. He loped down the broad steps toward the house and knocked on the back door.

Whistling softly through his teeth, he waited, eyeing the back veranda. A cluster of Indian corn and orange ribbon hanging on the wall; an oval brass plaque announcing, HARDING HOUSE; white lace curtains covering the window of an antique door; a new spooled railing painted yellow and blue; a new floor painted gray; a braided rug; and a crock in the corner holding a clump of cattails and Indian tobacco. Rumor had it Maggie wasn't afraid to spend money to dress up the place, and if the outside was any indication, she'd been busy at it. Even the tiny veranda had charm.

Eric knocked again, harder, and a male voice shouted, "Yeah, come on in!"

He stepped into the kitchen and found it empty, bright and transformed. His glance took in white cabinets with mullioned glass panes, rose-colored countertops, gleaming hardwood floors, a long, narrow drop-leaf table with a scarred top, a long lace runner, and a knobby basket of pinecones with a fat pink bow on its handle.

From another room a voice called, "Hullo, you lookin' for the missus?"

Eric followed the sound and found an electrician who looked like Charles Bronson hanging a chandelier in the ceiling of the empty dining room.

"Hi," Eric greeted, pausing in the doorway.

"Hi." The man glanced back over his shoulder, his arms upraised. "If you're looking for the missus, she's upstairs working. You can go on up."

"Thanks." Eric headed across the dining room to the entry hall. By daylight it was impressive: newly refinished floors still smelling of polyurethane and freshly plastered walls giving the impression of wide white space anchored by unbroken stretches of lustrous wood. A massive bannister dropped from above and from somewhere up there, a radio was playing.

He started up, paused at the top and glanced down the hall with all its doors open. He moved toward the music. In the second doorway on the left, he stopped.

Maggie knelt on the floor, painting the wide baseboard moulding on the opposite side of the room. She and the tunebox and the paint can were the only three things in it. No other distractions. Just Maggie, on all fours, looking refreshingly artless. He smiled at the soles of her bare feet, the paint smears on her sacky blue jeans and the tail of her sloppy shirt trailing on the lip of the paint can.

"Hi, Maggie," he said.

She started and yelped as if he'd sounded his boat horn at her ear.

"Oh my God," she breathed, sinking back on her heels, pressing a hand to her heart. "You scared the daylights out of me."

"I didn't mean to. The guy downstairs said I should come right up." He gestured with a roll of papers toward the hall behind him.

What was he *doing* here? Maggie knelt before him with her heart still erratic as he stood in the doorway dressed in loafers, jeans and a puffy black-leather bomber jacket with the collar turned up against his pale hair, just as he'd turned it up years ago. A little too fetching and a lot too welcome.

"I can come back some other time if—"

"Oh, no, that's fine . . . that's . . . the radio was on so loud . . ." Still on her knees, she stretched toward it and lowered the volume. "I was just thinking of you, that's all, and all of a sudden you said my name and I . . . you were . . ."

You're babbling, Maggie. Be careful.

"And here I am," he finished for her.

She got control of herself and smiled. "Welcome to Harding House." She spread her arms wide and looked down at her apparel. "As you can see, I'm dressed for guests."

To Eric, she looked utterly engaging, dappled with white paint, her hair tied away from her face with a dirty shoestring. He couldn't stop smiling at her.

"As you can see . . ." He held out his hands, too. "I'm not a guest. I just brought you some information about joining the chamber of commerce."

"Oh . . . great!" She laid her paintbrush across the can and with a rag from her back pocket scrubbed her knuckles as she got to her feet. "You want a tour while you're here? I have lights now."

He stepped further into the room and gave it an appreciative glance. "I'd love a tour."

"At least, I think I have lights. Just a minute." She hurried out into the hall and called downstairs, "Can I turn on the lights, Mr. Deitz?"

"Just a minute and I'll have this hooked up!" he called back.

She turned to Eric. "We'll have lights in a minute. Well, this is a guest room . . ." She gave another flourish. ". . . one of the four. As you can see, I'm using the original light fixtures because they're made of solid brass. I found out, after I started examining them closer, that they were all originally gas lights—did you know this town didn't get electricity until the 1930s?"

"Really?"

"So everything's been converted. I love the old fixtures because they're authentic. When Mr. Deitz gets the electricity back on, you'll see how pretty they look, even in daylight."

They stood beneath the gas fixture, looking up, close enough to smell each other. He smelled like crisp air and leather. She smelled like turpentine.

"And didn't my floors turn out beautifully? Wait till I show you the one downstairs in the main parlor."

He glanced down. Her feet were bare below baggy denims rolled to mid-calf, familiar feet he'd seen tens of times aboard the *Mary Deare* that summer when they had practically lived in bathing suits.

"They look just like new," he said of the floors, then glanced around the bare room. "The decorating's a little austere though."

Maggie chuckled and buried her hands in her front pockets. "All in due time."

"I heard you'd moved back. You sold your Seattle house?"

"Yup."

"Where are your things?"

"In the garage. So far I've only taken out the kitchen furnishings and one bed for me to sleep on."

"The kitchen looks great, by the way. I can see you have a touch."

"Thanks. I'm anxious to get all the woodwork redone so I can move the rest of the furniture inside." She lifted her gaze to the wide cove moulding overhead and he found himself studying the curve of her throat. "I decided to paint all the upstairs mopboards and ceiling mouldings white, and leave those downstairs natural wood. As soon as I get them finished I can start the wallpapering, but everything takes so long to get. Three weeks for most of the paper out of Sturgeon Bay. When I've finished the painting I've decided to give myself a break and go to Chicago. I can get wallpaper there in one day."

"You're going to do the papering yourself?"

"Uh-huh."

"Who taught you how?" he asked, following her into the next bedroom.

"Taught me?" She glanced back and shrugged. "Trial and error, I guess. I'm a home economics teacher. Need I tell you how non-economical it is to hire paperers? Besides, I enjoy it, and I have all winter, so why not do it myself?"

He thought about coming over sometime in the dreary days of midwinter and helping her. Stupid thought.

"You know what I've decided?" Maggie asked.

"What?"

"To name each bedroom after Thaddeus Harding's children. This one will be the Franklin, that one the Sarah, and that one the Victoria. I'll get a little brass plaque for each door. Fortunately for me, Thaddeus only had three children, so this last room will get the name it deserves." She led Eric into the fourth room. "The Belvedere Room. How could it be anything else?" He stood beside her, surveying the room by daylight. Bright, white, furnished only with her bed which sat dead center in the room. It had neither been neatened this morning nor overly mussed last night. She slept—he noted—facing the window and the water. In one corner of the room a pair of vintage high-button shoes sat primly on the floor.

He grinned, glanced from her bare feet to the shoes and remarked, "Ah, so this is where you lost them."

Maggie laughed and looked down, swishing a bare sole across the smooth floor. "These floors feel like satin. I can't get enough of them."

Their eyes met and memories bedeviled again—both of them, this time—of summer days aboard the *Mary Deare*, barefoot and in love.

She looked away first, toward the window, and breathed, "Oh, look . . . snow!"

Outside great downy flakes had begun to fall, lining the maple branches and disappearing as they touched the water. The sky was hueless, sunless, a great blending of white-on-white.

"I've missed it," Maggie said, moving toward the window. "In Seattle it snowed up in the mountains, of course, but I missed watching it change the yard like this, or waking up that first morning when your bedroom would be so bright even the ceiling was lit and you'd know it had snowed overnight."

He trailed toward her and stood at her shoulder, watching the snow, wishing just once he and Nancy could enjoy it together this way. For Nancy, snow always signaled the beginning of the difficult traveling season, so she found little in it to appreciate, not even aesthetically. When she was home it seemed they never took time for the quiet things like this.

What are you doing here, Severson, making comparisons between Maggie and your wife? Give her the damned papers and get out!

But he stood at the window beside Maggie, watching the rough tweed of winter disappear beneath a powdery blanket of white.

"You know what it reminds me of?" Maggie asked.

"What?"

"A linen tablecloth the world puts on for Thanksgiving. It should be snowy for Thanksgiving, don't you think?"

She glanced up and found him very close, studying her instead of the snow.

"Absolutely," he answered quietly, and for a moment they forgot the view, and the presence of the electrician downstairs, and the reasons they should not be standing so close.

Maggie recovered first and moved away discreetly. "Should we go downstairs?"

On their way down she explained, "I found the high-button shoes in an antique shop in Chicago and I couldn't resist them. They'll add a quaint touch to one of the bedrooms, don't you think?"

Her sensible chatter ended the threat they had felt upstairs, and if for a moment they'd been tempted, and if for that moment they'd recognized it as mutual, they moved on through her house pretending it had not happened. She kept up a lively dialogue while guiding him from room to room, showing him her walls and her windows and her floors, especially in the downstairs parlor.

"I discovered this marvelous craftsmanship underneath an old musty rug." She knelt and ran a hand over the exquisite wood. "It's quartersawn maple. Look how it's laid, isn't it a lovely design?"

He squatted, too, knees snapping, and touched it. "It's beautiful. Is this the room where you intend to have the candy bowl and the cordials?"

"Yes. We could have some now," she remarked gaily, "if I had any candy or cordials in the house. Unfortunately, I haven't put in a supply. Would a cup of coffee do?"

"I'd love one."

Leading the way to the kitchen she detoured through the dining room where the electrician was working with a screwdriver at a wall switch. With the power still off and twilight settling in, the room was dusky. "Do you know Patrick Deitz?"

"I don't believe I do."

"Patrick Deitz, this is Eric Severson. He runs a charter boat out of Gills Rock. We're going to have some coffee. Would you like some?"

"Don't mind if I do, Mrs. Stearn." Patrick slipped the screwdriver into his pocket and shook hands with Eric. "But wait right here while I get the power back on."

He was gone only momentarily, leaving Maggie and Eric standing in the gloaming facing a wide bay window. It was all right this time: Deitz was nearby and they had weathered the moment of captivation upstairs. They watched the snow, drawn together by the emptiness of the house and the change of season which was happening before their eyes, and by the very coming of twilight.

"I'm going to love it here," Maggie said.

"I can see why."

Deitz returned, experimented with a dimmer switch on the wall, and said, "How's that, Mrs. Stearn?"

Maggie smiled up at the ornate fixture which gleamed from a recent polishing. "Perfect, Mr. Deitz. You were absolutely right about which bulbs to choose. The candle-shaped ones add exactly the right touch. It's a grand chandelier. Isn't it a grand chandelier, Eric?"

Actually, it was a rather ugly piece of metal, but the longer Eric studied it, the more he was able to appreciate its antique charm. First the snow, then the floor, now the chandelier. Though he'd warned himself against making comparisons, it was impossible not to, for he realized while walking through this house how little time Nancy took to appreciate things—

little things, simple things. Maggie, on the other hand, managed to make the mere coming of dusk into an occasion.

"Well, how about that coffee?" she said.

The three of them sat at the table where she served coffee in man-sized mugs, tea for herself, and a plate of cinnamon cookies, which she replenished twice. They talked about the Green Bay Packers' season; and how you couldn't buy fuzzy peaches anymore because hybridization had made them smooth; and which was the best way to cook salmon; and about Maggie's kitchen table which she'd found beneath the tools in her father's garage. They had a lively discussion about which were the best antique stores in Door County and Maggie heard numerous anecdotes about the people who owned them.

After thirty minutes Patrick Deitz checked his watch, clasped his knees and said he'd better pick up his tools, it was five-thirty already.

As soon as he got up, so did Eric. "I'd better go, too," he said while Deitz went into the dining room.

"Aren't you going to show me what you brought for me?" Maggie asked, pointing to the papers Eric had dropped on an empty chair.

"Oh, I almost forgot." He handed them across the table to her. "It's just some information about registering with the chamber of commerce. I'm a member, and we try to get around to all the new businesses as soon as possible. I guess you can consider this your formal invitation to join."

"Why, thank you." She glanced at the magazine. *The Key to the Door Peninsula.* On the cover was a summer lakescape. Inside was a gathering of tourist information and ads for food, lodging and shopping in Door County.

"That's a copy of last summer's *Key* and the extra sheet has information about what it costs to register. It would be impossible to run an inn in Door County without belonging. Most of your referrals will come from the chamber so you'll find it's the best advertising money you'll spend."

"Thanks. I'll look it over right away."

"I'd guess we'll probably be going to the printer in February or March with next summer's copy, so you'll have plenty of time to have an ad laid out. I have mine done in Sturgeon Bay at Barker's. They have a pretty good graphic arts department."

"I'll remember that, thanks."

They moved to the door and paused. "The members of the chamber meet once a month for breakfast at different restaurants around town. Nothing formal, just a way of touching base with the other businesspeople. Next month—on the fourth, I think—we're meeting at The Cookery. You're welcome to come."

"I may do that."

Deitz came through the kitchen with his toolbox. "Well, goodnight, Mrs. Stearn. Thanks for the coffee and cookies. They were real good."

"You're welcome."

"Nice to meet you, Eric." Deitz nodded.

"Same here."

Deitz moved between them and Maggie opened the door to let him out. When he was gone she stood in the cold air with the door still open.

"Well, think about the breakfast," Eric encouraged.

"I will."

"And thanks for the tour of the house."

"You're welcome."

"I really love it."

"So do I." The air continued blowing inside. She crossed her arms.

"Well . . ." He reached in a pocket for his gloves and drew them on slowly. "Good-bye, then."

Neither of them moved, only their eyes, to each other. She hadn't intended to say the words but they came out of nowhere. "Let me get my jacket and I'll walk you up the hill."

He closed the door and waited while she disappeared into the maid's room and returned wearing a pair of Reeboks without socks, shrugging into a fat pink jacket. She dropped to one knee in the middle of the kitchen floor, rolled down her pants legs, then stood, zipping her jacket.

"Ready?"

She looked up and flashed a smile.

"Aha."

He opened the door, let her pass before him into the five-thirty dark where the softly-falling snow created a halo around the back veranda light. The air smelled fresh, of first winter as they moved side by side in Deitz's tracks.

"Be careful," he warned. "It's slippery." Instead of taking her elbow he let his arm buffer hers, a touch of nothing more than insulated clothing, yet through two winter sleeves they were aware of one another as flesh and blood. Somewhere above them Deitz slammed his truck door, started the engine and drove away. When he was gone, they moved slower, up the broad steps that climbed to the road.

The snow fell in great weightless flakes, straight down, in air so still the contact of sky with earth could be heard like the soft tick of a thousand beetles on a warm June night. Reaching the second step, Maggie stopped. "Shh, listen." She tilted her head back.

He lifted his face to the milky sky . . . listening . . . listening . . .

"Hear that?" she whispered. "You can actually hear the snow falling."

He closed his eyes and listened, and felt the flakes striking his eyelids and cheeks, melting there.

You go on home now, Eric Severson, and forget about standing in the snow with Maggie Pearson. He never thought of her as Maggie Stearn.

He opened his eyes and felt momentarily dizzy watching the perpetual motion above him. A flake plopped on his upper lip. He licked it off and forced himself to move on.

She moved with him, close by his elbow.

"What are you doing for Thanksgiving?" he inquired, suddenly certain she'd be on his mind that day.

"Katy is coming home. We'll be at Mom and Dad's. How about you?"

"Everybody will be at Mike and Barb's. Ma makes the stuffing though. She's scared to death Barb might put a little store-bought bread in it and kill off the whole family."

They laughed, reaching his truck where they stopped and turned toward one another, suddenly taken by the snow between their feet.

"It'll be the first time Katy sees the house."

"She's in for a treat."

"I'm not so sure. Katy and I had a difference of opinion about my selling the house in Seattle." Holding a prolonged shrug, Maggie continued as if vexed with herself. "Oh, damn, I may as well be honest. We argued about it, and she hasn't exactly been cordial to me since. I'm a little uneasy about her coming. She thinks it's a mother's duty to keep the home fires burning, as long as the home is the one the kids grew up in. I went to Chicago a couple of weeks ago and took her out for dinner but the atmosphere was a little chilly, to say the least." She sighed. "Oh, kids . . ."

"My mother always says all kids go through a selfish streak somewhere between puberty and common sense, when they think their parents are damned fools who don't dress right, talk right or think right. I remember going through that stage myself."

Maggie innocently widened her eyes. "Did *I*?"

He laughed. "I don't know. Did you?"

"I suppose. I couldn't wait to get away from my mother."

"Well . . . there you go."

"Eric Severson, you're not the least bit sympathetic!" she scolded with mock petulance.

Again he laughed, and when it ended he turned thoughtful. "Count your blessings, Maggie," he remarked, suddenly serious. "You have a daughter coming home for Thanksgiving. I'd give anything to have one, too."

His admission brought a jolt of surprise followed by a discomfited sense of having been told a confidence to which she was not altogether sure she wanted to be privy. Something changed, knowing there was such a chink in his marriage.

"You know, Eric, you can't make a remark like that without leaving one obvious question in a person's mind. I won't ask it, though, because it's none of my business."

"Is it all right if I answer it anyway?" When she refrained from replying he went on. "Nancy never wanted any." He studied the distance as he said it.

After a moment of silence she offered quietly, "I'm sorry."

He moved restlessly, shoveling snow with his feet. "Aww . . . well . . . I probably shouldn't have said anything. It's my problem and I'm sorry if I made you uncomfortable bringing it up."

"No . . . no, you didn't."

"Yes, I did, and I'm sorry."

She lifted her eyes and resisted the urge to touch his sleeve and say, I'm the one who's sorry, I remember how you wanted children. To do so would have been unpardonable, for in spite of the rifts between Eric and his wife, the fact remained he was married. For moments only the snow spoke, ticking to earth all around them. She remembered kissing him, long ago, on a night such as this, on his snowmobile in the ravine below the bluff, tasting him and the snow and winter on his skin. He had stopped the machine and they'd sat in the sudden silence, faces lifted to the dark night sky. Then he'd turned and swung his leg over the seat and said, softly, "Maggie . . ."

"I'd better go," he said now, opening the truck door.

"I'm glad you came."

He glanced toward the house. "I'd like to see it sometime when the furniture is all in."

"Sure," she said.

But they both knew the prudent course would be his never coming back here again.

"Have a nice Thanksgiving," he wished, climbing into the truck.

"Same to you. Say hello to your family."

"I'll do that." But he realized he couldn't pass along her message, for what reason could he give for having been here?

The truck door slammed and Maggie stepped back while the starter growled . . . and growled . . . and growled. From inside the cab she heard a dull thump as Eric gave the vehicle a little encouragement, presumably with a fist to the dash. Then more growling and the sound of the window being rolled down.

"This damned old whore," he said affectionately.

While Maggie laughed, the engine caught and roared. He worked the foot feed, turned on the wipers and shouted above the sound, "So long, Maggie!"

"Bye. Drive carefully!"

A moment later his tire tracks funneled away into the darkness. She stood a long time, studying them, feeling sensitized and restless.

On Thanksgiving Day twenty people gathered around the Severson table, eleven of them Anna's grandchildren. Mike and Barb were there with their five. Ruth, the baby of the family, had come from Duluth with her husband, Dan, and their three. Larry, the second youngest, and his wife, Fran, had come from Milwaukee with three more, one of them still young enough to need a high chair.

When the carving knife was sharpened and the roast turkey sat before Mike at the head of the table, he quieted the group and said, "Let's all hold hands now."

When the ring of contact created an unbroken circuit, Mike began the prayer.

"Dear Lord, we thank you for another year of good health and prosperity. We thank you for this food and for letting us all be around the table again to enjoy it. We're especially grateful to have Ma who has seen to it one more time that none of us suffers from eating store-bought bread. And for having Ruth and Larry's families here this year, too, though we ask you to remind little Trish when she's had enough pumpkin pie and whipped cream, bearing in mind what happened last year after she had her third piece. And of course we thank you for this sturdy bunch of kids who are all going to pitch in after dinner and wash the dishes for their mothers. And one more thing, Lord, from both Barb and I. Sorry it's taken us so long to be properly grateful, but we finally saw the light and we trust you're doing the right thing when you give us one more to oversee. Next year, when we hold hands around this table again and there are twenty-one of us, let us all be as healthy and happy as we are today. Amen."

The youngest children repeated, "Amen."

Nancy shot a glance at Eric.

The others stared at Mike and Barbara.

Nicholas finally found his tongue. "Another one?"

"Yup," replied Mike, picking up the carving knife. "In May. Just in time for your graduation."

As Mike cut into the turkey all eyes swerved to Anna. She unceremoniously helped her nearest grandchild mash a candied yam and remarked, "There's something nice and round and satisfying about an even dozen grandchildren. Barbara, you gonna get those potatoes and gravy started down there or are we gonna sit here staring till the food gets cold?"

One could see the visible relaxing of tension around the table.

The day left Eric feeling quietly despondent. Being with his brothers and sister again brought back lush, picturesque recollections of his boyhood in a family of six—the noise, the commotion, the bandying. He had assumed his whole life long that he would re-create the same scene with his own offspring. Accepting that it would never happen took some acclimating; it took, too, the punch of unfettered happiness out of this year's festivities.

Surrounded by noise and celebration, Eric lapsed often into periods of silence. Sometimes he'd stare at the TV screen without registering the touchdowns being made there. The others would cheer and rouse him from his reverie, tease him about napping. But he hadn't been napping, only brooding. Sometimes he'd gaze out the window at the snow and remember Maggie turning to say over her shoulder, "Thanksgiving should have snow, don't you think?" He pictured her at her parents' house having her Thanksgiving dinner and wondered if she'd settled the discord with her daughter. He recalled the hour spent in her house and realized he had been happier there than he was today, surrounded by people he loved.

He found Nancy studying him across the room and reminded himself of the true meaning behind today's observation. Taking his cue from Mike, he set firmly in his mind the things for which he should be grateful: this family surrounding him, the continuing good health of them all, his livelihood, the boat, the house, a hard-working, beautiful wife.

Arriving home at eight o'clock that night, he made a resolution to stop thinking about Maggie Stearn and to keep away from her house. As Nancy opened the front closet door he caught her and from behind, doubling his arms around her ribs, buried his face in her neck. The collar of her white wool coat smelled like a spicy garden. Her neck was warm and supple as she tipped her head aside and covered his arms with her own.

"I love you," he murmured, meaning it.

"I love you, too."

"And I'm sorry."

"For what?"

"For saying no the last time you wanted to make love. For shutting you out these last couple weeks. It was wrong of me."

"Oh, Eric." She swung around and came hard against him, clasping her arms around his neck. "Please don't let this baby thing come between us."

It already has.

He kissed her and tried to put the realization from his mind. But it remained, and the kiss—for Eric—became bleak. He buried his face against her, feeling bereaved and very frightened. "I'm so damned jealous of Mike and Barb."

"I know," she said. "I saw it on your face today." She held him, petting the back of his head. "Please . . . don't. I've got four days at home. Let's make them happy."

He would try, he vowed. He would try. But he recognized something he carried deep inside him, something new and disturbing and destructive. That something was the first seed of bitterness.

Katy Stearn left Chicago after her one o'clock class the day before Thanksgiving. She drove alone, giving her ample time to fret and build offenses against her mother.

I should be flying back to Seattle with Smitty. I should be meeting the gang down at The Lighthouse and checking out who's getting fat on cafeteria cooking at college and who's fallen in love already and who's still a nerd. I should be showing off my Northwestern sweatshirt and my new haircut and checking out old Lenny— find out if he's dating anybody at UCLA yet, or if I broke his heart for good. I should be driving down familiar streets and waiting for friends to call and sleeping in my old room.

She was newly eighteen and typical and considered herself not selfish, but wronged by her mother's sudden decision to move to Door County.

She had purposely avoided asking the location of Maggie's new house and drove instead directly to her grandparents', arriving shortly before seven.

Vera answered the door. "Katy, hello!"

"Hi, Grandma."

Vera accepted a hug while glancing at the empty porch. "Where's your mother?"

"I haven't been there yet. I decided to stop here first."

Pulling back she scolded, "Good gracious, child, where are your rubbers? You mean to tell me you drove all the way from Chicago without any rubbers in the car? Why, you'd catch pneumonia if you broke down and had to walk."

"I have a brand new car, Grandma."

"That's no excuse. New cars break down, too. Roy, look who's here, and without rubbers!"

"Hi, Grandpa."

"Well, little Katy." He came from the kitchen and gave her a bear hug. "Imagine you being old enough to drive up here clear from Chicago. How's school?"

They visited as they ambled back toward the kitchen. Vera asked if Katy had had supper, and when she said no, opened the refrigerator door. "Well, I have some leftover soup I'll warm up for you. Roy, move your junk aside. You've got it strewn all over the table." She began warming soup while Katy and Roy sat at the table and he asked her about Chicago and school.

When she had first made plans to go away to college, this was the scene she had imagined happening with her mother when she returned home. If she'd gone to her mother's first, it *would* be happening there. But that *strange* house in this *strange* little town! How could her mother have done this to her? How? Her mother accused her, Katy, of being selfish when Katy viewed Maggie's move as a rash act of selfishness.

Vera came with the soup, crackers, cheese and lunch meat and joined them while Katy ate. Afterward she began cleaning up the kitchen and Roy drew his work back to the center of the table.

"What are you making, Grandpa?"

"A whole Victorian town. I make a couple buildings each year. The first year I did the church, and I've done nine since then."

"What are you doing this year?"

"A house. A model of your mother's actually." Watching him piece together two delicate pieces of wood she became filled with a mixture of longings she did not understand. To be with her mother; to be free of her. To see the house; never to see it. To love it; to despise it. "She's bought herself quite a beautiful place, you know."

Vera spoke up from the sink. "I told her she was crazy to buy a place that big. And that *old*, for heaven's sake, but she wouldn't listen to me. What a single woman wants with a house that size is beyond . . ."

Vera went on and on. Katy stared at the replica and tried to understand her complex emotions. Roy spread glue on a miniature window frame and applied it to the house. What would the finished house look like? The upper half, the roof?

". . . hasn't got a stick of furniture in the place, so I don't know *where* you're going to sleep if you *do* go over there," Vera finally ended.

The scent of the glue filled the room. At the sink, Vera shined the faucets. Without glancing up from his work, Roy told his granddaughter, "I wouldn't be surprised if your mother is waiting for you right now to show it to you."

Katy's eyes began stinging. The tears blurred Roy's hands as she watched him spread glue along another piece and hold it in place. She thought of Seattle and the house she knew so well. She thought of a house across town where not a single memory dwelled. She must go to this place she resented, to this mother with whom she'd fought, whom she missed so hard it hurt her chest.

She waited until Vera went upstairs to the bathroom.

In the quiet kitchen Roy continued piecing his model.

"Grandpa?" Katy said quietly.

"Hm?" he replied, giving the impression his only concern was completing another building for his Victorian town.

"I need some directions to find it."

He looked up, smiled like a tired Santa Claus and reached across the table to give her hand a squeeze. "Good girl," he said.

The road was steep and curved. She remembered it vaguely from years ago when they'd occasionally come here for a summer vacation and would drive up the hill to look at the summer homes of the "rich people." The cliff, on the left, and the overhanging trees on the right hemmed in the road itself. No streetlights lit it, only an occasional light from a back porch, and in places even these were held back by walls of thick evergreens. The car lights picked out stone walls, frosted with snow, and the steep gabled roofs of garages that appeared to have more character than many modern homes.

She spotted her mother's car easily and pulled up across from it beside a tall wall of evergreens. Shifting to neutral, she stared at the vehicle with its cap of snow, at the strange garage, the flat white surface of the tennis court and the delapidated arbor seat about which her mother's letters had been filled. She felt strangely remote, confronting these things that already meant something to her mother. Again came the sense of abandonment for she, Katy, was no part of anything around her.

A glance to the right revealed the thick hedge that cut off her view of the house. Reluctantly, Katy switched off the lights, killed the engine and left the car.

She stood for moments at the top of the walk between the pungent shrubs, looking down on the backside of a house where the light on a small rear veranda beamed a welcome. There was a door with a window, and beside it another window, long and skinny, throwing a slash of gold across the snow. She glanced up at the looming roofline, but made out only great bulk with no detail visible in the shadows.

At last she started down the steps.

On the veranda she paused, her hands pushed deep into her pockets, staring at the lace on the window and the unclear images beyond. She felt as if her own needs, like the image seen through the coarse lace, had become obscure. She did not need her mother, yet her absence hurt. She did not need to come here for the holiday, yet going to Seattle without family was unthinkable. She glanced at the Indian corn and the brass plaque, prepared to dislike the place, cataloguing instead its welcoming charm.

She rapped on the door and stood back, waiting. Her heart hammered with both expectation and trepidation as she saw, through the lace, a figure move deep in the room. The door opened and there stood Maggie, smiling, wearing a pair of modish gray acid-washed bib overalls and a shirt styled like pink underwear.

"Katy, you're here."

"Hello, Mother," Katy replied coolly.

"Well, come inside." Embracing Katy, who more or less allowed it, Maggie thought, *Oh, Katy, don't be like Mother. Please don't turn out like her.* Released, Katy stood with her hands in her pockets, behind a barrier as palpable as a steel wall, leaving Maggie to search for enough social graces for two.

"So, how was your ride up?"

"Fine."

"I expected you much earlier."

"I stopped at Grandma and Grandpa's. I had supper with them."

"Oh." Maggie carefully concealed her disappointment. She had prepared spaghetti and meatballs, cheese bread and apple crisp—all Katy's favorites. "Well, I'm sure they loved that. They've really been looking forward to your coming."

Pulling her wool scarf from around her neck, Katy glanced at the kitchen. "So this is the house." A room with warmth and hospitality but so different from the house in which she'd grown up. Where was their old kitchen table? Where had this new one come from? And when had her mother begun dressing like a coed? So many changes. They gave Katy the impression she'd been away for years instead of weeks, that her mother had been perfectly happy without her.

"Yes, this is it. This was the first room I had redone. That's an old table of Grandpa's, the cabinets are new, but the floor is original. Would you like to see the rest of it?"

"I suppose."

"Well, here . . . take your jacket off and we'll walk through."

As they moved through the empty rooms Katy asked, "Where's all our furniture?"

"Stored in the garage. When it arrived I hadn't had the floors refinished yet."

It became apparent, as Katy was led through the house, that her mother had no intention of unearthing the relics of their past, that she would furnish the entire house with strange pieces. Katy's resentment prickled once again, although even she was forced to admit their traditional furniture would look puny and out of place in this house with its ten-foot ceilings and generous rooms. The structure demanded pieces with bulk and character and a long history.

They reached the Belvedere Room, and there at last was the familiarity for which Katy so longed: her own bed and dresser, looking ridiculously dwarfed in the immense space. The bed was covered with her familiar blue daisy spread, looking faded and ill chosen, and Maggie had unearthed several giant stuffed toys to set beside it. On the dresser were a jewelry box Katy had received as a Christmas gift when she was nine and a basket holding the mementos of recent years: beads and perfume bottles and the pom-poms from her roller skates.

She stared at it, feeling a lump form in her throat. How childish everything suddenly looked.

Behind her Maggie spoke quietly. "I wasn't sure what you'd like put out."

The blue daisies grew wavery and the awful weight of change pressed upon Katy. She felt her throat constrict. She wanted to be twelve again, and have Daddy alive, and not have to grow accustomed to changes. Simultaneously she liked being a college freshman, taking her first step in the world and being free of parental constraints. Abruptly she spun and threw herself into Maggie's arms.

"Oh, Mother, it's s . . . so hard gr . . . growing up."

Maggie's heart swelled with love and understanding. "I know, darling, I know. For me, too."

"I'm sorry."

"So am I."

"But I miss the old house and Seattle so m . . . much."

"I know you do." Maggie rubbed Katy's back. "But it, and all the memories associated with it, are part of the past. I had to leave them and make room for something new in my life, otherwise I would have withered away, don't you understand?"

"I do, really I do."

"Leaving there doesn't mean I've forgotten your father, or what he meant to both of us. I loved him, Katy, and we had the best life I could imagine, the kind I'd wish for you and your own husband someday. But I discovered that when he died, I'd died, too, for all practical purposes. I sealed myself away and mourned him and stopped caring about things it's not healthy to stop caring about. Since I've been here, I've felt so . . . so alive again! I have purpose, don't you see? I have the house to work on, and spring to look forward to, and a business to get on its feet."

Katy saw it all, this new side of her mother, a woman of tremendous resilience who could lay aside the straits of widowhood and bloom anew, immersed in fresh interests. A woman of eclectic tastes who could store away a houseful of traditional furniture and, eager-eyed, thrust herself into the gathering of antiques. A businesswoman who greeted new challenges with surprising confidence. A mother who was facing a catharsis as consequential as that which Katy herself was feeling. Accepting this new side of Maggie meant saying good-bye to the old one, but Katy realized she must do so.

She pulled back, still sniffling. "I love the house, Mom. I didn't want to, but I can't help it."

Maggie smiled. "You didn't want to?"

Mopping her eyes, Katy complained, "Well, damn it, I hate antiques! I've *always* hated antiques! And you start writing to me about armoires and brass beds and I start getting curious, and now here I am, picturing them and getting excited!"

Laughing, Maggie drew Katy into her arms again and the two rocked from side to side. "That's called growth, dear—learning to accept new things."

Katy pulled back. "And what is this called . . ." She plucked at Maggie's shirt sleeve. ". . . my forty-year-old mother dressed like a teenybopper. Is this growth, too?"

Maggie buried her hands in her deep overalls pockets, rolled back on her heels and looked down at her clothes. "You like them?"

"No. Yes." Katy threw her hands in the air. "Cripes, I don't know! You don't look like Mom anymore. You look like one of the girls in the dorm! It's scary."

"Just because I'm a mother doesn't mean I have to dress like Harriet Nelson, does it?"

"Who's Harriet Nelson?"

"Ozzie's Harriet, and by the way, I like being forty."

"Oh, Mom . . ." Katy smiled and hooked Maggie's arm with her own, turning her toward the stairs. "I'm happy for you, really I am. I doubt that this will ever feel like home to me, but if you're happy, I guess I should be glad for you."

Later, when they were getting Katy settled in the Belvedere Room, she observed, "Grandma's not too happy about your buying this place, is she?"

"What has Grandma ever been happy about?"

"Not much that I can remember. How did you end up so different from her?"

"With a conscious effort," Maggie replied. "Sometimes I pity her, but other times she absolutely infuriates me. Since I've moved out of her house and into this one I've only gone over there once a week, that's the only way we can get along."

"Grandpa is sweet though."

"Yes, he is, and I regret that I don't see him more. But he stops over here quite often. He loves the house, too."

"What about Grandma?"

"She hasn't seen it yet."

Katy halted in surprise. "What!"

"She hasn't seen it yet."

"Haven't you invited her?"

"Oh, I've invited her, but she always finds some excuse not to come. I said she infuriates me, didn't I?"

"But why? I don't understand."

"Neither do I. We've never gotten along. I've been trying to puzzle it out lately and it's almost as if she doesn't want others to be happy . . . I don't know. No matter what it is that anyone mentions, if it makes them happy, she has to either put it down or scold them for something that's totally unrelated.''

''She scolded me the minute I came in the house, because I didn't have my boots on.''

''That's the kind of thing I mean. Why does she do that? Is she jealous? It sounds ridiculous, but sometimes she acts as if she is, though I don't know of what. In my case, maybe it's my relationship with Dad—he and I have always gotten along fabulously. Maybe about the fact that I *can* be happy, even in spite of your dad's death. There's certainly *some*thing bothering her about my buying this house.''

''So I take it we're eating Thanksgiving dinner at her house?''

''Yes.''

''And you're disappointed?''

Maggie summoned a bright smile. ''Next year we'll eat here. How about that?''

''It's a date. Without any grief from me.''

Maggie put her mother from her mind. ''And when summer comes, if you want to, you can come and work for me cleaning rooms. You'd have the beach right here and I know some young people I can introduce you to. Would you consider doing that?''

Katy smiled. ''I might.''

''Good. Then how about some apple crisp?''

Katy grinned. ''I thought I smelled it when I walked in.''

Maggie linked an arm around Katy's waist. It had been three months of antagonism between them. Having the weight of it lifted was the only thing Maggie had needed to make her Thanksgiving happy. Side by side the two of them ambled toward the kitchen.

Chapter 9

❧

They had withstood Thanksgiving day with Vera. Katy stayed four days and promised to return to spend at least the first half of her winter break with her mother, after which she planned to fly to Seattle and stay with Smitty.

December arrived, bringing more snow and virtually no tourists until after the holidays when the cross-country skiers and snowmobilers would begin invading Door County once more. The Door changed colors—blue shadows on white land; black draping hemlocks and here and there the scarlet berries of the sumac bushes like plumes of fire above the snow. The birds of autumn stayed—the jay and chickadee and kinglets; the nuthatches, hanging upside down and racing around the tree trunks. The lake began to freeze.

Maggie drove uptown one day shortly before noon to pick up her mail.

The streets had ample parking now so she pulled up to the curb halfway between the post office and the general store. She was just stepping up onto the sidewalk when somebody called, "Maggie! Hey, Maggie!"

She looked around but saw no one.

"Up here!"

She raised her head and shaded her eyes against a piercing noon sun. A man stood in the bucket of a boom truck, high overhead, waving.

"Hi, Maggie!"

He was dressed in a parka and held a giant red Christmas bell in one hand. The sun caught in the tinseled greenery which cascaded over the edge of the bucket to a light pole on the opposite side of the street.

"Eric, is that you?"

"Hello! How are you?"

"Fine! What are you doing up there?"

"Putting up Christmas decorations. I volunteer every year."

She smiled, and squinted and felt improperly glad to see him again. "They look good!" She glanced along Main Street where swags of garland already created a canopy effect above the street and red bells decorated the poles clear to the curve at the east end. "My. Such impressive civic pride!" she teased, glancing up again.

"I've got plenty of time on my hands. Besides, I enjoy it. Puts me in the holiday mood."

"Me, too!"

They smiled at each other several seconds before he called, "How was your Thanksgiving?"

"Fine, and yours?"

"Okay. Did your daughter come home?"

"Yes."

From the sidewalk below the boom another man yelled, "Hey, Severson, you gonna hang that thing or should I go take a lunch break while you decide?"

"Oh, sorry. Hey, Dutch, you know Maggie?"

The man peered at Maggie from across the street. "Don't believe I do."

"This is Maggie Stearn. She's the one who bought Harding House. Maggie, Dutch Winkler. He fishes."

"Hi, Dutch!" she called, waving. Dutch returned the wave as a red Ford drove past, veering to avoid the boom truck that was blocking one traffic lane. The driver of the Ford waved to Dutch and touched his horn.

When the truck had passed, Maggie craned to look at Eric again. "Don't you get dizzy up there?"

"Who me? A fisherman who stands on a rocking deck all day long?"

"Oh, of course. Well, it's nice of you to volunteer and make the town festive for the rest of us."

"You get to see all the pretty girls from up here and they don't know you're watching," he teased.

Had he not been shouting so anyone on the street could hear, she'd have guessed he was flirting. She felt her cheeks grow warm and decided she'd dallied long enough.

"Well, nice to see you. I'd better go get my mail and my milk. Bye!"

"Bye!" He watched her from above, following her dark head and her pink jacket.

Pink jacket!

It struck him at that moment how she'd always favored pink. He'd forgotten. Now it came back, how he'd teased her, and given her small pink things. Once a pink teddy bear he'd won at a carnival. Once a pink peony from one of his mother's bushes, which he'd stuck in the vents of her school locker. Another time, pink tassles for her ice skates. But the time he remembered best was that spring they were seniors. The orchards had been in full bloom, and he'd borrowed Mike's car to take her to a drive-in movie. On his way, he'd stopped out in the country and picked pink apple blossoms, whorls of them, and had stuck them behind the visors and in the handles of the wing windows, and behind the clothes hooks and even in the ashtray. When he'd gone to pick her up he'd parked two houses away from hers, afraid her mother would see and think he was crazy; Vera was always gawking out the window when he came to get Maggie. When Maggie saw the blossoms she'd covered her mouth with both hands and gotten all flustered. He remembered hugging her—or she hugging him—in the car on her street before he'd started the engine, and the smell of the blossoms heady around them, and the spring evening pale at the windows, and being in love for the first and most wondrous time in his life. They'd never made it to the movie that night. Instead they'd parked out in Easley's orchard, beneath the trees, and they'd opened the car doors to let their blossoms mingle with those crowding the roof of the car, and there, for the first time, they'd gone all the way.

Standing in a manlift twenty feet above Maggie on a frigid winter day, Eric watched her pink jacket disappear into the post office and remembered.

When she was gone, he returned to work, distracted, keeping one eye on the post office door. Momentarily, she reappeared, shuffling through her mail as she walked toward the general store a half-block away. When she drew abreast of him she waved again—a waggle of two fingers—and he lifted a gloved hand, wordlessly. She disappeared into the store and he finished hanging the plastic bell, then peered down over the edge of the bucket. "Hey, Dutch, you getting hungry?"

Dutch checked his watch. "By golly, it's nearly twelve o'clock. Want to break for lunch?"

"Yeah, I'm ready."

Riding down, to the hum and shudder of the bucket, Eric kept his eyes on the door of the general store.

You're chasing her, Severson.

What do you mean? Everybody eats lunch.

The store was busy. Busy for Fish Creek in December. Everyone in town knew what time the mail came in: between eleven and twelve each day. And with no home delivery within the city limits, noon brought a daily deluge of people who walked uptown to get their mail and pick up whatever they might need at the store. If there was a social time in Fish Creek, mail time was it.

When Maggie entered the general store, most of the customers were up front. At the rear meat counter, nobody waited. She peeked around the high deli case.

"Hey, what's going on back here?" she inquired teasingly.

Roy looked up and broke into a smile. "Well, this is the nicest thing that's happened today. How're you, angel?" He left his chopping block and came to bestow a hug.

"Mmm . . . good." She kissed his cheek. "Thought I'd have you make me a sandwich as long as I'm here."

"What kind?"

"Pastrami. And make it thick, I'm hungry as a bear."

"Wheat?"

"No, rye." He pulled out a rye bun while she investigated the contents of the display case. "What've you got good in here? Oh, the herring barrel's in!" She rolled back the heavy glass door, lifted a chunk of herring on a slotted spoon and popped it into her mouth with her fingers. "Mmm . . . now I *know* Christmas is coming!" she mumbled with her mouth full.

"You want to get me fired, picking in there with your fingers?"

"They're clean," she declared, licking off her fingertips. "I only scratched my armpit once."

He laughed and shook a huge French chef knife at her. "You're taking liberties with my livelihood, young lady."

She pranced over, kissed his forehead, and leaned saucily against the butcher block. "Nobody'd fire you. You're too sweet."

On the other side of the deli case someone remarked dryly, "Well, I *was* going to order some herring."

Maggie swung around at the sound of Eric's voice.

"Hello, Eric," Roy greeted.

"It's hard to keep a Scandinavian's fingers out of the herring barrel, isn't it?"

"I told her she's going to get me fired."

"Whatever you're making there, make two," Eric ordered.

"Pastrami on rye."

"Fine."

Maggie moved back to the meat case, crooked a finger and said in a stage whisper, "Hey, Eric, come here." After a stealthy glance toward the front of the store, she appropriated another chunk of herring and handed it to him over the top of the tall, old-fashioned cooler. "Don't tell anybody."

He ate it with relish, tipping his head back and grinning, then licking his fingers.

"All right, you two, take your sandwiches and get out of my herring!" Roy scolded good-naturedly just as Elsie Childs, the town librarian, came around the corner. "I got business to tend to. What can I do for you today, Elsie?"

"Hi, Elsie," Maggie and Eric greeted in unison, taking their sandwiches and making a quick escape. Maggie grabbed a carton of milk and they paid up front, then left together. Outside, Eric asked, "Where were you planning to eat?"

She glanced at the long wooden bench against the store wall, where in summer tourists sat licking ice cream cones. "How about right here?"

"Mind if I join you?"

"Please do."

They sat on the frigid bench with their backs against the white wooden wall, facing south, warming in the radiant rays of sun pelting their faces. Wearing thick-fingered gloves they unwrapped toppling sandwiches containing an inch-high layer of meat, struggling to open their mouths wide enough to accommodate the first bites.

"Mmm . . ." she praised through her first mouthful.

"Mmm-hmmm!" he seconded.

She swallowed and asked, "Where's Dutch?"

"He went home to eat with his wife."

They continued their meal, conversing between bites. "So did you get your disagreement settled with your daughter?"

"Yes. She loves the house and wants to come and work with me this summer."

"Wonderful."

She reached in the brown paper bag for the milk carton, opened it and took a swig.

"Want some milk?" she offered, handing him the carton.

"Thanks." He tipped his head back and she watched his Adam's apple bob as he drank. He lowered the carton and backhanded his mouth with a gloved hand. "It's good." They smiled at one another and she shimmied aside so he could set the carton between them.

With their legs stretched out, their booted feet crossed, they ate on, leaning back lazily against the wall. Elsie Childs came out of the store and Eric drew back his feet as she passed in front of them.

"Hello again," he said.

"You two look comfortable," she commented.

They replied in unison.

"The sun is warm."

"Yes we are."

"Enjoy yourselves." Elsie continued toward the post office.

They finished their sandwiches while townspeople came and went before them. They drank last gulps of milk and Maggie put the half-empty carton back in the sack.

"Well, I should go home."

"Yeah, Dutch will be back soon. We have about six more swags to hang."

But neither of them moved, only sat with their napes to the wall, soaking sun like a pair of lizards on a warm rock. In the bare locust tree across the street a pair of chickadees sang their two-note song. Occasionally a car would pass, its tires singing *shhhh* in the slushy street. The wood beneath them grew as warm as the sun on their faces.

"Hey, Maggie?" Eric murmured, as if preoccupied with his thoughts. "Can I tell you something?"

"Sure."

He remained silent for so long she looked over to see if he'd fallen asleep. But his squinted eyes were fixed on something across the street, his interlaced, gloved fingers draped across his belly.

"I never did anything like this with Nancy," he said at last, rolling his head to face her. "She would no more sit on an icy bench and eat a sandwich than wear Reeboks without socks. It just isn't in her."

For moments they studied one another, the sun beating so brightly upon their faces it paled their very eyelashes.

"Did you do things like this with your husband?" Eric asked.

"All the time. Spontaneous, silly things."

"I envy you," he said, rolling his face once more to the sun, letting his eyes drift closed. "I think Ma and the old man used to sneak away and find things like this to do, too. I remember when they'd go out on the boat sometimes after dark, and they'd never let us kids come with them."

He opened his eyes and watched the chickadees. "When they'd come home, her hair would be wet and Mike and I used to giggle because we knew she never took a bathing suit. Now I think it's like that for Mike and Barb. Why is it some people find the secret and some people don't?"

She took a moment to reply. "You know what I think?"

"What?" He glanced at her again.

She allowed several beats of silence before giving her opinion. "I think you're allowing one dissatisfaction to magnify others. We all do that some- times. We're upset with someone about one specific thing, and it makes us dwell on all the other insignificant or irksome things the other person does. We blow them up out of proportion. What you have to do when you're unhappy about one thing is to remember the good. Nancy has dozens of attributes that you're letting yourself forget right now. I know she does."

He sighed, slumped forward, elbows to knees, and studied the sidewalk between his boots.

"I suppose you're right," he decided after some thought.

"May I offer a suggestion?"

Still hunkered forward, he glanced back over his shoulder. "By all means."

"Invite her." Maggie's eyes and voice turned earnest as she sat forward, shoulder to shoulder with Eric. "Let her know it's the kind of thing you'd love to do with her. Get out her warmest jacket, bundle her in it and order two sandwiches from Daddy, then take her to your favorite spot and let her know that the joy you get from it is as much from being there with her as it is from the novelty of eating a picnic in the snow."

For several beats of silence, he studied her face, the face he was coming to appreciate far too much. Often at night, between lights-out and sleep, it visited him in the dark. At length he asked, "So, how'd you learn all this?"

"I read a lot. I had a wonderful husband who was willing to try things with me, and I've taught a Family Life unit in home ec, which means taking a lot of psych classes."

"My mother didn't read a lot, or take psych classes."

"No. But I'd be willing to bet she overlooked a lot of minor shortcom- ings in your dad and worked damned hard at her marriage."

He looked away and his voice grew brittle. "Saying you don't want a family is more than a minor shortcoming, Maggie. It's a monumental deficiency."

"Did you talk about it before you and Nancy got married?"

"No."

"Why not?"

"I don't know. I just assumed we'd have kids."

"But if you didn't talk about it, whose fault is it that it's come between you now?"

"I know. I know." He jumped to his feet and went to the edge of the sidewalk where he hung from the curb by his heels, staring at the empty lot across the street. She'd put her finger on the thought that had rankled him countless times.

She studied his back, picked up her sack of milk and rose from the bench to stand behind him.

"I think you need a marriage counselor, Eric."

"I suggested that. She said no."

How sad he looked, even from behind. She had never realized how sad stillness can seem.

"Do you have any friends you could both talk to who might help? Sometimes having a mediator helps."

"That's another thing that's struck me lately. We don't have any friends, not as a couple. How the hell can we make friends when we scarcely have time to ourselves? I have friends, and I can talk to Mike—I already have. But Nancy would never open up to him or to any of the rest of my family. She doesn't know them well enough, probably doesn't even *like* them well enough."

"Then I don't know what else to suggest."

He turned to face her. "I'm some cheery company, huh? Every time we're together I manage to dampen your spirits."

"Don't be silly. My spirits are resilient. But what about yours?"

"I'll be okay. Don't worry about me."

"I probably will, the way I used to worry about my students when they'd come to me with some family problems from home."

They walked toward her car.

"I'll bet you were a damned good teacher, weren't you, Maggie?"

She gave some thought to her reply. "I cared a lot. The kids responded to that."

He found her modesty becoming, but suspected he'd guessed right. She was bright, insightful and unbiased. People like Maggie taught others without even being aware they were doing so.

They reached her car and stepped onto the street together.

"Well, the lunch was fun anyway," he said, trying to sound cheerier.

"Yes, it was."

He opened her car door and she set the milk on the seat.

"And your dad makes a walloping delicious sandwich. Tell him I said so."

"I will."

She got into the Lincoln and he stood with his hands curled over the top of the open door.

She looked up at him and for a moment neither of them could think of a thing to say.

He still had the most beautiful eyes of any man she'd ever met.

She still looked wonderful in pink.

"Here comes Dutch. You'd better get back to work."

"Yeah. Well . . . take care of yourself."

"You, too."

"So long." He slammed the door and stepped back as she put her key into the ignition, then stood in the street until the car began moving, and raised a gloved hand in farewell.

That night, alone in her kitchen, Maggie took out a carton of milk to pour a glass. She popped open the pouring spout and Eric's image came back as he had looked that day—his chin tipped up sharply, blond hair flattened against the store wall, his eyes nearly closed and his Adam's apple marking each swallow as his lips cupped the carton. She ran a fingertip over the edge of the pouring spout.

Resolutely, she forced the image from her mind, filled a tumbler and slammed the carton away in the refrigerator.

He's married.

And unhappy.

That's justifying, Maggie, and you know it!

What kind of wife would refuse to have her husband's babies?

You're making judgments, and you've only heard one side of the story.

But I feel sorry for him.

Fine. Feel sorry for him. But stay on your own side of the street.

The warning stayed with her while she counted down the days until the chamber of commerce breakfast, making her ambivalent about attending. As a woman, she thought it wisest to avoid further meetings with Eric Severson, while as a businesswoman she recognized the importance of not only joining the organization, but of taking an active interest in the group and getting to know the other members. In a town the size of Fish Creek, their referrals could bring in a lot of business. From a social point of view, if this was to be her home, she had to start building friendships someplace. What better place than at such a breakfast? And as for seeing Eric again, who could fault them if they both just happened to be at a breakfast attended by nearly every businessperson in the county?

The Tuesday morning of the breakfast she arose early, bathed and dressed in trousers of hunter-green wool and a winter-white sweater with a jewelry neckline, patch pocket and shoulder pads. She put on a string of pearls, replaced it with a gold chain and discarded the chain in favor of a gold pendant watch which she pinned over her left breast. In her ears she wore tiny gold loops.

When her hair was arranged and her makeup applied she caught herself spritzing perfume for the second time and glanced up sharply at her own consternated eyes in the mirror.

You know what you're doing, don't you, Maggie?

I'm going to a businessmen's breakfast.

You're dressing for Eric Severson.

I am not!

How many times have you put on mascara and eye shadow since you've lived in Fish Creek? And perfume? Twice, yet!

But I'm not dressed in pink, am I?

Oh, big deal.

Irritated, she slammed off the lightswitch and hurried from the bathroom.

She drove to the breakfast realizing that already things around town reminded her of Eric Severson. In the steel-gray morning Main Street appeared to have a brightly lit cathedral ceiling, the one he had hung. The front steps of the community church brought to mind their first surprised perusal of one another the day of Gary Eidelbach's wedding. The white bench before the general store brought back the memory of them sitting there at high noon, sharing lunch.

His pickup was parked on Main Street and Maggie could not deny her reaction to seeing it there—the full-body flush and the speeding pulse so like when she was first falling in love with him years ago. Only a fool would declare it was anything but anticipation.

Stepping into The Cookery, she picked him out immediately, from a good two dozen people in the room, and her heart gave a leap that warned she must consciously avoid seeking him out. He stood across the room, talking with a group of men and women, dressed in gray trousers and a dusty blue sport coat over an open-collared white shirt. His blond hair was neatly combed and he held a paper in his hand as if they'd been discussing something written on it. He glanced up immediately, as if her entry had activated some sensor warning him of her presence. He smiled and came to her directly.

"Maggie, I'm so glad you came."

He shook her hand—a firm, hard handshake, absolutely correct, not even a trifle lingering, yet she felt stunned by his touch.

"You have new glasses," she remarked, smiling. They made him seem the faintest bit a stranger and for a moment she indulged in the fantasy that she was meeting him for the first time.

"Oh, these . . ." A mere strip of gold held up the rimless lenses that set off his clear, blue eyes. "I need them for reading. And you have a new coat," he noted, stepping behind her as she unbuttoned the winter-white Chesterfield.

"No, it's not new."

"I was watching for the pink jacket," he admitted as he stepped behind her and took the coat as it slipped from her shoulders. "You always did look best in pink."

She threw a sharp glance over her shoulder and in the instant their eyes met she discovered that a room full of businesspeople was no protection at all, for his words resurrected memories she'd thought only *she* had fostered, and gave the lie to any pretended indifference she might have assumed. No, he was no stranger. He was the same person who had given her pink trinkets when they were young, who had once said their first baby would be a girl and that they would paint her room pink.

"I thought you had forgotten that."

"I had, until the other day when I stood twenty feet above your head and watched you walk into the post office wearing a pink jacket. It started a lot of old memories rolling back."

"Eric—"

"I'll hang this up and be right back."

He turned, leaving her rattled and trying to hide it, leaving her clinging to the subtle essence of his after-shave and admiring his shoulders and the line of his head as he carried her coat away.

Momentarily he returned, touched her elbow. "Come on, I'll introduce you."

If she had expected any false displays of indifference from him she had done him an injustice, for he was alarmingly straightforward in playing her personal host. Before the meal he kept her circulating, meeting members, then he seated her beside himself at a round table for six. He asked the waitress to bring a pot of tea without inquiring if she preferred it to coffee. He inquired whether her wallpaper had come yet. He said, "I have something for you," and belled out the front of his sport jacket, reaching for the inside pocket.

"Here." He handed her a newspaper clipping. "I thought you might be interested in this. There should be a lot of antiques."

It was an ad for an estate sale. Reading it, her eyes grew bright and avid.

"Eric, this sounds wonderful! Where did you find this?" She flipped it over and back.

"In the *Advocate.*"

"How did I miss it?"

"I don't know, but it says there's a brass bed. Isn't that what you want for the Belvedere Room?"

"And a Belter settee upholstered with French tapestry!" she exclaimed, reading on. ". . . and antique china, and beveled mirrors, and a pair of matched rosewood chairs . . . I'm going for sure!" THURSDAY NINE TO FIVE, 714 JAMES STREET, STURGEON BAY, the ad said. She looked up, beaming, excited. "Oh, thank you, Eric."

"You're welcome. Do you need a truck?"

"I might."

"The old whore is temperamental, but she's yours if you want her."

"Thank you, I just might."

"Excuse me," a male voice interrupted.

Eric looked up. "Oh . . . Mark, hello." He pushed back his chair.

"I take it this is the new owner of Harding House," the man said, "and since I'll be introducing her today, I thought I should meet her first." He was already extending his hand to Maggie. She looked up into a long, slim fortyish face framed by brown, wavy hair. The face might have been attractive but Maggie was distracted by the fact that he immediately brought it too close to hers, and wore a cologne so overpoweringly sweet it caused a tickle in her throat.

"Maggie Stearn, this is Mark Brodie, president of the chamber. Mark . . . Maggie."

"Welcome back to Fish Creek," Mark said, shaking her hand. "I understand you graduated from Gibraltar High."

"Yes, I did."

He held her hand too long, squeezed it too hard, and she guessed within ten seconds of their introduction that he was unattached and scouting the new female in town. He effectively monopolized her for the next five minutes, giving vibes of interest as unmistakable as his geraniumy-smelling cologne. During those five minutes he managed to confirm the fact that he was a divorcé by choice, that he owned a local dinner club called the Edgewater Inn, and that he was more than a little interested in seeing both her and her house sometime in the near future.

When he left to assume his duties as the head of the group, Maggie turned back to the table and took a drink of water to clear the taste of his cologne out of her throat. The others at her table were listening to a woman named Norma tell an anecdote about her nine-year-old son. While they were preoccupied with the story, Eric leaned back in his chair and glanced at Maggie.

"Brodie's a real go-getter," he remarked.

"Hm."

"And unattached."

"Hm."

"Runs a successful business, too."

"Yes, he made sure I knew."

Their eyes met and Eric's remained absolutely expressionless. He sat back with one finger hooked in the handle of his coffee cup while Maggie wondered what to make of his remarks. The waitress arrived and stepped between them to set their plates on the table.

After breakfast Mark Brodie called for quiet and took care of a couple business items before introducing Maggie.

"Ladies and gentlemen, we have a new member with us today. She was born and raised right here in Fish Creek, graduated from Gibraltar High School and is back with us opening our newest bed and breakfast." Mark leaned closer to the microphone. "She's mighty pretty, too, I might add. Everybody, say hello to the new owner of Harding House, Maggie Stearn."

She rose, feeling her face color. How dare Brodie put his mark on her before the entire town! The entire county for that matter! Her introduction signaled the end of the breakfast and she was immediately surrounded by members who reinforced Mark's official welcome, wished her well, and invited her to call on them for any help or advice she might need. In the congenial exchange, Maggie became separated from Eric, and looked up some minutes later to see him with a group of others, donning his coat and gloves near the exit. Someone was talking to her, and someone was speaking to him as he pushed open the plate-glass door and headed outside. Just before the door closed he glanced back at Maggie, but his only farewell was a slight delay in allowing the door to close behind him.

Mark Brodie wasted no time confirming Maggie's first impression of him. He called that evening.

"Mrs. Stearn? Mark Brodie."

"Oh, hello."

"Did you enjoy the breakfast?"

"Yes, everyone was very cordial."

"I wanted to talk to you before you left, but you were surrounded by people. I was wondering if you'd be interested in going on a sleigh ride on Sunday evening. It's for the young people's group from Community Church and they've asked for volunteers to act as chaperones."

Was he asking her for a date or not? How cagey of him to put it in such a way that she couldn't be sure. She decided to hedge.

"A sleigh ride—you mean there's enough snow for a sleigh ride?"

"Barely. If not, Art Swenson will take the runners off his rig and put the rubber tires on. It starts at seven and we'll be out about two hours. What do you say?"

Maggie weighed the possibilities and decided Mark Brodie was not her style, whether he intended the invitation as a date or not.

"I'm really sorry, but I have plans for Sunday night."

"Oh, well, maybe some other time then," he replied brightly, sounding not the least bit nonplussed.

"Maybe."

"Well . . . if there's anything I can do to help you settle in here, just let me know."

"Thank you, Mr. Brodie."

She hung up and stood beside the phone recalling his overbearing smell and his overbearing mien, and thought, *No* thank you, Mr. Brodie.

He called again the next morning, his voice overtly cheerful and loud in her ear.

"Mrs. Stearn, it's Mark Brodie. How are you today?" He sounded like an over-zealous used-car salesman on a TV commercial.

"Fine," she replied automatically.

"Are you busy Monday night?"

Caught off-guard, she answered truthfully, "No."

"There's a theater in Sturgeon Bay. Could I take you to a movie?"

She frantically groped for a reply. "I thought you owned a supper club. How can you get all these nights off?"

"It's closed Sundays and Mondays."

"Oh."

Undaunted by her sidestepping, Brodie repeated, "So, how about the movie?"

"Ah . . . Monday?" No excuse popped into her mind. None!

"I could pick you up at six-thirty."

"Well . . ." She felt embarrassed at her lack of excuses, but her mind remained blank.

"Six-thirty. Say yes."

She released a nervous laugh.

"If you don't, I'll only call again."

"Mr. Brodie, I don't date."

"All right. I'll show up at your door with supper in a brown paper bag some night. That won't be a date."

"Mr. Brod—"

"Mark."

"Mark. I said I don't date."

"So, pay your own admission to the movie."

"You're very persistent, aren't you?"

"Yes, ma'am, I am. Now how about Monday?"

"Thank you, but no," she replied firmly.

"All right. But don't be surprised when you hear from me again."

The man had hubris enough to fill a hayloft, she thought, as she hung up.

The phone rang again on Wednesday afternoon and she answered it with an excuse all prepared. But instead of Mark Brodie, it was Eric who opened the conversation without identifying himself, "Hi, how are you?"

She smiled broadly. "Oh, Eric, it's you."

"Who were you expecting?"

"Mark Brodie. He's called twice already."

"I told you he was a go-getter."

"He's becoming a pest."

"You have to expect that in a town of this size that hasn't got many single women, much less pretty, rich ones."

"Mr. Severson, you're embarrassing me."

He laughed and she felt totally at ease with him. "Can you hold on a minute while I wash my hands?"

"Sure."

She returned in moments, saying, "There, that's better. I was a little pasty."

"You're wallpapering?"

"Yes."

"How does it look?"

"Absolutely great. Wait till you see the Belvedere Room, it . . ." She interrupted the thought, realizing the implications of such familiarities.

"It—?" he encouraged.

It's a dusty shade of pink and you'll never see it. We must both make sure of that. "It's nearly finished, and the paper is going up like a dream."

"Wonderful. So what did you decide about the truck?"

The truck. The truck. She hadn't given it another thought, but she had no other means of transporting furniture.

"If you're sure you don't mind, I'll take it."

"Could you use a little company?"

She'd expected to simply borrow the truck and drive it herself. She stood in the kitchen feeling undermined, wondering how to answer, staring at the handle on the refrigerator door and picturing his face. When she failed to reply, he added, "I thought, if you bought anything big you could probably use some help unloading it."

How awkward. To object on the grounds of impropriety put motives in his mind of which he was perhaps not guilty, yet to accept might give him reason for believing something of that sort had possibilities. She decided to do the honorable thing, no matter how indelicate it sounded.

"Eric, do you think that's wise?"

"My day is free, and if it's all right with you I'll stop by Bead & Ricker and pick up something I ordered for Nancy for Christmas. They called to say it's in."

The mere mention of Nancy acquitted them both. "Oh . . . well, fine then."

"What time should I be there?"

"Early, so I don't miss any of the good stuff."

"Are you a breakfast eater?"

"Yes, but—"

"I'll pick you up at seven and we'll eat on the way. And, Maggie?"

"Yes?"

"You'd better wear boots. The heater in the old whore could be a little more efficient."

"I will."

"See you in the morning."

She hung up and propped her forehead in her hands, her elbows on her knees and sat there hunched over, staring at the kitchen floor. For a full two minutes, just staring, waiting for common sense to take over, thinking stupid things about widowed women making fools of themselves.

She leaped to her feet, cursed under her breath and picked up the phone to call him back and cancel.

She slammed it back down and sat on her stool again.

You know what you're getting into here.

I'm getting into nothing. This is the last time I'll see him. Honest.

She awakened the following morning with the thought singing through her mind: I'll see him today, I'll see him! She rolled to one side, snuggling her jaw deep in the feather pillow, wondering exactly how much contact with a married man constituted a friendly liaison. She lay thinking of him—his hair, eyes, mouth—and rolled to her back with her eyes closed and her arms curled tightly over her stomach.

She dressed in the most unattractive clothes she could find—blue jeans and a grotesque gold sweatshirt that made her a walking ad for Ziebart, then ruined it all by fussing with her makeup and doing the gel routine with her hair.

His truck pulled up precisely at seven and she met him halfway down the sidewalk, bundled in boots and her pink jacket, carrying four folded blankets over her arms.

"Good morning," he said.

"Good morning. I brought some blankets to pad the furniture with, in case I buy any."

"Here, I'll take them."

He took the blankets as they walked side by side to the truck.

"All set to find some buys?"

"I hope so."

Everything so platonic on the outside, while a forbidden glow was kindled by his very presence.

He stowed the blankets in the bed of the pickup and they got under way. The sun had not risen. Inside the cab the dash lights created a dim glow and on the radio Barbra Streisand sang "Have Yourself a Merry Little Christmas."

"Remember the time . . ."

They talked—had there ever been a person with whom she could talk with such ease?—about favorite Christmases of the past and a particular one, in the sixth grade, when they'd both been in a Christmas pageant and had had to sing a carol in Norwegian; about making snow forts as children; about how candles are made; how many varieties of cheeses come out of Wisconsin; how giving away cheese at Christmastime had become a tradition. When they grew tired of talk, they found equal ease in silence. They listened to the music and the weather forecast—cloudy with a sixty-percent chance of snow—and laughed together at a joke made by the deejay. They rode on in companionable silence as a new song began to play. They felt the rumble of occasional ice patches beneath the tires, and watched ruby taillights sparkle on the highway ahead, and observed the coming of dawn—a gray, somber dawn that made the interior of the truck feel insular and cozy.

A red-and-green neon sign appeared on their right, announcing, THE DONUT HOLE. Eric slowed the truck and turned on the blinker.

"You like doughnuts?" he asked.

"At this hour of the morning?" She pretended disgust.

He angled her a grin as he made a right-hand turn and the truck bumped into an unpaved parking lot. "It's the best time, when they're fresh out of the grease." A tire dropped into a pothole and Maggie slapped the seat to keep from tipping over.

She laughed and said, "I hope their food is better than their parking lot."

"Trust me."

Inside, plastic Santas and plastic wreaths decorated fake brick walls; plastic poinsettias in plastic bud vases adorned each plastic-covered booth. Eric directed Maggie to a booth against the right wall, then slid in the opposite side and unsnapped his jacket all in one motion, the way he had unsnapped his letter jacket a hundred times in days gone by.

A buxom waitress with coal-black hair came over and thumped down two thick white saucerless mugs, then splashed them full of coffee. "It's a cold one out there this morning," she said, leaving the thermal pot. "You're gonna need this."

She was gone before the coffee stopped swirling in the mugs.

Maggie smiled at the woman's retreating back, glanced at their drinks and remarked, "I guess we ordered coffee, huh?"

"I guess so." Picking up his mug for a first drink, Eric added, " 'The Hole' isn't classy, but it's got good country cooking." The menus stood between the sugar jar and the napkin dispenser. Eric handed her one and suggested, "Check out the Everything-in-the-World Omelette. It's more than enough for two if you'd like to share."

It took Maggie a full thirty seconds to read the list of ingredients in the omelette, and by the time she finished she was bug-eyed.

"They're serious? They put all *that* in one omelette?"

"Yes, ma'am. And when it comes, it's drooping over the edge of the platter."

"All right, you've sold me. We'll share one."

While they waited they reminisced about Snowdays dances in high school and the time the principal dressed up like Santa Claus and Brookie had taken a dare to hold a piece of mistletoe over his head and kiss him. They refilled their coffee cups and laughed about the fact that no pieces of silverware on their table matched. When their omelette arrived they laughed even more, at its sheer size. Eric cut it and Maggie served—a delectable concoction filled with three kinds of meats, two cheeses, potatoes, onions, mushrooms, green peppers, tomatoes, broccoli and cauliflower. He ate his with two enormous homemade doughnuts, and she with toast, and neither of them heeded the fact that they were again building memories.

Back in the truck, Maggie groaned and held her stomach as the pickup jounced out of its parking spot. "Oh, easy, please!"

"You just need tamping down," he teased, and, doing a speed shift, tromped on the gas and fishtailed across the parking lot, bouncing both of them around like corn in a popper. Maggie's head hit the roof and she shrieked, laughing. He gunned the engine, cranked the wheel in the opposite direction and she flew from the door against his shoulder, and back again before he finally lurched to a stop at the approach to the highway.

"S . . . Severson, you're cr . . . crazy!" She was laughing so hard she could scarcely get the words out.

He was laughing, too. "The old whore's still got some spunk in 'er yet. We'll have to take her out on the ice someday and do doughnuts."

In their younger days all the boys had "done doughnuts" by the dozens: driven their cars out onto the frozen lake and spun in controlled circles, leaving "doughnuts" in the snow. Then, as now, the girls had shrieked and loved every minute of it.

Sitting in Eric's truck, laughing with him while they waited for an oncoming car from the left, Maggie experienced a flash of *déjà vu* so profound it rocked her.

Maggie, Maggie, be careful.

But Eric turned and flashed her a wide, happy smile, and she ignored the voice, teasing, "You have a doughnut fetish, you know?"

"Yeah? So sue me."

In her younger days she would have slid across the seat and tucked herself under his arm, and felt its weight on her girlish breast, and they would have ridden that way, with the contact ripening their want for one another.

Today, they remained apart, linked only by their eyes, knowing what was happening, feeling helpless to stop it. A car rushed by from the left, leaving a gust of sound that faded away. Eric's smile diminished to a grin and he shifted lazily to first, still with his eyes upon Maggie, then turned his attention to the road and entered the highway at a respectable speed.

They rode on for some time, sorting through a welter of feelings, wondering what to do about them. Maggie stared out her window, listening to the hum of the snow tires on the blacktop, watching tan weeds and snowbanks pass in a blur.

"Maggie?"

She turned to find his eyes on her as they rolled down the highway. He returned his attention to the road and said, "It just struck me how seldom I've laughed in the last few years."

There were tens of replies Maggie might have made, but she chose to remain silent, digesting the unspoken along with the spoken. She was getting a clearer and clearer picture of his marriage, his loneliness, the loosening mortar between the bricks of his relationship with Nancy. Already he was comparing, and Maggie was clear-sighted enough to understand the implications.

In Sturgeon Bay he found the address with no trouble and they were waiting when the attendant unlocked the front door of an immense eighteenth-century house overlooking Sawyer Harbor. It had been built by a wealthy shipbuilder nearly a hundred years ago, and many of his original furnishings were still in it. With the death of a recent heir, the property had passed to those remaining who were scattered across America and had decided to sell the estate and divide the moneys.

The antiques were eclectic and well-preserved. Eric watched Maggie as she moved through the rooms, making discoveries, exclaiming, "Look at this!" She'd grab his sleeve and haul him toward a find. "It's bird's-eye maple!" she'd exclaim, or, "It has a burled inlay!" She touched, admired, examined, questioned, sometimes dropped to her knees to look underneath a piece. Through it all she showed an enthusiasm upon which he doted.

Nancy admired fine things, too, but in a wholly different way. She maintained a certain reserve that held her just short of animation over the small excitements of life. At times that reserve bordered on hauteur.

Then Maggie found the bed, a grand old thing made of golden oak, with a serpentine-designed headboard seven-feet high, replete with scrollwork and lush bas-relief carving.

"Oh, look, Eric," she breathed, touching it reverently, staring at its intricacies as if mesmerized. "Oh my . . ." She ran her fingertips over the oak-leaf detailing on the footboard. "This is why I came, isn't it?" She neither expected nor received an answer, did not even draw her eyes from the piece. From the doorway he watched her caress the wood, his thoughts

trailing back years and years, to a night in Easley's orchard when she had
first touched him that way. "This is a wonderful bed. Old, sturdy, solid
oak. Who do you imagine did all this carving? I can never see a piece like
this without wondering about the craftsman who made it. Look, there's
not a mark on it."

"The other pieces match," he pointed out, meandering into the room
with his hands in his pockets.

"Oh, a washstand and a cheval dresser!"

"Is that what you call it? My grandma used to have furniture like this."

He stood beside her, watching her open the doors and drawers of the
other pieces.

"See here? Dovetailed drawers."

"They won't come apart for a while."

She knelt, opened a door and poked her head inside. Her voice trailed
out hollowly, like a note from a woodwind.

"Solid oak." She emerged and looked up at him high above her.
"See?"

He squatted beside her, adulating as expected, enjoying her more with
each passing minute.

"On this piece I would set a pitcher and bowl, and I'd hang huck towels
on the bar. Did I tell you I've been doing huck toweling?"

"No, you didn't," he replied, grinning indulgently, still squatting beside
her with one elbow on a knee. He had no idea what huck toweling was,
but when she smiled about it the dimple in her chin became as pronounced as if carved by the same artist who'd done the bedroom suite.

"I had a devil of a time finding patterns. Oh, won't they look lovely
hanging on that bar?" On her knees, with eyes agleam, she turned to face
him. "I want the whole set. Let's find the man."

"You didn't check the price."

"I don't need to. I'd want it if it were ten thousand dollars."

"And it's not a four-poster or a brass bed."

"It's better than a four-poster or a brass bed." She fixed her eyes on
his. "Sometimes when a thing is right you simply must have it."

He did not look away.

The rose in her cheeks matched that in his. Their hearts experienced
a beat of disquiet. In that unwary moment they let their susceptibilities
show, then he gathered his common sense and said, "All right. I'll get
the man."

As he began to rise she grabbed his arm. "But, Eric?" Her brow fur-
rowed. "Will the old whore hold it all?"

He burst out laughing. The vulgar name was so inappropriate coming
from her.

"What's so funny?" she demanded.

"Just you." He covered her hand on his arm and gave it a squeeze.
"You're a delightful lady, Maggie Stearn."

She bought more than a truckful. They arranged for delivery of the
pieces they could not take and hauled away only the three she most
prized. Maggie supervised the loading with amusing zealousness. "Be careful of that knob! Don't rest the drawer up against the side of the truck.
Are you sure it's tied tightly enough?"

Eric glanced over at her and grinned. "Just because you're a ragman and I'm a stinkpotter doesn't mean I can't tie a decent knot. I've sailed a boat, too, in my time."

From the opposite side of the truck she gave a mock nod, and replied, "I beg your pardon, Mr. Severson."

One final yank on the knot and he said, "Come on, let's go."

They had spent the hours at the estate sale blithely forgetting his marital status, but their next stop would be at Bead & Ricker, and his mission there brought back reality with a sharp sting. By the time they pulled up at the curb before the store a somberness had fallen upon them both. He shifted to neutral and sat for a moment with his hands on the wheel, as if about to say something, then seemed to change his mind.

"I'll be right back," he said, opening the truck door. "It shouldn't take me long."

She watched him move away—the one she could not have—loving his stride, the way his hair brushed his upturned leather collar, the way his clothing fit, the colors he chose to wear. He entered the jewelry store and she sat with her gaze fixed on the window display—scarlet velvet and gems beneath bright window lights, trimmed with holly leaves. He had ordered his wife something custom-made for Christmas. She, Maggie, had no business feeling despondent knowing this, yet she did. What was he buying Nancy? A woman that beautiful was made to wear things that glistened and shone.

Maggie sighed and turned her attention across the street, to the entrance of a hardware store where two old women visited. One of them wore an old-fashioned woolen scarf and the other carried a cloth shopping bag with handles. One pointed up the street and the other turned to look in that direction.

Maggie closed her eyes and dropped her head back. *You shouldn't be here.* She lifted her head and caught sight of Eric's black leather gloves lying beside her. Gloves—shaped like his hands, the fingers curled, the fleece lining undoubtedly flattened from the contours of his palms.

Only a very foolish woman would have the urge to touch them, to slip them on her own hands.

A very foolish woman did. She picked them up and put them on, surrounding her hands with the worn leather that had surrounded his. Her hands felt dwarfed; she closed her fists, savoring the contact, in lieu of that which was forbidden her.

Eric came out of the jewelry store, and she put the gloves back where he'd left them. He climbed into the truck and tossed a silver foil bag on the seat. Maggie's eyes involuntarily followed it and glimpsed inside a small box wrapped in identical foil, trimmed with a red ribbon. She looked away, at a starburst in the side window where a rock had hit it long ago. She waited for the truck to begin rolling. When it didn't, she glanced back at Eric. His bare hands rested on the steering wheel and he stared straight ahead. The expression on his face resembled that of a man who's just heard a doctor say, all we can do now is wait. For a full minute he sat, unmoving. Finally he said, "I got her an emerald ring. She's crazy about emeralds."

He turned his head and their eyes locked.

"I didn't ask," Maggie replied quietly.

"I know you didn't."

In the silence that followed neither of them seemed able to summon the wherewithal to look away.

It was back, as strong as before. Stronger. And they were courting disaster here.

He turned to stare out the windshield again until the silence grew unbearable, then, letting the breath rush out between his teeth, he fell back into the corner of the seat. He propped an elbow on the window ledge and put the pad of his thumb against his lips, his face turned away from her. There he sat, staring at the sidewalk with the unvoiced admission jangling between them.

She didn't know what to say, do, think. As long as neither of them had voiced or displayed their attraction overtly, they'd been safe. But they were safe no longer, though not a definitive word had been spoken, not a touch exchanged.

Finally he sighed, centered himself behind the wheel and put the truck in gear.

"I'd better get you home," he said resignedly.

Chapter 10

❧

They drove back to Fish Creek in constrained silence.

She understood clearly: his displeasure lay with himself, not with her. He was the picture of a man torn. He drove the entire twenty-five miles scarcely moving a muscle, angling a shoulder into his corner of the seat, frowning at the highway. Not until they turned onto the switchback did he finally square his shoulders and settle himself behind the wheel. He parked the truck at the top of her walk, grabbed his gloves and got out without a word. She did likewise and joined him at the rear of the truck, waiting while he dropped the tailgate.

"Would you mind helping me carry it upstairs?" she asked, breaking their lengthy silence.

"It's heavy for a woman."

"I can handle it."

"All right, but if it's too heavy, say so."

She would not have said so had her discs slipped, although she couldn't have said why. A return to business between them, perhaps. Two delivery persons hauling freight, putting it in place with the impersonal demeanor of United Parcel Service employees.

They hauled up the washstand first, then the cheval dresser, marching back downstairs in dual silence—hers careful, his testy. She knew instinctively she would not see him again after today. His decision had been made in the truck in front of Bead & Ricker with an emerald ring between them. They took the bed up last, the headboard and footboard bolted together onto a pair of two-by-eights. When they'd set it down, he said, "If you've got some tools I'll put it together for you."

"That's not necessary. I can do it myself."

He confronted her head-on for the first time since their miserable ride back. "Maggie, the damned headboard weighs sixty pounds by itself!" he snapped. "If it falls over and splits you can kiss your antique value good-bye. Now get me a wrench and a screwdriver."

She got him a wrench and a screwdriver, then stood back and watched him bend on one knee and use the tools to separate the pieces of the bed. He worked at it with singular intensity, his collar turned up, head bent, shoulders hunched within the black leather jacket.

He freed one set of bolts, moved to the other and applied the screwdriver again.

"Here, hold this or it'll fall," he ordered without a glance in her direction.

She held the pieces upright as they came free of their support block. He rose, knees cracking, slipped the screwdriver into his rear pocket and moved about the room, laying the wooden side rails in place on the hardwood floor and coming finally to relieve her of the footboard, carrying it six feet away before kneeling again to hook the pieces together.

She tried not to watch him, to dismiss the attraction of his form as he bent and knelt while performing the peculiarly masculine task.

When the frame was assembled, he stood in the middle of it. "Well . . . that's it. How about the mattresses?" He glanced briefly at her single bed at the edge of the room.

"They're stored in the garage. Daddy can help me with them."

"You're sure?"

"Yes. He won't mind."

"Well then . . ." He drew his gloves from his jacket pockets, making no second offers. "I guess I'd better go."

"Thank you, Eric. I really appreciate the use of the truck and all your help."

"You got a good buy," he stated with finality as they left the room.

"Yes, I did."

They descended the steps side by side, rounded the newel and headed for the rear kitchen in an awkward emotional void. He moved toward the door straightaway, and she opened it politely, saying, "Thanks again."

"Yup," he replied, clipped, impersonal. "See you around."

She closed the door firmly, and thought, well, that's that. The decision has been made. *Have some tea, Maggie. Go up and admire your new furniture. Wipe today from your mind.*

But the house seemed gloomy and she suddenly had little taste for the antiques that had been so exhilarating earlier in the day. She wandered to the kitchen sink, turned on the hot water and clacked a kettle beneath it, switched on the stove burner and put the water on to heat; got down the teapot from the top of the cupboards and desultorily stared into a canister of tea bags, caring little what flavor they were.

Outside, Eric mounted the steps at a jog, vehemently slammed the tailgate shut, strode around to the driver's side, flung himself behind the wheel and heard the seatcover rip. He rolled to one buttock, reached behind himself and muttered, "Shit."

He skewed at the waist to look. Maggie's screwdriver had torn a three-corner rip in the vinyl.

"Shit!"—more exasperatedly, thumping the butts of both hands on the steering wheel. So angry. So trapped by his own emotions.

He sat for a long minute, his forearms on the wheel, gloved thumbs pressed to the corners of his eyes, admitting to himself what he was really angry about.

You're acting like a damned heel, taking it out on her when it isn't her fault! If you're going to walk out of here and never come back you can at least do it gracefully.

He lifted his head. The wind had picked up. It rattled the loose blade of a windshield wiper and spun last week's snow across the road. He scarcely noticed as he stared straight ahead, loath to go back to her door, yet spoiling for one last glimpse of her.

What do you want, Severson?

What does it matter what I want? All that matters is what I have to do.

Abruptly he started the truck engine and left it running: assurance that he'd be back up this hill in sixty seconds or less, heading home where he belonged.

At her door he knocked hard, as hard as his heart seemed to be knocking in his chest. She opened it with a tea bag in her hand and they stood like a pair of cardboard cutouts with their gazes locked.

"This is yours," he said finally, handing her the screwdriver.

"Oh . . ." She took it. "Thank you."

She spoke so quietly he could scarcely hear the words, then stood with her head hanging while he studied her downturned face.

"Maggie, I'm sorry." His voice held a note of tenderness now.

"It's all right. I understand." She wound the tea bag string around the screwdriver, her eyes still downcast.

"No, it's not all right. I treated you as if you've done something wrong, and you haven't. It's me. It's . . ." At his hips his gloved fingers closed, then opened. "I'm going through some troubled times and I have no right to drag you into them. I just wanted you to know I won't bother you again."

She nodded disconsolately and dropped her hands to her sides. "Yes, I think that's best."

"I'm going to . . ." He gestured vaguely toward the truck. "I'm going to go home and do what you said. I'm going to concentrate on the good. What I mean to say is, I want my marriage to work."

"I know you do," she whispered.

He watched her struggle to hide her emotions, but her cheeks took on a flush. The sight of it made his throat and chest feel as they had one time when the *Mary Deare* had gotten caught in a sudden summer gale and he thought she was going down. He spread his gloved fingers wide and pressed them to his thighs to keep from touching her.

"Well, I just wanted you to know that. I didn't feel right, leaving the way I did."

She nodded again and tried to hide the fact that tears were springing to her eyes.

"Well, listen . . ." He took one step back and said huskily, "You . . . you have a nice Christmas, and I hope everything works out with this place and your new business."

She lifted her head and he saw the tears glimmering in the corners of her eyes. "Thanks," she said, forcing a timorous smile. "You have a wonderful Christmas, too."

He backed to the edge of the steps and for a heart-wrenching moment their gazes spoke clearly of the want and need they were feeling. Her brown eyes appeared magnified by the tears that trembled on her lashes. His blue ones showed the depth of restraint he placed upon himself to keep from taking her in his arms. He closed and opened his hands once more.

"Good-bye." His lips moved, but no sound came out, then he turned and walked resolutely from her life.

During the days that followed, he avoided the post office at noon, bought his groceries anywhere but at the Fish Creek General Store and ate his lunches at home. Mornings, however, he continued his trips to the bakery and on his way down the hill often fantasized about walking in and finding her there, picking out a morning sweet, turning at the sound of the bell on the door and smiling when she saw him enter.

But she preferred eggs for breakfast; he knew that now.

The bay froze over completely and he rode his snowmobile out to go ice fishing every day. Often, sitting on a folding stool on the ice, staring down into the hole at the deep water, he thought of Maggie, wondered if she liked fried fish and remembered her stealing a piece of the silvery herring from the wooden barrel in her father's cooler. He thought about taking her a fresh lake trout; after all, he caught more than he could use. But that would only be an excuse to see her, he admitted, and took the trout to his mother and Barb instead.

He made a toboggan for Mike and Barb's kids for Christmas and gave it six coats of marine varnish. When it was done and he showed it to Nancy, she pushed her glasses down her nose, gave it a far shorter perusal than she gave her finished makeup each morning, and said, "Mmm . . . nice, dear," before returning to her bookwork.

He cut down two spruce trees on Mike's property, put one in a stand for Ma and hauled the other one home. When it was standing in the corner of the living room, aromatic and pungent, he stood before it with his hands in his pockets, wishing someone were there to share it with. On the weekend, when Nancy came home, they trimmed the tree together with clear, plain twinkle lights, clear blown-glass balls and clear glass icicles—the same decorations they used every year. The year she had come home with them—purchased in some fancy store at The Plaza in Kansas City—he had withheld his misgivings all the while they decorated the tree. When it was done, he'd studied it in dismay and said, "It's a little colorless, isn't it?"

"Don't be déclassé, darling," Nancy had chided. "It's elegant."

He didn't want an elegant tree. He wanted one like Ma's, hung with big multicolored lights and trimmings he and his brothers and sister had made in elementary school; and some that had been on Ma's tree when she was a little girl; and others that had been given to the family by friends over the years. Instead he had a tree that left him as cold as the teakwood fruit Nancy kept in the middle of the kitchen table. So, often on weekday evenings he went out to Ma's or to Mike's and enjoyed their trees, and ate popcorn and home-smoked fish and pulled taffy and teased the little ones and held them on his lap in their feet pajamas and watched the tree lights tint their faces many colors and listened to them speak with awe about Santa Claus.

Staring at the tree lights, Eric thought of Maggie and wondered what Christmas would have been like if he'd married her instead of Nancy. Would he have children of his own? Would they be together now near their own Christmas tree? He pictured Maggie in the big house with its bay windows and gleaming floors and the kitchen with the old, scarred table, and recalled the day he and Deitz had had coffee with her, and he missed her terribly.

During those same days and nights, she thought of him, too, and her sense of loss lingered, unaccountable though it was, for how could one lose what one had not possessed? She had lost nothing except the daily longing for Phillip which had magically dissipated since her return to Fish Creek. With some shock Maggie realized it was true—the feelings of self-pity and deprivation had mellowed into velvet memories of their happier times together. Yes, the loss of Phillip hurt less and less, but the one she missed now was Eric.

As the holidays approached she spent many bittersweet evenings recalling the recent occasions they'd shared: the first night in the dark, poking through the house with a flashlight; the day he found her painting in the Belvedere Room and the snow had begun outside; the day they'd eaten their sandwiches on the bench on Main Street; their trip to Sturgeon Bay. When had it begun, this insidious building of memories? And was he remembering, too? She had only to recall their last minutes together to feel certain he was.

But Eric Severson was spoken for, and she tried to bear that in mind as she filled her days and prepared for Christmas.

She called her father, and Roy came to help her carry in the mattresses from the garage, and move the twin bed down to the maid's room, and to rejoice with her over the new furniture for the Belvedere Room, and to praise her wallpapering efforts.

She made up the great hand-carved bed for the first time with eyelet sheets and a puffy down comforter, then fell across it to stare at the ceiling and miss a man she had no right to miss.

Mark Brodie called and invited her out to his club for dinner and she declined his invitation once again. He persisted, and she finally said, "All right. I'll go."

He did his best to impress her. A very private booth in a remote corner with discreet and gracious servers, linens, candlelight, crystal, champagne, escargot, Caesar salad mixed tableside, hot popovers, fresh abalone (which he'd had flown in especially for the occasion since it was not on the regular menu), and afterward Bananas Foster, again flamed tableside and served in fluted-stem glasses.

The entire meal, however, seemed flavored by his cologne.

He was attentive to a fault and a brisk conversationalist, but he liked to talk about his own success. He drove a Buick Park Avenue that smelled inside exactly like him—spicy sweet and suffocating. When he took her home she almost leapt from it in relief and gulped the cold night air like a person coming up for the third time.

At her door he took her shoulders and kissed her. French-kissed her. For damn near half a minute while she tested herself, resisting the impulse to shove him away, spit and wipe her lips. He wasn't a masher. He wasn't bad-looking, unkempt, obnoxious or ill-mannered.

But he wasn't Eric.

When the kiss ended he said, "I want to see you again."

"I'm sorry, Mark, but I don't think so."

"Why?" He sounded exasperated.

"I'm not ready for this."

"When will you be? I'll wait."

"Mark, please . . ." She drew away and he released her without further coercion.

"If I may be so gauche, I'm not a fortune hunter, Maggie."

"I never thought you were."

"Then why not have some fun together? You're single. I'm single. This town doesn't have a lot of others like us."

"Mark, I have to go in now. It was a lovely dinner, and you have a lovely restaurant and a great future, I'm sure. But I have to go in now."

"I'm going to break you down, Maggie. I'm not giving up."

"Goodnight, Mark. Thank you for tonight."

She called Brookie the next day and they made a trip to Green Bay to shop for lace curtains and Christmas presents, and to have lunch.

She admitted, "Brookie, I'm lonely. Do you know any single men?"

Brookie said, "What about Mark Brodie?"

Maggie replied, "I let him kiss me last night."

"And?"

"Did you ever eat a mouthful of geraniums?"

Brookie choked on her soup and ended up doubled over the bowl with laughter and tears and split peas nearly doing her in.

Maggie ended up laughing, too.

When Brookie could speak again she asked, "Well, did you go in afterward and make meatballs?"

"No."

"Then maybe you ought to ask him to change cologne."

Maggie thought about it the next time he called and she turned him down. And the next . . . and the next.

Katy called and said she'd be heading home on December 20, right after her morning classes. Maggie put up her tree in the parlor and made fancy cookies and a rum-soaked fruitcake, and wrapped gifts and told herself it didn't matter that she had no man of her own to buy for this year. There were her father and mother and Katy and Brookie. Four people who loved her. She should thank her blessings.

The weather warnings began on Tuesday morning but skeptics, meeting on the street, grinned and reminded one another, "They said the last two blizzards were headed our way, but we barely got enough snow to keep the winterkill off the shrubs."

The snow began at noon, sweeping out of Canada across Green Bay, fine shards that skittered like live things across ice-slicked roads and grew into a biting force mothered by fearsome thirty-mile-an-hour winds. By two o'clock schools closed. By four o'clock businesses followed suit. By seven o'clock maintenance crews had been pulled off the roads.

Eric retired at ten P.M. but was awakened an hour later by the shrill of his bedside telephone.

"Hello?" he mumbled, still half-asleep.

"Eric?"

"Yeah?"

"Bruce Thorson at the sheriff's office in Sturgeon Bay. We've got a critical situation on our hands, travelers stranded on the roads all over the county and we've had to pull the plows off. We could use every able-bodied snowmobiler we can get."

Eric squinted at the clock, sat up and ran a hand through his hair in the dark. "Sure. Where do you want me?"

"We'll be dispatching Fish Creek volunteers through the Gibraltar Fire Station. Bring any emergency equipment you can spare."

"Right. I'll be down there in fifteen minutes."

He hit the floor hurrying. On his way downstairs he buttoned his shirt and zipped his pants. He put water in the microwave for instant coffee, found a large black garbage bag and threw in candles, matches, flashlight, newspapers, a bobcap, Nancy's snowmobile suit and helmet (which she'd worn exactly once), a sack containing two leftover doughnuts, a bag of miniature Butterfinger candy bars and an apple. He pulled on his own silver snowmobile suit, boots, gloves, ski mask and helmet. A quick fill for the thermos, topped off by two glugs of brandy and he stepped outside looking like an astronaut ready for a moonwalk.

In the shelter of the house the storm appeared overestimated. Then he moved off the back steps and sank into a drift to his hips. Halfway to the garage, the maelstrom hit him full in the face and he floundered, falling sideways as he struggled on. He shivered and waded to the garage door where he was forced to shovel with his feet and hands to find the handles. Inside, the building was frigid—always more frigid on concrete than in the insulating snow. The sound of his own felt-lined boots on the icy floor reverberated in his covered ears. He filled the gas tank on his machine, tied a shovel and the bag of emergency supplies on the passenger seat, started the engine, and pulled outside. Already it was a relief to put his back to the wind while closing the overhead door. Shrugging and shivering, he faced the wind once more, boarded his machine and lowered his Plexiglas face shield, realizing it would be a long time before he climbed back into a warm bed.

The winds had escalated to near gale force, driving the snow in sheets that obliterated everything. Even from a block away, the red-and-blue Christmas lights on Main Street were invisible. Not until he was directly below them did Eric make out the eerily illuminated rings of blue and green in the swirling haze overhead. He drove down the middle of a Main Street which had disappeared, using the Christmas lights to guide him. Occasionally, on either side, a blob of white light would pierce the haze— a sign for a shop, or a streetlight.

Halfway to the fire station he heard the roar of an engine off to his left and glanced over his shoulder at a specter looking much like himself, only dressed in black and riding a Polaris. He raised one hand and the other driver saluted back, then the two drove side by side until out of the swirling white maze the red light of the fire station guided them in.

Two other snowmobiles were parked out front. Eric left his machine idling. He threw a leg over the seat, raised his face shield and called, "Hell of a time to be rolled out of bed, 'ey, Dutch?"

"God, you said it!" Dutch's muffled voice came from behind his face shield before he flipped it up. "She's a real piss-cutter, ain't she?" Dutch plowed his way to Eric and the men slogged toward the brick building together.

Inside, Einer Seaquist was parceling out emergency supplies to two other drivers. To one of them, he ordered, "Get over to Doc Braith's as quick as possible. He's got insulin for you to take out to Walt McClusky on County Road A. And you, Brian," he ordered the second driver, "take County Road F down to Highway Fifty-seven. They closed it at the other end, but as close as we can figure there are three cars out there that never reached their destinations. Dutch, Eric, glad you boys could help out. You can take your pick—County Road EE or Highway Forty-two. Damn drivers don't know when to pull into a motel. We think we've got stalled cars still out there. If you find anybody, do the best you can. Take 'em anywhere— motel lobbies, private homes, or bring 'em back here. You need any supplies?"

"Nope, got what I need," Eric replied.

"So do I," Dutch seconded. "I'll take EE."

"I'll take Forty-two," Eric said.

They left the fire hall together, plowing down the steps where the wind had already obliterated the tracks they'd made coming in. Straddling the seat of his machine Eric felt the reassuring vibrations of the engine rise up to meet him and thought of how much faith men put in machinery. Dutch, too, straddled his seat, reached for his faceguard and shouted, "Steer clear of barbed wire, Severson!"

"You, too, Winkler!" Eric returned, pulling his ski mask down and dropping his own faceguard.

They put their machines in gear and drove side by side, westward, along the length of Main Street, beneath the murky Christmas lights, then through the break in the bluff where Highway 42 climbed out of town. Up above, in open country, they followed the telephone poles, and some-times the tops of fence posts, the dip and rise of their headlights piercing only a limited distance ahead. In spots they glimpsed the highway, swept clean by the merciless winds; on other stretches they'd not have known the blacktop was beneath them without the posts and poles to mark it. Once their headlights picked out a mound they thought was a car. Eric spotted it first and pointed. But when they pulled up and started digging, they found it was only the boulder dubbed "the Lord's Rock," upon which the message, *Jesus Saves*, had created a landmark along Highway 42 for as long as Eric could remember.

On their machines again they drove as a pair until reaching the spot where Highway 42 intersected with County Road EE. There, with a salute of farewell, Dutch veered off to the left and disappeared into the storm.

After Dutch's departure, the temperature seemed colder, the wind keener, the snow sharper as it struck Eric's face mask. His lone headlight, beaming first high, then low, like that of a train engine, seemed to be searching for the mate that had been beside it until now. The snowmobile rocked, sometimes bumped, sometimes flew, and he gripped the throttle harder, welcoming the shimmy of motion that climbed his arms and vi-brated beneath his thighs—the only other sign of life in the vast, swirling night.

In time his limbs grew weary of shifting and balancing. The thumb of his left hand began to freeze. His eyes began to hurt and he grew dizzy from squinting into the kaleidoscopic motion before him. Monotony dulled his senses, and he feared he might have passed a stalled car without observing it. A stretch of blacktop swept along his left flank and he swerved toward it, realigning himself with the center of the road. Deep in his mind, beyond conscious thought echoed Dutch's warning, "Steer clear of barbed wire!" Unwary snowmobilers had been decapitated hitting barbed-wire fences. Others who lived through it wore a red necklace of scars for the rest of their lives.

He wondered where Nancy was. She hadn't called tonight. Fargo, if he remembered right. Did the storm system stretch that far?

He hoped Ma was all right, that her fuel oil barrel was full. Damn ornery woman wouldn't let Mike and him put in a new furnace for her. *The oil burner heats as good as ever,* she insisted stubbornly. Well, when this was over, he was going to buy her a furnace whether she liked it or not. She was getting too old to live in one hot room and five cold ones.

He hoped everything was okay with the baby Barb was carrying. This would be one hell of a time to sprout any trouble along those lines with only one hospital in the whole county, and it clear down in Sturgeon Bay.

And Maggie . . . all alone in that big house with the wind howling in off the lake and the old rafters creaking beneath the weight of the snow. Was she sleeping in that carved bed they'd carried in together? Did she still miss her husband on nights like this?

Eric might have missed the car altogether, had the driver not been wise enough to tie a red scarf onto a ski and ram it upright into a snowdrift. The wind snapped the scarf out at a right angle to the earth, it and the pole the only visible clues that a vehicle lay submerged nearby. Speeding toward it, Eric rose anxiously on one knee, his heart hammering. People died of asphyxiation in stalled cars. Or of exposure when they panicked and left them. He could not tell hood from trunk; it was all one smooth mound. No engine ran, no door had sliced off the top of a snowdrift. No snow had been cleared from around the tail pipe.

He had once pulled a drowning child out of the water at Stalling's Beach, and the feelings of that day came back—controlled terror, fear of being too late, adrenaline forming a stricture around his chest. He experienced a sense of phantasm, as if he were moving through molasses when he was actually covering distance like a cyclone, jumping off his machine before it had quite stopped moving, fumbling to free the shovel, wading through waist-deep snow in the beam of his headlight, fighting the elements with demonic passion.

"Hello!" he shouted as he gouged shovelfuls of snow and speared through with one hand to ascertain it was, indeed, a car underneath.

He thought he heard a muffled, "Hello," but it might have been the wind.

"Hold on! I'm coming! Don't open the window!" Impatiently he threw back his faceguard, scooped five times, hit metal, scooped some more.

This time he heard the voice more clearly. Crying. Distressed. Wailing muffled words he couldn't make out.

The shovel struck a window, and he shouted again, "Don't open anything yet!" With a gloved hand he scraped the snow from a small square of glass and peered through at a blurred face and heard a woman's voice crying, "Oh, God, you found me. . . ."

"Okay, just crack the window to let some air in while I free the rest of the door," he ordered.

Seconds later he opened the car door, leaned in and found a panicky young woman with tears streaming down her face, dressed in a jean jacket, with a leg warmer tied around her head, a pair of gray socks covering her hands, and various sweaters and shirts tucked around her lap and legs.

"Are you all right?" He removed his helmet and ski mask so she could see his face.

She was sobbing and could hardly speak, "Oh God . . . I w . . . was . . . so . . . scared."

"Did you have any heat?"

"Until I r . . . ran out of g . . . gas."

"How are your feet and hands? Can you move your fingers?" He bit off his gloves, unzipped a pocket of his snowmobile suit and pulled out a small orange plastic packet. He opened it with his teeth and slipped out a white paper pouch. "Here, this is a chemical hand warmer." He scrubbed it between his knuckles as if it were a dirty sock. "All you have to do is agitate it to get it warm." Kneeling, he reached for her hand, pulled off the sock and a thin wool glove underneath. He put the pouch in her palm, folded her hand between his own much larger ones, and brought them to his lips to blow on her fingers. "Move your fingers for me so I know you can." She wiggled them and he smiled into her teary eyes. "Good. Feel that heat starting?" She nodded miserably and sniffed, childlike, while tears continued streaking down her cheeks.

"Keep it in your glove and keep squishing it around. In a minute your hands will be toasty." After finding a pouch for her other hand he inquired, "Now, how about those feet?"

"I can't f . . . feel them any m . . . more."

"I've got warmers for them, too."

She had pulled two pairs of leg warmers over her thin leather flats. Removing them, he asked, "Where are your boots?"

"I . . . left them at sch . . . school."

"In Wisconsin, in December?"

"You s . . . sound like my g . . . grandma," she replied, making a feeble attempt at rescuing her humor.

He grinned, finding two larger pouches, agitating them to generate the chemical heat. "Well, sometimes grandmas know best." In moments he had the pouches against her feet, and a pair of thick wool socks holding them in place, and had forced her to drink a good shot of brandy-laced coffee, which made her choke and cough.

"Ugh, that stuff's awful!" she exclaimed, wiping her mouth.

"I have a spare snowmobile suit. Can you get it on alone?"

"Yes, I th . . . think so. I'll try."

"Good girl."

He produced a snowmobile suit, boots, mitts, mask and helmet, but she moved so slowly he helped her. "Young lady," he chided while doing so, "next time you go out on the highway in the middle of winter I hope you'll be better prepared."

Her sniffles had stopped and she'd warmed enough to become slightly defensive. "How was I supposed to know it got this bad? I've lived in Seattle my whole life."

"Seattle?" he repeated, pulling the woolen mask onto her head and snapping a helmet strap under her chin. "You drove all the way from Seattle?"

"No, just from Chicago. I go to Northwestern. I'm on my way home for Christmas."

"To where?"

"Fish Creek. My mother runs an inn there."

Seattle, Chicago, Fish Creek? Standing beside the stranded automobile with the wind whipping whirlwinds of snow about them, he peered at what was visible of the girl's face behind the mask and helmet.

"Well, I'll be damned," he murmured.

"What?"

"You wouldn't be Katy Stearn, would you?"

Her surprise was evident even behind the ski mask. Her eyes opened wide and stared at him.

"You know me?"

"I know your mother. By the way, I'm Eric."

"You're Eric? Eric Severson?"

It was his turn to be surprised that Maggie's daughter would know his last name.

"She went to the prom with you!"

He laughed. "Yes, as a matter of fact, she did."

"Wow . . . " Katy said, awed at the coincidence.

He laughed again and said, "Well, Katy, let's get you home."

He slammed her car door and led her toward the snowmobile, blazing a trail for her. Before boarding, he asked, "You ever ridden one of these things before?"

"No."

"Well, it's a little more fun when the windchill isn't fifty-five below zero, but we'll get there as fast and warm as we can. By the way, are you hungry?"

"Famished."

"Apple or candy bar?" he asked, digging in his emergency bag.

"Candy bar," she replied.

He produced the Butterfinger and started the engine while she bit into it, then straddled the seat and ordered, "Get on behind me and put your arms around my waist. All you have to do is lean to the inside when we go into a turn. That way we'll stay on the skis, okay?"

"Okay." She climbed on board and wrapped her arms around his waist.

"And stay awake!"

"I will."

"All set?" he called over his shoulder.

"All set. But Eric?"

"What?"

"Thank you. Thanks a lot. I don't think I've ever been so scared in my life."

He thumped her mittened hands in reply. "Hang on!" he ordered, putting the machine in gear and heading for Maggie's house.

The name thrummed through his head—Maggie. Maggie. Maggie—while he gripped the throttle and felt her daughter's firm hold around his waist. Supposing they'd been a little less lucky in Easley's orchard, the girl behind him could have been theirs.

He pictured Maggie in her kitchen, lifting aside the lace curtain on the door and peering out into the storm. Pacing the room with a sweater wrapped over her shoulders. Checking the window again. Calling Chicago to inquire about Katy's departure time. Making tea which probably went undrunk. Calling the state highway patrol office to learn the plows had been pulled off the road and trying not to panic. Pacing again with nobody to share her burden of worry.

Maggie, honey, she's okay. I'm bringing her to you, so keep the faith.

The wind was an enemy blowing straight at their faces. Eric hunkered behind the windshield, rode the drifts with his leg muscles burning. But he didn't care—he was heading for Maggie's house.

The snow fell heavier, thicker, more disorienting. He followed the telephone poles and gripped the throttle and knew he'd find the way. He was heading for Maggie's house.

He put the cold from his mind, concentrated instead on a warm kitchen with a long scarred table, and a woman with auburn hair waiting behind a white lace curtain, throwing open the door and her arms when she saw them coming. He had vowed to stay away from her, but fate had dictated otherwise, and his heart filled with sweet exhilaration at the thought of seeing her again.

Maggie had expected Katy around five or six o'clock, seven at the latest. By nine she'd called Chicago. By ten she'd called the highway patrol. By eleven she'd called her dad who could do little to ease her concern. By midnight, still alone and pacing, she was near tears.

At one o'clock, she gave in and went to bed in the maid's room—the closest one to the kitchen door. The attempt at sleep proved futile, and she got up after less than an hour, put on a quilted robe, made tea and sat at the table with the window curtain thrown up over the rod. She propped her feet on a chairseat and stared out at the white vortex whirling around the veranda light.

Please let her be all right. I can't lose her, too.

Eventually she dozed, her head propped on a swaying arm. She awakened at 1:20 to a faint faraway sound, a dull rumble approaching on the road above. A snowmobile! She put her face to the window, cupping a hand around her eyes as the sound grew louder. A headlight scanned her arborvitaes, then swept the sky like a searchlight as the machine seemed to climb the opposite side of the drift. Suddenly the light became real. A machine appeared atop the great curl of snow, then took a steep downward plunge and headed straight for the back door.

Maggie was up and running before the engine stopped.

She threw open the door as a rider swung off the rear of the seat and a muffled voice called, "Mother!"

"Katy?" Maggie stepped out into snow up to her knees. The creature plowing toward her was covered in silver and black from head to foot, her face hidden by a plastic shield, but her voice was unmistakable.

"Oh, Mom, I made it!"

"Katy, darling, I've been so worried." Tears of relief stung Maggie's eyes as the two exchanged an awkward hug, hampered by Katy's bulky clothing.

"My car skidded off the road . . . I was so scared . . . but Eric found me."

"Eric?"

Maggie pulled back and looked at the driver who'd cut the engine and was swinging off the seat of the sled. He was clad in silver from head to foot, his face shielded as he moved toward the veranda steps. Reaching them, he pushed up his face shield, revealing three holes in a black ski mask. But there was no mistaking those eyes, those beautiful blue eyes, and the mouth she had recently watched at close range, drinking from a milk carton.

"She's okay, Maggie. You'd better go inside."

She stared at the unearthly creature and felt her heartbeat grow erratic. "Eric . . . you? . . . why? . . . how . . ."

"Go on inside, Maggie, you're freezing."

They all thumped inside and Eric closed the door. He pulled off his helmet and mask while Katy talked nonstop. "The drifting got so bad, and it was blowing so hard you couldn't see anything, and then the car spun out and I hit the ditch, and I sat there with only a tablespoon of gas left and . . ." While Katy prattled she futilely tried to remove her helmet, still wearing thick gloves. Finally she cut herself short and demanded, "Damn it! Will *somebody* help me get this thing off!" Eric stepped forward to help, laying his own helmet on the table before unsnapping hers and pulling it off her head along with her mask.

Katy's face emerged beneath a mop of flattened hair. Her lips were cold-burned, her nose red, her eyes snapping with excitement now that the danger was over. She flung herself into her mother's arms.

"Gol, Mom, I've never been so happy to be home in my whole life!"

"Katy . . ." Maggie's eyes closed as she hugged Katy close. "It's been the longest night of my life." Breast to breast, they rocked, until Katy said, "But, Mom?"

"What?"

"I gotta go to the bathroom so bad, if I don't get out of this moonsuit pretty soon I'm going to embarrass myself."

Maggie laughed and stepped back, reaching to help her daughter with the trio of zippers on the one-piece suit. They seemed to be everywhere, down the front and up both ankles.

"Here, I'll do that," Eric said, nudging Maggie aside. "You've got snow in your slippers. You'd better get it out."

He went down on one knee and helped Katy negotiate the ankle zippers and untie her thick boots, while Maggie went to the kitchen sink and dumped the snow from her slippers. She dried her feet on a hand towel while Eric helped Katy strip off the ungainly snowmobile suit.

"Hurry!" she pleaded, dancing in place. The suit came off and she hit for the bathroom, stocking-footed.

Eric and Maggie watched her go, amused.

Around the corner the door slammed and Katy yelled, "*You* can laugh! He wasn't feeding you coffee and brandy for the last hour!"

At the kitchen sink, Maggie turned to face Eric, the laughter melting away gradually to be replaced by a caring glow as she studied him with her lips tipped up softly.

"You didn't just happen to be out for a ride in this blizzard."

"No. The sheriff's office called for volunteer rescuers."

"How long have you been out?"

"A couple of hours."

She moved toward him while he stood before the door looking twice his size in the silver suit and the felt-lined boots. His hair was disheveled, he needed a shave, and into his ruddy cheeks was pressed the knit weave of his face mask. Even rumpled, he was her ideal.

He watched her cross the room to him, a mother who had kept vigil through the wee hours, barefooted, wearing a quilted rose-colored robe, her face devoid of makeup, her hair hanging lank and curlless, and he thought, *Sweet Jesus, how did this happen? I love her again.*

She stopped very close to him and looked up into his eyes. "Thank you for bringing her home to me, Eric," she said softly and lifting up on tiptoe took him in an embrace.

He folded his arms around her, held her firmly against the sleek silver surface of his snowmobile suit. They closed their eyes and remained where they had wanted to be for weeks, padded full-length, unmoving.

"You're welcome," he whispered and continued holding her while his heart thundered. He spread his hand on her back and let his feeling for her swell while they remained motionless, listening to one another breathe, and to their own pulses hammering in their ears; smelling one another—fresh air, cold cream, a hint of exhaust fumes, and orange pekoe tea.

Don't move . . . not yet!

"I knew you'd be up, worrying," he whispered.

"I was. I didn't know whether to cry or pray or both."

"I pictured you here . . . in the kitchen . . . waiting for Katy while we rode back."

Still the embrace continued, safeguarded by the presence of another person a mere room away.

"She never wears boots."

"She will after this."

"You've given me the only Christmas present I want."

"Maggie . . ."

In the bathroom the toilet flushed and they reluctantly parted, standing close, studying one another's eyes while Eric gripped Maggie's elbows and wondered at the ambiguity of her statement.

The bathroom door opened and Maggie bent to pick up the snowmobile suit, mask and gloves, hiding her flushed cheeks.

"Whew! What time is it anyway?" Katy asked breathily, returning to the kitchen, scratching her head.

"It's going on two," Maggie replied, keeping her face averted.

"And I'd better be going," added Eric.

Maggie turned back to him. "Would you like something hot to drink first? Something to eat?"

"No, I'd better not. But if I could use your phone I'll call the dispatcher at the fire station and see if they still need me."

"Of course. It's right over there."

While Eric made the call, Maggie stacked the extra clothing on the table. Then she got out a variety of holiday-colored tins and began filling a plastic bag with an assortment of cookies. Katy followed her back and forth along the cabinets—an eternally hungry college student, sampling from each tin as it came open. "Mmm . . . I'm starved. All I had was a candy bar Eric gave me."

Maggie gave her a squeeze in passing, and said, "I've got soup and cold ham for slicing, and meatballs and herring and cheese and fruitcake. Take your pick. The refrigerator's loaded."

Eric's phone call ended and he turned back to the women.

"They want me to make one more run."

"Oh, no." Maggie turned to face him, distraught. "It's unfit for humans out there."

"Not when you're dressed right. And I warmed up while I was in here."

"Are you sure you wouldn't like some coffee first? Or soup? Anything?" Anything to keep him a while longer.

"No, I'd better go. A minute can seem like an hour when you're stranded in a cold car." He picked up his ski mask and slipped it on, followed by his helmet. He zipped his suit to the throat, donned his gloves and she watched him disappear beneath the disguise.

When he looked up, she felt a sharp thrill at the sight of his eyes and mouth so prominently highlighted while the rest of his face was hidden. His eyes—as blue as cornflowers—were unqualifiedly beautiful, and his mouth—ah, that mouth that had taught her to kiss, how badly she wanted to kiss it again. He resembled a burglar . . . a burglar who'd crept into her life and stolen her heart.

He picked up the extra clothing and she went to him with her offering—the only bit of herself she could think to send into the storm with him.

"Some cookies. For the road."

He took the bag in his clumsy glove, then glanced into her eyes one last time. "Thank you."

"Keep safe," she said quietly.

"I will."

"Will you . . ." Maggie's consternation showed in her eyes. "Will you call and let us know you got in safely?"

He was astounded that she'd request such a thing with her daughter listening.

"Sure. But, don't worry, Maggie. I've been helping the sheriff's office for years. I take every precaution and I carry emergency supplies." He glanced again at the cookies. "Well, I've got to go."

"Eric, wait!" Katy interjected, her mouth full of cookies as she bounced across the room to commandeer him for a swift, impersonal hug, hampered by his heavy outerwear. "Thanks a lot. I think you might have saved my life."

He smiled at Maggie over Katy's shoulder as he leaned down in accommodation. "Just promise me you'll carry emergency supplies from now on."

"I promise." She backed away, smiled, and stuffed another cookie into her mouth. "Just imagine that—me being rescued by the guy my mom went to prom with. Wait'll I tell the girls about this."

Eric's glance passed between the two women. "Well . . ." He gestured with the cookies. "Thanks, Maggie. And merry Christmas. You too, Katy."

"Merry Christmas to you."

Call, Maggie mouthed for his benefit alone.

He nodded and went out into the storm.

They watched him from the window, their arms around each other, holding the curtain aside while beyond the glass the snow engulfed him.

He secured the emergency clothes in the bag on the rear of the sled, straddled the seat and started the engine. Through the wall they heard it rattle to life, felt the floor vibrate, and saw the exhaust stream away in a white cloud. He lowered his face shield, raised a hand, threw his weight to one side and circled away from the house. With a sudden burst of speed, the machine shot across the yard, climbed the bank and shot through the air like Santa's sleigh, then disappeared, leaving only a whorl of white.

"What a nice man," Katy remarked.

"Yes, he is."

Maggie dropped the curtain into place and changed the subject. "Now how about getting some hot food into you?"

Chapter 11

In the morning, Maggie awakened to a world of white, the wind still keening, the snow plastered to the screens. A sheet of it fell and she lay motionless, studying the shape that remained, its edge like delicate tatted lace. *Did Eric make it home safely? Will he call today as I asked?*

The house was silent, the bed cozy with the wind whistling along the eaves. She remained in her warm nest, reliving the moments in Eric's arms: his cold, stiff snowmobile suit against her face; his warm hand on her back; his breath on her ear and hers on his neck; the smell of him— ah, the smell of a man with winter on his skin.

What had they said during those few precious seconds? Only the permissible things, though their bodies had said more. So what was to happen?

Somewhere in a neighboring state Eric's wife waited to board a plane that would bring her home for Christmas. And sometime over the holiday he would hand her a small silver box and she would pluck from it an emerald ring. Would she slip it on her own finger? Would he? What return gift would she give? And afterward would they make love?

Maggie squeezed her eyes shut and held them so a long time. Until the image of Eric and Nancy faded. Until she had chastised herself for some wishes she had no right to be making. Until her scruples were securely back in place.

She flung aside the covers, donned her quilted floor-length robe and went to the kitchen to mix up waffles.

Around 9:30 Katy came scuffing into the room, wearing one of Maggie's nightgowns and a pair of leg warmers flopping over the ends of her feet like elephant trunks.

"Mmm . . . smells good in here. What are you making?" She hugged Maggie and wandered to the window.

"Waffles. How did you sleep?"

"Like a baby." She pushed back a curtain and squinted. "Jeez, it's so bright!"

"It'll be your first white Christmas."

The sun was out and the snow had stopped falling, but still swirled before a powerful wind. Up above, the bank was as high and curled as a Big Sur breaker.

"What about my things? If it's still blowing this hard, when will I get my suitcases?"

"I don't know. We can call and check with the highway patrol."

"I've never seen so much snow at one time in my life!"

Maggie followed Katy to the window. What a sight. Not a manmade mark anywhere, only unbroken white carved into caricatures of the sea. Mounds and swales below while above the trees were so whipped and bent by the wind that no shred of snow clung to them.

"Looks like we're still isolated. It'll probably be a while before you see your suitcases."

It was precisely thirty-five minutes before Katy saw her suitcases. They had finished their bacon and waffles and sat over tea and coffee in the kitchen, still in their nightwear with their heels propped on empty chairs, when, like a replay of last night, a snowmobile climbed the snowbank beside the road, plunged into the yard and roared to a stop six feet from the back door.

"It's Eric!" Katy rejoiced, bounding from her chair. "He's brought my clothes!"

Maggie leapt up and hit for the bathroom, her heart already pounding. Last night, with concern for Katy uppermost in her mind, she hadn't given her appearance a thought. This morning she frantically dragged a brush through her hair and snapped a rubber band around it. She heard the door open and Katy exclaimed, "Oh, Eric, you angel! You brought my suitcases!" She heard him stamp inside, then the kitchen door closing.

"I figured you'd want them, and the way this wind is blowing, it might be a while before the tow trucks can get out there to haul your car out of the ditch."

Maggie slashed lipstick on her mouth and wet some stray hairs above her ears.

"Oh, thank you *sooo* much," Katy replied ecstatically. "I just said to Mom . . . Mom?" After a pause, Katy's puzzled voice repeated, "Mom? Where are you?" Then, to Eric, "She was just here a second ago."

Maggie tightened the belt on her robe, drew a deep breath, pressed her hands to her flushed cheeks and stepped around the corner into the kitchen.

"Well, good morning!" she greeted brightly.

"Good morning."

He seemed to fill the room, dressed in his silver snowmobile suit, looking half again his size, bringing the smell of winter inside. While they smiled at each other she tried valiantly to appear collected, but it was altogether obvious what she'd been doing in the bathroom: her lipstick was bright, the sides of her hair wet, and she was breathing with a trace of difficulty.

"Goodness, did you get any sleep at all?" she asked to cover her self-consciousness.

"Enough."

"Well, sit down. I'll heat up the coffee. Have you had breakfast?"

"No."

"I don't keep doughnuts around the place, but I have waffles."

"Waffles sound wonderful."

Katy's glance darted between the two of them and Maggie turned toward the stove to hide her pink cheeks.

"Bacon?"

"Bacon would be good, if you're sure it's not too much trouble."

"It's no trouble at all." No trouble at all when you're falling in love with a man. He unzipped his snowmobile suit and pulled up to her table while she busied herself at the cupboard, afraid to turn around, afraid Katy would detect more than she already had.

"How are you this morning?" he asked Katy.

"Fine. I slept like the dead."

Maggie recognized a new wariness in her daughter's voice. Obviously, Katy was trying to puzzle out the underlying vibrations in the room.

By the time she turned around, she had managed to compose herself but bending before Eric to set a cup of coffee on the table, her heart seized up again. His face was still ruddy from the cold, his hair plastered down from the helmet. He flattened one shoulder back against the chair and smiled up at her, leaving Maggie with the startling impression that had Katy not been there, he would have wrapped an arm around her thighs and held her beside him for a moment. She left the coffee and retreated to the stove.

She felt wifely, cooking for him. Unforgivable, but true. Sometimes she had fantasized about it.

He put away two waffles, four strips of bacon and four cups of coffee while she sat across from him in her rose-colored robe and tried not to study his mouth whenever he spoke.

"So you used to date my mother," Katy remarked while he ate.

"Yup."

"Prom, too," Katy prodded.

"Uh-huh. With Brookie and Arnie."

"I've heard about Brookie, but who's Arnie?"

"Arnie and I were friends in high school. We were part of a group that all hung around together."

"The ones who set fire to a barn one time?"

Eric's surprised gaze swerved to Maggie. "You told her about that?"

Maggie gaped at her daughter. "When did I tell you about that?"

"One time when I was little."

Maggie confessed to Eric, "I don't remember telling her about that."

"It was an accident," Eric explained. "Somebody must've dropped a cigarette butt, but don't get the idea that we were intentionally destructive. We weren't. We did a lot of things that were just innocent fun. Did she ever tell you about how we used to get all the girls out in some abandoned house and scare the devil out of them?"

"And get cats drunk," Maggie reminded him.

"Maggie, *I* never got a cat drunk. That was Arnie."

"And who shot the chimney off Old Man Boelz's chicken coop?" she inquired, holding a grin in check.

"Well . . . that was just . . ." He gestured dismissingly with his fork.

"And rolled about fifty cream cans down the hill by the creamery at one o'clock in the morning and woke darn near the entire town of Ephraim."

Eric laughed and choked on his coffee. When he had stopped coughing, he said, "Now, damn it, Maggie, nobody's supposed to know about that."

They had forgotten Katy was there, and by the time they remembered, she'd glanced back and forth between them a dozen times, listening to their good humored interchange with growing interest. When he'd finished eating, he bundled up again and stood on the rug smiling at Maggie.

"You're a good cook. Thank you for the breakfast."

"You're welcome. Thank you for bringing Katy's things."

He gripped the doorknob and said, "Have a nice Christmas."

"You, too."

Finally he remembered to add, "You, too, Katy."

"Thanks."

When he was gone, Katy came at Maggie headfirst. "*Motherrrr!* What's going *on* between you two!"

"Nothing," Maggie declared, turning away, carrying Eric's plate to the sink.

"Nothing? When you rush into the bathroom and comb your hair and put lipstick on? Come on."

Maggie felt the beginning of a telltale blush and kept her back turned. "We've become friends again, and he's helped me get my zoning permit for the inn, that's all."

"So what was all that about the doughnuts?"

Maggie shrugged and rinsed off a plate. "He likes doughnuts. I've known that for years."

Suddenly Katy was beside Maggie, taking her by an arm and studying her face minutely.

"Mother, you've got a *thing* for him, haven't you?"

"He's married, Katy." Maggie resumed rinsing the dishes.

"I know he's married. Oh God, Mom, you wouldn't fall for a married man, would you? It's so tacky. I mean, you're a widow and you know how . . . well . . . you know what I mean."

Maggie looked up sharply, her mouth pinched. "And you know what they say about widows, is that what you were about to say?"

"Well, they do."

Maggie felt a spark of temper. "What *do* they say, Katy?"

"Jeez, Mom, you don't have to get so mad."

"Well, I think I have a right! How dare you accuse me—"

"I didn't accuse you."

"It sounded that way to me."

Katy, too, grew suddenly irate. "I have a right to my feelings, too, and after all, Dad's only been dead a little over a year."

Maggie rolled her eyes and grumbled as if to a third party, "Oh, I don't believe this."

"Mother, I *saw* how you looked at that man, and you were blushing!"

Drying her hands on a towel, Maggie faced her daughter angrily. "You know, for a young woman who plans to work in the field of psychology you've got a lot to learn about human relations and the manipulation of feelings. I loved your dad, don't you *ever* accuse me of not loving him!

But he's dead and I'm alive, and if I should *choose* to fall in love with another man, or even to have an *affair* with one, I certainly wouldn't feel obliged to ask for your approval first! Now I'm going upstairs to take a bath and get dressed, and while I do I'd appreciate it if you'd clean up the kitchen. And while you're doing so, you might give some thought to whether or not you owe me an apology!"

Maggie marched out of the room leaving Katy, gaping, behind her.

Her outburst put a strain on the rest of the holiday. Katy offered no apology, and thereafter the two women moved about the house with stiff formality. When Maggie went outside later in the day to shovel the sidewalk, Katy made no offer to help. When Katy rode off in a tow truck to retrieve her car, she didn't say good-bye. At suppertime they spoke only when necessary, and afterward Katy put her nose in a book and kept it there until bedtime. The following day she announced that she had changed her airline reservations and would be returning to Chicago the day after Christmas and from there flying to Seattle.

By the time Christmas Eve arrived, Maggie felt the stress culminating in an ache that spread from her shoulders up her neck. Compounding it was the fact that Vera had grudgingly agreed to come to the house for the first time.

She and Roy arrived at 5:00 P.M. on Christmas Eve, and Vera entered complaining, bearing a molded jello on a covered cake dish.

"I hope this isn't ruined. I used my tallest mold, and I told your father to take it easy around the corners, but when we were starting up the hill the cover slid to one side and it probably ruined the whipped cream. I hope you have room in your refrigerator." She sailed straight to it, opened the door and reared back. "Judas priest, what a mess! How in the world do you find anything in here? Roy, come here and hold this while I try to make room."

Roy followed her orders.

Vexed by Vera's autocratic attitude, Roy's blind submissiveness, and the whole wrong mood of the holiday, Maggie stepped forward and ordered, "Katy, take the jello from Grandma and put it out on the porch. Daddy, you can put the gifts in the parlor. There's a fire in there, and Katy can bring you a glass of wine while I show Mother the house."

The tour started off badly from the beginning. Vera had wanted them to gather at *her* house for Christmas Eve, and since they hadn't she made it abundantly clear she was here under duress. She glanced around the kitchen and remarked caustically, "Good lord, what do you want to look at that beat-up old table of your dad's for? That thing should have been burned years ago."

And in the new bathroom: "Why would you ever put in one of those old clawfoot tubs? You'll be sorry when you have to get on your hands and knees to clean under it."

And in the Belvedere Room, after boldly asking what the furniture had cost, she declared, "You paid too much for it."

In the parlor, only recently furnished, she made a few positive comments, but they were embarrassingly paltry. By the time Maggie left her mother with the others, she felt like there was TNT running through her veins. Vera found her minutes later, in the kitchen, slicing ham with enough vengeance to sever the breadboard. Vera came close, her wine glass in hand.

"Margaret, I hate to bring up unpleasantness on Christmas Eve, but I *am* your mother, and if I don't talk to you about it, who will?"

Maggie glanced up, bristling, thinking, *You love to bring up unpleasantness any time, Mother.*

"Talk about what?"

"Whatever's going on between you and Eric Severson. People are talking about it, Margaret."

"Nothing's going on between me and Eric Severson."

"You aren't living in a big city anymore, and you're a widow now. You have to be careful about your reputation."

Maggie began slicing again. Rabidly. This was the second time she'd been warned about widows' reputations by people who were supposed to love her.

"I *said* nothing is going on between us."

"You call flirting on Main Street nothing? Eating lunch together on a park bench, where the whole town can see you, nothing? Margaret, I'd have thought you'd use better sense than that."

Maggie became so angry she didn't trust herself to speak. "You're forgetting, dear," Vera went on, "that you were at my house the night he picked you up to go to that county board meeting. I saw how you dressed and how you acted when he came to the door. I tried to warn you then, but . . ."

"But you waited until Christmas Eve, didn't you, Mother?" Maggie stopped slicing to glare at her mother.

"You have no reason to be cross with me. I'm merely trying to warn you that people are talking."

The knife started whacking again. "Well, let them talk!"

"They say his truck has been spotted in front of your house, and that the two of you were seen early in the morning having breakfast in Sturgeon Bay. And now Katy tells me he came here during the blizzard on his snowmobile!"

Maggie threw down the knife and flung her hands up in exasperation. "Oh, for Christ sake! He offered me the use of his truck to get the furniture!"

"I don't care for that kind of language, Margaret!"

"And he rescued Katy. You know that!"

Vera sniffed and raised one eyebrow. "Frankly, I'd rather not hear the details. Just remember, you're not a teenager anymore, and people have long memories. They haven't forgotten that the two of you used to date in high school."

"So what!"

Vera pressed closer. "He has a wife, Margaret."

"I know that."

"One who's gone all week long."

"I know that, too."

After a moment's hesitation, Vera straightened and said, "Why, you don't care, do you?"

"Not about shabby gossip, I don't." Maggie started slapping ham slices onto a plate. "He's a friend, nothing more. And if people are going to make something of it they must not have enough in their lives to keep them busy." She shot a flat-eyed challenge at Vera: *that means you, Mother!*

Vera's shoulders slumped. "Oh, Margaret, I'm so disappointed in you."

Standing before her mother, holding the platter of Christmas ham, Maggie felt a grave disappointment of her own. The fight suddenly left her and tears sprang into her eyes. "Yes, I know, Mother," she replied resignedly, "I don't seem to be able to do anything to please you. I never have."

Only when she'd finally drawn tears did Vera step forward and place a hand on Maggie's shoulder.

"Margaret, you know I'm only concerned about your happiness."

When had Vera ever been concerned about anyone's happiness? What drove the woman? She actually seemed unable to tolerate the happiness of others. But why? Because she was so unhappy herself? Because over the years she'd forced her own husband's emotional and physical withdrawal to the point where they lived nearly separate lives—hers in the house, his in the garage? Or was it, as Maggie had often suspected, jealousy? Was her own mother jealous of Maggie's very happy marriage to Phillip? Of her career? Her life-style? The change she'd made in that life-style? Of the money she'd received after Phillip's death, and the independence that money had brought? Of this house? Was Vera so small that she rued her daughter having anything better than herself? Or was it nothing more complicated than her ceaseless compulsion to give orders and be obeyed?

Whatever the reason, the exchange in the kitchen cast a pall over the remainder of the night. They ate their meal wishing it were already over. They opened their gifts with animosities roiling beneath the veneer of politeness. They bid good-bye with Vera and Maggie lifting their faces but never quite touching one another.

On Christmas Day, Maggie accepted an invitation to go to Brookie's, but Katy said she'd rather not be with a bunch of strangers and went to Roy and Vera's alone.

The following day, when Katy's car was loaded, Maggie walked her up the hill.

"Katy, I'm sorry it was such a crummy Christmas."

"Yeah . . . well . . ."

"And I'm sorry we fought."

"I am, too, but Mother, *please* don't see him again."

"I told you, I'm not seeing him."

"But I heard what Grandma said on Christmas Eve. And I have eyes. I can see how good-looking he is, and how you looked at each other, and how the two of you enjoy being together. It could happen, Mother, and you know it."

"It won't."

During the dreary, anticlimactic days following Christmas, Maggie kept that promise firmly in mind. She turned her attention once more toward the house and the business, throwing herself into preparations for spring. She hung more wallpaper, attended two auctions, ordered an iron bed from Spiegel's, shopped by mail for bedspreads and rugs. The state health inspector came and inspected her bathrooms, dishwasher, food storage and laundry facilities. The fire inspector came and inspected the furnace, fireplaces, smoke alarms and fire exits. Her official bed-and-breakfast license arrived and she had it framed, then hung it in the parlor above the secretary where her guests would register. She received spring catalogues from suppliers and placed orders for blankets, sheets and towels from the

American Hotel Supply; made a trip to Sturgeon Bay and set up a charge account with Warner Wholesale who would supply her with soap, toilet paper, disposable drinking glasses and cleaning supplies. She scoured books for muffin and quick-bread recipes, tried some and ate them alone or with Brookie, who stopped by often when she came to town. Or with Roy, who had made it a practice to have lunch with her at least twice a week.

While her mind and hands were occupied, she found it easy to exorcise thoughts of Eric Severson. Often, however, when she paused between tasks for a cup of tea she'd find herself standing motionless, staring out a window, seeing his face in the snow. At night, in those vulnerable minutes before sleep, he would appear again, and she would recall the surge of elation she'd felt upon seeing him at her door, the giddy sensation of stepping into his arms and feeling his hand spread wide upon her back.

Then, remembering Katy's warning, she would curl up like a shrimp and force the images from her mind.

Mark Brodie invited her out to his restaurant for New Year's Eve, but she went to a party at Brookie's instead and met a dozen new people, played canasta, ate tacos, drank margaritas and stayed overnight and most of the next day.

During the second week of January, Mark invited her to an art gallery in Green Bay. Again she declined and also passed up the January chamber of commerce breakfast, daunted by the thought of encountering either Mark or Eric there.

Then one night in the third week of January, she was sitting at the kitchen table in her red Pepsi sweats designing a business brochure when someone knocked on her door.

She switched on the outside light, lifted the curtains aside and came face to face with Eric Severson.

She dropped the curtain and opened the door. No beaming smiles this time, no boundless joy. Only a reserved woman looking up into a man's troubled face, waiting with her hand on the doorknob.

They took fifteen wordless, weighted seconds to look into each other's eyes before he said "Hi." Resignedly, as if his being here was the outcome of a lost battle with himself.

"Hi," she said, making no move to grant him entry.

Somberly, he studied her, in oversized red-and-white sweats and stocking feet, with her hair pulled into a scraggly tail off one side of her head, with ragtail sprigs spraying away from it like fireworks. He had stayed away purposely, giving himself time to sort through his feelings, giving her the same. Guilt, desire, dread and hope. He supposed she'd run the same gamut and he had expected her cool behavior, the forced detachment so like his own.

"May I come in?"

"No," she replied, still barring the way.

"Why?" he asked very quietly.

She wanted to let her shoulders droop, to huddle into a ball, to cry. Instead, she answered levelly, "Because you're married."

His chin dropped to his chest and his eyes closed. He stood motionless for an eternity while she waited for him to leave, to release her from this yoke of guilt she'd been wearing since her daughter's and mother's accusations. To take himself beyond temptation, beyond memory, if possible.

She waited. And waited.

Finally he pulled in a deep breath and raised his head. His eyes were troubled, his mouth downturned. His pose was so familiar—feet planted firmly, hands in the pockets of his bomber jacket, the collar turned up. "I need to talk to you, please. In the kitchen—you sit on your side of the table and I'll sit on mine. Please, Maggie."

She glanced at his truck, parked at the top of the hill in the break between the snowbanks, his name and telephone number listed on the door as clearly as a newspaper headline.

"Do you realize I could tell you precisely how many days and hours it's been since you were here last? You aren't making it any easier on me."

"Four weeks, two days and ten hours. And who said it would be easy?"

She shuddered involuntarily, as if he had physically touched her, pulled in a shaky breath and rubbed her arms. "I find it difficult to deal with the fact that we're talking about this . . . this—" She flipped up her palms then caught her arms again. "—I don't even know what to call it—as if it's foregone. What are we doing, Eric?"

"I think we both know what we're doing, and we both know what it's called, and I don't know about you, but it scares the goddamned hell out of me, Maggie."

She was quaking inside, and freezing outside: the temperature was three degrees, and they couldn't stand in the open door forever. Stepping back, she surrendered to the awesome gravity he exerted over her. "Come in."

Once given permission, he hesitated. "Are you sure, Maggie?"

"Yes, come in," she repeated. "I guess we both need to talk."

He followed her inside, closed the door, unzipped his jacket, hung it on the back of a chair and sat down, still wearing the look of weary resignation with which he'd arrived. She began making coffee without asking if he wanted any—she knew he did—and a new pot of tea for herself.

"What were you doing?" he asked, glancing over the rulers, vellum and cut-and-paste books strewn over the table.

"Laying out an ad for the chamber of commerce booklet."

He turned her work to face him, studying the neat lettering and bordering, the pen-and-ink sketch of Harding House as it looked from the lake. He felt empty and lost and very unsure of himself. "You didn't come to the last breakfast." He forgot the paper in his hands and followed her with his eyes as she moved along the cabinets, running water, scooping coffee.

"No."

"Does that mean you were avoiding me?"

"Yes."

So he was right. She'd been through the same hell as he.

She turned on the burner beneath the coffeepot and returned to the table to push aside her papers, steering well clear of him. She put muffins on a plate, found butter and a knife and brought them to him; got down a cup and saucer and refilled her sugar bowl and brought these, too, to the table. The coffee began to perk, and she turned the burner down. Finishing her busywork, she turned to find him still watching her, looking tormented.

Finally she resumed her seat, linked her fingers on the tabletop and met his gaze steadily.

"So, how was your Christmas?" she asked.

"Horseshit. How was yours?"

"Horseshit, too."

"You want to tell me about yours first?"

"All right." She took a deep breath, fit her thumbnails together and gave it to him straight. "My mother and my daughter both accused me of having an affair with you, and after a couple of pretty awful fights, they both left here very upset with me. I haven't seen either of them since."

"Oh, Maggie, I'm sorry." On the tabletop he took her hands.

"Don't be." She withdrew them. "Believe it or not, the battles between us were less about you than about my growing away from them, becoming independent. Neither one of them likes it. As a matter of fact, I'm slowly coming to realize that my mother doesn't like much of anything about me, particularly my being happy. She's a very shallow person, and I'm learning to overcome my guilt for realizing this. And as for Katy—well, she's not over her father's death yet, and she's going through a selfish stage. She'll outgrow it in time. So tell me about your Christmas. How did Nancy like her ring?"

"She loved it."

"Then what went wrong?"

"Everything. Nothing. Christ, I don't know." He clasped his nape with one hand and tipped his head back to its limits, closing his eyes, sucking in a deep breath and blowing it out slowly. Abruptly he snapped from the pose, leaning his forearms on the table and settled his eyes on hers. "It's just that everything's collapsing in my mind, the whole marriage, the relationship, the future. It's all meaningless. I look at Barb and Mike and I think, that's how it's supposed to be. Only it isn't, and I realize it's never going to be."

In silence he studied Maggie, the lines of worry still dragging at the corners of his eyes and lips. On the stove the coffee perked and the aroma filled the room but neither of them noticed. They sat on opposite sides of the table, their gazes locked, realizing their relationship was taking an irreversible turn and frightened by how it would shake their lives and those of others.

"I just don't have any feelings for her anymore," he admitted quietly.

So this is how it happens, Maggie thought, this is how a marriage breaks up and an affair begins. Discomfited, she rose and turned off the burners, poured water in her teapot and filled his coffee cup. When she was seated again, he stared into his cup a long time before raising his eyes.

"I have to ask you something," he said.

"Ask."

"What was that at the door the night I brought Katy home?"

She felt a warmth in her chest at the memory that it was she who'd broken the taboo. "A mistake," she replied, "and I'm sorry. I . . . I had no right."

With his eyes steady on hers, he remarked, "Isn't it funny, it felt like you did."

"I was tired, and I'd been so worried about Katy, and then you brought her home to me all safe and sound, and I was grateful."

"Grateful? That's all?"

As their gazes clung she felt the underpinnings of her resolve crumbling.

"What do you want me to say?"

"I want you to say what you started to say when I walked in here a few minutes ago, that what we're talking about here is that we're falling in love."

The shock went through her like an electrical current, leaving her shaken and staring at him with her chest tight and her heart knocking.

"Love?"

"We've been through it together once before. We should be pretty good at recognizing it by now."

"I thought we were talking about . . . about having an affair."

"An affair? Is that what you want?"

"I don't *want* anything. I mean, I . . ." She suddenly covered her face with both hands, pressing her elbows to the tabletop. "Oh God, this is the most bizarre conversation."

"You're scared, Maggie, is that it?"

She slid her hands down far enough to look at him, her nose and mouth still covered. Scared? She was terrified. She bobbed her head yes.

"I told you, I am, too."

She clutched her teacup—anything to hang on to. "It's so . . . so civilized! Sitting here discussing it as if no one else were involved. But others are, and I feel so guilty even though we've done nothing wrong."

"You want something to feel guilty about? I've got a few things in mind."

"Eric, be serious," she scolded because she was bursting with desire for him and this was the damndest face-to-face confrontation to which she'd ever been subjected.

"You think this isn't serious?" He held out one trembling hand. "Look at me shake." He gripped his thighs. "It took me damned near five weeks to come back here, and I didn't know what I was coming to do. You should have seen me at home an hour ago, getting showered and shaved and picking out a shirt as if I were going courting, but I can't do that, can I? And the other alternative makes me slightly less than honorable, so here I sit, talking about it—my God, look at me, Maggie, so I know what you're thinking."

She lifted a face that was brilliant scarlet and encountered his blue, blue eyes, as troubled as before. She said what she knew she must say. "I'm thinking that the proper thing for me to do right now would be to ask you to leave."

"If you'd ask me, I would. You know that, don't you?"

She studied him for one pained moment, then whispered, "But I can't, and you know that, too, don't you?"

Their forearms rested on the table, fingertips inches apart. He dropped his eyes to her hand, then took it loosely in his own—her right hand, bearing a gold wedding band. He ran his thumb over it and her knuckles, then raised his gaze again.

"I want you to know this is not something I do all the time. That hug five weeks ago is the closest thing to unfaithful I've ever been to Nancy."

Maggie was human; she'd wondered. And because she had, she dropped her eyes guiltily to their joined hands.

"Let me say this once, then never again." He spoke solemnly. "I'm sorry, Maggie. For whatever pain this brings you, I'm sorry."

He leaned forward and kissed her palm, a long, lingering kiss that kept him doubled over as if awaiting benediction. She remembered him at seventeen, often expressing himself in dear, touching ways such as this, and she pitied the woman who knew him so little she'd somehow failed to tap this wealth of emotion. With her free hand she touched the back of his head, the hair that had darkened to a tarnished gold since the last time she had caressed it.

"Eric," she said softly.

He lifted his head and their eyes met. "Come over here . . . please," she whispered.

He left his chair and circled the end of the table, still holding her hand. She rose as he reached her, and looked up into his face, realizing he was right: they'd begun falling in love months ago.

She rested her hands on his chest and lifted her face as his descended, then his soft, open lips touched hers. Ah, that kiss, that long-awaited kiss, fragile as a new bloom, exquisite in its intentional reserve. They brought to it the charmed recollection of first times, of their timorous explorations of one another in years long past, and of a night in Easley's orchard. They let the bloom open slowly, let the stirring build, and the breathlessness mount until their lips opened wider, their tongues joined.

In time he lifted his head and their eyes met; they read it in one another's gazes—this is not going to be a simple affair; hearts are involved here.

Their eyelids began closing before their mouths met a second time. In one motion he gathered her close and her arms circled his neck. The kiss became wide, lush, and flavored with remembrance, a taking of one another on any terms. Their tongues met and welcomed a new fervor as they clung hard, his hands stroking her back, hers, his shoulders. When at last they drew apart their breathing was labored, their mouths wet.

"Ah, Maggie, I've thought about this."

"So have I."

"That night I brought Katy home . . . I wanted to kiss you then."

"I lay in bed that night and worried about you out in the storm . . . riding away from me . . . and I was sorry I hadn't kissed you. I thought, what if you died without knowing how I felt."

He kissed her throat, her jaw. "Oh, Maggie, you didn't have to worry."

"A woman worries when she feels this way."

He kissed her mouth—warm, mobile mouth waiting eagerly for his return. The fervor built, took them on a swell of feelings that set their hands in motion and made them avid for more. They tasted and tested, their lips moist and supple and impatient. He bit her lower lip, licked it and spoke into her open mouth. "You taste exactly the way I remember."

"How do I taste?" she murmured.

He drew back and smiled into her eyes. "Like Easley's orchard when the apples bloom."

She smiled, too. "You remembered."

"Of course I remembered."

Struck suddenly by a sluice of happiness, she fit herself tightly against him, wherever and however she would fit—her face to his neck, her arms around his trunk, her breasts flattened, giving herself license to love being body to body with him at last. "We were so young, Eric."

"And it hurt so much to leave you." His hands roamed down her spine and came up beneath her sweatshirt, scanning her warm back.

"I thought we'd eventually get married."

"So did I."

"And when we didn't, the years passed and I thought I'd forgotten all about you. Then I saw you again and it was like a kick in the gut. I just wasn't prepared for it."

"Neither was I."

She simply had to see his face. Had to. She pulled back, looking up, still flush against his hips. "It's pretty stunning, isn't it?"

"Yeah . . . pretty stunning." It was then he touched her breasts, as their eyes communicated all they felt, as she leaned back at the waist and felt him hard against her. Beneath the oversized sweatshirt he unclasped her bra, ran his hands around her ribs and took her in hand. Both breasts at once . . . warm and erect. Gently . . . lovingly . . . stroking her . . . all the while watching her face.

Her lips dropped open and her eyes closed.

It was spring again, and they were young and raring, and he had come to pick her up with apple blossoms bedecking his car, and the same wondrous urges they had felt then, they felt now. She swayed pliantly as he stroked her, and smiled with her eyes still closed. From her throat came a sound of delight, neither word nor moan, a mingling of the two.

He dropped to one knee and she lifted her shirt, watching from above as his warm, wet mouth opened upon her, renewing memories. His head swayed, his tongue stroked, then his teeth closed lightly upon her. She gasped and her stomach muscles contracted.

He put his face against her bare midriff and made a hot spot with his tongue.

"Mmm . . . you taste good."

"Mmm . . . I feel good. It's been so long and I've missed this."

He moved to her other breast, washed it as he had the first, then rubbed it with his hair. She cradled his head, drifting in sensation. In time he lifted his face and said in a gravelly voice, "Maggie, M'girl, I think we're framed in your lace curtains, and they don't hide much."

Cupping his jaws she urged him to his feet. "Then come with me to the bed we bought together. I've wanted you in it since the night you set it up for me."

His knees cracked as he rose and tucked her securely against his side. With their arms around each other they snapped off the kitchen light and climbed the stairs, their lazy steps giving lie to the anticipation coursing through them.

In the Belvedere Room she switched on a bedside lamp. The shadow from its silk-fringed shade swayed against the wall as she turned and found him close behind her. He reached for her hips, set them lightly against his own and asked, "You nervous?"

"Dying."

"Me, too."

With a smile he released her and began freeing the buttons of his pastel-blue shirt, tugging its tails out of his jeans. When she reached for the hem of her sweatshirt he caught her hand.

"Wait a minute." He grinned charmingly. "Could I do that? I don't think I ever did before, except in the dark, fumbling around."

"You did it on the *Mary Deare* the day after prom, and it wasn't dark and you weren't fumbling."

"Did I?"

"Yes, and you were very good at it, actually."

He smiled crookedly and reached out, murmuring, "Let me refresh my memory."

He slid the baggy shirt over her head taking the bra with it, and flung them aside, looking down at her in the lamplight.

"You're beautiful, Maggie." He brushed his knuckles along the sides of her breasts and over their uptilted nipples.

"No, I'm not."

"Yes you are. I thought so then, and I think so now."

"You haven't changed, do you know that? You always had a way of saying and doing sweet, tender things, like downstairs when you kissed my hand, and now when you touched me as if . . ."

"As if . . . ?" His gossamer caresses sent goose bumps up the backs of her legs.

"As if I were Dresden."

"Dresden is cold," he murmured, enfolding her breasts in his wide hands. "You're warm. Take my shirt off, Maggie, please."

What a heady pleasure it was, divesting him of the blue shirt, then the white one underneath, tugging it over his head, further disheveling his hair. When he was naked to the waist, she held his clothes like a nest in her hands, lowered her face to them, breathing in his scent, calling back another memory.

He touched her head, stirred unbelievably by her simple gesture.

She lifted her face and told him, "You smell the same. A person doesn't forget smells."

His belt came next. She had removed the belt of another man countless times during their years of marriage, but had forgotten the impact of doing so illicitly. Reaching for Eric's waist, she felt heat pounding everywhere in her body. She freed his buckle and the heavy metal snap at his waist, watching his eyes as she laid her hand flat upon him and caressed him for the first time through faded blue denim. Soft old denim over hard, warm man. Her first stroke closed his eyes. Her second brought him leaning forward, hard against her, reaching behind her, running his palms deep inside her red sweat pants.

"You have a mole," he whispered, running one warm palm to her belly. "Right . . . here."

She smiled. "How could you remember?"

"I always wanted to kiss it but I was too chicken."

She unzipped his jeans and murmured against his lips, "Kiss it now."

They finished undressing each other in a rush. That first moment of nakedness might have been strained but he put self-consciousness to rout by catching her hands, spreading them wide and boldly assessing her length.

"Wow," he praised softly, meeting her eyes, grinning appreciatively.

"Yeah . . . wow," she returned, admiring him in kind.

He dropped their hands. His expression turned grave. "I'm not going to stretch the truth and say that I always loved you, but I did then, and I do now, and I think it's important to say so before we do this."

"Oh, Eric . . ." she replied wistfully. "I love you, too. I tried very hard not to, but I couldn't help myself."

He caught her beneath the knees and arms, and laid her across the bed, touched her in the places he'd touched years ago—breasts, hips and inside where she was liquid and warm. She touched him, too, stroked and studied him in the amber lamplight and made him tremble and feel strong one minute and weak the next. He kissed her in all the places he'd been too shy to kiss in their younger days, along her ribs and her limbs, stained golden by the lamplight while she lay lissome beneath his touch.

She tasted him in return, reveling in his textures and responses, each passing moment trying their patience.

When the limits of desire had been tested, he braced above her and asked, "Do we have to be careful not to get you pregnant?"

"No."

"Are you sure, Maggie?"

"I'm forty years old, and luckily for both of us, I'm beyond that particular worry."

Their reunion was slow and supple, a mating of spirits as well as bodies. He took his time easing into her, all below billowing with feelings while the moment became prolonged pleasure. When they were wholly bound at last, they poised, motionless, making of the moment a prayer.

After so many years, lovers again.

How delicious their fit. How incredible their heat.

Momentarily he pressed back, found her eyes wide and gleaming. She girded his hips with her hands and set him in motion, silken and strong within her. He found her hands and clasped them against the bedding while she watched his face.

"You're smiling," he said huskily.

"So are you."

"What are you thinking?"

"That your shoulders are wider."

"So are your hips."

"I've had a baby."

"I wish it were mine."

In time she drew his head down and their smiles faded, drawn away by the wondrous gravity of sensuality. They shared some lust and some fine driven moments before he wrapped her close and took her with him, rolling to their sides. Squeezing his eyes shut he held himself deep within her. "It's so good," he said.

"Because we were first for each other."

"It feels like coming full circle, like this is where I should have been all the time."

"Have you wondered what it would have been like if we'd gotten married the way we planned?"

"Constantly. Have you?"

"Yes," she admitted.

He turned her beneath him and the rhythm resumed. She watched his hair tap his forehead, and his arms tremble as they bore his weight. She rose to meet him, thrust for thrust, and murmured pleasured sounds that he echoed.

He climaxed first, and she watched it happen upon his face, watched his eyes close, his throat arch, and his muscles tense; watched beads of sweat appear upon his brow in the moment before the wondrous distress shook and shattered him.

When his body had calmed he opened his eyes, still leaning above her. "Maggie, I'm sorry," he whispered, as if there were some preset order.

"Don't be sorry," she whispered, touching his damp brow, his temple. "You were beautiful to watch."

"Was I?"

"Absolutely. And besides," she added guilelessly, "I'm next."

And she was.

Next.

And next.

And next again.

Chapter 12

❧

At 1:20 A.M. Maggie and Eric sat in the clawfoot tub, in nipple-high bubbles, drinking root beer and trying to yodel. He took a swig, backhanded his mouth, and said, "Here, I got one!" Raising his face like a baying hound, he broke into song.

"Mockingbird singing, yodel-o-yodel-o-do-hoo . . ."

While he howled, Maggie rocked like an Irishman in a pub and thrust her mug in the air. He howled so loud she expected the mirror to shatter, and ended with a long, mournful note that stretched his lips toward the ceiling.

"There, how was that?"

She set her mug on the floor and applauded. "Remarkable! Now I've got one. Just a minute." She retrieved her mug, took a swig and wiped her mouth. After clearing her throat she tried a chorus of the "Cattle Call."

Woo-woo-woo-oo-oo-oo! Woo-woo-woo-up! A-woo-oooo . . .

When the chorus ended, he yelled, "Bravo! Bravo!" and applauded while she bowed over her updrawn knees and spread her arms wide, dropping suds on the floor.

"Let's see . . ." He squinted at the ceiling, took a drink and hummed thoughtfully above his mug. "Mmm . . . mmmmmmmm . . . yuh! I got it! An old Cowboy Copas tune."

"Cowboy who?"

"Cowboy Copas. You mean you never heard of Cowboy Copas?"

"Nobody ever heard of Cowboy Copas."

"Shows how much *you* know. When I was little we used to put on shows on the back porch. Larry was Tex Ritter. Ruth was Dale Evans and I wanted to be Roy Rogers, but Mike said *he* was Roy Rogers, I had to be Cowboy Copas. So I stood there and bawled. Had my little six-shooters strapped on, and my red felt cowboy hat with the string pulled up tight under my chin with a little wooden ball, and my Red Rider cowboy boots, bawlin' fit to kill 'cause I had to be Cowboy Copas. So don't tell me nobody ever heard of Cowboy Copas.''

She was laughing long before he cut loose with his pitiful rendition of "Shy Little Ann from Cheyenne."

When he finished, she suggested, "How about if we do one together?"

"Okay. You know 'Ghost Riders in the Sky' by Vaughn Monroe?"

"Vaughn Monroe?"

"You don't remember him either?"

"Can't say I do."

"Then how about 'Tumbling Tumbleweeds' by The Sons of the Pioneers."

"That I know."

"I'll lead off."

He drew a deep breath and began.

See them tumbling down . . .

They sang three verses, humming the parts where they'd forgotten the words, managing some dubious harmony and ending with a pair of notes rendered like a pack of yowling coyotes.

Drifting along with the tumbling tum-bull-weeeeeeeeeeeeeeeeeds!

When the last note died, they collapsed into gales of laughter.

"I think we missed our calling."

"I think we cracked your new plaster."

They fell back weakly and Maggie caught a faucet between the shoulder blades.

"Ow-woooo!" she howled, coyote-fashion again. "That huuuuuuurts!"

He grinned. "C'm'ere. I got a place that won't hurt."

"No spouts and knobs?" she inquired, setting her mug on the floor.

"Well, maybe a couple," he replied, settling her between his silky thighs. "But you're gonna like 'em, Miss Maggie, I can promise you that."

"Mmmm . . ." she purred, resting her forearms on his chest. "You're right. I do."

They kissed, growing aroused beneath the bubbles, his hands gliding over her naked rump.

After some time she opened her eyes and inquired lazily, "Hey, cowboy?"

"Ma'm?" he drawled, arranging his mouth in a triangular grin.

"You wouldn't want to kiss my mole again, would you?"

"Well now," he replied in his best sagebrush accent. "A gentleman ought not refuse a lady when she asks so sweet-like. I think we can take care of that little matter with no problem atall."

They took care of that little matter and a couple of others, and by the time they had done so it was after three o'clock in the morning. They lay on the rumpled bed in the Belvedere Room with their tired limbs twined. His stomach rumbled and he inquired, "What've you got to eat, Miss Maggie? I'm damn near stove in."

Hooking her heel on the far side of his leg, she asked, "What do you want? Fruit? A sandwich? An omelette?"

He turned up his nose. "Too sensible."

"What then?"

"Doughnuts," he declared, slapping his belly. "Big, fat, warm, yummy doughnuts."

"Well, you've come to the right place. Let's go." She grabbed his hand and hauled him off the bed.

"You're kidding!" he exclaimed. "You really have doughnuts?"

"No, I don't, but we can make them."

"You'd start making doughnuts at 3:15 in the morning?"

"Why not? I've been collecting quick bread recipes till they're sticking out the drawers. I'm sure in some of those books we'll find doughnuts. Come on. I'll let you choose."

He chose orange drop doughnuts, and they built them together, she wearing her rose quilted duster, exclusively, he wearing blue jeans, also exclusively. It took them longer than warranted: she put him to work squeezing an orange and he tried to do so against some unorthodox places that brought about a good-natured scuffle, ending with the two of them rolling and giggling on the floor. While he was grating a rind, he scraped off the end of a knuckle, and its doctoring included enough kisses to delay the making of doughnuts for a good ten minutes. When the batter was finally mixed, it had to be tasted, resulting in an arousing round of finger sucking from which Maggie surfaced with the lazy warning, "If you don't let me go my grease is going to catch fire." His reply rocked them both with laughter that dwindled eventually and left them leaning against cupboards like a pair of surfboards stored in a corner. He planted his feet, locked his hands over her spine and studied her face with a growing sense of wonder. The laughter fell away.

"My God, but I love you," he said. "I'm halfway through my life and it took me till now to find out how it really ought to be. I do . . . I love you, Maggie, more than I planned on."

"I love you, too." She felt full with it, reborn. "During the past couple of months I've imagined this night finally happening, but I never imagined this part of it. This is special, the laughter, the sheer happiness. Do you suppose if we'd gotten married when we were fresh out of school we'd still be this way?"

"I don't know. It feels like it."

"Mmm . . . yes it does." She smiled up at him. "Isn't it nice? We not only love each other, we like each other as well."

"I think we've found the secret," he replied.

He studied her face, tipped up at an acute angle, her delicate chin with its distinctive dimple, her adoring brown eyes and softly smiling mouth. Upon it he placed a lingering, unurgent kiss.

When it ended she murmured, "Let's finish our doughnuts so I can curl up next to you and turn over while I sleep and feel you there behind me."

At 4:05 they fell into bed exhausted, with orange doughnuts on their breath. Eric curled behind Maggie, his face in her hair, his knees cupped behind hers, one hand on her breast.

He sighed.

She sighed.

"You wore me out."

"I think it's the other way around."

"Fun though."

"Mm-hmm."

"Love you."

"Love you, too. Don't leave without waking me."

"I won't."

And like two who'd been together for years, they slept in utter peace.

He awakened to the feel of their moist skins joined and his hand lying lax on her belly, lifting and falling with each breath she took. He lay still, filling his senses: her rhythmic breath on the pillow; rumpled eyelet sheet covering their shoulders; her naked rump sealed to his thighs. The smell of her hair and something flowery somewhere nearby; sun and snow indirectly lighting the room; dusty-rose paper covering the walls; the noiseless motion of white lace curtains in the forced air from the furnace. Warmth. Contentment.

I don't want to leave here. I want to stay with this woman, laugh and love with her and share the thousands of mundane tasks that bind lives. Carry the things that are too heavy for her, reach the things that are too high, shovel her walk, shave in her bathroom and use the same hairbrush. Stand in a doorway in the morning and watch her dress, and in the same doorway in the evening and watch her undress. Call home to say, I'm on my way. Share unshaven Sundays and rainy Mondays and the last glass of milk in the carton.

I want her with me when I put the boat in the water for the first time, to understand spring as a season of the heart as much as of the calendar. And in summer when I pass by on the water, to watch her turn with a trowel in her hand and wave from the yard at the sound of my horn. And in autumn to understand my sadness when I lay up the Mary Deare *for the winter. I want for us some fine things—an occasional Dom Perignon, two weeks in Acapulco, chateaubriand by candlelight; and some less than fine—graying hair and lost keys and spring colds.*

No, I don't want to leave this woman.

He knew the precise moment she awakened by the change in rhythm of her breathing, and the slight tensing of muscles that fell just short of a stretch. He spread his hand on her stomach and touched her back with his nose. She reached behind and slipped her hand between his legs. Stroked him—once, twice—tight, deft, certain, and his flesh sprang alive in her hand. She smiled—he knew it as certainly as if he could see her face—and curled forward, tucking him inside her, then reaching around with an arm and drawing him flush against her. He gripped her hips and said good-morning-I-love-you in an age-old, wordless way.

When they had shuddered and stilled, and the moisture lay drying upon their skins, she turned, their bodies still precariously linked, and hooked her legs over his thighs.

The smile he had earlier divined, he saw and met with one of his own. He crooked an elbow beneath his ear and fit the fingers of his free hand between hers. They lay studying one another's eyes while morning brightened the sills of the room. His thumb drew lazy circles around hers. The furnace clicked off and the curtains stopped fluttering. She reached to smooth a tuft of hair on his head, then linked her hand with his as before and resumed the lazy stirring of thumbs. No word was spoken, no promises lent, but during that silence they both said the most meaningful things of all.

. . .

A half hour later they sat at the table, holding hands, wishing useless wishes. He emptied his coffee cup and rose reluctantly, drawing his jacket from the back of the chair. He slipped it on slowly, delaying the inevitable, his head hanging as he reached for the bottom snap. She came to him and brushed his hands aside, usurping the task. One snap. Another. Another. Each drawing them closer and closer to parting. When all but the top snap were closed, she raised his collar and held it against his jaws with both hands, drew his face down and tenderly kissed his mouth.

"I would not have traded last night for Aladdin's lamp," she told him softly.

Closing his eyes, he wrapped both arms around her.

"It was better than when we were kids."

"Much better." She smiled. "Thank you."

They drifted into the somber silence of pre-parting.

"I don't know what's going to happen," Eric told her. "What I feel is strong, though. It'll need some kind of resolution."

"Yes, I suppose it will."

"I don't think I'll live too easily with guilt."

She spread her hands on the supple leather covering his shoulder blades and felt the need to make of this parting not a mere good-bye but a valediction.

"Let's not feel we must make promises to one another. Instead, let's believe this was predestined, like our first time in Easley's orchard. A lovely, unexpected gift."

He drew back, studied her serene brown eyes and thought, you're not going to ask, are you, Maggie? Not when you'll see me again, or if I'll call, or any of the questions I have no answers for.

"Maggie M'girl . . ." he said lovingly. "It's going to be very hard for me to walk out that door."

"Isn't that the way it should be when two people become lovers?"

"Yes." He smiled and brushed her jaw with his knuckles. "That's the way it should be."

They said good-bye with their eyes, with the lingering touch of his fingertips on her throat, and hers on his jacket front, then he bent, kissed her lightly, and whispered, "I'll call you."

She moved through the day vacillating between gladness and gloom. Sometimes she felt as if she radiated a halo of well-being, something shining and discernible. If a deliveryman were to come to the door, surely he would raise his eyebrows in surprise and ask, "What's that?" and she would reply, "Why, that's happiness."

Other times she would be struck by a wave of melancholy. It would stop her in the middle of a task and leave her with her eyes fixed on some inanimate object on the opposite side of the room. *What have you done? What's going to happen? Where will this lead?* To certain heartbreak, she was convinced, not for two people, but for three.

Do you want him to come back?

Yes.

No.

Yes, God help me, yes.

. . .

He moved through the day experiencing intermittent flashes of grievous-ness and guilt that would stop him cold and draw the corners of his mouth down. He'd expected it, but nothing this heavy. If he were to drive out to Mike's, his brother would frown and ask, "What's the matter?" and Eric would undoubtedly confess his wrongdoing. He had broken his mar-riage vows, had wronged a wife who, in spite of her shortcomings, de-served better, and a mistress who, given the grief she'd recently suffered, also deserved better.

Are you going back there?

No.

Yes.

No.

By noon he missed her so badly he called simply to hear her voice.

"Hello," she answered, and his heart thrust harder in his chest.

"Hello."

For moments neither of them spoke, only pictured each other and ached.

"What are you doing?" he asked at last.

"Brookie is here. She's helping me hang a wallpaper border strip in the dining room."

"Oh." Disappointment seemed to crush him. "Well, I'd better let you go then."

"Yes."

"I just wanted to tell you that I don't think I'd better come over to-night."

"Oh . . . well . . ." Her pause told him little of what she felt. "That's okay. I understand."

"It isn't fair to you, Maggie."

"Yes, I understand," she said quietly. "Well, just call whenever you can."

"Maggie, I'm sorry."

"Good-bye, then."

She hung up before he could explain further.

For the remainder of the afternoon he walked around hurting. Listless. Staring. Torn. It was Wednesday. Nancy would be home on Friday around four; the two days stretched before him like a bleak, featureless desert, though her arrival would bring him face to face with what kind of man he was.

He went upstairs and lay down on the bed with his hands stacked under his head, his insides quivering. He thought about going out to Mike's. Or Ma's. Talk to somebody. Yeah, he'd go out to Ma's. Fill her fuel oil barrel.

He rose and took a shower, shaved and put after-shave on his face. And his chest. And on his genitals.

The eyes in the mirror accosted him.

What're you doing, Severson?

I'm getting ready to go out to Ma's.

With after-shave on your pecker?

Goddamn you!

Come on, man, who're you kidding?

He slammed the bottle down and muttered a curse, but when his eyes lifted, the same alter ego regarded him from the mirror.

Go there one more time and you'll go there a hundred, then you'll have a full-blown affair on your hands. Is that what you want?

I want to be happy.

You think you'll be happy married to one woman and consorting with another?

No.

Then go to Ma's.

He went to Ma's and stalked in without knocking. She turned from the kitchen sink, wearing maroon double-knit slacks and a yellow sweatshirt sporting a green pickerel leaping after a lure.

"Well, look who's here," she said.

"Hi, Ma."

"You musta smelled my Swiss steak clear in town."

"I just stopped for a minute."

"Yeah, sure, and a snake's got toenails. I'll peel another couple of potatoes."

He filled her fuel oil burner. And ate a chunk of Swiss steak and a mound of mashed potatoes and some detestable green beans (these as penance). Then he sat on her lumpy sofa and watched one game show and an hour and a half of championship wrestling (an even greater penance) and one detective show, which brought him safely to ten o'clock.

Only then did he stretch and rise and wake Ma, who sat slumped in her favorite rocker with the pickerel folded in half across her flaccid breasts.

"Hey, Ma, wake up and go to bed."

"Whuh? . . ." she muttered, the corners of her lips wet. "Mmm . . . You going?"

"Yeah. It's ten o'clock. Thanks for the supper."

"Yeah, yeah . . ."

"Goodnight."

"Yeah, g'night."

He got into the old whore and drove at the speed of a glacier, telling himself if he burned up another half hour, by the time he reached Fish Creek it would be too late to drop by Maggie's house.

When he got to town he told himself he'd only head up Cottage Row to see if her lights were on.

When he drew abreast of her snowbanks he told himself he was only crawling along so he could peer down the path as he flashed past, make sure she was all right.

When he caught a quick glimpse of lights in the lower level, he ordered himself, keep going, Severson! Just keep your ass going!

Twenty feet beyond her house he braked and sat motionlessly in the middle of the road staring at the tip of someone's roof and a dark dormer window.

Don't do it.

I've got to.

The hell you do.

"Son of a bitch," he muttered as he slammed the truck into reverse, flung an arm along the back of the seat and careened backward at thirty miles an hour. He swerved to a halt at the top of her sidewalk, killed the engine and sat studying Maggie's kitchen windows between the high snowbanks—pale gold ingots of light drifting from somewhere deeper in the house. Why wasn't she asleep by now? It was going on eleven, and any woman with a lick of sense would have stopped waiting for a man by this time of night. And any man with an ounce of respect would leave her alone.

He threw open the truck door and slammed it vehemently behind himself, bounded down the steps and arrived breathless at her back door. Angrily, he knocked, then waited on the dark veranda feeling as if someone had driven a wedge into his larynx, watching for her approach through the darkened kitchen.

The door opened and she stood in a veil of night shadows wearing a long quilted robe.

He tried to speak, but couldn't—apology and appeal trapped in his throat. In silence they confronted one another, their own vulnerability and this terrible, magnificent greed they felt for one another. Then she moved, hurtling against him with a faint, lost cry, throwing her arms around his neck and kissing him as women kiss men who have returned from war.

"You came."

"I came," he repeated, lifting her free of the veranda floor with her feet trailing inches above his as he hauled her over the threshold. He elbowed the door shut with such force the lace curtain caught in the weather stripping. In the semidarkness they kissed, openmouthed and ravenous, abandoning grace and reserve, clawing at clothing and dropping it where it fell. Their impatience was a lightning bolt carrying them from one forbidden pleasure to the next—a puddle of clothing upon a kitchen floor; untrammeled seeking; an almost manic compulsion to find, touch, taste everywhere; his mouth upon her breast, belly and mons; hers upon him; her back against the kitchen door; his arm clamping her waist and hauling her down to her knees atop their discarded clothing, a frantic coupling and the racking of limbs, accompanied by the baring of teeth and their rasping cries of release.

Then two people panting and wilted, waiting for their breath to return.

It ended where it had begun, beside the kitchen door, with both of them astounded by their own abandon, still trying to sort through the maelstrom of emotions.

He fell to his back, watched her roll away and sit beside him running a shaky hand through her hair. The only light in the kitchen came from the opposite end of the house, barely illuminating her silhouette. A lump of clothing bored into his waist and a cold draft threaded in beneath the door.

"You said you weren't going to come over tonight," she said, almost defensively.

"And you said, 'okay,' as if it didn't matter one way or another."

"It mattered. I was afraid to let you know how much."

"Now I know, don't I?"

She felt like weeping. Instead she got up and padded to the small lavatory around the corner.

He lay where she'd left him while the light snapped on. The water ran. He sighed, then got up and followed. He stopped in the open doorway and found her standing naked, staring at the sink. It was a tiny room with an angled ceiling, papered in dusty blue with a border strip following the ceiling. It contained only the sink and the toilet, on opposite walls. He spied a box of tissues and moved inside to stand back to back with her, tending to necessities. "I didn't want to come back tonight. I went out to Ma's and stayed there late enough that I thought you'd be in bed. If the house had been dark I never would have stopped."

"I didn't really want you to come over either."

She turned on the water and cupped some against her face. He flushed the toilet, then turned to study her rounded back bent over the sink. She reached up blindly, found a towel and buried her face in it while he stroked the hollow between her shoulder blades and asked, "Maggie, what's wrong?"

She straightened and drew the towel to her chin, meeting his eyes in the mirror, an oval mirror mounted high on the wall, cutting off their reflections at shoulder level. "I didn't want it to be this way."

"What way?"

"Just . . . just lust."

"It's not just lust."

"Then why did I think about it so much today? Why did that just happen in the kitchen, just what I thought would happen if you came back?"

"You didn't enjoy it?"

"I loved it. That's what scares me. Where was the spiritual element?"

He fit his body close behind hers, slipped both arms below her breasts and dropped his lips to her shoulder.

"Maggie, I love you."

She aligned her arms with his. "I love you, too."

"And what happened in the kitchen was the result of frustration."

"I don't think I'll be very good at this . . . having an affair. I'm already an emotional wreck."

He lifted his head. For moments they studied one another's troubled eyes.

"May I stay here tonight?"

"Do you think that's wise?"

"You didn't question wisdom last night."

"I've done some thinking since then."

"So have I. That's why I went out to Ma's."

"And I'm sure we came up with the same conclusions."

"Nevertheless, I want to stay."

He spent that night and the next in her bed, and on Friday morning when he prepared to leave, the same pall fell upon them. They stood at the back door, his hands on her upper arms, hers at her sides. She had armored herself by assuming a mood of dispassion.

"I'll see you next week," he told her.

"All right."

"Maggie, I . . ." He struggled again with his great inner conflict. "I don't want to go back to her."

"I know."

He felt some confusion at her lack of clinging. She remained cool, almost remote, lifting tearless brown eyes, while he was the one who felt like crying.

"Maggie, I need to know what you're feeling."

"I love you."

"Yes, I know that, but have you thought about the rest of your life? About ever marrying again?"

"Sometimes."

"About marrying me?" he asked simply.

"Sometimes."

"Would you? If I were free?"

She paused, afraid to answer, because in the last three days she'd had time to consider how rash this had all been, and where it was taking her life.

"Maggie, I'm very new at this. I've never had an affair before, and if I seem unsure it's because I am. I don't know what comes first. I can't be intimate with two women at the same time, and she's coming home, and it's decision time. Oh, hell, this is awkward."

"For both of us, because I've never had an affair either. Eric, please understand. I *have* thought about what it would be like to be married to you. But it's been . . ." She paused, seeking honesty. "It's been more fantasy than anything else. Because we were first for each other, and if things had gone differently we might have been married all these years. I suppose it was natural that I idealized you, and fantasized about you. And then suddenly you came sweeping back into my life like a . . . a knight on a steed, a sailor at the helm, blowing your air horn and making my heart plunge. My first love."

She rested her hands on his leather jacket at the level of his heart. "But I don't want us to make commitments we can't keep, or demands we have no right to make. We've been together only three days, and—let's be honest—the way the sex has been, we may be reasoning with our glands right now."

He drew a deep breath and let his shoulders sag. "I've told myself the same thing at least a dozen times a day, and to tell the truth, I was afraid to bring up marriage for exactly the same reasons. Everything is happening so fast. But I wanted you to know before I left here that I've made a decision and I'm sticking to it. I'm going to tell Nancy tonight that I can't live with her anymore. I won't be one of those men who keeps stringing two women along."

"Eric, listen to me." She took his face in her hands. "There's a part of me that loves hearing you say that, but there's another part that sees very clearly how people in this situation do the thing that's ultimately wrong for them. Eric, think. Think very hard about your reasons for leaving her. They must be because of your relationship with her, not because of your relationship with me."

He studied her brown eyes, thinking how wise she was and how unclassic their responses: he supposed in most cases such as theirs, the single one would be clinging, the married one evasive.

"I told you before this started, I don't love her anymore. I haven't for months. I even talked to my brother, Mike, about it last fall."

"But if you've made the decision to leave her and you did it impulsively, there's a good possibility you're reacting to the last three nights instead of the last eighteen years, and which should bear more weight?"

"I said I've made my decision, and I'll stick to it."

"All right. You do what you must, but do it understanding that I have just embarked upon a new phase of my life. I have this house, and a business I've barely begun, and some things to accomplish on my own." More quietly, she added, "And I still have some healing to do."

For some time they stood separately, untouching.

"All right," he said at length. "Thanks for being honest with me."

"I've read," she told him, "that in order to buy a handgun you must fill out an application and wait three days. The lawmakers think it eliminates a lot of shootings. Perhaps they ought to make a similar law about leaving wives when affairs begin." Their eyes met, Eric's dismayed, Maggie's drawn with concern. "Eric, I've never considered myself a potential homewrecker, but I've got my guilts over what happened, too."

"So what do you want to do?"

"Would you agree to put off doing anything for a while, and during that time, staying away from me? From here?"

He studied her, beleaguered. "For how long?"

"Let's not set a time limit. Let's just consider it a commonsense time."

"Could I call you?" he asked, looking like a little boy chastised.

"If you think it's wise."

"You're putting it all on me."

"No. I'll only call you if I think it's wise, too."

He looked sad.

"Now smile for me once, before you go," she requested.

Instead, he clutched her close against him. "Aw, Maggie . . ."

"I know . . . I know . . ." she soothed, rubbing his back.

But she didn't know. She had no more answers than he.

"I'll miss you," he whispered. His voice sounded tortured.

"I'll miss you, too."

A moment later he spun away, the door opened and he was gone.

Chapter 13

Nancy had had a trying trip up from Chicago and arrived irritable. The roads had been icy, the weather frigid and the store clerks temperamental. When she opened the kitchen door and stepped inside, burdened by luggage, Eric was there to meet her. The aroma in the room immediately took the edge off her temper.

"Hi," she said, catching the door with her heel while he reached for her suitcase and garment bag.

"Hi."

She lifted her face toward his but he grabbed her things and carried them away without the customary kiss. When he returned to the kitchen, he moved straight to the refrigerator and reached inside for a bottle of lime water.

"It smells good in here. What have you got in the oven?"

"Cornish game hens with wild-rice stuffing."

"Cornish game hens . . . what's the occasion?"

Guilt, he thought, but answered, "I know they're your favorites." He closed the refrigerator, twisted off the bottle cap and opened a lower cabinet door to drop it into the garbage. She was close behind him when he turned.

"Mmm . . . what a nice homecoming," she said invitingly.

He raised the bottle and took a swig.

She caught him in the circle of her arms, pinning his elbows to his sides. "No kiss?"

He hesitated before giving her a quick one. The look on his face set off an alarm bell in Nancy.

"Hey, wait a minute . . . is that all I get?"

He eased free. "I've got to check the birds," he said, and picked up a pair of pot holders off the countertop before shouldering around her to reach the stove. "Excuse me, I have to open the oven."

Within Nancy the alarm bell sounded again, more insistently. Whatever was bothering him, it was serious. So many excuses to avoid a kiss, a glance. He checked the birds, drank his bottle of lime water, set the table, served her favorite foods, inquired about her week, and maintained eye contact for a grand total of perhaps ten seconds through the entire meal. His replies were distant, his sense of humor nonexistent, and he left half the food on his plate.

"What's wrong?" she asked at meal's end.

He picked up his plate, carried it to the sink and turned on the water. "It's just these winter doldrums."

It's more, she thought as a frisson of panic ricocheted through her body. It's a woman. The truth struck her like a broadside: he had begun changing the day his old girlfriend came back to town. Nancy added it up again—his distraction, his uncharacteristic quietness, the way he'd suddenly begun avoiding physical contact.

Do something, she thought, say something that will forestall him.

"Honey, I've been thinking," she said, leaving her chair, fitting her body behind his and twining her arms around his belt. "Maybe I'll ask to have my territory split so I could have a couple more days a week at home." It was a lie. She hadn't considered it for a moment, but, driven by desperation, she said what she hoped he'd want to hear.

Beneath her cheek she felt his back muscles working as he scrubbed a plate.

"What do you think?" she asked.

He continued moving. The water ran.

"If you want to."

"I've also been doing a little more thinking about having a baby."

He went still as a threatened spider. With her ear against his back she heard him swallow.

"Maybe one wouldn't be so bad."

The water stopped running. In the silence, neither of them moved.

"Why the sudden change of heart?" he asked.

She improvised as fast as her thoughts could race. "I was thinking since you don't work during the winter you could take care of it then. If I went back to work we'd only need a baby-sitter for half the year."

She ran a hand down his jeans and curled it against the warmth of his compressed genitals. He draped the butts of his hands against the edge of the sink and said nothing.

"Eric?" she whispered, beginning to stroke him.

He swung around and seized her against him, wetting the back of her silk dress, clutching her with the desperation of a mourner. She sensed she had stumbled upon some moment of crisis and felt certain she knew what it was: guilt.

He was rough with her, giving her no chance to desist, stripping her from the waist down as if afraid she—or he—might change their minds. There was a small sofa in the living room around the corner. He hauled her to it and without giving her the opportunity to take precautions, made short order of putting sperm within her: without kisses or tenderness their coupling could be called little else.

When it was over, Nancy was angry.

"Let me up," she said.

In silence they moved to separate parts of the house to put themselves in order.

In their bedroom upstairs she stood a long time in the dim light from the hall, staring at a knob on a chest of drawers, thinking, if he made me pregnant, so help me God, I'll kill him!

In the kitchen he stood for minutes. At length he sighed, resumed cleaning off the table, abandoned the job midway and returned to the living room to sit in the gloom on the edge of a chair with his elbows on his knees and reflect upon his life. He was so damned confused. What was he trying to prove by manhandling Nancy that way? He felt like a pervert, guiltier than ever after what he'd done. Did he really want her pregnant now? If he walked into the bedroom at this moment and said, I want a divorce, and she said okay, wouldn't he walk right out of this house and go to Maggie without a second thought?

No. Because he, not his wife, was the guilty party here.

The house remained so quiet he could hear the kitchen faucet dripping. He sat in the gloom until his eyes discerned the outline of the sofa where the cushions remained askew in one corner where he'd thrown her.

He rose disconsolately and straightened them. Went upstairs, climbing with heavy steps. In the doorway of their bedroom he stopped and looked into the darkened room. She was sitting on the foot of the bed beside the garment bag he'd brought up earlier. On the floor nearby sat her suitcase. He thought he would not blame her if she picked them up and walked out.

He shuffled in and stopped beside her.

"I'm sorry, Nancy," he said.

She remained motionless, as if she had not heard him.

He touched her head heavily.

"I'm sorry," he whispered.

Still sitting, she pivoted to face the far wall and crossed her arms tightly. "You should be," she said.

He let his hand slip off her head and drop to his side.

He waited, but she said no more. He searched for something further to offer her, but felt like a drained vessel without a single droplet left to offer her for sustenance. After some time he walked from the room and isolated himself downstairs.

On Monday forenoon he went out to Mike's, driven by the need for a confessor.

Barb answered his knock; round as a dirigible and wholesomely happy. She took one look at his glum face and said, "He's down in the garage changing the oil in his truck."

Eric found Mike dressed in greasy coveralls, lying on a creeper beneath his Ford pickup.

"Heya, Mike," he said cheerlessly, closing the door.

"That you, little bro?"

"It's me."

"Just a minute, let me get this oil draining." There followed several grunts, a metallic grating, then the ping of liquid hitting an empty pan. The creeper bumped along the concrete floor and Mike emerged, wearing a red bill-cap turned backward.

"You out slumming?"

"You guessed it," Eric obliged with a halfhearted grin.

"Looking like a whipped spaniel, too," Mike observed, rising, wiping his hands on a rag.

"I need to talk to you."

"Woa! This *is* serious."

"Yes, it is."

"Well, hang on. Let me stick a couple chunks of wood in the stove." In one corner of the garage a barrel-sized cast-iron stove gave off warmth. Mike opened its squeaky door, thrust in two pieces of maple, returned to Eric, and overturned a green plastic bucket. "Sit," he ordered, dropping onto the creeper with his legs outstretched and his ankles crossed. "I've got the whole damn day," he invited, "so shoot."

Eric sat still as a rock, his eyes on a toolbox, wondering how to begin. Finally his troubled gaze shifted to Mike.

"Remember when we were little and the old man would whip our asses when we did something wrong?"

"Yup. Whip 'em good."

"I've been wishing he was around to do it again."

"What have you done that you need whipping for?"

Eric drew a deep breath and said it plain. "I'm having an affair with Maggie Pearson."

Mike's hairline rose and his ears seemed to flatten. He took the news without comment at first, then turned the bill of his cap to the front and remarked, "Well, I see why you wish the old man were here, but I don't think a licking would do much good."

"No, probably not. I just had to tell someone because I feel like such a lowlife."

"How long has it been going on?"

"Last week, that's all."

"And it's over?"

"I don't know."

"Oh-oh."

"Yeah. Oh-oh."

They mulled a while before Mike asked, "So you intend to see her again?"

"I don't know. We agreed to stay away from each other for a while. Cool off a little and see."

"Does Nancy know?"

"She probably suspects. It was a hell of a weekend."

Mike blew out a long breath, removed his cap, scratched his head and replaced the cap with the bill low over his eyes.

Eric spread his hands. "Mike, I'm so damned mixed up. I think I love Maggie."

Mike studied his brother thoughtfully. "I figured this was going to happen, the minute I heard she was moving back to town. I know how you were with her in high school. I knew you two were getting it on back then."

"You knew?" Eric's face registered surprise. "Like hell you knew."

"Don't look so surprised. It was my car you were borrowing, remember? And Barb and I were getting a little ourselves, so we guessed about you and Maggie."

"Damn it, you're so lucky. Do you know how lucky you two are? I look at you and Barb, and your family, and how you turned out together and I think, why didn't I grab Maggie back then, and maybe I'd have what you've got."

"It's more than luck, and you know it. It's damned hard work and a lot of compromise."

"Yeah, I know," Eric replied disconsolately.

"So what about you and Nancy?"

Eric shook his head. "That's a mess."

"How so?"

"In the middle of all this she comes home and says, *maybe* she'll have a baby after all. *Maybe* one wouldn't be so bad. So I put her to the test. I jumped her then and there without giving her a chance to take any precautions, and she hasn't talked to me since."

"You mean you forced her?"

"I guess that's what you'd call it, yeah."

Mike peered at his brother from beneath his bill-cap and said quietly, "Not good, man."

"I know."

"What the hell were you thinking?"

"I don't know. I felt guilty about Maggie, and scared and angry that Nancy waited all this time to finally consider having a family."

"Can I ask you something?"

Eric glanced at his brother, waiting.

"Do you love her?"

Eric sighed.

Mike waited.

Beneath the pickup the oil gurgled once and stopped running. The smell of it filled the place, mixed with the smokehouse scent of burning maple.

"Sometimes I get flashes of feeling, but it's mostly wishing for what might have been. When I first met her it was all physical attraction. I thought she was the greatest-looking woman on the face of the earth. Then after I got to know her I realized how bright she was, and how much ambition she had, and I figured someday she'd succeed at something in a big way. Back then all of that mattered as much as her looks. But you want to know something ironic?"

"What?"

"It's the very things I admired her for that are driving me away. Her business success somehow came to matter more to her than the success of our marriage. And, hell, we don't share anything anymore. We used to like the same music, now she puts those headphones on and listens to self-motivation tapes. When we were first married we'd take clothes to the laudromat together and now she has her dry cleaning done overnight while she's in hotels. We don't even like the same kinds of food anymore. She eats health food and carps at me about eating doughnuts all the time. We don't use the same checkbook, or the same doctors, or even the same bar of soap! She hates my snowmobile, my pickup, our house—Christ, Mike, I thought when people were married they were supposed to grow *together*!''

Mike crooked his arms around his updrawn knees.

"If you don't love her you have no business trying to persuade her to have a baby, much less jumping her without a condom.''

"I know.'' Eric hung his head. In time he shook it forlornly. "Aw hell . . .'' He stared at the stove. "Falling out of love is a bitch. It really hurts.''

Mike rose and went to his brother, clapping an arm around Eric's shoulders. "Yeah.'' They remained that way a while listening to the snap of the fire, surrounded by its warmth and the familiar smells of hot cast iron and motor oil. Years ago they had shared the same bedroom and an old iron bed. They had shared both the praises and punishments of their parents, and sometimes—when it was dark and neither of them could sleep—their hopes and dreams. They felt as close now at the crumbling of one of their dreams as they had upon disclosing them as lads.

"So what do you want to do?'' Mike asked.

"I want to marry Maggie, but she says I'm probably thinking with my glands right now.''

Mike laughed.

"Besides, she's not ready to get married again. She wants to be a businesswoman for a while, and I guess I can't blame her for that. Hell, she hasn't even taken in her first customer yet, and after all the money she sank into that house, she wants a chance to see it go.''

"So you came to me asking what you ought to do about Nancy, but I can't answer. Would it bother you to let it ride for a while?''

"It just seems so damned dishonest. I had a hell of a time keeping from telling her this weekend and making a clean break, but Maggie made me promise I'd give it some time.''

After a moment's thought, Mike squeezed Eric's shoulder. "Tell you what let's do.'' He turned Eric toward the truck. "Let's get this oil changed and take the snowmobiles out for a ride. That always clears the head.''

They were men who'd been born in the north where winter makes up nearly half the year. They'd learned young how to appreciate the bright blues and stark whites of it, the sturdiness of skeletal trees, the beauty of snow-draped branches, of purple shadows and red barns against the white landscape.

They drove south, to Newport State Park, and along the shoreline of Rowley's Bay where the harbor appeared as a jigsaw puzzle of ice, the beach a crescent of white. Swells of water had surged beneath the frozen lake and raised great windrows, which eventually fell beneath their own weight, and cracked into great sheets that shifted back and forth, the cracks enlarging to ponds where goldeneyes, mergansers and buffleheads consorted. The ice hit upon itself and chimed in the empty bay. White-winged scoters swam along the ice-edge and dove for food beneath the glass. From the distance came a garbled yodel. *"O-owaowa-wa-wa."* A flock of birds lifted from the water, their long, thin tails trailing behind like giant stingers—old squaws, summer residents of the Arctic Circle on southern holiday in Door County.

Inland, the riders passed sumac and dogwood whose red berries shone like jewels against the snow, then on beneath a cathedral of hemlock and white pine branches, and into a copse of yellow birch laden with seed catkins where redpolls were having a repast. They followed a deer trail of dainty footprints where the animals had been dallying, and eventually came upon great pock marks where the deer had broken into a run and plunged down a steep dune where their bounding hooves had left great explosions of white, like giant doilies, upon the snow.

Blue jays swooped before them, scolding in their unpretty voices, and for a time a pileated woodpecker led them from one bend to the next. They found craters where deer had slept, a running spring where mink, mouse and squirrel had drunk.

They drove on to an ice-covered reservoir near Mud Lake where a beaver lodge rose like an untidy hairdo wearing a hat of white.

They sat for a time on a bluff above Cana Island with the forest at their backs and the horizon flat as a blue string in the distance, broken only by the spire of the island lighthouse. Nearby, a nuthatch sang its tuneless note while the ice below shifted and belched. A woodpecker hammered in a dead birch. Somewhere on the south end of Door County the frantic pace of the winter shipyards signaled their busiest season, but here, only calm prevailed. In it, Eric felt the essence of winter salve his soul.

"I'll wait," he decided quietly.

"I think that's wise."

"Maggie doesn't know what she wants either."

"But if you take up with her again you should make the break with Nancy right away."

"I will. I promise."

"Okay, then, let's go home."

January advanced. He said nothing to Nancy and kept his promise not to call or see Maggie, though he missed her with a hollow-bellied intensity. In early February he and Mike attended the Sports Show in Chicago where they rented a display booth, passed out literature, pitched prospective customers and booked charters for the upcoming fishing season. They were long, tiring days when they talked until their throats were sore, stood until their feet hurt, lived primarily on hot dogs available from venders on the showroom floor, and slept poorly in strange hotel rooms.

He returned to Fish Creek to an empty house, a note from Nancy out-lining her itinerary for the week, and the telephone only a reach away. A dozen times he passed it and thought how simple it would be to pick it up and dial Maggie's number. Talk about the show, the bookings they'd made, his week, her week—the things he should be talking to his wife about. In the end he resisted.

One day he went uptown to get the mail and passed Vera Pearson on the sidewalk. It was a windy day and she hurried with her head down, holding a scarf against her chin. When she heard his footsteps approaching from the opposite direction she looked up, and her footsteps slowed. Then her expression turned hard as she quickened her pace and moved on without any further acknowledgment.

During the third week of February he and Mike went to the Boat, Sports and Travel Show in Minneapolis. On the second day there a woman came into the booth who resembled Maggie. She was taller and had paler hair, but the resemblance was uncanny and brought Eric a sharp sexual reaction. He closed the button on his sport coat as he moved toward her.

"Hello, may I answer any questions?"

"Not really. But I'd like to take your brochure for my husband."

"Sure. We're Severson's Charters, and we run two boats out of Gills Rock in northern Door County, Wisconsin."

"Door County. I've heard of that."

"Straight north of Green Bay, on the peninsula."

Facts, pertinent questions, answers and a polite thank you. But once, while they talked, their eyes met directly and though they were total strangers, a recognition passed between them: in another time, another place, given other circumstances, they would have spoken of things other than salmon fishing.

As she left the booth, the woman glanced back one last time and smiled with Maggie's brown eyes, and Maggie's cleft chin, leaving him with so strong an impression of her that it distracted him for the remainder of the day.

That night after he'd showered and switched off the television set, he sat on the edge of his bed, a white towel girding his hips, his hair damp and finger-rilled. From the nightstand he picked up his watch.

10:32

He laid it down and studied the phone. It was beige—did any hotel in America buy phones in any other color?—the luckless color of things once alive. He picked up the receiver and read the instructions for long-distance dialing, changed his mind and cracked it back down.

Maggie knew him well, knew that even this indiscretion would create twinges of conscience.

In the end he dialed anyway and sat waiting with the muscles in his stomach seized up like a prize-fighter's fist.

She answered on the third ring.

"Hello?"

"Hello."

Silence, while he wondered, is her heart slugging like mine? Does her throat feel like there's a tourniquet on it?

"Isn't it curious," she said quietly, "I knew it would be you."

"Why?"

"It's 10:30. I don't know anybody else who'd call me this late."

"Did I wake you?"

"No. I've been gathering data for my income taxes."

"Ah. Well, maybe I shouldn't bother you then."

"No, it's all right. I've been at it a long time. I needed to put all these papers away anyway."

Silence again before he asked, "Are you in the kitchen?"

"Yes."

He pictured her there, where they'd first kissed, where they'd made love on the floor.

Another halting silence while they wondered how to proceed.

"How have you been?" she inquired.

"Mixed up."

"Me, too."

"I wasn't going to call."

"I halfway hoped you wouldn't."

"Then today I saw a woman who reminded me of you."

"Oh? Is it anyone I know?"

"No, she was a stranger. I'm at the Radisson Hotel in Minneapolis— Mike and I—we're here for the sportsmen's show. This woman walked into our booth today and she had eyes so much like yours, and your chin . . . I don't know." He closed his eyes and pinched the bridge of his nose.

"It's terrible, isn't it, how we look for traces of each other?"

"You do the same thing?"

"Constantly. Then berate myself for doing it."

"Same here. This woman . . . something strange happened when she walked in. We couldn't have talked for more than three minutes, but I felt . . . I don't know how to put it . . . threatened almost, as if I were on the brink of doing something unholy. I don't know why I'm telling you this, Maggie, you're the last person I should be telling this to."

"No, tell me . . . "

"It was scary. I looked at her and I felt . . . aw, shit, there's no other way to say it. Carnal. I felt carnal. And I realized that if it weren't for you and our affair, I might have struck up a conversation with her just to see where it would lead. Maggie, I'm not that kind of man, and it scares the hell out of me. I mean, you read about male menopause, guys who've been devoted husbands for years, and then in their forties they just lose it and start acting like morons, chasing kids young enough to be their daughters, having one-nighters with perfect strangers. I don't want to think that's what's happening to me."

"Tell me something, Eric. Could you ever admit a thing like that to Nancy—about that woman, I mean?"

"Christ, no."

"That's significant, don't you think? That you can tell me but not her?"

"I suppose so."

"While we're baring our insecurities, let me confess one of my own: that I'm a sex-starved widow, and you were my feast."

"Aw, Maggie," he said softly.

"Well?" she demanded, self-deprecatingly, remembering the night on her kitchen floor.

"Don't worry about it."

"But I do, because I'm not a user either."

"Maggie, listen, do you know why I called you tonight?"

"To tell me about that woman you saw today."

"That, too, but the real reason is because I knew I couldn't get to you, that it was safe to call you from three hundred miles away. Maggie, I miss you."

"I miss you, too."

"Next Friday makes four weeks."

"Yes, I know."

When she said no more, he sighed, then they listened to the electronic hum of the telephone line. Eric broke the silence.

"Maggie?"

"Yes, I'm here."

"What are you thinking?"

Instead of answering, she asked a question of her own. "Did you tell Nancy about us?"

"No, but I told Mike. I had to talk to somebody. I'm sorry if I violated a confidence."

"No, it's all right. If I had a sister, I'd probably have told her, too."

"Thanks for understanding."

They listened to each other breathe for some time, wondering what lay ahead for them. Finally she said, "We'd better say goodnight now."

"No, Maggie, wait." His voice turned abject. "Aw, Jesus, Maggie, this is hell. I want to see you."

"And what then, Eric? What will come of it? An affair? A messy breakup of your marriage? I'm not sure I'm ready to face that and I don't think you are either."

He wanted to beg her, make promises. But what promises could he make?

"I . . . I really have to go now," she insisted.

He thought he heard a tremor in her voice.

"Goodnight, Eric," she said gently.

"Goodnight."

For fifteen seconds they pressed their cheeks to the receivers.

"Hang up," he whispered.

"I can't." She was crying now, he could tell, though she did her best to disguise it. But her words sounded thick and quavery. Sitting on the bed, doubled forward at the waist, he felt his own eyes water.

"Maggie, I'm so goddamned much in love with you that I hurt. Like I've been bruised, and I'm not sure I'll make it through another day without seeing you again."

"Good-bye, darling," she whispered and did what he was unable to make himself do. She hung up.

He moved through the next day believing he would never see her again; her parting words had been sorrowful but final. She'd had a full, happy life with her husband. She had a daughter and a business and new goals in her life. She had financial independence. What did she need with him? And in a town the size of Fish Creek, where everybody knew everybody else's business, she was right to be cautious about involving herself in a relationship that was certain to bring her sideward glances from a segment of the population—whether they had an affair or he left Nancy for her. Already she'd suffered the censure of her own daughter and mother. No, their affair was over.

He had a miserable day. Walked around feeling like someone had stuffed a wad of rags down his chest cavity and he'd never draw another unrestricted breath. He wished he hadn't called her. It was worse since he'd heard her voice. Worse knowing she'd lived through the same four weeks as miserable as he. Worse knowing there would be no solace for either of them.

He went to bed that night and lay awake, listening to the sound of traffic on Seventh Street below, now and then a siren. Thinking of Nancy, and

Maggie's admonition to judge his marriage on the basis of it, and not his affair. He tried. He could not. To picture his future in any context was to picture it with Maggie. The hotel mattress and pillows were hard as sacks of grain. He wished he was a smoker. It would feel comforting to abuse his body with a little tar and nicotine right now, to suck it in and blow it out and think, to hell with everything.

His watch had an illuminable face. He pressed the stem, and checked it: 11:27.

Is this what articles mean when they talk about stress? Don't men my age have heart attacks when they get into a situation like this? Worried, undecided, unhappy, not sleeping or eating properly? On a sexual tight-rope?

The phone rang and he jumped so hard he skinned his knuckles on the headboard. He rolled up on one elbow and found the receiver in the dark.

"Hello?"

Her voice was soft and held a touch of penitence. She spoke without preamble. "I'd like very much to make dinner for you on Monday night."

He sank back on the pillows, his heart drumming hard, the knot of yearning exploding into a thousand smaller knots that bound him in the unlikeliest of places—temples, fingers, shoulder blades. "Maggie, oh, Jesus, Maggie, do you mean it?"

"I never meant anything more."

So what's it to be—an affair or marriage? It wasn't the time to ask, of course, and for now it was enough to know he'd see her again.

"How did you find me?"

"You said the Radisson in Minneapolis. There are four of them, I discovered, but I finally got the right one."

"Maggie . . ."

"Monday night at six," she whispered.

"I'll bring Chardonnay," he answered simply.

When he'd hung up he felt as if he'd been dragged free of a mudslide and flung up on solid ground, realizing he'd live after all.

On Monday night at six when he reached the top of her sidewalk, she stepped onto the back veranda and called, "Put your truck in the garage."

He did. And closed the doors before heading to the house.

He forced himself to walk, to descend the sidewalk at a casual pace, to climb the porch steps slowly, to keep his hands at his sides while she stood before him with her arms crossed, shivering, the light pouring from behind her and turning her into a celestial being with a halo.

They stood watching each other's breath puff out like white streamers in the chill February air, until he finally thought to say, "Hello, again."

She tipped her lips up and gave a timorous laugh. "Hello. Come in."

He followed her inside and stood uncertainly on the rug before the door. She had dressed in pink silk—a lissome raiment that seemed to move without prompting—and had hung a cord of pearls upon her deep, naked throat. When she turned back to face him the beads, the dress, and she seemed to tremble. But by some unspoken compact this greeting was to be the antithesis of the last. She accepted his green-glass offering and they tended to conventions.

"Chardonnay . . . lovely." This as she examined the bottle.

"Chilled." This as he removed his storm coat.

"I have the perfect glasses."

"I'm sure you do."

She stowed the wine in the refrigerator and he let his eyes drop down her legs. She was wearing high heels the exact shade of her dress. In the bright light of the kitchen they glistened. She closed the refrigerator door and turned to face him, remaining across the room.

"You look elegant," he told her.

"So do you." He had chosen a smoke-blue suit, pale-peach shirt and a striped tie combining the two colors. Her eyes scanned it and returned to his face. This, too, by unspoken agreement: lovers in finest feather, each seeking to please the other.

"We dressed," she said with a fey smile.

He offered a grin. "So we did."

"I thought a little candlelight would be nice." She led him into the dining room which was lit by only six candles, smelled of roses and had places set for two—the two at the near end, facing each other, at a table that would have held a dozen.

"You've finished the room. It's beautiful." He glanced around—ivory wallpaper, swags above the window, china in a built-in glass-doored cabinet, the gleaming cherrywood table.

"Thank you. Sit here. Do you like salmon or do you only fish for it?"

He laughed, and they continued appraising one another, playing the game of restraint as he took the chair she indicated.

"I like it."

"I guess I should have asked you. Would you like your wine now or later?"

"Now, I think, but let me get it, Maggie."

He began to rise, but she touched his shoulder. "No, I will."

He watched her leave the room and return in the shimmering dress that caught the candlelight and sent it radiating along her curves. She poured the wine, and took her place across from him, beyond a white-lace runner and a low crystal basket holding an arrangement of fragrant coral roses. She had arranged them all at their end of the table, as if the remaining length of it did not exist, and had placed the candelabrum carefully to one side.

"So, tell me about Minneapolis," she said.

He told her while they drank their wine and studied one another in the candlelight. While they lingered over tart endive salad and French bread so crusty the crumbs flew when they broke it. Once she wet a fingertip with her tongue, touched two crumbs and carried them to her mouth while he watched in fascination.

"When will you open Harding House to the public?"

She told him while he refilled their glasses, then buttered another hunk of bread, ate it with great relish, and wiped his mouth on a flowered napkin, which her eyes followed.

In time she served him blushing salmon in apple-cider sauce; cheesy potatoes tubed into a garland of rosettes, browned on the tips; and spears of asparagus arranged like the stems of scarlet roses which she'd somehow carved of beets.

"Did you do all this yourself?" he asked, amazed.

"Mm-hmmm."

"Does one eat it or frame it?"

"One does whatever one wants with it."

He ate it, savoring each mouthful because it was the first gift she'd ever given him, and because across the table her eyes shone with promise, and because in the candlelight he could study her to his heart's content.

Later, when their plates were removed and the Chardonnay bottle drained, she came from the kitchen bearing a single, exceedingly heavy, hat-sized chocolate-frosted doughnut on a footed Fostoria cake plate with a floating candle rising from its center in a matching Fostoria stemglass.

"Ta-daa!" she heralded.

He turned at her approach and burst into laughter, leaning back in his chair as she placed her *coup de grace* before him.

"If you can eat it all you win another of the same size."

She leaned before him to set it down, and his arm circled her hips as together they laughed at the gargantuan doughnut.

"It's a monster. I love it!"

"Think you can eat it all?"

He looked up, still smiling. "If I do, I'd rather name my prize."

His arm tightened and the laughter slipped from their faces.

"Maggie," he whispered, and drew her around until her knees struck his chair seat. "This month has seemed like a year." He pressed his face to her breasts.

She closed her arms about his head, her eyes against the candlelight.

"This meal has taken days," he added, muffled against her.

Her only answer was a smile, delivered while bending low over his hair, which smelled faintly of coconut.

"I missed you," he said, "I want you. First, before that doughnut."

She lifted his face, and holding it, told him, "My days seemed pointless without you." She kissed him as she had so tried not to think of kissing him during their separation, his face raised as she bent above it. Freeing his lips she stroked his cheek with the backs of her fingers and felt the wretchedness of the past four weeks dissolve.

"How foolish and self-deluding we were to believe we could will away our feelings for each other simply to avoid complicating our lives."

In the Belvedere Room her pink raiment drifted to the floor, and his suit was relegated to a small sewing rocker. Then, gladly, they gave up their wills to one another and celebrated the end of their self-imposed agony. Much later, lying with their limbs plaited, they spoke of their feelings during exile. Of feeling torn and lorn and incomplete when apart; of stepping into a room where the other waited and becoming immediately total, whole again.

"I read poetry," she admitted. "Searching for you in it."

"I rode the snowmobile, trying to get you off my mind."

"Once I thought I saw you uptown, from the back, and I ran to catch up with you, but when I got close and realized it was someone else, I felt tragic, like crying right there on the street."

"I thought of you most in those hotel rooms, when I couldn't sleep and I wished you were with me. God, I wanted you with me." He touched his index finger to the cleft in her chin. "When I stepped into this house tonight, and you were here, waiting, in your pretty pink dress, I felt . . . I felt like I suppose a sailor feels when he comes home from years at sea.

There was nothing more I wanted or needed than to be in that room with you, looking at you again.''

"I felt the same. As if when you left you took some part of me, like I was a puzzle, maybe, and the piece you took was right here . . ." She laid his hand over her heart. "And when you walked in, that piece fell into place and I came back to life again.''

"I love you, Maggie. You're the one who should be my wife.''

"And what if I said I would be?''

"I'd tell her. I'd end it then and there. Will you?''

"Isn't it odd? I feel as if the choice isn't really mine, loving you the way I do.''

His face became amazed. "You mean it, Maggie?''

She flung her arms about him, smiling against his jaw. "Yes, I mean it, Eric. I love you . . . love you . . . love you.'' She punctuated her pronouncement with kisses upon his collarbone, cheek, eyebrow. "I love you and I'll be your wife . . . as soon as you're free.''

They clung together and celebrated, rolling side to side.

In time their exuberance changed to wonder. They lay on their sides, close, studying each other's eyes. He carried her hand to his mouth and kissed its palm.

"Just think . . . I'm going to grow old with you,'' he said softly.

"What a lovely thought.''

And at that moment, they really believed it would happen.

Chapter 14

Nancy pulled into the driveway at 6:15 Friday night. Dusk had fallen, and from the kitchen window Eric watched her headlights arc around and disappear into the open garage. She'd always hated that garage door. It was old-fashioned, cumbersome, a son of a bitch to budge. Though it lowered with much less effort than it raised, he was nevertheless waiting to close it when she emerged from the garage.

A sharp wind bit through his shirtsleeves as he stood watching her lean into the backseat for her suitcase. She had good legs, always wore extremely expensive hosiery—aqua-green tonight, to match her suit. There had been a time when the sight of her legs had had the power to arouse him. He viewed them now with a sense of sorrow for his lost ardor, and with an unspoken apology for his stubborn insistence about this house— even this garage—which she'd hated so much. Perhaps if he'd given in on that one point alone she'd have given in on one, too, and they would not have reached this brink of dissolution.

She emerged from the car and saw him.

Immobility struck her: the lag-time of silence like that following a distant puff of smoke from a rifle before the sound catches up. These stagnant pauses had grown common to both of them in the weeks since his ill-advised sexual assault.

Nancy moved again. "What are you doing out here?"

"I'll take that." He stepped inside the garage and reached for her suitcase. She leaned into the backseat for a second load, coming up with a briefcase and a garment bag which she hoisted over her shoulder as he slammed the car door.

"Did you have a good week?" he asked.

"Fair."

"How were the roads?"

"Okay."

Their conversations had become sterile and halting since that night. They walked single file toward the house without attempting any further exchange.

Inside, she set down her briefcase and reached for her suitcase.

"I can take it upstairs for you," he offered.

"I'll take it," she insisted, and did so.

While she was gone he stood in the kitchen feeling shaken and apprehensive because he knew leaving her was the right thing to do and he dreaded the next hour.

She returned, dressed in a straight teal woolen skirt and a long-sleeved white silk blouse with a gold rose pinned at her collarbone. She crossed the room without meeting his eyes. He waited, leaning against the sink, watching as she lifted the lid from a pot of simmering chile, found a ladle, spoons, bowls, and began to fill them.

"None for me," he said.

She glanced up with the flat expression she had perfected since the night he'd drilled her on the sofa.

"I ate already." He hadn't, but the hollow within could not be filled with food.

"What's wrong?"

"Eat your chile first." He turned away.

She set the bowl on the table and remained standing beside it, her stillness tinged with caution.

"First before what?"

He stared out the window over the kitchen sink at the dirty snow and the late-winter dusk. Nerves jumped in his stomach and bleakness weighted him like a heavy yoke. This was not something one did blithely. The major part of his life was invested in this marriage, too.

He turned to face her. "Nancy, you'd better sit down."

"I'd better sit, I'd better eat!" she retorted. "What is it? Tell me so I can!"

He crossed the room and pulled out two chairs. "Come on, will you please sit?" When she had, stiffly, he sat across from her, forearms on the table, studying the wooden fruit he'd always disliked. "There's no good time to say what I've got to say—before you eat, after you eat, after you've had a chance to kick back. Hell, it's . . ." He linked his fingers and fit the pads of his thumbs together. Lifting his eyes to her, he said quietly, "I want a divorce, Nancy."

She paled. Stared. Fought the sudden onslaught of panic. "Who is she?"

"I knew you'd say that."

"Who is she?" Nancy shouted, rapping a fist on the table. "And don't tell me nobody, because I tried calling here twice this week, and when you're not home at eleven o'clock at night, there's somebody, so who is it?"

"This is between you and me and nobody else."

"You don't have to tell me because *I know*! It's your old high school girlfriend, isn't it?" Her head jutted forward. "Isn't it?"

He sighed and pinched the bridge of his nose.

"It's her, I know it! The millionaire widow! Are you screwing her, Eric?"

He opened his eyes and leveled them on her. "Nancy, for God's sake . . ."

"You are, aren't you? You were screwing her in high school, and you're screwing her now! I saw it the first day she came to town. She wasn't on those church steps five minutes and you had rocks in your shorts, so don't tell me this is between you and me and nobody else! Where were you at eleven o'clock Wednesday night?" She thumped the table again. "Where?"

He waited wearily.

"And last night!"

He refused to answer her anger with anger, which only incensed her further. "You son of a bitch!" She lunged forward and slapped his face. Hard. So hard two chair legs lifted off the floor. "Goddamn you!" She rocketed around the table and swung again, but he feinted and caught only the end of her fingernails across his left cheek.

"Nancy, stop it!"

"You're screwing her! Admit it!" He caught her by the forearms and they grappled, bumping the table, spilling chile, sending wooden pears rolling to the floor. His cheek began bleeding.

"Stop it, I said!" Still sitting, he gripped her forearms.

"You're spending nights with her, I know it!" She had begun to cry. "And it didn't just start this week because I've called here before when you weren't home at night!"

"Nancy, cut it out!" A drop of blood fell onto his shirt.

Locked like combatants, he watched her struggle for control and find it. With tear-streaked cheeks she returned to her chair and sat facing him. He rose and got a dishcloth to wipe up the spilled chile. She watched him move from the table to the sink and back again. When he was seated, she said, "I don't deserve this. I've been faithful to you."

"This isn't just about being faithful, this is about two people who never grew together."

"Is that some platitude you read in the Sunday paper?"

"Look at us." He pressed a folded handkerchief to his cheek, looked at the blood and asked, "What's left anymore? We're apart five days a week and unhappy the two we're together."

"We weren't until that woman moved back to town."

"Could we leave her out of it? This began long before she moved back to Fish Creek and you know it."

"That's not true."

"Yes, it is. We've been growing apart for years."

He could see her initial anger being replaced with fear, which he had not expected.

"If this is about my working, I said I'd ask about getting my territory cut."

"But did you mean it?"

"Of course I meant it."

"Have you done it?"

She hadn't. Both of them knew it.

"And even if you did it, would you be happy? I don't think so. You're happiest doing exactly what you're doing, and I've finally come to realize that."

She leaned forward earnestly. "Then why can't you just let me continue doing it?"

He released a huge, weary sigh and felt as if he was talking in circles.

"Why do you even want this marriage? What did we ever make of it?"

"You're the only one who thinks this marriage is a mistake. I think it's worth fighting for."

"Aw, for heaven's sake, Nancy, open your eyes. From the time you started traveling, we started losing it. We stored our possessions in the same house, and we shared the same bedroom, but what else did we share? Friends? *I've* got friends, but *we* don't. I've come to the sad realization that we never made any because making friends takes an effort, takes time, but you never had the time. We didn't entertain because you were always too tired by the time Saturday night came. We didn't go to church because Sunday was your only free day. We didn't have a beer with the neighbors because you considered drop-ins gauche. And we never had kids of our own, so we never did the regular kind of stuff like taking turns in a car pool or going to recitals or Little League games. I wanted all of that, Nancy."

"Well, why didn't you—" She bit off the sentence.

"Say so?"

They both knew he had.

"We had friends in Chicago."

"When we were first married, yes, but not after you took the selling job."

"But my time was so limited then."

"That's what I'm telling you—not that what you want is wrong, or what I want is wrong, but that what we want is wrong for each other. And what about pastimes? Yours is work, and mine—well, hell, we both know you've always considered my pastimes too unsophisticated to suit you. To ride a snowmobile you'd have to mess your hair. Fishing is too unrefined for an Orlane rep. And you'd as soon have a root canal as walk in the woods. What do we share anymore, Nancy, what?"

"When we started out we wanted the same things. It was *you* who changed. Not me."

He considered, then admitted forlornly, "Maybe you're right. Maybe it was me who changed. I tried the city life, the art galleries, the orchestra halls, but I found it more satisfying to look at a real wildflower than a painting of one. And I think there's more music at the Ridges Nature Sanctuary than in all the orchestra halls in the world. I was miserable trying to be a yuppie."

"So you forced me to move here. Well, what about me? What about what *I* wanted and needed? I loved those galleries and orchestra halls!"

"What you're saying is what I'm saying: Our needs and wants are too different to make this marriage work, and it's time we admitted it."

She rested her forehead on eight fingertips and stared at her bowl of chile.

"People change, Nancy," he explained. "I changed. You changed. You weren't a sales rep then, you were a fashion merchandiser, and I didn't know my father would die and Mike would ask me to come back here and run the charter service. I admit, I thought back then that I wanted to be a corporate executive, but it took some years of experiencing corporate life before I found out it wasn't what I thought it would be. We changed, Nancy, it's as simple as that."

She looked up with fresh tears in her eyes. "But I still *love* you. I can't just . . . just turn away from that."

The sight of her tears grieved him and he looked away. They sat for some moments in silence before Nancy spoke once more.

"I've said I'd consider having a baby, too."

"It's too late for that," he said.

"Why?" She leaned across the table and clutched the back of his hand. He let it lie lifelessly beneath hers.

"Because it would be a desperation move, and it's not right to bring a child into a marriage to hold it together. What I did that night was unforgivable, and I want to apologize again."

"Eric . . ." she appealed, still appropriating his hand.

He withdrew it and said quietly, "Give me a divorce, Nancy."

After a lengthy stretch of consideration, she replied, "So she can have you? Never."

"Nancy . . ."

"The answer is no," she said firmly and slipped from her chair and began gathering the wooden fruit from the floor.

"I didn't want this to turn into a fight."

She dropped four teakwood pears into the bowl. "I'm afraid it's going to. I may not like this place, but I've got an investment in it, too, and I'm staying."

"All right." He rose. "I'll go to Ma's for the time being."

Abruptly she softened. "Don't go," she pleaded. "Stay and let's try to work it out."

"I can't do that," he said.

"But Eric . . . eighteen years."

"I can't," he repeated in a choked voice and left her, with the pleading look on her face, to go upstairs and pack.

Ma's house was empty when he reached it. The light was on over the kitchen sink, spotlighting a dirty mixing bowl, a pair of beaters and two discolored, dented cookie sheets.

"Ma?" he called, expecting no answer, getting none.

In the living room the television was black, her crocheting lay in a pile on the davenport with the hook projecting from the ball of thread. He carried his suitcases on through, up the creaky stairs to his old room under the eaves. It was a bleak room, by most people's standards, with faded scatter rugs on a linoleum floor and worn chenille spreads on its two beds. It smelled faintly of bat droppings; brown bats had lived under the eaves and behind the shutters for as long as he could remember. Occasionally one would get in and they'd bring it to the ground with a landing net. But even as children they'd never been afraid of the animals. Ma had always insisted they put them out instead of killing them. Bats eat mosquitoes, she'd said, so treat them gentle.

The dry, aged-attic smell of the bats was distinctly nostalgic, comforting.

He switched on a dim lamp in the "boys' room," wandered through into "Ruth's room"—the two arranged shotgun fashion so that Ruth had always had to pass through the boys' barracks to reach her own. Back then a flowered cotton curtain had served as a door between the two sections; it had since been replaced by a wooden door.

In Ruth's room he wandered aimlessly to the window. Through the naked trees, from this high vantage point he could see the lighted windows of Mike and Barb's house, undoubtedly where Ma was. She went over sometimes for supper. He had no desire to join them tonight. Instead he returned to the boys' room and flopped onto his back on one of the beds.

There in the gloom, he mourned the marriage that had for years seemed vacant; the mistakes he himself had made during it; his childlessness; the investment of years that had tallied only disappointment and regret; Nancy's refusal to end the relationship that had no future; the turbulence that lay ahead.

He reminisced about moments when he and Nancy had been wholly happy. Reflections flashed in his mind as vignettes upon a screen, each sterling in its clarity. The time they'd bought their first piece of furniture—a stereo, which they'd purchased on time. Certainly not the most practical first piece, but the one they both wanted most. They'd hauled it into the apartment together, then lain on their backs on the floor, listening to the two albums they'd chosen—Gordon Lightfoot for him, the Beatles for her. Those old albums were still around somewhere; he wondered if they'd each take their own when they parted. They'd lain on the apartment floor, feeling the music vibrate through them, and they'd talked about the future. Someday they'd have a whole houseful of furniture, all the best, and a house to put it in, too—all glass and redwood, in some affluent suburb of Chicago, probably. She was right. He'd let her down there.

Another time when they'd impetuously flown to San Diego—counted their money and decided on a Friday noon (via telephone between their two offices) and by ten that night were checking into a hotel in La Jolla. They had walked its hilly streets holding hands, and drunk cocktails in open-air lounges while watching the sun set over the Pacific, and had eaten famous split-pea soup at some restaurant in a windmill, and had explored Capistrano Mission, and made love in broad daylight in a hidden cove on the beach near Oceanside, and had promised one another they would never grow predictable, but would fly away often that way, at the drop of a hat. Now their lives were as predictable as the lunar cycle and Nancy traveled so much there was no incentive for impromptu weekends away.

Another memory came. It was their second year of marriage when Nancy fell one day on an icy sidewalk and sustained a concussion. He recalled his sick fear while waiting in the emergency room for the results of her X rays, the emptiness of their bed during the night she'd remained in the hospital for observation, and the relief he'd felt at her return. In those days a single night apart had been a trial for both of them. Now, five days apart was the accepted norm.

He should have worked harder at finding a compromise that would have kept them together more of the time.

He should have built her a glass and redwood house.

They should have talked about children before they were married.

Lying on his boyhood bed, he found his eyes stung by tears.

He heard Ma come in downstairs, her footsteps pausing in the living room.

"Eric?" She'd seen his truck parked outside.

"Yeah, I'm up here. I'll be right down."

He knuckle-dried his eyes and rose, blew his nose on his bloody handkerchief and clumped down the steep, wooden stairs, breaking his headlong plunge with both hands on the wall above which seemed permanently soiled from the thousands of descents it had slowed.

She was waiting at the bottom, dressed in a quilted nylon jacket of Halloween orange and a cotton scarf covered with dreadful purple cabbage roses, tied tightly beneath her chin. Her glasses were steamed. She raised them onto her forehead and peered at him curiously. "What the devil were you doing up there?"

"Smelling the bat shit. Remembering."

"You all right?"

"I've been crying a little, if that's what you're asking."

"What's wrong?"

"I'm leaving Nancy."

"Ah, that's it." She studied him silently while he realized how little she'd cared for his wife and wondered what she felt. She opened her arms and said, "Come here, son."

He walked against her, took her short, stubby body against his much taller one, breathed the smell of late winter from her jacket, and the faint scent of fuel oil from her scarf and whatever Barb had cooked for supper from her hair.

"I'll need to stay awhile, Ma."

"As long as you want."

"I'll probably be a little grouchy."

She pulled back and looked up at him. "That's your right."

He felt better after the hug. "What happens to people, Ma? They change."

"That's part of life."

"But you and the old man didn't. You made it straight through."

"Why of course we changed. Everybody changes. But we didn't have as many complications in them days. You young people now, you got two dozen different experts telling you how you ought to think and feel and act and how you ought to *find* yourself." Long-lipped, she stretched the word. "Stupid expression . . . *fiiind* yourself. Give each other *space.*" Again she made mockery of the word. "In my day, a man's space was beside his wife, and a wife's was beside her man, and what you gave each other was a helping hand and a little bit of loving if you weren't too tired at the end of the day. But nowadays they'd have you believing that if you don't come first you're doing it wrong, only marriage don't work that way. Oh,

I'm not blaming you, son. I'm saying you were born in a time that was tough on marriages."

"We always got along, Nancy and I. On the surface things seemed okay, but underneath we've been at odds for years about the most important stuff—jobs, kids, where we lived, what we lived in."

"Well, sometimes that happens, I guess."

He'd expected her to show maternal favoritism and was surprised by her neutrality, though he respected her for it, realizing again that she'd never warmed to Nancy.

She heaved a sigh and glanced toward the kitchen. "Have you eaten yet?"

"No, Ma, I'm really not hungry."

Again she surprised him by not nagging. "Yeah, sometimes strife dulls the appetite. Well, I'd best get upstairs and change them sheets. They've been on since Gracie and Dan slept in 'em at Christmas."

"I can do that, Ma. I don't want to be any trouble to you."

"Since when was any of my kids a trouble to me?"

He went over and got her in an affectionate headlock, appreciating her with a freshness that healed.

"Y' know, the world could use a few more like you, Ma." For good measure he gave her skull a knuckle-rub, the way they all had when they were boys.

"Let me go, brat!" she blustered.

He released her, and they went upstairs together to change the bed.

They'd put on the bottom sheet when he told her, "I don't know how long I'll be here, Ma."

She snapped the second sheet in the air with two deft flicks and replied, "I didn't ask, did I?"

He went by Maggie's the next day at midmorning.

"Hi," he said, looking forlorn.

"What happened to your face?"

"Nancy."

"You told her?"

He nodded resignedly. "Come here," he said. "I need to hold you."

Against him, she whispered, "I need to hold you, too, while you tell me."

Each time he came to her their moods seemed a reflection of one another, as if a chord ran through both their hearts. Today they came together for reassurance. Passion had no place in their embrace.

"The news isn't good," he said quietly.

"What did she say?"

"She won't hear of a divorce."

Her hand moved lightly on his back. Her eyes closed. "Oh, no."

"I think she's going to make it as tough on us as she can. She says if she can't have me, you won't either."

"How can I blame her? Could I give you up if you were mine?"

He drew back, his hands on the slope of her neck while brushing the corners of her lips with his thumbs. He studied her soulful eyes.

"I've moved into Ma's, so things are still up in the air."

"What did your mother say?"

"Ma? She's the salt of the earth. She gave me a hug and said stay as long as you need to."

She pressed close to him again. "You're so lucky. I long for a mother I can be honest with."

Each Tuesday afternoon Vera Pearson volunteered her time at the Bayside Nursing Home where she played piano while the old folks sang. Her mother had been a devout Christian who instilled in Vera the importance of charity, both at home and in the community. So on Tuesdays she played piano at Bayside; on Saturdays she arranged altar flowers at the community church; during springtime she helped with the church rummage sale; in autumn she helped with the bake sale; she attended regular meetings of her church circle and the garden society and the Friends of the Library. If at each of these functions Vera garnered any gossip that the *Door County Advocate* had missed, she regarded it as her beholden duty to spread it.

On this particular Tuesday afternoon Vera had whispered to one of the nurses that she'd heard the middle Jennings girl, only a junior in high school, was pee-gee. "It's no wonder," she added, "like mother, like daughter."

After the music they always had "teatime." The coffee was absolutely delicious today, and Vera had one cup with her chocolate-frosted cupcake, two more with a slice of orange bundt cake and another with some coconut cookies.

She was in the restroom behind one of the two beige metal doors, struggling with her control-top panty hose when she heard the big door open and two women entered, conversing.

Sharon Glasgow—one of the nurses at Bayside—said, "Vera Pearson's got a lot to talk about. Her own daughter is having an affair with Eric Severson. Did you hear he left his wife?"

"No!"

The adjacent stall door closed and Vera saw a pair of white shoes beyond the partition.

"He's living at home with his mother."

"Are you kidding!" That was Sandra Ecklestein, a dietician.

"I guess they went together when they were in high school."

"He's really good-looking."

"So's his wife. Have you ever seen her?" On the other side of the partition a toilet flushed while Vera remained still as a broken watch. The dividing wall quivered as it was thumped by a door, and the white shoes went away. Another pair appeared. The faucet ran and the hand dryer whined and the routine was repeated while the two women went on to talk about other things.

When the room grew quiet, Vera hid a long time in her stall, afraid to go out until she was certain the two women had gone elsewhere in the building.

What did I do wrong? she thought. I was the best mother I knew how to be. I made her go to church, I set a good example by staying with one man my whole life, I gave her a clean home with good food on the table and a mother always in it. I set curfews and report card standards and made sure she never hung around with any riff-raff. But the minute she came back she ran off to that town meeting with him.

I warned her this could happen! Didn't I warn her?

Vera didn't drive. In a town the size of Fish Creek she didn't need to, but, trudging up Cottage Row on foot, she wished she did. Reaching Maggie's door, she was winded.

She knocked and waited, her purse handle over both wrists, which were pressed against her rib cage.

Maggie opened the back door and exclaimed, "Mother, this is a surprise! Come in."

Vera marched inside, puffing.

"Let me take your coat and I'll put on some coffee."

"No coffee for me. I've just had five cups at the home."

"The weekly sing-along?"

"Yes."

Maggie put the coat in the maid's room and returned to find Vera perched on a chair with her purse on her knees.

"Tea? A Coke? Anything?"

"No, nothing."

Maggie took a chair at a right angle to Vera's.

"Did you walk up?"

"Yes."

"You should have called. I would have come down and gotten you."

"You can take me back down after . . ." Vera paused.

Her tone warned Maggie something was wrong. "After?"

"I'm afraid I've come here on unpleasant business."

"Oh?"

Vera pinched her purse clasp with both hands. "You're seeing that Severson boy, aren't you?"

Taken aback, Maggie took some time in replying. "If I said yes, Mother, would you be willing to talk about it with me?"

"I *am* talking about it. The whole town is talking about it! They say he's left his wife and moved in with his mother. Is that true?"

"No."

"Don't lie to me, Margaret! I didn't raise you that way!"

"He *is* living with his mother, but he left his wife because he doesn't love her anymore."

"Oh, for heaven's sake, Margaret, is that how you excuse yourself?"

"I don't need excuses."

"Are you having an affair with him?"

"Yes!" Maggie shouted, jumping to her feet. "Yes, I'm having an affair with him! Yes, I love him! Yes, we plan to get married as soon as he gets a divorce!"

Vera thought of all the women in the altar society and the garden society and the church circle and the Friends of the Library, women she'd known her whole life long. She relived the sting of embarrassment she'd felt in the lavatory at the home this morning.

"How will I ever face the ladies of my church circle again?"

"Is that all that matters to you, Mother?"

"I have been a member of that church for more than fifty years, Margaret, and in all that time I've never had the slightest thing to hang my head about. Now this. You're not back in town but a few months and you're involved in this scandal. It's disgraceful."

"If it is, it's my disgrace, Mother, not yours."

"Oh, you're very smug, aren't you—just listen to yourself, believing everything he tells you, like some fool. Do you really think he intends to divorce his wife and marry you? How many women do you think have been told that line over the years? He's after your money, Margaret, can't you see that?"

"Oh, Mother . . ." Maggie dropped to a chair, overcome with disappointment. "Why couldn't you just once in your life be a support to me instead of tearing me down?"

"If you think I'd support such goings-on—"

"No, I didn't think you would. I'd never think that, because in all my life you've never given me credit for anything."

"Least of all good sense." Earnestly Vera learned forward and rested an arm on the table. "Margaret, you're a rich woman, and if you aren't wise enough to realize that men will be after you for your money, I am."

"No . . ." Maggie shook her head slowly. "Eric is not after my money. But I'm not going to sit here and defend him or myself because I don't have to. I'm an adult now, and I'll live my life the way I please."

"And embarrass your father and I without the slightest thought for our feelings?"

"Mother, I'm sorry for that, truly I am, but I can only say again, it's my affair, not yours or Daddy's. Let me take responsibility for my feelings, and you take responsibility for yours."

"Don't talk to me in your high-brow counselor's talk! You know how I hate it."

"Very well, I'll ask you something straight out, because I've always wondered." Maggie looked her mother square in the face. "Do you love me, Mother?"

Vera reacted as if someone had accused her of being a Communist. "Why, of course I do. What kind of a question is that?"

"An honest one. Because you've never told me."

"I kept your clothes clean, and the house perfect, and good meals on the table, didn't I?"

"A butler could do that. What I wanted was understanding, some show of affection, a hug when I came home, someone to take my side now and then."

"I hugged you."

"No. You allowed yourself to be hugged. There's a difference."

"I don't know what you want of me, Margaret. I guess I never have."

"For starters, you could stop giving orders. To both me and Daddy."

"Now you're blaming me for something else. A woman's place is to keep the home running smoothly."

"By dictating and criticizing? Mother, there are better ways."

"Oh, now I've done that wrong, too! Well, your father hasn't had any complaints, and he and I have been together for forty-five years—"

"And I've never seen you hug him, or ask him if he had a good day, or rub his neck. Instead, when he comes home, you say, 'Roy, take off your shoes, I just scrubbed the floor.' When I come home you say, 'Why didn't you let me know you were coming.' When Katy drove up for Thanksgiving you scolded her because she didn't have boots. Doesn't it strike you, Mother, that we might like something more in the way of a greeting? That now, at this rather emotional time in my life, when I could use someone to confide in, I might appreciate your coming to me to ask how I feel instead of accusing me of shaming you and Daddy?''

"It strikes me that I came in here confronting you with your loose actions, and you've managed to turn the blame on me for something I've never done. Well, I can only repeat, in forty-five years your dad has never complained.''

"No," Maggie returned sadly. "He's just moved into the garage.''

Vera's face turned crimson. Roy was the wrong one for moving into the garage! And she didn't dictate and criticize; she only kept things in line. Why, if it were left to Roy the floors would be full of scuff marks and their meals would be eaten at any ungodly hour and they'd be late to church every Sunday. And here was this ungrateful child, whom Vera had given every advantage—hand-sewn dresses, Sunday school, a college education—telling Vera she could use improvement!

"I thought I raised you to respect your parents, but obviously that's another area where I've failed." Summoning her shattered pride, Vera rose from her chair wearing a hurt look on her face. "I won't bother you again, Margaret, and until you're ready to apologize to me, you needn't bother me, either. I can find my coat.''

"Mother, please . . . can't we talk about this?''

Vera got her coat from the maid's room and donned it. Returning to the kitchen she attended to pulling on her gloves, never glancing at Maggie again.

"You needn't take me down the hill. I can walk.''

"Mother, wait.''

But Vera left without another word.

Closing the door upon her daughter, she felt her heart would surely break. That's all the thanks a mother gets, she thought, as she headed down the hill toward home.

That evening when Maggie saw Eric she said, "My mother was here this morning.''

"What did she say?''

"She demanded to know if I was having an affair with 'that Severson boy.' ''

He snapped shut a carpenter's rule and stepped down off a chair seat to gather her close. They were standing in one of the guest bedrooms where he was helping her insert a molly screw to hang a large-framed mirror.

"I'm sorry, Maggie. I never wanted that to happen.''

"I told her yes.''

He drew back in surprise. "You *told* her that?''

"Well, I am, aren't I? I chose to." With her fingertips she touched his cheek just below the fingernail marks where thin scabs had formed. "I can accept it if you can.''

"An affair . . . aw Maggie M'girl, what am I putting you through? What more will I put you through? This isn't what I wanted for you, for us. I wanted it to be legitimate.''

"Until it can be, I'll settle for this.''

"I filed for divorce today," he told her. "If everything goes right, we could be married a half year from now. But I've made a decision, Maggie.''

"What?"

"I'm not staying here overnight anymore. It looks too tacky, and I don't want people gossiping about you."

In the weeks that followed, he came to her most days. Mornings, sometimes, bringing fresh doughnuts; often at suppertime, bringing fish. Sometimes weary, falling asleep on her sofa, other times happier, wanting to eat, laugh, drive with the truck windows down. He came the day of ice-out, when the debacle on the lake signaled winter's end. And the day she got her first unexpected guests who'd gotten her name from the Door Chamber of Commerce and simply walked up to the door asking if she had a room. She was giddy with excitement that night and lit a fire in the guest parlor, making sure the candy bowl was filled and that there were plenty of books and magazines on hand. Her guests returned from having dinner uptown and knocked on the closed kitchen door to ask some questions. When Maggie introduced Eric by only his first name, the man shook his hand and said, "Nice to meet you, Mr. Stearn."

He helped Maggie put the dock in and built a new arbor seat which she'd decided she wanted at the end of the dock instead of clear back by the tennis court, which had lost much of its charm as a parking lot. When the last nail was driven they sat on the new arbor seat holding hands and watching the sun set.

"Katy has agreed to come and work for me this summer," she told him.

"When?" he asked.

"School is out the last week in May."

Their eyes met and his thumb stroked the back of her hand. After a wordless exchange she quietly laid her head on his shoulder.

He came the day he put the *Mary Deare* in the water, sailing in below the house and bleating his horn, bringing Maggie flying to the front porch to wave and smile as he'd often pictured.

"Come on down!" he called, and she raced down the verdant spring grass between rows of blossoming iris, and onto his deck to be borne away over the waves.

And again, later, when the Montmorencies and McIntoshes were in full bloom, he came in his battered pickup, cleaned both outside and in for the occasion and bedecked with blossoms that held Maggie momentarily in thrall, then brought tears to her eyes. He took her to an orchard in full bloom, laden with scent and color and birdsong, but once there they shared only a melancholy silence, sitting wistful, holding hands again.

May arrived and with it warm enough weather to paint the unheated apartment over the garage. He helped her prepare it for Katy, furnishing it with familiar pieces from the Seattle house.

Mid-month brought a steady stream of tourists and fewer times together, then their last night before Katy came home for the summer.

They said good-bye on the deck of the *Mary Deare* at ten after one in the morning, loath to part, surrounded by blackness and the soft swash of waves against the hull.

"I'll miss you."

"I'll miss you, too."

"I'll come when I can, in the boat, after dark."

"It'll be hard to get away."

"Watch for me around eleven. I'll blink the lights."

They kissed farewell with the same anguish they'd suffered when college had forced them apart.

"I love you."

"I love you, too."

She backed away, holding hands until their outstretched fingertips no longer touched.

"Marry me," he whispered.

"I promise."

But the words were mere pining, for though he'd filed for divorce immediately after leaving Nancy, the correspondence from her attorney remained unchanged: Ms. Macaffee would not agree to a divorce, but desired instead a reconciliation.

Chapter 15

❧

Katy had made up her mind she'd give her mother the benefit of the doubt. Grandma had written and said, your mother is having an affair with a married man, but Katy had decided she'd ask her mother straight-out. She was sure Grandma was wrong; it was something she only suspected. After the words they'd had at Christmas, she didn't see how her mother could possibly have done anything except refuse to see her old boyfriend again.

She stopped in Egg Harbor and put the top down on the convertible. It was a hot spring day and she had to admit, it felt wonderful to leave Chicago behind. Living by the lake might not be so bad after all, though she wasn't too sure how she'd like being a cleaning lady. But what other choice did she have? Until she graduated from college her mother controlled the money, and her mother had not invited Katy as a guest. She'd invited her as an employee.

Cleaning. Shit. Scrubbing the pots after strangers had used them, and changing sheets with curly black hairs in them. It was still beyond Katy why her mother wanted to be an innkeeper. A woman with a million dollars in the bank.

Her hair whipped in the wind and she glanced around to make sure nothing was in danger of sailing out of the backseat.

She returned her eyes to the road, the countryside ahead. Crimeny, it *was* a pretty place. Everything getting green and the orchards in full bloom. She *did* want to get along with her mother. She *did*. But her mother had changed so much since Daddy died. All this independence, and it seemed as if she just forged ahead and did things without considering Katy's feelings. And if what Grandma had said was true, what then?

Fish Creek was back in full swing. The doors of the shops along Main Street were standing open, most without even screen doors. Tulips were in bloom out in front of the post office, and down by the town docks sailboats were already moored.

Up on Cottage Row the summer places had been reopened for the season and a man was out trimming shrubs beside a stone entry into one of them.

At her mother's, a new sign hung: HARDING HOUSE, A BED-AND-BREAKFAST INN. Next to the garage Maggie's Lincoln was parked beside another with Minnesota license plates. Katy pulled in next to them, got out and stretched, and grabbed a load from the backseat.

She wasn't halfway down the steps before Maggie came charging out, smiling, calling, "Hi, honey!"

"Hi, Mom."

"Oh, it's so good to see you."

In the middle of the walk they embraced, then Maggie took one suitcase and they headed toward the garage, chatting about the trip up, the end of school, the nice spring weather.

"I have a surprise for you," Maggie said, leading Katy up the steps that climbed the outside wall of the building. She opened the door. "I thought you'd like a place of your own."

Katy looked around the room with wide eyes.

"The old furniture . . . oh, Mom . . ."

"You'll have to use the bathroom facilities in the house, and eat there with me, but at least you'll have some privacy."

Katy gave her mother a hug. "Oh, thank you, Mom, I love it."

Katy loved her lodgings, but her enthusiasm quickly changed to dismay when she was faced with the realities of having guests in the main house, moving about at all hours. Maggie kept the kitchen door to the hall closed so that the portion of the house reserved for their private use seemed hemmed in. That afternoon there were no less than five knocks on the hall door, bringing bothersome questions from guests. (Can we use the phone? Where can we rent bicycles? What restaurant would you recommend? Where can we buy film, bait, picnic food?) The telephone rang incessantly and the overhead footsteps seemed an intrusion. In late afternoon a new party checked in and Maggie had to interrupt meal preparations to show them upstairs and get them registered. By suppertime Katy was totally disenchanted.

"Mother, are you sure this was the right thing to do?"

"What's wrong?"

Katy gestured toward the hall door. "All the interruptions. People coming and going and the phone ringing."

"This is a business. You have to expect that."

"But why are you doing this when you have enough money that you wouldn't have to work for the rest of your life?"

"And what else should I do with the rest of my life? Eat chocolates? Go on shopping sprees? Katy, I have to be occupied by something vital."

"But couldn't you have bought a gift shop or become an Avon lady— something that wouldn't bring your customers into the house?"

"I could have, but I didn't."

"Grandma says this was a foolish move."

Maggie bristled. "Oh? And when did you talk to Grandma?"

"She wrote."

Maggie took a bite of chicken salad without remarking.

"She said something else that's been bothering me, too."

Maggie rested her wrist on the table edge and waited.

Katy looked square at her. "Mother, are you still seeing that Eric Severson?"

Maggie took a drink of water, considering her answer. Setting the glass down, she replied, "Occasionally."

Katy dropped her fork and threw up her hands. "Oh, Mother, I don't believe it."

"Katy, I told you before—"

"I know you told me to butt out, but can't you see what you're doing? He's married!"

"He's getting a divorce."

"Oh, sure, I'll bet that's what they all say."

"Katy, that was uncalled for!"

"All right, all right, I apologize." Katy held up her hands like a traffic cop. "But I'm appalled just the same, and I think it's a hell of a shameful situation." She jumped to her feet, took her plate to the garbage and spanked it clean with three loud whacks of a fork.

Maggie forgot about finishing her supper. She watched her daughter moving angrily to the sink. How was it that since last fall they had been on this merry-go-round of aggravation with one another? No sooner did they reach some truce, than up flared the tempers again. Other parents went through this during their children's teenage years, but for the Stearn family those had been surprisingly calm. Maggie had thought she'd made it through raising Katy with unusual luck only to find the distress beginning now at the time she'd thought they'd be most close.

"You know, Katy," she said reasonably, "if we're going to be at each other like this all the time, it'll make for a very long summer. Furthermore, our guests can sense if there's friction in the house, and they deserve to be greeted with genuine smiles. There'll be times when you'll be the one greeting them, so if you don't think you can handle it, tell me now."

"I can handle it!" Katy snapped and left the room.

When she was gone Maggie sighed, propped her elbows on the table and massaged her forehead with eight fingertips. She sat for some time, staring down at her plate and the unfinished chicken salad.

Suddenly the pieces started swimming and a tear plopped onto a leaf of wilted lettuce.

Damn, not again! Why am I doing this so often lately?

Because you miss Eric and you're tired of all the duplicity, weary of fighting your family and afraid that maybe he never will get free.

She was still sitting there wet-eyed when a guest knocked on the hall door. *Go away,* she thought, *I'm tired and I need this cry.* Tired—yes, she'd been so tired lately. For a moment as she pushed to her feet her head felt light. Then she swiped her eyes with a sleeve, put on a cheerful face and went to answer the knock.

It became apparent with Katy's first day of work that maintaining discipline as an employer of one's own daughter would present problems for Maggie. Like the parent giving her own child piano lessons, she found her orders taken lightly and followed sluggishly:

"I'll be there in a minute."

"You mean I have to dust the furniture every *day?"*

"But it's too hot to clean all three bathrooms!"

Though Katy's dilatory attitude incensed Maggie she refrained from badgering in hopes of minimizing the tension between them.

Then on the third day after Katy's arrival, her listlessness received a shot of adrenaline. She was stuffing soiled sheets into a canvas laundry bag when a lawnmower roared past the window, pushed by a shirtless young man dressed in red shorts and sockless Nikes.

"Who's that!" Katy exclaimed, staring, stalking him from window to window.

Maggie glanced outside. "That's Brookie's son, Todd."

"Mowing *our* lawn?"

"I hired him as my handyman. He comes two days a week to do the heavy work—mow, trim, clean the beach, take care of the garbage."

Katy strained to watch him, her forehead bumping the screen as the mower moved beyond range and decrescendoed.

"Wow, he's cute!"

"Yes, he is."

Katy made the dust bounce for the remainder of the morning and found countless opportunities to step outside: to shake the dust mop and rugs, to sweep the porches and carry trash up the hill to the dumpster beside the garage. She finished her cleaning in record time and careened downstairs, halting, breathless, beside Maggie who sat at her desk in their personal parlor.

"I scrubbed all three bathrooms, changed the beds, dusted the bedrooms *and* the guest parlor, including the windowsills. Can I be done now?"

Their agreement had been that Katy would work each day until two o'clock and after that would take turns with Maggie being available to check in arriving guests. During neither of her first two days had she completed her work by two; today, however, she was done by 12:15.

"All right, but I need to buy groceries sometime this afternoon, so be back here by three."

Katy scudded across to the garage, appearing minutes later in the yard wearing clean white shorts, a red halter top and fresh makeup with her hair in a neat French braid. Todd was emptying grass clippings into a black plastic bag.

"Here, I'll hold that for you," Katy called as she approached him.

Todd glanced over his shoulder and straightened. "Oh, hi."

Wow, what a build. And magnificent black hair, and a face that probably stopped girls in their tracks all the time. His bare torso and brow were beaded with sweat and he wore a white headband.

"Hi. You're Brookie's son."

"Yeah, and you must be Maggie's daughter."

"My name is Katy." She extended her hand.

"Mine's Todd." He shook it with a hard, dirty hand.

"I know. Mother told me."

She held the bag open while he dumped the grass inside. Standing close to him she caught the scent of tropical suntan lotion mixed with the green scent of the fresh grass cuttings.

"I saw you come outside before," he told her, stealing a glance at her bare midriff.

"I clean for my mother."

"So you're going to be here all summer?"

"Yup. I'll be going back to Northwestern in the fall, though. My second year there."

"I'm going into the Air Force in September. Thanks." He took the bag from her and knelt to replace the grass catcher on the mower.

From above, she studied his tan, sweating shoulders, the slope of his vertebrae and the wet black curls at his nape. "Sounds like our mothers were pretty good friends."

"Yeah. I suppose you heard the same stories I did."

"The Senior Scourges, you mean?"

He glanced up and they laughed. She loved the way his face crinkled when he did that. He rose to his full height, wiping his palms on his shorts while they looked each other over and tried to appear as if they were not, then let their interest ricochet toward the lake.

"Well, I'd better let you get back to work," she said reluctantly.

"Yeah. I've got another yard to do this afternoon."

She turned her head and caught him eyeing her bare midriff again. Abruptly he lifted his eyes and they both spoke at once.

"I'll be—"

"Where do—"

He flashed her a quick grin and said, "You first."

"I was just going to ask where the kids hang out around here."

"And I was going to say that I'll be done with my afternoon job around five. If you want I could take you out to City Beach and introduce you around. I know just about everyone in Door—everyone but the tourists, that is, and I even know a few of them."

She flashed him a bright smile. "Okay. I'd like that."

"After supper we pretty much hang out at the C-C Club down on Main Street. They have live bands in there."

"Sounds fun," she replied.

"I could come and pick you up around six."

"Sounds great! See you then."

Maggie noticed the change in Katy immediately. Her temperament mollified; she hummed and talked to her mother; she called a cheery good-bye upon leaving the house with Todd.

But by two A.M. Maggie hadn't heard Katy come in to use the bathroom. The following day Katy slept until ten and arose only under duress. For the next three nights she went out with Todd again, arising later and later each day, and when Sunday came, she grumbled about having to work at all. "It's Todd's only day off and we wanted to go to the beach early."

"You can go as soon as your cleaning is done."

"But, Mom . . ."

"It would have been done already if you'd gotten up when you should have!" Maggie snapped.

During the days that followed, while Katy saw more and more of Todd, Maggie burned with indignation, not over her dating—Todd was a pleasant boy, a hard worker, prompt and unfailingly polite—but because of her daughter's cavalier attitude about work. Maggie resented being put in the position of having to revert to mothering tactics that harked back to Katy's young teen days. She resented becoming the night watch. She resented Katy's blithe assumption that she could bend her hours to suit her personal needs.

There was something else that bothered Maggie, too, something she had not expected. She missed her privacy. After so few months of independence she found she'd grown accustomed to eating—or not eating—when she wished; to finding the bathroom the way she'd left it, her cosmetics where she'd put them; to having the radio on the station of her choice, and the kitchen sink free of dirty glasses. Even though Katy slept in the garage apartment the house was not her own anymore, and many times she felt small and guilty for her reaction. Because she realized that it might all be a subterfuge to disguise the one greatest imposition Katy's presence had created; it had forced an end to her evenings with Eric.

Maggie wished she could talk to someone about these complex feelings, but her own mother had put herself off limits, and since Todd was involved, Brookie was out.

Then one night eight days after Katy's arrival, Eric came.

Maggie jolted out of a deep sleep and lay tense, listening. Some sound had awakened her. She'd been dreaming she was a child, playing Red Rover in the tall grass beside a square yellow-brick schoolhouse when the school bell rang and awakened her. She lay staring at the black ceiling, listening to the midnight chorus of crickets and frogs, until finally it came again—the faint ting not of a school bell, but of a ship's bell, close enough to be heard, distant enough not to disturb. Intuition told her it was he, calling her with the familiar brass bell hanging above the *Mary Deare*'s cabin.

With racing heart she leapt from bed and scrambled through a dresser drawer, yanking on the first shorts she found, beneath her hip-length nightshirt. The clock said eleven. Running through the dark house, Maggie felt her heart clubbing in anticipation. She slipped like a wraith down the hall and out the front door, across the deep front porch and down the steps between the fragrant bridal wreaths that hung with great white ropes of flowers; toward the vast blackness of the lake where the soft chug of the *Mary Deare*'s engines rippled the night water and diffused the reflection of the moon; downhill . . . barefoot . . . across the dewy grass . . . beneath the black lace of maple arms until she heard the engines cut, then the light swash of waves against the dock pilings, then her own bare heels thumping on the wooden platform, feeling it buck as the boat hove against it.

He appeared as an apparition in white, as silent and ghostly as the *Mary Deare* itself, waiting at the rail with arms uplifted as she sailed into them like some lost pigeon homing at last.

"Oh, darling, I've missed you. Hold me, please . . . hold me."

"Ah, Maggie . . . Maggie . . ."

He hauled her tight against his bare chest, against the white trousers rolled to mid-calf. Spraddle-legged, he braced against the faint roll of the deck, kissing her as if to do so were to heal from some awful abuse.

Like a sudden tropical shower, her tears came, bursting forth without warning.

"Maggie, what is it?" He drew back, trying to lift her face, which she, abashed, hid against his shoulder.

"I don't know. It's just silly."

"Are you all right?"

"Yes . . . no . . . I don't know. I've been on the verge of this all day, for no good reason. I'm sorry, Eric."

"No, no . . . it's all right. You go ahead and cry." He held her loosely, rubbing her back.

"But I feel so silly, and I'm getting your chest wet." She sniffled against his slick bare skin and gave it two swipes with the butt of her hand.

"Go ahead, get it wet. It won't shrink."

"Oh, Eric . . ." After a halfhearted snuffle she began calming and settled comfortably against his widespread thighs. "I don't know what it is with me lately."

"Bad week?"

Her nod bumped his chin. "Could I unload on you, please?"

"Of course."

It felt so good to lean against him and spill out her feelings. "It's not working out, hiring Katy," she began. She told him everything—about Katy's late-night hours and how it affected her work; about the difficulty of supervising one's own daughter; about being unable to discuss it with Brookie; and her own sense of being trapped in a phase of motherhood she thought she'd outlived. She confessed her own abnormal irritability lately and her heartsoreness at losing even the thinnest line of contact with her own mother. She told him, too, that Katy knew she was seeing him and that they'd had words about it.

"So I needed you tonight . . . very badly."

"I needed you, too."

"Did you have a bad week, too?"

He told her about the grand hoopla at Mike and Barb's house this past week, first on Saturday when the whole tribe pitched in to throw a big graduation party for Nicholas; and last night when Barb had had a baby girl—two weeks late, but big and healthy and named Anna after her grandmother.

"In one week they send off one child into the world and bring another one into it," he reflected sadly.

"And you have none—that's what's bothering you, isn't it?"

He sighed and shrugged it off, held her by both arms and looked down into her face. "Something else happened last weekend."

"Tell me."

"Nancy came out to Ma's, begging for a reconciliation, and today my lawyer advised me it won't set well with the courts if I refuse to at least try a reconciliation when my wife is asking for one."

Maggie searched his face, consternation on her own.

"Don't worry," he added quickly, "I love you. You're the only one I love, and I promise I won't go back to her. Not ever." He kissed her mouth, tenderly at first, then with growing ardor, his tongue wet and sleek upon hers.

"Oh, Maggie, I do, I love you so." His voice sounded tortured. "I ache to be free so I can marry you, so you don't have to suffer your daughter's scorn and your mother's."

"I know." She took her turn at comforting him, touching his face, tracing his eyebrows. "Someday."

"Someday," he repeated with an edge of impatience. "But when!"

"Shh . . ." She calmed him, kissed his soft mouth, and coerced him into forgetting, for a while. "I love you, too. Let's make some new memories . . . here . . . underneath the stars."

The moon cast their shadow onto the wooden deck—one long spear against the lighter boards as they drew close and became one unbroken line. He opened his mouth upon hers, drew her hips flush to his, and ran his hands down the slope of her spine, flaring out and catching her buttocks to force her up hard against him. She lifted on tiptoe, running her nails up his skull, then down his naked shoulders. He captured her breasts beneath the loose-fitting T-shirt, caught her beneath the arms and lifted her toward the stars, holding her suspended as he closed his mouth upon her right breast. She winced and he murmured, "I'm sorry . . . sorry . . . I get too impatient . . ." Softer, he opened his mouth upon her, wetting her shirt, and her skin, and the deepest reaches within her. She put her throat to the sky and felt his arms quivering, and herself quivering, and the night air quivering around them, and she thought, Don't let me lose him. Don't let her win.

When she slid down his body, her hand led the way, skimming his chest and belly, then cupping him, low.

"Come on," he whispered urgently, catching her hand and leading her fore, where a canopy sliced off the moonlight and the panel lights illuminated their faces with a pale phosphorescence. Starting the engine, he perched on the hip-high stool and settled her between his thighs, facing Green Bay, slipping one hand inside her underwear, caressing her intimately as he took them away from shore.

Reaching back, she stroked him through his trousers, riding over the star-kissed waters, absorbing its slap and lap against the hull, and the smell of his warm hide and the brush of his hair as he lowered his face to the slope of her shoulder.

A mere twenty-five feet offshore he dropped anchor. They made love on the cool wooden deck, in a lunge and lift that matched the motion of the boat on the pliant night waves. It was as consuming as always, but beneath its wonder was an underlying thread of sadness. For he was not hers, and she was not his, and this above all they desired.

When it was over, he lay above her, his elbows braced on either side of her head. She studied his moon-shadowed face, what she could make out of it, and felt love inundate her once again with an immeasurable force. "Sometimes," she whispered, "isn't it hard to express it? In words powerful enough or meaningful enough?"

He touched her moonlit brow, stretched her auburn tresses upon the decking until they lay like a nimbus around her. He searched for ways he might express it, but he was no poet or philosopher.

"I'm afraid 'I love you' will have to do. That says it all."

"And I love you."

They carried the thought back to shore, captured it within for the days of separation ahead, reiterated it with their farewell kiss, clung to it as she bid him good-bye and left him standing on the end of the dock watching her up the hill.

At the top she turned and waved, then resolutely plodded up the front porch steps.

From the shadows came a voice. Hard. Condemning. "Hello, Mother."

Maggie started. "Katy!"

"I'm here, too, Mrs. Stearn."

"Oh . . . Todd." They'd been necking in the dark. It was obvious even without benefit of light. "You two are out rather late, aren't you?"

Katy's clipped response dared her mother to challenge her. "Seems everybody is."

From below came the sound of the *Mary Deare*'s engine as she skimmed away from the dock. Maggie realized Katy had had a clear view of the dock and as her eyes adjusted to the shadows of the front porch, she saw Katy staring at her nightshirt and bare feet, judging, reprehending. Maggie blushed and felt guilt come nettling. She wanted to say, *But I'm older than you, and wiser, and I fully understand the vagaries of this course upon which I've embarked.*

All which served as a harsh reminder to Maggie that she was setting a double standard when she should instead be setting a good example.

After that night, the thought troubled her. She had not before given much thought to promiscuity. It was something against which girls were warned during adolescence, but upon maturity Maggie had considered the affair her choice and hers alone.

Perhaps it was not.

With an impressionable eighteen-year-old daughter in the house, dating a handsome, undoubtedly virile young man, perhaps it was not.

Katy's late nights continued and Maggie awakened often to lie and worry, wander to the bathroom and through the dark house, wondering if she should talk to Brookie about it after all. But to what avail?

Her interrupted sleep began telling, and she grew sluggish, occasionally queasy, sometimes weak. She had never been a snacker, but began snacking thoughtlessly, a nervous reaction to the stress, she figured. She gained five pounds. Her bras didn't fit. Then one day she realized the oddest thing: her shoes didn't fit.

My shoes?

She stood beside her bed, staring at her feet which looked like a pair of overgrown potatoes.

My ankle bones don't even show!

Something was wrong. Something was very wrong. She added it all up: fluid retention, tiredness, irritability, sore breasts, weight gain. It was menopausal, she was sure—the symptoms all fit. She made an appointment with a gynecologist in Sturgeon Bay.

Dr. David Macklin had had the perspicacity to have the ceiling of his examination room painted with a floral motif. Lying on her back on the examination table, Maggie distracted herself by identifying the flowers. Tulips, lilacs and roses she knew. Were the white ones cherry blossoms? In Door County, how appropriate. The lighting was diffuse, illuminating the ceiling indirectly from the pale lavender walls, a restful room that put a patient as much as possible at ease.

Dr. Macklin completed his examination, lowered Maggie's crackling paper gown and gave her a helping hand.

"All right, you can sit up now."

She perched on the end of the table, watching him roll his stool to a wall-hung desk where he wrote in a manila folder, a mid-thirtyish man balding too young but wearing a great, bushy brown moustache, as if to make up for Nature's slight on his dome. His eyebrows, too, were thick and dark, dropping like parentheses beside his friendly blue eyes. He glanced up and asked, "How long ago was your last period?"

"My last real period—right around the time Phillip died, almost two years ago."

"What do you mean by real period?"

"The way it always was. Regular, a full four days."

"And after his death it stopped abruptly?"

"Yes, when I started experiencing the hot flashes I told you about. I've had some spotty periods off and on, but they didn't amount to much."

"Have you had any hot flashes lately?"

She considered before answering, "No, not lately."

"How about night sweats, any of those?"

"No."

"But your breasts have been tender?"

"Yes."

"How long?"

"I don't know. A couple of months maybe. I really don't remember."

"Do you get up fairly often in the middle of the night to urinate?"

"Two or three times."

"Is that normal for you?"

"No, I guess not, but my daughter lives with me and she's been staying out rather late. I have trouble sleeping soundly until she gets in."

"How has your temperament been lately? Have you been irritable, depressed?"

"My daughter and I seem to argue a lot. It's been a rather stressful situation with her living at home again."

Dr. Macklin hooked an elbow on the desk behind him and relaxed against it. "Well, Mrs. Stearn," he said, "I'm afraid this isn't menopausal, as you thought. Quite the opposite, as a matter of fact. My best guess is that you're approximately four and a half months pregnant."

Had he produced a ten-pound maul and bounced it off her head, David Macklin could not have stunned Maggie more.

For seconds she sat slack-jawed, gaping. When she found her voice it was incredulous. "But that's impossible!"

"Do you mean you haven't had intercourse in the past five months?"

"No. I mean, yes, I have but . . . but . . ."

"Did you take any precautions?"

"No, because I didn't think it was necessary. I mean . . ." She laughed—a short, tense call for understanding. "I'm going to be forty-one years old next month. I started having signs of menopause nearly two years ago and . . . and . . . well, I thought I was beyond that."

"It may surprise you to learn that a good ten percent of my patients nowadays are women in their forties, and many of them mistook their symptoms for menopause. Perhaps it would help if I explained a little bit about it and how it begins. Menopause is brought on by the body decreasing its output of the female hormone, estrogen. But the reproductive system doesn't close shop overnight. In some cases it may last over a period of years, causing the system to vary from month to month. Some months the ovaries function normally and the body produces enough estrogen to bring on a normal period. But at other times the ovaries fail to produce adequate hormones so ovulation does not occur. In your case, obviously, on one given month when you experienced intercourse, your system produced adequate estrogen to trigger ovulation, so here you are.''

"But . . . but what about the hot flashes? I told you, I went to the emergency room thinking I was having a heart attack, and a nurse and an intern watched the hot flash happening and identified it. They watched the color climbing my chest and they told me what it was. What about that?''

"Mrs. Stearn, you must understand, hot flashes can be caused by conditions other than menopause. Your husband died a rather dramatic and untimely death. I imagine the newspapers were hounding you and there were lawyers involved, and a daughter to console, legalities to get in order. You were under a great deal of stress, weren't you?''

Maggie nodded, too upset to trust her voice, feeling her eyes begin to tear.

"Well, stress is one of the culprits that can trigger hot flashes and undoubtedly it did at that time. Because you were informed, and because you were of the age where you could expect menopause to begin, you took it for that. It's an understandable mistake and, as I said, a common one.''

"But I . . .'' She gulped and swallowed. "Are you sure? Couldn't you be mistaken?''

"I'm afraid not. All the symptoms are there—the wall of your cervix is slightly bluish in color, the genitals are swollen, your breasts are enlarged and tender and the veins highly colored, you've been experiencing water retention, tiredness, increased urination, weight gain, and probably a grab bag of other discomforts—cramps, heartburn, constipation, lower-back ache, leg cramps, maybe even a temper tantrum or two and a few unexplained tears. Am I right?''

Maggie recalled her many bouts of irritation with Katy, the outgrown bras and shoes, the nocturnal trips to the bathroom and the night she'd stepped onto the *Mary Deare* and burst into tears for no apparent reason. Glumly, she nodded, then dropped her eyes to her lap, abashed by the fact that she had begun to cry.

Dr. Macklin rolled his stool nearer and fixed his sympathetic attention upon her.

"I take it from your signs of distress that you're single.''

"Yes . . . yes, I am.''

"Ah . . . well, that always complicates matters.''

"And I run a bed-and-breakfast inn.'' She lifted brimming brown eyes and spread her hands in appeal. "How can I do that with a baby in the house, waking for his night feedings?''

Dropping her head, she swiped at the tears with the side of her hand. Macklin plucked up three paper tissues and handed them to her, then sat nearby, waiting for her to collect her emotions. When she'd calmed, he said, "You realize, of course, that you're beyond the stage of fetal development where abortion is either safe or legal.''

She lifted beleaguered eyes. "Yes, I realize that, but it wouldn't have been a consideration, in any case.''

He nodded. "And the baby's father—is he in the picture?''

She met his kind, blue eyes, dried her own then rested her hands in her lap. "There are complications.''

"I see. Nevertheless, I must advise you to tell him as soon as possible. In these days of human rights awareness, we realize that fathers have the right to know of the baby's existence and to have the opportunity to plan for its welfare, just as the mother does, and as soon as the mother does."

"I understand. Of course I'll tell him."

"And your daughter—how old did you say she is?"

"Eighteen." At the thought of Katy, Maggie braced an elbow on her belly and dropped her face to her hand. "How ironic. Here I've been lying in bed at night worrying about this happening to her, wondering if I should bring up the subject of birth control. Oh, Katy's going to be appalled."

Dr. Macklin rose and stood beside Maggie with a hand on her shoulder. "Give yourself some time to adjust to the fact before you tell your daughter. It's your baby, your life, your ultimate happiness you should be concerned with. Certainly a barrage of accusations is not what you need right now."

"No . . . it's . . . I . . ." Maggie's thoughts became disjointed by the enormity of her plight. Sadness and panic besieged her by turns. Myriad concerns flashed through her mind, one upon the other, in no specific priority.

I'll be fifty-seven before this child finishes high school.

Everyone will know it's Eric's and he's still married.

What will Mother say?

I'll have to close the business.

I don't want this responsibility!

Dr. Macklin was speaking, instructing her to eliminate all alcohol and over-the-counter drugs from her intake, inquiring whether she smoked, handing her sample vials of prenatal pills, advising that she cut down on the use of salt and increase her intake of dairy foods and fresh vegetables, rest periodically with her feet elevated, do moderate low-impact exercise such as walking, and make an appointment for a return visit.

She heard his voice through a haze of thoughts that ran like gurgling currents through her head. She replied distractedly, yes, no, all right, I will.

Leaving the clinic, she experienced a feeling of displacement, as if she'd assumed the identity of another, fluttering above and behind the woman below like some watchful angel, while that woman whose pumps clicked along the sidewalk was the one who had just learned she was carrying a child out of wedlock and would inherit all the complication of such a situation.

Suspended above herself she could remain aloof from the cares of the other. She could know and watch but remain beyond direct involvement, enveloped in this anesthetized state of observant dispassion.

For a while she felt almost euphoric, divorced from the cloudburst of emotion she'd undergone in the doctor's office as she passed two sweaty towheaded boys licking strawberry ice cream cones and riding skateboards, as she moved from sunshine into shade along the city sidewalks and crosswalks, smelling the peculiar mixture of smells emanating from the open door of a drugstore and the adjacent dry cleaner's.

In the parking lot she paused beside her car, feeling the summer heat radiate from its metal body even before she reached to unlock the door. Inside, the trapped heat seemed to have speed, so powerfully it struck.

The steering wheel felt oily, as if it were being dissolved by the sun, and the leather seat burned through her clothing.

She started the engine, turned on the air conditioner, but as it emitted a hot blast, a wave of nausea struck accompanied by a billow of blackness, as of a curtain lowering behind her eyes. The sensations brought the bewildering truth back with vicious ferocity: *You* are the one who's pregnant! *You* are the gullible one who saw only what you wanted to see in the symptoms. *You* are the one who should have taken precautions and didn't, who *chose* an extramarital affair with a married man. *You* are the one who'll be attending school conferences in your forties, and be pacing the floor at night in your fifties waiting for your teenager to return from his first date. And you are the one who'll suffer the smalltown disdain of women like your mother for years to come.

The cold air rushed from the vents as she lowered her forehead onto the hot, hot steering wheel, and the hot, hot tears continued seeping from her eyes.

Four and a half months.

Four and a half, and I never even suspected—me, a Family Life teacher who spent years teaching high school students about contraception only to blithely ignore it myself. How stupid I was!

So what're you going to do, Maggie?

I'm going to tell Eric.

Do you think he can get divorced and married to you before this baby is born?

I don't know . . . I don't know . . .

Propelled by the hope that he could, she started the engine and headed home.

Chapter 16

Maggie had never called Eric at home, not since the previous summer when she'd been depressed and had unwittingly started all this at Dr. Feldstein's prompting. Dialing the phone that afternoon, she felt transparent, vulnerable. What she feared, happened: Anna answered.

"Yeah, Severson's Charters," came her gruff voice.

"Hello, Anna. This is Maggie Stearn."

"Who?"

"Maggie Pearson."

"Oh . . . Maggie Pearson. Well, I'll be jiggered."

"How are you?"

"Me, I'm fine. Got a new granddaughter, you know."

"Yes, I heard. Congratulations."

"And a grandson just graduated."

"One of Mike's."

"Yup. And a son living back at home."

"Yes, I . . . I heard that, too."

"But fishing's good, business is good. You oughta come out some time and try it."

"I'd like to, but I don't get much free time anymore since I've opened the inn."

"I hear your place is doing good, too, huh?"

"Yes. I've had guests nearly every night since I opened."

"Well, that's just swell. Keeping 'em happy, you know, that's what brings 'em back. Ask me and my boys."

A lull fell and Maggie could think of no way to break it but to inquire baldly, "Anna, is Eric there?"

"Nope. He's got a party out. What did you want?"

"Could you have him call me, please?"

"Oh . . ." After a startled blank Anna added, "Sure. Sure, I'll do that. Expecting him in around six."

"Thank you, Anna."

"Yuh, well, bye then."

"Bye."

When Maggie hung up, her hands were sweating.

When Anna hung up her mind was clicking.

Eric docked the *Mary Deare* at 6:05. Anna watched from the office window as he joshed with the guests, led them to the fish-cleaning shack, gutted their catch and hung seven salmon on the "brag board" for photographing.

At 6:30 he breezed into the office, inquiring, "Anything to eat, Ma?"

"Yeah. I fixed you a roast beef sandwich and there's iced tea in the fridge."

He patted her on the butt as he circumnavigated the counter.

"Thanks, Ma."

"Oh, by the way, Maggie Pearson called. She wants you to call her."

He stopped as if he'd run into an invisible wall, and wheeled around, suddenly tense.

"When?"

"Oh, about four or so."

"Why didn't you call me on the radio?"

"Why should I of? You couldn't call her till you got in anyways."

He slapped the doorframe and hurried off with impatience in every movement. While the returning fishermen came in for cigarettes and potato chips, she heard him making the call from the kitchen, though his words were indistinct. Minutes later, he came out to the office, frowning.

"Hey, Ma, have I got a seven o'clock party?"

"Yup," she replied, checking a clipboard. "Party of four."

"How about Mike?"

"Mike? No, he's open."

"When's he due in?"

"About a quarter hour or so."

"Would you call out and ask him if he'd mind taking my seven o'clock for me?"

"Don't mind at all, but what's so important it comes before customers?"

"I gotta run into town," he answered vaguely, already hustling toward the kitchen. Minutes later she heard the ancient water pipes thumping as he filled his tub for a bath. When he came through the office fifteen minutes later he was freshly combed and shaved, smelling good enough to lick and dressed in clean white jeans and a red polo shirt.

"Did you get Mike?"

"Yup."

"What did he say?"

"He'll take 'em."

"Thanks, Ma. Tell him thanks, too."

He slammed out the front screen door, jogged all the way to his pickup and took off spraying a rooster tail of gravel while Anna, with raised eyebrows, stared after him.

So that's the way the wind blows, she thought.

Maggie had said she'd meet him out at a little Baptist church in the country east of Sister Bay. The Door County countryside was dotted with churches such as this—tallspired, belfried, white wood structures with four arched windows on either side, a pair of pines standing like handmaidens beside it, and an adjacent graveyard slumbering peacefully amid the weeds and wildings. On Sunday evenings the windows would be open and from them would drift the voices of worshippers raised in song. But it was Thursday night, no evening services in session, no cars save hers in the gravel patch out front. The church windows were closed and the only vespers were those being offered up by a pair of mourning doves calling dolefully from their perch on a nearby wire.

She was squatting on her heels beside one of the grave markers when he pulled up. She studied him as he opened the truck door, then returned to her preoccupation as she bent forward with her dress of lettuce green spread about her.

He paused, savoring the sight of her in the streaked light of evening, pouring water from a shoebox onto a clump of purple flowers, rising to wend her way between the ancient, lichened headstones to a black iron pump where she refilled the cardboard box before carrying it, dripping, back to the chosen plot. She knelt once more and watered the flowers while overhead the doves mourned, the day retreated, and the scent of wild sweet clover grew heavy in the gathering damp.

He moved without haste, across the crackling gravel that had trapped the day's heat, onto velvet grass which foretold the night's cool, picking his way toward her between the loved ones from the Old Countries whose names could scarcely be read on the weatherworn markers.

Reaching her, he stood in the long shadows and touched the top of her head.

"What are you doing, Maggie?" he asked, his tone low, in keeping with the doves.

Still kneeling, she looked up over her shoulder. "Watering these poor withering phlox. This was all I had to carry water in."

She set the damp cardboard box at her knee and bent forward to pull two scrawny weeds from among the purple blooms.

"Why?" he asked, kindly.

"I just . . ." Her voice broke, then resumed, pinched with emotion. "I just . . . n . . . needed to."

How quickly her distress could disturb him. The sound of her choked voice brought an anxious tightness to his chest as he squatted on his heels, catching her elbow gently, urging her to face him.

"What's the matter, Maggie M'girl?"

She resisted, keeping her face lowered, and rambled, distraught, as if to postpone some besetting subject. "Don't you wonder who planted these? How long ago? How many years they've been coming up and surviving, unattended? I'd hoe around them a little bit if I had something to do it with, and try to get the qu . . . quack grass up. It's ch . . . choking them."

But she was the one who was choking.

"Maggie, what is it?"

"Do you have anything in your truck?"

Confused by her obvious distress and her reluctance to talk about it, he relented. "I'll see."

His knees cracked as he rose and headed for the truck. A minute later he returned with a screwdriver and handed it to her before dropping again beside her to watch as she worked up the rocky soil and tugged at the crowded roots. He waited patiently until the pointless task was finished, then stilled her hand with his own, closing it over her fingers and the tool.

"Maggie, what is it?" he asked in a near whisper. "Will you tell me now?"

She sat back on her heels, rested the backs of her hands palm-up on her thighs and lifted somber brown eyes to his. "I'm going to have your baby."

The shock ripped across his features, caught him like a kick in the chest and set him back on his heels.

"Oh, my God," he whispered, turning white. He glanced at her stomach, back up to her face. "You're sure?"

"Yes, I'm sure. I saw a doctor today."

He swallowed once. His Adam's apple jumped. "When?"

"In about four and a half months."

"You're that far along?"

She nodded.

"So far that there's no mistake? And not much risk of losing it?"

"No," she tried to whisper, though no sound came out.

A smile of sheer hosannah caught his face. "Maggie, this is wonderful!" he exclaimed, flinging his arms around her. "This is incredible!" He shouted to the sky, "Did you hear that? We're going to have a baby! Maggie and I are going to have a baby! Hug me, Maggie, hug me!"

She could do little else, for he'd wrapped himself around her like a bullwhip. With her larynx flattened by his shoulder her voice came out reedy. "My hands are dirty, and you're crazy."

"I don't give a damn, hug me!"

Kneeling in the grass, she hugged him with her dirty hands pressing the middle of his back—screwdriver and all—soiling his red shirt. "Eric, you're married to another woman who refuses to give you a divorce and I'm—*we're*—forty years old. This isn't wonderful at all, it's horrible. And everyone in town will know it's yours."

He set her back by both arms. "You're damned right they will, because

I'll tell them! No more dragging my feet over that divorce. I'll have her off like an old shirt, and what's forty anyway? Jesus, Maggie, I've wanted this for years and I'd given up hope. How can you not be happy?"

"I'm the unmarried one here, remember?"

"Not for long." Giddy, he held her hands and rushed on, his face radiant. "Maggie, will you marry me? You and the baby? Just as soon as it's legally possible?" Before she could answer he was on his feet, pacing excitedly, the knees of his white trousers stained green. "My God, four and a half months only. We've got some plans to make, a nursery to get ready. Don't we take some . . . some Mazda classes or something."

"Lamaze."

"Lamaze, yeah. Wait'll I tell Ma. And Mike. Man, is *he* going to be surprised! Maggie, do you think there's enough time that we could have another baby, too? Kids should have sisters and brothers. One of each would be—"

"Eric, stop." She rose and touched him, a cooling touch of common sense. "Listen to me."

"What?" As still as the markers around him, he stared at her with an expression of utter innocence, his face flushed with exuberance, the same rosy gold as the western sky.

"Darling, you seem to be forgetting that I'm not your wife. That privilege," she reminded him, "belongs to another woman. You can't . . . well, you can't just go around shouting hallelujah all over town as if we were married. It would be an embarrassment to Nancy, don't you see? And to our parents as well. I have a daughter to consider, and she has friends. I understand your being happy, but I have reservations."

He sobered as if some fatal accident had happened before his eyes, chilling his joy.

"You don't want it."

How could she make him understand? "It isn't a question of wanting or not wanting. It's here"—she pressed her hands to her stomach—"and it's nearly half-term already, which is much farther along than your divorce. And it will mean a tremendous interruption in my life, probably the end of the business I've been working so hard to get established. I'm the one who'll carry it from now until you're free, I'm the one who'll get the curious glances on the street, I'm the one who'll be called a home-wrecker. If I need some time to adjust to these things, you'll have to be tolerant, Eric."

He stood motionless, digesting her remarks, while overhead the doves continued mourning.

"You don't want it," he repeated, decimated.

"Not with the unconfounded joy you do. That'll take some time."

His face grew hard and he pointed a finger at her. "You do anything to get rid of it, and it'll kill me, too, you understand?"

"Oh, Eric," she lamented, drooping. "How could you even think such a thing?"

He turned away, paced to a maple tree and stared at its smooth, gray bark. For seconds he remained stiff and unmoving, then slammed the tree with an open palm. Leaning against the trunk, he hung his head.

The stunning summer sunset continued to praise the sky. Among the sumac scrub on the rim of the adjacent wood a green, whiskered flycatcher repeated his burry *fee-be, fee-be.* Beside the nearest headstone the phlox flowers nodded against the granite, while spiders and beetles hurried through the grasses and tiny green worms dropped on webs that shone like glass threads in the failing, final rays of the day. Life and growth flourished everywhere, even in a graveyard that marked the end of life and growth, even within the woman whose heavy heart, amid all this summer splendor, seemed misplaced.

She studied the man she loved—the bowed back, the rigid arm, the sagging head.

How disconsolate he looked, lifted to the heights one minute, then mired in despair upon being forced to consider their dilemma.

She moved behind him and laid her palms upon his ribs.

"Conceiving it was an act of love," she told him quietly, "and I still love you, and I'll love it, too. But bringing it into the world outside of marriage is less than it deserves. *That's* what I'm unhappy about. Because I'm reasonably sure Nancy will give you enough resistance to keep us unmarried until long after this baby is born."

He lifted his head and said to the tree, "I'll talk to her this weekend, and tell her that a reconciliation is out of the question. I'll talk to my lawyer and give orders to get this thing going." He turned to face Maggie, held from touching her by some new and unwanted constraint. He realized how prosaic their situation was, how classic his response appeared on the surface: a married man stringing his mistress along while keeping her pacified with promises of divorce. Yet she'd never accused him of lagging, never insisted, or demanded.

"I'm sorry, Maggie, I should have done it before."

"Yes . . . well, how could we know this would happen?"

His expression turned thoughtful. "How did it, Maggie? I'm just curious."

"I thought I was safe. I'd had certain signs of menopause for over a year. But the doctor explained that even when regular periods stop, there are still times when a woman can be fertile. When he told me I was pregnant I felt . . ." She glanced at her hands self-consciously. "I felt so stupid! Coming up unexpectedly pregnant at my age after I *taught* Family Life, for heaven's sake!" She turned away, chagrined.

He studied her back, the way she hugged herself, the way her palegreen dress pulled taut across her shoulder blades. The dark, uncompromising truth settled upon him. Sadly, quietly, he asked, "You really don't want it, do you, Maggie?"

She seesawed her head—more of a shudder than an answer. "Oh, Eric, if only we were thirty and married, it would be so different."

It was different for her, he realized; she'd had a family. She couldn't begin to comprehend the impress of this child upon his life versus the relative unimportance of his age, or hers. Once again disappointment deluged him.

"Here." She turned and handed him the screwdriver. "Thank you."

The reserve remained between them, distancing them for some reason he could not fully fathom.

"I promise I'll talk to Nancy."

"Please don't tell her about the baby, though. I'd rather she didn't know yet."

"No, I won't, but I need to tell somebody. Would it be okay if I told Mike? He's no blabbermouth."

"Of course, tell Mike. I may find myself telling Brookie, too, very soon."

He smiled uncertainly, longing to reach for her, but they remained apart. This was silly. She was carrying his baby, for God's sake, and they loved each other so much.

"Maggie, could I hold you? Both of you?"

With a tiny cry that caught in her throat she flew to him and released them from their agony as she went up on tiptoe and clasped her arms across his neck. He held her hard and felt his heart begin beating again.

"Oh, Eric, I'm so scared," she admitted.

"Don't be. We're going to be a family. We will, you'll see," he vowed. He closed his eyes tightly and ran his hands over her pregnant body— her back, buttocks and breasts. He dropped to one knee and, cupping her stomach, pressed his face against it.

"Hello, little one," he said, muffled against her soft, green dress. "I'm going to love you so much."

Through her clothing his breath warmed her skin. Through her sadness his words warmed her heart. But as he stood and closed her gently in his arms, she knew it wasn't enough. Enough was nothing less than becoming his wife.

There were times, Nancy Macaffee had to admit, when Door County was nearly tolerable. Now, in summer, at the end of a hot, hard week, return- ing to it wasn't quite as distasteful as in dead winter. It was, admittedly, cool here with the breezes wafting over the water surrounding the pen- insula, and she liked the shade trees and the profusion of flowers in both likely and unlikely places. But the people were peasants: old women still went uptown in scarves and curlers and old men still wore their bill-caps tipped to one side. Fishing and the fruit crops were the primary subjects of palaver when locals met on the street. Grocery shopping was deplorable and the house she lived in was an abomination.

How could Eric have *liked* the decrepit little cracker box? When he'd moved her into it—nothing else was available—he'd promised it was tem- porary. Was it her fault she wanted something better? Returning to it when he was there, it had been almost tolerable. Now that he was gone, she found it disgusting, but her lawyer had advised her to stay in it for legal reasons, and to do anything else would have meant a disruption in her life which she didn't need at this time.

Returning home on Friday night she cursed, trying to open the damned garage door. Inside, the kitchen smelled stuffy. The same stack of junk mail lay where she'd left it on the kitchen cabinet last Monday. Nobody had washed the rug by the kitchen sink where she'd dropped a spot of mayonnaise. No game hens or chile were cooking. Nobody offered to carry her suitcase upstairs.

But on the kitchen table was a note from Eric: *Nancy, I need to talk to you. I'll call you Saturday.*

She smiled and flew upstairs. All right, so he hadn't bought her a gleam- ing condo in Lake Point Towers with a view of the Gold Coast and all of Chicago at her feet, but she missed him, damn it! She wanted him back. She wanted someone to open the garage door, and to have supper cook- ing, and to take care of servicing her car and mowing the lawn and having the coffee perked on Saturday mornings. And when she slipped into bed, someone to reaffirm that she was a desirable woman.

Upstairs she threw her suitcase on the bed and stripped off a champagne-pink linen suit. Though sunset flooded the room, she snapped on the lights around her makeup mirror and leaned close, examining her pores, touching her face here, there, flicking a piece of fallen mascara from her cheek, testing her throat for tautness. She found a tiny brush and fluffed her eyebrows straight up. She traded that brush for another, removed her barrette and dropped it among the clutter on the dressing table, brushed her hair vigorously, bending sharply at the waist so its feathery tips whisked her shoulders.

Discarding the brush, she watched herself in the mirror, stripping off a peach-colored petticoat, bra and panties, letting them drop at her feet like petals at the feet of a Madonna.

She ran her hands over her flat belly, down her thighs, up her ribs, catching her cone-shaped breasts and lifting them high, pointing the nipples straight at the mirror.

Oh, how she missed the sex. They'd been so good at it.

But the thought of distorting her body with pregnancy remained repugnant. Some women were made for it and some weren't. Why couldn't he have accepted that?

In the cramped, ugly bathroom she drew a bath, laced it with bubbles and immersed herself with a sigh. Eyes closed, she thought of Eric and smiled. Tomorrow was too long to wait. She'd put on her new Bill Blass jumpsuit, and a spray of Passion—which he liked best—and she'd go out there to find out if he'd changed his mind.

Waiting for someone to answer her knock, Nancy glanced around in distaste. If there was one place she hated worse than her own house it was this stinking place. Fish—Jesus, she detested the very word. She could hardly eat a filet of mahimahi since she'd been subjected to the smells around here. How anybody could work in such a stench was beyond her. The whole damned woods stunk!

Anna answered her knock, looking as tacky as ever in a horrible T-shirt emblazoned with the words *Grandma's Marathon '88.*

"Hello, Nancy."

"Hello, Anna." Nancy perfunctorily rested her cheek on Anna's. "How are you?"

"Oh, you know . . . the boys keep me busy. Fishing's been real good. How about you?"

"Busy, too. Lonely."

"Yeah . . . well . . . sometimes we have to go through that. I imagine you came to see Eric. He's down at the fish-cleaning shed shutting down for the night."

"Thank you."

"Be careful in the dark in those high heels!" Anna called after her.

Nancy crossed the graveled area leading to the dock and outbuildings. It was ten P.M. Beneath the trees all was dark, but near the fish-cleaning shed a single bulb beamed under a cymbal-shaped reflector. Inside the crude building another bulb oozed weak light onto the concrete floor and the rough board walls. Approaching it, Nancy covered her nose with her wrist and breathed the scent of Elizabeth Taylor's Passion.

Down near the lake a bullfrog belched relentlessly. Crickets whined everywhere. Insects buzzed and beat at the lights. Something hit Nancy's hair and she cringed and thrashed it away frantically. From inside the cleaning shack two men's voices could be heard while hose water smacked the concrete floor covering the sound of Nancy's approach on the gravel.

She stopped within feet of the door and listened.

"Well, she's not exactly ecstatic." That was Eric.

"You mean she doesn't want it?"—and Mike.

"She doesn't want the interruption in her life."

"Well, you can tell her from me that we didn't want it either, but now that we've got Anna we wouldn't trade her for the world."

"It's a little different for Maggie, Mike. She doesn't think she can run an inn with a baby waking up and crying in the middle of the night, and she's probably right."

"I hadn't thought of that."

"Besides, she thinks we're too old to have a baby."

"But shit, man—doesn't she know you've wanted one your whole life?"

"She knows, and she says she'll love it. It's just the shock."

"When is it due?"

"Four and a half months."

Nancy had heard enough. She felt scalded. In the dark her cheeks flushed and her heart bumped crazily. The water still splattered as she turned and retreated, leaving their voices behind. Beneath the shadows of the maple trees she slipped back to her car, closed the door stealthily and sat gripping the wheel with her eyes stinging.

He'd made another woman pregnant.

Decimated, she dropped her forehead to her knuckles and felt the blood rush to her extremities. Fear, shock and anger coursed through her. Fear of the unknown turmoil ahead, the uprooting of their home and their finances and their life pattern, which she'd wanted changed— yes—but by choice not by duress.

Fear of losing a man she had captured in her twenties and of being unable to catch another in her forties.

Shock because it had truly happened, when she had been so sure she could somehow get him back, that her beauty, sexuality, intelligence, ambition and her position as incumbent wife would be enough to pull him back to her after he'd come to his senses.

Anger because he'd turned his back on all that and made a laughing-stock out of her with a woman everyone recognized as his old sweetheart.

How dare you do this to me! I'm still your wife! The tears came, burning tears of mortification for what she'd suffer when people found out.

Damn you, Severson, I hope your stinking boat sinks and leaves her with your bastard! She wept. She thumped the steering wheel. The spurned woman. The one who'd let herself be dragged back to this loathsome place against her will. The one who'd given up life in the city she loved so he could come here and play Captain Ahab. The one who went out on the road five days a week while he stayed behind to screw another woman! If she lived in Chicago nobody would know the difference, but here everyone would know—his family, the postmaster, the whole damned fishing fleet!

When her tears slowed, she sat staring at the bleak light of the shack doorway as the men's shadows crossed and recrossed it. She could give him what he wanted, but she'd be damned if she would. Why should she make it that easy for him? Her pride was annihilated and he was going to pay for it!

She dried her eyes carefully, blew her nose, and flicked on the dome light and checked her reflection in the mirror. In her purse she found an eyeliner wand and did a quick repair job, then snapped out the light.

Down in the fish-cleaning shack the water stopped plopping and the light flicked out. As the brothers stepped outside, Nancy left her car, slamming the door.

"Eric!" she called, friendly, approaching the two men across the patchy darkness beneath the trees. "Hi. I found your note."

"Nancy." His tone was cool, unwelcoming. "You could have just called."

"I know, but I wanted to see you. I have something important to tell you." As an afterthought she tossed out, "Hi, Mike."

"Hello, Nancy." Turning away, he added, "Listen, Eric, I'll see you tomorrow."

"Yeah. Goodnight."

When Mike left, silence fell, broken only by the nightcalls of thick summer. Standing within her approachable radius, Eric felt threatened, impatient to be beyond her scope.

"Give me a minute to wash my hands and I'll be right back." He stalked away without inviting her to wait inside. Hell, he'd finally admitted she'd never liked his mother or his mother's house. Why should he be noble at this late date?

He returned five minutes later, wearing clean jeans and a different shirt and smelling of handsoap, striding toward her as if he wanted to get this over with.

"Where do you want to talk?" he asked before reaching her.

"My, so brusque," she chided, taking his arm, resting her breast against it.

He removed her hand with deliberate forcefulness. "We can talk down in the *Mary Deare* or in your car. You name it."

"I'd just as soon talk at home, Eric, in our own bed." She rested a hand on his chest and again he removed it.

"I'm not interested, Nancy. All I want from you is a divorce, and the sooner the better."

"You'll change your mind when you hear what I have to tell you."

"What?" he snapped, with as much indulgence as a father removing his belt in the woodshed.

"It's going to make you happy."

"I doubt it. Unless it's a court date."

"What have you always wanted more than anything in the world?"

"Come on, Nancy, quit playing games. I've had a long day and I'm tired."

She laughed, forcing the sound from her throat. She touched him again on the arm, knowing he resented her doing so, wanting the satisfaction of feeling the shock strike him. She had a momentary flash of doubt: what she was doing was reprehensible. But what he'd done was, too.

"We're going to have a baby, darling."

The shock hit Eric like high voltage. He struggled for breath. Backed up a step. Gaped at her.

"I don't believe you!"

"It's true." She shrugged with convincing nonchalance. "Around Thanksgiving time."

He did a quick calculation: that night he'd taken her on the living room sofa.

"Nancy, if you're lying—"

"Would I lie about a thing like this?"

He grabbed her wrist and hauled her to her car, opened the door and pushed her inside, then followed, leaving the door open so the dome light shone down.

"I want to see your face while you say this." He gripped her cheeks and held them, forcing her to meet his eyes. To his great dismay he could tell she'd been crying, which increased his dread. Still, he'd make her repeat it so he'd be sure.

"Now tell me again."

"I'm three-and-a-half-months pregnant with your baby, Eric Severson," she said somberly.

"Then why doesn't it show?" He released her cheeks and passed a dubious glance down her length.

"Take me home and look at me naked."

He didn't want to. God forgive him, he didn't want to. The only woman he wanted to be that close to was Maggie.

"Why did you wait so long to tell me?"

"I wanted to make sure it wasn't a false alarm. A lot of things can happen in the first three months. After that it's safer. I just didn't want to get your hopes up too soon."

"So why aren't you upset?" he grilled her, his eyes narrowing.

"About saving my marriage?" she asked reasonably, then did a superb job of acting puzzled. "You're the one who seems upset, and I don't know why you should be. After all, this is what you wanted, isn't it?"

He sank back against the seat with a sigh, pinching the bridge of his nose. "But goddamn it, not now!"

"Not now?" she repeated. "But you're always pointing out that we're not getting any younger. I thought you'd be pleased. I thought . . ." She let her voice trail away piteously. "I thought . . ." She conjured up several tears which prompted the response she expected. He reached over and took her hand from her lap and held it loosely, stroking its back with his thumb.

"I'm sorry, Nancy. I'll . . . I'll go in and get my things and come back home tonight, okay?"

She managed to sound even more beleaguered and pitiful. "Eric, if you don't want this baby after all the years we've—"

He silenced her lips with a touch of his finger. "You caught me by surprise, that's all. And considering the way our relationship has deteriorated, it's not the healthiest environment to bring a child into."

"Have you really stopped loving me, Eric?" It was the first sincere question she'd asked. She was suddenly terrified at the idea of being unloved, of having to build a relationship from the ground up with some other man and go through all the exhausting groundwork it took to reach an amicable married status. Even more terrified that she wouldn't find one to do it with.

She received no answer. Instead, he released her hand and said heavily, "Go on home, Nancy. I'll be there soon. We'll talk tomorrow."

Watching him disappear into the shadows she thought, what have I done? How can I hold him once he learns the truth?

Walking back to the house, Eric felt as he had when the old man died— helpless and despairing. More: victimized. Why now, after all the years of coercing and convincing? Why now when he no longer wanted her or a child by her? He thought he might cry, so he went out onto the dock and stood beside the *Mary Deare*. The aftershock quivered in his belly. He doubled forward, hands to knees, submitting to abject despair, letting it shake him so that he might move beyond it toward unemotional reasoning.

He straightened. The boat lay listless in the water, the rods upright in their quivers, the mooring lines drooping to the dock. He arched, looked high at the constellations which the old man, with wisdom brought from the old country, had taught him to identify. Pegasus, Andromeda, and the Fishes. The fishes, yes, they were in his blood, in his lineage as surely as the color of his hair and eyes, passed down from some blond, blue-eyed Viking long before Scandinavians had last names.

She still hated his fishing.

She still hated Fish Creek.

She still wanted to be a career woman gone from home four nights a week.

Since he'd been at Ma's he'd done a lot of soul searching and talking with her and Barb and Mike. They had admitted to having difficulty liking Nancy all these years. He had admitted that the joy he'd known with Maggie made him realize what a state of quasi-happiness he'd lived in with Nancy all these years.

Now Nancy was pregnant . . . and resigned if not happy about it.

And so was Maggie.

But he was Nancy's husband, and he'd been begging her for years to have this baby. To abandon her now would be the height of callousness and he was not a callous man. Obligation pulled with a gravity as powerful as the earth's: the child was his, conceived by a woman who would make a formidable mother, if not a disastrous, absentee one; whereby Maggie— loving, kind Maggie—would in time welcome her baby, and would be everpresent, and guiding and judicial in its rearing, he was sure. Of the two children, Nancy's would need him more.

He turned forlornly and shuffled up to Ma's house to pack and face his purgatory.

Chapter 17

He slept little that night. Lying beside Nancy he thought of Maggie, her image appearing keenly in a dozen remembered poses: with her chin raised, yodeling in a bathtub; laughing as she served him a plate-sized doughnut; kneeling before a clump of withering flowers in a country graveyard; lifting her somber countenance while rocking his world with her news; gravely predicting that Nancy would keep them apart until well after Maggie's baby was born.

How right she'd been.

He kept to his side of the bed. Stacking his hands beneath his head, he made sure not even his elbow touched Nancy's hair. He thought of tomorrow; he would, of course, tell Maggie then, but he would not compound his wrongdoing by going to her fresh from even the slightest intimacy with the woman beside him.

He closed his eyes, assessing himself and the hurt he would bring to Maggie, suffering already at the thought of inflicting it upon her. His eyelids trembled. This was no venial offense. He was answerable to both women, guilty of all accusations, lower than either of them could even express. He could handle Nancy's wrath—and it would be vile when she learned the truth—but what of Maggie's hurt?

Aw, Maggie, what have I done? I wanted so much for us. You were the last one I wanted to hurt.

In the midnight blackness, he agonized. Some little creature scurried along the roof—a mouse, probably—leaving a trail of ticks as of acorns rolling down the shingles. Down on Main Street some teenager with a loud muffler let out his clutch and rapped his pipes up the deserted thoroughfare. Beside Eric the clock changed a digit with a soft *fup*.

Nancy's baby was one minute older.

Maggie's baby was one minute older.

He thought of the unborn children. The legitimate one. The bastard— what a harsh word when applied to one's own offspring. What would they look like? Would they have traces of the old man? Ma? Himself, surely. Would they be bright? (Coming from Maggie and Nancy, it seemed a certainty.) Healthy or sickly? Contented or demanding? What would Maggie's wishes be? To let her child grow up knowing who'd sired him or to conceal the father's name? If the child knew, he'd know, too, who his half brother or half sister was. They'd meet on the street, at the beach, in school, likely as early as in kindergarten. Somewhere along the line some kid would ask him, How come your dad lives with that other family? At what age do children become aware of the stigma of illegitimacy?

He tried to imagine himself taking both his children out in the *Mary*

Deare and putting fishing lines into their hands, teaching them about the water, and the constellations, and how to read the depth finder screen. He'd boost them up, one on each knee (for they'd be small yet), and hold them by their bellies so their inquisitive hands could grip the wheel while he faced them toward the monitor and explained: *The blue is the water. The red line is the bottom of the lake, and that white line just above it is a school of alewife. And that long white line . . . that's your salmon.*

On a more real plane, the idea seemed unlikely, ludicrous even, that two mothers of two of his children would be so bending as to allow such a flaunting of tradition, even in today's enlightened era. How stupidly self-serving of him to even imagine it.

Well, he'd know tomorrow. He'd see Maggie tomorrow, would suffer right along with her.

Saturday dawned unseasonably chilly, with cloud racks scudding before a brisk wind. Nancy was already at work in her office as Eric prepared to leave the house. He stopped at her door, drawing on a windbreaker, his arms leaden from lack of sleep.

"I'll see you tonight," he said, his first words to her since rising. He'd fallen asleep sometime after four o'clock, and had overslept and awakened to find Nancy already dressed and downstairs. She looked very *downtown*, in oversized spectacles, a knobby linen jumpsuit with a belt that looked like coconut shell, two pounds of earrings, a container of yogurt at her elbow and her hair belling out behind her ears like a hoopskirt. At his appearance she sat back and raised the eyeglasses onto her hair. "What time?" She picked up the yogurt and ate a spoonful.

"If this weather keeps up, early, maybe even this afternoon."

"Great!" She arched a wrist and the spoon flashed. "I'll fix us something loaded with calcium and vitamins." She patted her stomach. "Have to be extra careful about proper nourishment now." She smiled. "Have a nice day, darling."

Mentally, he cringed at her endearment and rebelled at the reminder of her pregnancy.

"You, too," he returned and headed for his truck.

The weather suited his mood. Rain began falling when he was halfway to Gills Rock, smacking the windshield with a sound like breaking plastic. Thunder grumbled and rolled an unbroken circle around the flickering horizon. He knew well before he reached Ma's that the morning's charters would already be canceled, but he drove on anyway, checked in with Mike and Ma, had a cup of coffee but passed up a piece of sausage, too preoccupied to eat. For a while he studied the soiled kitchen phone, the phone book on its string, with Maggie's Seattle number still written on its cover, remembering the first time he'd called her.

Ma repeated a question then yelped, "Boy, you got rutabagas in your ears or somethin'!"

"Oh . . . what?"

"I asked you if you wanted something else—some oatmeal maybe or some lunch meat on toast?"

"No, nothing, Ma. I'm not hungry."

"Not revving on all cylinders this morning either, are you?"

"Sorry. Listen, if you don't need me for anything I've got to run back to Fish Creek."

"Naw. Go ahead. This rain looks like she's settled in for good."

He hadn't told either of them why he'd decided to move back home with Nancy, and though Mike calmly leaned against the sink, sipping coffee, watching Eric appraisingly, Eric chose not to enlighten him yet. Besides, Ma knew nothing about Maggie's pregnancy and he couldn't bear telling her yet. Maybe he never would. Guilt again: withholding the truth from Ma, who always found out everything, as if she had hidden antennae that twitched whenever her boys were bad.

When he was eight—he remembered the age clearly, because Miss Wystad had been his teacher that year, and it was the year Eric had been experimenting with his first cussing—he had laughed and poked fun at a boy named Eugene Behrens who had come to school with a hole in the seat of his overalls and bare skin showing through. Eugene also had a home-style bowl-and-scissors haircut that made him look like one of the Three Stooges.

Bare-ass Behrens, Eric had called him.

"Hey, Yoo-gene," Eric had hollered across the playground. "Hey Yoo-gene Bare-ass Behrens, where's your underwear, Yoo-gene?"

While Eugene turned away stoically, Eric had taunted in a singsong,

> Yoo-gene Behrens' ass is bare
> He ain't got no underwear
> Looks like a stooge in his bowl of hair!

While Eugene broke into a run, crying, Eric turned around to find Miss Wystad five feet behind him.

"Eric, I think you and I had better go inside," she'd said sternly.

Of that conversation Eric remembered little, except his question, "You gonna tell my Ma?"

Miss Wystad hadn't told Ma, but she'd meted out a strapping that stung yet, as he remembered it, and had made him stand before the class and apologize to Eugene aloud while he was still red-faced and hurting and humiliated.

How Ma ever found out about the fiasco Eric never knew—Mike swore he hadn't told her. But find out she did (though she never alluded to the incident) and her punishment was even more ignominious than Miss Wystad's. He'd come home one day after school to find her cleaning out his chest of drawers. She had culled out some of his underwear, socks, T-shirts, corduroys. As he stood watching, she added to the stack a new T-shirt, his favorite, across its front a picture of Superman in flight. As she stacked the clothes, she spoke offhandedly. "There's a family named Behrens—real poor, got ten kids. One of 'em's in your room, I think. A Eugene? Anyway, their Pa got killed in an accident at the shipyards a couple years ago, and their Ma's got quite a struggle to raise 'em. My church circle's taking up a collection of used clothing to help them out, and I want you to take these to school tomorrow and give them to that boy, Eugene. Will you do that for me, Eric?" For the first time she glanced flat at him.

He'd dropped his eyes to his Superman shirt and gulped down a protest.

"You'll do that, won't you, son?"

"Yes, Ma."

For the rest of that school year he'd watched Eugene Behrens come to school in his Superman shirt. He'd never again poked fun at anyone less fortunate than he. And he'd never again tried to withhold his misdeeds from Ma. If he got into a scrape, he'd march straight home and confess, "Ma, I got into trouble today." And they'd sit down and work it out.

Driving to Maggie's through the downpour on a black summer day, he wished for the simplicity of those problems again, wished that he could simply go to his mother and say, "Ma, I'm in trouble," and they could sit down and work it out as they'd always been able.

The recollection made him blue, and he forgave Eugene Behrens for wearing his Superman shirt, and wondered where Eugene was now and hoped he had a closet full of nice clothes and enough money to live in luxury.

At Maggie's the lights were on: yellow patches upon a purple day. Whipped by the strong wind, the arborvitaes swayed and danced. The wet yellow paint on the house had darkened to ocher. The daylilies beside the back stoop were beaten flat by the water sheeting from the roof. As he ran down the steps droplets plopped from the maples in great, cold blobs that struck his neck and head and shattered on his blue windbreaker. The rag rug on the back veranda squished as he leaped onto it. Inside, the kitchen was empty but bright.

To Eric's dismay, his knock was answered by Katy, wearing a curious expression that soured into censure the moment she saw who stood outside.

"Hello, Katy."

"Hello," she replied tightly.

"Is your mother here?"

"Follow me," she ordered and went away. He hurriedly removed his tennis shoes and watched her disappear along the short passage into the dining room from where voices could be heard. He hung his head, shook the water from his hair and followed to find Katy waiting just inside the dining room doorway, the table surrounded by guests, and Maggie, at the foot.

"Someone to see you, Mother."

The conversation ceased and every pair of eyes in the room settled on him.

Caught by surprise, Maggie stared at Eric as if he were an apparition. Her face turned brilliant crimson before she finally gathered her poise and rose.

"Well, Eric, this is a surprise. Won't you join us? Katy, get him a cup, will you?" She moved over to make room for him beside her while Katy got a cup from the built-in hutch and belligerently clattered it onto the place mat. Maggie tried to rescue the moment by performing introductions. "This is a friend of mine, Eric Severson, and these are my guests . . ." She named three couples but in her embarrassment forgot the names of the fourth and colored again, stammering an apology. "Eric runs a charter boat out of Gills Rock," she informed them.

They passed him the footed china coffee urn, and the plate of pumpkin muffins, and the butter, and a glass of pineapple juice which one of them poured at the far end of the table as if this were one big happy family.

He should have called first. Should have considered that she'd be with her guests over breakfast, and that Katy would be here and openly antagonistic. Instead, he found himself subjected to thirty minutes of chitchat with Maggie tense as a guy-wire on his right, and Katy bristling with animosity on his left, and an audience of eight attempting to pretend they noticed nothing out of the ordinary.

When the ordeal ended, he had to wait while Maggie accepted checks from two of her clients, answered several questions and quietly gave orders to her daughter to clean up the dining room and go on with her daily work. "I won't be long," she ended, finding a long gray sweater and tossing it over her shoulders as she hurried with Eric through the rain toward the truck.

When the doors slammed, they sat in their soggy clothes, breathing hard, staring straight ahead. Finally Eric blew out a great breath. His shoulders wilted.

"Maggie, I'm sorry. I shouldn't have come here at this time of day."

"No, you shouldn't have."

"I never thought about you being at breakfast."

"I run a bed and breakfast, remember? Breakfast happens every morning here."

"Katy wanted to slam the door in my face."

"Katy's been taught some manners, and she knows she'd better remember them. What's wrong?"

"Can you come for a ride? Someplace away from here? Just out in the country a ways? We need to talk."

She laughed tensely. "Obviously." Rarely had he seen her upset, but she was—with him—as she glanced toward the house where Katy's image could be seen moving about the kitchen beyond the lace curtains. "No, I shouldn't leave. I have work to do, and there's no sense getting Katy any more antagonistic than she already is."

"Please, Maggie. I wouldn't have come if it wasn't important."

"I realize that. That's why I came outside with you. But I can't leave. I only have a minute."

A man came out, the guest whose name Maggie had forgotten, carrying two suitcases, running through the downpour to his car across the road.

"Please, Maggie."

She expelled a breath of exasperation. "All right, but not for long."

The engine sputtered, caught, and blustered as he pumped the gas, then put the truck in gear and drove up the switchback with the tires hissing like brushes on a drum, and the windshield wipers thumping like a metronome. He drove the opposite direction of town, south onto Highway 42, then east on EE until he came to a narrow gravel track leading off into a copse of scrubwoods. At the end of the trail where the trees gave onto a fallow field, he pulled to a halt and cut the engine. Around them the heavens dripped, clouds glowered, and the heads of wildflowers drooped like penitents before a confessor.

They sat momentarily, each enveloped by his own thoughts, adjusting to the metallic resonance of rain on the cab, the absence of flapping wipers, the blurred landscape whose focal point was an abandoned farmstead viewed through ribbons of rainwater branching down the windshield.

In unison they turned their heads to look at one another.

"Maggie," he said, forlornly.

"It's something bad, isn't it?"

"Come here," he whispered hoarsely, catching and holding her with his cheek and nose against the pleasant mustiness of her wet hair and wool sweater. "Yes. It's bad."

"Tell me."

"It's worse than the worst you've ever imagined."

"Tell me."

He drew back, met her brown eyes with an earnest, apologetic gaze. "Nancy is pregnant."

Shock. Disbelief. Denial. "Oh, my God," she whispered, pulling away, covering her lips, staring out the windshield. Quieter still, "Oh, my God."

Her eyes closed and he watched her battle with it, pressing her fingertips harder and harder against her lips until he thought her teeth must be cutting them. In time her eyes opened, and blinked once in slow motion, like an antique doll with lead-weights in its head.

"Maggie . . . oh, Maggie-honey, I'm sorry."

She heard only a roar in her ears.

She had been a fool. She had played into the hands of a man who was typical, after all. She had not questioned or demanded, but had taken him at his word that he loved her and was seeking a divorce. Her mother had warned her. Her daughter had warned her. But she'd been so sure of him, so absolute in her trust.

Now he was leaving her for his wife, leaving her nearly five months pregnant with his child.

She did not cry; one cannot weep ice crystals.

"Take me home, please," she said, sitting straight as a surveyor's rod, donning a veneer of dignity.

"Maggie, please don't do this, don't turn away."

"You've made your decision. It's clear. Take me home."

"I've badgered her for all these years. How can I divorce her now?"

"No, of course you can't. Take me home, please."

"Not until you—"

"God damn you!" She swung, slapped his cheek hard. "Don't you issue ultimatums to me! You have no more rights over me, no more say over what I choose to do! None! Start the engine this instant or I'll get out and walk!"

"It's a mistake, Maggie. I didn't want her to get pregnant. It happened before you and I even knew what we wanted, when I was so mixed up and trying to decide what to do about my marriage."

She flung open the truck door and stepped into soggy grass. Cold water oozed into the lacing holes of her shoes. She ignored it and headed along the dirt track knocking aside a clump of tall milkweed which wet her slacks to mid-thigh.

His truck door slammed and he grabbed her arm. "Get back in the truck," he ordered.

She pulled free and stalked on, head high, eyes dry of all but rainwater which plastered her hair to her forehead and leached through her eyelashes.

"Maggie, I'm a damn fool but your baby is mine and I want to be its father!" he called.

"Tough!" she called. "Go back to your wife!"

"Maggie, goddamn it, will you stop!"

She marched on. He cursed again, then the truck door slammed and the engine started. Killed. Started again, roared like a hungry giant before the truck shot backward, spraying wet muck onto its underbelly. She trooped along the worn track, as dogged as a foot soldier, preventing his bypassing her.

Bumping along behind her, in reverse, he hung his head out the window.

"Maggie, get in the damn truck!"

She gave him the flying finger, marching headlong toward the road.

He changed his tack, tried cajoling. "Come on, Maggie."

"You're out of my life, Severson!" she yelled, almost joyously. When she reached the blacktop he squealed backward onto the pavement on two tires and changed directions with a grinding shift that dropped the truck's guts.

The engine killed for good. The starter whined five times without results. His truck door slammed. Maggie strode on, picturing him standing beside it with his hands on his hips.

"You goddamn stubborn woman!" he yelled.

She raised her left hand, bent the fingers twice: *bye-bye,* and tramped on through the rain.

He stood staring after her, absolutely flabbergasted and angrier than he ever remembered being. This was the reaction he'd expected from Nancy, not from his sweet-tempered Maggie. Damned unpredictable hussy, flipping him off like that. So she was pissed off. Well, that made two of them! He'd let her stew for a couple of weeks until she got good and lonesome for him, then maybe he'd get treated civilly!

He watched until he was certain she had no intention of turning around, then kicked the truck tire, opened the door and pushed the damned old whore to the side of the road. When she was listing toward the ditch, he slammed the door and studied Maggie again, so distant he couldn't tell the color of her clothes.

Go then, you stubborn little twit! But you'll have to talk to me sooner or later. I've got a kid to support and it's bouncing along in the rain with you! You'd better—by God—take good care of it!

Maggie stopped at the first farmhouse she came to and asked to use the telephone.

"Daddy?" she said, when Roy came on the line. "Did you drive to work?"

"Yes, but what—"

"Could you please come out and get me? I'm at a farm out on EE just a little east of Forty-two . . . just a minute." She asked the greasy-haired adolescent girl who'd let her in, "What's the name here?"

"Jergens."

Into the phone she inquired, "You know where the Jergenses live, out south of town?"

"I know it, yeah, Harold Jergens' place, used to belong to his folks."

"I'm there. Can you come and get me, please?"

"Why, sure honey, but what in the world—"

"Thanks, Daddy. But hurry. I'm soaking wet."

She hung up before he could question her further.

When they were riding back to town together they encountered a hitch-hiker just a short way down EE.

Roy began decelerating, but Maggie ordered, "Drive on, Daddy."

"But it's raining and—"

"Don't you dare, stop, Daddy, because if you do, I'll get out and walk!"

They passed the man with his thumb up and Roy glanced over his shoulder.

"But that's Eric Severson!"

"I know it is. Let him walk."

"But, Maggie . . ." Severson was shaking his fist at them.

"Watch the road, Daddy, before you put us in the ditch."

She grabbed the wheel and averted a disaster. When Roy faced front Maggie turned on the heater, fingercombed her hair and said, "Prepare yourself for a shock, Daddy. This one's going to knock your argyle socks off." She cast him a steady glance. "I'm expecting Eric Severson's baby."

Roy gaped at her in amazement. She reached for the wheel again to keep them on the road.

"But . . . but . . ." He sputtered like a one-cylinder engine and cranked around to see the road behind them, oblivious to their direction or speed.

"Mother's going to shit a ring around herself," Maggie said matter-of-factly. "I expect this will end our relationship for good. She's warned me, you see."

"Eric Severson's baby? You mean *that* Eric Severson? The one we just passed?"

"That's right."

"You mean you're going to marry him?"

"No, Daddy. He's already married."

"Well, I know that . . . but . . . but . . ." Roy again did an imitation of an old Allis-Chalmers.

"As a matter of fact, his wife is expecting their first baby, too. But if I've got it figured right, mine will be born first."

Roy braked to a stop in the dead center of the road and exclaimed, "Maggie!" with all due astonishment.

"Do you want me to drive, Daddy? Maybe I should. You seem a little shaken."

She was out and around the car before Roy could digest her intention. She shoved him over bodily. "Move, Daddy. It's wet out here."

He moved as if a door had slammed during his nap, scudding over into the passenger seat while Maggie put the car into gear and headed for town.

"We had an affair, but it's over. I have my own plans to make now and I may need your help from time to time, but I'm a strong person. You'll see. I've been through Phillip's death, and the move here, getting rid of the house in Seattle with all its memories, and all the hubbub of tearing apart the new house and starting the business, and I intend to make a go of it, baby or not. Do you think I can?"

"There's not a doubt in my mind."

"Mother *will* be upset, won't she?"

"There's not a doubt in my mind."

"She will probably, quite literally, disown me."

"Probably . . . yes. Your mother is a hard woman."

"I know. That's why I'm going to need you, Daddy."

"Honey, I'll be there."

"I knew you'd say that." His shock was ebbing, in light of Maggie's decisiveness and steel intentions.

"Have you ever heard of the Lamaze method of giving birth, Daddy? . . ."

"I've read about it."

She sidled him a glance. "Think we could do it? You and me?"

"Me?" His eyes grew round.

"Think you'd like to see your very last grandchild born?"

He considered a moment before answering, "It'd scare the daylights out of me."

"The classes would teach us both not to be scared."

It was the first time she'd admitted being so, while outwardly she continued as strong and dauntless as a steel I-beam.

"Your mother," he said, eyes twinkling, "would shit a ring around herself."

"Tsk, tsk, tsk. Such shocking language, Daddy."

They both laughed, conspirators with a sudden strong bond. Reaching the edge of town, Maggie confessed, "I haven't told Katy yet. I expect some trouble when I do."

"She'll get used to the idea. So will I. So will your mother. Anyway, my feeling is, you answer to no one but yourself."

"Exactly. And I've just learned that today." She pulled up at the top of her walk. The rain had stopped. Droplets quivered on the tips of leaves, and the air smelled like herbal tea—green, moist, earthen.

Maggie put the car in neutral and took her father's hand.

"Thanks for coming to get me, Daddy. I love you." How easily she could say it to him.

"I love you, too, and I won't say I'm not shocked. I think my argyles are someplace back there on EE."

When Maggie had laughed and quieted, Roy looked down at their joined hands.

"You amaze me, you know? There's so much strength in you. So much . . ." He puzzled before adding, ". . . direction. You've always been that way. You see what you want, what you need, and you go after it. College, Phillip, Seattle, Harding House, now this." He raised his eyes quickly. "Oh, not that you went after this, but look how you handle it, how you make decisions. I wish I could be that way. But somehow I always take the route of least resistance. I don't like it in myself, but that's the way it is. Your mother, she bulldozes me. I know it. She knows it. You know it. But this time, Maggie, I'm standing up to her. I want you to know that. This isn't the end of the world, and if you want that baby, then I'll go there to that hospital and show the world I got nothing to hang my head about, okay?"

The tears she had stubbornly dammed until now spurt into her eyes as she crooked an arm around Roy's neck and pressed her cheek to his. He smelled of raw beef and smoked sausage and Old Spice after-shave, an endearing and familiar combination. "Oh, Daddy, I needed to hear that so badly. Katy's going to be so upset. And Mother . . . I shudder to think of telling her. But I will. Not today, but soon, so you don't have to think I'd leave that job up to you."

He rubbed her back. "I'm learning something from you. You watch.

One of these days I'm going to make a move that might surprise you, too.''

She backed up and glowered at him. "Daddy, don't you dare go fishing with Eric Severson! If you do, I'll get a new Lamaze partner.''

He laughed and said, "Go on in the house and get into something dry before you catch a cold and cough that baby loose.''

Watching her go, he considered it, what he'd been considering for five years now. He'd see how Vera took the news, then he'd make up his mind.

Chapter 18

❧

Maggie Stearn had a stubborn streak longer than the Door County coast-line. She could do it! She'd show them all! She set about adjusting to the finality of this new, imminent presence in her life and to the fact that it would be raised in a fatherless environment. She fortified herself for the physical and emotional stamina it would take to do credit to both roles, those of mother and innkeeper. She altered her expectations to exclude a husband and groomed her courage to break the news to Katy and Vera.

A week went by, then two, but still she hadn't told them. She wore loose blouses, untucked, and beneath them kept her slacks unbuttoned.

One morning in early August, when Katy was less than a month shy of leaving for college, they awakened to the aftermath of a storm. The wind had strewn the yard with maple leaves and weeping willow branches from a neighbor's tree. Since Todd wasn't expected again for two days Maggie and Katy went outside to rake them up themselves.

Already at eleven A.M. the heat was sweltering, rising from the moist earth with tropical intensity while the breeze off the bay remained too warm to bring much relief. It brought instead the noisome odor of debris tossed onto the rocky shore by last night's storm, and more work: they'd have to rake up the seaweed and dead fish before the mess started decaying in the sun.

Maggie leaned over to scoop a handful of willow withes against her bamboo rake and straightened a little too fast. A twinge stabbed low in her groin and dizziness momentarily enveloped her. She let the twigs fall, flattened a hand to her pelvis and waited out the vertigo with closed eyes.

When she opened them, Katy was studying her, the rake idle in her hands. For seconds neither of them moved: Maggie caught in the classic pose of weary expectancy, Katy temporarily dumbstruck.

Katy's expression became quizzical. Finally she tipped her head and said, "Moth-*errr* . . . ,'' half questioning, half accusing.

Maggie dropped her hand from her groin while Katy continued staring. Her glance darted from Maggie's belly to her face, then down again.

When comprehension dawned she began, "Mother, are you . . . ? You aren't . . ." The idea seemed too preposterous to voice.

"Yes, Katy," Maggie admitted, "I'm pregnant."

Katy gaped at her mother's stomach, aghast. Tears sprang to her eyes. "Oh, my God," she whispered after some seconds. And again, horror-stricken, "Oh, my God . . . this is horrible!" The ramifications of the situation settled upon Katy one by one, changing her face by degrees, as a flower withered by time-lapse photography. From stupefaction to displeasure to outright anger. "How could you allow such a thing to happen, Mother!" she lashed out. "You'll be forty-one years old this month and you're not that stupid!"

"No, I'm not," Maggie replied. "There *is* an explanation."

"Well, I don't want to hear it!"

"I thought—"

"You thought!" Katy interrupted. "What you *thought* is altogether too obvious. You thought you could have your little illicit affair without anybody being the wiser, and instead you turn up pregnant!"

"Yes, some five months now."

Katy retreated as if something vile had insinuated itself in her path. Her face took on an expression of repugnance and her voice became sibilant with distaste. "It's his, isn't it? A *married* man's!"

"Yes, it is."

"This is disgusting, Mother!"

"Then you might as well hear the rest of it: his wife is pregnant too."

For a moment Katy appeared too stunned to reply. Finally she threw one hand in the air. "Oh, this is just great! I've made new friends in this town, you know! What am I supposed to tell them? That my mother got knocked up by a married man, who also, by the way, happened to knock up his estranged wife at the same time?" Her eyes narrowed with accusation. "Oh, yes, Mother, I know about that, too. I'm not ignorant. I've asked around! I know he hasn't been living with his wife since last winter. So what did he do, promise to divorce her and marry you?"

Stung by guilt and a sense of her own culpability, Maggie blushed.

Katy clapped a hand to her forehead, standing her bangs on end. "Oh, good God, Mother, how could you be so gullible? That line is as old as VD! Speaking of which—"

"Katy, I don't need any sermons on—"

"Speaking of which," Katy repeated forcefully, "you're *supposed* to use condoms, or hadn't you heard? It's the *in* thing to do if you're going in for promiscuous sex. I mean, holy cripes, Mother, the newspapers are full of it! If you're going to snuggle up with some Lothario who's hitting on women all over town—"

"He is *not* hitting on women all over town!" Maggie grew angry. "Katy, what's gotten into you! You're being purposely crude and cruel."

"What's gotten into me!" Katy spread a hand on her chest, her face incredulous. "Into me! That's a laugh! You want to know what's gotten into me when my own mother is standing in front of me five months pregnant with a married man's kid? Well, take a good look at yourself!" Katy railed. "Look at how you've changed since Daddy died! How do you expect me to react? You think maybe I should start passing out cigars and spreading the news that I'm going to have a new baby brother?" Katy's face became distorted by rage as she thrust her chin forward. "Well, don't hold your breath, Mother, because I'll *never* think of that bastard as my brother *or* my sister! *Never!*' She flung down the rake. "All I can say is I'm glad Daddy doesn't have to be here to see this day!"

Crying, she ran for the house.

The door slammed and Maggie flinched. She stood staring at it until her tears began, Katy's renunciation resounding through her head. A dense feeling overtook her chest: fault and apology, weighted by the burden of wrongdoing. She deserved Katy's every rebuke. She was the mother, expected to be a paragon of irreproachability, a worthy role model. Instead, look what she'd done.

Oh, Katy, Katy, I'm sorry. You're right on every count, but what can I do? It's mine. I have to raise it.

Heavy-hearted, she stood in the dappled yard, quietly crying, wrestling with guilt and an overwhelming sense of inadequacy, for she didn't know, at this juncture, how to fulfill her duties as a mother. No case studies she remembered, no self-help books she'd read set precedents for a situation such as this.

The irony of it: she, a woman of forty being preached to by her daughter on the subject of birth control. Her *daughter* crying out, "What will my friends think?"

Maggie closed her eyes, waiting for the oppression to lift, but it grew heavier until she felt as if it might drive her, like a steel spike, into the very earth. She realized she was still holding the smooth, warm rake handle. Turning listlessly toward the dock she let it slip from her hand and bounce to the grass.

She sat for a while on the wooden bench of the latticed arbor seat, the one Eric had built for her. During that time, while he'd worked on it, she'd had visions of waiting here for the *Mary Deare* at the end of the day. Of catching the mooring line as the engine died, and walking hip to hip with him, up to the house in the gloaming when the sky was pink and purple and the water as flat as a glass of cherry nectar.

The breeze was cooler here, out over the water. A pair of white-banded plovers came flapping by, scolding, *chur-wee, chur-wee*, landing on the rocks to forage amid the flotsam. Far out on the water a sailboat with an orange spinnaker rode the wind. Maggie had meant to buy a new sailboat immediately after settling here. There were times when she'd imagined herself and Eric taking weekend jaunts up to Chicago, taking in shows, eating at Crickets, and ambling with joined hands among the slips in Belmont Harbor, admiring the crafts that sailed in from points all around the Great Lakes. She'd meant to buy a sailboat, but now she wouldn't, for what pastime was lonelier than sailing alone?

She missed Eric in those moments with so intense a grip that it seemed to be crushing the breath from her. She wanted nothing so badly as to be strong, self-reliant, willful even, and she would be again, but in her weaker moments, as now, she needed him with a stultifying desperation.

She found this appalling.

What, after all, did one person know of another's intentions? Analyzing her and Eric's relationship, she realized he could have been amusing himself with her all along, without the slightest notion of leaving his extraordinarily beautiful wife. The story about Nancy's refusal to consider a family—was it false? After all, Eric's wife *was* pregnant now, wasn't she?

Maggie sighed, closed her eyes, and rested her head against the lattices.

What did it matter, his honesty or lack of it?

Their affair was ended. Absolutely. She had shunned him, had stalked away peremptorily in the rain, had refused his phone calls and icily asked that he not call again the once he'd shown up at her door. But her aloofness was a sham. She missed him. She loved him, still. She wanted to believe he had not lied.

The plovers flew away. The spinnaker became a black speck in the distance. On the road above, a car rumbled past. Life moved on. So must Maggie.

She finished the raking alone, bagged the sticks and returned to the house to find Katy gone, a note on the kitchen table.

I've gone to Grandma's. No signature. No further enlightenment. Certainly no love.

Maggie's hand, bearing the message, dropped disconsolately to her thigh. *Mother*, she thought wearily. She tossed the note onto the table, pulled off her gardening gloves, and left them, too, before ambling around the perimeter of her kitchen like someone lost, riding the smooth Formica edge with one hip and one hand, postponing the inevitable.

She came, eventually, to the telephone on the cupboard beside the refrigerator.

The last great hurdle.

She backtracked and washed her hands at the sink. Dried them. Studied the telephone at ten paces, as a duelist studies his opponent before raising his arm. Finding no more logical delays, she closed the hall door and sat down on a small white stool next to the instrument.

Go ahead, get it over with.

At last she picked up the receiver and punched out her mother's number, drawing a deep, full-chested breath as she heard the ring, picturing the house—flawlessly clean, as usual—and her mother with her neat, dated hairdo, hurrying toward the kitchen.

"Hello?" Vera answered.

"Hello, Mother."

Silence: *Oh, it's you.*

"Is Katy there?"

"Katy? No. Should she be?"

"She will be soon. She's on her way over, and she's very upset."

"Over what? Did you two have another fight?"

"I'm afraid so."

"What's it about *this* time?"

"Mother, I'm sorry to tell you this way. I should have come over and told you personally instead of dropping it on you like this." Maggie inhaled shakily, released half the breath and said, "I'm expecting Eric Severson's baby."

Stunned silence, then, "Oh, merciful Lord." The words sounded muffled, as if Vera had covered her lips with a hand.

"I just told Katy this morning and she left here in tears."

"Oh, merciful Lord in heaven, Margaret, how could you?"

"I know you're very disappointed in me."

The imperious side of Vera could not be stunned for long. Abruptly she demanded, "You aren't going to *have* it, are you?"

Had the moment been less monumental, Maggie would have registered her own dismay at Vera's callous reply. Instead, she answered, "I'm afraid it's far too late to do anything else."

"But they say his wife is expecting, too!"

"Yes, she is. I'll be raising this baby alone."

"Not here, I hope!"

Well, you didn't expect sympathy, did you, Maggie? "I live here," she replied reasonably. "My business is here."

Vera made the expected remark. "How will I ever be able to face my friends again?"

Staring at a brass drawer pull on the cabinets, Maggie felt the hurt mount. *Always herself. Only herself.*

Abruptly Vera launched into a tirade, her words crackling with censure. "I told you—didn't I try to tell you? But, no, you wouldn't listen, you just kept running around with him. Why, everyone in town knows about it, and they know his wife is expecting, too. I'm already embarrassed to face people on the street. What's it going to be like when you're parading around with his illegitimate baby on your arm?" Without waiting for a reply, she rushed on with more narrow concerns. "If you had no more self-respect than that, you might have at least considered your dad and I, Margaret. After all, we've got to live here for the rest of our lives."

"I know, Mother," Maggie replied meekly.

"Well, how can we ever hold our heads up again after this?"

Maggie hung her head.

"Maybe *now* your father will stop defending you. I tried to get him to say something to you last winter, but no, he turned a blind eye like he always does. I said, 'Roy, that girl is carrying on with Eric Severson and don't tell me she isn't!' "

Maggie sat silent, mollified, picturing Vera's face growing red and her wattle quivering.

"I said, 'You give her a talking to, Roy, because she won't listen to me!' Well, maybe *now* he'll listen after he gets the shock of his life!"

Maggie spoke quietly. "Daddy already knows."

From clear across town she could sense Vera bristle.

"You told *him*, but you didn't tell me?" she demanded.

Sitting in silence, Maggie felt a glimmer of retaliatory satisfaction.

"Well, isn't that just ducky, when a daughter can't even come to her mother first! And why didn't he say anything to me about it?"

"I asked him not to. I thought it was something I should tell you myself."

Vera snorted, then remarked sarcastically, "Well, *thank you* for the consideration! I'm deeply touched. I have to go now. Katy is here."

She hung up without a good-bye, leaving Maggie holding the receiver in her lap, leaning her head against the refrigerator, her eyes closed.

I won't cry. I won't cry. I won't cry.

So what is the lump in your throat?

Daddy said it best: she's a hard woman.

How did you expect her to react?

She's my mother! She should be my comfort and support at a time like this.

When was she ever a comfort or a support?

The electronic hang-up tone began whining but Maggie remained motionless, gulping at the wad in her throat until she'd mastered the compulsion to weep. From somewhere deep inside she found a reservoir of strength laced with a liberal shot of vexation and drew from it. Vehemently she replaced the receiver, picked up the phone book, found the number of the *Door County Advocate* and ordered, "Want ads, please."

After placing an ad under HELP WANTED, she emptied the dishwasher, changed four beds, cleaned three bedrooms, washed two loads of towels, swept the verandas, mixed up a batch of refrigerator muffins, staked up the daylilies that had been flattened by the storm, greeted two incoming parties, answered eight phone calls, ate a piece of watermelon, gave a final coat of paint to a piece of used wicker, took a bath, put on clean clothes (comfortable ones this time, the maternity clothes she'd been hiding) and at 4:45 P.M. refilled the parlor candy bowl. All this, staunch as a midwife. Without a leaked tear.

I conceived it. I'll accept it. I'll overcome it. I'll be superwoman. I'll do it all, by God!

Her staunchness continued throughout that night, while Katy failed to call or return, and into the next morning as Maggie began her second day of innkeeping without help; through a lunch-on-the-run (a turkey sandwich in one hand, a dustcloth in the other); through the sign-out of guests and the blessed hours of silence following their departure, before the new batch arrived.

She was still suffering under her rigid, self-imposed drought when, at two o'clock, the kitchen screen door opened and Brookie walked in. She caught Maggie leaning over the half-empty dishwasher gripping a sheath of clean silverware. Standing just inside the door, samurai-fashion, Brookie pinned Maggie with a look of monumental pugnacity.

"I heard," she announced. "I figured you could use a friend."

Maggie's fortifications crumbled like the pediments of a fortress under cannonade. The silverware clattered from her fist and she sailed into Brookie's arms, bawling like a five-year-old with a scraped knee.

"Oh, Brookieeeee," she wailed.

Brookie held her fast, fierce, her own heart bounding with sympathy and relief. "Why didn't you come to me? I've been so worried about you. I thought it was something I did, something I said. I thought maybe you weren't happy with Todd's work and you didn't know how to tell me. I imagined all kinds of things. Oh, Maggie, you can't go through this alone. Didn't you know you could trust me?"

"Oh, B . . . Brookieee," Maggie wailed, releasing all her despair in a blessed rain of weeping, clinging to Brookie while her shoulders shook. "I was s . . . so afraid to tell any . . . one."

"Afraid? Of me?" Cajolingly, "How long have you known old Brookie, huh?"

"I kn . . . know." Maggie's words were choppy with weeping. "But I m . . . must look like a t . . . total idiot."

"You're no idiot, now stop talking that way."

"But I'm o . . . old enough to know b . . . better. And I b . . . belieeveed hiiiiim." The words wailed like a siren as Maggie wept with abject totality.

"So, you believed him," Brookie repeated.

"He s . . . said he'd m . . . marry me just as soon as . . . he . . . he . . . c . . . c . . . could get a d . . . div . . ." Maggie's words dissolved into an unchecked spate of weeping that echoed around the kitchen like a bagpipe through a glen.

Brookie rubbed Maggie's palpitating back. "Bawl all you want. Then we're going to sit down and talk, and you're going to feel better."

Childishly, Maggie claimed, "I'll never f . . . feel better ag . . . gain."

Brookie loved Maggie enough to smile. "Oh, yes, you will. Now come on. You're getting snot all over me. Blow your nose and swab your eyes and I'll make some iced tea." She plucked two tissues from a box and guided Maggie to a chair. "Sit down there. Empty those bilge pumps and catch your breath."

Maggie followed orders while Brookie turned on the water and opened cupboard doors. During the making and drinking of lemon tea, Maggie gained control and spilled her emotions, omitting nothing, pouring out hurt, disillusionment and her own grave faults in one unbroken current.

"I feel so stupid and gullible. Brookie, I not only believed him, I thought I couldn't get pregnant anymore. When I told Katy she gave me a lecture on condoms and I was so embarrassed, I wanted to die. Then she screamed at me that she'd never consider my bastard her sister or brother, and now she's packed up and gone to Mother's. And Mother—God, I don't even want to repeat the tongue-lashing I took from her, and I deserved every word of it."

"You through now?" Brookie asked dryly. "Because I have a few comments to make. First of all, I've known Eric Severson all my life and he's not the kind who'd use a woman and lie to her deliberately. And as far as Katy goes, she's still got some growing up to do. She just needs some time to get used to the idea. When the baby is born she'll change her mind, just wait and see. And about Vera—well, nobody said raising our mothers was going to be easy, did they?"

Maggie gave a halfhearted smile.

"And you're not stupid!" Brookie pointed a finger at Maggie's nose. "I'd probably have thought the same thing about birth control if I'd had hot flashes and screwed-up periods."

"But people will say—"

"Piss on people. Let them say what they want. The ones that matter will give you the benefit of the doubt."

"Brookie, look at me. I'm forty years old. Aside from the baby being illegitimate, I have no business getting pregnant at my age. I'm too old for parenting and there's a real risk of birth defects at my age. What if something—"

"Oh, come on now. Look at Bette Midler and Glenn Close. They both had their *first* babies after forty, and no problems at all."

Brookie's positive attitude was addictive. Maggie cocked her head and said, "Yeah?"

"Yeah. So listen—what's it going to be? Natural childbirth? You need a coach or anything? I'm an old pro in a delivery room."

"Thanks for offering, but my dad's going to do it."

"Your dad!"

Maggie smiled. "Good old Dad."

"Well, good for him. But if anything comes up and he can't make it, just call on me."

"Oh, Brookie," Maggie said wistfully. The worst was over, the storm calmed. "I love you."

"I love you, too."

Those words, above all others, healed, replaced self-esteem and a brighter outlook. The two women sat at right angles, their forearms resting on the scarred tabletop near a crockery pitcher of cosmos and larkspur Maggie had picked during her earlier spurt of angry energy. Maggie said quietly, "I don't think we've ever said it before."

"I don't think so either."

"Do you think you just have to get old enough before you can say it comfortably to a friend?"

"I guess so. You just have to learn that it feels better said than unsaid."

They smiled and shared a moment of silent affection.

"You know something, Brookie?"

"Hm . . ."

Maggie rolled her cold glass between her palms, studying her iced tea as she admitted, "My mother has never said it to me."

"Oh, honey . . ." Brookie took one of Maggie's hands.

Maggie lifted her troubled gaze, allowing herself to come to grips with the tremendous void Vera had left within her. She had been raised Christian. Everything from television commercials to greeting cards had instilled in her the canon that to do anything less than love a parent was depraved.

"Brookie," she said solemnly, "can I confess something to you?"

"Your secrets are my secrets."

"I don't think I love my mother."

Brookie's unwavering eyes held Maggie's sad ones. She gripped Maggie's hand reassuringly.

"I'm not shocked, in case you expected me to be."

"I expect I should feel guilty, but I don't."

"What's so precious about guilt that we all think we should feel it at times like this?"

"I've tried very hard, but she returns nothing, gives nothing. And I know that's selfish, too. You shouldn't evaluate love based on the returns it brings you."

"And where did you read that, on some greeting card?"

"You don't think I'm degenerate?"

"You know me better than that. What you are is hurt."

"I am. Oh, Brookie, I am. She should be the one holding my hand right now. Am I wrong? I mean, if it were Katy pregnant, I'd never turn her away. I'd be there for her every minute, and I'd hide my disappointments, because I've realized something in the last year or so. People who love one another occasionally disappoint one another."

"Now, that's the kind of common sense I believe, too. It's much closer to reality."

"I thought, when I moved back here, that it would be a chance for my mother and I to build some kind of a relationship, if not overtly loving, at least accepting. I've always had the feeling she never accepted me, and now, well . . . she's made it clear she never will again. Brookie, I pity her, she's so cold, so . . . so closed off from anything nurturing or caring, and I'm so afraid Katy is becoming like her."

Releasing Maggie's hand, Brookie refilled both their glasses. "Katy is young and impressionable, but from what I see of her around Todd, you don't need to worry about her being cold."

"No, I guess not." Maggie drew wet rings on the tabletop with the bottom of her glass. "Which brings up something else I needed to talk to you about, the two of them. They're . . . well . . . I think they're . . ."

She looked up into Brookie's eyes and found a grin.

"Intimate is the word I think you're struggling for."

"So you've seen it, too."

"All I have to see is the hour he's coming in every night, and how he gulps his food at suppertime in a mad rush to get over here and pick her up."

"This is awkward. I . . ." Again Maggie stopped, searching for a graceful way of expressing herself.

Brookie filled in the gap. "How can you say to your daughter, be careful, when you yourself are carrying an unexpected bundle, right?"

Maggie smiled forlornly. "Exactly. I've watched it happening and said nothing, because I'd look like a hypocrite if I did."

"Well, you can stop worrying. Gene and I talked to him about it."

"You did? . . ." Maggie's eyes widened in surprise.

"Well, Gene did. We have an agreement—he'll talk to the boys and I'll talk to the girls."

"What did Todd say?"

Brookie flipped up a palm nonchalantly. "He said, 'Don't worry. Everything's cazh, Dad.' "

The two women's faces brightened and they found themselves laughing. They sipped tea awhile, filtering their parental experiences through memories of themselves and their first sexual encounters. At length Maggie said, "Things have changed, haven't they? Can you believe you and I are sitting here calmly discussing the active sex life of our children as if it were the rising price of fresh vegetables?"

"Hey, who are you and I to point fingers? We, who once risked discovery on the same boat?"

"We? You mean you and Arnie, too?"

"Yup. Me and Arnie, too."

As their eyes met, their memories harked back to a day after prom aboard the *Mary Deare*, when they were young and ardent and turning cornerstones in their lives.

Brookie sighed, leaned her jaw on a fist and absently rubbed the condensation off the side of her glass. Maggie took up a similar pose.

"Eric was your first, wasn't he?"

"My first and my only, besides Phillip."

"Did Phillip know about him?"

"He suspected." Maggie glanced up pointedly. "Does Gene know about Arnie?"

"No. And I don't know for sure about any of his old girlfriends. Why should we tell each other? They were meaningless. Part of our coming of age, but meaningless today."

"Unfortunately, my first one is not meaningless today."

Brookie pondered awhile, then ventured, "To think I was the one who gave you his phone number and said, 'Don't be silly, why can't you call an old boyfriend?' "

"Yeah, it's all your fault, kid."

They exchanged salty grins.

"So, how about if I dump the baby on you occasionally when I need to get away for an evening?"

Brookie laughed. "That's the first healthy thing I've heard you say about the baby. You must be getting used to the idea of it."

"Maybe I am."

"You know what? I didn't want the last two I had, but they have a way of growing on you."

Brookie's choice of phrases brought a second welcome laugh. When it faded Maggie sat up straight in her chair and turned serious again.

"I'm going to dump one more confession on you, then that's it for today," she said.

Brookie straightened, too. "Go ahead. Dump."

"I still love him."

"Yeah, that's the tough part, isn't it?"

"But I've given it some thought and I've decided it took six months for me to fall *in* love, I should give myself at least that long to fall out of it."

How does one fall out of love? The longer Maggie went without seeing Eric, the more she missed him. She waited for the withering as a farmer awaits it during weeks of drought, watching over his struggling crops and thinking, just die and get it over with. But like weeds that can survive without nourishment, Maggie's love for Eric refused to wither.

August passed, a hot, tiring, oppressive month. Katy went back to school without a good-bye, Todd left for basic training, and Maggie hired an older woman named Martha Dunworthy who came in daily to do the cleaning. In spite of Martha's help, Maggie's days were long and regimented.

Up at 6:30 to bake muffins, prepare juice and coffee, set the dining-room table and make herself presentable. From 8:30 to 10:30 breakfast was available and she made sure she sat with each of her guests for a brief time during the meal, realizing that her friendliness and hospitality was the charm that would bring them back. When the last one had eaten, she put the dining room in order, then the kitchen, checked out guests (often a lingering parting since most of them went away feeling like personal friends). She accepted payment, filled out receipts and sent them away with picture postcards of Harding House, her business card, and hugs on the back veranda. Checkout usually overlapped inquiry calls which began around ten A.M. (numerous since autumn was approaching, Door's heaviest tourist season). The short-distance calls weren't bad; they were usually from the chamber of commerce checking on room availability. The long-distance ones, however, were time-consuming and required answering dozens of repetitive questions before most reservations were made. When the guests were gone she recorded the day's take in her books, answered correspondence, paid bills, laundered towels (the linen service did only bedding), picked and arranged flowers, supervised Martha's cleaning and went to the post office. Around two P.M. the next night's guests began arriving with their inevitable questions about where to eat, fish and buy picnic supplies. Between these daily duties, there were Maggie's own meals to be prepared and eaten, banking to do, and whatever personal tasks she had set for herself that day.

She loved innkeeping—she really did—but it was exhausting for a pregnant woman. She was at the beck and call of others nearly around the clock. Midday napping was impossible given the constant interruptions. If the last guest didn't pull in until 10:30, she was still up at that hour. And as for days off, they didn't exist. At night when she'd fall into bed, her legs aching and her body weary, she'd rest a wrist across her forehead and think, I'll never be able to do this and handle a baby, too. The baby was due around Thanksgiving and she'd accepted reservations through the end of October, but some days she wasn't sure she'd make it until then.

If only I had a man, she'd think in her weaker moments. If only I had Eric. Thoughts of him persisted, ill-advised as they were.

Then, on September 22nd, Brookie called with some news that spun Maggie's emotional barometer.

"Are you sitting down?" Brookie began.

"Now I am." Maggie plunked onto the stool beside the refrigerator. "What is it?"

"Nancy Macaffee had a miscarriage."

Maggie sucked in a breath and felt her heart whip into overdrive.

"It happened in Omaha while she was there on business. But, Maggie, I'm afraid the rest of the news isn't good. Rumor has it he's taken her on a cruise to Saint Martin and Saint Kitts to patch up her health and their marriage."

Maggie felt her momentary hope plummet.

"Maggie, are you there?"

"Yes . . . yes, I'm here."

"I'm sorry to be the one to tell you, but I thought you should know."

"Yes . . . yes, I'm glad you did, Brookie."

"Hey, kiddo, you okay?"

"Yeah, sure."

"You want me to come over or anything?"

"No. Listen, I'm fine. Fine! I mean it. Why, I'm . . . I'm practically over him!" she claimed with forced brightness.

Practically over him? How could one ever get over the man whose only child you would bear?

The question haunted her during restless nights as she grew near term, when her body grew rounder and her sleep was interrupted by countless trips to the bathroom. When her ankles swelled and her face got puffy and she began attending Lamaze classes with Roy.

October came and Door County donned its autumn regalia—the maples blazing, the birches flaming, and the apple orchards hanging heavy with their blushing burden. The inn was filled every night, and all the guests seemed to be in love. They came by twos, always by twos. Maggie watched them saunter toward the lake, hand in hand, and sit in the arbor seat studying the reflection of the maples which burned like live flames on the blue, calm waters. Sometimes they'd kiss. And sometimes risk a brief intimate caress before returning upyard with a look of replenishment on their faces.

Watching them, Maggie would retreat from the window, cradle her distended abdomen and relive the days of requited touches with a bittersweet longing. Observing the rest of the world passing two-by-two, she anticipated the birth of her child as one of the loneliest things she would ever live through.

"We'll do fine," she'd say aloud to the one she carried. "We've got your grandpa, and Brookie, and plenty of money, plus this grand house.

And when you're old enough, we'll buy that sailboat, and I'll teach you to become a ragman, and *you and I* will sail to Chicago. We'll do fine.''

One afternoon in late October, during a spell of Indian summer weather, she decided to walk uptown to get her mail. She dressed in a pair of black knit slacks and a rust-and-black maternity sweater and left a note on the door: *Back at 4:00.*

The poplars and maples were already bare, and the oaks were shedding their leaves along Cottage Row as she headed down the hill. Squirrels were busy gathering acorns, racing across her path. The sky was intense blue. The leaves rustled as she walked through them.

Uptown the street was quieter. Most of the boats were gone from the docks. Some of the shops had already closed for the season, and those remaining open had little foot traffic. The flowers along Main Street were withered but for the marigolds and chrysanthemums which had withstood the first frost.

The post office lobby was empty—a tiny yellow space surrounding the service window, which was unmanned as Maggie entered. She went straight to her box, got her mail, slammed the door and turned to find Eric Severson not ten feet behind her.

They both came to a standstill.

Her heart began pounding.

His face flushed.

"Maggie . . ." he spoke first. "Hello."

She stood rooted, feeling as if the blood were going to beat its way out her ears and splatter the lobby wall. Spellbound by his presence. Absorbing the familiar—tan face, bleached hair, blue eyes. Decrying the unfamiliar—brown jeans, a plaid shirt, a puffy down vest—which created an absurd sense of deprivation, as if she'd been cheated of the time during which he'd acquired them.

"Hello, Eric."

His eyes dropped to her maternity sweater, belled out by the protruding load she carried.

Please, she prayed, *don't let anyone else walk in.*

She saw him swallow and drag his eyes back to her face.

"How are you?"

"Fine," she replied in a queer, reedy voice. "I'm just . . . just fine." Unconsciously she shielded her stomach with a handful of mail. "How are you?"

"I've been happier," he replied, studying her eyes with a look of torment in his own.

"I heard about your wife losing the baby. I'm sorry."

"Yes, well . . . sometimes those things . . . you know . . ." His words trailed away as his gaze returned to her girth as if it exerted some cosmic magnetic force. The seconds stretched like light-years while he stood rapt, his Adam's apple working in his throat. In the back room a piece of machinery rattled and somebody rolled a heavy cart across the floor. When he looked up her eyes skittered away.

"I understand you took a trip," she said, groping for reasons to linger.

"Yes, to the Caribbean. I thought it might help her . . . us, to recover."

Hattie Hockenbarger, a twenty-eight-year veteran of the postal service, appeared in the window, opened a drawer and replenished her supply of postcards.

"Beauty of a day, isn't it?" she addressed them both.

They shot her a pair of distracted glances, but neither of them said a word, only watched her depart around a high wall before returning to their interrupted conversation and their fixation with one another.

"She's having trouble getting over it," Eric murmured.

"Yes, well . . ." Finding little to say on the subject, Maggie lapsed into silence.

He broke it after several seconds, his voice throaty, verging on emotional, too soft to be heard beyond the quiet lobby. "Maggie, you look wonderful."

So do you. She would not say it, would not look at him, looked instead at the WANTED posters hanging on the wall while firing a smoke screen of chatter. "The doctor says I'm healthy as a horse, and Daddy has agreed to be my coach when the baby is born. We go to Lamaze classes twice a month, and I'm actually getting quite good at Kagel exercises, so . . . I . . . we . . ."

He touched her arm and she became silent, unable to resist the gravity of his eyes. Looking into them she became decimated because, clearly, his feelings hadn't changed. He hurt as she hurt.

"Do you know what it is, Maggie?" he whispered. "A girl or a boy?"

Don't do this, don't care! Not if I can't have you!

In a moment Maggie's throat would close completely. In a moment her tears would well over. In a moment she'd be making an even greater fool of herself in the middle of the post office lobby.

"Maggie, do you know?"

"No," she whispered.

"Do you need anything? Money, anything?"

"No." *Just you.*

The door opened and Althea Munne walked in, followed by Mark Brodie, who was speaking. "I heard Coach Beck is starting Mueller tomorrow night. Should be a good game. Let's just hope this warm weather . . ." He glanced up and seemed to go mute. He held the door open long after Althea passed into the lobby. His glance darted between Maggie and Eric.

She recovered enough poise to say, "Hello, Mark."

"Hello, Maggie. Eric." He nodded and let the door close.

The three of them stood in a tableau of awkwardness, observed closely by Althea Munne and Hattie Hockenbarger who'd returned to her window at the sound of the door opening.

Mark's eyes dropped to Maggie's stomach and his cheeks turned pink. He had not called her since the rumors began circulating about her and Eric.

"Listen, I have to go, I have guests coming in," Maggie extemporized, affecting a cheerful smile. "Nice to see you, Mark. Althea, hi, how are you?" She rushed out the door in a welter of emotions, red-faced and trembling, unspeakably close to tears. Outside, she bumped the shoulders of two tourists as she hurtled along the sidewalk. She had planned to stop at the store and pick up some hamburger for supper, but Daddy would surely see she was upset and ask questions.

She plodded up the hill oblivious to the beautiful afternoon, the spicy smell of the fallen leaves.

Eric, Eric, Eric.

How can I live here the rest of my life, running into him now and then like I just did? It was traumatic enough today; it would be untenable with his child's hand in mine. A picture flashed through her mind: herself and their child, a son, entering the post office two years from now and encountering the big, blond man with the haunted eyes who would be unable to tear his gaze off them. And the child, looking up, asking, "Mommy, who's that man?"

She simply could not do it. It had nothing to do with shame. It had to do with love. A love that stubbornly refused to wither, no matter how ill-advised. A love that, with each accidental encounter, would herald their feelings as unmistakably as these fallen leaves heralded the end of summer.

I simply cannot do it, she thought as she approached the house she had grown to love. *I cannot live here with his child, but without him, and my only alternative is to leave.*

Chapter 19

It had been a tense summer for Nancy Macaffee. Feigning pregnancy had put her on edge, and had not brought back Eric's affection as she'd hoped. He remained distant and troubled, scarcely ever touching her, speaking to her about only the most perfunctory things. He spent more time than ever on the boat, leaving her alone most of the weekends she was at home.

His only sign of remorse came when she had called him from "St. Joseph's Hospital" in Omaha to tell him she'd had a miscarriage. He had suggested the trip to the Bahamas to get her back on her feet, and had willingly canceled a week of charter bookings to take her there. On the islands, however, beneath the spell of the tropics, where their love should have reblossomed if it were going to, he remained introspective and uncommunicative.

Back at home she had taken a month off, willing to try domestic science in a last-ditch effort to regain his esteem. She spent her days calling his mother for bread recipes, putting fabric softener in their laundry and wax on their floors, but she hated every minute of it. Her life felt pointless without the challenge of sales quotas and the high-tension pace of weekly travel schedules; without dressing up each day and jumping into the mainstream of the retail business where people had flair and style and the same kind of aggressiveness upon which she thrived.

Her time at home proved futile, for Eric sensed her restlessness and said, "You might as well go back to work. I can tell you're going crazy here."

In October she followed his advice.

But she continued searching for ways to win him back. Her most recent campaign involved his family.

"Darling," she said, one Friday night when he'd come home at a reasonable hour. "I thought maybe we'd invite Mike and Barbara over Sunday night. It's been my fault we haven't had friendlier relations with them, but I intend to remedy that. How about inviting them for supper? We could do linguini and clam sauce."

"Fine," he said indifferently. He was sitting at the kitchen table doing company bookwork, wearing glasses and a fresh haircut that made him look militarily clean. He had a wonderful profile. Straight nose, arched lips, pleasing chin—like a young Charles Lindbergh. The sight of him never failed to tighten her vitals when she remembered how it used to be between them. Would he never touch her sexually again?

She squatted beside his chair, crooked a wrist over his shoulder and flicked his earlobe with a finger. "Hey . . ."

He glanced up.

"I'm really trying here."

He pushed up his glasses. The pencil moved on. "Nancy, I have work to do."

She persisted. "You said you wanted a baby . . . I tried that. You said I snubbed your family. I admit I have and I'm trying to make up for it. You said you wanted me to stay home. I've done that, too, but it didn't serve any purpose whatsoever. What am I doing wrong, Eric?"

Again the pencil stopped, but he didn't look up. "Nothing . . ." he answered. "Nothing."

She stood, slipping her hands into her skirt pockets, crushed by the admission she'd been denying all these weeks, an admission that made her seize up with dread and insecurity.

Her husband didn't love her. She knew that as certainly as she knew whom he did love.

Maggie awoke at one A.M. on November 8th with a strong, knotting contraction that opened her eyes like a slamming door. She cupped her stomach and lay absolutely still, wishing it away, realizing it was two weeks early. *Don't let anything happen to the baby.* When the pain ebbed she closed her eyes, absorbing the prayer which had imposed itself without her conscious will. When had she begun wanting this child?

She turned on the light and checked the minute hand on her watch, then lay waiting, remembering her first birth, how different it had been with Phillip beside her. It had been a slow labor, thirteen hours total. At home they had walked, then danced, laughing between contractions at her ungainliness. He had carried her suitcase to the car and had driven with one hand on her thigh. When a hard pain snapped her straight as a switchblade, he'd rolled down the car windows and run a red light. His was the last face she'd seen before being rolled into the delivery room, and the first upon waking in the recovery room. How reassuringly traditional it had been.

How daunting, this time, to face it husbandless.

Another pain built. Eight minutes . . . pant . . . pant . . . call Dad . . . call the doctor. . . .

Dr. Macklin said, "Get to the hospital."

Roy said, "I'm on my way."

Vera told Roy, "Don't expect me to show my face around that hospital!"

Reaching for his shirt and shoes, he replied, "No, Vera, I won't. I've learned not to expect anything from you at the times that count."

She sat up, her hairnet like a web over her forehead, her face pinched beneath it. "See what this has done! It's driven a wedge between us. That girl has disgraced us, Roy, and I can't for the life of me see how you can—"

He slammed the door, leaving her braced up on one hand, still haranguing him from the bed they'd shared for over forty years.

"Hello, honey," he said cheerfully when he got to Maggie's. "What do you say we get this little person into the world?"

Maggie had not thought she could love her father more, but the next two hours proved differently. A father and daughter could not go through so intimate an experience without learning each other's true mettle and being bound by new, even stronger tethers.

Roy was magnificent. He was all the things that Vera wasn't: gentle, infinitely loving, strong when she needed strength, humorous when she needed reprieve. She had worried about certain moments—when he'd have to witness her pain, when her body was probed in one way or another, and above all, that of baring herself before him for the first time. He proved dauntless. He took her nudity in stride—a surprise—talking her through the first minutes with a recollection while rubbing her abdomen, naked, for the first time.

"When you were little, oh, about five, six maybe, you delivered your first baby. Do you remember that?"

She wagged her head on the pillow.

"You don't?" He smiled. "Well, I do." His hand made soothing circles. "That was back when we used to make home deliveries from the store. If somebody was sick, or if an old lady didn't have a car or a driver's license, we'd deliver her groceries for her. So one day the doorbell rang and I went to answer it, and there you stood, with your dolly in a brown paper sack. 'I gots a delibery from the hostible,' you said, and handed it to me."

"Oh, Daddy, you're making this up." Maggie couldn't help smiling.

"No, I'm not. I swear upon this very grandchild, I'm not." He patted her big, stretch-marked stomach. "You must have overheard things about deliveries and hospitals and that's how you figured it was done, straight to the door in a brown paper sack like I delivered groceries."

She laughed but at that moment a contraction began, closing her eyes, forcing a breathiness into her voice. "I wish . . . it were . . . that easy."

"Don't push yet," he coached. "Breathe short. Hold those lower muscles tight . . . just for a while yet. That's it, honey."

When the contraction stopped he wiped her brow with a cool, damp cloth. "There. That was a dandy. Things are coming along real good, I think."

"Daddy," she said, looking up at him, "I wish you didn't have to see me in pain."

"I know, but I'll be strong if you'll be. Besides, this is pretty exciting for an old man. When you were born I didn't get a chance to watch 'cause in those days they threw the fathers out in a smoky waiting room."

She reached for his hand. His was there to grip hers tightly. For either of them to say I love you would have been superfluous at that moment.

On the delivery table, when she called out, then growled with the effort of pushing the child from her body, he proved even more stalwart.

"That's the way, honey. Give 'em hell," he encouraged.

When the baby's head appeared, Maggie opened her eyes between pains and saw Roy's eyes rapt on the mirror, a smile of excitement on his face.

He wiped her brow and said, "One more, honey."

With the next push they shared the moment in eternity toward which all of life strives. One generation . . . to the next . . . to the next.

The baby slithered into the world and it was Roy who rejoiced, "It's a girl!" then added reverently, ". . . oh, my . . . oh, my," in the kind of hushed tone often prompted by perfect roses and some sunsets. "Look at her, look at that gorgeous little granddaughter of mine."

The baby squawled.

Roy dried his eyes on the shoulder of his green scrubs.

Maggie felt with her hands the wet, naked bundle on her belly, touching her daughter the first time before the umbilical cord was severed.

Even before she was bathed they held her, together, the three generations linked by Roy's rough meat-cutter's hand which lay on the baby's tiny stomach, and Maggie's much more delicate one upon the infant's bloody, blond-capped head.

"It's like having you all over again," Roy said.

Maggie lifted her eyes and as they filled with tears, Roy kissed her forehead. She found, at that moment, the blessing within the burden brought about by this unwanted pregnancy. It was he, this kind, loving father, his benevolence and goodness, the lessons he would teach her yet—both her and this child—about love and its many guises.

"Daddy," she said, "thank you for being here, and for being you."

"Thank you for asking me, sweetheart."

Mike called on November 9th and told Eric, "Barb's cousin Janice called this morning when she got to the hospital. Maggie had a girl last night."

Eric sat down as if poleaxed.

"Eric, you there?"

Silence.

"Eric?"

"Yeah, I'm . . . Jesus, a girl . . ."

"Six pounds even. A little small, but everything's okay."

A girl, a girl. I have a baby girl!

"She was born last night around ten I guess. Barb thought you ought to know."

"Is Maggie okay?"

"As far as I know."

"Did Janice see her? Or the baby?"

"I don't know. She works on a different floor."

"Oh, sure . . . well . . ."

"Listen, I hope it's okay to say congratulations. I mean, hell, I don't know what else to say."

Eric drew an unsteady breath. "Thanks, Mike."

"Sure. Listen, you gonna be okay? You want to come out or anything? Have a beer? Go out for a ride?"

"I'll be all right."

"You sure?"

"Yeah . . . I . . . hell . . ." His voice broke. "Listen, Mike, I have to go."

After hanging up he walked around feeling bereft, glancing out window after window, staring at objects without seeing them. What was her name? What color was her hair? Was she lying in one of those glass cribs that looked like a big Pyrex bread pan? Was she crying? Being changed? Was she in Maggie's room being fed? What would they look like together, Maggie and their daughter?

His mind formed a picture of a dark head bent over a blond one, the infant nursing from a baby bottle . . . or a breast. He felt as he'd felt within the hour after his father had died. Helpless. Cheated. Like crying.

Nancy came in from grocery shopping and he forced himself to act normal.

"Hi, anybody call?" she asked.

"Mike."

"They're still coming tonight, aren't they?"

"Yes, but he asked me to come out and help him move Ma's old fuel oil barrel this afternoon. We're going to haul it out to the dump." They'd finally talked Ma into a new furnace. It had been installed the previous week. It was a logical lie.

"Oh, that's all?"

"Yeah."

He moved like a plane on automatic pilot, as if all will had been taken from him—upstairs to reshave, change clothes, recomb his hair and pat after-shave on his cheeks, thinking all the while, you're crazy, man! You keep your ass away from that hospital!

But he continued preparing, unable to resist, realizing this would be his only chance to see her. Once Maggie took her home it might be months, years before she was old enough to walk and he happened to run into them uptown.

One look, one *glimpse* of his daughter and he'd hightail it out of there.

In the bedroom before Nancy's lighted mirror, he checked his appearance one more time, wishing he could have worn dress trousers and a sport jacket. *To haul Ma's oil burner to the dump?* His white shirt was tucked tightly into his blue jeans, but he smoothed the front another time, then pressed a hand to his trembling stomach. *What are you scared of?* He blew out a big breath, turned from his reflection and went downstairs to find his jacket.

Shrugging into it, avoiding Nancy's eyes, he inquired, "You need any help with supper?"

"You're great with Caesar dressing. I thought I'd let you make it and toss the salad."

"Right. I'll be home in plenty of time."

He hurried out before she could kiss him good-bye.

He'd gotten a new Ford pickup. No advertising on its doors, nothing to disclose who owned it. Driving it through the drear November afternoon toward Door County Memorial Hospital he remembered a day much like this, only snowy, when he and Maggie had driven to Sturgeon Bay to attend an estate sale. That was the day they'd bought the bed on which their daughter had probably been conceived. The bed that stood now in the Belvedere Room at Harding House. Who was sleeping in it? Strangers?

Or had Maggie kept it as her own? And was there a cradle in one corner? Or a crib against one wall? A rocking chair in one corner?

Lord, all he'd miss. All the sweet ordinary paternal milestones he'd miss.

The hospital was on 16th Place, north of town where the buildings thinned, a three-story brick structure with the maternity ward on the first floor. He knew his way to it without asking directions: he'd been here six times to see Mike and Barb's newborn babies. A half-dozen times he'd stood before the glass window, studying the pink-faced creatures, thinking, long ago, that one day he'd have one of his own; realizing, as the years advanced, that the chances of that happening were diminishing. Now here he was, taking the elevator up from the ground floor, entering the double doors into the maternity ward, a father at last, and having to sneak to see his own child.

At the nurse's station a plump fortyish woman with a dime-sized mole on her left cheek looked up as he passed, watching him through thick glasses that magnified her eyes and tinted them pink. He knew the procedure—anyone wanting to view babies asked at the nurses' station for them to be brought to the observation window, but Eric had no intention of asking. Luck would either be with him or it wouldn't. He nodded to the woman and proceeded around the corner toward the nursery window without speaking a word. Passing open doors he glanced inside wondering which was Maggie's, telling himself, should he happen to catch a glimpse of her, he *would not* pause. But he felt an almost sick longing at the realization of how near she was. Within yards, behind one of these walls she lay upon a high, hard bed, her body mending, her heart—what of her heart? Was it, too, mending? Or did it still ache at the thought of him, as his did at the thought of her? If he asked her room number and stopped in her doorway, what might her reaction be?

He reached the nursery window without encountering anyone, and looked inside. White walls trimmed with colorful rabbits and bears. A window on the opposite wall. A clock with a blue frame. Three occupied glass cribs. One with a blue nametag, two with pink. From this distance he could not read the names. He stood terrified, sweating, feeling an overload of blood rush to his chest and a shortage of breath as if he'd been tackled and gone down hard.

The baby beneath the pink card on the left lay on her back, crying, her arms up and quivering like newly-sprouted shoots in a stiff breeze. He stepped closer to the window and withdrew his glasses from his jacket pocket. As he slipped them on, the pink card came into focus.

Suzanne Marian Stearn.

His response was as swift and as total as passion. Such a wave, like a powerful breaker sweeping him to the ceiling and slamming him back down. It roared in his ears—or was it his own pulsebeat? It stung his eyes—or was it his own tears? It left him fulfilled and yearning, satisfied and empty, wishing he had never come this far yet certain he would have broken the limbs of anyone who'd tried to stop him.

Fatherlove. Mindless and reactionary, yet more real and swift than any love he had ever before experienced.

Her hair was the length, texture and color of a dandelion seed. It erupted in a perfect crescent around her head, as blond as his in his baby pictures, as Anna's, as Anna's mother's before her.

"Suzanne?" he whispered, touching the glass.

She was red and disgruntled, her face tufted by temper, her eyes concealed in delicate pillows of pink as she cried. Within a white flannel blanket her feet churned in outrage. Watching, isolated by a quarter inch of transparent glass, he suffered a longing so intense he actually reached for her, flattening a palm upon the window. Never had he felt so thwarted. So denied.

Pick her up! Somebody pick her up! She's wet, or hungry, or she has a stomachache, can't you see? Or maybe the lights are too bright in there or she wants her hands uncovered. Somebody uncover her hands. I want to see her hands!

Through the glass he heard her squall, a faint mewling sound not unlike that of a killdeer heard at a distance.

A nurse came, smiling, and lifted Suzanne from the sterile glass crib, talking to the infant in a way that shaped her lips like a keyhole. Her nametag said Sheila Helgeson, a pretty young woman with brown hair and dimples, a stranger to Eric. She cradled the baby on one arm and freed Suzanne's trembling chin from the folds of the undershirt, facing her toward Eric. At the touch, the baby quieted with amusing quickness while her mouth opened and sought sustenance. When none materialized, Suzanne howled afresh, her face pruned and coloring.

Sheila Helgeson bounced her gently then looked up and smiled at the man beyond the glass.

"It's time to feed her." He read the nurse's lips and suffered an extraordinary deluge of loss as she carried the baby away.

Come back! I'm her father and I can't come here again!

He felt a thickening in his throat, a constriction across his chest closely resembling fear. He was grabbing air with quick, short breaths, standing with his entire body compressed in an effort at control.

He turned and walked away, his footsteps rapping like rimshots in the empty hall. A simple question was all it would take and he'd know Maggie's room number. He could walk in and sit beside her bed and take her hand and . . . and what? Mourn this impasse together? Tell her he still loved her? He was sorry? Burden her further?

No, the kindest thing he could do for her was to walk out of here.

In the elevator, riding down to ground floor, he leaned his head back against the wall and shut his eyes, battling the urge to cry. The doors opened and there stood Brookie, holding a big purple florist's sack.

Neither of them moved until the doors began closing, and Eric halted them, stepping out. The doors thumped together and the two stood before them, grave, uncertain what to say to one another.

"Hello, Brookie."

"Hello, Eric."

There was no use pretending. "Don't tell her I was here."

"She'd want to know."

"All the more reason not to tell her."

"So you've patched things up with your wife?"

"We're working on it." His face held no joy while admitting it. "What's Maggie going to do about her business?"

"She's closed the inn to guests for now. She's thinking of putting it up for sale in the spring."

Another blow. He closed his eyes. "Oh, Jesus."

"She thinks it's best if she lives someplace else."

It took a moment of silence before he could speak again. "If you hear she needs help—any kind of help—will you let me know?"

"Of course."

"Thanks, Brookie."

"Sure. Now, listen, you take care."

"I will, and please don't tell her I was here."

She lifted a hand in good-bye, careful to make no promises as she watched Eric head for the lobby doors. On her way to Maggie's room, she reflected upon her responsibility as a friend—to divulge or not to divulge—which would Maggie have her do? Maggie still loved Eric, but she was working hard at surmounting and surviving his loss.

Brookie walked into Maggie's room just as a nurse was putting the baby into her arms.

"Hiya, Mag, how they hangin'?" she greeted.

Maggie looked up and laughed, accepting the baby and a bottle.

"Not too bad right now, but in a day or so when the milk comes in they'll be hangin' like a couple of water balloons. But lookit here what I got."

"Ah, the long-awaited offspring." Brookie plunked down the plant and walked straight to the bed as the nurse left the room. "Hiya, Suzanna Banana, how does it feel to be in low humidity? My God, Mag, what a looker. Crossed eyes and everything!"

Maggie's laughter bounced the baby. "You brought flowers?"

"For the kid, not for you."

"Then open them, so she can see."

"All right, I will." Brookie tore open the purple paper. "Now look here, Suzanne, this is a gloxinia—can you say gloxinia? Go ahead, try it—glox-in-ee-a. What the hell, Maggie, the kid can't even say gloxinia yet? What are you raising here, a moron?"

Brookie always brought her own brand of love: impudence and humor. In time Maggie got a hug, and Brookie said, "Nice goin', kid. She's beautiful." A few minutes later Roy showed up carrying a teddy bear the size of an easy chair, and a bouquet of mums and daisies, which he discarded the moment he saw his granddaughter. They were all adulating the baby when Tani walked in followed fifteen minutes later by Elsie Beecham, a lifelong next-door neighbor of the Pearsons. Given all the commotion and visiting, Brookie never got the chance to tell Maggie about Eric's visit.

Maggie's happiness over the birth of Suzanne was shadowed by moments of great melancholy. During her hospital stay the absence of Vera cut deep. She'd tried to arm herself for it in advance, realizing it would be self-deluding to hope Vera might change her mind after all, but when Roy came on his second visit Maggie couldn't resist asking, "Is Mother coming?"

His face and voice became apologetic. "No, dear, I'm afraid she's not." Maggie saw how he tried to make up for Vera's cold indifference but no amount of fatherly attention could ease Maggie's hurt at being shunned by her mother at a time that should, instead, have drawn them closer.

Then there was the matter of Katy. Roy had called to tell her the baby had been born, but no call came from her. No letter. No flowers. Recalling

Katy's parting riposte, Maggie would find tears in her eyes at the idea of two sisters who would be strangers to one another, and a daughter who apparently was lost to her.

And of course she thought of Eric. She lamented the loss of him as she had the loss of Phillip when he died. She mourned, too, for *his* loss, for the anguish he must be suffering, undoubtedly having heard of Suzanne's birth. She wondered about his relationship with his wife and how the birth of this illegitimate daughter affected it.

Late in the afternoon of the second day she was lying resting, thinking of him when a voice said, "Ah, somebody loves you!"

Into the room came a pair of legs carrying a huge vase of flowers surrounded by green tissue paper. From behind it emerged a gray head and a merry face.

"Mrs. Stearn?" It was a hospital volunteer dressed in a mauve-colored smock.

"Yes."

"Flowers for you."

"For me?" Maggie sat up.

"Roses, no less."

"But I've gotten flowers from everyone I know." By now she was surrounded by them. They had come from so many unexpected sources— Brookie, Fish and Lisa (Brookie had called them), Althea Munne, the owners of the store where Roy worked, Roy himself, even Mark Brodie on behalf of the chamber of commerce.

"My goodness, there must be two dozen of them here," the volunteer chattered as she set them down on Maggie's rolling table.

"Is there a card?"

The grandmotherly woman investigated the waxy green tissue. "None that I can see. Maybe the florist forgot to include it. Well, enjoy!"

When she was gone, Maggie removed the tissue and when she saw what waited inside tears stung her eyes and she pressed a hand to her lips. No, the florist had not forgotten the card. No card was necessary.

The roses were pink.

He did not come, of course, but the flowers told her what it cost him not to and left her feeling bereaved each time she looked at them.

Someone else came, however, someone so unexpected that Maggie was stunned by her appearance. It was later that evening, and Roy had returned—his third visit—this time bringing Maggie a bag of peanut M&M's and a book called *A Victorian Posy*, a collection of quaintly illustrated poems printed on scented paper. Maggie had her nose to a page, inhaling the musky scent of lavender when she sensed someone watching and raised her head to find Anna Severson standing in the doorway. "Oh!" she exclaimed, experiencing an immediate flash of angst.

"I didn't know if I'd be welcome or not, so I thought I'd better ask before I came in," Anna said. Her curls were extra kinky for the occasion and she wore a red quilted nylon jacket over polyester double-knit slacks of painfully royal blue.

Roy glanced from Maggie to Anna but decided to let Maggie handle the situation.

When she found her voice again, Maggie said, "Of course you're welcome, Anna. Come in."

"Hello, Roy," Anna said solemnly, entering the room.

"How are you, Anna?"

"Well, I'm not exactly sure. Those damn kids of mine treat me like I haven't got a brain in my head, as if I can't figure out what's going on here. Makes a person get a little tetchy, don't y' know. I certainly haven't come here to embarrass you, Maggie, but it appears to me I've got a new grandchild, and—grandchildren being a blessing I'm particularly partial to—I wondered if you'd mind if I took a look at her."

"Oh, Anna . . ." Maggie managed before she started getting misty and raised both arms in welcome. Anna moved straightaway to hug her, soothing, "There, there . . ." patting her roughly on the back.

Roy's support had been welcome, but a woman's presence had been needed. Feeling the arms of Eric's mother close around her, Maggie felt some of the emotional void filled. "I'm so glad you came and that you know about the baby."

"I wouldn't of, if Barbara hadn't told me. Those two boys would've let me go to my grave none the wiser, the durn fools. But Barbara, she thought I ought to know, and when I asked if she'd drive me down here she was more than happy to."

Drawing back, Maggie looked up into Anna's seamed face. "So Eric doesn't know you're here? . . ."

"Not yet he don't, but he will when I get home."

"Anna, you mustn't be angry with him. It was as much my fault as his—more, in fact."

"I got a right to be angry. And disappointed, too! Heck, it's no secret that that boy's wanted a baby worse than anything I ever saw, and now he's got one and damned if he ain't married to the wrong woman. I tell you, it's a sorry situation. You mind telling me what you're going to do?"

"I'll raise her myself, but beyond that I'm not sure yet."

"You plan to tell her who her father is?"

"Every child deserves to know that."

Anna gave a brusque nod of approval then turned to Roy.

"Well, Roy, are we supposed to congratulate each other or what?"

"I don't know, Anna, but I don't think it would hurt."

"Where's Vera?"

"Vera's at home."

"She out of sorts over this, or what?"

"You might say that."

Anna looked at Maggie. "Ain't it funny how some people will act in the name of honor? Well, I'd sure like to see my new granddaughter. No, Maggie, you just rest. Roy, you don't mind walkin' me down there to the nursery, do you?"

"I don't mind a bit."

A minute later they stood together, studying their sleeping grandchild through a big glass window, an old man with a smile on his face and an old woman with a glint of tears in her eyes.

"My, she's a beauty," Anna said.

"She certainly is."

"My thirteenth one, but just as special as the first."

"Only my second, but I missed out on a lot with my first one, being so far away from her. This one though . . ." His fading words told clearly that he had plenty of dreams.

"I don't mind telling you, Roy, that I never been partial to the wife my boy picked. Your daughter would've made a better one all the way around. It breaks my heart that they can't be together to raise this baby, but that don't excuse him."

Roy studied the baby. "Things are sure different than when you and I were young, aren't they, Anna?"

"That's for sure. You wonder just what this world's coming to."

They thought awhile, then Roy said, "I'll tell you something that's changed for the better though."

"What's that?"

"They let grandpas in the delivery room these days. I helped my Maggie bring this little one into the world. Would you believe that, Anna?"

"Oh, pshaw! You?!" She looked at him wide-eyed.

"That's right. Me. A meat-cutter. Stood right there and helped Maggie breathe right, and watched this one get born. It was something, I tell you."

"I bet it was. I just bet it was."

Studying the baby again, they contemplated the wonder and the disappointment of it all.

Anna got home at nine o'clock that night and called Eric immediately.

"I need you out here. Got a pilot light out and I can't get the blame thing lit."

"Now?"

"You want that range to blow up and me with it?"

"Can't Mike check it?"

"Mike ain't home."

"Well, where is he?" Eric asked disgruntledly.

"How the deuce should I know? He ain't home, that's all, now are you comin' out here or not?"

"Oh, all right. I'll be there in half an hour."

She hung up the phone with a clack and sat down sternly to wait.

When Eric walked in twenty-five minutes later, he made straight for the kitchen range.

"There's nothing wrong with it. Sit down," Anna ordered.

He came up short. "What do you mean, there's nothing wrong with it?"

"I mean there's nothing wrong with it. Now sit down. I want to talk to you."

"About what?"

"I went to the hospital and saw your daughter tonight."

"You *what*!"

"Saw Maggie, too. Barbara took me."

He swore under his breath.

"I asked her to because none of my boys offered. This is a real fine kettle of fish, sonny."

"Ma, the last thing I need is to get my ass chewed by you."

"And the last thing Maggie Pearson needs is a baby without a father. What the devil were you thinking, to have an affair with her? You're a married man!"

He put on a stubborn jaw and said nothing.

"Does Nancy know about this?"

"Yes!" he snapped.

Anna rolled her eyes and muttered something in Norwegian.

Eric glared at her.

"What the heck kind of marriage you got anyway?"

"Ma, this is none of your business!"

"When you bring one of my grandchildren into this world, I make it my business!"

"You don't seem to realize that *I* hurt right now, too!"

"I'd take a minute to feel sorry for you if I wasn't so danged disgusted with you! Now I may not think the sun rises and sets on that wife of yours, but she's still your wife, and that gives you some responsibilities."

"Nancy and I are working things out. She's changing. She has been since she lost the baby."

"What baby's that? I had four of my own and I lost two more, and I know what a pregnant woman looks like when I see one. Why, she was no more pregnant than I am."

Eric gaped. "What the hell are you talking about, Ma!"

"You heard me. I don't know what kind of game she's playing, but she was no five months pregnant. Why, she didn't have so much as a pimple on her belly."

"Ma, you're dreaming! Of course she was pregnant!"

"I doubt it, but that's neither here nor there. If she knew you were stepping out with Maggie she probably told the lie to keep from losing you. What I want to make sure of is that you start acting like a husband—of which woman, I don't care. But *one at a time*, Eric Severson, do you hear me!"

"Ma, you don't understand! Last winter when I started seeing Maggie I had every intention of leaving Nancy."

"Oh, so that excuses you, huh? Now you listen here, sonny! I know you, I know how that new daughter of yours is working on you, and unless I miss my guess, you're going to want to hang around Maggie's and see that little one now and then, and play father a little bit. Well, fine, you do that if that's what you choose. But you start doing that, and you know what else will start up again. I'm not stupid, you know. I saw those roses in her room, and I saw the look on her face every time she glanced at them. When two people got feelings like that for one another and a baby, to boot, that's a pretty tough thing to control. So, fine, you go see your daughter and her mother. But *first* you get yourself free and clear of the woman you got! Your dad and I raised you to know right from wrong, and keeping two women is wrong, no matter what. Do I make myself understood?"

His jaw was set as he answered, "Yes, clearly."

"And do I have your promise that you won't darken Maggie's door again unless you got a divorce paper in your hand?"

When no reply came she repeated, "Do I?"

"Yes!" he snapped, and slammed out of the house.

Chapter 20

It took monumental control for Eric to keep from accosting Nancy with his mother's suspicions the minute he walked in the house. His emotions were too raw, his confusion too fresh, and as it turned out, she was asleep. He lay beside her, wondering if Ma was right, going back over the dates. It had been sometime in early July when she'd told him she was four months pregnant, and he'd commented about her not showing. What had she said? Some passing remark about him looking at her when she was naked. He had, in time, and he'd wondered at her continued thinness, but she'd explained it away by reminding him that she exercised daily, was extremely fit and diet-conscious and that the doctor had told her the baby was small. By late August when she claimed to have miscarried she would have been in her fifth month. He tried to remember what Barb looked like in her fifth month, but Barb was a bigger woman all around, and what man besides a father is assessing a woman's girth in terms of months? What about Maggie? She'd been almost five months pregnant when she'd stormed away from him in the rain, and, like Nancy, she hadn't been wearing maternity clothes either. Maybe Ma was wrong after all.

In the morning he went into Nancy's office under the guise of filing the stubs from the bills he'd paid three days earlier. He was standing before the open drawer of a tall metal file cabinet when she passed in the hall. "Hey, Nancy," he called, forcing an offhanded expression, "shouldn't we be getting a bill from that hospital in Omaha?"

She reappeared in the doorway looking trim and chic in a pair of gray trousers and a thick Icelandic wool sweater.

"I took care of it already," she answered, and started away.

"Hey, wait a minute!"

Impatiently, she returned. "What? I've got to be at the beauty shop at ten."

"You took care of it? You mean the insurance didn't cover it?" She had excellent insurance through Orlane.

"Yes, of course it did. I mean, it will when I send in the forms."

"You haven't done that yet?" Nancy was the most efficient bookkeeper he knew. For her to neglect paperwork for three months was completely out of character.

"Hey, what is this, some kind of inquisition?" she returned, piqued.

"I'm just wondering that's all. So what did you do, pay the hospital by check?"

"I thought we agreed, you take care of your bills and I'll take care of mine," she replied, and hurried away.

When she was gone he began searching the files more thoroughly. Because of her traveling it made sense for them to have separate checking accounts but since her paperwork had always been heavy they'd agreed that he'd take care of paying their household bills. The insurance was one of those gray areas that crossed boundaries since he too was covered on her policy, therefore the paperwork for both of them was filed together.

He flipped through the folder but found only their dental claims for the past several years, a two-year-old claim for a throat culture he'd had, plus those for her annual pap smears. He searched every folder in the four-drawer file cabinet, then turned and sat down at her desk. It was a sturdy, flat-topped oak piece probably eighty years old. She'd bought it at a bank auction years ago, and he'd never snooped in it for anything beyond an occasional paper clip or pen.

Pulling open the first drawer, he felt like a burglar.

He found her canceled checks with no trouble, neatly filed and labeled, the most recent covering the month of October. He went back to August's and opened up the summary sheet, laid it on the desk and scanned it. Nothing to St. Joseph's Hospital, or to any strange doctors or clinics. He scanned it again, just to make sure.

Nothing.

He checked September's. Still nothing.

October's. Still no hospital.

He took off his glasses and dropped them on the blotter, spread his elbows wide on the desktop and covered his mouth with both hands.

Had he been that gullible? Had she lied to him as Ma suggested, to keep him away from Maggie? With his misgivings mounting, he searched on.

Checkstubs from Orlane. Clothing receipts from stores he'd never seen. A correspondence file containing business letters with New York return addresses and carbon copies of her answers. Visa stubs from all her gasoline. Maintenance records for her car. And inside a hanging folder labeled *Sales Profiles*, a plastic zippered case stamped with the name and logo of some real estate company he'd never heard of: Schwann's Realty.

He zipped it open and recognized the computer printout of a hospital bill even before he withdrew it from the pouch. Extracting the folded sheets, he glimpsed code words—Pulse Oximeter, Disp Oral Airway—that immediately diluted his suspicion. He unfolded the four connected sheets, saw the name of a hospital at the top and breathed easier.

Wait a minute.

The hospital was not St. Joseph's in Omaha, but Hennepin County Medical Center in Minneapolis. The admit/discharge dates were not August 1989, but May 1986.

Three years ago?

What the hell?

He frowned over the codes and descriptions, but most of them meant little to him.

Halcion Tab 0.5 MG

Oxyto3 In 10U 1C3

Ceftriaxone Inj 2 GM

Drugs, he surmised, and read on, frowning.

Chux Pkg of 5

Culture

Delivery Room Normal
D & C Post Delivery

D & C? He didn't know what words it stood for, but he knew what it meant. She'd had a D & C in May of 1986?

Dread filled his throat as he read the remainder of the list. By the time he reached the end his insides were quaking. He stared at the corner of an aluminum picture frame on the opposite wall while tremors spread down his legs and up his arms. His lips were compressed. His throat hurt. The sensation spread until he felt as if he were on the verge of choking. After a full minute of escalating distress he leapt from the chair, catapulting it backward as he stalked from the room with the bill in his hand. Out to the truck. Started it angrily. Ramming it into reverse. Digging up brown grass as he backed from the yard. Roaring down the hill and around the corner doing thirty in first with the transmission howling. Speed shifting into second an instant short of blowing up the engine, then thundering down the highway like a World War II bomber on a runway.

Fifteen minutes later when he stormed into Dr. Neil Lange's office in Ephraim, he was in no mood to be waylaid.

"I want to see Doc Lange," he announced at the receptionist's window, his fingers rapping the ledge like a woodpecker at work.

Patricia Carpenter glanced up and smiled. She was plump and cute and used to help him with his algebra when they were in the ninth grade.

"Hi, Eric. I don't think you have an appointment, do you?"

"No, but it won't take more than sixty seconds."

She glanced at her appointment book. "He's really full today. I'm afraid the best we can do would be four this afternoon."

His temper erupted and he shouted, "Don't give me any shit, Pat! I said it would only take sixty seconds, and he's only got one patient left out here before he goes to lunch, so don't tell me I can't see him! You can charge me for a goddamned office call if you want to but I've got to see him!"

Patricia's mouth dropped open and her cheeks colored. She glanced toward the waiting room at an old woman who'd looked up from her magazine at Eric's outburst.

"I'll see what I can do." Patricia pushed back her rolling chair.

While she was gone he paced and felt like a goddamned heel, remembering how Pat used to have a crush on him. Tapping a thigh with the rolled-up papers, he nodded to the white-haired woman who gawked back as if she recognized his face from the WANTED posters.

In less than sixty seconds Patricia Carpenter returned to the front, hotfooting it a step behind a long-striding giant in a flapping white lab coat who pointed a finger at Eric as he strode past the receptionist's window. "Get in here, Severson!" He flung the door open, his face grim with anger, and thumbed toward the end of the hall. "Down there."

Eric stalked into Neil Lange's office and heard the door slam behind him.

"Just what the *hell* do you mean by coming in here and harassing Pat? I've got a mind to toss you out on your ass!"

Eric turned to find Neil with his hands on his hips, his lips pinched, his dark eyes irate behind square horn-rimmed glasses. He was the second generation Doc Lange, only three years older than Eric, had delivered all of Mike and Barb's babies, had diagnosed Ma's high blood pressure and had at one time dated his sister, Ruth.

Eric took a deep breath and forcibly calmed himself. "I'm sorry, Neil. You're right. She's right. I owe her an apology and I'll make sure she gets it before I leave, but I need to have you explain something for me."

"What?"

"This." Eric unrolled the computer printout and handed it over. "Tell me what this bill is for."

Neil Lange began reading it from the top down, giving it his total attention. When he reached the halfway point, he glanced up at Eric, then read on.

Finishing, he let the sheets fall into their accordion fold and looked up. "Why do you want to know?"

"It's for my wife."

"Yes, I see that."

"And it's from some goddamned hospital in Minnesota!"

"I see that, too."

In silence the two men stood face to face. "You know what I'm asking, Neil, so don't give me that look. Does D & C mean what I think it means?"

"It means dilation and curettage."

"An abortion, right?"

Lange paused a second before confirming, "Yes, it looks that way."

Eric stepped back and collapsed to the edge of Lange's desk, catching himself with both hands, dropping his chin to his chest. Lange folded the bill with his thumbnail and dropped his hands to his sides. His voice softened.

"You didn't know about it until now?"

Eric shook his head slowly, staring at the brown flecks in the thick Berber carpeting.

"I'm sorry, Eric." Lange put a comforting hand on his shoulder.

Eric lifted his head. "Could there be some other reason for her having it?"

"I'm afraid not. The lab indicates serum pregnancy and surgical tissue II—that always means abortion. Also, it was done in a county hospital rather than a private or religious-affiliated hospital, which generally don't perform abortions."

Eric took a minute to absorb the anguish before drawing a deep sigh and pushing to his feet. "Well, now I know." He reached tiredly for the bill. "Thanks, Neil."

"If you want to talk, call Pat and set up a time, but don't come barging in here this way again."

Chin down, Eric raised a hand in farewell.

"Listen, Eric," Lange went on, "this is a small town. Talk gets around, and if what I hear is true you need to get your life in order. I'd be more than happy to talk about it, even away from the office where there are no interruptions. If you prefer, forget about calling Pat. Just call me, will you do that?"

Eric lifted his head, studied the doctor with a look of flat despair, nodded once and headed out. At the reception desk he stopped.

"Listen, Pat, I'm sorry for that . . ." He waved the scrolled papers toward the other side of the window. "Sometimes I can be a son of a bitch."

"Oh, it's all right. It—"

"No. No, it's not all right. You like salmon? Smoked maybe? Steak?"

"I love it."

"Which kind?"

"Eric, you don't have to—"

"Which kind?"

"All right, steaks."

"You'll have 'em. I'll drop off a package tomorrow, by way of apology."

He drove home slowly, feeling bleak as the November day. Cars piled up behind him, unable to pass on the curving highway, but he rolled along unaware of them. Endings—how sad they were. Particularly sad to end eighteen years of marriage with a blow like this. His child . . . Jesus, she'd disposed of his child as if it were of no more consequence than one of her outmoded dresses.

He stared at the highway, wondering if it had been a boy or a girl, fair or dark, with any of Ma's features or the old man's. Hell, it would be riding a trike by now, begging to have stories read, riding on his father's hand high overhead, learning about the gulls.

The white center lines became distorted by tears. His child, her child, who might have grown to be a fisherman or a president, a father or a mother someday. Nancy was his wife, yet she cared so little about him that the life he'd sired was absolutely dispensable. Eighteen years he'd hoped, a good half of that time he'd begged. And when it had finally happened, Nancy had killed it.

She wasn't home yet when he arrived so he put her office in order, growing angrier by the minute now that his first spate of melancholy was gone. He packed her suitcases, unpacked them and packed his own (he wasn't giving her a single thing to come back at him on), loaded the truck and sat down at the kitchen table to wait.

She arrived shortly after one P.M., coming sideways through the door with her arms full of packages, her hair oriental black.

"Wait till you see what I bought!" she exclaimed above the crackle of bags as she set them on the cabinet. "I went into the little shop next to the—"

"Shut the door," he ordered coldly.

In slow motion she looked back over her shoulder. "What's the matter?"

"Shut the door and sit down."

She closed the door and approached the table warily, drawing off her leather gloves.

"Whoa, you're really bummed out about something. Should I get my whip and my chair?" she cajoled.

"I found something today." Icy-eyed, he tossed the hospital bill across the table. "You want to tell me about it?"

She glanced down and her hands stalled, pulling off the gloves. Her surprise registered as a mere tightening of her brow before she disguised it beneath a look of hauteur.

"You were going through my desk?" She sounded affronted.

"Yes, I was *going through your desk!*" he repeated, his voice rising, his teeth bared on the final word.

"How dare you!" She threw the gloves down. "That's *my* personal file, and when I leave this house I expect—"

"Don't you get high-handed with me, you lying bitch!" He leapt to his feet. "Not with the proof of your crime lying right there in front of you!" He jabbed a finger at the bill.

"Crime?" She spread a hand on her chest and affected an abused expression. "*I* go off to get my hair done, and *you* dig through my personal files, and *I'm* the criminal!" She thrust her nose near his. "I'm the one who should be upset, dear husband!"

"You killed my baby, *dear wife,* and I don't give a goddamn what the law says, in my book it's a criminal act!"

"Killed your baby! Don't be ridiculous."

"1986. D & C. It's all there on that bill."

"You have a fixation with babies, Eric, do you know that? It makes you paranoid."

"Then explain it!"

She shrugged and spoke nonchalantly. "My periods were getting irregular. It was a routine operation to straighten them out."

"Done secretly, in some hospital in Minneapolis?"

"I didn't want to worry you, that's all. I was in and out in one day."

"Don't lie to me, Nancy. It only makes you more despicable."

"I'm not lying!"

"I showed the bill to Neil Lange. He said it was an abortion."

She stretched her neck like a gander, her mouth taut, and said nothing. "How *could* you?"

"I don't have to stand here and listen to this." She turned away.

He spun her around by an arm. "You're not walking away from this one, Nancy," he shouted. "You got pregnant, and you didn't even bother to tell me! You made a decision to snuff out the life of our baby, the baby I begged you for years to have. Just—*pfft!*" He brandished a hand. "Scrape it out, like you'd scrape out some . . . some *garbage.* Killed it without a thought for what I was feeling, and you think you don't have to stand here and take this?" He grabbed her by the coatfront and pulled her to her toes. "What kind of woman are you anyway?"

"Let me go!"

He jerked her higher. "Can you imagine what I thought when I found that bill? What I felt? Do you even *care* what I felt?"

"You, you!" she shouted, shoving him away and stumbling backward.

"It's always you. What *you* want, when it's time to decide where we'll live! What *you* want when we decide what we'll live in! What *you* want when we crawl into bed at night. Well, what about what *I* want?"

He advanced nose first. "You know something, Nancy? I don't give a damn what you want anymore!"

"You don't understand. You never did!"

"Don't understand!" His face turned red with rage as he controlled the urge to smash a fist into her beautiful face. "Don't understand you having an abortion without telling me? Jesus Christ, woman, what was I to you all these years, nothing more than a good lay? As long as you got your orgasms that's all that mattered, wasn't it?"

"I loved you."

He pushed her away in revulsion.

"Bullshit. You know who you love? Yourself. Nobody but yourself."

Coldly, she demanded, "And who do you love, Eric?"

They faced each other in deliberate silence.

"We both know who you love, don't we?" she insisted.

"I didn't until you became unlovable, and even then I came back here and tried to make a go of it with you."

"Oh, thanks a lot," she said sarcastically.

"But you lied then, too. You were no more pregnant than I was, but I was so gullible I believed you."

"I lied to keep from losing you."

"You lied to suit your own twisted needs!"

"Well, you deserved it! The whole town knew you were the father of her baby!"

The fight left him and guilt tempered his voice. "I'm sorry about that, Nancy. I never meant to hurt you that way, and if you're thinking I did it deliberately, you're wrong."

"But you're going to her now, aren't you?"

He watched her mouth turn sad and said nothing.

"I still love you."

"Nancy, don't." He turned away.

"We each made some mistakes," she said, "but we could start from now. A new beginning."

"It's too late." He stared out a window without seeing a thing. Standing in the kitchen of the house he'd loved and she'd hated, he felt momentarily overwhelmed by sorrow at their failure.

She touched his back. "Eric . . . " she said imploringly.

He swung away from her and plucked his leather jacket from the back of a kitchen chair, pulling it on.

"I'll be at Ma's."

The zipper closed with a sound of finality.

"Don't go." She began to cry. To the best of his recollection he'd never seen her do that.

"Don't," he whispered.

She gripped his jacketfront. "Eric, this time I'd be different."

"Don't . . . " He removed her hands. "You're embarrassing both of us." He picked up the hospital bill and put it in his pocket. "I'll be seeing my lawyer tomorrow and giving him the order that either he gets this thing pushed through fast or I'll find another lawyer who will."

"Eric—" She reached out one hand.

He put a hand on the doorknob and looked back at her. "I realized something while I was waiting for you today. You shouldn't have a baby and I should never have tried to talk you into it. It would be wrong for you, just like it's wrong for me to be without a family. We changed— somewhere along the line both of us changed. We want different things. We should have seen that years ago." He opened the door. "I'm sorry I hurt you," he said solemnly. "I mean it when I say I never meant to."

He walked out, closing the door softly behind him.

There were no secrets in a town the size of Fish Creek. Maggie heard about Eric leaving Nancy within days and lived on tenterhooks after that. She found herself stopping and cocking her head each time a vehicle passed on the road up above. Whenever the phone rang her heart shot into double time and she scurried to answer it. If anyone knocked on the door her palms were sweating long before she reached the kitchen.

She trimmed the leaves from the pink roses Eric had sent and hung them upside down to preserve them, but they were dry and bound with a mauve ribbon and still she hadn't heard a word from him.

To Suzanne she murmured, "Do you think he'll come to us?" But Suzanne only crossed her eyes and hiccuped.

Thanksgiving came and still no word from Eric. Maggie and Suzanne spent the holiday at Brookie's.

On December 8th it snowed. Maggie found herself wandering from window to window, watching the white fluff cover the yard in a soft, level blanket, and wondering where Eric was and if she'd hear from him soon.

She began making Christmas preparations and wrote to Katy, asking if she'd be home. Her reply was a brusque note: "Mother . . . I'm going to Seattle with Smitty for Christmas. Don't buy me anything. Katy." Maggie read it fighting tears, then called Roy. "Oh, Daddy," she wailed. "It seems like I've made everybody unhappy having this baby. Mother won't talk to me. Katy won't talk to me. You're going to have a miserable Christmas. I'm going to have a miserable Christmas. What should I do, Daddy?"

Roy replied, "You should put Suzanne in a snowsuit and take her for a buggy ride and get her acquainted with winter and spend a little time yourself looking around at the snow on the pines, and the sky when it's the color of an old tin kettle, and realize there's a lot out there to be grateful for."

"But, Daddy, I feel so bad that I've driven Mother away, and where does that leave you on Christmas?"

"Well, I may have to take a walk and look at the pines and the sky every now and then myself, but I'll get by. You just see after yourself and Suzanne."

"You're such a good person, Daddy."

"There, you see?" Roy replied with jocularity in his voice. "That's one thing you've got to be grateful for right there."

So Roy and Brookie saw her through.

For Maggie it was a Christmas of mixed blessings—with a new daughter but without the rest of her family. And still with no word from Eric. She spent the holiday at Brookie's again and on New Year's made a resolution to put Eric Severson behind and accept the apparent fact that if she hadn't seen him by now she wasn't going to.

One day in January she was taking Suzanne to the doctor for her two-month checkup, sitting at a red light in Sturgeon Bay when she glanced idly to her left and found Eric staring down at her from behind the wheel of a shining black pickup. Not a finger, not an eyelid moved on either of them.

Maggie stared. And Eric stared.

The middle of her breastbone ached. Drawing the next breath became a milestone.

The light changed and behind her a car horn honked, but she didn't move.

Eric's gaze shifted to the pair of tiny hands beating the air with excitement—all that he could see of Suzanne, who sat strapped into her infant seat, watching a paper cutout revolve in the breeze from the windshield defroster.

The car horn honked again, longer, and Maggie pulled away from the light, losing sight of his truck when he made a left-hand turn and disappeared from her rearview mirror.

Desolate, she told Brookie about it later. "He didn't even wave. He didn't even try to stop me."

For the first time, Brookie had no words of consolation.

The winter grew harsher in every way after that. Harding House seemed oppressive, so big and empty with only two in it and not a prospect of more. Maggie took up needlework to fill her time, but often dropped her hands to her lap and rested her head against the back of the chair. *If he's left her, why doesn't he come to me?*

February was bitter and Suzanne got her first cold. Maggie walked the floor with her at night, haggard from loss of sleep, wishing for someone to take the baby from her arms and nudge her toward bed.

In March letters began arriving requesting reservations for the summer and Maggie realized she'd have to make her decision about whether or not to put Harding House up for sale. The best time to do so, of course, would be when the spring rush began.

In April she called Althea Munne and asked her to come over and appraise the house. The day that the FOR SALE sign went up in the yard, Maggie took Suzanne and drove clear down to Tani's in Green Bay because she couldn't bear to look at the sign and wait for strangers to come poking and prodding through the place into which she'd poured so much of her heart.

In May Gene Kerschner came and hitched up the dock to his big green John Deere tractor and rolled it back into the water for the summer. The following day while Suzanne was taking her afternoon nap, Maggie set to work giving it a coat of white paint.

She was on her knees with her backside pointed toward the house, her head wrapped in a red bandana, peering up at the underside of the arbor seat when she heard footsteps on the dock behind her. She backed up, turned, and felt an explosion of emotion.

Coming down the dock, dressed in white jeans, a blue shirt and a white skipper's hat was Eric Severson.

She watched him moving toward her while adrenaline shot through her system. Oh, how the appearance of one person could change the complexion of a day, a year, a life! She forgot the paintbrush in her hand. Forgot she was barefoot and dressed in faded black sweatpants and a baggy gray T-shirt. Forgot everything but the long-awaited sight of him approaching.

He stopped on the opposite side of the paint can and looked down.

"Hello," he said, as if heaven had not suddenly shown itself to her.

"Hello," she whispered, her pulse drumming everywhere, everywhere.

"I brought you something." He handed her a white envelope.

It took moments before she could force her arm to move. She took the envelope wordlessly, staring up at him as he stood silhouetted against a sky of crayon blue—the same blue as his eyes. The sun glinted off the black visor of his cap, lit his shoulders and the tip of his chin.

"Open it, please."

She balanced the paintbrush on the edge of the can, wiped her hand on her thigh and began opening the envelope with trembling hands while he stood above her, watching. Watching. She drew the papers out and opened them—a thick white sheaf that wanted to spring together at the folds. As she read, the tremor from her hands twitched the corners of the sheets.

Findings for Fact, Conclusion of Law, Order for Judgment, Judgment and Decree.
She read the heading and lifted uncertain eyes.

"What is it?"

"My divorce papers."

The shock rushed up pushing tears before it. She dropped her chin and saw the lines of typing wash sideways before two huge tears plopped onto the paper. Abashed, she buried her face against it.

"Aw, Maggie . . ." He went down on one knee and touched her head, warm from the sun and bound by the ugly red hanky. "Maggie, don't cry. The crying's all over."

She felt his arms pull her close and realized he was on his knees before her. He was here at last and the agony was over. She threw her arms around his neck, weeping, confessing brokenly. "I th . . . thought you weren't c . . . coming back."

His wide hand clasped the back of her head, holding her fiercely against him. "My mother made me promise I wouldn't until I had my divorce papers in hand."

"I thought . . . I thought . . . I don't know what I thought." She felt childish, babbling so, but she'd been totally unprepared, and the relief was so immense.

"You thought I didn't love you anymore?"

"I thought I'd b . . . be alone for the rest of my l . . . life, and that Suzanne would n . . . never know you, and I d . . . didn't know how to face it without you."

"Oh, Maggie," he said, closing his eyes. "I'm here and I'm staying."

She cried awhile, her nose against his neck, his hand stroking her hair beneath the scarf.

At length he whispered, "I missed you so much."

She had missed him, too, but adequate words had not been coined to express the complexity of her feelings. To have him back was to taste the bitter turn to sweet, to feel the missing piece of herself settle into place.

Drawing away, she looked into his face, her own glossy wet in the sun. "You're really divorced, then?"

He dried her eyes with his thumbs and answered quietly, "I'm really divorced."

She attempted a quivering smile. His thumbs stopped moving. The pain left his dear blue eyes and his head slowly lowered. It was a tender first kiss, flavored with May and tears and perhaps a tinge of turpentine. His mouth dropped soft and open upon hers—a tentative first taste, as if neither could believe this reverse of fortune, while he held her face in his broad hands. Their tongues touched and his head moved, swaying above hers as their mouths opened fully. Still kneeling, he drew her hips flush against his and held her there as if forever. Great cotton clouds moved across the blue sky above, and the breeze touched her hair as he removed her scarf and cupped her head firmly. To kiss was enough—to kneel beneath the May sun with tongues joined and feel the agony of separation dissolve and know that no law of God or man stood between them any longer.

In time he drew back, found her eyes, told her eloquent things with his own, then folded her against him more loosely. For moments they remained so, motionless, empty vessels no more.

"I went through hell after I saw you in Sturgeon Bay," he told her.

"I wanted you to stop me, force me over to the side of the road and carry me away."

"I wanted to leave the truck there in the middle of the street and get into your car and drive off someplace, to Texas or California or Africa where nobody could find us."

She chuckled shakily. "You can't drive to Africa, silly."

"I feel like I could right now." With an open hand he rubbed her spine. "With you I feel like anything is possible."

"A thousand times I stopped myself from calling you."

"I drove past your house night after night. I'd see the light in your kitchen window and think about coming in and sitting with you. Not kissing you or making love, just . . . just being in the same room with you would have been enough. Talking, looking at you, laughing, the way we used to do."

"I wrote you a letter once."

"Did you send it?"

"No."

"What did you say?"

With her eyes upon a thin white cloud she answered, "Thank you for the roses."

He sat back on his heels and she followed suit, their hands linked loosely between them.

"You knew, then."

"Of course. They were pink."

"I wanted to bring them myself. There was so much I wanted to say."

"You did, with the roses."

He shook his head sadly, remembering that time. "I wanted to be there when she was born, come and visit you and claim her and say to hell with the world."

"I dried the roses and saved them for Suzanne when she gets older, in case . . . well, just in case."

"Where is she?" He glanced toward the house.

"Inside, sleeping."

"Could I see her?"

Maggie smiled. "Of course. It's what I've been waiting for."

They rose from their knees, his cracking—in her deepest aloneness she'd even missed the sound of his knees cracking—and they walked hand in hand to the house, through the gold-bright rays of midafternoon, across the rolling lawn where the maples were leafing out and the irises already blooming, up the wide front veranda and inside, up the staircase they'd climbed together on so many occasions.

Halfway up, he whispered, "I'm shaking."

"You have a right. It's not every day a father meets his six-month-old daughter for the first time."

She led him into The Sarah, a south-facing room trimmed in yellow with billowing white lace at the deep, wide box window where a giant wooden rocker sat. A guest bed stood against one wall. Opposite, was the crib—spooled maple with a tall peaked canopy cascading with white lace. The crib of a princess.

And there she was.

Suzanne.

She lay on her side, both arms outflung and her feet tangled in a pastel quilt covered with patchwork animals. Her hair was the color of clover honey, her eyelashes a shade paler, her cheeks plump and bright as peaches. Her mouth was most certainly the sweetest one in all of creation, and as he studied it, Eric choked up.

"Oh, Maggie, she's beautiful," he whispered.

"Yes she is."

"She's so big already." Studying the slumbering baby he rued every missed day that had passed since he'd seen her through a plate-glass window.

"She has one little tooth. Wait till you see it." Maggie leaned over and gently brushed the baby's cheek with one finger. "Suzaaanne,". she crooned softly. "Hey, sleepyhead, wake up and see who's here."

Suzanne flinched, poked a thumb into her mouth and began sucking, still asleep.

"You don't have to wake her, Maggie," Eric whispered, content to stand and watch. For the rest of his life, just stand and watch.

"It's all right. She's been napping for two hours already." She stroked the baby's fine hair. "Suza-aaaane . . ." she singsonged softly.

Suzanne opened her eyes, shut them again and rubbed her nose with one fist.

Side by side Maggie and Eric watched her come awake, making faces, rolling up like an armadillo, and finally coming up on all fours like a shaky cub bear, peering at the strange man standing beside the crib with her mother.

"Oops, there she is. Hi, sugar." Maggie reached into the crib, lifted the sleepy baby out and perched her on her arm. Suzanne immediately curled and rubbed and burrowed. She was dressed in something pink and green and her backside was puffy. One of her socks had slipped down, revealing a small, pointed heel. Maggie tugged it up while Suzanne finished her rooting.

"Look who's here, Suzanne. It's your daddy."

The baby looked up at Maggie with her lower eyelashes clinging to the soft folds of skin beneath, then shifted her regard to the stranger again, still a little shaky on Maggie's arm. As she stared, steadying herself with one hand against Maggie's chest, her thumb kept crooking and straightening against Maggie's T-shirt.

"Hi, Suzanne," Eric said quietly.

She remained as unblinking as a fascinated cat, until Maggie bounced her a time or two on her arm and rested her face against Suzanne's downy head. "This is your daddy come to say hello."

As one mesmerized, Eric reached and took his child, lifting her to eye level where she hung in the air and stared at his black, shiny visor.

"My goodness, you're a little bit of a thing after all. You don't weigh as much as the salmon we catch off the *Mary Deare.*"

Maggie laughed while one happiness seemed to crowd in upon another.

"And you're no bigger around either." He brought the baby close and touched his dark face to her very fair one, and caught the infant scent of her powdered skin and soft clothing. He set her on his arm, braced her back with one long hand and rested his lips upon her silky hair. His eyes closed. His throat seemed to do the same.

"I thought I'd never have this," Eric whispered, his voice gravelly with emotion.

"I know, darling . . . I know."

"Thank you for her."

Maggie put her arms around both of them, laid her forehead against Suzanne's back and Eric's hand while they shared the sacred moment.

"She's so perfect."

As if to prove otherwise, Suzanne chose that moment to complain, pushing away from Eric and reaching for her mother. He relinquished her but hovered close as Maggie changed her diaper and pulled up her stockings once again and put on soft white shoes. Afterward, they lay on the bed, one on each side of the baby, watching her untie her shoes and blow spit bubbles and grow fascinated with her father's shirt buttons. Sometimes they studied the baby, and sometimes each other. Often they reached across the baby to touch one another's faces, hair, arms. Then they would lie still, with contentment dulling the need to move at all.

In time Eric took Maggie's hand.

"Would you do something for me?" he asked softly.

"Anything. I would do anything for you, Eric Severson."

"Would you go for a ride with me? You and Suzanne?"

"We'd love it."

They walked outside together, Eric carrying Suzanne, Maggie bringing a bottle of apple juice and Suzanne's favorite blanket—enchanted beings still somewhat awestruck at the grandeur of happiness in its simplest form. A man, a woman, their child. Together as it should be.

The breeze touched the baby's face and she squinted her eyes.

A warbler trilled in the arborvitae hedge.

They ambled slower; time was their ally now.

"You got a new truck," Maggie remarked, approaching it.

"Yup. The old whore finally died." He opened the passenger door for her.

She had one foot on the running board before she looked up and saw the blossoms.

"Oh, Eric." She touched her lips.

"I could have asked you back there in the house, but with all the cherry trees in bloom, I thought we might as well do this right. Get in, Maggie, so we can get to the best part."

Smiling, beset once again by the urge to cry, she climbed into Eric Severson's shiny new truck and gazed around at the cherry blossoms stuck behind the visors and the rearview mirror, jammed behind the backseat until they nearly covered the rear window.

Eric climbed in beside her. "What do you think?" he asked, grinning at her, starting the engine.

"I think I adore you."

"I adore you, too. I just had to think of a way to tell you so. Hang on to our baby."

They drove through the Door County springtime, through the blossom-scented air of late afternoon, past sloping orchards rimmed with rock walls and birches shining white against new green grass, past grazing cows and bright-red barns and ditches filled with singing frogs. And came at last to Easley's orchard, where he stopped the truck between the billowing cherry trees.

In the quiet after the engine had stilled, he turned and captured her hand on the seat between them.

"Maggie Pearson Stearn, will you marry me?" he asked, his cheeks flushed, his eyes steady upon hers.

In the moment before she answered, all the sweet bygones came rushing back, filling her senses—the place, the man, the smell of the orchard around them.

"Eric Joseph Severson, I would marry you this very minute if it were possible." She leaned across the seat to kiss him, with Suzanne on her knees, struggling to reach the blossoms in the ashtray. He lifted his head and they searched each other's eyes, smiled their gladness once more before Eric braced up and dug into the left pocket of his tight white jeans.

"I thought about buying you a great big diamond, but this seemed more appropriate." He came up with his class ring and took her left hand to slip it on her ring finger, where it still fit loosely. Holding the hand aloft, she studied it, adorned as it had been twenty-four years before.

"It looks so familiar there," she said, smiling.

"All except for the blue yarn. I don't know what happened to that."

With the beringed hand she touched his face. "I don't know what to say," she whispered.

"Say, 'I love you, Eric, and I forgive you for all you've put me through.' "

"I love you, Eric, but there's nothing to forgive."

They attempted one more kiss, but Suzanne interrupted, wriggling off her mother's lap to stand on the seat between them. When she was on two feet she closed one chubby fist around a branch overhead and flailed the air with it, a sharp point of one stick narrowly missing Eric's eye.

He pulled back—"Whoa there, little lady!"—and planted one hand beneath her diaper, another on her chest and returned her to her mother's lap. "Can't you see there's a courtship going on here?"

They were both laughing as he reached for the ignition and headed back toward Fish Creek, holding Maggie's hand.

Chapter 21

They were married five days later in the backyard of Harding House. It was a simple ceremony on a Tuesday evening. The groom wore a gray tuxedo with lilies of the valley in his lapel (from the bed on the north side of the house), the bride wore a pink walking suit and carried a bouquet of apple blossoms (from Easley's orchard). In attendance were Miss Suzanne Pearson (wearing Poly Flinders and eating Waverly Wafers), Brookie and Gene Kerschner, Mike and Barb Severson, Anna Severson (having forsaken slogans in favor of blue polyester from Sears, Roebuck) and Roy Pearson, who walked his daughter down from the front veranda to the yard while from the porch came a scratchy monophonic recording of the Andrews Sisters singing "I'll Be with You in Apple Blossom Time."

On the fresh spring grass stood an antique parlor table holding a bouquet of pink apple blossoms in a milk-glass vase. Beside the table a judge waited in a black robe, its sleeves filling and emptying as breezes drifted in off the bay. When the song ended and the wedding party stood before him, the judge said, "The bride and groom have requested that I read a poem they've chosen for this occasion. It's of the same vintage as the house, and it's entitled 'Fulfillment.'

> *"Lo, I have opened unto you the*
> *gates of my being*
> *And like a tide, you have flowed*
> *into me.*
> *The innermost recesses of my spirit*
> *are full of you*
> *And all the channels of my soul*
> *are grown sweet with your presence*
> *For you have brought me peace;*
> *The peace of great tranquil waters,*
> *And the quiet of the summer sea.*
> *Your hands are filled with peace as*
> *The noon-tide is filled with light;*
> *About your head is bound the eternal*
> *Quiet of the stars, and in your heart*
> *dwells the calm miracle of twilight.*
>
> *I am utterly content.*
>
> *In all my being is no ripple of unrest*
> *For I have opened unto you the*
> *Wide gates of my being*
> *And like a tide, you have flowed into me."*

After the reading, Eric turned to Maggie. She laid her apple blossoms on the table and he took both her hands. In the late, low sun her face appeared golden, her eyes the pale brown of acorns. Her hair was drawn back from her face, and her ears held delicate pink pearls. In that moment she might have been seventeen again, and the branches she'd laid aside were those he'd first picked to express his love. No single act of his life had ever seemed so appropriate as when he spoke his vows.

"You were my first love, Maggie, and you will be my only love for the rest of our lives. I will respect you, and be faithful to you, and work hard for you and with you. I will be a good father to Suzanne and any other children we might have, and I will do all in my power to make you happy." Softly, he ended, "I love you, Maggie."

In the brief silence that followed, Anna wiped her eyes and Brookie fit her hand into Gene's. A glint appeared in the corner of Maggie's eyes, and her lips held a wistful smile.

She dropped her gaze to Eric's hands—broad, strong fisherman's hands; looked up into his blue eyes, the first she'd ever loved, blue as blooming chicory; into his dear windburned face that would only grow dearer in the years ahead.

"I love you, Eric . . . again." The merest smile touched their eyes and disappeared. "I will do all within my power to keep that love as fresh and vibrant as it was when we were seventeen, and as it is today. I will keep our home a place where happiness dwells, and in it I will love our child and you. I will grow old with you. I will be faithful to you. I will be your friend forever. I will wear your name proudly. I love you, Eric Severson."

Out over Green Bay a pair of gulls called, and the sun rested at the end of a long golden path on the water. Maggie and Eric exchanged rings, plain gold bands which seemed to catch the fire from sunset and warm beneath it.

When the exchange was complete, Eric lowered his head and kissed the backs of Maggie's hands. She did likewise, and they moved to the scroll-footed table, accepted a pen from the judge and signed their names to the wedding certificate. Their signatures were witnessed by Brookie and Mike and the simple ceremony was over less than five minutes after it began.

Eric smiled at Maggie, then at the judge, who extended his hand and a hearty smile. "Congratulations, Mr. and Mrs. Severson. May you have a long and happy life together."

Eric scooped Maggie into his arms and kissed her.

"Mrs. Severson, I love you," he whispered at her ear.

"I love you, too."

The circle around them closed. Brookie was crying as she kissed Maggie's cheek and said, "Well, it's about time."

Gene embraced them each and said, "Good luck. You deserve it."

Mike said, "Little brother, I think you got a winner."

Barbara said, "I couldn't be happier. Welcome to the family."

Anna said, "It's enough to make an old woman cry. At my age, getting a daughter-in-law and a new grandbaby all in one day. Here, take her, Eric, so I can hug Maggie." When she'd handed Suzanne to her daddy, Anna told Maggie, cheek-to-cheek, "I seen this day coming when you were seventeen years old. I can see you made my boy happy at last, and for that I love you." Hugging Eric, she said, "I wish your dad was alive to see this day. He always favored Maggie and I did, too. Congratulations, son."

Roy told Maggie, "You look pretty as a picture, honey, and I'm awful glad this all happened." Thumping Eric's back, he said, "Well, I finally got me somebody to go fishing with and, by golly, I plan to do it!"

They turned toward the house, everyone happy and chattering as they ambled up the front lawn. Suzanne rode on her daddy's arm, with her mother pressed close to his side.

In the dining room champagne and cake waited.

Mike proposed a toast. "To the happy bride and groom who started on our back porch when they were seventeen. May they be as much in love at ninety as they are today!"

There were gifts, too. From Brookie and Gene a pierced-work tablecloth long enough for the mammoth dining-room table, with ten matching napkins. From Barb and Mike a pair of antique candleholders of etched crystal with six white fluted candles to fill them. Anna brought a grab bag: embroidered dish towels, crocheted doilies, six pints of Eric's favorite thimbleberry jam and a china tea set that had belonged to Eric's Grandma

Severson. The latter brought tears to Maggie's eyes and a great big hug for Anna. Roy's offering was a small Louis XIV antique chair for the front parlor, which he had stripped, refinished and reupholstered. It also earned him a hug from his daughter and a round of enthusiastic inspection and compliments from all the guests. There was, too, something from Suzanne (though nobody would confess to having brought it): a greeting card with a picture of a Victorian family—father, mother and child—setting a toy boat asail beside a grassy-banked pond with a willow tree in the background. Inside, someone had written, *To my mommy and daddy on their wedding day . . . With lots of love, Suzanne.*

When they'd read it, Maggie and Eric exchanged a look of such expressive love that every eye in the room became misty. They were sitting on the window seat of the dining room at the time, with their gifts strewn about them and Suzanne nearby in her grandpa's arms. Eric touched Maggie's jaw, then reached for the baby.

"Thank you, Suzanne," he said, taking her, kissing her cheek. "And thank you all. We want you to know what it's meant to us to have you all with us tonight. We love you all and we thank you from the bottom of our hearts."

Suzanne started rubbing her eyes and whining, and it seemed an appropriate time to end the festivities. Each good-bye was emotional, but Roy lingered till last. Hugging Maggie, he said, "Honey, I'm so sorry your mother and Katy weren't here. They both should have been."

There was no denying their absence hurt. "Oh, Daddy . . . I guess we can't have everything perfect in this life, can we?"

He patted her shoulder, then drew back. "I want you to know something, Maggie. You've taught me a lot during these last few months that I wish I'd have learned when I was a much younger man. Nobody can make you happy but yourself. You've done it, and now I'm going to do it. I'm going to start by taking a little time off work. You know, in all the years I worked at that store I don't think I took more than four vacations, and I used all of them to paint the house. I'm going to be gone for a few days—take a little time for myself."

"Isn't Mother going with you?"

"No, she isn't. But I don't want you to worry. I'll talk to you when I get back, okay?"

"Okay, Daddy. But where—"

"You just keep on being happy, will you, sweetheart? It does my heart good to see you that way. Now I'd better say goodnight." He kissed Maggie, rubbed Suzanne's head and thumped Eric between the shoulders. "Thank you, son," he said with tears in his eyes, and left.

They stood on the back veranda and watched him climb the steps to the road, Eric holding Suzanne, Maggie with her arms crossed.

"Daddy is troubled," Maggie said reflectively.

Eric dropped an arm around her shoulders and tipped her against his side. "Not about us though."

She smiled softly and looked up. "No, not about us."

For a moment they lingered in each other's eyes before Eric said, low, "Come on. Let's put Suzanne to bed."

Suzanne was tired and grumpy and fell asleep before her thumb reached her mouth. They stood awhile looking at her, holding hands.

"I feel like I've never lived before," he said quietly. "Like everything began with you . . . and her."

"It did."

He turned her into his arms and held her in a loose embrace. "My wife," he whispered.

She pressed her cheek against his lapel and replied in matching quietude, "My husband."

They stood motionless a moment, as if receiving a blessing, then walked across the hall to the Belvedere Room where the great carved bed waited.

Roy Pearson drove home slowly. He went the long way around, by way of the switchback, up the hill from Maggie's, and out between the up-country fields, then down the curving highway to the stop sign at Main. He turned right, passed the store where he'd worked all of his adult life, recounting its sights and sounds and smells—aging fruit and garlicy sandwich meats, the tangy stink of pickled herring. The rumble of the old-fashioned door on the meat case when it rolled open. The *bing* of the cash register up front. (Actually, the old cash register had been gone four years and the new one went *dit-dit-dit-dit*, but when Roy thought of cash registers he still thought of bells.) Helen McCrossen coming in every Tuesday, promptly at eleven A.M., so promptly you could set your watch by her, asking, "How is the liverwurst today, Roy, is it fresh?" The feel of the cleaver in his hand, thudding against the butcher block. The cold, tallowy smell of the cooler.

He would miss the store.

At home, he pulled around the rear, parked before the closed garage doors and crossed the backyard to the house. The grass was dewy and his shoes got wet—Vera would scold if she were up. But the house was quiet and dim. He disregarded the back rug and crossed the kitchen floor, heading directly for the storage space beneath the stairs. He emerged with a flimsy cloth suitcase and a cardboard box which he carried upstairs to his bedroom.

Vera was awake, swathed in a hairnet, reading by the light of the bed-lamp which was clamped to the headboard above her shoulder.

"So?" she said as one might order a dog. "Speak!"

Roy set down his suitcase and box and made no reply.

"Well, she's married to him, then."

"Yes, she is."

"Who was there? Was Katy there?"

"You should have come and seen for yourself, Vera."

"Hmph!" Vera returned to her book.

Roy snapped on the ceiling light and opened a dresser drawer.

For the first time Vera noticed the suitcase. "Roy, what are you doing?"

"I'm leaving you, Vera."

"You're what!"

"I'm leaving you."

"Roy, don't be a fool! Put that suitcase away and get to bed."

He calmly began emptying drawers and loading the suitcase. The box. Carried three hangers from the closet and laid them across the foot of the bed.

"Roy, you're going to wrinkle those trousers and I just ironed them yesterday. Now, put them away this minute!"

"I'm all done taking orders from you, Vera. I've been taking them for forty-six years, and now I'm done."

"What in the world has gotten into you! Have you gone crazy?"

"No, you might say I've come to my senses. I have at the most maybe ten, fifteen good healthy years left, and I'm going to try to get a little happiness out of them the way my daughter did."

"Your daughter. She's behind this, isn't she?"

"No, Vera, she's not. You are. You and all forty-six years of being told where to take off my shoes, and how to put the Christmas tree in the stand, and how much fat to trim off the pork chops, and where I can't put my feet, and how loud the television can be, and how I never did a thing right. I want you to know I didn't just decide this overnight either. I've been thinking about it for five years. It just took Maggie's courage to finally make me work up a little courage of my own. I've been watching her the last year, forging ahead, making a new life for herself, making herself happy against all odds, and I said to myself, Roy, you can learn something from that young woman."

"Roy, you're not serious!"

"Yes, I am."

"But you can't just . . . just *leave*!"

"There's nothing here for me, Vera. No warmth, no happiness, no love. You're a woman who's incapable of love."

"Why, that's ridiculous."

"Is it? If I asked you right now, Vera, do you love me, could you say it?"

She stared at him, tight-lipped.

"When have you ever said it? Or shown it—to either me or Maggie? Where were you tonight? Where were you when Suzanne was born? You were here, nursing your bitterness, congratulating yourself on being right once again. Well, I made up my mind when that baby was born that I'd give you just so long to come to your senses and be a mother to Maggie and a grandmother to Suzanne, and tonight when you failed to go to your own daughter's wedding, I said to myself, Roy, what's the use? She'll never change. And I don't believe you will."

Roy laid a folded shirt in the suitcase. Vera stared at him, incapable of moving.

"Is there another woman?"

"Oh, for pity's sake. Look at me. I'm old enough to collect Social Security, I'm damn near bald, and I haven't had a good hard-on in the last eight years. What would I do with another woman?"

It began to dawn on Vera that he really intended to leave.

"But where will you go?"

"For starters, I'm going down to Chicago to see Katy and try to talk some sense into her and make her see that if she keeps on the way she is, she's going to turn out just like her grandma. Then I don't know. I've quit at the store, but I asked them not to say anything about it up till now. I may just retire and collect that Social Security after all. I may take my tools and set up a little fix-it shop somewhere and make doll furniture for my new granddaughter. I'd like to do some fishing with Eric. I don't know."

"You've quit the store?"

He nodded, stuffing a stack of socks into the box.

"Without even telling me?"

"I'm telling you now."

"But . . . but what about us? Are you coming back?" When he continued packing without looking up, she asked in a quiet, shaken voice, "Are you saying you want a divorce?"

He looked at her sadly. His voice, when he replied, was quiet and deep. "Yes, I am, Vera."

"But can't we talk about it . . . can't we . . . can't we . . ." She made a fist and pressed it to her lips. "Dear God," she whispered.

"No, I don't want to talk about anything. I just want to go."

"But, Roy, forty-six years . . . you can't just turn your back on forty-six years."

He latched the suitcase and set it on the floor.

"I've taken half the money out of our savings account, and cashed in half of our certificates of deposit. The rest I left for you. We'll let the lawyers work out details about our retirement account. I'm taking the car but I'll be back when I find a place, to get the rest of my clothes and my power tools. The house you can have. It was always more yours than mine anyway, the way you kept me from soiling and using things."

Vera was sitting up on the edge of the bed, looking bewildered and scared. "Roy, don't go . . . Roy, I'm sorry."

"Yes, I'm sure you are now. But it's a few years too late, Vera."

"Please . . ." she pleaded, with tears in her eyes as he left the room to collect some toilet articles in the bathroom. He returned in less than a minute and dropped them into the cardboard box.

"One thing you should make sure you do right away, Vera, is get yourself a driver's license. You're going to need one, that's for sure."

Vera's eyes looked terrified. She had one fist folded tight between her breasts. "When will you be back?"

"I don't know. When I decide what I want to do next. After Chicago I may check out Phoenix. They say the winters down there are mild and there are a lot of folks our age down there."

"Ph . . . Phoenix?" she whispered. "Arizona?" Phoenix was on the other side of the world.

He propped the box on one hip and picked up the suitcase with his free hand.

"You never asked, but Maggie and Eric had a real nice wedding tonight. They're going to be mighty happy together, and our granddaughter is a real beauty. You might like to walk up there and meet her someday." The last time he'd seen Vera cry this way was when her mother passed away in 1967. He thought it was a good healthy sign: she might manage to change after all.

"I imagine the minute I walk out the door you'll want to call Maggie and cry on her shoulder, but for once in your life would you think of somebody else first and remember it's her wedding night? She doesn't know I'm leaving you. I'll call her in a few days and explain to her." His glance circled the room once and came to rest on her. "Well . . . good-bye, Vera."

Without an angry word or a trace of bitterness, he left the house.

He surprised the daylights out of Katy when he rang her from the lobby of her dorm. "This is Grandpa. I've come to take you out to breakfast."

He took her to a Perkins Restaurant and bought them each a ham and cheese omelette and told her with a great deal of caring in his voice and eyes what he'd come to say.

"We missed you at the wedding, Katy." He waited, but she made no response. "It was a real nice wedding, in your mother's backyard by the lake, and I don't believe I've ever seen two happier people in my life than your mother and Eric. She wore a pretty pink suit and carried apple blossoms, and they said their own vows. They just kept it simple, then afterwards we had some cake and champagne. It was just a small group—the Kerschners, Eric's mother, and his brother and wife . . . and me." Roy took a sip of coffee and added, as if it just occurred to him, "Oh, there was someone else there, too." He leaned forward and laid a photograph on the table. "Your little sister." He sat back and hooked a finger through his cup handle. "Myyyyy, that's a darling little girl if I do say so myself. She's got that Pearson chin all the way. Cute little dent in it just like yours and your mom's."

Katy's downcast eyes remained riveted on the picture and her cheeks turned pink.

The waitress came and refilled their coffee cups. When she moved away, Roy leaned his elbows on the table.

"But that's not the reason I'm here. I came to tell you something else. I've left your grandma, Katy."

Katy's eyes shot to his, disbelieving.

"Left her? For good?"

"Yes. It's all my idea, and she was feeling pretty bad when I left her. If you could find the time to run up there one weekend soon, I think she'd really love to see you. She's going to be pretty lonesome for a while . . . she'll need a friend."

"But . . . but you . . . and Grandma . . ." It was inconceivable to Katy that her grandparents could part. People their age just didn't!

"We've been married forty-six years, and during that time I watched her grow colder and harder and more unforgiving, until it seems like she finally just forgot how to love. That's a sad thing, you know? People don't get like that overnight. They start in little ways—fault-finding, criticizing, judging others—and pretty soon they think the whole world is mixed up and they're the only ones who know how it ought to be run. Too bad. Your grandma had a nice chance lately to show a little compassion, to be the kind of person other people like, but she turned your mother away. She condemned Margaret for something that nobody's got the right to condemn another for. She said, if you don't run your life the way *I* think you ought to run it, well . . . then that's it, I don't want anything to do with you anymore. She never visited your mother in the hospital when Suzanne was born and she hasn't visited her since. She hasn't even seen Suzanne—her own granddaughter—and she refused to go to the wedding. Well, a man can't live with a woman like that, I know I can't. If your grandma wants to be that way, she can be that way alone." He ruminated awhile and added as an afterthought, "People like that are bound to end up alone eventually because nobody likes to be around bitterness."

Katy had been sitting for some time, staring at the table. When she looked up, tears lined her eyelids.

"Oh, Grandpa," she whispered in a trembling voice, "I've been so miserable."

He reached across the table and covered her hand. "Well, that should tell you something, Katy."

The tears magnified her eyes, growing plumper until they finally tumbled over and streaked her cheeks.

"Thank you," she whispered. "Thank you for coming and for making me see."

Roy squeezed her hand and smiled benevolently.

On the Saturday following their wedding, Maggie was feeding Suzanne her lunch and Eric had been gone since early morning. The infant seat perched on the kitchen table and Suzanne's mouth was lined with applesauce when the phone rang.

Maggie answered it holding the jar of warm baby food in her free hand. "Hello?"

"Hi, honey."

"Eric, hi!" she replied, breaking into a smile.

"What're you doing?"

"Feeding Suzanne her applesauce."

"Tell her hi."

"Suzanne, your daddy says hi." Into the phone Maggie said, "She waved a fist at you. Are you in for lunch?"

"Yup. Had a good morning, how about you?"

"Uh-huh. I took Suzanne out in the sun with me while I thinned the day lilies. She really seemed to . . ." Maggie stopped speaking, midsentence. A moment later her voice returned in a stunned whisper. "Oh, my God . . ."

"Maggie, what's wrong?" Eric sounded alarmed.

"Eric, Katy is here. She's coming down the sidewalk."

"Oh, honey," he said understandingly.

"Darling, I'd better go."

"Yes . . . all right . . . and, Mag?" he added hurriedly. "Good luck."

She was dressed in blue jeans and a Northwestern sweatshirt, a thin purse strap over her left shoulder. Her convertible was parked at the top of the hill behind her, and as she descended the steps her eyes were fixed upon the screen door.

Maggie stepped to it and waited.

At the foot of the veranda Katy stopped. "Hello, Mother."

"Hello, Katy."

For the moment only the most mundane question came to Katy's mind. "How are you?"

"I'm happy, Katy. How are you?"

"Miserable."

Maggie opened the screen door. "Would you like to come in and talk about it?"

Head down, Katy entered the kitchen. Her eyes went immediately to the table where the baby sat in ruffled blue britches with suspenders, sucking one fist, her ankles crossed and a bib flaring up around her ears. Letting the screen door close softly, Maggie watched Katy halt and stare.

"This is Suzanne. I was just feeding her her lunch. Why don't you sit down while I finish?"—painfully polite, as if a church elder had come to call.

Katy sat, mesmerized by the baby while Maggie stood beside the table and resumed spoon-feeding Suzanne whose regard was centered on the strange newcomer in the room.

"Grandpa came to see me on Wednesday."

"Yes, I know. He called."

"Isn't it awful about him and Grandma?"

"It's very sad to see any marriage break up."

"He told me some things about Grandma, about what kind of person she is . . . I mean . . ." Katy stammered to a stop, her face a reflection of anguish. "He said . . . he said I'm just like her, and I don't want to be. I really don't, Mom."

She was half-woman, half-child as her eyes began to glisten and her face crumpled.

Maggie set down the baby food and went around the table with open arms.

"Oh, Katy, dear . . . "

Katy fell against her, crying. "I was so awful to you, Mom, I'm sorry."

"This has been a trying time for all of us."

"Grandpa made me see how selfish I've been. I don't want to lose the people I love like Grandma did."

Holding her daughter, Maggie closed her eyes and felt another of the complex joys that were so much a part of motherhood. She and Katy had been through such a catharsis in the past two years. Bitter at times, sweet at others. While Katy clung, all but the sweet dissolved.

"Darling, I'm so glad you've come home."

"So am I."

"Katy, I love Eric very much. I want you to know that. But my love for him in no way diminishes my love for you."

"I knew that, too. I was just . . . I don't know what I was. Confused and hurt. But I just want you to be happy, Mom."

"I am." Maggie smiled against Katy's mousse-stiff hair. "He's made me so incredibly happy." The exchange, like a solemnization, brought the proper moment for Maggie's next question. "Would you like to meet your sister?"

Katy backed up, drying her eyes with the edge of a hand. "Well, why do you think I came?"

They turned toward the baby.

"Suzanna Banana, this is Katy." Maggie took Suzanne from the infant seat and perched her on her arm. Suzanne's blue eyes fixed upon Katy with uncomplicated curiosity. She looked back at her mother, then at the young woman who stood by uncertainly, and finally gave Katy a spitty smile and a gurgling sound of approval.

Katy reached out and took the baby from Maggie's arms.

"Suzanna, hiiiii," she said wonderingly, then to her mother, "Oh, wow, lookit—Grandpa was right. She's got the Pearson chin. Gol, Mom, she's just beautiful." Katy held the baby gingerly, bounced her experimentally, gave her a thumb to hang on to, and smiled into Suzanne's rosy face. "Oh, wow . . ." she said again, captivated, while Maggie stood back and felt favored by all the right forces.

The two were still getting acquainted when a truck door slammed outside and Eric came down the walk.

Maggie opened the screen door and held it while he approached.

"Hi," he said with uncharacteristic quietness, dropping a hand on her shoulder blade.

"Hi. We have company."

He stopped just inside the door, let his eyes find Katy, and waited. She stood on the other side of the table, her face a mixture of somberness and fear while Suzanne's broke into a smile at his appearance.

"Hello, Katy," Eric said at last.

"Hello, Eric."

He laid his skipper's cap on the cupboard. "Well, this is a nice surprise."

"I hope it's okay that I came."

"Of course it is. We're both happy you're here."

Katy's eyes flashed to Maggie, then back to Eric. Her lips quirked up in a doubtful smile. "I thought it was time I met Suzanne."

He let his smile shift to the baby. "She seems to like you."

"Yeah, well, that's a miracle. I mean, I haven't been too likable lately, have I?"

An awkward pause fell and Maggie stepped in to fill it. "Why don't we all sit down and I'll fix us a sandwich."

"No, wait," Katy said. "Let me say this first, because I don't think I'll be able to swallow anything until I do. Eric . . . Mom . . . I'm . . . I'm sorry I didn't come to your wedding."

Maggie's eyes met Eric's. They both looked at Katy and searched for some reply.

"Is it too late to say congratulations?"

For a moment nobody moved. Then Maggie shot across the room and put her cheek to Katy's while Katy looked over her shoulder with tear-filled eyes at Eric. He followed his wife across the room, and stood uncertainly nearby, studying the face of the young woman who looked so much like his infant daughter perched on her arm.

Maggie drew back, leaving Eric and Katy poised, caught in one another's regard.

He was not her father.

She was not his daughter.

But they both loved Maggie, who stood between them with her lips trembling while Suzanne studied the scene with wide-eyed innocence.

Eric made the final step and laid one hand on Katy's shoulder.

"Welcome home, Katy," he said simply.

And Katy smiled.

FORGIVING

Chapter 1

❧

Dakota Territory, September 1876

The Cheyenne stage was six hours late, putting Sarah Merritt into Deadwood at ten P.M. rather than in the late afternoon. The rig rumbled away and left her standing in the dark on a muddy street before a crude saloon. Several crude saloons. An entire streetful of them! The noise was appalling—a mixture of shouts, laughter, banjo music and brawling. And the smell—ye gods! Did nobody pick up the animal dung? Horses and mules lined the hitching rails; nearby, one of them was snoring.

Sarah backed up and squinted at the sign overhead. Eureka Saloon. She glanced down at the place—a frame building, unpainted, roughly constructed and crowded by a similar structure on the left and a log building on the right. The door to the Eureka was closed, but through its window murky coal-oil lantern light tumbled down a set of wooden steps leading directly from the building to the mud, without the benefit of a boardwalk.

Sarah glanced down at the trunks and bandbox sitting at her ankle, wondering what to do. Before she could decide, three gunshots cracked, a mule brayed, the door of the Eureka flapped open and a crowd of rowdies burst from inside and stumbled down the steps into the street. Sarah snatched her bandbox and scuttled to the shadow of the saloon wall. "Kill that claim-jumper, Soaky!" someone bellowed. "Fix his face so only his mama could love him!"

A fist smacked against a jaw.

A man stumbled backward and somersaulted over Sarah's trunks, picked himself up and vaulted at his opponent without noticing over what he'd stumbled. The rabble milled this way and that, shouting, brandishing their fists and beer mugs. A man thumped into the side of a mule, which brayed and skittered sideways.

"Kill the sonofabitch!"

"Yeah, kill him!"

Two onlookers clambered onto Sarah's cowhide trunks to get a better view.

"No! Get off there!" she shouted.

When she moved, one of the drunken revelers spotted her.

"Mother of God, it's a woman! You hear me, boys, it's a *woman!*"

The fracas ended as if a firebell had clanged.

"A woman . . ."

"A woman . . ." The word was passed from one man to another as, like fog, they crept close, hemming her in.

She stood with her back to the saloon wall, the hair on her nape prickling, clutching the ribbons of her bandbox while the men gawked at her skirts, hat and face as if they'd never before seen a female.

Summoning a note of bravado, she greeted, "Good evening, gentlemen."

Silent, they continued gawking.

"Could anyone tell me where to find the home of Mrs. Hossiter?"

"Hossiter?" a croaky voice repeated. "Anyone heard of a woman named Hossiter?" The crowd mumbled and shook their heads. " 'Fraid not, ma-'am. What's her husband's name?"

"I'm afraid I don't know, but my sister's name is Adelaide Merritt, and she works for them."

"Nobody named Merritt around here. Nobody named Hossiter either. Can't be more than twenty-five women in the whole gulch, and we know every one of 'em, don't we, boys?"

A murmur crescendoed and faded.

"What's your sister do?"

"Domestic work, and she distinctly said the name of her landlady was Mrs. Hossiter."

"Landlady, you say?" A spark of deeper interest perked up the fellow's voice. He spread his arms wide and pressed back the throng. "Here, boys, don't crowd the little lady, let her move out into the light where we can see her better. My name is Shorty Reese, miss, and I'll do what I can to help you find your sister." He doffed his hat, took her elbow and drew her to the foot of the steps where the lantern light ranged from the open door. By it she noted he was middle-aged, with dirty clothing, seamed face and one missing tooth.

"If you'll let me through, those trunks are mine. I have a picture of my sister. Maybe one of you will recognize her."

They stepped back and allowed Sarah to open the buckles of one of her trunks, from which she produced a sepia daguerreotype of herself and Adelaide, taken five years before. She handed it to Shorty Reese. "She's twenty-one and has blond hair and green eyes."

He turned it toward the light, cocked his head and studied it. "Why, this is Eve," he pronounced, "one of the upstairs girls at Miss Rose's, and she don't have no blond hair. Her hair's as black as the end of Number Fourteen stope."

"Eve?"

"That's right. Ain't this Eve, boys?" The picture was passed around.

"That's Eve, all right."

"Yup, that's her."

"That's Eve." The picture returned to Sarah. "You can find her up at Rose's, the north end of Main Street on the left. You mind my asking, miss, if you plan to work as an upstairs girl, too?"

"No, sir. I plan to start publishing a newspaper."

"A newspaper!"

"That's right, as soon as my press arrives, if it hasn't already."

"But you're a woman."

"Yes, Mr. Reese, I am." Sarah returned the picture to the trunk and buckled the straps. "Thank you very much for your help. Now if you could point me in the direction of a hotel, I'd be ever so grateful."

"Help her with her trunks, boys!" Reese shouted. "Let's get her over to the Grand Central!"

"No, please . . . I . . ."

"Why, it'd be our pleasure, miss. We don't get a chance to see a lady hardly at all. Like I said, can't be more than a couple dozen of the fairer sex in Deadwood, if that."

Though she little relished making her entrance into Deadwood in the company of the Eureka Saloon's clientele, she had no idea how she'd carry two trunks to the hotel on her own. It struck her, too, that as a newspaperwoman, she would be prudent to avoid alienating any of the townspeople on her first night in town. This was a gold town. Gold spelled money, and money meant rowdiness. Any one of these men could be the owner of the lot she might want to buy, or the building she might want to rent, or a member of the town board, for that matter.

"Thank you, Mr. Reese, I appreciate your help." She found herself buffeted along by the noisy lot, who hoisted her trunks onto their shoulders and escorted her to the other end of the block.

"You're in luck," Reese said, climbing the steps of a tall, false-fronted building with the first boardwalk she'd seen. "The Grand Central just opened last week." They took her right inside, across a Spartan lobby to the desk where they formed a circle around her, grinning, while presenting her to the night clerk. "Got a customer for you, Sam. This here's Miss Merritt, just came in on the Cheyenne stage."

"M—mmiss M—Merritt." His face grew scarlet as he extended a hand which was limp and moist as cooked cabbage. He was a chinless little man with round spectacles and an effeminate manner, dressed in a brown plaid suit with his hair parted in the middle. "I'm happy to m—make your acquaintance."

"This is Sam Peoples," Shorty filled in for Peoples, who was too flustered by her appearance to supply his own name.

"Hello, Mr. Peoples." His blush made him look combustible and for a moment he forgot to withdraw his hand. Self-consciously, Sarah withdrew hers, unaccustomed to creating such a stir.

"She's gonna start up a newspaper."

"A newspaper—my, my. Then we'd better take good care of her, hadn't we?" Peoples forced a nervous laugh. He dipped a black pen and extended it her way while revolving the hotel register to face her. Signing, Sarah felt the entire gallery of men watching.

When she finished she gave Peoples a smile and the pen.

"Welcome to the Grand Central," he said. "That'll be a dollar fifty for the night."

"In advance?"

"Yes. In gold dust if you please." He touched the gold scale at his elbow and left it nodding.

She stood straight as a lodgepole and fixed her eyes on the clerk's spectacles. "Mr. Peoples, I've just spent six nights and five days on the stagecoach from Cheyenne. Given all the robberies that have been happening along the stage routes, do you honestly believe I'd be fool enough to carry my money with me in the form of gold?"

Peoples' face turned brighter and he glanced helplessly at the men. "I'm s—sorry, Miss Merritt, I'm just the n—night clerk here. I don't own the hotel. But it's our p—policy to accept only guests who pay in advance, and gold dust is our legal tender out here."

"Very well." She set her bandbox on the desk and began untying its ribbons. "All my money is in the form of Wells Fargo certificates. If you can cash one into gold dust, I'd be happy to pay in advance." From a black organdy pouch she extracted a one-hundred-dollar certificate and offered it to Peoples.

Again, he glanced at the men, his face crimson. "I don't keep that k—kind of gold around either. You can c—cash it in the morning at the bank, however."

"And in the meantime?" She fixed him with a determined stare.

One of the onlookers said, "You gonna let a lady sleep on the street, Peoples?"

"Mr. Winters g—gave me orders." The more flustered the clerk became the more he stuttered. "Sh—she c—could sleep in the l—l—l—lobby, but it's the b—b—best I can d—do."

"Lobby!" A leather pouch landed on the desk beside the gold scale. "Take it out of there." Another pouch joined it—"Or out of here"—and another and another until there were nearly a dozen lying on the high counter.

Sarah turned to the men behind her, with a hand spread on her chest. "Thank you all so much," she said sincerely, "but I can't accept your gold."

"Why not? There's plenty more where that come from, ain't there, boys?"

"Hell yes!"

"El Dorado!" They punched the air in hallelujah and let out a roar. Several of them *hoo-rahed,* lifting their beer mugs, then took swigs.

Sam Peoples selected a pouch and carefully weighed out the gold—at twenty dollars per ounce, a dollar and fifty cents' worth scarcely looked like enough to have created this embarrassing contretemps. When the pouches were reclaimed by their owners, the gold proved to have come out of the sack owned by a tall, lanky man with thinning dark hair and a bleary-eyed smile. He had a prominent Adam's apple, watery red eyes, and he wove back on his heels as if struck by a wall of wind.

"Thank you, Mr.—?"

The man continued weaving and grinning in his alcoholic euphoria.

"Bradigan," Reese told her. "His name's Patrick Bradigan."

"Thank you, Mr. Bradigan."

Bradigan listed toward Sarah wearing an expression like a scratched cat, his squinting eyes scarcely registering what he saw.

"I shall repay you tomorrow as soon as I've visited the bank."

He gave a floppy salute and someone stuffed his gold pouch into his pocket.

"Where can I find you?"

"Least I can do fer a pretty lady," Bradigan mumbled.

"Bradigan tipped a few tonight," one of his cohorts explained. "He won't know the difference whether you pay him back or not."

They would have carried her trunks upstairs to her room but for the protests of Sam Peoples. "You'll w–wake up all my customers! Gentlemen, pl–please—get back to the saloon where you belong."

"All your customers are still *in* the saloons!"

"Then get back and j–join them." He sent the boys shuffling off with a doffing of hats and a chorus of goodnights for "the pretty little lady," which Sarah was not. She was five foot ten in her stocking feet, with plain brown hair, a nose she considered a trifle too long and lips too thin to be remarkable. She did have passably attractive blue eyes, vivid and thick-lashed, still nobody with all their faculties would mistake her for pretty. She was a long-faced woman who in all her life had never attracted as much male attention as during the last quarter hour.

"I'm giving you a room on the third floor. It's warmest up there," said the ingratiating Peoples, carrying the first of her trunks. He led her through a building whose primary recommendation was size. Big it was, but raw in every sense of the word, without a plastered wall in evidence, not even in the lobby, where the windows were bare of curtains and the only spots of brightness were provided by the china cuspidor and the calendar behind the desk, sporting the picture of a waterfall. The floors were constructed of bare pine planks, still emitting the smell of newly milled lumber. The walls were of green studs still oozing sap, between which the clapboard siding showed, replete with knotholes that seemed to peer back like empty eye sockets.

The stairs, situated just behind the desk, led up to the mouth of a dark, narrow hall. Midway along it, a single coal-oil lantern hung from a wall bracket; on the floor beneath it sat a covered china slop jar. He led her to a room a third of the way down on the left and opened a door made of planks on a Z-shaped frame.

"Water's in the c–can outside the door, mornings only, and you can dump your sl–slop in the jar down the hall. Matches are on the wall to your left. I'll be right back with your other trunk."

When he was gone, she found the tin match holder and lit the lantern beside her bed. By its smoky orange light she perused the room. *Lord in heaven, what have I gotten into?* The walls were as stark as those in the lobby, bare planks pocked by knotholes through which drafts blew. Overhead, the ceiling rafters showed. The window and floor were unadorned, the bed made of tubular brown tin, the ordinary table beside it holding only the lamp—no runner or doily, nothing to appeal to the feminine eye. Not even a coverlet on the bed, only the spruce green woolen blanket and a pillow which—thank heavens—had a muslin slipcover. She turned back the blanket and found muslin sheets and a real mattress stuffed with straw and cotton, and breathed a sigh of relief. There was a commode stand with a pitcher and bowl on top. She opened the door beneath and peered inside to find a covered china commode.

She had just closed the door when Sam Peoples returned with her second trunk. "I haven't eaten since noon," Sarah told him. "Would there be anything to eat?"

"Our d–dining room is closed, I'm sorry. But we'll be open for break-fast."

"Oh," she said, disappointed.

He backed toward the door. "There aren't many w–women in Dead-wood, as you know. You'd best b–bar the door." He indicated a heavy wooden four-by-four standing in the corner. "Good night then. May I say it's a pl–pleasure having you."

"Thank you, Mr. Peoples. Good night."

When he closed the door she studied the crudely hewn wooden brackets on either side. The bar was heavy. She struggled to lift and drop it into place, then turned to face the room with a sigh. She dropped to the edge of the bed, bounced once tentatively and fell back with one arm crooked above her head. Her eyelids closed. Of Sarah's five nights on the road, only two had been spent in beds. Two she'd slept wrapped in her own blanket, on the floors of log shacks serving as stage relay stations, and one on board the stagecoach itself, folded like a carpenter's rule on the hard horsehair seat. Her last filling meal had been yesterday noon at Hill City, where she'd had bread, coffee and venison. Today's fare had been bacon and cold coffee at breakfast, and at noon dry biscuits accompanied by water from Box Elder Creek. She'd taken her last bath in St. Louis nine days ago and smelled—she realized—like an old horse's hoof.

Get up, Sarah. Your day's not over.

Suppressing a groan, she forced her tired body to bend and shoved herself to her feet. The pitcher and bowl were empty. Out in the hall, the water tin was, too: *mornings only,* she remembered and went back inside to whack the dust from her woolen suit as best she could, recomb the sides of her hair and wipe off her face with a dry cloth. She replaced her hat, rammed the pin through her chignon, took her organdy pouch containing the Wells Fargo certificates, her father's watch, and her pen and ink, and left the room.

As she passed through the lobby, she startled Peoples, who advised, "Ma'am, you shouldn't be out on the street alone after dark."

"I've traveled clear from St. Louis alone, Mr. Peoples. I'm perfectly capable of taking care of myself. Furthermore, my sister is someplace in this town and I haven't seen her for five years. I intend to do so tonight if I have to wake her up to do it."

Outside, the din from the saloons still rattled up and down the thoroughfare. The boardwalks proved intermittent, built or not built at the whim of each lot-owner who'd erected a building. Striding down the center of Main Street, she made a mental note to write an editorial about standardizing the height and width of the boardwalks and making them compulsory for every building along Main. And streetlamps—the town needed streetlamps and a paid lamplighter to tend them at dusk and dawn. Ah, her work was cut out.

In spite of the clamor, the town had an eerie feeling lit solely by blobs of light from the saloon windows falling onto the rows of sleeping horses. She looked up. Only a narrow corridor of starlight shone overhead. The sides of the gulch hung like a widow's curtains, closed against intrusion, isolating Deadwood from the rest of the world. In the dark she made out the blacker shapes of pines high on the steep slopes, separated from town by the paler spots where the hills had been denuded. A few pines straggled in places to the very edges of the street. The wind whistled through them and down the ravine, a cold late-September wind that fluttered her skirt and stirred the scent of fresh animal droppings. Sarah covered her nose as she hurried along, formulating yet another editorial.

She passed a tin shop, grocer's, barber's, tobacconist, hardware, uncountable saloons and (surprisingly) a huge theater, the Langrishe, where lamps were lit and the bill announced "Flies in the Weed" by John Brougham. Smiling, Sarah paused and reread the bill. A hint of culture, after all. To her amazement, in the next block on the opposite side of the street she passed *another* theater, the Bella Union! Her spirits took their first upswing since she'd arrived in Deadwood. But where was the church? The school? Surely in a town this size there must be *some* children. She would make it a point to find out how many.

At the far end of Main, where it took a swing to the right, the wooden structures petered out and the gulch bottlenecked from three streets into one. Beyond that point fires glimmered in the distance, dots of hazel light between the paler squares of lantern-lit tents that lay scattered along the cut like the beads of a broken rosary. Where the three streets of town merged, foot traffic picked up. Men . . . all men. They stared at Sarah and stopped in their tracks as she passed. Men . . . noisy men, milling about the last string of buildings on the left whose doors opened and closed constantly, releasing peals of piano music and laughter.

All six buildings looked alike—narrow, unadorned, with heavy draperies drawn across the windows; windowless doors. There must be some mistake, she thought, stopping before Rose's, glancing at the names of the adjacent establishments—The Green Door, Goldie's, The Mother Lode, The Doves' Cote and Angeline's. They appeared to be saloons.

Nevertheless, she decided the safest course was to knock on the door of Rose's. She did, then clutched her money packet against her jacket buttons with both hands and waited. Given the noise inside, it seemed little wonder nobody answered. A creek purled somewhere behind her. A man left the place next door and disappeared into the dark in the direction of the tents. Unaware that she stood behind him, he broke wind noisily, pausing and canting his left buttock before the sound died and he moved on.

She knocked again, harder.

"Nobody knocks on the door at Rose's," a deep voice said behind her. "Go right on in."

She jumped and spun, pressing a hand to her heart. "Good heavens, you scared me!"

"I didn't mean to." A tall man stood close behind her. The dark hid his face.

"Tell me . . . is this the only Rose's in Deadwood?"

"The one and only. You're new in town," he speculated with a grin in his voice.

"Yes. I'm looking for my sister, Adelaide. I'm told she's an upstairs maid at Rose Hossiter's, but it seems she's changed her name to Eve."

"I know Eve."

"You do?"

"I know Eve very well, as a matter of fact. So you're her sister."

"Yes—Sarah Merritt. I've just arrived from St. Louis." She extended her gloved hand. He took it in a hard, protracted squeeze while she peered up trying to make out his face in the deep shadow of his ten-gallon hat.

"Noah Campbell."

"Mr. Campbell," she returned politely. When she would have withdrawn her hand he continued gripping it. "Well, Miss Merritt, this is an unexpected pleasure. Allow me to escort you inside and introduce you to

Rose. She'll know just where your sister is." As if executing an allemande-left, he opened the door and swung her inside, dropping her hand as the door thumped shut behind them.

"Welcome to Rose's, Miss Merritt," he said at her shoulder, flourishing an open palm at the room.

As if plunged into a nightmare, she stood rooted, absorbing impressions—hazy lantern light, garish parlor furniture, a parrot sidling left and right on a perch, squawking, "Dollar a minute! Dollar a minute!" Thick, tassled draperies, the smell of stale whiskey and hard-boiled eggs, the sting of cigar smoke, a lot of men in stages of semidrunkenness and one blowsy woman dressed entirely in emerald green with carmine lips and a feather in her red hair. She possessed an acre of cleavage resembling a baby's bare buttocks: an obese woman with a smoking cigar between her teeth who stood with her arm around the shoulders of a big, bearded man while he fondled her rump.

Sarah spun to Noah Campbell. "There must be some mistake. This isn't a private home."

"No, ma'am, hardly."

For the first time she saw his face. He had a bushy auburn mustache, a roundish nose with a faint dent at the end and grinning gray eyes that lighted on Sarah's and lingered. "Come along, I'll introduce you to Rose."

He put a hand on her spine and she balked. "No! I told you, my sister is an upstairs maid and her landlady's name is Mrs. Rose Hossiter. And please remove your hand from my back!"

He obliged, then stood back, studying her indulgently while his grin lingered. "Getting last-minute jitters, are you?"

"This place is horrible. It looks like a brothel."

He glanced idly at the woman in green, then back at Sarah. "Tell you what." His eyes roved lazily down her torso and back up. "I'm a pretty conventional fellow—Rose will vouch for me. I like it straight, no rough stuff, no more than two or three drinks beforehand. I pay good, in pure gold, I don't have any diseases or lice. *And,* I already took my bath. You can tell Rose that you've already lined up your first customer. How would that be?"

"I *beg your pardon!*" Sarah felt the blood surge to her face. The skin across her chest felt taut as a sausage casing, and it took superior poise to keep from slapping his face.

"I understand," he added in a confidential tone, taking her arm as if to guide her toward Rose. "Your first night in a new place and you're bound to be nervous—but there's no reason to make up stories about Adelaide being your sister."

"Adelaide *is* my sister!" She wrenched her arm free and turned upon him furiously. "And stop touching me, I said!"

He raised both palms as if she'd drawn a six-shooter. "All right, all right, I'm *sorry.*" His voice turned irritated. "You women are all so damned quirky. Never met a one of you who wasn't."

"I am *not* one of *those* women!" she spit, mortified.

Several men had risen and encroached. "Hey, Noah, what you got there?"

"Hooey, she's a tall one . . . nice long legs . . . I like them long-legged ones."

" 'Bout time we was gettin' some fresh flesh around here."

"What's your name, sugar?"

One of them with a beard like a billy goat reached out as if to touch her and Sarah recoiled, bumping back against Campbell, who gripped her arms to steady her. She lurched from his touch and hid a shudder, fighting the urge to crouch and raise her fists. The men inched closer. They were for the most part loud and ogling, with wet lips and florid cheeks; hair that needed cutting, nails that needed cleaning and necks that needed scrubbing. Most were old and brazen, but some were pitiably young and blushing as much as she.

At the sudden stir Rose glanced over and raised one eyebrow.

"Hey, Noah," one of the men asked, "where'd you find her?"

"Out on the street," Noah replied, "but back off, Lewis, tonight she's spoken for."

Rose was bearing down on them with one hand on her fat hip and her breasts leading the way like a pair of pink cannonballs. Her face wore an expression of hauteur and she carried her cigar in the crook of one finger. She parted the crowd as a plow parts soil, stopped before Sarah and assessed her coldly—one pass, down and up—with contemptuous, putty-colored eyes. She drew a mouthful of cigar smoke, let it slither up her nostrils and spoke, breathing a gray plume like the top of an Indian tee-pee.

"What've you got here, Noah?"

Sarah spoke up angrily. "Are you Rose Hossiter?"

At close range Rose's skin had the texture of cottage cheese, and her mouth was ludicrously enlarged. The kohl on her eyelids had gathered in the cracks and oozed to the inner corners where it collected in two black beads. One of her teeth was cracked off and her breath stank of cigars, though the smell was muddied by that of lily-of-the-valley perfume.

"That's right. Who wants to know?"

"Sarah Merritt. I'm Adelaide's sister."

Rose's hard eyes perused Sarah's flat brown felt hat and high-collared wool traveling suit, pausing on her inconsiderable breasts and hips. "I'm not looking for any new girls. Try next door."

"I'm not looking for a job. I'm looking for Adelaide Merritt."

"There's nobody here by that name." Rose turned away.

Sarah raised her voice. "I was told she goes by the name of Eve."

Her remark stopped Rose. "Oh?" The madam turned back. "Who told you that?"

"He did." She nodded sideways at Campbell.

Rose Hossiter flicked the wet tip of her cigar with a thumbnail and considered a while before asking, "What do you want with her?"

"I came to tell her our father died."

Rose took a pull on her cigar and swung away. "Eve is working. Come back tomorrow afternoon."

Sarah took one step forward and demanded, "I want to see her now!"

Rose gave Sarah a view of her broad posterior and her brassy Grecian topknot. "Get her out of here, Noah. You know we don't allow her kind in here."

Campbell took Sarah's elbow. "You'd better leave."

She swung around and swatted his hand with her money packet. "Don't you *ever* touch me again, do you understand?" Her eyes grew dark with indignation. "This is a public place, as public as a restaurant or a livery stable. I have as much right to be here as any man in this room." With one finger she drew an invisible arc spanning half of them.

"Rose wants you out."

"Rose will have me out when I'm satisfied about whether or not my sister works here and what she does. You expect me to believe that an upstairs maid works at this hour of the night? I'm not quite that naive, Mr. Campbell."

"Upstairs *girl*, not upstairs maid," he said.

"There's a difference?"

"In Deadwood there is. You're right. Your sister is a prostitute, Miss Merritt, but around here we call them upstairs girls. And Rose"—he nodded at the woman—"we call her kind landladies. This end of town is referred to as the badlands. Now, do you still want to see your sister?"

"Yes," Sarah declared stubbornly and marched away from him to take a seat between two very bad-smelling men on a horrid beet-colored settee with carved mahogany arms. One of them smelled like dried sweat, the other stank like sulfur. She perched stiffly, folding her hands over her money packet on her knees. She was neither a tearful nor a fearful type, but the realization that her sister was upstairs at this moment, probably servicing a man, brought a lump to her throat. The men beside her began crowding her thighs, and her heart started hammering.

The fellow on her left took out a twist of chewing tobacco and gnawed off a piece. The one on her right stared at her while she fixed her eyes on the parrot.

"A dollar a minute! A dollar a minute!" he squawked.

Presently Noah Campbell cut off Sarah's view of the bird. Her chin snapped up and her lips pruned. He hadn't even the grace to remove his hat or gun indoors, but wore the one pulled low over his eyes and the other strapped low on his hip.

"If you're not one of the upstairs girls," he advised, "you don't know what you're up against here. Since I'm the one who brought you in, Rose asked me to escort you out. Now the choice is up to you, but if you don't leave, you'll have to tangle with Flossie." He nodded at a figure moving toward them. "I doubt that you'd want to do that."

The Indian woman appeared silently, an amazon well over six feet tall, with a face that looked as if it had been hewn from a piece of redwood with ten whacks of an ax, then set afire and stomped out by hobnail boots. Her eyes were tiny, black and expressionless. Her skin was as coarse-grained as a strawberry, her stringy hair clubbed at the nape, her arms the circumference of a Civil War cannon.

"You," she pointed. "Get ass out."

Fear burned a hot path up Sarah's chest. She swallowed and stared into Flossie's unwavering, compass-point eyes, afraid to look away.

"My father has died. I haven't seen my sister in five years. I want to talk to her, that's all."

"Talk tomorrow. Now, get skinny ass out." Flossie leaned forward, gripped Sarah's upper arms and lifted her bodily from the red couch, extending her arms parallel to the floor until Sarah hung like a union suit on a clothesline.

"Put me down, please," Sarah requested in a trembling voice, her shoulders meeting her earlobes. "I'll leave on my own."

Flossie opened her hands and dropped Sarah like a discard. Caught unprepared, her knees buckled and she stumbled forward before catching herself on the arm of a chair and regaining her balance.

"Flossie!" a new voice shouted. "Leave her alone!"

Sarah straightened, tugging at the peplum of her jacket. Halfway down the uncarpeted stairs that dropped from above into the middle of the room, a woman stood with one hand on the rough rail. Her hair was jet black, hacked off parallel with the earth at jaw and eyebrow level, flaring out at the bottom as if its ends were split. Her skin was white as cornstarch, her eyes ringed by kohl and her lips a slash of scarlet. She wore a chemise and pantaloons of white covered by a transparent black kimono sporting two large red poppies, strategically placed. Wearing an expression as cold as Rose's, as foreboding as Flossie's, she advanced toward Sarah and stopped before her.

"What the hell are you doing here?" she demanded icily.

"I believe I should be the one asking that question."

"I work here, and I don't like to be bothered when I could be entertaining customers."

"Entertaining! Adelaide, how could y—"

"My name is Eve!" she snapped. "I've done away with Adelaide. As far as I'm concerned she never existed."

"Oh Addie, what have you done to yourself?" Sarah reached toward the brittle black hair at her sister's jaw.

Adelaide jerked back. "Get out of here," she ordered through set teeth. "I didn't ask you to come here. I don't want to see you."

"But you wrote to me. You told me you were here."

"Maybe I did, but I never thought you'd come traipsing after me. Now, get out."

"Addie, Father is dead."

"Get out, I said!"

"Addie, did you hear me? Father is dead."

"I don't give a damn. Now get out!" Addie spun away.

"But I came all the way from St. Louis."

Sarah found herself reaching for Addie's retreating back as her sister moved toward a cluster of men swilling whiskey at a round table.

"Snooker—you're next, honey. Sorry for the delay." Addie ran her palm across the shoulders of a middle-aged man wearing a red plaid shirt and suspenders. He craned his head around to peer at Sarah. Addie put a hand on his cheek and turned his face toward her own. "What're you gawking at her for? She's nothing." She leaned down and opened her garish red lips over Snooker's much older ones and Sarah turned away.

Noah Campbell reached for her elbow as if to escort her out.

"Don't touch me!" she ordered, once again jerking away from the man who, apparently, was another of Adelaide's customers.

Gathering her dignity and her broken heart, she headed toward the door.

Chapter 2

❧

Back at the hotel, she lay in bed, wide awake, stiff beneath the blankets. She was not a green waif, ignorant of what went on in the world. Hadn't her mother run off with a lover when she was seven and Addie three, never to be seen again? Hadn't she learned young that carnality can drive people to extremes?

Furthermore, she was twenty-five years old and had begun typesetting for her father at the age of twelve, writing articles at the age of fifteen. In the years since, she had been exposed to every kind of repugnant story imaginable. She had learned to control her personal reactions to them, to release her choler or her compassion only in ink on newsprint. *To care too much is to lose your objectivity,* her father had warned, and because there was not a person ever walked the earth whom she had respected more than Isaac Merritt, she had absorbed his every word. In doing so, she had become inured to the seamy side of life, to the frequent cruelties of humankind, to their immorality and greed and callousness and lust.

But this was personal. This was her little sister, Adelaide, with whom she'd shared a bed as a child, with whom she'd had the mumps and the chickenpox, and to whom, in lieu of their mother, she'd taught the basics of reading, writing, manners and housekeeping. Adelaide, who had always had such difficulty being happy after Mother left. Adelaide, in that repugnant place, doing repugnant things with repugnant men.

She pictured the brothel again with its wet-lipped clientele, its cigar-smoking madam and its degeneracy. What had prompted Adelaide to work there? How long had she been there? Had she been a prostitute ever since running away from home?

Five years. Sarah closed her eyes. Five years and all those nights and all those men. She opened her eyes: five years or five nights—was there a yardstick by which to measure depravity? She relived the initial rush of shock upon seeing Addie in those unchaste clothes, a good twenty pounds heavier, with her face painted and her hair dyed black, gone wiry. The last time Sarah had seen Addie, her sister had been a trim young girl with elbow-length silky blond hair and a shy smile she rarely showed. She had been a devout Christian, an obedient daughter and a loving sister. What had changed her?

By the devil, I aim to find out!

In the morning Sarah awakened to the tinny clang of someone replacing the cover on the water canister in the hall. Her eyes snapped open to the sight of the naked ceiling joists above. The memory of last night returned, and with it a zeal to get her sister out of Rose's.

She bolted from bed, flung open her trunk, rooted for clean clothes and tossed them across the bed. She unbarred the door, peeked into the hall and, with her enamel pitcher, hurried to the water tin. Poking a finger inside, she muttered wryly, "Oh, grand . . . just grand," dipped her pitcher anyway, carried it back to her room dripping, and in spite of the cold water, put the soap and the privacy to good use. Thirty minutes later, still shivering, with her hair in a doughnut at the back of her head, dressed in high-top black shoes, a brown broadcloth skirt, a no-nonsense brown shirtwaist and a double-breasted wool jacket, she stepped out of the Grand Central Hotel.

The September morning was chilly. Standing on the shaded boardwalk, she shuddered again, squinting up and down the street, drawing on her gloves, her money pouch clutched beneath one arm, a two-penny notebook between her teeth. She walked to the end of the boardwalk, her heels playing a tomtom beat on the hollow floor, and peered up a side street. It ended behind the hotel where Whitewood Creek brattled along just beyond the point where Deadwood Creek fed into it. On the far side of the water the gulch wall rose sheerly, holding back the sun. Taking a bearing from the shadows, she deduced the gulch ran in a northeasterly by southwesterly line. She and the Grand Central were at the southwest end; the "badlands" and her sister were at the northeast.

Out on the street, she lifted her eyes to the cerulean sky and turned in a circle. The canyon walls were dizzying, leading to a brownstone ledge high above the creek bed, and on one side, a stretch of towering white rocks, like great shark's teeth taking a bite out of the blue firmament. The rocky outcroppings were connected by stands of ponderosa pines blanketing the hills in great rolling stretches, then trailing down ravines and draws in jagged green-black fingers. Alive, the pines towered; dead, they crosshatched the depression in thatches of gnarl, lending Deadwood Gulch its name.

The town itself looked like an extension of the deadfall, as if tumbled down the ravine by centuries of weather. It started as a collection of tents and huts high up in the hills and straggled down to a bottleneck wide enough at one point to accommodate only a single street—Main—and it a disappointment. Its buildings were a sorry lot, thrown up hastily by the prospectors and merchants who'd come to cash in on the gold rush begun only that spring. Before coming out here, Sarah had read articles in Eastern newspapers claiming that Deadwood cabins were springing up faster than teepees on the Little Bighorn. There were accounts of lots being purchased on Monday and by Saturday holding frame buildings open and stocked for business. They looked it! Between these unpainted structures, brush wickiups and canvas tents served as temporary shelters for new arrivals who waited their turn for lumber or logs. Adding to the haphazard appearance of the town were the sluice boxes that poked their long snouts down the hillsides into the creeks, looking like giraffes with their feet splayed and their heads dipped to drink.

Sarah walked the length of Main Street, whose only spots of color shone from the shingles of newcomers heralding their practices and products: butchers, lawyers, doctors, a second hotel (the Custer), assayers, gambling halls (the Montana Club and the Chicago Room proving to be two of the largest buildings in town, filling the full size of their lots—which she estimated at twenty-five by one hundred feet—and boasting signs saying their doors never closed); gunsmiths, barbers, brewers, saloons (she lost count of these after thirteen); bakery, hardware and, of course, the badlands. As she had feared: everything for the adventuring male, but nothing for his lady. Not even a single mercantile store.

The two theaters, however, offered the promise of refinement, though by daylight the Langrishe proved to have wooden walls and a canvas roof! The liberty pole down on the corner of Main and Gold Street gave evidence that the country's centennial had been celebrated in some way on the Fourth of July. Also encouraging was the fact that someone had begun constructing what appeared to be wooden water ditches to convey water from some unseen spring to the town for domestic use.

Already at seven-thirty Deadwood was busy. Everywhere Sarah went, men's heads snapped around for a second look. Some of their mouths dropped open. Some flushed. Others mechanically doffed their hats. Along the creek men were working with cradles over open placer mines. All-night gamblers stumbled from the gaming houses with bags beneath their eyes. From the bakery came the smell of bread baking, making Sarah almost light-headed from hunger. Wranglers were hitching up horses at a livery stable. Out in front of a miners' supply store, a man with the longest arms Sarah had ever seen was hanging out gold pans on an overhead wooden grid where the breeze set them tinging like glockenspiels. Up the street she discovered a bathhouse—a bathhouse! she rejoiced. In the empty lot beside it two men were lighting a fire under an enormous black pot. She paused and watched awhile, coveting the idea of hot water—enough hot water to submerge oneself in. She was surprised when she saw them drop clothing into the pot and begin stirring it with long sticks.

"Good morning!" she called.

The pair turned and reacted like all the others, gaping as if she were an apparition.

"Good morning," they chorused after an awed pause.

"Are you a laundry or a bathhouse?"

"Neither, ma'am. We sell rags," said the shorter of the two.

She would need rags; there was always ink around a printing press.

"Oh, wonderful. That's what you're boiling there?"

"Yes, ma'am. The miners they come into the bathhouses carrying new clothes and they leave their old ones behind. Same up at the whorehou—" His buddy punched him with an elbow. "Ah, up at the badlands, that is, if you'll excuse our saying so. We pick them up free and delouse them and sell them again."

"How enterprising. I'll most certainly be one of your customers. Well, have a nice day, gentlemen."

"Wait!" they shouted when she turned away.

She paused and faced them.

"Who are you? That is, I mean to say . . . I'm Henry Tanby and this is Skitch Johnson." Tanby, the shorter of the two, removed his hat and held it in both hands over his chest. He had the features and neckless build of a bulldog.

She approached them and shook hands. "Mr. Tanby, Mr. Johnson." Johnson was young, skinny, pimply-faced, and apparently tongue-tied. "I'm Sarah Merritt from St. Louis. I'll be printing the first issue of my newspaper as soon as I locate my press."

"Newspaper. Well, I'll be. You come in on the stage?"

"Last night."

"Well, I'll be," Tanby repeated, then seemed to go blank, smiling into her face, forgetting to don his hat. Finally he remembered. Johnson was still standing with a gaping smile. Tanby nudged him in the ribs. "He's got no manners. Gawks like he never seen no woman before. 'Course the truth is we don't see many of 'em up here in the gulch."

"So I've heard." A self-struck woman would have reveled in all the attention she was getting; it merely amazed Sarah, who'd never before in her life made heads turn. "Well, I must move on, gentlemen."

As she turned away Tanby called, "You need anything, just ask! Always happy to help a lady!"

"Thank you, Mr. Tanby! Nice to meet you, Mr. Johnson."

Johnson came out of his stupor long enough to return her wave. Walking away, Sarah felt a fresh flash of surprise at receiving so much male attention. She was honest enough, however, to realize the underlying reason for it. She'd known there was a dearth of females in the goldfields, but had never guessed its extent. It put her in a rather advantageous position, she admitted, and decided she wasn't above utilizing that advantage when necessary. As a single woman in a new town, inaugurating a newspaper, there'd be times when she'd need help, guidance and support. Tanby, Johnson, Reese and Bradigan: she would remember the names of those who'd shown overt friendliness.

The town, she learned during her walk, held several faro banks but only one for use by the general public. She found it with no difficulty. It went by the very high-sounding name of Pinkney and Stahl's Merchants and Miners Emporium of Gold, Bills and Exchange. Its verbose marquee also boasted: "Greenbacks Exchanged . . . Loans Given . . . The Only Large Sized Iron Safe in the Diggings . . . We Take Gold Dust for Safe Keeping." She was waiting when its doors opened at the odd hour of eight-twenty. A short, overfed man dressed in a pressed black suit and four-in-hand tie unlocked the double-paned door and his eyebrows flew up when he saw her outside.

"Whu—am I seeing things?" He was bald and pink as a June plum.

"Not at all. I've come to cash some Wells Fargo certificates."

"Well, come in, come in." He ushered her in solicitously and extended his hand. "My name is Elias Pinkney, at your service."

He fixed her with an eager smile, though he was forced to look up to do it.

"I'm Sarah Merritt."

"Miss Merritt . . . well, well . . ."

Again she was compelled to extricate her hand. Pinkney seemed to follow the hand as she withdrew it, moving so close she took a step backward. "I must say you're a welcome sight. A welcome sight."

Did he repeat everything?

"I've just arrived in town and I need some gold dust so I can buy a meal."

"You don't need gold dust at all if you'll allow me to buy you breakfast. I'd be honored. Most honored."

His undisguised pressing startled Sarah, who was totally unversed in rejecting men's advances. She groped for a gracious refusal. "Thank you,

Mr. Pinkney, but I have a lot of business to transact today. I'm going to be printing Deadwood's first newspaper."

"A newspaper. That *is* good news. Very good news. In that case, I could introduce you up and down the street."

"Thank you, but I don't want to take up your valuable time. And I do need gold dust, if you'd be so kind."

"Of course, of course. Right this way."

She saw immediately that Mr. Pinkney, in spite of his overt interest in her, was a shrewd businessman. She exchanged one of her Wells Fargo certificates for gold dust, which she accepted in a buckskin pouch, Mr. Pinkney having extracted the customary five percent for the bank's fee; she deposited the remaining certificates in the bank safe, agreeing to pay a rate of one percent for the first month's service. Before leaving, she struck a barter with Pinkney whereby in the future she would have the use of his safe without charge and he would have free advertisement in her newspaper.

"So you're a woman with a good head on her shoulders."

"I hope so, Mr. Pinkney. Thank you."

She would have foregone a parting handshake, but he forced the issue, extending his hand first in a small breach of etiquette. Once he captured her hand, he retained it beyond the point of discretion, looking up at her from his diminutive height.

"The invitation to dinner stands open, Miss Merritt. You'll be hearing from me soon. Very soon."

With gold dust in hand at last, she escaped, hurrying, breathing easier once she was out of the bank. What a repugnant little man. Rich, no doubt, and wearing fresh laundry, but so certain that his money and social position would woo the first single woman to hit town. She found herself relieved that she'd been wearing gloves during all that handshaking.

With her stomach growling, she stopped at the first eating establishment she could find, a crude frame building called Ruckner's Meals. The place was filled with men who, by turns, stared, murmured, whistled, passed close to her chair for no good reason, doffed hats, spoke in undertones with their heads close together and chuckled. None of them, however, settled in the tables adjacent to hers, but left a ring of unoccupied chairs with her highlighted in its center.

A boy of perhaps sixteen came to take her order, grinning all the while.

" 'Morning, ma'am. What can I get for you?"

"Good morning. Could you fry a beefsteak so early in the day? I haven't eaten since yesterday noon."

"No beef, ma'am—sorry. Not much space for the beef to graze around here. We've got buffalo, though. It's just as good."

She ordered a buffalo steak, fried potatoes, coffee and biscuits, realizing every man in the building heard her do so. After the boy went away she donned a tiny pair of oval spectacles, opened her notebook, extracted a pen and a vial of ink from her organdy pouch and, trying to ignore the fact that she was being openly ogled, began composing her first article for the *Deadwood Chronicle*.

"$1.50 in Gold Dust Welcomes Editor of Deadwood Chronicle." In it she paid credit to all who had been solicitous in helping her the previous evening.

She was still writing when her food arrived.

" 'Scuse me, ma'am." A suspendered man stopped at her elbow with a platter of sizzling meat that smelled heavenly.

She glanced up and closed her notebook, removing it from the table-top. "Oh, excuse *me*. Mmmm . . . that looks delicious."

"Hope you like the buffalo. You could sure have beef if we had it." He set down the plate and remained at her elbow while she capped her ink and removed her spectacles. "My name's Teddy Ruckner, ma'am. I own this place." He was thirtyish, blond, dimpled and handsome in a boyish way. He had bright blue eyes and a likable smile that never wavered from her face.

"Mr. Ruckner." She extended a hand. "I'm Sarah Merritt. I've come to Deadwood to publish a newspaper."

When their hands parted he remained, wiping his palms on his thighs and nodding at her notebook. "Figgered you for a smart one when I saw you writing. It's sure good to see a woman around here. Where are you setting up business?"

"I'll have to locate a place. For now I'm staying at the Grand Central."

"There's one boardinghouse. Loretta Roundtree's. You could try there."

"Thank you, perhaps I will."

She picked up her fork, hoping he'd leave—her stomach positively ached—but he lingered, asking her several more questions, until she be-gan to feel additionally conspicuous as the focus of his overeager attention. Though she was not a woman prone to blushing, she blushed. Finally he realized he was delaying her meal and backed away. "Well, I'd better let you eat. Anything else you want, you just let me know. There's plenty more coffee where that came from."

She was in the restaurant for the better part of an hour and during that time not one customer left. More came in, however; perhaps two dozen more—quietly, unobtrusively, slipping in like children to see a sleeping infant, pretending to pay her no mind when it was obvious the word had spread she was there and they'd all come in to give her a gander. The chairs filled and still they came, standing to drink their coffee while in an immediate circle about Sarah the chairs remained vacant. Their furtive glances made her feel dissected. She kept her eyes on her plate and the article, on which she continued to write as she ate. Others—she could feel their eyes—studied her more overtly, probably assessing her as the sister of "Eve" from up at Rose's. Her coffee cup couldn't get a quarter empty before Teddy Ruckner refilled it: the only one brave enough to venture near her. When her plate was empty he came again with a piece of dried-apple pie. "On the house," he said, "and it's the house's pleas-ure—the whole meal, as a matter of fact."

"Oh Mr. Ruckner, I couldn't possibly accept without paying."

"No, I insist. You're about the most welcome thing we've seen around here since the last piece of fresh fruit came in. Enjoy the pie."

Self-conscious once more at being the center of attention, she concen-trated on her pie. She had eaten half the slice when she heard repeated greetings of "Mornin', Marshal."

"Mornin', boys," came the reply as the newcomer moved through the crowd. He shuffled to a stop on the far side of Sarah's table, taking a stance with his feet set wide and his hands on his hipbones. Even with her eyes downcast, Sarah saw his black trousers and the gun at his hip and sensed who stood before her.

She raised her eyes slowly to the silver star on his jacket, the rusty mustache, the black cowboy hat he declined to remove. In the clear light of day he was freckled as a tiger lily—she'd never been partial to either mustaches or freckles. He looked strong as a mule and about as pretty, with gray eyes and that notch at the end of his nose. She supposed some women might find it boyishly attractive. She, however, was put off by everything about the man, starting with his effrontery.

"Mr. Campbell," she said, cool, even as her blood began to rise.

He touched his hat brim. "Miss Merritt. Just wondering what all the hullabaloo was about in here."

"Hullabaloo?"

"Anytime the men start flocking to one spot it's my job to find out what's drawing them. Usually it's a fistfight."

Her blush continued glowing, fired by the realization that the marshal of Deadwood frequented its whorehouses, had carnal knowledge of her sister, and had offered to buy the services of Sarah herself last night within an hour after her arrival in town. Distasteful and cocksure, he stood before her with his Colt .45 strapped to his hip, daring her to make something of it.

"So it's Marshal Campbell, is it?"

"That's right."

She laid down her fork and met him eye to eye, speaking loudly enough to be heard in every corner of the room. "Is it common out here on the frontier for the town marshal to frequent its whorehouses instead of trying to shut them down?"

The big ox hadn't the grace to be affronted. Instead, he threw back his head and laughed while half the room laughed with him. When he'd finished, he pushed his hat to the back of his head and hooked a thumb over his holster belt.

"You're a regular little spitfire, aren't you?"

Incensed by his cavalier attitude and his amused eyes, she removed her spectacles and rose to her feet. "If you'll excuse me, Marshal, I've got a newspaper to get started." She gathered her belongings, stood beside her chair and raised her voice. "Gentlemen," she announced to the room at large, "my name is Sarah Merritt. I've just arrived from St. Louis and I plan to publish a newspaper here in Deadwood. I'm looking for two things, and I'd be very grateful if any of you could help me find them. First, I need a building to either rent or buy—preferably one made of wood instead of canvas. Secondly, I need news. No editor can print a newspaper without it, so please . . . feel free to stop me wherever you see me and tell me what's happening up and down Deadwood Gulch. I want the *Deadwood Chronicle* to be *your* newspaper."

When she finished speaking, someone in the far corner cried, "What do you say, boys, how's about a welcome for the little lady?" A cheer rose from dozens of male voices (all but Campbell's) and at last they closed in, offering their hands to be shaken, introducing themselves—men with names like Shorty and Baldy and Colorado Dick and Potato Creek Johnny; men with broken teeth and unwashed clothes and hands as rough as the terrain they mined; men with tintypes in their pockets and wives back home; women-starved men offering obeisance.

They told her where to find Craven Lee about available property, Patrick Bradigan about the $1.50 he'd loaned her, and where to find her printing press, which had arrived by mule train and was stored at the freight office run by a man named Dutch Van Aark.

Throughout their welcome, Marshal Campbell stood by observing, leveling her with his distracting watchfulness, speaking one last time as she headed for the door.

"See me about getting a license for that newspaper of yours."

She flounced out disregarding him, thinking, *I'll see you in hell first, Campbell!*

She began with Craven Lee, who'd laid out the lots for the town and acted as its realtor. She found him in a log cabin on Main Street, but learned he could do nothing for her at the moment. The list of prospective buyers, it seemed, was as long as a Norwegian winter, and the best he could advise was for her to stay where she was. At least she had a roof overhead and a bed at night.

She went next to find Bradigan at the Buffalo Hump Saloon, where he had begun his morning imbibing to ward off the trembles from the previous night's round. She marched in and once again made heads turn—all but Bradigan's. He was facing the bar with a glass in his hand.

"Good morning, Mr. Bradigan," she said behind his shoulder.

He cranked his head around slowly before removing his elbows from the bar and straightening in the bone-by-bone way of the seasoned drunk.

"Good morning, Miss Merritt." She was surprised he remembered. He aimed for his hat but never quite touched it.

"I owe you a dollar and a half in gold dust." She found her pouch and tugged at the drawstring.

He watched her with bloodshot eyes, digesting her message for some time before replying in a heavy Irish accent that came as slow as a spring thaw. "No, pretty colleen. Mine was the lucky pouch. ' Twas my pleasure, most sortainly."

Not by the longest stretch of the imagination did Sarah consider herself a pretty colleen. "Mr. Bradigan, please . . ." she returned quietly, flashing a glance at the bartender and several patrons who were watching and listening. "I pay my debts, and last night I wasn't altogether sure you knew your money was being taken."

He lifted a forefinger, gave a wobbly smile and turned back to his glass of whiskey. Hoisting it, he saluted her. "Welcome to Deadwood, Miss Sarah Merritt."

Realizing she would not get Bradigan to accept her gold, she handed the pouch to the bartender. "Here. Please take out a dollar fifty's worth and buy Mr. Bradigan whatever he wants."

Before she left, she said, "Thank you again, Mr. Bradigan." He faced her foursquare and silently bowed over his whiskey glass.

It was one o'clock by the time she stepped back onto the street. One o'clock and hopefully the residents of Rose's were up. Sarah headed toward the badlands with great trepidation, doffing her jacket and carrying it on her arm. It had warmed considerably and flies buzzed above the dung in the streets. A constant stream of wagons moved up and down

Main Street competing with the foot traffic. Of the dozens of faces she saw, none were female. She began to understand why both she and girls of her sister's ilk were such attractions in Deadwood.

At Rose's the front door was unlocked—a surprise. She'd expected to have to find a rear entrance or bang on the door until her knuckles were bruised to get an answer. Instead, it opened at her touch and she entered the same dim, smoky room as last night. Not a soul was in it. The smell of stale whiskey and unwashed cuspidors permeated the place, accompanied by the the strong sulfuric stench she'd detected last night. The room was unlit. The red tassled draperies were drawn against the noon sun with only a thin triangle of light filtering in at the bottom where the tassles brushed the floor. In the gloom, Sarah looked around, observing what she'd only glimpsed last night: the picture of a fleshy nude reclining on a fainting bench with a veil twined between her thighs and her private hair showing; a sign on the wall with a finger pointing toward the hall, saying BATHS REQUIRED; another with the heading MENU. She moved up close and read it.

THE BATH
THE TRIP
THE FRENCHY
THE HALF & HALF
THE SHOW DATE
THE OUT DATE

Startled, Sara realized the menu had nothing to do with food. Feeling debauched, she looked away.

A door to the left of the stairs stood open and she proceeded through it, to a long hall with an opening at the far end where voices, window light, clinking dishes and the smell of food announced a dining room. As she moved toward it, the sulfuric smell grew stronger. She reached its source—a room off the hall to the left, with a huge copper bathtub, wooden barrels of water, an iron stove for heating it and damp wood floors. Her revulsion freshened when she realized the required baths were laced with carbolic acid . . . for delousing.

With pinched nostrils she continued toward the far end of the hall, where she stopped just short of the doorway and listened.

" . . . could tell he never did it before. The bulge in his pants was bigger than a ham bone, so I says to him, I bet you hung like a bull, sugar. Get that big guy out here and let's have a look at him."

"Did he?"

"Too scared. Just stands there with his Adam's apple jumpin' and his face redder than a branding iron so I had to take control. I take his hand and put it on hisself, just to see what he do and he—"

Sarah stepped to the doorway. "Excuse me."

The story stopped. Everyone turned to stare at Sarah in the doorway.

Adelaide sat at a table with four other women—Flossie among them—wearing a royal blue dressing gown and eating chicken stew and dumplings. At a cast-iron stove on the far wall a fat woman tended a coffeepot. The black woman who'd been speaking let her glance move from Sarah to Eve and back.

"Adelaide, I'd like to talk to you."

Adelaide's face hardened. "What are you doing here! I told you last night I didn't want to see you. Now, get out." She resumed her eating.

"I've come a thousand miles to find you and I'm not getting out until we've had a chance to talk."

"Flossie." Adelaide signaled with her fork. "Get rid of her."

The Indian woman pushed back her chair and Sarah experienced another bolt of fright. But her father had taught her a newspaperwoman's first qualification must be courage. "Now, just a minute!" she said firmly, entering the room with her heart clunking, pointing a finger at Addie. "I'm not one of your customers you can have bounced onto the street. I'm your sister, and I'm here because I care about you. You can have me thrown out or probably beaten if you wish, but I'm not going away. Our father is dead and I've brought you your share of the inheritance. I've also brought his printing press and I'm setting up business in Deadwood, so you can either talk to me now or have me plaguing you persistently. Which will it be?"

Her show of bravado stopped Flossie and emboldened Sarah, who pinned her sister with an unremitting gaze. When Addie stared back stubbornly Sarah said, "Furthermore, I have a message for you from Robert. In that regard you have three choices. I can deliver it to you in front of your friends, or print it in the first issue of the newspaper, or you can take me to someplace where we can talk privately. Which will it be?"

Adelaide set her teeth, threw down her fork and lurched to her feet, rocking her chair onto its back legs. "All right, dammit, but five minutes and that's all! Then you either get out of here under your own steam or Flossie will help you out. Is that understood?" She stalked out the kitchen door, down the hall and up the stairs with her royal blue wrapper flapping, leaving Sarah to follow.

Before leaving the kitchen, Sarah pointed a finger at Flossie's nose and said, "You ever lay a hand on me again and you'll be sorry."

Upstairs, Addie led her along a skinny dark hall into the third room on the left. The door slammed behind them and Addie swung to face Sarah, her arms crossed tightly beneath her breasts.

"All right, make it quick."

Since temerity had worked so far, Sarah tried a little more. "If this is the room where you do your work, I refuse to speak to you in it."

"This is my own room. I work next door." She nodded sideways. "Now get on with it because I'm getting mighty impatient with you, big sister or not!"

"This is where you live?" Sarah surveyed the grim little room with its single cot, a curtain of the roughest unbleached muslin on the window, theater posters tacked to the rough walls. There was a rug, a coverlet, a cheap dressing table, mirror and one chair, a commode stand, and on the floor beside the door a china washbasin. A line of hooks on the wall held a collection of sleazy, bright-colored costumes much like the one Addie had been wearing last night. The only objects to warm the room in any way were some faded paper roses on the wall and, on the bed, a stuffed cat made of red, shaggy fox fur. The sight of it plucked at Sarah's heart: it was the only hint of the Adelaide she remembered: as children they'd never been without a pet cat.

"I see you still have a cat," she remarked with a reminiscent smile, shifting her regard to Addie, who raised one eyebrow and kept her arms crossed.

"Say what you have to say."

What Sarah wanted to say was, Why? Why this place? This profession? This apparent hatred for me, who never did anything but be the mother you never had? But she'd get no answers yet; that was clear.

"Very well, Addie." She spoke quietly, all traces of harshness gone. She opened her organdy pouch. "Father died last spring. I sold the house and the furniture and the Market Street Building. All I kept was the press and his desk and the few things I'd need to set up business. Here is your half of the money."

"I don't want his money!"

"But Addie, you could leave this place."

"I don't want to leave this place."

"How could you not want to leave this place? It's horrible."

"If that's all you came for, you can take his money and get out."

Sarah studied her sister sadly. "He never got over your leaving, Addie."

"I don't want to hear about him!" Addie insisted. "I told you I don't give a damn about my father!"

In spite of Addie's virulence Sarah forced herself to continue. "He contracted the bronzed disease about a year after you left. At first I only noticed that he was looking a little feebler, but then his mind became weak, his appetite grew capricious and in time his digestion ceased functioning. By the end he was unable to hold anything down and he suffered an extreme amount of pain. The doctors treated him with everything that's been rumored to help—glycerine, chloroform, chloride of iron— but Father's debility only grew worse until he shriveled up like a baby bird. He was always a proud man; it was very hard on him. I was managing the paper alone by then. Before he died, he made me promise I'd try to find you. He wanted us to be together, as we should be." With added tenderness Sarah said, "Addie, you're my sister."

"An accident of birth." Addie turned away and stared out the window.

"Why did you run away?" When Addie refused to answer, Sarah entreated, "Was it something I did? . . . Please, Addie, talk to me."

"Women who work in places like this don't talk to outside women. You'd best learn that."

Sarah studied Addie's shoulders for a long time before asking softly, "Was it something Robert did? He's wondered just as I have."

The back of Addie's hair was coarse as boar's bristles, uncombed, showing sections of her skull where her natural blond showed like the white at the throat of a purple iris. The sight of it brought a sorrowful expression to Sarah's eyes.

"You hurt Robert so badly, Addie. He thought you loved him."

Addie said, "I wish you'd go." The choler had left her voice; it was as quiet as that of a doctor asking a visitor to leave the bedside of one gravely ill.

After a stretch of silence Sarah said softly, "Robert has never married, Addie. That's what he wanted you to know."

Facing the window, with her arms crossed stubbornly, Adelaide Merritt felt threatened by tears, but refused to let them form. Behind her, she heard Sarah move toward the door, heard the doorknob turn and the hinges squeak. She knew Sarah was standing in the open door studying her, but she refused to turn around.

"I haven't found a building for the press yet," Sarah said, "but I'm staying at the Grand Central. You can come there anytime to talk to me. Will you do that, Addie?"

Addie gave no indication she'd heard.

Sarah studied her sister's blue wrapper and felt an immense clot of sorrow settle in her throat. On this mortal coil there was no other blood relative than Addie, and Sarah needed very badly to touch her once. They had sprung from the same womb and been sired by the same father. She crossed to Addie, laid a hand on her shoulder blade and felt it stiffen.

"If not, I'll come back again soon. Goodbye, Addie."

When the door closed, Addie stood a long time, staring out the window at a dry buff ledge where a poor misguided kinnikinnik bush had taken root far from its usual habitat. Its few berries were withering from waxy white to brown, unlike Addie—poor misguided Addie—who had gone from a healthy brown to a waxy white, living within walls where the sun never touched her skin, shut away from decent people, a prisoner by choice if not by circumstance. She had changed her name, and her hair color and her mode of dress and her persuasions. She had run half the length of the country, hoping never again to confront a soul from home. Now here came Sarah to unearth the past with all its promise and sordidness and secret guilt. To bring word of Robert, that wholesome young man of the clean skin and the sinless spirit who had seen in Addie only what he wanted to see. Robert . . . who had kissed her once with lamblike innocence . . . Robert . . . who had not married.

Tears were a luxury Adelaide had given up years ago. What good were tears? Could they change the past? Could they heal the present? Could they alter the future?

Blinking away the few that had formed, refusing to reach up and dry even the corners of her eyes, Addie dove onto her bed and curled her body around the fox-hair cat, clenching up until her knees nearly met her forehead. With her face against the furry stuffed animal she squeezed her eyelids tightly shut. Her bare, dirty feet were overlapped, her toes were curled and her stomach muscles quivering. For minutes only her fingers moved in the cat's fur. Then, still coiled, she made a fist and drove it into the mattress. Again. And again. And again.

Chapter 3

♣

Five minutes after leaving Rose's, Sarah found Dutch Van Aark's freight office. It was located in a log building which served as a miners' supply, grocery and, today, a post office. A corpulent man with a walrus mustache was serving a cluster of customers gathered beneath a sign announcing: LETTERS—JUST ARRIVED— ¢. When the group became aware of Sarah's presence they parted to let her near the counter.

Van Aark saw her and smiled. He had yellow teeth and a bun-sized lower lip that drooped, exposing his gums.

"I'll bet you're Miss Merritt and you've come for your printing press."

"Yes, I am."

"Well, it's here, out back. Come in on a ox train couple weeks ago along with all the rest of your stuff. I'm Dutch Van Aark."

He introduced her around and explained, when she inquired, about the mail. It had come in on yesterday's stage and since the town had no post office, anyone could buy the mail from the stage driver, then sell it to the recipients for a small profit. She recorded the interesting tidbit in her notebook along with the correct spelling of Van Aark's name. While she was writing, a woman entered the store—wide-beamed, with a workaday face, around thirty-five years old, wearing a homemade dress and cotton bonnet. It took little more than a five-second glance to ascertain she was a typical housewife.

The two women smiled at one another like long-lost cousins.

"Mrs. Dawkins, come in and meet the newest lady in town."

Sarah moved toward Mrs. Dawkins and the two clasped hands.

"Mrs. Dawkins and her husband run the bakery here in town."

"Hello, I'm Emma Dawkins."

"And I'm Sarah Merritt."

Their joy in meeting was genuine and the two exchanged a flurry of questions and answers. The Dawkins lived above their bakery and had three children. They had come to Deadwood from Iowa, leaving their families behind. Emma Dawkins was in the freight office today, hoping to find a letter from her sister back home.

"No letter, Mrs. Dawkins, I'm sorry," Van Aark told her. "But now that Miss Merritt is here, maybe we'll have more than letters to read." After the exchange of pleasantries the entire troop went outside to inspect Sarah's printing press. They found it in a wagon, covered by canvas, broken down into pieces, the smaller of them crated but the largest—the frame—standing free, lashed to the side of the wagon with leather straps.

When the canvas was folded back Sarah touched it reverently—her father's old Washington Hand Press—a thousand pounds of steel on which she'd learned her trade side by side with him. With it were his massive rolltop desk and packing crates containing the type cases, furniture cabinet, newsprint, ink and other paraphernalia she'd packed that summer in St. Louis. She counted the crates and found them all accounted for. Her eyes took on a glow of excitement. "I'll need a block and tackle to unload it tomorrow."

"I've got those in the store," Van Aark replied.

"And a tent, and a lantern and a few other things. If I make you a list can you have them ready in the morning?"

"You bet, Miss Merritt."

After the arrangements were made, Sarah spent a long while talking with Emma Dawkins, learning a great deal about the town and its residents and accepting an invitation to have supper with the Dawkins family the following night. Upon leaving Emma, she looked up the boardinghouse of Loretta Roundtree, located on a path that angled up the west side of the gulch where the buildings were perched on narrow terraces with their rear ends buried in the mountain. Though Mrs. Roundtree, bluff and big-faced, said she'd have loved to rent a room to Sarah if only for the female company, she regretfully turned her away, claiming she had a waiting list of over fifty.

Sarah made a note to that effect, and spent another hour walking up and down Main Street asking questions and taking additional notes on the status of the town before returning to her hotel room in the late afternoon.

There, once again she took out pen and ink, drew her bedside table near the window and sat down to keep a promise.

Dakota Territory.
September 27, 1876
Dear Robert,

I take pen in hand as I promised I would when I arrived in Deadwood, which I did yesterday. This is a particularly sordid settlement which, like a boy of fourteen, is outgowing its breeches and experiencing growing pains. If all is true that I've heard, the population of this gulch and all its tributaries is presently around 25,000.

Many of the men are rich, but more have not struck the big gold. These struggle along doing whatever jobs they can find. Others are now mining high-grade quartz, pulverizing it by hand using mortar and pestle. I have thought how odd that a town so rich resorts to such archaic methods.

But enough about the commercial aspects of Deadwood. You asked me to tell you if and how I found Adelaide, my dear sister and your remembered sweetheart.

She is here in Deadwood, but how my heart breaks to tell you what I must. Oh Robert, I fear our hopes for her were optimistic. She is not the same winsome young girl we last saw when she was sixteen. Dear Robert, do fortify yourself for a cruel blow which I so extremely regret delivering. Your fear was that I would find Adelaide married, but the truth is much worse. My sister has become a prostitute. Here in Deadwood they call her kind upstairs girls, soiled doves, similar euphemisms, but the unvarnished truth is as I said. Adelaide has become a prostitute.

She has changed her name to Eve and works for a procuress named Rose Hossiter, an uncivil and odious bawd who raises shivers along my arms as I force myself to recall her. Our Adelaide has blackened her hair, kohled her eyes, rouged her lips and allowed herself to grow obese during her prodigal years. I shall not torment you with details of her reprehensible mode of dress. These external changes are, however, only manifestations of the inner, more disturbing metamorphosis from the darling we once knew to a woman of granite expression and stone heart.

Though she has resisted my every overture, I will be here for Adelaide and will make every attempt to win her over and with the power of the printed word, to close down these dens of vice and corruption that turn decent, wholesome young girls like Addie into the poor, misguided, morally impoverished souls who deserve our pity.

I grieve for your disillusionment and sorrow upon receiving this letter, and for the loss of your dreams which you have held so long and faithfully, but in all earnestness, I implore you to move forward with your life, find some deserving young woman worthy of your devotion and, of Addie, to carry the memory, not the dream.

I shall post this by the Pony Express, which is much faster than the Cheyenne Stage, whose service is still only bi-weekly into Deadwood, and hope that it reaches you in all due haste. May your spirits not languish long, Robert, for you are too kind and good a man to suffer so unjust a sentence.

> Yours in friendship,
> Sarah Merritt

After she'd folded and sealed the letter she sat a long time, despondent, looking out her third-story window in the direction of Rose's. She thought she made out the tip of the building's false front, though Addie's window faced one side.

Oh Addie, you could have had such a fine life with Robert. How I envied you his favor, but he had eyes for no one but you. Even after you left, his mourning allowed him to see no other woman. You could be married to him now. Instead, there you are, in that horrid place, having run off just like our mother did, abandoning Father and me. After the hundreds of times you and I talked about the hurt she caused us, I could not believe you'd do the same.

The memories of those first days after her mother's abandonment were still vivid to Sarah. She had been sleeping soundly on a gray morning in November when her father, instead of her mother, had come in to awaken her for school.

"Where's Mama?" she'd asked, rubbing her eyes, and he'd told her Mama had gone away to visit her sister in Boston.

"In Boston?" There had never been talk of any aunt in Boston. "When will she come back?"

"Oh, I'm sure she'll be back in a week or so."

But a week had passed, then another; a month, and Addie started wetting the bed again, and crying for their mother at bedtime, and Sarah stood for hours looking out the window up Lamply Street, watching for a glimpse of the familiar dark-haired figure. A woman named Mrs. Smith was hired as their temporary housekeeper, but stayed on, and Father grew dour and his back became bowed, though he was still a very young man. Not until Sarah was twelve did she learn the truth from Mrs. Smith, who told her one day in the kitchen where they were pickling beets. "Your mother won't be back, Sarah," Mrs. Smith had said. "It's time you knew the truth. She ran off with a man named Paxton—Amery Paxton— who worked for your father as a typesetter. Where they went, nobody knows, but she left a note saying she loved Paxton and was going off to marry him. Your father never heard from her again, and of course he's never remarried, because he has no idea whether it would be bigamy or not."

Sarah had started collecting words that day, an acquaintanceship that would become the backbone of her life's work. *Bigamy,* she had entered in a blue-lined journal, *when one woman is married to two men. I know now why my mother left us.*

To this day Sarah could not eat beets or tolerate the smell of vinegar.

Sitting in her dreary bedroom in the Grand Central Hotel, she looked down at another journal, filled with notes she had taken since her arrival in Deadwood. She sighed and drew out a clean, loose sheet of paper. When things are troubling you, her father had often said, write.

She wrote, laboring under an intense commitment to create as accurate a picture of today's Deadwood as it was possible to paint with words. The inaugural issue of her paper would undoubtedly be preserved for all time. In a town where history was being made, this was bound to be true.

She worked until midnight, composing the articles for her first issue of the *Deadwood Chronicle.* Along with the one she'd begun in the restaurant at breakfast, the headlines included: MAIL ARRIVES AT VAN AARK'S STORE; CHEYENNE STAGE—DAILY SERVICE TO DEADWOOD EXPECTED BY OCTOBER; TELEGRAPH LINE COMPLETED AS FAR AS HILL CITY; SCARCITY OF WOMEN PREVAILS IN DEADWOOD; GRASSHOPPERS STILL PRESENT IN MINNESOTA; SEVEN BUILDINGS UNDER CONSTRUCTION ON DEADWOOD MAIN STREET; MSS. BELDING & MYERS CONSTRUCTING WATER CONVEYANCE DITCH FROM WHITETAIL TO THE HEAD OF GOLD RUN; PROSPECT ON #82 WHITEWOOD: $200 PER DAY. On her own behalf she composed a want ad announcing that the editor of the *Deadwood Chronicle* was looking for a place to set up her business and to lodge. But she worked the longest over an editorial entitled "Close the Heathen Brothels of the West." It was lengthy and impassioned and ended by saying, "We must purge this city of this scandal and bring the keepers of these houses under the lash of the law. But how shall we do so when the very representative of the law itself is frequenting the fair and frail? Surely public opinion can be brought to bear against this source of moral and physical disease."

By the time Sarah removed her glasses her eyes burned and her shoulders ached. Addie would be angry when she read the editorial, but that was a risk Sarah had decided she must take when she made her decision to attack the disease rather than the symptom. Shut down the houses and you shut down the prostitutes. Not a popular stand, given the conspicuous acceptance of the brothels, but a journalist's call—Isaac Merritt had taught his daughter—was not to be popular, but to be effective in forcing change where change was necessary.

In the morning Sarah stepped outside to discover there'd been rain— both a bane and a boon, for though the streets had turned to Dakota gumbo, the absence of dust, to a printer, was the greatest blessing of all. She was surprised to find she'd missed the storm, which had left tree limbs in the street, but a blue sky above and the promise of a perfect autumn day. The smell of the newly moistened dung in the street, however, had intensified.

She picked her way around it and posted her letter at the Pony Express office, then headed for Van Aark's store, gathering up an entourage on the way. They followed like children after the Pied Piper: Henry Tanby, Skitch Johnson, Teddy Ruckner, Shorty Reese and finally Dutch himself, all of them eager to help her move her printing press.

"Where do you aim to put it?" Dutch asked as he hitched a horse to the wagon.

"Follow me," she said and led them to the spot she'd chosen beneath an immense ponderosa pine whose bole was imposing enough to have put a gooseneck in Main Street down near the Number 10 Saloon: public property, she was sure, yet protected from traffic by the tree trunk itself and shaded by its branches.

"Here," Sarah proclaimed, looking up.

"Here?"

"We need a branch sturdy enough to support the weight of the press. That one will do."

"On the street?" Van Aark's lower gums showed pink as his mouth hung open.

"Until I can find an office, yes, this will do fine."

"But it's practically the middle of the street!"

"Public property though, right? And am I not the public? Are not you and I—all of us—the public? Who does a newspaper serve if not the public? Now if you'll help me, gentlemen, I'll have your first edition thumping off the press before nightfall."

They raised a cheer while a crowd gathered to watch Skitch Johnson swing himself from Henry Tanby's shoulders into the tree. Within minutes the block and tackle were mounted and the rope was reeved. As it dropped down through the sheave, eager hands waited to catch the steel hook and attach it to the frame of the printing press. The frame swung up and others leveled the earth beneath with flat spades and laid down a square plank as a stabilizer. The men strained at the ropes and, piece by piece, the press took shape: legs onto frame, frame onto plank, track onto frame, tympan frame onto track. Sarah gave instructions, lifting her arms to guide the pieces into place, securing them herself with shear pins and bolts. Some shimming was required before the entire setup stood firm and level, but when it did, she demonstrated the ease of operating the machine by cranking the empty bed and lowering the platen one time. Another cheer rose.

"All we need now is type, paper and ink and we'll be in business," Sarah declared.

"How about your tent, Miss Merritt, you want we should set that up, too?"

"I'd be so grateful if you would."

In no time they had her small tent standing taut and inside it her newsprint up off the damp earth. Outside, in bolder light, they uncrated all of her typesetting paraphernalia: furniture font, typecase, composing stick and leather apron. Once it was unearthed and arranged on the packing crates, she glanced around in satisfaction and brushed off her hands. "Thank you so much." She shook hands with each man who had helped. Meanwhile, the crowd had multiplied until it hampered traffic movement in the street. Fascinated, they remained, ogling the press, waiting to see it in operation. "I appreciate the muscle and the goodwill. You've given me a very warm reception, all of you."

"When will the first copy come off the press?" someone shouted.

"Find me another typesetter and I can be rolling ink by noon."

When the crowd failed to disperse, she removed her jacket, rolled up her sleeves and began setting type while they watched. If they had been fascinated before, they were transfixed now. Her right hand moved so fast the onlookers could scarcely follow it with their eyes. Over the years, setting type had become second nature to Sarah, and she did it in whirlwind fashion, often plucking the individual characters from the grid-shaped typecase by feel. She filled the composing stick in a matter of seconds, transferred the block of three lines to a flat tray called a galley, and began again.

Meanwhile, the crowd grew.

Two blocks away, Marshal Noah Campbell sat in his tiny office filling out more stinking licenses. Damn, how he hated paperwork! But when the town government was officially formed two weeks ago he'd agreed to take on all the duties of city marshal as prescribed by the newly drafted ordinances. Among them was the issuing of licenses and the collection of taxes from every company, corporation, business and trade in Deadwood.

Beaudry, Seth W., Gunsmith, he wrote arduously. *$5.00 Licensing Fee, Fourth Quarter, 1876, City of Deadwood.* He sat back, mumbling, scratching his mustache, eyeing his work. Shit and shit twice. Looked like a drunk chicken had walked through the barnyard and across the form. He could handle a gun and a horse and any drunk who wanted to start slinging fists, but a pen and ink had the power to discommode him.

Noah Campbell, he signed, then blew on the ink and added the license to the finished stack. He was dipping his pen to fill in the next one when he heard an ox whip. His head snapped up and he listened. The sound came again. There was no mistaking it, nor the bellowing of the skinners that drifted in through the closed door. Noah dropped his pen and his chair screeched back. In a half-dozen long strides he plucked his black Stetson off the wall hook and reached the door.

Smiling and eager, he stood on his front step, facing the opening of the gulch, watching the lead pair of dun-colored oxen plod toward him while the sound of the ox whips cracked against the gulch walls—*fap! fap! fap!*—like a stack of lumber dropping. They snaked along, ten, twelve, fourteen spans, while the cartwheels creaked and the lead bullwhacker let fly a string of profanity.

"Gee, I said, you sons of a whorin' bitches! You mothers of whorin' bitches! You grandmothers of whorin' bitches! Whaddya need, gunpowder up your asses b'fore you'll move! I'll ram it in with my own fist and light the fuse with this here cigar between my teeth if you don't—"

The rest was lost in the echoing crack of an ox whip as Noah leaned back and laughed. Good old True Blevins, he knew how to put on a show. Kept the whole street laughing every time he pulled in.

Noah and his family—mother, father and brother—had made the trip into the Black Hills beside True's ox train in May. It was a common practice for families unable to hitch up with a wagon train to move through the hostile Indian territory in the company of one of the bullwhackers, who charged a price for the concession.

In Noah's case the price had been worth it: he and True had become friends.

True wouldn't be too happy, though, to hear the news that he'd have to pay a license fee of $3.00 per wagon before he could unload his freight.

The cavalcade drew abreast of Noah and moved on as he waved to True and the drivers of the successive carts. Suddenly, up ahead, he heard the bawling of the oxen and the unmistakable voice of True, cussing fit to kill. The oxcarts halted and there was more cussing down the line. From the step of his office Noah could see a bottleneck up the street near the Number 10 Saloon. Leveling his hat, he leaped into the mud and headed up that way.

"Let me through," he ordered, squeezing between men's shoulders, bumping people aside as he forced his way through the crowd. He saw, even before he reached her, what was causing the traffic jam. None other than Miss Sarah Merritt, with her printing press set up practically in the middle of Main Street. Damn, but the woman was an aggravation. Dressed all in brown, with her sleeves rolled up and her hair in a doughnut, tall and skinny as a bean pole, she was busy dropping type into a metal stick while the onlookers appeared to have settled in for the day, waiting to see history in the making.

"What the Sam Hill is going on here?" He scowled and broke through the edge of the crowd.

Sarah glanced back over her shoulder and kept clicking pieces of type into place.

"I'm laying out a newspaper."

"Have you got a license to do that?"

"A license?"

"I told you yesterday you needed one."

"I'm sorry, I forgot."

"Furthermore, you're holding up a whole freight train and causing a road jam. You'll have to get this stuff out of here."

"I'm on public property, Mr. Campbell."

"You're a public nuisance, Miss Merritt! Now, I said you'll have to move!"

"I'll move when I find a building to rent."

"You'll move now or I'll throw you in jail!"

"This town hasn't got a jail. I've walked every inch of it and I know."

"Maybe not, but it's got an abandoned tunnel dug into the side of the hill behind George Farnum's grocery store and don't think I won't throw you in it—woman or not. I've got a job to do, and I intend, by God, to do it.''

"Incarcerating me might prove to be an unpopular move on your part.'' She glanced at the onlookers. "These men are anxious to see the first copy of their town paper come off the press.''

Campbell turned to the crowd. "You men, move on! You're holding up traffic here. Go on now, git!''

A miner with a gold pan and wheelbarrow raised his voice. "You really gonna throw her in jail, Noah?''

"Absolutely, if she doesn't obey the laws.''

"But, hell, she's a woman.''

"We made the laws for women as well as for men. Now move on so True can lead his train on through!''

He turned back to Sarah, standing with both hands akimbo, his big black Stetson worn level with the earth. "Miss Merritt, I'll give you one hour to get this paraphernalia packed up and moved off the street.''

"I'm not in the street.'' She finally stopped setting type and swung to face him. "I'm beside it on public land.''

"If you're not gone in one hour, I'll come back and see to your removal myself. And the *next* time I see you set up for business . . .'' He pointed a finger at the bridge of her nose. "You'd better have a city license hanging on your wall.''

He pivoted on the ball of one foot and stalked off with his cowboy boots rearranging the mud on the street. Glaring at his back, with her lips curled tight, Sarah gave one frustrated kick that fanned her skirts. Before the brown muslin had settled into place, she was back at her typesetting.

"Show's over, folks,'' Campbell cried to the malingerers. "Go on back to work.'' Waiting for the crowd to disperse, he drew a dollar-sized stem-winder from his vest pocket and checked the time: 11:04. He'd be back under that pine tree at four minutes after twelve, and that tall, bullheaded pain in the ass had better have pulled up stakes or there'd be hell to pay. She'd end up in a hole behind Farnum's grocery and he'd have every woman-starved male in the gulch harassing him for arresting her. But what choice did he have? He couldn't have her setting up her business anyplace she damn well pleased, stopping traffic, clogging up the street, thumbing her nose at their ordinances. Let her get by with that and the next thing he knew there'd be fistfights breaking out and men shot. In a town that lacked women the way this one did, it was bound to happen sooner or later. It might anyway, even after she moved her rig. Any way he cut it, Campbell realized he stood to look like a heel for stopping Sarah Merritt from printing the town's first newspaper. Sonofabitch, this was going to get sticky.

The crowd began breaking up.

Stalking toward the lead oxcart, Noah faced his next unpleasant task. "True!'' he bellowed, reaching the bullwhacker, "True, I've got to hold you up a minute.''

True stopped his freight wagon and spit a stream of tobacco juice into the mud, then swiped his stained mustache with the edge of one cracked hand. He had skin like venison jerky and only one eyebrow. He'd lost the other one in a close call with a bullet some years before.

"Noah, how're you doing, boy? How's your ma and pa?''

"Last time I saw them they were fine, but the Indians still raise occasional hell out there in the Spearfish, and to make matters worse, the farmers out there have to go out of the stockade to harvest. I worry about them some."

"Yuh." True adjusted his sweat-stained hat. "Bet you do. Well, you tell 'em hey from old True."

Noah nodded, rested a hand on the cart and squinted up at True. "Listen, True . . . the town set up some ordinances since you were here last, and I've been appointed the marshal."

"The marshal!" True raised his face and bellowed with laughter.

"What's so funny about that?"

"Why, hell, you ain't mean enough nor ugly enough to be no marshal. Well, on second thought, you just might be ugly enough."

"At least I got two eyebrows."

"You better watch what you say or you won't for long." True took aim at Noah's brow with a forefinger.

Noah laughed, then got serious. "Listen, True, I've got to charge you three dollars a wagon to let you unload your freight."

"Three dollars a wagon!"

"That's right."

"But we been hauling freight in here since spring. Hell, if it wasn't for us skinners this town wouldn't have windows or stoves or beans to boil! For that matter, if it wasn't for us, who would you and your ma and pa have rode up here with last spring when the damned Indians were trying to keep everybody out?"

"I know, I know. But I didn't make the ordinances, I just enforce them. Three dollars per wagon, True, from every one of you, and I've got to collect it."

True spit. Wiped his lip. Scowled at the ox yoke. "Well, shit and dance around it," he mumbled. He picked up his ox whip, made it whistle and smack, and bawled, "Git goin', you lazy no-good hunk of guts!" As the train began to move, he said without glancing at Noah, "We'll pay up at the freight house."

It took Noah the better part of an hour to collect the license fees from the entire ox train. The drivers had to be contacted and their gold weighed out, their names taken down and recorded for the city clerk and treasurer.

It was one minute after twelve when he left the gold at the city treasurer's and headed down the street toward the pine tree, where a crowd was again gathered watching Sarah Merritt defy his orders. He shouldered his way through the throng, tall enough to see above the surrounding heads that she was rolling ink, loading the press and cranking it by hand. When the process was finished she lifted a printed sheet. A roar of applause rose: shouting and handclapping and hooraying enough to be heard on the other side of the mountain.

"Gentlemen! The first copy of the *Deadwood Chronicle!*" Sarah shouted. "It's only a single page but the next issue will be bigger!" The cheers doubled as the sheet, with its ink still wet, was passed from hand to hand. Those who couldn't read asked those who could what it said. The men whose names were mentioned for helping Sarah on her first night in town became fleeting celebrities, patted on the back by their fellow townsmen. The editorial about the brothels was eclipsed by the feeling that each man there had taken a personal part in bringing the press to Deadwood.

Sarah Merritt had produced a second copy and was rolling ink for the third by the time Noah reached her.

"Miss Merritt," he shouted above the din, "I'm afraid I'll have to put an end to this."

She set down her brayer, closed the frisket, cranked it into place and lowered the platen with a lunge of one hip. "Tell *them!*" she challenged. She opened the press, plucked another printed sheet from it, the ink still gleaming, and handed it to him. "Tell them why you want to shut me down, Marshal Campbell! Tell them where I saw you the first time, and what you were there for, and why you want to restrict my freedom of speech!"

He glanced at her headlines. One jumped out at him. CLOSE THE HEA-THEN BROTHELS OF THE WEST.

Before the blood hit the crown of his head she was appealing to the crowd. "Gentlemen! Marshal Campbell is here to arrest me because he claims I'm on public land. But ask him what his real reason is! Ask him! I'm not the first newspaper publisher to be silenced because I speak the truth, and I won't be the last."

"What does she mean, Noah?"

"Let her be, Noah—"

"Town needs a paper, Noah—"

Noah knew the signs. Covertly he reached down and unsnapped his holster strap while shouting to them, "I warned her an hour ago she couldn't set up this press in the middle of the street. We've got new laws and I've been hired to see that they're obeyed."

"But you can't arrest no woman!"

"I don't like it any more than you do, Henry, but I took an oath to faithfully and impartially perform my duties, and she broke two ordi-nances that I can see. Ordinance number one, section two, regarding licenses, and Ordinance number three, section one, on nuisances and junk in the streets and alleys, to say nothing of disturbing the peace and obstructing traffic—which she and every one of you are doing when you refuse to break up this gathering."

"All we come to do was see the first copy getting made!"

"All right, you've seen it, now move along!"

"What's she talking about, Noah? You got other reasons to shut her down?"

"I'm not shutting her down, only forcing her to move!" Turning to Sarah, he ordered tightly, "Get your jacket and come with me."

"No, sir, I will not."

"All right, have it your way." He grabbed her by the back of the neck as if to shepherd her away.

"Get your hands off me!" She struggled.

"Get those feet moving, Miss Merritt!" He pushed.

"But my ink! My press!"

"Throw the canvas over it if you want to, but that's it. I gave you an hour to move it and you chose not to. Now get going!"

He pushed her.

A hunk of horse dung hit him on the shoulder.

"Let her be, we said!"

"Yeah, let her alone! She ain't hurting nothing!"

Another chunk of dung knocked Noah's hat off. He released Sarah and spun to face the crowd. They were surging forward, expressions black, fists clenched.

"You men, get back! She can run her press. She just can't run it here!"

"Get him, boys! He can't manhandle no woman like that!"

Everything happened at once. The sky began raining horse dung. The militants shoved forward. Noah drew his gun. Someone's fist struck him on the jaw. Sarah screamed and Noah stumbled back. His pistol fired and a half a block away True Blevins slumped over and fell across the freight he'd been unloading. Noah went down on his back, crushing his hat. Like a disturbed anthill, the men swarmed, fists first.

Sarah screamed, "Stop this! Stop!" and fell into the fray, grabbing an arm, hauling back on it. She caught glimpses of fists smashing into Campbell's face and screamed again, trying to protect the downed man. "Stop it! Oh please, no . . . Listen to me!" She screamed till her veins bulged.

"Listen to me!"

Her screaming finally registered, and the inner circle of attackers heeded. Their shouts stilled. They looked about for her. She knelt among them with her face ferocious, her hair awry.

"Look what you're doing!" she screamed raspily. "He's your friend, your marshal, and he was only doing his job! This is my fault!" She pressed her open hands to her chest. "Mine! Please, let him up."

Several men still crouched above Noah, their fists poised. They glanced from Sarah to the lawman. Realization filtered through them. Their hands relaxed. Murmurs began. "Let him up . . . yeah, let him up . . ." Sheepishly they shuffled to their feet. "You all right, Noah?" One of them offered Noah a hand. He knocked it aside and struggled to his feet, bleeding from one ear and his nose and mouth, cradling his ribs with his left arm. Already his face was beginning to swell.

In the stillness a voice called from down the street. "True Blevins has been shot!"

"Oh Jesus," Noah whispered and began shoving his way through the crowd, which parted as he came. Before he reached True, he was running. He vaulted onto the oxcart and took True's shoulders, turned him over gently on the sacks of cornmeal he'd been unloading.

True's eyes were bleary, but he gave a murky grin.

"Y' got me, boy," he croaked.

"Where?"

"Feels like everywhere." True's weak voice ended in a cough, followed by a groan as his eyelids closed.

"Get a doctor!" Noah hollered, and saw the blood on True's dirty leather vest. Softly he said, "True, I'm sorry. Hang on now, buddy. Don't you go die on me." Frantically, Noah stood and shouted, "I said get a doctor, goddammit!"

"He's coming now, Noah," someone beside the oxcart said in a hushed voice. "Here, you want to use this?" A handkerchief was handed toward Noah.

"No! Nobody touches him with anything dirty!" Dan Turley approached at a run, carrying his black bag. "Hurry, Doc!" Noah cried. "Help him up!"

A tall, gaunt man in shirtsleeves clambered aboard the oxcart and bent over True. "Get this cart rolling," Turley ordered as he turned back True's vest and unbuttoned his shirt. "Take us to my place. Noah, how about you? You need attention, too?"

"No, I'm all right, Doc." An ox whip cracked. The cart lurched and began rolling.

"Then I believe you've got business to attend to. You won't be any help hovering over me, so go keep yourself busy. I'll send word to you as soon as I know anything."

"But Doc, I'm the one who shot him!"

"He's in good hands, Noah." Doc took a moment to raise a no-nonsense gaze to Noah. "Go!"

Noah took one last look at True, touched the skinner's hard hand, and said, "True, you hang on, hear?"

Noah jumped off the oxcart and watched it roll up the street. His Adam's apple bobbed twice and his chest felt like drying rawhide. *Don't you go and do anything foolish, True.*

In time he sniffed, rubbed the back of one hand beneath his nose, and felt his concern for True give way to furor. He turned toward the great ponderosa pine where the crowd waited, becalmed by tragedy. As he strode toward them, their eyes dropped guiltily. They shuffled in place and joined their hands like mourners around a grave. A path cleared as he hit straight for Sarah Merritt, feeling rage building with each footstep. In his entire life he'd never felt the urge to strike a woman, but he felt it now, the unholy lust to drive a fist into that long, skinny face in retaliation for True. To see her crumple and whimper and be laid low just as True had been. What a stupid, senseless loss, if True died, all because of this self-righteous do-gooder who refused to obey a simple city ordinance.

She waited, stilled like the others, standing straight as the liberty pole behind her, holding Noah's Colt .45 Peacemaker on the flat of her hands as he approached.

"I'm so sorry," she whispered, solemnly handing him the gun. His left eye was swollen shut and rivulets of blood had painted rusty tracks down his chin.

"Shut up!" he barked, grabbing the Colt, suppressing the urge to crack it across her cheek. "I'm not interested in your pitiful condolences."

"Is he dead?"

"Not quite." He rammed the gun into his holster and bent over to sweep up his flattened hat. "But you'll have some answering to do if he gets that way. *You men!*" he roared, whirling on them, fanning at them with the hat. *"I'm telling you for the last time—clear out of this street!"* Like disturbed roaches, they scuttled off. Campbell punched a fist into the crown of his Stetson and it popped out, a mangled mess. "Sonofabitch," he mumbled, disgusted. When he spoke, the skin around his lips quivered and he rested his eyes anywhere but on the woman. "Sarah Merritt," he pronounced, glaring at the liberty pole in the distance, concentrating on what it symbolized in an effort to control his urge to drop her where she stood, "you're under arrest for disturbing the peace, operating a business without a license, and inciting a riot, and I hope to hell you put up another fight, because nothing would please me more than to tie and gag you and drag you through the streets by your hair!"

"You won't have to do that, Mr. Campbell," she returned meekly, picking up her notebook, jacket and organdy pouch. "I'll come with you."

His cork finally blew. *"Now* you'll come with me!" he shouted, glaring at her, pointing to where the oxcart had stood several minutes earlier. "Now that my friend's be●n shot, you'll come with me! God *damn* it!" He threw down his hat. "What ever happened to public whippings!"

She stood before him chastised, her mouth drawn, waiting. Beside her, her printing press was already covered by canvas.

"I can only repeat, I'm sorry, Mr. Campbell."

He studied her for several beats of silence and she thought she had never seen hatred more clearly illustrated than by his grim expression.

"If I have my way, you'll be a lot sorrier before this is over. Get moving," he said coldly.

She did as ordered, allowing herself to be ignominiously herded down the length of Main Street while the townspeople stared and whispered in her wake. He took her to a wooden frame building fronted by a set of steps and a covered boardwalk.

"Inside," he ordered, nudging her between the shoulder blades. They entered a store where customers stood as motionless as the cracker barrels around them, only their heads turning to follow Sarah's passage. A sleeping dog rose from behind a potbellied stove and nosed their heels desultorily as Sarah advanced through the premises with Marshal Campbell one step behind. They passed fresh apples and eggs, tinned goods and sacks of dried beans. And farther along, a vinegar barrel with a wooden spigot giving off the acrid smell Sarah so disliked. At the rear of the store a long counter faced the front and behind it stood a bearded man wearing a white apron, suspenders, sleeve garters and a dapper black derby hat.

"Noah," he greeted gravely.

"George," the marshal returned, "I need to use your tunnel for a while."

"Of course." There was no question: everyone in the place knew what had happened on the street and that the downed man was a friend of the marshal's.

"Is the lantern still back there?"

"Hanging on the hook in the passageway."

Campbell gave Sarah another nudge and followed her around the counter, through a back door into a short windowless walkway that smelled like a potato bin. When the door closed behind them, absolute blackness descended. Sarah felt a shiver of fear and balked. Campbell poked her again, propelling her forward three halting steps.

"Wait there."

She heard the clink of a lantern handle, then a match whisked and flared, illuminating his face as he plucked the lantern from the nail and lit the wick.

He nodded sideways and said, "In here."

She proceeded timorously into the abandoned mine. It was no bigger than a pantry and contained a wooden chair and a pile of straw covered with a holey horse blanket. It took a valiant effort to keep her voice steady as her eyes darted around the dirt walls.

"This is your jail?"

"This is it." He set the lantern on the floor beside the chair and headed for the door.

"Mr. Campbell!" she called, panicked at the thought of being left alone.

He turned and fixed his cold gray eyes on her but refused to speak.

"How long do you intend to keep me in here?"

"That's up to the judge, not me."

"And where is the judge?"

"Haven't had one assigned yet, so the town appointed George out there as acting judge."

"George? You mean the *grocer?*"

"That's right."

"So I'm to be tried by a kangaroo court?"

He pointed a finger at her nose. "Now, listen here, sister! You come in here and cause a man to get shot and now you're not happy with the accommodations. Well, that's just too bad!"

"I have rights, Mr. Campbell!" she shot back, her spunk returning. "And one of them is to present my case before a territorial court."

"You're in Indian territory now, and the territorial government is powerless here."

"A federal court then."

"The closest federal court is in Yankton, so all we've got is George. But the miners themselves picked him as the fairest man they know."

He turned toward the door again.

"And a lawyer!" she interrupted. "You cannot incarcerate me without a lawyer!"

"Oh, can't I?" He glanced back over his shoulder. "You're in hell-roaring Deadwood now. Things are done differently here."

On that ominous note he walked out and closed the door behind him. The last thing she heard was the key turning in the lock.

Chapter 4

♣

She stared at the door and listened to the hiss of the lantern, the only sound in the silence. Her pulse thumped, filling her throat. The top of her head felt tight. The backs of her arms felt tingly, a sure sign of impending panic. How long would she be left here? Would anyone come to check on her? What kind of vermin lived in that straw pile? What if the lantern went out?

She fixed her eyes upon it, the only other semblance of life in the room, and perched as near to its warmth as possible, on the edge of the chair seat. With her hands pinched between her knees, she concentrated on the flame until her eyes began to ache, then tightly closed them and chafed her arms. It was so cold in here, and she was hungry; she had not eaten at noon.

Who cared enough to come to her? Addie didn't seem to, and anyway, who'd tell Addie? What would happen to Father's printing press, sitting there under the tree? And her precious newsprint, which had survived the trip clear from the railhead without getting wet, and the type she valued so dearly because it was the same her father had used all his life? Neither it nor her brayer had been cleaned. There hadn't been time in the chaos. The brayer would be ruined.

When she was released from this mineshaft, what would she face? Suppose the oxcart driver died, could the blame possibly be pinned on her even though she hadn't touched the gun? What recourse had she if Campbell failed to send a lawyer? And what would happen if she had to face their "judge" unaided? Was the assault on the marshal serious enough to be called insurrection, and would she be liable for that, too?

She kept seeing his face with the knuckles battering it, feeling anew her horror at how spontaneously things had gotten out of hand, hearing the voice from down the street crying that a man had been shot. *I didn't mean to cause all that! I only meant to stand up for my rights!* Again the squeezing began, in her throat and scalp and down her arms, which began to feel numb.

Remember a newspaperman's first qualification, Sarah.

Resolutely, she found her father's watch, opened it and laid it on the floor beside the lantern. She rose from the chair, fetched the horse blanket and shook it. Lifting it to the light, she checked it for movement and saw none discernible. On the chair again, she draped it over her lap, removed her spectacles from the organdy pouch, donned them and opened her notebook and ink vial.

She contemplated a long time before dipping the pen and writing her first words.

Riot in the Street: Man Shot, Newspaper Editor Jailed.

With the unshrinking veracity instilled by her father, she set about writing an impartial account of what had happened on Main Street during the last two hours.

Doc Turley's office was a frame structure which doubled as his house. It was located a short distance beyond Loretta Roundtree's, where the buildings began to climb the steep sides of the gulch. The path to it angled up the side of the sheer slope like the footpath of a mountain goat. After the rain it was slippery, but Noah Campbell negotiated it with long strides and arrived at Turley's door worried. He entered without knocking, directly into Doc's waiting room, which was furnished with a few pole-and-hide chairs, all empty.

"Doc?" he called, advancing toward the rear.

"Come on in, Noah!"

Noah followed Turley's voice into his examination room, which had walls finished with a layer of pine boards over the studs—a rarity in Deadwood. A glass-fronted cupboard held probes and pinchers and a bevy of other intimidating instruments. In an enamel basin a bullet swam in some bloody water along with a needle and a pair of tweezers. On a leather-covered examination table lay True, out cold while Doc cut bandages for his right shoulder.

"How is he, Doc?"

"I had to chloroform him to take the bullet out, but unless I miss my guess, he'll be cussing at those oxen within a week or so."

Noah blew out a huge breath and felt the tension leave his shoulder blades.

"That's the best news I've had today."

"He's a crusty old bugger. His hearty condition will stand him in good stead now. Come and help me roll him over while I tie this gauze strip. I made an alum poultice to stop the bleeding."

Horsehair stitches held True's skin together and protruded like cat's whiskers in the area where Doc had done surgery. Noah had to cock his head to one side and watch with his good eye while Doc covered the wound with a white pad and looped gauze strips over True's shoulder and around his trunk.

"How long will he be out?" Noah carefully rolled True onto his left side.

"Chloroform only lasts ten or fifteen minutes at most. He should be coming around soon. He'll be groggy, though." Doc completed the bandaging and poured water in a clean basin before beginning to wash his hands. "He'll need someplace to recuperate. You got any ideas?"

"He can have my room at Mrs. Roundtree's."

"Where would you go?"

"Hell, I can sleep anyplace. I can bunk on the floor of my office or even throw up a tent for a couple weeks. The weather's warm enough yet."

"He's going to need some attention, and I doubt that Loretta Roundtree's got the time to be looking after a convalescent on top of running that boardinghouse. Furthermore, knowing True, he'd come to his senses at Loretta's and get up out of bed looking for his ox whip before the blood is dry in these wounds."

Noah considered for several seconds. "You think he could make the trip out to the Spearfish?"

"After a couple days he could."

"Then put him at Loretta's for now and I can look in on him a couple times a day when I'm making rounds to see how he's doing. Maybe you can do the same."

"I can."

"When you think he's well enough I'll run him out to the valley. My ma will pamper the piss and vinegar out of him." Doc laughed, drying his hands. "Matter of fact," Noah continued, "she'll give me a dressing down if she finds out True needed help and I didn't give her a chance to provide it."

Setting aside his towel, Doc said, "As long as you're here, I'd better take a look at that face of yours."

Noah submitted to Doc's examination while Turley asked, "What about those Indians out in the Spearfish?"

"Well, on that score, we just have to hope for the best. The treaty is signed, now we'll just have to see if they honor it. Oww! What the hell you doing, Doc?"

"Making sure you can still see out of that eye."

"I can see! Now let go!"

Doc released Noah's eyelid and peered into his ear. "Might have punctured the eardrum. Usually that's the case when you bleed from the ear. Cover the other one and tell me if you can hear me. Eardrums heal, though, most of the time. They get a little scar tissue that cuts down the hearing somewhat, is all."

"I can hear."

"Good. Did you lose any teeth?" Doc reached toward Noah's mouth, but the marshal reared back.

"I've got all my teeth, now quit your infernal prodding!"

"Testy, aren't you?"

From the patient came a mumble as his eyes fluttered open, then closed. Noah turned to the table and stood beside it, waiting. After several seconds True mumbled again and opened his eyes. They were blue as cornflowers, surrounded by deep grooves.

"Hey, you old hornswoggler. 'Bout time you were waking up."

"Take more'n a bullet t' put me t' sleep." His words were slurred.

"Doc's got the damn thing out. He's makin' soup with it."

True managed a weak grin. "What the hell'd you run into—Sitting Bull?"

"You just shut up about what I run into or I'll have Doc plaster a little more chloroform against your mouth, you old buffalo hoof." Noah smiled the best he could with his puffy lips, then said, "Listen, True, we're going to put you at Mrs. Roundtree's till you get a little stronger, then I'm going to take you out to the valley and let my ma feed you some of her good cooking and sass you back, just the way you like. How does that sound?"

True let his eyes close and spoke sleepily. "Can't. Got a train to unload."

"Oh, no you don't! You just forget about unloading trains for a while."

True's blue eyes opened quite wide this time and fixed on the younger man leaning over him. He spoke with surprising irascibility. "Some sonofabitch charges me three dollars for a license to unload my freight, now he says forget about it. What kind of town you running here, boy?''

"The unloading's all taken care of. You need rest now."

"Rest, hell . . ." True grunted and attempted to rise. Only one of his shoulders cleared the examination table before he fell back, panting. The marshal and the doctor exchanged glances.

Turley stepped forward. "True," he ordered, "you lay still or I'll tie you down. You want that?" True waggled his head while his eyes remained closed. "All right then. Sleep while you can, because that shoulder's going to hurt like a son of a gun tonight. Noah will come back later and help me get you over to Mrs. Roundtree's, then in a couple days when you're stronger he'll take you out to the Spearfish."

Noah thought True had drifted off again and said quietly to Dan Turley, "I'll be back. I've got to clear that woman's stuff out of the street."

True opened his eyes. "Met your match with that one, didn't you, boy?" he said.

"Yeah, well, she's not talking so smart right now. I've got her locked up behind Farnum's."

True smiled and nodded as if speculating to himself. "Yup," he said, "she's a hellcat. Look out you don't get scratched."

Heading away from Doc's, Noah considered True's words. Sarah Merritt was a hellcat, all right, and though his wrath had diminished somewhat upon learning True would live, he had every intention of letting her mildew in that mole hole until she'd learn a damned good lesson about the value of freedom, *and* about harassing the local lawman! By now she was bawling so hard she was probably treading brine. Well, let her tread! Let her consider what kind of a disaster her bullheadedness had nearly caused. Let her wonder when she'd see the light of day again, and how hungry she was going to get, and how long it would be before anybody remembered she was in there! No damned gangly female troublemaker was going to sashay into Marshal Noah Campbell's town and get by with the kind of shit she'd pulled.

So just what in thunderation was he supposed to do with that rig of hers anyway? He should be making his rounds right now; instead he had a thousand pounds of steel to get moved, and a tent to fold up and all that other paraphernalia she'd unloaded in the middle of . . .

Where the hell is it?

Rounding a corner onto Main Street, he gaped at the big pine tree. Her outfit was gone! Press, crates and tent . . . gone! Nothing left but the depressions in the mud where they had stood, and those obscured by boot-and hoofprints.

His pulse began to thump as he glanced up and down the thoroughfare. She'd have something to say about this. Somebody stealing her equipment from the middle of Main Street, where the marshal should have set somebody to guard it. But who'd think anyone would have the audacity to take something so big from such a public spot? And how hard could it be to find? The press alone was as tall as a man and weighed half a ton! *Goddammit!* As if he didn't have enough to contend with today, now this!

He spent an hour searching and turned up nothing. Not in alleys or at the freight office or at his own office. Grumpily, he plunked down in his chair and filled out a few of the sonofabitchin' licenses—what they needed licenses for was beyond him. He knew every person who'd paid their tax and every person who owed.

In the middle of the third form he threw down his pen and cursed silently, wrapped one fist around the other, forgot he was hurt and pressed them against his mouth; yelped and cursed once more. Checked his watch. Going on five-thirty and Farnum would close up at six.

All right, so she'd requested a lawyer. Given his druthers, he'd leave her to stew till morning, but it might not look good, his jailing her without legal counsel. Section two of the Deadwood City Ordinances laid out clearly what constituted the Common Council of Deadwood City and its legal ramifications. Not only was it made up of the mayor and six of his fellow townsmen, it stated unquestionably that the council could sue and *be sued*. It wouldn't bode well if within two weeks of the town's official formation its marshal got the city council sued. And he had no doubt that self-proclaimed muckraker would do it.

So he'd find her a damned lawyer. The town was full of them—seven licensed at last count—all hard-up for business because of the absence of an appellate court and the fact that there were no lawbooks in town yet.

He made a grab at the coat hook, but his hat was missing, left in the mud after that fracas. Cursing, he stormed outside and headed for the office of the closest lawyer, a bearded, sniffling fellow named Lawrence Chapline, who had set up shop in a tent. When Campbell turned back the flap and entered, Chapline was in the midst of wiping his nose on a damp handkerchief. He took one look at the marshal and exclaimed, "What in blazes happened to *you!*"

"Got tangled up in that street riot earlier today. The woman who started it wants a lawyer. Are you interested?"

Chapline had his hat on before the question cleared Campbell's lips. They walked back to Farnum's store and found it full of curious customers who knew there was a female incarcerated in the mine out back. Some of them nodded silently as the lawman and the lawyer passed. Others called, "What you going to do with her, Noah?" and "Are you defending her, Chapline?"

Businesslike, they proceeded through the store into the passageway leading to the tunnel. Campbell opened the door expecting to find Sarah Merritt engulfed in tears. Instead she was sitting on the hoop-backed chair, diligently writing in her notebook. She looked up, and the picture she made riled him all over again because there were no oceans of tears in sight. No weak, wailing female terrified of her straits. Instead she sat calmly on a chair and looked up through small oval spectacles that magnified her blue eyes and gave her the appearance of a schoolmarm correcting papers. Her lap was covered by the horse blanket, and her brown hair had been neatened as best she could manage. She might have been sitting at a table on a raised platform with five rows of school desks before her. Calmly, she closed her book, capped her pen and laid them on the floor. Her militancy had disappeared and in its place was strict politeness.

"Marshal Campbell, you're back," she said, removing her spectacles.

"I brought you the lawyer you asked for. This is Lawrence Chapline."

"Mr. Chapline." She rose, folded the horse blanket over the back of the chair and extended her hand. Immediately when she'd taken care of courtesies she asked of Campbell, "How is your friend?"

"Alive and ornery."

She rested a hand on her heart. "Oh, thank the Almighty. He'll live, then?"

"Looks that way."

"I *am* relieved. I've been so upset thinking I might have been responsible for an innocent man's death. And what about you? Are you all right?"

"Nothing serious. Maybe a punctured eardrum."

"Oh," she said, her mouth a small circle of regret while she looked up at his eye, which had swollen up like a toad's throat at twilight. And after a lull, "I stand before you remorseful and prepared to pay whatever fines may be imposed."

Oddly, Campbell had been more comfortable with her ire. Her newfound contrition put him on uncertain ground. He shifted his weight and said, "You'd better talk to Chapline while you have the chance. I'll be back in a while."

Left alone with the lawyer, Sarah said, "Thank you for coming, Mr. Chapline. What's going to happen to me?"

"Why don't you sit down, Miss Merritt, while I give you a little background about the law here. I think it will help you to understand."

"I've been sitting for quite some time. If you don't mind, I'll stand."

"Very well." Chapline rubbed his nose with his damp hanky and studied the floor for several seconds. He was perhaps thirty-five years old, bony and round-shouldered, with thinning brown hair as fine as a one-year-old's. It drifted above his dome as if it hadn't enough weight to lay flat. His nose was red and his eyes watery—a man who presented not at all the picture of one in whom you'd place your confidence when your well-being was threatened. But he had a voice that rumbled with authority. It vaulted up from his depths like the resounding crash of falling timber and seemed to shake the very sand loose from the walls of the mine as he continued speaking.

"We have a rather peculiar history of the process of the law here in Deadwood. The stampede of gold prospectors brought population before civilization, you might say, at a rate so incredible it nurtured lawlessness along with it—claim-jumping, saloon brawls and theft, to name a few.

"So the residents instigated a miners' court and decided that each session would be presided over by one of the seven lawyers in town, with the 'judge' changing from session to session."

Chapline again scrubbed at his nose and paced.

"You heard about the unfortunate shooting of Wild Bill Hickok here last month, I presume?"

"Of course."

"It was a shock to all of us, and if ever there was a town that wanted to see justice done, this was it! However, the trial turned out to be a travesty of justice in spite of all our efforts at jurisprudence. Better than half the men on the jury were suspected of having been part of the bunch who hired Jack McCall to kill Wild Bill. They handed down a verdict of not guilty and we had to let McCall go scot-free. Nobody liked it, but what could we do?

"A lot of us weren't happy about our court system, but before we could come up with a better one we had another homicide take place, this one three weeks ago. Fellow named Baum was shot. This time all seven of us lawyers volunteered our services, and my colleague, Mr. Keithly, acted as judge. Trouble was, we didn't have any lawbooks, and it created one heck of a predicament.

"It was decided then and there that not only would we order a complete law library for Deadwood, we'd suspend all trials until they got here. In the meantime we've begun organizing ourselves as a city, which is the only way we can expect to have an appellate court established here with a real federal judge."

"Have your lawbooks arrived yet?"

"No, they haven't."

"Oh." Sarah's shoulders wilted slightly. "Then it sounds bad for me."

"Not necessarily, because in the meantime small disputes are being settled by our new mayor, George Farnum, and that was agreed upon by the whole town when they elected him. Now, before you jump to conclusions, why don't you give me your version of the events leading to your arrest."

"That's easy." Sarah picked her notebook off the floor and handed it to Chapline. "I've written it all down for my next issue of the newspaper. This is exactly how it happened."

Chapline spent the next several minutes sitting on the chair, reading the account, his shoulder slanted toward the lantern light. When he finished, he wiped his nose and looked up.

"Did you refuse to move your printing press?"

"Yes."

"Were you operating it without a license?"

"Yes."

"Were you informed by the marshal that you needed a license?"

"Yes."

"Did you incite a riot?"

"Yes."

"Intentionally?"

"No."

"Did you yourself strike Marshal Campbell?"

"No."

"Did you encourage others to do so?"

"No. I tried to stop them."

"Did you see the freight driver, True Blevins, get shot?"

"Yes."

"Who shot him?"

"Marshal Campbell."

"It was an accident?"

"Absolutely."

"Were any other guns drawn?"

"No. It happened too fast."

"Did you resist arrest?"

"The first time, yes. The second time, no."

"Would you be willing to pay any and all damages, get a license to operate your newspaper, and agree to put off further publication until your equipment is under proper cover on private land?"

"Absolutely."

Chapline studied her silently for some time, sitting on the chair with his knees apart, clasped by his bony hands. Finally he inquired, "Do you think you can repeat those answers verbatim if I asked you the questions again?''

"Yes."

"Do you have the money to pay for the damages?''

"Right here." She patted her waist above her left hip.

"Excellent." Chapline rose to his feet. "Then what I think we'll do is appeal to Farnum's sense of fair play, making no excuses for what you've done, simply pointing out that your intentions were not dishonorable, nobody was irreparably hurt, and you are remorseful—which you've already demonstrated to Marshal Campbell. When we go out there, just make certain you keep the same contrite tone you've displayed so far. Regretful but not groveling.''

She nodded.

"All right, let's see what we can do." He gave her a bracing smile while rapping on the door.

Campbell opened it.

"We'd like to talk to Farnum," Chapline told him.

"Come on out." He stood back, waiting for Chapline and Sarah to precede him through the tunnel. To Sarah, the light at the end of it looked like the exit from purgatory. The sound of voices was as welcome as a spring thaw. From the musty smell of sunless earth she emerged into that of coffee beans and smoked jerky and vinegar (which seemed less offensive than before). From dark into light; from dampness into freshness; from solitariness into a crowd whose murmurs silenced as she appeared.

Behind the counter, Farnum stood, watching the procession move through the back door. Campbell halted just inside. The other two went around to the front of the counter.

"Mr. Farnum," Chapline said, "in view of the fact that our law library hasn't arrived yet, and a decent jail hasn't been built, and the town has voted you the authority to settle minor disputes, Miss Merritt asks if you would do so now, so she won't have to spend an indeterminate length of time locked in that abandoned mine.''

Farnum replied, "Well, I don't know. That's sort of up to the marshal here, whether he thinks the charges against her need those lawbooks or not. Marshal?''

Campbell uncrossed his arms and cleared his throat. Before he could answer, Chapline spoke up. "Miss Merritt has no intention of underplaying her guilt, but neither does she consider herself a dangerous criminal who deserves being jailed without recourse. Perhaps you would both read this and then decide. It's an article she wrote for her newspaper, and I think her candidness will speak for itself.''

Farnum removed his white apron and laid it across the counter with all the pomp of a judge donning black robes. Campbell moved behind the mayor's shoulders and the two read the article together. When they finished, they traded glances and in the following seconds each seemed to be waiting for the other to speak first. Again Chapline filled the gap.

"As you can see, Miss Merritt is not trying to whitewash her role in today's unfortunate incident, indeed, she's prepared to report it to the entire town in her own newspaper. Gentlemen, if you'll allow me, Miss Merritt has agreed to answer a few simple questions, and afterward you can make your decision.''

"All right," Farnum said, "go ahead. I don't see what harm it can do to listen."

Chapline ran through his questions, ending by extracting from Sarah the promise that she would be willing to pay any and all damages, including the doctor bills for True, and for Marshal Campbell, if there were any; she would pay whatever fines were imposed, and would get a license to operate her newspaper, and agreed to put off doing so until her press was under proper cover on private land. In that regard, Chapline asked them to consider that she had valuable property sitting out in the street and exposed to the elements and which needed her immediate attention.

At the mention of her property, which he still had not located, Noah shifted his feet. He glanced past Sarah at the curious faces watching and listening and realized a detailed description of these events would spread up and down this gulch faster than an epidemic of smallpox. Not a soul who heard it would feel Noah was in his rights to keep this woman locked in a hole in the ground when none of what had happened was provoked by her intentionally, and when she had virtually thrown herself on their mercy and was offering to make recompense to whatever extent was fair. None of that spoke as loudly, however, as the fact that she was female, single, and a non-prostitute—a rarity in Deadwood. Wouldn't he have a time explaining her incarceration to twenty-five thousand woman-starved miners?

The proceedings were moving on. Where the *jumping hell* was her press? For a moment he was tempted to lock her up simply to give himself time to find it.

"What do you think, Marshal?" the mayor was asking.

"She's caused one devilish amount of trouble today."

"Yes, she has, but I believe in this case the real court might be lenient. After all, she is a woman, and that mine is no place to stick a member of the fairer sex."

"How and when is she going to pay?"

"Here and now," Sarah interjected, slipping her hand into the side placket of her skirt and coming up with her buckskin sack of gold dust. "Just tell me what I owe."

Campbell's eyes met Sarah's. She had the damnedest, most disconcerting way of looking straight at a man. He had a feeling she knew he'd been standing there hoping she couldn't come up with the dust on such short notice. He was the first to look away.

"Whatever you say, Mayor," he allowed grudgingly.

Farnum imposed a twenty-dollar fine for disturbing the peace and another ten-dollar fine for operating a business without a license. He said he'd trust Sarah to pay the doctor bill and that she could settle that with Turley tomorrow. When the gold was weighed out, including an additional ten dollars' worth for her first quarter's license to operate a printing office, Sarah put away her gold dust and extended her hand to Farnum.

"Thank you, sir. I would have disliked spending the night in that mine." She pumped his hand hard, once, and turned immediately to Campbell. "Marshal."

She didn't offer her hand. Instead she hit him with a hard, direct gaze. It struck him how different she was than her sister—direct, focused, a fighter.

"I suppose it's something in my nature, but I expect we'll bump heads again," she told him.

In about two and a half minutes, he thought uneasily, watching her turn toward Chapline as if this meeting were concluded and she had been the one controlling its tempo all along. "Thank you, Mr. Chapline. I'll come by tomorrow and settle up with you." When she was halfway to the door Campbell called, "Miss Merritt, wait." Again she faced him squarely, putting him on edge. At times she seemed able to control her very impulse to blink, as now, when she simply stood waiting for him to move toward her. "I, ahh . . . I need to talk to you about another matter. Outside," he added, conscious of the onlookers.

"Very well. We'll walk together." She turned and led the way from the store, opened the door herself without waiting to see if he'd do it (he'd had no such intention), stalked out into the middle of the street without concern for her hems (he'd never seen a woman so indifferent to mud) and headed in the direction of the ponderosa pine with her notebook pressed to her left breast (what there was of it). Here, too, she was different from her sister—not much in the way of femininity at all.

They advanced up the street and he spoke up before she could catch sight of the tree.

He said it straight out, as if it were no fault of his, because he knew damned well it was.

"Someone stole your printing press."

"What!" She halted and spun on him.

"It disappeared while I was at Doc Turley's checking on True."

"Disappeared? Half a ton of machinery *disappeared?* What are you trying to pull here, Campbell?"

The thought had never occurred to him she'd suspect him of skulduggery.

"Me? I didn't—"

"Where have you hidden it?"

"Now, listen here—"

"Don't tell me this isn't your doing—!"

"I was down at Doc's—"

"Because nobody else in this town—"

"You can ask him!"

They stood in the middle of the street, shouting at each other, nose to nose. It was nearly suppertime; the streets were busy with hungry men heading for the food saloons; many stopped walking to rubberneck.

". . . have no right to impound my press!"

"I didn't impound it. Someone stole it!"

"What for?"

"Hell, I don't know!"

"What about my type and my ink and paper?"

"It's all gone, even the tent."

Her mouth tightened and she looked as if she'd like nothing better than to sock him in his other eye and give him a matched pair.

"You're the most unscrupulous reprobate in this town, and the pity is you've got them all bamboozled! To think they all elected you!" She tromped off angrily, still clutching her notebook, her free hand curled into a fist. By the time he reached the tree she was standing beneath it throwing glances in a wide circle.

"You'd better find it, Campbell, and do it quick!"

"That'll take some time."

"Then spend it."

"And search every building in this gulch?"

"You're the marshal, aren't you? That's your job! That press means my livelihood, and the type is the same my father began on. They mean far more to me than just the tools I work with, but of course you wouldn't—"

"Miss Merritt?" The youthful male voice interrupted Sarah's diatribe. A boy with a curly crop of black hair had approached. He was about sixteen, comely, with a shy mien and the first shadow of a beard beginning to sprout beneath his nose. He wore dome-toed boots, worn wool britches and a shabby green plaid jacket. His hands were in the jacket pockets.

"Yes?"

"Mr. Bradigan sent me. He's got your press and he says you should come with me."

"Mr. Bradigan!"

"Yes."

"But why? And where?"

"He'll explain if you'll just come along."

Sarah looked to Noah but he only shrugged. "I'd better come along and see what Bradigan is up to."

"What's your name?" Sarah asked as they struck off behind the lad.

"Josh Dawkins." He glanced back briefly.

"Dawkins? Are you Emma's boy?"

"That's right."

"Oh, goodness, I just remembered, I'm supposed to be at your house for supper. It must be almost that time now."

"She'll hold it till we get there. You've got to do this other first."

"Do what?"

"You'll see."

He led them to a small frame building on the southwest end of Main Street. Facing east, it was already blanketed in shadow from the canyon wall; within, lantern light glowed. Inside, Sarah came to a halt while her glance snapped from wall to corner to wall. There before her were all her prized possessions—her press, her furniture cabinet, her typecase, her father's desk, the crates containing her ink, brayers, newsprint and wood engravings—all set up in perfect working relationship to one another. The oily smell of ink combined with the tang of turpentine hung in the air like printer's perfume. On a wooden table along the right wall four stacks of printed pages were drying. At the press, wearing a black-blotched leather apron, Patrick Bradigan was cleaning today's type with a turpentine rag. He turned when they entered, gave a slow, wobbly smile, and an even slower, wobbly bow.

"Miss Merritt," he said in his rich Irish brogue. "Welcome to the office of the *Deadwood Chronicle.*"

She moved forward as if mysticized, her eyes taking a more lingering tally of the setup before returning to him. Stopping before him she said, "Mr. Bradigan, what have you done?"

"Found you a building and gotten your first issue ready for the streets, with the help of young Dawkins here. Patrick Bradigan at your sorvice, ma'am. Have composing stick, will set type." He whisked his composing stick from a breast pocket as if it were a cigar. She could tell immediately he was inebriated. Nevertheless, she was grateful.

"Mr. Bradigan, Master Dawkins, though it's inexcusable in a newspaperwoman, I must admit to being speechless."

Young Dawkins stood by beaming while Bradigan sported a pie-eyed grin.

"We ran three hundred twenty-foive copies."

"Three hundred twenty-five!"

"You'll sell every one of them, just wait and see. Tomorrow young Dawkins intends to help you."

She turned her full attention on the boy. "Thank you for the help you've already given."

"Ma sent me over when she heard about the fracas in the street. Word got to the bakery that Mr. Bradigan was going to take over getting the first issue out, and she said I should come and help however I could. I put the paper in the frisket while Mr. Bradigan rolled the ink. It was fun!"

She smiled, recalling the first times her father had allowed her to do that, how fun it had been for her, too.

"Perhaps we'll teach you the rest and make an apprentice out of you—would you like that?"

"Yes, *ma'am!* Would I ever!" he exclaimed with a huge smile.

She took another scan of the premises—raw wood walls, but four of them, sturdy, with a solid roof overhead, and a wide front window facing east for good morning light during her favorite composing time of the day. "Is the building yours, Mr. Bradigan?"

"The building's yours, to rent or buy, whatever you choose."

"But why . . . and how?"

"A gesture from the townspeople who want their first newspaper to begin operating full steam ahead as soon as possible. You can see Elias Pinkney about it. His bank built it on speculation."

"But aren't there others waiting in line to buy it? That's what I was told."

Bradigan cleared his throat and scratched the back of his neck. "Ahh . . . well, you see, those others were men, Miss Campbell, not eligible young colleens like you."

The implication left the unpretentious Sarah at a loss for a reply. *Gracious,* she thought. *Mr. Pinkney again.* Fatter than a Christmas goose and forty years old if he was a day, with his glowing pink head upon which Sarah looked down from her superior height. How discomfiting to rationalize Mr. Bradigan's remark while Marshal Campbell looked on, drawing his own conclusions.

She quickly changed the subject. "Well, luckily for all of us, I've paid my licensing fee. Marshal, have we done everything legally this time?"

"As far as I can see. If you have no complaints about Bradigan usurping your press, I'll leave you."

"No complaints at all."

He turned toward the door and she called, "Just a moment, Marshal." From the table she swished one of the newly inked sheets and folded it in half with the edge of her hand. "Any changes in the content, Mr. Bradigan?" she inquired.

"No. Just as you laid it out."

"A complimentary copy, Mr. Campbell," she said, offering it to him with the editorial faceup. Given all the hubbub today, she knew he hadn't read it. Her contrary side felt a thrill of satisfaction when he took it and said, "Well . . . thank you."

He glanced down and she watched his eyes find the headline. He read a line or two, then lifted his eyes. They were gray and flat as riverbed stones. "You do enjoy butting heads, don't you?"

"It's my job, Marshal."

He regarded her for several seconds before handing the newspaper back to her. "Give it to someone who's interested," he said, and left.

Chapter 5

❧

From the moment Sarah entered Emma Dawkins' kitchen, she knew she'd found a friend. Emma flew from her black iron range across the room and enfolded Sarah in her arms.

"Mercy, what you've been through today. I heard it all, and no woman should have to go through that. Well, you just sit right down and have a good strong cup of coffee while the girls help me dish up. A nice hot meal will take the jitters out of your stomach. These are my daughters, Lettie, she's twelve, and Geneva, ten, and this here is my man, Byron. Everybody," she addressed the group, "this is Sarah Merritt, the new woman I told you about."

Lettie was a thin, black-haired beauty with skin like eggshell, a feminine version of her brother. Geneva still wore her adolescent fat and had overstated dimples that would soon be beguiling the young boys around town. Byron looked as ordinary as a fresh-rolled noodle, his skin so naturally pale it appeared to carry a dusting of flour from his day's work. He was thin, with even paler skin along the insides of his wiry blue-veined arms, and had lanky brown hair and a clean-shaven face. Looking at him and Emma, Sarah wondered where Lettie's and Josh's dark-haired beauty came from. Byron came forward and shook Sarah's hand with a diffident nod of his head, then rested his hands along his thighs.

"Welcome," he said simply. "Won't you sit down?"

The meal was delicious, cabbage rolls filled with a mixture of venison and rice, richly flavored with onion and allspice, accompanied by an endless supply of warm bread. There was, however, no butter. Emma explained that the shortage of grazing land made dairy farming impossible except in the upland valleys, thus goat milk was widely used. The dearth of cattle created a butter shortage, too, so the town made do with salted lard for their bread.

Sarah made a memorandum to this effect in her notebook, adding that the butcher shop handled mostly wild game and fowl.

For dessert they had a marvelous tart stuffed with cinnamon and apples, accompanied by coffee.

The girls did the serving and clearing, without waiting for orders from their mother, and Sarah found herself impressed by their good manners and willingness. The Dawkins were a warm family who talked and laughed at the table; Sarah's presence was accepted as if she were a longtime friend. During the meal Sarah learned that all three of the youngsters helped their parents in the bakery and that none of them had attended school since the previous year in Iowa.

Sarah added another scribble in her notebook on a page with a heading, *Need for School.*

"How many children would you guess are in the gulch?"

This led to a ticking off of family names in which all the Dawkins took part while Sarah wrote down a list, including the locations of their homes.

When all but the coffee cups were cleared away, Sarah said, "I want to thank you both for sparing Josh to help Patrick Bradigan get my office set up."

"No need to thank us. He was only too willing, and the day's work was done at the bakery."

"Nevertheless, it was very kind of you to send him over. He did a respectable job, too. He helped Bradigan handle the press, and together they turned out three hundred twenty-five copies of the newspaper."

"Three hundred twenty-five!"

"That's what *I* said. But Bradigan assures me there'll be no trouble selling them all. As a matter of fact, Josh has applied for a job as my newsboy."

Across the table, Josh's brown eyes widened. When nobody spoke, Sarah went on. "Josh tells me he's interested in learning the printer's trade. If you thought you could spare him from the bakery, I'd be willing to pay him fifty cents a day to help around the newspaper office."

Josh's jaw dropped. His parents exchanged glances while Sarah pinned her earnest gaze on the boy. "He's a willing worker and Bradigan seemed to think he had a good, steady rhythm at loading the paper. On the day an issue comes out I could use him selling copies on the street if he wanted to. Also, once frost comes, I'd need him to go down to the office and start the fire early in the morning to thaw the ink."

"Pa, could I?" Josh's eyes shone with excitement.

Byron glanced from his son to his wife. "Emma, what do you think?"

Emma turned to Josh. "You'd rather learn that than be a baker like your father?"

Josh leaned forward eagerly. His glance darted between his parents and came to rest on Emma.

"Fifty cents a day, Ma," he said longingly, "and Miss Merritt says she could teach me how to set type."

"And perhaps to write articles, in time," Sarah added. "It's not school, but until we can get one here in Deadwood, it's as close as he can come. He'll be working with words, and—think!—is there any power greater than the power of the written word? My father always said, a man who can make words behave can make men behave. You would be giving Josh a wonderful opportunity."

"Well . . . I suppose since we still have the girls to help in the bakery . . ." Emma remarked as if convincing herself.

Byron said, "If that's what you want, son, I guess we have no right to stop you."

Josh pushed back his chair and leaped up, beaming. "I can do all those things and more. I can sell subscriptions door to door, and sweep up the shop at the end of the day, and shovel out front for you in the winter and carry in your wood and take messages for you when you're out. I promise you won't be sorry you hired me, Miss Merritt!"

"I'm sure I won't," Sarah told him with a smile.

Later, when Sarah and Emma had the kitchen to themselves, Sarah said, "I'm awfully lucky to have met Josh so soon after I came to town. He's going to be an asset to me, I can tell."

Emma was darning a sock stretched on an old wooden bed knob. She wove her needle in and out between the hand warping and spoke without lifting her eyes. "It's sad to see your young ones grow up. You know you've got to let them go, but when it happens, you're not quite prepared for it. Josh now, leaving us to earn his first money on his own . . ." She stopped darning for a moment and let the thought trail off.

Sarah leaned forward and covered Emma's hand. The women's eyes met.

"Should I have asked you first?"

"Aw no, it's not that. Josh is a real bright boy. If you want to know the truth, I never thought mixing bread dough would be enough for him."

Relieved, Sarah sat back. "Watching his eagerness tonight brought back memories of how I first helped my father. I was twelve when he first allowed me to set type. The piece was a very short filler about how to dry flower seeds for winter storage, and it had about fifteen lines or so. When I was done setting it my father was full of praise and he asked me how I'd done it so fast. Well, the secret was, I'd been "playing printer' whenever I could sneak into his office and do so. He'd be busy at his desk or pulling a proof and I'd be doing what most children do—imitating. He'd hear the type clicking and he'd call to me, "Be sure you put them back in the right places, Sarah.' So by the time he let me do it officially for the first time, I already had a rudimentary knowledge of the typecase layout and could actually find some of the letters without looking."

"So you were close to your father then?"

Sarah's expression became tender with reminiscence. "Always."

"And your mother?"

Sarah looked down into her coffee cup. "My mother ran away with another man when I was seven years old. I have only vague recollections of her."

"Oh Sarah. Oh my, how sad."

"We got along. We had a housekeeper, and Addie and I still had Father."

Emma studied her with sympathetic eyes before returning to her darning. "So you do have a sister." From Emma's tone it was clear she'd heard rumors.

"Yes."

"Is it true that you came here to look for her and found her working up at that place called Rose's?"

"It's true." Sarah's gaze became distant. "I just wish I knew why."

"Forgive me for asking."

"No, Emma, I don't mind, and what's the difference? The whole town knows anyway."

"Isn't it odd how two children can end up so different from one another?"

"Mmm . . . my sister and I were always different." Sarah brushed absently at the tablecloth, remembering. "From the time I first became aware that there was such a thing as physical beauty, I knew that was the biggest difference between Addie and me. It went without saying—she got the beauty and I got the brains. All through school, all through our growing-up years, she was the one old ladies patted on the head and I was the one they patted on the shoulder—there's a difference, you know."

Emma glanced up and waited for Sarah to go on.

"Children always wanted to be her friends, boys and girls both, while they somehow always stood back from me as if I cowed them. I never meant to. It was just the way I was. When the others would go out to play, I preferred to read. Boys pulled Addie's pigtails but they asked me how to spell the hard words. Addie won the prize for the prettiest-child contest and I won the spelling bees. Father even treated us differently. He babied her. I'm the one he took to the printing office with him. I'm the one he taught to set type. I'm the one who became his apprentice, his right-hand man. And don't get me wrong—I was proud to be. But I used to wonder sometimes why Addie didn't have to go to the office and work, too. Now, of course, I realize I was the lucky one. If Addie had learned a trade she might not be doing what she is."

"It's not your fault she ended up at Rose's."

"Isn't it? I sometimes wonder. Was it something I did or didn't do that made her run away from home? She wasn't happy there and I knew it, but I was so busy helping Father that I didn't take time to sit down and talk to her. From the time Mother ran away she was a sad little girl, but during her teen years she became even more quiet and withdrawn. I thought it was just growing pains."

"Now, don't you go blaming yourself," Emma said. "I haven't known you long, but what I do know tells me you had a hard row to hoe, growing up without a mother."

Sarah sighed and sat up straighter. "Goodness, haven't we gotten morose?"

Emma brightened and refilled their coffee cups. Clacking the pot back on the stove, she inquired, "So what do you think of our marshal?"

Sarah shot a glance at Emma. "Did you just see the hair bristle on the scruff of my neck?"

Returning to her chair, Emma laughed and took a sip of hot coffee. "There are a lot of rumors flying around about the two of you."

"They're not rumors. They're all true. We quite despise one another."

"What started it?"

"*He* started it!" Sarah became incensed. "The first night I came into town looking for Addie, who do you think was the first man I encountered going into Rose's? Your honorable marshal, that's who!"

"He's single, in the prime of life. What did you expect?"

"*Emma!*" Sarah's eyes and lips opened in astonishment.

"I'm only being realistic. We just got finished naming the families in the gulch. Us few married women, plus you and the upstairs girls are the only females for three hundred miles around. And men will be men."

"He's paid to uphold the law, not to flaunt it!"

"That's true, and I'm not excusing him. I'm talking about the nature of men."

"You are *too* excusing him!"

"Well, perhaps I am."

"Why?"

"Because I think he's a fair man when it comes to the law and he's got a hard job, taming this town."

"What if it were Byron who was frequenting Rose's? Would you be so forgiving then?"

"But it's not."

"But if it were."

"Byron and I have talked about it. He's happy at home."

Sarah had no idea married people discussed such subjects. She found herself discomfited and hid behind her coffee cup.

"Well." Emma set down her mending and slapped a hand down on the tabletop. "It seems we've had our first disagreement. This will tell us how good a friends we can be."

"I espouse causes, I know. Sometimes I become too zealous."

"I suppose that's how it ought to be for a woman in your business. But for a woman in mine it pays to look plainly at the temptations the world holds for a man and to see to it that *my* man has no reasons to seek them out."

They grew quiet for a while, studying each other, realizing they had been uncommonly frank with one another in this first private discussion.

"So . . ." Emma said.

"So . . ."

"Friends?"

"Yes, friends."

Emma squeezed the back of Sarah's hand on the tabletop.

The exchange lingered on Sarah's mind as she walked back to her hotel. Before coming to Deadwood if she had bumped heads with a woman over the subject of men frequenting brothels she'd have shunned the woman ever after. But she liked Emma, respected her in spite of her outlandish stand, and valued her newfound friendship, which Sarah was sure would grow in the years ahead. Emma was a wife and mother, a respectable woman who had a respectable marriage, and still she took a liberal stand on the issue of the marshal's peccadilloes.

How surprising that Sarah still respected Emma.

Perhaps she was still growing up.

The thought came with some surprise, for she had always considered herself years ahead of her age in maturity, thrust into it by the early loss of her mother, her sister's dependence on her at home, and her father's dependence on her in business, and he certainly had depended on her, more and more the older she got. Oddly, however, by depending, he had made her independent, for he had afforded her the opportunity to demonstrate her capabilities at an age when most young girls were still at home stitching samplers. Serious-minded as she was, she had thrived upon both the challenge and the success. The more her father praised her, the more diligently she had worked, in the end acquiring a master trade, a rarity for a woman.

So it was true; she'd been playing a grown-up role for so long she hadn't realized she had some maturing to do. Yet within two days of arriving in Deadwood she had bumped up against situations and people who had already begun to force her to a new plateau of growth.

Adelaide, of course—and who knew what mellowing would be required on Sarah's part before coming to terms with Adelaide's situation?

The marshal—she'd already run such a gamut of emotions due to that man, she felt years older after the confrontations.

And now Emma—a good, wholesome wife and mother who had reached out a hand in friendship but who—Sarah was certain—aimed to teach Sarah a thing or two about tolerance.

Well, she'd concede that Emma had the right to hold whatever views she chose about Deadwood's representative of the law visiting whorehouses instead of shutting them down, but she, Sarah, intended to use her considerable power as both a woman and a newspaperwoman to bring him to heel *and* to shut down the houses and clean up this town.

The following morning she awakened early, took a set of clean clothes and went to the bathhouse, where she sank into a copper tub of hot water to her armpits. Reclining, she let her hair trail into the water behind her and emptied her mind of all but the unaccustomed luxury of being warm, clean and drifting. She washed her hair, towel-dried and twisted it into a knot, dressed, and rolled up her dirty clothes to be dropped off at the laundry. She opened the door, stepped out into the hall and came face to face with Noah Campbell, holding his own roll of dirty clothes.

They both came up short.

He looked like a herd of buffalo had stampeded his face. It was eight shades of blue, purple and rose. His left eye was split like an outgrown tomato skin and his lower lip was bigger than Dutch Van Aark's. No hat in sight either, to help hide the damage. A single glimpse of Campbell and Sarah felt her collar grow tight.

"Marshal," she said stiffly.

Campbell nodded, stiffly, too.

"I'm sorry about that."

"I'm sure you are," he replied sarcastically.

"How is your friend Mr. Blevins?"

"Let's get one thing straight, Miss Merritt." Beneath his mustache his mouth was shrunken into a tight knot. "I don't like you and you don't like me, so why pretend to make polite chitchat when we run into each other? Just stay out of my way and let me do my job, and we'll pretend to tolerate each other."

He turned and stalked off up the hallway, leaving her to stand red-faced with embarrassment.

When he disappeared her mouth got just like his had been. *Insufferable, despicable, freckle-faced boor!*

She was so angry she went to Emma's to blow off steam. Emma wiped her hands on her white cobbler apron and said, "What's got you upset this morning?"

"The marshal, that's what!"

"You run into him already this morning?"

"At the bathhouse. He's despicable!"

"He probably thinks the same thing about you. Here, have a warm bun and cool down. You two are going to be bumping into each other pretty regular in a town this size, so you might as well get used to it.''

Sarah tore off a mouthful of bun and chewed it in a totally undignified manner. "I'm going to put a stop to him or to the brothels or both, Emma, mark my words!''

Emma laughed and said, "Well, good luck.''

Josh appeared and Sarah was forced to cool down.

" 'Morning, Miss Merritt.''

"Hello, Josh. Why don't you call me Sarah.''

"I'll try.''

She smiled. Emma and Byron had raised some fine kids.

"I was just heading for work," Josh said.

"So was I. Let's walk together.''

Sarah took some extra buns and the two headed toward the *Chronicle* office. It was a pretty day, the town was bustling, and she forced the marshal from her thoughts.

"I've been thinking," she said to her new apprentice, "this first issue of the paper—it might be good for business to make it a complimentary copy. What do you think?''

Josh was surprised at being consulted. "But—gosh!—if you sold them for a penny apiece you could make three dollars and twenty-five cents!''

"But if I gave them away free, and gained goodwill in return, then went to two sheets next issue, I could perhaps get three cents, or four, or even a nickel. Now what do you think?''

They decided the first copy would be complimentary.

At the office Sarah fixed Josh up with a canvas shoulder bag to carry the papers. As he headed out she ordered, "Leave one on every doorstep, and at every business, then go up and down the gulch and give them to the miners.''

"Yes, ma'am." He opened the door.

"Oh . . . and, Josh?''

"Yes?''

"Every business but the badlands. I don't want you anywhere near those buildings.''

"Yes, ma'am." He turned to go.

"And one more thing," she called. "Make certain that the marshal gets one. You hand it to him personally, do you understand?''

"Yes, ma'am.''

When Josh was gone, Sarah checked her watch. She had agreed to give Patrick Bradigan a try as a typesetter and had made arrangements to meet him at the office at eight A.M. It was already eight-twenty and no Irishman in sight.

He arrived at eight-fifty, red-eyed and affable, dressed in a brown tweed frock coat with his composing stick in his pocket and a red muffler tied jauntily around his throat.

"Top o' the morning to you, Miss Merritt," he offered, doffing an aging black top hat and bowing from the waist.

"Good morning, Mr. Bradigan. Am I mistaken, or did we agree on meeting at eight o'clock?''

"Eight o'clock, is it?" He pronounced his *t*'s crisply. "I thought it was nine. I says to meself, a pretty young thing like Miss Merritt must be getting at least that much beauty sleep to have eyes as bright as highland bluebells.''

"And you've been kissing the Blarney stone, Mr. Bradigan.'' He was a likable fellow, but she took his flattery with a grain of skepticism, realizing that the footing upon which they started was the one upon which they would proceed. In a tone of light reproof she told him, ''If you want to work for me you'll have to understand from the start that I won't abide your oversleeping, or arriving late, or missing appointments. When I commit myself to printing two newspapers a week I must know that I can rely on my staff to be here when I expect them.''

He doffed his hat again and held it over his heart, bowing deep. (She already recognized he was a great one for bowing.) ''My apologies, young miss, and I'll remember.''

"Good. Then permit me—may I ask a few questions?''

Returning his hat to his head and tapping its top, he said, ''You may.''

"How old are you, Mr. Bradigan?''

"I'll be thorty-two on the Feast of St. Augustine.''

"You're a journeyman printer?''

"I am.''

"Where have you worked before?''

"From Boston to St. Louis and a dozen towns in between.''

"What kind of presses have you worked with?''

"The wee ones—Gallys, Cottrells, Potters—and the big ones, too—the Hoe Ten Cylinder. I've even had a chance to operate one of the new Libertys that won the gold medal in Paris last year.''

"Ah, and how was it?''

" ' Twas a beauty. Printed clear as a Kilkenny brook and distributed the ink perfectly. And that treadle saved on me poor tired back.''

"Then why did you leave it?''

"Well now, you see . . .'' He cleared his throat and scratched his temple. "There was a sortain young lady who broke me heart.'' He placed his hand over it and gave the ceiling a gaze of dejection.

A likely story, thought Sarah. *He probably showed up inebriated for work once too often and got fired. Or woke up in a stupor at noon one day and decided it was time to move on.*

"How fast can you work?''

"I can set two thousand ems an hour.''

Her left eyebrow rose. ''Two thousand?'' That was fast.

"Mignon,'' he added, naming the style of type.

"As you saw yesterday, I use Caslon, primarily, for the body type. It's what my father used.''

"Caslon's all right. I've worked with it, too.''

"I'll give you a try, then, Mr. Bradigan, at a dollar fifty a day if that's agreeable, and you'll work from eight until six.''

"Those terms are acceptable.''

"Agreed, then.'' She extended her hand. When he took it she felt the early-morning tremor in his. ''To the success of the *Deadwood Chronicle,*'' she said, giving two hard pumps.

"To the success of the *Chronicle,*'' he seconded, and she withdrew her hand.

Leading the way toward the rear, she said, ''Before we do anything else

I want to get Father's clock hung up. I learned to the sound of its ticking, and I miss it."

"I spied it yesterday, when we were setting up. I'll be knowin' just which crate it's in."

With Bradigan's help, Sarah unearthed the familiar Waterbury in its fine walnut case, with its eight-day movement, ornamented pendulum and detailed hand carving. When it hung on the wall she set the hands to 9:09, closed the glass door and set the pendulum swinging. Standing back, she looked up at it.

"There, that's better. Wait until you hear it chime. It has a splendid cathedral gong that strikes on the quarter hour."

"Ahh," he responded, rolling back on his heels.

For several seconds they listened to the *tick-tocks,* then Sarah inquired, "Is there any plaster in this town, Mr. Bradigan?"

"Plaster, you say?"

"The clock looked so much better on our plastered walls in St. Louis. I miss them."

"Not that I know of. Not a soul I know's got plastered walls."

"Then let's be the first," she proposed. "I shall order some by Pony Express Mail today. Have you had your breakfast, Mr. Bradigan?"

"Me breakfast?"

"I've brought some buns from the bakery. Would you like one?"

When she offered one, he backed off with both palms raised. "No, no, none o' that for me. Me belly can't take it so early in the mornin'. But if it's all the same to you I will have a tot o' the rye—to oil the hinges, don't you know." From the capacious pockets of his frock coat he withdrew a small flask of whiskey and, with two fingers raised, took two deep swallows.

Watching him, she knew it would be useless to protest. Much as she disliked his imbibing, especially in so forthright a manner, she suspected that if she remonstrated with rules about his alcohol consumption she would lose a 2,000–em-per-hour typesetter. He was what she'd suspected— a tramp printer who'd wandered in off the stage with his composing stick in his pocket, and who would wander off again without notice, in a year or less, following the pattern of the majority of his ilk. The country was full of them, men who by virtue of the tedium of their trade had turned to the "ardent spirits" to break the monotony of routine, talented men who could set type like dervishes once they had several shots under their belt, but whose hands, without benefit of alcohol, shook as if palsied. She'd seen dozens of them come and go from her father's newspaper office over the years. Since Patrick Bradigan had seen the need to "oil his hinges" before so much as touching type for the first time today, she supposed he'd need the same lead time every day to allow the insidious stuff to calm his hands.

She turned away to find the article she'd written about yesterday's riot and subsequent arrest. Handing it to him, she inquired, "Can you read my writing?"

"As clear as me old mother's prayer book."

"Good, then I'll leave you to your task, since you know where everything is."

Covertly she glanced at the clock—9:13—and set about unpacking her books and small tools while pretending to pay him no mind. He did all the proper things, all in the fashion taught her by her father: removed his outerwear and rolled up his sleeves, a must where restricted movement meant inefficiency and a starched cuff could cause pied—spilled—type. He measured the width of yesterday's columns; set his composing stick to the correct length; dropped in the proper-length slug; settled it in his left hand with the thumb inside, fingers folded across the bottom—faultless form. Though Sarah turned away, she was wholly conscious of the *snick, snick, snick,* as he began plucking type—left elbow tilting, bringing the stick to meet the type in the most proficient fashion. *Snick, snick snick:* spacing, justifying, with scarcely a syncopation in rhythm.

He hadn't been lying. He was fast. Three lines were filled and transferred to the galley before the clock struck the quarter hour. Even the sound of the chime didn't distract him.

"You're right—splendid," he remarked at the reverberation, his hands flashing.

Patrick Bradigan went on creating the music Sarah loved while she unpacked her possessions and smiled at her good fortune. She thought of her father and how they'd worked together companionably this way, years ago; of her future and all she hoped to build here with this newspaper.

She thought of Noah Campbell and wondered if he'd read her editorial yet.

She thought of Addie, probably asleep in her room after a night of men like Campbell.

There were reforms needed in this town and she, Sarah, was here to make them.

Bradigan finished typesetting the article and slid it onto the composing stone, framed it with the chase, filled it with the furniture, locked it into place with quoins and tilted it to check the justification before carrying it to the press and pulling a proof. He used a pallet knife to spread a strip of ink, rolled it even on the brayer and inked his type with exactly four passes of the tool—the perfect number for greatest efficiency. He loaded the frisket, pulled the proof and brought it to Sarah for inspection.

"Thank you," she said quietly, then put on her spectacles and looked it over slowly. He had chosen Gothic Sans Serif for the headline—an appropriate matchup for Caslon body type. His indentations were uniform, justified edges clean; no misspellings or omissions. Flawless, fast work.

She removed her glasses, returned the proof and gave him a smile. "I think we'll get along just fine, Mr. Bradigan."

Sarah spent the morning setting up the remainder of her shop and greeting townspeople who came in to welcome her and the newspaper to Deadwood. Josh returned from distributing the papers and said he needed more, so he and Patrick got the press running again while she went to make calls on Lawrence Chapline and Dr. Turley. She paid the doctor and learned that True Blevins was progressing nicely. She went next to Elias Pinkney's bank to withdraw some gold dust and inquire about the wording on his advertisement. When he saw her enter the building he leaped from his desk chair and met her with his hand extended.

"Miss Merritt, my my, how lovely to see you again."

"Thank you, Mr. Pinkney." His name truly was appropriate: his cheeks, pate and mouth were all as pink as a baby's belly; pinker than ever as he continued smiling ingratiatingly and appropriating her hand.

"Everyone is talking about the first issue of your paper. Everybody. We're awfully proud to have it *and you* in Deadwood."

"I understand I have you to thank for making it possible."

"It is absolutely my pleasure to be of service to you."

She forcefully freed her hand from his grip and discreetly wiped it on her skirt. "The building is perfect and I'd love to keep it on whatever basis it's available. I can either rent or buy."

"Come, Miss Merritt." He appropriated her elbow. "Have a chair, please." He seated her beside his desk and concentrated on her eyes as if they were pools of blue water and he a man finishing hard labor on a hundred-degree day. For a moment she imagined him shucking off his clothes and getting ready to jump. The picture was distasteful. He was pudgy all over and had hairless, pink, feminine hands to go with his hairless, pink, feminine face.

"The rent, Mr. Pinkney." She put on her most professional mien. "Shall we settle that?"

"Oh, there's no hurry." He waved away her concern and sat back in his chair. "Your newspaper is the talk of the town. It's very well done. Very well done."

His repeating drove her crazy. She considered replying, "Thank you, thank you." Instead she told him, "I've hired some good help—Mr. Bradigan and Josh Dawkins. Without them I'm afraid I couldn't have gotten the first issue out nearly as fast as I did."

"How often do you plan to publish?"

"Twice a week."

"Ahh . . . industrious. Very industrious." He leaned close enough that she caught whiffs of his breath. It smelled like cloves, and she found herself wondering if he'd popped one into his mouth since she'd entered the bank.

"I thought perhaps we could set down the wording of your ad while I'm here."

"Of course! Of course!" he said eagerly. While they did business he smiled so broadly, attended her so ingratiatingly, that she felt claustrophobic. She brought up the subject of the building three more times, but he refused to name a price. Though he had a clerk to do so, he personally fetched her gold dust from the safe, and touched her hand while returning her pouch. She scarcely controlled the urge to recoil, but thanked him politely and bid him good day.

"One moment, Miss Merritt," he said, detaining her with a grip on her elbow. She knew instinctively what was coming and scrabbled through her mind for a graceful refusal.

"I wondered if some evening you'd do me the honor of allowing me to buy you supper."

But I'm looking down on the top of your bald, pink head.

"I do thank you, Mr. Pinkney, but I have so much to do these days, getting the business set up and acquainting myself with the town. Why, I still don't have a decent place to live."

"Perhaps I could do something about that, too."

"Oh no. I wouldn't want any more favors. My fellow townspeople might begin to resent me when the waiting lists are so long."

"I own a lot of property in this town, Miss Merritt. Where would you like to live? I'm certain something can be arranged."

And all I have to do is go to dinner with you. And let you fondle my hand and breathe cloves on my chin (the level where his mouth reached).

"Thank you again, Mr. Pinkney, but I'll wait my turn. The hotel really isn't so bad."

He smiled and extended his hand for a shake. She gave hers reluctantly and he held it in his damp palm. "The offer still stands. Supper anytime you're free."

Leaving the bank, the light dawned. He was bribing her! Free rent and a place to live, and all she had to do was submit to his attentions. Her face grew red and her temperature boiled. Why, he was no better than Campbell! He only disguised his proposition behind a façade of graciousness.

She had no delusions about herself and her pulchritude. She was a plain woman with too long a nose, overly tall, with more intelligence than most men wanted in a female companion. But she was—after all—female. No other qualifications were necessary in a town with the dearth of distaff that Deadwood suffered. It would have made some women feel heady. Sarah felt insulted. If a woman shortage was the only reason the men in this town wanted her, they could all go lick!

She returned to the newspaper office in a lather and had scarcely caught her breath when the door opened and the marshal walked in.

She knew in a moment that he had read the editorial.

She faced him squarely as he propelled himself across the room with clunking steps that said he'd as soon plaster the walls with her as speak to her.

"Your license," he said, without preliminaries, dropping it on a table where she'd begun arranging her wood engraving cuts.

"Thank you."

"See that you keep it posted on your wall."

"I will."

The two words hadn't cleared her lips before he was halfway back to the door, slamming it behind himself. No "Good day, Miss Merritt," no greeting for Patrick or Josh, just *clunk, clunk, hang this, clunk, clunk, bang!*

Sarah, Josh and Patrick were still exchanging surprised glances when the door opened and Campbell stormed in again. Standing two feet inside the entrance, he jabbed a finger at Sarah and said, "You owe me for a hat, lady!"

On his way out he slammed the door so hard the clock door drifted open.

"He must've read your editorial," Patrick said.

"Good!" she said, and threw down a woodblock with enough force to send two others jumping out of the case. With steps as aggravated as Campbell's she strode past the clock, closed its door, continued to her desk, collected what she needed and whisked toward the door.

"I have some errands to do. I'll be back in a couple of hours."

She was *sick and tired* of the men in this town!

At Tatum's Store she marched in and found herself ogled by a half-dozen more of them as she advanced toward the hats along the right. The store owner approached. He resembled a beaver, with prominent teeth, a rather receding, flat nose and thick hair that grew very low on his brow

and was slicked straight back with pomade. His smile was broad and ingratiating.

"Miss Merritt?"

"Yes."

"I'm Andrew Tatum. Much obliged for the newspaper."

"You're welcome, Mr. Tatum. I hope you enjoyed it."

"Most certainly did and we're happy to have you in town."

"Thank you."

"Are you interested in a hat?"

"Yes, I am."

"I'm sorry to say we don't carry hats for ladies."

"No, not for myself. It's for a man."

"A man's hat?" he repeated, surprised.

"That's right."

"What color?"

"Black . . . no, brown." She'd be damned if she'd buy him the color he
preferred.

"What size?"

"Size?" She hadn't given size a thought. Something for a bullhead, she
supposed, considering the man's insufferable attitude.

"It's for Marshal Campbell." Six pairs of ears pointed her direction
from all around the store.

"Ahhhh . . ." Tatum elongated the sound and rubbed the underside of
his nose. "I'd guess Noah wears about a seven and a half."

"Fine."

"Now this one . . ." He took one off a block and donned it on his
knuckles, pointing out its features with his free hand. "This one's called
The Boss of the Plains, and there isn't a man alive wouldn't be proud to
own this hat. It came clear from Philadelphia. It's a J. B. Stetson, made
of one hundred percent nutria fur, with a silk band and lining. Crown is
four and a half inches and the brim, four. But look here—it weighs only
six ounces . . ." Holding it by the brim, he bounced it in both hands. "Yet
it'll hold off the sun and the rain, and it's tough enough to be used as a
whip if need be, or a pillow, or for watering your horse, or for fanning a
campfire." Again, he demonstrated. "I believe Noah would be more than
happy with this hat."

"Fine. I'll take it." Everyone in the store was gawping by now. Sarah
wished Tatum would pipe down and get to his gold scale.

"Don't you want to know how much?" he inquired, loud enough to be
heard by J. B. Stetson himself, clear out in Philadelphia.

"How much?"

"Twenty dollars."

Twenty dollars! She swallowed her surprise and went with Tatum to the
scale, where he weighed out the full ounce of gold while speculative murmurings began among his other customers. When the purchase was complete, she inquired, "Can you deliver it, Mr. Tatum?"

Tatum appeared nonplussed. "Well, I guess I can, though I suspect
Noah is in his office right now, and it's only a few doors down."

"Thank you so much. I'd appreciate it if you would do that for me.
Tomorrow will be time enough."

"And what should I say about who's sending it to him?"

"Tell him Miss Merritt always pays her debts."

"You bet I will, Miss Merritt. You bet I will."

Leaving Tatum's store, she was certain she was blushing, which left her displeased with herself. She wished she were a man. Only those of the spear side could hope for any degree of anonymity in this male-dominated town. Not only was she a woman, but a newspaper publisher as well, and both virtues magnified her visibility. She had no doubt the news would spread faster than spilled water that the editor of the *Chronicle* had bought a new hat for the marshal, who had locked her in an abandoned mine the day before. Certainly there would be speculation about why. Well, let them wonder! She herself knew why. Because she wanted the books cleared between them so he'd have nothing to come back at her with. Her debt to Noah Campbell was paid in full. No further byplay need pass between them ever again.

Her temper had scarcely dimmed by the time she reached Rose's. This time the door was locked and she had to knock. Flossie answered.

"What you want?"

"I want to see my sister."

Flossie took a long, disparaging look at Sarah's pinched mouth and proper clothes, then thumbed over her shoulder. "Out back."

Sarah went down the center hall, passed the kitchen and found Addie collecting dry underwear from a clothesline in a tiny square of space behind it. The area was enclosed by a crude bark fence and held some water barrels and a huge woodpile that rested against the rear of the building. Addie's hair was wet and she wore a faded green dressing robe. Sarah watched for a moment and went down four wooden steps before speaking.

"Hello, Addie."

Addie glanced back over her shoulder before resuming her work. "What do you want?" she asked crossly.

"I brought you a copy of my first newspaper."

"I heard about it."

"It looks much the same as Father's. The same type and layout. I thought it might bring back some happy memories for you."

Addie plucked the last garment and dropped it into a wicker basket. She propped the basket on her hip and brushed past Sarah on her way up the steps. "You can keep your memories and keep your paper."

"Addie, please, why are you so bitter?"

Addie paused in the doorway, looking down on Sarah. "I'm surprised you come around here, a hoity-toity newspaperwoman like you. Don't you care about your reputation?"

"It's your reputation I care about."

"So I heard. You've been writing editorials."

"One, yes. I want you to read it." Sarah held out the paper.

"Leave me alone," Addie said and went inside, closing the door behind her.

Sarah studied the entrance for some time, then glanced down at the copy of the *Chronicle* in her hands. This made two times in as many days that she'd been told to keep her newspaper. She released a sigh and her shoulders sagged. What was she fighting for? For a sister who wanted to remain a harlot? For a dumpy, dirty town she didn't even like? To be accepted as a decent woman by a bunch of men who didn't have the faintest notion how to treat a lady?

She was sorry she'd come here. Sorry she'd found Addie. Sorry she'd left St. Louis. Disillusioned and very, very tired, Sarah reentered the brothel, left the newspaper on one of the tables in the reception room and quietly went away.

Chapter 6

🦋

Noah Campbell had read Sarah's editorial, all right. Read it and wanted to go over to that newspaper office of hers and run her through her own press a few times. The damned woman was a pain in the ass . . . and the eye and the lip and the ear, for that matter. One was black and blue, one was swollen and the other had a hole in it, all because of Sarah Merritt. To top it off, she wasn't content to get him mauled in the street, now she was mauling him in print. A hundred and fifty men probably went through *one* of those whorehouses in a night and she singled out *him*, Noah Campbell, the marshal of Deadwood, to hold up as an example of tarnished virtue!

For two cents he'd use her rag to light a fire in his office stove, but he'd be in trouble with his mother if he did. If Carrie Campbell found out the town had its own newspaper and Noah went out there without a copy—look out! And he *was* going out to the Spearfish, probably tomorrow.

Meanwhile, Noah had to find someone to fill in for him while he was gone. It was only an eighteen-mile drive, but he'd decided to stay overnight and get in a visit with his family while he was there.

On the morning following his starring role in Sarah Merritt's muck column, he was interviewing young Freeman Block with an eye to deputizing him when Andy Tatum came into his office wearing one hat and carrying another.

"Noah . . . Freeman," Andy greeted. "Mighty pretty weather we've been having, isn't it?"

"Sure is," Noah replied. "So pretty I'm fixing to take a ride out to the Spearfish and leave Freeman here in charge."

Freeman grinned and pointed at the brown Stetson. "You worried there's going to be a hat shortage, Andy?"

Andy chortled and needlessly brushed at the crown of the hat with his knuckles. "No. This is a delivery for Noah. From the new lady in town." Andy extended the hat.

Noah went stone-still. His expression turned dyspeptic.

"For you," Andy said. "Take it."

Noah leaned forward in his desk chair and reluctantly took the hat. "Do I understand you correctly? It's from that Merritt woman?"

"That's right. She said to tell you she always pays her debts."

Noah looked at it as if it might bite him.

"It's a damned good hat, too." Andy tugged up his pants.

"I can see that."

"Twenty dollars' worth."

Freeman whistled.

Andy was enjoying himself. "She didn't bat an eye when I told her how much it cost. Well, aren't you going to try it on?"

Noah settled the hat on his head very gingerly, using two hands.

"It fits," Freeman noted.

"Looks good, too," Andy said.

"Spiffy," Freeman added. "I wish I had some woman giving *me* hats."

"Aw, now, just a minute. There's no love lost between that bean pole and me."

Freeman's expression turned to one of lascivious speculation. "Any woman ever give *you* a hat, Andy?"

"Nope. The most any woman ever give *me* was a bad case of the crabs. 'Course, Noah ain't gonna have any of those from now on since he's gonna be staying away from the badlands."

While Freeman and Andy hooted and slapped their thighs, Noah glowered. "Now listen, you two, don't you go spreading any rumors about Sarah Merritt and me. Why, we can hardly be in the same room together without a pair of whips."

"Spreading any rumors! Hell, there were half a dozen men in my store when she walked in and picked out that hat and said plain as the sky for me to deliver it to you. Who's spreading rumors? My guess is she's got an eye for you, Noah. I'd put money on it. Why, hell, how many men do you figure there are up and down these gulches? Ten thousand? Twenty? And about two dozen women, which gives that little newslady a few to pick from. So who does she buy a new hat for? Noah Campbell, that's who."

"Must be his shiny tin badge," Freeman put in, smirking.

Noah took the hat off and flung it on the desk. "Now, Freeman, goddammit, watch yourself!"

Andy winked at Freeman. "I think it's that hairy mustache, myself. Some women like those things, you know. Me, I never could see why a man would want to hang a scrub mop beneath his nose, but it takes all kinds."

Freeman considered the marshal's upper lip with mock seriousness. "You think it's the mustache, huh? I heard a rumor about something that happened up at Rose's the first night that newspaper gal came to town and—"

Noah jumped to his feet and pointed at the door. "Freeman, goddammit! Do you want the job as deputy or not? 'Cause I can find plenty who do!"

"I sure do, Noah. I sure do." Freeman puckered, still chuckling silently.

"Then shut the hell up!"

"Sure thing, boss."

"And, Andy, I don't give a damn what your customers heard at the store. That woman and me get along like hot grease and water."

"As you say, Marshal. I'll do my best to stifle the rumors."

When the two were gone, Noah stomped around his office, kicked a chair and glared at the hat, still lying on his desk. If it were any other woman, in any other occupation, with any other kind of temperament, he might be interested. Lord knew it was lonely enough out here. But not

that tall, gangly four-eyes, with her forked tongue and her pointed editorials! He'd continue at Rose's, thank you. But he'd wear the hat. Why
shouldn't he? He'd earned it, by God.

He picked it up, creased the crown to his liking and plunked it on his
head. On the floor in the corner lay a saddlebag. From it he took a small
mirror and checked his reflection. Looked good. Looked damned good,
if he did say so himself. His eyes dropped from the hat to his black eye,
down his very Scottish nose to his bushy mustache, which he smoothed
with his free hand.

All right, so what the hell was wrong with mustaches!

The next day Noah rented an American Beauty runabout with tufted,
sprung seats and plenty of legroom—the most comfortable buggy available at Flecek's livery barn. In it he and True Blevins set out for the Spearfish Valley.

They'd ridden for some time, talked about the wonderful fall weather,
the peace treaty the Indians had finally signed, the high market value of
animal feed in the gulches and the relative merit of chewing tobacco.
True helped himself to a fresh twist and offered some to Noah.

"No, thanks."

They rode on companionably, enjoying the balmy day, the blue sky, the
peace. Their route followed Deadwood Creek northeast out of the gulch,
then swung northwest, following the outer rim of the Hills through tran-
quil pine-and-spruce-covered mountains where quick streams flowed over
shiny brown rocks. Beside these, peach-leaved willows flourished. Wild
currants and serviceberries gleamed ripe in the autumn sun with black-
billed magpies flying among them in sudden flashes of white.

After a long stretch of silence, Noah said thoughtfully, "Hey, True?"

"What?"

"What do you think about mustaches?"

"Mustaches?"

"Yeah."

"Hell, I got one, ain't I? What do you think I think of 'em!"

"No, I mean, do you think women like them?"

"Women! What brought this on?"

"Aw, hell, forget it."

True spit over the side of the buggy, then wiped his soup strainer.

"You got something stuck in your craw? Like that newspaperwoman
maybe?"

"Ha."

"I told you to look out for her."

"She's the last female I'd cotton to. Why, hell, did you read that editorial she put in her paper? She might as well have come right out and
said it was the marshal of Deadwood she ran into up at Rose's her first
night in town."

"What do you care? Ain't a single man in the gulch don't use the
badlands."

"Yeah."

"Me, I was plannin' on gettin' a little myself soon as I had my train
unloaded, but after Doc got done puncturin' me a little bigger I wasn't
sure my system could stand it."

They rode awhile longer, then True asked, "So what about her sister, the one named Eve—you done it with her?"

"Who hasn't?"

"Man, them two don't look atall alike, do they? That Eve, she's soft where a woman's got to be soft. And her face ain't too bad either."

Noah tossed a partial grin True's way. True had something there.

"I've been thinking . . ." Dropping the thought, Noah remained silent for so long True had to ask, "About what?"

"Oh, I don't know. Women. You know—the other kind. You ever done it with one that you cared about?"

True stretched his legs out and caught one wrist on the backrest behind Noah. He studied the ridge ahead and got a faraway look in his blue eyes.

"Yeah, I sure did. I was eighteen at the time. Had me a little gal that wanted to marry me in the worst way—Francie was her name. I was hauling freight for the Army then between Kansas and Utah, while they were trying to subdue those stubborn Mormons. She was one of them, a Mormon. I swear, for a while there, I was thinking about taking up the religion."

"What happened?"

"Her family had already promised her to one of her own. When she married him he already had two other wives. I swear, Noah, I never got over that. Hell, she loved me. She *said* she loved me. And I loved her, too, then she went and did a thing like that, married a man as old as Methuselah who already had more than his share of wives. I tell you, it soured me on *honest* women forever."

"How old are you now, True?"

"Forty."

"And you never met another one you cared for?"

"Nope, and I didn't want to neither."

"What about kids? You ever want kids?"

"A man like me's got no business wanting kids . . . never in one place, hauling freight and cussing at oxen. Hell, what would I do with a family? Nothing but a hobble on a man's leg."

If Noah detected a wistful note in True's words he refrained from saying so.

Shortly before ten A.M. they entered the Spearfish Valley. A natural amphitheater, it stretched out below them like an amethyst in a ring of jade. No wonder the Indians fought to prevent the white men from obtaining a foothold here. Not only was it beautiful, but fertile, with fast-running streams of pure cold water fed by melted snows and crystal springs. These streams coursed down from rockbound canyons in roaring torrents flecked with foam, a living, leaping source of health, wealth and happiness.

Noah's father, Kirk Campbell, had taken one look and decided the Spearfish Valley was destined to become the cradle of agriculture of western Dakota. Not for him the quick, fickle wealth of a mining claim, but the surer source of permanent prosperity to be found in a well-tilled farm.

Upon his arrival in the Black Hills in early May, Kirk had visited the valley's first white settler, James Butcher, who had already been forced by the hostile Indians from his original cabin and had built his second dwelling three miles east, near the spot where False Bottom Creek left the hills. Later in May, a large party of additional settlers arrived from Bozeman, Montana. Seasoned mountaineers, they were inured to hardship and Indian wars, fully capable of whipping any number of Indians daring to attack them. Along with them, Kirk Campbell settled in the Spearfish Valley. Immediately they had begun operations for securing ranches and water rights. They built a common stockade where they stored their provisions and ammunition and into which they drove their livestock at the close of each day. Through the summer Indian raids had continued sporadically, but the settlers—fully mindful of the shortage of arable, flat lands in this mountainous region, and of the insatiable demand for stock feed due to the influx of prospectors—posted guards and set about seeding their outlying fields.

Those fields lay ripe now at the turn of September into October, checkering the vista below with a range of hues from wheat gold to corn green. In the distance stock grazed—the great Montana herd—its population swelled by additional horses brought out from town each day to eat their fill at contract price. Drovers on horseback rode the perimeter of the herd, with one eye on the animals and one on the spine of the hills for any sign of Indians. In the patchwork fields the reapers worked, plying their scythes, followed by the shockers, leaving behind squares of tan earth tied by darker knots of brown—the shocks—like yarn in a crazy quilt.

Scattered across the valley were the farms themselves with the faint fuzz of failing fires drifting from the cabin chimneys, smudging the vast blue welkin above. Modest-sized outbuildings dotted the distance and from these, cart paths led like webbing toward the common stockade, which appeared to be made of toothpicks in the distance.

Down among the reapers Noah drove his rig, along the pummeled route the herd took each day, emerging from the foothills into the flat gold of an oats field where men raised their arms in greeting and women with their hair bound in kerchiefs paused to shade their eyes.

"Hello, Zach!" he called once. "Hello, Mrs. Cottrell!"

True waved, too, with his good arm.

"Looks like Mrs. Cottrell is pregnant," Noah remarked.

"Sure does."

They rode on until they came to the field south of the Campbell place, where the family was putting up hay—Kirk, his wife, Carrie, and Noah's younger brother, Arden. They were working with their backs to the approaching buggy, Kirk and Arden advancing side by side with their scythes swinging while Carrie followed with a curved wooden hay rake.

The three stopped working to watch the buggy approach.

"Anybody need a helping hand?" Noah called.

"Noah! . . . and True! Hello!"

They all came forward, smiling, dropping their tools and removing their gloves. "Well, this is a surprise." Noah's mother reached him first and rubbed her kerchief back off her hair before swabbing her face with it. "Holy Mother of God, what happened to you?"

Noah touched his eye. "I tangled with a woman."

Arden affectionately whapped Noah across the arm with his leather gloves. "Who was she, Calamity Jane?"

Kirk shook his son's hand, surveying the battle damage—"I'd like to see the woman that gave you this shiner." Next he glanced at True's slung arm. "The same one get you?"

True laughed and scratched his eyebrow with the edge of a horny index finger. "Not quite."

Kirk Campbell was a tower of a man, with hands as big as bear traps and a grip' to match. He sported a bushy orange beard, bushy orange eyebrows and a faceful of fiery freckles to boot. His eyes, amidst all that color, shone bright as the bluebells of his homeland.

Carrie, on the other hand, was dark-haired and gray-eyed, though her skin took the sun much better than her husband's and had burnished over the summer. She was pudgy and pretty and only as tall as her sons' shoulders.

"A woman, huh?" Carrie repeated.

"It's a long story, Ma, but I brought True out here to recuperate for a week or so. Think you could feed him and keep him tied down?"

"Just watch me."

Noah put his mother in the buggy and sent her back to the house with True while he took her place with the hay rake. There was a measure of contentment to be found in working behind his father and brother, stepping off the lengths of the field to the rhythmic *shhhppp* of their scythes, to the greeny smell of fallen hay, scooping it into a windrow with the rake tines vibrating beneath his hands. For a day or two he enjoyed it. But always it became confining and he longed for the commerce and company of town.

"So, have you decided to come back to farming after all?" his father asked.

"Just for today."

It had been a disappointment to Kirk Campbell when his older son had decided to take the job in town instead of settling in the valley with the rest of the family.

"I suppose you know the Indians signed the treaty, Pa."

"Yup. News reached us."

"But you still have lookouts posted."

"We do, but we haven't had a raid since midsummer. Hardly ever see them on the ridges anymore. My guess is it's a lot less risky living out here these days than it is living in town. By the looks of you anyway. I'd sure like to hear what you did to get that purple eye."

So Noah told the story.

His father and brother exchanged inquisitive glances. Kirk asked, "How old is she?"

Arden asked, "What does she look like?"

At sunset, around the kitchen table, his mother asked, "Is she married?"

True answered, "Nope," and stabbed himself another piece of bread.

"Did you bring us one of her newspapers?"

Noah said, "I did, but if I let you read it I don't want any guff out of any of you."

When Carrie had read it she pronounced, "This is a smart woman and an honest one. You could do worse."

Noah nearly choked on his mutton stew.

"For Chrissakes, Ma!"

"You know I don't abide cussing at the table. You're not getting any younger, you know. How long do you think a single woman will last before somebody else snaps her up?"

"They can have her!"

"That's how your father felt about me the first time he saw me. I laughed at his red hair and freckles and told him he looked like a frying pan that had been left out in the rain. Six years later we were married."

"Ma, I told you, this woman is like a bad case of hives. She's making my life miserable."

"The next time you come out here bring her along. If *you* don't want her maybe your brother would be interested in her."

"I'm not bringing her out here! I don't even like the woman!"

"All right then, I'll go take a look at her next time we come to town."

"Don't you dare!"

"Why not? I want some grandchildren before I die."

Noah rolled his eyes. "Jesus!" he muttered.

"Didn't I say no cussing at the table?"

Arden said, "Ma's right. If you don't want her I just *might*."

"What's the matter with you! You talk as if she's the last pork chop on the platter and all you have to do is reach over and stab her with your fork."

"Well, I could use a wife. I want a farm of my own," Arden replied. "And now that the Indian Treaty is signed, a woman would be more anxious to live out here."

"Then you'd better move to town and get in line, because half the men in Deadwood are eyeballing her everywhere she goes. But I wouldn't get my hopes up if I were you. The way she's running that printing press I doubt that she's the kind who'd want to be a farmer's wife. Besides, she's older than you."

"I thought you said you don't know how old she is."

"I don't. I'm just guessing."

"Twenty-five, you said."

"Thereabouts, yes."

"Well, I'm only twenty-one."

"That's what I said! She's older than you."

"So what?"

This was the damnedest conversation Noah'd ever heard! What did he care if his mother came into town and looked over Sarah Merritt, or if Arden came and poked her with his fork? Let them do what the hell they wanted! He, on the other hand, would stay out of the woman's way.

Which he did until three days later, the first Monday of October, when the first city council meeting—as prescribed by their new organizational policies—was scheduled to be held at seven P.M. in Jack Langrishe's theater.

Since the theater troupe would begin a performance at nine, the council members met promptly at six fifty-five in hopes of clearing up all business in the two hours allotted.

Noah was standing in the center aisle between the rows of chairs, with his arms crossed, waiting for the proceedings to begin, listening to a conversation between George Farnum and a group of others. The subject, as usual, was the Indian Treaty and the recent news that Chiefs Sitting Bull and Crazy Horse refused to comply with it. "Spotted Tail promised the commissioners that he would be answerable for Crazy Horse making peace, but he says Sitting Bull has a bad heart and that no one could answer for him."

"But the treaty's already signed. The Black Hills belong to the United States now."

"That won't stop Sitting Bull. We took his last sacred lands."

"Then it's our duty to impress upon the money centers of the East the value of the gold coming out of these hills. Let them put pressure on the federal government and demand military protection for the Hills. I for one still worry about—"

Noah glanced idly down the aisle and lost the drift of the conversation.

Sarah Merritt was advancing toward the group, her notebook pressed to her ribs.

When their eyes met, his arms uncrossed and her footsteps faltered. Her gaze shifted briefly to his new Stetson as she continued toward the knot of men. "Excuse me, gentlemen," she said, passing within inches of Noah's chest on her way toward the front of the auditorium.

She took a seat in the second row next to a miner whose name he couldn't remember. The miner looked up and leaped to his feet as she nodded to him, then the man resumed his chair and sat gawking at her profile. Noah watched the back of her head as she opened her notebook, got out a pen and ink, donned her spectacles and sat still as a stork, waiting. She was dressed in the same fusty brown suit as always. Her hair was pinched into a tiny knot that stuck out no farther than a nose on the back of her head. A tight, prissy hairdo for a tight, prissy woman. Glancing around the theater, he noted with acerbity the majority of the men ogling her as if she were a single mouse in a roomful of cats.

When the proceedings commenced, he took his place at a table up front with the mayor, the aldermen and the town clerk, Craven Lee, who also acted as ex-officio treasurer. George Farnum called the meeting to order and business began. Craven reported the election results, including the establishment of this very council and the town ordinances. Next came his treasury report, then Noah stood to deliver his report on what new licenses had been issued, including that to Sarah Merritt for the operation of the town's first newspaper. He avoided looking at her while reading his chicken-scratching, glancing her way only briefly as he resumed his seat. She sat correctly, spectacles downcast, taking notes.

After that, Noah sprawled back in his chair with his shoulders slanted and one forearm on the tabletop, trying to ignore her.

An issue was raised by the floor: the possibility of converting valuable cross streets into city lots. It was voted down.

A chimney rule was voted in: all future chimneys built within the city limits of Deadwood, South Deadwood and Elizabethtown were to have walls no less than four inches thick of brick or stone, completely imbedded in lime mortar and plastered on the inside with a smooth coat of the same.

A burning rule took effect: no shavings, hay or other combustible matter were to be set afire in any street, alley or thoroughfare nearer than twenty feet from any building, unless by direct permission in writing from the town council.

A dispute arose over the fixing of license rates. The lawyers and butchers in town protested that theirs were too high and should be lowered, and that those of the lucrative saloons should be raised. The rates remained unchanged.

Farnum asked if there was any more business.

Sarah Merritt stood up, removing her spectacles. "Mr. Mayor, if you please . . ."

"Miss Merritt," Farnum allowed.

Sarah's blue eyes were bright with conviction as she began to speak. "During the week I've been here I've noticed several situations that bear rectifying. The first—and in my estimation, the most important—is the lack of a school. I've taken it upon myself to begin a census of the families in the gulch, and by my count there are twenty-two children of school age residing in the area. That is indubitably enough that their education should be of primary concern to all of us. Most of them were severed from institutions of formal education in the cities they left behind. Some of them are being tutored by their mothers, but not all the mothers are literate, which throws the burden—I say, responsibility—back on us, the general, taxpaying populace of this town. Add to those the six children still too young for school, plus the Robinsons' infant, the first one born here on the Fourth of July, over whose birth I'm given to understand there was much rejoicing—and you can see the present need for a school. The future bears consideration as well. The signing of the Indian Treaty has already prompted safe passage of the first stagecoach into Deadwood. It, and soon the telegraph, combined with the news about the Peace Treaty, will bring even greater numbers of families here. I propose that by next spring, when that influx regenerates, we should have a teacher hired and a school established.

"Secondly, there's the matter of the animal offal in the streets. Not only is it unsightly and odoriferous, it poses a health hazard. We all know where cholera comes from, don't we? Our standards of sanitation are sorely in need of improvement. This town should hire a street cleaner and hire him now.

"Thirdly—though admittedly of minor importance—we might consider putting up streetlamps and combining the jobs of street cleaner and lamplighter into one.

"Fourthly comes the issue of boardwalks. Obviously no thought was put into their uniformity. Some of the businesses have them and some don't. Main Street is aesthetically repugnant, to say nothing of inconvenient. To traverse it one is forced to either progress like a jackrabbit beside the businesses or resort to slogging through the offal down its center. In a town so dominated by males, this is no surprise. However, gentlemen, if you want to encourage ladies—with their heel-length hems—to live here, I suggest you consider remedying this situation. To this effect, I propose passing an ordinance that not only makes boardwalks mandatory, but standardizes their height.

"Next I approach the obvious need for a suitable jail. The lockup you currently use is appalling. You have blacksmiths in this town. Put them to use building bars and appropriate whatever funds are necessary for the construction of a decent jail. Even a criminal deserves light and air.

"Lastly—and little thought is necessary for all of us to agree on this— we need a church. I understand your feeling that it will be difficult to woo another minister out here after the unfortunate slaying of Preacher Smith in August, but it is imperative that we try, and that when and if we get one, we have land and means set aside for the building of a church. We might consider constructing one building to temporarily serve as both church and school.

"That's all for now, gentlemen. I thank you for listening."

Miss Sarah Merritt calmly took her seat, hooked her glasses behind her ears and resumed her note-taking, presumably covering the issues she had just raised. The members of the city council exchanged glances, dumbfounded by such articulate rhetoric coming from the only female in the room. In the gallery, necks were stretched so men could get a better view of the woman up front. The miner next to Sarah puffed up with reflected importance, just sitting next to her. Noah took a good gander at her himself, as amazed as the rest of his constituents.

George Farnum broke the spell by chuckling and rubbing the back of his neck. "Well now, Miss Merritt, that's quite a bit of fat to chew."

She raised her eyes. "Yes, it is, Mr. Mayor."

"And we've got only so much money to work with."

"But we live in the richest pocket of land in America. I've heard that when news arrived here about the Peace Treaty being signed, miners rejoiced by scattering gold dust promiscuously in the very streets."

"That's true, but most of them are single men without families. They'd undoubtedly raise objections to being tithed for the building of a school. The land alone is going to come dear."

"Ask one of your wealthier property owners to donate it, then organize a school raising. Better yet, I'll organize the school raising. It will be easy for me since I have the newspaper at my disposal, and since I've already done the school census and know which families would be most likely to donate their time and muscle for the benefit of their children."

"That's very generous of you. And the land—do you have a solution as to where to get the land?"

"I've only been a resident of Deadwood for one week. No, I don't. But I know education is paramount. It *should* not and *can*not be delayed."

It was decided the issues would be thrown open for public discussion at the next town meeting, and that the board would announce this in the *Chronicle*. Also, it was voted that the minutes of each town meeting be reported in the *Chronicle* in the issue immediately following such meetings.

When the council meeting adjourned, Sarah became surrounded by men. They swarmed around her like flies around a raw steak. Miners and business owners; clean, dirty, old, young, the more-favored and the less: none, it seemed, were unsusceptible to the fact that she was dressed in skirts. The crowd included Teddy Ruckner, Dutch Van Aark, Doc Turley, Ben Winters, who owned the hotel where she resided, Andy Tatum and Elias Pinkney, who nudged his way through the press and appropriated her hand with an unmistakable air of possession.

Noah observed with a rancorous eye, then left his chair up front and made his way down the crowded aisle. As he eased through the knot of men around Sarah she looked up. Their eyes met. He gave a curt nod, she returned it and he moved on.

To Noah's intense dismay he found himself thinking of her in bed that night, the way he'd last seen her, surrounded by all those men, who fawned over her like besotted pups. Men could be such fools when faced with a woman shortage. Why, hell, she was about as curvy as a twelve-year-old boy, and she wasn't even pretty. Her face was too long and her nose too thin. Those spectacles made her appear bookish, and there was something distinctly off-putting about looking a woman in the eyes at the same height as your own.

She had good eyes, though. When she took those glasses off and set those bright blue eyes on you, you felt it clear to your toenails.

And Ma had one thing right. Sarah Merritt was bright. And gutsy to boot. How many women would attend a city council meeting, much less stand up before a roomful of aldermen and bombard them with criticism on their town, then offer suggestions for its improvement? Certainly the editor of any town newspaper had the power and the means to become a leader. But for a woman to do so . . .

Her temerity startled him.

The following morning dawned gloomy and cold. Noah awakened, peered at the window and drew the covers up tightly beneath his chin. He heard the clang of the iron range below as Mrs. Roundtree built a fire. From an adjacent room came the sound of snoring and he stayed a while longer in his warm cocoon.

Now why in the Sam Hell was he thinking of Sarah Merritt again?

He put her from his mind, sat up and stretched, donned his trousers and boots and made the trip outside. Back in his room, he washed and shaved with icy water—so icy that it drew his belly nearly to his backbone. He wet his hair, parted it on the side and combed it back uselessly. It seemed to have a will of its own. By the time it dried it would be sprigging up all around his hatline.

The smell of frying meat and boiling coffee drifted up from below and the house grew warmer. Footsteps sounded in the hall and down the stairs. Noah donned a red flannel shirt, a black leather vest, pinned on his star, left his gunbelt hanging on the back of a chair, and went down to breakfast.

Two steps into the dining room he came to a dead halt.

Sarah Merritt was seated at the table, taking a bite out of a biscuit.

Their eyes collided and her hand lowered. Slowly. Around her the other boarders stopped eating. She stared at Noah for several seconds, swallowed, then wiped her lips with a napkin.

"Well . . ." He continued toward the table. "This is a surprise. Good morning, everyone."

"Good morning," they chorused—all but Sarah Merritt. He seated himself in his usual chair, directly across from hers, and reached for an oval platter of meat. Only then did Sarah echo, quietly, "Good morning."

Mrs. Roundtree swept in from the kitchen—a buxom, red-faced woman with a mole the size of a watermelon seed on her right cheek. She set a bowl of fried potatoes on the table. "I believe you two know each other."

"Yes," Noah replied. "We've met."

Sarah found her voice. "You live here?"

"Ever since Loretta opened for business."

Loretta filled Noah's cup from a blue granite coffeepot. "Miss Merritt moved in yesterday."

"What happened to McCooley?" Noah asked, glancing up while the coffee gurgled into his cup. Yesterday morning a tinsmith named McCooley had been sitting in Sarah's chair eating his breakfast.

"Got lonesome for his family and went back to Arkansas. I thought it'd be nice to have some female company around this place, so I told Miss Merritt she could have the room."

Noah got himself busy spreading jam on a biscuit, cutting his meat.

Tom Taft, at Noah's left, said, "We were just talking about the play at the Langrishe. Miss Merritt says it's good."

"You stayed for it?" Noah asked her, making an effort for propriety's sake at being civil.

She picked up his lead and answered, civilly, too, "Yes. I thought I would write a review of it for my next edition of the paper, let the outside world know we do have a touch of culture here in Deadwood. Jack Langrishe's troupe is, after all, one of the most renowned and respected in America. I found *Flies in the Weed* very well done. Have you seen it, Mr. Campbell?"

"Yes, I have." He glanced up and found her face as red as his own felt. "What did you think of it?"

"I liked it, too."

"Well, at last we find something upon which we can agree."

Their eyes met again while he chewed and swallowed a mouthful of food.

"Maybe more than one thing," he mused.

"Have we agreed on something else?"

"The points you raised last night at the city council meeting. I couldn't agree more. Thank you for putting in a word about the need for a jail."

"There's no need to thank me. It's the truth."

"You were very convincing."

"I should be, don't you think? I have firsthand knowledge." She cocked her left eyebrow.

"I wouldn't be at all surprised to see you get every improvement you asked for."

"It's been true throughout history that wherever men go first, they reface. Then the women come along and refine."

Once again he was impressed by her eloquence.

"You really intend to act as organizer for a school raising?"

"Absolutely. I thought I'd begin by writing an editorial about the need for a schoolhouse, and for land to build it on. If nothing turns up, I have an idea of whom to solicit for a land donation."

"Busy, busy," he said wryly, lifting his coffee cup.

"But without the board approving the funds to pay a teacher it will all be useless."

"I'd guess a teacher's salary would be—what? Five dollars a day and found?"

"Seven. We'd want a good one."

"Seven I should think we could manage. Fines alone bring in good revenue, plus licenses."

"Yes, I know about both from personal experience."

To Noah's surprise a faint glow of mischief shone in Sarah Merritt's eyes. Without her glasses, they glinted like polished sapphires. The meal continued while they talked of the other reforms—the street cleaner, lamps and lamplighter, the boardwalks. By the time breakfast ended,

Noah realized they had dominated the conversation to the exclusion of the other men at the table. Pushing back his chair, he admitted with some amazement that he'd conversed with Sarah Merritt for a full thirty minutes and had come very close to enjoying every one of them.

Chapter 7

♣

Sarah's second issue of the *Chronicle* expanded to two pages. The first included the headlines: EDITOR OF *CHRONICLE* JAILED AND FINED; COMPLETE LAW LIBRARY EXPECTED IN DEADWOOD SOON; CAPITAL NEEDED TO BUILD STAMP MILLS; PROSPECT GOOD ON BEAVER, BEAR, SAND CREEKS; WILD GAME SCARCE AS BUFFALO, ELK, DEER RETREAT WESTWARD; BREWERY OPEN IN ELIZABETHTOWN; *DUTCH LOVERS* OPENING AT BELLA UNION THEATER; LANGRISHE TROUPE'S *FLIES IN THE WEED* CRISPLY AMUSING.

Elias Pinkney's ad ran on the second page along with Sarah's report on the city council meeting and an editorial about the need for a school. In it she suggested that if even a small portion of the gold funneling into the brothels of the badlands was channeled instead into a church/school fund, the building could be up in no time. She requested that all children be officially registered at the newspaper office so an accurate census could be obtained.

The *Chronicle* office got busier. Merchants came in to place ads. Mothers came in to register children. Miners came in to report their prospect. Everyone came to buy copies of the paper itself.

October made an angry entrance. One unseasonably bitter, snowy day early in the month, Sarah was leaving the building as a rider on a piebald horse drew abreast of her steps. The stranger drew rein and sat trembling, teetering low over the horse's neck.

"A doctor . . . ma'am . . . I need a doctor."

"We have seven of them. Up the street—Rathburn and Allen have tents on your left. Bangs and Dawson are in log buildings on your right, farther up. Henry Kice is in a tent around the corner on your right." She didn't bother naming the other two, who'd take more time to reach. "Can you make it, sir?" He appeared on the verge of tumbling from his mount.

"Thank you," he mumbled and, bobbing over his saddlehorn, urged his horse on.

She watched him turn right toward Henry Kice's.

Later that day she went to Kice's herself, wondering if the stranger had suffered a gunshot wound, and if so, under what circumstances. A stagecoach robbery perhaps?

Henry Kice said, "No, he's just a gambler from Cheyenne, name of Cramed. Got a bad case of lung congestion complicated by poison ivy. Undoubtedly the sudden change of weather caught him on horseback between Cheyenne and here and he caught a dilly of a cold. I ordered him to bed. I think he checked into the Custer Hotel."

Three days later Cramed's cold and poison ivy were both worse. A week after that, five additional cases of "poison ivy" were reported in town, three of them by residents of the Custer.

Sarah's headline asked, IS POISON IVY CONTAGIOUS?

Then Cramed died.

Sarah decided it was time somebody took some action. She stopped in the marshal's office one morning after Josh came to work and reported that his sister Lettie had fallen ill overnight. Campbell was at the rear of his office, speaking with a burly, bearded man Sarah recognized as Frank Gilpin, a local blacksmith. (It appeared the town was about to get a jail.)

Campbell looked over his shoulder when Sarah closed the door. He and Gilpin turned. Gilpin smiled and doffed his misshapen cap. Campbell came forward.

"Scouting for news this morning?" he asked.

"Could I talk to you when you're free, Marshal?"

"Of course. You know Frank Gilpin?"

Gilpin joined them, bringing the smell of body odor and a jovial if disjointed greeting.

"The young lady writes the newspaper, yes. Hello, so good to see you. We read about the jail, what you write, and Noah has me here. We see how many bars he needs and if these stingy miners got enough gold to pay for them, yes?"

She smiled and nodded, unsure of what she was concurring with.

"I go, leave you two to talk. Noah, you tell me yes or no, I make the bars in three, four days." Gilpin added something in a foreign language— presumably a farewell—and left.

"So you'll get your jail soon?" Sarah remarked.

"Hopefully after the November town meeting. Just finding out what it'll cost. Is that what brought you in here?"

"No. Another matter entirely. Tell me, Marshal, what do you know about smallpox?"

"Smallpox?" He frowned. "Why?"

"Because I'm going to write an editorial and I don't want to start any panics the law would frown upon. One run-in with you was enough."

"The poison ivy?" he asked.

"Exactly. Lettie Dawkins just broke out, plus five others, and Henry Kice is asking us to believe it's poison ivy. Rathburn, meanwhile, is claiming one of the other cases is the great pox."

"Syphilis?"

She nodded. "Could it be that Kice made the wrong diagnosis and is afraid to say so?"

"And Rathburn too?"

They considered silently awhile.

"What are the chances of two of them being wrong?" Campbell asked.

"I don't know. I only know poison ivy isn't contagious, and a young girl like Lettie wouldn't have syphilis. So what is it?"

"You think we have the start of an epidemic?"

"I've done some questioning. All the cases have started the same—three days of fever followed by a generalized eruption. One death already."

"Smallpox . . ." Campbell breathed and ran a hand over his curly hair.

"It might not be, but suppose it is. The entire gulch would already have been exposed."

"What do you suggest?"

"That every qualified doctor in the diggings be called upon to consult together and present a determination about the nature of the disease. If the consensus is smallpox, we must send for vaccine points immediately, by Pony Express, and build a pesthouse for the afflicted. Also we must arrange for some sort of isolation shelters for those who've already been exposed but haven't broken out yet."

"Where would we get the money?"

"The funds would have to be solicited from the citizens, and anyone who is financially able to contribute but declines would have his name published in the newspaper. I'll need your permission, of course, before I do such a thing."

"What is the incubation period of smallpox?"

"Ten to sixteen days."

"How long ago did Cramed come to town?"

"Thirteen days."

"Have you talked to anyone else about this?"

"No."

"George Farnum should know." Campbell broke for the coat pegs on the wall. "I'll tell him and call on the doctors immediately. Don't print anything until one of us gets back to you."

It was after five P.M. when Campbell entered the *Chronicle* office with a drawn look about his mouth. Patrick was picking through the wood engravings, searching for a border design, and Josh was sweeping around the woodbox at the rear. Sarah turned at the sound of the door opening and left her chair immediately. She met Campbell some distance from the others where they could speak without being heard.

"It's virulent smallpox," he said in an undertone.

A skitter of apprehension zipped through her. She removed her spectacles, pushed a thumb and forefinger against her closed eyes and whispered, "Lord, have mercy."

"I've sent a rider to the telegraph crew. The lines are up about halfway between here and Hill City so the message will go out yet tonight. If there are vaccine points in Cheyenne we'll be in luck. If not . . ." He shrugged. "We'll just have to wait and see."

"We'll need quarantine cards."

"Can you print them?"

"Of course. I'll have Patrick typeset them right away. And some kind of notice to call the miners in for inoculation as soon as the points arrive. What about the infirmary?"

"George has called an emergency meeting of the council for tonight. He asked if you'd attend."

"Absolutely."

"Eight o'clock at the Number Ten Saloon. Both the Langrishe and the Bella Union have early shows scheduled."

"I'll be there."

"Thanks." He took one step away and stopped. "Oh, and keep Josh here tonight."

"I'd already thought of that."

For a moment their gazes held, grave with responsibility and worry. In that instant Sarah felt an accord with Campbell, tied as they were by this momentous discovery. She thought he was going to offer something reassuring. Instead he said, "I'll see you later," and strode toward the door.

Patrick and Josh had quit working, sensing something amiss.

"What's wrong?" Josh asked.

"I'll need you both a while longer tonight."

"What is it?" Patrick said.

"It's very bad news, I'm afraid. The doctors have determined that we have smallpox in the gulch."

"Smallpox . . ." Josh repeated. He glanced toward home, back at Sarah. "You mean Lettie?"

"I'm afraid so, Josh."

He headed for the coat tree, but she caught his shoulder. "No, Josh. You'll stay here tonight."

"I gotta go home. If Lettie's sick she—"

"No. The safest place for you is away from there. I'll speak to Mrs. Roundtree and see if you can sleep on the settee in her parlor until the vaccine points arrive. The marshal has sent for them. Besides, I'll need you tonight . . ." She looked to Bradigan. "You too, Patrick. We'll need to print quarantine cards and notices about the inoculations. You'll stay, won't you?"

Patrick simply bowed.

"But my mother . . ." Josh said worriedly.

"I'll let her know. Now let's get busy."

When Sarah left the newspaper office the press was running. She went to Emma's and spoke to her from the ground below the kitchen window. Emma's face was wreathed with worry for her stricken daughter. Sarah could not help picturing Lettie, whose whole life lay before her, the girl's beautiful face with its flawless skin, suddenly vulnerable to scars, at the very least.

The two women lingered after the most important messages had been imparted, each wishing to go to the other and exchange a hug of comfort. Instead they stood separated by the height of a building.

"She'll be all right, Emma. I know she will." With her head tipped back, Sarah sent her friend a look of commiseration.

"Say a prayer, Sarah," Emma said plaintively.

"I will. And I'll take good care of Josh."

With a lump in her throat Sarah walked away.

At eight o'clock the emergency meeting convened in the Number Ten Saloon. Word had spread and the saloon was filled. All the members of the town council were present as well as the seven doctors from Deadwood and two others from the adjacent camps of Lead and Elizabethtown, which fell under the jurisdiction of the Deadwood City Council. Businessmen and interested parties had shown up also.

Before the meeting adjourned, the council had officially set up the Board of Health of the City of Deadwood, and they were given jurisdiction over all decisions regarding the control and treatment of the smallpox epidemic. Both Sarah and Noah agreed to sit on the board along with doctors from all three towns, the mayor and two leading businessmen. Before they left the saloon the groundwork was laid for the battle ahead.

A pesthouse would be built in Spruce Gulch, where all the afflicted would be taken. (Reaching this decision took three of the four hours' meeting time while various factions argued about where the pesthouse should be, nobody wanting it in *their* vicinity.) The lumber for it would be appropriated from the sawmills, which would be given official notice by the marshal of the board's priority status. All miners, merchants and businessmen able to contribute funds for the building of the shelter would be ordered to do so, contributions to be made to the town treasurer, shirkers to be openly listed in the *Deadwood Chronicle*. Volunteers would be sought to put up the building as well as quickly constructed shelters of brush and hide for the internment of the exposed. Volunteers would also be sought to nurse the sick. Dawkins' Bakery and the Custer Hotel would be placed under quarantine until the board lifted it. The brothels of Deadwood would be closed (this to be enforced by the marshal) until all their residents could receive the vaccine and the general quarantine was lifted. A special issue of the *Chronicle* was to be printed the following day to announce these decisions.

By the time the meeting adjourned it was past midnight. Noah and Sarah, both weary, headed for Mrs. Roundtree's together. The town was oddly quiet, even the saloons and gambling houses, as if in respectful acknowledgment of the disastrous news. The theaters had closed and their lanterns had been extinguished. The hitching rails were nearly empty. The sky wore a milky blanket of clouds that held out all starshine and moonlight. Main Street wore a crust of frost on its rutted wagontracks. Beneath, it was soft from the day's commerce. A wind chased down the ravine, bringing the distant call and answer of two owls, and off to their right the creek rustled.

They climbed the path to Mrs. Roundtree's with heavy footsteps, up the crude zigzagging steps to one landing, then another, and finally to the front door. Noah opened it and let Sarah enter before him. In the parlor a small oil lamp burned. Josh was asleep on the settee, half on his belly, with one leg cocked. A brown blanket had slipped toward the floor.

They studied him awhile in silence, reminded again that his loved ones were some of those most threatened.

"Poor Josh," Sarah said softly.

"Yeah. Who knows what'll happen."

"Don't say that, Noah." She bent to pull the blanket over the boy's shoulders. "I've come to love his family, especially Emma."

When she turned she found him watching her with a strange look on his shadowed face. She had called him Noah without realizing it. The look fled and he said, "Don't worry. They'll be fine."

"They're such good people."

"Yes, they are."

Another silence while their antipathy slipped another cog.

"You go up first," he said. "I'll turn off the lantern."

She was halfway up the stairs when the light went out behind her. In the blackness she faltered, reached out for the wall and ran her hand along it for guidance. She heard his footsteps behind her, tiptoeing on the creaky wooden steps.

She stopped. Behind her, so did he.

"Mr. Campbell?" she whispered.

"Yes?"

"Do you pray?"

Silence . . . then, "Sometimes."

Silence again before she whispered, "Tonight would be a good time."

The thought settled around them. Somewhere the house cracked and she continued up the stairs with him at her heels. Her door came first, on the left. She located the knob and turned it, then herself . . . to face him.

"Good night," she whispered.

It was as black as the earth around a tree root. She had a sense of Noah Campbell close enough to touch, were she to reach out. In the absolute lightlessness she caught the smell of leather from his vest and a hint of coal smoke from the extinguished lantern.

"Good night," he whispered. "See you in the morning."

The last thing she heard was his hand rubbing along the wall, guiding him to his door, which opened and closed.

The whorehouse looked different in broad daylight. Noah had never been here in the morning before. When Flossie let him in, the light from the open door flashed across the dim parlor, then disappeared, leaving them in gloom. He followed Flossie through the room, through the smell of last night's cigar smoke and whiskey, past the nude who smiled down from the murky shadows, past the bathing room with its strong stink of sulfur and saturated wood, to a room on the left where Rose Hossiter was sprawled on a dingy settee, snoring.

Flossie passed a cluttered desk and snapped up a green windowshade. Sun exploded into the room.

"What the hell . . ." Rose shielded her eyes and rolled like a walrus, trying to see behind her. "What the goddamn hell you doin', Flossie!" She scooped up a whiskey glass from the floor and flung it at the Indian woman. It crashed against the desk. "Get out!"

"Marshal's here," the Indian woman said and left the room.

Rose's unfocused eyes found the man at the door. "Marshal . . ." She struggled to rise. Her elbow caught the sheeny pink fabric of her robe and dragged it down, exposing one fleshy breast. She scraped it into place with a rubbery movement. The kohl she'd applied last night had taken a journey down her face. Her brassy hair listed in a scraggly knot behind one ear. She dished it to her skull with two pathetic pats but it sagged again and a hairpin bounced to her shoulder. Her mouth formed a wavery line as she smiled.

"Little early in the morning, isn't it?"

"Sorry to wake you, Rose."

She yawned and the smell of her fetid breath filtered across the room. "What time is it?"

"Ten-thirty."

She grunted and sat up, dropping her wide, bare feet to the floor. "Middle of the night," she said and bent forward toward an oval table. Her robe gaped to her waist as she reached for a skinny cigar and lit it with a stick match. Smoke poured from her nostrils and mouth as she sat back and said, "Well . . . haven't seen you around here in a while."

He made no reply.

"Some problem, Marshal?"

" 'Fraid so. I'm going to have to shut you down for a while."

"Shut me d——!" In the middle of the word she started hacking. The sound cracked in her throat twice. She had a disgusting way of sticking her tongue out when she coughed. Finally she got control.

"What do you mean, shut me down?"

"You and all the others along here. We have five cases of smallpox in town."

Rose got to her feet, closing her robe. "What the hell do I care about smallpox?"

"With the business you run, you'd better care."

"Now, listen, Marshal, you know we put our customers through a carbolic bath. Probably keep 'em from getting the damn pox."

"You know as well as I do that won't kill smallpox."

"Aw, come on, Marshal, have a heart."

"Can't," he said. "The town council made the rule and I've got to enforce it. I've got to quarantine you, Rose."

"For how long?"

"Couple of weeks, probably."

"A couple of weeks! And what we supposed to live on for a couple of weeks?"

"Now, Rose, I've been in here enough to know how much gold comes through that door each night. You could shut down for a couple of months and not feel it."

She studied him awhile, put down her cigar in an ashtray and sidled across the room to him. "Tell you what, Marshal." She took him by his lapels. "I'll make you a real sweet deal. You shut the others down and hang your quarantine sign out front, but leave my back door open. I'll cut you in for ten percent of the take for as long as I'm open exclusively."

He removed her hands from his jacket.

"I can't do that, Rose. We're trying to prevent an epidemic here."

She advanced again, one hand on a hip. "I'll throw in anything on the menu, no charge—anything you want and as much of it as you want for the duration. How about that?"

"Rose . . ." He held up both palms.

"Who's your pick? Eve? You always took a shine to Eve."

"I don't want Eve. I don't—"

"One of the Frenchies then. How about Ember? Ember ever had her mouth on you, Marshal?"

"I don't want any of them."

"I'd come out of retirement myself. Haven't been with a man for a while but I haven't forgotten what you fellas like. I could do you good, Marshal." She reached for his crotch.

He caught her wrist in a steel grip. His stomach lurched.

"No deals, Rose. Tell your girls as of now you're shut down."

"You're a handsome man, Noah . . ." She reached to caress his face with her free hand. His head jerked back. Their eyes locked while Rose's hand froze, halfway to its destination. She pulled free of his grip and yanked her bodice in place. Her expression turned contemptuous. "All right—get out of here, you sonofabitch, and take your fucking star with you."

She spun and retrieved her cigar. When he left the room she was blowing smoke toward the ceiling.

Outside, he sucked the clean air and felt as though he needed a carbolic bath himself. All the while he nailed the quarantine sign to her door his mind kept returning to that room and the sight of her rolling up from sleep looking like a bad case of winterkill; her callousness and dissipation, the stench of her, her pathetic attempt to appear seductive, her soulless eyes when he'd recoiled.

He shuddered once, as if she'd reached him.

That night at supper he was already seated when Sarah Merritt entered the dining room. She took her place across from Noah. She said hello to everyone else, finally to him . . . quick, quiet, with scarcely an encounter of eyes. Her face was clean. Her hair was wet on the sides, drawn back into its tidy, tiny twist. On either side of a center part a shallow natural wave nudged her forehead. Her blouse was gray with a white standup collar and sleeves with puffy tops and tight white cuffs.

Looking at her seemed to remove the sullied feeling he'd worn since morning.

The vaccine points came in by Pony Express from Sidney, Nebraska, in time to ward off a full-scale epidemic. Nevertheless, Sarah and Noah had two of the hardest weeks of their lives. She, with a paper to run, also acted as organizer for the inoculation clinic and the volunteer nurses. He, with the law to maintain, acted as organizer for the volunteer carpenters and tried to keep the whorehouses under quarantine. Two more people died—a miner known as Bean Belly Kelly and a Kentuckian named Yarnell whose occupation remained uncertain. They were buried in Mt. Moriah Cemetery near Preacher Smith and Bill Hickok.

Sarah felt obliged to attend their funerals. Without a preacher in town, it fell to the general public to give the men a proper send-off with a decent show of mourners. On the afternoon of Yarnell's burial, however, she was working at the pesthouse herself and missed the ceremony. She went up later with a crepe-paper rose to pay her respects.

It was peaceful as she climbed the steep incline to the cemetery that hung on the mountainside southeast of town. The earth was snowy and the smell of the pines keen. Their trunks—rusty red and scaly—stood straight as compass needles in the windless, overcast day. A bluejay scolded and left a bough bobbing. A porcupine waddled up the path before her. A squirrel, alerted, stopped munching a pinecone and waited as she passed.

She reached the top of the incline and stopped.

There were the gravestones, and sitting beside one, with his head hanging and a whiskey bottle wavering on one knee, was a man. He was dressed in dirty buckskin. His blond hair hung in unkempt ribbons, the same dull mushroom color as the fringes on his jacket. It covered his face while he sat in sodden slumber, one leg outstretched, the other forming a triangle against the earth. The snow beneath him had melted as if he'd been there for some time.

Sarah approached silently. Passed him. Read the grave marker—William Butler Hickok—and proceeded to the fresh mound beyond, where she laid her paper rose. After a moment of reverence she returned the way she'd come, circling wide to leave the drunk undisturbed. But a twig snapped as she passed and he lifted his head.

The drunk was a woman.

The bottle teetered on her knee as she stared at Sarah.

"Guess I fell asleep," she mumbled.

"I'm sorry I disturbed you."

"S'all right. I was jss . . ." Her words trailed away and she stared blearily at Sarah's skirt. In time she lifted her chin and asked, "You know me?"

"You're Miss Cannary."

"S'right. You know what they call me?"

"Calamity."

"S'right." She sat awhile, weaving, then remembered her manners.

"Want a drink?" She lifted the bottle.

"No, thank you."

"I'll have one myself then." A strand of hair got caught between her lips and the bottle. She strained the liquor through it, then smeared the whiskey off her lips with the back of a hand.

"You come fer the funeral?"

"No."

"You know 'im?" She gestured with the bottle toward Yarnell's grave.

"No."

"Me neither. I come to see Bill." She leaned forward from the waist and peered at Sarah. "You know Bill?"

"No, I'm sorry, I didn't."

She pointed with the mouth of the bottle at the stone behind her. "This here's Bill." She pivoted around, dragging her legs in the mud to drape a hand on Hickok's headstone. "Say h'lo to the lady, Bill. A real lady, not a whore like me."

Sarah stood transfixed, feeling like an intruder.

Jane leaned her face against the stone, closed her eyes and gave a great sigh. "He left me. Promised to marry me but he never did. Hell, I could ride and shoot as good as him 'n' skin mules 'n' drink any man under the table . . . but it wasn't good enough for him . . ." Tears seeped from her eyes and she curled herself to the gravestone. "Why'd you leave me, Bill . . . God, why din't you face that door . . . you always faced the door. . . ." Her pitiful weeping moved Sarah. She went to the woman and knelt, taking her arms.

"Miss Cannary, please . . . you'd better get up. Let me help you."

Jane drew her head up heavily, sniffed, and scraped the edge of her hand beneath her nose.

" 'Ass all right. I'm jss an old drunk. Leave me alone."

"You've been sitting on the ground. You're all wet. Please, let me help you up."

Jane lifted bleary eyes. "What you wanna help me for?"

Because the sight of you breaks my heart, sitting here grieving against your lover's headstone.

"It's time to go down now. You need dry clothes."

Sarah helped Jane to her feet and held her upright until she caught her balance. When she stood erect, Sarah gently took the bottle from her hands. "Here, let's leave that."

"Yeah, leave it fer Bill . . . he liked his whiskey neat."

Sarah hid the bottle behind Hickok's headstone and returned to take Jane's arm. As they started down the hill Jane waved back over her shoulder and said, "See y' around, Bill. Save me a place."

The downhill grade was steep. Sometimes Jane stumbled and Sarah would reach out to steady her. On Main Street they paused before the newspaper office.

"I have to go in here," Sarah said. "Do you have a place to go?"

"Yeah . . . I got me a place . . ." Jane gestured up the gulch as she stood weaving.

"Wait here," Sarah said. "Will you wait?"

Jane nodded as if her chin were weighted.

Sarah went into the *Chronicle* office and came back out with a packet containing some gold dust.

"Go take a hot bath," she said, handing it to Jane. "Then get yourself a good meal. Will you do that?"

Jane nodded and stumbled up the street. Sarah hurriedly returned to the *Chronicle* office, unwilling to watch Jane to learn if she used the gold for a bath and supper or a saloon.

The following day news reached Sarah that Calamity Jane showed up at the pesthouse, clean and sober, and worked there helping the sick until well past dark. From then until the quarantine was lifted the story was the same—Calamity Jane, who dressed in buckskins, rode like an Indian, swore a blue streak and drank like a man, proved herself a woman of kind and generous nature by giving the tenderest of care to the sick and afflicted.

Though Sarah occasionally encountered her, Jane would never speak. She would nod, and her eyes would linger warmly, but her silence seemed to say, you're a lady, I'll keep my distance.

A headline appeared in the *Deadwood Chronicle* when they knew the smallpox had been licked. MARTHA JANE CANNARY SELFLESSLY HELPS THE SICK.

Chapter 8

The lifting of the quarantine brought great joy to Deadwood. The brothels reopened, relieving some of the pressures that had led to increased belligerence among the men. Noah was called upon to break up fewer saloon fights. True Blevins returned from the Spearfish, collected his oxen and headed toward Cheyenne. The Dawkins family was reunited, grateful to have Josh back beneath their roof, even more grateful that Lettie had survived her ordeal with smallpox, though it appeared her face would bear several scars. Sarah returned to being a full-time newspaper publisher, and Calamity Jane returned to the saloons.

The telegraph brought word that Rutherford B. Hayes and William A. Wheeler had been elected president and vice-president, and it sent word that the quarantine of Deadwood had been lifted. Traffic resumed, bringing a marked increase in freight, the ox trains carrying in a stout supply of winter stores for the remote area before the big snows fell.

The women of Deadwood were particularly thrilled when a headline in the *Chronicle* announced the first mercantile items for them: bolts of cloth, spools of ribbon and even shoes of a smaller size. The article went on to note that future generations might diary the domestication of the town by the change in its incoming freight: seeds for spring, along with a barrel of tulip bulbs, which created a stir. Sarah's plaster arrived—much more than she had ordered, brought by two brothers named Hintson, a pair of plasterers with the perspicacity to realize that the first plastered building would signal a chain reaction and their business would flourish. There came a selection of framed pictures and broadloom rugs to complement those first white rooms, factory-made furniture, and a single umbrella of a color other than black. It was pistachio green with white stripes, and stopped every woman who passed the window of Tatum's Store.

But of all the freight that arrived, none was looked upon as a more certain sign of domestication than the load of forty housecats. They arrived in crates aboard a spring wagon, brought in by a speculator from Cheyenne who, within twenty-four hours of his arrival, sold the entire load at the preposterous price of $25 per head.

Though Sarah had no opportunity to announce the arrival of the felines before they were snapped up, she did, however, manage to buy one of them herself. It was a short-haired white female with one blue eye and one green. From the moment she picked it up—a placid, full-grown, overtly affectionate creature—she fell in love with it. The cat squinted, nuzzled and bumped the bottom of Sarah's chin with the top of its head, inviting attention. Sarah scratched its neck and it began purring.

"Hi, puss," she murmured. "You look just like old Ruler." Ruler was the cat she and Addie had grown up with, so named because they had all agreed he'd ruled the roost. "You like that scratching, huh?"

Much as she would have loved to keep the cat herself, she took it to the office only temporarily, where it immediately stopped the presses. Josh and Patrick left their work to take turns holding and scratching the new arrival, examining its colorful eyes, then turning it loose to nose around the perimeter of the room, where it explored the base of the press and sniffed the oily ink containers. Eventually it jumped up on Sarah's desk chair, licked its shoulders a few times, curled its paws to the inside and rounded up like a plumped pillow.

Josh was entranced.

"We can *use* a mouser around here. What're you going to name it?"

"I'm not. I'm going to give it to my sister."

"Aww . . . really?"

"Really. She always loved cats, and I've noticed there are other pets around that place. There's even a green parrot."

"Gosh! Really?" Josh's eyes grew excited. "I'd like to see that!"

"No you don't, young man. I told you once before, you stay away from there. But you know cats. This one won't take any time at all before she'll have a family of her own, and I intend to tell Addie that we want the pick of the litter. You're right. We could use a hunter around here to keep the mice from eating the newsprint."

She set out for Addie's late that afternoon. It was a gray, glowering day with snow threatening again. Above the surrounding rock walls fat-cheeked clouds seemed to whistle and spit gusts of wind down the ravine. It lifted Sarah's coat hem and sent shivers up her spine as she hurried along with the cat tucked below her chin, inside her woolen coat, with only its white face protruding. Though at their November meeting the town council had approved the building of a jail and a church, they had voted down standardizing the boardwalks, so it was up and down, up and down, as Sarah walked along the shelter of the building walls. Head down, she was climbing the steps at the end of a section of walk when she bumped smack into a body going the opposite direction.

"Whoa! Careful there!" Two gloved hands closed over her coat sleeves, and she looked up into a face with a familiar auburn mustache. He was wearing his new brown Stetson and a sheepskin jacket that made him appear half again his normal girth.

"Marshal, I'm sorry. I wasn't looking where I was going."

He released her and grinned down at the cat. "What've you got there?" He reached out one thick-gloved finger that dwarfed the cat's head.

"I'm one of the lucky ones. I managed to get one."

"So I see." He attempted to scratch the cat's chin, but the animal was frantic and wide-eyed, squeezed as it was inside the coat.

"Look," Sarah told Noah, lifting the creature's head. "She's got one green eye and one blue eye. Isn't that odd?"

They inspected the cat for some moments. "Sometimes cats with two different-colored eyes are deaf," Noah told her.

"Really?"

"Mm-hmm. I remember one when I was a kid, belonged to an old man named Sandusky who had a candle shop. He used to kick the cat out of his way when it didn't hear him coming. Always made me want to kick old Sandusky back. So where you going, kitty?" he asked the cat.

"I'm taking her to Addie."

Standing close on the windy boardwalk, they finally allowed their eyes to meet. Sarah had one hand folded around the cat's head to keep it from leaping, while Noah's gloved finger remained at its nose.

"That's nice of you. I imagine you'd like it for yourself."

"We always had cats when we were children, and I think Addie misses them. She keeps a stuffed cat on the bed in her private room."

Looking into Noah Campbell's gray eyes, Sarah wondered if he still frequented Rose's, particularly if he still saw Addie. The idea of his doing so created a queer lump in her chest. It came so suddenly she hadn't time to reason why.

Her attention returned to the cat. "This one is the same color as our old pet, Ruler."

"She'll like that."

"I hope so. I hope she'll *accept* it. She still won't talk to me civilly, or ingratiate herself to me in any way, yet I think she's terribly lonely."

Noah had never imagined the prostitutes being lonely. They were brash and forward and lived in their cloister with each other for company, days, and no letup to the incoming company, nights. But of course they must be lonely. How blind of him not to realize it until Sarah Merritt pointed it out.

Before he could remark, she went on. "I'm her only sister, and in spite of her fallen state, we could be friends again if only she'd let me. It hurts very much, being shut out when all I want to do is help."

Noah studied the part in Sarah's hair, what little bit showed in front of the woolen scarf tied around her head; he studied her smooth forehead, her thick eyelashes and pretty blue eyes, her downturned face as she concentrated on the cat. She was so absolutely untarnished. By contrast, he recalled Rose the morning she'd tried to seduce him, with her hair sagging and her gown gaping, and her general look of dissipation. He hadn't been back to any of the brothels since that day, hadn't even wanted to go.

"Maybe she's ashamed of having you see her there."

"She doesn't act ashamed. She acts brazen."

"I'm sorry. I can't explain it. But I think she'll love the cat."

Two men came by. Sarah and Noah stepped aside to let them pass. When they were alone again, she returned her attention to the cat, resumed her scratching. "Mr. Campbell . . . ?" It was on the tip of her tongue to pose a question beyond all impertinence. It had been on her mind for some time to ask him if Addie had ever spoken to him about home, if she'd given any clue to what had driven her away. In the end Sarah could not muster the courage to inquire about anything that had passed between her sister and this man while they were customer and courtesan.

"Oh, nothing," she said. "I guess I'll have to figure out Addie for myself." Sarah looked up and snapped out of her pensive mood. "I see the hat fits." It was the first time since she'd given it to him that it had been mentioned. He never wore it to the table at the boardinghouse, but she hadn't seen him anywhere else without it. The rich brown felt was almost the same color as his auburn hair, which quirked up below the hatband at his temples. By now she was quite familiar with it.

"Yes, it does. It's a dandy hat—thank you." He felt silly for not having said that a month ago, but a month ago they weren't speaking.

"And your eye is all healed."

"Oh that . . ." He waved a hand in disregard.

"And your hearing? Was it bothered?"

He cupped an ear and shouted, "What?"

They both laughed, then fell still and a little amazed, watching the change in each others' eyes before their gazes parted.

"Well," she said, increasingly ill at ease, "I'd better be on my way. It's cold out here."

"Yes . . . see you tonight at supper." He touched his hat brim and they moved off in opposite directions.

Twenty feet up the boardwalk, Noah gave in to the impulse to turn around and look back at her. He stopped, turned and found her doing exactly the same thing—standing on the boardwalk looking back at him with the cat tucked beneath her chin.

For several seconds they stared. And grew conscious and self-conscious by turns.

Then, simultaneously, they spun and hurried off, wishing they had not turned around in the first place.

. . .

Sarah had not seen Addie since the outbreak of smallpox. She hoped that the ensuing weeks might have mollified Addie and her reception might be warmer. Standing in the hall outside Addie's room, Sarah unbuttoned her coat, perched the cat on one arm and knocked.

Addie called, "Who is it?"

"It's Sarah."

After a length of silence the door opened narrowly. "What do you want this time?" Addie was wearing the same dressing robe as the day she'd been collecting clothes from the line.

"I wanted to make sure you're all right."

"I am."

"I've brought you something."

Addie's eyes dropped to the cat and the hard lines of her face melted. "For me?" The door opened more.

"A fellow from Cheyenne brought a load of them in this afternoon and it was a mad scramble, but I managed to get one. Here . . ." Sarah held out the creature. "She's for you."

"Oh . . ." Addie reached out as if mesmerized.

"She rode here buttoned inside my coat, so she's probably a little skittish right now."

"Ohhh, look at you . . ." Addie cooed to the cat, taking it beneath its front legs and drawing it near her body. "You look just like old Ruler." She turned, taking the cat inside. Sarah followed uncertainly, remaining near the open door. Addie cuddled the cat, settling it on her arm and dropping her face down to rub its head until the cat grew cautious and leaped onto the bed.

Addie followed, sitting on the edge of the mattress, stretching out a hand to entice the creature to come close and allow itself to be petted. When it did, she gathered it onto her lap, set to work giving its throat a two-handed workover.

"You came all the way from Cheyenne? Hey, we're going to take good care of you and keep you away from that nasty old parrot."

All of her antipathy had vanished. She spoke to the animal affectionately, even maternally. Looking on, Sarah glowed within. To see Addie with her veneer of antagonism finally dissolved had been Sarah's dearest hope.

"What's its name?" Addie asked, still lavishing attention on the beast.

"It hasn't got one that I know of."

"Maybe I'll call it Ruler."

"I was hoping you would." It was the first memento of the past Addie had allowed. Sarah inched into the room and stood near the foot of the bed a good distance from her sister. Though she wanted to sit down beside Addie, Sarah resisted the urge. Though she wanted to flop onto her stomach and lie side by side with Addie, admiring the cat, she refrained. She was wise enough to realize she could not force a return of affection; it would take time and nurturing to draw Addie from her indifference.

"It's a female, and I expect it'll have a litter someday. When it does, I wouldn't mind having one of her kittens to keep in the newspaper office."

For the first time since Sarah had presented her gift, Addie looked at her.

"You wanted Ruler for yourself, didn't you?"

"No. I bought her for you. But I took her over to the office to show the fellows, and Josh fell in love with her."

For a while their gazes held. The room seemed filled with tremulous feelings not unlike those preceding a first kiss—that moment of uncertainty and hope when two people poise on a brink that will forever change their sentimental climate.

"Who's Josh?" Addie finally inquired.

It was the first sign of interest Addie had shown in Sarah's doings. Encouraged by it, Sarah perched on the bed at the far end from her sister. Addie let her.

"Josh is a young boy who works for me. His parents own the bakery."

"And the other fellow is Pat Bradigan?"

"Yes. He's a tramp printer, but a good one."

Sarah was happy Addie didn't say, I know him. She called him Pat instead of Patrick—that was clue enough that he, too, had probably been one of Addie's customers.

"He drinks a lot, and someday I know he'll simply not show up for work and I'll never see him again, but meanwhile I don't know what I'd do without him."

Addie said, "I read your editorial."

"What did you think?"

"Rose didn't like it."

"I really don't care whether she did or not. I mean to close her down, and all the other houses in the badlands."

"And then what happens to me?"

"You'll be out of here, I hope."

Addie got to her feet, taking the cat with her. "Well, what if I don't want to be?"

"Please understand, Addie, there are things I must say, as a newspaperwoman. Father taught me that."

"Father, Father—I wish you'd stop talking about him!"

Studying Addie's back, Sarah sensed their thin reconciliation crumbling. She rose. "I think I'd better go now and preserve what little headway we've made today. Take good care of Ruler."

Addie stubbornly said nothing.

Sarah moved toward the door.

Suddenly Addie spun. "Hey, Sarah?"

Sarah stopped and met her sister's eyes.

"Thanks."

Sarah smiled, lifted a hand in farewell and left.

Outside, the late afternoon weather was abominable. It had begun to sleet. The sides of the gulch were obliterated by the downfall, which seemed to isolate any pocket of life afoot. The occasional lamplight falling from windows shimmered and fragmented across the glazed boardwalks. From inside the saloons the sounds were muted, and Sarah felt sorry for the animals left to stand in the elements with icicles forming on their manes and tails. She gripped her collar shut and stalked along with her head down. Her emotions were in a state of flux and she needed someone to talk to about both Addie and the marshal. It had been an unnerving afternoon. Patrick could close up the office for the day so she need not return there, and she had no desire to face Noah Campbell across a supper table. So she headed instead for Emma's, hoping for a supper invitation.

She found her friend, as expected, preparing the meal for her family in the warm, redolent kitchen above the bakery. Lettie answered her knock and smiled when she saw it was Sarah.

"Hello, Miss Merritt."

"Hello, Lettie, how are you?"

"Better." But Lettie hung her head.

Sarah tilted Lettie's chin up and spoke looking square into her striking brown eyes. "You are a beautiful girl, Lettie. Never forget that. Beauty is a thing that starts deep in the depths of one's soul and shines forth with an unmistakable glow from the eyes and the smile. You still have that glow, believe me. I, for one, would sign indenture papers if I could have your pretty face."

Lettie blushed—a healthy sign, Sarah thought. "I've interrupted your game. I'm sorry. Hello, Geneva."

Lettie rejoined Geneva at the kitchen table, where a game of rummy was in progress.

Geneva smiled and Sarah said, "Hello, Emma. May I come in?"

"What are you doing out on a nasty afternoon like this?" At the stove, Emma turned over a chop in a skillet, sending up a sizzle and a mouthwatering smell.

"I just came from visiting Addie."

"Girls, put your cards away now and go fetch your father. Tell him supper's just about ready." When they were gone, Emma inquired, "So how are things with your sister?"

"Thawing." Sarah began unbuttoning her coat without invitation.

"Well, hallelujah."

"Save your rejoicing. I haven't melted her yet."

"Sit down. Tell me what happened today."

"I bought her a cat."

"You paid twenty-five dollars for one of those cats!"

"It was worth it to see the look on Addie's face. It's the first time I've seen even a glimpse of the old Addie. She said she's going to name it Ruler, like the cat we had when we were children. Do you know, Emma, that's the first reference to our life back in St. Louis that hasn't soured her and made her grow hateful? And just before I left she thanked me."

"Sounds to me like you're getting through to her."

"Maybe . . . though we did have words about my stand on the brothels, which seemed to put us back on shaky footing. She's so distant, Emma. So guarded, as if showing any emotions toward me would belittle her in some way. I simply can't understand it."

Emma lifted a cover, sending up a cloud of steam. She tested a potato with a two-pronged fork. "I'm afraid I can't shed any light on it either."

"Marshal Campbell says maybe she's ashamed to have me see her there."

"Oh?" Replacing the cover, Emma glanced at Sarah and raised one eyebrow. "You've been *talking* to the marshal?"

"We've been talking for some time."

"Not voluntarily."

"We ran into each other on the street this afternoon."

"You mean you actually carried on a civilized conversation?"

"Quite a civilized one, as a matter of fact."

"It must have been, if you could bring up such a touchy subject as your sister." Emma went to a bureau and found a flowered tablecloth.

"What do you think of him, Emma?" Sarah inquired pensively.

"He's got a hard job." Emma flared the tablecloth and let it settle on the table. "Seems to come from decent folks. He's a fair man, I already told you that. What do you think of him?"

"I think he's stubborn—still he was very cooperative during the epidemic. I think he respects the work I do, but almost against his will. I think he believes women are much more suited to Addie's profession than to mine."

"Here"—Emma handed Sarah a stack of plates—"set the table, would you? Something happen between you two you aren't telling me about?"

Sarah began setting the plates around. There was one extra, as she'd hoped.

"Nothing, really."

"Then why all the cogitating?"

"No reason. We've gotten a little less contentious since we worked together on the health board. Today we just talked about the cat and laughed a little bit."

"And then?"

"And then when I was walking away . . . oh, it's nothing."

Emma dropped a cluster of silverware on the table. "What? Spit it out."

"Well, like I said, we were walking away from each other and I just turned around to look at him for some reason, and he was standing there on the boardwalk staring back at me."

With her hands on her hips Emma studied the younger woman, who was carefully placing each fork and knife on the table. "That's not nothing. That's an interested man."

"Oh Emma, don't be silly. I've irritated him since the first day I came into town."

"You wouldn't be the first couple in history who started out hating each other."

"We're not a couple. If anything we're adversaries."

"Not since the smallpox fight. You just said so yourself."

The women's gazes held, Emma's matter-of-fact, Sarah's troubled. "Emma, I'm very confused about him." At that moment Josh came stomping in. "I'm home, Ma. Oh hi, Sarah."

"Hello, Josh," Sarah replied, regretfully dropping the subject of Noah Campbell. "Is everything all right at the office?"

"Yup. All closed up."

"Sarah's staying for supper. Get your hands washed," his mother ordered, "the others will be here in a minute."

The family gathered and there was no more time for private talk. After supper Sarah helped with the dishes, but the children remained in the kitchen until seven o'clock when she left for home, affording no further opportunity for her and Emma to pick up the threads of their earlier conversation.

Still, Noah Campbell remained on her mind as she walked home. Why had he been looking back at her? He was an unlikable, outspoken man of loose morals who had made it plain she'd better step wide around him.

She was a woman of uncompromising morals who would never, never overlook a man's prurient bent. Why had she been looking back at him? Granted, they'd swallowed their antipathy out of necessity while they'd joined forces to fight the smallpox. But the fight was won; it was back to business as usual, and that business meant the two of them on opposite sides over the issue of closing the brothels.

The wind was still howling and the sleet had turned to snow. The night sky was inky but for the sheets of white that came down sideways. Sarah passed the newspaper office and tried the front door from force of habit. It was locked as it should be so she continued toward home. She took a side street and climbed the foot trail up the side of the gulch to Mrs. Roundtree's. She was ascending the steep steps to the front door when a voice from above startled her.

"Well, you're back."

"Marshal, what are you doing out here?" She stopped two steps below him, looking up. How distracting to encounter him after he'd been so strong on her mind.

"Smoking."

Smoking was, however, allowed inside the house; the parlor was provided with giant free-standing ashtrays. Furthermore, he'd never felt the need to do his smoking—what little of it he did—outside before. She got the distinct impression he'd been waiting for her.

"You missed supper," he said.

"Yes, I ate with the Dawkins."

"How is Lettie?"

"Self-conscious of her scars."

"That'll pass."

"Perhaps. Perhaps not." Sarah knew from personal experience that self-consciousness over one's shortcomings in the beauty department did not pass. For some reason she'd been dwelling on hers often lately.

He took a drag of the cigarette, and the wind tore the smoke from his mouth as he flicked the butt away. He peered off into the distance, as if the weather were of capital interest to him.

"Nasty night," he remarked.

She took the plunge. "You weren't worried about me, were you?"

"It's my job to worry about the residents of Deadwood."

"Well, I'm all right, so you can go back inside."

She climbed the last two steps and reached for the doorknob. Before she could turn it he asked, "So how did your sister like the cat?"

"She loved it. She's going to name it Ruler."

"Well . . . that should make you happy."

"Yes." They stood close in the windy, black night with the sound of her skirts luffing against his ankle and the fine shards of snow ricocheting off his hat brim and her forehead. She held her coat closed at the throat and he had stuffed both hands into his jacket pockets. If there was an embryonic attraction between them, it pleased neither of them.

"Well, good night, Mr. Campbell," she bid finally.

"Good night, Miss Merritt."

In her room she lit a lantern and built a fire in her tiny six-plate iron stove. Standing before it, with her palms extended, she wondered about him. Had he, indeed, been waiting for her? Could Emma be right about his being interested? Surely not. Then why had he turned to study her on the boardwalk? All right, supposing he was interested, what was her own reaction? This afternoon on the boardwalk, when she'd run into him there had been a moment—a brief moment, granted—of exhilaration when their eyes had met. He had been as surprised as she, and while he'd stood there gripping her arms she had looked into his gray eyes with their spiky auburn lashes and found them unduly attractive. His face no longer put her off. His freckles had faded over the autumn, and his cheeks had looked ruddy from the wind. Funny, she had even grown accustomed to his mustache. And his nose—well, his nose was Scottish, and very appropriate for a man named Campbell.

So, what of your feelings for him, Sarah?

She had, her entire life long, been a thinker; it was natural for her to dissect and rationalize rather than admit offhand that her feelings for him might possibly be changing. The truth was, she did not *want* her feelings for him to change. It could lead to nothing but an awkward situation, given that he'd been Addie's lover and probably still was.

The room warmed. She removed her coat and hung it on the wall pegs but found herself restless, pacing the confines of her sleeping space, thinking of Addie, wondering things about Addie and Noah Campbell that she had no right to wonder. She imagined Addie with her fingers in Noah's hair. He had the most beautiful head of hair she'd ever seen on a man, with enough natural curl to spring up and twine around a woman's fingers. Sarah had never in her life had her fingers in a man's hair.

She withdrew from her reverie and went to the mirror to take down her own hair. She brushed it vigorously, donned her nightwear and found a small hand mirror. In it she studied her Elizabethan nose, covering the end of it to imagine what she'd look like if it were shorter. She studied her lips. Too thin, not plump and seductive like Addie's. Her eyes—they still pleased her, vivid, blue and sparkly when she need not wear her glasses, but the moment she put them on, she looked frumpish and lackluster.

She sighed, set aside her mirror in favor of pen and ink and tried working on an editorial about the need to preserve the last of the great buffalo herds which were now centered in the valley east of the Big Horns. But often she'd snap out of a lapse to find the ink dried on the pen nib instead of the paper, and a picture of Noah Campbell's hair in her mind.

At breakfast the following morning she was uncomfortably aware of him across the table. In spite of her previous night's rationalization, the fact remained she and Noah had been seeing each other with disturbing regularity for quite a few weeks already—two meals a day and in between— and she had memorized things about him that a sensible woman would not have noticed. She had come to recognize the stubborn refusal of his hair to remain obediently sleeked down, and the various hues—from mahogany to nutmeg—that it took on as it dried each morning during breakfast. She had grown familiar with the hatline that dented it even when his hat wasn't on, and the curls that sprang up below it, at the temples, like the tail feathers on a mallard.

She had come to appreciate the faint scent of his shaving soap which he brought down to breakfast with him, accompanied by the shine of his freshly bladed skin above and below his mustache. She was familiar with all his shirts—he wore a clean one each morning under his black leather vest—the red flannel he'd been wearing the first morning; a green plaid with a collar badly in need of turning; two blue cambrics—one with a neatly sewn patch on the right elbow, the other newer; a tan one that looked terrible with his ruddy complexion; and the white one he wore on Sundays.

She knew his mealtime preferences: coffee black, salt and pepper over his entire plate before he even tasted it, a second helping of fried potatoes with his morning eggs; no cabbage, rutabagas or turnips—these he disliked—but any other vegetable offered; a huge puddle of gravy if it was on the table, two additional cups of coffee during the course of the meal, and a cigarette afterward instead of a sweet.

She knew his mannerisms, too. He always nodded to the men as he said good morning. Never nodded when he said it to her. When he was listening most intently, he rested a forefinger along his upper lip. When he said something humorous he often tugged at his right earlobe. He seemed comfortable using a napkin while some of the men used their cuffs.

Leaving the dining room when breakfast was finished, Sarah realized, to her dismay, that she had memorized no such things about Mrs. Roundtree's other boarders.

He had grown familiar with her, too. She wore mostly shades of brown—skirts, shirtwaists and jackets—and pinned her pendant watch in precisely the same spot upon her left breast each morning. She carried her dirty laundry downtown on Monday mornings and back home on Tuesday afternoons. She was a creature of utter punctuality, leaving her bedroom at precisely the stroke of seven-thirty each morning, appearing at supper on the dot of six. Ironically, she cared little for the food itself but ate only because she must, leaving food abandoned when her mind was preoccupied with a story. He recognized her preoccupation by the way she took little part in the mealtime conversation and the way she stared at the sugar bowl. Sometimes she'd have to be called twice before realizing she was being spoken to, though in print, she never missed a detail that was newsworthy, be it obvious or incidental. She was acute at picking out and printing items that would have seemed banal to the average ear, but beneath her skilled hand became articles of pertinence to both Deadwood residents and the country beyond the hills. The middle finger of her right hand was misshapen from overusing a pen, and most times it bore a faint black crescent of ingrained ink. She had arresting blue eyes that won a second glance from him whenever he encountered her without her glasses. She was a woman without artifice—no kohl on her eyes, no carmine on her lips—but he thought if she were ever to show up at the table wearing these, he would be outraged. Her coiffure scarcely changed from day to day except when the bump at the back was slightly off-center, as if she'd secured it without benefit of a mirror. Her nails were clipped short and she owned a single pair of unbecoming shoes, as far as he could tell—lace-up, brown, blucher-style boots that saw her through mud, snow, sleet, and the dung on the street, about which she continued to badger in each issue of her newspaper. He suspected, if the town had a church, the same shoes would appear there with her Sunday clothes. One fact he was aware of above all others: ever since the day they'd spoken on the boardwalk she had stopped looking him directly in the eye when she spoke to him. Instead, she fixed her attention on the star on his chest.

. . .

Sarah Merritt's and Noah Campbell's jobs put them into contact with one another on a regular basis. In collecting news, she consulted him for items about arrests and the law. In making his rounds, he walked into businesses at random—hers included.

Whenever they met she greeted him formally as "Marshal Campbell," and he did likewise, calling her "Miss Merritt."

If, as the days passed, they encountered each other more often, they credited it to necessity and nothing more.

A week after their encounter on the boardwalk, Sarah and her staff were working in the newspaper office when a short, pudgy woman entered. She was brown as an old saddle and had dark hair with a few streaks of gray curving away from a center part. Her gray eyes were direct, if not quite piercing, and she zeroed in on Sarah as if the others were not present.

"So you're her!" the woman said in a voice that rang through the room like a dinner triangle.

Sarah rose from her desk, removed her cuff guards and left them behind.

"I'm Sarah Merritt," she said.

The woman stuck out a hand. "I'm Noah Campbell's mother, Carrie."

Sarah saw the resemblance immediately—the gray eyes, the tiny knob that ended the nose, the high, round cheekbones.

"Hello, Mrs. Campbell." She shook the woman's hand.

"He told us about you. About this place, too. Thought I'd come and have a look-see for myself. Howdy." She nodded to Patrick and Josh without pausing to allow introductions, all the while giving the premises a blatant assessment. "By the sound of it you're a regular go-getter. Noah admires that."

"He does?" Sarah was doing her best to hide her surprise.

"I says to him, Noah, why don't you bring her out here sometime, but you know how sons are. Once they leave home you've got the triple dickens trying to get them back themselves, much less bring any of their friends."

Friends? This woman thought Sarah was Noah's friend?

"So I says, all right, I'll just go into that newspaper office myself and say hello. My other son, Arden, he'll probably be in here sometime today, too. Kirk, now—he's my man—he's got better things to do, since we don't come into town too often, but Arden and me, we were just plain curious since Noah he talked so much about you when he was out last time."

He did? Sarah was conscious of Patrick listening, all the while he manned the press, and Josh, too, as he did the inking.

"Sounds like you're a bright lady, running this newspaper like you do. Me, I have a struggle just to read, let alone write, but Noah, he brought us out a copy of your paper, and though I had to muddle through it, I have to admit it was downright exciting to read what's going on in the rest of the country, as well as here in town."

"You live out in the Spearfish Valley, I believe?"

"That's right."

"Would you mind answering a few questions about it?"

"Why . . ." Carrie Campbell's eyebrows rose. "Why, no, though I don't know what I'd have to say that you'd be interested in."

"The Spearfish was the last stronghold of the Indians. The rest of the country is watching it carefully to see if the Indians uphold their part of the treaty."

The ensuing interview reiterated to Carrie Campbell how bright Sarah Merritt really was. Her questions touched upon the quality of this year's harvest, which particular crops had been grown, the number of bushels yielded per acre, the current price of stock feed, the overall weather conditions including rainy days versus sunny during the past growing season, the number of families residing in the Spearfish, their ethnic background, their geographic background and what if any social events took place there.

When all of Sarah's questions had been answered, Carrie watched the younger woman remove her oval spectacles and lay them aside, wondering what the deuce her boy Noah was waiting for. The girl wasn't much to look at, but she was smarter than a few men Carrie could name. Furthermore, she'd come all the way out here and opened up this business, hadn't she? That took spunk. And though she was skinny, she looked healthy enough to bear a few grandchildren, and probably bright ones at that!

"When the piece is written, I'll be sure to send a copy out with Noah," Sarah offered.

"Yes, I wish you would, unless of course you'd care to bring it out yourself, maybe stay for dinner along with Noah."

"Thank you, Mrs. Campbell, but I'm afraid I'm very busy keeping the paper running. I gather all the news myself, you see, and write the articles, too, besides selling ads and attending whatever local functions and meetings need to be covered. I have very little time to myself, I'm sorry to say."

"Sure . . . well . . . it's been a pleasure meeting you." Carrie extended her hand again. "You take care of yourself now."

"Thank you. You do the same."

When she was gone, Sarah felt Patrick's eyes following her around the office. She avoided them. He got out his flask, took a nip and went back to work.

At ten minutes to twelve someone else entered the newspaper office. He was dark-haired and cute and several years younger than Sarah.

"Hi," he said, removing his hat. "Are you Sarah Merritt?"

She suspected who he was even before she answered. "Yes, I am."

"I'm Arden Campbell, Noah's brother. I came to ask if I could take you out to dinner."

She stood staring at him for five seconds, stupefied, then burst out laughing.

He laughed, too, then asked, "Well, could I?"

"Mr. Campbell, I don't even know you."

"Well, I know that. That's why I asked you out to dinner, so we could *get* to know each other. I'm harmless, and a lot more friendly than my brother. I'm twenty-one and I like pretty women and I haven't had the pleasure of one's company since we moved out here, and we both have to eat a noon meal, so why not do it together?"

"I don't think that's a good idea, Mr. Campbell."

"Why? Has Noah got dibs on you?"

"No." She felt herself begin to blush.

"Has somebody else?"

"No."

"Then why not?" He lifted his left arm and sniffed beneath it. "I smell bad or something?"

Again she laughed. "Mr. Campbell—"

"Call me Arden."

"Arden, there aren't a lot of women in this town. I think we would start a lot of gossip if I ate lunch with you."

"Why, shee-oot, who's afraid of gossip! Come on . . ." He took her by an arm. "If they say Arden Campbell's out sparking the new woman in town I'll spit in their eye and say damned right."

She found herself being hauled toward the door, and resisted. "But I don't know you, I said!"

"You're going to! Now get your coat, or your pocketbook or whatever you need, because you're going to dinner with me whether you like it or not."

It was quite a meal. He dragged her down the street to Ruckner's and deposited her in a chair and glued his eyes to her, removing them only long enough to cut his elk roast. He jabbered like a magpie and made her laugh so often she had to keep covering her mouth with her napkin to keep food from flying out. He volubly greeted every man who entered the place, calling out, "You've met Sarah Merritt, haven't you?" He said he was a Christian, and looking for a wife, and intended to be farming his own place inside of two years, and have a family inside of three, if he had to send for a mail-order bride to do it, which he hoped he would not have to do. He said he could sing like a nightingale, fight like a terrier, dance like a highlander and cook flapjacks better than his ma. He told her one day he'd like to whip some up for her. He claimed he found life too serious to be serious about, and thought the best way to get through it was to laugh whenever you could. He told her he was tough, and honest, and hardworking and lovable—just that he'd never been around a woman long enough to prove it. He *told* her he was coming into town Saturday night to take her to the play at the Langrishe, and gave her no option to refuse. He'd pick her up at seven, he said, leaving her, somewhat overwhelmed, at the door of the newspaper office.

Chapter 9

Noah heard the news before Arden came into his office.

"Hey, big brother!" Arden greeted with a wide smile.

"Big brother, my foot! What the hell's the idea of taking Sarah Merritt out for dinner?"

"I told you I was going to."

"And I told you to keep away from her."

"I asked her if you had dibs on her and she said no."

"You did *what!*" Noah came up out of his chair.

"I asked her if you had dibs on her and she said no. I asked her if anybody else did and she said no again, so I'm courting her."

"Courting her! Why, you just met her two hours ago!"

"We got along real well in those two hours, though. I had her laughing fit to kill. I'm taking her to the Langrishe Saturday night."

"The hell you are!"

"I don't know what you're getting so upset about. *You* don't want her."

Noah didn't, so he dropped back into his chair. "Does Ma know?"

"Not yet, but she'll be happy. She went over and checked Sarah out, too."

Noah clutched his head. "Judas priest."

"Ma invited her out to the house for a meal sometime. I wouldn't be surprised if she comes."

"What about Pa? I suppose he went to gawk at her, too."

"Pa's in the saloon getting happy. He'll be patting Ma's butt while she's fixing supper tonight." Arden laughed. "You see him yet?"

"Yeah, I talked to him and Ma both, earlier." After a pause he said, "Listen, about that woman—forget what I said, and whatever you do, don't tell her I said it!"

"Don't worry. I've got better things to do with Sarah Merritt than talk about you."

For the remainder of the day Noah stewed over the turn of events. He remembered Arden's grin when he'd said he had better things to do. Exactly *what* better things? Hell, the brat was only twenty-one! But recalling himself at twenty-one, Noah scowled. Unless he missed his guess, Sarah Merritt was one hundred eighty degrees from her sister in the worldliness department. She wouldn't be accustomed to fending off randy young whelps with hubris the size of a barn loft and precociousness to match.

At suppertime that night Noah stood inside his bedroom with his hand on the doorknob and his watch in his palm. At the dot of six he heard a door open down the hall, opened his own and snapped his watch shut.

"Well . . . hello," he said, feigning surprise as he overtook Sarah Merritt from two doors down.

"Hello."

"You had quite a day."

"Yes, I did."

"By the sound of it, you met my whole family." He loitered in the center of the hall, forestalling her progress toward the stairs until he'd said what he was disinclined to say before the big-eared audience around the supper table.

"Not quite. I didn't meet your father. The other two were charming though."

"Obviously."

"So you heard about my going to dinner with Arden."

"The whole town heard about it."

"Well . . . he's a persuasive young man."

"Obviously."

"I imagine you know that he's taking me to the theater, too."

"Do you think that's a good idea?"

"The bill has changed. Mr. Langrishe's troop is performing *Only a Far-mer's Daughter,* which I must see anyway in order to review it. I may as well take the opportunity with your brother."

My brother who's only twenty-one and keeps you laughing fit to kill? The thought was irksome because Noah was much more suited to her age and he'd never seen her laughing fit to kill. That once on the boardwalk she had let go briefly, but usually she remained serious, almost contained, around him.

What could he say?

"That makes sense," he replied. With a flourish toward the stairs he said, "Shall we go down? I think I smell onions."

For the remainder of the week he continued to stew.

On Saturday evening he retired to Mrs. Roundtree's parlor immediately after supper and parked himself there with the only reading material he could find, a copy of the Montgomery Ward Catalog for Fall and Winter of 1875–76. He really should be uptown. Saturday night and Sunday, when the miners all came to town for liquor, baths and whoring, were the row-diest days of the week in Deadwood. Many Saturdays Noah skipped his supper or gobbled it and ran back on duty, for he'd discovered that his mere presence on Main Street put qualms in the way of most belligerent fist-slingers. So it might look fishy, him sitting here in the parlor when he'd normally be uptown, but he sat nonetheless, scanning all the tempt-ing bargains as if he cared one iota.

Spring beds for $2.75.

Farm wagons for $50.

Seventy-two dozen buttons for 35¢.

The haberdasher, Mr. Mullins, sat for a while with him, then went away. Tom Taft stuck his head in and said, "Staying home tonight, eh, Mar-shal?" Taft continued out the front door. In the kitchen, Mrs. Roundtree clattered dishes.

Shortly before seven, Sarah Merritt came downstairs and entered the parlor.

"Hello again," she said quietly, taking a seat on a maroon horsehair settee.

Noah looked up and said nothing. She had used some contraption to make her hair look like chain, all quirked up and kinked in peculiar squiggles around her face. Low at the rear, it was clumped loosely with a few wormy-looking strands crawling down her neck. She wore the same brown coat he'd seen dozens of times, but where it fell open he saw a bluish, striped skirt he'd never seen before. And damned if she didn't smell like lavender!

"Ordering buttons, are you, Mr. Campbell?" she inquired, tilting to-ward him to eye the open catalog. He slapped it shut and tossed it aside.

"So you're going to review the play."

"Exactly."

He linked his hands over his vest and drew doughnuts with his thumbs.

She had never seen this precise pursed expression on his face before, like that of a headmaster facing a naughty student. It made his mustache beetle out in the most unattractive fashion.

"Is there some reason you object to my going to the play with your brother, Mr. Campbell?"

"Object? Me?" Wide-eyed, he tipped his thumbs toward his chest. "Why would I object?"

"I don't know. That's what puzzles me, yet earlier this week you asked me if I thought it was a good idea, and tonight, here you are, waiting in the parlor like some grousing father. *Have* you some objection?"

"Hell no!" He shot from the chair, flapping both arms heavenward. "I have no objection at all. I was just sitting here letting my supper settle before I went back to work." He plucked his jacket and hat from a tree in the corner and clapped the latter on his head while opening the door. "I've got enough drunks to tussle with that I don't need to do it with you!"

He met Arden coming up the path, wearing a smile as wide as a miner's pickax, smelling sweet enough to corrode metal at fifteen paces.

"Hey-a, big brother, what's n——"

"H'lo, Arden."

"Hey, wait a minute!"

"It's Saturday night. They'll be raising hell in town." Noah stalked on downhill at a bone-jarring clip.

"Well, cripes, can't you even stop to say hello?"

"Nope. I've got work to do!"

"But Ma sent these shirts she mended!"

"Just put them in my room. Mrs. Roundtree won't mind. And tell Ma thanks!"

Continuing down the hill, with the smell of Sarah's lavender water and Arden's bay rum lingering in his nostrils, Noah thought, *I hope the two of 'em choke each other!*

Entering the parlor, Arden Campbell seemed to bombard the room. There was no description for him as apt as *cute*. He had a face shaped like an apple, with round, boyish cheeks and the faintest notch in the chin. His black sparky eyelashes gave his deep blue eyes a look of perpetual excitement. His mouth looked as though it had been sucking on a very sweet peppermint stick for a long, long time: lips slightly puffed, pink and shiny, wearing the expression of a man very pleased with the world.

When he smiled—and he smiled most of the time—one could imagine that he'd taken in some effervescent substance that filled and vivified him. He had the ability to focus all his radiance in one direction—for the present on Sarah—and gave the impression nothing else of importance was happening within at least a hundred miles.

His comeliness quite startled Sarah.

"Hello, Sarah! I thought tonight would never come!" he bellowed. "Gosh, you look pretty! Let's go!" Without wasting time on polite parlor talk he commandeered her hand, linked it through his arm and took her from the house. Luckily she was wearing her coat or he might have herded her off without it, he was so eager.

The night was brisk and clear, but she had little chance to appreciate it. He walked as he did everything else, at the clip of a buck deer at rutting season. She had to quick-step to keep up with him.

"So how have you been? How's the paper doing? What have you heard about the play?"

"Fine. Wonderful. Nothing yet—Mr. Campbell, would you please slow down!"

He did so with a laugh, but it lasted only a dozen steps before he was towing her again at his enthusiastic stride.

At the Langrishe, he led her right up front to the third row, bellowing out hellos that drew additional attention their way. He solicitously helped her with her coat, draped it over her shoulders, then sat forward in his seat without using the backrest, as if preparing to spring from it. During the performance he hooted uproariously at the humor, and at the end of each act not only clapped but stuck two fingers in his mouth and whistled, nearly puncturing Sarah's right eardrum.

When the play was over he tucked Sarah's hand in the crook of his arm while walking her home.

"Did you like it?" he asked.

"No, I'm afraid I didn't."

"You *didn't!*"

"The way I saw it, it poked fun at the rural community, and I intend to say so when I review it."

"I'm more rural than you, and I didn't feel like they were poking fun at me."

"We all have a right to our own opinions. I could see you enjoyed the show very much, and that's fine, but consider the humorous lines again— don't you think they portrayed farmers as slow-witted dolts?"

He considered a while and answered, "Maybe in some ways, but a person has to be able to laugh at himself."

"At himself, yes. But should he draw the line when others do so at his expense?"

They had a lively discussion on the subject, and by the time they reached the path leading to Mrs. Roundtree's house he was holding her hand. At the foot of the stairs leading up to the house he tugged her to a halt. "Wait." He captured her other hand and tipped his head back. His palms were hard and smooth as boot soles. "We've got some great stars tonight. Stars this great deserve to be admired, wouldn't you say?"

She gave them her attention. "Do you know what George Eliot calls stars? Golden fruit upon a tree all out of reach." She lowered her chin and met his eyes. "Eloquence has always touched me."

He gazed at her. "You're the smartest girl I ever met."

"I'm not a girl, Arden. I'm twenty-five years old. Most women my age are married with families already."

"You want to be?" He grinned.

"Not particularly. I just meant to point out the difference in our ages."

He transferred his hands to her neck and began rubbing it through her coat collar. "Let's see if it makes any difference."

Her heart did a little dance of curiosity as he tipped his head and kissed her. The pressure of his mouth was warm, moist and brief. It turned her cheeks warm. She had never smelled bay rum at such close range, nor had her lips wet by any tongue but her own. It was a startling but grand sensation.

He drew back and said, very close to her mouth, "Nobody ever done that to you before?"

"A time or two."

"How old were you?"

"Eleven, I believe."

He laughed, landing a puff of moist breath on her nose. "And truthful, too."

"I must go in, Arden."

"Not so fast. One more."

What a one more. He used both arms, both hands and opened his lips wider than before. With his tongue he encouraged her to do the same. Bedeviling sensations skittered everywhere through Sarah. When he turned her loose he said, *"That's* how it's done. Now what do you think?"

She was surprised to find herself slightly breathless as she answered, "I think I'd better say goodnight and thank you for a lovely evening."

"Can I see you next Saturday night again?"

"I don't think it would be a good idea to make a regular thing of it."

"Why? You didn't like the kissing?"

"The kissing was interesting. I enjoyed it."

"Interesting! Is that all?"

"Actually, no. It was a lot more than interesting."

"Well, then . . ." Had he been a rooster his neck feathers would have been ruffled.

"Good night, Arden. Let's not rush things."

He attempted to waylay her for one more kiss, but she turned him around and waited until he'd retreated down the path. She climbed ten steps, turned at a landing and climbed another thirteen before reaching the final landing where she came up short.

"What are *you* doing out here?"

"Having a last smoke before bed." In the deep shadow of the house with its unpainted exterior, Marshal Campbell blended into the dark, propping his spine and the sole of one boot against the wall behind him. He drew on his cigarette and made a bright red dot in the blackness.

"Shouldn't you be making your rounds?"

"Quiet tonight. Town's starting to settle down since we got our ordinances."

"Marshal, let's get one thing clear. I resent your spying on me."

He blew out some smoke and chuckled once so quietly it scarcely carried to her.

"I'm twenty-five years old!" she said, piqued. "Quite old enough to take care of myself, and I can spend my evenings with whom I *choose!*"

"You're absolutely right," he answered levelly, still leaning indolently against the wall. "Good night, Miss Merritt."

She left him as he was, smoking alone, and went to her room to lie down and evaluate kissing his brother. It had been, she decided, a thoroughly pleasant distraction.

Given the amount of attention Sarah's presence had generated since her arrival in Deadwood, even she had been surprised that no other male than Arden Campbell had dredged up the nerve to come calling on her. His doing so, however, seemed to release a ground swell. On the Sunday following her date with him no fewer than three suitors appeared at Mrs. Roundtree's asking to see her.

The first was a total stranger—middle-aged, thick-waisted, with heavy-lidded eyes and a face like a bumpy gourd—who introduced himself as Cordry Peckham and said he was a wealthy man; he'd struck a rich vein early in the summer on Iron Creek and would be pleased to buy her the best the town had to offer of whatever she'd like if she would only come for a ride with him in his buggy.

She thanked Mr. Peckham but told him it would be unacceptable for her to ride out with a man she'd never before met.

The second was Elias Pinkney, who looked up into her face and turned the color of his name and got great sweat dapples on his bald head as he invited her to his home for supper. He had a thirteen-stop organ, he said, which she would be welcome to play, and a stereoscopic viewer with a large collection of photos of such wonders as Niagara Falls, Covent Garden and the Taj Mahal. He owned, too, a lap harp, a priceless chess set carved of Indian ivory, a respectable collection of books, any of which she was welcome to borrow, and a wonderful curiosity called a kaleidoscope which must be seen to be believed. She would, he believed, find a number of entertainments if she'd accept his invitation.

She thanked Elias as graciously as possible, feeling a measure of pity for the poor sap, and subdued the urge to find a handkerchief and dry his dripping pate.

The third caller was Teddy Ruckner, who invited her to his restaurant for supper that evening. He had, he said, been hoarding a roast of beef, which he would prepare along with the vegetables of her choice and warm bread pudding (which he already knew was one of her favorite desserts). Teddy seemed like a sensible young man. He had always appealed to her; they were more suitable in age; she ate most of her noon dinners at his place and thought he would be pleasant company. Also, she thought it prudent on her part to demonstrate to Arden Campbell that her evening with him was not to be construed as any sort of assignation. Furthermore, real beef sounded heavenly.

She accepted Teddy's invitation.

They passed a most enjoyable evening. He cooked the beef with bay leaf, onion and sherry, and served it with rich, dark gravy and a bevy of vegetables. As she'd guessed, he was an engaging fellow. Not only did he make a special effort to please her with the meal (he had closed his eating saloon to all but them and had produced a coral-colored tea cloth, matching napkins and a candle for their table), but they passed three thoroughly enjoyable hours discussing a variety of topics: *Only a Farmer's Daughter,* which he, too, had seen the previous night; the unpalatable habit of snuff-chewers expectorating in the street; his origins (he had left an aging mother and father behind with a married sister in Ohio to come here and make his pot of gold); her origins; the rumor that someone was planning to build the first much-needed stamp mill for the reduction of ore in the gulch; the domestic economy of blowing out a candle by holding it above you, thereby preventing the wick from smoldering down as it does when blown from above. He claimed the latter and demonstrated to his companion, ending their meal with a laugh when he proved himself correct.

When he walked her home he made no attempt to hold her hand, but at the foot of her steps he stopped and asked, "Would you mind if I kissed you, Sarah?"

She had suffered a dearth of male attention throughout her growing-up years, and thought she deserved this superabundance of it. Furthermore, she was curious to know whether her reaction would be as agreeable as it was to Arden's kiss.

Teddy, however, was much less impulsive than Arden. His kiss was executed without the use of his tongue. It was more of a gentle settling of his mouth over hers, and a small parting nibble. She found herself faintly disappointed.

"Good night," he said quietly when it ended. "I've enjoyed it."

"I have, too. Thank you, Teddy."

Much to Sarah's relief, Marshal Campbell had taken her at her word and stopped his spying. She encountered him nowhere on her way through the house.

At breakfast the following day they exchanged forced good mornings, establishing a status of edgy neutrality.

Later, she arrived at the newspaper office to find Patrick Bradigan already there working.

"Good morning, Patrick, are you turning over a new leaf?" she teased. "It's only eight o'clock."

"Y' might say that, miss, yes."

He didn't look exactly well, she realized upon closer scrutiny. His eyes were abnormally bright and his color high. "Patrick, aren't you feeling well? You look terribly flushed this morning."

"I'm feelin' fine. Well, perhaps a wee bit murky."

"Why, Patrick, what is it? If you're ill you certainly needn't have come to work." She approached him and touched his forehead. "You should be resting if—"

"I'm not ailin' with the smallpox, so y' needn't fret yourself on that score." He caught her wrist and held it, rising from his chair. No whiskey tainted his breath, but his eyes were bloodshot.

"Then what is it?"

"Ah, well . . ." A sheepish half-grin tilted his lips. " 'Tis the daft wishes of a lovestruck man." He took her hand in his and studied it. "I thought perhaps I'd best be askin' y' now before one o' those other young swains pops the question and y' decide to jump the stone with him. I was wonderin', pretty colleen, if you'd do me the honor of becomin' me wife."

Her lips dropped open in surprise. "Why, Patrick . . ."

"I know this is sudden, but hear me out. I've turned over a new leaf. You see, I haven't tipped the barley bottle once today. No, don't pull your hand away." He gripped it tighter. "From the minute I laid down me gold t' pay your first night's lodging I says to meself, Patrick me boy, there's the girl of your dreams. And when you turned out to be in me own trade, I says to meself, faith and begorra, the match was made in heaven!"

"Oh Patrick—"

He took her head and kissed her, halting her words.

She stood still as a newel post and allowed it. None of the pleasant amplification of Arden's kiss followed, only disenchantment accompanied by a wish to have it over. His mouth was wetter and more desperate than either Arden's or Teddy's and she could feel the trembling in his hands.

When he drew back, still holding her head, he vowed, "I can give up the drink, you'll see."

"Of course you can, with or without me."

"Then say yes."

She drew back, forcing him to drop his hands. "I'm not Catholic, Patrick."

"What does it matter clear out here? We'll likely be married by the circuit judge when he comes through, and later by a man of the cloth, whatever cloth comes first."

"I'm sorry, Patrick," she told him softly, "but I don't love you."

"Don't love me! But how could y' not love me when I can set type at two thousand ems a minute and print a page in forty-five seconds?" He grinned boyishly.

"Patrick, please," she pleaded quietly. "Don't make this more difficult for either one of us. I don't want to lose you as an employee, but I cannot marry you."

She watched his need for a drink escalate as he stood soberly before her, chagrined and trying not to show it, heartbroken and attempting to laugh it off.

"Ah, well . . ." With a wave of the hand he turned aside. "What you lose on the swings, y' gain on the roundabouts. I won't have t' buy a house then, and a wagonload o' furniture, will I? I wasn't just sure how I'd manage that." He returned to work, but within minutes she noted him sipping from his flask, and by midmorning he wore the effulgent glow of an Irish sunset.

When Josh came in he sensed the tension and asked, "What's wrong?"

"Nothing," Sarah replied.

There was, of course, something wrong between Sarah and Patrick from that morning on. The equanimity they'd shared over their work was strained as never before. However, she silently thanked Patrick for one consideration: he had pronounced himself in the privacy of the office so nobody else need ever know, for as the week progressed, the male attention continued and Sarah began to feel more than ever like a prize specimen under a bell jar. Men came into the newspaper office and offered her everything from their mothers' lockets to shares in their gold mines. In return they sought her company at dinner, supper, plays, the gambling tables, picnics (it was November, for heaven's sake!), and more than likely at breakfast, too, if any could be so lucky. She turned them all down, for she had business to do.

On Saturday, Arden Campbell showed up with the pistachio and white striped umbrella and presented it to her with his full-moon smile.

"I can't accept this, Arden."

"Why not?"

"Well . . . because."

"Because people might know it's from me and think you're my girl?"

"Yes, as a matter of fact. Besides, it's the middle of winter. What would I do with it?"

"Save it till spring. Now, I'm taking you out to dinner tonight and I won't take no for an answer."

"Yes, you will."

"No, I won't. I paid a half an ounce of gold for that bumbershoot. You owe me."

She laughed and snapped the umbrella open, gave it a twirl and watched the stripes blur. "Arden, you're incorrigible."

"Damned right. Now shut that thing up and let's go."

She went with him and had a lovely time. He made her laugh as no other man she'd ever known. He teased—something new for her—and brought out a humorous side she'd never known she possessed. And at the end of the night, he kissed her again and turned her stomach to frogs' eggs, and dazzled her with his tongue, and tried to touch her breasts and nearly convinced her to let him.

She went, the next afternoon, to Addie's where her initial reception was halting but became more genuine as the two shared some affectionate exchanges about Ruler, scratching her and letting her act as the bridge between them. In time Addie sat cross-legged near the pillows on her bed where Ruler gamboled with a string of red glass beads. Sarah sat at the foot. It was a dingy afternoon and a small lamp was lit—the perfect setting, Sarah thought, for two sisters to exchange confidences and thereby begin rebuilding trust.

"I seem to have an admirer," Sarah began.

"The way I hear it, you seem to have a whole townful."

"Well, one in particular."

"Who?"

"The marshal's brother, Arden Campbell."

"Ohhh . . . the cute one."

"Yes, he is, isn't he? But he's four years younger than I. Do you think that matters?"

"You're asking me?" Addie exclaimed. "Why?"

"Because you've always seemed to know about these things. Even when we were young you knew how to act around boys. I was busy helping Daddy publish a newspaper when I should have been learning the fundamentals of . . . well, of, of dalliance."

"Dalliance?" The prudish word caught Addie and brought out a laugh. "For a woman who always seems to be able to pull a thousand words out of a hat to suit any occasion, you had some trouble saying that one, didn't you?"

"Don't laugh at me, Addie. I'm four years older than you but I'm ten years behind in matters of concupiscence."

"It doesn't strike you as unfitting that you should be asking me when you know what I am? What I do?"

"I'm asking you to forget for a while what you do and not let it come between us. I don't know any other way for us to become sisters again. Besides, I need your advice."

Addie stopped sidewinding the beads, and the cat took up swatting at a fold in her dressing robe. For moments neither sister spoke, though their gazes remained earnestly locked.

"So what do you want to know?"

"Three men have kissed me recently. Should I have let them?"

"I don't see why not."

"Because one is my employee, one is not anyone I'm particularly attracted to, and the other one is four years younger than me and altogether too attractive for his own good."

"What did you think of it?"

"It was an interesting comparison."

"It'll be more than interesting once the right one kisses you."

"How do I know the right one hasn't?"

Addie looked very wise. "Because when the right ones does, he'll make you feel like you're a thimbleful of fondant, and you're going to wish you were, and that he'd lick the last drop from you or die trying."

"It was a little like that with Arden, but Arden is too young and much too eager to suit me. He wants everything to happen last week. Teddy Ruckner isn't that way at all. We simply had a good time together. We talked about so many things, and he fixed me the most delicious supper, then walked me home. But his kiss was rather flat and disappointing. Then there was Patrick . . . that one was embarrassing and we've both been self-conscious ever since. But what I wonder, Addie, is this—is it fair to a man to accept his invitations for dinner and plays when you're accepting the invitations of others as well?"

"Of course. If they want to spend their money on you, let them. But just remember one thing: if you want them to marry you, keep your bloomers buttoned."

The newspaper was growing. Sarah was putting out four sheets twice a week, the current edition announcing that the office of the *Deadwood Chronicle* was the first plastered building in Deadwood; an exceedingly rich quartz lode had been discovered on Black Tail Gulch and the owners were making grub by pounding the ore in mortars and afterward panning out the precious metals for lack of quartz mills and arrastras. At Claim #3 above discovery on Deadwood Gulch, Pierce & Co. was taking out an average of $400 per day, while the cold weather had put a stop to surface mining on many of the creeks until next spring. The telegraph was completed to within twenty-five miles this side of Custer City, and by next week the poles would be set as far as Deadwood. A party was planned at the Grand Central when the long-awaited wires reached the city. The Black Hills Country would soon have a reliable map, as Mr. George Henkel, well-known civil engineer, had been engaged all summer upon a survey and would soon have his maps completed. A two-hundred-dollar reward for the arrest of road agents operating on the Cheyenne & Black Hills Stage road was offered by Wyoming Governor Thayer and a number of county commissioners. No new cases of smallpox had been reported. Land for a combined church/school building had been donated to the city by Elias Pinkney, the amount of money to be appropriated for construction of the building to be put to a vote of the general public on December 4. An ad for a schoolteacher for next term would be placed in larger city newspapers as soon as the telegraph reached Deadwood.

Sarah was reading over the proof sheets of the edition on a cold afternoon in late November. A fire burned in the potbellied stove at the rear of the office, which was so much brighter with the lanterns reflecting off its new white walls. At a worktable Patrick was teaching Josh the rudiments of setting type as they composed the program for the Bella Union's next play. The room was pleasant with the smell of printer's ink and burning pine. The sound of the male voices murmured on while now and then the soft clatter of wood sounded as they selected furniture or maple engravings for their project.

The door opened and Sarah turned in her swivel chair.

A man had entered and stood smiling broadly at her. He was dressed in a beaver bowler and a dark plaid woolen greatcoat with attached cape. She removed her spectacles to see him more clearly.

"Hello, Sarah."

"Robert!"

Her heart did a doubletake as she bolted from the chair and met him in a fond embrace halfway across the room. In all the years she'd known Robert Baysinger they had never touched more than hands in a formal greeting, but his unexpected arrival chased propriety from both their minds. "What in the *world* are you doing here?" she asked, quite crushed in his arms.

"I received your letter."

He released all but her hands, gripping them firmly as they stood back to study one another.

"Oh Robert, it's so good to see you." From the first time he'd come to their house as a very young boy, she had thrilled at the sight of him. But he'd had eyes for no girl but Addie.

"It's good to see you, too. You look very well."

"So do you." She had never seen him in such rich clothes before. He had grown a beard and mustache—those old dislikes which on most men looked shoddy. On Robert they look distinguished, and immediately she loved them. "How I've longed for a glimpse of someone from back home, and here you are, stepping into my office as if you'd only crossed the street."

"Believe me, I crossed more than a street." They laughed and he released her hands reluctantly. "Is there somewhere we can talk privately?"

"Oh goodness . . ." She thought fast. "Yes, at Mrs. Roundtree's, where I live. There shouldn't be anyone in the parlor at this time of day. But first come and meet some friends of mine." She led the way toward the others, who'd been watching with unconcealed interest. "Patrick Bradigan and Josh Dawkins, I'd like to introduce an old friend, Robert Baysinger, who's just arrived from St. Louis."

During handshakes Sarah explained, "Patrick is my typesetter and Josh is our apprentice." The three exchanged pleasantries while Sarah fetched her coat and tied an unadorned brown wool bonnet on her head. "I'll be gone for a while. Lock up if I'm not back before closing time."

With her hand tucked securely in the crook of Robert's arm, the two of them made their way to Mrs. Roundtree's.

"You gave me such a surprise, Robert."

"Undoubtedly. But not unpleasant, I hope."

"Of course not. How have you been?"

"Heartsore. Wondering if what I'm doing is the right thing."

"You've come here to see Addie of course."

"Of course. I made the decision as soon as I received your letter, but it took some time to get arrangements made."

"She's not the same, you know."

"Perhaps not, but I find I cannot live in peace until I make an attempt to get her out of that sordid life she's fallen into. Call me a fool—I know, I am—but I've never been able to forget her. So I persuaded a group of investors to back me and I've come to the hills to build a stamp mill."

"A stamp mill! Oh Robert, you'll be rich in no time."

He laughed. "I dearly hope so."

"We need one so badly here."

"Which you implied in your letter. That's what put the idea in my head."

"What do you know about it?"

"Not a lot, but I'm learning. I've been to Denver and bought the stamps themselves and learned what I could there. It's a relatively simple procedure, and I'll be relying on the experienced miners to help me set it up."

They had reached Mrs. Roundtree's. In the parlor, Robert politely helped Sarah remove her coat.

"Thank you," she said, slipping from it, watching as he hung it on the tree along with his own. It had been a long time since a man had performed this courtesy for her. Robert did it with the naturalness of a true gentleman. He had been her ideal and still was. How ever could Addie have run away from him?

He waited until she sat before doing so himself on an adjacent chair.

"Now tell me about Addie," he said.

"Oh Robert . . ." She sighed, her expression doleful. "You mustn't expect to see the same woman or to be welcomed with any degree of warmth. She's become very hard, remote most of the time, wearing a sort of shield to ward off any sort of closeness to other human beings."

"She's still that way with you?"

"I've made some progress. I bought her a cat—it looks just like old Ruler. You remember Ruler, don't you?"

"Yes, of course I do."

"That seemed to break the ice infinitesimally. I've been allowed to sit in her room and visit with her briefly, but she refuses to come and visit me at either my newspaper office or here. I've never run into her on the street, and she won't talk about the past. So if you intend to change her, you have a big job ahead of you."

"Thank you for the warning. I'll move with the utmost caution."

She felt pity for him, for his undying devotion to a woman who did not deserve it and who would undoubtedly hurt him far more deeply than even she, Sarah, had been hurt.

"Oh Robert," she said, leaning forward in her chair and reaching a hand to cover one of his. "It's so very good to see you again."

He turned his hand over, gave hers a squeeze and said, "That goes both ways." After several beats of fond silence they sat back. "So tell me all about you, your newspaper, the people here and all that gold. The reports continue to astound the rest of the country."

They had a long, friendly visit, lasting until nearly suppertime, when the other boarders started clumping in.

"Where are you staying?" she inquired as he rose to leave.

"At the Grand Central Hotel."

She rose and stood facing him. "I understand some of its rooms are getting plastered. Maybe you'll be lucky and get one."

The door opened and Noah Campbell stepped into the room, dressed for the weather in his thick sheepskin jacket and Stetson. As he closed the door his eyes, unsmiling, scanned Sarah . . . Robert . . . returned to Sarah for no longer than it takes a flint to spark. He nodded curtly and hit for the stairs.

"Just a minute, Marshal," she called.

He turned back and stopped several paces from them, his boots planted wide, his hat still on.

"This is Robert Baysinger, who's just arrived from St. Louis." Sarah added for Robert's benefit, "Noah Campbell, our marshal. He lodges here, too."

"Baysinger."

"Marshal."

The men shook hands. Robert smiled. Noah did not.

"Mr. Baysinger intends to open up a stamp mill here."

"Good luck," Campbell said and withdrew abruptly enough to appear unpardonably rude.

"Your marshal doesn't seem to like me," Robert ventured when Noah's bootsteps sounded in the upstairs hall.

"Think nothing of it. He doesn't seem to like anybody. I think he has a dyspeptic stomach."

They chuckled softly in parting and Robert touched his cheek to hers.

"I'll be seeing you soon."

"You know where to find me."

"Wish me luck with Addie."

"Good luck."

At supper Noah remained aloof. He talked with the others, joked and laughed, but whenever he glanced Sarah's way his face turned passive. Afterward she went upstairs to fetch her coat and returned to her office to finish the proofreading she had abandoned earlier.

There were still coals in the stove, and the clock kept her company with its soft, metronomic *tuk, tuk, tuk.* She had been reading at her desk for fifteen minutes when the door opened and Noah Campbell entered.

She removed her spectacles, swiveled her chair and remained sitting. "Yes, Marshal, is there something I can do for you?"

"I'm just making my rounds."

She sat back, holding her eyeglasses upon her knee by their wire bows. "I'm sure you could see through the windows nothing is amiss here."

"You don't usually come down here after supper."

"Am I required to get your permission before doing so?"

"No."

"Then I shan't." She turned back to work, waiting for him to leave. Behind her all remained quiet while the clock continued its message.

Out of the blue, Campbell inquired, "Where's Baysinger?"

Again she swung to face him. Again she removed her spectacles, made a triangle of them and tapped her knee. "You were very rude to him, you know."

"Who is he?"

"An old friend."

Campbell's mouth took on the shape of one who is trying to bite a poppy seed in half with his incisors. After staring at her for several seconds he shifted his weight to the opposite foot and said, "You're getting to have quite a few of those, aren't you?"

"Must I get permission for *that?*"

"Don't get impertinent, Sarah, you know what I mean!"

To the best of her recollection it was the first time he'd used her given name.

"I'm afraid I *don't* know what you mean. Would you care to elucidate?"

"People talk, you know! It won't take long and they'll be saying you're cut from the same bolt as your sister if you keep on the way you have been."

"Keep on doing *what?*"

"Spending time with every Tom, Dick and Harry who comes along, that's what!"

"Are you lecturing me on my morals, Mr. Campbell?"

"Well, somebody's got to! Baysinger makes four men you've spent time with in the past two weeks! What do you think that looks like, for God's sake?"

"Are you forgetting where you were the first time I met you?"

"That has nothing to do with this!" He jabbed a finger at the floor.

"Oh, doesn't it! You frequent the local whorehouse, but I cannot even meet self-respecting men in public places without getting evangelized! If our situations were reversed, would you appreciate being lectured to by me?"

He glowered at her for some time before throwing up his hands. "I don't know why I bother wasting my breath."

"Neither do I. In the future, why don't you just save it? Now if you'll excuse me, Marshal, I have work to do."

She presented her back while he stood for several seconds glaring at it. Then his footsteps clunked toward the door and he slammed it with unnecessary vehemence, leaving her to stare at the cubbyholes of her desk with her heart tripping fast in confusion.

Chapter 10

❧

Up at Rose's it was dinnertime for the first shift. Cook had made chicken and dumplings this noon. The aroma drifted upstairs and made Addie's mouth water. Garbed in her dressing gown, she picked up Ruler and left the room. "Come with me, missy, and I'll get you some gravy." There wasn't much good to say about *the life,* but the food was one of them. They ate like royalty. Had the freshest foods available, and their own cow boarded at a livery (after all, they *needed* the butter!) and all the milk, cream, sugar and mashed potatoes and pies and cakes it took to keep a covey of confined females happy. Glorianne was a good cook and didn't skimp on anything.

In the kitchen doorway Addie met Ember, one of the Frenchies.

Addie's expression grew vengeful. "What're *you* doing down here? You're not allowed in here with us!" She passed the woman shoulder-first, making sure not even her cat's hair brushed Ember's arm.

"Don't get your tits in an uproar, Eve baby. I just came down to fill my butter bowl."

"Fill it on your own dinnertime!"

"You don't own the kitchen, bitch!"

"If I did you wouldn't be working here at all!"

They had their social stratum which segregated them at mealtime: the

Frenchies, who specialized in oral sex, ate after the straights, who disdained what the Frenchies did upstairs. The ill feelings between the two groups spawned verbal sniping at the best of times, killings at the worst.

In the last house where Addie had worked, a straight girl named Laurel had put ground glass in the douche of a Frenchie named Clover.

Addie had friends here, though—good friends. Jewel, Heather and Larayne were already at the table when she entered the kitchen with the cat on her arm. Flossie was there, too, but Flossie never said anything, only ate without bending over and left the room with a belch.

"I'd watch that cat around Ember," Heather warned. "She's jealous 'cause you got it."

"She touches this cat and she's a one-nipple whore."

Everyone but Flossie laughed, then they spooned up. On the floor beside the table, Ruler was treated to her own helping of chicken and dumplings, and gravy made of pure cream, while around the table four overweight women ate their fill, followed by enormous servings of thick chocolate cake with butterscotch-nut filling, topped with whipped cream. Prompting them all to eat more, more, more was Glorianne, an immense white woman who played no favorites, so was loved by all. Glorianne was the mother some of them had never known, the grandmother some of them remembered and the provider of the greatest solace in their sordid lives: food. They ate this way every noon, gorging. At suppertime, just before the customers started arriving, they didn't eat much at all.

"Girls, you done me proud," Glorianne approved as she waddled around the table refilling their coffee cups.

Flossie got up, burped her way to the door and left without a word.

"Have you ever seen Flossie smile?" Larayne inquired of the others.

"Never," Jewel answered.

"A couple of times when she scratched Ruler she looked like she was threatening to," Addie said. "but I guess it was just gas bubbles after all."

Larayne reached down and picked up Ruler. Holding her near her face she said, "I wish I had a cat."

Jewel said, "I wish I had a man."

"How many you want?" put in Addie. "At six o'clock they'll be pouring through the doors."

It was a hackneyed joke with many variations. They had laughed at it a hundred times. Dutifully, they laughed once more.

Scratching the cat, Larayne grew wistful. "Someday one of those miners is gonna walk in here with his pockets bulging and—"

"Oh—his *pockets* are going to be bulging." Jewel's interruption got the requisite laugh from Addie and Heather.

"—and he's going to say to me, Larayne honey, let's go buy us a farm down in Missouri and raise some cows and some babies and some chickens and listen to the mourning doves coo while we sit on the porch in the evening."

The group had grown quiet. The cat's purring filled the room.

"That what you want? A farm in Missouri?" Jewel asked. "Me, I'd take a big city—Denver, maybe. My man would run a bank or a jewelry store maybe, and we'd live in one of them grand houses with the porches and roofs like a witch's hat, and there'd be a carriage house out back where the help would live, and on Sundays we'd drive along the thoroughfare like I heard the gentry do."

"Would you have kids?"

"Mmm . . . one or two maybe."

"How 'bout you, Heather? Where would you live?"

"I'd live where you could see the ocean, and my man and me we'd saddle horses and ride in the surf. We'd have a lot of flowers around the house, and sometimes when my back was tired he'd rub it and that's all he'd want . . . just to do that for me without asking anything in return."

They thought about it awhile . . . a man who asked nothing in return. A man who'd deliver them out of this life into one of marital love. It was the fantasy that propelled them from day to day.

"How about you, Eve?"

Addie's expression grew brittle as hard-crack taffy. "You and your men. That's all you think about—well, you're wasting your time. Nobody's going to come in here and carry you off, and if they did, you'd be sorry anyway. There's not one of them worth daydreaming for."

No matter how often they indulged in fantasies, they could not lure Addie. She alone remained cynical.

At that moment Rose bustled in, dressed in a red wrapper. "Time to pack it upstairs, girls, and let the others eat."

They gave her the usual grumblings. "We're still drinking our coffee . . . let 'em wait . . . you're a hard woman, Rose . . ." Nevertheless, they vacated the room, taking the cat and their cups with them.

Addie spent the afternoon ironing her cotton underclothes. She stitched up some popped seams in her gowns and corsets, mixed up a new batch of hair dye and made three poor charcoal sketches of the cat in various poses. At five o'clock she lit her lamp, debated about hairdos— Oriental or French?—heated the hair tongs, arranged her hair in a high pompadour, trimmed it with a feathered aigrette, floured her chest, vermilioned her lips, kohled her eyes and lashed herself into a corset that barely covered her nipples. Beneath it she wore cotton bloomers; over it, the black robe with scarlet poppies, and on her feet, scarlet satin slippers—the girls who wore red shoes turned the most tricks, without fail.

The talk about husbands had, as usual, brought a backlash of depression. As she checked her reflection in the mirror, Addie's mouth was tight, her eyes lifeless.

There was time to go downstairs and have a piece of cake: Glorianne's healing chocolate cake with butterscotch-nut filling.

In the kitchen she cut a piece and stood beside the woodbox, eating it. Larayne came in, drank a dipperful of water and found an oatmeal cookie.

Rose bustled in, trussed in a sapphire-blue surah dress, its twills worn flat from overuse.

"Fella out there askin' for you, Eve. Better get out there."

"Oh damn. Who is it?"

"Never saw him before."

"I'm having a piece of cake."

"Can't keep the customers waiting."

Addie slammed down her plate. On her way toward the door Rose gripped her arm. "Put away the egg timer for this one, Eve. Judging by the way he's dressed, he's worth a lot more than a dollar a minute. You peek his poke first, understand?"

"Yes, ma'am," Addie answered. In this business there were no such things as set fees. For the familiar men who breezed in and out in a matter of minutes, the egg timer was used, but when a new man showed up, a girl was expected to visit first and use her seductive wiles to get an idea of the fellow's worth, then sap him to the limit. Sometimes if a man had no money, his gold watch would do, or whatever of value he happened to have. Once Addie had entertained a trick for a bag of dried beans.

This one, Rose had said, looked rich.

Addie saw him first from behind. He was standing in the murky lounge reading their "menu" when she entered and caught a glimpse of him through the hand railing of the stairway.

Though no one at Rose's called her Addie, there were times since Sarah had shown up in town that she thought of herself by that name: Addie as she'd been before age twelve, holding Ruler, feeding the cat beside her chair, in the company of her friends. She was as close to Addie as she'd ever be again. But the moment she began moving toward the man in the parlor she became Eve.

She loosened the belt on her dressing gown.

Strolled with rocking hips.

Lowered her eyelids.

Opened her lips.

Spoke in a smoky contralto.

"Hello, sugar. You lookin' for little Eve-ey?"

He turned . . . slowly removed a bowler from his head. "Hello, Addie," he said quietly.

Her smile collapsed. Her heart plunged and the blood dropped from her face. The last time she had seen him he was nineteen. Five years had transformed him into an adult with thick side whiskers, a fuller face and a neck to match. He was taller, too, and his caped greatcoat gave the impression of substantial width and acquired wealth. He wore kid gloves and held the expensive beaver hat.

"Robert?" she whispered.

He hid his dismay well. She was nearly unrecognizable, fleshy and half-dressed, with brittle hair and kohl on her eyes. At fifteen she'd been shy and girlish, at sixteen she'd disguised her young breasts behind dresses with large half-moon yokes bordered by ruffles. Now she had breasts the size of cantaloupes, exposed nearly to the tips, the skin as coarse and loose as bread dough.

He smiled sadly. "Yes, it's me."

"What are you doing here?" she asked, closing her dressing gown with one hand. His eyes followed, then dropped politely to the hat in his hands.

"Sarah wrote to me when she found you. I asked her to." Not until her clothes were adjusted did he raise his eyes. Her face had grown red with chagrin.

"You shouldn't have come here."

"Perhaps not. Sarah said the same thing. I found, however, that I could not seem to get on with my life until I had settled this matter of you in my mind."

"Forget me."

"I wish I could," he whispered earnestly. "Don't you think I wish I could?"

"I'm nothing. Less than nothing," she claimed flatly.

"Don't say that."

"Why not? It's true."

"No," he said simply.

For a moment they exchanged gazes, silent and confused.

"It's true," she repeated.

"You were the center of all my hopes and dreams. You were sweet and innocent and caring."

"Well, I'm not anymore!" she snapped. "Now, why don't you just get out of here?"

"I'm not the one who should get out of here, Addie. You are."

"What is this, a conspiracy? First Sarah comes poking her nose into my life, now you! Well, I don't need either one of you! I'm a prostitute, and a damned good one! I earn more money in one week than she'll earn with that goddamned newspaper press in a year, and I don't have to work half as hard to do it! I eat like a queen and lay on my back and get paid for it. How many people do you know that have a life so soft?"

He stood a while before replying quietly, "So coarse, Addie. Are you trying to show me your worst side to scare me off?"

She gazed at him as if he were a sliver on the board wall behind him. "I've got paying customers to get ready for. You'll have to excuse me." She turned toward the stairs.

"You're not getting rid of me that easily. I'll be back."

She climbed the steps without a backward glance, rocking her hips, holding her head high.

"Do you hear me, Addie? I'll be back!"

In her room she closed the door and flattened her spine and palms against it. Her chest ached. Her eyes stung. She squeezed them shut, riveting herself against the door, breathing as if someone had just broadsided her.

He came here to find me!

There wasn't a prostitute in the universe who didn't have dreams like the girls had been voicing this noon: a man coming to take them out of the trade. No matter how tough they talked, how they hated men, how they disdained men every chance they got, they all wanted to be rescued by one and transformed by his love into a woman of virtue. And Addie was no different.

Oh Robert, I didn't want you to see me like this, here in this place where I've become soulless. I've had to—don't you see?—to survive. Now here you come to rake up guilt and confusion and wants that a woman like me doesn't deserve.

She relived the shock of seeing him downstairs. He had been reading the list of aberrations performed in this place on any man who requested them. Did he think she did all that? What the Frenchies did? In spite of it, he had removed his hat. Oh, he had removed his hat. Still pressing the door, she opened her eyes to the blurred rafters. How long had it been since any man had removed his hat in her presence unless it was to sail it out of the way from the middle of a bed? She saw again the shock Robert had almost been able to hide at the sight of her scarcely covered breasts. She saw his cheeks growing florid as he dropped his gaze, and the hurt in his eyes at her purposely coarse language.

Don't come back, Robert, please. I wasn't worthy of you then and I'm not now. It will only hurt you more if you make me tell you why.

Downstairs the piano player struck up "Clementine." Addie had heard it so many times it made her ears jangle. Thrusting herself away from the door, she bolted across the room to her mirror, swiped at the smears of wet kohl dripping down her face and poured water from her pitcher into her bowl. When she had washed her face she applied fresh kohl to her upper and lower eyelids, painted her mouth with carmine paste; glued a black velvet mole on the high inner side of her left breast; atomized her neck, cleavage and thighs with orange blossom cologne; checked the results in the mirror and went to the room next door.

There, she lit a lantern, put a clean flannel pad on top of the counterpane, wound the clock on the table beside it, stationed it beside the egg timer, glanced at the butter bowl to make sure it was amply filled, moved it over to within easy reach of the bed, filled the pitcher and bowl from the tin in the hall, splashed two inches of water into the china chamberpot beside the door, replaced the pitcher and bowl on the wash table and smoothed her corset over her round stomach.

She glanced over the room and discovered Ruler had followed her. She picked up the cat and said, "Come on. You don't belong in here." With the care she displayed for no other living creature, she gently put the cat back in her private room, curled its tail around it on the bed, kissed its face and left it there where it could not witness the degrading side of her life.

Downstairs the men were waiting. One named Johnny Singleton brightened and hurried to the foot of the steps as she descended.

"Hello, Johnny-boy. You're back."

"You betcha, Eve-ey. To see my favorite."

With practiced ease she led him to believe she liked him, felt seduced by him and would rather be with him than with any other man on earth. She teased him in the proper tone, dredged up laughter when it was required, inquired in a seductive whisper if he'd had his carbolic bath, took him upstairs to the room she had prepared, turned over the egg timer, performed the rite with enough false relish to make him feel bullish and virile, collected seven dollars in gold dust when it was over, gave him a goodbye kiss, closed the door behind him, squatted over the china pot to give herself a quick finger douche, washed her hands, dumped the basin in the slop jar in the hall and replaced the pad on the bed with a clean one.

Downstairs, she deposited the gold in the drop box near the kitchen door, made an *x* and two *l*'s on a paper (*x* equaling five dollars, *l* equaling one dollar), signed her name and deposited it, too, then went back to the parlor to smoke a cigar and wait for her next trick.

By four A.M. she had performed the ritual twenty-two times. Beside the bed the butter bowl was nearly empty. In a wooden hamper lay twenty-two soiled flannel pads. In the box downstairs was $236 she had put there.

But Adelaide had had no part in it. Eve had done it all, had lain beneath man after man in the dreary room where the bedding was never turned down. Had laughed and coaxed and joked and stroked. Had drawn from them guttural sounds matching others that could be heard through the thin walls. Had satisfied their needs while pretending she was slicing peaches for a family of four; picking colorful flowers in a dooryard while dressed in white organdy; following a collie out to meet a man walking up a lane, a man who looked very much like Robert; ridden in the surf behind him on a galloping horse . . . whatever fantasy it took to escape the room and the man . . . all the fantasies she refused to divulge when the others daydreamed aloud.

And when all twenty-two had expunged themselves within her body, when she had cleansed herself one last time with a potash douche to kill their seeds and had bathed the smell of their secretions from her skin, she slipped into her own room and coiled herself around the warm, purring cat who demanded nothing of her, who neither used, accused, abused nor asked questions.

Ruler . . . warm, purring sweet Ruler . . . don't ever leave me . . .

The following day Addie roused toward noon, her thoughts indistinct. There was something she was going to do today. She tried to grasp it, but the images that drifted through her mind appeared smudged, as if viewed through a fingerprint.

Her eyes flew open. Oh yes—Sarah. She was going to set Sarah straight today.

Shortly after two o'clock that afternoon Sarah was helping a customer, Josh was gone on an errand, and Patrick had his hands full, cleaning type with a turpentine rag when the door opened and Addie stepped into the *Chronicle* office.

Sarah glanced up and smiled. "I'll be with you in a minute."

Addie waited near the door, wearing a navy blue brimmed hat with a veil drawn down to the chin and tied at the back, partially concealing her face.

Sarah accepted a nickel for a copy of the paper, bid good day to the customer and followed him toward the door. He eyed Addie warily as he passed her, giving Sarah the distinct impression he knew her but was reluctant to admit it in broad daylight in a respectable place of business. Neither did Addie glance his way but waited, stiff as a dagger.

When the door had closed behind him, Sarah gave Addie a second glad smile.

"Addie, I'm so happy you've come!"

"Well, don't be!" Addie snapped. "It's the first and last time I'll set foot in here."

Taken aback, Sarah felt her smile wilt. "What's wrong?"

"You sent for Robert!"

"No."

"Don't lie to me. He's been to see me and he told me you wrote to him."

Across the room, Patrick—bless his soul—kept his back turned, put his rag away, released the quoins from a chase and began to put type away. The sound of metallic clicks created a welcome sound in the otherwise silent room while the two sisters faced each other.

"Yes, I wrote to him because he asked me to. But the truth is, I advised him not to come."

"Well, he has, and it's all because of your meddling."

"Addie, he simply asked me to let him know if you were all right. He was worried about you."

"Seems everybody is lately—him, you—I'm getting more visitors than an Irish wake! Well, I'm not some freak show you can come and stare at whenever you want, so stay away! I don't know what you came nosing around for in the first place. I don't need him and I don't need you. You're not going to reform me, if that's what you have in mind, so you can give up that idea. I said it to him and I'll say it to you—I have a soft life and I don't have to lift a finger to have it. Just stay away—do you hear me—just stay away!''

Addie whirled, yanked open the door and slammed it as she left.

Behind her, Sarah remained rooted, bewildered and hurt, her mouth small, her cheeks burning. She felt the insidious sting of tears build behind her nose and knew in a moment her eyes would be brimming. Patrick had stopped putting away type and stood watching her with a long face, his work forgotten.

She walked primly to the hat tree beside her desk. If she met Patrick's eyes she would embarrass them both. She kept her own downcast while methodically donning her coat and plain brown bonnet.

"I hope you can manage alone for a while, Patrick," she said quietly.

"Sure," he replied with equal quiet. "You just go."

She went. Retreated. Hid. In her room at Mrs. Roundtree's where she sat on a hard chair beside the window and let her tears flow at last. She cried silently, motionlessly. Her hands lay listlessly in her lap, the teardrops plopping between them and making dark circles on her brindle-colored skirt.

Addie, Addie, why? I only want to be your friend. I need a friend, too, don't you see? We share bonds that cannot be broken, no matter how you try. The same mother, father, memories. On this entire earth we are the only blood relatives to one another. Does that count for nothing?

How consuming, the loneliness of the discarded. To reach out in love and have that love flung back hurt as nothing Sarah had experienced before. She felt an aloneness as deep as that of the orphaned, or the aged who have outlived their offspring. Sitting at her window, depleted, motionless, she felt as if the tears rolling quietly down her cheeks drew from her her last reserves of strength. With a great sigh she rose and stretched across the bed to escape in sleep.

The window had darkened to the blue of early gloaming when Sarah awakened. Someone was knocking.

"Yes?" she called. "Who is it?"

"It's Mrs. Roundtree. Are you all right in there?"

Sarah sat up unsteadily. "I'm fine."

"Supper's been on the table for ten minutes already. Aren't you coming down?"

She made a muddled mental search for a time reference—What day? What hour? Why am I in my dress?—and answered, "I'll be right there." She dragged herself to the edge of the bed and waited for reality to return. Her head hurt. Her entire body felt shaky. Her pulsebeats seemed to be magnified until they jiggled the bed. Horrible feeling, coming out of a deep sleep that way and groping for crisp edges.

As those edges returned she stood, moved about in the gloom, touching her tender eyelids, straightening her hair, wetting the sides with a comb, brushing at her skirt, tugging at her sleeves. When she'd put herself in reasonable order she descended into the light below. Entering the dining room, she felt each man turn and look.

"You all right, Miss Merritt?" Mr. Mullins asked. She had come to be regarded as an ingenue over whose welfare all the men presided.

"I'm fine, really. Go on with your meal."

She took her chair across from Noah Campbell and saw his hands stall over his food as he studied her wrinkled shirtwaist and puffy eyes. Without speaking, he reached for a platter of fried fish and extended it her way. "Thank you," she said, avoiding his eyes. The others resumed their mealtime chatter. Noah Campbell took no part in it but watched Sarah surreptitiously as she nibbled at the food on her plate, leaving much of it untouched.

"Why, you haven't eaten enough to keep a sparrow alive," Mrs. Roundtree chided as she collected plates.

"I'm sorry. It's very good, really, but I just don't seem to have an appetite tonight."

"There's blackberry sauce for dessert."

"No, none for me," Sarah replied. "If you'll excuse me, I have some writing to do." She rose and left the room.

The marshal watched her go, guilt-stricken for having brought this on with his outburst last night in her newspaper office. He hesitated less than five seconds before hastily rising, sending his chair scraping back. "No sauce for me either. Good meal though, Mrs. Roundtree."

He took the stairs two at a time and reached the upper hall just as Sarah's door was closing.

"Miss Merritt," he called, "could I talk to you?"

She reopened the door and stood waiting, the room behind her black, only one lantern shedding dim light from its wall bracket two doors down. "Yes, Marshal?"

He stopped before her, hatless, gunless, the star on his black leather vest catching the light. "I'll be going out again to give the town the once-over. If you need Doc Turley I can send him up."

"Mr. Campbell, I'm not certain I can handle all this concern from you. Have you taken it upon yourself to become my personal guardian angel?"

"I got a little heavy-handed with you last night. I'm sorry."

"Yes, you did."

"I'm trying to apologize," he said.

She looked square into his eyes and saw the potential of a good man. "Apology accepted."

Eye to eye, they stood and felt their misgivings beginning to slip, uneasy as they so often were when this happened. Foes . . . friends . . . antagonistic . . . sympathetic. It seemed they could not find an even emotional keel with one another.

"Now, about Doc Turley . . ."

She gingerly touched her eyelids. "Do I look like I need him?"

"Well, something's wrong, I can tell."

"I've been crying," she admitted point-blank. "I don't do it very often, I can assure you."

His eyes settled on hers and stayed. "Was it about your sister?"

Sarah nodded.

"There was scuttlebutt in town that she came out of Rose's and went to see you today."

"Yes, at the newspaper office. It was about Robert Baysinger. By now you probably know who he is."

"No, I don't."

"We all grew up together in St. Louis. He was Adelaide's first suitor when she was sixteen years old."

"Adelaide's?"

"Yes. When I left there Robert asked me to write him and let him know if I found Addie, and how she was. I did that after I arrived in Deadwood, never suspecting that Robert was planning to come here himself. When he showed up yesterday no one was more surprised than I. Except, perhaps, Addie."

"I can imagine."

"I don't know what passed between them, but he went to see her at Rose's, and she came to me today accusing me of bringing him here to try to reform her."

"Did you?"

"No. I told you, I had no idea he was even coming. He simply arrived unannounced."

"At Rose's, too, I take it."

"Exactly."

Noah crossed his arms and leaned a shoulder against the doorframe. "What does he want from her?"

"I don't know, but she's so angry at me and I don't understand why."

"Ask her."

"I have. It's as if she doesn't hear me. For a while I thought I was making some progress. I didn't push her, but I didn't let her forget I was here. I went to visit her regularly and thought if I just let her know I cared, that I was here for her to rely on if she needed anything, it would effect a slow healing of whatever it was that had come between us." She paused thoughtfully before continuing. "For a while it seemed to be working. Especially after I gave her the cat. She actually let me sit on the foot of her bed. She named the cat after . . . oh, I already told you that, didn't I? Well, I took it as a good sign. The first memory of our childhood she allowed, you see. But today . . ." Sarah's expression became dejected and she leaned against the opposite doorframe. "I'm afraid I just don't know what to do anymore."

They stood facing each other, their enmity forgotten for the moment. After some silent reflection Noah said, on a sigh, "Ahh, sisters and brothers . . ." He gave a mirthless chuckle. "We're reared being told to love them, but sometimes it's hard, isn't it?"

Tom Taft and Andrew Mullins came upstairs and excused themselves as they went by the couple at the near end of the hall. Noah removed his shoulder from the doorway to give them room to pass, then resumed his pose.

"Addie and I have always been so different," Sarah continued, as if the interruption hadn't taken place.

"So have Arden and I."

"You and I are the older ones. We're supposed to set a good example, but even when we do they don't always follow it, do they?"

"Not at all."

They spent some time pondering before Sarah went on. "When we were girls I always worked and Addie never did. Our father made me learn the newspapering trade while she was never required to do anything. I couldn't understand why he babied her so, why she didn't have to at least run errands for him. Now I see that I was the lucky one. She told me this afternoon that she has no intention of reforming, because she has a soft life with no work.''

''She said that?''

Sarah nodded.

He left the doorframe, settling his weight on both feet. ''At the risk of treading on forbidden ground, I don't think the life of those women in the badlands is soft. The men who go there aren't always gentlemen. I know because I've been called up there more than once to arrest some of the customers.''

''For . . . for hurting the girls, you mean?''

He leveled his gaze on her without replying.

''Answer me, Marshal.''

He did so reluctantly. ''It happens, whether you want to believe it or not.''

Sarah closed her eyes and rubbed her forehead. She looked at Campbell again and asked, ''Then why won't she leave it?''

''Maybe she feels caught. Where would she go? What would she do?''

''I'm here. She could help me with the newspaper.''

''No offense, Sarah, but your sister isn't exactly . . . well, let's say she'd have to go some to get as bright as you.''

''I could teach her.''

''Maybe you could, but how much would she earn?''

''Enough to live decently.''

''I don't think she ever could live decently, not in the sense that you mean, not in the town where she knows all the men the way she does. The women would shut her out.''

''What women? There are only twenty of us here and I think they'd give her a chance out of respect for me if I asked them to.''

''There'll be more coming and you know it. Besides, I think you overestimate the extent of the ''good women's' forbearance.''

''I suppose you're right. So what should I do . . .'' With a hand on her heart, Sarah thrust her head forward. ''. . . let her live there and do what she does and pretend she's not my sister?''

''I don't know. Sometimes we just have to let people make their own mistakes. It's the same with Arden. He never thinks things through, just charges headlong when he gets an idea before he takes time to think it through. I try to tell him, Arden, if you're going to survive in this world you'd better take time to think about the consequences of your actions *before* you move.''

''Does he ever listen to you?''

Again the marshal relaxed against the doorframe. ''No, hardly. When we were pups he'd be the one with all the reckless ideas—jump off the riverbank before you knew if there were rocks underneath, tease a wild badger before you knew how fast he could run. Arden would get hurt and I'd catch hell for it. Ma would get on me something awful without waiting for me to explain. But he's one of those guys—hell, you just can't hold 'em down.''

''So I noticed.'' They exchanged a long, placid look.

''I never asked before, but how did the two of you get along?''

''The way you'd expect. He ran two steps ahead of me all night long. I was much too breathless for comfort.''

Noah thought about remarking that they'd been neck and neck when Arden escorted her to the bottom of the steps, but refrained. He studied her shadowed face, realizing that at some time during the past two months he had grown accustomed to her tallness, to her eyes being nearly on a plane with his, to her utilitarian mode of dress and her long thin face which no longer put him off. At some point in their acquaintanceship his respect for her had come to supersede these superficialities.

"He says he's going to ask you out to the place sometime. You going?"

She looked him straight in the eye. "Actually," she replied, "I'd rather go with you."

Her honesty caught him by surprise though he continued lounging against the doorframe with his weight on one hip.

"I think that could be arranged."

"Your mother intrigued me and I'd like to meet your father."

"They're good people."

"You're very lucky to still have them."

"Yes, I know."

They sent each other timid half-smiles and she realized that at some time since she'd lived here she had begun anticipating mealtimes with him across the table, she had ceased objecting to his unannounced appearances at the newspaper office and had grown to feel secure because he was always sleeping down the hall.

After a moment he said, "We could go out some Monday. The town's usually quietest then."

"I'd like that."

He drew away from the wall. "Well . . . I'd better get my jacket and hat and go make my rounds. I could walk you up to the newspaper office if you're going back up there."

"I'm staying home tonight. I'm going to write in my room."

After a hesitation beat, he said, "Well, good night then."

"Good night."

He headed for the opposite end of the hall.

"Mr. Campbell?" she called after him.

He turned and paused directly beneath the lantern, which put rich rust highlights in his hair and mustache.

"Thank you for offering to get Dr. Turley."

He smiled, becoming a male reflection of his mother.

"Don't worry about your sister. She'll make out all right."

He turned and continued away while she quietly closed her door.

Chapter 11

The following evening Mrs. Roundtree knocked on Sarah's door. "You have a caller, Sarah."

"Thank you. I'll be right down."

She capped her ink, looked in the mirror, patted her hair and went downstairs.

"Robert," she said with a glad smile. "I was hoping it would be you."

"I thought perhaps we might go out for a walk so we could talk privately." There were three men in the parlor.

"Of course. Let me get my coat and I'll be right back down."

The November night was clear and brisk. A quarter moon hung like a lopsided smile, trimming the edges of objects with a rim of silver. The shadows of the gulch walls were as black as printer's ink. He took her arm as they headed down the path and followed Deadwood Creek to the spot where it intersected with Whitetail Creek, then up the incline toward Lead.

"You saw Addie?" Sarah opened.

"Yes."

"And you got no further than I did."

"No."

"Depressing place, isn't it?"

"How can she live there? And do that?"

"I don't know. Did you see her room?"

"No. The lobby was bad enough."

"They refer to it as the parlor."

"Parlor . . . ha."

"My feelings exactly. My skin crawls each time I walk through it."

"There was a list on the wall."

"Yes, I've seen it."

No more was said on the subject. They walked along through the shadows.

"Are you sorry you came?" Sarah asked.

"Yes. And no. Seeing her for myself—the way you described her—was a shock. But with two of us working on her, maybe we'll be successful in making her leave that life. And I came for one other reason."

"To get rich."

"Yes."

"You always said you would."

"You remember how it was in my family . . . so many mouths at the table that my mother didn't even peel the rutabagas. The skins were too precious. Well, I made up my mind early that I'd never be like that. I wouldn't have to worry where the next meal was coming from, or the next stick of wood. I want to be rich so I never have to go through what my parents did. Does that sound avaricious, Sarah?''

"Not at all. And I'm sure you'll do it."

"I have a good head, and I've never been short of ideas. When you wrote about the need for the stamp mills I *knew.* I just *knew* it was the opportunity of a lifetime. If I could get financial backing to build one I'd see my dream come true, and I will. The men behind the stamp mill have placed great trust in me and I aim to see that trust pay off for them and for me.''

"And what then, Robert?"

"What then?"

"If you could get Addie to leave Rose's, would you marry her?"

"I don't know. While I was traveling out here, I thought about it. I pictured myself taking her out of that brothel and making her into the sweet girl she used to be. I guess I fancied myself some kind of noble cavalier. But facing her as she is today, I really don't know."

"It would take a very special man to forget her past."

"To tell you the truth, Sarah, I'm not sure I ever could."

She thought, *If you cannot, I'll be here waiting. Perhaps one day you will finally notice.*

"But enough about me," Robert said, changing the mood. "What about you? Tell me everything that's happened since you've been here."

"Well, I haven't gotten rich, nor do I want to, but I'm happy running Father's press. I started with a single page and have already expanded to four. The paper is paying its way, and of course I print everything from the theater bills to "wanted' posters, which also bring in good money. I've attracted many of the merchants to advertise in the *Chronicle,* and I have excellent help in Patrick and Josh. I don't know what I'd do without them."

"And what about your social life? Considering how few women there are in this town, I imagine the men sit up and take notice."

"Well, yes . . . actually. I've had offers to play a thirteen-stop organ and look at the Taj Mahal through a stereoscopic viewer."

They laughed, and Sarah went on. "I've been cooked a real roast beef dinner, which is hard to come by here, and I've been given a green and white striped umbrella in the middle of November by a man four years my junior who made me an offer of marriage—sort of."

"Sort of?"

"You'd have to know Arden to understand. But that's not all. I've also been arrested for causing a riot, thrown in jail for causing a man to get shot, threatened by the marshal who said he'd like to drag me down the street by my hair, and tried by a local grocer. It certainly hasn't been dull."

"Sarah, is that all true?" Robert stared at her agape. They had returned to town and stopped before the doorway of her shop.

"Every word."

"And you aren't going to enlighten me?" His eyes were wide with amazement.

"Of course, but it'll take awhile. Would you like to come inside where it's a little warmer?"

In the newspaper office she lit a wall lantern and put a stick of wood on the glowing coals. Robert sat on Patrick's tall stool and Sarah on her swivel desk chair. They talked for two hours.

Marshal Campbell saw the windows of the *Chronicle* office glowing and crossed the street on foot. His exchange with Sarah last night had been as close to pleasant as any so far. At breakfast today she'd been friendly, and at supper congenial. He'd just step into her office and say hello, let her know he was on the job, maybe pass a few minutes chatting. She was interesting to talk to, involved as she was in all the news of the town. She had opinions about everything, and though sometimes they weren't the same as his own, he'd come to appreciate the amount of thought she put into her views.

He reached her window, glanced inside and stepped back into the shadows.

She was there all right, but so was Baysinger, settled comfortably on a high stool while she—on her chair with one foot on an open desk drawer—rocked left and right as they talked. Their coats hung on the bentwood coat-tree as if they'd been there for some time. There was no evidence of interrupted work. The cover of Sarah's desk was rolled down. Her pen and ink were nowhere in sight.

Noah Campbell stood at the edge of the window light, coming to grips with a small pang of jealousy.

Jealousy? Where had that come from?

Baysinger said something, pointing to the plastered walls, and she laughed. He laughed, too, then she rose and went to the rear of the room where she opened the stove door. He followed and took over the job of sticking another piece of wood in the stove. With her back to the window, Sarah crossed her arms. Baysinger slipped the fingers of both hands into the rear waist of his trousers. They stood together that way, facing the stove, presumably talking.

Campbell watched until he grew tired of waiting for them to move, finally doing so himself, walking away without ever entering the *Chronicle* office.

Robert and Sarah had made a pact. Every day, without fail, each of them would visit Addie. No matter how bald her rejections, no matter how repugnant her domicile, they would pursue a campaign of invitations. To dinner. For a walk. To the newspaper office. For a ride. They would take her small gifts. They would—they vowed—break her down with love.

Meanwhile, the town of Deadwood reveled in the news that it was to have its first stamp mill. Robert Baysinger's name was spoken with near reverence even before Sarah put an article in the *Deadwood Chronicle* announcing his arrival and intent. Robert had brought the stamps themselves—there were forty of them—from Denver. Construction got underway immediately on a steep sidehill of Bear Butte Creek. A sturdy wooden structure was built to support the great steel shoes, which were driven by a steam engine. The shoes raised and lowered upon a sheet of mercury-coated copper, to which the smaller gold particles adhered while the larger ones rolled on down the hill to be collected below. The mill would do contract work, keeping ten percent of all the gold that was stamped.

Robert had no trouble finding employees to build and work in his mill; not everyone in the gulches had "seen the elephant." There were many whom the color had eluded, or who had lost their diggings at the gambling tables, or whose claims had petered out.

Because he brought a service to the goldfields that had been much needed, while at the same time providing steady work for over two dozen employees, Robert became a prominent and well-liked man.

He settled into the Grand Central Hotel, returning to it without fail at four o'clock every afternoon to wash and shave, splash his face with bay rum, don a clean white shirt with a new linen collar, his gray and brown striped cassimere suit, his heavy caped coat and his freshly brushed bowler. As a finishing touch, he carried an ivory-headed walking stick each day when he set out for Rose's, making certain he arrived well in advance of the evening customers.

"Good afternoon," he would say politely to Flossie when she answered the door. "May I see Miss Merritt, please?"

Addie would come downstairs, often in a state of semidress. He would ignore her exposed skin and ask, looking straight into her cold eyes, "May I buy you a piece of pie, Addie?" or "Do you have a night off when I might take you to the theater, Addie?" or "Would you like to ride out with me to see the stamp mill, Addie?"

Addie would answer, "Only if you buy me off the floor."

He would reply politely, "No, not that way. Perhaps another day you'll feel like getting out." And he would hand her some token—a bright blue jay's feather he'd found by the mill, an abandoned bird's nest he'd plucked from a pine, an exceptionally pretty rock with pink stripes running through it, a humorous drawing from some old publication, a braided clump of dried sweetgrass he'd found out in the hills which could be burned to scent the air.

He never took her anything of monetary value, only offerings he thought of as "gifts of the heart."

She never refused them, but she never said thank you.

Sarah went, too, each day around noon when Addie was likely to be up and on her own time. She would offer news about Robert's enterprise— "The mill is going up fast," or about neutral subjects—"Everyone in town is talking about the telegraph coming." She would bring offerings, too: a fresh bun from Emma's bakery, the latest issue of her paper, an origami bird Patrick had folded from a sheet of newsprint, the raisin-filled cookie from last night's supper. She would keep her smile intact while Addie offered none, and at the end of the visit would remind her sister, "I have work for you anytime you want it, Addie, and a room at Mrs. Roundtree's we can share."

If the way to Addie's heart was by showing they cared, Sarah and Robert believed that one day their method would work.

On December 1, 1876, the telegraph line reached Deadwood from Fort Laramie, where it connected with Western Union. The town went crazy. It was a clear, mild winter day and everyone piled into the streets to watch the final wire being hung in midafternoon. When the connection was made, the man on the pole raised his arm and a deafening cheer rose. Sarah was standing below with Patrick, Josh, Byron and Emma. Hats flew in the air. The roar became immense. Byron picked up Emma and swung her off her feet. Someone did the same to Sarah and she hugged him hard and shouted in his ear, "Isn't it wonderful?" He set her down and kissed her hard on the mouth—a miner whose name she did not know—then they laughed and cheered with the rest of the town.

"Come on, Patrick, we must get to the telegraph office!" she shouted above the din.

They pressed through the crowd to the tiny office where the town's first telegraph operator, James Halley, was sitting at his spanking new desk with his finger on the brass telegraph key. It was too crowded inside for two more bodies, so Sarah tapped on the window and a man named Quinn Fortney raised it so Sarah could hear what was being said as the mayor of Deadwood sent a message to the mayor of Cheyenne.

"Shhh! Shhhh!" The signal hushed the crowd while those nearby heard the first *tap-t-t-tap* come back with a congratulatory message. When it was complete, James Halley came out onto the telegraph office steps and read it loud enough for those a block away to hear.

"Congratulations, Deadwood. Stop. Now a copper wire connects the fabulously rich goldfields of the Black Hills with the world at large. Stop. Expect great progress to follow. Stop. Congratulations. Stop. R. L. Bresnahem. Stop. Mayor of Cheyenne. Stop."

Another cheer rose. Men were hugging men. Patrick was hugging Sarah. Somewhere a banjo played. Men danced jigs. Patrick kissed Sarah, and she was too excited to consider objecting.

"Just think, Patrick!" she shouted joyously. "We can get news from all over America the same day it happens!"

"And you'll go to six pages, then eight, and me fingers'll be nubbins keepin' up with y'."

She laughed happily. "No, not for a while. Now let me go. I must get people's impressions during all this excitement."

She wove through the crowd asking the question, "What does the arrival of the telegraph mean to you?"

Dutch Van Aark said it meant he could place an order one day and have it arrive by stage three days later.

Dan Turley said it could mean saved lives, as in the instance of the smallpox outbreak they'd just had, when the disease could have been identified faster and the vaccine points ordered in one day instead of three.

Shorty Reese said it meant the miners would get the going rate for their gold dust.

Teddy Ruckner said it meant he could let his relatives in Ohio know he was all right without having to write letters.

Benjamin Winters said it meant he was throwing the biggest party the town had ever seen at his Grand Central Hotel starting *immediately!* He ended with a fist in the air, raising a roar of approval. He led the way toward his establishment with a surge of men following. "Hey, everybody, party at the Grand Central! Get that banjo player!"

In the midst of the crowd, Sarah turned and found Noah Campbell behind her.

"Marshal, isn't it wonderful?" Her smile was broad as a sickle blade.

"I hope so. We'll see if this crowd gets out of order before it's all over."

"Oh, they're just celebrating. It's the biggest day in Deadwood's history.

Tell me, Marshal, for the *Deadwood Chronicle*—what does the coming of the telegraph mean to you?"

"Means I can get any news about stagecoach holdups while the trail's still hot. Maybe pick me up a couple of rewards, huh?" He grinned mischievously, which she'd never seen him do before. "But right now it means I'm going over to the Grand Central to join the celebration, whether it gets out of hand or not. How about you? Do you know how to celebrate or is that all you do is work?"

"Oh, I know how to celebrate. I'm actually quite good at it."

"Then let's go."

"I'd love to, but I must find Patrick and Josh first and tell them I'm closing the office for the day."

"Then you'll come over yourself?"

"Yes."

"*Without* your notebook and pen?"

"Well, I can't promise that."

"You can't dance with your inkpot open."

"How do you know I can dance at all?"

"You'd better be able to when you're a woman and there's a banjo playing in this town."

"We'll see," she said, and left him in the middle of the street with the crowd milling and the sound of the banjo moving his way.

Patrick and Josh were nowhere to be found, so she hung a sign on the office door saying CLOSED FOR THE DAY, and locked it behind her. The street was still clogged with people, all gay and excited, more than ready to regale until the wee hours.

On an impulse she detoured to Mrs. Roundtree's. If this was to be her first party in Deadwood she had no intention of spending it dressed in her puce-brown skirt and workday shirtwaist. Though it was nearly suppertime, the house was empty: even her landlady was somewhere in the crowd downtown, kicking up her heels.

In her room, Sarah washed, put rosewater beneath her arms, brushed down her hair and tucked it back behind her ears with a pair of shell side-combs, then, at her forehead, squiggled six strands with the curlings tongs. She hooked on a sturdy jean corset, topped it with two white petticoats, tied on her crinoline bustle for the first time since coming to Deadwood and dressed in her only good suit—a forest-green polonaise jacket over a rose and green striped nansook skirt with a square-pleated ruffle at the hem.

Before the mirror she neither simpered nor quailed, only gave herself a parting glance and went out to join the fun, leaving her pen and notebook at home.

Up at Rose's it was later than usual when Robert arrived. The piano player was plunking desultorily in the parlor, and Rose was playing solitaire at a table, with a burning cigar in the corner of her mouth. Though it was time for customers to be arriving, none were.

Addie came downstairs when summoned, and for once she was fully dressed, though the cerise garment left much of her chest unveiled.

Robert was waiting at the foot of the stairs. "Addie," he said, "have you—"

"My name is Eve."

"Not to me. Have you heard the news, Addie? The telegraph has arrived. Benjamin Winters is throwing a party at the Grand Central Hotel. Will you come with me?"

"Sure. But an outdate'll cost you plenty."

"This is a social invitation, not a business one."

"I don't accept social invitations."

"Make an exception for an old friend."

"Are you crazy?"

"Not at all. Will you come to the Grand Central with me for the evening?"

"I've got to work."

"No, you don't. There aren't any customers. They're all down at the Grand Central. Now, go upstairs and get rid of the raccoon eyes, and put on a decent dress and come with me."

A fleeting expression touched Addie's face, making it momentarily vulnerable. Her eyes met his and stayed. He sensed her resolve weakening, and saw a first crack form in her veneer of heartlessness. Then Rose dropped her cards and pushed back her chair. Sauntering over to Robert with the smoking cigar crooked in her finger and a hand on her hip, she said, "You're suckin' wind, mister. Eve told you she's working, and she is. Where would I be if I let my girls walk out of here with cheapskates like you who expect their attentions for free. I'm running a business here, Baysinger. Either dig out your gold dust or leave."

His glance encountered Rose. It struck him that although the girls were not locked here physically, she held them with a grip more restraining than any steel lock. She fed them a daily diet of self-recrimination and intimidation cleverly disguised as tact. *We keep off the streets because nobody wants to see us there.* She kept her girls off the streets so they wouldn't get a taste of what they were missing.

Coming to this conclusion, Robert let his glance slide away from Rose as if she were an insect in his soup.

"Addie?"

"Do as she says."

"All right. But you must have *some* time to yourself. You need to get out of here, Addie. You can't live your entire life shut inside this building. Think about it, and I'll be back."

He extended his hand and she took it. Under the guise of a handshake he transferred to her palm something small and soft.

"I liked your hair much better when it was the color of cornsilk. Goodbye, Addie. I'll see you again soon."

When he was gone she returned upstairs. Alone in her room she opened the small square of tissue and found within it a lock of hair he had snipped from her head many years ago. She touched it—soft, golden, slightly curled—and reminiscence flooded back. She had been what—fourteen? Fifteen? He had come one evening in spring to play dominoes, and had brought her a red tulip he'd stolen from his mother's garden. She had told him, "I don't have anything to give you in return."

"I know something," he'd said.

"What?"

"A lock of your hair."

He had taken the scissors himself and snipped it from the nape of her neck while they had chuckled secretly and, afterward, had kissed and forgotten all about playing dominoes.

In her room on the second floor of Rose's, Addie touched her nape and recalled the exquisiteness of his youthful admiration. She looked into her mirror and reality returned in the form of the coarse black pelt hanging square-cut below her ears. Rose had said, dye it. Too many blondes this far north. You want to make money as a blonde, you go south where most of the women are black-haired. You want to make money up north, you go black.

Studying her reflection in the mirror, Addie wondered what it would be like to return to blonde after all these years.

The Grand Central was mobbed when Sarah arrived. Someone had hung bunting on the front porch rail and decked the inner hall with pine boughs. In the lobby the furniture had been pushed back against the walls, and three pails of sand had been used to anchor fake telegraph poles connected by ropes which were also festooned with garlands of evergreen. The banjo had been joined by a fiddle, and the dancing had begun, with every available woman pressed into service. Emma was there, as well as her daughters, and Mrs. Roundtree, and the butcher's wife, Clare Gladding, and Calamity Jane, in buckskin. Those men who could neither resist the music nor find a female partner danced with each other. A portion of the dining room had been cleared for dancing also and the two musicians roamed through the crowd, spreading the music as they went. Against one wall a long table held an array of food. Before Sarah could see what it held, she found herself swept up by Teddy Ruckner, who appropriated her without asking and danced her into a two-step to the tune of "Turkey in the Straw."

"Teddy, slow down!" she exclaimed, laughing.

"Not tonight! Tonight we go full-tilt!"

"I'm not used to this!"

"You will be! These men are going to dance the soles off your shoes."

Their execution of the two-step was graceless but gusty. Whirling and stomping in Teddy's arms, Sarah caught a glimpse of Noah Campbell, eating a sandwich and watching her. People came between them and she lost sight of him. The dance left her and Teddy laughing and winded. When it ended, Sarah was snapped up by Craven Lee, and after him, Shorty Reese. When the third song ended she found a queue of others waiting to partner her.

"Gentlemen, I need a break . . . please."

They regretfully backed off and allowed her to escape toward the food table. Reaching it, she murmured, "Oh, my stars!" She had not seen such an array of food since leaving the East. Sliced roasts of wild game and a mountain of buns, whole baked fish, their eye sockets filled with cranberries, fricasseed rabbits and roasted chickens. Breaded parsnips, dark and light breads, hot rice cakes, a bevy of hot vegetables and every pickled thing imaginable from herring to tomatoes to watermelon. There were macaroon cakes, brandied peaches, apple fritters and an English walnut cake.

And in the center of the table—presided over by Ben Winters himself— a washtub half-full of pale amber liquid. Ben was adding brown sugar to the tub when Sarah drew up at the table to admire the spread.

"Miss Merritt—help yourself. Plenty to eat, and this here's a little posset for ladies and gentlemen alike."

"Posset, Mr. Winters?" She smiled knowingly. "If it's posset, where's the milk?" Sarah knew perfectly well the genteel lady's drink was made with milk.

Winters grinned and stirred the mixture with a long-handled spoon. "Oh, all right, call it a peach cordial then. Or call it a rum punch. But have some. It's not every day our town gets a telegraph. Running that newspaper, you've got more reason than most to celebrate."

"If it's all the same to you, Mr. Winters, I'll start with a little food. It looks wonderful." While she selected tidbits from the table, Sarah saw rum, brandy, nutmeg and water go into the tub. Nevertheless, she accepted a cup of the punch when Ben handed it to her and sipped it in an effort to cool off. It *was* slightly peachy in flavor and quite delicious.

She was lifting the cup for a second drink when someone clasped her elbows from behind.

"Sarah! I found you!"

She looked over her shoulder. "Arden, how did you hear the news?"

"Gustafson rode out to the Spearfish this morning and said the connection with Western Union should be made by tonight. Guess we missed the grand event, but we sure found the party! Let's dance, Sarah!"

He stole her plate and punch cup and abandoned it on a table, hauling her amidst the dancers with his usual impatience. "Arden, you might ask a girl instead of telling her," she chided when he had her bobbing fit to shake her bones from their sockets.

"You came, didn't you?"

"Arden Campbell, I'm not sure I like your cocky attitude."

"Like it or not, I've got you now and I'm *keeping* you." He hauled her close and executed two galloping turns while her cheekbone bumped his jaw and from across the crowd his brother and mother watched. Oh, gracious, his mother was here! Probably his father, too, if the red-bearded man between them was the family member she hadn't met.

"Arden, let me loose," she insisted and got her wish, but by the time the dance ended, she felt as if she'd been through Robert's stamp mill.

"Come on, meet my father."

Again she had no choice. She was hauled off so abruptly her teeth clacked. Arden brought her to a halt before the trio of Campbells.

"Pa, this is Sarah. Sarah, meet my father, Kirk Campbell."

They shook hands while she tried not to stare at his freckles and red beard. She'd never seen a face so big and orange or had her hand gripped by one any larger.

"Hello, Mr. Campbell."

"So you're the one my boys been talking about. And Carrie, too."

"Hello, Mrs. Campbell," Sarah added while Noah stood by with his arms crossed over his chest, offering nothing.

"This is some shindig, isn't it?" Carrie Campbell said. "I said to Noah, it's a good thing you've got that jail because you'll probably have some drunks to throw into it tonight."

A delicate subject, Noah's jail. It brought a dead end.

"That newspaper of yours looks mighty good," put in Kirk. "I imagine this new telegraph will be a good thing for you."

"Yes, sir, it will be."

They talked about the telegraph, and the food, and the expected growth of the town, come spring. All the while, Noah stood silently while Arden shifted from one foot to the other and finally demanded, "You can talk about all that later. Now we've got to dance. Come on, Sarah!"

Once more she was unceremoniously hauled to do his bidding. Over Arden's shoulder her eyes caught Noah's and she thought, *Please rescue me.* But at that moment someone tapped him on the shoulder and apparently asked him to follow, for he turned and went into the crowd at the far end of the lobby. When the song finally ended she glanced across the crowd and saw Noah heading her way, but before he reached her, Robert appeared.

"Miss Merritt," he asked, very properly, "may I have the next dance."

"Of course, Robert. I don't believe you've met Arden Campbell." When the two men had exchanged cordialities she danced off at a much more sedate pace with Robert. Arden watched dolefully and she'd lost sight of Noah.

"Well, Robert, I haven't seen you for a few days."

"I've been very busy at the mill."

"And I at the paper."

"Are you making any progress with Addie?"

"None. Are you?"

"I think I might have cracked through to her tonight." After that their talk centered on Addie, and his mill and the telegraph, of course. They danced three dances, then retired to the punch bowl and Sarah had her second cup of the "peach cordial."

The party grew livelier and Sarah got slightly giggly. She danced, it seemed, a good twenty-five dances, with everyone in the place except Noah Campbell. Every time it seemed he was heading her way, someone interrupted. Once a gunshot rang out and he was called upon to make an arrest and was gone for some time, locking the merry-doer in jail as Carrie had predicted.

When he returned it was after midnight and she was near the door, taking her coat from a rack. He walked up behind her.

"Are you leaving?" he asked.

She turned, smiling disjointedly, her cheeks abnormally flushed. "I do believe, Marshal, that I've had too much to drink."

"So have a lot of others. I'd better walk you home."

She leaned close to his ear and whispered, "Thank goodness. I wasn't sure how to get rid of Arden."

She was having some difficulty finding her sleeve with her arm, so he helped. Arden approached, breathless after hunting up his own jacket. "Noah . . . I'm walking Sarah home."

"I'll take care of that," Noah informed him.

"Now, wait a minute!"

"Ma and Pa are looking for you. I think they're ready to start for home."

"Good night, Arden," Sarah added as Noah took her elbow and ushered her out the door.

"But Sarah . . ."

"Good night, Arden," Noah added, closing the door between them.

"I think I must apologize, Marshal."

"For what?"

"Tippling. It isn't very ladylike to be caught in this condition."

"You had a good time, didn't you?"

"Oh, I did. All except for your brother. He dances like popcorn!"

Noah laughed while she hurried two steps ahead, swung about and lifted one foot straight at him. "Look! Do I have any soles left on them?"

"Some."

"Well, that's a miracle. It's hard work being one of only twenty women in a town like this."

They walked side by side without touching. She was actually quite steady on her feet.

"You were a good sport. The men loved it."

"I thought we were going to dance, you and I."

"You were quite busy."

"Didn't you dance with *any*body?"

"I was quite busy, too."

"I'll bet you don't know how. That's it, isn't it?"

"You guessed it. I'm worse than Arden."

She laughed, then pressed her palms to her cheeks. "Goodness, my cheeks are so warm."

"Rum does that to a person."

"Ben Winters told me it was posset."

"You didn't believe him, did you?"

"No. I saw him put the liquor in. I just decided to have a good time, like everybody else."

"You'll probably have a headache in the morning."

"Oh dear."

"It helps to drink a little coffee. Maybe we could find some in Mrs. Roundtree's kitchen."

They were climbing the long steps to her house by this time. From behind and below, the faint noise of celebration could still be heard. Noah opened the door and they entered the dark parlor.

"Just a minute," he said. She stood in the dark, unbuttoning her coat while he found a match and lit a lantern. "Come on," he said, picking it up, leading the way to the kitchen.

He set the lantern on the table among a collection of wooden bowls, a lard crock, and a saltcellar. The fire in the stove had long since gone out and the room was chilly. He hefted a coffeepot and gave it a swirl. "There's something in here." He stepped into the dark pantry and reappeared pouring the cold coffee into a heavy white mug.

She sat at the table. "Aren't you having any?"

"I'm not drunk."

"Oh, that's right." She smiled, accepting the cup as he stepped over and handed it to her, then returned the pot to the cold iron range. He angled a chair away from the table, sat down to her right, dropping an elbow on the table edge and crossing an ankle over a knee. He was dressed in his thick sheepskin jacket—unbuttoned—and the hat she'd given him.

"Your father is the orangest man I've ever seen."

Noah burst out laughing.

Sarah covered her lips with a finger. "Shhh! You'll wake up the whole house."

"Orangest?"

"Or should that be orangiest?"

They'd begun whispering.

"My mother says when she first met him she told him he looked like a frying pan that had been left out in the rain."

She giggled, suppressing the sound behind her fingers, then took a gulp of cold coffee.

"Oh yuk . . . this stuff is terrible."

"Drink it anyway."

She grimaced and followed orders, then shuddered and wiped her mouth with the back of one hand.

"You'll live through it," he said, grinning.

The room grew quiet. Their eyes met. Hers dropped.

"I like your hair that way . . . loose."

Her blue eyes lifted, wide and somewhat surprised. Self-consciously she hitched a wisp of hair back behind one ear.

"I've got awful hair."

"No, you don't."

"Addie's the one with the pretty hair. You should see it when it's blond. You never saw anything so shiny or bright."

He sat calmly studying her, an elbow on the table, his fingers twined loosely before him, his silence a gentle rebuff for her belittling herself in favor of her sister. Another lull fell and she groped for a topic of conversation.

"You have a nice family," she said, no longer whispering, speaking very softly. "I envy you."

"Thank you."

Again came quiet. She filled it. "The cold air and the coffee helped. I feel much steadier."

"Sarah, could I ask you something?"

"Yes?"

"What are you to Baysinger?"

"A friend."

"That's all?"

"Yes. I told you that before."

"The two of you are together a lot."

"Yes. We talk easily, and both of us are interested in Addie's welfare. Why do you ask?"

"Because I'm considering doing something." He got up from his chair, took her empty cup and deposited it in the empty dishpan beside the water pail. He crossed his arms and ankles and leaned his backside against the dry sink, regarding her from across the room. "I've actually been considering it for some time, but I thought it was only fair to warn you before I did it."

"Did what?"

"Kissed you."

Her jaw went slack and her eyes forgot how to blink. She couldn't think of one darned thing to say.

"Would that be all right?" Noah Campbell asked.

"I guess so."

He boosted off the dry sink and came across the wooden floor, stopping beside her with a shuffle of his boots. Leaning one hand on the back of her chair and one on the tabletop, he bent forward and tipped his head so the brim of his Stetson would miss her head. He kissed her once, quite dryly and briefly on the lips, so dryly and briefly neither of them bothered to close their eyes. He straightened his elbows and their eyes met. "I thought I should ask first," he said. "Knowing how you felt about me in the past."

"Yes. That's all right. It's . . . uh . . ." She cleared her throat. She was not a woman given to stammering. "How long have you been thinking about it?"

"Since the day you took the cat to Eve."

"Oh."

"Well . . ." He straightened fully and began buttoning his jacket. "It's late."

"Yes. I should get to bed."

"And I should get back uptown and make sure the night ends peaceably."

He picked up the lantern and waited for her to rise and move before him through the kitchen doorway into the dining room to the foot of the stairs.

"Good night, Sarah," he said, without a smile.

"Good night, Noah."

"See if the lantern is on up there."

She climbed to the landing and saw that the hall lantern had been left burning on its bracket.

"Yes, it is."

"Good. See you in the morning."

He went out and she went up and sat on the edge of her bed in somewhat of a daze. What did it mean when a man considered kissing a woman all that time and finally did it with as much thought as if he were taking a test. Or giving one?

Chapter 12

❧

In the morning Sarah was relieved to find the marshal did not appear at breakfast. She'd heard him come in near four o'clock and imagined he, as well as several others of the meal's absentees, was still asleep.

Sarah seated herself gingerly at the breakfast table and accepted a cup of coffee but declined eggs and toast. Her head buzzed and her neck ached. Food sounded repulsive. Not only had she been imprudent at the punch bowl, she hadn't slept any more than Noah Campbell. Instead, she'd lain awake thinking about that kiss.

It hadn't been particularly romantic, but she supposed Noah Campbell wasn't a particularly romantic man. Still, for a prosaic kiss, it certainly had lingering power.

She thought about it a good half dozen times that day—while she and

Patrick laid out an extra issue of the *Chronicle* announcing the arrival of the telegraph and telling about the celebration at the Grand Central; while she ate an enormous dinner at Teddy Ruckner's and reminisced with Teddy about what a good time last night had been, and declined his invitation to the Bella Union for that evening; while she limped back to the newspaper office on her poor tired feet and tried to keep from nodding off at her desk during the afternoon; while she waited for the marshal to pop into the newspaper office and he didn't.

They met at suppertime.

Sarah had changed to a clean shirtwaist, combed her hair and used a touch of rosewater at her throat. She was dismayed to find Noah acted as if the kiss had never happened. He was friendly, but no friendlier than to the men. They all talked about last night's party, but his eyes never once passed her any ulterior message, nor did he speak to her any more directly than to the others.

She supposed she'd failed the test.

Christmas was approaching. Jack Langrishe came into the *Chronicle* office one day three weeks before the holiday. He was a dapper man with a dark goatee and mustache, and always wore a square-crowned black silk hat.

"Good morning, Miss Merritt." His voice held the rich tenor of distant thunder, and his elocution was flawless.

"Mr. Langrishe, how nice to see you. You've come for the new theater programs. They're all ready."

"Not specifically. I've come about Christmas."

"Christmas?"

"I decided to approach you first because you've been the most outspoken citizen of Deadwood regarding our lack of a church and a minister."

"Have I offended you, Mr. Langrishe?"

"Not at all. Quite the opposite. I feel as you do, that this town needs both. Since we have neither, and since the holiday is upon us, I propose to offer my theater for a Christmas Eve program and pageant which might stand in lieu of an official church service."

Sarah smiled. "What a marvelous idea. How generous of you to offer your facilities once again."

"I want to include the children."

"Of course."

"And as many adults as we can charm into taking part."

"I believe we'll have more luck with the children." She chuckled.

"Undoubtedly."

"Still, their mothers are more than eager to see anything organized for their benefit. We might entice some of them onto the stage."

"I hope so, and fathers, too. We'll use the theater troupe, of course, but I'd like to see the other members of this town become an integral part of the production."

"How can I help?"

Jack Langrishe touched a corner of his mustache and inquired, "Can you sing, Miss Merritt?"

She laughed self-deprecatingly. "Not as well as I can write."

"I need someone to organize the children and direct their musical renditions."

"I can try."

"I *knew* you'd come through!" He emphasized with a fist.

"We'll need to announce it in the paper."

"Yes, that was going to be my next request."

"I'll have Patrick lay out the announcement right away."

Jack Langrishe was a magician. He charmed not only Sarah into directing the children's choir, but Elias Pinkney into carting his thirteen-stop organ down to the theater to join the piano already there, and a blacksmith named Tom Poinsett into constructing eight large triangles out of drill steel. He found a xylophone musician named Ned Judd to practice playing several numbers on the triangles, and talked Mrs. J. N. Robinson, the mother of the only infant in town, into playing the part of the Madonna and allowing her baby to represent baby Jesus. (As luck would have it, the Robinson child was a boy.) From the Langrishe troupe's supply of costumes came angels' gowns, shepherds' crooks, kings' crowns and more.

It was Sarah's idea to use the occasion to appeal for money for the construction of the church/school building, and to incorporate its collection into the pageant. (What better time to ask men to open their purses than when their ears are filled with the sounds of children's voices, their heads are full of memories of home and their hearts are brimming with holiday charity?) Though the gulch had no frankincense and myrrh, it had more than its share of real gold. They would collect it in a replica of a gold casket which Jack found among his theater props, and the three "kings" would offer it to the infant "Jesus" as part of the pageant itself.

Word spread that Jack Langrishe and Sarah Merritt had some lavish plans for the Christmas production, and sixteen children showed up to be in the choir. So many adults came that Jack actually had to audition and select from among them.

Rehearsals were held in the early evenings to allow Jack time to prepare his troupe for their regular nine o'clock performances of the current play, *Othello*.

On the evening of the first practice, Sarah excused herself from the supper table early. Noah Campbell glanced up and said nothing. The second evening he said, "Rehearsal again?"

"Yes," she replied and hurried away.

The third evening he stopped by the theater shortly before eight o'clock. By now the building had a wooden roof and two cast-iron stoves. The door squeaked as he entered. He inched it shut behind him, closed the latch soundlessly, removed his hat and stood at the rear to listen. Sarah was up front, her back to the door, directing the small fry of the town as they sang "Oh, Come, Little Children." She wore a dark green skirt and white shirtwaist with a string tie gathering it into a ruffle on her spine. Her hair was done in a tidy chignon. She stood very straight, directing with tiny movements of her arms, occasionally nodding her head to encourage the children not to lag. Their voices—a mixture of clear and off-key—carried through the room and touched a soft spot in Noah's heart.

> *Oh, come, little children*
> *Oh, come, one and all*
> *Draw near to the cradle*
> *In Bethlehem's stall*

They sang the verse while Noah's eyes remained on Sarah's back. He imagined her mouthing the words, bright-eyed and enthusiastic for the children's benefit. The verse ended, her arms stilled, and she said, "Very good. Smaller children, stay where you are. Older ones, circle to the outside and get the candles. No whispering now while Mr. Langrishe reads the verse."

They all followed orders—for the purpose of rehearsal, small wooden spindles were being used for candles. While these were being distributed, Jack Langrishe read the Christmas passage from the Bible in his resounding voice, and townspeople drifted onto the stage—uncostumed tonight, but clearly playing the parts of Mary, Joseph, the shepherds and wise men. Mrs. Robinson laid an empty rolled-up blanket in a wooden cradle and stood looking down at it. On the opposite side of the cradle stood Craven Lee, equally pious. Three men left a rear row of chairs and moved up the aisle; the last, Dan Turley, placed a small gold box at the foot of the cradle. A chime sounded, slowly, three times (one of the steel triangles), and Sarah raised her hands. As the last reverberation faded, she gave the children the downbeat for "Silent Night." They sang one verse alone, then she turned as if to direct the audience to join the second verse, singing herself.

She saw Noah and missed some words.

He nodded and her cheeks took on a slight flush before she resumed singing. He took a deep breath and joined in.

Shepherds quake at the siiiight . . .

He sang full-out, experiencing an unexpected accord with Sarah Merritt as he did. It was the strangest thing he'd ever done with a woman, but it felt good. Mighty good.

Christ the saviour is born
Christ the saviour is born . . .

The song trailed into silence and their gazes dovetailed for a moment before Sarah turned to attend the children. Jack Langrishe's voice returned. Noah remained at the rear of the theater, watching the woman in green and white, jarred by the realization that he was, in all likelihood, falling in love with her. She touched a blond head, bent and whispered an order in a child's ear. For a moment he imagined the child was his and hers: she was good with the children, he could see that. She was educated and bright and brave and moral. What a mother she'd make!

What a mother?

Whoa there, Noah, you're getting a little ahead of yourself.

He'd kissed her once, and sung a Christmas song with her and already he was imagining her as the mother of his children? That was Arden's fancy, always talking about having a wife and a family, not Noah's! The idea of being so abruptly swayed to that way of thinking brought him a backwash of denial tinged by panic.

Nevertheless, he waited until the rehearsal ended, following Sarah Merritt with his eyes, dissecting his newfound feelings. She raised both palms in the air, calling for attention. "Children, you sounded like angels from heaven. You may go home now, and the next time we'll practice with our costumes and the lighted candles.''

She came down the aisle, retrieving her coat and a small bonnet from a chair near the rear. He smiled and waited for her.

"Good evening, Marshal."

"Hello, Sarah. Here, I'll help you with that."

"You have a very fine voice," she said, slipping into her coat while he held it for her.

"So do you."

"So if we cannot dance together, at least we can sing," she said, smiling, closing the button at her throat. He handed her the bonnet, watching as she tied it beneath her chin. How amazing: he had difficulty tearing his gaze away from the curve of her throat and jaw while she tied the ribbons. She finished and began drawing on gloves, suddenly lifting her head and flashing him a full smile that seemed to catch him beneath the ribs. He struggled to recall exactly when she'd begun to change in his eyes, when her tallness had become elegance, her plainness purity and her ordinary face his ideal.

"I've come to walk you home."

"All right. But I need to stop by the newspaper office on the way."

"Fine."

Outside it was cold and windy. He wanted to take her arm but refrained. What had come over him? He'd done tens of things more personal with tens of women in his day, yet he was wary of taking her arm.

"The children need wings. I'm going to see what I can do with some newsprint and flour paste. Didn't they sound wonderful?"

"Angelic. They certainly like you."

"I like them, too. I've never worked with children before. It's a surprise how responsive they can be."

At the newspaper office she lit a lamp. He waited while she gathered a roll of paper, then helped her tie it with string.

"I wish I could think of some way to make the wings glitter," she said.

"Mica," he suggested.

"Mica . . . why, of course, that's it!" she exclaimed.

"A mortar and pestle would break it up fine enough, and if you sprinkled it on while the flour paste was wet it should stick."

"What a wonderful idea!"

"If you want I'll go out and find you some.''

"Would you really?"

"Sure. I won't have time tomorrow, but I'll do it the next day. I'll even break it up for you."

"Oh Noah, thank you." Her blue eyes sparkled with genuine gratitude.

He smiled and nodded, pleased with himself and with the glow created by her approval.

"Ready?" he asked, picking up the roll of paper and reaching toward the lantern.

"Ready."

He lowered the wick and followed her to the door.

As she opened it, he said, "Sarah, wait a minute."

She paused and turned, pulling on her gloves. "What is it?"

With his free hand he pressed the door closed, sealing them inside the dark, quiet newspaper office.

"Just this . . ." he said, tipping his head and moving toward her. His hat brim bumped her bonnet. They chuckled while he backed off and removed his Stetson. "Could I try that again?"

She answered quietly, "Please do."

His second aim was perfect, and their mouths joined lightly, remained so while the pendulum clock ticked away ten . . . fifteen . . . twenty unhurried seconds. With his hat in one hand and the roll of newsprint in the other, he had no means of holding her. She might easily have slipped away after a brief touch of their lips, but remained near, tilting her face in compliance. In the dark, their sense of touch became magnified. Soft became softer. Warm became warmer. His breath fanned her cheek, hers fanned his. They waited, in counterpoint, to see what the other would do. He opened his lips and touched her with his tongue and she met it with her own. They sampled each other, still somewhat surprised, with their mouths slightly open. The kiss ended as cobwebs break, with a reluctant drifting apart.

The clock ticked several times before Noah spoke.

"Something happened tonight when I was singing with you."

"It was such a surprise when you did it."

"It was a surprise to me, too. I've done a lot of things with women, but that was the first time I ever sang with one. Did you know you blushed when you turned around and saw me standing there?"

"Did I?"

"Yes, you did. And that's when it happened."

"What?"

"The same thing that's happening now."

"What's happening now?"

"My heart is racing."

"Is it really?"

"Isn't yours?"

"Yes . . . but I thought . . ."

"What?"

"I thought the first time you kissed me, I failed a test."

"What test?"

"I thought you were testing me . . . to see if you liked it, and you didn't."

"You were wrong, Sarah."

"I would not have known it. After that kiss, you looked at me no differently than you looked at the men."

"I was trying to do what was proper."

"I'm not sure this will ever be proper—you and I."

"Why?"

"Because of my sister."

"Your sister means nothing to me."

They remained close, acclimating to honesty and the reaction they set off in one another.

"Sarah, would it be all right if I set down these things I'm holding?"

"If you want to."

He squatted and set them on the floor. Rising, he took her by the upper arms and they listened to the faint, fast fall of one another's breathing. He drew her to his breast and found her mouth once more and kissed her as neither of them had believed would ever happen, with a lush embrace and a thorough blending of tongues. He spread a hand upon the back of her scratchy woolen coat while she did likewise on the back of his rough sheepskin jacket. Buffered by the two garments, they indulged in the time-honored intimacy that rattled them with disbelief.

They parted as reluctantly as before, still somewhat stunned.

"Noah, this feels so strange."

"I know."

"It doesn't feel as if it could be you and me."

Standing close in the dark, they thought about it awhile—their rocky beginning and how they had disliked one another, now this.

She surprised him by requesting, "Could we do it again, Noah?"

"Why, Sarah Merritt," he said with a smile in his voice. "You surprise me."

In the darkness he took her head in both hands, and she found her mouth fully inundated, and her senses captivated by the smell of his shaving scent, which had been wooing her across the breakfast table all these weeks. His mustache was soft, his tongue even softer as it touched her, wet and warm, within. She returned his kiss in full while his embrace grew powerful enough to lift her onto tiptoe.

When her heels once more touched the floor, both of them were slightly breathless.

"I think we'd better go home now," Sarah whispered.

"Of course. It's late." He retrieved his hat and the paper roll and followed her out of the building, waiting while she locked the door. They found curiously little to say to one another on their way up the hill. At Mrs. Roundtree's she climbed the steps ahead of him and paused at the top, a woman uncertain of how such things proceeded. Were doorstep kisses expected now?

"I'll go out and find the mica on Thursday," Noah said, halting her with words instead.

"Thank you . . . yes, the children will love it."

"I'll bring it by your office."

"All right."

She reached for the doorknob but he detained her with a touch on her sleeve.

"Sarah, I'm not very good at saying things, but . . ." He released her arm and shifted his weight from one foot to the other. "It was a good feeling, singing 'Silent Night' with you tonight."

"Yes, it was. You have a beautiful voice, Noah. Perhaps when we get our church you'll be in the choir."

"If you direct it, maybe I will."

It was brighter beneath the starry night sky, bright enough for him to make out her face, though his remained hidden by the shadow of his hat brim. She gave a short smile and said, "Well, I'd better go in."

"And I'd better make one more round." He handed her the paper roll.

"Good night, Noah."

"Good night, Sarah."

"See you at breakfast."

She prepared for bed slowly, perplexed by her changing sentiments for him. When she'd donned her nightgown she wrapped herself in a shawl and got out her journal in an effort to sort out her feelings.

I have been kissed, truly kissed, by a man who has carnal knowledge of my sister, a man I once avidly hated. I am the only eligible young woman in this town, and I've been trying to be very honest with myself about whether that is the reason for his attentions, but I think not. I believe our feelings for one another are genuinely changing, but to what end I must ask myself now. The women in my family have set a precedent—first my mother, and now Addie. Have I the inborn predisposition to be like them? Does he think I am easy game? I should not like to think so, yet how can the doubt not crop up, considering that I met him the first time in the entry to a brothel? Is this the kind of man I should encourage? What would Father advise? Supposing Noah Campbell's intentions are honorable, let us even suppose he falls in love with me and proposes marriage. How awkward it would be to lay with him and realize my sister had come before me. . . .

In the morning she was still confused. Facing him across the breakfast table, she was torn by the wish to meet his eyes and the equally strong one to avoid them. Thankfully, he treated her no differently than at any other breakfast. They lived, after all, in the same boardinghouse, on the same floor, with only two doors between them. By unspoken agreement they observed the same polite conventions they'd shown one another all along. It was the same at supper that evening, and during the following day's breakfast.

The afternoon of the second day, however, he brought her the ground mica, as promised. Patrick was working at a table near the front of the office when Noah came in and went directly to Sarah at her desk and handed her a drawstring bag.

"Here's your mica," he said, looking pleased and a trifle expectant.

"Thank you." Sarah was surprised to find a tightness around her heart as she accepted it. She glanced at Patrick, easily within earshot, then said to Noah, "I've been experimenting with the wings. Would you like to see them?"

"Sure."

She led him to the rear of the office, where three various shaped wings of paste-laden newsprint were drying over barrels. They stopped with their backs to Patrick.

"I like this one," Noah said. "If angels really do have wings, I bet they'd look like this."

"With mica on them they'll be even more seraphic. Thank you again for getting it."

"It was no trouble. Are you making them all?"

"No, Emma volunteered to be in charge of the costumes. I'm only making the prototype."

A lull fell. He could tell by her downcast face she'd had some sort of change of heart since the last time they'd been in this office together.

"Noah, I've been thinking . . ." she said quietly, toying with the drawstring bag.

"What?"

"About you . . . and Addie." She looked square into his eyes. She had not removed her spectacles, and with them appeared vulnerable.

"There's no point in you and I . . . well . . ." She gestured with one hand and returned her attention to the bag. "It's pointless, that's all."

"Sarah, I haven't—"

From behind them Patrick called, "Sarah, would y' be wantin' me to use a cut of a horse and sleigh on this ad for Tatum?"

"Yes, that would be fine," she replied, raising her voice; then more softly, "I really must get back to work. Thank you again, Marshal."

He studied her somberly for five seconds—so it was back to Marshal again.

"All right, Sarah, if that's the way you want it." Not a muscle moved on his face as he stared at her, then touched his hat brim and left.

He bowed to her wishes between then and Christmas, making mealtime tense as they sat in their customary chairs across from one another. They became adept at passing platters without meeting glances; at joining in the mealtime conversations without exchanging any but the most una- voidable words with each other; at leaving the table at separate times so they need not walk up the stairs together.

One morning, while it was still dark outside and she'd just rolled from her warm bed, she opened her door and encountered him heading for the same place as she. They froze, each of them disheveled from sleep, with their outerwear thrown on carelessly. The top of his underwear showed behind his sheepskin jacket. She held her coat closed over her nightgown. His whiskers were shady, his hair stood on end. There were sandmen in her eyes, and her hair looked untamed.

" 'Morning," he said.

" 'Morning."

Still neither of them moved. Or smiled. Or breathed.

Finally, he found his voice. "You go first. I can wait." He turned and hurried back to his room.

On Christmas Eve afternoon it snowed. Sarah made a trip to the bath- house, spread rosewater on her skin and donned her best bustled suit with the polonaise jacket. At home she crimped her hair, added a rat to the back, left tendrils trail at the hairline and pinned her locket at the throat of her high-collared white blouse. Before the small mirror she paused, lifted a wrist to her nose and thought of Noah Campbell, probably down the hall changing clothes at this very minute.

I miss him.

She picked up the gift she had made for Addie—a delicate tussie-mussie made of dried flowers tied in a punchwork doily by a lavender grosgrain ribbon. She studied the gift sadly, wondering about the two of them, to- gether up at Rose's. *And how many others, Noah?*

She sighed, stared out the window where the snowflakes fell like goo- sedown. The sky was lavender, like the ribbon she held. Each time she thought of Noah and Addie it was like touching an old bruise. When had he last seen her? Did he go there regularly? Did he kiss Addie in the same lingering way he had kissed her?

If she, Sarah, were to allow the kisses to go on, would he expect, in time, to do with her the other things he had done with Addie?

Despondently she donned her coat.

Outside, the gulch wore an ermine cape. Miners were arriving already from the hills, leaving their mules at the hitching rails and entering the eateries. Many of them greeted her by name.

At Rose's the parlor was deserted. Sarah went straight up to Addie's room and knocked. Addie was holding Ruler when she opened the door. The sight of her with only the cat for company created a lonely prospect on Christmas Eve.

"Merry Christmas, Addie," Sarah said. "May I come in for a minute?"

Addie stepped back, silent.

"I brought this for you."

Addie looked down at the gift. "I don't have anything for you."

"I don't need anything. Here . . . take it."

Addie let the cat go and reached for the nosegay. Her face was sad and downcast. "You never let up on me, do you?"

"It's Christmas. I wanted to give you something."

Addie stared at the tussie-mussie and said nothing.

"I know that you've heard about the Christmas program we're putting on at the Langrishe tonight. I'm directing the children's choir and I'd like very much for you to come."

"I can't."

"Of course you can. You simply put on a coat and hat and walk down to the theater with me."

"And let them throw stones at me?"

"No one will throw stones."

"You live in a dream world, Sarah. I couldn't go back to a normal life even if I wanted to."

"So you won't even try?"

"No."

Disappointed, Sarah studied Addie. "Have you seen Robert?"

"Nearly every day. He won't let up on me either."

"So accept one of his invitations. Become his friend again."

"He lives in a dream world, too."

"Addie . . . ?"

Of all the times she'd visited Addie, Sarah had never seen her sister as approachable as now. There was a question she deeply wanted to ask. If she did so at this moment she would get the truth, she was sure. *Addie, does the marshal still come here to see you?* Her mouth opened to ask it, but the words lodged in her throat.

In the end, afraid of the answer, she could not ask.

"Nothing . . . I hope you like the tussie-mussie. I must get on to the theater. The children will be arriving soon."

Addie's expression grew more forlorn.

"Merry Christmas."

"You too."

They stood separated by a mere four feet, each longing for something the other could not give. Suddenly Sarah rushed forward and caught Addie in a hug, their cheeks joined.

"Oh Addie, will we ever be sisters again?"

For a moment Addie hugged her back.

"You'd better not count on it."

"Please come tonight."

"I can't, but good luck with your program," she said.

Sarah spun from the room before she could cry. Sixteen children were counting on her to be exhilarated and smiling. She could not let them down.

. . .

The Langrishe was filled with men in an appropriately subdued mood for the first religious observance ever held in Deadwood. The stage was trimmed with pine boughs. The cradle was lined with straw. The children were scrubbed and eager. The mothers were nervous. The pageant members were in costume.

The marshal was not there.

Sarah's disappointment outweighed anything so far as she peeked from behind the curtain, searching the crowd for his familiar mustache and gray eyes. She saw Robert, and Teddy Ruckner, Mrs. Roundtree, Mr. Mullins, Mr. Taft and dozens of others she recognized. But not Noah. In spite of her misgivings, it was he of whom she'd thought as this night approached, he for whom she wanted the children to perform well, he whose eyes she would seek when she turned to face the audience and direct them in the last song. She supposed he had gone out to the Spearfish to spend the holiday with his family.

The program began with a rousing rendition of "Adeste Fideles," sung by all, accompanied by Elias Pinkney on the thirteen-stop organ and the xylophone musician, Mr. Judd, on the eight triangles. There followed an original reading by Jack Langrishe, leading into a series of vignettes of Christmases in other lands. Sarah sat to one side of the stage with her angel choir, watching the door. The reading of the Christmas story had just begun when it opened and Noah came in.

Sarah's heart gave a leap.

His eyes scanned the stage, found her and stopped.

Hello.

Hello.

Their silent communion was unmistakable. For the first time that night she caught the spirit of the season.

The children sang well. The Robinson baby fussed very little. Everyone loved the chimes. Jack Langrishe's voice was dynamic and his costumes rich with authenticity. The miners filled the king's casket with so much gold dust a second container had to be employed.

And when Sarah turned to direct the last verse of "Silent Night," she and Noah sang to each other.

The thunder of applause at the program's end set forth a round of jubilant hugging onstage and handshaking among the audience. Above the heads that separated them the eyes of Sarah and Noah found each other time and again. Robert located her, gave her a crushing hug and a grand smile, but he had come to seem less extraordinary to Sarah than she'd once thought. Over his shoulder she watched Noah. There were punch and cookies for the adults, and for the children sacks of popcorn and hard candy. The crowd, made up mostly of single men separated from their families, was reluctant to break up and end the evening, so began a round of informal caroling accompanied by the organ. In the midst of the celebration costumes had to be collected and clothes changed backstage. Reluctantly Sarah went off to gather angel wings and find Jack Langrishe to ask about a place to store them till next year, fearing all the while that when she returned to the theater floor Noah would be gone. He was still there, however, and they began working their way toward each other. A cluster of Norwegian men struck up a carol in their native language. A roulette wheel clicked: someone had rigged it up with gifts for the children substituting for numbers. Amidst the singing and the clicking and the sound of happy voices, Sarah and Noah met.

For a while they only looked at each other without smiling.

Finally he said, "It was a wonderful program."

"Thank you."

"The children sounded as good as they looked."

"Everyone loved their wings, thanks to you."

They tried for timid smiles and found them. The Norwegians ended their song, which sparked another by a group of Swedes, louder than the previous one, so loud it drowned out everything else.

"I thought you weren't coming," she said.

"What?" He dipped his ear near her mouth. She caught a whiff of something sweet from his skin.

"I said I thought you weren't coming. You were late."

"I had to wait in line at the bathhouse."

"Oh."

"Everybody in the gulch must've taken a bath tonight."

"I got mine early enough that I missed the crowd."

"Good for you."

A lapse fell while they tried to think of some reasonable subject of conversation to give them an excuse to remain together.

"I don't see your family here," she said.

"No, they didn't come. I'm going out there in the morning."

"You're lucky. A lot of these men are missing their families tonight, I think."

"Sarah?"

She waited, with her eyes lost in his.

"I was wondering if you'd want to come with me."

"I'm sorry. I've made other plans."

Their silence lasted several seconds while they read the disappointment in each other's eyes. "Well, maybe some other time."

Finally he thought to ask, "Could I get you some punch?"

"Yes, I'd love some."

He went away and returned bearing two cups filled with red liquid, handing her one.

He raised his. "Merry Christmas."

"Merry Christmas."

The rims of the cups clinked. After he drank he glanced over the crowd while drying the bottom fringe of his mustache with the edge of an index finger. He caught her watching him and she looked away.

He leaned close enough to be heard. "Looks like you'll get your church and school building after all."

"I hope so."

"How much do you think they collected?"

"I couldn't even guess."

Emma appeared with her brood. "Time we were getting home. Have you seen Byron?"

"He's over there." Sarah pointed.

"Go get your father, Josh. Tell him we're ready to go. Marshal, Merry Christmas."

"Same to you."

"Sarah, we'll see you tomorrow then."

"Yes."

"Dinner will be ready at four."

"I'll be there."

When they'd gone off, Noah said, "You're spending tomorrow with them?"

"Yes. You didn't believe me, did you?"

He shrugged and looked down at his cup.

She kept thinking about missing the chance to go out to the Spearfish with him. When she spoke, her voice held passionate disappointment. "Why didn't you ask me earlier?"

"I wasn't sure you'd want to."

"But you could have asked, Noah."

"You haven't called me Noah since the night I kissed you."

"I've been very mixed up."

His unsmiling eyes took hers and kept them. "You don't make it easy on a man, Sarah."

"I know," she replied meekly. "I'm sorry."

He seemed to consider awhile, then he set down his cup, and his face took on a look of remoteness. "Well, I have to get an early start in the morning."

"Yes, I suppose you do." She set hers down, too, while he glanced off across the room and made no move to leave, obviously troubled.

They both spoke at once.

"Sarah—"

"Noah—"

In the silence that followed, with their eyes locked, she took courage.

"Could we walk home together?" she asked.

"Where's your coat?"

"In one of the dressing rooms backstage."

"Did you wear a hat?"

"No."

"Stay here," he said, leaving her. She waited despondently while he disappeared, thinking this was one of the more difficult struggles with which she'd ever dealt, developing feelings for a man she felt obligated to shy away from. The missed opportunity to spend Christmas with him and his family crushed her, took all the joy out of her plans for tomorrow. He knew her well enough to recognize her coat in a jumble; it seemed significant that they'd spent that much time becoming friends. So what did she want of him? Of herself? Alas, she did not know.

He returned with her coat, held it while she slipped it on, then guided her toward the door, both of them wishing and being wished Merry Christmas several times on their way.

Outside others were walking home. At the hitching rails the blankets and saddles on the animals were covered with snow. Two mules plodded up the street bearing riders who called out holiday greetings in the dark.

Sarah and Noah replied in unison, Noah raising one hand. In silence they traversed the boardwalks—up one set of steps, down another, across a street, up steps again. Occasionally their elbows brushed but they did not speak. At a corner they turned onto a side street and began climbing the steep hill.

Suddenly, in the still night, a musical note sounded, stopping their footsteps.

"What was that?"

It came again and they lifted their faces to the night sky.

"The chimes," she breathed.

From somewhere up high above the gulch the notes struck and reverberated, bouncing from wall to wall, down the chasm, shimmering up their spines.

"It must be Ned Judd. He's playing 'Adeste, Fideles,' " Sarah whispered.

They stood in place and listened as each note echoed and re-echoed. The night came alive with music that seemed to have an almost celestial splendor as it resounded through the wondrous acoustical chamber around them. It filled their ears and seemed to skitter out the tops of their heads while, enraptured, they held still.

When the song ended, Noah said, "Where do you suppose he is?"

"On one of the ledges. He must have carried the triangles up there. What a Christmas gift for us all."

Another song began. "Away in a Manger."

Noah found one of Sarah's hands and tucked it tightly beneath his elbow. They turned and continued toward home, bound once again by music. On the top landing at Mrs. Roundtree's, she and some of her boarders stood with their faces lifted, listening too, as the carol seemed to emanate from the rocks, the pines, the very heavens themselves. Noah discreetly released Sarah's hand and they climbed the stairs and joined the others, elevating their faces, too.

The song ended and a mutual sigh rose, like that following a burst of fireworks.

"For a Christmas that started out to be the loneliest one a lot of us has ever faced, it sure turned into something special," Mrs. Roundtree said.

A murmur of voices concurred.

"Thanks to Mr. Poinsett's triangles."

"And Mr. Judd's playing."

They mingled awhile, remarking on the pageant, the children's choir, the angel wings, complimenting Sarah on her part. The heavenly concert continued, but in time they tired and drifted inside, bidding one another goodnight as they shuffled upstairs, moving like a slow tide, each to his own door. In the sluggish current of night-going, Sarah lost Noah without a private farewell—a disappointment—surrounded as they were by others.

In her room she undressed in the dark, hung up her outerwear and donned a thick flannel nightgown. She removed the pins and rat from her hair, took her brush and a warm blanket, opened the window and sat before it on a wooden rocker. Two songs played. Three. She brushed her hair slowly to their rhythmic bonging, unwilling to submit to sleep until the last note had been savored. The winter air threaded inside. In time she drew her feet up and hooked her heels on the chair seat, tipped her head back and listened to the soulful sound of the carols ricocheting through Deadwood Gulch.

In his room down the hall, Noah Campbell, too, opened his window. He lit a lamp, removed his jacket, boots and shirt, sat down in his stocking feet, trousers and long underwear, and rolled a cigarette. He lit it from the lamp flame and watched the smoke linger at the window opening before it drifted back inside. He smoked two cigarettes, listening to the lovely, lonely chimes, before his fingers grew cold.

He extinguished the lamp, pulled the rocking chair near the bed, resumed his seat and propped his calves on the mattress, covering his front with a blanket. Thinking. Thinking. Of Sarah Merritt and himself singing face to face across a crowded theater, of Sarah Merritt and himself trying to avoid each other's eyes across the breakfast table, of Sarah Merritt and himself kissing in her newspaper office with a great deal of uncertainty, then afterward pretending it had never happened.

He rose, stretched, stood before the open window, rubbing the back of his neck.

If she were one of the girls up at Rose's he'd know how to approach her. But she wasn't a woman with whom a man trifled.

He stood for some time considering before he crossed to his door, opened it silently and shut it just as silently behind himself. In stocking feet he ventured down the hall and paused before her door.

He tapped quietly and waited.

Momentarily her door opened a crack. Her room was dark, leaving her only a suspicion in the blackness.

"Yes?" she whispered.

"It's Noah."

"Noah . . . what do you want?"

"I can't sleep. Can you?"

She paused warily before answering, "No."

"What were you doing?"

"Sitting by the open window, listening to the chimes."

"Me too."

The implication sneaked through the crack in the door even before he said, "We could listen to them together."

No reply.

"Could I come in, Sarah?"

"No, I'm dressed for bed."

"Put on a robe."

"Noah, I don't think—"

"Please."

She remained motionless for a long time before stepping back. He touched the door and it swung freely. He stepped into her room and closed the door without a click. By the faint light of the new-fallen snow he could see she had backed off several feet and stood clutching a blanket around her shoulders.

"You shouldn't be here," she told him.

"No."

"What if somebody heard you?"

"Everybody's asleep, and I'm stocking-footed."

He took a step toward her and she fled to her chair, drawing her knees up tightly to her chest and wrapping them with the blanket. He went to her bed and sat down in the deeper shadows while the midnight snow turned the side of her face and hair and blanket into a pale wash.

For a while they listened to the triangles playing "O Sanctissima."

At length he spoke out of the dark. "Sarah, I don't know where to go with you," he said, as if the admission were the accumulation of all his thoughts during his vigil down the hall. "Do you know?"

"I don't know what you mean."

"Yes, you do. I've kissed you twice and both times we've enjoyed it, but the next day we look at each other and get spooked."

"You too?"

"Yes, me too."

"I'm sorry. I . . ." She had no idea how to reply.

"I think about you a lot, yet I'm scared to death of you. It's the damnedest thing I've ever been through."

"You? Scared of me?"

"You're a very intimidating woman."

"I didn't know that," she whispered, chagrined.

"Well, you are. You're better than most men at what you do, and you're one hell of an organizer and a reformer and a choir director and an editor and . . ." He paused.

"And?"

"And I want to know what you think of me."

Her reply came in a quiet, fearful voice after long moments of silence. "I'm afraid of you, too." He made no reply, so she continued. "And I think of you, too, more than I believe is advisable. You see, you're not at all the sort of man I thought I'd . . ." She stopped.

"You thought you'd what?"

"Be attracted to." There, she'd said it. She supposed her cheeks must be glowing in the dark.

"What sort am I?"

She regretted having to say it. "The sort who visits brothels."

"I haven't been back to Rose's since the first night you came to town."

"But the fact remains you've been there . . . with my sister."

"Sarah, I'm very sorry about that, but I can't change it."

"And I can't change how I feel about it. It will always be there between us."

"I said I haven't been back and it's the truth. Ask your sister."

"My sister is lost to me because of your kind."

"No! I'm not the reason she is what she is!"

"Hold your voice down."

Softer, he repeated, "I'm not the reason she's a prostitute."

"Then what is? If only I understood it."

She dropped her head to her knees and for a while only the sound of the chimes filled the room. When he touched the back of her hair she started and threw back her head. She hadn't heard him move to the front of her chair.

"You must leave," she whispered, panicked.

"Yes," he agreed, "I must leave. I have known your sister in the biblical sense, so I must leave. Anything you or I might feel for each other should be shunted aside because of something that happened before we ever met, is that right?"

"Yes." Her eyes were wide, her heart hammering.

He gripped her arms and drew her to her feet. "That's bullshit, Sarah, and you know it." His head lowered and their mouths joined—his opened, hers closed. He waited, but she would not relent and allow herself to kiss him back. In time he lifted his head.

"I'm in no hurry," he whispered. "Take your time deciding."

He returned to his preoccupation with her lips, wetting them languidly with his tongue, undeterred by her tightly crossed arms and her refusal to comply. He was very adept, very patient, very convincing.

She trembled and tightened her grip on the blanket.

Lifting his head, he remained close, kneading her shoulders through the thick wrap of wool while her wide eyes fixed upon his: light pricks of contact in the darkness.

He slipped his hands through the break in the blanket and found her hips, rested his hands on their notches and drew her against him. Like the pause between lightning and thunder, he allowed a hesitation before tilting his head for another kiss.

She took part primly, with her arms wedged against his chest, her body canted back at the waist. After a stretch of persuasion which bore no results, he retreated and they stood facing each other in the half-embrace.

"You want to enjoy it, don't you?" He lifted his hand to stroke the hair from her temple, and she shivered. "Let yourself . . ." In slowest motion he kissed her eyelids, her cheek, earlobe, the underside of her jaw, stealing her wariness, setting her heart a-hurry. He kissed her mouth once more, spreading the flavor of smoke upon her tongue, bringing the texture of silk where his mustache rode her skin. His hands slipped behind her, low, where her nightgown lay full and loose, made faint movements that sent it whispering across her skin like a curtain across a sill. He spread his hands wide and brought her flush against him.

With a despairing cry she conceded, flowing to him like a breaker to a shore, throwing her arms up and veiling them both with the blanket. Their warm, full lengths joined and he held her in place without moving, their hearts beating crazily.

She had not known simply standing so against another could make mockery of all one believed. Again a sound formed in her throat, trapped, fearful. From outside came the dying peal of the last chime. It seemed to ring within her body and shimmer outward to all the surfaces he embraced.

She freed her mouth. "Noah . . ." Her eyes had closed. "This is wrong."

"This is human nature," he said. "It's how men and women find out what they think of each other."

"No . . . you must go," she said feebly.

"Poor Sarah . . ." he whispered. "So confused." He went on kissing her neck, where the faint taste of rosewater remained . . . descending until his breath warmed a path through the coarse flannel of her nightgown to her right breast.

"Stop!" she whispered, straining away, pushing on his shoulders. "Please . . . I cannot. Please . . ." She lost her grip on the blanket. It slipped to the floor as she wedged her arms between them, took fistfuls of his underwear and pushed him away. Tears were raining down her cheeks. "I'm not like Addie! I will not be like her! And my mother . . . my mother, too. Please, Noah, stop!"

He went motionless, his hands still touching her, but without insistence.

"Please, Noah . . ." she whispered once more.

He stepped back, beleaguered by guilt. "I'm sorry, Sarah." She stood with her arms crossed like a bandolier, protecting her breasts.

"Please go."

"I will, but I want your promise that you won't think less of yourself.

It's all my fault, I should have gone back to my room when you told me. Sarah, I didn't know about your mother.''

She turned away to the window, hugging herself—no chimes now, the magic all gone.

Apologetically, he retrieved her blanket from the floor, took it to her and draped it across her back, leaving his hands curved over her shoulders.

"I want you to know something, Sarah. I'm as surprised and bewildered about what's happening between us as you are. I don't think either one of us planned to have any feelings for each other. As a matter of fact, I think we're both fighting it. But I'm honest enough to admit that I didn't just walk into your room tonight because I was randy. There's more to it than that. I've come to admire you for dozens of reasons—you're bright, and hardworking, and plucky, and you fight for what you believe in. Churches, schools, boardwalks, stopping an epidemic of smallpox, even closing the brothels. I know you're going to doubt my honesty once I leave you, but it's true. Even when I was locking you up in that mine I thought you were one of the spunkiest human beings I'd ever met. Spunky and fearless. Since then you've shown me I was right. And lately I've been enjoying other things about you—the way you are with the children, how hard you worked on the pageant—all right, so laugh at me—but even singing "Silent Night' with you changed something between us. All that came first before tonight. Sarah . . . please look at me." He forced her to turn and face him. "What happened here is nothing to cry about.''

Her tears continued nonetheless. "What we did is not allowable. It cheapens what we feel.''

"I'm sorry you feel that way.''

"I do.''

"In that case I promise it will never happen again." His hands dropped from her shoulders and he stepped back.

"Well . . . I'll go now.''

With his head hanging, he moved toward the door. She felt bereft and wanted to reach out toward him and say she was sorry too, but she couldn't, because she was right and he was wrong to have come in here and forced the issue. Good, honorable men didn't.

At the door, he turned. "Merry Christmas, Sarah. I hope I didn't ruin it for you.''

"I enjoyed the chimes," she said sadly.

He studied her silhouette against the dim window light, opened the door and soundlessly disappeared.

Chapter 13

At midnight on Christmas Eve, Rose Hossiter's brothel was crowded with lonely miners who sought company to relieve their Christmas desolation. Kithless, they had watched the Christmas pageant and thought of home— of mothers, fathers, siblings, sweethearts and friends left behind in the cities as large as Boston, Munich and Dublin; or in rural communities with names too obscure to bring the light of recognition to a listener's eye. They thought of familiar hearths and mothers' bread and their old pet dogs, maybe long since dead. Some of them thought of the children they'd abandoned and the wives they'd send for, come spring.

Some were drunk.

Some were tearful.

All were lonesome.

The triangle bells of Tom Poinsett were the greatest boon to the flesh business since the discovery of gold itself. While they played, the tide of lonesome males, fresh from giving gold dust to the infant Jesus, brought the remainder of it to be exchanged for any soft, warm, sympathetic breast upon which they might lay their sorrowful heads and forget their homesickness.

Robert Baysinger was among these.

Remaining at the theater until the lanterns were being extinguished, he had watched Sarah leave with the marshal; the Robinsons leave with their baby; the Dawkins with their family; even Mrs. Roundtree with a group of her lodgers. As the theater emptied, Robert's solitariness closed in. Who was there for him in this town, save one for whose company he must pay? Damn the woman for her continued aloofness. He should disdain her, but found himself unable. He had, after all, come here largely because of her.

Forlornly he donned his coat and hat, took up his cane and went from the hall into the street, where the sound of the chimes lifted his face to the sky and seemed to widen the spaces between his bones. He stopped a minute, pulling on his capeskin gloves, letting the hymn shimmer through him. At home there had been church spires with bells that tolled the hour. Sometimes, as a child, they would awaken him in the mornings.

Three in a bed they'd slept—he, Walt and Franklin. Seemed like there were never enough beds, nor food, nor money. Sometimes not even enough love. Perhaps he was wrong about that: maybe the shortness had not been of love itself, but of the time to show it.

When he remembered his parents, he pictured them overworked and weary. It seemed they'd never had time to relax. His father labored fourteen hours a day in an effort to scrape together enough money to provide for his outsized family, which seemed to increase by one head per year. Ten hours a day Edward Baysinger worked as a trunkmaker at Arndson's Leather Factory; evenings, in a tiny shop behind their house, he fashioned wooden stocks for brushes on a foot-powered wood lathe. Sometimes he sharpened knives and shears. Sometimes he repaired chair rungs. Sometimes he bought and sold bone. Always he collected fat and tallow which his wife, Genevieve, brewed into yellow lye soap and sold to supplement the family's income, which never seemed adequate.

Whatever the secondary labor, the boys were always expected to help. They carted wood; sold wood shavings for kindling; fashioned bone handles for toothbrushes; begged waste fats door to door; peddled soap door to door, and as each one grew old enough, went to work in Arndson's Leather Factory. The only job the boys escaped was stirring and cutting the soap, which fell to the two girls of the family, who also helped their mother with the never-ending laundry and cooking for the tribe of thirteen.

By the time Robert was twelve he knew he wanted something better for himself than the endless toil and struggle he witnessed in his parents. His mother looked haggard and shriveled by the time she was thirty. His father's disposition became grumpier and more cynical in relationship to his growing responsibilities.

Though school was considered a luxury by Genevieve and Edward Baysinger, their son Robert fought for the right to continue his studies at the age when the others went into the factory. It was at school he met the Merritt girls. And later, when he was old enough to go begging grease and fat from the back doors of kitchens for his mother's soap pot, he knocked one day upon a strange door and to his surprise, it was answered by Adelaide Merritt.

"Why, Robert!" she had said. "Hello!"

He was chagrined to have to ask one of his schoolmates for the runoff from their frying pans, but Adelaide was sweet and friendly. She took him inside to a wondrously uncrowded kitchen where an uncorseted, buxom woman named Mrs. Smith found a good-sized tin of leftover grease and offered it along with fresh apple cakes and cold milk. These Robert shared with Addie Merritt at a grand round table covered with a crocheted cloth and decorated with a bouquet of daisies and fresh, red, pungent basil, which the housekeeper said kept the spiders and ants from visiting her kitchen.

From the first Robert was taken with all that space for only four people. Space, order, fastidiousness and quiet. Such marvelous quiet. Where he lived total quiet prevailed only in the deepest hours of the night, and even then the place was likely to rumble with snoring from one quarter or another. Around Addie's table were only four chairs instead of thirteen. On the range was one teakettle instead of three. In a cookie jar on the sideboard was an entire *batch* of snickerdoodles of which he was invited to partake at will after he finished his apple cake. In his entire life he'd never known such plenty, for at the Baysinger house cookies were rare and never lasted long enough to be stored in a jar.

And Addie's house was so clean! The floor had no footmarks, the windows no handprints, the curtains were starched and the rag rug at the kitchen door looked as though no one had ever stepped on it. In the parlor the antimacassars were perfectly centered on the sofa, the reading materials were stacked in bookshelves and folded in magazine racks; Mr. Merritt's pipes and tobaccos were neatly housed in a smoking stand, and there was space enough for a fern wider than the spread of a man's two arms. The room also held the ultimate luxury: a spinet. Robert tried to imagine his parents ever accumulating enough extra money to afford a spinet. The idea was preposterous.

Beside the piano stood a high chest of twenty skinny drawers containing sheet music. Addie selected some and played for him—a mazurka, "Für Elise" and "Londonderry Air"—sitting straight as a gopher with her fingers curled precisely over the keys. Her blond hair was looped up from her ears into a plaid moiré ribbon from which it flowed down her back in gentle curves. She was wearing a blue dress with a white lace collar. His eyes were equally taken by the girl, the room and the spinet. A large white cat came padding in and preened himself against Addie's ankles. She stopped playing to scoop him up and introduce him as Ruler before handing him to Robert and resuming her song.

Everything about that evening remained indelibly in Robert's memory. Addie's quiet reserve—so much greater than that of most girls her age that it made her seem older than her nine years; the obvious quality of every furnishing in the house; the tranquillity which prevailed. Even when Mrs. Smith came into the parlor and announced that it was late and time for Robert to leave and for Addie to retire, Addie accepted the order with grace far above her years.

She saw him to the front door, took Ruler from his arms and invited him to come back anytime. Without compunction, as if the difference in their ages and class did not exist, she said, "I'll let you know when Mrs. Smith has another batch of grease saved up and you can come and collect it."

Though Addie turned a blind eye to the differences in their class, Robert was stung afresh as he walked away. No, his parents would never have a spinet, nor luxuries of any kind, but from that first evening Robert spent in the Merritt house he vowed he would have them aplenty.

The next time he went there Sarah was at home. At fourteen, she was one year older than Robert and so much better acquainted, since on alternate years they had shared the same teacher and classroom—their school was arranged with two grades per room. Sarah was a brain. She won every spelling bee ever held, partook in every essay contest (often winning first prize), finished all her schoolwork in the time allotted, so carried books home only by choice. She often helped the children of the younger classes with their arithmetic, and when the teacher left the room was appointed monitor.

At home she spent all her time reading, or writing in a composition book, which she carried with her at all times. She had to be encouraged to play a duet on the spinet with Addie, doing so finally with a humph and a sigh as if put upon. Once she joined the music, however, she seemed a good sport (though she was not as natural on the piano as Addie), and after that, when Robert visited, the three of them formed a trio of friendship that made his visits there even more anticipated.

Addie—he discovered—was moody. At times she would be morose and withdrawn, taking all of Sarah's and Robert's best efforts at clowning to draw her from her glumness and make her laugh. They went on picnics together in the summer, Mrs. Smith providing them with enticing delicacies packed in a wicker basket with a linen liner: cucumber and minced ham sandwiches, cheese straws, raspberry tarts and a delectable specialty called chutree, made of vinegared, sugared and spiced strawberries, favored particularly by Robert, who (while the girls turned up their noses) spread the chutree on Mrs. Smith's crusty white bread and thought it the finest treat oné could hope to eat.

In winter they skated on Stepman's millpond, where large groups of young people met and built fires and drank hot peach punch spiced with cinnamon sticks. Many evenings Robert and Addie studied together while Sarah wrote in her journal. Often Sarah and Robert both helped Addie, who was much slower to learn and never quite understood many of the advanced mathematics problems they solved for her, nor how to properly parse a sentence, nor the reason for learning any of these things.

Their father was seldom home. When he was, the trio of young people would leave him to whatever room he chose—parlor or kitchen—moving to the opposite room to carry on whatever activities they were pursuing. Sarah introduced Robert to Isaac Merritt the first time.

"Father, this is our friend Robert Baysinger. He's come to study. We're helping Addie with her numbers."

"Robert," the older man had said, offering a handshake. He was an impressive man with straight, tall stature and a clean-shaven face, wearing a three-piece business suit trimmed by a linked gold watch fob. "Welcome. It's always seemed to me that Sarah never invited enough young people to the house. I'm glad to see she's made a new friend."

His assumption that Robert was there primarily as Sarah's friend went uncorrected, for at the time he was as much her friend as Addie's. Anything else would have been improper, given Addie's age. Yet the undercurrent of attraction between the younger two was already beginning to bloom.

Addie bloomed, too. Robert watched it happen, remaining the soul of propriety while her thinness took on the first gentle turns of puberty and the fuller curves beyond. Her hair touched her waist, curling at the tips like white wine hitting the bottom of a glass. Her face lost its childish appeal to the greater one of adult beauty. But as she grew older she seemed to distance herself from him and Sarah. More often she retreated into the puzzling realm of reticence and cheerlessness. She played the spinet with a look of disassociation—by now she was playing Mendelssohn—breaking into occasional passages when she displayed a nearly vitriolic passion. The first time it happened Robert became frightened and touched her shoulders to stop her. "Addie, what is it that's bothering you?"

She withdrew her hands from the keyboard as if it had suddenly burned her and tucked them into the folds of her skirt.

"Nothing." The word emerged toneless.

Sarah was seated by the gas lamp, wearing her spectacles, writing in her composition book. Mrs. Smith was in the kitchen, stitching beside the stove. Robert rubbed Addie's shoulders.

"I think I'll leave now. Walk me to the door," he requested.

Addie rose from the piano stool, lifeless but correct.

"Good night, Sarah," Robert called.

She looked up. "Oh . . . good night."

In the shadows of the front entry where the stairwell emptied down from above, he buttoned his jacket while Addie waited with that same remote look on her face, her eyes fixed upon the carved work on the umbrella stand.

"Addie," he told her, "perhaps I shouldn't come anymore."

Her ennui vanished. "Oh no, Robert!" Her eyes widened in distress. "Whatever would I do without you!" Without warning, she threw her arms around his neck and gripped him quite desperately. "Dear Robert, you're the best thing in my life, don't you see?" Her breath came fast, almost terrified. He closed his arms across her back and held her for the first time ever. She was fifteen at the time, he eighteen, and miserable with unexpressed love. He had at some time during their friendship decided he could not openly court her until she reached age sixteen. By then he might even have prospects and could ask her to marry. Meanwhile, he resisted the flare of desire and kept his hands on her back.

"Sometimes you don't seem to remember I'm in the room."

"I do . . . oh I do. Come again on Thursday the way you always do. Please, Robert, say you will."

"Of course I will. But I want to make you happy, and more often lately, I don't know how."

"You do, Robert. Please believe me."

Heroically, he put her from him. How beautiful her eyes and mouth, even when dismayed. In the deep shadows where they stood she gazed at him with undisguised affection and true fear at the thought of losing him.

"You do make me happy. I should die if I were to lose you."

He thought he should die if he could not kiss her.

"Addie," he whispered, touching her face with both hands, holding it with exquisite tenderness. He lowered his head and she stretched to meet his first kiss as if she, too, had suffered waiting for it. He felt her mouth tremble beneath his, though he stood carefully disjoined from her body, bending to reach her. Tens of times he had resisted this impulse and the greater one that followed. He embraced her fully, opened his mouth, and to his delight, she responded ardently.

With an effort he ended the kiss and stepped back.

Even in the subdued light he could tell she blushed.

"I think you should go now, Robert."

He tried to lift her chin, but she pulled it sharply aside and said, "Don't!"

"But Addie—"

"Don't, I said." She wouldn't lift her head. "We must not do this anymore."

Five months passed before they kissed again. They did so on a bitter cold January night out beside the woodpile where they'd made excuses to go. She had thrown on an unbuttoned coat; he had followed in his shirt-sleeves. She had bent forward to begin stacking logs on her arm when he gripped her elbow and said, "Addie . . ."

She straightened, swinging about, meeting his eyes with a mixture of alarm and innocent craving. There wasn't a doubt in the world what was on both their minds.

He took the stovewood from her arms, piece by piece, and tossed it onto the pile.

"No," she whispered. "Robert . . . no . . ." She wedged the butt of one hand against his chest as he gripped her arms in a manner indicating he'd brook no refusal.

"I kissed more girls before I was thirteen than in all the years since. Because of you, Addie . . . because I was waiting for you. Ever since the first day I came into your house and you played the piano for me I've been waiting for you to grow up. Well, you're almost there, so don't say no, Addie."

The kiss began as a struggle and ended in submission.

As with the first time, their years of repression came to bear upon them, lending their juncture a desperation.

He cupped her head.

She gripped his shirt.

He opened his mouth.

She opened hers.

He opened her coat and stepped against her.

But he denied himself the places he would touch, clasping her against his tumescent body with only the consolation of freeing two buttons between her shoulder blades, slipping his hand inside against her warm back, circling her waist with the opposite arm, kissing her mouth passionately.

She stopped it, tearing away, averting her face, the top of her head to his chest. They were both panting.

He kneaded her shoulders while rebellion built in his throat.

"Don't do that, Addie. You did that last time. Why should you feel ashamed?"

She swung her head remorsefully. He struggled to understand her disproportionate remorse. He struggled with anger that boiled up out of nowhere because he could not understand her, nor stop loving her.

"Addie, I've kissed you, nothing more. What's wrong with that?"

"Nothing." She was crying . . . silently . . . all by herself . . . crying with her sweet-smelling hair against his chest while he was left to wonder and soothe.

"Has your father warned you against this? Is that it?"

She made negative motions with her head.

"Are you afraid I'll go further? Addie, I wouldn't, not unless you wanted to, too."

The head wagging continued.

"Are you afraid we'll be discovered, or that Sarah might know, or be jealous, or what? What is it, Addie? You wouldn't cry like this over just a kiss."

She pulled back and dried her eyes as if she'd gathered a reserve of implacability from deep within. "You take the wood in, Robert, will you please? Tell Sarah I'm not feeling well and that I went upstairs to bed."

"Addie, wait . . ."

She'd already put space between them, walking backward toward the side of the house and the front door.

"It's not you, Robert, it's me. Please believe me, you've done nothing wrong."

"Addie, I promise I won't kiss you that way again . . . please, don't go in . . . Addie, I'm sorry . . . I love you . . . Addie? . . . Addie, please stay."

She had reached the corner of the house and paused, still facing him, her dark coat like a bloodspill on the dead, snowless grass. "You'd better not love me, Robert. You'll be sorry if you do."

He took a step toward her and she ran around the corner while he gave up the chase before it began, wilting with frustration, arms hanging loosely, head lolling back while he closed his eyes. He didn't understand her. How could he when she refused to confide the source of her fears? Perhaps she feared a total physical relinquishment and its probable outcome. What woman would not, considering the disgrace of pregnancy without wedlock? He was eighteen already and she only fifteen, not a woman at all, but a nubile young girl, afraid of her own budding sexuality. She kissed like a woman who loved it, yearned like a woman who wanted more, but backed off like the girl she was.

Nevertheless, he'd promised to respect her wishes. So why had she admonished him against loving her?

The probability struck him as if the woodpile had collapsed on his head.

She was dying! Most certainly that was it. His precious Addie was ill with some fatal disease for which no cure was known. Why else her gloomy introspection and her lapses at the piano while she played with despair in every note? Why else her bursts into impassioned fortissimos as if at the unfairness of fate? Why else her withdrawal from his kisses when he knew she had feelings for him? And her withdrawal even from Sarah, whom he knew Addie loved unquestionably?

If Sarah wondered why Addie returned to the house via the front door that night, and Robert not at all, she tactfully refrained from asking.

Robert went home without his jacket, sick with worry and shivering from chill in the fifteen-degree January night.

The following morning after Mr. Merritt had left for his office he knocked on the back door. Mrs. Smith answered.

"Why, Robert, whatever are you doing out there without a coat in this weather?"

He offered no explanation. "Would you get it for me, Mrs. Smith? I left it on the hall tree."

"Well, of course, but . . . land sakes, come inside. You look like you're freezing to death."

When Mrs. Smith returned with the garment, he inquired, "Is Addie all right this morning?"

"Addie? Why, I think so. She's off to school as usual. Why do you ask?"

If Addie was dying of some invisible disease, Mrs. Smith certainly acted blasé about it.

"Don't tell her I said anything, will you? We had an argument last night, that's all."

"Mum's the word," she promised with an affectionate glint in her eye. Mrs. Smith had always been their ally and had held a soft spot in her heart for Robert from the first night he'd come asking for grease. Since then he had fought his family for the right to attend school, had completed twelve grades and taken a job in a bank down on Market Street, where he was clerking for good wages, saving them and meeting the moneymakers of St. Louis. From them he was learning more than any college could have taught him about how the rich get richer. Though he had only one jacket to his name, he knew Mrs. Smith respected his frugality and the reason for it. She believed, as he did, that one day he would make his mark on the world.

When his jacket was buttoned, he lingered, silently composing and re-composing a question about Addie's health. In the end, with a lump in his throat, he blurted it out.

"Mrs. Smith, is Addie dying?"

Mrs. Smith's jaw dropped. Her double chin hung like forgotten bread dough over the edge of a pan.

"Dying?"

"Something's wrong with her—something serious. I know!"

"Goodness gracious, *I* don't know," Mrs. Smith whispered.

"She scarcely speaks to Sarah and me, and sometimes she gets terribly silent and stares at us like she's on a ship that's drifting away into a fog. Last night she . . . please, Mrs. Smith, forgive me for being blunt, but I kissed her and she cried for no reason at all and said that if I were to fall in love with her I'd be sorry. Since I'm reasonably sure she loves me too, and since I have every intention of marrying her someday, I can't think of why I might be sorry unless she were to die."

Mrs. Smith plopped into a chair, pinching her lower lip, and stared at some kitchen corner.

"Oh dear me, I've known something was amiss, too, but I never considered this."

Robert sat on the opposite side of the table, tense in the face of Mrs. Smith's commensurate worry.

She looked up. "Did you ask her? What did she say?"

"No, I was afraid to. That's why I came to you."

"I simply don't know. If there is something wrong with her, neither she nor Mr. Merritt have confided in me. I think, perhaps, he's the one we should ask."

"Together?"

"Why not? We're both worried about her, aren't we?"

They did so that afternoon while the girls were still in school. Robert asked for an hour off work and they met at the newspaper office, clasping hands and exchanging grave glances before entering together.

Isaac Merritt sat in a cubicle of glass and mahogany, his name in gold leaf on the window of the door. When he saw the unlikely duo approaching, he rose and rushed forward with anxiousness bending him toward them.

"Mrs. Smith, Robert, what is it? Has something happened to the girls?" Twin lines dented the plane between his eyebrows.

"Nothing immediate," Mrs. Smith replied, "though young Robert has come to me with some concerns and we thought it best to speak to you about it."

Baffled, Merritt looked from one to the other and belatedly offered, "Most certainly. Come in." They all sat but Robert, who stood beside Mrs. Smith's chair, facing Addie's father behind the desk.

"Please," the older man said, "don't keep me in suspense. If one of my daughters is in some trouble, I want to know about it."

"It's not exactly trouble, sir, it's . . ." Mrs. Smith began, then groped in her sleeve for a handkerchief and pressed it to her mouth as her chin began to tremble. "It's . . ." Mrs. Smith broke into weeping.

"Well, good God, out with it!" Merritt exploded, overwrought with concern.

Robert spoke up.

"We were hoping that you could tell us, sir, what's wrong with Addie."

"*Wrong* with her?"

"Yes, sir. Some things she's said lately, and her increasing despondency led us to believe she might be ill. Perhaps gravely so."

"What has she *said?*" Merritt's voice hissed. Inexplicably, his anger seemed to flare.

Robert hesitated, swallowed. He glanced to Mrs. Smith for guidance.

"Go on, tell him. He's a fair man."

"She said, sir, that if I were to fall in love with her I'd be sorry, but I'm afraid it's already too late. I *am* in love with your daughter and I would very much like to marry her when she comes of age. I had intended to wait until she was sixteen to declare myself, but this . . . this curious condition seems to have taken hold of her and I thought, since I have reason to believe Addie loves me, too, there must be something very serious wrong with her to make her say such a thing. The only thing I could think of was some dread disease."

Isaac Merritt's face had grown red. His lips were compressed.

"What do you know about this, Mrs. Smith?"

"Only that she hasn't been acting herself lately. She is a sad young lady, and—"

"I'm speaking of this man and my daughter!" Merritt snapped. "I've left her in your care and you've obviously allowed her to indulge in improper tête-à-têtes with a man three years her senior when she is nothing but a girl barely out of pinafores!"

Mrs. Smith stared at her employer in surprise.

"Why, Mr. Merritt, whatever . . . why, you know Robert. He's been the girls' friend for years."

Merritt rapped his knuckles on the desktop. "I thought he was Sarah's friend, not Addie's!"

"He's that, too, sir. He's both of their friends."

"But while Sarah is of marriageable age, you've allowed him to spend time privately with Addie, who is not!"

Mrs. Smith got spunky. "With the deepest respect, too, I'll be bound, which he's earned from me who knows him nearly as well as I know your own daughters. Why, he's come here to speak to you honestly about his feelings, which took a good deal of courage, considering he thought—and I did too—that Addie might possibly be ill, very ill, maybe even dying. For you to attack him this way when he was sick with worry is not like you, sir."

Merritt calmed himself and replied quietly, "You're right, Mrs. Smith. Robert, I'm sorry. There is nothing physically wrong with Addie. If she'd seen a physician, even without my knowledge, I'd surely have known, for wouldn't I have received a bill? She has, I'm afraid, inherited her mother's temperament—moony and distracted by turns, which made my wife very difficult to live with, and makes Addie much the same. Though I appreciate your concern, take it from me, it is ill-founded."

Both Robert and Mrs. Smith relaxed.

"Ooo, sir, I'm happy to hear it," she said, passing a hand over her forehead.

"I apologize, too, for implying that you've done less than a good job with the girls. Your care for them has been impeccable, better perhaps than their own mother could have provided, had she stayed."

"Why, thank you, sir."

"I believe, though, that we must allow for Addie's moods. She isn't the intelligent girl her sister is nor has she the wit and personality to attract friends easily. She's always preferred to be alone, and loners must be granted their curious shifts of temperament, must they not? She is a young girl standing on the threshold of womanhood. Let's give her time to step into it gracefully without badgering her to cheer up, shall we? She'll do so in all due time, I'm sure."

"Perhaps you're right, sir." Mrs. Smith crossed herself. "I'll say a novena for her, that's what I'll do."

"Thank you, Mrs. Smith. Now if you wouldn't mind excusing us for a moment, I'd like to talk to young Robert alone."

"Of course." She worked herself out of her chair with no small effort. Over the years she'd grown rounder. "I've got some marketing to do, and since Robert's going back to the bank from here, I'll bid you both good afternoon."

When she was gone, Isaac Merritt waved a hand toward her chair. "Sit down, Robert."

Robert did so.

Merritt sat, too, joined his hands, steepled his fingers and tapped them against his lips. He studied Robert silently for some time, then let his joined hands drop to his lap.

"So you love Addie, do you?" He sounded remarkably calm, considering his earlier vehemence.

"Yes, sir, I do."

"And you want to marry her."

"When the time is right."

"Ah, yes . . ." Merritt reached for a humidor and extracted a cigar. "When the time is right." He snipped the end. "And when is that?"

"As soon as her schooling is done, I thought, although I'd always intended to let my intentions be known when she was sixteen."

"Next year."

"Yessir."

"And you'll be nineteen then, is that right?"

"Yessir."

Merritt lit his cigar and blew smoke toward the ceiling. Leaning back in his chair, he said, "I thought it best not to expound upon the subject while Mrs. Smith was here, but you're old enough for a man-to-man talk." He leaned forward, bracing his elbows on the desk, studying the cigar while rolling it between his fingers. "I've been eighteen myself, Robert. I know the"—he thought a moment—"the impatience a man feels at that age." He looked up. "Like a ripe watermelon waiting to be dropped, eh?"

Robert blushed but his gaze held steady. "In spite of what you may think, sir, Addie and I have never been alone together by design, and when we are there've been no improprieties between us."

"Of course not. But you've kissed her, I suppose."

"Yessir, but nothing more."

"Of course not, only the struggle with yourselves."

Robert could not in all honesty deny it.

"I would imagine that a girl of fifteen is of an age to be kissed—in my day they were. But think, Robert, of the exigencies it places upon her. You are eighteen already . . . a man. Old enough to be married, should you choose; to have a family, a home of your own, the freedoms of the marital state. You've begun treating Addie as a woman, yet she knows she is not one. So is it not believable that she should react as she has? With periods of despondency and gloom? She feels guilty, believing she is holding you back. And in spite of your declarations of honor, in spite of your good intent, and in spite of the fact that I believe you, the best thing for both you and Addie might be for you to see her less until she's reached the age where she *can* marry."

Though Robert felt downhearted he admitted he'd had the same thoughts himself at times.

"Two years isn't so long," Merritt went on. "I understand you're learning under the big boys over at the bank. In two years you'll know nearly as much as they. Undoubtedly you'll be saving your money and investing it under their tutelage. I'll be the first to admit I wouldn't mind having a daughter married to an up-and-coming banker who will—I have every reason to believe—be a prosperous leader of his community one day. Mrs. Smith's faith in you is not ungrounded. I've asked around about you and what I've learned is most impressive. I was, however, as I said earlier, under the impression that it was Sarah who'd caught your eye. Forgive me for admitting I'm disappointed that it isn't. With her plain looks and her bookishness, Sarah will have some difficulty finding a husband. But since it's Addie, perhaps you and I could reach an understanding.

"During these next two years, you tend to learning all they can teach you at the bank. Make a good solid start for yourself, invest your money— I'll even advise you on that if you wish—but ease away from Addie. See her occasionally, of course, but offer logical excuses for having less time to devote to her. And when she's seventeen I'll be more than happy to give my blessings at your wedding."

Robert felt relieved in a dampened way. Two years of avoiding Addie; how could he do it when he'd seen her almost daily for years?

"I have your permission then, to propose when she's sixteen?"

"You have it."

"Thank you, sir."

Robert rose and extended his hand. Merritt shook it solidly.

"You won't be sorry," Robert promised. "I'll work damned hard during the next two years to give Addie the kind of home she deserves."

"I'm sure you will. And I'll be keeping my eye on you, whether you're aware of it or not."

Robert smiled and released his future father-in-law's hand.

"You just watch me. I'm going to be as rich as you someday."

Isaac Merritt laughed as the younger man headed for the door.

"Oh, one more thing, Robert." Robert paused and turned. "I see no reason to trouble Addie by telling her of this conversation. We must, after all, allow her to do her own choosing when the time comes."

"Certainly, sir."

"Good luck to you, Robert."

"And to you, too, sir. Thank you."

There had followed the most miserable six months of Robert's life, avoiding Addie—and thereby, Sarah, too—giving up their friendship while offering plausible excuses for his absences. He lived with the fear that Addie would lose her feelings for him. Once he spoke to Sarah about it, inviting her out for a walk and confessing his loneliness and confusion, and his hurt over Addie's earlier withdrawal. He told Sarah he was working to secure his future and hinted it was Addie's future, too, but he was bound by his promise to Isaac Merritt to keep his intentions secret.

Were there other boys at school who'd caught her attention? No, none Addie spoke of, Sarah assured him. Had she confessed to Sarah that her feelings for him had waned? No, Sarah had replied. Does she speak of me at all? he'd asked with longing in his eyes. Sarah had simply refrained from answering, returning his look with one of shared dismay.

Addie's birthday fell in June. Two weeks beforehand he sent her a note, asking for the pleasure of her company on the Sunday preceding it. They would picnic at the Botanical Gardens.

He rented a rig for the first time ever and picked her up with great pomp and ceremony. He had bought for the occasion a vested linen suit the hue of oatmeal and wore a choking, high collar under a painstakingly knotted tie. She wore an airy dress of lavender dotted Swiss, a wide-brimmed straw bonnet, and carried a white lace parasol. From the moment they regarded one another at the door they recognized a mutual somberness, a sorrow-wasted state bordering on melancholy which accompanied them to the carriage. He helped her embark and she held her skirts aside as he seated himself beside her.

"Would you like the bonnet up?" he asked.

"No, my parasol is fine."

He flicked the whip and the bay trotted off briskly, its hooves making the only sound as the two of them rode side by side in silence.

"How have you been?" he asked, and she replied, "Fine."

They had dressed in finest regalia—his first costly summerweight suit, which had set him back dearly; her first grown-up bonnet and the dress with its rustling petticoats such as full-grown women wore. They had breached some indefinable line between callowness and majority that had nothing to do with age, but having breached it they found it execrably silencing.

At the gardens he helped her alight and took up their picnic food, tied in his mother's dish towel: though he'd outlayed cash on a fine suit which would enhance his image at the bank, he would not get rich spending money on wicker baskets.

"I thought we would try the arbor seat just beyond the orangery. Have you been there?"

"Yes. My father has brought us here many times."

They walked together in the sun, along gravel paths between shoulder-high delphiniums the color of sky, past velvety purple petunias that turned the air to nectar, between a pair of magnificent copper beech trees as wide as houses with great drooping arms of shade, into the sun again along a rose path and through an ornate glass orangery where lacy palm trees thrived in the humid warmth; back into the cool between high boxwood hedges and through a topiary arch that brought them to a circular green enclosure surrounded by more square-edged boxwood hedge. Within it beds of white petunias, brilliant red celosia and purple ageratum formed a starburst design. In its center, painted white and draped with thick emerald grapevines, waited the double-benched arbor seat.

Reaching it had taken ten minutes of walking while neither Robert nor Adelaide spoke a word.

She stepped up onto the painted floor and took a seat; her skirts covered the width of the wooden bench, leaving Robert little choice but to seat himself opposite.

He waited for some sign, and with his eyes called her, but she looked up at the leaf-screen overhead and remarked, "It's cool here."

Her remoteness hurt. He didn't know how to perforate it, to force her to bend or mend or end this indifference she had espoused.

"It's been a long time since we were on a picnic."

"Yes, it has."

He untied the dish towel. "It's not as fancy as Mrs. Smith's, but it's what I could manage. Corn gems, currant preserves, cheese and ham." He piled a selection on a cloth napkin and offered it.

"Thank you." She arranged the napkin on her crackling skirt, toying with it distractedly, bringing points up like mountains surrounding a valley. She studied the food instead of him, but showed no interest in eating anything. He chewed some cheese, which seemed to lodge in his throat, then gave up the effort.

"You aren't eating," he said.

She rested a hand on her ribs and flashed him a glance. "I'm sorry. I'm not really very hungry."

"Neither am I."

He set aside their napkins and sat watching her gaze at tne gardens sparkling in the sun. He bent forward, bracing his forearms on his knees.

"Happy birthday, Addie," he said quietly.

Her attention shifted to him and stayed. For a moment he saw undisguised yearning in her eyes and the same affliction that had narrowed his throat, but she quickly hid it, dropping her gaze.

"I'm sorry I'm not more cheerful. I know you meant this to be a festive occasion. You've gone to all this trouble, and I . . . I . . . ."

Her eyes could no longer refrain from resting upon his. They returned, illuminated with regret and hurt he could not comprehend.

"What's the matter, Addie?"

"I've missed you."

"You don't act like you've missed me."

"I've missed you, Robert, so very much."

"May I come and sit beside you?"

"Yes." She lifted her skirts, and when he sat, they covered most of his trouser leg. His knee pressed her thigh within the voluminous petticoats as he took her hand.

"I love you, Addie."

She closed her eyes and dropped her chin, though not before he caught a glimpse of tears.

"I love you too," she said to her lap.

He touched the crest of her cheek. "Why does that make you cry?"

"I don't kn–know." She had begun to sob quietly, her shoulders curled forward. Her sorrow reached within him and seized him about the heart.

"Please, Addie . . . don't cry . . ." He took her in his arms but the embrace was awkward, complicated by her wide hat. "Addie, darling . . . shh . . ." He had never before used the endearment; it resounded in his own head and gave his stomach a clenched feeling. "There's no more reason to cry, because everything is perfect. I've asked your father permission to marry you and he's said yes."

She drew back, her wide eyes streaming. "He did?"

"Yes, a year from now when you've finished school." He reached up and removed her hat. The pin clung to her topknot of curls and disheveled them, trailing one strand, like a drop of honey, down the side of her neck.

His news released a fresh flow of tears. He felt helpless in the face of them, groping for the proper means to end them, certain it was not within his power. Nevertheless, he took her face in one hand and drew her to his side, where his hammering heart at last pressed against her arm. "What is it, Addie? You're breaking my heart and I don't know what to do for you anymore. Don't you want to marry me?"

"I can't . . . you must not ask m–me."

"But I am asking. One year from now, tell me you'll marry me."

She pushed back and said, "No."

His fear became brittle, intense. He reacted instinctively, gripping her arms and forcing her into his embrace, kissing her with furor, need, and an unholy terror unleashed by the possibility of living without her when he had known since he was thirteen that he would marry her one day. Her resistance vanished and the kiss became a terrible thing, a heavy-hearted trade-off of uncertainty and desire, a lament, an exquisite end of their vernal longings, with her arms about his neck and their mouths wide. He flattened her breast with one hand and she whimpered against his tongue.

"Addie, let's go where we can be alone."

"No . . ."

"Please . . ." He kissed her again, openly caressing both her breasts through the crisp dotted Swiss and layers of softer underclothes.

"Robert, stop. We're in the middle of the public gardens."

He knew where they were: he had chosen it to preclude the possibility of just such a scene.

"Come with me, Addie, please." His voice was hoarse.

"Where?" Hers was thin.

"I know a place. I delivered plant stakes here once for my father."

"No."

"How can you say no when you feel yes?"

"We can't."

"Please . . . where we can see each other. I want to see you, Addie."

Voices drifted to them from beyond the boxwood hedge, and footsteps sounded on the gravel, coming their way. Robert released Addie, keeping her stirred with an intense gaze while reaching for her hat.

"Put it on. Let's go."

Protected from view by Robert and a partial cascade of grapevines, she adjusted two hairpins and rammed a pin through the straw hat. He handed her her parasol, took her elbow and left via the only path, exchanging inane greetings with the intruders. Beyond the boxwood border he took her hand and led her at a rush through floral lanes to a break in the greenery where they were forced to dip low and remove Addie's hat to make their way through. Beyond lay a cart path in a patch of uncultivated woods, leading to a white shed with crossbucked doors. Before it stood a pony cart filled with the heads of flowers plucked by the gardeners from the plants the previous day.

Robert tried the doors. They were unlocked, but inside, the shed was crowded with gardening tools, buckets, lath and trellis wire, leaving a little patch of floor, and it strewn with garden soil.

"Damn." Robert swept a glance over the woods around them. He struck off toward the front of the pony cart, hauling Addie along behind him, stepping over the wagon traces, which rested on the ground, tilting the cart forward and spilling its load in an array of wilting color. Down upon it he took her, already kissing and embracing her as they fell to the resilient floral cushion.

"Robert," she managed, "your new suit . . ."

"I don't care." The stains of rose petals and marigolds and larkspur had already soiled his elbows during the fall.

"But someone will come."

"It's Sunday. The gardeners are all at home."

He kissed her as Adam had kissed Eve before she found the apple tree, then rolled her to her back and leaned over her, studying her face in the dappled shade, framed by fading flowers and wilting greenery that gave up a spicy redolence.

"Oh Addie, you're so pretty."

He sat up and stripped off his jacket, tossed it aside and took her in his arms, rolling to his back with her atop him. Many long, wet kisses later, when his knee had forced her skirts high between her legs, and their mouths were swollen, they paused for breath.

"Addie, I love you so much," he breathed.

With their gazes locked, he rolled her to her back.

"Robert," she whispered, "my new dress . . ."

A petal fell from his hair onto her face, where it remained as he spoke. "Let's take it off too." Her green eyes fixed upon his and she swallowed as if with great difficulty.

He struggled to his knees, drawing her after him by one hand, the petal from her cheek drifting to her skirt. When she sat, he got behind her, freed a long row of buttons and turned her dress down to her waist. Beneath it she wore a white cambric shift gathered at a scooped neckline. He kissed the slope of her bare shoulder, then moved around to face her on his knees. Her shift was held together by a white center bow. It disappeared at his tug, the ribbons falling to the depression between her breasts. He put his face there and pressed her back down, kissed her breasts first through white cambric, and saw them naked for the first time as she lay upon the wilting flowers of yesterday.

"Robert, we can't," she whispered breathlessly when they'd kissed again with their legs plaited.

He continued his seduction, wooing and weakening her with touches and kisses while the spent blossoms lifted their haylike scent into the cool green woods. Her murmurs and flushes and closed eyelids spoke of acquiescence until he brushed her skirts up and touched her beneath them.

She uttered a cry and pushed his hand away, but he persisted. She was wearing stockings and garters and one bright tear in the corner of each closed eye. Her jaw was clenched.

As his hand found its destination she cried out and recoiled, scrambling away from him as if in revulsion.

"Stay away from me!" She was on all fours, sliding down the tilted wagon, taking dead flowers with her. Her eyes were wild and rabid.

"Addie, where are you going?" He sat up.

"Stay away!"

"I'm sorry, Addie." He reached out one hand in appeal. "I thought you wanted to."

"No!" She lurched back, posed on all fours, like a dog, her eyes dark and terrified.

"I won't hurt you. I promise I won't touch you again. Dear God, Addie, I love you."

"You don't love me!" she screamed. *"How could you love me and want to do that to me!"*

Her voice rang through the clearing, carrying to the public gardens, he was sure. People would come running if she continued.

"Addie, what's wrong with you?"

He could see she was in a state of irrationality as she struggled to her feet and stood hunkered forward, like a Neanderthal brandishing a spear, while attempting to draw her shift into place with her other hand.

His throat was tight with fear. "Let me help you with your dress. I won't touch you anyplace else, I promise." He moved toward her warily, but she backed up and yelped, "No! Stay away, I said!" tripping on her dress, soiling the hem and stumbling.

He stood by helplessly while she began babbling, scrabbling her bodice into place, her eyes searching the ground as if confused about the litter of dead flowers. ". . . all these roses . . . must get home . . . shouldn't have come here . . . birthday . . . Sarah will know . . ." She scuttled backward some distance before turning and running with her clothing still disheveled.

"Addie, your hat! Your umbrella!" He grabbed them and jogged after her. "Addie, wait!"

The last he saw of her was her stained dress, opened up the back as she lifted her skirts and ran as if red lava were at her heels.

The following morning she was gone.

Chapter 14

❧

And now it was Christmas Eve, five and a half years later. All that time he had carried guilt and confusion as well as the memories of their unresolved love. He needed resolution; absolution, maybe—he was not sure.

He sat in the parlor at Rose's, in a stuffy room with thick velvet curtains, a round black iron stove and a good two dozen lonely men. He alone, among them, seemed sober. The cigar smoke hung like fog. The beer-soaked floorboards emitted a malty smell. He imagined he detected, too, the odor of human secretions and felt befouled by his surroundings.

The menu on the wall seemed to leer at him; he turned his head to look at something else. A brassy-haired bawd was petting the buttocks of a man with a large boil on the back of his neck. The old harlot who ran the place was smoking a cigar and squinting at him through the haze. Robert shuddered and studied his knees. Another whore came down the stairs. The harlot came to him and said, "Ember is free now. How 'bout her?"

"No, thank you. I'll wait for Eve," he replied, the name strange on his tongue.

"You're sure about that bath now, honey? We don't want our girls catching nothing."

"I'm sure. I took one this afternoon."

He waited a total of forty minutes, wondering what Addie's customer would look like when he came down, imagining sordid pictures of Addie ministering to someone who resembled the thickset miner with the boil on his neck.

He watched every man who came downstairs, guessing which one was Addie's. He guessed right—she descended minutes after a tall, scraggly fellow with skin the color of a mushroom who came down running his thumbs under his suspender straps. Addie disappeared into the hall momentarily as every girl did after every descent—presumably depositing her earnings under the gimlet gaze of her employer. Returning to the parlor, Addie was signaled over by Rose, who spoke while nodding in Robert's direction. Addie's head snapped around even before Rose finished speaking.

Across the smoky, stuffy room tension immediately stretched between the two of them like a turnbuckle. He nodded, sitting straight on a hard chair with his hat and cane on his knees.

She stared at him, her expression unreadable, before beginning to thread her way across the room.

His palms got sweaty. Surely his chest would implode. He thought, *I'm not at all sure I can do this, not to her and not to me.*

She wore an open kimono, sheeny and black, with large orchid flowers; stockings, garters and black slippers with high heels. Her underwear showed in the break down the middle.

"Hello, Robert."

"Hello, Addie."

"Rose doesn't like it when you call me that."

He cleared his throat and said, "Eve," and after an interim, "Merry Christmas."

"Sure. What can I do for you?"

He knew nothing of whorehouse protocol. Was he expected to pick a selection from the menu here and now?

"I'd like to go upstairs."

"I'm working, Robert."

"Yes, I know."

Ten seconds of electric silence, then, "I can't do any favors for old friends."

"I don't expect any. I'll pay whatever is required."

She studied him with a deliberately flat expression, then turned away. "Get one of the other girls." He caught her arm and swung her around.

"No! You!" His expression was grim, his grip indurate. "It's time we had this over with!"

"This is a mistake, Robert."

"Maybe so, but only one in a long line of many. Where do I pay?"

The madam and a huge, menacing Indian woman were already moving toward them. He dropped Addie's arm and the pair fell back.

"Upstairs," Addie answered. "Follow me."

In the midst of the crowd Rose halted Addie with a pudgy, beringed hand. "Don't forget now, Eve—no special considerations for old boyfriends. He pays like all the rest."

"Don't worry, Rose. I wouldn't dream of cheating you." And to Robert, "Come on."

Her hair was cropped straight across the forehead and bottom, Oriental fashion. He watched it refuse to sway as he followed her upstairs and through a door on the left. Inside, his eyes took a quick flight around the room—the pad on the bed, the egg timer beside it, the butter bowl, the gold scale, the clock, the pot beside the door: an airless, windowless cubicle where he was one in a progression of thousands.

Addie said, "I'll take your coat." She hung it on a tree in the corner and laid his hat and cane on a hard, armless wooden chair that had probably been used for more than a hatrack. He resisted the urge to pluck it off and hang it on the tree, too.

She returned to the door and closed it, lounging back upon it, watching his eyes search for locks.

"No locks here, honey," she said in a cornsilk voice. "But don't worry. Nobody will come in unless I scream." The implication chilled him. He wondered how many times she had, and how badly she'd been hurt before anyone reached the door.

"I have a request, Addie."

"Eve."

"Eve," he repeated. "Please don't call me honey."

"Sure." She still lounged against the door. "Anything else?"

"No."

An immense silence passed while she stood against the door and he tried to pretend she was a stranger.

"This your first time in a place like this?" Addie inquired.

"Yes."

"We're required to ask—did you take a bath?"

"Yes, this afternoon."

"Good. This we're not required to ask—is it your first time?"

A moment, then, quietly, "No."

She boosted away from the door and said on a gust of breath, "Well, then . . . about the business."

He reached in his pocket for his pouch of gold dust, but she came to him and pressed his hand to detain it. "Not so fast. We can talk a minute first." She circled him, running her hands over his trunk, making broad swipes that crossed his watch fob from above to below and back again. He clenched his stomach and held it taut.

"If you collect the money first, then fine. I'll do like everyone else."

"Just relax, Robert . . . relax. We'll get to that in a minute. We need to talk about what you want."

He wanted her to stop rubbing him the way she rubbed every other man who entered this room. He wanted her to grow back her beautiful blond hair and put on a decent dress that covered her. He wanted to scrub the filth off her face and take her to a church somewhere and kneel beside her and put this sordid room behind them forever.

"What do you want, Robert, hmm? This is the way it's done. You tell me what you want and I'll tell you how long it takes and that way neither one of us gets surprised in the end. How does that sound, hmm?"

"Fine." He dropped his hand from his gold pouch pocket.

"We can do it quick and slick. See the egg timer? It's a dollar a minute that way."

Sweet savior, an egg timer. How many men could churn through here in intervals that short? Without time for even a pretense of affection?

"Otherwise we can do the trip. Most men like the trip. It's got just about everything and it'll take about forty minutes. Tell me what forty minutes of heaven is worth to you, Robert. We'll start out nice and slow . . ." She reached down his trousers and stroked him indolently, and to Robert's chagrin he was turgid. He grabbed her by both elbows and held her away. "Please, Addie . . . Eve. I'll pay whatever you ask, just don't . . . don't . . ." Don't be so facile and practiced. "Could we just get on with it in a straightforward manner?"

"Sure." She backed off and dropped the seductive act, exchanging it for cool detachment. "Let's say twenty dollars. In advance."

Twenty dollars, twenty minutes or thereabouts. Could he get her to talk in twenty minutes? He'd been unable to do so in the weeks that he'd been here. What purpose would it serve if he put them both through this and she shed no light on that time five years ago?

She accepted his gold pouch and weighed out a full ounce, returned the pouch to him and waited while he stood uncertainly.

"Would you like to kiss me, Robert?" she asked.

He swallowed and answered honestly, "No."

"Would you like me to kiss you?"

"I'd like to talk, Addie. Could we just talk?"

"Of course." She took his hand and led him to the bed. They sat on the edge and she pulled one knee up on the mattress, turning to face him. "But I won't talk about the thing you came here to talk about. Anything else, but not that. Are you lonesome, Robert, because it's Christmas? Is that it?"

The words he wanted to say were trapped in his throat.

"You miss your family?" Her voice seemed genuine with caring for the first time since his arrival in Deadwood.

"No. I never was close to them. Well, maybe my brother Franklin."

"I never met him. I never met any of them."

"I wanted you to."

"Well, sometimes things just don't turn out." She reached out and stroked his lapels. "You've done very well for yourself, haven't you, Robert. You're rich, just the way you always wanted to be."

"I wanted to be rich for you, too, didn't you know that? It's why I was away from you so much during that time when—"

She covered his lips with a finger. "Shh . . . nothing about that."

He gripped her hand and held it against his breast. "Why?" he asked passionately.

She shook her head slowly, breaking into tiny pieces inside, Eve and Addie warring with one another. She had survived the minutes since spotting him in the parlor by reverting to Eve, by hardening herself to all human emotion. She could get through this if she kept Addie locked up and out of sight. Vulnerable, aching Addie, who was weeping inside her right now, who wanted to cover herself and hide in Robert's arms and beg his forgiveness, beg him to excuse her from this unspeakable act that would reduce them both beyond redemption.

"Why, Addie?" Robert repeated. "I deserve to know after all this time. I've been through seven hells believing it was my foolish advances that forced you to run, but I've never fully understood the rest of it. You were young, I know, and I was old enough to realize you weren't ready, but why did you desert your family? Do you know how your father suffered? How Sarah did?"

"I did too," she said poignantly.

"Then why? Why this?" He passed a hand through the air of the sleazy room.

"Because it's the only thing a woman knows."

"No. Don't tell me that because I won't believe it! You were a virgin that day we were in that cart of flowers. I know it just as surely as I know tonight that you're not. You were terrified of what nearly happened between us. That's why none of this fits!"

Addie begged, *Tell him.*

Eve said, *Get it over with.*

Her expression glazed over. She glanced at the clock beside the bed. "Robert, I have to start timing you from the minute the door closed. We've already used up five minutes. You've got fifteen more to go. Are you sure you want to spend it talking?"

Any sentimentality she'd shown had vanished; there would be no further answers, he could tell.

He rose from the bed and began loosening his tie: two brusque yanks while the skin on his facial structure seemed stretched so tightly the bones showed through. His mouth was rigid, his eyes dispassionate.

"All right, let's get on with it."

He removed his jacket, hung it on the coat-tree. Then the watch fob. The vest. The suspenders. His shoes and socks, sitting on the bed as if he were the only person in the room. His shirt, standing with his back to her. His trousers. Down to his wool union suit.

He turned to face her. "Well, are you going to sit there all night on my twenty dollars?" She hadn't moved a muscle. Her eyes were wide like that day on the flower cart.

"Well?" he snapped.

Don't, Robert, please. "Sometimes the men like to undress us."

"I have no desire to undress you. Do it yourself," he ordered.

His union suit was opened to his navel. He dropped his arms to his sides and waited, little understanding why he wanted to humiliate her. Perhaps because he himself was humiliated to be here, to be engaging in this depravity which with each passing moment was approaching the time of least grace.

"I'm waiting, Eve," he ordered.

She rose and stood before him, as straight as St. Joan's stake, her eyes fixed unwaveringly upon his. She removed her kimono, tossed it to the bed. Slipped off her satin shoes. Garters. Stockings. The corset: its hooks came free in a series of lunges which he followed with his eyes, breast to belly. It dropped to the floor. She opened her chemise and dropped it, too. Beneath it the skin was crosshatched in a pattern of wrinkled cotton. His eyes perused the wrinkles, lifted to her naked breasts, lingered, then rose to her face while she worked the button at the waist of her pantaloons. One glinting tear had formed in each of her eyes, hovering at the outer corner like dew at the tip of a leaf.

His throat filled. Inside him, something rended.

"No, Addie, not this way," he whispered, stepping forward and hiding her against himself, pinning her arms at her sides. "I cannot do it this way." His eyes were closed, his eyelashes wet. "Not for gold. Not with you hating me and me hating myself. Forgive me, Addie."

She let herself be held and hidden, standing limply in his arms while Addie crept out of isolation and tapped at the door of a hurting heart.

"Aw, Addie, what have we come to?" He caught the back of her head in an open hand and held her while they cried together silently, too close to see faces, too shaken to speak. A door closed down the hall. Someone laughed. Downstairs the parrot squawked. The clock beside the bed ticked off two costly minutes . . . three . . . still they remained, her hair meshed with his beard, two of her bare toes stacked upon his big one.

"Put your clothes back on, Addie," he whispered hoarsely, moving as if to release her.

"Wait." She clung, hiding still. "I have to tell somebody. I can't live with it any longer."

He resumed the pressure of his arms around her shoulders and waited. Her throat was caught on his shoulder. He felt her swallow.

"It was my f–father," she whispered at last, with her fists closed in the scratchy woolen underwear on his back. "He used to c–come into my b–bed at night. He used to make me d–do all these things with him."

The splash of shock caught him like scalding water. His stomach took up some slack he had not known was there. Denial sprang to mind—*Somehow you've misunderstood, Robert.*

"Your father?" he whispered.

She nodded, bumping his shoulder, holding her sobs inside so they palpitated against his stomach.

His hand went to her head and pulled it more tightly to his neck. Could he have made of himself a complete circle to shield her from every side, he would have done so.

"From the time my mother left."

"Oh Addie . . ." He had not known pity could reach such immense proportions.

"I used to sl–sleep with Sarah, and then Mother left and I st–started wetting the bed so Father put me in a room of my own and that's when it st–started. He used to tell me that if he rubbed me down there I w–wouldn't wet the bed anymore. It was very lonely without Mother and at f–first I liked having him climb in with m–me and h–holding me."

Robert's tears fell on Addie's hair while the two of them remained sealed together like blades of wet grass.

"You were just a child."

"It was long before I knew you. Long before I fell in love with you." Her words were distorted against his collarbone.

"He forced himself on you? Totally?"

"Not at first. That began when I was twelve."

"Twelve . . ." *Twelve . . . sweet heavens, twelve.* He had known her at twelve. He had watched her play the spinet with that haunted solitariness that kept drawing her away. She had owned a green plaid dress with a white pilgrim collar that hung down nearly to the points of her budding breasts. He had sometimes sneaked glances at them while her eyes were on the music. Remembering, he felt guilty for even so small an infraction.

"Just at the time you began to mature."

"Yes," she whispered.

"About the time I began noticing you growing up, too."

She remained silent.

"It got worse then, because of that, didn't it?"

Still she said nothing.

"Didn't it, Addie?"

"It wasn't your fault. You didn't know."

The world behind Robert's eyelids was blood red with agony. "Oh Addie, I'm sorry."

"You weren't the cause. It had begun long before you."

"Why didn't you tell someone . . . Mrs. Smith, Sarah . . ."

"He warned me nobody would believe me. I would be laughed at and pointed at. What we did was forbidden. I knew it by that time, and they might even take him away, he said, and then Sarah and I would have nobody to take care of us. I believed him and I was afraid to tell Mrs. Smith. And how could I tell Sarah? She would never have believed me. Father was her hero."

Some hero. Robert's shock began congealing into anger at the bestiality inflicted by Isaac Merritt upon a child of utter innocence, too young and indoctrinated with fear to have means of combating it.

"And all that time, while you were growing away from me, I thought it was something I was doing. At one point I believed you were dying of some deadly disease, you had changed so much and seemed so frail with worry. Did he ever tell you I spoke to him about it?"

She drew back to see his face. "You did?"

His hands remained curled around her shoulders. He spoke directly to her eyes. "He told me it was the differences in our ages, yours and mine, and that you undoubtedly felt pressure to allow my advances when all the time he was the one preying upon you."

"Oh Robert . . ." She rested her hands on his chest. "I could see the heartache I was causing you and Sarah, and so many times I ached to confess to you."

"Not confess!" he insisted. "Never confess. To confess implies guilt when you were guilty of nothing." Robert's rage thickened.

"But you loved me and I was unlovable and unworthy."

"That's what he wanted you to think. Did he pump you full of those ideas too?" He could read the truth in her face, could imagine how Merritt had manipulated her by fear and debasement, infiltrating her mind with whatever lies it took to keep her quiet and submissive. Robert's rage came full force and brought with it a passionate fury. He swept Addie's robe from the bed onto her shoulders. "Get dressed, Addie. You don't ever have to disrobe for a man again. Your ordeal is over." As if to a third party, Robert cursed while donning his trousers. "God damn him to hell. What *fools* we were, all of us! Why, I played right into his hands. I went to him asking permission to marry you when you were seventeen and he said yes. After that you drifted farther and farther away. I see it now. It all fits."

Addie had donned her robe. He gripped her hands so hard her fingers overlapped. His eyes blazed as he spoke. "Do you know what I would give to have him alive for one hour? I would cut off his testicles and stuff them in his mouth like a roast pig!"

"Oh Robert . . ." She could think of nothing else to say.

"What does it take to get you out of here for the night?"

"Robert, you can't—"

"What does it take!" he repeated more demandingly.

"You have to buy me off the floor."

"To the tune of what?"

"Two hundred dollars."

He gave her his gold pouch. "Measure it out."

"Two hundred dollars? Robert, that's silly."

"I'm a damned rich man. Measure it out."

"But Rose will—"

"We'll fight with Rose later." He was hurriedly donning the remainder of his clothes. "It's Christmas Eve, Addie. I'm not leaving you in this whorehouse on Christmas Eve, and if I have it my way you won't be back at all, so weigh the gold!"

When his clothes were in order she was still facing the bureau with the gold pouch held limply in one hand. From behind her shoulder he took the pouch and told her quietly, "I'm sorry I shouted at you, Addie. Here, I'll finish that while you get dressed. Pack only what you need for decency sake. I want you to take nothing away from this place."

He suddenly realized she was standing with her back to him, crying quietly. He turned her to face him. "Addie, don't cry. The time for crying is over."

"But Robert, what can I do? I've lived behind these doors so long . . . you don't understand."

How many times could a man's heart break? "You're afraid?" he said gently. She had since the age of three never lived a normal life. Walking out with him would be an act of normalcy, but more—of courage. "My poor, poor girl, of course you're afraid. But I'll be there with you. Now come . . . get dressed. Do you have street clothes?"

She nodded forlornly.

"Where are they?"

"In my room next door."

"We'll get them."

He carried the remainder of her garments and they closed the door on the wretched room he vowed she would never enter again. In the dark next door he said, "Where's the lamp?"

"Straight ahead."

When he lit it a white cat lifted its head off the bed and squinted at him over its left shoulder.

"Can I take Ruler?" she asked.

"Absolutely. He's the only good thing in this place."

"And my tussie-mussie from Sarah?"

"Of course."

Her clothing hung on pegs, little of it suitable for polite company. He chose the plainest dress he could find and waited with his back to her as she put it on. When he turned, she was waiting, her makeup run, blurring her face like an impressionist's painting. He wet a cloth in a nearby basin and held her chin while gently washing away the diluted kohl from her eyes and the carmine from her lips.

"You won't need this anymore either, Adelaide Merritt," he vowed softly, and when he was done, stood before her studying her familiar green eyes, which were swollen from crying. "How I've longed to see the Addie I remember. Little by little we'll bring her back."

"But Robert—"

He silenced her with a touch on the lips. "I don't have all the answers, Addie, not yet, but how can we find them if we don't start searching?"

Downstairs she deposited the two hundred dollars in gold dust in a drop box in the hall, and told Rose as she passed, "Robert is buying me off the floor."

"Twenty-four hours and not a minute more, you hear me, Eve?" Rose called after her, then added, louder, "Where are you taking that cat?"

With Ruler in her arms and Robert at her side, Addie walked into the cold Christmas air.

Above them, "O Sanctissima" was ringing through the gulch.

"Could it be a sign?" Robert asked, lifting his face as they strode in long, matched steps.

"Heaven doesn't send signs for prostitutes," Addie replied.

"Don't be too sure," Robert replied, slipping his hand around her elbow.

At his hotel the desk was abandoned. A note, tacked to the pigeonholes, said, GONE HOME FOR CHRISTMAS. Robert stepped behind the desk and selected a key.

"Who says there's no room at the inn?" He smiled as he returned to Addie and touched her back, directing her toward the stairs. On the second floor he opened a door, went inside and lit a lantern. The room was plain but plastered, and there was a curtain of sorts on the window. He opened the door of a round iron stove and knelt before it.

"But Robert, we haven't paid for this room."

"I'll catch up with Sam in the morning or whenever he gets back."

She stood uncertainly near the open doorway as he rose and turned. "I have to go out back for some wood. You'll find a tin in the hall with water, if it isn't frozen. It should be empty enough for you to lift by this time of the day. Get the whole thing and bring it to the stove, will you, Addie? I'll be right back."

She released Ruler, who explored the room. Robert returned in minutes with an armload of wood, knelt and built a fire, closed the squeaky stove door and adjusted the grate. He rose once more, brushing off his hands as he faced her.

"When you've finished your bath, knock on the wall. We can talk then if you like."

"Thank you, Robert."

He smiled. "I'll bring you a nightshirt, just a minute."

She listened to his footsteps fade and return. He re-entered and handed her a folded nightshirt. It was blue and white striped flannel. The stripes quavered as she looked down at them through fresh tears and repeated, "Thank you, Robert."

He stepped nearer and lifted her chin with a knuckle. "Knock," he whispered, and left her, closing the door behind him.

The room had a rocking chair. She dropped to it and doubled forward, burying her face in the blue flannel stripes. She sat a long time, motion-less, acclimating to freedom, wondering what Robert's intentions were, if any. The water began to sizzle and she rose with a sense of wonder to stir it with her finger. The only bathing vessel present was the bowl beneath the pitcher. She made do with it, and afterward hung her towels carefully and stood beside the radiant stove, warming her skin, feeling fear bake out of her. She dressed in the nightshirt. It felt like crawling into Robert's skin, where everything was normal and secure and you had a sense of purpose. She brushed her hair and recalled how he disliked it black, so reclaimed her damp towel and bound it turban-fashion around her head before quietly tapping on the wall.

She heard his door open and close, and his footsteps approaching. Her door opened and he said, "Your room is warmer than mine. May I come in?"

"Of course."

He stepped inside and closed the door without compunction. He was dressed in his black woolen trousers, white shirt and suspenders. High-topped shoes, too. He took her hand and led her near the lantern. "Well, look at you . . ." He took her head in both his hands and placed her clean-scrubbed face in the direct yellow glow. He studied her minutely, a faint smile on his lips. "It's really Addie Merritt after all. How do you feel?"

"Much better. Amazed. Adrift. Afraid."

He dropped his arms. "Would you rather be alone, Addie?"

"No, I . . . it's Christmas Eve and who wants to be alone on Christmas Eve? I would like to talk, Robert, really I would, but it wouldn't be good for you if word got out that you'd been in my room with me. Up at Rose's is one thing, but here . . . this is a respectable establishment, I'm sure."

"Addie." He took her hand and led her to the bed. "You need to start concerning yourself with things that really matter."

He cocked her pillows against the headboard, ordered "Sit," and when she did, "Move over." Atop the coverings he took his place beside her, put both arms around her and snuggled her against his side. He stretched out his legs, crossed his ankles and said, "Listen . . . the bells have stopped."

They both listened.

A coal sang a sizzling note in the stove.

Across the hall someone was snoring.

Ruler vaulted up onto the bed and picked his way onto Robert's lap, settled himself square atop his fly buttons and curled up like a jelly roll.

Robert and Addie laughed.

"Well, I guess that settles that," he remarked.

She laughed again and ended with a sigh. "Oh Robert, I don't know where to begin."

Somehow they found the place. She began with her disillusionment when her mother ran away, the feeling after that of being different from other children who still had mothers. Those years of lonely longing, after Mrs. Smith came, when Sarah and she would stand at the window looking down Lampley Street, still believing their mother would return. Her child-ish chagrin when she began wetting the bed, and her fear when Sarah's complaints about it prompted Addie's move to a room of her own where the loneliness took on space and intensity. Her relief the first time her father had slipped in, in the dark to comfort her. The hazy area between puerile ignorance of what was truly happening and the dawning of revulsion followed by sexual guilt. The clearer recollections of begging to sleep with Sarah, who most often argued, "But you kick and take the covers and talk in your sleep. Go sleep in your own room." Begging for a lock on her bedroom door while her father declared before both Sarah and Mrs. Smith that the way to cure Adelaide's problems was not through locking out bogeymen but by leaving the door open and realizing there were none. Going to bed before her father got home, lying rigid with eyelids trembling, pretending to be asleep in hopes he'd pass right by her room and go to his own. Studying hard in hopes she'd become smarter and would be taken under Father's publisher's wing as Sarah had been, and so please him that he would reward her by leaving her alone in the bedroom. Learning to hate her physical beauty, which she blamed for the perverted attention it sparked.

And the advent of Robert himself into her life.

Her immediate gravity toward him. Her relief when Isaac had allowed Robert's visits. Her occasional jealousy of Sarah, who, with her intelligence more matched to Robert's, could offer him so much more by way of stimulating discussion and even humorous exchanges. Then puberty and the onset of Isaac's forced intercourse. The added shame it brought. The arrival of her uncontestable love for Robert, confounded by guilt at her lack of virginity and fear that even if and when they either married or became lovers he would discover her unchaste state and hate her for it.

"I felt so helpless," she said. "He would tell me that if I ever told anybody no man would want me, and I believed him."

"Of course you did. He stripped away all your feelings of self-worth."

"I felt like I was wearing a coat of shame, and no matter where I went everyone could see it, especially you."

"I never guessed, never."

"When I told you tonight, you were shocked, weren't you?"

"I felt like I'd been poleaxed."

"So imagine my fear of your guessing it when I was only fifteen or sixteen years old. You would have been revolted, just the way my father said."

"Maybe I would have. Who's to say now?"

"Every time after you kissed me, I went to my room and cried."

"And that day in the flower cart . . ."

"I thought you'd be able to tell I wasn't a virgin if we did anything. I was so afraid of losing you."

"So you ran away and I was the one who lost you."

"I thought I didn't have a choice. I couldn't stay with him any longer, and I couldn't go to you."

"You left two very confused and worried people behind—three counting Mrs. Smith."

"I'm sorry I had to do that."

"Where did you go? First off, I mean."

"I started in Kansas City, but one of the girls there got pregnant and gave the baby out for adoption, and that sort of ruined everything for all of us so I moved on to Cheyenne for a change of scenery. There one of the girls put ground glass in one of the other girl's douches—there was a lot of jealousy over the good-paying customers. The girl nearly died. She was my friend—or as close as you can get in the business. So anyway, after that I came up here when the gold rush started. But the houses were all the same. I really only exchanged one prison for another. The difference was I hated men and could get even with hundreds of them for what one had done to me." They lay in silence awhile before she finished, "You should know, Robert, I still hate men."

He accepted her remark without comment, even though she was still beneath his arm with her head on his shoulder and her hand on his chest. He supposed she had a right.

In time he asked quietly, "Does Sarah know about Isaac?"

"No."

"Do you intend to tell her?"

She rolled away from him. "What good would it do?"

He pulled her back where she'd been. "It would help her understand, just like it did me."

Addie sat up and hugged her knees. "But it would hurt her."

"Yes, it would hurt her."

Silence settled, a long, trying silence. She broke it as if Robert had argued.

"But I'd be so ashamed to tell her."

"Then he's still got a hold on you, even though he's dead."

She dropped her forehead to her knees and said, muffled, "I know . . . I know."

He had planted the seed; let it bear fruit or not, as it would.

"Come . . . lie back, Addie. You don't have to decide tonight."

She returned to the lee of his arm, lying silent and thoughtful. He lay as before with his ankles crossed, but gave her arm a squeeze. She sighed and stared across his chest at the doorframe, where lamplight and shadow created a sharp edge of gold and gray. Her eyelids grew heavy and blinked . . . grew heavier . . . blinked again and remained closed. Shortly, his followed suit.

She awakened to find the room sunny and smelling of an oil-fed wick that had run out of fuel, the bedding flipped from the outsides toward the middle and Robert sleeping with his back to her.

She yawned and tried to stretch without waking him.

Robert made minuscule waking movements, eventually looked back over his shoulder and said, " 'Morning."

"Closer to noon, I think."

He rolled to his back and yawned, great big, stretching with his hands behind his head, making the mattress tremble. When his mouth closed he turned his head, grinned at her and said, "Let's go give Sarah a Christmas surprise."

She smiled and said, "All right, let's."

Chapter 15

❧

Christmas began for Sarah with a bittersweet cast, her first without her father; without Addie, too. Though she was looking forward to dinner with the Dawkins family, they were not her own. Furthermore, the day seemed to stretch interminably toward four P.M., the time of her invitation. Meanwhile, Mrs. Roundtree's felt forlorn, filled with men missing loved ones back home, crowding the parlor until it became stuffy, reminiscing about pung rides or lutefisk or oyster stuffing, depending upon the geographic location or nationality from which they'd hailed.

To her credit, Mrs. Roundtree did her best to offer a festive air. There was the tree in the parlor and a special late-morning breakfast of ham and potato pancakes, herbed eggs and assorted sweetbreads with a rare delicacy: real butter. Mealtime, however, lacked attraction due to Noah Campbell's absence.

Sarah had awakened thinking of him, of something Addie had once said about certain men making a woman feel like a thimbleful of fondant. Last night in her room she had for the first time begun understanding the treachery of such feelings. Kissing him, breast to breast, she had felt the hollow hand of temptation reaching to be filled. For those few minutes—seconds?—she had felt voluptuous. He had said inviting such feelings was natural, but there were Commandments against such situations. Now she understood why.

He remained in her thoughts, vivid and imposing, the key to her day's brightness or eclipse. She supposed, much to her dismay, that she loved him. In her childish fantasies she had imagined that falling in love was like being lifted by seraphs to a supreme plane where roses trailed forever at one's feet and the soul so radiated joy that it lit the space around it. Instead, it resembled falling off a horse—a stumble, a roll, and reproach with herself for having chosen poorly and tumbled when she might as easily have drawn a Pegasus and flown.

No, this was not flying. This was picking one's way through the morass of cans and cannots, do's and don'ts, must and must nots that had been fixed in her conscience years ago by a good Christian father who took her to church every Sunday and so respected that church's laws that he clung to his marriage vows until death, even in the face of his wife's desertion.

She wished Isaac were here now. How comforting it would feel to sit in the same room and confide in him, "Father, I'm so confused."

Instead, she went to her room and penned a letter to Mrs. Smith.

Deadwood, Dakota Territory
Christmas Day, 1876
Dear Mrs. Smith,

> The blessed holiday is here, spreading its beneficence on Dead-
> wood Gulch.

She went on to describe the pageant, then wrote:

> It has been exciting to be a part of the growth of Deadwood. The
> *Chronicle* not only succeeds, it thrives. I'm up to six pages now and
> having no trouble filling them with the freshest news: the telegraph,
> you see, has arrived at last. When Mr. Hayes and Mr. Wheeler take
> their oaths of office next month, I will be reporting their inaugural
> addresses at the same time the rest of the nation reads them. Imagine
> that.
> Addie is well. I see her daily, though we don't live together. I am
> still residing at Mrs. Roundtree's boardinghouse, though I believe it's
> time I purchase a house of my own since I know I'll be staying in
> Deadwood indefinitely.

Now where had that come from? She didn't recall consciously making
such a decision, but once the words were on paper she reread them and
found the idea splendid. A home of her own with furnishings of her
choice and more than a mere parlor to move about in, where she wasn't
engulfed by men or crowded into a lonely cubicle. She spent time imagining it, and afterward, her day felt brighter.

> I'm afraid I must abbreviate this, for I am invited to the home of
> friends—the Dawkins—for Christmas dinner. Dear Mrs. Smith, I
> hope this finds you hale and hearty. You linger on my mind often
> with the fondest of regard. Please do write back soon to let us know
> you are as wholesome and happy as we remember you.

> > Your loving,
> > Sarah

Upon rereading the letter Sarah found the description of the Christmas
program suitable for publication with minor revisions and some additions.
She made these, recopied it for Patrick, and was proofreading the final
draft when a knock sounded at the door.

She opened it to find Mrs. Roundtree in the hall, looking as if all her
sphincters were cinched.

"Visitors for you downstairs."

"Visitors?" Sarah was surprised.

"I'd as lief they wouldn't come here again," the landlady added sourly.
"You might tell them that. Not him, just her. Mind you, I run a respectable place here."

"Who is it, Mrs. Roundtree?"

"Mr. Baysinger and one of them from up at the badlands, judging from the look of her, and marching into my parlor as bold as brass. What are my men going to think!''

Sarah's heart began pounding. "Tell them I'll be right down.''

"I don't speak to her sort, thank you, and if you want to you'll have to do it somewheres else besides in my house.''

"Very well,'' Sarah snapped, flushing with indignation at the woman's captiousness. "I shall do exactly that. Thank you for your *charitable* attitude, Mrs. Roundtree, especially in this season of love!''

Mrs. Roundtree swung away in a self-righteous huff. Sarah snagged her coat and hat and clattered down the stairs with excitement brimming in her throat.

Robert and Addie stood just inside the parlor door, flanked by a roomful of gawking men with faces red as scalded pigs. Robert looked wonderfully at ease, maintaining a light hold on Addie's elbow. Addie fixed her stare on Sarah's descending form as if petrified to swing her eyes aside.

Sarah walked directly to her, extending both hands, smiling so hard her molars showed. "Addie, darling . . . merry Christmas.'' She squeezed Addie's hands and suggested, "Let's go,'' as if a plan had been previously made.

Outside, beneath the two o'clock sun, Sarah gave her sister an immense hug. "Oh Addie, you've come at last. Now my happiness is complete.'' After a moment she turned to do the same to their longtime friend. "And Robert . . . you've brought her. I always knew I loved you and now I know why. Thank you from the bottom of my heart.''

"I thought you two sisters should be together for the holiday.''

"Absolutely. And with you here, too, our gathering is complete.''

Addie said, "Your landlady didn't like me in her parlor.''

"My landlady has a worm up her posterior—you'll forgive my vulgarism, especially today, but her superciliousness galls me!''

"Sarah!" Addie said in amazement.

Robert laughed heartily while Sarah secured her outerwear.

Addie was still too shocked to linger over the snub. "I've never heard you talk like that in my whole life!''

"Hadn't you heard?'' Sarah tugged on her gloves, leading the way down the endless stairs to the path below. "I'm a firebrand. You have to be to run a newspaper that's worth anything at all. What have you planned for the day?''

"Nothing. We just came to see you,'' Robert replied, following both women.

"Wonderful. I can offer you a cup of coffee at the newspaper office.''

"Fine,'' he said.

Sarah sensed that somehow Robert had talked Addie out of Rose's, but that Addie had capitulated reluctantly. A keen thread of understanding ran between her and Robert: they would win Addie over by keeping her off-guard. At the bottom of the long steps each of them captured one of Addie's arms and they walked along linked three abreast.

"Addie stayed overnight at my hotel last night.''

"You did!'' Sarah came up short, bringing the others to a halt. "Does this mean you've left Rose's for good?''

Addie and Robert answered simultaneously.

"I don't know."

"Yes."

Robert spoke as they moved on. "I've told her I don't want her to go back there and I think she'd be willing if we came up with a plan."

Addie said, "And I've told Robert that he doesn't know how terrifying it is to face a world of people who cross to the other side of the street when they see you coming. Besides, I don't know anything else. What would I do?"

"You'd live with me."

"At Mrs. Roundtree's? Don't be absurd. You saw how she treated me."

"Not at Mrs. Roundtree's. We'll get a place of our own. Why, I was just thinking this morning that it's time I did that. I even wrote to Mrs. Smith and told her so."

Robert put in, "And I'd subsidize you in return for . . . oh, let's say darning my socks. How good are you at darning socks, Addie?"

Addie pinched back a smile. "I've never darned a sock in my life and you know it."

"That's right. Mrs. Smith did things like that, didn't she? Then cooking. How good are you at cooking? I'd pay you handsomely for a home-cooked meal now and then."

"I don't cook either."

They reached the newspaper office and went inside.

"If you'll light a fire, Robert, I'll go out to the pump and get some water. Addie, will you grind the coffee?"

"I just realized," Addie said forlornly, "I've never done that either."

Sarah said cheeringly, "Well, it's easy enough. Just put the beans in and crank. Maybe we'll make a domestic of you yet."

At a small rectangular table near the rear of the office Addie found the coffee grinder and the sack of coffee beans. "What do I catch them in?" she asked.

Whisking out the rear door, Sarah answered, "On a piece of paper will be fine." When she returned, Robert had the fire started and Addie was still grinding.

"How many?" she asked.

Sarah set the pot on the stove and said, "Oh, about a quarter of the amount you've already ground." The two sisters looked at each other and laughed. Abruptly Addie's face fell and she said, "I'm so ignorant. I just don't know anything."

Sarah went to Addie and clasped her cheeks lightly. "Just think of how exciting your life will be from now on—you'll learn something new every day. Robert and I will teach you, just as we did when we were children, and I think I know someone else who'll help, too."

"Who?"

"Stay here. I'll go ask her."

Sarah headed for the door.

"But Sarah, where—"

"Just wait here for me. Robert will show you how much coffee to put in that water and when I come back I'll expect a cup."

She went out without further enlightening them, straight to Emma's, where her knock was answered by Lettie, swathed in a cobbler's apron with a glow on her cheeks.

"Sarah, it's you already! Merry Christmas."

"The same to you, Lettie."

"Who is it, Lettie?" Emma called.

"It's Sarah already. Come in, Sarah."

Emma came to the door, wiping her hands on her apron. "You're a little early, Sarah, but if you don't mind we sure don't."

"I'm leaving again in a minute, and I'll come back at four, but I had to talk to you first."

"Sure, come on in."

The room smelled delicious, of garlic and onion and roasting meat. Of cinnamon and apples and the green tang of fresh-cut cabbage. At a work-table, Geneva wielded the grater. The windows were opaque with steam that collected in beads and painted clear stripes to the sill. Byron wandered in and said, "Well, if it isn't our children's choir director. Those young ones sounded good enough to be in one of Langrishe's stage shows."

"Oh Byron, you always say the nicest things. They *were* wonderful, weren't they?"

Josh followed his father into the room and announced, "Next year I want to sing in the choir, too."

"You'll be more than welcome." They rehashed last night's affair before Sarah spoke of the business at hand. "I'm glad you're here, all of you, because I've come with a very special request."

Emma said, "You just name it."

"I believe you all know Robert Baysinger, my childhood friend from St. Louis. He's finally convinced my sister to leave the brothel. They're at my newspaper office now, and if it's at all possible, I'd like to bring them here with me for Christmas dinner." Before anyone could speak, Sarah hurried on. "I know it's presumptuous of me to ask, especially considering how late it is, and the food is already prepared, but she was very badly snubbed at Mrs. Roundtree's this morning. I'd like to show her that there are people who'll still treat her decently, that's why I've come to you. But I'd only bring her if all of you are in agreement . . . and if there's enough food, of course."

Emma spoke for all. "What kind of Christians would we be to close our door in judgment? Of course you can bring her, and Mr. Baysinger too."

Sarah's shoulders slumped in relief. "Emma, you're a true friend—all of you are. Thank you." Her eyes touched each of them in turn. "There are some things you should know. We're still trying to convince Addie not to go back, so her acceptance here will be especially encouraging. She believes that nobody will treat her civilly, but after today she'll realize that not everybody is like Mrs. Roundtree. Also, Emma, Robert and I have been racking our brains trying to come up with some reasonable form of occupation for Addie. She's no good with words at all, or I'd put her to work at the newspaper office. I've been thinking, if she and I took up housing together she might simply act as our housekeeper, but she doesn't know anything about that either. Would you help?"

Emma beamed, her cheeks red from kitchen heat. "You've come to the right woman. These girls of mine can already cook durn near as good as their mother. Bring her on and watch us make a new woman out of her!"

"Oh Emma . . ." Sarah crooked an elbow around the good woman's neck. "Perhaps I've never told you that I love you. All of you . . . Byron . . ." She hugged him and each of the others in turn. "Josh, Lettie,

'Neva. I simply don't know what I'd have done without you. You've been the family I didn't have since I've lived here in Deadwood.''

"Well, you've got one now, and we're going to do all we can to see that you don't lose your sister again. Now go on back there and get those two."

"Yes, ma'am," Sarah answered with her heart full. "You're sure there's enough food?"

"Josh shot the goose. Josh, you think that honker will feed eight?"

"You bet!" Josh replied proudly. "He went a good fourteen, maybe sixteen pounds."

As Sarah left, Emma was ordering, "Girls, grate a little more cabbage."

The newspaper office smelled like coffee when Sarah returned. Addie and Robert had pulled up a pair of chairs near the stove and sat sipping from Patrick's and Sarah's mugs. They turned as Sarah closed the door and reached for her bonnet strings.

"You'll both be very happy with my news."

"What?"

"You're invited to my friends the Dawkins' for Christmas dinner."

Robert smiled.

Addie shrank.

"Oh no."

"What do you mean, oh no?"

"I'd rather go back to Rose's," she said into her cup.

Sarah briskly crossed the room and took her sister by the shoulders. "Listen to me, Addie. The Dawkins are good people. Emma and Byron have raised three wonderful children who've had a good example set by their parents. None of them will walk a wide berth around you. Granted, Mrs. Roundtree did, and I'm not saying others won't. But not Emma, and not her family. You have to start somewhere, Addie, and Christmas dinner with them is far from the worst occasion you could draw."

"You went there and asked them if I could come, didn't you?"

"Yes. You and Robert both."

"I don't want to trail along on your skirt tails."

"I do," Robert put in jovially. "For a homemade Christmas dinner in a real home, I don't mind how I get invited."

Addie looked unconvinced. "Addie, listen," Sarah reasoned, "Emma Dawkins knows a lot of people in this town. What she does is noticed by others. Most of the women see her nearly every day to buy bread from her. If she accepts you, chances are many of them will follow her lead. You must come."

"I can't."

Sarah grew stern, backing off with her hands on her hips. "Honestly, Addie, sometimes I grow so peeved with you! *And* with Father! If he hadn't spoiled you silly you might have had more gumption. All you ever had to do was pout a little bit and feel sorry for yourself and you got your way."

"I did not pout!"

"You're pouting now, just like a child."

"And I did not get my way!"

"You certainly did. While I was made to go to the newspaper office and work, you stayed home and dawdled."

"Well, maybe I wanted to go, too. Maybe I wasn't allowed!"

Robert sat silent and watchful.

"We'll argue about this later when Robert isn't here. For now I'd like you to give me just one good reason why you won't accept Emma's invitation."

Addie's chin got stubborn. "I thought I shouldn't go where there are children."

"Emma's children know what a brothel is. How could they live in this town and not? Why, I've been warning Josh not to deliver papers up there at the badlands since the first day I hired him. If Emma's not afraid they'll be jaded by your presence, why should you be?"

Addie had no retort. She stared at her sister, who went on authoritatively.

"And let's get one more thing settled—I won't have you at the Dawkins' unless you have every intention of never going back to Rose's again."

"But if I don't—"

"If you don't you and I will live together here at the newspaper office until we can find a house, which we'll start searching for the moment Craven Lee opens his door tomorrow morning. I have no intention of renting from a snob like Mrs. Roundtree, who shuns my sister with one hand and takes my gold with the other. She has a lot of nerve expecting me to. So we'll get some cots and sleep here until other arrangements can be made. That way Josh can sleep later in the mornings since he won't have to come in and light the fire to melt the ink. And I won't have to be running back and forth up that infernal set of steps, or traipsing out in the cold before the sun is even up in the morning. We'll eat at Teddy's until we can find a house, and when we do—well, I hope you'll learn how to cook, and if not, we'll live on a lot of fried eggs. Now what do you say?"

Addie considered silently for some time, glancing from Addie to Robert and back again.

"You mean we'll sleep here tonight?"

"No, not tonight. We'll have to think of something else for tonight. Not only you, but me. I refuse to sleep one more night at Mrs. Roundtree's after the way she treated you."

"What about Addie's room at the hotel?" Robert put in. "Couldn't the two of you share that for a night or two?" He understood that Sarah was determined to stick beside her sister to make sure she didn't backslide to Rose's.

Sarah replied, "We could if it's all right with Addie."

Addie said doubtfully, "I guess it would be all right. But I'd have to go back to Rose's to get the money she owes me from last night."

"Absolutely not!" Sarah yelped.

"But—"

"I won't have you taking one more penny from that hog ranch!"

"But she owes me a hundred dollars' worth of gold from Robert alone!"

Sarah's eyes widened and her cheeks took color. She shot a discomfited look at Robert.

"Oh, you mean . . ." She stumbled to a halt.

"I bought her off the floor," he admitted.

"For two hundred in gold," Addie added. "Why should Rose get all of that? She owes me half."

"All right, you go get it—but one hundred and not a flake more. And Robert will go with you."

"Absolutely," Robert put in.

Now that the decision was made, Sarah could see Addie quailing. "Rose will be very angry," the younger woman said.

"That's why he should go along. I want to make sure you come back out of there once you go in. I don't trust that big hulking Indian woman or that bawdy madam. What do you think, Robert, should you go now before the evening traffic picks up over there? Then Addie would have it behind her and could enjoy her dinner without worrying about having to face Rose. And while you're over there, I can go back and collect a few things from Mrs. Roundtree's."

"Now is fine with me if Addie agrees."

"Addie?" Sarah leveled her sister with a straightforward gaze.

Addie looked slightly pale. "Now?"

Robert took her hands. "Sarah's right. Then you'll have it over with and you can think about your new tomorrows. Just think, Addie, a future with possibilities—all you have to do is hand Rose your walking papers. As for the money, I don't care about that. Leave it there if you want."

"But I earned it fair and square. And if you don't want it—well, it's the only thing I have to give to Sarah toward my keep."

"Very well, we'll take it and you do just that, give it to Sarah. But let's go now."

Beneath his direct gaze she turned docile and replied meekly, "All right, Robert, if that's what you want me to do."

The sun had retired behind the western rim of rock and pine as they walked toward the badlands. Main Street lay in shadow, nearly deserted. Somewhere a chickadee sang his repetitive two-note song and off in the distance a burro brayed.

As they neared their destination Robert felt Addie gripping his elbow tighter.

"Are you afraid?" he asked.

"Rose won't be able to find another girl so easily in the middle of the winter, and without girls she loses money."

"Has she ever threatened you?"

"No, not directly, but she's a hard woman. They're all hard women there, especially when they're angry."

"I'll stay with you all the time."

They walked awhile before she asked, "Are you afraid, Robert?"

"Yes, but I have conviction on my side."

Staring straight ahead, Addie told him, "I don't deserve your kindness, Robert, not after what I've done."

"Nonsense, Addie."

"They call us the fair and the frail, but you can't be frail to survive there, and if you're fair at first, that soon changes. Why are you doing this, Robert?"

"Because everyone deserves happiness, and I could see you weren't happy there. And for Sarah, and myself, too, because we couldn't bear the thought of the girl we used to know doing work like that."

"You must forget her, the girl you used to know. She doesn't exist anymore."

They'd reached Rose's. Robert turned to Addie.

"Maybe she does and you just don't know it. Let's go in and get this unpleasantness behind us."

Inside, the smell was awful—carbolic water, cigar smoke and liquor. Living in it day in and day out, Addie hadn't realized how cloying it was, but after a single day away, entering Rose's parlor, she covered her nose with a glove. There were three men sitting at a table, desultorily sipping drinks. Rose herself was with them, packed into a satin dress the color of a bottle fly's wings. She swung her head, fixed her pewter eyes on Addie and drawled, "Well, look who's back, and bringing her rich little daddy along with her." To Robert she said, "Just can't get enough, can you, sugar?"

Addie said, "Could I talk to you in your office, Rose?"

The madam's eyes took a slow walk down Robert's trousers and back up to his neatly trimmed beard. "Why, sure," she replied belatedly and pushed herself up from the table. To the trio at the table she said, "Be right back, boys, and I'll bring a new bottle."

Addie led the way toward the far end of the hall. Just short of her office door Rose turned and poked four fingers against Robert's chest. "No men allowed back here, sugar. It's private, you unnerstand."

Robert looked beyond Rose to Addie, who unobtrusively waggled her head. Addie entered Rose's office, asking over her shoulder, "How was the take last night?"

Rose followed, answering, "Big. Damn big. Best I ever done, matter of fact. Now today's another story, so far anyway. Everybody gettin' *Christian* on me, holing up and becoming do-gooders."

"I missed the divvying up this morning." Every morning Rose tabulated the previous night's take and gave each girl half of what she'd taken in. "I'll take mine now."

Rose went to her desk and opened a drawer. "Sure, Eve. You did all right. A hundred from that Jake alone. You must have something he likes." Rose tossed her a bag of gold dust.

Addie called, "Robert, would you come in here, please?"

Robert stepped around the doorway into the room.

Rose scowled. "Now just a minute! This is private, and no man puts foot in here unless I invite him!"

"Robert has come to escort me away. I'm leaving, Rose."

"Leaving? What does that mean—leaving?"

"For good."

Rose raised her big face and bellowed, "Ha! You might think so, Evie-honey, but you'll be back."

"I don't think so."

"You will be. Wait till those holier-than-thou women out there lift their skirts aside so they won't brush against you. Wait till the men who soaked their dinks in you treat you like you're invisible when they meet you on the street. Wait till one of them grabs you in an alley and thinks he'll get a little free. Wait till you run out of money and wish you could earn a dollar a minute without lifting a finger. You'll be back. Mark my words."

Addie's expression remained stolid. "I won't be taking any of my things. You can give them to the other girls."

"So you take up with him instead?" Rose shouted. "You think you won't still be a whore? Well, I got news for you, sister, you spread your legs for one or a hundred, it's all the same. Whether they give you gold or a place to live, you're still their whore! So go live with him then. Be his private whore! I don't care!"

"Goodbye, Rose."

"Don't you goodbye Rose me, you ungrateful bitch! You owe me!" Rose struck like a snake, grabbing Addie's hair. "Leaving me high and dry with an empty—"

Addie screamed.

"—bed and losing my money when I took you in and—"

Robert picked up a marble penholder and cracked Rose across the forearms.

"Mraaawk!" she squawked, releasing Addie. *"Flossie!"* she screamed, her face turning red as her hair. "Get the hell in here, Flossie!"

Robert said calmly, "We'll be going now." He put an arm around Addie's shoulders. "If you make any attempt to stop us, I'll break your arms—both of them. Tell your Indian woman the same goes for her. Tell her to let us pass."

Flossie had appeared in the doorway. Robert turned to her and ordered, "Step aside. Miss Merritt is leaving."

Flossie took one menacing step forward and Robert struck her with the marble penholder across the back of her left hand. She cried out and buckled halfway, couching the bruised hand against her thigh and moaning quietly.

"Excuse us, please," Robert said, reverting to his usual impeccable manners, herding Addie around Flossie.

"Stop them!" Rose shouted.

Flossie continued moaning and coddling her hand.

"I'll have the law on you, Baysinger! You can't barge in a person's home and assault them and think you can get away with it just because you own a goddamned stamp mill!"

Robert paused in the doorway and said to Rose, "I'd welcome the opportunity to recount before a circuit judge the scene that just happened here. Please do call Marshal Campbell. If he needs me he can find me at the home of Emma Dawkins having Christmas dinner. Merry Christmas, both of you."

In the parlor, the three men were sitting on the lips of their chairs, gaping at the hall. Robert set the hunk of marble on a table as he passed. "Good day, gentlemen. This belongs to Mrs. Hossiter. She'll be back to get it in a minute, I'm sure."

He and Addie were outside within three minutes of their arrival, the break made, the threats quelled. To Robert's amazement, they had strode no more than four steps when Addie folded and dropped, covering her face with both hands as she broke into intense weeping. He squatted beside her, curling a hand around her sleeve.

"Addie, what is it? Why are you crying?"

"I don't know . . . I don't kn–know . . ."

He drew her to her feet and put both arms around her, her face still covered with her gloved hands.

"Are you doing this against your will?"

"No . . ." she wailed.

"Do you want to stay?"

"No . . ." she wailed again.

"Then why are you crying?"

"Because . . . it's all I c–can do. They're my only fr–friends."

"I thought you said they were hard."

"They are, but they're my friends, t–too."

"I'm your friend. Sarah's your friend, and soon the Dawkins will be."

"I know . . . but I'm such a useless person. What good am I on this earth? I'll only be a burden to Sarah and to you."

"Shh. You mustn't talk that way. The burden was knowing you were in that place. Knowing you're making a clean break is lifting the burden, don't you see?"

She peered at him through streaming eyes. "Is it really, Robert?"

"Absolutely. And I never want to hear you say again what good are you on this earth. Whatever would it have been like for me if you hadn't been on it?"

"Oh Robert . . ." Behind her gloved hand her mouth trembled while a new waterfall of tears appeared. On the street before Rose's she flung both arms around his neck and repeated, "Oh Robert . . ." And after a moment, still sniveling, "Robert Baysinger, you'll make an honest woman of me yet."

He rested his hands on her waist and smiled, then pressed her away. "Would you like to stop at the hotel and wash your face before we go to the Dawkins'?"

She gave him a quavery smile, a nod, and he took her arm.

While Addie and Robert were checking her out of Rose's, Sarah was doing the same at Mrs. Roundtree's. Returning to the house, she packed a trunk, which she left, and a valise and bandbox, which she carried downstairs. She found her landlady in the kitchen, peeling apples into a crock bowl on her lap as she sat at a worktable.

"Good afternoon, Mrs. Roundtree," Sarah said from the doorway.

The woman looked up, her lips downdrawn. "I hope you told your sister not to come around here again."

Sarah replied brusquely, "I'll be vacating my room now, Mrs. Roundtree. I'm sure you'll have no trouble finding another renter. I'll send someone after my trunks first thing in the morning."

Mrs. Roundtree's mouth dropped open. "Well, there's no need to be hasty."

"My decision was made the moment you spurned my sister."

"What decent woman wouldn't after she's been soiling herself up there with the rest of those doves and taking money for it?"

Sarah pinned her with an audacious stare. "Charity, Mrs. Roundtree. Charity for those less fortunate than ourselves—I'd advise you to adopt it. My sister wants to reform, and I intend to do everything in my power to support her, beginning with my leaving here. While you're taking such a high-handed position, you might consider the intended spirit of this holiday. Is it *selective* love for mankind that Christmas stands for, or unbiased love for all?" Sarah tugged on one glove. "If in the future you should recognize yourself in one of my editorials, don't be surprised." She tugged on the other. "If anyone should ask, I'll be lodging at the Grand Central with my sister for a while. Good day, Mrs. Roundtree."

She left the house feeling the ardent zeal that so often drove her when she espoused a new cause.

The trio who arrived at the Dawkins' at four P.M. were in the formation that seemed to symbolize their relationship throughout their young lives—Addie in the middle, flanked by Robert and Sarah. Ever it would be, it seemed, the two stronger ones shoring up the weaker.

Emma, always the spokesman for her family, met them at the door and offered a handshake when introduced to Addie.

"Miss Adelaide," she said, "welcome. These are my children, Josh, Lettie and Geneva, and this is my man, Byron. We're awful pleased you could join us for supper. Mr. Baysinger . . ." She shook his hand. "You too. We're very fond of Sarah, and it just wouldn't do to leave her out of the holiday celebration. Your being her dear ones, well . . . shoot. This is right where you belong."

Emma's welcome assuaged the first of Addie's misgivings. Each family member followed with a welcome, the girls' shy, Josh's wide-eyed with curiosity, Byron's quiet but sincere.

They gathered at a table whose seating had been extended with planks between the chairs. Byron said a simple grace.

"Dear lord, we thank you for this food, these friends, and this wonderful Christmas season. Amen."

They ate a delicious meal of roast goose, mashed potatoes, apple dressing, cole slaw, candied yam pie and a bevy of breads and sweetmeats. Though Addie took little part in the conversation, she was neither excluded nor included to any greater degree than anyone else. The primary topic was last night's Christmas program and the impromptu triangle serenade that had taken the whole gulch by surprise.

Geneva said, "Mother let us leave the windows open and listen after we went to bed. Did you leave yours open, too, Sarah?"

"Yes, I did," Sarah answered, then grew pensive, remembering what had followed, wondering what it was like in the Spearfish Valley where he was, if he, too, was eating Christmas supper, when he would return, and if he was thinking of her at this moment.

Emma interrupted her reverie. She was speaking to Addie. "Your sister tells me you'd like to set up housekeeping but you don't know much about it. Well, that's all right. Most of us have a lot to learn when we do that. Anytime you want to learn to mix up a batch of bread, you just come on over to the bakery about five A.M. Heck, we might even put you to work!"

"Five A.M.?" Addie repeated dubiously.

"Shouldn't take you but three or four times and you'll get the knack."

"That's terribly early, isn't it?"

"Got to start that early to get the bread baked by nine."

"Thank you. I—I'll remember that when we find our house."

"No time like the present to get started, then by the time you find a place of your own you'll be as comfortable around the kitchen as these girls of mine."

"They bake bread?" Addie glanced in wonder at Lettie and Geneva.

"They don't need to with us owning the bakery. But they know how, and they know their way around a cookpot, too, don't you girls? Why, they made the cabbage salad and the sweet potato pie and helped with prett' near the whole meal. You're a little late getting started, but don't you worry, Miss Adelaide. We'll teach you what you need to know."

When they'd thanked the Dawkins and were heading to the hotel, Addie said despairingly, "Those young girls know more than I do."

"Well, of course they do," answered Sarah. "They've had a mother to teach them. Don't worry, though. If Emma says she can teach you, she can. And you won't have to learn everything overnight. Heavens, we don't even have our house yet."

At the hotel they parted in the hall. Robert gave them each a kiss on the cheek and said, "It's been a wonderful Christmas, thanks to you both. I won't be seeing you in the morning. I'll be going out to the mill early."

Addie watched him abjectly as he proceeded along the hall to his adjacent room. At his door he lifted a hand, sent them a smile and went inside.

Sarah watched and waited. After a long moment, Addie turned toward her. Sarah gave an understanding smile. "Without him, you're afraid again, I know. But I'm here for you, too, and you must not doubt that within yourself there is a strong, resilient person waiting to spring back and show the world her spirit. Come . . ." She held out a hand. "Let's go to bed, just as we used to when we were very small and afraid of the dark. Together."

Addie put her hand in Sarah's and they opened the door of room 11.

Chapter 16

♣

True Blevins happened to be in town, so Noah took him home to spend Christmas with his family. They rode out on horseback, since horses were faster and surer than a wagon at this time of year. They moved single file, in silence for the most part. The Spearfish Canyon was incredibly beautiful beneath its quilt of snow. Spearfish Creek, still open, whispered beneath thin-edged ice, then gurgled into the sunlight, breaking into a million reflected pinpoints of silver. Sometimes it disappeared underground to re-emerge later and become a surface stream again. Banks climbed from it, immense tumbles of great brown rocks amidst which an occasional mouth of a cave would appear, with animal tracks having worn away the snow at its door.

The pine-shrouded hills loomed up in silent majesty, the black-green branches of the ponderosas drooping like old shoulders clad in heavy ermine capes while overhead they hobnobbed with the very blue Black Hills sky. Here and there splashes of color appeared—a covey of red crossbills working among the conifer branches extracting seeds from pinecones; the brighter green of dog-haired pine growing in crowded, stunted clusters; the flash of a bluejay; the straight red pillars of the ponderosas themselves.

The silence was broken by the dull thump of the horses' hooves, the taunting of a crow, the chatter of the open water. A solitaire spiraled above the treetops singing its clear, musical warble. A doe came crashing through a thick stand of deerbrush in an old burn area, heeled sharply when surprised by the horses and bounded off the way she'd come.

True's mount whickered and sidestepped. Behind it, Noah's did too.

True said, "Easy, girl," then moved on as before.

Noah did likewise, then relaxed in the saddle and took up thinking of Sarah Merritt again.

The woman had him in a tizzy. He should have dropped her to the bed last night and found out whether she was capable of melting or not. No, he shouldn't have. He'd done the right thing. But doing the right thing was so damned fustrating! So how the hell was a man expected to proceed with such a woman?

Sarah Merritt—her face came to him in vivid detail—*I don't know what to do about you.*

It struck him that for the first time in his life he wanted to court a woman and he didn't know how.

Court her?

The idea still terrified him.

He wanted to court a woman who was so excessively virtuous she could not allow herself to kiss a man without tearful recriminations? *He,* whose first sexual liaison had taken place at sixteen? *He,* who had since enjoyed women wherever he could find them? *He* wanted to marry a woman whose Puritanical virtue would in all likelihood lead to a lifetime of frugal caresses and dutiful subservience at bedtime?

It wasn't supposed to happen like this. If you fell in love with a woman she was supposed to get short-breathed and willful, like you. She was supposed to touch your face and your hair and your body like the soiled doves did, look into your face the way they did, only meaning it.

Instead, Sarah Merritt recoiled.

Yet she'd admitted she was attracted to him.

There was the puzzlement. If she was, and last night was an example of what he could hope to expect, where could it lead? Not every girl in Noah's past had been paid for. Some had been good, wholesome girls who favored him to the extent that denial became difficult. They were chaste girls like Sarah, yet they'd had what he considered a normal curiosity and appetite for seduction. If Sarah had acted like them—tempted rather than threatened—he'd be less confused, but she seemed to have the distorted idea that intimacy presumed wantonness, which was not true.

Nevertheless, he couldn't stop thinking about her. He pictured himself returning to the boardinghouse, knocking on her bedroom door and leaving it wide open while he said point-blank, *Sarah, I love you. Do you love me?*

The truth was he was deathly afraid she'd say no and he'd be decimated. Kissing a girl the way he'd kissed Sarah last night was supposed to give a man a clue to her feelings. Instead, the experience left him even more unsure and vulnerable than before, frightened because he was actually getting serious about the idea of marriage.

True slowed and waited until Noah came up on his left flank, then they walked their horses, side by side.

"You're quiet today," True remarked.

"Sorry."

"Actually, I don't need a man gabbin' my ear off to be comfortable with him."

"Guess I'm just tired. Those bells kept me awake last night."

"Me too. Sounded pretty though, didn't they?"

"Yup."

True turned and studied Noah lazily, as if waiting for Noah to say more. When he didn't, they rode on in silence. Soon they scaled a hogback and ahead of them stretched the Spearfish Valley with its hayfields lying like great white linens on a fallen clothesline. Chimney smoke rose in lazy plumes. Haystacks appeared like snow-covered hummocks in the unbroken expanse of white.

At his parents' house Carrie hugged them, Kirk took their jackets and Arden asked, "Have you seen Sarah? How is she? Is she seeing anyone?"

True's eyes nonchalantly passed to Noah, who ignored the question.

"Well, tell me!" Arden demanded.

Removing his hat, Noah replied, "Yes, fine, and I don't know."

"What do you mean, you don't know. You know everything that happens in that town. You make it your business to know!"

"I don't know."

"Well, that's a fine how-do-you-do!" Arden threw his hands in the air.

"Arden, for pity sake, quit nettling your brother," Carrie chided.

"I saw her at the Christmas program last night," Noah offered—a crumb in hopes of shutting Arden up. "She directed the children's choir."

"She did?" Obviously a crumb wasn't going to do the trick. "How'd she look? What was she wearing?"

"Hell, I don't know—True, how did she look?"

True said, "Like an angel."

"Damn! I knew we should've gone in and seen it. Didn't I tell you, Ma, we should go?"

"That's a long ride in there and back again the same day when Noah was coming out here anyway, and a person never knows about the weather at this time of year. Besides, I told you both, you and your pa, I didn't want to be in any hotel on Christmas Eve."

They had to recount every particular about the Christmas program. Noah left most of the telling to True, who went into surprising detail in describing Sarah's green jacket, her hair, even the angel costumes.

Noah turned to stare at True. What the hell was going on here? How did True remember all that? True's gaze rested on Arden throughout the recital, but from all he said Noah supposed True had seen him leaving with Sarah. If he did, he never mentioned it.

For Noah it was a flat day, in spite of True's presence, Carrie's home cooking and being with his family again. All the while he was in the valley, he kept wishing he were back in town. All the while he sat at his mother's table he kept wishing he were at Mrs. Roundtree's. All the while he faced Arden across it, he kept wishing he were facing Sarah instead.

Often he'd find himself taking no part in the conversation around him, remembering given moments during the last three months: the day Sarah had given him the Stetson and Andy Tatum had said, my guess is she's got an eye for you, Noah; the day he'd run into her on the boardwalk when she was taking the cat to her sister; the night he'd first kissed her in Mrs. Roundtree's kitchen.

They stayed overnight, he and True, and started for town at midmorning, beneath a sky turned turgid with gray-cheeked clouds that scudded and scowled, each one seeming to bear a face with a warning that their return trip would be colder than their trip up had been.

True again rode lead with Noah's gray gelding close on the mare's wind-whipped tail, closing rank even when Noah attempted to rein him back. In the deep canyons and creek-bottoms the wind eddied and whistled like a morning teakettle. It arched the tips of the pines. It lifted great sheets of snow from their branches and scattered them like puzzle pieces on the earth below. It plucked Noah's voice from his lips and hurled it at the back of True's head.

"Hey, True, you mind if I ask you something?"

True cranked his head ninety degrees to the right. His cheek bumped his upturned collar.

"Ask!" He had to shout to be heard above the wind.

"Remember that little Mormon girl you told me about, the one you wanted to marry?"

"Francie?"

"Yeah, Francie."

"What about her?"

"How did you know you loved her?"

Noah watched True bob up and down in the saddle. They were trotting on a fairly flat stretch of trail with a patch of paper birches on their right. True's hat was pulled low over his forehead. His wool collar nudged it from behind. Once again True turned his head to be heard.

"I knew 'cause making her happy in bed seemed less important than making her happy out of it."

Noah thought about that some. "You mean you took her to bed—a Mormon girl?"

"Nope. Never did. Wanted to, but I never did. I wouldn't've done that to her unless we were married."

They rode a while in silence, Noah feeling guilty for placing so much importance on Sarah Merritt's aversion to sex. All right, so that part shouldn't matter so much. If you were really in love the other things mattered more—respect, friendship, being able to talk to one another, enjoying a few of the same things, looking forward to being in the same room together.

"Hey, True?"

"Yeah?"

"Were you scared when you asked her to marry you?"

"Nope. I only got scared after I asked her and she said no—thinking about spending the rest of my life without her." The mare picked its way down a rocky incline and the gray gelding followed. True hollered back, "You get a little scared ever, thinking about spending the rest of your life without that little newspaper lady?"

"I figured you knew it was her."

"Doesn't take much guessing, watching the two of you in the same room. Like a pair of witching sticks above water."

"I didn't know it was so obvious."

"I saw you leave with her on Christmas Eve."

"I figured you did. Thanks for not telling Arden."

"Any fool could see she's not for Arden." True bobbed several more times before he shouted over his shoulder, "So you gonna ask her or not?"

"I've been thinking about it."

"Got that lump in your throat, do you? Like a cud caught sideways?"

"Yeah." The lump was there as Noah answered. He tried to swallow it but it stuck, even as he hollered at True's back. "She's scared of what happens in the bedroom, True. Real scared. Says she doesn't want to be like her sister."

True cocked himself sideways in the saddle and cranked his head clear around to cast a long glance back at his companion. The horses trotted along. Their manes lifted in the wind. Finally True faced front again.

"Now that's a problem," he called.

Back in town, Noah slowed his horse to a walk as he passed the office of the *Deadwood Chronicle.* Inside, the lanterns burned. He could see Bradigan and the Dawkins boy moving about, but not Sarah. Absurd, this overwhelming sense of disappointment, just because he'd expected to see her head beyond the gold leaf printing on the window when he passed by. He found himself looking in every window he passed, hoping to catch sight of her if only fleetingly.

He checked in at his office. Freeman Block, now a salaried deputy, reported that things had been quiet. No saloon fights, no trouble in the gambling halls, scarcely any traffic on the street yesterday.

Noah sent Freeman home and returned his horse to the livery barn, stopped by Farnum's store, bought six sticks of jerky and returned to his office to gnaw them and do paperwork.

The afternoon seemed to crawl. Sometimes he'd find himself staring at the street, wishing she'd walk by so he could make an excuse to go out and bump into her, talk a little bit, see her face and try to figure out if asking her to marry him was the right thing to do.

Sometimes he sat with his face in his hands, miserable for reasons too complex to unsnarl.

He left the office a good fifty minutes before suppertime, went up to Mrs. Roundtree's and took a sponge bath, combed his hair, shaved meticulously, trimmed the lower edge of his mustache with a scissor, splattered a little sandalwood vegetal on his cheeks and neck, put on clean clothes clear down to his hide and checked his pocket watch.

Ten minutes to supper.

He dropped the watch into his vest pocket, returned to the mirror and assessed his face. Funny-looking face—what would a woman see in it? Everything too round and high to turn a woman's head, plus that silly-looking dent in the end of his nose. Well, hell, it was the best he could do.

It felt like he'd been away from her for two months instead of two days. The five minutes before he left his room and clattered downstairs put grasshoppers in his stomach.

In the dining room the men all said hello, how had his trip out to the Spearfish been, how was his folks, was they getting snow up that way?

Mrs. Roundtree brought in a huge brown crock full of baked beans, a platter full of venison chops, a bowl full of pickled beets, a plate of sliced bread.

Noah glanced at Sarah's empty chair.

Mrs. Roundtree plunked into her own place at the head of the table and said, "There you are, gentlemen. Go to town."

Again Noah studied the chair where Sarah usually sat. So she was a little late. Unusual, but it *could* happen.

The venison platter came from Noah's left, went around the corner and took a long pass over Sarah's empty seat.

"Aren't we waiting for Miss Merritt tonight?" Noah asked.

"She moved out," Mrs. Roundtree replied tartly, looking down her nose as she stabbed a hunk of bread and passed it on. "Lock, stock and barrel."

"Moved out! When?"

"Last night. Sent the Dawkins boy after her trunks this morning."

"Where?"

"I didn't ask. Have some beets and pass them on."

"But why?"

Mrs. Roundtree leveled her disapproving gaze on Noah. "It's not my business to ask people why they come and go. You're holding up the proceedings, Mr. Campbell. Mr. Mullins is waiting for the beets."

Noah passed them on woodenly. She was gone! On the night when he'd pretty much decided to take her out for a walk and ask her to marry him, Sarah Merritt was gone. He figured he knew exactly why.

Supper tasted like fodder. He ate because he was expected to: to leave the table and run to find her would look most peculiar. All the men seemed to be casting him surreptitious glances, gauging his reaction to her absence. He avoided looking at her empty chair.

After supper he went upstairs to collect his gun and make his evening rounds. The *Chronicle* office was black. He stood a long time, looking in, feeling black himself. He could see the outline of his hat reflected in its windowglass, but could not make out his features.

You know perfectly well why she moved out of Mrs. Roundtree's, Campbell. She didn't want to deal with a rounder like you coming into her room in the dark of night and pestering her.

He pivoted and headed toward the next boardwalk, past the sound of a tinkling piano muffled by closed doors, past the laughter of men at the gaming tables, stopping beneath the overhanging roof of the boardwalk across from the Grand Central Hotel. She'd probably moved back there. If he stood here long enough she might come out. And he might cross the street and say, Hello, Sarah. Then what? Everything he imagined happening after that made him look like a lovesick fool, so he stomped into the Eureka Saloon, had a double belt of Four Feathers whiskey and went home to bed.

In the morning he awakened surly, remained surly through breakfast, and while he returned to his room for his gun, jacket and hat, and while he resolutely returned the Stetson to its peg on the hat tree, and while he plucked it off again and slammed it on his head, and muttered, "All right, I'll wear the sonofabitch."

They'd had snow overnight. He shoveled the boardwalk in front of his office, went inside and made a checklist of all the license taxes that needed collecting at the turn of the quarter, added wood to his stove, drank a cup of coffee that tasted like buffalo piss, stood staring out the window at the ruts in the street, sighed and gave up.

He needed to see her. Needed to spill what was on his mind. Needed to find out what was on hers. Needed to rid his gullet of this great lump of nothingness he'd felt since leaving her room on Christmas Eve.

There were four people in the newspaper office when he opened the door: Patrick Bradigan, running the handpress; Josh Dawkins, inking it with a brayer; Sarah's sister, Eve, folding newspapers at a long table on the side; and Sarah herself, wearing a leather apron, squatting over a bucket of turpentine, cleaning a hunk of metal with a brush. He passed the typesetter and apprentice, nodding to them. He passed Sarah's sister, saying quietly, "Hello, Eve." He gave them the barest edge of his attention. It was all for Sarah, who looked up and went very still when she saw him approach. She released the brush and rose, wiping her hands on a rag, her face smileless.

"Hello, Noah," she said.

He removed his brown Stetson, held it in both hands and asked, "Could I talk to you outside a minute, Sarah? It's personal."

"Of course." She set the rag aside and untied the leather thongs at her spine, took off the apron and donned a coat from the hat tree beside her desk.

She headed for the front door but Noah asked, "Could we go out back instead?"

Her gaze collided with his and slid away. "All right."

Her hair was pinned up in a neat coil, and the smell of turpentine followed her.

Outside the weather was much like yesterday, the wind picking up last night's snow and pelting it against her skirt and his trouser legs. She held the neck of her coat closed and turned to him as the wind whipped a strand of hair from its moorings into the corner of her mouth. She reached up and scraped it away, but it blew back immediately into her face.

He faced her with his hat pulled low, collar up, gloved hands joined before him like a ball and socket. He dropped them to his sides as he said, "I missed you at Mrs. Roundtree's last night."

She hesitated a beat before replying, "Yes, it was a rather sudden move. How was your Christmas?"

"It was . . . all right."

"And your family?"

"They're fine. Arden asked a thousand questions about you."

Her lips smiled, but her eyes remained fixed on Noah's as if she scarcely registered the remark.

"Aw, hell, Sarah, the truth is my Christmas was terrible. I kept wishing I was with you and I couldn't wait to get back, then when I did I found out you'd moved. You didn't have to do that, Sarah." He lifted one hand and let it fall. "I shouldn't have come into your room that night after you asked me not to, but I told you it wouldn't happen again, and I would have kept that promise."

"You think that's the reason I moved?"

"Well, isn't it?"

"No."

"Then what—"

"It's because of Addie. She's left Rose's for good."

"For good?"

"That's what she says."

"Well, that's . . . that's good news."

"At least we're hoping it's for good, Robert and I. He talked her out of there and brought her to see me, and we all had a delightful Christmas dinner at Emma's. But Mrs. Roundtree treated Addie abominably and told me if I wanted to visit with her I'd have to do it somewhere else from now on because she didn't want women like that in her house. So I got angry and . . . and I suppose a little bit retaliatory—after all, if a woman like Addie wants to reform and nobody will help her, what chance has she got? I gave Mrs. Roundtree the sharp side of my tongue and moved into a room at the Grand Central with Addie for the time being until we can buy a house of our own."

"A house of your own?"

"I've already talked to Craven and he thinks he may have one for us, but in the meantime, I'm so afraid Addie will go back that I won't let her out of my sight. That's why she's here folding papers. But as soon as we can find a house, Emma's going to teach her how to do housekeeping. That should keep her out of trouble."

He digested it all, watching the wind make flags of her hair, watching her scrape a strand of it away from her eye.

"I'm so relieved. I thought you were moving out to get away from me."

"No . . . not at all."

She met his eyes. For a while neither of them spoke.

"Can I tell you the truth, Sarah?"

She waited.

"I thought about you all the time I was gone, and I kept blaming myself over and over again, and telling myself that you're not like the women up at Rose's, and I should have known better than to go to your room. Sarah, I'm sorry for what I did . . . but on the other hand, I'm not, you see . . . hell, I don't even know how to say what I mean."

"I think you're doing quite well, Noah."

"Am I?" He looked rather miserable. "You're the one who's good with words. Sometimes when I try to say things to you they don't come out the way I intend them to."

"What you're trying to say is that you missed me."

"Yes . . . yes, I did."

"I missed you, too." The wind lifted a few strands of her hair straight up and settled some down across her forehead. "Christmas at Emma's was wonderful, but I kept wondering what the Spearfish Valley looked like, and where you were and what you were doing."

"Did you, Sarah?"

She nodded silently, looking square into his eyes.

The lump reappeared in his throat and breathing took a tremendous effort.

"This isn't the time or the place I'd planned to say this, not . . . not here in the alley by your woodpile. I thought I'd take you out walking up toward Mount Moriah some night when it was quiet and the owls were calling and . . . and . . ." He stumbled to a halt. Her blue eyes appeared silver, reflecting the leaden sky, waiting. "I think I love you, Sarah."

She seemed to lose her grip on her jacket front. Her lips parted and her eyes went wide and motionless. It took some time before she spoke in a voice airy with surprise.

"You do?"

"And I think we should get married."

She stood dumbstruck while he presented his case. "I thought about it all through Christmas, and I believe it's the right thing to do. Now, I know what you're thinking, that I've been around the horn a few times, and I have, but that doesn't mean a man can't change. And as for your sister, I swear to you, Sarah, from this day forward I'll treat her like she was my own sister. I know it's asking a lot of you to forget what . . ." He gestured toward the world behind his shoulder. ". . . well . . . what's gone on up at Rose's, but that was before I knew you, and everything's changed since then."

"Noah, I don't know what to say."

He studied her face with his heart racing while she stood utterly still, only her hair lifting and falling like loose cobwebs. "Well, for starters, you might tell me if there's any possibility that you love me too."

Her cheeks got very red and she dropped her gaze. "I think there's a very good possibility of that, Noah."

"But you've been fighting it, right?"

She tactfully refrained from replying.

"Well, so have I," he admitted. They stood a while with the wind eddying around them, wondering where to go from here.

"It didn't happen anything like I expected it to." He reached out his gloved hands and took her by the upper arms, remembered how she disliked being touched and dropped his hands. He glanced at the woodpile, pushed a stick of firewood in line with those beneath it. Pushed a few others. "You weren't what I expected. I wasn't what I expected—I mean, the way I acted."

"How did you think it would be?"

He gave up his preoccupation with the wood and faced her. "I don't know, but I didn't think I'd be walking around miserable like this all the time."

"Well, if it's any consolation, I'm miserable, too."

His voice softened. "But then I see you and it feels like everything falls into place."

"Yes," she replied, "for me, too."

Silence passed.

He smiled.

She smiled back.

"Well?" he said quietly.

"Well . . ." she replied.

Their uncertain smiles remained while at his side his gloved hand worked a piece of bark, then dropped it and became still.

"I know what I promised in your room on Christmas Eve, Sarah, but is there any chance you'd like to kiss me?"

A tender, half-sad smile touched her lips. "Oh Noah," she said quietly, and moved toward him.

He moved, too—a step from each and their heads tipped, their mouths joined. It felt like starting at the beginning, standing in the brisk winter wind, tasting each other with cold lips and warm tongues, while a well-spring of emotion flooded their breasts. Their embrace was chaste, by anyone's standards, with his hands on her sleeves and hers on his jacket front. When the kiss ended they drew back to study one another's eyes while wind whistled between them.

"So what do you think?" Noah said at last. "Would we be less miserable together?"

Her hands remained on his heavy jacket. "Could I have some time to think about it, Noah?"

His spirits fell. "How much time?"

"Until I can be sure Addie won't backslide. If I told her now that I want to marry you, she'd have the perfect excuse to go back to Rose's. She's very unsure of herself, you see. In there—strange as it seems—she felt secure. She was paying her own way and she was accepted. Nobody pointed fingers at her. Out here, none of those things are true."

"How long will it take?"

"I don't know. I must find us a house—I think I should do that and get her accustomed to fending for herself. She doesn't know anything, Noah, not how to cook or to wash clothes or how to handle herself in gracious company. She never had to learn. Who'll teach her if I don't?"

"And if you buy a house, what about us? Are you saying that's where you'd want us to live?"

"I don't know. I hadn't thought that far ahead. Where did you think we'd live?"

"I haven't thought that far ahead either, but it wouldn't work for all three of us to live in the same house."

"No, of course it wouldn't. But there's no rush, is there? Why, we don't even have a preacher yet."

He hadn't thought of that either.

"So what are you saying? Yes, you'll marry me, but after we get a minister and after Addie's settled into a house of her own?"

She opened her mouth to say I guess so when she thought of her newspaper.

"What about the *Chronicle?*"

"You can still run it, can't you?"

"Not if we have a house and a family."

"Would you want a house and a family?" he asked. He was really asking if she wanted a family.

"Why, of course. When you get married those things just happen."

"But would you *want* them? *My* house and *my* family?"

The idea was new. She needed some time to think about becoming a mother. She would be as green at it as Addie was at housekeeping, yet who was there to teach her?

"Noah, one hour ago we were both rebelling against the idea of falling in love with each other, now we're discussing details that . . . that . . . oh Noah, I don't have answers for everything. Not this quickly."

He stepped back, feeling rebuffed. "All right, we'll let it ride for a while. Would you like a locket or a pin or anything like that?"

A puzzled frown crinkled her eyebrows. "A locket or a pin?"

"To seal the engagement? There's enough gold in this town to make you whatever you want."

He wasn't so much different from his brother after all. He suddenly seemed in a hurry.

"You want to make it official? You're sure?"

"If you do."

"Very well . . . a locket or a pin."

"Which one?"

"You choose."

They remained awhile, feeling some of the joy dribble out of the moment. "But Noah . . ." She touched his sleeve. "I would have to hide it for a while, otherwise Addie might feel she was holding me back."

His disappointment grew. He'd always imagined betrothals occasions for great celebration. Hell, if it were up to him he'd be proud to have her print in her newspaper that Noah Campbell and Sarah Merritt were engaged to be married and would do so as soon as the town got a preacher.

Nevertheless, he had to admit, "Yes, that's probably a good idea. I need time to tell my family first, too. Arden is going to be upset."

"It's strange, isn't it, how this all started? You with my sister and me with your brother while you and I found each other intolerable?"

"Well, somehow things worked out, didn't they?"

The sound of a whinnying horse carried to them on the wind while they stood in the shelter of the building, close enough to touch, but refraining.

"I'll miss you at the boardinghouse," Noah said.

"I'll miss you, too," she replied.

Her blue eyes wore an expression of longing that set off a reaction in his heart; still he waited, tethered by self-imposed restraints, afraid to assume he had the right to kiss her, even as her espoused.

"I've wanted to tell you something for the longest time," she whispered.

"Te—" His voice broke and he cleared his throat. "Tell me."

"I think you have the most beautiful hair I've ever seen."

"Oh Sarah . . ." They moved as one, into a swift embrace, her arms around his neck, his around her back, kissing open-mouthed while impatience pressed upon them like a gale. She clung, fitting her tongue to his, and her body to his, and her will to his. The first kiss ended and he held her head, taking a journey across her face with his mouth, strewing it with tiny bites and kisses.

"Oh Noah," she whispered, her eyes closed, her head thrown back as he kissed her throat. "All my life I thought I would live alone. I thought I would never have this . . . that no man would ever ask me to be his wife. I was so afraid of being unloved."

"Shh . . . no . . . no . . ." he whispered. "There's so much good in you it makes others good, and you're pure and fine and bright and brave. And you have the most beautiful blue eyes I've ever seen."

She opened her eyes and encountered his at close range. "Really?"

"Really." He smiled, still holding her head in his gloved hands.

A sluice of joy struck her. She beamed, and kissed him once more in celebration . . . then in yearning.

When their mouths were wet and their propriety threatened, he drew back, breathing erratically, and put distance between them.

"You'd better go inside now, Miss Merritt, and I'd better go back to work."

"Must we?"

"Yes, we must. But Sarah?"

"Hm?"

He kissed her nose. "Please hurry and get your sister settled."

They exchanged an intimate look that said the wait would be long, regardless.

"I'll try," she answered, and bidding him a reluctant goodbye returned to the newspaper office wondering how the others could possibly miss the glow that must be radiating from her like a nimbus.

Chapter 17

❧

Craven Lee found them a house with miraculous speed, eliminating the need for Sarah and Addie to take up temporary lodging at the rear of the newspaper office. A man named Archibald Mimms had moved into the gulch the previous spring and built the house for his wife and family who were to follow. In the meantime his wife had taken ill and been unable to travel. Two days after Christmas Mimms received a telegram bearing the news that his wife had died back in Ohio, and he left on the stage the next day to return to his children. To Craven Lee, he said, "Sell it with everything in it. I ain't never coming back to this hellhole. If I hadn't left Ohio in the first place my wife would still be alive."

The house had two rooms up, two down, and was cubic and unglamorous. Mimms had furnished it with only enough to get by, though he had taken advantage of the plastering craze in hopes of pleasing his wife. The plastered walls cut down drafts and added brightness, but the place lacked any other charm. One bedroom and the parlor were totally bare. The only covered windows were the two in the bedroom Mimms had used; they were covered with sacking that had been nailed to the window frames. The kitchen had a sparse collection of tinware and dishes, an oak table and four chairs, a dry sink and a good Magee range.

Sarah took one look at the place and decided two women with a sizable chunk of inheritance money could certainly dress it up enough to make it homey. Mimms had the gold dust in his pocket before he left on the stage, and four days after Christmas Addie and Sarah were outfitting for domestic life. More accurately, Sarah was outfitting, for Addie refused to accompany her sister when she went uptown to make purchases.

"The men all know me," Addie said, standing in their room at the Grand Central Hotel.

"So what?"

"They act strange when they see me away from Rose's, like I've got two heads or something. And there might be women in the shops."

"Addie, you have as much right to be there as anyone else."

"No . . ." Addie shrugged sheepishly. "You go."

"But Addie, what good did it do to break free of Rose's if you make yourself a prisoner here?"

"I'm not a prisoner. I'll go . . . sometime soon, but not just yet."

Sarah felt disappointed, but realized she could not force her sister back into the mainstream of life overnight. "Very well, I'll go alone. May I get you anything?"

"Some yard goods for dresses. Robert made me leave all mine behind. And some thread and chalk and needles. And buttons, I guess."

"There's a tailor in town. Why don't you just go see him?"

"I'd like to try making them myself. I can't do much—I can't darn Robert's socks—but after all the samplers Mrs. Smith made us stitch, I think I can make a dress. But I want you to use my money, please, Sarah."

They'd already butted heads about buying the house with the inheritance money, which Addie claimed she didn't want, but there was no other answer, of course. Still, Sarah understood Addie's necessity to cling to some figment of pride. "All right, Addie, I'll try to pick out something you'd like. Something blue if Andrew has it." Addie had always loved blue.

"Blue would be nice."

Sarah waited while Addie fetched the money from beneath her pillow. Accepting it, she tried to think of it not as tainted lucre, but as a contribution toward Addie's solid future.

"I'll have arrangements made for everything to be delivered to the house later on this morning. You'll be there?"

"Yes."

It was almost a test for Addie to leave the hotel all by herself and walk the few blocks to their house: in the five days since she had left Rose's this would be the first time she was left totally alone.

Sarah had her hand on the doorknob when Addie said, "Oh Sarah, please . . . one more thing?"

Sarah turned.

"Could you bring something to bleach out this dye?" Self-consciously, Addie plucked at her coarse black hair. "Robert just hates it."

Sarah returned to Addie and embraced her, feeling hopeful and happier than she had since Addie ran away from home. "I'll bring back the whole apothecary!"

Before she was done, Sarah had to enlist the help of Josh and Patrick to rent a wagon at the livery and bring it around to Tatum's General Store, followed by Parker's Apothecary, the meat market, Emma's bakery and the Grand Central, where they collected Sarah's possessions.

Mimms' clapboard house was located about halfway up the hill toward Mt. Moriah on the side of the gulch that caught the afternoon and evening sun. Mornings, it would be shrouded in shadow until ten o'clock, but at two o'clock when Sarah and her entourage arrived, it was awash in sunlight, reflecting off the snow. Smoke lifted from the chimney, and inside, Addie was happily washing windows while Ruler nosed the water in the bucket.

Patrick and Josh greeted her with smiles, carrying in a carved maple bed. "Hello, Miss Addie."

"We've nearly cleaned out Tatum's!" Sarah announced, breezing in behind them, "to say nothing of the apothecary and Farnum's Store."

Sarah had bought a wagonful. For the kitchen, a rocking chair, wash-tubs, a copper boiler, a hand wringer, Pearline washing compound, castile soap, brushes, floor oil, a broom, a supply of rags from Henry Tanby and Skitch Johnson, a willowware set of nested baskets, a pie safe, a good iron spider, a spice mill, a granite roaster, a set of Marlin dinnerware, a bone-handled carving set, tinned steel tableware, a glass vinegar crewet, and for the wall, a tin matchbox with matching comb case painted with crowing chanticleers in bright reds and oranges on an écru background.

For the front room, a three-piece upholstered parlor suite, an oval pie-crust table, two banquet lamps, a large Smyrna rug, a library table, and to drape it with, a tapestry table cover, complete with tinseling and tasseled edge.

For upstairs there was new furniture for Addie's room, plus pillows, blankets, linen sheeting, brass wall hooks, bedwarmers, a peerless enamel chamber pot and Scotch crash for toweling.

For Sarah's own bedroom (the one previously used by Mimms) a fine drop-front desk and a center-draught bracket lamp for the wall beside it.

As Addie watched it all being carried in, her eyes grew wide. "So much! Should you have bought so much, Sarah?"

"Father did very well in St. Louis. He would have wanted us to have a nice home here."

Addie's face became expressionless as she stooped down to brush the seat of the divan.

The men came through and said, "Well, that's it!"

"Thank you, Patrick and Josh," Sarah said.

"We'll get that wagon back to the livery."

When they were gone, Sarah said, "Addie, come see the sewing supplies I bought you."

For the only occupation in which her sister had expressed an interest or a hint of confidence, Sarah had admittedly overindulged. There were twenty yards of white goods, a length of woolen druggeting in ink blue, another in deep cranberry with tiny flecks of bone-gray, some plain home-spun in two designs, tinted muslin, a small piece of beaver cloth cloaking, satin surah for lining, buttons, dress braids, hooks and eyes, ribbons, cord-ing, elastic, dress reeds, lead dress weights, brass pins and an ebony sewing box containing eight spools of cotton, a thimble and a pincushion shaped like a strawberry.

When the packages lay strewn about the parlor, Addie seemed pleased and said, "Thank you, Sarah. I'll try to do Mrs. Smith proud."

"I've bought us each something special—something just for ourselves."

Addie rose, sweeping a hand over the collection. "This isn't special?"

"No, not really. This is mostly things we need, and they're not nearly as good as anything we had in St. Louis. I'm only sorry I couldn't buy you a spinet. But if the railroad ever comes through here, you can be assured I will. Meanwhile, I thought we should each have something very elegant and personal to remind us that we were brought up among good taste and fine things." Sarah held out a package. "For you."

Addie reached out reluctantly.

"Oh Sarah . . ."

"Sit down on our new divan and open it."

Addie perched gingerly on the dusty-rose divan and placed the parcel in her lap. From its wrapping of cotton wadding she withdrew matching glove—and handkerchief-boxes of fine, translucent opal glass. On their covers hand-painted florals were surrounded by raised, gilded rococo or-namentation. When Addie had run away from home she had left behind many such pretties, gifts from their father, or from Mrs. Smith, or from Sarah herself. The pieces were expensive and finely crafted. She ran her fingers around and around the gilded rim of one cover.

Watching her, Sarah said, "Two times now you've been forced to leave your personal belongings behind. These you'll have for keeps."

"Oh Sarah, they're beautiful."

Across the cluttered room, Sarah felt a wisp of maternal care just as she'd experienced many times after their mother left, in those days when she would try in any small way to make up for the loss. Addie truly wasn't very bright, but she had always loved bright things and had felt comforted by having them around her.

"Addie . . ." Sarah called quietly. Addie looked up from the handker-chief box. "I'm sorry I said what I did about you being spoiled and not having to work at the newspaper office when we were young. I loved it there, truly I did, just as I knew you didn't. And I was good at it, just as I knew you weren't. What I said was cruel and self-serving. Forgive me."

Addie set down the handkerchief box and replied, "It doesn't matter. It's all behind us now."

Abruptly shifting moods, Sarah said perkily, "Would you like to see what I got?"

Addie found her smile. "Not a glove or hanky box, I'm sure."

Sarah laughed. She had never been the glove-box type. From another roll of wadding she took a flint-crystal writing set with two silver-capped ink bottles and a pair of fine pens on an embossed silver base.

"For my new desk." She held it aloft.

"It's very pretty," Addie said. "But I'm glad I got my handkerchief boxes instead."

Again they laughed. With the good mood restored, Sarah put her writ-ing set on the library table, pushing aside other items. Turning, she searched the parcels on the floor. "And I did stop by the apothecary as you asked." She found the correct bundle, dropped to her knees and began rooting through it while the inquisitive cat came to investigate the crackle of paper and paw at the tangle of string. "I'm not sure what will get rid of hair dye, so I brought everything . . ." Item by item, she set them on the floor. "Salts of lemon, oxalic acid, lye, Borax, salts of tartar, dry ammonia, carbonate of soda, Fuller's Earth Water, and if none of those work, something called Magic Annihilator, which Mr. Parker said truly does work miracles—if it doesn't rot your hair out of your skull."

"I can't wait! Will you help me, Sarah?"

"As soon as we get our house in order."

The two women set about unpacking the purchases, putting their fur-niture in place, making a home out of a house. They put dishes on Mimms' crude kitchen wall shelf, food in the pie safe, a blue and white checked cloth on the kitchen table. In the late afternoon they made a pot of coffee and spread lard on slabs of Emma's bread, cut cheese and shared their first repast. Afterward, they sat down with needles to hem sheeting for their beds, then made them up in tandem. They hung Sarah's new wall lantern, filled it and a table lamp for Addie with coal oil, set out their new ornaments and stood back to admire their rooms. On Sarah's new desk the pen set reflected the lamplight. On Addie's new bureau the glass boxes added a touch of femininity. Ruler had already curled up on Addie's bed.

She stood in the doorway, perusing the room, genuinely excited for the first time since leaving Rose's.

"A room of my own . . ."

From the opposite doorway Sarah added, "And a room of my own. Now I won't have to spend so many evenings at the newspaper office."

Addie remarked, "We need some rugs."

"We'll get them, and some curtains and maybe even some wallpaper when spring comes and the freight wagons start rolling again."

"And we'll plant some flowers around the kitchen door the way Mrs. Smith used to."

"Absolutely." Sarah took it as a good sign: Addie was planning a future.

Addie turned to Sarah and asked, "Now could we work on my hair?"

With evening fallen and the lamps lit, they hung sheeting over their kitchen windows, stripped Addie down to her shift and set about bleaching the dye out of her hair. First they tried plain glycerine soap; next, oxalic acid mixed with salts of lemon. The rinse water looked murky, but Addie's hair remained black as tar. Next they tried the Magic Annihilator. It smelled like it could rot the heads off nails but removed no more dye than the other solutions had. Finally they dissolved lye, Borax, salts of tartar and dry ammonia in hot water. It stung Addie's eyes and nearly stopped her breath, but the color began fading. Addie leaned over the dry sink while Sarah dipped cup after cup of the acrid mixture over her hair and massaged it through the strands.

"Addie, I think it's working!"

"Is it really?" Addie said, upside down.

"Look at the water!"

"I can't. If I open my eyes I'll go blind."

"The water's all black. Wait—I'm going to dump it and make another batch." Sarah took the basin and slung it in the yard. She mixed up a second batch of the fetid brew and watched it grow darker and darker with each trip through Addie's hair.

During the third batch she reported enthusiastically, "You're getting gray, Addie! And grayer and grayer!"

"Oh Sarah, hurry! I'm dying to see!"

Finally Sarah threw away the last basin of solution and rinsed Addie's hair with plain water, then with Fuller's Earth Water. She wrapped her sister's head with a length of their new toweling, jostled it around a few times and ordered, "All right, take a look."

When the towel fell away, Addie took up a hand mirror to examine the results. Her hair stood up in spikes—not exactly blond, but certainly not black. Rather midway between—the color of old nickel.

Looking forlorn, Addie plucked at the spikes as if stripping seeds from them.

"It's not blond."

"But it's lighter than it was."

"But I wanted it to be blond."

"Sit down, let me comb it."

Addie sat, looking in the mirror while Sarah attempted to draw a comb through the snarls. It took some doing. When the comb would finally cut through, Sarah opened the oven door and said, "Pull your chair back here." Addie moved her chair near the warmth, slumped low on the seat and closed her eyes while, in silence, Sarah combed her hair.

During those minutes of silence, while the older sister ministered to the younger, they recovered something of what they had lost as siblings. The room was cozy—lamplit, curtained, quiet. Some soot tumbled down the stovepipe in a rush of muffled ticks. The teakettle hummed softly. Upstairs, the cat slept.

"Sarah?" Addie said.

"Hm?"

"I've been thinking . . ."

"About what?"

"Robert."

"Mm . . ."

"He invited me to go out with him on New Year's Eve, first to supper and then to the Langrishe."

"And what did you say?"

"Nothing yet. But I don't want to go."

"Robert will be disappointed."

"I was thinking . . ."

Sarah continued combing. "You were thinking . . ."

"That maybe I could invite him here instead."

"Well, of course you can. You don't need my permission."

"I thought maybe I could invite him for supper, but I don't know how to cook."

"Certainly I'll help you, if that's what you're asking."

Addie boosted up and cranked around to look back at Sarah. "You will?"

"I'm not the world's most experienced in the kitchen, but I know a little from watching Mrs. Smith, and what we can't figure out we can ask Emma. Now, about that hair. The ends are snagged. Should I try trimming them?"

"Do you know how?"

"No better than you probably. No worse either."

"Should I trust you?" There was an actual gleam in Addie's eye.

"No," Sarah replied, grinning as she went to find the shears.

Addie submitted and Sarah went to work, dropping nickel-colored floss on the floor. When she was finished, Addie swept up the trimmings and stitched them into a small piece of cheesecloth. She coiled her hair around the rat, flattened it against the back of her head and with four deft stabs hairpinned it into place.

"There are some things, Addie, that you do a hundred times better than me. A remarkable improvement."

Addie looked pleased. "Do you think Robert will approve?"

"He'll love it. You look like a hausfrau."

Addie checked the hand mirror once again. "I do, don't I? I never really liked the black either."

"It's late. I'm tired, how about you?"

They replenished the woodbox from the pile Mimms had left in the backyard, stoked the range, set the dampers and retired to their rooms upstairs. Ruler came into Sarah's room while she was getting ready for bed, did a turn around her ankles, checked out her bed and returned to

Addie's room for the night, where—it was apparent—the feline would make her permanent nest.

When the lanterns were extinguished the two women settled into their rooms beneath their crisp, new sheets which smelled faintly like clean-picked flax in a dry bin.

Sarah lay for some time, looking at the dark ceiling, unable to feel drowsy in the strange bed, with the window in a strange place, and the faint snow-light coming in from an odd angle.

She thought of Noah, of how much she'd missed him over Christmas, and of how her face had grown hot when she'd looked up and seen him entering the newspaper office, how her pulse had leaped and her hands had gone motionless. She relived the minutes out by the woodpile before he'd kissed her, all the insurgent feelings that had risen up and deluged her, the wondrous shock when he'd said he loved her and had proposed marriage.

How incredible that she, who in her first twenty-five years attracted no more male attention than a garden scarecrow should, within three months of arriving in Deadwood find herself in love and loved by a man who wanted to spend the rest of his life with her.

"Addie?" Sarah called quietly. "Are you awake?"

"Yes."

"Would you mind if I invited the marshal for New Year's Eve?"

After a pause, Addie answered, "Why should I mind?"

"I just thought I should ask."

"The marshal's a very nice man, Sarah, and I have no claims on him."

Sarah smiled. "We'll make it supper for four then."

On New Year's Eve Sarah closed the newspaper office at four and went by Emma's to pick up bread, and by the butcher shop where, to her great delight, she found a rare supply of beef. Back then to Emma's to find out specifics about how to cook a roast.

At home she entered to find their kitchen transformed.

"You've made curtains!" she exclaimed.

"You like them?"

"Oh Addie, they're wonderful!" They were far less glamorous than any they'd had in Missouri, but so few buildings in Deadwood had curtains that any were a luxury. Addie had simply hemmed long rectangles of white sheeting, sewn lace on the fourth side, driven nails into the upper corners of the window frames and draped the curtains over them as swags. Below she'd used flat pieces the size of the window opening with buttonholes worked into the top corners. When Sarah entered, they hung on nails to the left of each window.

"We can cover them at night . . . see?" Addie demonstrated, stretching a curtain across a window and catching the buttonhole on the far nail.

"Ingenious! And ever so much easier than tacking up sheeting every night. And a bouquet, too . . . Adelaide Merritt, what a regular domestic you're becoming!" On their blue and white checked tablecloth Addie had put a bowl of pine sprigs.

"I thought we should have something special for tonight."

"You went out," Sarah noted, pleased.

"Just up to the cemetery. Nobody goes up there much in winter."

"It's a start. The kitchen looks lovely, Addie, truly it does. But listen—we must hurry. I've brought a roast of beef and Emma told me just what to do with it."

Sarah showed Addie how a roast is seared, and smothered in onion and bay leaf and covered with its own drippings and baked in the oven. They peeled potatoes and scraped carrots and cobbled up some tinned peaches and left them baking in the oven while they went upstairs to dress.

Addie wore a new dress she'd stitched from the blue wool druggeting. It was simple, collarless, with sleeves gathered onto dropped shoulders and a skirt gathered onto an unadorned bodice. She drew her nickel-colored hair into a tasteful French roll and left her scrubbed face unpainted.

"I look terribly pale this way, don't you think?" she asked, coming around the corner into Sarah's room. "Why Sarah . . ." Addie's face went flat with surprise. "While I'm bleaching myself outyou're turning into a butterfly. Where did you get it?" Addie took a turn around Sarah's burnt-orange dress. It was made of silk and had a bustled rear, swagged like the kitchen curtains and gathered up onto three covered buttons at the lumbar bend.

"It's an old one I haven't worn since I've been here. I got it for Christmas two years ago, but I hardly ever had an occasion to wear it afterward."

"And your hair. You've curled your hair?"

"Just a little, with the tongs, yes." Sarah laughed at Addie's astonishment. "Well, I *have* curled it before, you know. And after all, it's New Year's Eve. I wasn't going to wear my leather apron and my sleeve guards."

Addie's expression turned amused. "The marshal's going to drop his rocks."

Sarah laughed. "So is Robert. Your dress turned out heavenly. And wait till he sees your hair."

"Don't change the subject, Sarah. What's going on between you and the marshal?"

"The same thing that's going on between you and Robert—nothing. We're simply going to enjoy a festive New Year's Eve together."

The gentlemen arrived promptly at seven P.M., meeting on the street leading up the hill. Noah bore a bottle of port and Robert another of sherry.

"Fancy meeting you here, Baysinger," Noah said when the two found their paths merging. "Are you going where I suspect you're going?"

"Up to Addie's."

"And I'm going up to Sarah's. Looks like we're spending New Year's Eve together, eh?"

The two had never been cordial, largely on Noah's part, because he'd never lost the suspicion that Baysinger held a great attraction for Sarah. He set his antagonism aside, however, as the two climbed the street toward their destination.

"I was surprised to hear about Addie leaving Rose's. Sarah is pleased."

"So am I."

"You talked her out of there, did you?"

"I did."

"The men of this town won't thank you."

"Does that include you?"

"Not anymore it doesn't."

"That's good, because Addie is an old friend. Her welfare is far more important to me than the whims of a bunch of randy miners."

They reached Mimms' house and approached the door together. Pausing, each allowed the other the opportunity to knock. With a flourish of one hand Noah gave Robert the go-ahead.

His knock was answered promptly by Sarah.

"Hello, Robert. Hello, Noah. Come in."

Robert looked dumbstruck, gazing at her. Up. Down. Up again. At last he moved toward her. "Sarah—you look wonderful!" Without compunction he kissed her cheek, which she willingly offered.

"Why, thank you, Robert."

"I'll double that," Noah put in, swallowing his jealousy as he received only her hand in greeting.

"Thank you, Noah. May I take your coats?" She hung them on brass wall hooks beside the door.

"For you . . ." Noah said, handing her his bottle.

"Also for you," put in Robert, doing likewise.

"My goodness . . ." She lifted the bottles to examine their labels. "Spirits."

"Allowable, I believe, to toast the new year," Robert said.

"Certainly. Thank you both." She gave each a smile. "Addie's still upstairs. She'll be here in a moment." She raised her voice and called, "Addie, the gentlemen are here." And to the men, "Please sit down."

Noah did, on the edge of the divan. Robert, however, took a turn around the room, remarking, "You two have been busy, haven't you?"

"As beavers. What do you think of it?"

"I approve. Ah . . . this looks familiar." He opened the cover of the family Bible which lay on the library table.

"I brought it over from the newspaper office. I thought it belonged in the house."

Noah watched and listened, jealous once more because he could share nothing of Sarah's past as Baysinger could.

"There's your father's writing. Sarah Anne, born May 15, 1851. Adelaide Marie, born June 11, 1855. Ahh, we ate a lot of Mrs. Smith's sourcream cakes on those days, didn't we?"

Noah had not known until that moment the date of Sarah's birth, much less celebrated it with the sour-cream cake of the revered Mrs. Smith, nor could he recognize the writing of Sarah's father. He wondered if there would ever be, between himself and Sarah, the easygoing closeness she shared with Baysinger.

"Hello, Marshal. Hello, Robert," Addie said at that moment from the doorway.

Robert glanced over his shoulder. The Bible cover fell from his fingertips and plopped shut. For a moment he thought someone else stood at the foot of the steps. Her hair was nearly silver, swept back simply and becomingly. Her dress was dark, with Puritan lines. There was no paint on her face.

"Addie?"

"It's me."

"Your hair . . . it's not black anymore."

"Sarah did it." She touched it, tipping her head. "It didn't get quite

as light as we'd hoped, but it'll have to do until it grows out or until some
fresh lemons come into town.''

Robert went to her, took her by the arms and scrutinized her at close
range. "Well, *this* is cause for celebration.''

They had a lighthearted evening, enjoying each other's company with
increasing relaxedness. Noah found, much to his surprise, that the longer
he was around Robert the more he liked him. Baysinger had a ready smile,
an artless way with both women, and he laughed easily. To Noah's increasing amazement, he found that the three of them acted like unilateral
friends. If there was another side to the relationship of Robert with either
woman, it certainly didn't show. They teased one another, told amusing
stories about their youth, and, as Noah laughed with them, his jealousy
faded.

Supper itself was plain fare, but a joy to eat among the company of
friends his own age and in the kitchen with its cheery atmosphere.

"I envy you," Noah said to the three at one point. "Still such good
friends after all these years.''

"Envy us no more," Robert said, raising his glass. "Join us. To a long
and endearing friendship among the four of us! Let tonight be the first
of many such nights to come.''

"Hear, hear!" Four glasses clinked and they all sipped sherry. When
the meal was finished and the dishes set aside, they played Parcheesi. As
the competition became good-naturedly cutthroat, the men removed their
sack coats, unbuttoned their vests and rolled up their sleeves.

At five minutes before midnight they refilled their glasses and counted
down the hour with Noah acting as clock watcher, holding his pocket
watch in his hand.

"Five, four, three, two, one . . .''

"Happy new year!" they chorused, exuberantly clinking glasses together,
partaking of port before exchanging a round of kisses across the kitchen
table.

Robert kissed Addie.

Noah kissed Sarah.

Then Robert kissed Sarah and Noah kissed Addie.

The men shook hands.

The sisters hugged.

"Should auld acquaintance . . ." Robert began, and the others joined in.

When the song ended, the silence was tinged with melancholy.

Robert spoke for all of them. "We all have old acquaintances we've left
behind, acquaintances we miss, but, thanks to all of you, especially you
ladies for gathering us all together, it's been the best night I've spent
since coming to Deadwood. Here's to a promising year ahead, and happiness for all of us.''

"Hear, hear!''

After emptying his glass, Noah drew a deep breath and said, "I'm sorry
to break this up, but I promised Freeman I'd spell him at midnight so he
can do a little celebrating himself. Walk me outside, Sarah?''

As they rose, Robert tactfully decided, "I think Addie and I will have
one more glass of port.''

Outside, Noah said, "Thank you. It was fun, and I like Robert.''

"I'm glad." She hung her head back. "That way the four of us can do
more together. Oh my, look at those stars. Aren't they heavenly?''

"Mmm . . ." He gave them a glance. "What did you tell Robert and Addie about us?"

"Nothing. Only that we're friends." Her head still hung as if on a rubber support. "Heavenly stars . . ." She giggled.

He peered at her more closely. "Why, Miss Merritt, are you tipsy again?"

She drew her head up with a great effort. "Why, I believe I am, Mr. Campbell, and it's quite delightful." Another lilt of mirth escaped her.

"You're giggling!"

"So I am, but it's all your fault. You brought the port."

"So the woman I'm going to marry occasionally overindulges, does she?" He found himself grinning.

"Mmm . . . disgraceful, isn't it?"

"Absolutely."

"So arrest me." She flung her arms around his neck and let her body thump against his. "You've got the gun and the star. Go ahead, arrest me, Marshal Campbell," she challenged, an inch from his nose.

He kissed her, full and hard upon the mouth, and when it ended they were both breathing like stopped trains. Her giggling was gone. His grin was, too.

"It's freezing out here," he said, unbuttoning his sheepskin jacket and holding it open. "Get in here with me."

She had come outside without her coat and went willingly against him, sliding her arms around his trunk where it was warm and the sheepskin furry and his body very solid. He folded his jacket around her shoulders and doubled his arms around her.

"I like this new side of you," he said, the words caught low in his throat.

"I'm shameless."

"Then always be shameless," he replied as his lips covered hers again and he drew her hips flush to his. They tasted port upon one another's tongues, and felt the heat of two bodies straining together in the chill of the night—breasts, bellies, knees—until delightful suppression became agony, and he sensibly broke away.

He groaned a little and took in a big gulp of air.

"I am shameless," she whispered against his jaw, the scent of his leather vest and his skin warm in her nostrils.

"No, it's just the port."

"Something remarkable has happened, Noah."

"What?"

"Anxiety. All the while I sat across the table from you, calmly playing Parcheesi, I was worrying that we wouldn't get a moment alone."

"I was anxious, too, because I brought you something."

"What?"

He produced it from his pocket, wrapped in an envelope of velvet. "To make it official."

"A brooch." She withdrew from inside his jacket, took the brooch and held it up as if to catch the starlight. "My betrothal brooch . . ."

"Yes."

"I can't see it."

"Here." He found a wooden match in his pocket and struck it on his bootheel, then held it cupped in his hands. By the meager light she examined the pin. It was shaped like a wishbone with a rose on its left branch.

"A wishbone . . . it's beautiful, Noah." She had begun to shiver.

"And a rose, for love. I know you can't wear it where Addie can see it, but you'll find a hidden place, I'm sure." The match burned short and he shook it out.

"I will. I'll wear it every day. Thank you, Noah."

"You're shivering. You'd better go in before you catch a cold."

"Yes . . . Addie and Robert will be wondering."

"Thank you for the supper."

"Thank you for the brooch . . ." She smiled. "And the port."

He went away several steps, returned and kissed her softly on the mouth.

"I love you, though it still amazes me."

"I love you, too."

Chapter 18

Eight days later, on a Sunday night, Robert and Noah had supper with the Merritt sisters again, setting a precedent for the weeks that followed. The foursome met often after that, to share a meal, or popcorn, play games or visit. Sometimes they had long discussions that lasted late into the night on such varied topics as true happiness; men's right to expectorate on the street; women's revulsion at men who expectorate in the street; the possibility of raising lettuce in the dead of winter using a cold frame; what makes popcorn pop; and the effect of weather upon human emotions. As the winter advanced, their friendship became cemented, taking the edge off the dreary season with its short days and bleak snows.

Meanwhile Sarah's newspaper reported the events of the new year, 1877. In Washington, a new president and vice president took their oaths of office. In Philadelphia, the U.S. Centennial Exhibition closed down. In Minneapolis the state's first telephone switchboard opened at the city hall. In Colorado a naturalist named Martha Maxwell discovered a new species of bird called the Rocky Mountain screech owl, while another woman named Georgianna Shorthouse was sentenced to three years in prison for performing an abortion. Out of New York came the remarkable news that a woman could detect when she was pregnant by keeping careful daily measurements of her neck, which would swell immediately upon her getting in the family way. Electric clocks, run by batteries, invented by a German named Geist, were beginning to appear in American homes. Throughout all of America, trade in cattle hideshad completely replaced that in buffalo hides.

Closer to home, the legislature of Dakota Territory convened in Yankton, the capital, while in Washington the national legislature did the same, their ratification of the Indian Treaty finally and officially opening the

Black Hills to legal white settlement. The inclement weather brought a respite from robberies on the Deadwood Stage Line.

In Deadwood itself offerings at the Langrishe changed weekly. Flour was selling for $30 per hundred. A fellow named Hugh Amos shocked the town by committing suicide, apparently due to loneliness. Another fellow named Schwartz slipped and fell on the boardwalk in front of the Nugget Saloon and sued the owner over his broken arm. Local businessmen were encouraged to spread wood ashes on their boardwalks to prevent such mishaps from occurring. The females of Deadwood were invited to meet at the office of the *Deadwood Chronicle* to form a Ladies' Society whose functions would be both social and charitable.

The formation of such a group had been on Sarah's mind for some time. Not only did the local women need to socialize; by banding together they could have a domesticating influence on the entire gulch. The town needed a library. Until a school was built, children—and adults, as well— needed a source of reading material. What a wonderful head start a library could give their school when it was eventually built. Sarah saw a women's group as the perfect organization to begin collecting and cataloguing books for the cause.

The problem of men spitting on the street was more than aesthetic. Not only did the women's hems trail in the effluvia, it spread disease. Since the smallpox epidemic Sarah had written one editorial about the health hazards engendered by the habit, but she'd seen little improvement. A women's group could work on a campaign to educate the men about hygiene and perhaps make anti-expectorating signs and post them around town.

On the social side, the women might discuss books, read poetry, exchange seeds for their spring gardens, plan Fourth of July celebrations, perhaps invite a temperance advocate to speak.

It was Sarah's hope, too, that she might use the group to inveigle Addie out of the house and into the good graces of the townswomen. However, on the night of the first meeting Addie refused to go.

"I'm not ready yet," she said.

"When will you be?"

"I don't know. Maybe when my hair grows out." Addie's natural blond was beginning to show at the roots.

"If they see you there beside me, in *my* newspaper office, joining a group whose intent is to do charitable work, who'll cast stones?"

But Addie refused to go and the group was formed without her. At their first meeting they avidly embraced Sarah's suggestion and dedicated themselves to their first project: the collection of books for the Deadwood Public Library. Sarah offered to keep the volumes in the *Chronicle* office and put Josh in charge of lending them out until other arrangements could be made.

The ladies agreed with Sarah that when the town found a schoolteacher he would be overjoyed to discover the citizens had been forward-thinking enough to have already established a lending library. They believed, too, that the building of a school should be of primary concern to all of Deadwood, since it would draw more families to the town, come spring.

Yes, they agreed, the school should come first before a church.

In early February, however, a telegram arrived from a man named Birtle

Matheson, who agreed to become Deadwood's minister. He was a Con-
gregationalist and would be arriving in early April.

The news caused a great stir of excitement, not the least of which was
displayed by Noah Campbell, who, upon hearing it, went directly to the
Chronicle office.

"Sarah, can you come with me for a few minutes?"

"Certainly. What's going on?" She got her coat and they headed outside, striding side by side down the boardwalk.

"Deadwood's getting a minister."

She halted in her tracks. "When?"

"The first of April. A fellow named Matheson from Philadelphia. A
telegram just came in this morning."

"Well," she said on a puff of breath, leaving an undecided note in the
air.

"We can set a date now," Noah said.

"But what about Addie?"

"Addie can take care of herself."

"She still refuses to leave the house."

"Then it's time you force her."

"How?" Sarah resumed walking and Noah stayed with her, step for step.

"Stop babying her. Stop delivering everything she needs to her doorstep. Stop going to the butcher shop, and the grocer's, and Emma's every
day for bread. The agreement was that she'd take care of those things for
you, but you've continued to do it all and run the newspaper, too. Does
she even cook?"

"She tries." Addie did try, but her cooking was abysmal.

"Maybe Robert and I have added to the problem by providing just
enough social diversion to keep Addie happy without having to leave the
house. Maybe we should insist on the four of us going to the theater
sometime instead of holing up the way we do."

"I confess, I'd rather hoped that Robert might ask Addie to marry him
and our problem would be solved, but he seems quite content with a
platonic relationship. Has he mentioned anything to you?"

"Nothing. Which brings us back to you and me and setting a date."

Sarah was torn. What would Addie do if forced to live alone?

"I feel a responsibility toward Addie."

"And none toward me?" His voice took on an edge.

"I didn't say that."

"You're not her mother, Sarah."

"No, I'm not. But if she had one, chances are she wouldn't have gone
astray, so who cares about her? Who helps her? Now that I've gotten her
out of Rose's shall I simply abandon her?"

"Living across town isn't exactly abandoning her."

"Living where?"

"I've found us a place."

"You have?"

"Amos's."

"Hugh Amos's?" She came to a stop.

"It's for sale."

"But Noah . . ."

He turned around and went back to her. She wore an expression of
wide-eyed repugnance.

"He didn't kill himself in the house, Sarah, he did it out at his mine."

"I know that, but . . ." Hugh Amos had used his shotgun. Sarah had reported the suicide. How could Noah blame her for balking?

He mulled awhile, looking annoyed. Abruptly he grabbed her hand and ordered sternly, "Come with me." They were three doors from his office. He hauled her to it, took her inside and closed the door behind them. At the rear two new jail cells stood empty. A blue granite coffeepot stood on the chrome fender of a small, oval woodstove. It was warm in the room, and private.

Noah swung around and clamped Sarah by the shoulders. "All right, I want to know the truth. Do you want to marry me or not?"

"It's not that simple."

"Yes, it is that simple. Either you want to or you don't."

"I want to, but—"

"Dammit, Sarah, you find enough reasons to put it off ! You won't tell Addie because she might go back to Rose's. You don't want Amos's house because he shot himself. You won't set a date because we don't have a preacher. Well, now we've got one, and I'm asking you to make it official. I want to set a date and tell my family and tell your sister and get on with our lives."

His insistence left her silent. There were times when she recognized in herself hints of dispassion. If not dispassion, certainly a more controlled passion than his, coupled with a reluctance to commit to all that marriage would entail: the sudden overturning of her life, which had just achieved a satisfying orderliness; sexual submission, which filled her with a certain amount of dread; and along with sexual submission, children, whose arrival would signal the exchange of her leather apron for a cotton one; the end of her newspapering—at which she was very capable—in exchange for daily domesticity, at which she was only minimally capable; the relinquishment of her financial independence, which she also found satisfying.

"Do you love me, Sarah?" he asked, sounding a little hurt and confused. "Because some days I'm really not sure. I know it was a little slow in coming—I realize that. Remember the day I first told you I loved you? I asked if there was any possibility that you loved me too, and do you know what you said? Not I love you, Noah, but, I think there's a very good possibility of it. Well, I think it's time we clarify that matter. Granted, I resisted falling in love with you, too, but now I have and I'm not afraid to say it. I love you, Sarah, and I want to marry you and live with you. I'd like to know if you feel the same way about me."

His eyes were dark with intensity, his voice was earnest as he fixed her with an unwavering gaze that demanded the truth. She did love him in return. She *did*. But she had known him only five months and he had to understand that she had accepted his proposal conditionally; that condition was Addie.

"I do love you, Noah." The worry remained in his eyes. "I do," she whispered, embracing him tightly. "And you're right. I'm not Addie's mother. Sometimes I forget that, but I've grown accustomed to mothering her over the years. Please understand that and give me the time I'm asking for. I have to see some progress in her before I walk out of her life, because no matter what you say about living across town, when I leave that house she'll feel abandoned."

He said nothing, only held her.

"Noah," she told him, "we've only known each other since September. Shouldn't we give ourselves a little more time, too?"

He drew back and studied her eyes. His remained somber. She wondered what he was thinking.

He kissed her, holding her by the upper arms, a tender-sad kiss that made her wish she could concede to his wishes and marry him without delay. Because she could not, she put her arms around his neck and gave him a kiss of apology.

In the middle of it, Freeman Block opened the door and walked in. "Well, what have we here?"

"Get out," Noah ordered, keeping Sarah where she was.

"Do I have to? This looks pretty interesting."

"Dammit, Freeman!"

"You forget, I work here."

"Go work somewhere else for half an hour."

Freeman chuckled. "You and Sarah, huh? I told you, didn't I? The day she bought you that hat, I says, Noah, that gal's got eyes for you."

"Freeman, damn your mangy hide!"

"All right, I'm going."

When the door slammed, Noah sighed and released Sarah. "Well, it won't be a secret anymore."

"Perhaps you're right. Perhaps it's time I tell Addie anyway."

"Against your wishes?"

"Let's call it a compromise. I'm not ready to name a date yet, but I'll wear your brooch where it can be seen. Maybe if Addie knows about my upcoming departure she'll prepare herself for it."

Studying her, Noah thought, *She's always so rational, so in control of every situation. I wish sometime she'd lose that control.*

"Now I really must go back to work, Noah. I'll have to write up the news about the new minister coming."

"Should I walk you back?"

"No, you don't need to."

"Let me know what Addie says when you tell her."

"I will."

He gave her a brief kiss, wishing once again that she felt the same reluctance at parting as he. Wishing just once she would fling her arms around him and declare she would miss him, would give anything if they could spend the rest of the day together, the rest of their lives, starting now. But Little Miss Containment had things to do that were probably of equal importance to her as lollygagging with him, so he had to be content with her brief display of affection and the one promising kiss that had been interrupted by Freeman.

When she was gone, Noah went over to the stove and tipped the coffeepot above a white enamel mug, but only a tablespoon of thick black sludge ran out. He lifted a stove lid and tossed the dregs inside. A plume of smoke rose. A hiss. The smell of charred coffee. He stood a long time staring into the coals.

If she loved him she'd want to marry him, it was as simple as that. He loved her and that's what he wanted to do—speak vows, set up a house, sleep together (lord, yes), have babies. That's how it was done, dammit. He didn't understand loving without being impatient for these things. He didn't understand how she could put her feelings for her sister before her feelings for him. It wasn't enough for Noah that Sarah conceded to wear his betrothal brooch only when forced to by Freeman Block's wagging tongue. She should have been wearing it all along in plain sight because she was so excited she wouldn't consider doing anything else!

But it had never been that way with Sarah.

His mother had a theory that in every marriage there was one who loved more. Well, in his it seemed obvious who that one would be.

He put two sticks of wood in the stove and returned to his desk. Five minutes later he'd done nothing but stare at a bunch of papers.

He needed to talk to somebody.

He chose Robert, that night, at a table in a corner at the Eureka Saloon. It was smoky and loud, and somebody nearby had horse manure on his boots. But in all the noise nobody paid them any mind.

"What do you think of Sarah?" Noah asked Robert.

"Salt of the earth. Honest. Moral. Hard worker. Probably the most intelligent woman I know."

"Probably a damn sight more intelligent than me."

"Hell, Campbell, that wouldn't take much."

They laughed good-naturedly. They could do that now.

Noah tipped his chair back on two legs. He studied Robert from beneath his hat brim. "I'm going to marry her."

Robert's cheeks went flat with surprise, then lifted in a smile. "Well, I'll be damned. You've already asked her?"

"Yup."

"And she said yes?"

"Sort of."

"Sort of?"

Noah's chair came down on all fours. "She's not willing to name a date yet. I've given her a betrothal brooch which she's agreed to wear, though."

Robert set down his beer and gripped Noah's hand. "Congratulations! This is good news."

Noah smiled wryly. "I hope so."

"What's the matter? You don't look very excited."

"Oh, I'm excited. Sarah's the one who's not."

"Well, she said yes, didn't she?"

Noah studied the rim of his beer mug, then leaned forward with an elbow on either side of it.

"She's an odd woman, Robert, totally different than Addie. Sometimes I get the feeling that she's so smart, there's so much going on in her head, so much she wants to *do* that she hasn't got time for marriage. It's the *other* thing she'll do when she finally gets time. Sort of takes the edge off the excitement, if you know what I mean."

Robert took a sip of beer and waited.

"There's a preacher coming to town and I want to get married as soon as he gets here but she's dragging her feet. It's as simple as that."

"Hell, you haven't even known her half a year, and half that time the two of you fought like two roosters slung over a clothesline."

"Yeah, I know." Noah sighed and rubbed the back of his neck. "There's something else."

"I'm listening."

Noah studied his beer mug. Scratched its handle with a thumbnail. Met Robert's eyes.

"I think she's scared to death of being touched."

"I told you she was moral, didn't I?"

"It goes beyond that. It's all mixed up with what Addie was. Sarah says, 'I don't want to be like Addie.' "

"Can you blame her?"

"I don't expect her to be. What I mean is I . . . well, I got carried away once. Just once. I tried something with her and she made it very clear she wasn't that kind of girl. So since then I've been what I believe is called a perfect gentleman. I don't even kiss her very often and half the time she acts like she's scared to death to do that. Now, dammit, Robert, that's not natural. Not when two people are supposed to love each other. Saying goodnight should be torture, that's how I see it."

"Are you sure you love this woman?"

"I think about her day and night. She's driving me nuts!"

"But do you love her?"

"Yes. Against my better judgment, yes."

"Then don't worry about it. Women want a marriage certificate first."

"You want to know something funny?"

"What?"

"I thought for a while it was you she loved."

"Me!"

"I was jealous as hell when you first came to town."

Robert laughed. "No, it was always Addie for me. Sarah and I were just friends."

"So what about you and Addie? You got any plans?"

Robert settled back in his chair, drew a huge breath and blew it out with his cheeks puffed. "Addie's still a mess."

"She's scared as hell to go out of that house, isn't she?"

"Not only that. Believe it or not, I think there are times when she misses the whorehouse."

"Oh Robert, come on."

"I know it sounds ridiculous, but think about it. She lived the life for five years. She made good money. All her needs were taken care of. She didn't have to cook, clean, work, worry. The men loved her. I think she was good at what she did—hell, you'd know about that better than I would."

"She was good."

"And *you're* jealous of *me?*" Robert said wryly.

"That was business, Robert. Nothing but, and I gave that up when I fell for Sarah."

Robert took a long swig of beer, studying Noah over his glass. "It's a damned miracle you and I ever got to be friends, you know that?"

Noah answered with a slow grin. When it passed he asked, "So do you love Addie or what?"

"The truth is, I don't know. I care enough about her to want her to have a decent life, but taking on a woman with her kind of past is scary. It makes you wonder if one man will ever be enough for her. Or if one man is too many. Because the odd thing is, though she might miss the life, she hated it, too. She hated the men all the while she pretended to love them, did you know that?"

Noah had never thought about it before. The idea was mildly shocking.

That night after supper while Sarah and Addie lingered over coffee, Sarah said, "I have something to tell you. I hope it won't upset you."

"Upset me? Is it something bad?"

Sarah's smile dawned and set in rapid succession. "No, it's not bad." She leaned her elbows on the table and said, "Noah has asked me to marry him."

Consternation flitted across Addie's features. At first she said nothing, then rose and went to the stove to get the coffeepot.

With her back to Sarah, she said, "My goodness."

"What do you think, Addie?"

"You and the marshal—I don't know what to think."

"Addie, come here. Sit down."

Addie turned slowly and returned to the table, leaving the coffeepot behind. She sat down on the edge of her chair.

"We haven't set a date yet."

Addie nodded, her eyes fixed on her full cup.

"But a telegram came in today with the news that Deadwood will be getting a minister in early April."

Addie's gaze shot to Sarah. "Early April!"

"I didn't say I was getting married then, I said that's when the minister will get here. But Addie, you must face reality. It will happen sometime and when it does, I'll be going to live with him."

"Why can't you live here?" Addie asked plaintively.

Sarah touched Addie's wrist. "I think you know the answer to that."

"Oh." With the quiet word Addie dropped her gaze. "Then what would I do?" she asked forlornly.

"You would make a life of your own. You must start now, Addie, by leaving this house like a normal person, by going uptown and doing the shopping and seeing people again."

"I had a life of my own, but you and Robert took me out of it," Addie retorted with a sudden burst of anger. "If neither one of you wanted me, why did you make me leave Rose's? I was happy there, can't you understand that?"

"Addie, don't say that."

"I *was!* Happier than I am here being a nothing. I can't cook, I can't write articles, I hate washing clothes and blacking stoves! I'm not even good enough to be Robert's wife, because if I was he would have asked me by now. Instead he treats me like a pet sister. Well, I don't want to be his pet sister and I don't want to be your house slave, so just go ahead and marry the marshal and move wherever you want to!"

Like a petulant child Addie ran from the kitchen, up the steps and slammed her bedroom door.

Sarah remained behind, stunned. Of all the ungrateful, self-indulgent, moronic women in the world, her sister took the prize! Addie couldn't see beyond her narrow concerns to what it was she and Robert had done for her. She wouldn't make an effort to become self-reliant, to become proficient at anything that smacked of hard work. Instead she would blame them for not sacrificing themselves further so she could remain in her ivory tower, disdaining the rest of the world.

Sarah rose and clanked her empty cup into a dishpan. She poured hot water from the teakettle, added cold, began washing their supper dishes with enough vehemence to be heard through the ceiling.

Well, let her sit up there and bawl!

Sarah felt like bawling herself. She loved Addie, had left St. Louis for her, had made the fearful trip out here into the unknown, had set up a business and a home and sprung Addie out of Rose's meat hole and all she got for it was blamed!

Well, so be it.

When the preacher came she'd be the first one married and let Addie run back to Rose's and stay there till the syphilis got her out once and for all!

Of course the anger burnt itself out. By ten o'clock, when each of the two women had listened to the house noises for three hours, when their self-imposed exiles had begun to grow lonely, when antipathy lost its buoyancy and became a burden, Sarah extinguished the kitchen lantern and felt her way up the stairs. They creaked. At the top she paused to study the thin blade of light showing beneath Addie's closed door. Sadly, she turned to her own.

She had just lit her lantern when Addie's door opened and she came to Sarah's doorway, pausing one step inside.

"Sarah?"

Sarah turned.

"I'm sorry. I didn't mean it."

The two exchanged gazes across the quiet room. Sarah rose and the two rushed together to hug.

"Oh Addie . . . I'm sorry, too."

"You didn't do anything wrong. You have every right to marry the marshal, and you should. I'm just scared is all. I don't know what's going to happen to me."

Taking Addie's hand, Sarah led her to the bed and they sat down.

"You'll be fine," Sarah said.

"How? How can I be fine when no man will have me, not even Robert, who loves me? I know he does."

"Have you ever stopped to think, Addie, that Robert may be waiting to see that you *don't* need him before he decides he *does* need you?"

Addie looked puzzled. "That doesn't make any sense."

Sarah took her hand. "What man would want to marry a woman who believes she's better off in a brothel? You've got to show him, Addie. You say you can't do anything, but that's not true. There *are* things you can do. You just don't want to because most of them are hard work and you've never had to work hard before. You live in a town that's ninety-nine-percent men, for heaven's sake! There are dozens of jobs that women do better than men, or that men wouldn't dream of doing for themselves. You could clean their houses, mend their shirts, launder their sheets, cut their hair—I don't know exactly what it is. You're the one who must decide. But I know one thing: there's enough money in this gulch, and enough womenless men, that any woman has a distinct advantage when it comes to business. If you were to open up a shop and a man opened up the same kind right across the street, he'd probably go out of business because you'd get it all."

It was obvious Addie had never pondered the possibility before.

"I'm asking you to use your head, Addie. Stop hiding behind the excuse that you're not as bright as I am and find something you can do better than me. When you find it, my guess is that Robert will pop the question. He didn't break you out of Rose's for nothing."

"You really believe that, Sarah?"

"Yes, I do. Robert loves you as surely as trees are green. He's just waiting for you to become worthy of him."

"Oh Sarah, I love him so much, but he's never even kissed me since the night he took me out of Rose's."

"Give him time. But more importantly, give him a reason to."

Addie's countenance remained sober. After lengthy thought she said, "All right. I'll try."

It seemed there would be a church raising. The next issue of the *Chronicle* announced not only the hiring of the minister, but the fact that lumber was needed, and each mine—and landowner was requested to donate one tree, delivered to the Beaver Creek Sawmill. The mill donated the cutting time to the cause while the butcher shops donated venison to feed the crew. Teddy Ruckner said he would cook it, and the Ladies' Society, which had already held several weekly meetings, volunteered to serve it.

The event was planned for the first weekend in March.

"Are you coming with me tomorrow?" Sarah asked Addie the night before it.

Addie took a deep breath and answered, "Yes."

Sarah smiled. Addie smiled, though not as confidently as her sister.

The day of the church raising dawned clear and warm. As if the project were blessed by some omnipotent force, the chinook winds came over the Rockies and turned winter to spring. The morning temperature was just below freezing, but by noon it had reached the sixties.

Everyone turned out—merchants, miners, men, women, children and one ex-prostitute, wearing a scarf tied backward over her gray and blond hair. When Addie showed up beside Sarah, she brought more than one person up short. Some of the men, after jolts of recognition, mistakenly-greeted, "Hello, Eve," to which she replied, "My name is Addie now." Most of the women stiffened, but out of respect for Sarah offered perfunctory greetings when Addie was introduced. Emma, of course, led the vanguard of acceptance, thumping an arm around Addie's shoulders and ordering, "Come with me. I need someone to help me carry bread over from the bakery."

On their way they ran into Noah, heading toward the church lot dressed in dungarees and a red flannel work shirt, carrying a wooden toolbox.

"Addie!" he exclaimed in surprise. "You're helping today?"

Addie offered a dubious smile. "Sarah talked me into it."

"That's wonderful!" he exclaimed, beaming.

"So you're going to marry my sister."

Emma exclaimed, "What!"

"That's right. Soon, I hope, now that we've got a preacher coming."

"I guess that'll make us relatives."

"I guess so."

"Well, I can stand that if you can."

He laughed. She followed suit, and they stood awhile facing each other in the street, aware that the situation could be awkward if they'd let it, determined they would not let it.

"Congratulations," Addie said.

"Thanks, Addie."

"Why hasn't Sarah told us?" Emma put in.

"It hasn't been official very long. My family doesn't even know yet."

Emma thumped him on the arm. "Well, that's just grand news, Marshal, just grand."

"I think so, too. Well . . . I'd better get up there and lend a hand. I hear hammers pounding already."

They parted, Noah to pitch in with the carpenters, Emma and Addie to get the bread. Upon their return to the church site, Robert found them. He, too, held tools and wore rough work clothing.

"I heard you were here today," he said to Addie. He looked pleased. "You keeping her busy, Emma?"

"You bet. No slackers allowed in Deadwood when there's a church to raise. Where's Sarah?"

"Over there, making coffee."

Emma climbed onto a nail bucket and spied Sarah working with the women while nearby Noah helped the men. Emma formed a megaphone with her hands. "Listen, everybody! Let's get this thing built right, 'cause the first ones married in it's gonna be the marshal and Sarah Merritt!"

Sarah and Noah were separated by fifty feet, but their heads snapped around and their eyes met. The resulting hoorah put color in Sarah's cheeks.

"Noah Campbell, you old sonofagun you!" Somebody banged Noah's shoulder blades.

"Had to throw her in an abandoned mine to get her to say yes though, didn't you, Marshal?"

"And she give him a black eye for it, as I recall!"

"I'd treat you better than that, Sarah! You wouldn't have to give me no black eyes!"

The jovial ribbing went on and on until Sarah spun away to help the women make coffee over the open fire.

At midmorning a wagonload of Spearfish Valley farmers arrived, among them Noah's family. They heard the news before they reached the heart of town. Carrie was the first off the wagon.

"Where's that son of mine? I want to hear it from his own lips!" When she found Noah she bellowed, "Is it true? You marrying that young newspaper gal?"

"It's true, Ma."

"Where is she?" Louder she hollered, "Lead me to my future daughter-in-law!"

The crowd produced Sarah, nudging her forward while Carrie bore down on her from the opposite direction with her son in tow.

"Gal, you've made a mother happy! When's the glorious day?"

"I . . . I'm not sure." Sarah barely got the words out before she was enarmed by Carrie and found herself confronting Noah over her shoulder.

"Well, it can't happen too soon to suit me. I'm just mighty happy about the turn of events. Kirk, Arden, here she is!" She heralded them over. "Here's Sarah! And Noah, too!"

Kirk arrived with Arden trailing. Noah's father gave Sarah a bear hug that nearly popped her spleen. "Well, this is something," he said, "this is certainly something. You have our blessings." He released her and shook Noah's hand. "Congratulations, son."

It was Arden's turn. He tried for a smile but it barely bent his lips. "You broke my heart, Sarah," he said, kissing her cheek. "I asked you first."

He did the correct thing, however, with Noah: shook his hand and said for the whole town to hear, "I guess the best man won."

Noah and Sarah found no privacy until sometime later when she came by offering him a cup of coffee. He held a cup while she poured.

"I guess everybody knows now." His statement assumed the unasked question, *And what do you think of that, Sarah?*

She righted the coffeepot, gave him a smile and caught him by surprise by saying, "Then I guess it's time we set a date."

The church went up with the grace and precision of a staged dance. The floor first. Then one wall, and another and two more, followed by the roof joists, white as bone china. On the ground an eight-man crew was designing a belfry with a pointed steeple. At another station a crew was building a pair of matched doors. Nearby some older men were riving shingles while the children bundled them twenty to a pack and tied them with twine for easy lifting up to the rafters. Soon the carpenters appeared in silhouette against the blue March sky, balancing on the skeletal building, plying braces and bits and joining the sturdy structure with pegs. Meanwhile the women kept the coffee coming.

At noon the venison was carved over the open pit where it had cooked, and served with fresh bread, baked beans and corn cakes at tables made of planks and sawhorses. Afterward, the women worked on the cleanup while the men returned to their labors. In the late afternoon, with the structure framed and enclosed, the belfry was hoisted up and set in place to the accompaniment of cheers. At suppertime platters of cold venison sandwiches appeared, accompanied by more hot coffee and dried-apple pies.

At twilight the tools were stored for the night, lanterns came out and a keg of beer was tapped. Someone produced a fiddle, someone else a mouth organ, and an impromptu dance began on the fragrant, freshly milled floor of the church. Every woman was pressed into service as a partner, but still there weren't enough. A number of good-natured men played the parts of women by appropriating the ladies' aprons and tying them on while dancing to "Turkey in the Straw" with partners of their own gender.

There was much laughter and camaraderie. No females were allowed to play favorites, but were whirled and swirled from one man to the next.

Passing through Arden's arms, Sarah heard, "If he doesn't treat you right, you know where to come!"

Passing through Noah's, she heard, "I'm going to walk you home when this is over."

Only one clinker spoiled the night. When Addie was reeling from the dance floor, breathless, at the end of a number, she was confronted by Mrs. Roundtree, who hissed in an undertone, "You have your nerve, mixing with honest, God-fearing folks in *this* building. Go back to the whorehouse where you belong!"

Sarah overheard and rounded on the woman. "Do you call yourself a Christian!"

Robert found Addie later, outside, standing apart from the others, staring into the bonfire, which still burned.

"What's the matter? Why did you leave the dance?"

"There are some who don't want me there."

"Who?"

"It doesn't matter."

"Who?"

She refused to answer.

"Did one of the men say something?"

"No, one of the women."

"The women will be harder on you than the men. It'll take some time."

"I can't say I wasn't expecting this. It just hurts a little more than I thought."

"So are you going to knuckle under and hide in your house again?"

She looked up into his face, which was illuminated by the shifting firelight. "No. I'll be back tomorrow to finish what we started."

He smiled and said, "Atta girl, Addie. Come on, I'll walk you home."

The dancing was short-lived: everyone was tired; they'd worked hard today. No beer was allowed inside the church, and the single keg that had been tapped emptied fast. The Spearfish Valley folks went home. Those with children had packed them off to bed. Robert and Addie had disappeared. Noah took Sarah's hand and repeated Robert's words. "Come on, I'll walk you home."

They climbed the steep hill where the day's melt-off was still gurgling downhill. A half-moon had risen and rimed the gulch with silver. The night had the raw-earth smell of near-spring. Below, the new church steeple and rafters stood out like a drawing on a blackboard.

Between Sarah and Noah, everything had changed. Everyone knew. Soon the church would be complete and there would be a minister. Sarah had said she'd name a date.

Neither of them spoke until they reached her doorstep. Noah took both her hands and said a single word. "When?"

She'd expected the question and had prepared an answer on her way up the hill.

"How about the first Saturday in June?"

His grip tightened on her hands. In the moonlight she made out his swift smile.

"You mean it, Sarah?"

"Yes, I mean it, Noah."

He kissed her in jubilation. Then in speculation, the mood changing as he angled his head and opened his mouth. He drew back, sent a silent message into her eyes and lowered his open mouth to hers once more. She moved against him and opened hers, too, and felt ardor dawn as a wondrous, impulsive force. It fed upon itself and gave way to outright temptation, fueled by the touch of his tongue upon hers and the caress of his hands on her back, her ribs, her breasts. She shuddered once in pleasure, amazed that it should be so, that she could allow the intimacy and revel in it. How different it felt, sanctioned almost, by their plans to be married in a mere three months.

But when his hands moved to her throat as if to free buttons, she halted them.

"No, Noah, we mustn't."

They stood in the grip of the silent impasse with his hands detained by hers. She folded his much longer hands between hers and kissed his fingertips.

"Not because I don't want to," she whispered.

He relented, releasing an unsteady breath against her face.

"I won't apologize this time."

"There's no need to," she replied, and for the first time said the words without prompting.

"I love you, Noah."

Chapter 19

There was one thing Addie had done since leaving Rose's that had brought her both pride and pleasure: making the curtains. A service with questionable potential, curtain-making, but one she could, in spite of her limited sewing skills, perform with a degree of self-confidence. Why wouldn't it succeed? The womenless men of Deadwood Gulch lived in bare-bones houses, lacking the time and know-how to dress them up. Might they not pay someone else to do so for them? Furthermore, everyone in town was predicting a deluge of settlers when spring came, prompted by the continued excellence of the gold prospect, the presence of the telegraph, daily stagecoach service and now the church, with a school sure to follow by autumn. Deadwood had all the earmarks of a boomtown destined to live on. When the ladies started flooding in, Addie's Window Dressings would be there waiting for them.

From Mr. Farnum's suppliers of yard goods and sundries she ordered a selection of ginghams, poplins and calicos, braiding, tassles and lace. They arrived on True Blevins' first ox train in late March, along with twenty other carts loaded to the heckboards with everything from ice boxes to windowglass to a twenty-four-inch-diameter brass bell for the First Congregational Church of Deadwood. Addie placed an advertisement in the *Deadwood Chronicle:* "Fine quality, hand-stitched curtains made to order for your windows from my large supply of material and trimmings. See Miss A. Merritt, Mt. Moriah Road."

Her first customer was the future Mrs. Noah Campbell, who ordered curtains made for the house she would occupy with her husband, come June.

Her second was the Reverend Birtle Matheson, who arrived by stagecoach in early April.

Addie had finally decided to join the Ladies' Society, who took it upon themselves to outfit the log house and have it all homey when the new minister arrived. They scrubbed and cleaned it, polished its windows, blacked its stove and wove rugs for its floor. Addie, meanwhile, had volunteered to make the curtains.

She got the flu, however, which lasted two days and put her under the weather. By the time she felt well again and completed the curtains, the Reverend Matheson was already installed in his house.

The day she delivered them it was feeling like spring. The sun was bright and the air was filled with the scent of rain-washed pine from the previous night. It was warm enough to leave her coat behind and wear only a fringed shawl over her blue dress. She packed the new curtains into a basket, along with a hammer, hooks and a cluster of dowels to use as curtain rods.

She knocked on the door of the parsonage, expecting a middle-aged man to answer. Instead, the door was opened by a man only a few years older than herself. He wore brown trousers and a white shirt, open at the throat, with the sleeves rolled to midarm. He had attractive eyes, beautiful wavy hair the color of cherry wood and, overall, a set of unexpectedly handsome features.

"Reverend Matheson?" she inquired.

"Yes." He smiled, showing perfect teeth.

"I'm Adelaide Merritt. I'm a member of the Ladies' Society and I've brought the curtains for your house."

"Miss Merritt, come in." He reached out and shook her hand, then drew her up the last step and over his threshold. His door faced south. He pushed it back against the wall, letting the sun flood his front room. He hitched his hands onto his hipbones and stood regarding her in the comfortable, wide stance. "What a beautiful day. And what a beautiful surprise!" She had the startling impression he was not speaking only of the curtains in her basket. He smiled at her with his whole face, raining upon her the considerable force of his attention.

His youth came as a shock. Perhaps it was his name—Birtle—that had led her to believe he'd be old, a widower perhaps, for they'd been forewarned he had no wife. Addie had asked Sarah, who'd already met him, what he was like, but Sarah had only said he was a very nice-looking man.

He was all that and more as he stood before Addie alert and attentive with no cleric collar in sight.

"Curtains, you say?"

"Yes. I've started a business making them, and I volunteered to make yours. I'm sorry they weren't up when you got here, but I had the flu."

"The flu . . . I'm sorry. You're feeling better, I hope."

"Yes. Much."

He smiled at her long enough to make her uncomfortable, then moved abruptly, as if just remembering he hadn't done so for a while.

"Well, come in. Let's have a look." He took the basket from her hands and set it on a square table. "Show me what you've made."

While she took them from the basket he said, "You must let me pay you."

"Oh no, it's my contribution. I'm not much of a cook, so I didn't bring any cakes. And I don't care much for rug-making so I didn't help with those, but curtains I'm getting a little familiar with. I've also brought some things to hang them with."

The curtains were of broadcloth, white on white, with a design of ivy leaves woven within vertical stripes. "The white will show the soot more than a color would, so they'll have to be washed regularly, but this cabin is rather dark. I thought it could use brightening up.''

"Indeed, it can, Miss Merritt. It is *Miss* Merritt, isn't it?''

Her glance returned to his Mediterranean-blue eyes. "It's Miss,'' she answered, and his smile unabashedly doubled in candlepower.

"Miss Merritt,'' he repeated. A lull followed, charged with his attention and her discomfort at being its object. "Well!'' He clapped his hands once and rubbed them together. "Can I help you hang them?''

It was one of the most bizarre hours of her life. Birtle Matheson acted like no minister she'd ever imagined. He took her shawl and folded it over the back of a chair. In his rolled-up shirtsleeves he stood on a chair and drove the hooks into the window frames where she told him to. He conversed in loquacious fashion, punctuating his speeches with frequent laughter, asking her a hundred questions about herself and the town, supplying information about himself. He was fresh out of the seminary and determined to do well in this his first assignment. His father was a minister in Pennsylvania, his mother was dead—her maiden name had been Birtle—and he had two sisters back east, both older and married. He had once had ringworm and lost half his hair and promised God that if he'd just let it grow back, he would follow in his father's footsteps and become a minister. He had answered the Deadwood advertisement because he saw it as an opportunity to build a church from the ground up and form a strong bond with his congregation. He liked to fish, read Dickens, sing and watch sunsets.

"You won't be able to watch sunsets here,'' she told him.

"Of course I can. They just happen a little earlier.''

He had a contagious optimism and when he rested his unsettling eyes on her she found it difficult to look away.

"Perhaps sometime we can watch one together,'' he suggested, again facing her directly with his hands on his hips.

"I don't think so.'' She handed him a curtain shirred on a dowel.

He stepped onto the chair, hung it and stepped down, resuming his forthright stance—a stance with which she was rapidly becoming familiar. "Why not?''

"Ask anyone in town,'' she replied, turning away, heading to retrieve her basket and shawl now that the last curtain was hung.

He followed, said at her shoulder, "I've been unpardonably rash. Forgive me, Miss Merritt. Now you're running away.''

She flipped her shawl around her shoulders, put her hammer in the basket, the basket over her arm and turned to face him.

"You're forgiven,'' she said. "And I'm not running away. The curtains are all up. I must be going now.''

"You're sure you're not running?''

She was, but lied. "I'm sure.''

"All right. Then thank you, Miss Merritt,'' he said, detaining her by offering his hand for shaking. She obliged. He squeezed her hand hard, his smile entering her eyes like rays of blue sun. "Will I see you tomorrow at services?''

"Yes, I'll be, there.''

"Till tomorrow, then.''

She went away feeling stunned. A minister! And a bold, young, attractive one at that. It had been so long since an ordinary man had shown an interest in her. It felt very good, being admired and wooed, exchanging repartee with a man the way young people were supposed to. It was a part of life she'd missed. Of course, he had no way of knowing her past. He'd find out soon enough.

The following morning, Sarah and Addie attended church with Noah and Robert, a prearranged plan. When they arrived, Reverend Matheson was standing out in front shaking hands with his new congregation.

"Ahh, Miss Merritt," he said, shaking Sarah's hand first, recalling her from earlier. Likewise Noah, whom he greeted by name. "Soon to be my first nuptials. How nice to see you here together." They moved on. "And the other Miss Merritt, who brightened my house yesterday." There was no denying he retained his hold longest on Addie's hand, and his smile was specially bright and steadfast upon her. In his black suit and white cleric collar he was an eye-catching sight. The sun radiated off his auburn hair and his perfect teeth. "The curtains add a real touch of hominess. Thank you again."

"You're welcome."

Behind Addie, Robert observed, feeling a riffle of annoyance at the man's undisguised interest in her.

"I thought perhaps one day soon I might call on you and your sister, pay an official greeting, as it were, on the founders of the women's group, which I'm sure will play an important role in both the charitable and social future of our church."

"Sarah founded it, I didn't."

"Have I your permission nonetheless?" he inquired.

"Yes, of course. We'd be happy to receive you. May I introduce you to our friend Robert Baysinger?"

Matheson shook Robert's hand firmly and offered a smile, but Robert's smile was a veneer, short-lived, scarcely touching his eyes.

"Reverend Matheson," he said.

When they moved on, Robert spoke quietly at Addie's ear. "Seems you've made an impression on our new minister."

"All I've made, Robert, are his new curtains." They entered the church at that moment, cutting off the possibility of further exchange.

Matheson gave a thumping, exuberant speech—hardly a sermon—thanking the town for their rousing welcome, Mr. Pinkney for the donation of the land, the men for the spanking new church, the women of the Ladies' Society for his comfortable house, and especially Miss Adelaide Merritt for his new curtains. He gave a thumbnail sketch of himself, gaining a round of laughter (from everyone except Robert Baysinger) when he told the story of how he was drawn to the ministry by a case of ringworm. He announced plans to begin a children's Bible study class immediately, and to visit the homes of the townspeople and even venture out to the mines to personally invite those outside the town limits to join the parish. He invited the Ladies' Society to affiliate themselves with the church and use it for their meetings. He announced a hymn, then led all in a voice so true and enthusiastic, the combined chorus fairly loosened the pegs holding the building together.

After services, Matheson again took up his post at the church door. Robert, however, steered Addie around him without pausing.

She pulled her elbow free and remarked, "Robert, how rude!"

"You keep away from that man!" Robert ordered.

"Ro-*bert!*" Indignant, Addie drew to a halt. "He's a man of the cloth! And furthermore, I don't take orders from you!"

Robert appropriated her arm and forced her on. "Keep walking, Addie. People are staring."

"I don't doubt it, with you storming out of church and giving the minister the cold shoulder on his first Sunday in town! Let me go! I'll walk on my own."

She did. All the way home. While Robert stalked along beside her, glowering. When they reached the house she stopped on the doorstep and turned to him, plainly to prevent him from following her inside. "I don't like your proprietary attitude, Robert. Thank you for walking me home, but you don't need to do that anymore either if you can't be civil to the people who are civil to me."

She turned and entered the house, leaving him simmering on the step. He spun and marched down the hill, meeting Sarah and Noah coming up.

"Robert?" Noah said as the other man strode past with a stormy expression on his face. "Hey, Robert, what's wrong?"

Robert spun around and ordered Sarah, "Tell your sister, *Fine!* If that's the way she wants it, that's fine by me!"

Executing a brisk about-face, he stalked away.

Sarah gaped at Noah. "What do you suppose that was all about?"

"Probably the new minister. He seems a little moonstruck by Addie."

Birtle Matheson came to call that very afternoon. Addie answered his knock and had difficulty hiding her shock. "Why, Reverend Matheson!" He was dressed in his black suit with the white cleric collar. His eyes were quite as blue as the sky behind him, and his eyelashes were the kind that make old ladies say, he should have been a girl.

"It was a little lonely in my house all alone. I hope you don't mind that I came unannounced."

"No, not at all."

"May I come in?"

"Sarah's not home. She and Noah have gone over to their house to do some cleaning."

"Perhaps we could walk then."

"Walk?" Wouldn't Mrs. Roundtree have a field day with the news that Eve, the ex-prostitute, had spent her Sunday afternoon walking with the new Congregational minister?

"It's a lovely day." He squinted at the sun. "Feels like spring. I think I heard some peepers down by the creek." He transferred his most convincing smile to her.

"I think not," she answered.

"Why?"

"It wouldn't be good for you."

"Let me be the judge of that."

"Please, Reverend Matheson, I cannot walk out with you."

"Because you used to work at Rose's?"

Addie's face paled. She stood stalk-still, waiting for the blush that was sure to follow. Not a reply came to mind.

Birtle Matheson put his hands on his hips, caught one shoe on the threshold. "I did some inquiring after your remark yesterday afternoon."

"Then you know how inappropriate it would be for the two of us to be seen together."

"Not at all. Judge not, lest ye be judged."

She studied him in amazement. "You're crazy," she whispered.

"I think you're a very pretty lady, Adelaide Merritt, and you're single, and I'm single, and it's a beautiful spring day and I should very much like to take you for a walk. Now what's crazy about that?"

She stared at him, speechless. She no longer thought of herself as pretty. When she looked in a mirror she saw an ex-prostitute who'd known for years she was fat, who had shorn her hair to an unfashionably short boyish cap of blond curls to get rid of the last of the gray, who wore high-collared plain dresses and could not get the man she loved to propose marriage.

When Birtle Matheson looked at her he saw a woman whose white-blond hair puffed around her face in the unspoiled, slightly curled fashion of a child's. He saw a woman who had been eating her own terrible cooking for four months and had trimmed to an attractive silhouette. He saw clear skin, clear eyes, and clear amazement that he should find her attractive, the latter which attracted him even as much as her considerable physical attributes.

"A simple walk," he reiterated.

They went on a walk, heading away from town, following the creek for a while, then heading into the woods, over hills and along tributaries swollen with melted snows, where wild creatures were nesting in the banks and willow branches had turned brilliant red in preparation for leafing. They spoke about the town, its people, the haunting Christmas triangle concert, about Sarah and Noah and their rocky beginning, about nature, the possibility of there being trout in the mountain streams. They sat on a sandstone outcropping in the pleasant afternoon sun and watched a water ouzel walk underwater as it fed. Birtle said, "Tell me about this Mr. Baysinger who accompanied you to church this morning."

She told him, "Robert is our friend from back home. I've loved him since I was a girl."

Birtle remained silent a long time. Somewhere in the trees behind them a chipmunk clucked. "All right," he said at length. "Now I know what I'm up against."

Meanwhile, Noah and Sarah were busy at the house they would share as husband and wife. In the yard, Noah knelt, running a brush through the black stovepipe while a black-billed magpie looked on and cocked his head in curiosity, then rose in a flash of white to a better vantage point. Above him, Sarah finished washing an upstairs window, lifted it and knelt with her elbows propped on the low ledge, looking down on Noah. She was dressed in a brown muslin skirt, a white blouse with the sleeves rolled up and a bibbed apron.

Noah sat back on his heels and looked up. "All done?" he asked.

"With the windows. But I'd like to turn the mattress over."

"Hold on till I finish this and I'll be right there."

He went back to work while she remained at the sill in the warm sun, watching the magpie, who was soon joined by another; smelling spring lifting from the warming earth; glancing off toward Elizabethtown where the willow trees looked swollen with buds. She turned her gaze on Noah, watching his russet head bent over his work, his shoulders flexing as he plied the brush and lifted the pipe to peer inside. He set it down, got to his feet and washed his hands in an enamel bucket, dried them on a rag from his hind pocket and entered the back door.

She heard him come up the stairs and rose from her knees.

"Here I am," he said, coming around the corner into the room. "Let's turn that mattress." He wedged between the bed and the wall and together they flipped the mattress end over end.

"Feels heavy as a bag of oats," he said.

"Cotton batting," she explained, leaning over to whack at the rope marks on the blue and white ticking.

He circled the foot of the bed and stood behind her. "We'll need sheets and blankets."

"I'll take care of that." She whacked the mattress again.

"And pillows."

Whack! Whack! "I'll take care of those, too."

He glanced down at her backside while she thumped the mattress and made her skirts stir. "And a coverlet."

She glanced back over her shoulder and quickly straightened. "Noah," she reprimanded.

He looked up and grinned. "On the other hand, who needs sheets and blankets and pillows."

She was on her back beneath him so fast the mattress bounced. Dust motes rose around them. Outside, the magpies chattered quietly while inside all was still. His eyes, above hers, were dark with mischief that slowly faded, replaced by a certain kindling as he braced on his elbows and considered her facial features in turn—eyes, nose . . . mouth.

"Noah, we—"

"For once, Sarah, don't say it. I know what the rules are."

He leaned down and kissed her once, lightly, an unhurried sample and warning before lifting his head to meet her eyes briefly. Dipping down again, he toyed with her lips, nipping first one, then the other, leaving touches of dampness and the faint whisk of his mustache before settling, eventually, at an angle, kissing her with deliberate voluptuousness.

In time he raised his head and let their gazes meet while his fingertips grazed her neck and they considered where this could lead. Where it must not lead. Her lips were open and wet and she was breathing fast. The next kiss was unrestrained, his mouth wide and his arms surrounding her as he rolled them to their sides. He kissed her as if there were no rules. Kissed her the way young swains have been kissing their maidens in springtime since there has been a springtime. Kissed her until they felt like the buds on the willows outside.

It became an ardent battle, each of them fighting for a fuller, wetter, warmer fit. With their mouths locked, he found her breast within her blouse and apron bib. He caressed and reshaped it, raising a pleasured sound in her throat. He pressed a knee high within her skirts and went on petting her until petting would no longer suffice. The ropes gave a single creak as he fit their bodies together and held her with an arm across her spine. They stopped kissing and lay entwined, breathing on one another's faces in labored puffs.

Finally they fell apart, distancing themselves enough to regain composure.

"Oh Noah," she whispered, "you make it so difficult."

"Do I?"

"Oh yes."

"It's never seemed difficult for you before."

"It's difficult today."

He smiled and touched her chin. "That's what I've been waiting to hear."

They lay awhile, enjoying each other's eyes, the warmth of the sun as it crept another inch up their bodies, the simple linking of their hands between them. Once she touched his mustache. Once he tucked a strand of hair back from her temple.

Finally they fell to their backs, hands upthrown, and studied their ceiling.

He rolled his head to look at her. "I'd better get that stovepipe back inside," he said.

"And I'd better get some sheets on this bed."

They smiled and he sat up and tugged her after him.

The Reverend Birtle Matheson's immediate pursuit of Addie Merritt had the town buzzing. Everywhere Robert Baysinger went, he heard murmurings behind his back or was asked outright questions about it: "Is it true he's sparking her? What's between you and Addie? Folks figured the two of you for a pair after you took her out of Rose's. Doesn't seem right, a minister and a soiled dove."

His hackles rose at each new comment he heard. He grew irascible with the world. At the stamp mill the men remarked grouchily that the boss must've breathed too much mercury vapor and it had poisoned his system. Robert even snapped at Noah one noon when they were eating dinner at Teddy Ruckner's together and Noah mentioned, "I heard Matheson's planning some kind of spring fair to raise funds for hymnals and pews."

Robert thumped a fist on the table and barked, "Goddammit, Noah, do I have to hear that man's name everywhere I go?"

Taken aback, Noah replied cautiously, "Sorry, Robert. It was just an innocent remark."

"Well, *don't* make any more innocent remarks, not about Matheson! He's nothing but a goddamned lecher!"

Noah waited a while, ate a hunk of venison chop, drank some coffee, cut another piece of meat, watched Robert chew his as if it wasn't dead yet.

At length Noah took another swallow of coffee and asked, "How long since you've seen Addie?"

"What business is it of yours?"

"How long?"

Robert glared at Noah and said, "Three and a half weeks."

"Three and a half weeks." Noah paused. "You gotten any smarter?"

Robert's eyes flashed to his friend's. He threw down his fork. He pointed a finger. "Listen, Campbell, I don't need any lip from you!"

Noah affected an expression of righteous astonishment. "You need it from somebody! Everybody in town is talking about how you're growling at them when they so much as say hello on the street. Half the men at the mill are ready to quit because you've been such a damned bear to live with. I'm ready to kick your ass clear up to your armpits. Don't you know what's wrong with you, Robert? You're in love with Addie.''

Robert stared at him.

"You've been in love with her since you were fifteen years old, and you're so damned scared to admit it you're willing to let Matheson sashay into town and sweep her off her feet, and never go banging on her door to call a halt to it.''

"She told me not to bother her anymore.''

"Hell yes, she did, after you acted like a horse's ass that first Sunday Matheson was in town. Why do you think she did that?''

"How am I supposed to know? Who the hell can figure out the woman?''

"You don't suppose she was trying to scare you into something, do you?''

"Noah, she told me point-blank she didn't want to see me anymore.''

Noah threw up his hands. "You're so damned ignorant. Open your eyes, man! The woman loves you!''

Robert glowered while Noah preached on.

"Why do you think she left Rose's? Why do you think she let her hair go blond? Why do you think she started sewing curtains and joined the Ladies' Society and became respectable again? To be worthy of you, only you're so dim you can't see it. Have you got any idea how much courage it took her to do any one of those things in this town? Everywhere she goes she runs into men she's been in bed with and women who know it, but she's willing to face them down and say, that's over, I'm changed, I want a decent life now. So are you going to let her have it or what?''

"I think she wants it with Matheson.''

"Bullshit.'' Noah threw down his napkin. "But if you're not careful, she will, because that man's showing her some fevered pursuit, and her head's likely to be turned by it sooner or later. Especially given the fact that he's the minister. Why, can you imagine what a victory it would be for a woman like Addie to marry such a man after what she was? She could thumb her nose at the entire town.''

"Addie wouldn't thumb her nose at anybody. She's not that kind.''

"There! You see? See how well you know her? See how you jump to her defense?''

Robert thought awhile, then shook his head. "I don't know, Noah. She dropped me flatter than a stove lid the minute she laid eyes on him. That hurts.''

"Well, maybe it does. Maybe she hurts, too, you ever thought about that?''

When Robert refused to answer, Noah leaned forward, resting his forearms on the edge of the table. "Remember once I told you I was jealous because I thought there was something between you and Sarah? Do you remember what you said? You said it had always been Addie for you. So put your claim on her, man. What are you waiting for?''

Robert slept little that night. He thought about Noah's words. He thought about how pretty Addie looked with her hair back to its natural color, and how slim she'd gotten since she'd left Rose's, and how she dressed as normal as any housewife, and how she'd overcome her fear of leaving the house, and had started up a perfectly respectable business.

What man wouldn't sit up and look twice?

Noah was right. If he didn't move fast he was going to lose her, and the idea was unthinkable!

The following afternoon at quarter to four Robert stood before the shaving mirror in his room at the Grand Central Hotel. He had just returned from the bathhouse and Farnum's store. Every garment on his body was brand spanking new. His beard and mustache were neatly trimmed. His hair was slick as an otter's. He smelled like geranium vegetal.

He used a sharp-toothed comb on his beard, mustache and eyebrows. His mustache again. He dropped the comb, tugged at his waistcoat, frowned at his reflection, drew a great breath, blew it out, adjusted his new lapels, his starched wingtip collar, his gray and maroon paisley tie and finally dropped his hands to his sides.

Go ask her, Robert. Before that preacher does.

He donned his beaver bowler, left his cane but took a clump of blue flag—wild iris—out of a glass of water and left the room.

Outside it was one of those balmy days that come along maybe twice in a springtime, the kind you wish you could bottle and keep, so still a man could hear his own whiskers growing, so perfectly temperate it was hard to resist flopping down beneath a tree and looking for pictures in the clouds.

He'd chosen the time carefully—four o'clock when Sarah would still be at the newspaper office and Addie would have the bulk of her day's work done.

On his way up the hill he rehearsed what he would say.

Hello, Addie, you look lovely today. How perfectly transparent. He'd have to do better than that.

I've come to apologize, Addie, and to say you've been brave and wonderful and I've been a perfect fool. No, that sounded silly.

Hello, Addie. I've come to see if you'll go for a walk with me. (She must love walks; she'd been taking enough of them with that preacher!) But he didn't want to run the risk of being interrupted by people, so a walk wouldn't do.

Hello, Addie. I've brought you some wild irises. The men found them up in the creek this morning.

The door was wide open when he approached it, with sunlight angling across the floor inside. He could smell supper cooking but not a sound came from inside. He knocked and waited with his heart in his throat.

He heard chair legs scrape and in moments her footsteps approaching on the pine floor.

After all the rehearsal, upon seeing her again the prepared words fled.

She appeared before him wearing a blue and white striped skirt and solid blue shirtwaist with a high white collar and deep starched cuffs, also of white. Over this she wore a white bibbed apron tied at the back, with some fancy stitching across the bib and pocket. On her right middle finger she had a silver thimble. Her white-blond hair curled softly around her face, only a finger-length long. Her face was thinner and her curves had returned, accented by the waistband of the apron and the gentle swell of the bib above. She stopped on the threshold and stood very still.

"Hello, Robert," she said quietly.

He removed his hat. "H——" He cleared his throat and tried again. "Hello, Addie." The words sounded wheezy and unnatural.

She waited without fidgeting. Her skin was very fair. It was easy to see the faint blush that rose to her cheeks. Ruler came padding from somewhere and sat down in the sun to look up at the two of them.

"What are you doing here?" she asked.

"I came to see you," he replied stupidly.

"Yes, I see that. Is there something you wanted?" She was so calm, so quiet-spoken.

"Yes, to apologize, first of all."

"There's no need to apologize."

"The last time I saw you I was very upset. I was rude to the minister and sharp with you. I'm sorry."

"You're forgiven."

He stood in the spring sun, she in the shadow of the doorframe with the sun slicing across her right shoulder and down her skirts. Seconds ticked by and neither of them said anything.

Finally she glanced down. "Are those for me?"

"Oh . . . yes!" He handed her the flowers. The stems were crushed. His palm was green. "From up in the stream above the mill. They grow wild up there."

"Thank you. They're very beautiful." She lowered her face to smell them while he watched the sun glance over her shining hair for a second. When she lifted her head her upper body again retreated to full shadow. "I should put them in water. Come in, Robert." She turned and walked sedately away.

He followed, feeling callow and earnest and wistful, past two patches of sunlight that fell through her curtained windows, into the kitchen, where her stitchwork was lying on the bare table beside a pincushion and a cup half-filled with coffee. Ruler watched them go, then padded slowly after them and took up a post near the range. Addie poured a dipperful of water into a clear glass and put the irises in it and brought them to the table.

"Sit down, Robert. Can I get you some coffee?"

"No. No coffee."

He sat and she sat, at right angles. He laid his hat on the table beside her closework. A fly came in and landed on the edge of her cup and she waved it away, again with the collectedness he found so terrifying. After a vast silence he asked, "How have you been, Addie?"

Their eyes met. "Fine . . . just fine. Busy. I've gotten a lot of orders."

"Good."

"Yes, it is. Better than I ever imagined. Would you mind if I keep sewing while we talk?"

"No, go right ahead."

She picked up her work, draped it across her lap and began stitching. So calm, so remote, so indifferent it made a lump form in his throat. She was treating him exactly the way he'd treated her since she'd lived in this house. How stupid he'd been!

"You look very good."

Her eyes flashed up, returned to her work. Stitch. Stitch.

Good? She looked incredible. She made the flowers look garish, the sunlight wan. He couldn't peel his gaze off her.

"Are you still seeing the minister?"

"I have been, yes."

"Do you have feelings for him?"

She gave him another glance, the duration of one stitch, then dropped her eyes. "I consider that private, Robert."

"What I mean to say is . . ."

Stitch. Stitch. Her needle went on tunneling.

"What I mean to say is, do you have any feelings for me?"

She stopped stitching. Her eyes remained downcast. The needle moved on.

"I've always had feelings for you, Robert."

"Then would you . . ." He reached over and covered her right hand to stop it. "Would you look at me, Addie?"

She wouldn't. He waited several seconds, but she wouldn't. He left his chair, removing the work from her hands, placing it on the table before going down on one knee beside her chair. He took both her hands and looked up at her beautiful, pale face.

"Addie, I came here today to tell you I love you. I've loved you for so long, I don't remember a time when it wasn't true."

She lifted her beloved green eyes. They were brimming.

"You do?"

"Yes. And I want to marry you."

She swallowed once, trying very hard to hold her tears in check. "Oh Robert," she whispered, "what took you so long?"

Their reunion was swift and fierce. He caught her hard against him, so hard the impact sent her tears spilling. Her arms doubled around his neck and for a moment they merely clung, their eyes closed, his bearded cheek pressed against her pale jaw. At length he drew back and lifted his face to kiss her, kneeling yet with his trousers lost in the folds of her white apron. She held his face in both her hands, forgetting she still wore the thimble on one of them. What a long, long, long-awaited kiss, flavored of coffee and geranium vegetal, open and wet and tempered by all those years, and all that history that had brought them to this moment of truth. When the kiss ended he laid his face against her apron bib and breathed, "Oh Addie, I love you so much. I've been so miserable these last three weeks."

"So have I." She continued caressing the back of his head, his neck, his shoulders, while he pressed kisses wherever his lips touched her starched clothing. "I thought I'd have to marry him to finally get you to realize you loved me."

"You've known it?" He drew back to see her eyes.

She nodded, stroking his hair back from his temples, the expression in her eyes loving and uncomplicated for one of the first times in their lives. "For quite some time."

"Noah gave me a good talking-to yesterday. He told me I was going to lose you if I didn't pull my head out of the sand."

"Hooray for Noah," she replied softly.

They kissed once more, Robert still kneeling while Addie's palms covered his silken beard. They tasted each other shallow and deep, letting time drift by unheeded. When the kiss ended he remained for a while with his forehead against her chin, her left hand softly skimming his shoulders while he held her right and discovered the thimble still on it.

He sat back and looked down at it, fitting and refitting the thimble on the tip of her finger.

Finally he looked up into her eyes. "You haven't said you love me."

"But I do."

"I want to hear you say it."

"Oh Robert, in all my life I've never loved another man but you."

"Then you'll marry me?"

"Of course."

"Even though Birtle Matheson will have to perform the ceremony?"

"Even though."

"He won't like it."

"He knew all along how I felt about you. I told him the very first day he took me out walking that I loved you."

"You did?"

She nodded, lifting one hand to sculpt the hair above his right ear, following its contour with her fingertips while his face was lifted to receive the love in her gaze.

"We've come through some hell to get here, haven't we, Addie?"

"That's all over now." She kissed him as if to promise only heaven ahead, leaning down and slanting her mouth over his, running her palms over the scratchy new wool covering his back. He rose, drawing her to her feet, fitting their hips together and holding her close while his head tipped and their open mouths joined. He made a sound, throaty and passionate, an ode to the end of their separateness while he locked her ever tighter to his mouth and body.

The thimble dropped to the floor. Ruler shot out from beside the stove and batted it against a chair leg while above her the man and woman went on kissing. On and on the thimble rolled—across the bare floor, against a mop board, across the floor again—creating the only sound in the otherwise quiet room.

In time Robert lifted his head. His face was flushed and his breath sketchy. He touched Addie's face—as flushed as his own—and, looking into one another's eyes, they laughed.

In joy.

And wonder.

And relief.

"Won't we have some stories to tell our grandchildren?"

"Robert, you wouldn't."

"Maybe I wouldn't. But it would be a convenient threat to keep you in line with."

"You won't need to keep me in line. I'm in it and I'm staying."

"We should tell Noah and Sarah."

"They'll hardly be surprised."

"Did everybody in this town know how I felt before I did?"

"Just about."

"Should we tell them tonight?"

"Let's. I'm trying not to ruin an elk roast. Why don't you run and find Noah and ask him if he can come up here for supper and we'll tell them then."

He beamed, happier than he had ever imagined being.

"Don't worry. I'll find him."

Chapter 20

Robert brought champagne, which was plentiful, given the number of saloons and the amount of wealth in town. Addie's elk roast turned out passably good, accompanied by roast potatoes and carrots and surprisingly light cornbread. The mood around the supper table was festive even before the announcement was made. The foursome had spent many hours together before Robert and Addie's rift, making the reunion in itself cause for celebration.

When their plates were full and the meal in progress, Robert refilled their glasses and lifted his own in one hand while capturing Addie's hand on the corner of the table.

"Addie and I have an announcement to make, though it may not come as much of a surprise to either one of you. But we wanted you to be the first to know . . ." His eyes lit on Addie and stayed.

"We're going to be married," she finished.

Sarah and Noah spoke at once.

"Oh Addie . . . Robert . . . this is wonderful!"

"Well, it's about time!"

"Congratulations! I couldn't be happier." Sarah rose and circled the table to hug them both.

Noah followed suit. "The same goes for me. I spread it on a little thick yesterday, Robert. I figured I'd either lose a good friend or shock some sense into your head. So when's the big day?"

"When *is* the big day?" Robert asked Addie. "We haven't had a chance to talk about it yet. We just decided three hours ago."

"Soon." Addie smiled. "I hope."

"So do I," Robert seconded.

Sarah said, "You're going to be married in the church, I suppose."

"Yes."

"By Matheson?" Noah asked.

"He's the minister," Robert replied.

"Well, I propose a toast." Noah lifted his glass. "To Robert and Addie, who absolutely belong together if ever two people did. May your wedding day be sunny and your lives be the same."

They had a lot to talk about—two weddings, two homes, four futures which would be inexorably entwined, to the delight of all. They discussed dates and celebrations and the disposition of the house in which they presently dined, deciding it would work out beautifully for Robert and Addie to be married the week following Sarah and Noah's wedding and make this their home after Sarah moved out.

They laughed about Robert's stubbornness, and how long it had taken him to pop the question to Addie. They speculated on what Birtle Matheson's reaction would be when asked to perform the service for the girl he'd been sparking. They even talked about Rose's—all of them felt it was a healthy sign they could do so—and the possibility of inviting some of her girls to Addie's wedding. Wouldn't all those doves have stars in their eyes? Wouldn't Mrs. Roundtree have venom in hers?

Their meal was long finished, the dishes removed to the dry sink, awaiting washing, and the four of them were still lolling at the table sharing lazy and pleasant conversation, winding the evening down. Robert leaned forward, half-sprawling on the table, his jaw propped on the butt of one hand, comfortable and relaxed with his friends. He turned his glass round and round with his fingertips, watching it catch the tablecloth and drag it into a pinwheel.

"What you said is true, Noah. I can't think of another couple who belong together the way Addie and I do. We've been through it all and put it all behind us—her running away, her working at Rose's, what her father did to her—what could be tougher to face than all that? But we did it, and the way I see it, after overcoming all those hurdles, marriage will be a breeze."

Into the silence that followed, Sarah spoke with an edge to her voice. "What her father did to her?"

Robert gave up his preoccupation with the glass and lifted his head off his hand. Addie was making surreptitious shushing motions, a horror-stricken expression on her face. He straightened slowly.

"What did her father do to her?" Sarah asked Robert.

He glanced from one sister to the other. "Doesn't she know?"

Addie's face had gone ashen. "Let's just forget it, Robert."

"Know what?" Sarah's glance darted between her sister and Robert.

"Nothing," Addie said, reaching for her dirty cup and saucer and jumping to her feet.

"Addie, sit down," Sarah ordered quietly.

"The dishes are getting all dried on."

"Addie, *sit down.*"

Noah sat unmoving, wondering what the hell this was all about.

Addie returned to her chair, set down the cup and saucer and fixed her eyes on them.

"Would you care to explain?"

Addie said, "This is something between Robert and me. He shouldn't have brought it up."

"But he did. Now I want to know what it's all about. What did Father do to you?"

Addie's eyes grew glittery. She banged a fist on the table, making the cup and saucer dance. "Robert, damn you! You had no right!"

"Addie, I'm sorry. I assumed you told her a long time ago, right after you told me. Why, hell, if she doesn't know, how could Noah have found out?"

Noah spoke up. "I'm afraid I don't know what you're talking about."

"Of course you do. You alluded to it one night when you told me you were going to marry Sarah, remember?"

"No, I don't, Robert, I'm sorry."

"You told *Noah?*" Addie cried, aghast.

"No, I didn't tell Noah. I thought he knew! I thought Sarah had told him. We were talking about you women, that's all."

"Enough of this!" Sarah put in. "I want to know what it was Father did to you that's causing all this distress!"

Addie pinched her folded hands between her knees and dropped her eyes to the cup and saucer. "You don't want to know," she whispered.

"Robert?" Sarah snapped officiously.

Robert said quietly, "I can't tell you. Addie has to."

"Very well then, Addie."

Addie continued staring at the tabletop with tears lining her eyelids. Noah sat with his arms crossed, an innocent observer.

"Will somebody tell me!" Sarah shouted, again banging a fist on the table. A massive silence followed.

After several seconds Robert's contrite voice broke it. "This is my fault, Sarah. I'm really sorry. Please, just let it ride."

"I cannot any more than you could if it were your father being discussed in such dire tones. Now what did he do?"

Robert reached over and squeezed Addie's shoulder. "Tell her, Addie. Tell her and be done with it."

Noah began to rise. "If you'll excuse me, this seems like a family matter."

Addie caught his arm. "No, stay. If we're all going to be related you might as well hear it, too."

Noah glanced at the faces around the table—Sarah's, looking pinched with displeasure as she stared at Addie; Robert's, looking penitent and concerned for his fiancée; Addie's, looking sad while asking him to remain. He sank back to his chair.

Addie rested her forearms on the table and wrapped both hands around her empty cup. There was a silvery track from a tear on her right cheek, but she was no longer crying. She appeared outwardly calm, resigned, studying the cup. "When Mother ran away, Father forced me to take her place . . . in bed."

Robert laid a hand on Addie's wrist and stroked it with his thumb.

Noah spread a hand over the bottom half of his face and gripped the hollows of his cheeks.

Sarah gaped at her sister.

"I don't believe you!" she whispered at last.

Addie met her eyes for the first time. "I'm sorry, Sarah. It's true."

"But . . . but you were only three years old!"

"That's right," Addie said sadly. "I was only three years old. And then I was four, then five and ten and eleven and twelve. And when I was sixteen I knew I couldn't stand it anymore, so I ran."

"But our father was a good, wholesome, God-fearing man. He wouldn't do such a heinous thing."

"He was a good, wholesome, God-fearing man around you, but he had two sides, Sarah. You only saw the one he wanted you to see."

Sarah shook her head, her eyes wide with shock. "No. I'd have known, I'd have . . . you'd have . . ."

"Given it away somehow? He made me promise not to at first and later I was too ashamed to."

"But how could he . . ." Sarah's lips hung open. She seemed to be silently begging for help.

"He pretended he was just comforting me because I missed Mother so much. He said it was our little secret and I must not tell anyone. He made you believe he was moving me into a room of my own because I was wetting the bed, but the real reason was so he could slip into my room without being suspected. Why do you think he never let Mrs. Smith live in with us? She would have—"

"No!" Sarah screamed, leaping to her feet. "I won't listen to any more! You're lying!" Tears rained down her face. Her eyes were wide, her face blanched. "Father wouldn't do such a thing! He loved us and took care of us! You're . . . you're defaming him and he's not here to defend himself!" She was sobbing as she ran from the room up the stairs.

"Sarah!" Noah ran after her, taking the steps two at a time, ignoring the fact that he was trailing her to her bedroom. He followed the sound of her weeping and found her in a room to the left. She had thrown herself across the bed in the dark.

"Sarah," he said gently, sitting down beside her.

"Get away!" Twisted at the waist, she struck back at him blindly. "Don't touch me!"

"Sarah, I'm sorry . . ." He found her shoulder and tried to turn her over so he could take her in his arms.

"Don't touch me, I said! Don't you ever touch me again!" she screamed. He withdrew his hand while she sobbed into the mattress and made the entire bed tremble. He remained awhile, uncertain, aching for her, wanting to hold her and help her through this ordeal.

"Sarah, please . . . let me help you."

"I don't want your h–help. I don't w–want anything. Just leave me alone!"

He rose and stood looking down at her dim form while she wailed and sobbed by turns. He went and stood by a window, looking out at the night, feeling bereft and helpless and shocked himself. Her father, sweet Jesus, her father. The man she'd patterned her entire life after, the man she quoted and imitated and adulated. He'd been more than a parent to her, he'd been her mentor and emancipator as well. Not only had she learned his trade, she had adopted his strict code of morality in that trade—she thought.

My God, how devastated she must be.

He thought of Addie, below. Poor, beautiful, abused, unbright Addie, who had carried that knowledge all these years and protected her sister from it. She had run from a father into a life of degradation and he, Noah, had been one of the men who'd compounded her self-abasement. What should he say to Addie when he went downstairs?

And to Robert, who unwittingly had uncovered this nest of maggots? Robert was a man who would not knowingly hurt a soul.

Noah wanted to remain here in the dark until harmony had been restored and the sorrow in this house had been eased, but what kind of friend hides in times of need?

Sarah's keening had become high and grieved and had begun a queer, resonant quaking in his stomach.

He tried again. "Sarah," he said, returning to the bed, sitting beside her and touching her heaving back. "Sarah, what he was to you can never be changed."

She shot up, swinging on him, screaming, *"He was my father, don't you understand! He was my father and he was a liar and a filthy hypocrite! An ani-mal!"*

He didn't know what to say, so he sat on the bed and tried to put his arms around her.

"Get out!" she screamed. *"Le . . . ea . . . eavvve . . . meeeee alllllooooone!"*

Her vehemence abashed and terrified him. He withdrew and stood uncertainly beside the bed while she sat on the edge of it with her entire body drooping and her frame convulsed by great heaving sobs.

"All right, Sarah. I'll leave. But I'll come by tomorrow and see how you're feeling. Would that be all right?"

His only answer was her continued weeping.

"I love you," he whispered.

She remained as before, drooped and crying as he left the room.

Downstairs, Addie was huddled in Robert's arms near the dry sink with the dishes forgotten beside them. A dish towel was slung over Robert's shoulder as the two exchanged murmured conversation. When Noah entered the kitchen they turned to watch him cross the room but remained linked with their hands upon one another, as if afraid to break apart.

Noah stopped near them and the three stood in a tangled silence.

"She's in a bad state," he said quietly.

"Let her cry for a while and then I'll go up to her," Addie said.

"She won't let me touch her."

"She needs to be alone awhile."

Noah nodded, then stood forlornly. "Addie, I'm really sorry," he finally said.

"Well, who isn't, but what can we do about it except try to overcome it and make our lives happier?"

"I never knew . . . I mean, when I used to come and see you up at Rose's . . ." His eyes flashed to Robert, back to Addie. "This is awkward, but I figure it needs saying. I wouldn't have come there if I'd known. I thought you girls were . . . well . . . I thought . . ."

She took pity and touched his arm. "Yeah, that's what everybody thinks. That we're just crazy about it. But listen, Noah, it's not your fault, what the old man did to me. I don't want you feeling guilty about it, too. I think there's been enough guilt around here for one day."

Noah shifted his eyes to meet Robert's.

"Robert," he said, and paused, searching for words.

Robert said, "Some big mouth I've got, huh?"

"Hell, you didn't know."

"That doesn't help Sarah any though, does it?"

They stood awhile, quiet, until Noah put one hand on each of their necks, forging them into a circle.

"You two are good people. You're going to be happy, I know it. And Sarah and I are going to be happy, too. We'll all get over this and be two old married couples who play cards every Sunday night."

They narrowed the circle and stood with their heads touching in a clumsy three-way embrace. Noah broke it up.

"Listen, I've got to go. Tell Sarah I'll be by tomorrow. You'll go up to her soon, won't you, Addie?"

"Yes, I promise."

He nodded and gave her a little smile of gratitude.

"Robert," Noah said by way of parting.

The two clasped hands, necks—a silent communion, gripping each other, reluctant to let go. Finally they parted, clearing their throats. There'd been more emotion expended in this house tonight than any of them were comfortable with.

"I'll see you both tomorrow."

Up in her room, Sarah lay lifelessly on her side, her hands limp, one of them holding a damp handkerchief. Her lips felt puffed and glossy. Her eyes hurt. Her body was inert but for an occasional residual sob that shuddered through her.

The pieces all fit now. Everything.

Father, abandoned by his wife for another man, never marrying or even seeing other women. Addie, after Mother left, inconsolably sad, wetting the bed, getting a room of her own but growing sadder as the years advanced and she should have gotten over Mother's absence. Father's first approval when Robert entered their lives, his later antipathy when Robert reached puberty and began noticing Addie as a girl. Addie's disappearance followed by Father's immediate failing. Addie, taking up the oldest profession as an extension of her role at home; her adamant refusal to speak of their father or accept any inheritance money from him. Even Addie's being excused from having to work at the newspaper office the way Sarah had. Sarah understood now the true reason.

How lucky she'd been.

Sarah, the smart one.

Addie, the pretty one.

She groaned and dragged one heavy arm closer to her face, guilt-struck because she'd complained about Addie not having to help the way she did. Ruler appeared out of the darkness, jumping up behind her with a soft "Mrrr?" as if asking what was wrong. She reached an arm back and hauled her over her hip, settled her in a silky, vibrating curve against her stomach. Funny how when she really needed her the cat stayed, even though her first loyalty was to Addie.

For a while Sarah erased tonight's revelation from her mind, concentrating on the cat's purring, the warmth of her body, the milky smell of her fur, the comfort of having her close, just as Addie must have been comforted by her when she worked at Rose's.

Rose's.

Father.

The ugly truth returned, bringing a shudder that closed Sarah more tightly around the cat until her mouth touched her head.

Was this how Addie had felt, night after night, alone and wretched after their father had done his dirty work?

No. Much worse . . . immeasurably worse. Guilty and frightened and filled with hatred and despair and helplessness, for whom could she have turned to? Who would have believed a child so young, given the sterling reputation of Isaac Merritt, who was respected from one end of St. Louis to the other?

The faint light from the lower level went out and footsteps came up the stairs in the dark . . . into Sarah's room . . . to the bed. Sarah remained silent, facing the wall. Addie lay down behind her, matching the curves of her body to those of Sarah's, hooking an arm around her waist and finding Ruler on the far side, then locating the back of Sarah's hand. She fit her own over it and squeezed hard, her fingertips digging into Sarah's palm, the younger sister now succoring the older, protecting her from what she herself had never had protection from.

Sarah's tears came again, stinging her sore eyes. She felt Addie's face pressed between her shoulder blades. They lay motionless a long time, like twins in a womb, until Sarah could contain her despair no longer.

"All this time," she said in a croaky voice, "I thought it was something I'd done that made you run."

"No. Never you. You were my bulwark, didn't you know that? You still are."

"Some bulwark. I feel like I've been struck by a big fist right here where Ruler's lying against me. I'm unable to move or to . . . to reason."

"Maybe it's better that you know."

"It doesn't feel better."

"I know it doesn't right now, but in the long run."

"Now that I do, I'm surprised it took me this long to figure it out except I . . . I never knew . . ." Sarah swallowed a new lump forming in her throat. "I never knew f–fathers . . ." She couldn't finish.

"Shh . . . don't cry anymore." Addie petted Sarah's hair. "It's not worth it. It was over a long time ago and I've come through it all right. Look, we all have. Like Noah said, soon we'll be two old married couples playing cards on Sunday night."

Sarah touched her knuckles to her lips, her eyes still streaming.

After a while Addie said, "Robert said to tell you he's sorry."

Sarah made an effort. She blew her nose. She took a deep, shaky breath, turned to her back and settled Ruler between herself and Addie.

"Dear Robert . . . how he must love you."

"He loves you, too. He felt terrible about hurting you."

"How long ago did you tell him?"

"Christmas Eve."

"Christmas Eve . . ." The night things had started between herself and Noah.

"It was a terrible night. He came to Rose's wanting to hire me for the night, but in the end he couldn't make himself do it for money. I ended up crying and telling him about Daddy and that's when he made me leave Rose's. He said I should tell you then. He thought you should know, but I didn't see any reason. You always loved Father so much and thought he was some kind of a god. I knew this would happen when you found out. But Sarah, you have to forget it. If I can be happy with Robert, that's all that matters."

"It's not all that matters. It matters that my father was a hypocrite, preaching one thing and living another, that he was a filthy bestial criminal, preying on his own daughter and ruining her life. I feel so guilty, Addie, for not knowing, for not helping, for . . . for criticizing you because you never had to go to the newspaper office and help." Sarah rolled to her side, facing Addie. "Don't you see, Addie? He took everything away from you and gave me everything. How can I live with that?"

"By remembering what you did for me. You came here to find me, you brought me Robert. If it wasn't for the two of you I'd have died in that whorehouse thinking that I wasn't worthy of anything better, because all those years I thought I was a low, foul person, the scum of the earth. I thought all I was good for was that one act. But Sarah, I don't think that anymore. You and Robert have given me back my self-respect."

They lay awhile in silence, thankful for the dark, each with a hand on the cat's fur, linked by her comforting presence.

"Addie, did Father . . ." There were so many questions Sarah wanted to ask, needed to ask, was afraid to ask.

"You can ask me, Sarah, if you want. Anything. I'm not ashamed anymore because I know now I was innocent. But what good will it do you to hear the truth? I'll tell you this much. The real stuff didn't start till I was twelve. Till then it was a lot of him touching me and kissing me. Now think good and hard before you decide to ask me more."

The room remained quiet a long time, the darkness impacted with unwanted visions. Finally Sarah replied, "All right, I won't ask, but I have one more confession to make. May I?"

"What could you have to confess?"

"I was always jealous of how beautiful you were."

Their fingertips touched on Ruler's fur.

"And I was always jealous of how smart you were. I used to think if I could just get smarter he'd let me go to the newspaper office the way you did and he wouldn't need me for that other reason."

"Oh Addie . . ." Sarah reached up and put her hand around the back of Addie's head and drew it near so their foreheads touched.

"The world's not a very perfect place, is it?" Addie said. After her staunchness through Sarah's weeping, she now sounded on the verge of tears herself.

Sarah became the strong one. She patted Addie's short, silky hair and left her hand curved protectively around Addie's nape. "No it isn't, dear one. Far from it."

They fell asleep where they were, fully dressed and exhausted from the surfeit of emotion. In the deep of night Addie awakened, removed her shoes and those of Sarah, who mumbled, "Addie? . . . whm . . . ?"

"Get under the covers and go back to sleep."

The next morning Sarah overslept and arrived at the newspaper office late, her face looking like an overstuffed pillow. Patrick glanced at her sideways and took a swig from his flask. Josh stared at her head-on and said, "You look pure awful, Sarah! Are you sick?"

Her head felt like she'd boiled it. Her eyes ached and her nose was swollen. Concentrating was impossible. She stayed until nearly eleven A.M., when she finally gave up and went back home to bed.

Addie came to her room much later and gently shook her shoulder. "Sarah, wake up."

Sarah opened her bleary eyes and tried to recall why she was in bed in the middle of the afternoon.

"Ohhh . . ." she groaned and rolled to her back with a hand covering her eyes.

"Noah is here." Sarah struggled to become lucid. "You've been sleeping four hours already. It's the third time he's been here and I thought I should wake you. Do you want to see him?"

Sarah pushed herself up shakily. "No, not really." She scraped a hand over her tousled hair and glanced around, orienting herself. The sun was on the windowsill. Ruler was near her feet. At her desk her journal lay closed and the crystal penholder sat beside it.

"What time is it?"

"About quarter after three."

Sarah boosted herself to the edge of the bed and dropped her feet over. "How are you today?"

"I feel wonderful, actually. What shall I tell Noah?"

"Tell him I'll be down in five minutes."

"All right." Addie swept toward the door. She pointed to the pitcher and bowl. "I brought you some warm water."

Sarah rose, feeling unsteady as a newborn colt. She washed her face, combed her hair and winced at her reflection in the mirror. She looked no better than she had this morning. Her eyes were bloodshot, her skin saggy and purple around the eyes. Even her lips looked swollen. Yet Addie seemed revitalized. Perhaps Robert had been right: revealing her secret, Addie had at last become free of it. If so, Sarah felt as if the burden had been transferred to her shoulders.

She changed her wrinkled dress and went downstairs to face Noah. He was sitting on the parlor settee wearing his work equipment—gun, holster, brown leather vest and star. He held his hat in his hands—the one she'd given him—and rose immediately when Sarah entered the room.

"Hi," he said with an uncertain pause. "How are you?"

"Puffy and shaky and a little incohesive."

"I was worried when I went to the newspaper office and you weren't there."

"It was a bad night."

"I imagine. You and Addie talked?" Addie had retreated to the kitchen to give them privacy.

"Yes."

Noah left his hat on the settee and went to her, taking her by the upper arms while she crossed them and fixed her eyes on an armchair to her left. Neither of them spoke.

At length, she pulled back so he was forced to release her. "I'm not very good company today." The damnable tears threatened once more and she turned away to hide them. "I'm sorry. I know this must seem bizarre to you. It does to me, too. I'll need a little more time to get my emotions in order."

"Of course you will," he said quietly. "But don't worry about me. I've got plenty to keep me busy at work. When you're rested up and want to see me, let me know."

"Thank you, Noah, I will."

She recognized the coldness in herself immediately—her unwillingness to meet his gaze, a reluctance to be touched by him, relief when he dropped his hands. His visit was absolutely correct, even thoughtful, yet she could not conjure the slightest sense of gratitude for his attempt at comforting her.

Rebuffed, he withdrew, collecting his hat and leaving the house with the careful footsteps of one retreating from a wake.

When he was gone, Sarah sat on a stiffly upholstered side chair, her eyes closed, her arms crossed, imagining this must be what it felt like to be in a coma, chilly and removed from the life around you, hearing it but not heeding it.

In the kitchen Addie clamped a handle on a hot iron and laid it on a damp cloth over a curtain-in-progress. It sizzled. Out on the back doorstep Ruler meowed to get in. Addie went to the door, opened it and said,

"Well, are you coming in or not?" The door closed and the iron clanked again, hitting the stove. Outside, a wagon passed on the road, rearranging the gravel. Some birds chirped.

The way you treated Noah was unpardonable.

I am suffering.

Maybe he is, too.

His suffering, if it existed, was of little import to Sarah beyond that brief thought. She struggled to merely open her eyes, to rise from the chair, to proceed with normality. How could Addie be ironing curtains in the kitchen as if the axis of the world had not tilted?

Sarah moved to the kitchen doorway. Addie looked up.

"Noah has gone?"

Sarah nodded.

"He's very worried about you."

"Is there any coffee?"

Addie blinked in surprise at Sarah's response. "Yes, I believe so."

Sarah poured some and took it upstairs without a further word about last night or about Noah. Leaving the kitchen, she only said, "I'm not very hungry tonight, so don't fix much for supper."

She returned to work the next day, submerging herself in daily duties and trying to keep unwanted images from her mind, but they persisted, horrid vignettes of her father hunkering over Addie. They came at frequent intervals and Sarah would snap from her involvement with them to find her hand clenched on a pen and her stomach muscles quivering. Though she was ignorant of the machinations of copulation, she had once seen a pair of dogs mating. A woman had run out of her house with a broom and had beaten on the male, shouting, "Get off her! Get off her, you big thing!" to no avail. The two had remained sealed together for an ignominiously long time in the woman's front yard, until every child in the neighborhood had witnessed the spectacle.

Sometimes Sarah imagined herself with the broom in her hand, flailing her father, whom she pictured in the pose of the male dog. The image might have lasted only a second or two, but it would leave her feeling soiled and shaken.

It persisted at night, too, before sleep came, while she lay in the room next to Addie's and nursed an anger for her father that grew to immense proportions. She began having nightmares, awakening from them with her heart hammering and the visions from her dream already evaporated before she could see them.

Four days passed and she had not seen Noah. Five, and she still hadn't seen him. Six, and he appeared beyond her window glass, standing outside the newspaper office, raising a hand in silent hello. She raised hers, too, but returned to work without going out to invite him in.

A week after that fateful betrothal supper, he came to the house while making his early-evening rounds.

Addie answered his knock. She and Robert had been sitting on the settee making wedding plans while she stitched her own bridal dress.

"Noah!" Addie exclaimed happily, "come in!"

"Noah!" Robert jumped up from the settee and came to greet him with a handclasp. "Where have you been? We were just talking about you."

"I've been keeping out of Sarah's way. How is she?"

"Remote."

"From you too?"

"From all of us, I'm afraid."

Noah sighed and looked worried. "Is she here?"

"I'll get her," Addie said.

Sarah was sitting at her desk writing when Addie announced from the doorway, "Noah is downstairs. He'd like to see you."

Sarah looked over her shoulder. She was dressed in a white long-sleeved nightgown topped by her old pumpkin-colored shawl. Her hair hung in a loose braid down her back. Some seconds passed while she contemplated. Finally she answered, "Tell him I'll be down."

Five minutes later she emerged from upstairs wearing a wine-colored dress and high-button shoes with her hair secured in a fastidious bun at the back of her head. When she entered the parlor all conversation ceased. She stopped near the foot of the stairs and returned the regard of the other three, who were seated on the settee and an adjacent chair.

Noah rose, holding his hat.

"Hello, Sarah. I haven't seen you in a while."

"Hello, Noah."

Neither of them smiled.

"Could I talk to you a minute?"

"Surely."

"Outside," he suggested.

She led the way, stopping perhaps ten feet from the door, which Noah closed. He stopped behind her and replaced his hat on his head. It was dark; no moon, only the light from the windows falling across the rocky surroundings of the house. The faint tang of dying wood fires lingered in the air from the nearby chimneys. Down below, the lights of the saloons along Main Street created a faint glow.

He didn't know how to begin.

"I thought I'd hear from you," he finally said.

She made no excuses, said nothing at all.

"Addie said you've been quiet, not talking to her either."

"Addie's been with Robert a lot."

"That's why you're not talking to her? Because she's been with Robert?"

"I've been . . . evaluating, let's say."

"Me?"

"No, not you. Life."

"And what have you discovered?"

"That it is fickle."

"Sarah . . ." He touched her shoulder but she flinched away. Hurt, he withdrew his hand and waited. When she refused to face him he walked around her and confronted her face to face.

"Why are you shutting me out?"

"I'm not shutting you out."

"Yes, you are."

"I'm healing."

"Let me help you." He reached for her, but she squirmed away and held up both hands.

"Don't!"

"Don't?" he repeated sharply, hurt by her continued rebuffs. "I'm supposed to be the man you love and you say don't when I try to touch you?"

"I simply can't stand it right now. All right?"

Noah considered, then said, "I'm not him, Sarah, so don't blame me for what he did."

"You don't understand! What he did was monstrous. I cannot simply blink my eyes and get over it. I loved him unquestionably all those years, then in one moment my illusions about him were shattered. If I need time to get over that, you'll simply have to understand."

"Time? How much time? And while you're getting over it, do you intend to keep pushing me away?"

"Please, Noah," she whispered.

"Please what?" he snapped.

She hung her head.

"Please don't touch you? Please don't kiss you? Please don't marry you?"

"I didn't say that."

He studied her downcast face, his mouth small, his throat constricted, so confused and hurt he didn't know what more to say to her.

"Matheson wants to talk to us about the wedding."

She looked off into the distant dark. "You talk to him."

He let out a chunk of sound resembling a laugh, only short and hurt. It shot into the night like a knife thrown into a tree. He turned away, stood facing the town, sensing only doom ahead.

"Do you want to call it off, Sarah?"

It took her some time to answer. "I don't know."

"Well, you'd better decide, because it's only two weeks away."

She stepped near him and laid a hand on his shoulder blade.

"Poor Noah," she said. "I know you don't understand."

"The hell I don't," he said deep in his throat and stalked away, leaving her standing alone in the night.

He told Robert, who told Addie, who talked to Sarah the next night.

"What are you doing, Sarah? You love Noah, you know you do!"

"Nothing's been decided yet."

"But he told Robert you wouldn't go talk to Birtle Matheson about the wedding."

"That doesn't mean I'm not marrying him."

"Are you then?"

"Quit badgering me!"

"Badgering you!" Addie plunked down on the edge of Sarah's bed and pushed down the book Sarah had been reading, forcing Sarah to meet her eyes. "You know what you're going to do? You're going to let our father ruin your life next. Nobody that wicked should have so much power over another human being, especially not from his grave."

Without a further word she left the room.

Two days passed. On the third, Noah sent a note via Freeman Block.

Dear Sarah,

Could I take you out to supper tonight? I'll come to the house to get you at seven o'clock.

Love, Noah.

"Tell him yes," she said to Freeman.

. . .

Sarah had thought about what Addie said. Her father should *not* have the power to ruin her life, especially after he'd ruined a good portion of Addie's.

She dressed in a fine lawn dress of solid white, with two lace-trimmed petticoats underneath and her engagement brooch pinned at her throat. It was a stunning May evening and she wanted to please Noah, and be unflinchingly in love again and feel exhilarated by the sight of him, and revel in the innocent kisses and caresses that she'd come to enjoy only days before this disaster had befallen.

He wore the new suit he had bought for their wedding, crisp and black and proper with a winged collar catching him high beneath his chin, and a silvery-gray tie as wide as an ascot, stuck through by a pearl pin. On his head, not the Stetson, but a flattering black topper with a bell-shaped crown.

When she saw him on the doorstep her heart fluttered. When he spoke, the words sounded tightly controlled, as if he were afraid to release them from his throat.

"Hello, Sarah."

"Hello, Noah."

"You look pretty."

"So do you."

They smiled stiffly.

"Are you ready to go?"

"Yes."

They walked down the hill, looking straight ahead, without bumping elbows, exchanging only the most stilted dialogue. They dined at the Custer on the finest fare the town had to offer—deviled clams, pheasant in claret sauce, parsnip fritters and that rarest of delicacies: fresh, cold glasses of real cow's milk. Though each of them relished every drop of their milk, neither ate more than half the food on their plate.

After dinner he took her to the play at the Langrishe. It was a farce called *Hanky-Panky,* which elicited great laughs from all the crowd. They sat through it without even registering what was happening on the stage.

Afterward, he walked her home through the pleasant spring night. A slim crescent moon had cleared the mountains, and above the ravine a corridor of stars glittered. When they reached the house, the windows were dark, the door closed. They stopped before it and Noah turned toward Sarah.

"I realized tonight that we haven't done much of this."

"Of what?"

"Courting. The real thing—me inviting you and coming to pick you up and the two of us fussing up for each other. It felt like this is the way it's supposed to be."

"Yes, it did."

"You felt comfortable with me?"

"Yes, I did."

"And if I kiss you? Will you still feel comfortable with me?"

She had known it was coming, had been preparing herself all night. How intimidating that she'd *had* to prepare herself for it. What had happened to the woman who'd lain on a newly turned mattress in the sunlight and enjoyed this man in a wholly physical way? Why, as he stepped nearer, did her heart clamor with unreasonable fear? He was gentle, understanding, patient, and she loved him. How confusing: she truly loved him . . . as long as he kept his distance.

In the shadows beside the front steps, he rested his hands on her shoulders, giving her fair warning. She knew full well that all his preparations for tonight—his written invitation, all their finery, the meal, the play—had been merely a prelude to this moment of truth.

"You're not Addie and I'm not your father. Think about it."

He laid his mouth upon hers very lightly. She felt smothered but waited for the sensation to recede. Instead it advanced, taking on magnitude as the kiss became fully realized. She submerged her resistance and saw it through, put her hands on his breast and opened her lips when his tongue touched them, and tipped her head aside in response to his head tipping, and tried to recapture the innocence and trusting they'd built between them.

It didn't work.

She felt a sob building deep within, pushing panic along before it. When it erupted she pushed him hard with the butts of both hands, and he stumbled back.

"I can't!" She was breathing as if chased, gulping air and crying. "I can't," she whispered, spinning away, clamping a hand over her mouth, terrified and abashed because she was humiliating and hurting him. What should she do? How could she cure this ungrounded fear? How could she love him and be repulsed by him? She understood clearly, he was not her father, he would not hurt or abuse her, yet she could not control her revulsion at even this simplest intimacy.

"Damn you, Isaac Merritt!" she shouted. "Damn you to eternal hell!"

Her shout echoed once from the wall of Mt. Moriah above them and left an awful stillness afterward.

Noah stood behind her, out of his depth. She had annihilated all hope for them. Who was to blame?

"I'm so afraid," she said. She was not crying but her voice quivered.

"There's nothing to be afraid of anymore."

She turned, her hands still at her chin. "You're leaving me."

"No, you left me. The minute you found out why Addie ran away from home, you left me."

"I didn't mean to . . . I couldn't . . . it was . . . oh Noah, I don't want to lose you."

"Yes, you do. You've been fighting your feelings for me since the first time I kissed you. Well, now I know, and maybe I'm a little relieved. It's not any fun being the one who's always asking for affection. When it really works, it's supposed to flow both ways. So let's just put an end to this misery, okay, Sarah? I don't think . . ." He paused, sighed, raised his hands and let them drop. "What difference does it make? We could never make this work."

She stood mute while her future withered.

"Do you want to cancel things with Matheson or should I?"

"Noah, maybe if I . . ." She had no further words, no idea how to help herself or him.

He said, "I'll tell Matheson." After another silence he added, "Well, I guess this is it then. I want to say good luck, but the words stick in my throat."

"Noah . . ." She reached out one hand.

He turned and walked away. She watched the weak moonlight pick out the rim of his new top hat, his shoulders which dropped away from her with each downhill step he took. At the bottom of the path he stopped dead still for a full fifteen seconds. As if losing a battle with himself, he turned and called quietly, "Good luck, Sarah," before resuming his walk out of her life.

Chapter 21

And so it was that Adelaide Merritt and Robert Baysinger were to be the first ones wed in the Congregational Church of Deadwood. Their wedding day dawned cloudy, but by nine o'clock the blue sky had broken through, reminding Sarah of Noah's toast on that evening before her world had crumbled. *May your wedding day be sunny and your lives be the same.*

She would see him today. The two of them would be standing up for Addie and Robert while the entire town wondered why their own engagement had been canceled. She had carefully tucked away her betrothal brooch between layers of cotton in a tiny inlaid box of tulipwood which she kept on her desktop.

Addie's wedding was scheduled for ten A.M. Shortly after nine Addie came into Sarah's room carrying her curling tongs, dressed in her chemise and petticoats.

"I want to fix your hair."

"I should be fixing yours. It's *your* wedding day."

"I'm better at it. And besides, mine's all done."

"It looks beautiful."

"I know it does. Sit down."

"But Addie—"

"Don't but Addie me. I'm going to make you ravishing."

"An Eleventh Commandment couldn't make me ravishing."

"Sit down, I said."

Sarah sat. "I know why you're doing this, but it won't work. It's over between Noah and me."

"I once thought it was over between Robert and me, but look where I'm going today. Just sit still so I don't burn you, and tip your head when I say tip." She removed the lamp chimney, struck a match and began heating the tongs.

Twenty minutes later Sarah's hair was drawn to the crown of her head, secured by a wide mother-of-pearl barrette, and cascaded past her collar in a froth of springy ringlets.

"Oh Addie, it's so obvious!"

"It's your sister's wedding day. You're expected to primp."

"But what will Noah think?"

"He'll think exactly what I *want* him to think. That he'd better think again!"

"Addie." Sarah turned and caught Addie's arm. "You don't need to try to make amends. It was Noah's and my decision to break off our engagement. You're not responsible."

Addie saddened. "I know. But Robert and I feel so awful about it."

"Enough about that. It's your wedding day. I won't have you spoiling it by getting blue. Now let's go to your room and I'll help you into your dress."

Addie's dress had its flaws—stitching together gussets and tucks was more difficult than making flat curtains—but what the garment lacked in perfection it made up in flattery. High-necked, V-waisted (front and back), with corkscrew sleeves and a brief pleated train, it gave Addie a fairy waist. Its whipped-honey hue nearly matched her hair, into which she had pinned some wild plum blossoms which matched those she would carry along with six red tulips from Emma's yard.

When the last wrist button was closed, Sarah offered a moment of silent adulation before kissing Addie's cheek. "In spite of what you think, this is one of the happiest days of my life. Noah was very right when he said you and Robert belong together. You truly do."

Noah came to collect the women in a rented rig. When he knocked on the door Sarah's duty, as handmaiden to the bride, was to answer. She calmed herself, pressed a palm to her stomach and approached the door with careful control and a cardboard smile.

"Hello, Noah," she said as if his appearance had not created a rent in her heart. He was dressed in the black suit he should have worn for their own wedding. His cheeks were shiny, his mustache neatly trimmed, a rich dark wing above his familiar mouth. The sight of him made her tongue dry.

"Hello, Sarah. How have you been?" So proper it was numbing. No smile, no second glances.

"Fine." Proper, too. "I believe Addie is all ready. I'll get her."

They rode to the church in a carriage for four, with Addie insisting on sitting in the backseat alone. Proximity, however, had no effect on the estrangement of the two up front. They rode as if a great-aunt sat between them.

At the church Robert waited, dapper and smiling, reaching up to help his betrothed alight from the carriage, to accept a touch of the cheek from his future sister-in-law, a handshake from his friend.

To Noah, aside, he said, "Take notes today. You're going to need them, mark my words."

The wedding was short and simple. Birtle Matheson carried it off in a manner that gained him only further respect from his new congregation, who knew he'd had eyes for the bride himself. The attendees packed the church and included three of Rose's girls, who watched the proceedings with bald yearning in their eyes; many single businessmen in town who chided themselves for never seeing the possibilities in the woman they'd known as Eve; Patrick Bradigan, who was sober for the occasion; the Dawkins family and more.

When Robert spoke his vows he clutched Addie's knuckles so tightly white rings appeared below his thumbs.

"I, Robert Baysinger, take thee, Adelaide Merritt . . ."

Sarah stood behind them, painfully conscious of Noah, six feet away, his hands linked, standing straight and still as an obelisk, watching the proceedings.

It came Addie's turn.

"I, Adelaide Merritt, take thee, Robert Baysinger . . . to be my wedded husband . . ."

Addie displayed a smile of singular radiance as she looked into Robert's eyes. A tear formed in Sarah's, and as she lifted a handkerchief to wipe it away, Noah turned his head to watch. His glance lasted no longer than it would have taken the tear to fall, but in that moment when their gazes met she saw that it was no more over for him than it was for her.

The ceremony ended. Addie walked down the aisle on Robert's arm. Noah took Sarah's. For the duration of the exit they touched, but it was the only contact they shared that day. At the church door he released her. Throughout a dinner in the churchyard and a dance beneath the June sky they remained carefully aloof. Through the thousands of touches and words exchanged with familiar people, they exchanged none with each other. Sometimes, across the crowded yard Sarah would see him, drinking beer or talking, dancing with Emma or Addie, but if their eyes chanced to meet they parted in the same breath. Once he danced with Geneva Dawkins, who wore a profuse blush, and once with one of Rose's girls, whom he seemed to find highly amusing. He threw his head back and laughed at something she said. How excruciating to watch the play of sun on his hair and mustache, to relive moments when his laughter had been shared with her, to realize it would not be again. *Who knows? He might even start frequenting Rose's again.* The possibility brought Sarah an actual physical pain.

For a while he watched a game of mumbletypeg whose knife-flippers were all lads Josh's age. When he glanced up and saw Sarah watching him, she turned away.

The town had grown. Unfamiliar faces dotted the crowd. She put her time to use introducing herself to each one, taking down names for the "Welcome" column of the *Chronicle,* inviting the new women to join the Ladies' Club, the new men to attend the town meetings. But her zest for the work seemed a thing of the past.

Near the end of the afternoon, Sarah searched out Emma.

"I have a big favor to ask you."

"Ask away."

"I need a place to stay tonight."

"You've got it."

"A pallet on the floor will do. I know your place is crowded."

"You've got it."

"I thought I should leave the house to Addie and Robert. You see, the original plan was that—"

"I know what the original plan was."

"I'd rent a hotel room for the night, but they're full and—"

"Are you going to quit apologizing? We're your friends. You'll stay with us and no questions asked."

She found Addie and told her. Addie said, "I feel like I'm putting you out of your own house."

"It's your wedding night. If we had a train, you'd be on it, heading somewhere for a honeymoon. Since you can't be, I'm going to Emma's."

At Emma's, after all the others had retired for the night, the two women sat in the kitchen, sipping something Emma called "teakettle tea," little more than weak tea diluted with a lot of hot milk.

"It was a nice wedding," Sarah said.

"Yup."

"And Addie was a beautiful bride."

"She was that."

"Matheson didn't bat an eye."

"No, he didn't."

"I've never seen Robert so happy."

"We going to chitchat all night about junk like that or are you going to spill what's on your mind?"

"You know what's on my mind . . . Noah."

"I thought that was over."

"It's supposed to be, but I still love him."

"I saw him staring at you a time or two when you weren't looking, too."

"You did?"

"Me and about five hundred others. So what happened between you two?"

"Oh Emma, it's so complicated."

"I'm not simple, you know. I might be able to shed some light if you give me a chance."

Sarah considered, sipped her teakettle tea. She wanted to confide in Emma, but now that the opportunity presented itself, she wondered about loyalties.

"I'd be telling you without Addie's permission so I must have your word of honor it'll go no farther than this."

"You got it."

Sarah told the entire story. When she reached the part about Addie and their father, Emma put a hand over her mouth and squeezed hard. Above it, her eyes seemed incapable of blinking.

". . . and so ever since then, every time Noah touches me . . . I don't know . . . something happens inside me and I stiffen up. I know he's not my father, I *know* that, but somehow I feel threatened and I freeze up and . . . and I feel so stupid and guilty and . . . Oh Emma, what am I going to do . . ." Sarah was in tears as the last word wailed through the kitchen.

Emma, appalled and out of her depth, found it easiest to draw Sarah from her chair and clamp her in a hard embrace to avoid meeting the younger woman's eyes. A father and his own daughter. Dear lord, in all her born days she'd never heard of anything so vile. Poor Addie, and this poor one here, worshiping the damned old swine all those years. Who could blame her for backing off from anything wearing pants after getting a shock like that? But what should she tell her? How should she comfort her when Emma's own reaction was so horrified she was having trouble coming to grips with it herself.

Sarah sobbed and clung as she would to a mother. Emma patted and rubbed her shoulders.

"Oh, my dear, dear girl, what a terrible thing for you to go through."

"I love him, Emma. I want to be married to him, but . . . Oh Emma, how can I change . . . ?"

Emma had no notion what to advise. Such convoluted relationships were beyond her scope of experience. She had fallen in love with a plain man, married him, had his children, worked hard and lived by the Good Book. She'd thought that's how most lives worked. This disgusting story though . . .

"You've got to give it some time is all. Isn't that what they say heals all wounds?"

"But I hurt Noah so. I pushed him away when all he wanted to do was help me. He'll never come back."

"You don't know that for sure. Maybe he's just giving you some time to heal."

"I don't want time. I want to be married to him now and be as normal as everybody else."

Emma patted her some more, rubbed her shoulders, felt like crying herself, but could think of not one word to ease this pitiful creature.

"Oh me," she sighed. "I wish I could help you."

Sarah dried her eyes and Emma refilled their cups. When the two women were reseated, Sarah spoke, gazing forlornly at Emma.

"He danced with that girl from Rose's today. I saw them laughing together."

Emma could only squeeze her hand in silence.

In the house on Mt. Moriah Road, the bride and groom entered their bedroom. Robert set the lantern down, closed the curtains and returned to Addie. He smiled, reaching to the top of her head. "Your flowers are wilted." He took the plum blossoms and put them beside the lantern.

She rolled her eyes up and touched her hair self-consciously. "I'm surprised they didn't fall out. There's hardly enough hair to hold them."

"There's enough," he said, drawing her hands down, keeping them.

They had been among a crowd for ten hours, jovial, smiling, celebrating, while this singular hour waited like winter-locked violets await the spring.

"How do you feel?" he asked.

"Nervous."

He laughed. "Why? We've only waited six years for this, or is it seven?"

"More like twelve," she said. "Since we were children."

"Very young children, and I came to your door begging for fat drippings and thought you were the most beautiful creature God ever put on this earth." He took her face in both his hands. "I still think so."

"Oh Robert." Her glance dropped.

How amazing, he thought, *she's timid with me.*

He dropped his hands to her shoulders.

"Mrs. Baysinger," he said, as if the word had some new, exotic flavor that he was testing on his tongue.

"Yes, Mr. Baysinger?" She looked up.

"Shall I kiss you first or unhook those fifteen hooks down your back?"

"How do you know there are fifteen?"

"I counted them today."

Her face lit with surprise. "How could you have counted them? They don't show."

"I can see I'll have to prove it. Turn around."

She turned, smiling at her window curtains while he counted aloud.

"One . . . two . . . three . . ."

"Robert?"

"Four . . . five . . ."

"How could you have counted them?"

"Your stitches show. Six . . . seven . . . eight . . ."

"Robert?"

"Ten . . . eleven . . ."

She waited through numbers twelve and thirteen before admitting, "I thought today would never end."

At *fifteen* the room fell into a vibrant silence, broken only by their breathing. The dress was open to her hips. He slipped his hands inside and rested them on her waist. He leaned down and kissed her gently between the shoulder blades, lingering, breathing her scent, while his pulse felt like hammerblows in his throat.

"I think I deserve a medal," he whispered, "for all the times I wanted to do this and didn't." At her waist his grip tightened. He straightened, drawing her back flush against him, speaking near her ear. "In that hotel room on Christmas Eve, and here in this house on a hundred occasions since then, when I sat across the table from you playing Chinese checkers, or eating apple cobbler, or listening to Sarah talk. Sometimes in the kitchen when we'd be doing dishes or you were sitting at the table stitching a curtain and I'd look at you and watch your hair change from gray to blond, and realize that I'd loved you since I was twelve years old and no other man in this world had as much right to you as I."

"Is that what you were thinking?" Her voice sounded breathy.

"I wanted you so much I felt pagan."

"And I thought it was just the opposite. All these months since you took me out of Rose's I thought you were remembering my past and trying to get beyond it."

The butts of his hands pressed down upon her hipbones, then rode her ribs to the hollow below her breasts before starting back down. "How could you think that? I've wanted you, wanted this since I was eighteen and I went to your father to ask his permission to marry you. And since Christmas Eve when I made the worst blunder of my life by offering you money. Addie," he whispered, "can you forgive me for that?"

She turned, forcing his hands to divert to her elbows. Fixing her shining green eyes on his, she whispered, "I will forgive you, Robert, if you'll end this torture and make me your wife."

The wait was over. He kissed her wholly, reaching deep around her until their bodies coiled like vines and his hands were inside the back of her gown, skimming her shoulders, waist and spine, sweeping lower still, filling with her petticoats and—faint within them—the swells of her flesh. Through tier upon tier of cotton, he learned her shape, moving the fabric and himself against her while their kiss became grand and avid.

When he lifted his head they were both breathing like runners. Her lips glimmered wet in the lamplight, her eyes were wide, the pupils dilated, fixed upon him. He gripped her right hand, hard, and kissed the butt of it with his intense gaze riveted upon hers. Brief as an exclamation point, that kiss, before he dropped her hand and stepped back.

"Don't move," he ordered, fiery-eyed as he began stripping off his jacket. "Don't touch a thing. I haven't waited all these years to watch you take your own clothes off."

"My shoes . . ."

"All right, your shoes."

She sat on the edge of the bed with a buttonhook while he rid himself of jacket and vest, then sailed his shirt toward a chair. It fell on the floor as he sat on the bed beside her and bent to his own shoestrings. Removing their footwear, they exchanged ardent glances, then he stood, shucked off his trousers, flung them aside and reached for her hand. "Come here," he said huskily, standing before her in his short-legged cotton union suit. She gave him her hand and let herself be drawn to her feet.

"Now I'm going to see you," Robert said.

He turned down her dress, unbuttoned the waist of her petticoat, freed her corset hooks and stripped the whole works to her feet, shucking garters and stockings along the way. He rose, offered his hand, and she stepped from the blossom of clothing, naked.

He let his eyes rove, let a smile put a single shallow wrinkle beside his mouth and said, "Aren't you the prettiest thing I ever saw."

He lifted his eyes to her face. "Why, Addie, you're blushing."

"So are you."

The smile reached his eyes. "Well, isn't that nice."

She touched the buttons at his chest and asked, "May I?"

He raised his palms and let them fall.

A moment later their blushes intensified.

He touched her the first time with four fingertips, just below her throat, on the firm, pale place above her breasts, as if to confirm her reality. From there straight down, over the tracery of lines left by her tight undergarments, then circling the perimeter of each full breast with a touch as faint as a dropping leaf.

As her eyelids closed he gently put his mouth on hers and murmured against her lips, "You're so beautiful," then picked her up and laid her on the bed.

The lantern light angled across her face as he braced on an elbow above her. It gilded her skin and sketched her eyelashes as sweeping dark curves that followed the line of her cheek, just as his hand followed the line of her breast and ribs.

"I love you, Addie," he whispered.

"Oh Robert, I love you too . . . so much."

He opened his hand on her stomach. She might never have been touched before, so fervid was her reaction, a shudder and soft gasp as she drew his head down and claimed his mouth with hers. Silence passed, a long, rich silence, while they became two in love, exalted by it.

He touched her low, made her lips part and her breath cease.

She took him in hand, made his eyes close and his heart plunge.

They opened their eyes and breathed once more, taking each other back to the beginning . . . Robert and Addie, children again, innocents, trudging through the days of acquaintanceship. Robert and Addie, adolescents, studying each other with changed eyes, imagining this day. Robert and Addie, husband and wife, pure in intention, taking their due, sharing an imperfect love made perfect by forgiveness.

It was, for Addie, all she had missed, and for Robert, all he had dreamed.

When their bodies joined it became triumph. He was kneeling with her folded around him—a damp leaf around a stem—her arms crossed upon his shoulders, his caught below her hips.

Pressed together wholly, they stilled in wonder. He lifted his face and met her lambent gaze. All those years . . . how incredible that they'd never before known each other this way. How perfect that nature had provided this accolade for two who loved as they did.

They kissed. And created motion. And made it lithe and graceful as flight.

In time her head hung back and she shuddered, calling out his name . . . half of his name . . . the remainder drifting off into infinity.

He took her down beneath him, beat an ardent rhythm upon her and watched her eyes adore his countenance, watched a smile steal upon her face as his left to make way for the clench and flush of climax.

Afterward, he rested upon her heavily.

The hair on his nape was wet. His limbs were sapped and lifeless. His breath was sketchy. Onto their sides he rolled them, keeping her close with one heel, then folding an elbow beneath his ear. He touched her nose with a fingertip and let it trail over her lips and chin.

"How do you feel, Mrs. Baysinger?"

She smiled and closed her eyes. "Don't make me say it."

"Say it."

She opened her eyes; in them, quiet satisfaction. "Like it was my first time."

He waited, thought some about what to say, drawing patterns on her throat. "It was," he said, and sketched a grapevine around her left breast.

They loved with their eyes, and after a lengthy spell of silence she said, "Robert?"

He was too content to reply.

"There's something I must say. It's about my other life."

He stopped sketching grapevines. "Say it."

"Just this once, and then I'll never talk about it again."

"Say it . . . it's all right."

"When I was with others," she told him, looking squarely into his eyes, "I had this place I escaped to, this other person I became. I was Eve, and being her was the only way I knew how to survive. But tonight, with you, I was Addie. For the first time in my life I was Addie."

He clasped her to himself full length, his chin caught on her shoulder, holding her strong.

"Shh."

"But you have to know, Robert, how much I love you for giving me back to myself."

"I know . . ." he whispered, pulling back to look into her eyes. "I know."

"I love you," she told him once more.

He accepted her statement without diluting it by returning the words. And anyway . . . she knew. She knew.

She surprised him by declaring next, "I want to have your babies."

He asked, "Can you?"

"Yes, I can."

"I didn't know for sure. I supposed there must have been something you did to prevent it all those years. I didn't know if it was permanent."

"No, it wasn't."

He kissed her, taking her neck in his hand and petting her hair afterward as if it were a scarf upturned by the wind.

"Robert?"

"Hm?" He continued smoothing her hair.

"I want a lot of your babies. More than this house will hold."

He smiled and boosted himself above her. Just before their lips met he said, "Then we'd better get busy making them."

Chapter 22

❧

With the loss of Noah, the fervor had gone out of Sarah's life. Always, before his advent, she had enjoyed a passion for her work that energized and drove her. Whatever the demand placed on her by the exigencies of newspapering, she placed an even greater one upon herself. She had been a fomenter, an inciter, a zealot who oftentimes charged in with horns lowered, her enthusiasm stemming from some source she had not questioned, had not actually known she enjoyed until it disappeared.

In the weeks following the wedding, she lowered her horns no more. She went to the newspaper office each day, but her work there seemed of little consequence. She composed articles, set type and proofread, but her labors seemed trite if not pointless. She scouted news, sold advertising and reviewed plays but admitted that in the long run what she did made very little difference in the grand scheme of the world.

At home she retired early to her room, feeling like an interloper downstairs where Addie and Robert, paragons of marital bliss, snuggled on the settee, held hands and sometimes dropped quiet kisses upon one another. Though she rued them none of their happiness, witnessing it left her feeling bereft.

In her room, she began articles that often lay unfinished while some transient memory would bring forth a line of poetry. Sometimes she composed an entire poem, other times only the one line; sometimes she poured out her loneliness in her personal journal, other times stared at the grain of the tulipwood box until her hand reached out and opened it, removed her engagement brooch and held it, rubbing it with her thumb. Afterward, she would cover her face with her palms and dwell upon her shortcomings as a woman.

Who would ever love her, a frigid shell unable to accept human warmth? If she could not accept it from a man she loved, what hope was there of overcoming her disastrous strait? Sometimes she imagined herself going to Noah and instigating a liaison, carrying it through to its end, simply to test herself. But she was too ignorant to visualize such endings, and after recounting what little she did know of sexual encounters, she would always emerge feeling guilty and dissolute.

How ironic that once she had pushed Noah away, crying, "No! I will not be like Addie!" while now she prayed to become more like her, only to find herself instead an aberration, a freak. It seemed the greatest of cruelties that nature had given her the need to be loved while robbing her of the ability to accept its most profound manifestation.

Often she damned her father, that once-admired pillar of propriety, whose licentious acts had brought her to this impasse. Despising his memory only added to her grief, turning her lonelier and more retiring at home, more bitter and fault-finding at work, where, daily, she was forced to touch the tools she had once so valued for having been Isaac Merritt's.

One day in mid-July when the newspaper office was hot and pervaded by the smell of animal dung from the street, she made a regrettable scene. She had been counting the number of times Patrick got out his hip flask and tipped it up. She'd also been listening to the speed with which the type clicked into the composing stick. It seemed to have gotten slower as the afternoon progressed. A clunk and skitter sounded behind her, followed by a curse. She looked over her shoulder to find Patrick mumbling under his breath and perusing pied type that was scattered over the galley tray. Rather than begin sorting it, he reached for his flask again. She swung about and knocked the flask from his hand.

"That's right! Drink some more! That'll fix the pied type, won't it!" she shouted. On the floor the flask whirled twice and gurgled out its contents.

Patrick tipped back on his heels. His cheeks were flushed and his gaze somewhat glassy. " 'M sorry, Miss Sarah. Didn't mean t——"

"You didn't mean," she scoffed. "You poison yourself day after day with that . . . that *swill* while it slows down your work and fills the very air with fumes! Well, I'm sick of it, Mr. Bradigan, do you hear me! Sick of it and of you stumbling around here inept in the afternoons!"

Her shrill words echoed in the room as she spun and stormed out the door, leaving Patrick and Josh staring after her. The puddle of liquor was soaking into the floorboards. The bottle had stopped gurgling. Josh crossed the room and picked it up, handed it to Patrick apologetically.

"She didn't mean it, Patrick."

"Yes, she did." Patrick studied the bottle in his thin, knobby hands. He sniffed loudly. "I drink too much and I know it."

"Naw. You do all right. You set type faster than anybody she's ever seen. She's told me so."

Patrick shook his head abjectly, staring at the bottle. "No . . . she's right. I'm nothing but a rock around her ankle."

He looked so forlorn Josh didn't know what to say by way of comfort. "Come on." He draped an arm over Patrick's back. "I'll help you pick up the type. We'll have it all sorted by the time she gets back."

Sarah, however, did not come back before closing time. When Josh and Patrick left for the day they locked the door.

She returned shortly after six P.M. to find the pied type straightened, the galley meticulously filled and lying on the composing stone with the furniture locked into place around it, ready to be printed.

The room smelled of turpentine and was stiflingly hot, the back door closed, cutting off drafts. The front door was open to the street sounds that seemed remote and lonely. Sarah stood beside the printing press feeling as if the platen had just been lowered on her chest. She had lashed out at Patrick when it was not he with whom she was displeased, but with life. She had treated him unforgivably, and had no excuse. Granted, Patrick drank, but he managed his work in spite of it, and pied type only rarely. *Anyone* who worked around type long enough would pie it occasionally: this afternoon's spill could have been caused by Josh or herself as easily as by Patrick. The three of them had established a wonderful working relationship. If anyone was threatening it lately it was she, not Patrick; she with her quick temper and sullen moods and her inability to be pleased, no matter how the others tried.

She dropped to her chair, let her head fall back against it and closed her eyes.

Oh Noah, she thought, *I'm no good without you.*

The next morning Patrick failed to show up. Sarah's apology waited on her lips, but by eight-thirty, when no Patrick appeared, she suspected she'd have no opportunity to express it. She looked up often, watching figures passing on the street, but by nine o'clock he still hadn't arrived. She took the broom and went out to sweep her boardwalk, pausing several times to gaze up the street in the direction of the hotel, hoping to see his tall, curved frame come shambling toward her. Still no Patrick.

She went inside and asked Josh, "What did he say yesterday?"

Josh shrugged and studied the toes of his boots.

"You can tell me, Josh. I know I was in the wrong and I'm very sorry for it. I only hope I get a chance to say so to him. What did he say?"

"He said he knows he drinks too much and that he's a rock around your ankle."

Sarah bit her lips to keep them from trembling, turned toward the window and murmured affectionately, "Oh Patrick."

By noon, when he still hadn't appeared, she knew he was gone, knew even as she hustled over to the Grand Central Hotel to ask Sam Peoples if he knew where Patrick was.

"He paid up this morning and left," Sam told her.

"On the stage?"

"I'm afraid so, Miss Merritt."

She turned away quickly to hide the tears that sprang to her eyes. *Patrick, come back. I didn't mean it. You were always so good to me, from the first night I came to town when you laid down your gold for me right here in this lobby and paid for my room. Please, Patrick, I'm so sorry.*

Patrick didn't come back of course. He had vanished the way all tramp printers vanish, as she had early on expected him to, but as she had in later months believed he never would, for she had come to rely on him so completely she'd been unable to imagine running the paper without him. He'd been there at its inception. He'd set her first type and run her first copies under the big pine tree the day she'd been locked in that mineshaft. He'd been around here for months, singing amusing Irish ditties, training Josh—and a patient teacher he'd been—and manning the office whenever Sarah left it. And once he had even kissed her and asked her to marry him.

One didn't lose a friend like Patrick without regrets.

• • •

Summer advanced and August came on—hot, dusty and dry. The underground quartz mining bore immense riches not only in gold, but in silver as well, while the prospect in placer mining continued at record highs. The shipments leaving Deadwood were valued in the tens of thousands of dollars. The James gang was raiding all over the upper central corridor of the country, and a kid named Antrim chalked up his first victims down in Arizona. Then one day in late August, a Deadwood freight wagon was found ten miles southwest of town with its driver and guards all dead and its thirty thousand dollars' worth of gold and silver gone.

Within an hour after the news reached town, Noah Campbell mounted a buckskin gelding in front of his office, signaled to the men who'd volunteered to ride with him and dug his heels into the horse's sides. A cloud of dust rose as the riders galloped down Main Street with guns strapped to their hips, rolls behind their saddles and their buckskin bonnet strings cinched up tightly by wooden beads.

The street was crowded with people who'd heard the news and had gathered to watch the posse off. Noah rode through them with his eyes leveled on the horizon and his expression grim. His glance shifted only once, when he passed the office of the *Deadwood Chronicle,* where Josh Dawkins, Addie Baysinger, Sarah Merritt and her new printer, Edward Norvecky had gathered to watch the departure. Of the four, he saw only one, Sarah Merritt, dressed in her leather apron with her arms crossed tightly over the bib of it and her eyes following him, only him, intent and worried as he shifted his eyes from her and riveted them straight ahead as he galloped past.

Robert rode with him, and Freeman Block, and Andy Tatum and Dan Turley and Craven Lee, and a delegation of three miners, plus an ex-army tracker who went by the name of Wolf. They rode out toward Lead, across the forested hills of Terry Peak, through the limestone plateau, a high escarpment of buff and pink rock and invariable ponderosa pine. They spent their first night in a cave at the foot of the cliffs, continuing the next morning across "the racetrack," a red valley of sandstone, clay and shale that entirely circled the hills, its soil so salty and dry no tree could survive in it and no man wanted to. Across the barren racetrack to the hogback ridge—the outer rim of the hills—traveling through eerie graveyards of petrified wood that dropped eventually to the arid stretches of the Great Plains beyond. And so into the plains themselves where water was scarce and food scarcer.

The August sun scorched their skin. The wind dried their eyes. Their tongues felt swollen. Their mounts plodded listlessly, and they stopped often, pouring water from their canteens into their hats to water their horses, drinking sparingly themselves, gnawing on jerky to replace the salt in their systems, redonning their hats to feel the welcome coolness on their heads dry within minutes as they pushed on again.

A hundred and fifty miles to the west lay the Bighorns, the probable destination of their prey, but little more than a blue haze on the horizon. The men plodded toward it. Their lips cracked. Their beards grew. Their skin stank. It became difficult to recall why they were out here in this purgatory.

Their fourth night out they camped in the open on hard earth, saddle stiff and disheartened, with prickly pear and yucca for company.

When they were bedded down on their comfortless bedrolls with their heads on their saddles, studying the stars, Robert said, "What's wrong, Noah?"

"We're never going to catch those murderers. The sonsabitches are gone and they left three dead men behind."

"No, I mean, what else is wrong? You've ridden for four days and haven't said a dozen civil words to anyone."

"It's too goddamned dry out here for talking."

Robert let that pass. "They say in town you've gotten sour and heartless, that you'd as soon throw a drunk in jail as point him toward home. You never used to be that way."

"If you don't mind, Robert, I've got some shut-eye to catch."

"It's Sarah, isn't it?"

Noah snorted. "Sarah . . . shit."

"She's just as bad as you. What the hell are the two of you trying to prove?"

"Robert, shut up, will you? When I want your advice I'll ask for it."

"You saw her out there in front of her place when we rode out, worried sick about you, don't pretend you didn't. Are you two going to stay stubborn for the rest of your lives?"

Like a spring, Noah sat up. "Robert, goddammit, I've had about enough of you! Sarah Merritt is out of my life, and I'll run my jail any way I see fit, and I'll run this posse any way I see fit! Now shut the hell up and leave me alone!"

With an angry lurch, he flung himself on his side and yanked his blanket to his shoulders, turning his back on his friend.

That night while Noah slept, something bit him, some crawling creature, no doubt—a spider maybe, Doc Turley said, examining the welt in the morning. Turley broke a yucca spine and smeared some slimy juice on the bite, but it remained scarlet and swollen and left Noah feeling dizzy and fevered. Wolf, the tracker, returned from a brief scouting trip and said it was no use going on, they'd lost the trail. The murderers were on their way to the Bighorns while the posse was exhausted and hungry and sunburned. It was time to go home.

The whole town saw them return, looking like a bunch of convicts, drooping in their saddles, with scraggly beards and dusty clothes and no prisoners in tow. Sarah went to the window of the *Chronicle* office and watched them ride by, relief slumping her shoulders. The hat she'd given Noah looked as though it had been sifted with flour. A dirty handkerchief hung around his neck, and his eyes, fixed straight ahead, appeared small and wincing in his sunburned face while his hands rested on his saddlehorn.

"Looks like they didn't catch 'em," Josh said, at her side.

"No."

"They look pretty rough, don't they?"

"Eight days is a long time."

"You going to interview the marshal about it?"

More than anything in the world, Sarah wanted to be that close to Noah once again, if only to ask him questions. The posse rode out of sight. Sarah drew a deep breath and turned to Josh. "If I draw up a list of questions, how would you like to do it?"

Josh's eyes bugged. "Really?"

"You've got to start sometime."

"Well, if you think I can."

"You interview the marshal, then we'll work on the story together."

"Gosh, thanks, Sarah!"

That night at supper, Robert supplied the story in its entirety, while putting away enough food for two men.

"Noah's changed," he remarked at one point.

Sarah refused to ask. Instead she waited for Addie to do so.

"He's got the disposition of a wounded boar," Robert said. "He's surly and silent most of the time, and when he does talk everybody wishes he wouldn't."

Sarah decided it was time she left the table. "Well . . . I've got some words to get on paper. Thank you, Robert, for filling me in."

"Sure."

When she had escaped the room Robert and Addie looked at each other and Addie asked, "Do you think either one of them will ever break down?"

"Hell, I don't know. I took enough abuse trying to talk some sense into him without getting into it with her, too."

Over the summer the town's population had leaped, as predicted the previous fall. It was no longer an uncommon sight to see women, even single ones of marriageable age, on the street. The arrival of women brought the arrival of the first ready-made clothing store for them, its first milliner, its first sidesaddles, its first sewing machine, which was purchased by Robert Baysinger for his wife's curtain-making enterprise.

Sarah Merritt had inaugurated a women's column in the *Chronicle*.

It seemed there was never a shortage of news.

A schoolteacher named Amanda Searles was hired and would begin teaching in September. An assayer from the Denver mint, named Chambers Davis, opened a full metallurgical laboratory with one furnace for the melting of gold dust and two for crucible assays of ore. In the same building the town's second stamp mill opened for business along with the first bathing arrangement with both hot and cold running water—the latter at the encouragement of Davis's well-liked, socialite wife, Adrienne. A man named Seth Bullock, who'd run for sheriff in the fall and lost, was appointed to the position by Governor John Pennington. The Deadwood Post Office was established and the town was named the county seat. A judge named Murphy moved to town and built the first brick house in all of the Black Hills. The nearby village of Gayville was destroyed by fire, prompting the organization of the Pioneer Hook and Ladder Company— again, the first in the hills. A bigamist and soiled dove named Kitty LeRoy was shot and killed by her fifth husband, a faro dealer named Sam Curley, who then turned the gun on himself.

Beyond the hills, the national bicycle craze took fire in the East with the first mass production of Colonel Albert Pope's "Columbia" safety bicycle. Cycling clubs formed everywhere and started badgering for better roads, begging the newspapers to back them up in their efforts. Adrienne Davis had a bicycle shipped into Deadwood and stopped traffic everywhere when she was seen riding it in skirts shorter than her ankles.

Meanwhile, James J. Hill was busy buying up land to lay down the foundations of his railroad empire while President Marvin Hughit of the North Western Railroad assured the mayor of Deadwood that the rails would head their way as soon as the survey showed it to be practical.

By the end of August the grasshoppers left Minnesota.

In September child labor became an issue in Massachusetts.

In October the Evans and Hornick ox train arrived in Deadwood from Fort Pierre with a record-breaking 300,000 pounds of freight.

Over the stretch of that summer and autumn the face of Deadwood changed dramatically. The brush wickiups were replaced by frame buildings, many of them sporting exterior paint. Through their windows curtains could be seen. The flowers planted by the incoming women trimmed yards and fences. The town now employed a lamplighter/street cleaner who made the main thoroughfare a more pleasant place by both night and day. A new school building was erected. Children were seen walking to it in the mornings and from it in the afternoons.

Deadwood had been domesticated.

So had Addie Baysinger. One evening in late November, with supper over and her hand tight in Robert's beneath the table, she smiled at Sarah and said, "We're going to have a baby."

Sarah's coffee cup never made it to her lips. It clicked onto her saucer as her eyes went round. For moments she only stared. At last she found her tongue.

"Oh Addie, how perfect."

"We're so happy. Aren't we, Robert?" Addie turned her adoring gaze on Robert, who brought her hand from beneath the table and kissed her knuckles.

His smile verified it even before he spoke. "Absolutely happy. We want a boy."

Sarah covered their joined hands with both of her own, squeezing hard. "This is wonderful news. I'm so happy for you. Congratulations." Their countenances radiated such uncomplicated joy, the sight of them beaming at one another gripped Sarah's heart. Her little sister and dear, kind Robert—they'd weathered every setback and emerged victorious.

Truly, their happiness was a victory. Living with them, Sarah had observed its effects firsthand as the two of them settled into the routine of married life like contented birds building a nest. Now that nest would be filled, and it was time—Sarah realized—that she herself moved out of it.

"When is the happy event?"

Addie shrugged excitedly. "I don't know for sure. Sometime in late spring, I think."

"The perfect time. Warm days and cool nights, and a while before the worst of the mosquitoes come out."

"As far as I'm concerned, any time would be the perfect time," Addie said.

"Also the perfect time for me to move out," Sarah added.

Addie's brow furled. "But Sarah, we have plenty of room. Why, this little feller won't need more than a clothes basket to sleep in."

"It's time," Sarah said simply. "I've been thinking about it for a couple of months already. I appreciate your letting me live with you for as long as I have, but this is *your* home, and it's time I left it to you."

Addie and Robert spoke together.

"But Sarah—"

"You know we don't—"

Sarah held up her hands. "I know." She rested them on the table. "You would allow me to stay until I grew too old to climb the stairs if I were silly enough to put you out that long."

"We love you, Sarah," Robert said earnestly. "We don't want you to leave."

Sarah smiled at him tenderly and squeezed the back of his hand once more. "Thank you, Robert, but *I* need to go. I need to have a place of my own, roots of my own, some sense of belonging somewhere for life."

"But the house is yours as well as mine," Addie said.

"It was bought with Father's money, but so was the newspaper office. So we're even, aren't we? Now, I don't want to hear any more about it." Sarah rose, collecting empty coffee cups. "I've decided I'll start looking immediately and will hope to have a place of my own by the first of the year. I'll stay here through Christmas, but that's all." As she carried the cups away, Robert and Addie exchanged glances that admitted, while they were reluctant to see Sarah go, the idea of living alone was undeniably inviting. Robert rose and followed Sarah to the dry sink where she set the cups down. He took her by the shoulders and turned her to face him.

"As long as you know you're always welcome here."

There was no question in Sarah's mind. She also knew as she looked into Robert's eyes that he still felt guilty for causing the breakup between herself and Noah, and that, as penance, he would keep her beneath his wing forever if she would let him.

"I know, Robert. I'll only be across town somewhere, and I'll come back often to see that little boy of yours. I'll probably spoil him silly."

He squeezed her arms and kissed her cheek. The touch of his mustache brought the memory of another and made Sarah already feel like a lonely maiden aunt.

Shortly thereafter, Addie began wearing loose-fitting dresses without waists. She was the healthiest expectant mother imaginable, with a new glow in her normally pale cheeks, her gold hair shiny and grown to collar length, and a contentment level that sometimes brought Sarah a pang of envy. Having grown up as she had in a motherless home, Sarah had never witnessed marital bliss. During those winter days while Christmas approached—short days when dark fell early and the favorite place was near the kitchen range—both she and Robert took to coming home earlier. He would enter the house smiling and go directly to Addie, wherever she was, whatever she was doing. He would kiss her forehead, mouth or ear and ask how the little fellow was doing in there, and would glance lovingly at Addie's round stomach. She would show him the tiny clothes she'd made—the sewing machine was constantly clunking—or exclaim that she'd read in *Peterson's Magazine* some tidbit about the preparation of baby foods or diaper care or teething. Once Sarah found them standing facing a kitchen window at dusk with Robert behind Addie, his chin on her shoulder and his arms doubled around her midriff below her breasts. Addie's arms covered his and her head was tilted to one side. Neither of them spoke, only rocked blissfully left and right. Sarah watched them for some time, then tiptoed away, leaving them undisturbed to stand by herself at the front-room window and stare out at the dusky tones of twilight, thinking of Noah and aching for all they had missed.

Addie and Robert were painfully aware of Sarah's increasing despondency and withdrawal. At night, in bed, they whispered about it and wondered how to help her.

One night in December, when supper was over and Sarah had retired early to her room, Robert went to Addie where she sat stitching in the parlor in a straight-backed side chair which had grown more comfortable as her girth increased. He bent down and braced his hands on the arms of her chair and said, looking into her eyes, "I'm going to Noah's."

When they had exchanged a prolonged gaze she somberly touched his cheek and said, "Good luck, dear."

It was almost eight-thirty by the time he approached Noah's kitchen door. Noah answered his knock and for moments neither man spoke.

Finally Noah said, "Well, this is a surprise."

"You still pissed off at me?" Robert asked, point-blank.

"No. I got over that long ago."

"Am I disturbing anything?"

"Hardly. Just having a late supper. Come on in."

Inside, Noah said, "Take your coat off, sit down."

The room looked barren and lonely but for the yellow flowered curtains that Addie had made last spring, the only woman-touch in the room. Noah's interrupted meal consisted of beans and bread on a blue enamel plate. The table had no cloth; the room no pictures on the wall, ivies at the windowsill, nor rug beneath the table. Noah's boots stood by the woodbox, his hat lay on the table, his gunbelt hung on the back of his chair and his heavy leather jacket hung on a peg by the door, alone. It wrenched Robert's heart to see his friend so lonely.

"So how've you been?"

Noah shrugged. "Oh, you know. Same as always." He sat down and resumed his meal. "I hear you and Addie are going to have a baby," he remarked.

"That's right. Sometime toward spring. She's one happy woman."

"I hear you're one happy man, too."

"That's a fact."

"Well that's good. I'm damned happy for you both."

Silence fell. Noah ate a forkful of beans. Robert sat back in his chair with one elbow on the table and his ankle over a knee, studying his friend.

"How come we never see you up at the house anymore?"

Noah stopped eating. "You know why."

They measured each other awhile. "So," Robert said, "you avoid her and you avoid us, too."

"It's not intentional. I figured you'd know that."

"Well, for what it's worth, we miss you around there."

Noah set down his fork and studied it in silence.

"I came over here to tell you something."

Noah met Robert's eyes and waited.

"Sarah says she's moving out the first of the year."

Noah's eyes remained expressionless while he absorbed the news. "So?"

Robert spoke with fire. "So she's going to find some house and live in it alone, and you're going to sit up here eating your beans alone at eight-thirty at night and it makes no goddamned sense at all!"

"She doesn't want me."

"She wants you so damned bad she's dying inside."

Noah snorted and looked away.

"Jesus Christ, man, she had a shock. I know because I'm the one who gave it to her. And, yes, she needed some time to get over it, but not the rest of her life!"

Noah snapped a look at Robert. "She wrote me off and I'm not crawling back to her to get kicked in the teeth again. Twice is enough!"

Robert studied Noah awhile and asked quietly, "You love her, don't you?"

Noah threw his head back, pushed away from the table edge with both hands and exclaimed to the ceiling, "Sheece!"

"Don't you?"

Noah leveled his chin and shot a withering glance at Robert from the corner of his eye.

"So how many other women have you been seeing lately?"

"How many other men has she been seeing?"

"None. She sits in that house at night watching Addie's stomach get bigger and tiptoeing around to try to keep out of our way, and I never saw a lonelier sight in my whole life than her trying to pretend she's happier without you. Unless, of course, it's you up here with your beans, trying to pretend you're happier without her."

Noah tipped forward, clunked his elbows on the table, joined his hands in a hard knot and pressed them to his mouth, staring at an empty chair on the opposite side of the table.

Robert let the silence go, let Noah stare and think awhile. On the stove a teakettle sizzled. In the firebox a coal popped. Noah's eyes got suspiciously glisteny. He held them wide, careful not to blink.

Finally he closed them, dropped his forehead to his thumb knuckles and whispered, "I can't."

Robert reached out and put his hand around Noah's forearm. "I know," he said softly, "it's hard. But it's hard for her, too." He let some seconds pass before adding, "Chambers and Adrienne Davis have invited Addie and me to their place for dinner next Saturday. We'll be leaving the house at seven o'clock." He squeezed Noah's arm once, let his hand fall away and rose, buttoning his coat.

Noah lifted his head and stared at the chair as before. Robert put on his hat and gloves.

"Sometimes a person can suffocate on his own pride," he said, then left his friend sitting there in his silent kitchen with his elbows braced on either side of a plate of cold beans.

When Robert was gone Noah remained at the table a long time, his wounds freshly opened. The last seven months had been hell: lonely, painful, tormented. She had rejected him, emasculated him, and left him still loving her. Love? Was this love? This colorless movement through days that seemed to have neither crest nor trough but rolled along doldrumflat? This searching the faces on the street for a glimpse of her, then crossing to the other side if she appeared up ahead? This dwelling on the memories he had of her instead of making new ones with someone else? This wanting, one minute, to go to her and shake her till her head snapped, the next pitying her to the point of misery?

He had moved through his first twenty-six years with relative clear-mindedness, quite sure of himself, his motives, his desires, his goals. Since Sarah Merritt had come into his life and left it, he had become like the habitual drinker who says, I can quit anytime I want to, then gets drunk by noon every day. She was his liquor, the thing he declared he could live without, but dwelled on with debilitating regularity.

Perhaps this was true because he was the spurned one and his ego was wrinkled. But if that were the case, he would have hied himself over to Rose's and gotten his ego starched months ago. Instead, he had felt no predilection toward that pastime in which he'd once so blithely indulged; the revelations about Addie's sorry past had taken care of that.

There were other women in Deadwood now, decent women he might have pursued, but none seemed to appeal, nor could he shake the feeling that he still owed monogamousness to Sarah Merritt, broken betrothal or not.

He wondered if he would go through life without ever marrying, one of those pitiable creatures about whom the locals, when he was seventy and bent, would say, he never got over his broken heart, just holed up there in that house they bought together, and let those yellow curtains she'd put up hang there till they were nothing but holes, and ate his meals alone.

Robert was right, eating his beans alone was one of the most pathetic rites he'd ever experienced. Why did he do it? Why didn't he go up to Teddy's and have supper with people? Why didn't he say, to hell with Sarah Merritt, I have some living to do?

Because he'd been waiting for her to heal, to knock on his door and walk into this kitchen with regret in her eyes and say to him, Noah, I'm sorry. Noah, please take me back. Noah, I love you.

But would she? Could she? Or was he pining away for something she was incapable of doing?

He could go to her and do the pursuing once more, might even get her to say she'd marry him, but what then? An attempt at seducing her before marching her down the aisle was unthinkable. She had made it abundantly clear she would not abide it—and, hell, to tell the truth, the thought of laying a hand on her terrified him by this time. So . . . let Victorian mores dictate that she approach her wedding bed a virgin? But supposing she froze up on him then too? Supposing he took the jump and found himself committed to a lifetime of living with a frigid woman.

Noah Campbell sat with his elbows beside his beans, beleaguered by the dozens of unanswered questions that felt like hammerblows as they clanged through his head.

So what're you going to do when Saturday night comes, Noah?

I don't know.

You gonna go over there and let her turn you away again?

She might not.

That's right. She might not, but then again she just might.

Chapter 23

On Saturday night Sarah watched Addie bustling around the house getting dressed for her first social invitation since she'd married Robert. She pinned her hair up in a neat gold crown, polished her lips with petroleum jelly and donned a maternity frock covered by a hooded cape of periwinkle blue. Dressed totally respectably, she nevertheless stood before Sarah looking doubtful. "I wonder if Adrienne Davis knows about my past."

"My guess is she does, but she's willing to overlook it. She's a natural-born social leader, and tonight is going to be your ticket into acceptable society."

"Do you really think so, Sarah?"

Sarah kissed Addie's cheek. "You're Mrs. Robert Baysinger now." She tipped her chin up. "Be proud, and don't let the past matter."

When they left the house, Addie looked proud indeed, holding Robert's arm, excited and anticipatory. Sarah watched them go, feeling wistful and a little envious of their happiness.

When they were gone the house felt mournful. She wandered around listlessly, watered some houseplants, went up to her room, removed her shoes and replaced them with maroon felt carpet slippers. She pulled the combs from her hair and let it trail down her back, too lonely to care about brushing it. She released her throat—and cuff-buttons, wrapped in her favorite ugly pumpkin-colored shawl, took out her engagement brooch, placed it before her on the desk, donned her spectacles and got out her journal. In time she got chilled and found herself staring into the cubbyholes of the desk, writing little.

Around eight o'clock she took her writing materials downstairs. There was a Christmas tree in the parlor, but the room was dark as Sarah crossed through it on her way to the kitchen where she arranged her things on the table, the brooch within easy reach beside the journal with its marbelized cover and unlined white pages. She added two logs to the fire, poured herself a cup of leftover coffee and sat down once more to write.

The sounds in the kitchen—homey in times of fulfillment—tonight seemed lonely, and intensified Sarah's sense of solitude: the hiss of the teakettle in its customary nighttime spot at the cooler end of the range; the soft pop of the fire as it subsided to glowing coals; the creak of her chair as she leaned over the table; the scrape of her pen on the paper; the hiss of the lantern while she sat staring at the brooch, waiting for words to form in her mind; the quiet thump as Ruler jumped from a chair and stretched with her hindquarters raised.

Sarah sat back. "Hey, Ruler, come here," she coaxed, dropping her hand with the fingers pursed.

Ruler finished her stretch, seated herself in the curl of her tail and blinked at Sarah from five feet away. She studied the cat awhile, wishing she would leap up to her lap—a warm, living solace—but Ruler had other things to do. She started giving herself a bath.

It'd be nice to be a cat. All you'd have to be concerned with would be eating and sleeping and preening. There'd be no such thing as regrets or wishes or broken engagements. When the spirit moved you, you'd go out and hunker down and growl for half an hour, nose to nose with one of your ilk, and howl a little bit and leap around in the moonlight in the tall grass or the crusty snow, and when the moment was right, couple with your lady love, and the next day have no concern or memory of it.

Ruler moved farther away, leaped onto the rocking chair seat where she settled in the shape of a muff with her front paws hidden.

Sarah dipped her pen and wrote, "I wonder what it would feel like to be expecting a child, to don my cape over my bulging stomach and leave the house on Noah's arm, heading for a dinner with Chambers and Adrienne Davis, to be at last a part of the world that moves two by two." She dipped her pen again and held it above the page, staring at its black nib until the ink started drying, creating a marbleized design of peacock and copper on the curved metal.

In the front room, some needles fell from the Christmas tree onto the bare wood floor. Ruler's ears twitched, her pupils dilated, and she glanced sharply at the doorway.

Sarah sat watching her absently until Ruler settled back into a furball and squinted her eyes. Sarah turned her regard to the brooch, reached out and touched it with her fingertips, as lightly as if inspecting it for fine cracks.

In time she sighed, dipped the pen and wrote on. "I find myself fantasizing about Noah so often, picturing what it would be like if I were like Addie and could—"

A knock sounded on the front door.

Both Sarah and Ruler shot startled glances through the doorway. Sarah sat unmoving until it sounded again, then pushed back her chair and removed her glasses, leaving them behind as she gripped her shawl and headed for the dark front room. With one hand she clustered her disorderly hair at her nape, then let it spring back into disarray as she opened the door.

Noah stood on the step.

For seconds neither he nor Sarah spoke. Or moved. He studied her from beneath the brim of his brown Stetson, his hands at his sides, his features only a suggestion in the faraway light from the kitchen lantern. The lines linking his nose and mouth were deep grooves, disappearing into his dark mustache. His somber eyes were mere pinpricks of light.

She stood on the threshold above him, one hand gripping her aged shawl, the other, the doorknob, while only the ragtail outline of her hair was lit from the light behind her.

"Hello, Sarah," he said finally in a voice that sounded weary beyond belief.

"Hello, Noah."

Silence abounded while they waited for a miracle to bring ease between them.

"I think we should talk. Could I come in?"

"Addie and Robert aren't home. They're gone to the Davises'."

"Yes, I know, Robert told me. That's why I came."

She hid her surprise and said, "What good will talking do?"

"I don't know . . ." He dropped his gaze to the threshold and shook his head forlornly. "I don't know," he repeated, quieter. "I only know we've got to because we can't go on like this anymore."

She stepped back and freed his way. "Come in then."

He moved the way a farmer moves through his fields after they have been leveled by hail, entering the front room with its scent of pine and its total familiarity, even in the near dark. She left the door for him to close, placing herself a goodly distance away, waiting with her arms crossed, wrapped so tightly the weave of the crocheted shawl became distorted.

"I'll light a lantern," she said, heading toward a round parlor table between two chairs—three amorphous shapes in the dark.

"No, don't. The kitchen is warmer anyway." He moved toward it as if homing to some force beyond his control. In the doorway he paused, studying the room where he had shared meals and felicitations, laughter and games, and friendships whose absence had left a void in his life. Sarah had been writing: her things were scattered on the table. The room emanated a melancholy that struck him deep—the cat curled up on a rocking chair by the stove, the evidence of Sarah's singular occupation on a Saturday night when the others were off to happier pursuits, the betrothal brooch he had given her resting among her writing materials like a sad, powerless talisman. He stepped near the edge of the table and looked down at her empty coffee cup, the brooch, her glasses, the open book with her effortless angular writing, so different from his own labored scratching that never seemed to follow the horizontal line of the page. He touched the book, read the last sentence she had written and felt a great pressure in his chest.

From the doorway she watched him and remarked quietly, "It's not polite to read other people's journals."

He looked over his shoulder, studied her tightly crossed arms and smileless face. "You don't have any secrets from me, Sarah. Everything you're feeling, I'm feeling. I'd say we're a couple of pretty miserable people."

"Sit down." She came into the room and closed the book, set the penholder atop it and left the brooch where it was. He hung his jacket on the back of a kitchen chair, took off his hat, scooped the cat off the rocker and dropped to it himself while Sarah resumed her place at the table.

Ruler stayed on Noah's lap where she'd been put, giving their eyes a focal point while Noah scratched the creature's neck and head. In time he lifted his gaze and asked wearily, "So what are we going to do, Sarah?"

She put her elbows on the table, wrapped one hand loosely around the other and rested her cheek on them. "I don't know."

Some time passed before he said, "I missed you."

A smile touched her lips, then fled: her only reply.

"Say it," he said.

"I think it's better if I don't."

"Say it anyway."

"I missed you, too."

For a while they simply looked at each other, allowing the loneliness of the past months to show in their faces. Ruler began purring. Noah kept scratching.

"I've done some tough things in my life, but coming here tonight beats them all."

"So why did you?"

"Because I've been going through hell and hell's not my favorite place to be going through. How about you?"

"Yes. The same."

"This town's got some nice decent women now, but I'd as soon eat a dish of mud as take one of them out. Damn you for that, Sarah Merritt."

Her smile glimmered again, as sad as before.

Noah drew a deep breath, let it out with a faint shudder and dropped his head against the back of the chair. His eyes closed. He set the rocker in slight motion and breathed, "I'm so damned tired."

An urge flooded her as she studied him: to rise and cross the few feet that separated them, line his cheeks with both her palms and kiss his closed eyes, then rest her jaw against his forehead.

She rose instead and refilled her coffee cup without offering him any. "I suppose you've heard Robert and Addie are expecting a baby."

"Yes, I heard."

"Ironic, isn't it . . ." She stood facing the stove, a finger in the cup handle, without drinking. ". . . that I wish it were me."

He opened his eyes and studied her long back with the latticework of ugly pumpkin-colored knit covering her brindle-brown blouse, and her hair streaming over both, in bad need of combing.

"Do you?"

"Yes, very much. I envy them."

"That surprises me."

"Me, too. I always thought my newspapering was enough to keep me happy."

"And it's not?"

She refused to answer.

He sighed.

A long time went by before he asked, "Could we talk about your father, Sarah?"

"My father is no longer mentioned in this house."

"Your father's been mentioned in every word that you and I have spoken since that night you found out about him."

"I loved him more than any person on this earth and he betrayed that love in the most unforgivable way possible."

"And now I pay for what he did to Addie. How much longer?"

"Why don't you just go to one of those other women? It would be so much simpler for you."

"Because you're the one I'm stuck on. I told you that before. I stayed away from you for better than half a year hoping I could get over you but it didn't work. I still love you."

He watched her from behind, gauging her minute motions, the slight drop of her chin, the way she held the cup without drinking from it. She took it to the dry sink and set it down, untasted, then returned to her chair and her former pose with her cheek resting on her loosely joined hands.

"Marrying you would be sheer stupidity."

"But you want to, don't you?"

"Yes."

"What if I came over there and kissed you and touched you in a less than brotherly way, what would happen?"

She laughed ruefully, put ten fingertips over her face and wobbled her head left and right twice.

"See?" he said. "That's what I mean when I said coming here took some nerve. If you turned me away again it would be the last time. I could never come back again."

"I've had the most preposterous thought these last few months," she admitted, regarding him again over her joined hands. "It's absurd, sinful even, but I've had it nonetheless, during my weaker moments when I've missed you so much I wondered if I might die of it. I've thought, why couldn't I marry Noah and we would silently agree that he could continue going to Rose's as he did when I first met him? There. Now you know what kind of woman I am."

The corners of his mouth tipped up sadly. "Lonely, scared . . . just like me."

They studied one another while the lantern hissed and the stove radiated warmth, finding their point-blank honesty at once disconcerting and relieving.

"Now I'll tell you a deep, dark secret of my own, something I've imagined since we've been apart—coming here and hauling you upstairs and taking your dress off and kissing you in ten places and showing you that when you care about someone the way we care about each other, that's a natural part of it. Do you want to try it?"

She laughed aloud, briefly. "Of course not."

"No, of course not. If you'd said yes, you wouldn't be Sarah and I wouldn't love you and we wouldn't be sitting here across the room from each other, hurting this way. So what should we do?"

Her mouth got the tortured look that precedes tears. Her only answer was a shake of the head: "I don't know, I'm so afraid."

He put his feet flat on the floor and leaned forward, scaring the cat away. Resting both elbows on his knees, he fixed his eyes on Sarah's. When he spoke his voice sounded constricted and unnatural.

"Did you really miss me so much you thought you might die of it?"

"Yes," she whispered, feeling her chin grow hot where her joined hands touched it.

"Then meet me," he said and pointed at the floor halfway between them. "There."

She felt adhered to the chair, studying his earnest eyes, the slope of his shoulders leaning toward her, his squarish hands curved one around the other as he waited for her response. She had only to rise to be in his arms again and face the moment of proof. Her only other choice was to watch him walk out that door, never to return, to relive the purgatory she had suffered since they'd parted ways.

She had moved in a colorless, tasteless void these past seven months without him, but tonight he had merely to appear before her and she came back to life. He stepped into a room and her apathy vanished like frost from a lighted windowpane; she *felt* again.

To maintain this distance from him was agony. To watch his face reflect the torment on her own filled her with anguish. Was this passion? She so wanted passion, not for its own sake, but because without it she was doomed.

"Meet me," he repeated.

She swallowed the tears that were on the verge of forming and pushed back her chair, fear and want crushing her like a great hand that would prevent her from rising. She pressed her palms to the tabletop and rose against it.

He got up from the rocker and waited.

"I wish I were Addie," she whispered as she began to move toward him.

"No, you don't," he replied, moving, too, "because then there wouldn't be you and me."

They met at the corner of the table, pausing before one another before stepping into a tenuous embrace. They held each other loosely, acclimating to the tumult of feelings before he drew back and offered his eyes, then his mouth, softly. The great weight of loneliness lifted, and the kiss became a twining, the embrace a reclaiming of what each had given up. She put her arms about his neck and he drew her full-length against him. Heart to heart, they rested, their eyes closed, their fear of missteps dissolving in the grand rush of reunion. They kissed unbrokenly, testing each other, and themselves, letting the contact heat at will until their mouths opened and their tongues met. She made a small, pained sound in her throat and he replied with a tightening of his embrace. Suddenly their restraint vanished and their kiss became urgent, their bodies taken fire from the taste and touch of one another after the months of self-denial. He made a throaty sound, too, neither sob nor groan, but an agonized end of agony while their fists searched for a grip—his on the woolly weave of her shawl, hers on the smooth leather of his vest.

In time they halted to hold each other fast and let the torrent of feelings rush out.

"Oh Noah, I love you," she said. "I missed you, I was bereft without you."

"I love you, too. Tell me again."

"I love you, Noah."

He held her so tightly her heels left the floor. "I never thought I'd hear you say it again."

"I was always so stubborn about saying it . . . I'm sorry, Noah, but I do love you, I do, only I never thought falling in love would be so terrible."

"Or so wonderful."

"Or so frightening."

"Or so lonely. A hundred times a day I had to stop myself from walking past your newspaper office."

"I kept looking out the window, hoping to see you pass."

"And then we'd meet on the boardwalk and act like we didn't know each other."

"Nobody could live with me."

"Me either. I was angry at the whole world."

"I snapped at everybody and got so irritable and fault-finding. I scared off Patrick with my temper, and I miss him so much. And poor Josh— I've been awful to him, too. Nothing seemed right without you, nothing."

They kissed again, incautiously and deep, searching for motions to re-iterate all they felt. When it ended he had a two-handed grip on her hair, tipping her head back with the faintest tug on her scalp.

"I never want to go through that again," he said fiercely.

"Neither do I."

They let their eyes rove each other's face, sharing a very small space on the kitchen floor, with her maroon carpet slippers planted between his scuffed brown cowboy boots. He released her hair and began stroking it back from her temples.

"How do you feel?" he asked.

"As if I've been living underwater for a long long time and have just come up into the air."

"How else do you feel?"

With her head thrown back and her throat arched, the words came out strained. "I want you."

His hands stopped moving. "I'm going to do something. Don't be scared." He lifted her in his arms, threshold fashion, and ordered, "Turn off the lantern."

She reached and adjusted the ribbed brass screw, bringing darkness descending over the room, then linked her arms around his neck. He carried her to the rocker and put her on his lap with her legs draped over a wooden arm of the chair.

"Say my name," he whispered.

"Noah."

"Say it again."

"Noah."

"Yes, Noah . . . and I still want to marry you." He set the chair in motion, rocking gently, and resumed stroking her hair back from her left temple while his other hand curved up her back and closed lightly around her neck, toying with it beneath her hair. He kissed her mouth softly . . . softly . . . and went on rocking her, easing her, touching his lips to other fine places—her cheek, her eyebrow, her chin. He nuzzled her throat, felt her head hang back and the warmth of her hair leave his left hand. He touched her breast the way he had touched her hair, a finding in the dark, a mere grazing without demand. He heard her breath catch and went on caressing her with faint strokes of his thumb while his forearm rested along her stomach.

"I love you, Sarah," he whispered.

He felt tremors begin deep within her. They shimmied up through his arm as he caressed her breast and felt it bead up. She murmured something—a wordless sound that needed no words, sliding from her throat as she covered his hand with both of her own and clamped it tightly against herself. She drew her head up with an effort and brought his open hand to her face and kissed it in three places, then replaced it on her breast. She closed her eyes and sat very still, letting his hand play over her. When he found her mouth again, her lips were open, the breath hurrying from them in wonderful, soft gusts.

As the kiss ended, she whispered in wonder, "Oh Noah . . ."

His hand departed her breast and settled her in the curve of his shoulder with her forehead on his jaw. The rocking chair resumed its faint, rhythmic ticks against the floor.

"Oh Noah," she repeated, her breath warm against his neck.

In the darkness he smiled and continued rocking.

"So will you marry me, you stubborn woman?"

"Yes, I'll marry you, you incorrigible man."

"I won't go to Rose's."

"I don't think you'll have to," she replied.

He stopped rocking and kissed her—much less desperately than when they'd been on their feet, but leaning forward and coiling around her until his leather vest creaked. He kissed her in myriad soft ways, and, parting, let his lips linger.

"Did I see that betrothal brooch on your kitchen table?"

"Yes, you did."

"Do we have to light the lantern to find it?"

"No, of course not, I can find it in the dark. I've done it many times." She left his lap, retaining a fingerhold on one of his hands while reaching for the tabletop. Momentarily, she returned, and, sitting upright on his lap, pinned the brooch to her blouse, directly over her heart.

"There," she said, settling into the lee of his shoulder once more. "Everything's where it should be."

"Let's see," he whispered. He found the brooch, and if in finding it he touched her breast again, she objected no more than she had the first time.

Minutes later she whispered, "Noah?"

"Hm?"

They were rocking again, wishing Addie and Robert would never come home.

"That feels wonderful."

He chuckled and kept on rocking.

They were married on Christmas Eve at five P.M. by Birtle Matheson in a brief, quiet ceremony with only Addie and Robert as witnesses. Sarah wore a simple dress of ivory satin—made by Addie—and carried a tiny ivory Bible festooned with matching ribbon. Her hair was upswept in a modified pompadour—again by Addie—trimmed by a tiny spray of seed pearls, and her lips were painted, for the first time in her life, with a touch of coral.

Noah wore the black suit he'd bought months ago for this occasion, with its double-breasted vest, a white shirt with a wing-tipped collar and a black four-in-hand tie.

After the ceremony the four of them had supper at Addie and Robert's house, accompanied by champagne and a fancy ribbon cake baked for the occasion by Emma, who had gracefully accepted the news that the wedding was to be private and small, so small she herself would not be invited.

"You do it your way, Sarah," she had said, "and blessed be the day."

On her way home from Addie's, Sarah was thinking, . . . *and blessed be the night . . . please, oh please.*

The house where she would live as Noah's wife was as she remembered, plain and only partially furnished, awaiting her choices on what remained to be bought. Entering the kitchen, she exclaimed, "Why, it's warm in here."

"I hired Josh to come and stoke the fire."

"Oh, how thoughtful, Noah . . . thank you."

The lantern flared, then Noah came up behind her and took her coat from her shoulders. He hung it, along with his own, and his hat, then returned to her.

"I have another surprise for you. Come." He took her hand, and the lantern, and led her straight up the stairs to their bedroom, where he stepped back to let her enter first. In one corner, in a pail of sand, trimmed with embossed cardboard cutouts and red wax candles in tin clips, was a fragrant spruce tree.

"Oh Noah!" she exclaimed, delighted. "When did you do this?" She had been here earlier to bring her belongings, and the corner had been bare.

"This afternoon after you left. I'll have to confess, I hired Josh to go out and find it."

"It smells delicious. Can we light the candles?"

"Of course. But I'd better get some water up here first, just in case." He set the lantern on the dresser, took the pitcher from the bowl and said, "Be right back."

While he was gone, she put her hands to her cheeks and glanced at the bed, trying to be calm.

Noah returned in minutes with the full pitcher and some matches. He struck one on his heel and touched the wicks of ten miniature candles. The shadows of the pine needles danced on the ceiling and walls. They studied the flames in silence before he turned to look at her and said quietly, "Merry Christmas, Mrs. Campbell."

She looked into his eyes and replied, "Merry Christmas, Mr. Campbell." His thumb stroked hers . . . once, twice . . . then they prudently returned their gazes to the tree. Already the candles were dripping red wax onto the lower branches, and it was beginning to tick onto the floor.

"I'm afraid we'll have to blow them out."

"They were lovely while they lasted."

She blew out all ten flames and stood amidst the scent of smoking wicks. "You made us a beautiful memory, Noah. Thank you."

He retreated and she heard movement behind her. She turned to discover he had removed his jacket and was loosening his tie.

"You'll need help with your buttons," he said.

"Oh . . . yes." She turned her heated face away, presenting her back, and he stepped behind her to do the honors.

"Thank you," she whispered when the last button was freed.

He cleared his throat and said, "I have to step out back and put a couple more pieces of wood in the stove." At the sound of his retreating footsteps she glanced back over her shoulder. He paused in the doorway, said, "The water in the pitcher is warm," and disappeared without even taking the lantern.

She was so relieved her breath swooshed from her like a passing gale. He had said he'd visualized taking her dress off and kissing her in ten places, and she'd supposed that's how this interlude would begin, and in spite of the episode on the rocking chair, when her clothing had remained intact, she had worried that at the last minute she would be terrified and stiffen up and would ruin her wedding night. Instead, he proved himself romantic and considerate beyond her dearest hopes.

He gave her more time than needed. By the time he returned, her nightgown was buttoned up the front and tied at the throat, her face was washed and she was brushing her hair before the dresser mirror.

She glanced at the doorway the moment he stopped in it, and tried to hide a smile: he was wearing a red and white striped nightshirt.

"It's all right, you can laugh," he said, lifting his arms and glancing down. "I've never worn one of these things before. I thought you might appreciate it, but I feel like a damned sissy."

A sudden laugh doubled her forward with the back of the brush against her mouth. In none of her preconceptions had she pictured herself laughing on her wedding night. When she straightened, he was chuckling, too, studying his bare feet and rather skinny ankles.

"Good God," he muttered, then stood straight and jabbed a thumb at the bed. "Would you mind getting in there so I can pile in behind you and hide?"

She scrambled into the bed, still smiling, establishing her place closest to the wall. He *did* pile in right behind her, leaving the lantern lit and pulling the covers to their waists.

Settling onto her back, she thought, *He's wonderful. He knows how nervous I am and he's doing everything he knows to make this easy for me.*

He settled on his side, braced his head on one hand, and immediately found her hand, fit his fingers tightly between hers, closed them hard and kissed her knuckles.

"I know you're scared, but there's no need to be."

"But I don't know what to do."

"You don't need to know. I know."

He had ways, oh, he had ways. He used them, one upon the other, gentling her with a first tender kiss, sweet and moist, while finding her bare foot beneath the blankets and covering it with one of his own. His head swayed, and the smooth sole of his foot rubbed the top of hers, then hooked her leg from behind and held it captive. The kiss ended and he nuzzled her jaw, the soft hollow beneath it.

"How can you smell like roses in the dead of winter?" he asked.

"I put on some rose water while you were downstairs."

"Oh, you did?" He backed up and smiled, only inches from her face, and brushed her cheek with a knuckle.

"Did you put some roses here, too?"

She blushed brighter. "Do men always tease women when they're doing this?"

"I don't know. This one does. Does it bother you?"

"It's unexpected . . . it's . . . I . . . I'm not used to blushing."

"It's very becoming, though. I think I'll make you do it often."

"Oh Noah . . ." She dropped her gaze demurely.

He lifted her chin and kissed her so very lightly his shadow never fully darkened her lips. Then again, to one side of her mouth . . . and the other . . . then on her chin . . . and on her throat.

"Mmm . . . I remember this smell. You smelled like this one year ago tonight."

"And you smelled like this across the breakfast table at Mrs. Roundtree's every morning after you'd shaved."

He lifted his head, smiling. "I didn't know you noticed."

"I noticed a lot of things about you. I memorized every shirt you owned, and your favorite foods, and a lot of little mannerisms you have. But mostly I noticed your hair . . . I so love your hair, Noah."

He went perfectly still, fixing his gray eyes on her beautiful blue ones, leaning on one elbow, motionless above her.

"Touch it," he whispered.

She raised both hands and threaded them through his thick, lush hair, ruffling it, mussing it, living out a fantasy as his eyelids slid closed and he lowered his face to the eyelet lace between her breasts. While her hands continued moving, his breath warmed her, his mouth opened and he caressed her with it alone, nuzzling the inner swells of her breasts within her lace-trimmed gown.

Her eyes drifted closed, too, and her fingertips relaxed in his hair, becoming still as he found and covered the fullest part of her breast. "Ohh," she breathed, surprised by the swift sensation and her response to it. Her hands clasped his skull, drawing him more fully against herself, first one breast, then the other, where he bit her—bit her!—and sent a wondrous recoil clear to her toes.

Abruptly he rose, rushing up like a swimmer out of the deep, meeting her waiting mouth with his, matching their bodies while everything became urgent. Tangled in two nightgowns, they pressed as close as the folds of cotton would allow.

Suddenly he broke away, ordering, "Sit up," doing so himself, drawing her after him, scraping her pretty white nightie up until it caught beneath her hips. "Up again . . ." And with a shift and lift, she felt the garment swept away. It sailed over her head and landed on the floor, followed immediately by his own, and before the two had become a motionless puddle, his arm took her down with him, onto their sides, and his foot scooped her close once more.

They fell to the pillows with their eyes wide open, pressed skin to skin, with her left breast caught up high by his wide hand. When he spoke, his voice sounded gruff.

"If anything hurts, you stop me."

She nodded her head twice in rapid succession, wide-eyed and breathless.

Then he released her breast, and found her hip, and curved his hand behind to hold her while teaching her motion—fluid and rhythmic and altogether tempting. They kissed, all lush and lusty, propelled by the relentlessness only first times can bring. He caught her knee and drew it over his hip, and touched her intimately for the first time.

"Oh!" she cried, and "Oh" again, as she twisted her face against the pillow. In time he captured her hand, whispering, "Here . . . like this." And all she had thought to be sordid became exalted.

Wily, wonderful man, he had her welcoming him at the moment of union. And later, crying out aloud with her throat bowed. And later still, gripping his shuddering body with her heels.

When it was over they lay twined, depleted, breathing the scent of each other's dampened skins.

She laughed once in celebration, with her eyes closed and her face at his chest. He took her head in both hands and tipped it to a better angle, rubbed his thumbs near the corners of her eyes and said, smiling, "There, now you know."

"All that worry for nothing," she said.